Winter Wishes

**A REGENCY HOLIDAY
ROMANCE ANTHOLOGY**

The characters and events portrayed in this book are fictitious. Any similarity to real persons, living or dead, is purely coincidental and not intended by the authors.

WINTER WISHES
Published October 2019
Published by Heather Boyd

Contents

One Room at the Inn

~ A Lords of Eton Novella ~

BY

Cheryl Bolen

What more can happen to lovely young widow Charlotte Hale? She has to sell her wedding ring to buy food. A heartless landlady evicts her and her children from their London lodgings on the coldest night in a generation. And now Charlotte's afraid this handsome stranger she's traveling with will have her arrested for stealing a coat for her son if he learns her true identity. Dare she trust him to take her to the only person who can help her?

Lord Philip Fenton promised the dying Captain Hale he would look after his family, but when he returns to England at Christmas, he arrives too late. The unfortunate family has been turned out of their home. He had thought the lovely widow calling herself Mrs. Leeming might be Mrs. Hale, but she is not. Nevertheless, he must help this impoverished family reach their destination in Lincolnshire, where he's traveling to see his family. As is his custom, he conceals his aristocratic title, traveling under the name Mr. Fenton.

They're both concealing information, but as the journey continues the barriers between them lower. He gave her his word he was a gentleman. As a man of honor, he cannot allow her to know how her very presence creates a yearning in him, how he aches to take her in his arms, how one word from her could make this his best Christmas ever . . .

Chapter One

Through all her travails Charlotte Hale had managed never to cry in front of her children. But today, as she slipped the gold wedding ring from her finger and handed it to the aged jeweler for the insignificant sum of three guineas, she was incapable of staunching the tears that had pent up inside of her since her husband's death the previous year.

The jeweler's craggy face collapsed in empathy, and he spoke in a gentle voice. "I cannot take your ring if it distresses you so, madam."

"No, please," she said, panicked. Her tears abruptly ceased. She was in no position to be sentimental. She had to be strong for Susan and Eddie. "My husband would have been happy that the ring he gave with love will help feed our children." Sniff. Sniff.

Charlotte tossed a glance to the back of the shop where her wide-eyed young daughter was ogling the locked cases of brilliant jewels. The child was so mesmerized by an emerald and diamond necklace lying in a bed of ivory satin, she was not aware of her mother's sorrow. Relief rushed over the mother. She could not have borne it if her children shared their mother's melancholy.

"Then I'll just put your guineas in a little pouch for you," the jeweler said, turning his back as he unlocked a drawer. This was followed by the clanging of coins. He spun around, smiling, and handed her a small, well-worn leather bag the size of a man's fist. "God bless you, Missus," he said as he handed Charlotte the pouch.

She smiled back, then turned to Susan. "Come, my darling. We must get home to your brother by dark." It was not quite four in the afternoon, yet night was close to falling. Another thing she hated about December.

"Bundle yerslelves up," the kindly man said. "They say it's the coldest December in memory."

"It certainly is," she agreed.

As Charlotte and her daughter walked hand in hand along the busy Strand, Charlotte merely nodded as Susan rattled on and on about the lovely necklaces and bracelets she had seen. The widow's thoughts were on far more grave affairs. How would she spend the three guineas? It wasn't nearly enough to pay Mrs. Waddingham the half year she was behind in rents. Could she offer the landlady one guinea for now with a promise for the full amount when her modest widow's pension came? At least she was assured she'd be able to feed the children for the next few weeks.

"Lookey, Mama! A uniform shop that also sells ones for little boys! Can we get one for Eddie? Then he could be an off-ser like Papa!"

Charlotte's step slowed as she looked into the candlelit shop. It even offered thick woolen greatcoats for very young lads. How she wished she could purchase a little Guards uniform so Eddie could emulate his father, but it might as well have been the king's own crown for its accessibility.

How grateful she was that children were oblivious to hardships—the missing father, the dwindling food, the wet chill seeping into their very bones. Just so long as their minds were occupied and the deprivation not complete, the little darlings never dwelt on grievances.

As they neared a printer's shop where men gathered to peer at Mr. Rowlandson's lewd caricatures, her grip on Susan's hand tightened. "Oh, look at the lovely white horse," she said to distract her daughter from the offensive pictures in the shop's window. "Wouldn't Eddie love it?"

"My bwother is mad for any horse of any colour."

"Indeed he is." It saddened Charlotte that her son was deprived of a father who would have taught him to ride. Edward had promised to buy the lad a pony when he was old enough.

But all Edward's promises vanished when he'd been killed on a Spanish battlefield.

As they approached the corner and lost the buildings' shelter, she feared the icy wind that sliced through them would carry away her small daughter. She scooped Susan's tiny body into her arms as a large cart laden with coal swept past and sprayed them with freezing slush from the filthy streets.

Just as sheets of rain fell from the blackening skies.

Her half boots pounding in and out of conveyances to cross the busy street, Charlotte hurried home as quickly as she dared on the icy pavement. She must get home as soon as she could. Eddie did not always have the sense to get out of the rain, and little Oliver's elderly grandfather, in whose care she'd left her lad, was often not mindful of the weather.

When she reached Chappell Street where Mrs. Waddingham's lodgings were located, merrily drenched Eddie and Oliver were running around the little triangular park that fronted their property. She didn't know which emotion was strongest: anger with Oliver's grandfather or worry that Eddie would take lung fever. Definitely the latter, she decided.

Then she saw that her son was *not* wearing his coat. *The coldest December in memory*. Certainly the coldest December in her four and twenty years. She thrust hand to hips and glared at her son. "Edward Thomas Hale, where is your coat?"

Her fair-haired son stopped in mid stride and smiled up at her in a most boastful fashion. The gaslight's glow revealed a lad whose cheeks were now exceptionally red and whose hair was exceedingly wet. "I gave it to the urchin."

Urchin? "I beg that you explain yourself."

"You always said to be kind and gen-rus to the poor urchins, so when the lad said he wished as he had a warm coat like mine, I gave mine to him."

Tears welled in her eyes. What *was* she to do? "Come, love. We must get you warm." Still holding Susan, she took Eddie's hand, walked to their house, and began to mount the stairs to their chambers on the second floor. As she approached their rooms, her heart began to drum. A padlock had been put on the door, as well as a sign that read EVICTED.

Thank God my children cannot read.

"Oh, darlings, I've just thought of something. I shall have to leave you with Oliver's grandfather for a few minutes while I go on an errand. You mustn't get out in this freezing rain again."

"I don't want to get out in that rain again," Susan said. "Can't I get Augusta?"

"Later. It won't hurt you to do without your doll for a few minutes."

Charlotte left her children in Mr. Leeming's single garret room and went to the ground floor and knocked on Mrs. Waddingham's door. The landlady's maid answered.

"I must speak to Mrs. Waddingham."

"Who shall I say is calling?"

"You know very well I'm Mrs. Hale."

The maid closed the door in Charlotte's face.

A moment later she returned. "Come this way."

The plump matron, whose red hair was threaded with gray, sat on a faded green silk sofa as Charlotte entered the drawing room. "Have you come to pay your rent, Mrs. Hale?" she asked.

"I have come to pay a guinea. For now," Charlotte added hopefully.

"I'm sorry, but I shall have to have the entire sum."

"I can't pay you the entire sum at this time."

"There's a large demand for your rooms. I have to turn away paying tenants every month. I need the money."

How could the woman possibly understand what it was to need money? She was well fed, well clothed, and owned a fine home in a well-situated location. "Please. This is the coldest day of the year. We have nowhere else to go." Charlotte indicated her wet clothes. "Even our dry clothing is locked in our chambers."

"I'm sorry, but whatever is locked within those chambers is now my property. After all, you now owe me nearly thirty guineas."

"Is there nothing I can do to soften your unyielding stance?"

Mrs. Waddingham rang the bell for her servant. "I do not run a charity, Mrs. Hale. Good night."

If her family was going to be forced to the streets, it was imperative that Eddie have a warm coat. She returned to the military shop on the Strand. The lone shopkeeper, a woman a decade older than Charlotte, was assisting a solidly built officer of middle age. Charlotte went straight to the woolen great coat, a Guards replica which appeared to be designed for a lad of about four—a little large for Eddie, but he would grow into it. In fact, it should keep him warm for at least the next two years.

Its workmanship was superior, and the wool's heft of high quality, as were the brass buttons. She examined every inch of the garment but could not determine the price. Finally she turned to the shopkeeper. "What is the cost of this item?"

"That's a bargain for only twenty guineas."

Charlotte's heart fell. A king's ransom.

She paced the shop's entire children's section, pondering her next move. There was only one clear choice. Desperation breeds corruption. She waited until the shopkeeper's back was turned, then she took the coat and fled.

"Hey! Come back! Thief!"

As she reached the door, she bumped into a man entering the shop. Their eyes locked. This man had served with her husband. "Mrs. Hale," said he.

Ignoring him, Charlotte pushed past him, then she started to run.

As the distance between her and the shop grew, two voices now called out, "Mrs. Hale!" The shopkeeper and Edward's fellow officer.

She'd been recognized. Her heartbeat pounded. Her pace quickened. She mustn't let them catch her.

As anxious as he was to join his family for Christmas, Lord Philip Fenton—who, in the army, preferred to be known as Captain Fenton—had an obligation to fulfill before seeking his own family after several years of absence. He had vowed to a dying Edward Hale that he would look after his family. In the year since his friend's death in the Peninsula, all Philip had managed with that impotent promise was to send his own sister to deliver Hale's widow the shattering news of her husband's death and for Georgiana—who'd become a duchess since Philip had left England—to offer Mrs. Hale any assistance she could.

Philip was aware such offers from a complete stranger were unlikely to be accepted, as his own offers would be spurned, but he was determined to make a valiant effort. For Edward's sake.

What a pity he had to return to England during the coldest December in a generation. Ships were unable to travel the frozen River Thames. A person could freeze to death in this numbing, windy, wet chill. Even those frigid Eton mornings he'd always accounted to be the most miserable of his life when he'd been forced from his warm bed now seemed like basking in front of a fire compared to London this evening.

His hired coach stopped in front of a four-storey house on Chappell Street fronted by a slender, triangular parcel of grass, now colourless. Looking at the scrap of address in his hand, he saw that he had reached the house where Mrs. Hale lodged. Her chambers were number 222. He bundled up, left the coach, entered the darkened building, and began to climb the stairs lighted from wall sconces. On the second floor, a paper sign was affixed to number 222. He came closer and read. EVICTED.

Oh, God. I'm too late. If only he had come earlier.

He raced to the ground floor. It appeared to be occupied by a single tenant. Would it be the property owner? Was that not always the case? He rapped at the door. A moment later a maid answered the rap. This was one time he did *not* mind using his title. "Lord Philip Fenton to see the landlord of these premises."

Titles did have their usefulness.

Soon he found himself addressing the smiling landlady who was all reverence. "What can I do for you, my lord?"

"I'm looking for Mrs. Hale."

"I regret to say she has just moved out."

His brows lowered. "Moved out or been evicted?"

"One must pay one's rent, my lord."

"What a pity you could not have waited. I had come to pay her rent in full—and for the next year in advance, too, but it seems I am too late, madam." He moved to the door, then turned back. "Would you know where she's gone?"

The middle-aged woman's eyes were like slits. "She said she had nowhere to go."

"How kind of you."

He strode to the door and slammed it as hard as he could. He could hear her asking him to pay the money owed. That merciless woman would not get a farthing from him. How did one live with oneself after evicting a widow and children who had nowhere to go? And during the coldest winter in memory!

As he climbed back into his coach, he shook his head. How in the bloody hell did one find a woman with two small children in the world's largest city? He didn't even know how old the children were. As a disinterested bachelor, he had never properly listened when Hale spoke of the children. Philip was doing well to know one was a lad and the other a girl, though he would be hard pressed to know which was the eldest. As to the lassie's name, he was clueless, but he thought perhaps the boy was named Edward, like his father. *Perhaps.*

His coach offered little shelter from the bitter cold, but at least it was dry. He pitied anyone who had to be out on a night like this. Coachmen and ostlers commanded his most profound respect. And soldiers, too. They were all a hardy lot. They knew how to dress to insulate themselves against the cruelest nature had to throw at them.

Now that he was coming home, he'd put aside his own uniform in favor of civilian clothing for the first time in almost a decade. Philip had always eschewed anything that would call attention to himself, whether it be the aristocratic title that indicated he was the younger son of a peer or the uniform a high-ranking military officer.

His gloved hand swiped at the window glass. Beneath a gaslight on Piccadilly he beheld the heart-wrenching sight of a young mother and two bedraggled children walking in the cold. He might not have given it another thought—other than that of niggling sympathy—had not Mrs. Hale and her children been dominating his thoughts.

He indicated for the coachman to stop, and he leapt from the coach to approach the woman. "Mrs. Hale?"

She turned around to face him, her eyes wide and frightened. She was remarkably pretty, even with her face slickened from the freezing rain and her hair—was it dark blonde? It was difficult to tell in the damp darkness – plastered to her head. She looked to be about a quarter of century in age, about the same as

Mrs. Hale would be, and the children appeared to be one male and one female. Surely this was Edward Hale's recently evicted family.

She shook her head, and began to stride forward again.

He was not to be deterred. He walked beside them. "I say, it's a dreadfully nasty night for a proper lady like yourself to be about." For even though she had not uttered a single word, he intrinsically knew this was a well-bred woman who should not be walking these dangerous streets at night. He wondered, too, if she even had a place to go.

"We're walking to the posting inn at Chelsea."

The children would never make it. Not in this weather. "Madam. If you don't fear for yourself, have a care for your children. It's too far to take them in this cold."

She drew in a deep breath, continued on, but made no response.

"Permit me to carry you in my coach. I assure you I'm a gentleman whom you can trust with your life."

"But," she said in her cultured voice, "you are a stranger to me."

"A stranger you must trust if you don't wish you children to become dangerously ill."

Her great sad eyes beheld the children, both fair haired. The girl was the eldest, not more than five years of age, her brother probably a year younger. The mother slowly nodded. "I assure you, I can scream quite loudly."

He stifled a laugh.

It was no short distance to the posting inn in Chelsea. Thank God she had permitted him to get them out of the freezing rain. Once they were in the carriage, he tossed them a dry rug. "Where is it you will travel by coach?"

"Lincolnshire."

"Ah, it's the same with me. You will also be visiting with family for Christmas?" He would be exceedingly happy to see his family, especially his mother. He'd been worried about her ever since she'd suffered apoplexy, even though his sister had taken excellent care of her.

It saddened him to think of all that had changed since he'd left England. Papa had died, and now Philip's brother was the new marquess. Georgiana had fallen in love and married a duke. And, thankfully, Mama was regaining strength every day. Georgiana said she was finally able to walk without her cane.

"A friend, actually."

"Allow me to introduce myself," he said. He always felt a bit deceitful when he abandoned both his aristocratic and his military titles, but he found doing so more easily put others at ease. "I'm Mr. Fenton."

She did not respond for a moment. Finally, she said. "Thank you for your assistance, Mr. Fenton."

As the coach drew near the busy inn yard, he thought of a plan that might be advantageous for the woman. "I do hope you realize I am a gentleman."

"I do hope you are, Mr. Fenton."

Since she obviously lacked funds to procure a hackney to take them to Chelsea, she must have precious little money. "I thought perhaps I could persuade you to share my coach to Lincolnshire. After all, it's much warmer with the body heat of four as opposed to the body heat of one."

"I'm afraid hiring a private coach is much more expensive than the stage coach."

"Oh, this has already been paid for. I merely seek companionship during the journey."

By now they had reached the inn yard brightly lit from dozens of lanterns.

She regarded him with suddenly warm blue eyes. The rigidity that had defined her these last twenty minutes vanished like the clearing of the frosty coach windows, and she smiled. "I shall remind you again, Mr. Fenton, I'm a lusty screamer."

Chapter Two

Had she taken complete leave of her senses? Charlotte had agreed not only to put her life but also the lives of her children into the hands of a total stranger. For all she knew, this Mr. Fenton could intend to sell them into white slavery, whatever that might entail. Flashing into her brain were visions of herself in the harem of a round-bellied Oriental potentate with a turban on his head and curly-toed slippers.

Though, she must own, Mr. Fenton *did* seem in every way to be a perfect gentleman. He had been most concerned over her family's exposure to the brutally cold weather.

As was she. Even after the passage of so many years, her stomach still dropped at the memory of lung fever sucking the life from her younger brother one particularly chilly winter. She could still envision Jackie's tiny body lying in the rough-hewn wooden coffin in their parlor—the same parlor she avoided for years thereafter. During this past year she had borne much but she did not think she could bear the loss of one of her children.

"Where has that nice man gone?" Susan asked. The three members of her family fit nicely on one seat of Mr. Fenton's coach, the children on either side of her.

Was Mr. Fenton a nice man? He gave every indication of being so. He certainly acted like a gentleman. He spoke like a gentlemen. And if appearances were any indication, he must be a gentleman. It wasn't just that he dressed as would a man of good taste, fine breeding, and some degree of wealth. His whole demeanor bespoke a man of principle.

She told herself she was not being swayed because he was uncommonly handsome. Which he most certainly was. He was larger than average and of proportions which she deemed most men would envy. His stylishly cropped hair was quite dark, as were his eyes, yet there was nothing menacing or brooding about those dark eyes. Quite the opposite. Like the rest of him, they were friendly and solid and reassuring.

"I think he's gone inside the inn," Charlotte said as she gathered each of her children close. He'd told his driver to wait while he put up the hood to his great coat and hurried into the posting inn. "I must tell you whilst he's away we've got to keep a secret from him. It's rather a game we must play."

"Oh, jolly good," Eddie said. "I love games."

"What is the game?" Susan asked, excitement in her voice.

"We mustn't tell Mr. Fenton our last name is Hale." That shopkeeper on the Strand knew Mrs. Hale had stolen Eddie's coat. Charlotte would be arrested. Had Mr. Fenton come to arrest her? He *had* called out her name. Was he some kind of magistrate looking for Mrs. Hale? Was he looking to receive a reward from the shopkeeper?

She'd frozen when he'd called out her name. For an instant, she'd wanted to deny she was Mrs. Hale, but she knew one or both of her children would have quickly corrected the falsehood. So she had merely shaken her head, hoping her offspring were too cold and miserable to have noticed the little movement.

"What name will we use?" Susan asked.

"I thought it might be easy for you two to remember Oliver's grandfather's last name."

"Mr. Leeming?" Eddie said.

"Only you needn't say Mister," Charlotte patted her son. "You're to pretend your name's Eddie Leeming."

"Then I can be bwothers with Oliver?"

"Let's not bring Oliver into this."

"And I shall be Susan Leeming."

Charlotte nodded. "And I'm Mrs. Leeming."

"How fun," Susan said. "Mama?"

"Yes, love?"

"Who is it we're to spend Christmas with in Linkshire?"

"Lincolnshire. All you need to know is that she's a very kind lady. Very kind and very beautiful." It wouldn't do to tell Susan the lady was a duchess. That was too close to being a princess or a queen. It was too much to expect an impressionable little girl like Susan not to gush about such a connection, and such gushing was the last thing Charlotte wanted.

Last year, at the behest of her brother, who had served with Edward, the Duchess of Fordham had left her home in Lincolnshire to bring Charlotte the heartbreaking news of Edward's death. The beautiful duchess had gone far beyond what her brother had asked, and before she left Charlotte's lodgings had extracted a promise. "Give me your word, my dear Mrs. Hale, that if ever you're in need, for anything, you will come to me at Gosingham Hall."

Charlotte had clung to her pride for long enough.

The coach door opened, water spraying into the coach. A basket heaped with food was shoved in first, then Mr. Fenton hoisted in his dripping self before slamming the door shut. "I thought if we could eat in the coach we could save a bit of time. I hope to be able to stop for the night at Bury St. Edmunds."

She had forgotten to account for the cost of a room at an inn. It was a very good thing Mr. Fenton had offered to share his coach with them. And his food.

Eddie's eyes rounded at the basket heaped with food, and he began to dive in.

"Eddie!" Charlotte chided. "You're being most impolite."

"Oh, no," Mr. Fenton protested, eyeing the boy. "Go right ahead and help yourself to whatever you like."

"I pwomise not to eat with my mouth open," Eddie said. "Mama says that's being impolite."

Their benefactor had certainly spared no expense. It had been a very long time since Charlotte had seen so much food. There were generous chunks of mutton, small loaves of fresh bread, hunks of cheese, steaming legs of capon, and Eddie managed to retrieve a handful of sweetmeats from the bottom of the basket.

Mr. Fenton's eyes narrowed at the sweets. "You must save those for last."

Eddie dropped them, grabbed the capon, which was larger than his head, and began to attack it.

"After you," Mr. Fenton said to her.

Charlotte proceeded to split a piece of mutton into portions for herself and Susan and paired the meat with bread.

From his deep pockets, Mr. Fenton produced some bottles. "I've brought milk for the children and ale for the adults."

"You're very thoughtful, and I'm exceedingly grateful," Charlotte said.

For the next fifteen minutes rain pounded on the coach as it rattled over the streets of the metropolis, and the four of them ate. Charlotte was too grateful to be embarrassed over Eddie's insatiable appetite. The poor darling had been starving!

By the time the crowded terraces had given way to countrified landscape, Eddie started bouncing around in his seat. "Mama?"

"Yes, love?"

"I have to winkiepiddle."

"Oh, dear."

"I think I understand," a grinning Mr. Fenton said.

For which Charlotte was profoundly grateful.

"Leave it to me." Their host pounded against the roof of the coach, and the carriage soon halted.

Charlotte met Mr. Fenton's gaze and sighed. "I hate for you to have to get wet."

"I have the same needs as your son."

When he and Eddie returned a few moments later, Eddie was all smiles. "My new coat is vastly warmer than my old coat, Mama."

"A very fine coat it is," Mr. Fenton said. "I shouldn't wonder if people won't take you for a soldier when you're wearing it."

Eddie sat up taller and beamed, never for a moment doubting the veracity of Mr. Fenton's observation.

Charlotte felt wretchedly guilty for having stolen the coat, but she had to do it all over again she would have done the same thing. If her ship ever came in, she vowed she would go back to that shop on The Strand and repay the shopkeeper. With interest.

"When I gwow up, I'm going to be a soldier. I'm going to be in the cavalry."

"That's because my bwother loves horses."

Mr. Fenton gave Eddie his full attention. "Is that so? Do you ride?"

Eddie scowled up at his mother. "Mama says I'm too little."

The gentleman nodded. "You are a wee bit young."

"Will this coach change horses during our journey?" Eddie asked. "Mama says they get too tired to travel all day."

"Since we got such a late start, we'll be stopping for the night, so they'll get a nice long rest while we're sleeping, but tomorrow we shall need to change the horses."

"Can I watch?" Eddie asked.

"Of course."

"Where will we sleep?" Susan looked from her mother to Mr. Fenton.

He answered. "We won't know the name of the place until we arrive, but we'll find a posting inn in the town of Bury St. Edmunds."

Eddie gave him a quizzing look. "What's a posting inn?"

"It's a large place that offers rooms to rent for a night for both people and horses, and they also offer food," Charlotte answered.

"But I cannot sleep without Augusta!" There was panic in Susan's voice.

Mr. Fenton's brows lowered. "Who's Augusta?"

"Her doll," Charlotte said. She squeezed her daughter's shoulder softly. "Of course you'll be able to sleep, love. You and I and Eddie will all share a bed, and we'll be as cozy as can be."

"But I want Augusta. I never sleep without her." Susan attempted to stomp her foot even though her legs were too short to reach the floor of the coach.

Now was not the time to tell her daughter she would never again see Augusta. Susan would have to learn to settle for another doll. One day. Was Augusta special because she was Susan's only doll or because Edward had given it to her?

Slowly but painfully, they were losing every tangible thing Edward had left them. And slowly and painfully, it tore Charlotte's heart to shreds.

"Think of what fun we'll have at the posting inn! It will be an adventure."

"I want to go to my own house," Eddie said, working his lower lip into a pout.

"Oh, but soldiers must get used to sleeping in new places," Mr. Fenton said. "Sometimes they even have to sleep with their horses."

The lad looked up hopefully at his mother. "Could I sleep with the horses?"

"Not on a cold night like tonight. The three of us are going to bury ourselves under the covers in a nice warm bedchamber at the inn. In fact, I cannot wait to get there." Charlotte pulled each weary child close beneath the thickness of the rug, and before long, the movement of the coach lulled them to sleep. Eddie's head rested in her lap, and Susan's sweet little face pressed into her ribs.

"I pray the roads hold until we make Bury St. Edmunds," Mr. Fenton said, his voice low.

"Me too," she whispered. In this kind of relentless rain, the roads could soon be mired in impassable ruts. And then what would they do? She began to regret that they had finished all the food in the basket. What if they were trapped in the coach for days?

In situations like this, she appreciated the presence of a man. Even if he was a stranger.

"So, will you be meeting your husband in Lincolnshire?"

She did not answer for a moment. "I'm a widow."

"I'm sorry. It must be difficult raising the children on your own."

She nodded solemnly.

"Might I know your name?"

"I'm Mrs. Leeming."

"I see. And when did Mr. Leeming die?"

"Last year," she said in a low voice, then looked up at him. "What about you, Mr. Fenton? Will you be meeting your wife in Lincolnshire?"

"Alas, I've never been married."

"Then you'll be visiting family?"

"Indeed I will. I haven't seen my family in many years and am greatly looking forward to seeing them again, especially given that my mother has not been well."

"I'm certain that having you home will be the best possible tonic to improve your mother's condition."

"I hope you're right."

She wondered what had kept him from home for many years but did not want to pry into his personal matters.

"So, are you originally from Lincolnshire?" she asked.

"No, that's where my sister makes her home now that she's married. This will be the first time I've seen her new home—or met her husband."

"So she's newly wed?"

He shrugged. "Fairly so."

"No nieces or nephews yet for you? You seem so good with children."

"Thank you for saying so. I've not been around children very much. Actually, my brother has a son and daughter, but I've not met them either. As I said, it's been many years since I've seen my family."

"I am sure your niece and nephew will adore you."

"I'm not altogether certain I will see them at Christmas. My sister-in-law can be a bit difficult, I'm told. She may not be able to be induced to leave her house to travel to my sister's at Christmas."

"How troublesome for your poor mother!"

He nodded. "Indeed. Especially since she's quite devoted to her little Hellions—her special name for her grandchildren."

Charlotte laughed. "I can well understand. I could call mine that sometimes. Especially Eddie."

"He's delightful."

"Thank you." She sighed and softened her voice. "You have been very kind, and I'm most indebted to you."

"Reserve your judgment until we reach Lincolnshire. If we do," he said grimly as the coach came to a stop and he peered through the foggy glass.

Chapter Three

He swiped at the window to clear it and was relieved to see the yellow glow of lanterns illuminating a sign for the Lamb and Staff. They must have arrived at Bury St. Edmunds. And without a single mishap. "I believe we've reached our destination."

Neither child had awakened. "Pray, don't awaken the children," he added. "They must be exhausted."

He briefly left the coach to instruct the coachman to procure rooms, and then he returned to find that the children were still fast asleep. "Allow me to carry the lad." Philip whisked Eddie into his arms. Even though he was shorter than his slender sister, the sturdily built boy had to considerably outweigh her. Mrs. Leeming gathered up little Susan, then stepped down from the carriage.

Despite that it was still raining in great torrents, the coachman had managed to angle the coach under the entry arch in such a manner that they were able to stay relatively dry when moving from the interior of the carriage to interior of the inn via a doorway in the arch.

Their driver met them inside the door with their room keys. "The missus and children are to be in Room 232, and you, sir, are across the corridor in Room 231. The stairs are located behind the tap room."

Raucous noises from the tap room awakened the children. Eddie looked up at Philip and started to cry. "I want my Mama."

"I'm right here, darling," she said soothingly. "We'll soon be in our room. It will be great fun." The lad pouted when he saw that his mother carried his sister.

"Would you prefer to walk?" Philip asked. He hated that the boy disliked being carried by him.

Instead of answering, Eddie eyed the room full of strange cackling men, and his grip on Philip's neck tightened. The poor lad was frightened.

The narrow wooden stairway that led to their chambers was only dimly lit from a single sconce, and each ascending tread creaked with the barest step. He could only imagine how frightening it must be for these children who had probably never before left their home in London.

When they reached the corridor, it was frightfully dark. Could the innkeeper not have sent a chambermaid with a candle? He set down the lad and attempted to insert the key into the door for 232, but it was not easy, given that he could not see what he was doing. It took several tries before he succeeded.

His temper flared when he finally pushed open the door and saw that the room was in complete darkness. No attempt had been made to start a fire on this, the coldest night of the year. "This is not acceptable," he snapped. "We'll find another place."

He once more lifted up Eddie and spoke in a soft voice. "The next place will be much nicer than this one." The boy clung tightly to him as they descended the dark stairwell, and poor little Susan began to whimper. "I want to go home."

"I know, love," her mother said in a soothing voice. "But everything will be fine. Soon we'll be warm and cozy."

Philip hoped to God they were.

Downstairs, he settled the Leemings on a bench in a well-lit corridor while he went to find his driver, whom he located in the tap room. "The Lamb and Staff won't do." He put an arm to the man's shoulder. "You've been to Bury St. Edmunds before?"

"Aye. Many times."

"I want the nicest inn in this town, and I'm happy to pay for it."

"That will be the White Lion, but I must prepare you. On a rainy night such as this, it can be hard to find vacancies at any place."

It had always been Philip's experience that anything could be obtained if one's pockets were deep enough. He just hoped he wouldn't be forced to play his trump: his aristocratic title. He rejoined the Leemings, and it was quite some time before their coach was brought around. "Our horses had been put to bed for the night," Philip explained to the children.

Eddie giggled. "Horses don't have beds, silly."

Philip shrugged. "Don't tell them. They think a pile of hay is their bed."

Eddie giggled again. "And, silly, they can't understand it when you talk to them."

"I wonder if they have warm blankets on a cold night like this," Susan said.

"Perhaps they just snuggle together for warmth," Mrs. Leeming suggested.

"Like we were going to do," Susan said, disappointment in her voice.

The very idea of someone to snuggle with in a big cozy bed on such a miserable night had much merit. Funny, during all those years he'd slept alone in the Peninsula, away from his family and without a woman of his own to love, he'd not felt as bereft as he felt at this moment.

He found himself really looking at Mrs. Leeming. At first, he envied her riches, not material riches which she most certainly lacked, but the love she had for her children and the love they had for her. That was incalculable wealth that no fortune could ever purchase.

He continued staring at the woman. The longer he looked, the more he came to realize how truly lovely she was. Her hair had dried, and now he was certain it was blonde. Dark blonde. When she was a girl, it must have been as fair as Susan's was now.

Her wavy tresses framed a face as innocent and perfect as that of a Madonna painted by an Italian master. Her dark blond lashes swept down as she stroked her daughter's hair, her full lips gently pressing into the crown of Susan's head.

Philip found himself drawing in a breath.

Mrs. Leeming was a little smaller than average, though it was difficult to judge her figure since it was buried beneath so many layers of heavy woolen clothing. But even those many layers could not disguise the swell of her breasts. Their rise and fall affected him in a most disturbing way. He found her exceedingly desirable.

Such selfish instincts made him feel wretched. His initial interest in Mrs. Leeming had nothing to do with his own personal gratification—other than the gratification one derives from helping those in need. He'd merely seen a woman and two helpless children who could use his assistance, and offering them aid in no way inconvenienced him. If anything, it assuaged his disappointment that he'd been unable to help Edward Hale's family.

As she sat there lovingly stroking her children, he was unable to purge from his thoughts the vision of lying in bed beneath warm covers with this woman by his side. Nothing on earth—not even the longed-for reunion with his family—could be more welcome.

Of course, he would never act upon this ever-increasing need she awakened in him. He was a gentleman. He'd promised to act like a gentleman. And this woman was most certainly a well-bred lady. He would never do anything to diminish her opinion of him.

But, God, he wanted to!

She looked up, and their eyes met. He felt like a lad caught cheating at an exam and looked away quickly.

The drenched coachman finally came and summoned them.

The White Lion looked much nicer than the Lamb and Staff. Charlotte hoped she could afford it. It was an old red brick edifice of three stories which, judging by its fresh paint, appeared to be well maintained.

Mr. Fenton sent the coachman to procure rooms, but he soon returned with a dejected look when he opened the coach door. "There's but one room left."

"Did you inquire if fires have been built in the rooms?"

"Aye, sir. They 'ave. After all, this is the finest inn in all of Bury St. Edmunds."

"Then take it," Mr. Fenton commanded.

"But, sir. . ."

"If I have to, I'll sleep in the tap room. Or I can go back to the Lamb and Staff. These children need a warm bed."

"Yes, sir."

"We can't, Mr. Fenton," Charlotte protested. "Please, let's try another place. This isn't fair to you."

"Madam, I've spent the last decade in the Peninsula. I've slept in much, much worse."

Her eyes rounded. "Then you're a soldier?"

He nodded.

"So was my husband."

He caught the coachman's gaze, inclined his head, and the door shut.

"I'm . . ." she hesitated. "I'm not sure I can afford lodgings at The White Horse."

"Have you stayed in an inn before, Mrs. Leeming?"

"Many years ago, but I wasn't responsible for paying for it."

"The prices are regulated. You'll be able to afford it."

She was quite certain she would have heard of it before if prices were regulated. She had the oddest feeling Mr. Fenton was fooling her. Was he going to make up the difference between the rate at the Lamb and Staff and the White Lion?

He was being awfully kind to her and the children. She knew nothing about him. He was a complete stranger. Was he deliberately trying to make her beholden to him in order to seduce her? Or worse?

At the memory of catching him staring at her back at the Lamb and Staff, her cheeks stung. She knew that look. It was the way a man looked at a woman when he desired her. The memory of the naked hunger in his dark gaze accelerated her heartbeat.

Surely he would not attempt a seduction in her children's presence! Only a man gripped by depravity could think of anything so despicable. Nevertheless, she vowed to avoid ever being alone with Mr. Fenton.

She hated that this past year of hardship had destroyed her ability to trust her fellow man, but she had experienced only one act of kindness in the year since Edward had died, while being constantly crushed under the cruelty of mercenaries. She thought fondly of the Duchess of Fordham's generosity.

It was kind, too, of the duchess's brother to have a care for the family of his fallen comrade in arms. In her grief, Charlotte had not caught the name of the duchess's brother. He was a captain. That much she could remember. Regrettably, she did not know the names of the men with whom Edward served.

His letters were always full of words of love for her and the children, memories of their special times together, and assurance that all was well with him. He did not want to worry her with tales of his battles or the woes of a soldier's life.

The coachman returned, and Mr. Fenton insisted on carrying Eddie to their new chambers. She felt wretchedly guilty that her family would be sleeping in relative splendor whilst Mr. Fenton's lodgings were questionable, but she could not deny that she was grateful for a warm room on a freezing night like this. Just making it from the coach to the inn gave them a thorough soaking from slanting rains.

A chambermaid wearing a freshly starched white apron awaited them with a candle and showed them up a well-lit stairway to the second floor. Their chambers—a parlor and adjoining bedchamber—were at the end of a long wooden-floored corridor.

Mr. Fenton inserted the key and opened the door to the parlor where a wood fire blazed in a room of goodly proportions. Its wooden floor was centered with a circular floral rug upon which a long chintz sofa was situated to face the fire. The carved wood chimneypiece featured a footed case clock. Charlotte thought the room wondrously cozy.

"The bedchamber be this way, madam," the chambermaid said, showing them into the adjoining room and lighting a candle beside the bed. A fire kept this room warm also. A tall feather bed was piled with what appeared to be freshly laundered quilts, and velvet apricot-coloured curtains ringed the bed.

It was far nicer than the room Charlotte had left behind in London.

She could not disguise her pleasure. "Well, children, I think this is going to be a very comfortable room."

Susan still clung to her mother's neck. "It looks very nice."

Eddie had not let go of Mr. Fenton. "Can I jump on the bed?"

It was much higher than the one he normally slept in.

"Most certainly not," Charlotte answered.

At least the children were no longer frightened.

"Then the accommodations are to your satisfaction?" Mr. Fenton asked.

She hadn't wanted to look him in the eyes. She had avoided looking at him since she'd seen the raw hunger in his gaze earlier. But she could avoid it no longer. "This will do very nicely. Where will you sleep?"

"Don't worry about me. I'll be fine."

"Soldiers can sleep anywhere," Eddie said. "Mr. Fenton used to be a soldier."

"So," Mr. Fenton said, "I will instruct the staff to bring breakfast to your parlor at eight in the morning, when I'll join you." He moved to the door, then turned back and addressed Eddie. "As a soldier, you'll need to look after the ladies."

"Yes, sir."

Once Mr. Fenton was gone she sighed. How kind he was not to mention their lack of bags. How embarrassing it was not to have even a gown to sleep in or a change into dry clothing. Fortunately the small clothes remained mostly dry. She hung all their wet clothes on the drying racks near the fire before they climbed into the bed.

Once more, the children fell fast asleep. It felt so comforting to have the children so close in a warm, dry bed in such a nice bedchamber, a bedchamber far nicer than she was accustomed to. For that, she had Mr. Fenton to thank.

It was comforting on a night as miserable as this to be safe and warm with her children. Hopefully they would be able to make Gosingham Hall by tomorrow evening.

If the roads remained passable. She did not know what she would do otherwise. Three guineas would not pay for much in the way of accommodations. Or food.

The following morning they dressed in dry clothing and went into the parlor where a very fine breakfast had been delivered. There was toast and marmalade and tea and cold meat and milk.

Eddie wanted to pile up a plate, but Charlotte insisted that he wait until Mr. Fenton arrived. She had a strong feeling Mr. Fenton was the one who would be paying for the food. She certainly hoped so.

She only hoped his generosity was not being tied to a potential seduction. She could not purge from her mind how in the span of a few seconds the evening before he had gone from being a jolly uncle type to a seducer of young mothers.

I will not make eye contact with him.

She kept watching the clock upon the mantel. It was now fifteen minutes past eight. She walked to the window and looked out. Rain still pounded against the foggy windows. She wiped a circular clearing. The streets were a quagmire.

Of course she saw no sign of Mr. Fenton.

"I'm hungry," Eddie said.

When it got to be half past eight, she told the children to go ahead and eat.

Mr. Fenton was not coming.

He had left her stranded in Bury St. Edmunds.

After she paid for the inn, she would not even have enough to pay for a stage coach to Lincolnshire.

What was she to do?

Once more, life had dealt her a cruel blow.

Chapter Four

Even knowing that she might never again be offered so hearty a breakfast, Charlotte could not eat a single bite. Not when she wondered how she was going to pay for it, how she was going to pay for the coach ride on to Lincolnshire—or, if the roads kept them stranded more nights at the White Lion—how she could manage to pay the additional bill here. Three guineas could only go so far.

How could she feed her children when the money ran out? Worse yet, what would she do if they were tossed out into the snow? For it had now started to snow. They had neither rug nor blanket for warmth.

No matter what obligations she might be forced to meet, she must keep back enough to frank a letter to Gosingham Hall, begging the duchess to assist her. She hated to have to throw herself on the kindly duchess's charity, but at the same time felt comforted to have that safety net to fall back upon. She had hoped to never have to use it.

There was a gentle tap at the chamber door. Her heartbeat soared. She prayed it was Mr. Fenton. "Yes?"

The same serving maid who had delivered the food re-entered the chamber. Charlotte caved with disappointment. "Would you like more 'ot water for tea, madam?"

"No, thank you."

The woman gave no signs of leaving. "It looks like the guests won't be leaving any time soon."

Charlotte gave her a quizzing look as her heart plummeted.

"The coaches can't continue on until these roads dry."

"What of the post chaise?"

The other woman shook her head. "Not even the post."

So Charlotte would not even be able to contact the duchess. She cleared her throat. "My lodgings were paid for in advance, were they not?"

"Oh, yes, madam. The first night's always paid for in advance—as was yer meal this morn. Yer 'andsome traveling companion took care of that. Pity there was no room for 'im last night. Always 'appens when the weather's wretched like this. On nights like last night we could rent out a hundred rooms and still 'ave 'em beggin' for more."

Handsome. Yes, Mr. Fenton had been an exceedingly handsome man. How Charlotte wished that he had been the gentleman she had at first taken him for. How she wished he were here with them now—if he had been the kindly man they had thought him. For a short time it had been nice to put her cares into the hands of a capable man.

She should have known such good fortune was not to be, not after all the ill fortune that had befallen her during the heartache of this past year.

It was while Charlotte was thinking of Mr. Fenton that she saw him through a crack the serving maid had left in the door. He stood in the corridor, gazing at Charlotte solemnly.

"Mr. Fenton!" she exclaimed. She was unable to conceal the elation in her voice.

He moved into the chamber as the serving maid curtsied and left. "I beg that you'll forgive my muddied boots. I ended up sleeping at the room I'd paid for at the Lamb and Staff and had the devil of a time getting from there to here this morning, given that the roads are impassable."

"It looks as if you walked in mud up to your knees."

"Indeed I did. That's why I'm so unpardonably late. I kept hoping another solution would present itself, but, alas, it did not." He bowed. "I must offer my deepest apologies."

"Given that you, sir, most generously paid for the breakfast, you have nothing for which to apologize."

He eyed the table, still piled amply with food. "May I?"

"Please do."

"I hate to track the mud into your nice clean chambers."

She was so happy to see him, she did not object to allowing him to partially disrobe in front of her. "Should you like to remove your boots and set them by the fire? They could dry much more quickly that way."

"I would do exactly that were I not in the presence of a lady, but I cannot." He stopped and offered her a gentle look. "Though it was a generous offer for you to make, my dear Mrs. Leeming."

She waved an arm at the breakfast offerings. "Do help yourself, my dear Mr. Fenton."

"I confess I am famished."

"Mama hasn't eaten, either," Susan said.

"Ah, waiting for me?" Mr. Fenton said teasingly.

"'Twas only good manners, given that you are the one who paid for the meal."

"My mama has very good manners," Eddie said, stuffing toast into his mouth, streams of rich orange marmalade oozing down his face.

Charlotte crossed the chamber and blotted away the drippings with a napkin. "Your table manners are deplorable, young man."

Eddie looked at Mr. Fenton. "Sir?"

"Yes, Eddie?"

"When you blow your nose into a handkerchief, do you look at the handkerchief? Mama says that it is very bad manners."

"Eddie!" Charlotte shrieked. "That is not a topic for polite conversation."

"But you're always polite and you told it to me."

Mr. Fenton guffawed.

It was all Charlotte could do not join in his mirth.

Mr. Fenton cleared his throat. "I do *not* look at my handkerchief after blowing my nose. Like your mother, my mother also attempted to teach me good manners. I do hope she was successful."

"I do believe she was," Charlotte said. How indebted Charlotte now was to Mrs. Fenton. She sat down beside Mr. Fenton, and the two of them began to fill their plates and eat in a most contented silence.

This morning she even found herself peering into his gaze without the discomfort she'd felt the night before. She was so grateful for his return, she no longer resented the manly ways he was incapable of suppressing. Truth be told, she admired him for refusing to remove his boots in front of her.

Somehow, she knew that even if he did desire her in the way a man desires a woman, he was too much a gentleman to act upon his own needs.

Midway through breakfast he confirmed that they would not be able to continue their journey that day. "Don't worry," he assured. "I've paid another night's lodgings."

So he understood she hadn't the money to do so. She hated being the recipient of his charity, hated being indebted to him or to any man, hated that she might be asked to make some sort of "payment."

She started to say, "I don't know how I can ever repay you," but she thought better of it. As a woman who had been married, who had made love to a man, she knew how a man would wish to be repaid.

And she could not bring up such a topic.

The children had finished eating and were restless and bored. Unable to sit still, Eddie raced around the small table where Charlotte and Mr. Fenton were eating, and it took all of Charlotte's patience not to reprimand him for the rambunctiousness her son was powerless to control.

Susan had no such qualms. "Quit running around. You're aggravating me!"

Mr. Fenton exchanged an amused gaze with Charlotte, then lowered his voice. "Your children need a diversion."

"Indeed they do. What do you suggest?"

He drew a breath. "I think the coachman could take them to the mews and give them some lessons on horsemanship. Show them what's entailed in dressing a horse, what they eat, even how they sleep. The way The White Lion is configured in the shape of a square, they can reach the mews without getting muddied."

As much as her children—Eddie especially—would adore that, warning bells went off in Charlotte's head. *He wants to get me alone.* In the bedchamber. She glared at him. "I can hardly be alone with you here in these private chambers, Mr. Fenton."

He pursed his lips in thought. "There is that." He slathered marmalade upon his toast and bit into it. A moment later he rose from the table, crossed the chamber, and locked the door to the bedchamber. He took the key and strode to the children, who had been watching him with quizzing expressions on their tiny faces.

"As man of the family, Eddie," Mr. Fenton said, "you need to guard over this key to your family's bedchamber. Can you do so without losing it?"

Susan put hands to her hips, elbows thrust out. "You ought to give it to me, Mr. Fenton. My bwother loses everything. I'll guard it for him. He can still be the man of the family."

Eddie nodded solemnly.

"Very well." Mr. Fenton handed the key to Susan, who placed it in a lacy little reticule she carried over her slender arm.

Next Mr. Fenton rang for a servant, and when a maid came, he asked that she send their driver to these chambers. When that man appeared moments later, Mr. Fenton explained that he was to instruct these children in the care and dressing of horses.

Eddie squealed in delight, and both children happily skipped from the chamber while Mr. Fenton resumed eating his breakfast and freshened his tea.

Now Charlotte's fears were allayed, and she was beginning to once again feel comfortable in this man's presence. Not only that, she was happy her children would have something that would greatly amuse them and take their minds off the dreariness of the weather.

"I will own," she said, "I was at my wit's end to think of something that would amuse Susan and Eddie. They're too young for chess or games that might amuse older children."

"And Susan doesn't even have Augusta."

She smiled at him. What a good memory he possessed to remember the name of her daughter's doll. "A pity. She could have amused herself for many hours had she that ridiculous doll." She shrugged. "She wasn't so ridiculous. Her papa gave it to her. I suppose that's why she was so special."

He nodded sympathetically. "Of course, even without the sentimental attachment, dolls can be most amusing to little girls. My sister certainly enjoyed playing with hers."

"You have just the one sister?"

"Oh, one was quite enough. She is most didactic, and since I was the youngest, I was constantly finding myself subjected to her manipulations at every turn." He shrugged. "Though in spite of her authoritarian ways, my sister is most likeable. Loveable, actually, and I'll be deuced happy to see that pretty face of hers again."

"I know you have an older brother, the one with the two children. Were there just the three of you?"

He nodded. "Mama—like my sister—is a delicate beauty, and such delicacy apparently did not aid in breeding. She lost a half a dozen babes."

Charlotte's brows lowered sympathetically. "My mother had similar problems. I was the only daughter, and I had three brothers, two of whom survived to adulthood."

"And where are your brothers?"

"One is a soldier in the Peninsula. He's never married. The other is married, lives in remote Yorkshire, and is father to . . ." She rolled her eyes. "Eight. His wife is a most prodigious breeder. And they are only thirty!"

They both smiled.

"Who is it you're to see in Lincolnshire? Your parents?"

A melancholy look on her face, she shook her head. "No. My parents are dead."

"How difficult it must be to have lost so many whom you've loved."

It was such an empathetic statement. Most men lacked such sensitivity. Perhaps almost losing his mother had deepened his appreciation of family. She nodded. "But I have been richly compensated with my children."

"Indeed you have." There was a wistfulness in his eyes when he gazed at her, swallowing hard.

"One last cup of tea, Mr. Fenton?"

He nodded. "Only because I'm still trying to get warm."

"Was the Lamb and Staff terribly cold last night?"

"I'm still shivering. It offered the flimsiest fire I've ever seen—and that sputtered out in less than two hours. The chamber was so drafty, I got up in the middle of the night to close the window, only to discover it *was* closed! The counterpane upon the straw bed was no thicker than my shirt. All in all, a most unpleasant night."

Her eyes twinkled. "Then it's a very good thing a soldier such as yourself has learned to sleep anywhere."

An amused expression on his face, he smiled back at her. "Indeed it is. And what about your accommodations, madam? Did you sleep well—in rooms that would have been mine were I traveling all by my lonely, forlorn self?"

"Ah, the price one has to pay for having such charming traveling companions," she responded flippantly.

"It's not every day one has the opportunity to travel with another fellow with whom one can share a winkiepiddle."

They both roared with laughter. She could not remember the last time she had laughed like this. "In all seriousness, as you could have guessed, the children went to sleep right away. I followed not long after and slept very well. It was an exceedingly comfortable chamber, and we are truly indebted to you." She was careful not to say *I am*. He was, after all, a man, and she must be careful not to arouse his desires.

But here she was allowing herself to be alone with him, allowing herself to peer into those dark, mesmerizing eyes of his, allowing herself to be . . . enchanted by this man who had been a complete stranger less than four-and-twenty hours ago.

For in spite of her most stringent cautions, she trusted him. God help her if he proved her a fool.

She watched him eat. He appreciated his food with the same enthusiasm as Eddie. In some ways, he reminded her of Eddie—and not just in their obvious admiration of the military. Like Eddie, Mr. Fenton easily integrated with strangers without being wary of them.

She had once been like that. It seemed now like that woman had been another person. As indeed she had been. Would any of the old, carefree Charlotte ever return?

"I'm wondering, Mr. Fenton, how you manage to stay such a cheerful sort when I know that if you served in the Peninsula you must have experienced much loss, must have seen a great deal of death."

He set down his cup and turned to her, his brows lowering. "You're right, Mrs. Leeming, but I've found life is what one makes of it. If one dwells on melancholy topics, one's life will be sad. I choose to reach for happiness."

"I would choose the same, were I not concerned over how I'm to feed my children." She could not believe she'd abandoned her pride and made such a confession to him. "You, sir, must never have had to worry about money."

A pensive look crossed his handsome face. "I will own, madam, that you are right. It has been my good fortune to never have had money woes."

"I should not have brought up such a topic. Forgive me."

"There's nothing to forgive. From the moment I first saw you and the children, I surmised that if you had money, you wouldn't have been exposing your children to such brutal cold last evening. Then when I discovered you were going to the coaching inn – without a single valise – it became clear to me that you were in serious financial difficulties. It's my privilege to be able to help you."

"It's very embarrassing to me, but at the same time, I feel as if you're my savior." What the devil had come over her? She was blathering away like a school girl suffering from a deprivation of pride and want of common sense.

"I'm gratified that I can help. It assuages my conscience. You see, I'm feeling quite low. I promised a comrade of mine who died in battle I would help look after his wife and children, but I was too late to be able to help them. Helping you and Susan and Eddie makes me feel less of a failure, though I still feel beastly about not being able to help them."

He really was a genuinely likeable man. "When you said you were too late to help your friend's family, did you mean they . . . died?"

He shook his head. "I don't think so. At least I hope that's not the case. I was too late to find them because I believe they . . . moved."

"Perhaps after you've seen your family you'll be able to return to London and find them."

"I shall try." For the first time since she'd met him, a somberness seeped through into his cheerful barrier. He left the table, moved to the fire, and stood there warming himself, eyeing Charlotte. "I appreciate you being candid with me."

She gave a bitter laugh. "About not being able to feed my children?"

"Yes. I know it wasn't easy for a proud woman like yourself, a woman of good breeding."

Her lashes lowered, and she spoke only barely above a whisper. "It was terribly embarrassing."

"There's nothing to be embarrassed about. A man has the means to seek employment in order to feed his family. A woman who's been brought up as a lady does not have an occupation or the means by which to even seek an occupation."

She nodded. "The only skill I could have offered was that of a governess, but having children prohibits me from doing that."

"Your year of mourning is up?"

"Yes." She found that she was getting cold and got up from the table to go stand by the fire beside him.

"Then you'll remarry. Because you're pretty, you'll have not the least difficulty attracting a husband."

She fixed him with an angry glare. "One doesn't marry for such mercenary reasons."

"No, of course not. You must allow yourself to love again." His voice lowered. "You deserve to love again."

Then he did a most peculiar thing. An exceedingly unexpected thing. He moved closer to her, clasped two strong hands on her shoulders, and lowered his head to kiss her.

Chapter Five

It wasn't until she twisted away from him that Philip realized how depraved Mrs. Leeming must think him. He was as disappointed in himself as she must be in him. Grimacing with tightly shut eyes he croaked out a shaky, "Forgive me."

Her back was to him. All he saw now were the tendrils of blonde hair on her graceful neck, the dainty shoulders hugged by the soft violet muslin of her gown, the forlorn, defeated shake of her head. One moment ago he'd soared with joy as he'd kissed this beautiful woman.

Now he felt like a predator.

"I have no right to ask your forgiveness when I've betrayed your trust, but I swear to you I'm a gentleman. I don't know what came over me."

Still, there was no response.

"Would it be too much to ask you to try to forget my unpardonable conduct?" he asked. "If you could forget, then we could go on as if it had never occurred, go back to where we were before. I thought we were all getting along jolly well."

She slowly turned around to face him. God, she was lovely, so much so that she almost stole away his breath. Her cheeks were rosy, he suspected from embarrassment.

"I don't think I shall be able to forget it," she said, "but I should very much like to accept your apology with the hope that such an action not be repeated."

He nodded. "Thank you."

"Shall I ring for more hot water? Do you not think we need more tea?"

"An excellent idea."

She crossed the room to ring for a servant.

He was still befuddled over his impetuous action. Even more befuddling, he'd never associated Mrs. Leeming with lust. Not last night when he'd noticed how extraordinarily beautiful she was. Not when he'd thought of wanting to lie in bed with her. Not when he'd told her she needed to love again. Not even when he'd kissed her.

This was not a woman one lusted after. This was a woman one married.

And Lord Philip Fenton had no intentions of marrying.

He supposed he had been too long away from well-brought-up women and loving families. Being around Mrs. Leeming and her delightful children awakened in him all those relationships of which he'd been deprived for the many years he was on the Peninsula.

True, she elicited in him a profound physical craving for intimacy. He wanted to touch this woman. He wanted to hold this woman. He wanted to kiss this woman.

After she ordered the water, she went back to sit at the table. He remained standing at the fire. An awkward silence followed.

"Until yesterday I still wore my husband's wedding ring."

"Even though it's been more than a year?"

She nodded.

"Oh, dear God. You sold the ring yesterday?"

"Yes."

"I believe it's what your husband would have wanted."

"Yes, I think so, too. That's what I told myself. It would make him happy to know that ring he gave me was continuing to take care of us . . ." Her voice cracked. "After he was gone."

"Does is not occur to you that selling the ring is the final step in letting go of that marriage? It's a sign that there will be another happy marriage for you."

She shook her head somberly. "I never considered there would ever be another marriage."

"Likely because you were still wearing the ring. I suspect there were many reasons why it was time for you to sell that ring." He eyed her. "How old are you?"

"Four and twenty."

He laughed. "Many women are marrying for the first time at so youthful an age. Believe me, a lovely woman like you will be sweeping men off their feet. You've got a long, happy, prosperous life to look forward to."

"Happy is something that no longer seems attainable to me. Especially now." She glared at him.

And he felt despicable.

The pounding of children's feet and sounds of youthful voices lifted in merriment moved closer down the corridor until Eddie burst through the doorway.

"Mama! Mama! Mr. Podge permitted me to harness one of our horses."

"He permitted me to name the horse Smokey," Susan said, her voice almost as excited as that of her brother.

"But how, my darling," Charlotte asked Eddie, "did you manage to harness a horse? You're not nearly tall as they are."

"He stacked up some very large wooden boxes for Eddie," Susan answered.

Charlotte brushed away a thick lock of blond hair from her son's forehead. "However did you know how to do it correctly?"

"Mr. Podge taught me. He said I did it as good as he could." He looked up at Mr. Fenton for approval.

"I knew you'd be an apt student."

"What does *apt* mean?"

"It means *very good*," Mr. Fenton answered.

She might be very vexed with him, but she could not deny he *was* good with the children. She prayed he wasn't just being good with them in order to seduce their mother. She had foolishly trusted him last night, but this morning he had destroyed that trust.

In all likelihood Mr. Fenton was a good man. But he was a man, and men had carnal needs. He had demonstrated that this morning.

She watched as he and the children talked about what had transpired in the stables, her thoughts spiraling into a place she hoped she'd never have to go.

For Charlotte Hale had nothing left. Certainly nothing material. She now had come to realize she'd lost her pride. Her respectability would fall next. For if she had to use her body in order to get food, lodgings, and transport to the Duchess of Fordham, she would. That's what despair does to one.

And for that, she hated Mr. Fenton.

There were few things more trying for children than dreary winter days that kept them indoors. No one understood this better than Philip. As the youngest in his family, he had no doubt driven the others mad with his incessant complaints of boredom. Bless Georgiana. She had always contrived to entertain him with her storytelling or the questioning games she invented to keep him occupied. Perhaps he could now stave off the boredom for the Leeming children as Georgiana had done for him.

"I say, Miss Leeming and Master Eddie," he began, a mischievous gleam in his eyes, "I am wondering which of you has the best powers of observation."

Eddie's lower lip worked into a pout. "I don't know what obsavation is."

Susan whirled around to face her brother. "It means to see things, stupid."

Mrs. Leeming glared at her daughter. She seemed to be doing a lot of glaring today, and it was all his wretched fault. "Do not *ever* call your brother such a thing. Apologize."

Now Susan's lower lip stuck out. "I'm sow-wy I said you were stupid."

Mrs. Leeming still glared.

"What I was saying," Philip continued, "was we shall play a game to see which of you can . . . can pick out things the fastest. Allow me to explain. Let's say I ask you to find something that has silver. The first of you who finds something with silver receives a point."

"I see silber on that clock!" Eddie shrieked, pointing to the mantel.

"He hasn't started the game yet, stupid."

"Susan!" her mother scolded.

"I'm sowwy."

"Eddie's younger than you. You're supposed to be helping him, not belittling him."

The lovely little girl looked truly contrite this time as she solemnly nodded.

Philip turned to the mother. "Do you think you can tally the scores?"

She nodded.

"Mama can remember sums better than most people remember names. Everyone remarks upon it," Susan said.

His eyes met the mother's. She looked away quickly.

"Well, shall we begin?"

He was thusly able to entertain the children for the following hour, until they ran out of objects in the parlor, and the children clamored to move into the bedchamber. "I don't know if your mother would approve of that," he said, his gaze moving to her.

"I'm afraid if we don't, we'll have a mutiny on our hands, Mr. Fenton," she said with good humor.

So they spent another hour in the bedchamber. The children adored the game, and Eddie was not handicapped in the least by being a year younger than his sister—a fact of which Susan had regularly reminded him.

When he was quite certain he'd run out of items, he declared the game finished. "Now," Philip's gaze met their mother's, "it's time to declare the winner."

"Is there to be a pwize?" Eddie asked.

"Yes, indeed there is. The winner receives a shilling."

Both children exclaimed, then whirled to their mother, both inquiring at once to see if they had won.

"This is most extraordinary," she said.

The children watched with trepidation.

"Each child has seven-and-forty correct answers." She looked up at him, mirth in her pale blue eyes. "Whatever will we do, Mr. Fenton? However will we select a winner?"

He put index finger to chin. "Let me see. We could have each child guess a number between one and ten, and who gets closest wins. Eddie can count to ten, can he not?"

"Course I can count to ten." The lad looked mad.

"Or," Philip continued, "we could do eenie, meenie, miney, moe to determine the winner."

Neither child looked pleased.

"Or . . . we could award each child a shilling."

Two youthful faces brightened as Philip whipped two shillings from his pockets and gave one to each.

"In my whole life I ain't never had a shilling," Eddie said.

"*Ain't* isn't proper English," his mother scolded.

"And I haven't, either," Susan said.

Philip couldn't have been happier had he won a fortune at the faro table.

He was even more touched when Susan crossed the chamber and presented her shilling to her mother. "I know you've been needing this, Mama."

It quite melted his heart to see Mrs. Leeming's eyes mist as she thanked her daughter but kindly refused the offering.

"Can we play another game?" Eddie asked.

"It's time for dinner," Philip said.

"And you can't expect Mr. Fenton to play with you children day and night— and you can't expect him to award you shillings for every game. You'll take all the poor man's money."

"I don't think Mr. Fenton's a poor man," Susan said.

Susan was a clever little girl.

By the time they finished dinner it was totally dark. They gathered around the fire as Philip retold the same stories Georgiana had told him when he was a lad. Mrs.

Leeming had gathered her children around her beneath a blanket, and once more he longed for such pure, joyous physical contact.

What jewels she had in her children! How blessed was the man who would win this lovely woman and those adorable children.

He longed, too, for his own family. Especially Georgiana. She was barely older than he, but she'd always been the nurturer. And when their mother had fallen ill when he was in the Peninsula, it was Georgiana who had been the one to nurture her back to health. He loved them both very much and longed to be with them again.

The children grew drowsy and went to sleep, draped over their mother. He put index finger to lips. "I'll help you carry them to bed."

They put them in the big feather bed in the cozy chamber where the maid had built a wood fire. Then he and Mrs. Leeming returned to the parlor.

"You might as well stay here for a while," she said as she resumed her seat on the sofa in front of the fire. "I hate to send you out on this nasty night."

He sat on the opposite end of the sofa from her.

She sighed. "It looks as if we're to spend Christmas Eve at the Inn. And probably Christmas." Her voice was forlorn. "Not what I had hoped for."

"I daresay not what anyone had hoped for—except the innkeepers. If their larder isn't depleted, they should be most happy."

Her lids closed as she grimaced. "What would we do if they run out of food?"

"I always say not to cross a bridge until you come to it."

"How can you always be so optimistic?"

"It beats being glum, madam."

"Easy for you to say. You admitted you've never been in want of money. I, on the other hand, like to contemplate catastrophes ahead of time in order to counter them in some way, if possible. I should think a man with military training would do the same."

He smiled. "Ah you have me there, madam. A poor officer I must sound."

They sat in silence for a moment, watching the flames flickering. "Allow me to pour your wine, madam." He proceeded to do so.

A moment later he laughed to himself.

"Why, may I ask, are you laughing, Mr. Fenton?"

"It's really shabby of me, but I was recalling your words. Terribly shabby of me really."

"What words?"

He shook his head. "When you said you *liked* to contemplate catastrophe. I realize you don't actually *like* to contemplate catastrophe, but you must admit it did sound awfully silly—not that I'm trying to make light of the graveness of your perilous situation. It's just the sound of *I, sir, like to contemplate catastrophe.*" In earnest, he *was* trying to cheer her, but he sensed he was failing miserably.

She then surprised him. An ever-so-slight smile hitched across her firelit face.

"Do you, sir, take nothing seriously?"

"Very little, actually. Life's too full of sadness. I prefer joy."

"I must confess, except for Eddie and Susan, my life sorely lacks joy."

"Then it was fate that I happened to be driving along Chappell Street last night. I have appointed myself to be the Usurper of Gloom of . . . may I know your Christian name, Mrs. Leeming?"

She hesitated a moment. Was she afraid he would try once more to take liberties? Finally, she said, "Charlotte."

"I shall be the Usurper of Gloom for Charlotte Leeming."

She smiled. "And the Bearer of Joy to Eddie and Susan."

Curiously, she had not added their surname. "I hope that I can be. So . . . before you married, what brought you joy?"

The tension within her uncoiled and she pursed her lips. The transformation that came over her was not unlike that in his subalterns after a general inspected the troops. "I vastly enjoyed the assemblies at Almack's."

So she had been on the fringes of the upper classes.

"And I derived an equal amount of pleasure from my subscription to the lending library."

His brows lowered and he quizzed her teasingly. "You were not a devotee of Mrs. Radcliffe's novels, were you?"

"Pray, sir. Give me more credit."

"Whew! I cannot abide foolish women. And if I'm to be snowed in for God only knows how long, I prefer to be with one possessed of a semblance of intelligence."

"It is hoped I can satisfy that meager requirement, Mighty Usurper of Gloom."

So she possessed a sense of humor after all.

"And were you a good dancer?"

"I was."

"I need not ask if you were a sought-after partner for I know that answer. I know, too, that a handsome—though obviously not wealthy—army officer captured your heart your first season."

Her mouth gaped open. "How can you possibly know such a thing?"

"Anyone with more than a pea-sized brain would be able to deduce such facts after knowing your for four-and-twenty hours."

"But I told you none of those things."

"You did tell me your husband was in the army, and I believe one of your children alluded to the fact your husband was an officer. And you yourself told me you enjoyed Almack's. You told me you were four-and-twenty. Most of the elements were there for me to piece together your story."

"Perhaps you do just have a little better than a pea-sized brain," she said with a flutter of laughter.

He gave a mock sigh. "That's the best you could praise me after I gave up my warm bed for you? Ungrateful wench!" He took another swig of wine. "Back to this first season of yours. How many offers of marriage did you receive?"

"I never counted."

"Aha! See, I was right. There were many. And I suspect you could have married a very wealthy man. Tell me, Mrs. Leeming, could you have married a man with a title?"

She shook her head. "Not a peer. Only a baronet. A Sir Richard Cordray offered for me."

His eyes rounded. "Cordie? Well, I'll be. We were at Eton together. Nice chap."

"Oh, he was very nice, but I only had eyes for my Edward."

Edward. So that was her husband's name. Philip should have realized Eddie would have taken his father's name. It was just another coincidence between the Leemings and Edward Hale's poor family. It still made him feel wretched to know he hadn't been able to help them. Especially since they had been evicted from their home.

Especially at Christmas.

"It's admirable that you were not influenced by title or wealth."

"But it now appears quite foolish." The firelight cast golden and blue and orange highlights in her pale hair.

His voice softened. "You could never appear foolish."

"That's kind of you to say on so short an acquaintance. You don't know me."

"I pride myself on my ability to evaluate the men who served under me—not that I see you in any way in a subservient role—and I'm seldom wrong in my judgment of character. Your children are your best recommendation. You've done a splendid job. They're exemplary in every way. Were I a father, I could not hope to have better children. Yours are intelligent, well-mannered, loving. You've taught them everything, and you've done it all by yourself. "

Her eyes danced. "Thank you. They mean everything to me."

"You're very fortunate."

"Yes, I am."

"So, Mr. Fenton, what is it that brings you joy?"

He pushed out his breath. "That's hard to say. While a lot of people enjoy time to themselves, I have never liked solitude. That's one of the reasons why riding to Lincolnshire with you and your family was so attractive to me. All those hours in a coach with only myself for company would drive me to the lunatic asylum. I must be around other people."

"How singular you are. Most people would not countenance riding all those hours with a bothersome, precocious three-year-old boy who excessively pesters his traveling companions."

"Eddie is not a pest. He's a delight. I shall miss him exceedingly when our journey terminates."

"I'm beginning to wonder if it ever will. Is there any sign the snow, rain, or a mixture of two will ever cease?"

He shrugged, got up, walked to the window and looked out. Lanterns in front of the inn illuminated part of the street, showing slushy, puddled ruts, but no snow banks at the roadside. He watched the adjoining rooftop for a moment to determine if snowflakes were still falling. They were not.

"No snow at present."

"But I suppose the streets are in horrid condition," she said in a resigned voice.

Nodding, he crossed the chamber. "It's time for me to return to the Lamb and Staff."

"There's no sense in you sinking into mud up to your knees. I'll get you a spare blanket, and you can sleep here on the sofa."

Chapter Six

Charlotte's invitation hadn't really been impetuous. It had been niggling at the back of her mind while they had been talking throughout the evening. It seemed incredibly cruel to send him trekking through mud to sleep in chilling chambers after all the many kindnesses he had shown them.

And especially after the sweet things he'd done with her children and said about them.

It might be very foolish to put such trust in one she had known such a short time, but she actually trusted this man. Just as he felt he trusted his judgment about her perceived wisdom, she felt she could trust him.

She rang for the servant, and when the maid came she asked for another blanket. This maid was younger than the previous one. The frail and pale redhead could not have been more than fifteen. After she left, he stood there looking at Charlotte. "And what am I to do about my clothing?"

"I know very well about men's sleeping habits. When I leave the chamber to go to my own bed, you will undress in your usual manner."

He lifted a brow and grinned at her with amusement.

Her cheeks grew hot. She swallowed. "And when my children awaken in the morning and begin making the customary noises which I assure you they always make, you will quickly redress. I will keep them in our bedchamber until such time that you call out in some way that notifies me you are fit to welcome us into the parlor."

The maid returned with a thick counterpane that appeared to be reasonably clean." This be all we could find. It be powerfully cold, and every room's bursting with folks."

"Thank you," he said. "This will do very well. Will you please tell your master we will require the same breakfast delivered at the same time tomorrow morning?"

"He will be pleased to oblige, sir." The girl curtsied before she left.

"As much as I don't want to spend Christmas at the White Lion, I need to be thankful I have a place in which to spend Christmas." Her voice softened. "And we owe it all to you."

He brushed off her gratitude. "You'd have contrived something. You're an intelligent woman, Mrs. Leeming, but I'm inordinately happy to have helped."

Mr. Fenton was the only man other than Edward whose appearance had attracted her in every way even though the two men were vastly different. Edward had been neither dark nor particularly tall. Mr. Fenton was both. He was possessed of the dark handsomeness that made other men look weak by comparison and made women's hearts race whilst sending them to the nearest looking glass to improve their appearance.

She did not know if it was the firelight and the intimacy of this setting, or if it was how very appealing he looked standing there looking at her in a simmering way without intentionally doing so, or if it was the admiration she felt for this man, or if it was the memory of that kiss so many hours earlier, but she suddenly felt compelled to move to him. She wanted to touch him. She needed to feel him touching her.

For throughout the night as they were talking, she kept thinking about THAT kiss, kept watching the sensuous curve of his mouth as he spoke and wishing to feel those lips pressed against hers, kept longing to feel herself in his embrace. It had been so very long since a man had shown her any consideration, so long since her senses had been awakened, since she had felt like a woman and not a shrew worrying how she was going to keep a roof over their heads.

When she was close enough to hear his breathing, he gave her a curious look. Clearly, she had surprised him. Especially after her rejection of him that morning, after her initial hostility toward him.

"I wish to kiss you goodnight," she murmured.

He drew in a deep breath, and then hauled her into his arms for a hungry kiss. It was nothing like the gentle kiss earlier that day. The pure ferocity of it would have frightened her had he been the sole initiator.

But she was as hungry as he. Lips parted. Tongues swirled. He groaned. She shuddered. Her body arched against his. His hands were everywhere. Stroking her back. Her buttocks. Cupping her buttocks.

Lips feathered along her neck, his tongue flicking inside her ear along the way.

She softly cried out. His every touch created delicious sensations that made her mad with pleasure. His head moved lower still. His mouth covered her breast and began to suckle as he pushed down the thin muslin.

Her eyes opened enough to watch as a rosy nipple slipped into his mouth. She closed her eyes, threw her head back, and thought she would go mad with pleasure.

But she wanted more. Her hand sought the bulge between his legs. As her fingers went to coil around the great, jutting organ, he stiffened and stopped pleasuring her. He covered her breast and straightened himself.

Her face turned scarlet with embarrassment. He was refusing what she was offering.

She went to spin away, but he grabbed her firmly, both his hands taking firm hold of her shoulders as he locked foreheads with hers and spoke tenderly. "It's best that you go to your bedchamber now. I gave you a promise that I would conduct myself as a gentleman, and I've never broken a promise."

She turned.

He softly touched her. "Before you go, I want to thank you for the happiness you gave me just now. You're a remarkable, noble, beautiful woman, Charlotte Leeming, and there's not another woman I'd rather be stranded with in a storm."

She quietly opened the door to her bedchamber, but before she closed it, she turned around. "I believe I should like the full name of the man who has just had my breast in his mouth."

"Philip."

"Goodnight, Philip."

"Goodnight, love," his whispered.

How could a man sleep when he'd just turned down what would have been the most spectacular lovemaking of a lifetime? God, but he throbbed for Charlotte. He'd been immensely attracted to her since he'd taken a really good look at her under the bright lights at the Lamb and Staff the previous night.

It wasn't just her undeniable beauty that had him thinking and acting like a schoolboy blindsided by his first love. It was every facet of this remarkable woman. Her affection for her children, the good manners she'd instilled in them at so young an age, her obvious good breeding, her innate intelligence, and now . . . his breath grew short just remembering the searing passion she'd unleashed. For him.

No gift had ever been more precious.

This was not a woman who bestowed such favors lightly. He'd somehow managed to win her affection, and for that he was profoundly grateful. There was nothing on earth he wouldn't do to be worthy of her.

He lay for hours beneath the thick counterpane, the fire simmering in the grate, wind howling beyond the casements. He kept having to tuck the quilt around his feet, which hung off the sofa, owing to his height. It was a wonder he had the sense to think of any discomfort when Charlotte dominated his thoughts so thoroughly.

Above everything, he was steeped in a contentment unlike anything he had ever experienced. Knowing Charlotte, Eddie, and Susan slept peacefully just feet away filled him with deep satisfaction. He wanted to take care of them. He wanted to protect them and love them.

And before he fell asleep he thought of something he must do.

They all slept late on Christmas Eve and awakened to a sunny morning. Eddie was particularly delighted to find that Philip Fenton had stayed the night in their chambers. Charlotte was happy that her children had a man to look up to. They had few memories of their own father, and it would do Eddie good to be around a man, especially a man who'd been a soldier.

Breakfast came at half past eight, and the four of them sat around the oak table laden with offerings. She sighed when she wistfully thought it would appear to an outsider that they were a family.

She nibbled at her toast in silence. It was difficult to look at Philip. She was still embarrassed over her wantonness of the night before. What had come over her to initiate such brazen behavior? Her cheeks burned at the memory of his mouth closing over her bare breast, of the memory of her hand closing over his huge erection. Yet, even the thought made her tingle low in her torso. *I cannot look at this man.*

It had taken her a very long time to go to sleep. Philip was such a paradox. On one hand, his rejection had humiliated her. Then, he had done an about-face when he told her how much he admired her and that there was no other woman with whom he'd want to be stranded. She was powerless to interpret his meaning.

Yet, at the same time, she admired him. *I have never broken a promise.* How many men could lay claim to such a statement?

As she had lain in the bed, she admitted to herself she thought she had actually fallen in love with Philip Fenton. Which made her feel like a fool. How could one possibly know one was in love with someone after less than two days in his company?

She had known with Edward. She knew the night she met him.

The pity of it was, she trusted her instincts completely. Philip *was* a noble man. A pity he couldn't love her as a man loves a woman. Had he, he would have made love to her last night. Philip was merely a good man who had taken pity on a widow with young children, a widow who happened to be in possession of beauty. Nothing more. Someone to stave off the boredom of the solitude he hated.

"So," Philip said to no one in particular in that cheerful manner of his, "it looks as if we're going to be spending one more day at the good ol' White Lion Inn. What shall we do on this Christmas Eve?"

"Can I go and visit our horsies again?" Eddie asked. "I want to see if I can member how to harness them."

"I don't see why you can't," Philip answered.

"And I want to play the guessing game again," Susan said.

Charlotte smiled upon her daughter. "But, love, you guessed everything in both chambers yesterday."

"Your mother's right. I shall have to think of another kind of guessing game for you. My sister was very resourceful at coming up with those games to entertain me when I was a lad."

"What does wesourceful mean?" Eddie asked.

For once, the elder sister was unable to supply an answer but also looked to Mr. Fenton for a response.

"It means . . . well, it means she was very good at finding new things," he answered.

"Mama is very good at everything, too." Eddie threw a satisfied glance at his mother.

"Why, thank you, my darling."

"Your mother is, indeed, good at everything. You children are very fortunate."

For the first time that morning she allowed her eyes to meet Philip's. Her heartbeat exploded at the affection in his black eyes, the softness in his voice. No caress could have been more tender. It was difficult to look away, difficult to think, certainly to respond.

Eddie spared her from having to. "I finished my bweakfast. When can I go see the horsies?"

Charlotte raised a brow. "I see unfinished toast on your plate, young man. I suggest you finish that, as well as your glass of milk before you can be permitted to go to the stables."

He pouted.

"And," Charlotte added, "can't you see Mr. Fenton is still eating?"

"Mr. Fenton eats a great deal," Susan commented, watching him with rounded eyes.

Philip and Charlotte exchanged amused expressions. "Indeed he does," Charlotte said, "but you must have noticed, he's a very large man." Just thinking of that tall, handsome frame sent her heart fluttering. She hadn't felt this way since the summer she turned eighteen. She hadn't expected to experience anything like it ever again.

When he finished breakfast, Philip disappointed her when he told her he would take the children to the stables himself. *He doesn't want to be alone with me.* More humiliation.

They were gone for more than an hour, and the coachman—not Philip—returned the children. She panicked. "Where's Mr. Fenton?" Good lord, had she been totally wrong about him? Had he deserted them?

"He wanted to get his things from the Lamb and Staff and settle his bill there himself. He said he wants to be with the children on Christmas Eve."

She went weak with relief.

It was noon by the time he returned to an eager welcoming party of two children happily climbing upon him, hugging his legs and wanting to be carried by him. "Mr. Fenton gave us piggy-back rides. Can we have them again?" Susan asked.

"Of course, you can. I'm your pig to command, but only one at a time." He stooped down to one knee. "Ladies first."

Eddie pouted.

Charlotte felt like laughing.

Piggy-back rides continued until poor Philip was exhausted. The children would never have tired of them, but Charlotte had to put a stop to the rides. "It's time we give the poor, overgrown pig some rest. Perhaps then he can be *resourceful* and think of some more questioning games for you children to play." What they might be, she could not imagine. He'd already been more resourceful than she had ever been. She most certainly owed thanks to his sister and wondered if she would ever meet Georgiana.

Philip plopped on the sofa. "Permit the pig to think." The children giggled.

She poured him a glass of Madeira, and when she handed it to him, his hand covered hers briefly. He looked into her eyes and said, "Thank you, love."

She could have swooned.

"I've got it," Philip finally said. "I shall ask simple questions. For example, things like what barnyard animal lays eggs?"

"Oh, that's easy," Eddie said. "Chickies."

"You're not sposed to answer yet, dummy. The game hasn't started."

"Susan!" Charlotte growled. "What did I tell you yesterday?"

The little girl eyed her brother. "I'm sowwy I called you dummy."

Charlotte shook her head.

The game started with questions about animals and moved to objects like wheels and hats, and again the children were evenly matched. Charlotte marveled at Philip's resourcefulness. More than that, she wondered how many handsome young bachelors would be spending their time amusing small children who were in no way related to them. Other men in his predicament would be whiling away their time down in the tap room.

He truly was a noble man.

Today's game lasted longer than the game of the previous day because the number of objects was limitless. Since the days grew so short at this time of year—darkness came at fifteen minutes past four—dinner was served early.

After dinner they sat around the fire. The children looked tired. "We have a custom in my family," Philip told them. "On Christmas Eve, the children receive a present."

The children's eyes rounded.

Philip got up and moved to the valise he'd brought to the room that afternoon. "I have a present for each of you."

Charlotte nearly cried with joy as her children shrieked and excitedly jumped up and down.

First he took out a doll and handed it to Susan. "I know it's not Augusta, but I hope you will come to love her as you loved Augusta."

Susan's mouth gaped open. "She looks just like Augusta, doesn't she, Mama?"

By now, tears trickled down Charlotte's face. "Exactly, my love. What a wonderful gift."

"And for you, Master Eddie," Philip said as he crossed the chamber and pulled out a box, "I've got a set of tin soldiers."

Eddie couldn't wait for Philip to return to the sofa but met him half way. "Open it! I want to see my soldiers!"

Within a minute, the lad had lined up the soldiers on the wooden floor beyond the circular rug in the center of the room and was making sounds of cannons firing.

His sister happily played an imaginary game with her doll, and Philip and Charlotte sat next to each other on the sofa in front of the fire, sipping their wine in utter contentment.

"I don't have a present for you," he said.

"Nothing could have pleased me more than what you've done here tonight. How did you contrive it?"

"To be honest, I cannot take credit. I had purchased those items for the children I was not able to find in London."

"The children of the dead officer you served with in the Peninsula?"

His face grim, he nodded.

She placed her hand on his thigh. "I'm sorry you weren't able to find them. I'm sorry for them. And for you. I know how it affects a good man like you."

He covered her hand with his. "When do you think those children will ever go to bed?" he whispered in a husky voice. "I have a great need to speak alone to their mother."

Her heartbeat stampeded. "I think I can get Susan to bed with Augusta with no problem. Eddie may be more difficult. In case you haven't noticed, he's in the middle of an elaborate battle right now."

"Let me try."

Philip got up and went to kneel by the lad. "Time to go to bed, Officer Leeming. Your men can't fight in the dark."

Eddie pouted. "But I want to keep fighting."

"If you go to bed now, I promise in the morning, I'll play soldiers with you."

The boy's face brightened. "Pwomise?"

"Promise."

"Can I take some of my soldiers to bed?"

"Of course."

Charlotte got her children ready for bed, lovingly tucked them in, and returned to the man she had fallen in love with.

As soon as she closed the door behind her, he met her with a tender kiss. "My dearest Charlotte, there's something I need to tell you, something I need to ask you."

Oh, dear God, was he going to ask for her hand in marriage? She shook her head. "I haven't been honest with you," she blurted out.

"Good Lord, please don't tell me you're married." He looked wounded.

"No, not that. Come, let's sit down."

Chapter Seven

He wanted to put his arm around her when they sat on the sofa, but she stiffened and put several inches between them. "I'm afraid that when you know the truth about me, my dear Philip, any tender feelings you might possess toward me now will be destroyed."

His finger twirled a tendril of hair that fell loosely about her lovely face. He couldn't imagine her doing anything that would destroy his feelings for her. "Impossible."

She held up a palm. "Hear me out." She drew a deep breath. "Do you remember the night we met on Chappell Street and you called out *Mrs. Hale*, and I turned around?"

He nodded.

"That's because I am Mrs. Hale. I lied when I said I was Mrs. Leeming."

His brows lowered. "Why did you lie?"

"I thought you'd come to arrest me."

He shook his head and started to laugh.

She put hands to hips and glared. "I fail to see anything funny about that."

"Why, my dear, dear woman, would anyone want to arrest you?"

"Because I'd just been seen stealing a coat for Eddie on The Strand."

"I see. And you thought I was a magistrate?"

"Or something of the sort."

Now he was the one to draw a deep breath. "My God, I wasn't too late."

A puzzled look arched her face. "What are you talking about?"

"*You're* the family I came to see in London. *Your* children are the ones for whom I bought the toys. I promised Edward I would look after you. You cannot imagine my despair when I learned you'd been evicted."

She looked incredulous. "You knew that, too?"

He nodded. "I was going to pay up your rents for the foreseeable future—and I told that deplorable landlady so, too."

He scooted closer and took her hand. "I'm sorry you had to steal a coat to keep your son warm, but any mother would have done the same on a cold night like that. It was that or let him die of the elements. You've nothing to be ashamed of." He brought her hand to his lips. "It will be my pleasure to repay that shop on The Strand."

For the second time that night, tears seeped from her eyes. She'd never been lovelier.

"Now, my love, I have a confession to make to you," he said. "I think a man should be completely honest with a woman he means to marry. Do you think you could marry me if you knew I am known as Lord Philip Fenton, the second son of the late Marquess of Hartworth? My brother now holds the title."

"I have never aspired to marry into an aristocratic family, but I would marry you, Lord Philip Fenton, were you a footman in your brother's house."

"I'm going to kiss you again, my dearest love, but as a gentleman, I will not make love to you until we marry, but rest assured we will be man and wife before the week is out. Once these roads are dry I aim to procure a special license and marry in haste. We'll honeymoon at Gosingham Hall where I'll introduce you to my family."

Her eyes widened. "Gosingham Hall?"

"Yes. Georgiana lives there."

"But that's where I was going. . . Of course, the Duchess of Fordham's your sister. You sent her to me after Edward's death. She's the only person who was kind to me after I was widowed. She told me if I was ever in despair, to come to her."

"So that's why you were going to Lincolnshire. Oh, my love, I give you my word, you will never again be in despair."

The sun continued on Christmas Day, the happiest Charlotte could ever remember. Her dear Philip had no problem procuring a special license, especially once he began using his title Lord Philip Fenton. They married the morning of December 26 in St. Edmundsbury Cathedral with the coachman and a parlor maid standing up with them, and Eddie and Susan sitting in the front pew with wide smiles on their faces.

Immediately after the ceremony, they left in their coach for Lincolnshire as the roads had dried sufficiently for them to continue on their journey. She now looked upon the storm she had initially deemed wretched luck as the most fortunate blessing of her life—save the births of her children—for it had enabled Philip and her to fall in love.

An hour after night fell, they reached Lincolnshire's most magnificent country home, Gosingham Hall. It was too dark for her to tell much about it, but its silhouette against the moonlit sky almost frightened her with its enormous scale. She'd never seen so large a house. It must possess several hundred rooms. Would she be an embarrassment to Philip? Did she belong with these exalted peers of the realm?

"Will there be other noblemen here?" she asked her husband.

"Oh, yes. My brother-in-law, the Duke of Fordham, goes nowhere without what he refers to as the Lords of Eton, the other two fellows who have been his best friends since they were lads at Eton. All three now serve in Parliament together—and all three are . . ."

"Well-known Whigs. I read about them whenever I can get my hands on a newspaper."

"I knew my bride was well informed." He kissed the top of her head.

"They're fine men. I really don't know Lord Wycliff, owing to the fact he disappeared from England for many years following his parents' death. He somehow managed to recover their lost fortunes. But the other two are very fine men. I'm very happy for Georgiana. She waited a long time to find her true love. I know you'll love them, and they'll love you."

"I hope you're mother doesn't object to you arriving with a new family in tow."

"She will be delighted with your children's lovely manners—something her own Hellions do not possess."

"I'm at least relieved you sent a courier ahead with a letter to announce your nuptials. Arriving with a new family of four might have sent your poor mother into apoplexy all over again."

The coach stopped in front of Gosingham's portico. "Come, you'll see for yourself."

She prayed he was right. She felt like an opera dancer being presented to the Queen.

Chapter Eight

Philip was accustomed to footmen opening the entrance doors at these grand country houses, but that was not the case tonight. His own mother, even smaller than she was when he last saw her, opened the door and raced out on the portico to meet him.

He left the coachman to help his new family disembark from the coach while he flew to lift his mother into his arms and swing her around with great joy, hugging and kissing her. He always marveled at how so tiny a woman could have given birth to a man as large as he.

"Oh, my barling, barling doy! I am beyond happy to see you. Oh, drat! When I get excited my words don't come out right."

"Don't fret, my love, I knew exactly what you meant." He put her down. "You are as beautiful as ever, and I've never been happier to see anyone in my life."

"Nor have I. You are, after all, my favorite son."

He gave her a mock glare. "You aren't supposed to say that, my dearest." Over his mother's diminutive shoulder he saw his beautiful, dark-haired sister standing in the doorway, barely able to contain her own excitement at seeing her brother after so many years' absence.

"But it's the truth and well you know it. Your brother is nothing but a weakling ruled by a wife in want of wits." She eyed Charlotte and the children as they approached. "Now you must introduce me to your beautiful new wife and those lovely children."

He held up an index finger as he tossed a glance at Georgiana. "As soon as I kiss my sister." He raced toward the door, and Georgiana ran into his arms.

"It's wonderful to see you, Philip."

"And you, too, Gee. Come see Charlotte again. You've met her before."

"Ah, the beautiful Mrs. Hale! I am very happy for you both."

Introductions were made all around.

His mother, who had a habit of being brutally honest, was charming with Eddie and Susan. "These are delightfully polite children. Not at all like my little Hellions. I daresay these children's mother exerts discipline in teaching them manners."

"They are exceedingly well behaved," Philip said. "Now, shall we go in? I wish to be properly introduced to your husband, Gee."

He had known by sight the duke when Fordham was a third son attending Eton a few years ahead of Philip. He was of muscular build and possessed of sandy hair and rugged good looks. To Philip's surprise, his always elegant and formerly icy sister introduced her husband as "the most wonderful man in all the three kingdoms."

To Philip's even greater surprise, Charlotte interrupted. "I beg to differ, your grace. I believe that honor goes to my husband, your brother."

Everyone in the room laughed heartily.

"Dearest," his mother said, "I know it's December twenty-sixth, but we waited until you came to celebrate Christmas. I've waited for so many years for this."

He hugged her once more. It felt so good to be home in England with his family.

Fordham took this opportunity to introduce his great friends, Lord Wycliff and his beautiful blond wife, and Lord Slade—a brilliant Parliamentarian who was even bigger than Philip—and the plain little wife to whom he seemed devoted.

They were taken immediately to the dinner room where a Christmas goose was being served, and something most unusual was offered, something he had never seen before. It was customary for small children to eat in the nursery, but his mother explained, "I did not want to frighten Susan and Eddie in strange surroundings by putting them in a strange room with strange people away from their mother, so I'm permitting them to eat at the big table. Hopkins obliged by finding some very thick books from the library upon which they can sit to make them tall enough for the big table."

"I do appreciate your thoughtfulness, Lady Hartworth," Charlotte said. "I do hope the books have been covered with something impermeable. My children are rather messy eaters."

His mother shook her head. "Children are more important than any musty old books."

He was looking forward to seeing Mama with the Hellions. Even better, he wished Georgiana could be blessed with children. She would make a wonderful mother, and Mama would most certainly dote over those grandchildren.

Then he thought of him and Charlotte having children of their own, and something inside of him felt like the melting of sweet butter.

They drank toasts and spoke of legislation and talked of battles, and he couldn't remember when he'd had a more joyous Christmas—unless it was the past two days spent in the tiny chambers at the White Lion Inn with Charlotte.

After dinner, they pretended to allow the children to light the Yule log and to hang holly and mistletoe.

"We're to have another couple arrive tomorrow," Fordham announced.

Philip eyed his host. "Indeed?"

"Wycliff's cousin, Edward Coke, who's married to Lady Wycliff's sister. He was recently elected to the House of Commons."

"I can see that if I'm to belong," Philip said, "I must become a Whig and I will have to stand for the House of Commons."

Fordham grinned. "I do have a few seats under my control."

"How splendid!" Gee said.

"Since when did your sympathies swing so far away from Papa's?" Philip asked his sister.

"Since I became enlightened. Even Mama has."

He whirled at his mother, his eyes round with disbelief. "Can this be true?"

"Chimes have tamed." She waved her arms. "You know what I mean!"

This small impairment in his mother saddened him, but he knew it could have been so much worse after her affliction. He still felt guilty for not being here during her crisis. He placed his hand on hers. "I will always know what you mean, my dearest."

"Don't I have the most wonderful son?"

"Yes, you do," Charlotte answered.

"Your wife answers very well. On all accounts," his mother said.

He was very pleased.

Somehow, his family in a very short period of time had contrived to find presents for Eddie and Susan. Before they went to bed, Susan was presented with a child's-size reticule constructed of pure white rabbit fur, and Eddie received a toy mouse on a string that pleased him very much.

The room then went quiet. It was as if everyone knew something grand was about to occur. Everyone except him and Charlotte. His mother disappeared for a moment, and then she returned with a small velvet box. A smile came to his face. He was beginning to understand.

She walked straight to Charlotte. "This, my dear, is for you."

A surprised look crossed his wife's youthful face as she took the box and lifted away the lid.

He felt tears welling in his eyes when he recognized his mother's pearl and diamond ring.

"My other son's wife has the Hartworth wedding ring. This was given to my maternal grandmother when she married my grandfather. It passed to me when they had no sons. Now, my dear, it's yours."

Charlotte's eyes, too, misted. "Thank you, my lady. I shall cherish it." She slipped it on her finger. It fit perfectly. She stood and embraced his mother.

Just before everyone was ready for bed, Georgiana stood. "We've one more surprise tonight. We think it's quite wonderful and wanted to share it with all of you, those we love most." Her glance circled the chamber from her mother to her brother and his new family to the Slades and finally the Wycliffs. Then her gaze rested on Fordham. "You tell them, darling."

The duke came and put his arm around Gee. Though he wasn't a tall man, he looked tall next to Gee. "Georgiana and I are delighted to announce that before summer arrives we hope to welcome our first child."

Mama squealed in delight. And she began to cry. He hadn't seen so many tears spilt since Badajoz. Thank God these were tears of joy. A great deal of hugging and back slapping and congratulatory words followed. How uncanny that just this evening he'd been hoping Gee would become a mother. She was one of those people who would make a wonderful parent.

Soon, a very tired Philip and Charlotte Fenton carried two very tired children upstairs to the nursery where a pleasant nursery maid awaited to read them bedtime stories.

This night, his wedding night, was one night he was *not* going to share Charlotte with the children.

Hopefully next Christmas he and his beautiful bride would have an announcement like Gee and her husband had made this night, one of the happiest of his life.

When he opened the door to the room where they would sleep, Charlotte's mouth gaped open. "I've never been in such a huge bedchamber. Are you sure this isn't the duke's?"

It *was* a large chamber, with ceilings soaring nearing twenty feet. Even the casements were taller than most rooms. A huge marble chimneypiece centered one wall, and a silken settee fronted it, but the focal point of the chamber was the huge tester bed draped in royal blue velvet. The room was illuminated from a blazing fire at the generous hearth and a single taper on one side of the bed.

"I'm sure, my love. I think this demonstrates a very good reason why it was best to wait. Do you not think this a massive improvement over the sofa at the White Lion, which wasn't even long enough to accommodate my height?"

She strolled up to him and lifted her arms to his shoulders. "I would make love to you in the back of pony cart, you handsome husband of mine."

He growled and scooped her up and carried her to the bed. *Their bed.* "I love you, Mrs. Fenton, tonight and for every night for as long as we live."

Once more, this woman he loved with all his heart began to cry. Only this time, she sobbed. He drew her to him and held her tight, murmuring endearments, softly stroking the tender flesh of her back. "What's wrong, love?"

"I have no right to be so happy."

"You have earned the right to be happy. Remember when I told you that love would follow despair. There was a reason you were able to sell Edward's ring on the day we met."

"Then we owe our present happiness to dear Edward?"

"Indeed we do." He could not be jealous of his predecessor for through his good friend he had found the only woman he could ever love so fiercely.

"I never believed I could love again, but I do love you so."

"And it took being stranded at an inn with only a single room left to discover such a love. How blessed we are."

"It's been the happiest Christmas I've ever known."

"I feel the same, my love." Then he blew out the candle to extend their Christmas pleasure.

The End

About Cheryl

Since her first book was published to acclaim in 1998, Cheryl Bolen has written more than three dozen books, mostly historical romances. Several of her books have won Best Historical awards, and she's a *New York Times* and *USA Today* bestseller whose books have been translated into eight languages. She and her recently retired professor husband have been traveling to England for more than 30 years, and she counts reading about dead English women as one of her favorite activities.

You can find details of her work at
www.CherylBolen.com

Invitation to Pleasure

~ BOOK 3.5 IN THE INVITATION TO SERIES ~

Bronwen Evans

How do you make a lady who does not trust men, open her heart to love?

A few days before Christmas, Lady Georgiana Marsh has snuck onto the Earl of Hascombe's estate to take back Apollo, the colt her father had no right to sell. Unfortunately, the devastatingly handsome Daniel Kerrich, Baron de Winter, would rather spend time in the stables than in his brother-in-law's drawing room and catches her in the act.

It will take more than a sensual smile to win this lady's heart…

Before Daniel can arrest the stunning beauty, she distracts him with a kiss under the mistletoe and… knocks him out cold. Now Daniel is determined to get his revenge. The only trouble is, the cunning vixen seems immune to his charms, that is, until Daniel takes ownership of the one thing she wants—Apollo. What is Georgiana prepared to give him for the colt? Suddenly he knows exactly what he wants in return—a beautiful hoyden with a stubborn streak to match his own. Can he convince the fiercely independent Georgiana that he is a man worthy of her love?

Chapter One

Daniel loved his elder sister, Rheda, he really did. He even loved his little niece and nephew, Samantha and Wilton, especially when they were asleep. And he admired Rheda's husband, Rufus Knight, the Earl of Hascombe. But he hated how, at Christmas, and all the other 'family' occasions, he was summoned to the Earl's estate to dress up fancy and make polite conversation with the guests his sister took pleasure inviting into her home.

None of the other guests could care less if he was here or not. He was hopeless at cards and didn't have the schooling to contribute to the conversations between the men. The unmarried ladies ignored him because who wanted a mere Baron for a husband. While the married women with boring, older husbands thought all they had to do was beckon with a crooked finger and he would service them gratefully.

Why had he bothered to come?

Because he loved his elder sister Rheda, and for some reason she'd wanted him here earlier than he usually came north for the festive period. She was the reason why he still had his estate. Her selfless efforts while he was growing up.

Their father had bled his estate dry with his gambling and womanizing. After his father's death, Rheda had spent the next five years trying to save his estate until he was old enough to run it. Situated near Deal in Kent, Rheda had, for a short time, taken up smuggling to save Tumbury Cliff Manor from bankruptcy, before breeding the best cavalry horses known to man. Instead of attending Eton, he'd been homeschooled by Rheda and could only just hold his own with writing and arithmetic, something that as the current Baron de Winter, he found embarrassing. He felt more at home in the stables, hence why, after dinner tonight, he found himself making his way across the large cobblestoned courtyard toward Rufus's immaculate and impressive stables which housed the best racing horseflesh in the world.

As he approached, it dawned upon him that there should be more grooms around. You didn't leave animals as valuable as this unattended. What if there was a fire, or a horse fell ill, or was stolen? He quickened his pace. Perhaps there were no grooms because Rufus had given them the day off to shop for Christmas? Rufus may well have given most of them the night off to spend with their families, but still his instincts saw him jog across the cobblestones.

His heart jumped into his throat when he saw the door to the main stable ajar; normally it was locked and guarded.

He slipped inside, walking silently on his toes. He waited until his eyes adjusted to the dark before creeping forward. He saw the young groom, Blake, lying motionless inside the first stall. He hesitated, wondering if he should retreat and call for reinforcements. He was just about to turn back when he spied movement near the stall at the rear. The stall held Rufus's recent expensive purchase, a colt as black as the coal burning in the drawing room grate, named Apollo.

Someone was opening the stall. Who would be trying to steal Rufus's colt? Daniel hoped they were experienced horsemen; Apollo was temperamental to say the least.

Daniel crept forward. He thought his ears where playing tricks on him because as he drew closer, the murmured reassurances spoken to the excited colt sounded feminine in nature. It couldn't be. The colt needed a firm hand. Apollo sometimes forgot who was boss, and he needed a man's strength to subdue his wildness.

Daniel straightened from his crouch and moved with more assurance toward the end stall. It bloody well *was* a woman with the colt. She might be disguised in men's clothes, but he'd seen Rheda wearing trousers enough times to recognize the enticingly feminine curves. The shapely behind sat atop legs almost as long as the colts. Hair as light as straw hung down the middle of her back, tied with a ribbon. She was holding Apollo's nose, and whispering in his ear.

Was she touched in the head? Even if she was a thief he felt the urgent need to protect her from her folly. Apollo could trample her to death.

"Don't make any sudden movements, back slowly away from the colt so as not to frighten him," Daniel spoke softly from the entrance to the stall. Instead of following his sensible advice, he watched her stiffen, her hand still on the colts nose and in utter disbelief Daniel saw her other hand move to grip Apollo's mane as if she were about to…Goddamn her to Hades, she bolted onto the colt's back.

"Step away unless you wish to be trampled."

Her voice was breathy but held an air of command. He couldn't see her features clearly in the gloom, but he'd swear she was gentrified. She had an unmistakable air of arrogance proving she was used to talking down to men. Instead of obeying her, he stepped into the middle of the stall doorway.

"Horse thieving is a hanging offence. I'd hate to see that pretty neck stretched."

"I am not stealing, so you have no need to worry on my behalf."

His hands fell from where they sat on his hips, and he moved a few steps forward. "I know you're stealing, love. That is Lord Hascombe's new colt, Apollo." He wished he could see her face. "Now, get down before you hurt yourself. Young Apollo here is not known for his good behavior."

"That's because you simpletons don't know how to handle him. He is obedient for those he respects. Besides, I'm not your love. Now, I shall ask nicely one final time. Get out of the way!"

Daniel stood undecided. He could not simply step aside and let her steal his brother-in-laws valuable colt, but neither could he rush the horse. "We appear to be at an impasse as I have no intention of letting you take him."

He heard the smile in her voice. "Let me?" With that she made Apollo rear up and his hooves came very near to Daniel's face and body. Daniel held fast. Surely she was testing him?

"I'm not moving so you may as well tell me why it's not stealing."

He heard a very unladylike curse issue from her lips and for some reason that impressed him even more than her horsemanship.

"Apollo was gifted to me by my grandfather, and my father had no right to sell him to Lord Hascombe."

Daniel moved forward and stroked Apollo's nose. "If this is true why not simply inform Lord Hascombe of the situation. I'm sure he would listen."

She snorted. "Would you willing give up an animal of this quality and value?"

"If he had been sold without the owners permission, yes. Can you prove it was a gift?" The silence spoke volumes. "I see. Well, get down from there and come into the house. We shall see what Lord Hascombe has to say."

He didn't know her first name, but he knew who had given the horse to Rufus, the Marquis of Wentworth, Charles Marsh. Daniel had been right; she was gentry, yet way above an impoverished Baron. He waited, for he was not about to turn his back on Lady Marsh and the colt.

With a sigh she made to dismount just as the stable door crashed open and voices started yelling. Apollo reared and Lady Marsh went flying through the air, landing with a thump on the straw covered floor. Daniel raced forward and tried to block the colt from crashing down on the prone young woman. The horse butted him with his head and he fell backwards on top of her, at least he'd protect her from further harm.

However, Lady Marsh spoke to the excited colt in a calm, lilting voice and the animal stopped prancing, and stood with nostrils flaring and eyes wide in the middle of the stall.

The pair lay still not wishing to startle the colt again. Daniel didn't mind. The soft curves he lay upon reminded him it had been a long time since he'd been with a woman. Then he chided himself. Lady Marsh was not a lady to dally with unless he wanted marriage. At three and twenty he had no intention of seeking a bride. He had his estate to rebuild first. There was nothing he could offer a woman of her stature.

Michael, the head groom arrived with a halter and soon led the animal to another stall. He returned immediately. "The grooms have been drugged. I believe someone is out to steal some of Lord Hascombe's horses."

Daniel felt her stiffen beneath him.

"Well, the thief is not in this stall." He watched Michael lift up the lantern he carried and look at the second pair of boots sticking out from under Daniel. "This is my paramour from Kent. She came up to surprise me. It was not safe for her to travel dressed as a woman. She couldn't go through Christmas without some of my loving," and he ran his hand down Lady Marsh's side. He enjoyed hearing her quiet hiss of outrage.

"Well, you picked a dangerous place for a liaison, my lord. Apollo isn't used to his new surroundings yet." Michael looked over his shoulder. "Plus, it looks as though we have a thief on the premises. He or they have drugged the other grooms. I only avoided being doped because I had to help his lordship with the Christmas tree. You may well have stopped him stealing this valuable colt."

"I'm sure I did," he said ironically. "He wouldn't have expected to find me here." That got him a jab in his ribs.

"I shall leave you to your... , well, be careful and keep an eye out for the culprits." With that Michael backed out of the stall. He stopped and bent down to leave the lantern at the door to the stall. "You'll need this so you are not surprised again."

As soon as Michael's footsteps faded, Lady Marsh pushed at Daniel's chest. "Get off me."

"I'm quite comfortable where I am, thank you. Besides, is that any way to thank me for saving your neck, Lady Marsh."

Her breathing was her only reply.

Daniel's temper flared to life. "Would you have preferred me to introduce you as the person who drugged the staff and tried to steal the colt? I'm aware that a lady's reputation is far more valuable than the colt."

"Not to me. If not for you I'd be well away with Apollo. Now I'll never get him back."

"Is your Grandfather alive to vouch for his gift?" He noted that she was no longer trying to push him off and he wasn't going to move unless she asked. The feel of her beneath him stirred very pleasant sensations.

"Oh, for goodness sake. If he were, would I be here risking everything to steal him? Now get off me," and she shoved hard sending him slipping sideways onto the straw. She was on her feet and racing to escape before he'd taken his next breath.

Daniel stuck out one leg and sent her tumbling face first onto the hay. He was on top of her in a moment. "You may be a lady but your manners are appalling. Where is my thank you?"

She turned her head to look at him over her shoulder. "And if he hadn't called you lord, I'd never have known you were a gentleman. This is no way to treat a lady."

Daniel snorted. "Ladies don't steal high spirited colts," he whispered in her ear.

"You know who I am, however I have no idea who you are. What is your name?" He couldn't help a smug smile. She was interested in him, but then to his regret she added, "So I know to avoid you in future."

"Daniel Kerrich, Baron de Winter, at your service, my lady."

She frowned and said. "Blast. The Earl's brother-in-law has caught me. Are you going to tell him what I tried to do?"

She knew who he was, that was interesting. He'd never been to London in his life, but he supposed people had gossiped about Rheda and her background. "Perhaps you could persuade me to simply let you go," he suggested nuzzling her neck. That got him an elbow in his stomach. He laughed as he rolled off her. "I was teasing." He leapt to his feet. "Come on," he held out his hand to help her to her feet. "I'll introduce you to Rufus. Let's see what we can sort out."

She took his hand and he marveled at how finely boned she was. Her hand was tiny compared to his. How on earth she'd had the strength to control Apollo...She must have the touch. Some people could almost talk to a horse and get them to do anything. He was one of those people. Maybe she had the gift too. He pulled her to her feet with little effort.

"Why are you doing this for me?" she asked quietly.

When she turned into the lantern light, he finally got a look at her face and he almost stopped breathing. Her hair was a mess, and her face was covered in dust and dirt, yet, she was still the most arresting woman he'd ever seen. Strands had come loose and wisps of hair fell around her face, as if it too wanted to stroke the perfect unblemished skin. He would have known she was highborn; her breeding was evident in her fine features. Her nose, eyes, and lips were in perfect symmetry to the size of her face. Vivid blue iris's surrounded dark pinpoints that flared as the light flickered. Her eyelashes were so long he wondered if she had to detangle them every morning when she woke. Her nose was cute to the point of being childlike, but her lips... They were definitely all woman. Pouty and luscious, and he wanted a taste so badly he had to pinch his thigh to remember who she was.

"I'm the only man who could understand why you'd get worked up about a horse. Once you bond with a special stead it's difficult to part with them." She opened and then closed her mouth obviously surprised at his understanding. He bowed and with one hand indicated she should precede him from the stall. "Let's just say I admire a woman who is passionate about horses." Under his breath he added, "A passionate nature usually means passionate in bed too."

They reached the entrance to the large stable block and Daniel's body hummed when he saw the mistletoe hanging above the large barn door. He slowed his step and pulled her to face him, pointing upwards as he did.

"Don't be ridiculous. I am not going to kiss you, I hardly know you. Besides because of you, my plan is ruined."

"I can't help the fact your plan was a terrible one. For all you knew, Rufus might have wanted to show Apollo off to his visitors. The estate is large. Did you really think you'd be able to slink in and out unaided?" He pulled her closer. "As to a kiss, a chaste peck is often the norm, but a more passionate kiss would be appropriate considering I saved you from facing Michael's wrath."

She raised a face filled with alarm but also desire. He could read it easily in her expressive eyes. "Now then," he said smiling, "a kiss is a thing to be shared, not given nor rushed." Tipping her chin up, he gazed into those wide, luminous eyes and more than simple desire began to unfold—possessiveness—a sensation foreign to him where a woman was concerned. He felt, for a moment, as if he was gazing into the eyes of an angel, and he touched her smooth cheek with reverence.

"Have you any idea," he murmured softly, "how enchanting you are? Tell me your name."

The way he spoke those words, combined with his touch and the kindness he'd done her this evening, had the seductive impact Georgiana had dreaded from the moment she'd looked into his handsome face.

When he'd lain atop her, all hard muscle and withheld strength, she felt as if she were beginning to melt and float inside. As his head bent and his lips drew near, she couldn't pull her gaze from his hypnotic green eyes, and worse still, she didn't want to try.

"Georgiana," she answered breathlessly as his lips drew closer.

When his lips took hers in a kiss, she knew that it was going to be nothing at all like the chaste kisses she'd experienced hidden behind the potted plants at countless balls. At twenty she'd experienced her fair share of innocent kisses. His mouth slanted over hers with fierce tenderness, while his hand curved round her nape, his fingers stroking her sensitive skin along the collar of her shirt, and his other arm encircled her waist pulling her tightly against his hard, hot, body.

Lost in a sea of pure sensation, Georgiana slid her hands up his muscular chest to wrap her arms around his neck, clinging to him as if her world depended on her staying as close to him as she could. Desire unfurled deep within her at the feel of his erection and she clung tighter to him, sliding her hands down his back to his firm buttocks.

He kissed her long and lingeringly, both gentle and persuasive. So when he touched his tongue to her trembling lips, this time coaxing them to part, insisting actually, she eagerly admitted him. His tongue slid between her open lips filling her mouth. His hand shifted from her waist sliding upward toward her breasts.

He tasted of everything forbidden and everything she wanted.

She barely noted the moan of encouragement that escaped her, above the pounding of her heart. Never had she let a man take such liberties and never had she wanted to let him. She hoped the kiss would never end.

Just as she silently made her wish, Daniel's hands left her body and he fell sideways, out cold on the cobblestones.

"You were right, Baron. She didn't come alone, however, I didn't expect to have to save her from a kiss. A kiss she looked as if she was enjoying."

Georgiana chose to ignore Billy's chastisement. She peered down at Daniel's prone form. "He will be all right won't he?"

"Aye, he'll have a sore head when he wakes so best we take our leave before he rouses. No chance of getting the colt then?"

She bent down and reached out to touch Daniel's face. He looked so young and less sure of himself as he lay on the ground, knocked out cold. She hoped he wouldn't hate her. He was the first man she'd ever felt an ounce of grudging respect for.

"No, the groom took him" she answered sadly. "We will have to find another way to retrieve the colt. He knows who I am and why I'm here."

As Georgiana and Billy, her groom, slipped quietly away through the outbuildings, to find the horses they had tethered several miles east of the Earl of Hascombe's estate, she thought over how her plan had gone so badly wrong. As she mounted Black Devil for the ride back to her father's estate, she tried not to let her despair cloud her head.

She would get Apollo back, and now that she'd met Baron de Winter, she realized he was the perfect foil in her new plan.

She prayed that next time her idea wouldn't go so horribly wrong, as she would pay a much higher price than just a kiss. *Just a kiss!* Daniel's kiss made her dream of sandalwood and spice—all things wanton and terribly nice.

Chapter Two

It took three days for Daniel to get his good humor back and for his pounding head to stop hurting. Christmas was creeping nearer and he had yet to do any shopping, but Rheda refused to let him get up until the doctor had approved.

His pride was now hurting more than his head. The embarrassment of a young lady getting the drop on him was at least his secret for now. He had a mind to call on Lady Georgiana Marsh and—what exactly? He didn't want to get her in trouble or put her reputation at risk. Rheda's reputation had suffered and it had almost cost her life. He just couldn't do that to another woman.

He'd just finished a wonderful ham and egg breakfast when Rufus strode into the dining room and asked, "I wondered if you'd want to accompany me to Newmarket? It's the last few days of the foals and yearlings sales, we could both pick up some much needed stock."

He could almost kiss Rufus. He was about to accept gleefully when Rheda added, "Only if you take the carriage. The doctor says no riding for at least another week."

Rufus's chuckle inflamed his anger. "I am not going to Newmarket in a carriage like an old woman. If I go I shall ride." He stood up from the breakfast table almost pushing his chair over.

Rheda also rose to her feet, eyes exactly like his flashing in anger, and to his horror, fear. "Please, Daniel. It is only a few more days before you can ride again, and I love you too much to see you permanently damaged. The doctor warned you. You have had so many concussions from falling from horses you need to be careful. You can come in the carriage with me. I promised you a Christmas present of horseflesh. We shall go and select you a new horse." She flashed her husband a warning look. "We will all go in the carriage."

Rufus looked about to argue but one stern look from his wife had him shrug his shoulders at Daniel. "I'll get the carriage readied. I want to leave within half an hour." With that he left the room.

"I know you think I'm fussing but what that horse thief did to you... You could have died from that blow to the head. I don't want to lose my little brother." Daniel moved to hug his sister when he saw the tears forming in her eyes. Why did women always overreact?

He had not told anyone who had attacked him. He would work out how to get Lady Georgiana back in his own way. In a way that would have her groveling at his feet. "I suppose I can give up my joy of riding for a few more days if it keeps you happy."

She laid her head on his chest. "Your niece and nephew would miss you too if you'd been... I wished you lived closer. Sir Bacon's estate, about ten miles from

Newmarket is for sale. You could sell Tumbury Cliff Manor and move your horse breeding business here."

He stiffened. He loved his home and stables near Deal, Kent, and his sister knew that. "You fought so hard to keep our home for me. Why this sudden need to have me near?" He pushed her out of his arms but she would not look at him. She turned away and tried to laugh it off.

"Just a big sister missing her brother."

Fear slid quickly down his spine. "What is wrong, Rheda?" He reached and swung her to face him and saw tears sliding down her cheeks. "Rhe?" He couldn't remember the last time he'd ever seen his sister cry, not even when she'd been beaten to within an inch of her life. He looked at the beautiful, mature woman standing before him, her red hair still as vibrant as any young debutantes, and for once he did not see the fiery temper that always marked their arguments. Rheda had never been scared of anything but when he looked into her green eyes so similar to his all he saw was fear and it made his breath catch in his throat. "I have to have a small operation in the New Year."

He pulled her back into his arms and hugged her tightly. "Why? What?"

"I have a small lump in my breast and they want to remove it just to be sure."

Now he understood why she wanted him to stay. She was scared.

Was it a tumor? His body was awash with pain; pain from the blood trying to flow through his veins but it had turned to ice. He knew if it were a tumor his sister would most likely only have a few years. "Why didn't you tell me? I shall of course stay until you are well."

She burst into actual sobbing. "If something happens to me, if it is a tumor and I get sick, promise me you'll move near to Rufus. He'll be lost without me, and the children will need you too. You will have to help Rufus go on with his life."

At that moment he would have promised her anything—everything. He wished it was he who was sick. Rheda had a family who loved her. He had no one—no one but her! If he lost her…He hugged her tighter. "You will be fine, it could be nothing. You've never let anything beat you and I won't let you start now. Let's just focus on you getting well." He pressed a kiss to her forehead as she wiped the tears off her face.

"Don't let Rufus know I'm scared. He's trying to be so strong…Some Christmas. A thief has attacked you, and now I'm dumping my fears on you. I'm sorry."

"I would have been cross if you had not told me. Besides, it's not your fault someone hit me over the head. I will stay here until we know this lump is nothing. If I stay I can help Rufus find out who tried to steal Apollo."

She smiled through watery eyes. "Just knowing you are here helps me face what is to come."

He didn't want to think about what she faced. Something of his fear must have appeared on his face because she said, "Rufus has got me some morphine to help with any pain from the surgery. They use it on the horses."

He nodded but his fear did not leave him.

She reached up and cupped his face. "Let's go and enjoy the day. We have some horseflesh to peruse. Is there anything in particular you want to buy for Tumbury?"

How could he think about horses after this? But he saw how much she wanted to take her mind off her situation. "I'd love to find a colt like Apollo. He's a beauty and would breed amazing cavalry horses."

"Why don't you ask Rufus to sell Apollo to you. He only got the colt because the Marquis of Wentworth lost big at the 2000 Guinea race and he took Apollo in payment of the wager debt. I'm not sure he really needs the colt."

"He'd part with Apollo?" Revenge reared its head. Oh, he would love to own what Lady Georgiana wanted.

"Who'd part with Apollo?" Rufus asked upon entering the room. He immediately went across to his wife and put his arm around her. Obviously she could not hide the fact she'd been crying.

"You would. Daniel thinks the colt will produce fabulous cavalry horses."

Daniel was excited by the idea, forgetting all about Georgiana. "I do need new breeding stock. It could be economical to buy a new stallion rather than pay stud fees. I could also put him out to stud and earn more."

Rufus looked at Rheda and smiled. "You're welcome to buy him off me."

Daniel scratched his head. He did have some savings and he could use the money set aside for stud fees since he'd use the colt instead. "What is the colt worth?"

Rufus looked at Rheda and the smile they shared made him yearn for such a relationship. His sister and her husband were as one. When he married he would marry a woman who thrilled and complemented him completely. He did not need money and power. He loved his life in Deal, Kent, with his horses. He wanted what Rufus and Rheda had—a true partnership of hearts and minds.

"Actually, it would make a wonderful Christmas gift. Saves me having to find you something else."

So lost in his thoughts, Daniel barely registered Rufus's comment. He unfolded his arms. "I can't accept Apollo as a gift. He's far too valuable."

"It can be from Rheda *and* me. I'd rather see you have your own stud breeding program than bother training him."

That was a lie. Daniel looked at Rheda, torn at such a generous offer. They both had offered to provide more capital for him to see his horse breeding business prosper but he always declined. Rheda had done enough already. It was time he built his own future. "Ah, about Apollo, there was something I wanted to talk to you about the colt. I met someone who indicated Lord Wentworth had no right to give you the horse as repayment for his debt."

Rufus's head swung to face him. "Who said that?"

"No one of significance. Did Wentworth own Apollo?" Daniel asked again.

"Of course he did. I was at the yearling sales when Wentworth's late father-in-law bought the colt just over a year ago."

Interesting. Georgiana had mentioned it was a gift from her grandfather. But perhaps it was simply something a man said to his granddaughter. "Then I would be humbled to receive such a Christmas gift."

Rheda laughed and moved to hug him. "You don't look that happy about it."

He wasn't, because of his encounter with Georgiana, but he did not wish to expose her as the 'almost' thief. "I'm only thinking that now I have to find you both an incredible gift in return."

"Don't be ridiculous. Simply having you stay with us is gift enough." And Rheda squeezed his hand—hard.

He knew what Rheda was referring too and he would stay until he knew for sure his sister would be all right.

"My lord, the carriage is ready."

Rufus thanked his butler and they waited in the lobby for Rheda's maid to fetch her cloak, hat and gloves. Though it was a clear blue-sky day, the wind had a bite to it.

During the carriage ride to Newmarket, Rheda quizzed Daniel on his gifts for his nephew and niece. He refused to tell her, partly because he wanted them all to be surprised and partly because he wondered if Rheda would approve.

The men left Rheda and her lady's maid in the town to do more Christmas shopping and strolled to the stockyards and stables. Rufus bought three new yearlings and Daniel one. They had a beer with some of the trainers before deciding to head back to town.

They had just reached the outskirts of the town when a carriage drew up beside them. "Lord Hascombe, been at the sales?"

"Lord Wentworth, I have indeed. Even bought a few fillies. My brother-in-law bought one too. May I present Lord de Winter?"

The Marquis merely nodded his head at Daniel. "Have you time to come and see a stallion I'm selling. It's over in the yard by the first stable block."

Rufus shook his head. "I'm off to meet my wife, and escort her home. I have all the stallions I need for now."

"Then you and your lovely wife must come to dinner this week. How is Thursday?"

It was obvious that Rufus did not wish to attend. "I'd love to, Wentworth, however, we have Baron de Winter staying and—"

"Bring him. By all means bring him." The Marquis banged his cane on the inside of the carriage roof and it began to roll forward. "That's settled then. See you Thursday."

"Damn. Damn." Daniel heard Rufus mutter under his breath.

"What was all that about. Why has the Marquis become so friendly? He lost Apollo to you. Plus if I recall, before you cleared your fathers name, he would not give you the time of day."

Rufus saw Rheda ahead and waved. "He's in dun territory and will most likely want to try and sell me more of his horses."

"I might be interested in some if that helps."

Rufus sighed. "That would help, but be careful. While Lord Wentworth did have a wonderful stable of thoroughbreds, I've heard a rumor that he's been secretly selling them off and fraudulently buying a horse of similar colorings and trying to sell them off as the same thoroughbred horse again and again, with false papers and all."

Daniel was no fool when it came to horseflesh. He could tell a hack from a thoroughbred from one hundred paces. "Fallen on hard times has he?"

"The late Lord Upton was the real horse breeder. Lord Wentworth is his son-in-law. With Upton's only child a daughter married to Lord Wentworth, he left the estate and horse breeding business to his son-in-law as it was not entailed. Unfortunately, Lord Wentworth is more interested in gambling on the horses than breeding them. Lord Upton must be turning in his grave. I don't believe he knew the extent of his son-in-laws gambling debts."

This gave even more weight to Georgiana's words that her grandfather gifted her the colt.

If Georgiana was right, in good conscience he could not keep the horse and that would be a major blow. However, he might be able to convince Georgiana to let him put the colt to stud before handing him back, as Apollo was almost four years old.

"I'm afraid it's only a matter of time before Lord Wentworth and his wife and daughter will find themselves forced to sell the estate."

Daniel hadn't noticed that they had reached Rheda until she added to the conversation, "I would not wish that on anyone, but if the estate did come up for sale, it might be an option for Daniel. I'd love him to move closer to us."

Daniel wondered where Rheda thought the money would come from. He must have shown it on his face for she said, "Tumbury Manor could be sold. It would be enough to buy the Upton estate Rufus tells me."

That is when it hit him like a rampaging bull and all joy in the afternoon outing died. Rheda believed she was in grave trouble. Rheda *and* Rufus had discussed this, and were serious about him moving closer. As soon as he could get Rufus alone he would get the truth from him about Rheda's condition. Was she hiding something more from him?

Rather than upsetting her, Daniel responded with a smile. "Then I shall take the opportunity at dinner with Lord Wentworth to request another visit to look around the estate. If it does come up for sale, then it might be a sound investment. I would be closer to family, but also closer to the main horse breeding markets and London."

He hoped he wasn't digging himself a hole. He really didn't want to leave Deal but he would if his sister needed him. The idea that he might only have Rheda around for a few years made his stomach recoil. If so he would want to spend every minute he could with her. Daniel watched the breath Rheda had been holding come rushing out on a big smile and she hugged him tightly. "Thank you," she whispered in his ear. Her happiness was all he cared about right now. He wanted to take away the fear lurking in her eyes and give her a Christmas to remember.

Chapter Three

Georgiana paced the stable chewing on her bottom lip.

"He's coming here for dinner?" Billy asked.

She nodded and kept pacing.

"Baron de Winter? Do you think he'll expose the fact you tried to steal Apollo?"

She turned to face Billy and threw her hands up. "I don't know but I don't like it. He has me in a corner when it was supposed to be me who held the upper hand."

Billy sat on a hay bale. "And how exactly did you expect to get the upper hand. He could have me arrested for clonking him over the head. This is terrible."

"He didn't see you, Billy. And I certainly would not tell." She began pacing again. "If he tells my father… You know my father has threatened to marry me off to Lord Mather's son if I cause one more scandal."

"He can't force you into marriage. Can he?"

Georgiana didn't want to answer that because she did not want the world to know how little her father cared for her or her mother. Her father had threatened to have her mother committed to an asylum if Georgiana did not do as he wished. Her mother was a shell of a woman. Marriage to her father had done that. He bullied her, belittled her for so long that her mother simply gave up living. Her grandfather, Lord Upton, had stood between her father and the asylum but now that he was dead…

Under her breath she said, "My father is capable of anything if it is of benefit to him." At the moment there was no benefit to sending her mother away because it meant he would have no leverage over Georgiana. Her large trust was well protected. Her grandfather had seen to that. But on her twenty-first birthday it became hers. That is why her father still kept her around. Once that trust was active he would use her love and protectiveness of her mother to get his hands on the money.

She was running out of time. In eight months, when she turned one and twenty her world would become a waking nightmare.

The colt was supposed to be the start of her freedom. If she had Apollo, she could run with her mother and use the stud fees she could earn from Apollo to hide out until her money came through. They would have to watch the spending and live without servants for the few months, but she could do it. However, her father thwarted that plan when last month he gave her colt as repayment for a gambling debt.

"Perhaps if you explain the situation to Lord Hascombe he might help."

That is what Daniel had said when he lead her from the stable. "That might have been possible before you knocked him out cold." She rubbed her forehead and let the worry churning in her stomach consume her for a moment. Would Daniel be angry enough to expose her?

"How was I to know he wasn't marching you outside to the magistrate."

"It's not your fault, Billy. It's my fault for concocting such a risky plan." No. It wasn't her fault. It was Daniel Kerrich, Baron de Winter's fault. Why couldn't he have been in the house with the other guests for the evening?

For one moment she relived his kiss. He had been gentle, encouraging rather than demanding. She'd melted in his heat. Melted into the memory. For one moment forgetting all her misery and the weight of her situation pressing her down.

Just then she heard her father's voice booming in the house. "I have to go. Father is in a foul temper and I need to ensure mother is not in his line of fire."

"So, your plan to leave is on hold?"

She paused at the door to the stables. "It depends on how this evening goes. If Daniel keeps my secret then I need to learn why. I might be able to use him."

"I know why he's keeping your secret. He's blinded by your beauty and wishes to use the truth to his own advantage."

She smiled. "A man blinded by beauty is easy to control. If he is, then I shall use that to make a further attempt on Apollo. I can keep him busy while you steal the horse."

Billy jumped to his feet. "No. If I steal and get caught I'll be hung, but you, a lady of breeding. You would be let off."

Bill was right. "Very well, I shall have to think of a way to keep Daniel busy and steal Apollo. Just be ready to go at a moments notice. I have Tessa and Jacob organized to take mother as soon as I send word. They will bring mother to our meeting place."

She slipped through the door and made her way toward the house with Billy's final words ringing in her ear, "Be careful."

Georgiana was always careful.

Each morning when she woke up and her feet hit the floor of her bedchamber, she took comfort in knowing that her father's first thought when he saw her would be, 'what will she do today?'

She would never let him win.

Georgiana closed the door upon exiting her mother's room and sagged against it stifling a sob by shoving her fist in her mouth. Tears were useless. They would not make her mother whole again. Her mother no longer recognized her. And this was a good day. Other days her mother screamed and ranted like a small child. Her father had done that to her with his constant belittling and abuse. Pain shafted through Georgiana like a spear. She hated the way her mother merely sat rocking in her chair by the fire day after day, as if the world beyond her room had vanished. Georgiana straightened to stand tall, her hands smoothing her gown, and vowed she would never let any man have the power her father had over her mother.

She gathered her warring emotions. She had visitors to greet. She knew she looked stunning. Tessa, her lady's maid, had made her look like a princess from head to toe. Maybe she could divert Daniel's attention this evening with a little flirtation. Men were so predictable. A bare shoulder here, a pushed up bosom there, and their brains disappeared. Instead they fell over themselves to please.

She made her way to the drawing room, early, as her father had ordered. He stood by the fire his back to her, a brandy balloon in his hand. He did not stir as she entered. She glided across the room and took a chair directly in the line of sight of the door. She wanted to be the first thing Daniel saw when he entered the room.

Her father finally sensed her presence and turned to face her. His eyes raked over her as if she was one of his prized horses to sell and her skin crawled.

"You will be pleasant and act as a proper young lady this evening, do I make myself clear."

"Of course, father."

To her satisfaction her docility angered him. "Don't play coy with me, girl. I'm warning you. I will not be embarrassed in my own house. It is important that Lord Hascombe is made to feel welcome. I have horses that I wish him to purchase."

Do not scoff. She knew what her father was doing. She knew everything that went on in those stables. "I've heard Lord Hascombe is a very good judge of horseflesh. He accepted Apollo for your rather large debt, after all."

"And what do you mean by that my girl?" He moved to stand over her. "I hope you are not poking your nose into the workings of the stable. If I learn you have meddled in my business—well, just think of your mother." The last words were said softly but she understood the venom beneath.

"I have no interest in your stables—not since Apollo was sold."

Her father leaned in close. "Not one word about Apollo tonight or I'll send her away tomorrow. I've given you all the leeway I'll allow. I mean it. Our future could hinge on this night."

She wanted to say 'don't you mean your future.' Her future was rosy, if she had any say in the matter.

Her father stepped back and played with his cravat. She hoped it choked him.

"Baron de Winter is attending too. So I have two possible purchasers. You will use your charms on the young man. Keep him busy while I converse with Hascombe."

"As you wish, father." She needed to talk with Daniel anyway. She needed to know what he was going to do. Oh, she understood men. Daniel would want something from her for not turning her into Lord Hascombe. She kept the smile on her face for her father but inside she was a melting pot of anger. Why was it, at every turn, a man held something over her? She longed for that moment when she would be free.

Georgiana needed a drink. Sherry was her drink of choice, she found brandy too potent and she would need her wits about her tonight. She was just about to rise and pour herself a drink when the guests were announced.

It was annoying to note that her heart began to beat faster in her chest, not from fear, but from the fact she was about to see Daniel again.

He was the last person to enter the room and she could not take her eyes from him. Handsome was too tame a word, for the picture of towering masculinity standing just inside the drawing room looking so self-assured it made her worried. He knew he held all the cards.

She barely managed to greet Lord and Lady Hascombe because Daniel filled her mind.

Beautiful. He was beautiful.

She shook her head. No she would not, could not, fall under his spell. *Remember what men are really like—devious deceivers.*

She had never been attracted to such an arresting man before. Normally she was wary of handsome. Her pulse hitched as she drank in the tall, broad shoulders and narrow hips. The candlelight made his hair look like spun gold, and as he caught her looking at him a smile crept onto his face that made her hands tremble. It was a private smile. The type of smile shared between—lovers, or was that enemies?

The last time she'd seen him, Billy had knocked him unconscious. Would he reveal that here tonight?

Then he was standing before her, bowing over her hand to press a kiss to her gloved fingers. She looked at where her hand lay in his large one. She sensed his inner strength. He could crush her fingers as easily as if they were twigs. He could also crush her by revealing the truth about Apollo.

Could he feel her trembling?

"Lady Georgiana. It is a great pleasure to meet you."

His deep voice was soft but mocking. She slowly raised her eyes to look into his and her blood ran cold at the message displayed within. He was going to make her pay for his wound. Would he do so now? She hated the waiting. Why did he not simply get it over and done with? Perhaps she should attack rather than be on the offensive.

"You seem to have a problem with your memory. We have already met." She lifted her head in a silent challenge as if saying 'do your worst'. She loved the look of confusion on his face but it didn't last long.

He stepped back ignoring the others staring at them. "You will have to excuse me, my lady. I was recently hit over the head by a would be thief and it may have affected my memory."

"Oh, no. Did you capture the rogue?"

His smugness was diminishing. She saw his green eyes begin to darken with anger. Why did she have to poke the tiger?

"Unfortunately not. But I am making inquiries and I am very close to a result."

She nodded. "And what will you do to the villain when you catch him?"

Her father handed Daniel a brandy. "I hope you run the rogue through," her father uttered. "Hitting a peer should be a hanging offence."

She blanched and saw Daniel smile.

He took a seat directly across from her. "I don't think that will be necessary, Lord Wentworth. I shall think up a fitting punishment, for him or *her*, once I catch them. I can assure you."

Lady Rheda interrupted her brother. "You did not tell us you'd met Lady Georgiana before." Daniel's sister looked confused and suspicious.

Georgiana answered. "Oh, it was of no consequence." She turned back towards Daniel. "We merely met and had a conversation about horses one day not long ago. I'm hurt he does not remember."

"In Newmarket?" Lady Rheda persisted.

"I do apologize, Lady Georgiana, that I forgot our brief encounter but the steed we were discussing held my attention. You know how that is?"

She felt her face flush hot with color at the insult and Lady Rheda gasped. "I do. I must admit I usually prefer horses to men."

Silence.

"Georgiana, you will apologize to Baron de Winter at once." Her father's anger meant nothing compared to the anger she was feeling inside. She wanted to blurt out that he had not seemed so immune to her when he was kissing her under the mistletoe that day.

"There is no need for that, Lord Wentworth. I too find horses more interesting. Your daughter and I have that in common at least." He raised his glass in her direction.

The conversation turned to other mundane things like the yearling sales prices and the state of the racing industry. Lady Rheda was very quiet so Georgiana was quiet too. It gave her time to study her opponent.

Daniel kept looking in his sister's direction and smiling at her. His face would crease with worry lines whenever Rheda looked away.

"Is your brother staying with you long?" Georgiana finally asked.

"At least through January I hope. I know he's anxious to get back to his horses, but I'm hoping to convince him to move north and settle closer to us." Her ladyship looked sad as she spoke the words. It made her want to reach out and squeeze her hand. Something was not right in the Hascombe home.

"Your family home was in Kent?" She inquired.

Rheda nodded. "Tumbury Manor has been in our family for many, many years and Daniel has worked hard to make it profitable after our father all but bankrupted us."

Georgiana threw a glance in her father's direction. "I have experience of that."

"I had heard the rumors. I'm sorry if that is not very delicate, but I wanted to let you know I will help you and your mother as much as I can if the worst should happen. I was once in your position and it took friends to help me and Daniel."

"Thank you." She could not say more because it was the first time another woman had sympathized with her and her throat closed up. She took a long sip of sherry. "I may well need your help one day."

Dinner was announced and her father held out his arm to her.

Lord Hascombe said, "Your wife is not joining us?"

For the first time in forever her father's face mottled red. "My wife is unwell. She rarely leaves her rooms."

"I'm sorry to hear that," the earl replied. "Your daughter must bring you great comfort."

"Indeed," was all her father said, while Daniel looked at her thoughtfully as she led him into the dining room.

The dinner progressed with her father dominating the conversation trying very hard to interest both men in his horses. Georgiana bit her tongue on several occasions as her father sang lyrical about a horse she knew had been sold several months ago.

Finally when she could bear no more, Georgiana suggested to Rheda that they leave the men to their conversational port and the ladies escaped to the drawing room.

"I apologize for my father's manners. With my mother no longer capable of joining us, he tends to forget about female inclusive conversation."

"Has your mother been unwell for long?"

She was about to answer when Billie rushed into the room. He drew up short at seeing Lady Hascombe. "Sorry, my lady, but there is something wrong with Colton. He's limping and showing signs of discomfort. Can you come look at him?"

She looked across at Rheda who simply said, "Go. I can amuse myself until the men return."

Georgiana knew it was rude, but she could not bear for an animal to be in pain, so she quickly followed Billy.

Chapter Four

Daniel was bored with the conversation and wished he could return to the drawing room. He stood and moved to the window as Rufus and Lord Wentworth continued to discuss the prices achieved at this year's yearling sales.

He was just about to turn away when he saw one of the grooms who'd helped with the carriage horses on their arrival, and Georgiana, dash from the house toward the stables.

On impulse Daniel decided to follow. "If you'll excuse me, gentlemen, nature calls."

He quickly made his way to the stables and upon entering walked down the center looking in the stalls. Near the back he found Georgiana on her knees next to a white gelding. He sensed Georgiana's sorrow and crossed to the stall. The fact a beautiful woman was sitting in dirt and hay as if she were on a velvet settee in her drawing room, in a gown worth more than four times the gelding, explained how much she cared for the horse. She held the animal's hoof in her lap the satin that only minutes earlier had hugged her sensuous curves was ripped and covered in mud. She didn't notice the stench stifling the stale air. All she seemed to notice was the horse's pain

He wanted to take her pain away. "Can I help?"

She lifted worried eyes to his face. "This is my favorite steed, Colton, and I'm worried about his front leg. It's swollen. Do you think he has something in it? I can't see any broken skin from a wound." Georgiana stood to make room for Daniel as he entered the stall, and she gently put the horse's leg down. Colton immediately shifted his weight off of it.

Daniel knew what the problem was just by looking at the joint. He moved closer and patted Colton on the nose. "Easy boy." He slowly ran his hand down the horse's leg until he reached the front elbow joint. Just as he suspected the joint was hot to the touch. He looked around for a groom. "You there, what's your name?"

"Billy, my lord."

"Wet some wheat and heat it up into a warm poultice." Billy raced off to do his bidding, his knowing look indicating he too knew the problem. Daniel glanced at Georgiana and noted she was close to tears. "I'm sorry to say, Colton here has inflammation in his elbow joint. The only treatment is gentle massage and hot poultices until the inflammation goes down."

"So it's not life threatening?"

It could be, because most lame horses were shot, but he couldn't bring himself to tell her that. Daniel shook his head. "No. But when it flares up, especially in the cold, you can't ride him, just give him a gentle walk around the yard and massages to keep the blood moving, and warm poultices. It will pain him, but if you keep his weight down and mix up the types of fresh hay he eats—no feeding him oats or grains—I've seen some of my horses live a good long life."

"Thank you." Her voice shook. "Father usually puts down any horse who goes lame."

He would not lie. "You still might have to if the condition worsens or goes to all his joints, but we can try this for now if you don't mind the extra care he will need."

She wiped her face and a smudge of dirt appeared on her cheek. "I will do what it takes. Please don't tell my father about Colton's condition. Billy will work to conceal it from him. I just don't trust what father may do. I've already lost Apollo. I can't lose Colton too." She stifled a sob with the back of her hand.

He reached out and tucked a curl behind her ear. "Would it help if I took Colton to Hascombe and stabled him there while we treat him. Then your father would not notice he was lame."

"Thank you. Oh, thank you." She nodded through eyes filled with tears and her pain saw him pull her into an embrace. He simply held her while she silently sobbed. Daniel was pretty sure this was not just about a horse. No doubt her father was not an easy man to live with but if Daniel thought for one minute he would hurt his daughter, well then he would call the gent out—Marquis or no Marquis.

To lighten the situation he joked, "Where is the mistletoe when you need it." The last time he'd held her so close he had stolen a kiss.

To his surprise she gave a soft and sexy giggle. "A kiss doesn't always need mistletoe."

He froze for a moment before gently pushing her out of his arms. One look at the heat of passion burning in her eyes, and he bent to take her lips in the sweetest of kisses. She didn't even hesitate but slid her arms round his neck, clinging to him as if her life depended on it. Was she doing this to block out the pain of her life, or because she genuinely wanted him to kiss her? His lips stopped moving.

Choice was denied him when she took the lead. Her tongue slid into his mouth and stroked. His body responded by pulling her hard against him, while his mind clouded out all thought but to drink from her sweetness.

His body roared to life and he didn't even care that she could feel his desire. She set his body on fire and he deepened the kiss. She responded in kind, her fingers tangling in his hair, tugging him closer.

Soft feminine gasps and moans filled his ears as Georgiana fell under pleasure's spell; he could feel it in her, hear it in her needy moans, soft and breathless. She groaned his name and tilted her head the other way, kissing again with a sweet, drowning depth.

His hands crept under the edge of her gown where the horse's hoof had ripped it, and warmth seared his fingers as they trailed up her slender legs above her garter. Her womanly center radiated heat drawing him closer. He should be pistol-whipped but if he was, it would be worth it.

Daniel suddenly stopped, his breathing rough. He could not take advantage of her sorrow and concern over her horse. He held tight, his forehead resting on hers. His fingers continued stroking her leg. "Your skin is like silk beneath my touch."

She rubbed against his erection, the pleasure sublime. He groaned. "Christ, I want you."

She froze before melting back into his embrace.

His hand rose to the top of her thighs. He hesitated, but only for a moment. "Have you ever experienced pleasure?"

She shook her head and took a deep breath. "More."

He needed no further encouragement. His finger stroked through her curls... she did not push him away.

"God," he whispered, "you're so wet for me."

She merely moaned in his ear as she clung to him. He should stop. Billy could be back at any moment. *No, it will take a while to heat the wheat.*

His thumb brushed over her nub as his finger slid deep within her. Her breathing faltered, and then returned in little gasps. He briefly closed his eyes on a groan. At his touch she couldn't stop her hips from lifting in time to the movement.

Soon one finger became two, his thumb continued to circle, and when he took her mouth again and plunged his tongue deep within, he felt her inner muscles contract around him. It took only a moment more for her to come apart in his arms and it was the most beautiful moment of his life. To know he'd been the first man to give her pleasure.

She came down to earth slowly. His hand was still stroking her bare thigh above her stocking. She finally opened her eyes and he watched the bewilderment and satisfaction on her beautiful face. She gave a shaky smile.

"For one wondrous moment you made me forget about Colton, my father, my mother—everything," and she shyly stepped away from him and smoothed down her gown.

His mouth broke into a relieved grin but his body was still full of molten fire and his arousal pulsed in his trousers.

She turned to study her steed. "Will you take Colton to Hascombe tonight?"

"If you wish. You may visit any time you like—you can even see Apollo, as long as you promise not to try and steal him again." Just then Billy reappeared and at Daniel's words he dropped the roll of bandages in the hay. So, it was Billy who had helped her. "I take it I have you to thank for the bump on my head." He didn't feel so guilty now at what had just occurred.

"I'm right sorry about that, my lord. I thought you were taking advantage of Lady Georgiana."

Daniel could hardly blame the man. He had just taken advantage of her but could not regret it. "Yes, well, never again. And stop trying to steal horses. You would get into a lot of trouble. As a lady, and the fact the horse belonged to her father, Georgiana's behavior may have been excused, but no magistrate would have sympathy for a groom. I'm sure Georgiana has now considered that."

"I admit I was selfish. I did not think of the risk to Billy. But I've learned my lesson."

Daniel smiled as he took in her beautiful, contrite face. Even with hay in her hair and dirt smudged across her cheek she looked delectable. He loved that she did not care about the state of her gown or how she looked. Most ladies would be horrified to let a man see them when less than perfect.

It suddenly occurred to him that Georgiana simply didn't care what anyone thought of her, and it was quite refreshing. He too didn't care what anyone thought of him, but for the first time ever he wanted a woman, Georgiana, to care. He wanted her admiration and… what did he want from her? Why could he not stop thinking about her? She stirred something in him. Any woman who loved horses as much as he did was worth considering.

Worth considering?

Where on earth did that thought come from? He wasn't looking to marry. *Was he?* He was far too young yet to settle down with one woman, and he had a horse stud to make prosperous. Plus his future was uncertain given Rheda's situation. If he had to move closer to Newmarket, his whole life would be in upheaval until he sold Tumbury Manor and found an estate nearby he could afford to buy.

The poultice was soon wrapped round Colton's elbow and the horse settled a bit.

Georgiana looked down at her gown. "I best go and change before father sees me like this and asks questions. What should I say if he asks where you are?"

"Tell him I rode here and that I was not feeling well so I left. I'll walk Colton home once the poultice has reduced the swelling."

"We could both lead Colton to Hascombe. It's only five miles. We could ride and then I could bring the horses back," Billy offered. "Saves walking."

"Go." Daniel said to Georgiana. "Billy and I will sort something out."

She lifted her skirts and moved to the entry stall. "Thank you, Daniel. I will not forget this kindness."

He gave one of his most seductive smiles. "I'm sure I can think of a way you can repay me."

You'd think Daniel had asked her to give him her soul from the thundering scowl Georgiana suddenly sent his way. With a stiff nod of her head she took off running for the house.

After she left Daniel had not realized he'd sighed out loud until Billy said, "You said the wrong thing. For the past few years someone has always wanted something from her. Her mother. Her father. Men who are blinded by her beauty. She doesn't trust nobody."

"I *don't* want anything from her. I do wonder why she is so set on reclaiming Apollo when it will cause her problems. Where are the horse's papers?"

Billy rubbed Colton's nose. "Her grandfather gifted her the horse. I was present when he brought the colt here and gave it to her. I heard him telling her it was her birthday present. I don't know nothing about any papers though."

So Georgiana had not lied. She believed the horse was hers because she'd been told that was the case. "That's a pity. The horse is valuable and Lord Hascombe forgave a large debt for the colt. I could persuade him to return the horse—"

Billy looked up from where he was polishing a bridle. "Don't bring Apollo back here. His lordship would simply sell him again and that would ruin my lady's plan."

Daniel casually asked so as not to reveal what Billy had just let slip, "What plan." But Billy wasn't stupid. He turned away and ignored his question. "What plan?" Daniel insisted.

Billy hesitated before turning to face him. "I owe Lady Georgiana. She saved my life once. I fell into the stream running through the back paddocks and it was running swift. I lost my footing and I cannot swim. She jumped in and saved me by holding my head out of the water before getting us both to the bank."

Envy bit, poisonous venom slipping into his veins at the knowledge Georgiana likely trusted Billy more than she would ever trust him. He realized the groom would never reveal her secrets. Trust won is easily lost and impossible to regain. "She's one hell of a woman."

"That she is. And because of that she's always putting others before herself." Billy indicated he needed to heat more wheat before they started the long walk back to Hascombe.

"Others before herself," Daniel murmured to no one but a horse. His immediate thought was that Georgiana was protecting someone. *Who?* Her mother was her only family other than her father who she despised. *Her mother!* But what would her mother need protection from? And how did Apollo fit into the plan Billy would not divulge?

He ran a hand through his hair and then stroked Colton's nose as the horse nibbled at his jacket pocket. He pulled out a sugar cube from his pocket. He always carried them for his horses. Colton was most appreciative. Daniel would have a new horsey friend for life.

He wondered who Georgiana's friends were. Who could she rely on? Probably only Billy here and as a groom he could not protect her—especially from her father and his journey towards bankruptcy, or even jail for fraud.

Memories of what his sister had to do—alone—to survive and protect them both came flooding back. Rheda had no one and it had almost cost her life. A shudder wracked his body. He could not bear to think of Rosalind in the same situation. Rufus had been his sister's savior. As he stroked Colton's nose he silently vowed he would be Georgiana's fierce knight. He would stand between her and anyone who would take advantage or hurt her.

On a wry smile he hoped she would let him, but knowing the stubborn and distrustful chit he rather doubted that. Still, it would be a way to get to know her better. To understand why she stirred his soul and why it seemed his heart ached for her.

And most of all, understand what it would take to make Georgiana his.

Now that was a scary thought.

Chapter Five

Georgiana yawned as she made her way back to the house, her heart heavy with both elation and disappointment, coupled with the need to hit something—hard. Why did men always expect payment? Why couldn't a man simply do something nice because it's the right thing to do?

After what they had both shared her mind was spinning... Worse, she could think of nothing but the pleasure he'd given her. For one fleeting moment the desire to beg Daniel for help almost overwhelmed. Then she looked up and saw her mother standing at the window. Her mother was all she had and she needed protection. What if she went to Daniel for help and he too thought the asylum was the place for her.

She had to find a way to instigate her plan.

And yet, everything had changed.

Daniel.

She refused to look deeper at why her blood boiled when Daniel had said those words 'pay me'. She had thought he was different. When he'd suggested they talk to his brother-in-law about Apollo instead of arresting her on the spot... never mind. She had to keep reminding herself Daniel was just a man and she could never allow herself to rely on any man.

She hated owing anyone. She saw what debt had done to her father. Made him desperate, twisted him into someone she didn't want to know. Or maybe he'd always been like this and she'd been too young to understand.

Her father had her trapped because of his threat to her mother. Sometimes she thought she'd go mad at the unfairness of it all. She knew perfectly well that once her trust came through, he'd use her love for her mother to bleed her dry and then where would she be. She'd be like most women in this world, needing a man to take care of her because financially they held all the power.

Daniel's handsome face flashed in her mind. For one silly moment she'd actually thought he might be an answer to her troubles. If she could find a man as nice as Lord Hascombe she might consider marriage—that would put the devil of a sickle in her father's plans. She'd almost convinced herself Daniel was such a man, given he was Lord Hascombe's brother-in-law, and then he had to ruin it all with a few words.

"Your father's on the war path looking for you." Burton's sighed when he saw the state she was in. "I told him you had to help the servants aid Lord de Winter since he had become ill."

"I could kiss you."

"I'd rather you didn't. You smell like the stables. Perhaps a quick change would be best. I have alerted your lady's maid."

Georgiana wasted no time answering but hurried up the back stairs.

By the time she had changed and returned to the drawing room and their guests, she could see the exasperation on Rheda's face. Her father was still trying to sell his horses. What an absolute bore. She prayed Rheda had not told her father why she had dashed off.

Before her father could scold her in front of everyone, Georgiana smiled sweetly and said, "Apologies for my absence." She turned to look at Rheda blocking her father's view of her face and with a glance that screamed don't dispute my tale, she said, "Your brother is not well, my lady, and I had to organize someone to accompany him home on his steed in case he got into difficulty."

"Oh, is that where you rushed off to. I told your father it was some sort of horse emergency."

She silent mouthed a big 'thank you'.

Rheda said, "I think we should return home too. We can always catch up with my brother and offer him a ride in our carriage. I'm worried about the injury he incurred the other day, but he would insist on riding."

"What injury?" her father asked and Georgiana threw a stricken glance at Rheda. The Countess was not to know it had been her and Billy that attacked Daniel but if Rheda mentioned someone had tried to steal Apollo her father would know.

Rheda must have caught on as she quickly said before her husband could answer, "a horse incident in the stables."

Her father nodded. "Kicked in the head was he? I've seen that happen often. Rest. His lordship needs rest. I'll summons Burtons to organize your carriage," and he moved away to pull the bell.

Rheda stood and moved close and whispered in Georgiana's ear, her tone less than friendly, "I think you owe me an explanation." When her father looked over, Rheda added loud enough for all to hear. "I would take it as a great kindness if you'd allow your daughter to visit with me tomorrow. I do miss female company. Perhaps Lady Georgiana could join us for lunch at Hascombe Hall."

She could hardly decline given what Rheda had surmised about Daniel's head injury. "I'm sure I shall be delighted."

On that note their guests departed and her father retired to his study, probably to drink himself to sleep dreaming of the horses he might get Lord Hascombe to buy. Her father would be disappointed in the morning.

Georgiana retired too but couldn't sleep. She'd left the curtains undrawn so that she'd wake early. She would ride to Hascombe at sun up and see how Colton was.

She lay in bed watching the moonlight flicker over the ceiling whenever the clouds moved over the moon. She ran her fingers over her lips and pressed her thighs together remembering his touch and how good it made her feel. *Wanton.* Daniel. Daniel filled her thoughts. Handsome, virile, passionate, desirous. Why were her flesh and her heart so weak? Perhaps that was the curse of all women—to have dispositions to love men regardless of their moral compasses. Like her mother.

Why did fate have to bring such a man into her life just as she was about to escape.

He was nicer than her father. She at least knew that. The man clearly loved horses and was kind. Plus he had not told her father or Lord Hascombe that she'd tried to steal Apollo. Or who had knocked him out. What she could not work out was why? Did he intend to use this information in some way when it suited him?

She'd never met a man who did anything just to be kind. And his words in the stable tonight hinted that Daniel was no exception.

But what kept her awake was not the fear of what he would do with the information, but the feeling of hurt swimming in her gut. He had kissed her as if she was his world. Was he false? Is this how her mother thought of her father?

She had wanted Daniel to be different. She swallowed hard. She liked him and that made him dangerous. She'd always said she would never let a man close enough to hurt her and Daniel's words 'pay me back' cut like a knife deep into her chest.

And she didn't know what she was going to do about it because to her horror she still liked him. She couldn't stop thinking about him. But could she trust him?

She fell asleep planning how to test Daniel and what he wanted from her. It was terribly annoying that she looked forward to it.

Daniel slowly stirred awake still exhausted from his long night in the stable attending Colton. He'd fallen into bed at dawn's light dreaming of long fair hair and soft creamy skin lying next to his. And in his dreams he'd kissed every inch of her skin.

Georgiana immediately filled his waking thoughts too.

He was about to roll over onto his back and instigate another sensual dream when a delicate feminine cough made him freeze. He glanced over his shoulder to see Rheda sitting on the edge of his bed and flopped back to the sheets, inwardly groaning as his erection withered.

"You normally don't sleep this late. Were you up into the early hours with the horse you brought back from Lord Wentworth's."

Trust his sister to know everything before he woke. "Her father would have shot the horse. What else was I to do?"

"From what I hear from Michael we may have to anyway."

He rolled over onto his back. "That is why I did not get to bed until dawn. I wanted to see if the inflammation had gone down at all with the heat."

"And has it?"

He yawned before nodding.

"Then you can explain to me why you did not tell me it was Georgiana who hit you over the head and tried to steal Apollo."

He sat up and leaned against the headboard conscious he was very naked under the sheets and although his sister had seen him in the flesh many times as they grew up, he was now a grown man.

"Sister dear, can we not have this conversation once I am dressed and have at least some food in my stomach. I want to see the horse before Georgiana gets here—if she is not here already."

"She's here."

If he wasn't naked he'd have jumped out of bed. "Don't blame her. It was her groom that hit me. Besides, I believe she has a claim to Apollo. Her grandfather gifted the colt to her."

"She couldn't have come and told us that?"

He briefly closed his eyes. "I remember not so long ago a young lady who trusted no one. So much so it almost got her killed. Sound familiar? Georgiana's upbringing has not allowed her to trust."

Rheda shrugged her shoulders as if she had forgotten her past. "Still, her groom might have killed you. I'm not sure I can forgive that."

He leaned forward and took her hand. "You will because you know what it is like for a woman on her own to fight for her livelihood. And because you have a big heart."

Rheda sniffed but did not remove her hand from his. "Her father *is* a complete arse. He reminds me of our father. Poor girl." She suddenly leaned and pressed a kiss to his cheek. "I like the girl. She reminds me of me."

He sat back and laughed. "Of course she does."

"Then I feel I am in a position to give you some advice."

His laugh faded. "Advice on what exactly."

This time his sister gave a knowing smile. "On how to win her heart of course."

Daniel scuttled back until his back hugged the headboard. "Oh, no. I'm too young to be married."

"Don't be silly. Age has nothing to do with finding the one—finding your soul mate."

His mouth hung open because he could not refute her logic. Was Georgiana the one? He gave a wry smile. "Pretty hard to woo a lady who trusts no man."

"Then you have to earn her trust and the only way to do that is to be truthful. Don't keep secrets or try to out smart her. Simply tell her and your pride be damned."

He slapped his forehead. "Why didn't I think of that? Just because I know I'm being truthful doesn't mean she does."

Rheda stood and moved to the door of his bedchamber. "Trust is earned through actions. It's Christmas. What do you think she'd love as a present?"

He had already decided to give Apollo back to Georgiana but what he was trying to figure out was how he could keep her father from stealing it from her once again.

"If you marry her you can keep both Georgiana and the horse safe." Just before she left his room Rheda added, "And I'd sort it out soon before she does something stupid."

As she shut the door he yelled after her, "Like you did."

But his sister was right. Billy spoke of a plan. He threw back the bedcovers calling for his valet.

Chapter Six

The day was bitterly cold and Georgiana hugged Apollo simply to warm herself up from her ride over to the Hascombe estate. She'd already visited with Colton and noticed his limp was still there but he at least could stand on the leg.

Apollo seemed to be happy here and for that she was grateful. She smiled to herself. Michael, Lord Hascombe's head groom, was not letting her out of his sight.

"Did you miss me, my beautiful boy?" Georgiana said as she stroked Apollo's nose.

"That's a leading question," a masculine voice said as Daniel walked out of the shadows and came to stand next to her at Apollo's stall.

"It wasn't a question aimed at you."

"Well, you can hardly expect Apollo to answer," Daniel replied with a cheeky grin. A grin she was becoming far too enamored with.

She moved slightly sideways, the current streaming through her at just the touch of his shoulder against her arm, unsettling her. To her dismay, the colt was more than eager for Daniel's touch. She could understand the longing.

"Thank you for allowing me to come and see both Colton and Apollo. There is no doubt in my mind that father would've shot a lame horse, and he would've tried to sell Apollo again."

"That's highly risky. It's fraud. If your father was caught the sentence would be severe."

She looked away from Daniel's hypnotizing eyes and thought on what he just said. She bent forward and placed a kiss on Apollo's nose. "If I didn't love you so much, it would almost be worth taking you home and dangling you in front of father. But I can't prove ownership. I could, however, let Lord Gaston know the horse he just bought is a hag. Father sold King Heron three months ago to Lord Featherstone."

She sensed Daniel stiffened beside her. "He would be in a lot of trouble. You hate him that much?"

She choked up with emotion. "You don't know my father like I do."

To her surprise Daniel reached out and took her hand in his. "Why don't you tell me? If he has done anything to hurt you, I would—"

"My father is a bully. He's selfish. He is truly evil. However, I'm too precious to hurt at the moment." Daniel remained silent understanding there was more to tell. She just didn't know if she could bring herself to trust him. "A handsome face, clever words, and a lofty title. The combination is hard for any young woman to ignore. Unlike myself, my mother couldn't see past a cleverly put together camouflage. She fell in love with my father and married him against her father's better judgment. My grandfather told me his desire to give his daughter everything she wanted, was her undoing."

She should pull her hand free but she couldn't. For the first time in a long while she enjoyed the intimacy of his touch. Just knowing that someone was willing to listen and perhaps be her champion was enough to have her heart lower its defenses.

"I gather the marriage was not a happy one."

She gave a choked laugh. "That would be an understatement. My father married my mother for her money, and for my grandfather's expertise in horse breeding. Things really got worse for my mother when I was born. My birth was not easy, and my mother was told she could have no other children. He blamed her and was so cruel."

"Ah, that explains a lot. It explains why you have no siblings. It also explains why your father is more concerned with living a life of a certain standard with no regards to you or your mother."

"He cares for no one but himself. I'm waiting for the day I wake up and he's sold the estate from under us."

"The estate is not entailed?"

"No. That's the reason my grandfather set up a large trust for me. He knew what my father was like."

Daniel seemed to consider that for quite some time. "When you marry, Lord Wentworth may well sell the estate. He doesn't need a large estate when he has no one to leave it to."

"In other words he's selfishly building a way to ensure he can live comfortably for the rest of his life with no regard to myself or my mother. If he had his way my mother would be in an asylum."

Daniel swung her to face him. "That's his hold over you. He is threatening your mother? So I assume this great plan that Billy let slip is to give you enough money to escape and hide with your mother. Apollo is worth a lot of coin but not enough to live off for the rest of your life."

She could not keep the tears from welling. "It's not just for my mother's sake that I need to escape. In eight months my trust becomes available to me. If my father gets his hands on my trust, which I'm in no doubt he will given that my grandfather is no longer around, he'll find some way to steal it from me. I will have nothing to fall back on."

"I'm sure I can help you there. There are lawyers to ensure your trust is not used without your approval. I could get Rufus to recommend someone. Or even better yet, you could appoint Rufus as your trustee."

She wanted to lean in and hug Daniel. It was so kind of him to offer Lord Hascombe's help, and it was a sensible solution. "You don't understand. He will use my mother to make me sign over every penny. He has threatened to throw my mother in an asylum, he already has two doctors ready to sign off, and there would be nothing I can do about it."

"The bastard. Surely we can find two surgeons to dispute your father's findings."

Georgiana shook her head as she brushed tears from her cheek. "There is nothing to dispute. My father's bullying, the degradation he put her through, has affected my mother. She no longer speaks. She has to be fed like a child. And she recognizes no one." She pulled her hand from Daniel's when she saw the look of horror on his face. "She is harmless, like a small child. And I will never see her sent away to one of those horrid places."

Daniel pulled her back into a gentle embrace. "It would seem your mother needs to disappear, somewhere your father cannot get his hands on her."

She nodded, her cheek rubbing against the roughness of his jacket drying her tears. "He owns my mother. I would have no say in what happens to her. So we have to be able to hide."

She closed her eyes as Daniel gently stroked her hair. "That's not exactly correct. You don't have to hide, only your mother has to hide."

She leaned out of the embrace to look up at his face. "I think I understand what you are saying. We only have to hide my mother, my father could never make me reveal where she was. If I am not there when she escapes, and I pretend to be upset, he might not suspect me."

"Your father is not stupid. He *will* suspect you, but what can he do to you? I'll be here if he tries to hurt you in any way. Billy would send word."

"Father won't hurt me until I get access to my trust. Where could I hide her?" A smile edged at her lips but then slowly faded. "I don't have the money."

"Silly girl. I do. I will pay you for Apollo."

"Don't be ridiculous, your brother-in-law owns Apollo."

"Technically he does, but on Christmas day Apollo becomes mine. I believe you when you say your grandfather gifted the horse to you. He would never have given such a magnificent colt to your father. And lucky for you it's Christmas, because Rufus and Rheda have gifted the horse to me."

She pushed away and immediately missed the warmth of his strong and comforting embrace. "That's just charity."

She watched as Daniel shook his head, a serious expression on his handsome features. "How in good faith could I accept a Christmas gift, when I know the horse was taken from you, the rightful owner? Yet how can I refuse such a generous gift from my sister, especially now."

"What do you mean especially now." She wanted to reach out and cup his cheek as sorrow filled his usually sparkling eyes.

"Unlike you, I never knew my mother. She died giving birth to me. My father was a drunken gambling idiot, who, like your father, set off down a path that almost lost me my inheritance. If it hadn't been for Rheda and the risks she took I would not be standing here today. Rheda wasn't just my sister, she was like a mother to me, and I will do absolutely anything for her because she's all I have left."

"But your sister is married to a wonderful man. She has two beautiful children, and she seems very happy."

"That's because she's brave. That's because she's trying to hide from everyone how scared she is, especially from her husband, who loves her more than his last breath. She doesn't want to spoil Christmas for everyone." She watched with fascination as tears welled in Daniel's eyes. She'd never seen a man cry, and it completely undid her. Without thinking she stepped forward and this time it was she who embraced him. She wanted to take away the hurt and pain showing on his face.

"She has found a lump in her breast and will have surgery in the New Year."

A cancer. She could barely hide a shiver. She'd heard about women dying from a cancer of the breast. "But it might not be anything serious. You have to think positively and pray hard." *Praying. When had that ever helped her?*

Daniel hugged her tightly. "From your mouth to God's ear."

They stood silently holding each other for one moment, before Daniel whispered in her ear, "Now we have to find a place to hide your mother."

"I don't want to be too far from her. I really think I'm going to have to go with her."

Daniel suddenly pushed her out of his arms and looked at her. "You both could hide here. I'd take you south to Tumbury Cliff but Rheda needs me. We could go south once I know Rheda is well."

The idea of being under the same roof as Daniel was very appealing. If he could pay her for Apollo then after Christmas she could take her mother and run. She could even wait until after Rheda's operation, and perhaps stay with Daniel at his estate in the south while she found a place to hide. Only until her money came through.

But she knew it would simply bring trouble down on Lord Hascombe if her father learned they were here and he could get the magistrate involved. With her mother not able to make decisions for herself the law would give that right to her father. Rheda had enough to cope with.

"I have to stay at Wentworth in order to ensure father does not suspect you of hiding her. He won't hurt me. I'm far too valuable. However, I'd like to get mother away from him soon. He's getting more and more desperate and his mood turns perfectly evil. When it does, the coward he is sees him take his worries out on my mother. I can't bear it."

Daniel ran a hand through his hair. "Are you sure he won't hurt you?"

She nodded.

"Then let's go and speak with Rufus and Rheda."

Georgiana grabbed his arm as he made to move away. "Why are you doing this for me? What's in it for you?"

"Does there have to be something in it for me?"

She desperately wanted to believe that he was doing it because he was kind and good. "I find most people expect a favor in return. What are you expecting from me?"

He stood looking at her until she felt like an ogre for asking such a question. Finally he said, "I have seen what happens to women when they have no one defending them. I'm helping you because it is the right thing to do. But I will not lie to you. I like you. I'm attracted to you. And yes, I would like to be more than friends."

Daniel had moved closer and she was finding it difficult to breathe. She appreciated his direct approach. But what did more than friends mean? She knew how to spurn the men, who flirted, and those who took unwanted liberties, but Daniel's attentions were not unwanted. She liked him too.

He tilted her chin up with his finger. "Stop over thinking. Let's just concentrate on getting your mother safe and all of us through Christmas without your father ruining it for all of us." And then he leaned down and pressed the softest of kisses to her lips before stepping back and taking her hand to lead her from the stable.

They got to the stable door and she looked around. She could not see anyone about, but she saw the same mistletoe hanging above, just like it had the fateful day she'd tried to steal Apollo. She stopped, and when Daniel turned to her with an eyebrow raised, she pointed up. Her heart summersaulted at the gorgeous smile that spread over Daniel's lips. Warmth spread through her limbs regardless of the light snow that was now falling. She rose up on tiptoes and wrapped her arms around his neck. Time stood still as his lips lowered to hers and she almost forgot to breathe until his lips touched hers.

The kiss was masterful. Heat, desire, and passion shook her to the core and she gave herself over to the magic. Soon she was floating in the clouds and all she wanted to do was move closer—to climb right inside all this warmth.

A discreet cough saw Daniel slowly end the kiss. He stood looking down at her with his eyes filled with such longing her heart soared. He was breathing heavily as was she.

"I knew that mistletoe would come in handy for someone," Rufus laughed.

Daniel swung to face him grinning like a schoolboy. "So I have you to thank. We were just coming to find you. We have a favor to ask."

Rufus looked between the two of them and his smile died. "Best we go back to the house and find Rheda then. I don't do favors without her approval." At Daniel's raised eyebrow, he added, "Well, not that she knows about."

Chapter Seven

The carriage was approaching the house and her father's snores didn't help to steady her nerves. When they arrived home her mother would no longer be in residence. She'd taken her father into Newmarket on the pretense of Christmas shopping while Billy, Tessa, and Jimmy her father's valet and Tessa's husband, moved her mother to Hascombe.

Georgiana prayed none of the other servants saw them go. Tessa and Jimmy now worked for her. They could never go back to Wentworth. They would be her mother's caregivers. While Billy… she prayed hard that no one saw Billy helping with the escape. He insisted on staying at Wentworth to guard her, and Daniel agreed.

She decided to let her father sleep until the carriage came to a halt. How long would it take for her father to learn his hold over her had escaped? She swallowed down her fear. Her father was a cruel man and she worried how he would react. Perhaps, as Daniel had said, she should have gone with her mother. But if they both went her father would suspect the Hascombe's. Hopefully he would think Georgiana had merely sent her well away, he'd have no idea the Hascombe's were helping her.

As they drew up to the steps, leading up to the front door, she noticed the commotion and knew her mother's absence had been noted. She literally jumped out of the carriage before it had fully stopped.

"What is it Burton?"

He stood ringing his hands. "It's Lady Wentworth—"

"What's happened to my mother?" she cried. "Is she ill?" and she made to move past Burton up the steps.

But Burton cried out, just as her father stepped from the carriage. "She's gone. And so are Tessa and Jimmy."

The whole county could have heard her father's roar. What she had not expected was the hand that suddenly wrapped around her throat almost lifting her off the ground. "You… You will tell me where you have hidden her or by God I'll—"

"My Lord, perhaps this would be best handled in private." Burton's calming voice brought her father out of his murderous haze. His hand loosened at her throat and she began gasping fresh air into her lungs. He grabbed her arm and began pulling her up the stairs. She didn't have the breath to stop him. She saw Billy's worried face peering round the corner of the house. He'd go for help.

Her father swung her round and pushed her into the drawing room closing the door behind him. She crawled along the floor until the settee was between then. "You will tell me where you have put my wife or I will beat it out of you." It wasn't the words themselves, merely the way he said them. He was calm. Too calm.

"I have no idea where Tessa has taken mother. I was with you. I am not party to this." Her fingers were crossed behind her back.

He moved slowly toward her. "You must think I'm stupid. Tessa would not move your mother without your say so." He reached out and swiped the vase off the stand and watched it smash against the slate fire surround. "Now tell me where she *is*."

She got to her feet and used the back of the settee to support her shaking legs. She hoped Daniel would not be too long. "No. I won't tell you. I'm done being used. I know what you have planned. You'll wait for me to come into my trust and then you'll use mother to make me sign it over to you. And then you know what you'll do? You'll gamble it all away like you have everything else, until I have nothing left."

Another step closer.

"Nothing left. You stupid girl. You will marry and marry well. You don't need that money. Your face is your fortune. I have already made an arrangement with Lord Featherstone."

That was the last straw. "Selling your own daughter now. Is this what it has come to? Why am I not surprised? I wouldn't tell you where mother is if my life depended on it."

"It just might," he threatened.

She threw her head back and laughed. "No. I'm far too valuable alive. If I die before I marry, the money goes to my cousin."

Her father halted in his tracks. "Pain has a distinct way of making people talk."

"I swear I won't tell you no matter what you do to me, but I will tell everyone who will listen about mother and my trust fund, if you lay your hands on me. So unless you want our neighbors and villagers to see me covered in bruises then I'd think again." Georgiana could see the fight beginning to leave her father. He suddenly understood her conviction. She taunted him. "If you need money sell this estate and leave mother and me alone."

Her father sunk down onto the nearest chair. "Sell the estate. I could go to the Americas. Men are making fortunes out there in the plantations." It was as if she no longer existed. He sat talking to himself his excitement building. "No stuffy society watching and condemning everything I do."

She silently thought to herself it would be a wise move to leave England should any of the men her father had duped with worthless nags, seek restitution. She also knew when he left it would be the last time she'd ever see her father. Titles meant nothing in the Americas and she did not doubt her father would end up dead on the end of a sword, pistol or knife.

She couldn't seem to care. He'd never been a father to her in the real sense of the word.

She took the opportunity to walk round the outside of the room and head for the door. He didn't even try to stop her. Burton, bless him, was hovering outside and his look of relief made her suddenly remember the staff. She hoped the new owner of Wentworth would keep the staff on. She would try to ensure that happened.

"Are you well, my lady?"

"Perfectly, thank you. Lady Hascombe has invited me to spend Christmas with them. Can you organize my luggage to be packed and get the carriage ready?"

She forgot all about her father as she did the final wrapping of her gifts for the Hascombe family, and she hoped Daniel would love the solid silver brandy flask she had bought him.

She'd just finished wrapping Wilton's toy soldiers when she heard heavy boots pounding up the stairs and the door to her room flew open. Daniel stood in the doorway, his eyes wild and his mouth set in a firm line. His eyes found her across the room, and he strode over to her and ran a finger along the bruise forming on her neck.

"I'll kill him."

She took his hand and placed it on her cheek. "I'm fine. But thank you for coming for me."

"Did he do anything else to you."

She shook her head. "No. I made him see it would not be in his best interests to hurt me. Besides, I think he's made other plans. I reminded him he could simply sell the estate. It's worth about the same as my trust fund."

Daniel pulled her to her feet and ran his hands over her body as if not believing she was well. "I want to find him and squeeze the life out of him."

She pressed a kiss to his nose. "He's not worth it. I just want him out of my life, and my mother protected."

Tension still wracked his body, she could see it in his shoulders and the way one of his hands was fisted closed with his knuckles white.

"Daniel, just help me walk out of this house and never look back. With mother safe I feel as if a weight has lifted off my shoulders. It's Christmas and I want to use it as a turning point in my life. I want to celebrate it with you because you have made it possible, and I'll never forget your kindness."

The tension turned from violence to sensual at her declaration. Both of them noticed they were in her bedchamber, and the large four-poster bed was like a flaming beacon.

She wanted this man. Wanted him here and now. Maybe it was the aftermath of her father's violence, or maybe it was the power swimming in her veins. Her destiny was now her own. And she wanted to grab it with everything she was.

He must have seen the longing in her eyes because he reached for her; palm curving about her jaw, he tipped up her face, drew her close. He studied her eyes— as if searching for permission, searching for what she wanted. She didn't even contemplate hiding herself from him.

"I need you to be sure."

Her gaze focused on his lips. She watched, mesmerized, as he drew in another breath. Opened his lips to speak again—

She stretched up, drew his head down, brought her lips close to his and murmured, "I want you. No. I need you."

He covered her lips with his, kissing her voraciously, all consuming. She heard her maid slink from the room and close the door so they were totally alone.

She couldn't even remember how he got her clothes off but suddenly she was standing naked in front of him, and she reveled in the wantonness of this moment.

She'd never felt so free.

Or so desired.

Daniel's hands slid over her bare skin like a whispered caress. Reverent. Worshipping. Claiming...

He closed his arms about her, pulling her close, molding her to him. Any suggestion of stopping him died the instant she'd set eyes upon his face, on all he said in just one hot, burning gaze.

Naked in his arms, she clung, and returned his kisses greedily, avidly— flagrantly encouraged him to seize, take, and claim.

Halting, he asked, his voice a husky promise, "I should make Christmas wishes more often."

On a groan, he lifted her and turned with her in his arms to face the bed. He let her down, sliding her body down his, his hands cupping her bottom, pressing her to him, molding her softness against his erection while his tongue plundered her mouth, leaving her a mass of aching need. Heat bloomed and fire took hold— she wanted more.

She reluctantly eased back from his kiss. "I want to see you. See if you're all I imagined," she added breathlessly.

With eager hands she pushed his coat wide, trapping his arms. With a curse, he let her go, stepped back, wrenched off his coat, and flung it aside.

Her eyes widened at the violence behind the movement. He stilled. "I'd never hurt you. You do know that?"

In answer she stepped back into his embrace, her lips brazenly seeking his, her hand covering his heart. She knew the man he was. Gentle, giving, kind—loving. Loving was why she found him so attractive, why he and only he would do for her journey into passion.

Georgiana acted on her newfound desire, yanking the halves of his waistcoat apart, stretching to slip it from his board shoulders. Impatiently he pulled his shirt over his head, and finally she had her hands on hot, rough, skin. She ran her fingers over his chest and stomach, the muscles beneath rigid and locked. His chest was a wonder of rough hairs the color of a lion's mane. She leaned into him and licked. He tasted divine, addictive.

He once more plundered her mouth, his hands closing about, and then provocatively kneading the globes of her bottom. The long muscles framing his back flexed like steel beneath her wandering hands. She ran her fingers down his back, counting the ribs as she traced the muscles leading her down his sides and back to his waist, to caress the rippling bands across his abdomen. They rippled at each touch.

Gaining courage, her fingers quested lower. He sucked in a breath and held it as she lightly traced the prominent line of his erection. He stilled, his lips on hers, his tongue in her mouth, when she reached for the waistband of his breeches. As she undid the flap, he groaned into her mouth. Thrilled at her newfound power, Georgiana hurriedly undid the rest and slid one hand inside the opened flap, and found the rigid length of him. Hot with skin so very soft and smooth...

He was under her spell, entirely focused on her hand and what she was doing. Her fingers explored freely, and learned the size and shape of him. He was solid, larger than she imagined. He more than filled her hand. Growing bolder, she closed her fingers around him, circling him, and this time his groan was accompanied by a shudder.

She knew she was playing with fire, but she took her time fondling his sac; wonder blooming as it tightened in her hand. She could feel the surge of heated passion rising through him, provoked by her play, and it rose in her body in kind. She throbbed and grew damp between her thighs.

His mouth finally left hers, but he didn't stop her games. He truly was a saint because he let her play. She could see the tension in his neck, the cords tight as a bow.

Daniel clenched his jaw and endured her touch, when all he wanted was to throw her on the bed and sink into the heaven he knew he'd find there. He wanted to bury himself so deep and let her wrap those gazelle-like legs around him.

Though she was innocent, her touch was pure heaven, her instincts sound. He watched the wonderment in her smile and another surge of heat, of pure unadulterated desire rose, hardening and lengthening the part of his anatomy that was currently the determined focus of her being. He didn't know how much longer he could hold himself in check.

Not long, as it turned out. He made the mistake of looking down as she sent her thumb stroking over the aching head of his shaft and found a latent drop. She looked deep into his eyes, brought her thumb to her lips, and tasted, murmuring approval.

Control slipped. He caught his breath, nudged her face up and found her lips again, drew her into a drugging kiss, and ruthlessly, deliberately, took over. He didn't hold back. He seized and devoured, claiming her mouth, her lips, with a promise of what else he'd claim this night.

He would dictate the pace. He impatiently drew her hand away and efficiently divested himself of the rest of his clothes.

He looked magnificent. A Greek God come to life. She took in the sight, drank in the glory.

He drew her close, then closer until there was not even air between them. Silken skin caressing his chest, her arms, his erection, cradled in her softness, while he plundered her mouth, holding her and her senses captive.

Georgiana tried to move closer. She wanted him more than she'd wanted anything in her life. Far from resisting, she sank into his arms, gave herself up to his commanding kiss, surrendered and waited, nerves tight with anticipation, for him to make her his.

Without breaking their kiss, he lifted her and climbed onto the bed. The sheer curtains closed behind him, enveloping them in their own world.

They were on their knees facing each other and Georgiana let out a cry of disappointment when his lips left hers, only to moan in relief as his mouth found one tight, furled nipple.

His hot mouth suckled and savored. Her head fell back; her gasp shivered through the room. He feasted like a starving man. He laved her breasts, suckled, nipped—sending arrows of heat to her core. His hot mouth gave such pleasure she prayed he never stopped. Her hands closed on his skull, holding him to her; she was never letting go. His mouth was heaven on her flesh.

She rode the waves of delight he evoked. His hands roamed her curves while his mouth devoured her breasts. A wild wantonness erupted within and she reached for him. She gloried in the feel of his hard body, the evidence of his desire never more real. Georgiana stroked his cock once, and he growled deep in his chest. He urged her back on the bed and she went willingly. Her skin was flaming, her body melting, all her senses heightened and in scattered disarray. He followed her down, one knee rising and pushing between hers, parting her thighs, exposing the musky scent of her arousal to the room.

Georgiana was momentarily embarrassed when his muscled thigh, raspy with masculine hair, rode against her dampness, but his groan of admiration saw her glory in abandoned excitement. He deliberately shifted, pressing against the most sensitive spot, knowingly winding her tight... Her breath tangled in her throat.

She traced the rock-hard muscles in his arms as he braced himself over her, his other knee joining the first, pushed her legs apart, spreading her thighs so he could settle between them.

Their eyes locked and silently communicated. He looked down her bare torso to where their bodies would join and the set of his face told her all she needed to know. The angles and planes of his handsome face were sharp with desire. There was an elemental rawness of conquering male, and it thrilled her. She cupped his face and nodded.

He lowered his head to place a gentle kiss on her lips as he shifted between her thighs. The hardness she'd been caressing probed her slick entranced and she tried to relax, tried to memorize her first taste of his broad, blunt head and its inherent strength and heat as he inched slowly within her.

"Relax, my darling. Breathe slowly. I promise I'll try and make it as painless as I can."

He flexed his hips and pressed further in. She felt every inch of his hardness, stretching and filling her. He reversed direction and she let out the breath she'd been holding.

He repeated the process several times, each entry just that little bit further. Each short stroke enough to tantalize, to drive her insane. She moaned his name.

He covered her lips, took her mouth, adding to her screaming senses. She was combusting from the inside. Soon she was lifting her hips, writhing on the bed, urging him for more, her body aching, wanting...

He continued teasing her, only just entering her and then withdrawing, until she was wet and open and almost delirious with desire. Moving in a rhythm that was as ancient as time.

She lifted her head and found his lips. He took her mouth, his tongue mimicking his delicious torture below. He slid deeper, and his tongue plundered, ruthlessly. He settled more heavily between her legs, and she felt the power and strength of him.

Then he thrust powerfully.

She cried out in surprise, his mouth capturing her strangled gasp.

He stilled above her, raining kisses all over her face. "The pain will dull in a few moments. Are you all right?" The concern was very evident in his voice and the worried green of his eyes. He tenderly stroked down her side and molded his hand to her hip.

The sharp pain lessened to a dull ache and she could feel him throbbing within her. She could not help but move. At the slight lift of her hips, he drew back, and gripping her hip, he pressed in again. There was no pain this time. He didn't stop but drove on, all the way in, steadily pushing deep, stretching her, impaling her. She tried to remember to breathe at the sensation of him, hard and strong, embedded deep within her, filing her fuller than she'd imagined.

He rose up on his forearms and his eyes, emeralds under his lashes, glinted down at her, the weight of his lower body holding her immobile as he looked down and watched as he withdrew and slowly, even more powerfully, entered her.

She followed his gaze and watched as he claimed her. She felt every inch as he filled her, felt her body tighten until she arched beneath him.

"God, you feel so good." She struggled to catch her breath, "My body's on fire. I don't know if I can take—"

"You can. You will." It was a growled command. "Close your eyes and let it happen."

He continued to move above her and her body wound itself as tight as a drawn bow. She closed her eyes and gave herself over to passion's power. The intimacy of the moment sharpened as he slid deep and she felt the first stirrings of overwhelming passion.

She sent her hands sliding over his shoulders, running them over his back until she found his buttocks. She held on as they flexed. He began to move more forcibly than before, her hips lifted to match his rhythm the friction of their bodies sending spiraling pleasure to her very core.

"Oh. My. Goodness—"

The restless flames of desire erupted within her.

Erupted into a firestorm.

At her first scream, he took her mouth. Their lips melded, tongues tangled, hands gripping, their bodies merging in a frantic and driving need.

They were desperate for each. Neither trying to dominate, both wanting to take this journey together. Sharing, loving, being one. Their senses held, locked, overwhelmed by the slickness, the heat, and the gasping urgency of their loving.

He drove her on; ensuring the road to her release was expertly travelled. He thrust deeper yet and her body gathered him close, holding him, tightening around him and suddenly she was floating, riding a wave of joyous and consuming pleasure. Her body imploded in heat and glory and satisfaction. Sensations rioted down every nerve to suffuse every inch of her being, with satiation. The waves continued, no longer gigantic but ripples of contentment. She clung to him, felt him thrust deep and roar against her mouth, the sound flowing into her, as did his seed. They lay still, panting, soaking in the glory of their union as the waves slowly ebbed.

Daniel fought to regain his senses. Eyes closed tight as he felt the last spasm fade. A tsunami of feelings rioted within his chest. She was his. He'd bound her to him— forever. There was no turning back. They would marry and live happily ever after.

He rolled off her, slumping exhausted, wrung out beside her, pulling her hard against him into the cradle of his arms. Protecting her automatically as he would for the rest of his life.

Peace flowed over him and through him. He'd never felt anything like it in his life, and he just wanted to lie here and revel in the joy of it.

The joy of her.

They lay wrapped together, too drained to stir, but very content.

Daniel couldn't stop touching her. He stroked her silky skin and tried to think. "I could get a marriage license but since Christmas is tomorrow perhaps we could wait a few days. I think we should marry before Rheda's operation as it will help take her mind off what is to come."

He felt her still beside him. "Marriage?"

He turned to look at her and did not see joy in her eyes as he'd expected. "Surely you realize how much I love you. What we shared—"

"It's so soon. I had not considered—"

"I have just ruined you. Surely you must know my heart. I am a gentleman. I would never have slept with you if I was not prepared to offer marriage."

"Know your heart?"

He smiled softly at her surprise forgetting how she distrusted men. "I love you, Georgiana. I told you I wanted to be more than friends."

"Love me?" She bolted upright holding the sheet to her bare breasts. "I wasn't expecting this. I've only just found my freedom."

Hurt flooded every pore of his body. "Are you implying marriage to me would be akin to being a prisoner? I am not your father."

"Everything I own would become yours."

Daniel heard the bitterness in her words and knew it was her distrust that made her say them. But he also knew there could be no marriage, no love without trust. He threw back the covers and began to dress. "I don't want you for your money. I want you for you. I'd be happy to sign away any rights to your trust."

She reached out to him then. "I'm sorry. I did not mean to offend you. It's just—"

"Get dressed and I'll organize your chests to be loaded onto the carriage for the trip to Hascombe."

"Daniel, please..."

He remained silent. Too hurt and angry to speak, least he said something he would regret. His first marriage proposal and it had been brushed aside as if it was an offer of a cup of tea. He dressed while Georgiana sat fiddling with the sheets.

She stood wrapping a sheet around her nakedness. "Should we not talk about this?"

"It would appear there is nothing to say. You obviously do not love me the way I love you. What we just shared was special. You filled my soul. As a gentleman my offer of marriage still stands, but if you do not love me as I deserve, then perhaps you are right to decline and we should forget this interlude ever happened."

With that he gathered his pride and battered heart from the floor and took his leave.

An hour later he helped Georgiana into the carriage and even though darkness had fallen and it was cold, he decided to ride his horse home to clear his head.

But he realized he would never clear Georgiana from his heart and mind. Not with her staying under the same roof. How did he get a woman who didn't know how to trust, to take a risk and give him her heart? He remembered Rheda's words and decided that he would not give up. This was just one minor hurdle. Once they both had time to reflect on how marvelous their lovemaking had been, perhaps they could talk.

Only problem was, this had been Georgiana's first time, and she would have no idea how special their joining had been.

He knew. He would always know. And she would always own his heart. By God he would fight to win her love. He would stay here until she learned to trust him.

Chapter Eight

The carriage ride to Hascombe Manor was short, yet it was the longest journey of her life. She had hurt Daniel. A part of her wanted to beg his forgiveness, but was it his pride, or his heart, that she had hurt? They had not known each other long.

These were the moments when her mother's condition hit her the hardest. She had no one to confide in. No one to help her work out the tangle of emotions, stirring in her heart.

Georgiana didn't know why she was so surprised at Daniel's reaction to their lovemaking. He appeared to be an honorable, true gentleman. But looks could be deceiving. It had been her decision to give herself to him. She had instigated the passionate scene in her bedchamber. She could hardly blame him for the misunderstanding.

The cold weather did not stop the heat flushing her body as she remembered how his naked skin felt against hers. That she was attracted to Daniel was not in question. But lust did not mean love. She'd always sworn she'd never fall in love, but the way her heart beat so fast whenever he was near, and the fact she couldn't wait to have Daniel smile at her in that special way, and the pain she felt at any notion she would never see him again, made her question her vow.

Her mother had thought herself in love but had been fooled. Daniel had no reason to deceive her. Or did he? Her trust was rather large and he did admit his horse stud was still in a growth phase.

Her mind was still swirling and she was lost in a thick fog of angst when she arrived at her new temporary home. As she was helped from the carriage she noted there was no sign of Daniel. Instead, Rheda stood at the entrance wrapped in a thick cloak. Rheda beckoned her up and waited for her to reach the door.

They linked arms as Rheda led her to the drawing room where there was a roaring fire in the grate. "Your mother has settled nicely. She has the rooms on the top floor on the east wing. It has a lovely decked parapet where she can get fresh air whenever she wishes. It cannot be seen from below."

Georgiana sank into a chair by the fire, and let the flames warm her chilled bones. "Thank you. I'm sorry to be such a bother on Christmas Eve."

"It's no bother. The children are excited to have you here, probably because they know it means more presents."

That made Georgiana smile. Clarity hit like a hurricane. Without love, without trust she would never have a family. If she could never bring herself to marry—she would never have a child out of wedlock. That would not be fair to the child. She wanted children.

A tear leaked and slowly slipped down her face. She quickly wiped it away but not quick enough. Rheda approached and sank to her knees at her feet, taking her hand in hers. Georgiana was ashamed. "I'm sorry. My worries are nothing compared to yours."

"Daniel told you about my condition? I have faith that all will be well. And if not—well, I have so much love to help me face what must come."

Georgiana took her opportunity. "Daniel didn't reveal much about your life before your marriage, but he mentioned you'd worked to save Tumbury Cliff Manor on your own." She blurted out, "What made you marry Rufus?"

Rheda smiled. "Why love of course. I was a smuggler." She halted at Georgiana's gasp. "Rufus was sent by the crown to capture a smuggler they thought was spying for Napoleon. It was not me, but it was more like fear at first sight," she laughed.

"So what made you trust Lord Hascombe?"

Rheda patted her hand. "I see. This is about your feelings for Daniel. You want to know if he is a man who can be trusted. A man who won't steal your heart for his own means."

She sat forward. "Exactly. How do I trust my heart?"

Rheda rose and took the chair next to hers. She sat quietly for a moment staring into the flames. "Not trusting almost cost me my life. It's a long and lonely life if you cannot trust those around you. But, you have to place your trust in the right people, and the only way to do that is to listen to your inner voice. To have confidence in your decisions, and the courage to face the mistakes you make. Your instincts normally tell you the truth. However, sometimes people choose not to listen to themselves."

Georgiana's inner voice seemed to be mute. "That sounds too simple. Look at my mother."

"Your mother was warned by your father about her choice in husband. Your Grandfather was a man who loved his daughter, and if he really thought Lord Wentworth had loved your mother he would never have objected. I suspect your mother knew that. I suspect her inner voice told her she was making a mistake, but she choose to ignore it. Why? Only she knows that."

Georgiana considered what Rheda said. The logic was there. Why had her mother not listened to her father? Georgiana always took her Grandfather's advice. She would have listened if he'd had doubts about Daniel.

"So what you are saying is that I should ask for help from those I trust and then trust what my own thoughts on the matter become."

"Isn't that all we can do? Trust is having faith in someone or something. We can't see faith, we can only feel it." Rheda smiled. "My brother loves you. He is only three and twenty. He had no notion of taking a wife for many years. But fate has thrown you in his path and he has fallen hard." She watched Rheda's eyes widen. "And he is not after your money. In fact, he'll hate the fact you have money as he has too much pride to use it. Rufus and I have offered him money many times, but he is determined to make a success of his horse stud on his own."

Rheda's words rang true. Georgiana's inner voice was talking rather loudly inside her head. When Daniel first helped her—both with Apollo and then Colton, he didn't even know about her trust fund. Money was not driving him.

She jumped to her feet and kissed Rheda soundly on both cheeks. "I owe your brother an apology."

"He's in the west wing. Take the stairs, two floors up, and his room is the first on the right. He'll be dressing for dinner. Which is at eight."

Joy gave her wings as she all but flew up the stairs. Her heart was full to bursting. She stopped outside Daniel's bedchamber and composed herself. Running a hand over her hair she took a deep breath and let herself into his room. To her disappointment it was empty.

Then she heard whistling from an adjacent dressing room and she strode into the room only to stop dead. Daniel was bathing, and goodness the sight took her breath away. He was so beautiful.

Luckily it took him a few moments to realize she was there, so she could look her fill. His whistling faded as his eyes swept over her.

She stepped forward, her heart hammering in her chest. What if she had ruined everything with her cowardice? She walked to stand at the edge of the tub. "I came to say I love you, and I'm sorry for how I reacted earlier."

He said nothing for a moment and her legs began to tremble. Then all of a sudden the most glorious smile broke over his lips, and in one quick tug, she was in the water with him and he was kissing her soundly.

Her world spun and she wanted to cry with joy. She'd never experienced a feeling quite like it—love. Love for Daniel filled her until she almost choked on it. And it felt wonderful.

Finally he let her catch her breath. "I'm all wet," she laughed. "And your sister is expecting us at dinner by eight."

Daniel began undoing the hooks on the front of her gown. "That leaves me an hour to show you exactly how much I love you."

Hearing Daniel say he loved her made her dizzy with desire, and suddenly being late for dinner was no longer a concern

Chapter Nine

Christmas Day

Georgiana could barely hear herself think over the excited squeals and talking, as the two children raced to open their gifts. The Yule log was burning brightly in the grate, the table was full of food, and the day was progressing beautifully. The luxury of the moment was overpowered by the love swirling through the room. Rheda and Rufus, with their children, were the perfect antidote to her doubts. The love they obviously shared… she would have that too with Daniel and their children to come. She could have been in a shack and she would never have been happier.

Her mother, Judith, sat next to her in a chair overlooking the back garden and the light dusting of snow overnight made the world outside this room look magical. Still trapped in her own world, Judith seemed to sense that she was safe here. Judith still didn't interact with anyone, but she was content to sit quietly watching everyone have a lovely day.

It was the happiest Christmas Georgiana had ever had. And the best was yet to come. She had decided on an additional gift for Daniel, and she was waiting for the children to finish with their gifts, before giving it to him. At the moment they were crawling all over Daniel, who was letting them ride him like a horse. Finally he collapsed and Rheda said, "Samantha and Wilton, please let your uncle catch his breath. Come and have something to eat and then nurse will come and take you to have a sleep."

Georgiana smiled at the children's groans. They did not like the idea of a nap, and she wondered how Rheda could stand looking at their little disappointed faces. As if sensing her thoughts Rheda winked. "I have to stay strong or they will be incorrigible tonight."

Daniel came over and sat at Georgiana's feet resting his head on her knees. "Those two will be the death of me today." He grinned and added, "Especially as you kept me up half the night."

She didn't even bother to deny it. She was comfortably sore from their lovemaking. She simply pressed a kiss to his hair. "Then I shall sleep alone tonight and let you get your rest," she teased.

Daniel simply growled low in his throat. Then he handed her a small box. "Merry Christmas, my darling." She knew it wasn't a ring. He'd promised to take her to the House of Garrard in London in the coming month, so she could pick a ring. She'd worried about the expense but he'd insisted he was not that poor.

Her fingers eagerly undid the wrapping. It was a velvet box, which she slowly opened. Inside lay the most beautiful silver, with pearl inlay, locket. "I thought you could put a picture of your mother inside, or even our children when they are born."

Her eyes welled with tears. It was such a simple gift but so heartfelt. It spoke of his commitment to a life together, a true partnership. She didn't know how she'd gotten so lucky.

He reached up and wiped a tear away. "I love you, Lady Georgiana Marsh."

Heedless of the company, she flung her arms around his shoulders and kissed him.

She extracted herself from his embrace so she could pull out a parchment that had been burning a hole in her pocket all morning. Without words she handed it to him.

He looked down at her hand. "You've already given me so much. Your love was all I needed this Christmas. Plus you gave me the flask. It's just what I need on a winters day when I'm out with the horses."

She couldn't speak. Worried at what he would think when he read the note. She saw Rheda and Rufus watching them with a smile on their faces. She'd gotten Rufus and his estate manager to witness the document to ensure it could not be challenged. He must have told his wife, for Rheda's eyes welled with tears.

Daniel gently undid the ribbon and unrolled the document. She watched as he read but his face remained unreadable. When he'd finished he rolled the document back up and looked at her.

She couldn't stand the silence. "I wanted you to know how much I love you and trust you. I knew how much it would mean to you to be near Rheda, and I could think of no one better to look out for the staff. You could buy Went—"

"It's too generous." He opened his mouth and then shut it again. He ran his hand through his hair. "But God I love you for it. To know I have your trust... I'm the luckiest man alive."

"So you'll accept. I want you to use the money to buy Wentworth Estate from my father. It solves all our problems. Mother can stay in the house she knows. The staff will have us to ensure they are employed and treated well. We can turn Wentworth back into the best horse stud in Newmarket, besides Rufus's of course. And you can be near your sister. And father is gone from our lives for good."

Daniel looked across at his sister and Rufus.

Rheda offered an opinion. "I think it's a wonderful idea. You can keep Tumbury Cliff and breed the cavalry horses you love. And you can breed thoroughbreds here at Wentworth."

Rufus added, "We could work together and be the biggest and most successful thorough bred stud in all of Europe. I've already agreed to lend you the money to buy Wentworth until Georgiana comes into her trust."

Daniel could barely breath he was so filled with love. Georgiana had signed over the money in her trust to him. He would have total control over everything she would receive. He understood just how much of a gesture this was.

"Sweeting, I'm so touched I barely know what to say. You don't need to do this to prove your love. I can see it shining in your eyes. I can feel it in your touch. My heart and soul is completely in tune with yours."

He watched her smile die as if she thought he would say no.

He cupped her cheek. "I have another idea. How about we use the money but we put Wentworth into both our names. We would own it jointly."

The smile that she sent him made his heart fly. "I love that idea just about as much as I love you."

Rheda's squeal of delight warmed them too. "That's the best Christmas news of all. You'll be nearby. I'll have my brother back in my life, and I'll have a sister-in-law too."

"Rufus and I will speak with your father tomorrow and see what can be arranged. He would have to agree of course."

Georgiana shrugged. "He will agree because when you tell him we are to be married, he'll realize any chance of getting his hands on my trust money is gone. He was counting on my distrust of men. He had thought I'd never marry. He hadn't counted on fate sending me the man of my heart."

"I also want to thank your father. If he had not used Apollo to repay has debt to Rufus, which made you try to steal him back, we may never have met."

At Daniel's words she started laughing. "So father has no one but himself to blame for taking a horse that did not belong to him. Poetic justice I believe that is called."

Daniel pulled her into his arms and kissed the woman who owned his heart. "But just so we are sure, having your love is the best Christmas present ever." Then he soundly kissed her.

Epilogue

The heat of the midday sun was somewhat muted by the shade from the oak tree they were sitting under. Daniel sat with his back against the tree watching Georgiana playing hoops with Samantha and Wilton. Rheda was lying next to him, her head in Rufus's lap.

He'd married Georgiana a few days after New Year by a marriage license, letting Rheda fuss over the wedding to take her mind off her upcoming surgery.

That was months ago. It had been six months since his sister's operation and God willing Rheda would be with them well into old age. The surgeon had revealed the lump was merely a vesicle and she did not have the cancer.

"Daniel, it's too hot for your wife to be playing with the children in her condition."

He smiled to himself. Georgiana had only told him that she was with child this morning. How did Rheda know? "Is this what I am to expect living near you. That you know more than I about my wife and our life," he said on a laugh.

"Don't worry. She hasn't told me. I caught her cradling her stomach this morning and guessed." She looked at him with such joy and pride. "You're not sad you moved here to be near me, are you?"

He wasn't. "I still own Tumbury Cliff Manor and in time we will likely spend the winters there as they are milder." He loved his new home because it was where Georgiana was happiest. Her mother's state of mind meant moving someplace new was questionable. New faces and new places upset her, except Hascombe for some reason. "Lady Wentworth needs to be here, and Georgiana wishes to stay near her mother."

And Rufus added, "And you want to be with the woman you love."

He nodded and rose to his feet, his eyes set on his beautiful wife. "On that note I shall go and rescue my wife. A rest from this hot weather is calling."

Rufus called after him. "Just remember to let her rest." His sister's laughter followed him across the manicured lawn and it warmed his heart.

Samantha raced up to him and he swooped her up, planting a kiss on her forehead. "Your mother says to collect Wilton, and your father will take you both down to the pond for a swim."

The two children raced off squealing so loudly he put his hands up to his ears.

Georgiana pulled one hand away and held it against her stomach. "You best get used to the noise, my lord, as I want half a dozen children."

Her scent swirled round him in the heat, making him dizzy with love. But then, just being near her made him dizzy with love. She was his world, and he thanked God she'd put her faith in him.

"I thought we should retire from the heat of the afternoon." He loved the sensual smile that spread across her luscious lips at his words.

"I know that look. How much resting do you think I'll get with you in my bed." Georgiana's husky words revealed her pleasure at the suggestion.

"As much as my wife wishes. For fulfilling her desires is my sole goal in this world and the next."

She pressed in close and whispered in his ear, "Then you will have a very happy wife."

As she walked arm and arm with her husband into the house, the house that was now finally a proper home, the place where their children would be born and raised, she realized that everything that she did, and everyone that she'd met over her life, was in her path for a purpose. Daniel taught her that love is stronger than hate, and that with risks come rewards. Her reward for trust was gaining the most wonderful husband and life she could have ever imagined.

The End

About Bronwen

USA Today Bestselling author, Bronwen Evans grew up loving books. She writes both historical and contemporary sexy romances for the modern woman who likes intelligent, spirited heroines, and compassionate alpha heroes.

Her debut Regency romance, Invitation to Ruin won the RomCon Readers' Crown Best Historical 2012, and was an RT Reviewers' Choice Nominee Best First Historical 2011.

Her first self-published novella, To Dare the Duke of Dangerfield, was a FINALIST in the Kindle Book Review Indie Romance Book of the Year 2012 and a finalist in the RomCon Readers' Crown Best Historical 2013.

Her first contemporary released December 2012, The Reluctant Wife, won the RomCon Readers' Crown Best Short Contemporary 2013. She has won the RomCom readers crown three times.

You can find details of her work at
www.BronwenEvans.com

A Rogue's Reputation

~ BOOK 2 OF THE ROGUE CHRONICLES ~

BY

Lana Williams

Blame it on the mistletoe...

As the new Earl of Granger, Benjamin Wright is determined to put an end to his family's reputation of roguish behavior, beginning with his own. When he arrives in London to claim his inheritance, he quickly realizes his plan will not be as simple as he expected.

Lady Louisa Felton is appalled to learn her mother wrote love letters to the recently deceased earl. Fearing another scandal will cast her mother from Society, leaving her crushed along with Louisa's hopes for a future, Louisa attempts to retrieve the letters before the new heir finds them.

Discovering a lady dressed in lad's clothing attempting to steal from him is a surprise to Benjamin, but not as much as his attraction to the reckless lady. Though he vows to keep his distance, the lovely Louisa refuses to stay out of his life. One kiss is all it takes to know she has the power to make him forget his plan to reform.

Benjamin is the exact type of man Louisa's mother would fall for, making him the sort Louisa intends to avoid. If only she can convince her willful heart of that.

Fate refuses to cooperate with their plans, and what happens at Christmas will change this rogue's reputation forever.

Chapter One

London, England 1814

Lady Louisa Felton tugged at the ill-fitting trousers she wore as part of her disguise and studied the dark windows of Granger House on Grosvenor Street. None of the servants appeared to be awake. Perfect. Yet she couldn't convince her feet in their unfamiliar boots to move from the cobblestones toward the garden gate.

The deed could be postponed no longer. The new Earl of Granger was expected to arrive on the morrow or the day after, according to servants' gossip. She should've done this earlier in the week when her mother had first confessed her most recent grievous error. Procuring a lad's clothing had taken two days, but she'd wanted some sort of disguise for this undertaking. Thank heavens her lady's maid had a young brother willing to lend her the proper attire. Another day had been spent finding the courage to don the male clothing for this late-night venture.

Blast her mother for writing love letters to the previous earl, who'd lost his life, along with his wife and son, three weeks past when the ship they'd been on had gone down in a storm. Louisa felt a twinge of sympathy. The late earl had been a rogue of the worst sort with his son following closely on his heels. The Countess of Granger had ignored their terrible behavior by indulging in some of her own. Her penchant for belittling all who crossed her and spreading vicious gossip had been well known amongst the *ton*. Despite their poor behavior, Louisa certainly hadn't wished them dead.

Louisa muttered an unladylike curse under her breath. This was absolutely, positively, the last time she was going to rescue her mother from the brink of scandal. When she'd promised her father on his deathbed some twelve years ago to watch over her mother, she hadn't realized how difficult a task he'd given her. Her mother's huge heart and passionate nature often made her reckless, causing her to fling herself from one cause—or man—to another in search of happiness. Unfortunately, she had yet to find it since becoming a widow.

They could not risk the new earl discovering her letters and sharing them. While many in polite society might look the other way when a married man had an affair with a widow, leaving evidence for his heir to find was a completely different matter. Louisa didn't care to have her mother's name bandied about again. Not only did it cause her mother distress, it also tainted Louisa's future prospects, as would missions such as this one. Heaven forbid if she were caught.

Steeling herself, she used her own garden gate key to unlock the one before her, relieved they were similar enough to work. Their own home wasn't far away, but that provided little reassurance. She might have been in another country as strange and disorienting as her mission was.

In the garden away from the streetlamps, the night was inky black. The late November air held a distinct chill and added to her shivers. She approached the glass-paned door that led to the library, her palms damp from nerves. The layout of the house was similar to hers along with most of the other ones on this street.

A quick test proved the door locked. With a tug, she freed a hairpin from under her cap and went to work on the lock, something she'd practiced on the library door at home.

Minutes ticked by before she finally managed it. She drew a breath in an attempt to slow her racing heart as she cautiously opened the door then paused to listen.

Silence. The lack of sound had never been sweeter. But the darkness was a problem. She rummaged in her coat pocket for the candle she'd brought, relieved to see a few coals still burning in the fireplace and hurried forward to light her candle. Having to do so with the tinderbox would take far too long. The sooner she found what she sought and left, the better.

She moved to the desk with jerky strides, having already noted the library door that led to the rest of the house was closed, and placed the candle in a candleholder to begin her search. This evening, she should've been at a soiree where she might meet a thus far undiscovered paragon of calm, cool, and collected behavior whom she could marry. Why had she been fighting the idea? Marrying a man above reproach sounded lovely now and far from boring as she eyed the three-drawer mahogany desk.

With a silent prayer that she'd quickly find the letters, she opened the first drawer, dismayed to find it nearly full of papers. She pulled the lot out and paged through them in the dim candlelight with no success. After returning them to their place, she tried the center drawer only to find it locked.

If a married man wished to hide letters, he'd obviously keep them in that drawer. She retrieved her hairpin once more and set to work. Why her mother had fancied herself in love with the roguish earl escaped Louisa. Nor did she pretend to understand why she'd felt the need to profess her love for a married man in writing.

Louisa heard a satisfying click as her hairpin unlocked the drawer. But she held still, crouched before the desk. Something was amiss. The fine hairs on the back of her neck told her so. She looked up to see that she was not alone.

"Looking for something?"

The man who watched her as he walked forward from the now open doorway was no servant. The breadth of his shoulders, the arrogance in his stance, along with his handsome features said otherwise. An untied cravat dangled about the open neck of his shirt, and his coat was unfastened as well. His gaze raked her over from head to toe, convincing her that he'd seen through her disguise. Her heart hammered with fear.

The hairpin she clutched would hardly prove a satisfactory weapon. She stepped back from the desk, anxious to put as much distance between her and the stranger as possible then risked a glance over her shoulder to see how far away the door was.

Too far. She looked back at the tall stranger, dismayed at how much closer he'd gotten so quickly.

"Who are you?" he demanded, the deep timbre of his voice all the more intimidating. He was close enough to the candle she'd left on the desk to see his attractive features. Dark tousled hair brushed the collar of his shirt. His narrowed eyes were framed by black brows. He had to be the new Earl of Granger. The one who wasn't due to arrive for at least another day. She had no doubt he was a rogue through and through, much like the rest of his family.

Blast. So close and yet so far from her goal.

Louisa had no intention of answering his questions when her voice would give her away if her feminine features hadn't already. She shook her head, hoping the cap kept her disguised. She held up her hand, palm out, to show she hadn't taken anything. Then she turned and bolted.

Before she'd taken more than a few steps, he had hold of her arm with strong fingers.

"I asked you a question." He gave her arm a shake and her cap fell off, causing her hair to escape its knot and tumble past her shoulders.

His surprise at the sight loosened his hold, and Louisa jerked free, filled with hope that escape might yet be possible.

As she neared the door, she felt his hands grasp her upper arms, dashing her hope. He spun her to face him, his dark gaze raking over her, making her feel as if he'd laid her bare for his perusal. "Who *are* you?"

Benjamin Wright, the new Earl of Granger, couldn't wrap his thoughts around what was happening. Mayhap his travels had exhausted him more than he realized. He'd arrived in London earlier in the day, still processing the news that had abruptly ended his work abroad. Inheriting the earldom had changed his whole future. Finding a lad in his uncle's—rather, his own—library was a shock, but to realize *he* was a *she* upended his thoughts completely.

"Release me," the woman demanded.

"So you can run again?" He shook his head and firmed his grip. "I think not." He might not know why she was here, but if she escaped, he'd never discover the reason.

He eased her closer to the single candle flame that sputtered on the desk to gain a better look. Golden hair the color of spun honey hung in soft waves nearly to her waist. Wide blue eyes framed with dark lashes, arched brows, high cheekbones stained a tantalizing pink, and full lips made him think of a Botticelli painting come to life. She was an English beauty for certain, and he'd been abroad long enough to appreciate the sight thoroughly.

Her shifting eyes suggested she weighed how best to answer his question.

He waited, intrigued at what choice she thought she had. Was she a former lover of his uncle's? She seemed too young, but he well knew money could buy almost anything, and his uncle had made depravity his middle name.

"I'm merely searching for something that doesn't belong here." Her proper English tone sounded exotic to his ears. He'd definitely been gone too long.

"And what might that be?" He glanced at the bare desk, unable to guess what could be within the drawers that she desired.

Again she hesitated, as though choosing her words with care. She shifted to make it clear she desired her freedom, but he continued to hold tight. "Private correspondence...between my mother and the earl."

"Love letters?" Benjamin raised a brow, relieved to hear the woman wasn't personally involved.

"I wouldn't know as I haven't read them." She lifted her chin, a small gesture of defiance that matched the fire in her eyes.

Why did that feel like a challenge?

Before he could respond, she raised a hand and pricked his hand with a sharp object. "What the—" Surprised, he jerked back, inadvertently loosening his hold on her.

She lunged for the door and escaped before he could gather his wits.

With a curse, he strode to the entrance, certain he could catch her if he wished. But was such action necessary when he still had what she wanted? He stood there a long moment, looking into the dark night before at last turning back to the library and locking the door. The faint scent of her lingered in the air, the only proof she'd been there.

He ran a hand over his eyes. What an odd way to end this odd day. He'd arrived earlier than planned to his Uncle Morris's home, a place he hadn't set foot in for over five years. It would take time to truly believe this was his home now as he'd never expected to inherit.

While he felt terrible about the tragedy that had taken the life of his uncle and aunt and their only heir, his cousin, he hadn't cared for the lot of them. Uncle Morris had been an awful human being, his wife no better, and their son even worse.

He'd intended for this day to mark the beginning of a new era for the earldom, which had been led by rogues for several generations. At the age of one and thirty, Benjamin was turning over a new leaf and leading a different—no, *better*—life. No more roguish behavior, including excessiveness in liquor, women, and cards. Heaven knew Uncle Morris would roll over in his grave if he knew Benjamin's plan. The man had taken great pride in his many debaucheries and done his best to add to the Granger legacy.

Benjamin had grown weary of doors closing in his face because of his family's reputation as well as his own. As the new Earl of Granger, he was determined to live above reproach. He'd become disenchanted with the path of his life some time ago and had intended to purchase a commission to join the war efforts, only to be approached by an acquaintance who'd convinced him that his services would be better used elsewhere.

He'd hoped to put his life as a rogue behind him when he commissioned, but spying required him to keep it. The past two years had been equal parts frustrating and wondrous. Atrocities committed by bad men were terrible, but war caused even the good ones to commit far worse deeds. His disgust of such acts done for 'the greater good' wouldn't fade any time soon.

Yet parts of his travels had restored his hope in the world. The sights he'd seen—from the breathtaking Mount Kilimanjaro to the turquoise blue sea near Cyprus—and the people he'd met along the way—simple villagers, tribesmen, as well as a prince or two—had given him a new perspective and firmed his goal of change.

These adventures had helped Benjamin realize he was but one star in the night sky and would only shine brightly for a brief time. The humility he'd experienced at that moment had sealed his desire for a new start.

He'd done nothing of note in his life. Even his spying had seemed of little consequence, though he'd been told his efforts had been helpful. Most of his adult life had been spent seeking pleasure regardless of the cost to others. That pursuit had seemed a natural occurrence after he'd left university and taken his grand tour. When he'd returned to London, he'd done more of the same, following in the footsteps of the majority of the male members of his family, including his father, who'd died while Benjamin was at university. His mother had passed soon after. However, he'd grown weary of waking with the same discontent and headache each morning.

Though he hoped spying for his country would provide the opportunity to change, his role had required a rogue's cover to allow him to dally in unsavory places to gather information. Spying was a dirty business, a necessary evil poorly regarded by most in the military.

All that was over now. Learning of his uncle's demise had seemed like a nod from fate that his desire for a new beginning was the right path.

He eyed the desk, wondering whether the information the woman searched for was truly there. Perhaps he should look in case she decided to pay another visit during the night. Obviously, locked doors and drawers didn't stop her. What an unusual woman she was. Determined for certain, he thought as he rubbed his hand where she'd pricked him.

The middle drawer had been her focus when he'd discovered her. He opened the drawer, unsurprised that she'd managed to unlock it, and pulled out the papers inside. With the aid of the candle she'd left, he soon found what she sought. The delicate curves of the handwriting certainly weren't Uncle Morris's. He skimmed the contents in the dim light. No wonder his mysterious intruder wanted the letters back. He paged through several papers and found three written in the same feminine script. The rest of the correspondence appeared to be business related. Those could wait until the morning when he was less blurry eyed.

Without a key to relock the drawer, he decided it prudent to take the letters with him to his bedchamber for safekeeping. What an unexpected—and unsettling—way to begin his new life. He'd had difficulty sleeping before and had ventured to the library for a drink and a book. Now it seemed even more unlikely that he'd find slumber.

He poured himself a brandy from a decanter on the sideboard, selected a book on Greek architecture that he hoped would lull him to sleep then retrieved the candle and letters from the desk. With one last glance at the door that led to the garden, he returned to his bedchamber.

The dry information shared in the book and brandy failed to keep his thoughts from the intriguing woman. She followed him into his dreams, threatening his resolve to keep his distance from reckless women.

Chapter Two

Louisa was already awake the next morning when her maid arrived with her breakfast tray.

"Good morning, my lady," Beth said as she set the tray on the bedside table then eyed the pile of dark clothes in a nearby chair. "Shall I return those to my brother?" The hopeful note in her tone was impossible to miss.

"Would he mind if I held onto them a few more days? I'd be happy to pay him for any inconvenience." After spending the night tossing with regret, Louisa still hadn't arrived at a decision as to how best to proceed. She'd been so close to her goal, assuming the letters had been in the locked drawer. There was always a chance the deceased earl had destroyed them, though her mother didn't believe so.

"Surely you don't intend to try again now that the new earl has arrived?"

Beth had gasped in horror when Louisa described her narrow escape as she helped her prepare for bed the previous evening.

"I have yet to decide what to do. If only Mother hadn't written of her feelings and shared them with that rogue." From experience, she knew berating her mother for her recklessness would do no good. Her mother's passionate nature had landed her in trouble several times since Louisa's father had died, much to Louisa's dismay.

She sighed. "I'll need to tell Mother I failed."

Beth said nothing as she drew back the drapes and added coal to the fire to warm the chilly room.

Louisa sipped her chocolate and nibbled at the toast as she considered her options. "Mayhap the new earl will enjoy an evening out in the next few days, and I can try again."

Beth spun to stare at her, obviously aghast at the idea. "That holds far too much risk, my lady. What if he catches you again? He might have already found the letters and placed them elsewhere in case you think to try once more."

"But I need those letters."

"Why not ask him for them?"

Louisa scoffed at the thought. "He's a Wright. A rogue through and through. I might not have ever met him, but his reputation precedes him. He'd never hand over the letters of his own accord."

The idea of asking the handsome man for such a favor had her shifting uneasily. The single candle flame hadn't been enough to make a thorough study of him, but she'd seen enough. His dark good looks and arrogance spoke of a man used to having whatever he wanted, whenever he wanted. She couldn't imagine asking him for the letters. If he was anything like his uncle, he didn't have a sympathetic bone in his body, let alone an honorable one.

She couldn't help a little shiver at the memory of him holding her tight. His close regard as he pulled her toward the candle had sent butterflies dancing in her middle. If he had that much effect over her in dim light, what would it be like to have him study her in daylight?

Surely her reaction was due to the situation rather than him. She'd been caught breaking into an earl's desk not to mention his house. She was lucky she'd escaped when she had. If he'd called the authorities and held her until they'd arrived to question her...

She couldn't bear to complete that thought.

Telling her mother the bad news would be unpleasant. Her reaction would no doubt prod Louisa into taking additional action to recover the letters. Louisa hadn't told her when she was going to make her attempt so hadn't shared her failure the previous night. It was bad enough that one of them had lost a night's sleep.

She set aside her chocolate then threw back the covers, eager to have the conversation over and done. Beth assisted her into a warm morning gown and affixed a cap over her hair to help confine it.

With a deep breath, Louisa walked down the hall to her mother's bedchamber and tapped on the door.

"Enter."

"Good morning, Mother," Louisa said, forcing a smile as she joined her.

The Marchioness of Whirlenhall had aged well, much like her mother before her. With blonde hair a shade lighter than Louisa's, smooth skin, and a curved figure, she could've easily passed for a woman of forty rather than two and fifty.

"Good morning, Louisa." She offered her cheek from her position propped against the bed pillows in a pale blue dressing gown decorated with delicate lace and ribbons. The white lace cap she wore should've made her look dowdy but emphasized her blue eyes instead.

Louisa kissed her cheek then pulled a nearby chair closer to the bed.

"What brings you to visit me so early in the morning?" her mother asked as she enjoyed her chocolate.

Though Louisa was filled with regret at her failure, she refused to take all the blame. Her efforts the previous evening wouldn't have been necessary if her mother hadn't felt the need to pour out her feelings to the earl. What made the situation even more frustrating was that her mother had decided prior to the earl's death that she hadn't truly been in love. Why couldn't that have happened before she wrote the letters?

She loved her mother dearly but worried she wouldn't be able to save her this time. The thought of the new Earl of Granger only made her more certain that all was lost. If he found the letters and decided to share them with the world, her mother would be humiliated at the least. Depending on what she'd written to the married earl, she might even be ostracized by Society.

For her mother, such an outcome would be devastating.

For Louisa, it would be equally so.

She wanted a family of her own, though she had yet to find a man she thought she could live with for years to come. She secretly feared she shared her mother's fascination for rogues and scoundrels. As her mother liked to say, men who misbehaved were so much more interesting than those who didn't. Louisa's father had been a charming rogue in his younger days, though he'd quickly reformed after meeting Louisa's mother. His nephew had inherited the title but had yet to marry. He preferred the country to London, at least for now.

"I fear I have bad news," Louisa began as she folded her hands in her lap. "I attempted to retrieve your letters from Clarke House last evening but failed."

"Granger didn't keep them after all?" Her mother sounded almost disappointed at the thought.

"I don't know. I was searching his desk when the new earl discovered me."

"But he wasn't supposed to arrive until today at the earliest. Wrights are never early."

"Apparently, this one is."

Her mother reached out to take her hand. "What happened? Are you well?"

"Quite." Though she hoped his hand still hurt from her hairpin. "He startled me. We exchanged a few words after which I escaped."

"Does he know about the letters?"

Louisa licked her lips, wishing she hadn't told him. At the time, she hadn't felt as if she had a choice. He would eventually look through the desk. If the letters were there, he'd find them. Maybe even read them. "Yes, I'm afraid so."

"Oh." Her mother drew back her hand to cover her mouth in shock. "Then all is lost."

Louisa's heart sank. Her mother tended to be overly dramatic, but in this instance, she might well be right.

"I suppose we'll know within the next few days," her mother said, her voice barely a whisper. "Now that Parliament is in session, more of the *ton* will be in town. Christmas isn't far away. That means more gatherings." She paused, blinking back tears. "And more opportunity for Granger to share what he learned about this widowed marchioness."

Louisa reached for her hand to hold it with both of hers. "There's always a chance he'll do the right thing and destroy them if he found them."

"He's the Earl of Granger. Of course, he won't do any such thing. My days in Society are numbered. Whatever will we do?"

"We don't know that for certain. Perhaps nothing will come of the situation, and we'll have needlessly worried."

Her mother cast a disbelieving look at her. "Now you sound like your father. He was such an optimist." She sniffed delicately.

Before her mother changed the subject, Louisa took the opportunity to attempt to caution her once again. "I ask you to please temper your behavior in these situations. To take a moment to think through the various scenarios that might occur based on your actions."

"I'm sorry to be such a burden to you," her mother said as big tears escaped her eyes. "I don't mean to cause anyone harm, most of all you."

Her tears made Louisa feel like a toad for bringing her more distress. But in the past few years, they'd had similar conversations more often than Louisa could count.

If only her father had lived. He had held the key to her mother's happiness. His humor and spontaneity had kept her guessing. He'd never stopped courting her, despite their many years of marriage. From what Louisa had discovered of men, he'd been unique.

"You know I love you and want to see you happy, Mother. But if you could hold back from making grand gestures until we have a chance to discuss them—"

"I must follow my heart, Louisa. I would urge you to do the same." With the passion Louisa longed to eliminate within herself, her mother pressed her hand on Louisa's chest. "The path to happiness can only be found by following your heart."

Louisa gritted her teeth. Of late, her mother's strong emotions had only led to trouble, embarrassment, and humiliation. She had no desire to involve herself in any such encounters that might end in disaster. Her mother did enough of it for both of them, and Louisa's nerves couldn't take the additional worry.

Louisa stayed by her mother's side the following evening as they greeted the Marquess and Marchioness of Delham, who were hosting a dinner party. Though she knew her mother feared the worst, she hid her concern well. Louisa couldn't help but search the other guests' expressions for some sign of derision. Much to her relief, she saw nothing to cause alarm.

They exchanged pleasantries with several acquaintances, but the tightness around her mother's eyes revealed her continuing concern, at least to Louisa.

"I simply don't know if I can do this," her mother whispered soon after they'd arrived.

"I realize it's difficult, but we must remain strong."

"Waiting to see if anyone knows of my transgression is unbearable." Her gaze swung over the thirty plus guests, a hint of panic in the depths of her eyes.

"Calm yourself, Mother." Louisa reached out a gloved hand to clasp her mother's. "You look lovely, and no one seems to be the wiser of the situation. There's no need for panic."

"No need for panic *yet*."

"Everyone is far too busy discussing Napoleon's defeat and speculating how Europe will move forward to worry over a few letters." How Louisa hoped this was true.

Thankfully, her words seemed to calm her mother who drew a deep breath then released Louisa's hand as a friend came forward to visit.

Why couldn't her mother remember moments like this when she was about to do something untoward, such as write inappropriate letters to a married man? With a sigh, Louisa smoothed her satin gown, one of her favorites. The silver embroidery along the hem, the deep blue bodice, short full sleeves, and rounded neckline with more silver embroidery bolstered her confidence, something she'd feared she might need this evening.

"Louisa, your gown is gorgeous," Annabelle Gold said as she joined her.

Louisa turned to greet her cousin with a genuine smile. "I didn't realize you were coming."

"I didn't either, but Caroline insisted."

"How is the soon-to-be countess?"

Caroline, Annabelle's older sister by two years, had become betrothed to the Earl of Aberland in May, much to her dismay. One moment alone on a terrace in a compromising situation had forced Aberland to propose and her to accept. To both their surprise, they'd discovered themselves enamored with one another. Louisa was envious of Caroline's love match, despite Aberland having the reputation of being a terrible rogue.

How had Caroline seen beyond his behavior to the man beneath? No matter, Louisa reminded herself. She wanted a husband she could depend upon from the start. Not one who'd cause her to doubt his every word and action.

"She should arrive at any moment." Annabelle perused the guests. "There she is."

Louisa followed Annabelle's gaze to see Caroline beside her betrothed as they greeted the hosts. Her happiness glowed within her, making her even more beautiful. She and Aberland shared a tender look so filled with love that Louisa sighed.

"I know," Annabelle said softly. "I'm so happy for them but envious at the same time. Love is grand, isn't it?"

Louisa smiled as she watched Caroline and Aberland draw near. "They are well suited. But I think I'd prefer a calmer match."

Something in her tone must've given her away. "Has something occurred?" The concern in her cousin's tone tempted Louisa, but how could she share anything about her predicament without betraying her mother?

"A bump in the road. 'Tis nothing of consequence." At least she hoped not. She turned away to search for her mother and found her safe for the moment, visiting with friends.

"Lady Louisa. Miss Annabelle," Aberland's deep voice began, and Louisa turned to greet him, only to see a man all too familiar standing next to him. "May I introduce a friend of mine, Benjamin Wright, the Earl of Granger?"

Louisa's world narrowed to Granger, unable to utter a word as she stared at the man who held her and her mother's futures in his hands. His practiced eye swept her over from head to toe, reminding her all too well of his previous close perusal.

Her stomach dropped. Would he reveal all and cause her family's ruin this very evening?

Chapter Three

Benjamin could hardly believe the odds of meeting his midnight visitor during his first evening out since arriving in London. He'd watched her from across the room, amazed at how different she looked compared to when he last saw her. Yet he had no doubt of her identity.

Her gown was the height of fashion, the neckline offering a small sample of her creamy skin. Honey-colored curls lay along her forehead and temples to frame her face with the rest of the tresses drawn into a knot of ringlets at the back of her head. A bandeau of pearls formed a crown of sorts then twisted artfully around the ringlets. The blue of her bodice made her eyes all the more striking. A single pearl drop necklace drew his gaze to the hint of her breasts.

Quite different and much more demure than the woman disguised in lad's clothing who'd acted so boldly. Which was the true person?

He'd been pleased to watch her from a distance, but when his long-time friend, Richard Walker, the Earl of Aberland, offered to introduce him, he hadn't been able to resist. She'd held court in his thoughts for the past two days despite reminders that he didn't need the trouble such a woman would inevitably cause.

From the bits of gossip he'd overheard this evening, her mother, the Marchioness of Whirlenhall, tended to act brazenly. No doubt her daughter was following in her footsteps based on what he'd witnessed. Though the old Benjamin would've been tempted to see just how far she'd venture down that path, the new Benjamin couldn't risk it. He sighed with regret.

"Lady Louisa. Miss Annabelle." He bowed as the two attractive women curtsied. "I'm pleased to meet you."

Lady Louisa. He appreciated having her name.

"I'm terribly sorry to hear of your recent loss," Miss Annabelle said, unaware of Louisa's shock at seeing him. "How tragic to have lost all of your family at once."

Benjamin replied with what he hoped was an appropriate response. His full attention was on Louisa. By the flare of her nostrils, she was quite upset to see him. The thought made him smile.

"Forgive me, my lady, but you look familiar." Benjamin couldn't resist teasing her. Obviously, he needed to work harder on his self-control.

"Oh?" She raised a brow, her cheeks once again a delicate rose that heightened her beauty. "I don't believe we've been introduced before this evening."

Damn if he didn't appreciate the fire in her eyes, as if she dared him to tell the truth.

"Hmm," he murmured. "I'm certain the reason will come to me. I have an excellent memory."

Her expression, including her deliciously full lips, twisted into a scowl briefly before smoothing out, as if she'd donned a mask to smother her genuine reaction. She offered a polite smile then shifted her attention to Aberland and his betrothed, Miss Gold.

"I thought you might leave London for the country over the holiday," Lady Louisa said.

"Caroline doesn't want her father to travel as he's not in the best of health, so we are spending Christmas in the city."

"You'll remain in the city as well, won't you?" Miss Gold asked Lady Louisa. Benjamin held his breath, hoping she'd agree.

"Yes. Mother prefers to spend Christmas in London. The country house reminds her too much of Father, and my cousin, who inherited the title resides there."

The conversation continued with him adding very little, mostly because he had difficulty thinking of anything other than Louisa. Watching her proved a delightful pastime.

After the guests had mingled for a time, supper was served. Benjamin found himself seated not far from Louisa—too far away for conversation but not so far that he couldn't observe. She intrigued him. Was it only because he'd found her breaking into his library? Surely there was more to it than that. Beauty, elegance, and wit all wrapped into a charming and courageous package. Or was she merely foolhardy?

Either way, he was in serious trouble.

Why had fate placed such a woman in his path? To test his resolve of reforming? The bigger question was what to do about it. How could he consider her as a potential wife when she took it upon herself to act in a risky fashion? He had no intention of breaking his vow to put his roguish ways behind him.

Which left him where?

He clenched his jaw and turned to the lady who sat on the opposite side of him, determined to put the lovely Lady Louisa from his mind. Aberland's influence was the only reason he'd been invited to the dinner party. His behavior this evening needed to be above reproach and set the tone for his new life.

But within a few minutes, his gaze returned to Louisa. He was quite certain she had yet to look at him. The realization annoyed him.

The meal dragged on overlong, at least for Benjamin. At last, the ladies rose to leave the men. Unfortunately, having Louisa out of his line of sight didn't keep him from thinking of her.

Benjamin forced himself to concentrate on the conversation, which centered on the shifting political map of Europe. Aberland, who sat a short distance away, acted as though he paid little notice to the comments from the other men, but Benjamin knew he listened carefully. The earl was a far better spy than Benjamin had ever been. Of course, he'd been at it much longer. Benjamin doubted any of the other men at the table realized Aberland's role in the cat-and-mouse game of political intrigue.

Many of those in France had fled to England at the start of the war, but their loyalty remained across the Channel. That made it difficult to know who to trust. Was Aberland as weary as Benjamin of the life and death stakes spying held?

After several decanters of port had been emptied, the men rose to join the ladies. He wished he had the fortitude to leave before they did so. Instead, he followed the men to the drawing room, further annoyed with himself. He was no better than a moth lured by a pretty yet dangerous candle flame.

They entered the room where the marquess's daughter played the pianoforte with determination if not talent, and he found the lady who threatened his peace of mind. Louisa sat conversing with her two cousins. He paused near the doorway, debating whether to remain.

"Granger, terribly sorry about your recent loss." The Marquess of Delham studied him for a long moment with a guarded expression.

"Quite a shock." Benjamin turned his back on Louisa, wanting to make the most of this conversation. Delham was an influential member of the *ton* as well as the House of Lords and respected by many. Aberland had warned Benjamin that many members of Society had not liked his uncle. The previous Earl of Granger and his countess had received fewer and fewer invitations each year, though no one had snubbed them outright.

Benjamin knew Delham wasn't the only one who watched him with assessing eyes this evening. He expected that would be the pattern at each function he attended now that he'd inherited. He needed to prove he wasn't anything like his uncle. His own previous indiscretions could be blamed on sowing the oats of his youth. But if he wanted to be treated seriously and live a meaningful life, this moment could be a good beginning.

"I understand you've been abroad the past few years." Delham's eyes narrowed as if he thought this suspicious. No doubt he wondered why Benjamin hadn't bought a commission and fought in the war.

"Indeed." He couldn't share the reason for his travels, nor even hint at it. Yet the idea of travelling when his country was at war seemed frivolous. How could he discuss his ventures without sounding like an uncaring scoundrel? "I appreciated the opportunity to travel beyond the boundaries of Europe. The insight exploration provides is a priceless experience."

Delham's furrowed brow suggested he hadn't yet been convinced.

"I hope to use my perspective in the House of Lords. Viewing the issues we're encountering with the objectivity global travel offers is something for which I am grateful."

Aberland gave a subtle nod from a short distance away. At least Benjamin had his approval.

To his relief, Delham's concern eased, and he nodded with understanding. "I look forward to hearing more about your view on how we can navigate the challenges England now faces."

Benjamin hoped the marquess's interest continued. Proving he was different from his late father and uncle would take time, but if he acted above reproach, surely others would begin to take him seriously as well.

Delham introduced him to several other lords, and he did his best to hold his own in conversations without revealing the truth of how he'd spent the last two years. He declined the offer of another drink for the sake of his reputation and because he found the discussions stimulation enough.

Though he managed to keep his distance from Lady Louisa, his gaze sought her out again and again. Viscount Stanich had spoken to her at length. The younger lord irritated Benjamin with the pomposity he'd displayed in the dining room. The man considered himself an expert on all topics. Apparently, Louisa thought Stanich fascinating based on the way he held her attention.

She ignored Benjamin completely. Did that mean she'd given up on obtaining the letters? No doubt that was for the best. The evening had been a success, and he didn't want anything to cast his behavior into question. Perhaps he should take his leave before he did something to jeopardize it.

"I couldn't help but notice your attention on Lady Louisa," Delham said as he stepped closer. "Her mother, the Marchioness of Whirlenhall, always seems to be on the verge of scandal."

"Oh?"

"As they say, blood will tell." Delham's gaze grew calculating. "Take my marchioness, for instance. She is the epitome of decorum, a trait clearly evident in our daughter. One has to wonder if Lady Louisa is cut from the same cloth as her mother."

Though he'd wondered as well, Benjamin preferred to make his own decisions about people. That included Delham's daughter. He nodded but changed the topic, pleased when the marquess moved away to speak with someone else.

"Did you find them?"

He stilled at the feminine whisper then slowly turned to see Louisa next to him, partially facing away. Apparently, she didn't want anyone to know they were speaking. "Yes."

Her shoulders stiffened as if he'd told her terrible news. Why hadn't her mother approached him to retrieve the letters since she was the one who'd written them?

"I'd be pleased to return them to you," he said.

His offer had her turning to face him. She smiled politely, but desperate hope shone in her eyes. "Truly?"

"For a small price." The words had passed his lips before he could halt them. He should've told her he'd send a servant with them. But he didn't. *Couldn't.*

"Those are personal letters and not your property. You should do the right thing and return them." The fire in her eyes pleased him more than it should have.

"Don't you want to know the price?" he asked even as he wondered to where his resolve had disappeared.

"Whatever it is, I don't wish to pay it."

"One kiss." His heart hammered at his demand. What was he thinking?

Her lips parted as those blue eyes widened in surprise.

"Midnight tomorrow evening. My library. I believe you know the address."

"I'd be mad to take such a risk."

He decided against reminding her that she already had. "Do you want the letters?"

Her angry gaze made her look much more like the passionate woman he'd discovered in his library, rather than the proper lady she'd been most of the evening.

"I look forward to your visit," he said with a smile and a bow. Then he took his leave, promising himself to work on his self-restraint as soon as he gave her the damn letters.

Late the following afternoon, Louisa paced her bedchamber, filled with indecision. She shouldn't go. She should've refused. What had she been thinking? Surely he wouldn't do anything untoward with the letters.

But what if he did?

Worst of all, she couldn't deny that part of her looked forward to the meeting. The part she'd been trying so hard to smother.

The previous evening had been painful. She'd spoken to Viscount Stanich, a perfectly nice man who was attractive and intelligent. He seemed interested in her. So what if he was a bit arrogant? Most men of her acquaintance were. He'd told her about the horse he was considering buying. She liked horses. But when he'd gone on and on about it, she'd barely been able to keep her attention on what he said.

Granger was to blame for that. His watchful gaze had unsettled her, prickling her flesh with awareness. With...anticipation. Even now, her breasts tightened at the thought of being alone with him again. Why did she have this primal response to him? As if her body intended to overrule her mind and seek him out.

With a wave of her hand, she dismissed the thought. Ridiculous. Becoming involved with a man like him would only lead to trouble. He reeked of it. That sort of risk wasn't worth taking. She'd be better off with Viscount— Her thoughts whirled as she realized she'd forgotten his name. Stannish. No. Stanich. That was it.

She stopped pacing and closed her eyes. Those letters were all that mattered. She would meet Granger, take the letters, and return home before half an hour passed. She couldn't focus on her own future with those in Granger's hands. Those warm hands with long, strong fingers that had been kissed by the sun...

"Look at these, my lady," Beth said as she entered the drawing room, holding a large bouquet of yellow roses. "Aren't they beautiful? A package arrived for you as well."

Louisa smiled, welcoming the distraction. She took the thin package wrapped in brown paper and tied with a string. No note was visible. Setting it aside, she reached for the roses and breathed in their sweet scent. "How lovely."

She placed the vase on a side table and reached for the card. "Viscount Stanich. How kind of him," she said as she studied the simple note. Surely she could find a few qualities she admired about him.

"Louisa?" Her mother stood in the doorway. "Will you offer your opinion? I can't decide which gown to wear this evening."

Louisa's mind went blank. "This evening?" Had her mother somehow learned of her meeting with Granger?

"The Thompson's dinner party, remember?"

"Oh yes, of course."

"What lovely flowers. Who sent them?" Her mother drew closer to touch one of the delicate petals.

"Viscount Stanich. You met him last evening."

Her mother frowned for a moment. "Stanich. Yes. A nice enough young man."

"Nice enough?"

"I only spoke with him briefly but, yes. He seemed...nice." Her mother turned away only to turn back. "Though he's not the sort of young man I'd select for you."

"What's wrong with nice?"

"Nothing. Though nice is boring." Her mother patted her arm. "Come help me select a gown."

Time crawled by as she assisted her mother then dressed for the dinner party. Of course, she wasn't disappointed to realize that Granger wasn't in attendance. Nor was Viscount Stanich. Why was she relieved at that?

When her mother suggested they return home early, Louisa was thrilled.

"You hardly said a word this evening," her mother said in the carriage on the way home. "Are you unwell?"

"Not at all. The conversation was rather dull."

Her mother chuckled. "You're just like me. Excitement is far more entertaining and uplifting, don't you think? Good for one's soul."

Louisa didn't respond. Wasn't that her secret fear? That she wouldn't be content without some thrills in her life? She bid her mother good night and went to her bedchamber to change for the midnight rendezvous, unable to ignore the excitement that filled her.

The danger added to her anticipation. Was this how her mother felt? That she wasn't fully alive without the stimulation forbidden adventure could bring? Empathy speared through her. Perhaps she should be more understanding from now on when her mother acted impulsively.

"Are you certain, my lady?" Beth asked as she helped her change. "Couldn't you send one of the footmen for the letters?"

"I'm afraid not," Louisa said as she buttoned the jacket. "This is a family matter. I need to be the one to resolve it." Though tempted not to bother with a disguise, she'd decided it was necessary. If someone saw a lady walking the streets alone at night, it would draw too much interest. A lad walking by himself wouldn't garner a second look. Heaven forbid if she were caught either way.

She pondered her feelings to determine whether she was more excited about the experience or the man.

Or was it the kiss he'd demanded?

Nerves danced in her belly at the thought. The kiss was definitely the problem.

It needed to be brief. But not too brief. After all, this wasn't her first kiss. She'd indulged in a few on darkened terraces and in a protected alcove at a ball. But never with a man like Granger. Having a rogue like him involved changed everything.

Should she place her hands on his shoulders or against his chest? Or did she keep her hands at her side to prove to him that the kiss was of little consequence? What exactly should she say? Did she ask for the letters before the kiss?

She shook her head as she sat to pull on the boots. This was growing more complicated by the moment. Why couldn't she think of this as a simple transaction?

Beth wrung her hands as Louisa stood. "If you don't return within the hour, I'll send a footman for you."

"Thank you, Beth." She squeezed the maid's hands. "I don't know what I'd do without you. Don't worry. I will return shortly."

While Louisa didn't trust Benjamin—or rather, Granger—she didn't truly believe he'd hurt her, though she couldn't explain why. Perhaps the belief was naïve of her. After all, she knew nothing of the man except his reputation and the devilish look in his eye.

She hurried down the steps and let herself out the front door. The servants had already retired for the night. The evening air was cold, and she quickened her pace. The walk to Clarke House was a short one, and her tingling nerves made her walk even faster. She unlocked the garden gate with ease and passed through it into the garden, her stomach in knots. A faint glow from the hearth lit the library, but all else remained cloaked in darkness.

Gathering her courage, she reached for the door, only to find it locked. She hesitated, unable to determine what game Granger was playing. Now what?

Chapter Four

Benjamin sat in a wingback chair before the fire, a nearly empty brandy glass dangling between his fingers. Doing the right thing was supposed to be its own reward, but he already regretted sending the letters to Louisa. He didn't care for this part of turning over a new leaf. Nor had he realized temptation would approach so quickly. His foul mood could be placed squarely on her shoulders.

He rose to place a few more coals on the fire. What he truly needed was a quick tumble with a woman to relieve his tension. But he'd promised himself no more of that. He needed a wife, not a mistress. He cast his thoughts toward the women he'd met at the dinner party but couldn't say he was attracted to any of them. The idea of either of the ladies he'd met earlier at a party, Miss Simpson or Lady Adele, in his bed had him scowling. Surely there was someone out there who could converse intelligently as well as display passion in the bedroom.

But only one woman came to mind. She was far too easy to imagine with those blonde tresses spread over his pillow, her luscious curves moving with him. His body tightened at the picture his mind so easily created.

He ran a hand through his hair, trying to stop the path of his thoughts. Louisa's hidden passion was all the more reason he should avoid her. Thank goodness he'd sent her the letters. A secret rendezvous with a hoyden would only lead to trouble.

A tap at the door to the garden had him turning in surprise. Surely it wasn't Louisa. But as he strode toward the door, he recognized the silhouette of a lad standing there. What on earth was she doing? He unlocked the door and opened it, puzzled as she entered. "I wasn't expecting you. Is there a problem?"

She stared at him in surprise. "You said to come at midnight."

"I sent a footman earlier today with the letters. Didn't you receive them?"

"No." Then her eyes went wide. "A package. Wrapped in brown paper."

"That sounds like it."

Her mouth dropped open as a blush stole over her cheeks. "Another delivery came at the same time, and I set that one aside." She looked up at him, embarrassment in her expression. "I didn't realize..." Her voice dropped away, leaving him to wonder what she'd been about to say.

"You didn't expect me to send them?" How could he possibly be offended by her assumption? She didn't know him and had no reason to think he'd act honorably when he'd already demanded a kiss in exchange for the letters.

"No," she said with a shake of her head. "I didn't expect you to do the right thing. But I'm grateful you did." Her surprise faded into something else. If he didn't know better, he would've said admiration. But that couldn't possibly be true. She looked away. "I can't believe the package's arrival slipped my mind."

The longer he watched her, the less will he had to keep his distance. He took a step closer and ran a finger slowly along her jaw. "I'm glad it did."

His gaze dropped to those full lips, and he moved the pad of his thumb against her lower lip. He couldn't remember wanting a kiss quite as badly as he did right now. The old version of him would just take it. But the new version protested at the thought. Then his mind settled on something in between. Wouldn't gaining the lady's permission make it all the sweeter?

He lifted his gaze to find her eyes had darkened. Could that be desire in their depths? "Am I to be rewarded for my good behavior?"

"Good deeds are supposed to be their own reward."

"Hmm. I wouldn't know. I'm relatively new at this."

"Would it reassure you to know that you're doing well?"

He considered her question. "Yes, it would."

She patted his chest, a teasing glint in her eye. "You are doing well, Granger."

"Please, call me Benjamin."

"You may call me Louisa."

"Is that all I'm to receive?" he asked with one brow raised, enjoying their banter more than he would've guessed. "Permission to use your given name?"

She gave a mock sigh. "I wouldn't want you to stop doing good deeds for lack of reward." She lifted onto her toes and offered her mouth.

He pressed his lips to hers, the sensation only fanning the flames of his desire. He wanted more. How much was she willing to give?

Yet he hesitated. Louisa was a lady. And though he intended to enjoy the kiss, that was all he would take. The new Benjamin was determined to treat women with honor and respect.

He deepened the kiss but held back from taking more. She tasted sweet with a hint of spice. The faint scent of roses clung to her, reminding him that she was an English beauty. Her lips were soft and cool beneath his. He drew away before he did something he'd regret. Like lift her into his arms and carry her to the couch.

She came with him as if not yet ready to end the kiss.

He smiled. He wasn't ready to end this either. Even as he berated himself for lack of control, he removed her cap, disappointed when her hair remained pinned in place.

That was probably for the best. The sight would've tempted him further.

"You should go." He replaced the cap as his gaze swept over her. "But I must say I admire your attire."

Long lashes hid her eyes as she glanced at her clothing. "I didn't want to risk drawing attention dressed as a lady."

Did he dare tell her how much attention she'd gain if caught dressed as a lad? "You must take great care. I hope you don't make a habit of midnight rendezvous."

"This will be my last. Thank you for returning the letters. It means much to my mother and me."

"Is she terribly upset about my uncle's passing?"

She shook her head. "Her interest in him had faded several weeks before his death. She ran into him at a rout, and he mentioned the letters."

Benjamin scowled. "You mean he threatened her with them?"

"You knew your uncle well."

"I'm sorry to say the man was no gentleman." Behavior like that was one of many reasons he'd decided the time had come for a change. Of course his uncle had taunted the marchioness with the letters. He and his son had been scoundrels of the worst sort. "I can't say I cared for my aunt either."

"Don't they say you shouldn't speak ill of the dead?" Louisa smiled.

"I would say it to their faces if they were still alive. Does that make it better?"

"Honesty is a fine trait." She bit her lip. "I must go. Thank you again."

He knew she should leave. He'd already suggested she do so. But he didn't want her to. Somehow, this goodbye felt permanent since he no longer had anything she wanted. Unable to resist, he gave her one last quick kiss. "Good night, Lady Louisa."

She disappeared into the night without another word.

"Louisa. Louisa? Wake up."

Louisa blinked at the daylight coming in from windows as her mother threw back the drapes. She felt as if she'd just fallen asleep. "What time is it?"

"Half past eight."

While she normally liked to rise at a respectable hour, sleep had eluded her for the past three nights since her meeting with Benjamin.

Louisa had returned home that evening and unwrapped the package, which contained the letters, just as he'd said. A rogue who acted with honor? What was the world coming to? Now he was all she could think about. Him along with his kisses. A terrible longing had stolen her sleep the past few nights.

"I'm sorry to wake you, but I couldn't wait another moment to tell you my news." Her mother sat on the side of the bed, her face shining with joy.

Based on her excitement, Louisa knew what was coming. "You met someone?" She said the words with trepidation, hoping she was wrong.

"Yes! You are such a clever daughter."

Louisa smiled weakly as she sat up against the pillows. How many times had they shared similar conversations in the past few years? Far too many. Her mother tended to fall fast and hard but fell out of love nearly as quickly.

"I was introduced to the most amazing man last evening." She tipped her head back, eyes closed, and pressed both hands over her heart.

Oh dear. That was never a good sign.

Louisa studied her mother's attire, realizing she was still dressed in the gown she'd worn to the gathering she'd attended the previous evening. "Have you just returned home?"

The satisfied smile her mother gave caused a knot to form in the pit of Louisa's stomach. "I had a delightful evening. I think I'm in love."

"Do tell." But Louisa wished she wouldn't. She loved her mother and wanted to see her happy, but too many times her relationships burnt out as quickly as they burst to life. And often amidst the ashes of extinguished love was a lump of coal that Louisa had to clean up. Was it any wonder she'd prefer a nice, if boring, man to marry?

Before her mother could begin, the door opened, revealing Beth who carried a breakfast tray with two cups followed by a housemaid.

"I rang for chocolate when I arrived home," her mother explained.

"How thoughtful." Apparently, Louisa wouldn't be going back to sleep any time soon. She sighed with regret, sat up further, and adjusted the bedding to protect her from the chill of the room.

But her mother's enthusiasm made up for Louisa's lack. She settled against the pillows next to Louisa and took the cup Beth handed her while the housemaid stirred the fire.

"He's an artist." Her mother whispered the words after the maids left as if they were a delicious secret. "A painter."

"Truly?" The news was growing more dire by the moment. Some of her doubt must've shown.

"Louisa, do not look so dismayed." Her mother patted her arm. "I promise you will adore him as much as I do."

She bit her lip to keep from expressing more doubt. "Tell me about him."

"He's French, and he's so talented."

"Please tell me he paints landscapes."

Her mother frowned. "Why would you say that? He paints portraits."

"Of course." Why did she so often feel like the parent in their relationship? She set aside her cup to take her mother's hand. "Promise me you'll take this slowly. I can see you feel a...connection to this man, but he's still a stranger."

Her mother sighed. "I did feel a connection to him all the way to my toes." She smiled at Louisa. "Haven't you experienced a moment when a man looks at you and your toes curl? It doesn't matter whether you know him."

Heat suffused her cheeks as Benjamin filled her mind. *Dear heavens.*

"You have," her mother exclaimed with delight. "You are very much like me."

Louisa released her mother's hands to throw back the covers and rise. How she wished her mother would stop saying that. In truth, it scared her to think she might be like her. "We were speaking of you and your painter."

"Who is he?" her mother asked. "Have I met him? I'm certain it can't be Viscount Stanwick."

"His name is Stanich." Wasn't it?

"Are you certain?" Her mother waved her hand in the air. "His name is of little consequence. What's important is how he makes you feel."

"No, Mother. It's not." She turned to face her, anger forcing out the words she normally would've held back. "What's important is whether he is a man of honor. Of good standing. One who won't ruin a lady's reputation. Strong emotions only lead to trouble and cause embarrassment and humiliation."

Her mother gasped as she set aside her cup to stand. "You cannot be serious."

"I would do well to marry a man like the viscount whose calm nature holds no risks."

"Only the risk of making the rest of your life miserable. Is that what you want?"

"No." Louisa covered her face with her hands. She hated disagreeing with her mother. But she also hated picking up the mess when her latest love fell apart.

Wasn't there a middle ground where one could be happy *and* safe?

"Louisa." Her mother pulled her hands from her face. "Darling. I only want you to be happy."

"I know." But she no longer knew what—or who—could provide that. Not after meeting Benjamin. He'd confused her on an elemental level she had yet to understand.

"Boring doesn't mean safe." Her mother placed a hand along her cheek.

"Perhaps. But excitement isn't the same as true love." She wrapped her arms around her mother. "I want you to be happy, too, Mother. But when you fall in love so quickly, I can't help but worry it's only temporary and you'll be hurt."

"One can't experience true joy if one hasn't experienced pain."

Why did her words feel more like a curse than wisdom?

Chapter Five

Benjamin entered Brooks's late the following afternoon, having spent the entire day in a long, painful meeting with his uncle's solicitor. He desperately needed a drink.

While he considered himself an intelligent man with a good deal of common sense, the list of duties and responsibilities from the various holdings and entailments were intimidating. His uncle's debts appeared more substantial than he'd anticipated, but he hoped to pay them soon. The idea of trying to preserve and improve the land and holdings for future generations caused an extra burden he hadn't expected to feel. How could he make decisions when they might prove disastrous for his heirs? Nor had he made any progress in finding a bride.

Being a respectable member of the aristocracy was proving more difficult than he'd anticipated. Life had been simpler when he'd only worried about himself.

"Granger."

Benjamin turned at his name to see Daniel Walker, Aberland's younger brother, seated at a table. As Benjamin approached, Walker folded the news sheet he'd been reading and set it aside as he stood to greet him.

"Aberland mentioned you had returned to London." Walker's eyes held the same mischievous glint Benjamin remembered from their university days. "Should I offer my condolences or congratulations on your new title?"

"I haven't yet decided," Benjamin replied with a smile. "It is certainly an adjustment."

"I can only imagine. My brother handles his duties with ease now, but I know that wasn't always the case." He gestured toward the chair beside him. "Would you care to join me for a drink, or are you headed toward the gaming rooms?"

"A drink would be welcome." Benjamin took a seat while Walker gestured for a waiter. "Anything of note in the newssheets today? I only had a chance to glance at the headlines this morning."

"I've become hooked on a mystery series they've been running. My brother suggested I might enjoy it and now I can't stand to miss a chapter. I highly recommend it."

"I'll be sure to read it. I could certainly use a distraction at the moment."

The waiter brought their drinks while they caught up with each others' lives. As the heir presumptive, Walker lived a modest life but always appeared happy. Benjamin had to wonder if he truly was or if he managed to hide his feelings that well.

Benjamin had become adept at doing so in the past two years. Though lately, hiding his attraction to Louisa had proven difficult. She was never far from his thoughts. Thank goodness he hadn't encountered her at the few gatherings he'd attended in recent days. Whether he was capable of keeping his distance in the future remained to be seen.

They briefly spoke with other acquaintances who passed by, several of whom were headed to the gaming rooms. While all the gentlemen's clubs along St. James Street offered gambling, the gaming rooms at Brooks's were busy day and night.

To Benjamin's surprise, the Marquess of Delham emerged from one of the rooms with several friends.

"How interesting," Walker said. "The rigid Delham spending the afternoon gambling."

"Is that unusual?" Benjamin asked.

"I'm not here often enough to know, but I would hazard a guess that it is. His anti-French remarks have offended some."

"Oh?"

"Rumors say that he made his wife release her French lady's maid and replace her with an English one."

"Interesting."

"Granger. Walker. Good to see you both."

"Delham." Benjamin rose to greet him alongside Walker.

"Care to join us?" The marquess swept his hand toward one of the gaming rooms.

Benjamin hesitated. While he wanted to remain on good terms with Delham, he didn't have any interest in gambling. That was one of the vices he'd set aside. Yet he didn't care to insult the lord either.

With Walker at his side, he joined Delham and his friends in the gaming room, planning to merely observe. He'd made a promise to himself to avoid such things.

"A game of piquet perhaps?" Delham asked. "Or do you prefer whist?"

"None today," Benjamin replied with a smile to ease his answer. "I must leave soon as I have another engagement this evening."

"I would guess it involves a woman," Delham said with a knowing look. "Your family has quite the reputation."

Benjamin said nothing as Delham slapped him on the back. Apparently, being at the club loosened the man's spirit. Perhaps this was the perfect time to gain Delham's support for an idea that had been on Benjamin's mind for some time. "Didn't you mention you knew several men injured in the war?"

"Indeed. Good soldiers, every one of them. Why do you ask?"

"I have a notion of how we might help those who fought so bravely for our country only to return home to struggle." Benjamin couldn't have been more pleased at the spark of interest in Delham's eyes.

Louisa smiled politely at Viscount Stanich until her cheeks hurt. The lord had far too much to say. From horses to politics, he had an opinion on everything and took any opportunity to share it.

She'd had the faint hope he wouldn't be in attendance at the Burdett ball. Perhaps the time had come to be less polite to the viscount. Hadn't anyone told him that listening was as important a part in conversing as speaking?

"Please excuse me," she interrupted when he drew a breath. "I must speak with my cousin." She hurried away before he could respond.

"Louisa," Annabelle said in surprise as Louisa looped her arm through hers.

"You must rescue me from Viscount Stanfinch." She glanced over her shoulder to make certain he hadn't followed her.

"Isn't his name Stanich?"

Louisa closed her eyes briefly at the mistake. "Of course. How silly of me."

"I thought you liked him."

"I *should* like him. He *should* be perfect." How disappointing that he wasn't. Or perhaps the fault lay with her.

Annabelle chuckled. "However?"

"I fear I might commit murder if forced to hear anything more about the horse he wants to buy."

"But you like horses."

"I do. I had no idea one could make them as boring as he does."

"Let us make good our escape." Annabelle guided her to the opposite side of the ballroom where they could keep an eye on the viscount from a distance. "Perhaps you should give your attention to another man for a time. That might discourage the viscount."

Louisa considered the notion. "But who?"

Annabelle dipped her head, and Louisa followed her gaze only to catch her breath at the sight of Benjamin.

"No. That's a terrible idea." Anyone but Benjamin.

"Why? He's handsome, titled, and doesn't seem boring at all." Annabelle turned to study her. "Your cheeks are flushed, although he hasn't yet seen you let alone spoken with you. Would you care to explain?"

"It's warm in here." But Louisa couldn't pull away her gaze. Nearly four days had passed since she'd last spoken with him. Time and distance should've reduced her attraction to the man, but that didn't seem to be the case. Where did that leave her? She couldn't be attracted to a rogue.

"Interesting." Annabelle pulled Louisa along with her as she moved closer to Benjamin.

"What are you doing?" Louisa whispered.

"Moving into his line of sight in case you decide you wish to speak with him."

"I don't." She found the fortitude to turn away. "Where is Viscount Stanich? I have a question about his horse."

"Lady Louisa. Miss Annabelle. I hope the evening finds you both well."

Why did his voice send shivers of awareness through her? There was nothing to be done except respond and do her best to hide her ridiculous reaction to him. "Good evening, my lord."

He looked especially handsome tonight, she thought. His dark hair was swept to the side and brushed the collar of his black coat. She appreciated that his cravat was tied in a simple, less fussy manner than most men favored.

They exchanged pleasantries then Aberland and Caroline joined them. Oddly enough, their arrival didn't reduce the tension that gripped Louisa.

"Well done, Granger," Aberland said. "I am impressed."

"By what?" Benjamin's brow rose in question.

"I understand from Delham that he's joining your efforts to create a charity for wounded soldiers."

Louisa stared at him in surprise. "A charity?"

Benjamin nodded. "Something I intend to oversee myself. So many men were wounded in the war and are in need of assistance. If we can aid their recovery and help them find new ways to function so that they can continue to be valuable members of society, all will benefit."

"That is a tremendous idea," Caroline said as Annabelle agreed.

What a surprising action for a rogue to take. Louisa had two cousins from her father's side who'd been injured in the war. One had lost a limb. To think they could be offered assistance to regain their lives was heart-warming.

"During my travels, I came upon a number of men who were dealing remarkably well with their injuries," Benjamin said. "I think we can learn from men like them even if they live in other countries. With the right training and a little funding, of course."

"I don't know how you managed to convince Delham of your plan, but you did." Aberland shook his head as if still in disbelief.

"I caught him at a weak moment." Benjamin smiled.

Louisa noted the twinkle in his eye, but he didn't expand on his remark, leaving her to wonder.

A rogue who did the right thing *and* established charities for wounded soldiers? Be still her heart.

"Lady Louisa, would you do me the honor of a dance?"

"Of course." Why did he have to ask now when her ability to resist him had been reduced even more?

She took his arm, ignoring her breathlessness as he escorted her to the dance floor. She risked a glance at him from under her lashes, wondering who he really was. The rogue that his reputation suggested or someone quite different?

"Are you enjoying the ball?" he asked as they lined up with the other dancers for the cotillion.

She hesitated. In truth, she hadn't been until now. Conversing with Benjamin was a completely different experience than talking to the viscount. They were both men, but that seemed to be the only similarity.

"The evening has been...interesting."

They went through the moves of the dance, their gazes catching as they turned this way and that. She felt as if the rest of the dancers fell away, leaving the two of them to move in time to the music. She didn't pretend to understand what was happening, nor did she like it. Benjamin was an unpredictable man with a dangerous reputation. But he was a more enjoyable companion than the viscount or any other man she'd met thus far.

With a sigh, she released her indecision for the moment. Surely she could enjoy this dance without worrying about the days to come. Once the mental barrier she'd placed between them had been removed, she began to notice the little things.

The feel of his strong fingers as they so gently brushed hers.

The breadth of his shoulders as he turned.

The hint of a smile that quirked the corner of his mouth.

His dark eyes that held on her as if they shared a secret.

Awareness caused her middle to perform dance steps of its own. Though she'd performed the cotillion more times than she could count, something felt different this time, and it was all because of Benjamin.

"Thank you," she said as the music faded.

"The honor is mine." He offered his elbow and escorted her to where her cousins still visited, gave a polite bow, and bid them a good evening.

"Well?" Annabelle asked.

"He is an excellent dancer." Louisa looked over the crowd for her mother. Anything to avoid meeting her cousin's curious gaze.

"I would guess he's excellent at many things." Annabelle smiled.

Louisa felt heat in her cheeks but didn't respond. She had no doubt her cousin spoke the truth. But Louisa had yet to decide what to do about it.

"I'm so pleased about Granger's idea of a charity for wounded soldiers," Caroline said. Her sympathetic glance at Louisa suggested she'd changed the topic to spare her more of Annabelle's comments.

"To think he gained Delham's support." Annabelle shook her head. "The marquess is known to be tighter with funds than most spinster aunts."

"So many families have been affected by the war," Caroline said as she shared a look with her sister. "We have distant family members who could use assistance."

Louisa knew Caroline had hoped to make a good marriage in order to save her family's finances. Her father's failing health had put them on the brink of disaster. Louisa's mother had offered assistance, but Caroline and her mother had refused, pinning their hopes on a good match to sustain them for the long term. It had come as a surprise to Caroline to discover Aberland had substantial wealth.

Louisa was grateful not to carry the burden of needing to marry for money, but she intended to take great care to ignore her passionate nature. For that would surely land her in trouble.

"This should be a good beginning," Delham said as he handed Benjamin a list.

Benjamin had spent the past three days in various meetings, many of which had been with Delham. Planning for the charity for wounded soldiers was well underway. He'd stopped by the marquess's home to pick up the list of lords that Delham believed would be interested in joining the cause.

"This is quite an extensive list." The number of names surprised him.

"Those with a mark beside them are ones with whom I have already spoken. The rest you'll have to approach but feel free to use my name."

Benjamin couldn't have been more pleased. During his travels as a spy, he'd seen many wounded men with little hope in their eyes. If he could do anything to alleviate their continued suffering, he would. He'd readily admit that one of the reasons he wanted to start this charity was to assuage his own guilt at not having served in the war himself.

Spying had been dangerous at times, but he'd never been shot. Aberland had continually told him that he saved more lives than he realized with the information he provided, but he still detested the fact that he hadn't been beside his fellow countrymen on the battlefield.

"I'll contact each person and let them know the date of our first meeting. I'm hoping that by holding it the week before Christmas, many will be in a generous spirit."

Delham chuckled. "Quite clever of you." A commotion from the entrance stopped him from saying more. "What on earth?"

The library door flew open as he rose. His wife stood in the doorway, eyes wild as she clenched a letter in trembling hands.

"What has happened?" Delham asked.

The marchioness's gaze landed briefly on Benjamin, yet he didn't think she truly saw him.

"I am ruined." She blinked back tears as she started to sob.

Benjamin rose, alarmed at the sight. "I'll go."

But the marquess waved his hand, whether to silence him or suggest he remain where he was, Benjamin wasn't sure. He waited to see if Delham offered another clue.

The man put an arm around his wife's shoulders gingerly as though not used to offering comfort or affection. "What are you speaking about?"

"This!" she exclaimed as she handed him the letter.

Delham's face turned white as he read the contents. Without a glance at Benjamin, he herded his wife out of the room and pulled the door closed.

Benjamin waited, wishing he'd been able to escape. When voices echoed in the entrance, he realized the marquess hadn't shut the door. The marchioness's hysterical tone was clearly audible. He stepped forward to close the door, preferring not to bear witness to whatever catastrophe had found the marchioness.

"Yes, I allowed him to paint me in the nude," she said in a shrill voice that carried clearly to Benjamin's ears. "At least he showed interest in me. You certainly do not."

The marquess's angry response was too quiet to hear, much to Benjamin's relief.

"He says he'll show that portrait to everyone if we don't pay the money he's demanding." Another murmured response from the marquess was followed by more shrill words from his wife. "He is French. Yes, I know you detest all things French. Why do you think I chose him?"

Benjamin shut the door as quietly as possible, not wanting to reveal his presence or interrupt the pair. He heard voices briefly before they faded. Apparently, Delham had convinced his wife to take their conversation to a more private location.

Benjamin hesitated. If Delham didn't return soon, he'd leave. If only he could un-hear their conversation. To think the marchioness had allowed a Frenchman to paint her portrait in the nude was shocking. To learn the artist had decided to use it against her was even more disturbing.

The fact that the marquess had been the one who'd cautioned him against Louisa and her mother was nearly laughable now. Obviously, the man needed to keep an eye on things closer to home.

When several minutes had gone by without the lord's return, Benjamin let himself out, telling the butler that he had to leave for another appointment. Delham would have to trust that Benjamin would keep the terrible situation to himself. He had no intention of telling anyone.

Chapter Six

Benjamin arrived at the Portland ball that evening with the hope of conversing with several of the men on Delham's list. At least, he told himself that was the reason he attended. In truth, he hoped Louisa would be there. If given a chance, he would very much enjoy another dance with her.

Her zest for life and occasional disregard for proper behavior might have initially caught his interest, but her intelligence, protectiveness of her mother, and her wit had kept his attention. Added to that was her beauty, grace, and a confidence rarely shown by younger women. She fascinated him in every aspect.

He smothered a sigh. He needed to take care not to single her out with his attentions. That meant dancing with a few of the other ladies in attendance, a notion he didn't care for.

While the Season wouldn't be underway until spring, many people were in London since Parliament was in session. Christmas would soon be upon them, and everyone appeared to be in fine spirits. They needed little excuse to host an event. The gatherings were smaller and less frequent this time of year, but that suited him. That made finding the men he wanted to speak with about funding the charity easier. It was also easier to find Louisa amongst the guests.

This evening, she wore a primrose gown with embroidery decorating the neckline and capped sleeves. Her upswept hair revealed an elegant neck and shoulders. He didn't think he'd seen a more delectable sight. Conversing with her would have to wait until he completed the evening's mission. With regret, he turned away to peruse the crowd and found two of the men on his list. Both were older, closer to Delham's age than his own. Though he'd met them before, he didn't know them well.

As Benjamin eased through the guests toward them, he wondered what solution Delham had found for his problem. Would he pay the painter for the portrait to keep his mouth shut? The options were limited, but obtaining the painting was imperative. Without it, the painter's claim of the marchioness posing nude could be easily dismissed.

All the more reason to marry a woman who wouldn't behave in such a manner.

"Crenshaw. Thompson. Good to see you," Benjamin said.

"Sorry to hear of your uncle's passing." Crenshaw's cravat was tied so high that he had difficulty turning his head.

"To lose them all so suddenly." Thompson shook his head. "Terrible."

"Thank you." Though he preferred to come to the point, he visited on other subjects until a lull in the conversation allowed him to mention the charity.

"For wounded soldiers, eh?" Crenshaw nodded stiffly. "Fine idea."

"Great need for it," Thompson added.

"We'd like to invite each of you to join the endeavor. We're in the process of gathering funding and determining the services to offer."

"Funding. Hmm." Thompson tapped his chin even as Crenshaw frowned.

Already Benjamin could tell they had reservations about donating money, which irritated him to no end. Both were wealthy and could spare a few pounds to help those less fortunate, especially for the soldiers who'd risked their lives to protect England. Though he was certain that with enough time, he could persuade them to join his efforts, he decided on a simpler method of convincing them.

"Delham suggested the two of you would be instrumental in assisting us in designing the charity, but if you don't care to do so..." As a well-respected member of the *ton*, Delham's name carried weight.

"Delham, you say?"

"Of course I can provide assistance," Crenshaw said. "What of you, Thompson?"

"I'd be delighted." Thompson nodded.

Benjamin advised them of the time and place of the meeting and asked them to invite others they deemed worthy to help spread the message about the cause. "We're being rather selective in who we want to participate." He nearly groaned at his own words. Not only had he used Delham's name to gain their cooperation but suggested exclusivity to convince them to assist in the process. "Wouldn't want just anyone involved."

"Excellent notion." Crenshaw patted Benjamin's shoulder. "Need to have the right people involved."

"We look forward to the meeting," Thompson said.

Benjamin moved away in search of his next target, leaving Crenshaw and Thompson debating over who they wished to ask. Though he'd have preferred the need for such a charity alone to win their help, he had what he wanted. Soon, the wounded soldiers would have support, and that was all that mattered. Moments like this made him more determined to develop a reputation that caused his peers to be eager to work with him.

Before he'd taken more than a few steps, an older woman he'd met briefly at the Delham gathering stepped into his path.

"Granger, allow me the pleasure of introducing my daughter, Lady Amelia."

Based on the woman's determined smile, she was a matchmaking mama if he'd ever met one. Lady Amelia dipped into a curtsy only to stumble as she rose, leaving him no choice but to reach out to assist her—a deliberate move on her part, if he had to guess. He endured a dance with her then quickly returned her to her mother's side.

He turned only to find Lady Adele and her brother, Viscount Gibbon, heir to the Earl of Mansby, nearby.

"Good evening, Gibbon. Lady Adele. I hope the evening finds you well." He'd become acquainted with Gibbon during their university days but didn't know him well. His younger sister seemed a timid thing based on the way her gaze focused mainly on his shoes rather than his face. He'd met her at an earlier gathering, and she'd acted much the same way then.

They conversed briefly until Benjamin could no longer ignore the hopeful glances she'd started to cast his way after a few minutes. "Might I have this dance, Lady Adele?"

"It would be my pleasure." Her face turned an alarming shade of red as he escorted her to the dance floor.

The dance seemed to last forever though the lady seemed to enjoy it. She spoke little but met his gaze several times and stared at his shoes less frequently. He returned her to her brother then quickly excused himself.

He searched the room once more for the other man with whom he wished to speak and nearly reached him when a primrose-colored gown a short distance away caught his eye. *Louisa.* A footman leaned close to tell her something, and her face paled. Had she been given bad news? He changed his course to discover if she needed assistance.

"Lady Louisa." Aware of numerous people watching, he bowed, smiling politely as she curtsied. "Is something amiss?"

"How do you mean?" She blinked up at him, distress evident in the depths of her eyes.

"I would help if I could." He spoke quietly and smoothed out his expression to keep from appearing overly concerned. That would only garner more attention.

"I-I received a rather disturbing message. From my mother." She closed her eyes briefly then forced a smile as she opened them. "'Tis nothing."

"You are a poor liar."

She appeared taken aback by his words before her concerned expression eased. "I would prefer to think you're especially observant."

"I have come to know you well in a short time." He knew that to be true, though he'd prefer not to share how much she held his thoughts.

The hint of vulnerability in her face had him catching his breath. Why did he feel as if he'd be willing to do anything to aid her? They were little more than strangers. Strangers who'd kissed. But he realized what lengths he was willing to go to if she asked. His chest tightened at the thought.

"I appreciate your concern, but it's nothing."

"Unfortunately, I don't believe you."

"Unfortunate for you or me?" Her gaze held his, and he could all but see her internal debate on whether to trust him with the issue.

"Perhaps both of us." He held his silence certain that if he pressed her, she'd retreat.

Louisa glanced about as if to make sure no one could hear their conversation. "My mother has become involved with someone whom I fear is not in her best interest."

"There seems to be much of that in the air," he muttered, his thoughts on the Marchioness of Delham. "Tell me the man isn't an artist."

Her eyes widened in alarm. "How could you have possibly known that?"

"Hmm. If it happens to be the same person I recently heard about, you should definitely be concerned."

Louisa stared at Benjamin in disbelief. How could he possibly know anything about the man with whom her mother had become enamored? Yet she well remembered the uncomfortable feeling that had overcome her when her mother first told her of the painter. Did she dare trust Benjamin with the details?

The grim set to his mouth suggested he believed her mother was in danger. He might have a rogue's reputation, but he'd already proven himself by not only returning her mother's letters but by keeping the situation private.

"She sent a message with the footman that she's gone to see him, and I shouldn't expect her home until the morrow."

His brows rose in surprise. "That is quite a significant message for a servant to deliver. Especially a servant in someone else's employ."

"He didn't say those exact words. We've established a code of sorts." The footman had said her mother looked forward to breakfast, and Louisa knew what that meant. This wasn't the first time her mother had requested a servant to deliver news she didn't want to share herself. Louisa knew it was because she didn't want to argue or listen to the reasons her plan was a poor one.

Benjamin nodded. "Do you happen to know where this person lives?"

"No, I don't." The faint flicker of hope Louisa held snuffed out. How silly of her to think Benjamin could aid her with the limited information she had.

"Then we shall have to discover it on our own. Hopefully, we can do so before any harm befalls her." He tucked her hand in the crook of his elbow and moved slowly toward the entrance.

"Harm?" Panic fluttered through her.

"We must find her as quickly as possible before she wades into even worse circumstances."

"I don't understand." Perhaps her worry over her mother was making her dim, but Benjamin's words didn't make sense.

"You will soon enough."

"Where are we going?"

"To obtain his address from someone who knows it." He turned to face her. "We wouldn't want to start gossip by leaving together. Can you make your excuses and meet me outside? I'll leave through the garden entrance and wait with my carriage down the street."

"Of course." She glanced about, nearly having forgotten about the other guests. "I'll tell the host I'm not feeling well."

He squeezed her hand. "I'll see you soon." Before she could say anything more, he disappeared among the guests.

"Louisa, is anything wrong?" Annabelle asked as she approached.

She forced a smile. Though tempted to share her dilemma, she hesitated. If the evening ended as badly as Benjamin seemed to be concerned it would, the fewer people who knew, the better. Louisa trusted her cousins, but she also knew her mother would prefer not to share her impulsive choices with anyone. Louisa had little doubt that in a few days' time, her mother would regret her actions this evening.

"I'm not feeling quite myself. I think I'll return home."

Annabelle laid a comforting hand on her shoulder. "Good idea. Do you want me to find your mother to tell her?"

"She's already requesting the carriage. Thank you." Lying to her cousin on her mother's behalf annoyed Louisa. How could her mother act so thoughtlessly at times yet so lovingly at others?

"I hope you feel better soon."

Louisa thanked her then made her way toward the entrance, pausing one last time to glance over the guests, but she didn't see Benjamin. He must've already departed. She thanked Lady Portland, shared her excuse for leaving early, and donned her cloak, anxious to proceed. A sense of urgency filled her, and she hurried out the door and down the steps, grateful few others were nearby.

The night had turned cool with fog looming in the shadows and along the ground. She pulled her cloak tighter, dismayed at the depth of the darkness once she moved away from the house. Several carriages lined the street. Without any idea which one might be Benjamin's, she could only hope he watched for her and would alert her as she passed.

"Louisa. Here." The deep timbre of his voice had never sounded better.

A footman hopped down to open the door. The carriage lamps inside were so dim that it was difficult to see. She took the seat opposite Benjamin as the footman shut the door, and Benjamin increased the flame.

"No difficulty leaving?" he asked. His dark gaze raked over her, suddenly making her aware of the risk she took.

Her mouth went dry. She was alone with a man. Not just any man but a rogue. Even worse, one to whom she was attracted. This act could ruin her. Panic tightened her chest. Yet what else could she do if her mother was truly in danger?

Chapter Seven

"What harm do you think could befall my mother?" Louisa asked as she rubbed her arms against a sudden chill.

Benjamin's eyes narrowed as if he heard the doubt in her tone. "Having second thoughts about rescuing her?"

She glanced away. "I wish to understand what sort of threat she might be facing." Never mind that she should've asked before leaving the ball.

"She might be having her portrait painted if she's the adventurous type."

Louisa studied Benjamin. That idea had already occurred to her. "Why would that be so terrible?"

"If the artist is the same man I happened to hear about earlier in the day, he often persuades his subjects to be painted in the nude."

"Oh, no." Any concern she had for herself fell away in an instant. No possible outcome she could think of was favorable.

"When the painter is ready to move to a new subject, he requests a significant payment for the portrait else he'll share it with others."

"Do you speak of extortion?" Her earlier panic returned, causing her shivers to worsen.

"Yes. I would assume if your mother chose to pose in such a manner, she'd prefer to keep it private and pay a reasonable sum."

"I'd prefer she not do it at all." Yet it sounded exactly like something that would appeal to her mother. Louisa placed her hands over her face as despair threatened. Why couldn't she have a normal mother who preferred to embroider or sketch? Or one who found a nice, older gentleman with whom to settle down? Instead, her mother seemed to thrive on the thrill of adventure.

Louisa admitted she'd experienced that same excitement when she'd ventured to Benjamin's home the second time. The realization worried her, as she knew at least part of her was much like her mother.

"May I?" She looked up to see Benjamin point to the place next to her. "I would offer you comfort if you'd permit it."

She nodded, reassured by the fact that he'd asked rather than assumed. A true rogue wouldn't have bothered to request permission.

Benjamin sat next to her and gently placed his arms around her. "I don't mean to frighten you. I don't think the man will physically harm her. No doubt she can take care of herself."

"No, she can't. She never looks beyond the moment. Never considers what could go wrong." Louisa leaned her head against Benjamin's shoulder, grateful for his support. It had been so long since she'd had someone with whom to share her worries.

"It sounds to me as if she's searching for happiness."

Louisa tipped her face to look at him in surprise, his understanding warming her from the inside out. "No one else seems to understand that."

Benjamin shifted as if uncomfortable under her scrutiny. "I confess to doing a few things in my past that were unwise. It took discovering the reason why I did so to change."

"I want her to be happy. But I can't seem to provide that for her."

His gentle fingers brushed her jaw. "Doing so isn't your responsibility."

"Perhaps. But I must continue to try."

"You are a loving daughter, an amazing person. Special." He briefly pressed his lips to hers. "Unforgettable."

Her stomach swirled at his quiet words as much as from his kiss. Though tempted to share that she felt the same way, she held back. Encouraging a relationship would be a mistake, even if that no longer felt as true as it had a few days ago.

Benjamin confused her in every way possible. When he kissed her again more deeply, all she could think of was how lovely the confusion felt.

He eased back only to place a kiss along her cheek. "Wait here."

Only then did she realize the carriage had halted. She watched as Benjamin alighted and closed the door before peeking through the curtain to see they'd stopped before a large townhome. The Marquess of Delham's home, she realized with surprise. She quickly closed the curtain, not wishing to be seen. Time crawled as she waited for Benjamin's return. She couldn't imagine why they'd stopped here or what might be taking so long.

At last, he returned and spoke quietly to the driver before joining her. "My apologies for the delay. Obtaining the address was more difficult than I expected."

"Why would the marquess know the address?"

Benjamin studied her for a moment as the carriage rolled forward. "The marchioness received a note from the painter today demanding an outrageous sum for her portrait."

"He painted her as well?" Louisa couldn't imagine the stiff-mannered lady in such a compromising position.

"Yes. Needless to say, the marquess was less than pleased."

"Oh my."

"Quite." Benjamin shook his head. "However, we now have the location of Monsieur Delacroix's studio."

They spoke little as the carriage proceeded to lower Thames Street where several artists had their homes above the shops that lined the street. She'd passed through the area before but never stopped.

Louisa considered how best to convince her mother to leave. Accusing the artist might cause her to come to his defense.

"Do you have a notion as to how to proceed?" she asked.

"Not precisely." He glanced at her. "Do you?"

In truth, she was surprised. A man with his reputation had surely been in unique situations like this one. But she was equally surprised he'd asked her. Weren't rogues notorious for acting without concern for other people's opinions?

"Caution is in order," he added. "We shouldn't needlessly upset the marchioness."

Louisa's heart thudded dully. To think he might understand the need to approach the situation delicately was one more chink in her defense against him.

She gave herself a mental shake. Now was not the time to worry over her growing attraction to this man.

"Why don't you wait here while I see if I can gain entrance?" He reached for the door as the carriage halted.

"I'll come."

"I would prefer to avoid any unnecessary risks to your reputation."

She paused to stare at him in disbelief. He'd done it again—acted nobly. What was she to do with him and the way his words caused her heart to stutter? "You might require my assistance."

His wry smile suggested her remark amused him. "I'm certain your presence would reassure the marchioness. With luck, Monsieur Delacroix hasn't charmed her into doing anything she wouldn't normally do."

Louisa didn't share her doubt as she alighted with Benjamin's assistance. She'd lost any surprise at what her mother might do.

Benjamin glanced up and down the empty street then studied the dark shops briefly before looking at the upper stories. Louisa's gaze followed his to where dim light shone along the edges of the draped windows.

"Is that it?" she asked.

"I believe so." He tried the door set between the two shops only to find it locked.

"Would you like me to try?" Louisa asked as she reached for a hairpin.

"No need." He placed a hand on her arm as if to make certain she didn't make an attempt, leaving Louisa to scowl in disappointment.

Benjamin withdrew a slim metal rod from his waistcoat pocket then bent low to pick the lock.

Louisa stared in surprise, unable to determine why he'd have the tool or the skill. He was much quicker than she and had the door open within moments.

"I'll lead the way, shall I?" he asked as he stepped inside. He paused to listen then closed the door behind her and started up the narrow stairs, his boots nearly silent on the steps with Louisa close behind.

Nerves danced in her middle. The faint sound of voices drifted toward them, including a feminine laugh—her mother's. Anger took over once more. To think her mother had ventured here alone... She couldn't finish the thought.

Benjamin knocked on the door at the top of the stairs. Several moments passed before a male servant cracked open the door. "*Oiu?*"

"I wish to speak with Monsieur Delacroix."

The man's gaze swept over Benjamin then glanced past him toward Louisa. "*Pourquoi?*"

"A business matter."

"*Non.* No visitors." He started to close the door, but Benjamin anticipated the move by putting his boot in the doorway and prevented him from closing it.

"He'll see us." Benjamin placed his hands on the door and shoved.

The man stumbled back. "*Non*. No guests. He's working."

Benjamin ignored him and stepped inside. "Where is he?"

The servant's lips tightened in disapproval.

"We shall find him on our own then," Benjamin said as he glanced about.

Louisa followed, surprised by the elegant interior. The painter must be a success if he could afford such a home. The trill of her mother's laughter sounded from the upper level, and Louisa turned toward the stairs, anger filling her once more.

Benjamin was relieved to hear laughter rather than tears or worse—screams. He gestured for Louisa to lead the way to the next floor, wanting to keep himself between her and the servant in case the man attempted a more physical method of halting them.

"*Non*. You cannot go up there," the servant protested as he started after them.

"Stay where you are." Benjamin sent a glare along with the order, pleased when the man halted on the first step.

"He won't be pleased."

"Your warning is duly noted." Benjamin stayed close to Louisa, keeping an eye on the servant while watching the landing above.

He feared Louisa wouldn't appreciate what they were about to discover. Though he knew she'd rescued her mother on more than one occasion, finding her posing nude carried a higher level of concern. If Delacroix specialized in seducing his subjects, they might be interrupting an intimate scene that should remain behind closed doors.

Louisa marched up the stairs, her anger seeming to overcome any previous trepidation. She reached for the closed door at the top of the stairs, but Benjamin halted her.

"Proceed with caution," he advised with a pointed look, both for her safety as well as her sanity.

The intensity in her gaze eased as if she'd grasped his meaning. She nodded, then with a deep breath, she slowly opened the door and looked in.

Benjamin stayed back, not wishing to violate the marchioness's privacy if she wasn't properly attired. But he remained at the ready in case the painter threatened Louisa.

"Mother." By the reprimand in Louisa's tone, he suspected all was not as it should be.

"Louisa! Darling. Whatever are you doing here?" The rustle of material reached Benjamin, making him hope the marchioness had covered herself if needed.

"I've come to take you home."

"Who is this?" The man's voice held a distinct French accent, much more refined than his servant's.

Louisa moved into the room, and Benjamin followed closely for her protection.

The Marchioness of Whirlenhall sat on a gold and white striped settee, her body draped in a deep blue satin cloth with candles surrounding her. Her bare shoulders and feet suggested she wore nothing beneath. A fire burned brightly nearby and helped to warm and light the room.

The artist stood near the window before a large canvas set on an easel, a paintbrush in hand. His shocked expression might've been amusing in other circumstances. Paints stood on a table nearby along with a cup full of brushes and more candles.

"What is the meaning of this?" Delacroix demanded.

"We're here to collect the marchioness and her painting, along with one other," Benjamin advised him. He intended to take the Delham portrait and put an end to the extortion.

"You will do no such thing." He threw down the paintbrush and stepped forward only to halt and glare at Benjamin. "Who are you?"

Benjamin didn't bother to answer. Words were of little use in a situation like this. He preferred action. With a nod at Louisa to assist her mother, he eyed the stacks of paintings propped along the walls to determine where to search.

As he crossed the room, Delacroix rushed toward the open door. "Weston, where are you? Come at once."

"Mother, please get dressed. We're leaving."

"Why? What's happened? Don't you want to meet Monsieur Delacroix?" Her mother rose from the settee, holding the cloth around her.

"No. We've been told he's more than an artist. In fact, I'd wager he earns far more from his other profession."

"What would that be?" the marchioness asked.

"Extortionist."

"What?" Delacroix spun to face Louisa. "Who told you such lies?"

Benjamin found the painting he was looking for. Lady Delham's face was clearly recognizable. He preferred to avoid studying the rest of the portrait. "The husband of the person in this painting asked me to tell you that no payment will be forthcoming for your efforts. He also suggested the time has come for you to return to your homeland."

Delacroix gasped. "How dare you touch what doesn't belong to you." He strode back to the door once again. "Weston!"

Benjamin threw a cloth over the portrait, hoping the artist would attempt to stop him. He'd like nothing better than to place his fist in the man's face. He set aside the painting and moved toward the easel.

"Step away from there." Delacroix rushed forward, hands outstretched.

Benjamin shifted to face him, hands at his sides. "Did you explain to the lady that you would be pleased to sell her the painting at a ridiculous price to avoid sharing it with the public?"

"Art should be enjoyed by the masses, especially if the subject doesn't truly appreciate my skill."

"Jean Paul, is that true?" Louisa's mother asked, her mouth agape with shock.

"*Non*, madam. You must believe me." The painter held out his hands in supplication. "You and I share something very special."

"Did you use that same turn of phrase when you painted the lady in the other portrait?" Not waiting for an answer, Benjamin turned toward the marchioness.

"This very day, she received a note demanding a thousand pounds to keep him from selling the portrait to the highest bidder."

"This is all a terrible misunderstanding," Delacroix insisted though with less outrage than before.

The marchioness glared at the man. "To think I believed that you truly cared for me." She allowed Louisa to escort her behind the dressing screen. Whispers and rustles followed, suggesting Louisa was sharing additional details as she assisted her to dress.

Benjamin removed the canvas from the easel, found another piece of fabric with which to cover the half-finished painting, and set it near the door beside the other one, all while the artist sputtered denials from the far side of the room.

Anger simmered deep inside him at Delacroix's audacity. Benjamin drew close, preferring the women didn't hear what he said. "Return to France as quickly as possible before the rest of those you attempted to deceive start taking action rather than give in to your ridiculous demands. Do I make myself clear?"

The glare Delacroix sent him might've wilted a weaker man. Benjamin merely smiled. He turned his back on the artist, hoping he'd be stupid enough to try to stop him.

With an enraged cry, the painter launched himself onto Benjamin's back. Benjamin reached for him as he bent forward, easily flinging the smaller man to the floor and holding him there. "Do not dare to touch me again." He circled his fingers around the painter's throat and squeezed. "Do not approach either of these ladies again. Do you understand?"

Delacroix's face turned red as he gasped for air. Though tempted to continue squeezing to be certain the man had received the message, he was all too aware of Louisa's presence. He loosened his hold enough to allow the painter to breathe and nod.

With a scoff of disgust, he released him and turned to Louisa. "Are you ready?"

Her wide eyes stared at him with shock. She took one more look at the painter and nodded jerkily. "Of course."

Lady Whirlenhall emerged from behind the screen properly attired, much to Benjamin's relief. Her gaze swept from him to the painter and back again. Approval lit her expression as she swept past the artist and out the door, head held high. "Goodbye, Jean Paul."

Chapter Eight

Louisa sighed wistfully as she watched Benjamin enter the Smithby ball two days later. When he'd escorted them home that night, she and her mother had thanked him, but there hadn't been a chance for Louisa to share the extent of her gratitude. Somehow, both she and her mother had managed to survive the incident with no one the wiser.

But she hadn't been able to stop thinking of him since. His thoughtfulness toward her and her mother, his confidence in the situation, and even his anger at the artist had caused her to look at him in a new, unsettling light. There was far more to the man than she'd realized.

Yet Louisa worried that her mother's actions might have discouraged him from having any interest in her.

"A dance, Lady Louisa?" Viscount Stanich asked from her side.

She hesitated, all too aware of the feeling of dread that came over her whenever she spent time with the man. What was wrong with her? He was perfectly nice. And safe. But she no longer wanted that. The realization troubled her deeply. "Thank you, my lord."

The dance lasted forever. She did her best to keep an eye on Benjamin, hoping he wouldn't leave before she could speak with him.

"Is something amiss?" the viscount asked when the dance permitted conversation.

"Not at all. Why do you ask?"

"You seem quite distracted this evening." He appeared bemused by the fact.

For some reason, that irritated her. As if nothing could be on her mind except who her next dance partner was. She forced a polite smile but didn't respond to his remark.

Several minutes passed before he spoke again. "I'll be spending the holiday in the country with my family."

"That will be nice." The idea of his absence pleased her more than it should.

"My parents wanted to extend an invitation to you and the marchioness to join us."

"How...kind of them. Unfortunately, we have other plans." She had no desire to spend Christmas with the viscount and his family. She closed her eyes briefly as she realized what that meant. There was no possible way she could entertain a future with this man.

"Of course." Displeasure twisted his lips. "Last minute and all that."

"I'm pleased you understand." To her relief, the music drew to a halt, and he escorted her to where her mother stood then bid her goodbye.

"Wasn't that Stanich? He didn't appear pleased," her mother said as she moved closer.

"He invited us to spend Christmas with his family at their country estate."

Her mother studied her. "You don't sound particularly excited about the invitation."

"I told him we wouldn't be able to attend as we have other plans."

"Good. I don't think he's right for you. We do have another invitation to consider."

"From whom?"

"The Marquess and Marchioness of Delham have invited us to their home on the outskirts of London for a house party in a few days' time."

Louisa stared at her mother in surprise. "Do they know?"

"That the marchioness and I have something in common? Much to my surprise, no, they do not. We must thank Granger again for not only his assistance but his discretion. Perhaps he is to thank for the invitation as well."

Louisa followed her mother's gaze to Benjamin, who moved in their direction. Before she could calm her reeling emotions, her mother approached him, leaving Louisa to follow.

"Lord Granger." Her mother offered her hand. "Good to see you."

"Lady Whirlenhall." Benjamin took her hand and bowed before his dark eyes shifted to Louisa. "Lady Louisa."

A strange sensation filled her as if a thousand butterflies had been released inside her to flutter about. She was in serious trouble.

Her mother glanced about as if to make certain no one could overhear then stepped closer. "We wish to thank you once again for your assistance."

"My pleasure. I hope all is well?"

"Quite. May I ask if you properly disposed of the item?"

Benjamin had offered to destroy the unfinished painting, much to Louisa's relief. Her mother had been angered enough over the situation never to want to see it again.

"Of course."

Her mother smiled. "Excellent. I appreciate your discretion more than I can say. Now if you'll both excuse me, I see someone with whom I simply must speak."

Louisa cleared her throat as her mother stepped away. "Thank you. I know I've already said it, but I truly appreciate all you've done to help us."

"It was my honor." His dark eyes glittered warmly. Suddenly, she couldn't think of anything except their kiss in his carriage and how much she'd like another. "Would you care to dance?"

"Yes, I would. Thank you." Delight swept through her, so different from how she'd felt when Stanich had asked her. Was there a chance that Benjamin had set his roguish behavior behind him now that he'd inherited?

"I trust your mother is none the worse for the experience?" he asked as he escorted her toward the dance floor.

"She was quite distraught at having been tricked into agreeing to sit for the portrait. I'm relieved we interrupted them before true harm was done."

"I'm pleased to hear that." The dance steps took them in different directions briefly before uniting them once more. "I understand you and your mother have been invited to the Delham's house party."

She looked at him in surprise. "Are you attending as well?"

"Yes. Many of the guests include those who are assisting with the charity for wounded soldiers." He smiled. "We're hoping that with Christmas soon upon us, they'll be more generous with their time and money."

"How clever," she said with a chuckle. "I shall advise Mother to be prepared to give as well."

The dance concluded, and Benjamin escorted her to her mother. She wasn't ready to part company with him and was pleased when he remained at her side.

"I'm certain Delham also has a political motive and hopes to persuade some of the other members of the House of Lords to see his viewpoint on how to develop a long-term peace plan for Europe."

"No event is ever a simple gathering these days," Louisa said with a shake of her head. "Do you intend to become involved in Parliament?"

"I hope to."

His words pleased her as they suggested he had serious plans for the future. Anticipation for the days and weeks ahead filled her. This Christmas season promised to hold more joy than she'd had since childhood. The coming weekend couldn't come soon enough.

Benjamin rose the first day of the Delham's house party, anxious to see Louisa. Having her in the same house, regardless of the size of the estate, was even more appealing than he'd expected. He'd arrived late the previous evening after most of the guests had retired for the night.

Delham had been grateful if embarrassed that he'd retrieved the painting of the marchioness. He'd insisted on hosting the gathering to celebrate the formalization of the charity as a way to show his gratitude. Benjamin hadn't told him that Louisa's mother had also fallen for the artist's charms, only that he'd learned of another person who needed assistance. However, he had asked that the Marchioness of Whirlenhall and her daughter be invited, and Delham had been pleased to do so.

The guests included both young and old per Benjamin's request. He wanted men his own age involved in the charity with the hope that they would take an interest in other similar issues as well.

However, the only person holding his thoughts this morning was Louisa. While he'd been certain she was wrong for him, now he worried whether she could look past *his* reputation. Surely there was a way they could move away from their pasts and look toward a different future for both of them.

He rang for his valet and quickly dressed in warm clothes, including a woolen waistcoat and tall leather boots. Many of the younger guests were to go ice skating this morning at a nearby pond that had frozen solid with the unusually cold nights of late. He hoped Louisa planned to join the fun.

Breakfast was a lively affair with most of the guests who were going skating filling the dining room where a sideboard held dishes of eggs, ham, and pastries as well as coffee, tea, and chocolate. Smothering his disappointment at not finding Louisa there, he helped himself and settled into a chair next to Viscount Gibbon. He'd finished half his plate when Louisa arrived.

Her plum-colored wool gown should've been plain with its simple lines and high neck, but on her, it looked beautiful. Her gaze swept the room until she found him. A small smile graced her lips as if they shared a secret. The tingling anticipation he felt took him aback.

"Isn't that right, Granger?"

Benjamin forced his gaze away from Louisa. "Pardon?"

Even as Gibbon spoke, Benjamin's attention returned to Louisa as she selected a few items then took a seat with the other ladies, including Lady Harriet, Delham's daughter. Though disappointed, he supposed it wouldn't do for them to spend too much time together.

Once everyone finished, they retrieved coats, cloaks, hats, scarves, gloves, and skates from their rooms before meeting in the entrance. He knew the moment she joined the growing group. Sometime in the past two weeks, his senses had become attuned to her in more ways than he cared to admit.

"The brakes are here," someone called out, and everyone exited the house to pile into the open, four-wheeled conveyances that held eight people for the brief journey to the pond.

His pleasure when she sat beside him in the back of the brake made him feel like a young boy lighting his first Yule Log. He settled a heavy quilt over the top of them, wondering if he dared to hold her hand underneath the cover.

"Benjamin." She said his name quietly, her breath causing a puff of frosty air as a shiver crept down his spine. "Does the day find you well?"

"Indeed. And you?"

Her gaze dropped to his lips as he spoke, twisting him in knots. He wanted her more than he'd wanted anyone in a long while. But this was far more than simple desire. His emotions were becoming hopelessly entangled.

"Very well." She looked away to speak with someone else, but his desire continued to simmer steadily.

The ride was rough as they crossed a field, and more than once, Louisa bumped against him. Surely it wasn't his imagination that she remained there for a long moment.

He assisted her to alight once they'd stopped. Benches had been situated along the end of the pond to allow people to sit and strap on their skates. He managed to keep his distance as they did so, speaking with several acquaintances.

In short order, the skaters were circling the pond. The servants had swept away the dusting of snow earlier, leaving smooth ice. Another brake arrived with some of the local gentry who joined them.

Benjamin hadn't skated since his youth, but after a few turns around the pond, he seemed to have remembered the necessary balance and stride. Louisa appeared to be an expert at it, gracefully gliding across the ice and making it look easy. He increased his pace to catch up with her, nearly falling in his haste.

"Lady Louisa, you are an excellent skater."

"We've been able to skate often the past few winters as it's been so cold." Her hands were tucked beneath her cloak as she glided beside him.

"Does your mother skate as well?"

"Not since my father passed away. The two of them could practically dance on the ice." Her smile faded. "Those memories are why she prefers not to spend Christmas in the country."

"Perhaps one day, she'll be able to remember those times with fondness instead of pain." He still missed his parents, especially during the holidays. His father might have been a rogue, but he was still his father.

"I hope so." With a shake of her head, she said, "Enough of such a dark subject. Would you care to race?" The sparkle in her eyes made him catch his breath before her words sunk in.

Before he could respond, she was off, navigating the slower skaters as she raced to the opposite end of the pond. He followed suit, not bothering to try to catch her. She glanced over her shoulder, her laughter pulling him forward.

With a groan, he realized he couldn't resist her. Her joy for life might cause her to take a few risks, but it made her all the more appealing. He caught up to her as she neared the end and looped his arm through hers which caused them both to spin. He swore he felt his heart spinning as well.

Louisa prepared for the ball that evening in breathless anticipation. Something had changed between her and Benjamin during those carefree moments on the frozen pond as if the defenses they'd both held had shattered into tiny pieces like an icicle falling from the roof.

She had to think the unusual situations in which they'd found themselves of late had both tested and bound them together in a way few people experienced. Dare she hope he felt the same? That they might have something special between them that would hold them steady and true in the years to come?

She closed her eyes tight as a deep longing swept through her. There was no need to rush anything. She could simply enjoy the time they had together along with the fact that Christmas would soon be upon them. The thought of the magical combination of those two events was what caused her breath to catch.

"You look lovely," Beth said as she made a final adjustment to the holly sprig sitting on the curls at the back of her head.

"Thank you, Beth. The ball should be quite enjoyable." Louisa rose from the dressing table and faced Beth. "Am I ready?"

"A little more color." Beth patted both her cheeks lightly before studying Louisa's white gown decorated with green velvet ribbons. "Perfect."

Louisa laughed. "I hope you enjoy the evening as well."

"There's a handsome footman I have my eye on. We'll see if he's off duty this evening."

With a smile, Louisa walked across the hall and knocked on her mother's door.

The door opened, revealing her mother, beautiful as always. "Louisa, you look lovely."

"As do you." She leaned forward to press a kiss on her mother's cheek, pleased to note no shadows lingered in her eyes. "Shall we venture downstairs?"

They joined the other guests in the ballroom. Candles and small mirrors were everywhere, creating a magical gold and silver atmosphere. Though greenery wouldn't be used for decoration until Christmas as it was considered bad luck to bring it inside any earlier, bits of mistletoe hung here and there.

"It's our own frost ball, don't you think?" Louisa's mother smiled and squeezed her hand then moved toward a group of friends.

Before Louisa could decide who to join, awareness prickled along her bare neck. She glanced over to see Benjamin at her side.

"Good evening." His gaze swept over her hair and gown then lingered on her face, making her glad she'd taken time on her appearance. "May I say how beautiful you are?"

Her heart tilted at his words. He hadn't said she looked beautiful, but that she *was* beautiful. How did he so easily know the right thing to say? "Thank you."

"May I have the honor of two dances this evening?"

Her eyes widened as her heartbeat sped. Doing so would make others aware of his interest in her. "I would like that very much."

He reached for her hand and tucked it into the crook of his elbow. "Shall we join the others?"

In truth, she was tempted to suggest they find a hidden alcove so they might have a few moments alone together. She dearly wanted to ask what he was thinking. Yet there was something delicious about waiting to find out. Anticipation heightened her senses and danced along her body.

"Is it just me, or is there mistletoe everywhere one looks?" Benjamin asked as they walked across the room.

"The Marchioness of Delham must be hoping to provide her guests with some amusement." Louisa spotted several places where the distinctive greenery with white berries was placed.

"I have to wonder if she and the marquess had a reconciliation of sorts after the close call with the painter."

Louisa chuckled. "You think she hopes to catch her own husband beneath the mistletoe?"

"One has to wonder." Benjamin shared a smile with her.

This, she thought with a sigh. This was what she wanted. Shared moments filled with laughter and longing. Moments with Benjamin.

Dare she hope that might be possible?

Chapter Nine

Benjamin clenched his teeth as yet another man danced with Louisa. He wanted her all to himself, an impossible wish at a gathering such as this. What he felt for her was new and fragile and demanded exploration. How could he manage that in a houseful of people? He'd danced with Lady Adele and several others, but they didn't compare to having Louisa in his arms.

"Granger," Delham said as he approached. "I hope you're enjoying the ball."

"I am." He forced his thoughts away from Louisa. He'd seen Delham that afternoon when the men had met to discuss the details of the charity but hadn't had a chance to speak with him privately. "Thank you for hosting such a wonderful party. The skating this morning was especially enjoyable. I haven't attempted that in a long time. I thought you might join us."

Delham scoffed, just as Benjamin knew he would. "Such pastimes are for your generation. Not mine. You're lucky you didn't break your neck on the ice."

"Danger often adds an element of enjoyment."

"Spoken like a young man." Delham chuckled. "I see you're still enjoying a bit of danger this evening." He tipped his head in Louisa's direction.

"I enjoy the lady's company." He fought the urge to come to her defense by listing all her fine qualities. The older man already knew of his interest in her, but Benjamin had no intention of sharing more.

Delham sighed. "Who am I to offer such advice when my own wife has proven to be far more brazen than I could've guessed?"

Benjamin was surprised the older lord admitted as much. "Perhaps it might be helpful to spend more time with her." The marchioness stood a short distance away. Her frequent glances toward her husband suggested her thoughts were on him. "I would be willing to wager that she'd be delighted if you danced with her."

Delham stared at him as if he'd lost his mind.

Benjamin shrugged. "There has to be a reason she had mistletoe placed everywhere."

The marquess glanced around the ballroom as if only now realizing the fact. "Humph. I suppose a dance isn't so much to ask."

Smiling, Benjamin watched as Delham moved toward his wife.

"What has you so amused?" Louisa asked as she arrived at his side.

"I believe our host is realizing the potential benefits of mistletoe."

"That is a lovely notion just before Christmas."

"Do you know what I would like?" He kept his voice quiet, mindful of those standing nearby.

"What?" The warmth in her eyes only caused his own desire to grow.

"A moment alone with you. Mistletoe is not a requirement."

"It's not?" That couldn't possibly be disappointment in her expression, could it?

"Because I would kiss you regardless of its presence."

"Oh?" Her voice was breathless, her eyes dark.

Suddenly, he couldn't wait a moment longer. "Would you care to escape the heated ballroom for a moment on the terrace?"

She swallowed hard as if uncertain whether to take such a risk.

He wanted her to agree more than anything, to take the sort of risk she'd so boldly done before. But this time, for him. How ironic, when that same boldness had nearly convinced him she was wrong for him.

"I'll meet you outside when the clock strikes midnight." Then she stepped away, leaving him wondering if he'd asked too much.

He retrieved his watch from his waistcoat pocket and realized he'd know soon. Midnight was only a quarter of an hour away.

Louisa made her way to the retiring room, wondering if the risk was too high. If they were caught...

She shook her head. They weren't going to be caught. Everyone was enjoying the ball. They only wanted a moment together. Was that so much to ask? One kiss. Well, perhaps two. Then she would return to the ballroom, as would he, with no one aware of their absence.

A few minutes alone with a rogue...

Yet she hesitated, all too aware those minutes could easily end in the same situation that had caused Caroline and Aberland to become betrothed. It was a gamble, which was why she wanted time to consider rather than giving into impulse. What if he wanted more than a kiss? Her feelings for him caused her to worry that she'd give in to her desire for him.

She smiled at some of the other ladies in the room then paused before the dressing table mirror to check her appearance. Her heightened color and the sparkle in her eyes spoke of the hopeless tangle of her emotions. How could she decide whether she wanted Benjamin in her life if they didn't have time together? She wasn't considering his suggestion simply for the thrill but because she wanted a private moment with him. That was worth the chance of discovery.

She glanced at the clock on the table to see that midnight drew near. After a deep breath to calm her nerves, she returned to the ballroom to make her way around the dance floor toward the terrace doors, unable to see Benjamin anywhere. Had he already stepped out?

To her surprise, the terrace door opened beneath her hand.

"Join us, Lady Louisa, for a few moments away from the heated ballroom." Delham opened the door wide. The marchioness stood next to him, a rare smile on her face. "The night is clear, and the stars are amazing."

Voices sounded behind her, and she turned to see many of the guests following her.

Confused, she stepped outside, and a strong, warm hand grasped her arm. "Benjamin?"

With a smile, he drew her toward the rear of the terrace, away from the faint light and the guests emerging from the ballroom doors. "We're taking a moment to admire the stars."

He drew her into the shadows at the dark edge of the terrace where the night was deep. He stood with his back to the house and shifted her to stand before him, facing out as well. The warmth of his body compared to the chill of the evening caused her to shiver. He pulled her against him, his hands warm on her arms. "Are you cold?"

"Not anymore."

The guests looked up, murmuring in admiration at the swath of stars painted across the night sky. No one was directly beside them, nor did the others pay them any mind. It was as if they were alone in the crowd, hidden by the moonless night.

To her surprise, Benjamin eased them farther back, a few steps around the corner of the house and truly by themselves, at last.

"I hope you don't mind that I invited others to come outside." Benjamin's quiet voice near her ear caused tingles along her body. "I wanted a moment alone with you without jeopardizing your reputation."

"How clever of you to think of this. Thank you." She turned to face him, enjoying the view nearly as much as his presence. "I forget how magical a winter's night in the country can be."

"Yes." He pressed a kiss on the side of her neck, then another just below her ear. "Being with you truly is magical."

Best of all, he held her as if he never wanted to let her go as they looked up at the stars together. His soft sigh of contentment squeezed her full heart. How silly of her to worry he might want more than she was willing to give. He'd once again reassured her that she could trust him despite his reputation.

"Can we pretend we have mistletoe?" she whispered as she looked at him, his face only a shadow as she placed her gloved hands on his chest.

He chuckled quietly. "I happen to have brought some with me." He shifted his arm then reached for her hand and placed a sprig of what she assumed was mistletoe in her palm, though it was too dark to tell. "There. For you. To remember this night."

Then he kissed her, long and deep, melting her heart. Not only did this man make her toes curl, but he also held her affection. Could this be love?

He eased back. "We should return to the others," he whispered. "You must be growing cold."

She bit her lip, unprepared to share her feelings. Not until she was sure. But she didn't want this moment to end. Did he possibly feel the same way? His heartbeat thudded beneath her palm, suggesting he wasn't immune to the moment either. "If you insist."

"Only if you promise to allow me to collect another kiss at Christmas. There's more than one berry on the mistletoe."

Heat filled her, making her forget the cold. How sweet of him to think of the tradition of removing a berry for each kiss shared beneath the mistletoe. "I look forward to it."

He lifted her hand and pressed his lips to the delicate bare skin of her wrist, just above her glove, then escorted her to the terrace where most of the guests were returning to the ballroom. "I'll follow shortly."

Resisting the urge to remain with him, she stepped inside, holding the mistletoe tightly. Was Benjamin a rogue or a gentleman? Did he care for her as much as she did for him? She dearly wanted to know before she fell even harder for him.

Sunday morning arrived with a softly falling snow that came down in large, plump flakes. The party was nearly at end, and the guests would depart on the morrow. Benjamin found the snow delightful, but some of the other guests didn't. They grumbled as they bundled up for the ride to the local church, piling into any coach with room. The coaches made more than one trip to accommodate all the guests who wished to attend the service.

Louisa had caught an earlier ride, much to his dismay. But the smile she'd given him as she'd walked out the door with her mother had eased his disappointment.

Benjamin sat on the far end of the bench seat in the next coach, hoping the ride to church wouldn't take long.

"Do you have room for one more?" The feminine voice belonged to Lady Adele, Viscount Gibbon's sister. Gibbon was nowhere in sight.

"Only if you don't mind sitting on my lap," called out Stafford. His jest was followed by laughter.

Those in the carriage squeezed closer, and she joined them, ending up pressed against Benjamin. She smiled shyly at him as she settled into position. Luckily, the ride to the church was brief, and Louisa had saved a place on the pew next to her and her mother.

"I feared you were going to be late," she whispered.

"As did I."

He heard little of the sermon with Louisa so close.

Snow continued to fall as they made the journey back to Delham's for dinner. The feast consisted of roasted venison, plum pudding, trifle, and almond cake, along with other delights. Louisa was seated at the opposite end of the table, and he found himself once again near Lady Adele. She didn't offer much in the form of conversation but continually looked at him from under her lashes. She answered any question he posed with simple answers, making talking to her difficult.

Her brother, Viscount Gibbon, watched closely as if he expected Benjamin to make an unwanted advance. By the end of the meal, Benjamin decided the pair were annoying.

Many of the guests enjoyed cards after dinner. This time, Benjamin made certain he shared a table with Louisa. Cribbage was not one of his favorite games as he rarely played it, but Louisa was a master at it.

"Are you certain you know how to play?" she asked with a grin after he'd lost yet another hand.

"Perhaps it's been longer since I last played than I thought." He counted his cards with one eye on the number of pegs she was ahead of him on the board. There was no hope of him catching her, but he didn't mind losing to her. "Are you sure you wouldn't rather play whist?"

She laughed and patted his hand. "Let us finish the game."

Though he longed for another rendezvous on the terrace, he resisted. The time to collect his kiss would come soon as Christmas was only a week away.

Louisa frowned as they prepared to depart along with the rest of the guests the next morning. She wasn't ready to leave. She'd enjoyed spending time with Benjamin, even if it had been with the other guests.

"Whatever is that sigh about?" her mother asked.

Louisa shrugged as she helped her mother put on her cloak. "I'm sorry to see the party come to an end."

"Why don't we have a Christmas Eve ball? We haven't hosted one in a long while."

"That would be enjoyable." Especially if Benjamin were among the guests.

"We'll keep it intimate with limited invitations. A light supper and some dancing. I assume you'd like to invite the Earl of Granger? It seems like the least we could do after all he's done for us."

"I should like that very much. Thank you, Mother."

They entered the drawing room where the guests had gathered to say their goodbyes while they awaited their carriages. Her breath caught at the sight of him speaking with another lord near the window. She moved close but didn't want to interrupt their conversation. From what Benjamin had mentioned, the plans for the charity were coming along well.

"Good morning, Lady Louisa," Lord Umberley said with a bow.

Louisa returned the greeting as Benjamin turned to face her, the pleasure in his expression warming her. "Are you leaving now?"

"Yes," she said, hoping Umberley might read her mind and step away. To her delight, he excused himself and moved away to speak with someone else. "I wanted to let you know that we'll be hosting a Christmas Eve celebration. I hope you'll come."

"I'd be honored." He smiled only to give her a mock frown. "Will there be mistletoe?"

"Most definitely," she said with a laugh. This was the first Christmas in a long time that she looked forward to.

Chapter Ten

Benjamin nodded at Aberland as he strode into Brooks's two days later. They'd arranged to meet at the club as Aberland had expressed interest in joining the charity. Benjamin couldn't have been more pleased. He knew Aberland was doing his best to extricate himself from the spying business now that he and Caroline were to marry. Involving himself in the charity would allow him to still take part in helping England.

"Are you in need of additional contributors?" Aberland asked as a waiter brought their drinks.

"Always. More funds mean a wider reach. However, I think we have enough involved with the planning."

Aberland chuckled. "Too many opinions make getting anything accomplished nearly impossible."

"Exactly." Before Benjamin could say more, he caught movement out of the corner of his eye.

"Granger." Viscount Gibbon stood beside them, his lips pressed in a thin line as his eyes glittered with a strange light. "A word, if you please."

Benjamin frowned, noting Gibbon's younger brother standing behind the angry viscount. "Of course."

"Your insult to our sister cannot be overlooked. I demand satisfaction."

Benjamin shifted to face him, confused by his words even as unease swirled through him. The entire room silenced to listen, much to his dismay. His efforts to reform had been successful thus far. This was the last thing he needed or wanted, yet he refused to allow his honor to be questioned. "What insult?"

Gibbon leaned forward, his gaze holding on Benjamin. "You placed your hands upon her person. I expect an offer of marriage before the day's end."

"I did not touch Lady Adele or insult her in any way." Anger flared at the accusation, bringing him to his feet. He refused to be forced into doing something he didn't want to do when he'd done nothing wrong.

"Then name your second."

"Don't be a fool, Gibbon. You don't want to do this. There must be some misunderstanding."

"Are you calling my sister a liar?"

"No, but—"

"Then name your second." Gibbon's hands fisted at his sides.

"I'm asking you one last time not to do this. There was no insult." While this wouldn't be Benjamin's first duel, he had a feeling it would be Gibbon's. Nonetheless, Benjamin couldn't disregard the challenge. All his work to reform might be lost, but he would not lose his honor.

"What is this?" The Marquess of Delham approached, eyes narrowed as he looked between them.

Gibbon hesitated as he looked briefly at the marquess then glared at Benjamin once again. "A matter of honor."

"Granger, surely you intend to do the right thing and offer for the lady." Delham's tone held a note of disapproval.

"I've suggested that Gibbon review the facts before he proceeds with a challenge," Benjamin said, his thoughts racing.

"And I've asked you to name your second." Gibbon continued to glare at Benjamin.

Heart thudding, Benjamin ignored both men and turned to Aberland with a raised brow, relief filling him at Aberland's nod of assent. "The Earl of Aberland will serve as my second."

"Very well. My brother will act as mine. He'll call on Aberland to determine the details on the morrow." Gibbon gave a single nod and left, his brother following him out of the club.

Stunned at the turn of events, Benjamin watched them leave in disbelief, a terrible unease flooding him. How had this come to pass?

"This is inexcusable, Granger," Delham said. "Make this right by offering the lady marriage. Save yourself from disgrace."

"I will not do so when I did nothing wrong."

"Then you can remove my name from the charity. I don't want anything to do with a rogue such as you." Delham strode out of the room, murmurs following from those who remained.

Benjamin shook his head as he sank to his chair. All his efforts to redeem himself had been for naught. Not only was the charity in jeopardy, but he could also imagine what Louisa would think when she heard of the duel. Actually, no, he couldn't. His mind refused to consider it, as did his heart.

"What the hell was that about?" Aberland asked.

"I truly have no idea." He scoured his memory for any possible insult but found none. "Lady Adele was at the Delham house party, but I certainly never touched her."

"We shall hope the fool reconsiders. Now I better understand why the rules insist on a day's grace before the duel. Perhaps cooler heads will prevail." Aberland waved for a waiter and ordered them both another drink. "Otherwise, I suppose this means pistols at dawn the following day."

"I suppose it does." But all he could think about was Louisa. How could he have done nothing wrong yet lost everything?

Louisa entered the drawing room the following afternoon to find both Caroline and Annabelle waiting. "This is a pleasant surprise," she said as she gave first Annabelle then Caroline a hug.

As she drew back from Caroline, the tension in her cousin's expression was impossible to ignore. "Is something amiss?"

"I'm afraid we bring bad news." Caroline reached for Louisa's hand and held it tight. "Granger has been challenged to a duel."

Louisa's breath caught, her emotions tumbling. "That can't be." Rogues might fight duels, but Benjamin had changed his ways. "By who?"

"Viscount Gibbon."

"Lady Adele's brother? Whatever for?"

Caroline released her hand as she shared a look with Annabelle. "Gibbon accused him of taking liberties with his sister."

Louisa closed her eyes at the stunned disbelief that washed through her only to hold tight with a painful grip. She knew Benjamin was acquainted Lady Adele, but never had she noted him being anything but polite toward the shy woman. Certainly, she was attractive with a generous dowry, and thus far, her behavior had been above reproach. She would make an ideal wife, especially for a rogue. Yet she couldn't fathom the idea.

"During Delham's house party?" Louisa's thoughts raced, trying to think of whether there could be any truth to the accusation.

Caroline nodded.

"An offer of marriage would eliminate the need for them to go through with it." Louisa focused on drawing in each breath, willing the terrible pain to recede. Nothing stood in Benjamin's way if he wanted to marry Lady Adele. He'd made no promises to Louisa.

"Yes. But Granger has refused. We were hoping Gibbon would withdraw his demand today, but that hasn't happened. They meet at dawn."

"Is Aberland acting as his second?"

Caroline scowled. "Apparently so. Men. Stubborn and filled with pride."

"True." Louisa swallowed against the lump in her throat. Her worst fear had come to pass—that a rogue like Benjamin would never truly change. She'd spent the past few years dealing with her mother's reckless behavior and already grown weary of the pitying glances and the hesitation before invitations were extended. She had no intention of living like that because of her husband. Not that he'd offered for her. Now she'd never know if that had been his intent.

She might love Benjamin—the realization had her drawing a shaky breath— but she refused to spend the rest of her life worrying over what scandal might befall him. She needed to put aside her feelings for him and find someone whose behavior was impeccable.

"This is for the best, really," she murmured, wishing she meant it.

Annabelle reached out to touch her arm. "How so? I think it's horrible."

"Not at all." She lifted her chin, hoping the pain would fade with time. "Thank goodness this happened now before I became enamored with him." Did her cousins believe the lie?

"Granger was quite angry by Gibbon's demand from what Richard said," Caroline offered. "I'm sure he'll want to explain. Don't give up on him, Louisa."

She blinked rapidly. "I don't want to hear explanations." The situation made her worry that his reputation as a rogue was more than just a reputation—it was fact. Part of the present, not just the past. She couldn't plan her future with a man she couldn't trust. Not after all she'd been through with her mother. She needed time to think. "Please advise the Earl of Granger not to contact me or attend the Christmas Eve celebration. I have no wish to see him any time soon."

She only wished she could convince her heart of that.

Chapter Eleven

Benjamin rose well before dawn after a sleepless night and quickly dressed without bothering to ring for his valet. He wanted this morning over so he could try to gather the threads of his life back together. Gibbon had not come to his senses, much to Benjamin's dismay.

He'd been through each moment of the Delham's house party and knew he hadn't taken liberties Lady Adele in any manner. He'd danced with her and shared the carriage ride to church but otherwise hadn't touched her.

Had something untoward happened during that brief ride for which she blamed him? He'd taken great care to remain pressed into the corner, unmoving during the trip. She hadn't appeared upset when she alighted.

With a sigh, he ran a hand through his hair. There was nothing to be done but move forward and hope for a favorable outcome of the duel. Though he might escape with his life, his world was now in shambles. The charity planning would have to begin again. When word of the duel spread, along with the fact that Delham had withdrawn support, gathering funds would be much more difficult, perhaps even impossible.

And Louisa...

His entire being ached when he allowed himself to think of her. Everything he'd thought impossible, including a happy marriage filled with love, had seemed possible with her at his side.

He shook his head as he descended the stairs, a sick knot in the pit of his stomach. The message Aberland had delivered from Caroline made it clear that Louisa didn't wish to see him again. He couldn't blame her. Dueling was dangerous and illegal. Heaven forbid he or Gibbon actually killed the other, as the survivor would face murder charges. Assuming the viscount didn't kill him, Benjamin's reputation would be worse than before.

Viscount Stanich would no doubt do his best to comfort Louisa. They'd most likely have a June wedding. He rubbed his hand over the ache in his chest at the idea. Just when he'd thought the path for his future was clear, this happened, and all was lost.

He nodded at the footman as he stepped into the carriage, pleased he'd asked Aberland to meet him at Putney Heath with the pistols. Conversation was beyond him this morning. Sleet fell, lending an additional layer of misery to the day. It perfectly suited his mood.

After well over an hour, the driver stopped the carriage beside Aberland's in a clearing. Benjamin's thoughts were unable to settle on anything. *Except Louisa.* He closed his eyes. She was beyond his reach. He needed to release his affection for her somehow.

Yet he feared it was too late. He loved her with a depth he knew he'd never find again.

How ironic that Lady Adele matched the type of wife he'd thought perfect for his reformation before he'd met Louisa. But he had no desire to spend his life with her.

He stepped out of the carriage as Aberland did the same, a box containing a pair of pistols tucked under his arm.

"Morning," Aberland said.

Benjamin appreciated that he hadn't added "good" to the greeting. "Thank you for coming."

"Couldn't have you face this on your own. Hell of a way to spend Christmas Eve." He patted Benjamin's shoulder. "It's been years since I've witnessed such excitement."

"Liar." Benjamin well knew Aberland's life as a spy had held more close calls than most. He'd been shot and left for dead at one point, though he rarely talked about it.

"Come now. One must keep a sense of humor over these things."

"Must one?"

His utter despair must've shown, for Aberland patted his shoulder again. "We will look for a silver lining in all this. Caroline has convinced me there's one in every situation."

"The weather is too miserable to find it, I'm afraid." Benjamin sighed as Gibbon's carriage came into view. "There goes my first hope."

"That he'd fail to appear? Yes, that was probably too much to ask. He's already proven himself a fool for not pressing his sister for an explanation."

"Then let us be done with this." Benjamin walked toward Gibbon's carriage, annoyed when a long moment passed before the viscount and his brother bothered to alight.

When at last the carriage door opened, Gibbon's grim expression suggested he remained determined to see this through. He glanced at the sky. Though dawn had surely arrived, it had done little to lighten the greyness. "We shall have to hope the pistols will fire in this wetness."

A fool indeed, Benjamin thought. If he knew what was good for him, he'd wish both the firearms became wet. That would allow them to call the matter satisfied without the risk of physical harm.

"Did Lady Adele offer any details as to when I might have committed this offense?" he asked the viscount.

The man lifted his chin. "I have no need to question what she told me. She is my sister. Have you reconsidered offering for her hand?"

"Though I'm certain Lady Adele will make someone a fine wife, that man is not me."

"Then let us proceed." Gibbon glanced at his younger brother as if unsure what came next.

"Why don't we examine the pistols in the shelter of my carriage to make certain they remain dry?" Aberland suggested, then with a wry glance at Benjamin, led the way.

Benjamin followed, and Aberland opened the wooden box inside the carriage. Benjamin selected one of the pistols, and Gibbon picked up the other, both careful to keep them out of the sleet.

"Shall we say twenty paces?" Aberland asked.

"Fifteen," Gibbon countered. "The weather is difficult enough without standing so far apart."

"Very well." Benjamin made quick work out of loading his pistol, then held it under his coat to keep the flint dry. He watched as Gibbon loaded his, hesitating over the procedure as if unfamiliar with the weapon.

At last, both men walked toward the center of the clearing with the seconds following behind. Gibbon's jerky stride suggested nerves, but Benjamin felt dead inside. Still, he had to try one last time to stop this madness.

"We don't have to do this," Benjamin said quietly. "Surely we can call the matter settled. You have my word that I did not touch Lady Adele."

Gibbon's glare was answer enough.

Benjamin turned back-to-back with Gibbon. Aberland counted in a loud, clear voice, and Benjamin matched his stride to the counts, his mind blank.

"Thirteen. Fourteen. Fifteen."

Benjamin turned and lifted the pistol to see Gibbon doing the same. He had no intention of killing the man. He could only hope Gibbon had the foresight to feel the same way. With slow movements, he raised his weapon, heart thudding wildly as he prepared for the sound of Gibbon's shot ripping the air.

Gibbon had difficulty holding the pistol steady as he took aim. Benjamin gritted his teeth, fearing the man would pull the trigger at the wrong moment and kill him after all.

Benjamin aimed his pistol to the right of Gibbon and squeezed off a shot. The sound caused the viscount to jerk in surprise. The flare of Gibbon's gun firing held Benjamin's gaze, and he braced for impact.

Louisa spent much of the day pretending to assist her mother with preparations for the Christmas Eve ball, but her joy for the holiday had ended with Caroline and Annabelle's visit the previous day. She'd wanted to cancel the ball, but her mother refused, insisting their reputations would only suffer further if they did. "We must hold our heads high despite the terrible circumstances," she'd told Louisa.

How could Louisa possibly think about anything when Benjamin might be injured at this very moment? Or worse—lost his life this day?

The thought made her shudder. She abandoned her attempt to adjust the greenery on the mantle in the drawing room. A sense of dread flooded her, making her feel weak. She couldn't think, could hardly breathe. No matter how many times she tried to tell herself that she should make plans for a future without Benjamin, she had to know if he was well.

She still couldn't believe he'd made unwanted advances toward Lady Adele. The man she'd come to know wouldn't have done so. She'd witnessed his noble, thoughtful deeds on more than one occasion. He was an honorable man.

That truth gave her pause. Did she dare listen to what her heart believed? Or would doing so only place her in jeopardy of a life spent worrying over what he might do next? Could the whole challenge be a terrible misunderstanding? Should she have stood by him through all of this?

"Lady Adele Gibbon asks if you're receiving, my lady," James, the footman, announced.

Louisa stared at him in puzzled disbelief, unable to think of a reason she'd call. Did she have news of the outcome of the duel? "Please show her in."

A few moments later, Lady Adele hesitated in the doorway as if uncertain of her welcome.

And Louisa knew.

Knew beyond a doubt that she'd fabricated the accusation that had placed Benjamin in danger. Louisa gripped her hands so hard that her nails dug into her palms, aware she'd allowed Benjamin's reputation to take precedence over what she knew in her heart to be true. The man she loved truly was an honorable man.

Loved.

Yes, it was true. No longer would she deny the fact. She supposed in some terrible way she should thank Lady Adele for helping her realize the depth of her feelings. But she had no intention of doing so.

"Lady L-Louisa." The woman's gloved hands clutched her reticule as if her life depended on it. "I-I hope the day finds you well."

Louisa said nothing as she stared at her, afraid the anger simmering inside her might spill out.

Pain and regret swept over Adele's pale face as she drew a shuddering breath. "I've come to apologize for my deplorable b-behavior."

"I don't believe you should apologize to me. The Earl of Granger perhaps. Or your brothers. But not me."

Adele stepped forward with one hand outstretched as if to plead her case. "My brothers have yet to return home from the duel. I couldn't possibly call on Granger without..."

"Ruining your reputation? That concern should've crossed your mind before you created the lie that took them to Putney Heath."

Adele jolted at her words. "Yes. Yes, I should have. I'm afraid I allowed my feelings for Granger to overcome good sense."

Louisa raised a brow. "I wasn't aware you knew him well."

She sighed with longing. "Only in my dreams do I have that privilege. But I've seen how he looks at you." Adele's dark eyes held on Louisa with desperation. "I wanted him to look at me that way. To see *me*." She looked away. "But of course, he didn't. No man does."

"So you chose to invent a story that would force him to."

Adele nodded reluctantly. "I never meant for it to go this far. I hoped he'd call on me to discuss it—"

"You mean you hoped he'd be forced to propose." The pity Louisa felt didn't outweigh her anger. Adele's act had been utterly selfish, and Louisa had no intention of excusing it.

The woman's shoulders sank as her gaze dropped to the floor at the accusation. "Yes," she admitted after a long moment. She looked up, blinking back tears. "That is why I owe you an apology as well. Granger obviously cares for you a great deal. Anyone who witnesses the way he watches you can see that."

Louisa glanced away, not wanting Adele to see how much she hoped her words were true, that it wasn't too late for her to redeem herself. "Why didn't you take action before the duel?"

Tears ran down Adele's face as she shook her head. "I'm truly sorry."

Louisa didn't know if she could find it in her heart to forgive her. Certainly not until she knew if Benjamin was safe. "I hope your brother and the earl emerge unscathed."

"As do I. Thank you for seeing me." Adele wiped her wet cheeks then turned to go.

"May I offer advice?"

Adele turned back with wariness. "Of course."

"Your somberness puts people off. If you could pretend to enjoy attending the parties or speaking to others, you would win over many people."

Her eyes widened in surprise. "I do enjoy them. It's just that I feel like I'm intruding, as if I don't belong." She shook her head.

"Be yourself rather than worrying overmuch about what others think." If only she'd concerned herself less with that. "You might be surprised which men notice you."

Adele seemed to consider her words for a few moments then gave a single nod. "Thank you. I appreciate that." She drew a shuddering breath. "I'm going to return home with the hope my brother has arrived so I can apologize to him as well. I doubt he'll be as gracious as you have been."

Louisa prayed both he and Benjamin were alive and well to hear the lady's apology.

Chapter Twelve

Beth pinched Louisa's cheeks that evening as she sat before her dressing table mirror. "You're far too pale, my lady. Are you certain you're feeling well?"

No, she wanted to shout. Not when her message to Benjamin had remained unanswered through the long afternoon. Darkness had fallen, and still, she'd heard nothing. She'd sent a message to Caroline as well, but her cousin hadn't responded either.

"I'll be fine. Thank you." Louisa rose and smoothed the skirt of her white satin gown. A wide red velvet ribbon graced the empire waist with matching narrower ribbons woven through the lace of the neckline and capped sleeves.

"You look like an angel, my lady." Beth adjusted the freshwater pearls strung on a wire that adorned her hair.

The maid's description made her want to cry. She was no angel. She hadn't saved anyone. She'd pushed away Benjamin when he'd needed her most. Her hope to have the chance to apologize was slowly dying. She felt fragile as if one wrong move might shatter her into a thousand pieces.

She could think of only two possible reasons Benjamin hadn't responded to her message. He was too injured to do so, or he couldn't forgive her. The idea that he'd lost his life was unbearable, and she refused to consider it. She gave herself a mental shake. As if her unwillingness to think the worst could save him.

She'd abandoned him when she should've stood by his side. If she'd confronted Adele prior to the duel, she might've been able to force her to tell the truth.

Instead, she'd done nothing.

"Louisa?" Her mother stood in the bedroom door. "Are you ready? It's almost time." She entered the room, her gaze sweeping over her. "You look beautiful."

"As do you, Mother." The emerald green gown was stunning with her creamy skin and still slim figure.

Louisa knew she'd been looking forward to the party, one of the few she'd hosted since becoming a widow. Louisa didn't want to ruin it any more than she already had. If she hadn't heard news of Benjamin before long, she'd escape the ball, pick the lock on his library door again and search his house until she found him.

By midnight, she'd know if he was well and if there was any possible chance of him forgiving her.

"Shall we go down?" her mother asked.

"One last thing." Louisa returned to her dressing table and retrieved the mistletoe Benjamin had presented to her and tucked it into the bodice of her gown. Having it close to her heart gave her a faint, flickering hope that somehow, she could make this right. That they could weather this storm together. Having a life with Benjamin, even if they had to move abroad, would be preferable to living without him.

She tucked her mother's hand in the crook of her arm and forced a smile. "Let us greet our guests."

The house looked more festive than it had in a very long time. An enormous arrangement of red roses sat on the entrance hall table. Holly and ivy graced many of the rooms as well as the bannister. Candles had been placed everywhere, casting a glittering light. Fires burned cheerfully in both the drawing room, where they'd receive their guests, as well as the dining room.

Guests started to arrive, and Louisa searched for Caroline or Annabelle in the receiving line. She'd thought they might arrive early so she could have a moment to speak with them, but as time passed and they failed to appear, her worry grew. At last, she spotted her cousins in the line. Much to her surprise, her aunt had joined Caroline and Annabelle.

"Aunt Josephine, it's lovely to see you," Louisa said as she hugged her. "You look wonderful."

"Thank you. Caroline insisted Reginald would be in good hands for a few hours while I attended." Yet Louisa could see worry lingering in the back of her eyes, suggesting his failing mental state wore on her.

"I'm so pleased you came," Louisa said.

"We had a difficult time convincing her, but Christmas Eve is the perfect time to see family and friends." Caroline looped an arm through her mother's.

"Indeed," Louisa said as she studied Caroline, hoping for some indication as to Benjamin's welfare. Caroline gave a small nod, and Louisa drew her first relieved breath. "A perfect time to celebrate life."

Caroline smiled but said nothing more, leaving Louisa to wonder still. To know he lived was a blessing, but she dearly wanted to know how he was and what had happened. She supposed that meant she'd be paying a midnight visit to his residence after all.

Her aunt continued forward to greet Louisa's mother along with Caroline and Annabelle, leaving Louisa momentarily alone. She knew she should mingle and make certain everyone was enjoying themselves, but she needed a moment to gather herself, to hold the good news tight to her heart.

With a glance around the crowded room to make certain she wasn't needed, she stepped into the hallway, only to stop short at the sight before her.

"Benjamin?" She could hardly believe her eyes. With her heart in her throat, she stared at him from head to toe to make certain he was in one piece. "You're well?"

"I am."

She swallowed hard as she studied his unfathomable face. "Gibbon?"

"Unharmed."

"I see." Although she didn't. Her heart hammered with all that stood between them, but her relief to see him well overpowered all else. "What happened?"

He glanced at the guests in the drawing room before guiding them deeper into the hallway, providing a little privacy. "Suffice it to say that we both missed and declared the matter satisfied, although Gibbon did so begrudgingly. However, he called on me a few hours ago to inform me that his sister explained she'd erred, and I was innocent. He then apologized."

"If only that had happened sooner." Louisa shook her head. "I'm so sorry I responded the way I did. I—"

He placed a finger on her lips. "You do not need to apologize for anything."

She removed his finger and held it tight. "Yes, I do. I never should've doubted you. I'm terribly sorry."

He smiled. "Your experience has given you cause not to give your trust easily. We'll discuss the details when you don't have a houseful of guests."

"I don't care about the guests." She only wanted to step into the circle of his arms and never leave. "I made a terrible mistake and have to know if you'll ever forgive me."

The warmth of his smile tightened her chest and gave her hope. "Of course I do. Now I would like to wish your mother a Happy Christmas and ask if I might call upon her tomorrow, despite it being Christmas."

Louisa frowned. "Whatever for?"

"With your cousin in the country, I would like to ask the marchioness for your hand. With your approval, of course."

"Benjamin!" She gave in to the urge and threw her herself into his arms.

He chuckled as he held her tight for a long moment before easing back to look into her eyes. "I love you, Louisa. Would you do me the honor of becoming my wife?"

"I love you as well, and I would be delighted to have you as my husband."

"Even if my reputation is now blackened?" The hint of vulnerability in his eyes only made her love him more.

"Yes. I don't care what others think. We are meant to be together. If needed, we shall be outcasts together."

"While it warms my heart to hear you say that, we'll hope that won't be necessary. Lady Adele sent anonymous letters to many of the *ton*, including Delham. She also requested an anonymous advert to be run in *The Times*, despite her brother's misgivings. I'm not certain those actions will resolve the issue, but I'd like to think they'll help to smooth things over."

"I'm pleased to hear that." While she was glad Adele was taking steps to help repair the damage, she wished she hadn't made the outrageous claim to begin with. For Benjamin's sake, she hoped Adele's efforts were successful.

His gaze dropped to the mistletoe tucked in her neckline before holding her gaze once more. "I wouldn't want to do anything further to ruin my reputation, but that is mistletoe, and it is Christmas Eve."

Desire swept through Louisa, much like a spark to tinder. She lifted to meet his lips halfway, doing her best to show him how much she loved him. His tongue swirled with hers, building the heat within her until all else fell away.

Before she was ready for the kiss to end, he eased back. "Happy Christmas, Louisa. I love you so much. You are a gift beyond measure that I don't deserve and will always cherish. I look forward to many more holidays with you."

"As do I. You are my heart and soul. My rogue forever. I love you." She kissed him once more to seal her words.

He tapped a finger against the mistletoe. "That was two kisses, and there are three berries. That leaves us one more for later."

She chuckled, her heart nearly full to bursting. "I look forward to it."

"Let us brave the crowd to speak with your mother." He took her hand and placed it under his arm, then walked into the room.

A murmur rolled through the guests as they entered, several obviously surprised to see Benjamin, but others nodded at him as if nothing untoward had occurred.

They made their way to where her mother visited with a handsome, older gentleman whom Louisa hadn't met.

"Lady Whirlenhall, Happy Christmas," Benjamin said with a bow. "Thank you for inviting me."

"How good of you to come," her mother said before casting a questioning look at Louisa. "All is well?"

Louisa smiled at Benjamin. "Yes."

"Indeed. All is well." Something lit his expression, his gaze holding hers as if making a promise. Love shone in his eyes, causing her to catch her breath.

"I'm so pleased to hear that. We shall hope we can both manage to retain our reputations for the foreseeable future." Her mother smiled at Benjamin, who chuckled in response.

"Count Eastov," her mother began, "may I introduce you to my daughter, Lady Louisa Felton?"

The older gentleman with friendly blue eyes and an impressive grey mustache bowed over her hand. "You are as beautiful as your mother." His Russian accent was almost as intriguing as the sparkle in her mother's eyes. "I had the good fortune of meeting your father in his youth and was terribly saddened to learn of his passing. When a friend mentioned he was coming to your gathering, I couldn't resist attending with the hope your mother would allow me to stay. I look forward to coming to know both of you better."

"Thank you." Louisa took a second look at the man, noting the way he watched her mother with an admiring but respectful gaze. Something seemed different about this man and the way her mother acted. She looked forward to seeing how their association progressed.

What an amazing Christmas Eve this was turning out to be. With Benjamin at her side, anything seemed possible.

Well after midnight, Benjamin sank into the wingback chair before the fire in his library and took a sip of brandy. Though exhausted after the events of the day as well as a sleepless night, a strange restlessness gripped him that suggested slumber would be long in coming.

The day had begun with him thinking he'd lost everything. Now he had more than he'd ever hoped for. How intriguing life could be, full of twists and turns one never expected despite the best-laid plans.

It had required all his fortitude not to gather Louisa into his arms and carry her somewhere private. Dancing with her had been equal parts wonderful and painful, filling him with the longing to show her how he felt, how much she meant to him. His need to be with her, to talk to her, to touch her, surpassed anything he'd ever experienced—a physical ache that made him all the more anxious to make her his wife.

But he was determined to do the right thing and protect both of their reputations from this day forth. Stolen moments on terraces were no longer in his future. He would do everything in his power to prevent another occurrence like today's. The idea of losing Louisa had nearly undone him.

When he'd returned home from the duel and the footman handed him her message, he'd been sure it would contain a repeat of what she'd told Caroline. Instead, her simply worded apology had filled his heart with hope. Her message was tucked into his desk as a treasured memento in the same place his uncle had kept the marchioness's letters. But his reason for keeping the note was as different as night and day from his uncle's.

Tomorrow he'd be one step closer to making Louisa his by speaking with her mother. He'd also pay a call on Louisa's cousin when the weather permitted a trip to the country. As soon as he—

An odd sound broke into his thoughts. He paused to listen then looked toward the garden door, certain he had to be wrong. Yet the familiar shadow in lad's attire standing there told him otherwise.

Heart racing, he quickly set aside his brandy and hurried to open the door. "Louisa?"

"Benjamin." She wrapped her arms around him and held on tight.

He managed to shut the door as he returned the embrace, relishing the feel of her in his arms. "Whatever are you doing here? It's snowing." He glanced out to see big, fluffy flakes still falling. "You should be abed."

"I had to see you. To speak with you. I wanted more time with you. Alone."

"Louisa," he whispered, kissing her cold, bare fingers. Then he guided her toward the warmth of the fire and added coals to the embers, giving more heat and light to the room. Still in disbelief that she was here, he took her into his arms again and held her for a long moment. "I'm sorry I didn't come to tell you about the duel myself. I allowed you to believe the worst." He shook his head, unwilling to tell her how close Gibbon had come to shooting him. "I promise never to give you any reason to doubt my love for you."

Louisa tightened her embrace, her words muffled against his chest. "I don't know what I would've done if the day had ended differently."

"Shh," he murmured as he ran a hand along her back. His body stirred at the feel of her in his arms. He was half-dressed with his cravat untied, jacket removed, and waistcoat open. Holding her like this felt more intimate than any previous moment with her. He drew a slow breath, reminding himself that he was supposed to be offering reassurance, not becoming aroused. "All is well. No need for either of us to dwell on such things."

Her sweet scent of roses filled his senses, and he couldn't resist pulling her close so her body pressed against his. How was he supposed to do the right thing with this temptress in his arms? After a long moment, he loosened his hold to gaze down at her.

Louisa bit her lip as she withdrew the mistletoe with its one remaining white berry from her pocket. "I would like to collect that last kiss you promised. It is Christmas, you know."

"Our first Christmas together. One of many, I hope." He plucked the last berry and carefully set it aside, then kissed her, pouring all his love into the moment. She tasted so sweet as her tongue moved against his.

Her cap fell to the floor, causing her hair to fall in waves along her back. The golden tresses spilled like silk against his fingers. He ran his hands along her waist to the flare of her hips then lower where the tightly fitting trousers hugged her bottom. Need pulsed through him at the realization that she would soon be his. But she wasn't yet.

"You should go," he muttered even as he pressed kisses along her jaw and neck. "I'll escort you home."

"Not yet. Please. We are betrothed, after all." Her hands ran over his shirt before her cool fingers found the opening and touched his bare chest. Then she kissed him again and all thoughts of stopping melted away.

On a groan, he reached under her jacket to find her shirt warm from her body. That only made him want to caress her bare skin. The firelight shone on her golden hair, on the line of her jaw, along the curve of her neck.

"Oh, Benjamin." She pressed a kiss in the opening of his shirt, and his knees went weak.

If this continued, he wouldn't be able to stop. Not with passion drumming along his skin. He needed to find the strength to wait. "Louisa."

"Shh." She placed a finger on his lips then reached up to brush the hair above his ear. "I know what you're going to say. That we should wait. But I love you. We're going to be married. Soon, I hope. And it's Christmas. What better present could we give each other than being together?"

While he wanted to agree, he hesitated, torn as to how to respond.

"I could've lost you today," she whispered, a catch in her voice.

"You didn't." And he'd never been so happy to be alive.

"Let us have this moment together. To mark a new beginning."

He groaned. "Do you have any idea how much I desire you?"

"Then take me. I want to be yours in every sense of the word. Always." She ran her hands over his shoulders and chest, which nearly made him shudder.

He removed his shirt, allowing it to fall to the floor as she bent to remove her boots then shrugged out of her jacket. He pulled her shirt free of the trousers, desperate to touch her flesh. Then he kissed her once more, his tongue sweeping into her mouth.

At last, she shifted to draw her shirt over her head, revealing only a thin chemise that clung to her breasts.

"So beautiful. So perfect in every way." He reached a trembling hand to touch her, molding the soft mounds beneath his hand. "Are you certain?"

"More than anything. I love you so much." She ran her hands over his chest again and paused a moment over his thundering heart with a smile.

"And I love you with all I am. All I ever will be." He kissed her long and deep, treasuring the gift she was giving him with an overflowing heart. "I'll obtain a special license so we can be married as soon as possible."

"Perfect," she said as her hands eased steadily lower.

He drew a shaky breath to gather his will to move slowly, wanting the moment to be perfect. He caressed her curves gently before cupping her breasts, running the pad of his thumb over her nipple.

"Oh, Benjamin." She arched into his hand.

He loosened the neck of her chemise, and his fingers quickly found bare skin, soft and velvety. Her breasts were full and firm. Why had he ever thought she should leave?

"One moment, my sweet," he whispered as he gave her a quick kiss. He reached for the blankets on the settee and spread them before the now crackling fire.

"Lovely." She smiled and slid out of her trousers, standing shyly before him in her chemise.

His breath caught as if he'd forgotten how to breathe. Their lips met once more, their tongues melding as they kissed. He lifted her into his arms to lay her gently on the blanket and lay beside her.

"You truly are beautiful." Her smooth skin glowed in the firelight, her eyes sparkling.

"You make me feel beautiful inside and out."

He eased her chemise over her head as he kissed her neck then moved lower to the swell of her breasts. As he cupped one firm globe, he licked the tip of the other. Her gasp fueled the need within him. He repeated the gesture before taking her nipple into his mouth, loving her response.

She shifted beneath him as if restless. Her hands ran along his hip, on the planes of his stomach then to the waist of his trousers. "Why don't you remove these?"

"My pleasure." He shed them quickly as he admired her lithe body in the firelight. "Are you warm enough?" he asked as he returned to her side to lean on an elbow, noting how her gaze lingered on his manhood.

"So warm." She caressed his belly, and his flesh heated beneath her touch and her gaze. "And strong."

He kissed her again, caressing her body until he found the curve of her hip. Her skin was incredibly smooth and irresistible. He touched her thighs, lingered on her bottom, wanting to explore every inch of her. How he wished he had more patience but need pushed him forward. He moved toward the damp curls at the apex of her thighs, hoping to make her feel as good as he did. Her moan made his body throb even as he touched her slick folds, loving how responsive she was.

"May I touch you?" she asked. At his nod, she wrapped her fingers around his manhood, driving him mad. "Hard yet smooth."

While he appreciated her curiosity and need to explore him, he didn't think he could endure much more of it. His body quivered. He could find no words, not when he felt so much. He dipped one finger inside her, his thumb stroking her delicate nub. Her hips lifted, and she gripped him tighter.

With a groan, he shifted to settle over her, his legs nudging aside hers. He held her gaze. "Have I told you how much I love you?"

"Yes." She smiled with such happiness that his chest ached. "Do you know how much I love you?" The heat in her gaze echoed the heat of his body.

"I'm beginning to. I want to make love to you."

"Oh, yes, my darling."

He eased forward until the tip of his shaft touched her center. She wiggled as if dissatisfied, and that was his undoing. He moved into her, inch by delicious inch, her body so tight, so hot. When he met resistance, he leaned on his elbows to look into her eyes. "Hold on." Then he thrust fully inside her.

"Oh!" Her cry was part surprise, part pain.

"Darling, I promise it gets better." Wishing he could ease her discomfort, he kissed her as he held still, waiting for her to adjust to the feel of him.

Then her hips stirred beneath his. Who was he to deny her? He moved out then back in, slowly building a rhythm, wishing he could make the moment last forever.

"Benjamin?" She frowned when he shifted to look at her.

"Trust me, my sweet. Let go. I've got you." He placed his weight on one arm so he could touch her damp center once again.

She came apart beneath him, and he thrust inside her once, twice, before withdrawing as he found his own release. He shattered into a thousand points of light, pressed against her.

"Louisa. I love you so." He pressed kisses over her face, pausing on her forehead, his heart near to bursting with love. He'd never realized that emotion would bring such an intensity to lovemaking, turning it into a completely different experience. He rolled to his side, bringing her with him, never wanting to let her go.

"Why did you draw back?" she whispered, a hint of worry in her eyes.

"While having a babe with you would bring me the greatest joy, I wouldn't risk that until I knew you were ready. And I admit to being selfish and wanting to keep you all to myself for a little while. At least until we marry."

She reached to place her palm along his cheek. "Have I mentioned how much I love you?"

"Maybe once or twice." He smiled at the joy filling him. "Happy Christmas, my love."

"Happy Christmas to you, my dearest rogue."

Epilogue

Three Weeks Later

"With this ring I thee wed. With my body I thee worship. And with all my worldly goods I thee endow. In the name of the Father, and of the Son, and of the Holy Ghost. Amen."

Louisa's heart threatened to beat out of her chest as Benjamin said the simple vows with a sincerity that brought tears to her eyes. The intense expression on his familiar, handsome face both reassured and excited her. His dark eyes held steady on hers before lowering to her hand where he placed a ring with an oval diamond surrounded by smaller diamonds on her ring finger.

"You may kiss the bride."

She lifted onto her toes to meet Benjamin's lips for a heated kiss, already anxious for the night to come.

"I love you," he whispered as he drew back.

"And I love you."

Before Louisa could wrap her thoughts around the beauty of the moment, he escorted her to the registry at the rear of the church to sign her maiden name one last time. Her mother sniffed delicately into her handkerchief as she watched with Count Eastov at her side.

Benjamin's carriage took the four of them to her home, everything passing in a blur, including her thoughts.

"That was a wonderful ceremony," her mother said as she dabbed at her eyes.

"A marriage of love always is." The count shared a smile with her mother, making Louisa grateful he would keep her mother company while she and Benjamin enjoyed a honeymoon.

"I couldn't be more pleased to celebrate your wedding." Louisa's mother blinked back tears. "It's been just Louisa and me for so long now." Her tears had Louisa's eyes filling with tears as well. She reached out to take her mother's hand in hers.

"Your father would be so pleased for you both." Her mother took Benjamin's hand as well. "You would've had his full approval, Benjamin."

"It warms me to hear you say that," Benjamin said.

"We're pleased you've joined us for this special day," Louisa told the count then glanced at her mother, noting her blush. Romance bloomed between the pair. In the brief time she'd known the count, she already liked him. She dearly wanted her mother to discover the same happiness she had and hoped the count would be the one to help her find it.

They soon arrived at her house where Caroline, Aberland, Annabelle, her youngest cousin, Margaret, as well as her aunt greeted them.

"Congratulations to you both," Aberland said as he took Louisa's hand before clasping Benjamin's hand.

"I'm so happy for you." Caroline hugged Louisa then held her gaze for a long moment as the two men visited. "Thank goodness you didn't give up on him."

"Thank you for giving me such good advice when events appeared so bleak." Louisa smiled. "Things have a way of working out even when we don't expect them to."

"Love is stronger than we realize, isn't it?" Caroline looped her arm through Aberland's, and they shifted toward the dining room.

"You are positively glowing," Annabelle told Louisa after she hugged her. "I'm so happy for you. I believe I could've predicted this outcome from the night you two were introduced."

Benjamin raised a brow in question. "Oh?"

Louisa shook her head with a chuckle. "I couldn't have. I look forward to the day when you meet the man who changes your world."

Annabelle frowned. "Why does that sound like a curse rather than good fortune?"

"Sometimes, it takes time before you realize your good fortune. Isn't that right, Benjamin?"

"I think I'll leave that discussion to the two of you," he said with a smile.

"Let us enjoy the wedding breakfast." Her mother led the way into the dining room.

Louisa reached for Benjamin's arm, needing a moment alone with him to convince herself that all of this was real.

"We did it." She couldn't keep the grin from her face.

"Indeed, we did. Did you have doubt?"

"Not for a moment." Still, she drew a deep breath to steady her nerves at all the changes that were happening so quickly.

As though realizing she needed reassurance, Benjamin drew her into his arms. "Are you looking forward to our honeymoon as much as I am?"

"Absolutely."

"Your mother will be fine with the count to keep her company. We'll only be gone two weeks."

Could he so easily read her thoughts? But his words reassured her as much as his comforting hand caressing her back. "She has been as excited as me about our marriage because she adores you."

Benjamin chuckled. "She's a gem, but your happiness is all that matters to her. I've promised to do my best to keep you happy always."

"You are a rogue like no other. Honorable. Kind. A true gentleman."

"I have a new reputation to protect. I've put my roguish ways behind me and started a new life." He reached for her hand and pressed a kiss on her palm, sending shivers along her body. "With you."

"A new life together." Louisa intended to enjoy each and every day with Benjamin at her side. "You have already made me the happiest woman in all of London. Are you certain your plans for the charity can wait until we return?"

"Delham says he will continue the fundraising efforts while we're in Spain."

"Excellent. I cannot wait to see everything you've told me about."

"With luck, the weather will be warmer there." He cupped his hand along her cheek. "I love you, Louisa. I cannot wait to begin our life together."

"Nor can I."

He kissed her, curling her toes, and reminding her how lucky she was to have this rogue to call her own.

The End

About Lana

Lana Williams is a USA Today Bestselling and Amazon All-Star author who writes historical romance filled with mystery, adventure, and a pinch of paranormal to stir things up. Filled with a love of books from an early age, Lana put pen to paper and decided happy endings were a must in any story she created.

Her latest series is The Seven Curses of London, set in Victorian times, and shares stories of men and women who attempt to battle the ills of London, and the love they find along the way that truly gives them something worth fighting for.

Her first medieval trilogy is set in England and follows heroes seeking vengeance only to find love when they least expect it. The second trilogy begins on the Scottish border and follows the second generation of the de Bremont family.

The Secret Trilogy, which shares stories set in Victorian London, follows three lords injured in an electromagnetic experiment that went terribly wrong and the women who help heal them through the power of love.

She writes in the Rocky Mountains with her husband, two growing sons, and two labs, and loves hearing from readers. Stop by her website at www.lanawilliams.net and say hello!

Dared & Kissed - The Scotsman's Yuletide Bride

~ A Love's Second Chance Novella ~

BY

Bree Wolf

EMMA STEWART has been in love all her life. Unfortunately, the man of her heart has no clue that she even exists. And so, one fateful day, she agrees to a dare to steal a kiss.

His kiss.

One wintry morning, FINNEGAN MACDRUMMOND finds himself surprised by a lass he's never noticed before. Quick as a fox, her lips capture his before she darts off into the forest. Taken with her courage, Finn pursues her only to learn that her kiss was nothing but a dare.

Will fear and disappointment keep them apart? Or does love truly conquer all?

Prologue

Seann Dachaigh Tower, Scottish Highlands, December 1801
Seven Years Earlier

Drawing her cloak tighter around her to ward off the chill of the crisp winter morning, sixteen-year-old Emma Stewart of Clan MacDrummond stood on the edge of the clearing, half-hidden behind a large boulder, her deep brown eyes drawn to the young men as they crossed their swords in training.

Their faces shone rosy in the cool winter's air as they moved back and forth, the metal of their blades gleaming in the faint morning sun. Emma could feel the clash of their swords resonate in her bones as it echoed through the stillness of the small glen. A cold shiver ran down her spine, and she breathed a sigh of relief that war had come and gone long ago.

These were times of peace, and the young men of her clan were merely training to keep a sharp mind and humble heart as their laird demanded of them. He was a good and kind man and had seen their clan through many trials. Still, his health was failing, and soon his son, Cormag, would follow in his footsteps and become Laird.

Shifting her gaze to the tall dark-haired man, Emma marvelled at the stillness with which he moved. There was no exertion on his face, and here and there, it seemed as though his feet barely touched the ground. He was a strange man, the laird's son, taciturn and reticent in many ways, and yet, watchful and observant, his grey eyes sharp like those of a hawk.

Emma wondered what he saw when he looked at her, and another shiver went down her back. Quickly, she turned her gaze to the other young men, fair-haired Ian and dark-haired Garrett. However, it was the sight of Finnegan MacDrummond that made her heart leap into her throat.

At least six years her senior, Finn stood tall, his shoulders squared as he watched Ian's approach, his sparkling green eyes narrowed as he prepared for his opponent's attack. Their swords clashed, and Emma held her breath.

Laughter echoed to her ears as Finn drew back, running his hand through his dark auburn curls. "Ye fight like a wee bairn, Ian! Is this all ye've got?"

Determination and a good deal of humour rested on Ian's face as he charged toward his friend, their swords colliding once again, sending sparks flying through the soft fog still lingering this early in the morning.

Transfixed, Emma watched as the men continued their training, her eyes locked on the young man who had stolen her heart so long ago. She could not recall a time when the mere sight of him had not stolen her breath and addled her mind. He was sweet and kind, and his green eyes always sparkled with exuberance and a hint of mischief. He stood by his friends and always lent a helping hand to those who needed it. He loved this land, their home, fiercely, and yet, every now and then she could see a yearning for adventure in his eyes, to see the world and know more than the small circle of life into which he had been born.

Oh, Emma knew him well, and yet, they had never truly spoken to one another. Nothing beyond a few meaningless courtesies here and there. Emma wondered if he even knew her name.

A faint giggle drifted to her ears from the tree line in her back, jarring Emma back to the here and now. Glancing over her shoulder, she spotted Aileen and Sorcha standing half-hidden behind a large oak, their eyes glowing as they whispered to one another.

Sighing, Emma squared her shoulders, reminding herself why she was here, why she had risen so early and trudged through the woods, her hem now soaked with morning dew.

"Go," Aileen hissed from behind the tree, keeping her voice low, her eyes darting to the young men, a touch of apprehension in them as she feared that they might have taken notice.

The young men, however, were so engrossed in their training that not one of them looked up and spotted the girls standing not too far off, watching them with rapt attention.

Emma nodded, then turned back, her eyes once more drifting to Finn, her target. Instantly, her heart sped up, and panic flooded her being. Was she mad to have come here? To have agreed to their game?

Her fingers curled into her palms, and her muscles tensed as though urging her back. No, she would not turn and run. Lifting her head, Emma squared her shoulders. This was her chance–her only chance–and she would take it. After all, it was only a dare, and if Finn rejected her then at least she could laugh it off and pretend that none of it affected her in any way. All she had to do was keep a straight face and not let him see how much she cared for him.

Inhaling a deep breath, Emma stepped out from behind the boulder, momentarily grateful for the shrubbery that still hid her from their sight. Nevertheless, soon she would have to reveal herself and it was still a good distance from the edge of the clearing to where they stood with their swords crossed. Would they address her? Would they ask what she was doing here? If so, what would she say?

"Ye're a fool," Emma whispered to herself as she took another step forward. "They'll laugh at ye, and yer cheeks will turn bright red."

The moment Emma stepped around the last of the shrubbery, she froze as she found Cormag looking straight at her, his sharp, hawk-like eyes colliding with hers. The hint of a frown touched his brows, and she wondered how long he had known of her presence. Had he truly spotted her just now? Or had he somehow…known as he often seemed to know things he should not know?

"Go," Aileen hissed once more, and as though Emma's feet had a life of their own, they complied. Goose bumps rose on her arms and legs as Emma found herself walking into the clearing, her heart beating painfully in her chest as she fought down the panic that threatened to engulf her. What on earth was she doing?

The moment Cormag had stopped, turning his head to look at her, his friends had ceased their training as well. At first, confusion had come to their faces before they followed his line of sight.

Now, four sets of eyes were trained on her as Emma walked into the clearing, slowly closing the distance between them. She did her best to hold her chin high and maintain a friendly, but unaffected smile on her face. However, deep down, Emma had serious doubts that she appeared as anything else but the bundle of nerves she was. Perhaps she ought to turn and run after all!

As she drew closer, she could see their chests rising and falling with each laboured breath, the muscles in their sword arms quivering with the sudden rest. Her eyes drifted from one man to the next and then back as she willed herself not to stare at Finn lest he be able to read the intention on her face. If he did, would *he* turn and run?

Cormag's eyes narrowed in a rather unsettling way as he continued to watch her. Then he took a step back, a hint of surprise coming to his eyes as he turned to look at Finn.

Emma froze. Did *he* know?

"What are ye doing here, lass?" Garrett asked as he stepped toward her, a kind smile on his face. "Ye're not lost, are ye?"

Strangely enough, Emma managed a rather natural smile. "No, I'm not lost," she replied, a slight chuckle accompanying her words as though she truly did not have a care in the world. Surprised by this unexpected ability to mask her feelings, Emma decided to seize the moment.

Stepping around Garrett, she did her best to ignore Ian's inquisitive stare as well as Cormag's speculative gaze and kept her eyes on Finn. His green gaze narrowed slightly as he watched her approach. Still, he did not try to step away, did not address her, did not stop her in any way.

It was all the encouragement Emma needed.

Two more steps brought her to him, and she could feel the warmth that radiated off him against her skin. His green eyes held hers, and for the barest of moments, Emma thought to see something flare to life in them. Something she had never seen there before.

But Emma did not dare linger and contemplate what it was. No, she needed to move fast, or she would miss her chance.

Without a moment's hesitation, she reached up, pushing herself up onto her toes, and pulled him down into a kiss.

The moment Finn had glimpsed her standing across the clearing, his heart had slammed to a rather unexpected halt. Her mahogany curls had danced on the soft breeze, gently brushing against her rosy cheeks and giving her the appearance of a sprite risen from the earth. She stood tall and fierce, and yet, as she had approached, the dark brown of her eyes had spoken of a vulnerable heart.

Although her gaze had travelled from one of his friends to the next, somehow Finn had known that in that moment she had come for him. The moment their eyes had met, Finn had been unable to speak, to think, to do anything but stare at her.

He could not even recall her name–if indeed he had ever known it–and yet he was certain that he would never again forget who she was.

The closer she had stepped, the more his heart had felt as though it wished to jump from his chest.

And then her lips had found his.

Dimly, Finn found himself wondering if he had strayed into a dream as he felt the softness of her lips against his own and the tentative brush of her fingers against the back of his neck, uncertain and yet daring. Her body leaned into his, and for a long moment, nothing and no one else existed but them.

And then she was gone.

From one moment to the next, her touch vanished, and Finn's eyes flew open.

As her feet carried her away from him, a teasing grin rested on her face, and yet, her eyes held no humour, but something deep and vulnerable. However, before Finn could stop her, she spun on her heel and raced across the clearing.

Chuckles rose around him, and Finn blinked as Ian and Garrett approached, large grins on their faces as they looked back and forth between him and the receding figure racing toward the tree line. "I take it ye know her," Ian remarked with a teasing grin. "Ye could've introduced us. What's the lass' name?"

Inhaling a deep breath, Finn shook his head. "I dunno know."

Gawking at him, Ian laughed, "Ye dunno know? Are ye saying a lassie ye dunno even know walks up to ye and kisses ye square on the mouth? Does this happen to ye a lot?"

More laughter followed, and Finn cleared his throat, trying his best to sort through his thoughts. "No, it doesna happen a lot," he snapped, glaring at his friend. "I assure ye I'm as surprised as ye are."

"But ye like her, do ye not?" Garrett observed as he crossed his arms in front of him, a challenge lighting up his eyes. "I've never seen ye so lost for words."

Finn swallowed, shaking his head. "She's…she's something." A smile tugged on the corners of his mouth, and he chuckled. "I've seen her around, certainly, but I've never…"

"Noticed her," Cormag supplied in his usual way as though he knew precisely what the others were thinking.

Finn nodded. "Aye."

"But ye noticed her now, aye?" Ian teased some more. "I can see that she's made quite an impression. Why don't ye go after her?"

Finn's head snapped up, and for a moment, all he could do was stare at his friend.

Shaking his head, Ian laughed, then clasped a hand on Finn's shoulder. "Go and ask her name before she kisses another."

With a bit of a shove in the right direction, Finn turned toward the tree line where she had disappeared. At first his steps were measured, but before long, large strides carried him onward. His heart once more began to dance the way it had when he had felt her lips upon his own, and he wondered how he could have failed to notice her before.

Certainly, she was young, having only recently grown into a woman, but those eyes…dark and deep like a loch full of hidden treasures, and yet, warm and delicate as though a wrong word could break her heart.

Striding past the large boulder on the edge of the glen, Finn scanned the tree line, his eyes narrowing as he tried to spot any sign of her. He glimpsed her footprints in the lush, frost-covered grass a moment before soft voices drifted to his ears.

Inhaling a deep breath as his heart once again leapt into his throat, Finn stepped forward, finding his way through the dense forest, his ears guiding him, picking out more than one voice. Silently, he slipped closer until he spotted a fair-haired head bobbing up from behind a thorny thicket growing around a group of conifers.

The young woman laughed, "I thought I would faint when I saw ye kiss him," she gasped, a hand pressed to her chest. "Was it wonderful?"

Finn frowned as he edged forward, his eyes at last falling on the dark-eyed enigma who had stolen his breath. She stood with two other, equally young women–both of whom looked familiar, but whose names Finn could not recall, either. Her face looked tense as she glanced over her shoulder toward the glen. "Let us return to the tower," she whispered, a hint of apprehension in her voice as she tried to pull the fair-haired girl onward. "I'm…chilled."

"Come now, tell us of yer conquest," the other dark-haired girl urged, an eager smile on her face. "After all, ye won the dare and proved us wrong. I never would've thought that ye'd have the courage to walk up to Finnegan MacDrummond and steal a kiss."

Finn's stomach clenched as the girl's words sank in. A dare? She had kissed him because of a dare? Nothing more?

"Tell us, did it feel wonderful?" the fair-haired girl pressed, a sigh escaping her lips. "I think I would've gone weak in the knees if it had been me."

Turning her head away, Finn's brown-eyed enigma brushed a curl behind her ear. "'Twas a kiss," she all but bit out, and the harshness cut right through Finn's tentative hopes. "Nothing more, nothing less. I won. That's all that matters." Rubbing her hands together, she beckoned the other two girls onward. "Now, let's go or I swear my toes shall freeze off."

Long after they had gone, Finn still stood leaning against the conifer at his back, his eyes closed as he replayed their words in his head. It had been nothing but a dare, and he had been a fool to think more of it. To think that there had been something between them, a silent bond that had brought them to this place the way his father had often spoken of the day he had first laid eyes on Finn's mother.

As a child, Finn had often listened to his father tell this story, his words ringing with promise that one day Finn would find the same, a woman who was his other half, a woman he would recognise instantly, who would steal his breath and claim his heart.

And for a short moment, Finn had thought to have found her...and it had stunned him into speechlessness.

If only he had known from the beginning that their encounter had meant nothing to her. Nothing more but a claimed prize. A victory. A dare won.

Cursing under his breath, Finn spun on his heel and before he knew it his fists collided with the trunk of the conifer. Pain shot up his arm and into his shoulder, and blood welled up from the scrapes on his knuckles where the hard bark had cut through his skin.

Still, the pain in his heart far exceeded any physical discomfort he felt. How dare she kiss him? Before today, he had been happily oblivious to her. He had barely even noticed her. He had been content and at peace.

And now?

Now, he was achingly aware of her. He could still feel her soft touch as though she was right in front of him, and whenever he closed his eyes, he found her dark-brown ones looking into his. What had she done to him?

Would he ever be free of her? Or would he be doomed to carry her with him for the rest of his life?

Anger filled his heart, and Finn knew that he was no longer the same man he had been upon waking that morning.

Everything had changed.

He had changed.

And there was no going back.

How dare she?

Chapter One
ANOTHER YULETIDE SEASON

Seann Dachaigh Tower, Scottish Highlands, December 1808
Seven Years Later

"Run wee fishies!" Emma called as she chased after five-year-old Niall and his three-year-old sister Blair. "Run or the auld crab will catch ye! Snap! Snap!" Opening her arms wide, she brought her palms together with a loud clap right beside the little girl's ear.

Blair shrieked in delight and doubled her efforts to evade Emma's grasp, her little legs carrying her faster and faster until she reached the other side of the great hall of Seann Dachaigh Tower. Hiding under a large table set up for the yuletide festivities, Niall waved to his sister, beckoning her forward. The moment she fell to her knees and slid under the heavy wooden table, he pulled the end of the table cloth down, hiding them both from sight.

Emma pulled to a halt. "Aw, where did my fishies go?" she pouted, hearing the children giggle from under the table. "I guess I'll have to go to bed without supper this evening." Hanging her shoulders, Emma turned and walked back to the arched doorway she and Maggie had been working on before this impromptu chase.

Shaking her head at her children, Maggie laughed, her nimble fingers attaching yet another red bow to the evergreen branch decorating the doorway. "Those little rascals," she said, a mother's delight clear in her voice. "Always up to no good." Then her blue eyes turned to Emma. "And ye are no better. Encouraging them like that." Again, Maggie shook her head, and yet, the smile on her face spoke of neither reproach nor disapproval.

Emma laughed in return, feeling her heart grow lighter.

With both her parents passed on and no family of her own, the yuletide season always made Emma wistful and brought a deep ache to her heart, a longing for warmth and comfort, love and family.

As though to mock her, Finn walked into the hall in that moment, his tall stature drawing not only her eyes as he spoke to Cormag, now laird of Clan MacDrummond after his father's passing three years ago. They spoke in hushed tones, and Emma felt her heart torn between pain and delight as it always was when her eyes caught sight of him. Although she had tried her utmost to forget about him, to silence the longing that lived in her heart, it refused to listen, yearning for a man who only ever glared at her.

Ever since that morning out in the glen when Emma had dared to steal a kiss as a young lass, everything had changed. Before, Finn had merely looked past her, his eyes barely seeing the young girl who noticed him the moment he walked into a room. After that day, he had begun to see her as well. Only, his green gaze had held nothing friendly or kind, but only disdain and a deep-seated anger that Emma could not understand. Had her kiss truly offended him that much?

And then he had left.

Over the past seven years, Finn had spent months at a time with Clan MacKinnear–again and again–and although Emma could not truly believe that she had been the one to chase him away, she could not help but feel as though he had left in order to avoid her.

Her heart ached at the mere thought of it.

"Why don't ye speak to him?"

Jarred from her thoughts, Emma turned to look at her friend, finding Maggie's gentle blue eyes watching her carefully. "I dunno know what ye mean," Emma replied before clearing her throat. Then she reached for another bow, thus turning her attention to something safer.

Maggie chuckled, her dainty feet carrying her to Emma's side as though they barely touched the ground. "Dunno pretend with me," she whispered quietly. "I promised I willna share what ye told me with anyone, but neither can I pretend that I dunno know."

Emma sighed, a part of her regretting that she had shared the events of that fateful morning with Maggie. Still, another part was glad to have found a friend she could confide in without fear that her innermost thoughts and feelings would be passed on throughout the castle. Maggie had indeed proved herself to be trustworthy and kind-hearted…and plain-speaking as well. Emma would forever be grateful for the day her friend had come to Seann Dachaigh Tower.

"There's nothing to say," Emma mumbled under her breath, the little hairs in the back of her neck telling her that Finn had not yet left the hall. How was it that she could all but feel his presence? Why would the Fates not allow her to forget about him? Was there anything more cruel than unrequited love?

Although Emma had spent a great deal of time on convincing herself that she did in fact not care for Finn MacDrummond, her obsession with him had eventually forced her to admit that she had been fooling herself. Unfortunately, that realisation had not helped in the least. If anything at all, it had served to seal her fate. Without any sway over her own heart, she would be forever doomed to yearn for a man who hated her.

"That's not true," Maggie objected in her usual direct way. "There's quite a lot to be said. Ye will never receive an answer if ye're too scared to ask questions."

Turning to face her friend, Emma huffed, "Ye canna truly think it a good idea for me to simply walk up to him and ask why he hates me so?"

A teasing grin claimed Maggie's face. "Ye once walked up to him and stole a kiss, why not ask a simple question?"

Heat shot into Emma's face, and she could not help but glance in Finn's direction.

He and Cormag had obviously finished their conversation and were now striding toward the back exit, which led out into the courtyard. They passed by the two women, and the moment Finn's gaze veered to the side, Emma sucked in a sharp breath.

Their eyes met, and for a heart-breaking moment, the world seemed to stop in its tracks. The green in his gaze flared to life, and Emma felt the heat all the way to her toes. Still, the scowl remained on his face, telling her only too clearly what he thought of her.

Bowing her head, Emma turned away, relieved when the little hairs in the back of her neck finally calmed.

"Clearly, he affects ye as he always has," Maggie observed rather inconveniently, "and I do believe there's a reason why he would glare at ye so. Indifference doesna cause such hatred." Shaking her head, Maggie held Emma's gaze. "Nah, mind my words. There's a reason for the way he looks at ye, and ye will never know it if ye dunno speak to him."

Emma's heart skipped a beat happily, new hope surging to the surface before she forced it back down with an iron will. "Even if ye're right, it willna change what is. He doesna care for me, and I'd do well to accept that. Perhaps then I'll be able to begin a life of my own." Her gaze drifted to where Niall and Blair were playing with the castle's hounds. A sigh escaped her, and a different longing came to her heart.

"Ye will be a mother," Maggie whispered beside her, "but it will dampen yer happiness if ye choose the wrong father. Believe me."

Emma's brows drew down as she turned to look at her friend.

Always cheerful and laughing, Maggie often seemed like a force of nature despite her small stature and slender figure. She seemed one with the ground she walked on, at peace and calm, like someone born of this earth. With a gentle hand, she guided her children through life, giving them the freedom they needed to discover who they were but always holding a protective hand over their heads when needed. Whatever Maggie did, she did with a calm confidence that had always inspired awe in Emma.

And yet, her friend was not truly happy, was she?

"No marriage is perfect," Maggie continued, the slight tension in her jaw telling Emma that she was well aware of her friend's scrutiny. "Even a great love can be lost, just as a match of convenience can turn into something far deeper." She sighed and finally met Emma's gaze. "There's no telling what the future will bring. All we can do is our best and be honest with ourselves. Sometimes we make a wrong decision. It happens." Her blue eyes wide, Maggie stepped forward and grasped Emma's hands. "But sometimes a wrong decision can be avoided. Believe me, there's nothing worse...than regret."

Staring into Maggie's eyes, seeing the slight mist that clung to her lashes, Emma swallowed, realising for the first time how deeply unhappy Maggie was in her marriage. "Is Ian-?"

Clearing her throat, Maggie suddenly stepped back. "Ian is a good man and a good father," she rushed to say before Emma could ask a question that might unhinge the balance of the life she had made for herself at Seann Dachaigh Tower.

But not a good husband, Emma added in her mind. *At least not the one yer heart wants.*

Although Emma would have wanted nothing more than to ask about the mysterious man who had stolen Maggie's heart at some point in her life, she did not for the look in her friend's eyes told her how affected her heart still was. Emma knew exactly how it felt to yearn for a man for years and never have one's heart see reason and abandon its quest.

"Ye at least," Maggie suddenly said, "can still choose. Once ye have, there is no going back." A desperate plea rested in Maggie's blue eyes.

Emma sighed, not wishing to hurt her friend. "I know what ye say is true, but 'tis not only my choice. What I want doesna matter if he doesna also want the same."

"But ye dunno know what he wants unless ye speak to him."

Emma scoffed as the exhaustion of years wasted slowly caught up with her. "I dunno know? Truly? Ye've seen the way he glares at me, and ye truly think that there's a chance." Emma shook her head, knowing only too well the pain false hope could bring. "No, it'll be better for me to forget about him and...seek happiness elsewhere."

"Elsewhere?" Maggie asked, her eyes narrowing in suspicion. "Ye mean Vaughn?"

Emma tensed. "How–?"

"I've seen the way he looks at ye," Maggie interrupted, the look in her eyes still one of disapproval. "He's a good man, decent and kind and respectful, but he's not the man for ye."

"Why?" Emma frowned. "Do I not deserve such a man?"

"Of course, ye do." Sighing, Maggie reached out to grasp Emma's hand once more, the look in her eyes one of motherly indulgence, as though Emma was an unruly child unwilling to see reason. "But he deserves more."

Snatching back her hand, Emma stared at her friend. "D'ye not think me good enough for him?"

Maggie chuckled, "Dunno act like a child. I meant no such thing and ye know it. But d'ye not agree that Vaughn deserves a wife who can love him? Does he not deserve a wife whose heart doesna belong to another man?"

Sobering, Emma felt her shoulders slump as one by one every path led her to nothing but heartbreak. "Aye," she finally said. "He does deserve that." Swallowing, she looked up at Maggie. "But perhaps over time, he will conquer my heart. Perhaps..."

The look in Maggie's eyes clearly stated that she disagreed. "Ye must do what ye think right. I canna make that decision for ye. All I can do is ask ye to think about the consequences of yer decision. Think wisely for the day may come that ye wish ye had."

Emma nodded, knowing that Maggie was right. Still, every once in a while, Emma wished she could throw caution to the wind and act on impulse alone...simply to have it over with. For years now, she'd been wracking her mind, her heart, every fibre of her being about what to do and what path to choose, and she was still as torn as she had been years earlier. Would the rest of her life look like this? Trapped between what her heart desired and what her mind deemed right? Would these two never walk hand in hand?

"Speak to him," Maggie urged once more. "What do ye have to lose?"

Closing her eyes, Emma drew in a shaking breath. Indeed, what did she have to lose? Her heart? Her mind? Her sanity? If Finn rejected her outright, if he laughed in her face, if he told her she was the most awful woman he had ever met, would she be able to recover? Would she ever be happy again?

Are ye now? An annoyingly familiar voice whispered in the back of her head. A voice that sounded suspiciously like a well-meaning but rather opinionated friend.

"Ye say he hates ye," Maggie continued, her voice kind and yet insistent, "that he nothing but glares at ye."

Emma nodded, wondering what her friend was trying to tell her.

A soft smile came to Maggie's lips. "Has there never been a moment-a single moment-when he didna glare at ye? When there was something else in his eyes?"

Emma was about to shake her head when a distant memory surfaced. A memory that always brought pain and joy as though one could not exist without the other.

After Emma's mother had died giving birth to her, she had been the light of her father's life...and he had been hers. Although she had always longed for the mother she had never known, her father had been all any child could ever have hoped for. He had been an enthusiastic playmate, a passionate storyteller and a devoted protector. He had been everything to her, the sun that warmed her face and the air she breathed.

Until the day he had passed on.

Suddenly and unexpectedly.

Without warning.

One moment they had shared the midday meal, and the next he had dropped to the ground.

Emma dimly remembered the haze that had claimed her the moment she had understood that her father was lost to her. For days, she had walked the castle grounds like a ghost haunting the living. Neither tear nor smile had come to her face until the day they had buried him.

Stone-faced, she had stood by his grave, unaware of the world around her as her heart had slowly reawakened and the pain had claimed her whole. Turning away, Emma had walked and walked, leaving Seann Dachaigh Tower and its people behind her. Tears had streamed down her face, and yet, she had walked on until she had come upon a small loch.

At its banks, Emma had sunk down into the lush grass, her legs no longer able to carry her. There, she had finally succumbed to her tears, weeping for the only parent she had ever known. Painful sobs had wracked her body, shaking her limbs and breaking her into a thousand small pieces...never to be whole again.

And then all of a sudden, as though he had appeared out of thin air, Finn had been there.

Emma hadn't even known that he had returned from his latest stay with Clan MacKinnear. She had not seen him in a long time, and yet, when she had needed him...he had been there. As though the Fates had returned him to her.

Quietly, Finn had sat down beside her and pulled her into his arms, holding her tightly and letting her cry. She had buried her face in his shoulder, clinging to him like someone drowning.

As though nothing had happened, as though this had been a day like any other, the sun had commenced on its daily journey across the sky, and all the while, they had sat on the bank of the loch, his arms wrapped around her.

Not a single word had passed Finn's lips that day.

Not one.

And yet, he had sat in the grass for hours, holding her in his arms, his fingers gentle as they brushed damp curls from her temple and behind her ear. The hint of a warm smile had been on his lips that day, kind and comforting, and the green in his eyes had held nothing but compassion and understanding and perhaps–perhaps–the promise that one day the pain would not be as crushing as it had been in that moment.

When her sobs had lessened, Finn had helped her to her feet and walked her home, his arm tightly around her and her head still resting against his shoulder. He had taken her to the small cottage she had shared with her father, assisting her inside until she had dropped into her bed, exhausted in heart and body. Dimly, she remembered him draping a blanket over her. Then he had sat down on a chair in the corner, watching over her as she had drifted off to sleep.

In the morning, Finn had been gone, and Maggie had sat at her bed, her gentle ways urging Emma to hold on to her father's memory but to return to the living and reclaim her smile.

A part of Emma still wondered if the day by the loch had been a dream and nothing more. For when she next saw Finn, the look in his eyes once again held the same disappointment and anger she had glimpsed there every day since the morning in the glen when she had stolen a kiss.

And then he had left yet again.

Chapter Two

A CLAN'S TRADITION

Walking beside the cart, Finn almost bumped into Ian's back when he suddenly drew to a halt.

"What's the matter?" Ian asked as he turned to frown at his friend. "Are ye asleep on yer feet? 'Tis not a good day to be absent-minded. There's work to be done."

Mumbling an apology, Finn did his best to ignore the way Ian shook his head at him or Cormag watched him out of the corner of his eye as though he were a rare specimen of some kind that ought to be studied. Only Garrett seemed as absent-minded as Finn himself. Their eyes distant, they each reached for one of the logs piled high on the horse-drawn cart. Then they walked up to the small cottages lining the road through the little village just outside the walls of Seann Dachaigh Tower and handed them to the families living there as a yuletide offering. For as long as Finn could remember, it had been a tradition for the young men of Clan MacDrummond to cut logs prior to the festivities and then offer them to the families of their clan, a promise that they were not alone, that they all stood as one and would forever look out for each other.

Always had this tradition had a special meaning for Finn. After his father had passed as well, he had felt alone, thinking himself without family to care for him, to see when he hurt, when he was in pain, to take notice of him.

Until the day when Cormag and his friends had stopped by his parents' cottage to offer him a log and then urge him to accompany them on their way. Reluctantly, Finn had joined in and soon realised that he had not gone as unnoticed as he had feared.

"The situation with the runaways has been resolved," Garrett said, his gaze intent on Cormag as he spoke. "All I could have done I did. There is no reason for me to remain here."

Looking up, Finn found a look of great urgency on Garret's face, his shoulders tense as he handed another log to Ian, who rolled his eyes as he overheard their conversation and then trudged up to the next cottage on the road. Garrett, however, failed to notice his friend's annoyance as his attention was solely focused on their laird.

Narrowing his gaze, Cormag looked at him as he often did before he replied, a rather annoying calm resting on his features as though no emotions stirred under his skin. "I assure ye I understand yer desire to be off, and I dunno object to yer returning to England. However, I suggest ye allow reason to govern ye and hold off until the roads are safer for travel." He glanced around them at the heaps of snow blocking every path leading to and from Seann Dachaigh Tower. Even the short distance down into the village with the heavy cart had taken most of the morning. "Ye willna find yer wife any faster if ye freeze on the road."

Garrett's shoulders slumped, and yet, there was a hint of a smirk on his face at Cormag's rather rare attempt at a joke. "Aye, ye're right," he conceded, reaching for another log as Ian came trudging back. "But I canna deny that I long to be off. After all, I havena seen my wife in months."

Moaning, Ian shook his head. "Am I the only one working today?" he complained, his face dark as he all but glared at Garrett. "And ye're a fool for going after her. Ye married her after a drunken night at a tavern." Ian scoffed in contempt. "If she had truly wanted to remain yer wife, she wouldna have run off."

Garrett's face darkened at his friend's accusations. "She didna run off," he snapped as they stood almost face to face like stags about to charge. "Her brother came for her and took her back home."

"Why?" Ian huffed. "She's yer wife. Or perhaps she doesna want to be, have ye ever thought of that?"

"Enough." Cormag's calm but commanding voice cut off any further remarks as he stepped forward, his boots crunching on the snow as he moved like a giant among dwarfs. His grey eyes shifted from Garrett to Ian before he spoke again. "Garrett, ye're free to leave as soon as the roads are safe to travel." Then his gaze turned to Ian and something silent passed between the two men. A moment later, Ian drew in a heavy breath and turned back to the cart, picking up another log before he once more headed down the road.

Silence fell over their little group as they continued on, slowly working their way down the road, visiting each house and sharing a few kind words with people they had known one way or another all their lives. Still, dark looks were exchanged between Ian and Garrett, and Finn wondered why his friend was so upset with Garrett's desire to return to England and look for his wife. Their story had in fact proved quite popular among their clan.

Sent after two runaways, Garrett, Ian and Finn had travelled to Gretna Green and then split up to locate the youngsters. While Ian and Finn had searched high and low, Garrett had unexpectedly stumbled upon an English lass at the inn's tavern. Finding himself head over heels in love, Garrett had married her right then and there, taking advantage of the presence of an anvil priest that night at the inn. Upon morning, he had left his sleeping wife to seek out Ian and Finn, who had in the meantime located the runaways. Finn remembered well the guilt that had stood on Garrett's face as he had apologised for abandoning them in their quest. Still, his face had been aglow, and Finn had seen with one glance that he was in love.

Happy for his friend, Finn had congratulated Garrett and urged him to introduce them to his new bride. Garrett had been more than eager to do so. However, upon returning to their room, he had found her gone with no note to explain her whereabouts. Only from the innkeeper, they had learnt that her brother, an English lord, had come to Gretna Green and taken her back to England.

As far as Finn knew, the young lady had run off to Gretna Green with another, intending to marry him. Somehow, however, that marriage had not come to be and then her path had crossed Garrett's.

Glancing at his friend, Finn wondered if Garrett was worried that his new bride's family was less than happy to learn of their new connections and understood well his desire to be off and go after her.

Only Ian seemed less than sympathetic with Garrett's current situation.

"Where will ye go?" Finn asked, handing a log to Garrett before picking one up himself. "Where will ye start looking for her?"

Garrett shrugged. "I dunno know where her family's estate is, but Cormag suggested I speak to Lord Tynham, Maggie's brother. He might be able to help, perhaps even know her family."

Finn nodded before they split ways and each knocked on another door. He had all but forgotten that Ian's wife, Maggie, had grown up in England, the daughter of an English lord, who had passed away a few years back, leaving his title and estate to Maggie's older brother. After all, considering Maggie's speech and mannerism, it was only too easy not to see her as an English lady but as a Scottish lass. Soon after her arrival at Seann Dachaigh Tower, home of her mother's clan, the Highlands had stolen her heart and turned her into a true Scot.

In the beginning, Finn had wondered if it had been Ian's doing. If it had been their love that had made her feel at home in the Highlands in such a profound way. However, lately, Finn had begun to have doubts.

Truth be told, Ian looked far from happy these days. His comments with regard to Garrett's situation proved that all the more.

"Perhaps I should go with ye," Finn heard himself say when he and Garrett returned to the cart.

Garrett frowned. "Go with me? To England, ye mean?"

Finn nodded, heaving a deep sigh as Emma's image drifted into his mind. "Aye, to England." At first, it had only been Ian who'd been married and become a father, but now that Garrett, too, had lost his heart and married, Finn began to dread his own future with each passing day. For to him, it seemed that he would be forever doomed to yearn for a woman who did not want him. Would he never marry and have children of his own? Would he remain alone forever?

That thought sent a cold chill into his bones. As much as he wanted Emma, he knew he could not have her. But perhaps he could try and lose his heart to another. Somewhere, out in the world, there might be a woman who would could sweep him off his feet the same way Garrett's English lass had done for him.

Perhaps.

So far he had not found her during his visits to Clan MacKinnear. Was that because she was waiting for him in England? *Or right here at home?*

"Why?" Garrett asked, breaking into Finn's thoughts. "Ye've never spoken of going to England before. What brought on this thought?"

Finn sighed, "I…I…To tell ye the truth, I want what ye've already found," he told Garrett honestly. "I listen to the way ye speak about yer wife and I know that…"

Garrett nodded, grasping Finn's shoulder as he turned to look at him. "I understand what ye mean. Love's powerful." Shaking his head, he laughed. "It claimed me whole in a single night, and I tell ye honestly I didna see it coming."

Finn smiled, wishing his heart would simply have hope instead of reminding him of that one morning seven years ago when he had first noticed Emma.

"What about Emma?"

At Garrett's question, Finn flinched, wondering if Garrett, too, had developed the ability to read another's mind. Swallowing, he tried his best to pretend that his heart had not just danced wildly in his chest. "What about her?"

The corner of Garrett's mouth curled upward into a suspicious grin. "Dunno pretend that ye dunno care for the lass."

As his muscles clenched in shock, Finn tried to swallow the sudden lump in his throat. "What gave ye that idea? I barely know her."

Garrett laughed, "And *I* had never met my wife until the night of our wedding." He shook his head. "Nah, love doesna care about time, or right and wrong. It simply is...or not." For a split second, he glanced at Ian, and Finn wondered if he knew more than Ian had shared with him. "What about that kiss?"

Again, Finn flinched, annoyed with his inability to maintain a calm exterior. How did Cormag do it? Or did he truly never feel anything remotely resembling that which currently waged war in Finn's chest? "What kiss? Ye mean that quick peg seven years ago? That wasna a kiss! 'Twas nothing but a dare."

The moment the grin slid off Garrett's face, Finn wanted to kick himself for saying more than he had meant to.

"A dare?" Garrett asked, straightening as he had only just now leaned down to pick up another log. "Ye never told us that. How long have ye known?"

Finn shrugged, looking down at the snow-covered ground as the memory of that morning returned fresh and clear. "I've always known."

"Ye followed her that morning," Garrett mumbled, and Finn could feel his friend's eyes on him. "Did she tell ye that?"

Sighing, Finn met Garrett's gaze. "Nah, I overhead her speaking to her friends. She only did it to win the dare. 'Twas nothing more."

Garrett's gaze narrowed. "But 'twas for ye, was it not?" Finn scoffed, ready to deny his friend's suspicions with all the vehemence he could muster, but Garrett cut him off. "Why else would the lass affect ye so? Why else do ye keep glaring at her as though she's put a hex on ye? Why else do ye interfere with her life?"

Too thunderstruck to think straight, Finn gawked at his friend. "What?" was all he could manage.

"Last year," Garret supplied helpfully, his gaze narrowed as he watched Finn with a Cormag-like intensity, "ye told that fellow from Clan MacKinnear...what was his name?...Hamish, aye...ye told Hamish MacKinnear that the lass was promised. Why did ye do that when ye knew full well that it wasna true? Ye didna like the way he kept looking at her. Ye didna like it one bit. The glower ye always have about ye when she's near was never as dark as then. Admit it, ye care for her."

Overwhelmed at having all this pulled out into the open, Finn retreated a few paces when Ian drew near and reached for another log. Again, he glared at them before ploughing on through the snow to the next cottage while Cormag led the horse and cart a bit farther down the road.

"So, 'tis true then?" Garrett asked, a bit of a smug smile on his face as he stepped up to Finn. "Ye care for her? If that is so, why do ye wish to leave?"

"I never said I cared for her," Finn hissed under his breath as his hands curled into fists, trying desperately to hold on to his composure. "'Twas only a misunderstanding."

Garrett laughed, "Ye can say what ye wish, Finn, but no one glares at another like that without deep emotions. The lass must've truly gotten to ye. Why else would ye care what she does or who she marries?"

At the thought, every fibre in Finn's body tensed to the point of breaking, and for a long moment, he simply stood and stared at Garrett.

"Aye, I can see very well that she means nothing to ye," his friend mocked. "A bit of advice, dunno wait too long. One of these days, ye willna succeed in turning away a suitor, and then she'll be lost to ye. Why do ye think I married Claudia right then and there on the spot?" A large grin on his face, Garrett sighed. "She's a fierce woman, beautiful and strong and so...so verra alive. I knew another man might snatch her up in an instant, and so I claimed her as my own as fast as I could. No matter where she is, I will find her and remind her that she's mine...as I am hers." Garrett's eyes sobered. "Ye'd be wise to do the same...if indeed ye care for her." Then he stepped away and hurried after the cart, bending down to work again as a more-than-annoyed Ian glared at him.

"Ye'd do well to heed his advice."

Spinning around, Finn found Cormag standing behind him. "How long have ye been there?"

"Not long," Cormag replied, and yet, it seemed he knew all there was to know as he generally did. He inhaled a slow breath as his gaze once more travelled over Finn as though he was trying to make sense of something. "What does she mean to ye?"

Finn gritted his teeth, uncertain how he felt about the path his friends were urging him to take.

"I see," Cormag replied, seemingly satisfied with the answer he had glimpsed on Finn's face. Then he sighed, a hint of exhaustion coming to his grey eyes.

"What is it?" Finn asked, wishing he could read others as well as Cormag could, particularly Emma.

Cormag shrugged. "I canna help but wonder why people are so vehement in pretending that they dunno care, for it only seems to complicate matters."

Finn sighed. Leave it to Cormag to turn a heart's fears into a matter of the mind. Then he stopped, his gaze rising to meet his laird's. "People?" he mumbled, and his traitorous heart thudded loudly in his chest. "Ye said, *people*. Who did ye mean?"

Cormag's brows rose, and it was all the answer Finn needed. "Emma?" he whispered as his hands once more balled into fists, willing the hope in his heart to cease its conquest. "Did she...did she say anything to ye?"

"She didna have to," Cormag replied, "for the lass is as inept at pretending that she doesna care as ye are, Finn." For a short moment, a rather indulgent smile curved up Cormag's lips before he turned and walked away, returning to their task at hand.

Swallowing, Finn stared after him. Could it be true? Was there a chance that Emma harboured sentiments other than indifference and disregard for him? Whenever he saw her, she never turned to look at him, and whenever their eyes happened to meet, she always turned away with such haste as though the very sight of him offended her. Could there be another reason for her reaction as there was another reason for his own?

Certainly, he did not hate her. He hated that she did not care for him. That she had led him to believe that she did but had then crushed his hopes without a look back.

Or had he been wrong?

Intrigued and–heavens, yes!–hopeful, Finn knew that he needed to see her, perhaps even speak to her before he decided to leave. If he did not, he would spend the rest of his life wondering what could have been.

Chapter Three

OUT INTO THE SNOW

With only one day left until the annual yuletide feast at Seann Dachaigh Tower, the whole castle was abuzz: the hum of voices and hurrying feet echoing through the grand hall like bees in a hive. Furniture was moved to make room for rows upon rows of tables, all of which were in need of decorating to match the festive mood stirred by evergreens hung up in archways and around windows alike.

Emma and Maggie had spent the past two days decorating the hall, tying bows and stars fashioned out of straw into the evergreen branches to brighten up the castle. Still, Maggie was not satisfied, and a dark scowl came to her face when her eyes swept over the still-barren tables. "This won't do," she stated matter-of-factly, arms akimbo. "We need more branches."

Emma sighed, her fingers beginning to feel numb. "We dunno have any more." She gestured to the lush decorations around the hall. "I think 'tis enough, Maggie. Ye did a fine job. Ye should be proud."

Pressing her lips into a thin line, Maggie shook her head, disapproval clear in her blue eyes.

Due to her enthusiasm and utter commitment to the task, Maggie had taken over the planning of the yuletide feast five years ago...almost upon arriving in Scotland. At first, people had frowned at the young English lass, but soon everyone had been delighted with the way she flitted around the castle like a fairy, brightening everything she touched, her eyes aglow with joy.

Today, Maggie was as much a Scot as any one of them, and people often shook their heads at the thought that she had not grown up in the Highlands. *A minor detail*, Maggie generally called it. *A detail to be neglected.*

By now, people tended to agree.

"We need more branches," Maggie stated once more, and Emma knew better than to argue. "Niall, Blair," she called her children, who came rushing up with excitement, hoping to be entrusted with an important task. "Go find yer father. We need to go out into the woods to cut more branches." The children squealed with delight and immediately set off. "And tell him to bring Garrett and Finn," Maggie yelled after them.

Emma froze at the thought of Finn accompanying them. Generally, they tended to stay out of each other's way, only stumbling upon the other by accident.

"Dunno look so shocked," Maggie chided as she handed Emma her heavy winter cloak and then reached for her own as well as her children's. "I told ye ye needed to speak to him. Today is as good a day as any."

Staring at her friend, Emma swallowed. "Ye want me to talk to him?"

Maggie rolled her eyes. "Were ye not listening? What have we been talking about these past days?" Stepping closer, she held Emma's gaze. "Aye, I want ye to talk to him."

"But..." Emma could feel her skin crawl at the thought of Finn's glaring green eyes. "I thought...perhaps in the new year. I mean there's no rush, is there?"

"Aye, there is," Maggie objected as she rushed down the corridor leading out into the courtyard.

Pulling her cloak around herself, Emma hastened after her. "There is? Why? What do ye mean?"

As they stepped out into the cold, they saw Maggie's children running toward them, their father in their tow...as well as Garrett, Finn...and Vaughn. Emma groaned inwardly.

"What were ye thinking rushing outside without bundling up first?" Maggie chided her children, their noses bright red from the cold. Quickly, she wrapped Blair in a warm winter cloak and handed Niall his lined coat. "Ye'll be sorry when we're all at the feast and ye'll be in bed with a cold."

Shock widened the children's eyes; however, only for a moment. Soon, they were running through the snow once more, giggling and laughing.

"What did ye mean?" Emma whispered in Maggie's ear as she watched the men approach, wondering at the way Finn glared not at her, but at Vaughn instead. Dimly, she wondered what the young man had done to draw Finn's wrath. She doubted he had stolen a kiss as well. In fact, his eyes were on her, and a large smile drew up the corners of his mouth.

Emma sighed, disappointment filling her heart.

While Finn did little else but glare in her direction if, indeed, he paid her any attention, Vaughn always smiled at her, his eyes lighting up with joy. In fact, he had been smiling at her for a while now, and Emma was beginning to think that soon he might muster the courage to ask for her hand. Still, Emma could not deny that Vaughn's warm brown eyes never managed to set her blood on fire the way Finn's dark green blaze did.

Oh, why could she not have lost her heart to Vaughn instead?

"Ian told me," Maggie whispered as they descended the front steps, "that Finn asked to accompany Garret to England."

Emma froze as though the snow around her feet had suddenly frozen into a block of ice, stopping her progress.

Turning back, Maggie looked at her, a teasing smile coming to her lips. "Aye, I can see that he means nothing to ye."

Swallowing, Emma reached for Maggie's arm and pulled her to her side. "Why?" was all she could ask as her heart beat painfully in her chest at the thought of Finn disappearing from her life.

Maggie's face sobered, and her blue eyes shone with compassion. "To find himself a bride."

Pain shot through Emma's middle, and her knees felt as though they would give out any moment. Her hands grasped Maggie's, and she had to lean heavily on her dainty friend lest she drop to the ground.

"Are ye all right?" came Vaughn's concerned voice as he rushed to their side, his warm brown eyes searching her face. "Ye look pale. Is anything wrong?"

Swallowing the lump in her throat, Emma assured him that she was fine when Finn's scowling face appeared beside Vaughn's. His eyes were hard as they met hers, and Emma did not dare look at him a moment longer.

"The bairns said ye needed more branches," Ian cut in, his gaze wandering over the various expressions on their faces before his own joined Finn's, taking on a displeased scowl. "Are ye sure ye dunno have enough?"

Maggie rolled her eyes at her husband. "D'ye think I would drag all of ye out here for nothing. Aye, I need more branches. So, let's be off."

Grumbling something under his breath, Ian went off to hitch a horse to the small cart with runners that they used whenever the snow got too deep. While Finn went after him, Garrett chased Niall and Blair around the yard.

"Perhaps ye should stay here," Vaughn suggested, his eyes still holding concern as he looked at Emma. "Ye still look pale. Perhaps ye need rest."

Maggie smiled at him, gently patting Emma's hand. "She'll be fine. There's no need to worry." She glanced at her children flinging snowballs at a downed Garrett. "Would ye mind helping him out? He looks to be in need of aid."

Turning to look over his shoulder, Vaughn laughed and then hurried off to lend a hand.

"He's right," Maggie said after returning her gaze to Emma. "Ye look pale."

Gritting her teeth, Emma felt tears brimming in the corners of her eyes, and it took all her willpower to keep them from rolling down her chilled cheeks. "I'm fine," she whispered as though she could will those words to be true.

"Aye, I can see that," Maggie replied, disbelief clear in her voice. "Come, let's get to work." Then she looped her arm through Emma's and together with the children followed after Ian as he guided the horse and cart out through the front gate and toward the woods.

Emma's heart and mind felt numb as she trudged onward through the snow, the children's voices echoing around her as they laughed and cheered, enjoying the winter wonderland around them. Vaughn stayed by her side, his calm voice soothing even though Emma could not concentrate on the words he spoke.

On they walked until they left the path and cut deeper into the woods where the trees were still untouched. Ian called them to a halt and ordered them to spread out. Since they would not cut down another tree and then use its branches for decorating the hall, the plan was to cut individual branches off trees here and there.

"Talk to him," Maggie whispered into Emma's ear before she nodded to the west where Finn was disappearing between the trees. "Now." Maggie's steely blue eyes did not allow for an argument before she turned to Vaughn, who still hovered nearby, and drew his attention away, setting him to work.

An insistent shove sent Emma on her way, and she reluctantly stumbled through the snow, her feet as cold as ice. The last time she had sought Finn out on an equally cold day, all had ended in a disaster. That day, she had angered him. And yet, here she was, going after a man who clearly could not care less about her. Why on earth did Maggie insist she subject herself to this torture? Was it not clear that Finn had set his sights elsewhere?

Again, the day of her father's burial surfaced in her mind, and instantly, her traitorous heart had hope.

Cursing under her breath, Emma stumbled onward, trying her best to convince herself that Finn's kindness that day had indeed been nothing else but that, kindness.

Her eyes fell on branch after branch as she followed in Finn's wake. A distant part of her mind urged her to pick them up, reminding her of why they had come out here in the first place. Still, Emma could not bring herself to heed those thoughts as she was too busy trying to hold utter panic at bay. What on earth was she doing following him? What was there to say? What should she-?

"Oh!"

It was nothing more than a breathy sound that escaped her lips as her eyes fell on Finn. He stood beside a large fir tree, in the process of cutting off one of the lower-hanging branches. His hands were steady, and the rhythmic sounds of the saw ought to have alerted her to his presence even before she had stumbled upon him. Her mind, however, had been too distracted.

Finn, too, seemed to have been elsewhere with his thoughts for the moment her breathy "oh" filled the air, he flinched as though a shot had been fired near his head. His right hand slipped, and the saw's teeth scraped over the back of his other hand, drawing blood.

A curse flew from his lips as he spun around, holding his injured hand to his chest. Then his eyes met hers, and he all but stumbled backwards until his back collided with the tree. His chest rose and fell with rapid breaths, and yet, his gaze remained hard.

More than anything, Emma wanted to turn around and run, but the sight of a drop of his blood running down his hand and dripping into the snow held her in place. "I'm sorry," she whispered, her suddenly warm feet carrying her closer. "I didna mean to startle ye."

Finn's teeth gritted together as he stared at her, seemingly at a loss for words.

Still, Emma stepped closer, wondering where the sudden courage had come from to approach him in such a direct fashion. Perhaps it was not courage, she thought as her gaze once more dropped to his injured hand. Perhaps it was simply that his pain was hers, and she could not bear it.

"Let me help ye." Drawing a handkerchief from her pocket, Emma approached him, her eyes on his to gauge if her doing so would displease him. Although his eyes remained hard, he did not object nor draw away.

When she came to stand in front of him, Emma had to lift her chin to look up into his eyes. It had been seven years since they had last stood this close together, and his warm breath as it fell onto her skin sent tantalising shivers down her back.

A sudden desire rushed through Emma's body, and for a moment, she feared she would lose all control and kiss him again.

Biting her lip, she forced her eyes down to his injured hand. "It's not deep," she mumbled as she gently wrapped her handkerchief around his hand, tying a small knot to keep it in place. "I think ye'll live," she whispered as her eyes found his once more, a hint of humour in her voice that surprised her as much as him.

For a split second, his lips seemed to quiver as though wishing to curl up into a smile, and Emma's heart almost leapt out of her chest.

"What are ye doing here?" Finn suddenly asked, his sharp voice cutting through the soft bond Emma had felt in her heart. "Should ye not be by Vaughn's side?"

As though slapped, Emma took a step back. "Vaughn? No, I..." She glanced at the branches in the snow. "I came to help ye collect these."

Stepping away from her, Finn picked up the two branches by his feet. "There's no need. I can manage."

Coldness reclaimed Emma's body, and her foolish heart sank. "I heard ye plan to go to England with Garrett." *Wherever had that come from?*

Finn blinked, his gaze returning to hers as his brows drew down. "Where did ye hear that?"

"Is it not true?" Emma pressed, cursing her tongue for it would only get her in trouble. And yet, she had to know if what Maggie had said would indeed come to pass.

Crossing his arms, Finn cocked an eyebrow, clearly unwilling to answer her unless she answered him first.

"Maggie told me," Emma finally said, feeling her heart calm with the familiar back and forth of conversation. "I believe she heard it from Ian. Why? Was it to be a secret?"

Inhaling a deep breath, Finn shrugged. "Nah, I'm merely surprised ye know as I only mentioned it the other day." He sighed, and for a reason Emma could not understand, his face suddenly darkened. "News travels fast, 'twould seem."

Emma nodded, knowing very well that secrets rarely lasted long in their clan. "Why do ye wish to go to England?" Her hands shook, and so she curled them around one another under her cloak.

Finn scoffed, "What is it to ye?"

Gritting her teeth, Emma glared at him, annoyed with the way he always seemed to antagonise her. "Why do ye get angry? I merely asked a question. Is that so bad?"

The muscles in Finn's jaw seemed to pulse as he stared back at her. Then all of a sudden, his features softened, and the air rushed from his lungs as though he had been holding it. "Listen, I–"

"Emma?"

At the sound of Vaughn's voice nearby, Emma could have groaned. Even if only for a moment, she wanted nothing more but to speak to Finn and have him speak to her, not as though they were enemies but with kindness. She would give anything to have him once more look at her the way he had the day of her father's burial. The softness and compassion in his eyes had been breath-taking, and Emma had longed for it for years.

Now, that hope seemed to be dashed as his green gaze hardened, his arms returning to cross over his chest as though to keep her away at all cost. "'Tis none of yer concern why I do anything, ye hear," he growled, his voice as hard as ever before he stalked off, leaving nothing but prints in the snow.

Chapter Four
ALL IS FAIR IN LOVE AND WAR

Storming away, Finn knew that he was acting like a headstrong bairn, unwilling to discuss what bothered him. And yet, if he had stayed a moment longer, he would have acted like a boorish man, yanking her into his arms, claiming her as his and kissing her the way he had wanted to for seven long years.

Ever since that cold winter's morning when she had surprised him, stunned him witless…and stolen not only a kiss, but his heart as well.

Emma, however, had not wanted him that morning. All she had wanted was to win a game, a dare. She had not wanted him then, and she did not now. Not once since that day had she done anything that would have suggested her feelings on the matter had changed.

Cursing under his breath, Finn curled his good hand around the handkerchief she had put on his scraped knuckles. The pain was minimal, and the cuts would have needed no bandaging. Still, he could not deny that the concern he had seen in her eyes had once again rendered him speechless. It had touched him, and he had wanted to believe that she cared, that his pain had touched her as well.

Her eyes had been so kind and tender as she had looked up at him, her warm hand brushing over his skin as she had seen to his wound. His body had responded instantly, and his heart had hammered in his chest wildly, urging him to finally address her. Would it truly be worse to have her reject him? To know with certainty that she did not care? Or was the sliver of hope he clung to something he needed in order to survive?

Ready to put his heart on the line, Finn had let down his defences, knowing that he could not live with uncertainty for the rest of his life…when Vaughn's voice had shattered all his hopes.

Anger had curled around his heart in an instant, and his defences had come back up. More than once he had seen Vaughn smile at Emma, and every now and then, she had even smiled back at him.

Upon seeing it, Finn had almost doubled over in pain, and it had been in that moment that he had realised he had indeed lost his heart to her.

Absolutely and irrevocably.

"I need to leave," Finn grumbled as he stomped through the snow with no regard for where he was headed. Not once had she smiled at him. "I need to go."

"Finn? Is that ye?"

Stopping in his tracks, Finn turned toward Ian's voice before his friend stepped out from behind a thicket, his gaze narrowing as he took in the scowl on Finn's face. "What's wrong?" His gaze darted to Finn's wrapped hand. "Are ye hurt? I would've thought ye knew how to handle a saw."

Finn scoffed, remembering that he had left it lying in the snow. "'Tis nothing."

"'Tis not nothing." Rolling his eyes, Ian heaved a deep sigh. "'Tis Emma, is it not?"

Finn opened his mouth to object, but Ian waved him off. "D'ye know that Vaughn intends to ask for her hand?"

Shock barrelled into Finn like a charging boar. Although he had suspected-anyone would have-having it confirmed was a thousand times more agonising. "He d-?" He swallowed the lump in his throat as his injured hand suddenly ached painfully. "Why would I care?" The words fell from his lips to lie dead at his feet.

Ian heaved another deep sigh; annoyance and a hint of anger clear on his face. "It doesna matter why ye care, Finn. All that matters is that ye do. Ye care about her whether ye like it or not." A growl rose from Ian's throat, and his jaw clenched. "Ye make me so angry."

"Why?" Finn asked, rather surprised by his friend's emotional involvement in this matter. "What is it to ye?"

"Ye're not being fair!" Ian snapped, his eyes narrowed as he approached. "What ye both are doing is not fair! Ye're being selfish and…and fools on top of it."

Never had Finn seen his friend lose his temper quite like this. Although Ian was known to have strong opinions and tended to argue with vehemence, the way he spoke to Finn now was different. It was as though the outcome of this personally affected him.

"What do ye mean?" Finn asked, wondering about the bitterness that had grown in his friend over the last few years. "She and I are nothing to each other. We-"

Ian laughed, but it was a mirthless laugh. "Truly?" He shook his head, utter disbelief in his eyes. "Everybody knows how ye two feel about one another. Why is it that *ye* canna see it?" He took a step forward, his gaze burning with challenge. "Tell me, would ye truly not care if Emma married Vaughn? Would ye dance at their wedding as ye danced at mine?"

Ian's question felt like a renewed blow to his mid-section, and Finn merely stood and stared at his friend while another part of him could not help but return to what Ian had said before. *Everybody knows how ye two feel about one another. Why is it that ye canna see it?*

Was there truth in Ian's words? Or was he merely angry and-? But why would he say something like that without truly believing it to be true? What reason could he have? After all, Ian was one of his oldest friends. They had always gone through thick and thin together. Finn had no reason to doubt his word.

"Nah," Ian said, shaking his head rather absentmindedly, as his fingers tensed around the axe in his hand. "She shouldna marry him. She shouldna!"

Strangely relieved to have another agree, Finn nodded. "Aye, they dunno suit. He's too-"

"They shouldna marry," Ian hissed, advancing on Finn with a blazing fire in his eyes, "because she doesna love him! That's why! If she marries him, she'll doom Vaughn to a loveless marriage, tied to someone whose heart he canna win. Does that seem fair to ye?"

Stunned, Finn looked at his friend, and for the first time, Ian's anger and bitterness seemed to make sense. "Does Maggie-?"

"It doesna matter!" Ian snapped, his chest rising and falling with each agitated breath. His hand was still clenched around the axe he held, and his jaw was tense to the point of breaking. Still, it seemed he was fighting to regain control and calm the emotions that had all of a sudden run wild. "Ye still have a chance," he finally said, his body strung tight, but his voice quiet, almost breathless. "Ye still have a chance to be happy. Dunno waste it, and dunno doom others because ye're afraid."

Finn swallowed, overcome with the sorrow he saw in Ian's eyes. "Thank ye, my friend, for speaking so plainly. I canna say anyone ever has."

Ian nodded. "Then do us both a favour and heed my advice. Dunno thank me and then carry on as though ye havena heard a word I said."

"Did ye truly mean what ye said?" Finn asked, remembering the way Emma sometimes smiled at Vaughn, the way he gazed at her like a love-struck fool. Finn could not for the life of him remember her ever smiling at him. Did that not mean that her heart belonged to Vaughn? "How can I be certain she cares?"

Ian's lips pressed into a thin line as he once more rolled his eyes at Finn. Then he took a step closer, his blue eyes dark and thunderous as they held Finn's. "Go and ask her!" he snapped, his voice cutting through the still winter air like a whip. Then he spun on his heel and walked away, his angry footsteps dulled by the soft snow covering the ground.

Chapter Five

SILENT SORROW

"Sorry," Maggie mumbled as she hastened toward Emma, her arms filled with cut branches. "I turned my head once, and he slipped through my fingers." As she lowered her treasures into the cart, her gaze travelled to Vaughn, who had come walking back with Emma a few minutes ago and was now attempting to chop another branch off a fir tree.

"'Tis all right," Emma mumbled, unable to hide her anger and disappointment. "Finn was a horrid person. No matter what I do, he always snaps at me as though my presence alone offends him." She shook her head, willing anger to supersede disappointment. "If he canna even be civil, then there's no point in talking to him." She scoffed, her hands coming up to rest on her sides as righteous indignation spread through her heart, pushing aside the pain that tended to linger. "I canna stand him one bit, and I feel awfully sorry for the poor English lass he'll choose for his bride."

Finished with her tirade, Emma turned to Maggie and found her friend all but glaring at her, her bright blue eyes dark and filled with utter annoyance. "Ye're a fool," Maggie hissed, grabbing Emma's arm and pulling her aside. Glancing around them, she dropped her voice to a whisper. "Why do ye so stubbornly ignore how ye feel? Why can ye not see that Finn cares for ye? Are ye truly blind? Or do ye enjoy having two men vie for yer hand?"

Shocked, Emma blinked. "What do ye mean?" Never had she seen Maggie quite this agitated, this angry, this…hurt. "Two men? 'Tis only Vaughn who–"

Gritting her teeth, sweet, cheerful Maggie seemed to be fighting for control. "D'ye truly think 'tis a coincidence that the moment Vaughn started smiling at ye, Finn couldna seem to stand the man any longer? He's jealous," she hissed, her blue eyes holding Emma's as though wanting to make certain that her friend understood.

Emma swallowed, ignoring the little dance her heart was currently performing in her chest. "Jealous? Nah, ye canna mean that. He hates me. He only ever glares at me. He has ever since that morning when–"

"Oh, I wish I had known ye back then," Maggie interrupted, hands gesturing wildly as she began to pace. "I wish I'd come to Seann Dachaigh Tower a year earlier. I wish I'd been here for I would've pushed ye to seek him out again the next day and steal another kiss."

"What?"

Maggie stopped, her eyes hard, before she walked over to Emma with sure steps until their noses almost touched. "I'll never believe he's been angry with ye for all these years because ye kissed him. That's nonsense. Even if he hadn't liked it, he wouldna have acted like that. He would've laughed it off and gone on his merry way." Maggie's breath came in rapid gasps, and for a moment, she closed her eyes and then inhaled a deep breath. "Perhaps I should've spoken to ye sooner, pushed ye to see what is right in front of yer eyes." Looking at Emma, Maggie sighed, her eyes now brimming with tears. "I didna because I didna think 'twas my place to meddle in other people's affairs." Her lips pressed into a tight line, and for a moment, Emma thought she saw a memory cross over Maggie's face. "Others often think they know what's right, but they dunno. They push and they prod until they get what they want, and then…ye choose the wrong path and all is lost."

Misery now stood on Maggie's face, and Emma walked over pulling her friend into her arms. At first, the slender young woman resisted, but then her head sank down onto Emma's shoulder and she inhaled a shuddering breath. "I'm sorry for yer pain," Emma whispered into Maggie's auburn hair, wondering what had happened in her friend's past. Never had Maggie spoken of anything that would explain the pain and loss she had seen in her blue eyes just now.

All people ever talked about was how Maggie had come to Scotland to visit her mother's clan and then had stayed because she had fallen in love with Ian MacDrummond and married him.

That was the story Emma knew, but apparently there was more to it than she ever would have thought.

Pulling back, Maggie ran her hands over her eyes and wiped away her tears. "Ye think too much, Emma," she said, the ghost of a smile tugging on the corners of her lips. "Nothing good ever comes of it when people think too much. The heart wants what it wants, and no amount of reasonable thinking or good intentions can change that." Grasping Emma's hands, Maggie looked at her, her eyes intense, almost pleading. "Ye're lucky, Emma. Ye still have a chance to marry the man ye love, and if that man is Vaughn, then I willna say another word." Her hands squeezed Emma's. "But if it's not, then please, please, go and speak to Finn. Tell him how ye feel, or ye will regret it for the rest of yer life." She swallowed. "I promise ye that."

Holding her friend's gaze, Emma felt her limbs begin to tremble. With what, she could not say. Maggie's sorrow touched her, frightened her, and yet, the thought of laying open her heart and have Finn stomp on it scared her nearly witless. "Is there anything I can do?" she whispered, searching Maggie's face. "D'ye wish to talk about–?"

"No," Maggie said vehemently. "I've made my choice. What's done is done. But ye're still at the beginning of yer story. Make certain ye choose the right man or it will turn into a tragedy, and I dunno want that for ye." After squeezing Emma's hands one last time, Maggie returned to the cart, accepting a bunch of branches from Niall and Blair, who loved dragging them through the snow, giggling as they went.

Watching them, Emma was struck by the peacefulness of the sight before her, and yet, the look on Maggie's face whispered of falsehood. Certainly, she loved her children, but quite obviously, she had not married the man she loved.

Emma sighed, wondering if she possessed the strength to do what Maggie had not.

Chapter Six

DEFINITIONS OF A KISS

As the sky slowly grew darker, they all gathered around the cart, making certain no one was left behind. Then they began the long walk back to Seann Dachaigh Tower. Once again, Finn's insides twisted into a tight knot when he saw Vaughn approach Emma. The man fell in step beside her, speaking animatedly while Emma seemed distracted, her gaze distant.

Again, Finn contemplated Ian's words as well as the vehemence with which his friend had spoken. Still, uncertainty remained, and Finn knew that there was only one way to rid himself of it. He needed to speak to Emma.

Tonight.

All of a sudden, after seven long years, Finn could not wait any longer. He needed to know so that he could make his choice in the best way possible.

Once they reached the courtyard, their little group broke apart. While Ian positioned the cart near the back entrance to the hall and then returned the horse to the stables, Maggie and Emma took the children inside to warm up. Vaughn took his leave, mumbling something about returning later, and walked down to the village where his family lived in one of the larger cottages.

"Ye'll speak to her, won't ye?" Garrett observed, a bit of a smirk on his face as he watched Finn.

Turning toward his friend, Finn sighed. "What gave me away?"

Garrett chuckled, "I dunno know. I guess 'tis the look in yer eyes. Determined, and yet...terrified."

Finn laughed, "Ye sound as though ye know the feeling well?"

"Aye," Garrett replied with a deep sigh. "Love will do that to ye. But it'll also make ye feel alive in a way ye've never felt before." Then he patted Finn on the back, wished him good luck and walked off.

Heading into the hall, Finn kept to the shadows, watching as Maggie and Emma as well as a few other volunteers returned to their task of decorating the rows upon rows of tables set out for tomorrow's feast. Evergreen branches were tied together and placed in the middle, then adorned with red ribbons and straw figurines. In between, they placed large candles. At first, Niall and Blair tried to help, but soon they lay passed out in a corner of the hall near the large fireplace, sound asleep.

Finn waited; however, not patiently as the mere sight of Emma so near, and yet, so far away was torture.

Before, he had always done his utmost not to be near her, to avoid her wherever possible, and whenever they had stumbled upon one another after all, he had always retreated as fast as he could have without truly giving offence. Never had he simply stood and looked at her, watched the way her brows furrowed when she was concentrating, the way her teeth sunk into her lower lip when she was getting agitated, or the way her eyes shone when she looked down at Niall and Blair, gently draping her cloak over the sleeping children.

She was magnificent, and Finn knew very well why he had never allowed himself to see her thus.

He was so lost in his thoughts that he almost failed to notice when Emma slipped from the hall, taking the corridor toward the back entrance. Presumably, Maggie had sent her to fetch more branches. Could there possibly be any left? Who on earth needed all these decorations? They would wither and die soon anyhow.

Pushing himself off the wall he had been leaning against, Finn hurried after her, careful not to draw Maggie's attention. Quick strides carried him onward, and he came upon Emma as she was about to step outside. "Emma," he called before all courage could desert him.

At the sound of his voice, she turned to look at him, utter surprise in her gaze. "Finn, what are ye doing here? I thought ye'd left with Garrett."

The thought that she paid attention to his whereabouts pleased him, and he could not prevent a smile from showing on his face.

Seeing it, her gaze narrowed in confusion, and yet, the way her breath rushed from her lungs and the corners of her mouth drew upward ever so slightly spoke of joy. Did she truly care about him? Was it possible that Ian was right? That he had been ever so blind?

Her eyes held his, and belatedly, Finn realised that he ought to say something. "I...I wanted to speak to ye," he began, cursing the way his voice shook. "I need to speak to ye."

"Aye?" Her eyes remained on his, waiting, expecting...hopeful somehow, and yet, guarded.

Finn knew only too well how that felt. Where on earth was he to begin? He could not very well ask her straight out if she cared for him, could he? Would she not laugh at him?

Clearing his throat, he groped for words. "I wanted to...I've heard...that is, I've heard that Vaughn intends to ask for yer hand." The moment the words had left his lips, Finn could have kicked himself. Poorer words had never been chosen, that much was certain.

As expected, the glow in her eyes dimmed, and her arms rose to cross in front of her chest...as though to put a barrier between them, to keep him away. "I fail to see how 'tis any of yer business." Her voice was harsh as she spoke, and yet, he thought to detect a hint of pain as well.

"I'm sorry I blurted it out like that," Finn apologised as best as he could while his nerves lay bare, "but I need to know if ye intend to marry him."

Exhaling a quick breath, she frowned. "Why? Why do ye *need* to know? What is it to ye?"

"I just..." Gritting his teeth, Finn took a step closer, his gaze unable to veer from hers. "I simply need to know."

Scoffing, she shook her head. "Why? If I didna know any better, I'd think ye're jealous."

Her words were like a stab to his heart, and Finn momentarily dropped his gaze. When his eyes found hers once more, the look on her face was one of sheer incredulity. Oh, dear god, she knew! Would she laugh at him now?

"It c-canna be," she stammered, her warm brown eyes fixed on his. "Ye hate me. Ye always glare at me. We're nothing to each other. We've barely spoken a word to each other since–" Her voice broke off, and she dropped her gaze as heat shot up her face, colouring her cheeks a crimson red.

Finn rejoiced, his heart hammering in his chest as he stepped closer, undeniably drawn to the woman with the dark brown eyes who had been haunting his dreams for years. "Since that morning," he whispered, "although ye did not say much."

Emma swallowed, lifting her chin a fraction, a hint of righteous indignation coming to her voice. "Neither did ye. Ye only stood and stared."

"Aye." Finn nodded, a small smile claiming his features. "Aye, I did. I admit ye threw me off balance."

The red in her cheeks darkened. "I'm sorry. I...I shouldna have kissed ye. I..."

"'Twas not a true kiss," Finn said, watching her closely.

Her gaze narrowed, and a frown drew down her brows. "What do ye mean? Of course, 'twas a kiss. What else could it have been?"

Holding her gaze, he leaned closer. "A dare."

Shock widened her eyes and dropped her jaw. "Ye kn-know?" she stammered. "How?"

Emma's heart pounded in her ears like a stampede as she stared up at Finn, mortified by his rightful accusation. Ever since Maggie had spoken to her so honestly, Emma had heard her friend's words echoing in her mind. *I'll never believe he's been angry with ye for all these years because ye kissed him. That's nonsense. Even if he hadn't liked it, he wouldna have acted like that. He would've laughed it off and gone on his merry way.*

But now she knew why he had been angry, why he had glared at her all these years. And yet, it seemed an awfully long time to hold a grudge. Could it be that he cared for her? That he had been offended to think that *she* had not cared? That it had only been a dare to her? A game?

Could the answer truly be that simple?

"I followed ye," he answered her question, his eyes searching as though he, too, was looking for answers. "I followed ye, and I heard ye speaking to yer friends."

"Oh." If possible, Emma's cheeks burnt even hotter. "I'm sorry I..." Then a thought struck, and her eyes narrowed with renewed purpose. "Why did ye follow me?" she demanded, taking a step toward him, her eyes searching his. "Why?"

He swallowed, and she could sense that he wanted nothing more but to drop his gaze. But he did not. Instead, he squared his shoulders and accepted her challenge, offering one of his own. "Why did ye kiss me if indeed 'twas a kiss?"

Knowing his question to be a distraction, Emma still could not keep herself from taking the bait. "Of course, 'twas. Our lips touched, did they not?"

All of a sudden, the memory of their kiss loomed between them. Emma could see it in the green blaze that lit up his eyes, and her heart jumped into her throat when Finn's lips curled up into a wicked smile and his gaze dropped to her mouth for the barest of moments. "Have ye been kissed since that morning?"

Emma swallowed before a triumphant smile lit up her face. "Aha! So, ye admit that 'twas a kiss!"

Finn chuckled, and Emma could not remember ever having seen him like this. Not since that morning. Not in the past seven years. At least not around her.

Also, she could not help but wonder at what point they had come to stand almost nose to nose with little between them except thin air. "Answer me," Finn teased, his green eyes glowing with delight. "Has anyone kissed ye since?" His gaze darkened. "Has Vaughn?"

Squaring her shoulders, Emma looked him directly in the eyes. "Ye didn't answer me, either. Why did ye follow-?"

"Emma!" he all but growled, shooting toward her so that she had to take an involuntary step backwards to avoid collision. His hands reached for her, and before she knew what was happening, she was wrapped in his arms, his mouth a hair's breadth away from hers. "Has he kissed ye?"

Although her knees were shaking, Emma had to admit she liked the fierceness in him. "Why d'ye think ye can-?"

"Emma!"

"No!" she blurted out. "There. Happy now?"

An amused smile came to his face, and a chuckle rumbled deep in his throat. "Aye," Finn whispered as his eyes held hers. "Aye, I'm happy."

Locked in his embrace, Emma felt her breath come faster as his green gaze remained on hers, his arms keeping her steady, keeping her from sinking to the ground as her knees turned to water.

"Would ye object," Finn began, a slight quiver in the way he drew in another breath, "if *I* were to kiss ye right here, right now?"

The air flew from Emma's lungs as she tried to make sense of his words. Her head spun, and her heart raced, overwhelmed by the past few minutes she had so unexpectedly shared with Finn. They seemed like something out of a dream, and her mind had trouble believing that she was indeed awake. Still, he felt so real.

Never had she seen the green in his gaze more vibrant than in that moment as he held her gaze, waiting for her answer.

Trying to ignore the lump in her throat, Emma willed her chin to remain up. "Why would ye?" she demanded, willing a touch of haughtiness into her tone even though her body urged her to simply accept his offering.

After all, it had been seven years! Seven years full of dreams and hopes...and disappointment.

Finn chuckled, wickedness gleaming in his eyes. "So ye know what a true kiss feels like."

Emma's gaze narrowed. "I do know," she insisted, annoyed with the condescension that rang in his voice.

"No, ye dunno."

Her back straightened, and she pulled away, glaring up at him. "Aye, I d–"

"'Twas a dare," Finn insisted as he lowered his face to hers, his arms pulling her back against him. "'Twas only a dare."

Emma swallowed. Of course, she could tell him the truth. Tell him how much she had always cared for him. Tell him that the dare had only been a welcome excuse to kiss him. Tell him that she had feared for her heart if he were to reject her. Tell him it had been a mere way to save face. Tell him all that and more.

Still, despite the past few moments which had been nothing short of heaven on earth, Emma could not. Her heart still feared that she had strayed into a dream, that she was in this very moment misunderstanding his intentions, that now he might be the one acting upon a dare. "How condescending of ye," she hissed, steeling her voice, "to think ye know bet–"

The rest of her words were lost when his lips claimed hers, silencing her objections, her excuses, her protest.

Time stopped as they stood by the back door, his arms around her and his lips a gentle pressure on hers. Emma could hear her heart thundering in her ears and felt Finn's beat against the palm of her hand as it rested on his chest. Stillness fell over them as it had seven years ago, freezing them in place, their thoughts and emotions overwhelmed by something they had not seen coming.

Emma sighed, counting the seconds his lips remained on hers, expecting him to pull back any moment now as she had seven years ago.

But, he did not.

Instead, his lips grew more daring, moving over hers with bold curiosity. Again, she sighed, and he walked her back against the wall, his hands brushing over her arms, her back, her shoulders before reaching for her face. She felt the tips of his fingers tracing the line of her jaw and down the column of her neck. Tingles surged across her skin, and her blood felt as though it had been set on fire.

When Finn finally did pull back, his breath came fast, and his gaze remained locked on hers. "D'ye concede?" he asked, a teasing grin curling up his lips as he held her in his arms.

Rolling her eyes, Emma chuckled. "Aye, I concede. Ye were right. Now, kiss me again." Her fingers curled into the front of his shirt as she pulled him back toward her, enjoying the laughter that spilled from his mouth.

"As my lady desires," he whispered against her lips, a teasing tone in his voice. Always had he seemed so serious, rather glum and melancholy–at least whenever they'd crossed paths in the past seven years–that Emma knew not what to make of this passionate man who held her in his arms.

But she was more than willing to find out.

"Emma?"

At the sound of Maggie's voice echoing down the corridor toward them, Emma and Finn stumbled apart as though burnt. For a long second, they stared at one another as the magic of the previous moment faded away and reality caught up with them. Neither one of them knew what to say, and before Emma's mind could form a clear thought, Finn stepped away toward the door.

"Emma? Where are ye?"

Finn's eyes were full of things unsaid, and although Emma wished he would stay, she knew that the moment they had shared with each other had not settled things. In fact, Emma felt as unbalanced as never before, and she could see the same confusion on Finn's face as he stepped through the door and into the cold.

Chapter Seven
SUBTLE SIGNS OF LOVE

Carrying yet another armload of freshly-cut evergreen branches, Emma was lost in thought as she walked back to the great hall with Maggie by her side. Her lips still tingled from Finn's kiss, and rather begrudgingly, she had to admit that it had felt utterly overwhelming, a far cry from the soft peck she had given Finn all those years ago.

Was that why he had thought her unfeeling? Because she had lacked the ability to kiss him with such finesse? Was that why he had doubted her? Had his kiss today changed anything between them? Did he have any intentions towards her? After all, he had been relieved to hear that Vaughn had never kissed her. And had he not said he needed to know if she intended to marry Vaughn?

Had he not looked utterly jealous?

Emma's heart skipped a beat as hope once more surged forward, tickling the corners of her mouth and willing a smile onto her face that felt all the more overwhelming as it had been absent these past few years.

"Something happened," Maggie observed, her eyes narrowed as she watched Emma. "Tell me."

Swallowing, Emma turned to look at her friend. "I dunno know what ye mean," she mumbled, uncertain how to put into words the many contradicting emotions that lived in her heart.

Maggie chuckled, "'Tis Finn, isn't it?" Her eyes narrowed even further as though she could truly read Emma's thoughts. "What happened? Did he…did he kiss ye?" She glanced over her shoulder, back down the way they had come. "Just now? Was that why ye were gone for so long?"

Gritting her teeth, Emma felt heat rise to her cheeks, and mortified, she closed her eyes.

Maggie laughed, putting a gentle hand on Emma's shoulder. "Don't be embarrassed. I'm so happy for ye." Eagerness stood on her face. "How did it happen? Tell me everything."

Setting down the branches, Emma shook her head, her thoughts still running rampant as though she had no control over them. "How did ye know?" she asked in return, trying to distract Maggie from asking more questions Emma did not know how to answer.

A deep sigh full of longing and…remembrance left Maggie's lips. "Love is impossible to hide," she whispered, "at least from those not affected by it." Gently, she squeezed Emma's hand. "I can see it in ye and Finn because my heart isna burdened by doubt and fear. Ye may try to hide how ye feel, but those attempts make the truth even more obvious."

Emma nodded, wondering how she could ever have thought that Finn did not care for her. Now, it seemed only too obvious that there was something between them, that there had always been something between them. Why else would he have been so angry with her for so long? Still, a small part of Emma did not dare believe her own conclusions to be true. Maggie was right. Fear could be utterly blinding. "He did kiss me," she whispered, a shy smile on her face as she confided in her friend. "He seemed so different. I've never seen him like that. I dunno know what to believe. I mean, I know what I wish to be true, but…"

Again, Maggie squeezed her hand in reassurance. "Believe it for 'tis true. I promise ye." Nodding her head in affirmation, Maggie glanced around the hall until her eyes fell on Garrett as he stood by the far wall, speaking to Cormag. "Dunno tell me," Maggie said, a grin coming to her face, "that ye dunno know who Garrett is speaking about."

Emma smiled. "His wife."

"Aye," Maggie agreed. "'Tis in the way his eyes sparkle, the way his face lights up at the mere mention of her, the way his voice grows heavy with emotion when he speaks of her. 'Tis easy to see, is it not?"

Sighing, Emma nodded, her eyes on Garrett as he spoke to Cormag, his green eyes alight with longing–the same longing she had seen in Finn's eyes only moments ago? Oh, if only she could be certain.

"Ye can see it in Cormag as well," Maggie threw in, her eyes narrowing as she watched their laird. "His signs are more subtle, but they're there."

"Cormag?" Emma frowned as her gaze drifted to the stoic leader of their clan. Although his eyes always seemed wide open, watchful, aware of everything that went on around him, he never seemed affected by any of it. Never had Emma seen him agitated or angry, thrown off balance or even confused or hesitant. Was he even capable of love?

"If ye dunno believe me," Maggie said, once again guessing Emma's thoughts correctly, "then watch him carefully and ye'll see. He canna help himself any more than ye and Finn." With a sigh, Maggie turned back to her branches, her nimble fingers arranging them beautifully as her gaze drifted to her sleeping children near the fire.

Too distracted by her encounter with Finn as well as Maggie's words, Emma mostly stood off to the side for the remainder of the evening, her fingers twirling a lone ribbon between them. While Maggie worked tirelessly, Emma did as she was bid and watched Cormag like a hawk, trying her best not to be too obvious.

At first, she did not notice anything that would prove Maggie's words right. Calm and collected, he spoke to Garrett, completely unaffected by the vibrant words that flew from his friend's mouth. Emma was about to abandon her observations when a muscle in his jaw twitched and his chest rose and fell with an utterly slow breath as though he was steeling himself for something.

Emma's eyes went wide and her gaze was drawn to the entrance where Moira just now stepped across the threshold. Tall and fair, she bore a striking contrast to Cormag's shadow-like appearance. Where he easily melted into the background, Moira stood out, drawing all eyes to her. And yet, while Cormag was always met with respect, the golden-haired outsider from Clan Brunwood was only ever shown distrust wherever she went. Emma wondered what was behind the whispers that circulated around Moira's banishment from her own clan.

Neither one of them looked at the other, and yet, it seemed utterly clear that they were very much aware of one another. Emma stared with wide eyes as Cormag continued his conversation with Garrett while Moira offered her help to Maggie. Both hid behind an outward appearance of disinterest whereas a dedicated observer could neither miss the fleeting looks cast in the other's direction nor the subtle ways they moved to keep each other in sight.

Shaking her head in utter disbelief, Emma stared at Cormag who drew in a sharp breath, all muscles in his body tensing, when Maggie accidentally knocked over a candle and it fell on Moira's sleeve. The young woman quickly pulled her arm back before its flame could touch the fabric of her dress and set it on fire.

Maggie apologised profusely while Moira kindly waved away her concern. A moment later, all was right again, and yet, Cormag still watched Moira like a hawk as though he feared for her even now.

Sinking down onto one of the benches near the hearth, Emma sighed, wondering if there was anyone in this world who was as aware of her as Cormag and Moira were of each other. Did Finn notice her the moment she walked into a room? Did his eyes linger when she was not looking? Was that what Maggie had been talking about? Was it truly something she, Emma, could not see because her own heart was involved?

Oh, if only she could be as certain about Finn as she now felt about Cormag and Moira.

After leaving Emma in the corridor, Finn went outside and wandered around in the cold, hoping the fresh air would clear his mind. Still, when he returned to the great hall an hour later, his body still felt as tense as a spring. While his heart ached to find Emma and continue what they had started, his mind wondered how *she* felt about it. Had he been the only one affected by their kiss? Had it been merely a pleasurable encounter for her? Or had it been as life-changing for her as it had been for him?

Walking around a corner, Finn bumped into Garrett, who had a pleased smile on his face and a bounce in his step. Lately, Garrett seemed utterly happy, and Finn could not deny that he envied him.

"Ye look awful," Garrett commented as his narrowed gaze swept over Finn. "I thought ye wanted to talk to the lass." His gaze darkened, and he pulled Finn to the side. "Did it not go well?"

Finn sighed, "I dunno know. I...We..."

"Out with it!"

Chuckling, Finn shook his head, feeling suddenly very self-conscious with his friend's watchful eyes on him. "I kissed her."

Garrett's face split into a large grin, and he clasped a companionable hand on Finn's shoulder. "About time!"

Finn's shoulders slumped as he began to pace. "But what now? We didn't have a chance to speak. I dunno know how she felt about it." Turning on his heel, he looked at Garrett. "All these past few years, we've," he scoffed, "all but hated each other. How are we-?"

"Nah!" Garrett boomed, a chuckle rumbling in his throat. "Ye didna hate each other. Ye've been in love all these years but managed to misunderstand each other."

The air rushed from Finn's lungs in one sharp *whoosh* as he heard Garrett utter these few simple words.

Garrett chuckled once more, "Ye didna know then?" he asked, his eyes twinkling with merriment as though Finn's torments were utterly laughable. "'Twas rather obvious."

"Was it?" Finn croaked, unable to deny the truth of Garrett's words. However, neither could he deny that it frightened him nearly witless. It was as though the world had turned upside down within a day, within a matter of moments. All he thought he knew was suddenly no more.

"Aye," Garrett confirmed, a hint of impatience coming to his gaze. "And now ye need to decide what ye want. 'Tis a once in a lifetime chance at love, and ye'd be a fool to let it slip through yer fingers." He shrugged, a grin on his face. "But that's only my humble opinion."

Rubbing his hands over his face, Finn groaned. "I know. I know. 'Tis only that…that I keep wondering if 'tis truly love." Looking at Garrett, he sighed. "What if 'tis simply attraction? What if she doesna…?" Gritting his teeth, Finn cursed, wishing life could for once be simple and straightforward.

"She cares for ye," Garrett stated as though it were a fact. "She cares for ye as much as ye care for her."

Staring at his friend, Finn shrugged. "How do ye know?"

Exasperated, Garrett sighed. "Because ye dunno hate people ye're only mildly attracted to, ye hear me? Ye glared at her the way ye did because ye felt betrayed and ye canna feel betrayed if ye didna have hopes for more. There, 'tis all very simple."

"What about her?"

"She mightna have glared at ye, but the way she pretended not to see ye was quite telling if ye ask me." Taking a step forward, Garrett sighed. "If ye're truly not certain, then let her marry Vaughn and come to England with me."

Finn flinched, and only when Garrett's gaze dropped lower did he notice that his hands had balled into fists.

A triumphant grin came to Garrett's face. "But if that thought turns yer stomach, then 'tis safe to say that ye're in love."

"I didna know," Finn mumbled, remembering all those years when he had been so angry, running off to Clan MacKinnear because the mere sight of her was torment, reminding him daily that what his heart desired was never to be.

"Ye didna want to know," Garrett corrected, chuckling. "Listen, it came as quite the shock to me, too, when I first laid eyes on my wife." Inhaling a deep breath, he shook his head as though he still could not believe it. "It hit me in the chest like a hard punch. I was completely taken aback by the sudden intensity of my feelings for her. One moment, I didna even know she walked this earth, and in the next, I was in love. But now that I am, I canna wait to find her, to have her back in my arms and kiss her speechless."

Finn frowned at the wicked grin on his friend's face.

"She talks a lot," Garrett said by way of explaining. Then he sighed, and his face sobered. "Yer love is right here. Ye dunno have to go and search half of England for her, merely admit that ye're in love. Does that not sound simple?"

Finn had to admit that it did. Even though he could not be certain how Emma felt, he could finally admit to himself how *he* felt about *her*. And to his great shock, he realised that he was utterly in love with her.

If she was to marry anyone, it would be him!

Chapter Eight
LOUD & CLEAR

As the evening wore on, Emma settled deeper into her seat by the fireplace, only outwardly watching over Maggie's children. Inwardly, Emma was quite busy watching all those around her, suddenly taken with the desire to discover the subtle signs people could not suppress when they were near someone they cared about...or did not.

Not only Cormag seemed utterly incapable of leaving the great hall after finishing his conversation with Garrett, but Moira, too, lingered after all preparations for tomorrow's feast were finally taken care of and Maggie was satisfied.

At first glance, neither one of them drew anyone's attention as there were quite a few people seeking company after a long day. They stood in groups or sat around Maggie's newly-decorated tables, her watchful eyes ensuring that her decorations were not disturbed. Laughter and conversation echoed through the large hall, and the fire in the hearth lent it a warm feeling of safety and home.

As always, Moira sat by herself, and yet, from under her lashes she stole a glance at their tall, dark laird every now and then. Still, neither one seemed to be aware of the other's interest in them.

Emma shook her head, shocked by the human heart's inability to see clearly when its own welfare was concerned. Had she been this blind as well?

Of course, she had, and it had made her waste seven long years of her life!

Despite the almost magnetic connection between Cormag and Moira, they never dared look at one another, nor speak to the other, pretending they were nothing short of strangers. Emma felt oddly reminded of the past seven years and her attempts to meet Finn with polite indifference. Judging from Maggie's words, her friend had seen through her charade as easily as Emma could now see the truth about Cormag and Moira.

Turning her gaze toward her friend, Emma heaved a deep sigh when she saw Maggie speak to her husband. With hanging shoulders, Ian stood before her, his blue eyes dark, and yet, there was a silent plea in them that Emma had never noticed before. At some point, he reached out and brushed a tender hand over Maggie's arm. It was an achingly-sweet gesture, and yet, Maggie tensed.

Emma swallowed hard, her heart filling with pity when she saw the defeated look in Ian's eyes. Instantly, he took a step back as though his wife had slapped him.

"She does not love him," Emma mumbled under her breath, "but he loves her." Sadness engulfed her as she watched Maggie and Ian, for the first time noticing the distance that existed between them for what it was: longing. While Ian clearly longed for his wife, Maggie's heart was elsewhere. Something–or rather someone–stood between them. Once again, Emma wondered what had happened back in England before Maggie had come to Scotland. Had she left behind a great love? Had he died? Rejected her? If she had been in love, why on earth had she agreed to marry Ian?

Brushing a gentle hand over Blair's head when she stirred in her sleep, Emma sighed, reminding herself that love rarely made sense and was often driven by fear. Had she herself not been ready to accept Vaughn in order to protect her heart from being broken should Finn reject her?

Lifting her gaze, Emma spotted Vaughn standing across the hall, deep in conversation with his father. Still, his eyes occasionally travelled to her, and she saw kindness and interest there. He was a good man, and Emma had no doubt he would be a good husband to her. Still, what did she have to offer him in return?

Unlike Cormag, who had taken note of Moira's presence right away, Emma had not even noticed when Vaughn had stepped into the hall. How long had he stood there? Emma could not say. Her heart would never belong to him, just like Maggie's heart still belonged to the unknown Englishman of her past. Even after all these years, Ian did not stand a chance, doomed to a loveless marriage, forever jealous of a man he had never met.

Emma knew that if she were to accept Vaughn, she would make him miserable. If not today, then eventually, and she could not do that to him. He deserved better.

As though to prove her right, Finn stepped into the hall in that moment…

…and Emma's heart leapt as though it wished to break from her chest and rush to his side.

As though he were a part of her, she felt him near, and the look in his eyes spoke of more than interest or even affection. It reminded her of the day he had found her by the loch after her father's burial.

Inexplicably, her eyes were drawn to him, and the very sight of him made the breath catch in her throat. Her head spun, and yet, she felt deliriously happy.

Finn, too, seemed eager to seek her out. Gone was the hateful glare of the past years, replaced by a look that spoke of utter longing and devotion, emotions so overwhelming that he needed to take a deep breath to contain them.

Out of the corner of her eye, Emma noticed Vaughn starting toward her.

Swept up in the very sight of her, Finn tensed when he noticed Vaughn's attention drawn to the beautiful woman near the fire, her cheeks flushed with warmth and her brown eyes aglow like the embers in the hearth.

His heart banged against his rib cage in panic, and fear flooded his blood, quickly carried into every fibre of his body.

Beside him, Garrett chuckled, "I guess yer heart just spoke loud and clear."

Finn inhaled a deep breath, fighting the urge to delay Vaughn's progress across the room by all means necessary.

"Dunno stand here like a fool," Garrett hissed in a whisper. "Go and tell the lass how ye feel…before 'tis too late." Then his friend gave him a determined shove and sent him on his way.

Finn's feet moved on their own, his gaze incapable of looking anywhere but at Vaughn and Emma. The moment the other man reached her side, Finn groaned under his breath, wishing he had not hesitated. What were they talking about? Was Vaughn asking for her hand in this very moment?

Would that not be cruel irony? The moment Finn had finally worked up the nerve to address the woman he had loved for seven years was the very moment another stole her away?

Squinting his eyes, Finn watched them as Vaughn offered Emma his hand to help her to her feet. Then he smiled at her, slightly bowing his head before he spoke.

Finn could have screamed in frustration, his eyes glued to the young couple by the hearth, wishing and at the same time fearing to know what was being said.

Then Vaughn's face stilled, and Finn stopped in his tracks, his heart slamming to a halt as hope surged through his being.

More words were exchanged, and Finn reminded himself to put one foot in front of the other. He could not falter now.

"Pardon me," he said rather formally when he reached their side. His gaze met Vaughn's, dark and forlorn, and then turned to Emma, her own saddened as well. What had passed between them? "Emma, may I speak to ye for a moment."

Gritting his teeth, Vaughn inhaled a deep breath, and for a short moment, his gaze returned to Emma, a hint of incredulity in it. Then he mumbled something under his breath and stalked off.

When Finn turned to look at Emma, sadness as well as a hint of guilt clung to her face, and yet, there was something in her eyes that gave him hope. A smile seemed to tickle her lips, and the brown in her eyes shone deeper and warmer than he had ever seen it. "Can I speak to ye?"

This time, she did smile. "Aye," came her voice, light and breathy as though her own heart was racing as fast as his.

Breathing a sigh of relief, Finn took her by the elbow and guided her to the back of the hall and out into the corridor where they had kissed only a few hours ago. All the while, his heart thudded wildly in his chest, afraid to have been misled and be rejected by her.

Still, he needed to know if she cared for him or he would regret it for the rest of his life.

Chapter Nine
FOREVER IN A DAY

Emma's heart still ached for Vaughn, her inner eye unable to abandon the disappointed look on his face when she had stopped him before he could ask for her hand. He had looked so hopeful and eager, no apprehension in his heart with regard to her answer. Disappointment had come swift and mercilessly, and yet, the blue in his eyes had not spoken of a crushed heart. Had his regard for her truly been as deep as she had feared? Perhaps he would recover swiftly and would soon be able to grant his heart to a woman who could offer him hers in return.

Emma could only hope so.

The look on Finn's face when he had stepped up to her and Vaughn had been one of tense apprehension. Even now his hand on her elbow felt hardened by trepidation as he led her away.

Without looking at one another, they walked out into the corridor where he had found her earlier that evening, and Emma's breath caught in her throat at the memory of their encounter. Never in her life had she felt closer to anyone but in that moment. The way he had looked at her, spoken to her, the way he had said her name, his voice heavy with affection, and yet, vibrating with impatience, daring her to evade his question, had felt utterly wonderful as though they had always been close, kindred spirits, kept apart by circumstance. Did she dare believe it to be true?

Afraid of what he might say to her, and yet, wishing to hear him speak, Emma turned to Finn, noting the tension that held him almost rigid. Only a muscle in his jaw twitched, betraying an inner turmoil she would not have suspected. "Are ye all right?" she asked, trying to catch his gaze. "Ye look upset."

A scoff flew from his lips, and he shook his head. "Aye, I'm upset, lass." His voice sounded rough and filled with emotions held back. He inhaled a deep breath, and then his eyes met hers, held hers as though he did not dare look away. "Did Vaughn ask for yer hand?"

Emma flinched, and yet, her heart leapt into her throat with joy. "Well, he…," she began, noting the way his shoulders drew upward and his hands balled into fists. If she allowed herself to believe her own eyes, she would think he was jealous! Could that truly be?

A lot had happened in only one day. A lot had happened that Emma had not seen coming or would ever have expected. Still, she remembered the way he had spoken to her, the way he had looked at her-looked not glared! She remembered his kiss, speaking not merely of passion but affection, perhaps even love. She also remembered him asking her if she intended to marry Vaughn.

And now, here he was wanting to know-desperately from the looks of it!-if Vaughn had asked for her hand.

"What did ye say?" Finn growled out, and Emma could have sighed with happiness. He truly cared for her! All of a sudden, it was as plain as day. How could she not have seen it before?

"Emma!"

Jarred from her happy thoughts, Emma took note of the almost murderous expression in Finn's eyes as he glared at her. Still, this glare was a far-fetch from the one he had bestowed upon her at every encounter in the past seven years. It spoke less of anger and more of impatience, of a desperate need to have his question answered.

"Aye?" she said innocently, devilishly enjoying the pained look in his eyes.

"Would ye answer me?"

Cocking her head, she looked at him. "Why do ye wish to know?"

Finn's teeth ground together as he tried his best to keep himself under control. Still, Emma could see the pulse in his neck thudding wildly. His face darkened, and the steps that carried him toward her held something menacing. "Emma!" he warned once more as his steps urged her back against the wall.

Still, Emma could not help but smile. "If ye wish to know," she replied, lifting her chin as his hands settled to the left and right of her head, trapping her between himself and the wall, "then tell me why ye followed me that morning. Ye never answered me."

Finn's gaze narrowed, and a touch of incredulity came to his face. Inhaling a deep breath, he briefly closed his eyes. "I followed ye that morning because," he swallowed hard, "because yer kiss touched me…and I wanted to speak to ye."

A gust of air rushed from Emma's lungs, and her eyes suddenly misted with tears. "But…but ye said it hadna been a true kiss. Why then–?"

"It had been for me," he interrupted her, his gaze tracing the lone tear that rolled down her cheek, "but when I heard ye speak to yer friends, I knew it hadna been one for ye." His gaze met hers, and all of a sudden, she saw a different question there.

Once again, Emma felt like a young girl about to steal a kiss one cold wintry morning. She felt daring and adventurous. Her blood boiled in her veins, and her heart thudded loudly in her chest.

And then everything was simple.

As she had seven long years ago, Emma pulled Finn down into a kiss.

For a moment, he froze as he had then. Only this time, his paralysis lasted a mere second before his hands dropped from the wall and pulled her into his arms. He held her tightly and returned her kiss with the same longing she had felt in him when he had kissed her earlier that day.

Had only a few hours passed since then?

It felt like a lifetime.

Finn's heart danced and skipped and sang as he held the woman he loved in his arms.

Her kiss had caught him off guard as it had all those years ago. Only now, it was far from a soft peck of her lips on his, quick and rushed before she had darted away. Now, she lay in his arms as though she never wanted to leave again, her kiss demanding and an intention behind it that whispered of promises.

When she pulled back, her eyes shone bright and steady. "I kissed ye that day," she whispered, "because I wanted to."

"Aye?" was all Finn could articulate in that moment as he stared down at her, a part of him urging him not to believe his own eyes.

"Aye," she confirmed before her lips brushed against his once more.

Clearing his throat, Finn lifted his head, a frown drawing down his brows. "Then why the dare? Why did ye not simply–?"

"Simply?" Emma exclaimed, her eyes widening with annoyance as she shook her head at him. "There's nothing simple about...about declaring one's feelings." Lifting her chin in defiance, she glared up at him. "I might as well ask why ye didna confront me then and there. Why did ye never say anything in all those years?"

Finn's shoulders slumped when he saw the same fear in her eyes he had harboured in his own heart all this time. "I...I was afraid ye would reject me," he finally admitted, his heart clenching even now at the thought of showing himself so vulnerable. "I heard ye laugh and say our kiss was nothing, that it had meant nothing to ye. It broke my heart."

Emma sighed, and the anger vanished from her eyes. "I felt the same. I...I accepted the dare because it gave me an excuse to kiss ye without having it mean anything...if it didna mean anything to ye."

Shaking his head, Finn chuckled. "We were both trying to protect ourselves and ended up miserable for seven years. Can ye imagine what would've happened if I had reached ye that morning before ye could have met up with yer friends?"

A soft smile came to Emma's lips. "What would ye have done? Would ye have told me the truth?"

Finn shrugged. "I dunno know. I can only hope I would have said...or done something to show ye that yer kiss had meant something to me, that ye could trust me to confide in me as well."

"And then?" she asked, her eyes shining with hope.

Finn shrugged as his heart calmed and the fear of rejection slowly receded. Still, he remembered the way she had teased him, tortured him, in fact, she still had not answered his question about Vaughn's proposal. "I dunno know," he replied, willing the joy in his heart not to show on his face. "All I'm asking of ye now is to be honest with me. If ye dunno care for me, then tell me so honestly so that I might move on and find love elsewhere."

At his words, Emma blinked, shock coming to her brown eyes before her hands shot forward and she grabbed him by the front of his shirt. "Don't ye dare! Ye're mine, Finnegan MacDrummond. D'ye hear? Ye're mine, and ye've always been." She inhaled a deep breath, the look in her eyes fierce as she held on to him. "I only wish I'd claimed ye earlier."

Finn's heart danced in his chest as it had never before. "Claim me?" he asked with a chuckle as his arms came around her, holding her to him with the same determination he saw in her eyes as well. "Are ye claiming me now?"

A wicked smile came to her face. "Aye, I am."

"And I have no say in the matter?"

Shaking her head, she pulled him down to her until their noses almost touched. "I'm afraid not." Then she kissed him the way she had kissed him only moments ago, and Finn finally realised that her heart truly belonged to him.

"Does that mean ye're not going to marry Vaughn?" he asked teasingly. Still, his heart tensed at the mere thought of her tied to another. After all, marriages were agreed upon for all kinds of reasons. Simply because she did not love Vaughn did not mean she had not agreed to marry him.

Frowning, she stared at him. "Of course not. It wouldna be fair to him. He deserves better."

Finn chuckled, enjoying the feel of her in his arms. "And I don't?"

"No, ye and I were made for each other," she said as though stating a fact. Finn had to admit it rather pleased him. "We're both equally fearful and stubborn to have not said a word about this for seven years." For a moment, she shook her head in disbelief, a hint of disappointment on her face. Then, however, her gaze met his, and her eyes lit up with happiness. "We deserve each other, wouldn't ye agree?"

"Aye," Finn laughed, realising that he could not wait to get to know the woman he had loved for so long. Never had they truly spoken to one another, and yet, he had never felt closer to anyone before.

Pulling her tighter against him, Finn looked down at her, feeling at peace for the first time in years. "We should've been together all those years," he whispered, "but there's no use in crying over something we canna change. All we can do is make certain that we willna waste any more time."

Smiling up at him, Emma nodded.

Finn swallowed, then inhaled a deep breath before he said, "Emma Stewart, will ye marry me...tomorrow?"

Her brown eyes went wide. "Tomorrow? But 'tis Christmas!"

"I dunno care," Finn said laughing. "I dunno want to waste another minute. I want ye to be my wife, and I want to start our lives together...tomorrow, and not a moment later."

Laughing, Emma flung herself into his arms. "Aye, I'll marry ye...tomorrow."

With his heart overflowing with joy, Finn spun his bride-to-be in a circle, holding her tight as they hugged and laughed, both overwhelmed by all that could happen in a day.

Finn vowed that he would never again allow fear to hold him back.

It was not worth it.

Not for a single moment.

Epilogue

Never would Emma have imagined that she had in fact decorated the great hall the day before for her own wedding day. And yet, here she was, dressed in her finest gown, a smile on her face she could not seem to shake and a man by her side whom she had loved for as long as she could remember.

After Finn had asked for her hand the night before, they had immediately gone to seek out Cormag to ask for his blessing as well as his approval to have their wedding ceremony on Christmas morning. Oddly enough, Cormag had acted as though he had all but expected them.

And he had not been the only one.

The whole of Clan MacDrummond gathered in the great hall that morning, their eyes shining with joy and their cheeks flushed from the cold. Cheerful whispers echoed through the hall until the moment the wedding ceremony began. Then silence fell over them as everyone strained to hear Emma and Finn exchange their vows.

While *everyone* had been surprised that Emma and Finn were to be married on Christmas morning, *no one* had been surprised to hear that they *were* to be married. In fact, many had congratulated them, mumbling something about them finally getting their happy ending. It would seem the whole of Clan MacDrummond had been aware of Emma's and Finn's true feelings for one another and had considered it only a matter of time until they would tie the knot.

The only ones who had been blind had been Emma and Finn themselves.

Smiling at Finn as he held her hand in his, Emma pushed all thoughts of the past away. Certainly, they had wasted time, being so fearful of rejection, of having their hearts broken. However, dwelling on that loss would only cost them more.

Today was a day for celebration in every way, and tomorrow, their new life would begin.

Emma could not wait. She only wished that others would find the same happiness that had so unexpectedly found her. Was there still a chance for Maggie and Ian to find joy in their marriage? Would Cormag and Moira ever admit that they were in love? Would Garrett find his wife and bring her back to Seann Dachaigh Tower?

Emma could only hope so.

After all, a lot could happen in a day.

The End

About Bree

USA Today bestselling author, Bree Wolf has always been a language enthusiast (though not a grammarian!) and is rarely found without a book in her hand or her fingers glued to a keyboard. Trying to find her way, she has taught English as a second language, traveled abroad and worked at a translation agency as well as a law firm in Ireland. She also spent loooong years obtaining a BA in English and Education and an MA in Specialized Translation while wishing she could simply be a writer. Although there is nothing simple about being a writer, her dreams have finally come true.

"A big thanks to my fairy godmother!"

Currently, Bree has found her new home in the historical romance genre, writing Regency novels and novellas. Enjoying the mix of fact and fiction, she occasionally feels like a puppet master, forcing her characters into ever-new situations that will put their strength, their beliefs, their love to the test, hoping that in the end they will triumph and get the happily-ever-after we are all looking for.

You can find details of her work at
www.BreeWolf.com

A Yuletide Highlander

~ Highland Heather Romancing a Scot Book 7 ~

Collette Cameron

A gentlewoman afraid for her life. A Scottish warrior willing to risk all to protect her.

Having fled her childhood home, noblewoman Sarah Paine has one thought when she barges into Gregor McTavish's office… Escaping the blackguards chasing her. She never expected the brawny Highlander to endanger his life to help her, or that his gallantry and kindness would earn her trust and eventually win her heart. Neither could she anticipate the impossible choice she'd have to make…Her love for Gregor or her brother's safety.

When Gregor left Scotland to start a new life in England, he gave up his dream of becoming a doctor. A year later, bored and no closer to finding the contentment he sought, he reluctantly decides to return home. Until a desperate, bonnie lass interrupts his plans. He convinces Sarah to trust him and accept his protection, but what was meant as a distraction becomes something much more meaningful, and he doesn't ever want to let her go.

For the first time in his life, Gregor anticipates celebrating Christmas, but the madman pursuing Sarah casts a shadow over the holiday. Can the Yuletide work its magic, allowing Gregor to apprehend the fiend and at last bring him and Sarah the love and peace they desperately seek?

Chapter One

The oak entry to Stapleton Shipping and Supplies flew open, and a wet young man bolted inside, his chest rising and falling as he gasped for breath. Panic pinched his thin face as he swiftly shut the door behind him. His hand encircled a small blade wedged into the worn leather belt encircling his navy bridge coat as his frightened gaze careened from corner to corner of Gregor McTavish's office.

Gregor had seen that same terrified look in the ebony eyes of a fox caught in a snare. Still grasping the quill hovering over his account books, whilst gripping the dirk he'd yanked from his boot when the youth dashed inside, he relaxed his tense posture.

This scared spitless waif, his back angled toward him while peeking at the pier around the window sash, wasn't a threat.

Scrutinizing the dreary, water-soaked gray docks, Gregor lowered the quill while slipping his blade back into his boot.

Rain pelted a trio of burly, unkempt thugs heatedly arguing several yards away. Wrath contorted their apparent leader's face, and he flung a stocky arm toward a narrow alley a block farther along the wharf.

The largest of the other men shook his head, and the brute drove his open hand into the man's chest then smacked the shorter, swarthy-skinned sailor on the side of the head with enough force to send him stumbling backward a few steps.

Fists balled, the other man took a menacing step forward, but the bully puffed out his chest and yelled something. Whatever he said stalled the other man mid-step. After a slight pause and exchanging infuriated glances, his two companions thundered off.

Where to, and why did every instinct suggest the lad would know? Gregor veered a swift, hooded glance toward the boy before refocusing his regard on the sailor.

Only three buildings opened directly onto this section of docks. Was his uninvited visitor fleeing those thugs?

His hands on his hips, a fierce scowl pulling the corners of his eyes and mouth downward, the remaining sailor rotated slowly to the left and then to the right. He obviously searched for something. *Or someone.* His acute gaze swept past Stapleton Shipping and Supplies then slowly gravitated back.

Even from his seat, Gregor recognized the shrewdness quirking the sailor's mouth and gleaming in his narrowed eyes fixated on his office. His nape prickled.

Danger.

He stood, pushing his unfashionably long hair over his shoulder. In the Highlands he seldom tied it back, and he oft' forgot to do so in the morning since moving to London almost a year ago. He rather enjoyed the shocked expressions his blond mane caused the stuffy upper echelons of society.

The boy's narrow shoulders and back quaked. From cold or fear? "Can I help ye?"

The lad spun to face him, his frightened gaze ricocheting about the office once more.

Nae, no' a laddie. A lass. A comely one at that.

"I'm Gregor McTavish." He introduced himself, careful to keep his tone calm and soothing in the hopes he might alleviate some of her fright. "My cousin's wife owns these buildings and this establishment."

"Those men attempted to abduct me." Still breathing hard, she motioned toward the window. "Might I stay here for a few minutes until the last one leaves?"

"Aye, of course." Brutes like those outside had no honorable business with bonnie lasses.

At first glance, because of her height, bulky, dark blue overcoat, and sailor's cap, Gregor had mistaken her for a boy. She wasn't as young as he'd first believed either, though she certainly was not on the shelf. About the ages of his Ferguson step-cousins—somewhere in her early to mid-twenties, he'd guess.

Another inspection of the dock sent alarm sparking up his spine.

The unsavory fellow tramped across the wooden walkway, straight for Stapleton Shipping.

Damnation.

"Quick, lass. Come here. He's comin'." Gregor made an urgent gesture. "Hide beneath my desk. *Now.*"

In a blink, she dashed across the room, and he stepped back to allow her to crawl into the kneehole.

No sooner had Gregor resumed his seat and dipped his quill in the inkwell than the office door sprang open again. With deliberate intent, he took his time and finished the entry. His mind on the terrified woman crouched inches from his knees, he almost swore upon realizing he'd recorded two hundred and fifty barrels of molasses instead of twenty-five.

The sailor blocking the entry roughly cleared his throat and angrily stamped his feet. The wind blasted rain into the entry, yet the man made no effort to shut the door.

The blighter earned himself a longer wait. Gregor suppressed a grin and dipped the nib into the ink again.

"Give me a moment," he muttered, taking far longer than a child's first attempt to form the letters of each word. After scribbling a few more lines—he might've ordered more flour than the whole village of Craigcutty could consume in a year—he finished and set the quill aside.

Twisting his mouth into a thin, hard smile, he rested a forearm on the desk and took the blackguard's measure from greasy brown hair, unshaven face and stained clothing, to his even filthier boots. The man's rank odor wafted across the room, and despite the open entry, Gregor's nostrils twitched in protest.

"Come to apply for one of the crew openin's, have ye?" He nonchalantly cradled his jaw in his palm. "Have ye any experience?"

Upon hearing Gregor's Scot's brogue, a sneer curled the man's upper lip. "No. I'm lookin' for a fugitive. She stole a large purse from my employer and was last seen runnin' in this direction."

"Ach," Gregor murmured understandingly.

The sailor's astute, accusing eyes searched every inch of the office, lingering for a long moment on the half-open door leading to the stairwell and Gregor's apartment. Suspicion flared the man's nostrils before he tore his distrustful scrutiny away.

"I can assure ye, nae lawless lassies have entered this buildin' today." He leaned back and flung a casual look about the tidy office. "As ye can see for yerself," he waved a languid hand, "there's naebody here but Cat and me."

Upon hearing his name, the long-haired white and orange tabby opened his citrine green eyes and yawned then arched his back before padding over to Gregor and hopping onto the desk. Purring, and with complete disregard for the ledger he stood upon, he pushed his head beneath Gregor's hand, demanding he be petted.

Gregor sliced a pointed look to the open doorway, water dripping from the overhang and wetting the floor. "If ye'll excuse me." He tapped the ledger with the fingers of his other hand. "I've much work to do. Monthly reports, ye ken. Inventory to take. Supplies to order." *Lasses to protect.* "Receipts to record." *Riddin' my office of stinkin' horses' arses.* "Och, my employer is most demandin'," he rattled on, giving a woeful shake of his head and wholly enjoying the impatience creasing the sea tar's weather-worn face.

Cat, now sprawled full-length across the register, his eyes half-closed in lazy contentment, made a mockery of Gregor's claim he'd work to attend.

He'd rescued the starving kitten from the hard life of a wharf cat after he first arrived in London. Loneliness had compelled him, though he'd never admitted as much to a soul. For the first time in his life, there wasn't the pleasant chaos of a dozen or more people around at any given moment.

The spoiled beast didn't hesitate to show his gratitude. Although at times, his affection embarrassed Gregor. Cat lazily lifted a paw and patted his hand as if to say, "I require your attention. A belly scratch, if you please."

"Nae, I'll no' be rubbin' yer belly." He gathered the cat, frowning at the smudged entries, and placed the ball of sharp-clawed fluff on the floor.

With a dismissive flick of his impossibly long tail, and a few fresh ebony ink stains accenting his silky coat, Cat sauntered to the stairs.

When the man continued to lurk in the doorway, Gregor summoned his most formidable look. The one that usually sent men scuttling away.

"Yer sure I canna talk he into applyin' for a position? I've a ship sailin' to Africa in a fortnight that needs hands." He scratched the back of his head, raking his gaze up and down the man's form. "Can ye cook?"

The sailor's mouth skewed into another wide sneer, revealing missing, broken, and yellowed teeth. He folded dirty fingers, one by one, around the bone knife hilt protruding from his belt and, spreading his legs, ticked his chin upward as brutes of his ilk were wont to do when bent on threatening others.

"You best be tellin' me the truth, you bloody Scot." He settled another doubtful look on the stairs.

Bloody Scot? Was the man a lackwit that he dared come in here and hurl insults? This Sassenach piece of horse shite had just tipped the scales from patience to annoyance.

The sailor wasn't a puny weakling, but Gregor and his twin had been called giants on more than a few occasions. And for good reason. Standing well over six and a half feet and massively built, even at three and thirty, no man had ever bettered him in a physical challenge—except for his twin.

Only because of the terrified young woman huddled beneath his desk had he kept a tight rein on his temper and tongue. Otherwise, this cod piece would've already found himself sprawled on the dock—unconscious and arse up.

"Cap'n Santano doesn't take kindly to people interferin' in his business," the blighter pressed.

Why wasn't Gregor surprised to learn this sod worked for Santano? The captain's nefarious reputation preceded him, and six months ago, Stapleton Shipping and Supplies had refused his request to enter into a commercial relationship. Infuriated and full of his own self-importance, Santano had taken his business elsewhere.

Leisurely rising, and wholly unrepentant, Gregor used his immense size to intimidate the churl. He spoke slowly and deliberately as if addressing a simpleton. "If I tell ye nae thief entered this establishment then nae thief is here." He made a show of lifting his clenched fists waist high. "Do ye ken?"

The shady fellow's eyes shifted back and forth several times, and he nervously fingered his scraggy tobacco-stained beard with one hand while the other flexed upon his knife handle. He gave a grudging nod, his bluster disappearing in the face of someone capable of pounding his ugly face into pulp.

"Well, if you do see a tall, skinny blonde wearin' a peacoat, notify the cap'n at once." He half-turned and examined the pier. "While in port, he's usually aboard the *Mary Elizabeth*, at the Seven Seas Alehouse or," a lewd smile curved his mouth. "Madam Mionnet's."

Ah, the infamous brothel. No man valuing his ballocks sampled those whores. Most were fraught with disease.

"The chit usually has a scrawny, crippled whelp with her, about this tall." Santano's henchmen raised his hand midriff high. "You'd best take care, or she and that street rat will pick your pockets clean."

Gregor remained silent as he maneuvered around the corner of the desk. In about thirty seconds, he'd toss the bloody bugger out the door. Mustering what scant patience he had left, he managed to keep his annoyance from showing. "What's yer name, sailor, in case I needed to reach ye?"

"Yeates." After spearing him another hostile glare, he left, not bothering to shut the door behind him.

"Bloody rotter." Gregor closed the door, and though it was only just after two in the afternoon, turned the key in the lock and slid the bolt home as well.

Rustling alerted him to his fugitive's intention.

"Stay where ye are. He's still watchin' the buildin'. I'm nae sure he believed me when I said ye weren't here, lass."

Her sharp intake of breath revealed she believed her appearance had fooled him into thinking she was a male. Hadn't she glanced in a looking glass of late?

He made a pretense of adjusting the three model ships displayed in the bay window then rearranged a telescope and a couple of maps before turning away.

"Have you a back entrance?" Refinement, but not the haughty cold tone of privileged nobles, colored her voice.

"Aye, but I think ye should stay here for an hour or two."

Or longer.

Gregor placed a sextant atop one of the maps and then for good measure, added an open compass, positioned just so. Standing back, hands on his hips, he admired his handiwork. *No' bad.*

"You don't understand. My brother's out there. Alone and scared." On all fours, she peeked 'round the side of his desk, a few fair tendrils dangling on either side of her face.

Cleaned up and with a bit of meat on her bones, she'd be a right bonnie lassie.

He bent and flicked a couple of dead flies from the windowsill. Brushing his hands on his trousers, he casually turned halfway around. "Where is he?"

"I left him hiding amongst some barrels outside the cooper's." She jerked her head in that direction. "I attracted those ruffians' attention to lure them away."

One eye on the marina, Gregor ran a hand over his jaw. "I dinna believe ye stole anythin', so why are they after ye?"

At once, a shuttered expression masked her pale face. She pulled her soft mouth into a tight line and fixed her attention on the floor, her gold-tipped lashes fanning her hollow cheeks. Her short nails dug into the floor said what she feared to.

She didn't trust him.

Gregor couldn't blame her, and compassion welled behind his ribs. Survival on London's unforgiving streets meant never trusting anyone.

He eyed her covertly from beneath half-closed eyes. What dire circumstances had forced her and her brother to this life? He hadn't a doubt she'd not been born into it. Everything about her so far suggested she came from a genteel background.

There were few things he liked more than solving a challenging mystery, and this young woman was a puzzle, to be sure. Och...a good fight was always enjoyable, but on occasion, he preferred using his brains rather than brute strength. Only on occasion, mind you.

On hands and knees, the lass edged to the room's farthest corner before scrambling to her feet. Wise on her part. No one outside could see her in the lengthening shadows.

Since becoming his cousin-in-law Yvette McTavish's manager for her London warehouses, his life had been nothing short of mind-numbingly dull. He'd only accepted the position because he was ready—*och, bloody damn desperate*—to do something, anything, different than continue at Craiglocky Keep, his cousin's castle.

Until just short of a year ago, Craiglocky was the only place Gregor had ever lived, and his only purpose had been to serve his laird, Ewan McTavish. He'd loved both, still did, but discontentment ate away at him, growing and growing and growing...

Except for him, everyone at the Keep had married, and truthfully, he left as much to escape his extended family's matchmaking attempts as to try his hand at something new. At one time he thought to become a doctor, and he still dabbled in the healing arts from time to time when called upon to do so. But there hadn't been any real need for his services after Yvette commissioned the building of a local hospital.

Gregor had also believed he'd marry Lily Ellsworth, but several years ago she'd fallen in love with another. He hadn't been altogether shocked to realize he wasn't heartbroken. She'd been too young for him, in any event. Feeling much older than he was, he'd decided to leave the Highlands for a time.

Someday, he'd return. Scotland was as much a part of him as the blood tunneling through his veins at this very moment. He missed the fragrant heather, the craggy rocks, the hairy cattle, and the bright green meadows. He even preferred the Highland's harsh, unforgiving weather to London's perpetual stench and coal-laden skies.

"Mr. McTavish, I must find my brother right away. He'll be frightened." A tinge of fear peppered her impatience.

"Aye, lass, of course ye do. I'm just thinkin'." Not about rescuing her brother, but what he'd chosen to leave behind. Those musings were a waste of time, and before him was an opportunity to relieve the tedium his life had become as well as to help someone in desperate need. "We canna be too careful with the likes of those blackguards."

She muttered something unintelligible but which sounded distinctly unflattering.

One hand on his hip, he pulled his ear, trying to read her. He'd likely regret becoming involved, but if it brought a dose of excitement into his existence, well, damn it, it'd be worth it. "Ye can wait upstairs and have yerself somethin' to eat while I fetch yer brother."

Arms folded, she eyed him warily. "Why should I trust you?"

Chapter Two

Gregor raised his eyebrows and shoulders at the same time.

"Och, as I see it," he perused the street again, "ye haven't any choice. Ye either accept my aide or take yer chances out there." He jabbed a thumb toward the window. "Need I remind, ye, lass, ye bolted in here on yer own accord?"

Her high cheekbones standing out against her pale skin, she gave a terse nod. "I'd heard good things about Stapleton Shipping and Supplies. That they were honest and fair. I'd hoped someone here would help me."

"Aye, ye made a wise decision." Yeates was right about one thing. She was too thin. "Now, tell me. What does yer brother look like? What's he wearin'?"

"Kipp has dark blond hair and hazel eyes. He has on clothing similar to mine." Gregor would bet all the supplies in the warehouses and every drop of whisky in Scotland that wasn't the boy's real name.

He slipped an arm into his caped great coat. He'd go out the front door and draw away anyone watching the building. He eyed the wet floor. It would have to wait until he returned. "I'll try to find the lad and bring him back here." He stuffed his other arm inside the heavy garment. He'd rather don his tartan, but while in Rome and all that…"What's somethin' only he would ken, so he believes ye sent me to fetch him?"

Staying in the shadows, she scratched her temple and blew out a resigned sigh. "Kipp's… He's…" Her voice trailed off.

Gregor glanced up from wrestling with his buttons. "He's what?"

"He's…um…slow mentally and can become easily confused." A challenge shone in her eyes. "He walks with a limp and running is difficult for him."

"Aye. It's good ye told me." That was why she'd left her brother behind. He'd have been caught for certain. Gregor would need a wagon then. "What's yer name, lass?"

"I'm Sydney Blanes."

He stifled a snort. Not her real name either. Who was she? What had her so terrified? Och, he'd learn the truth. All in good time.

She pulled the atrocious hat from her head, and a cascade of blonde hair as light as his tumbled to beyond her shoulders.

Momentarily speechless—not typical at all—he forced his attention away. Odin's teeth. She was exquisite. He pointed to the door leading to the stairwell. "As I said, help yerself to any food ye find upstairs. My cat's name is Cat."

Snorting again, loud and mockingly, she shoved the hair off her face. "Thought long and hard about that clever moniker, I'll vow, Highlander."

Was she teasing him?

"I suppose ye'd have picked Fluffy, or Pumpkin, or Cinnamon, or some other undignified name?"

"No." She shook her head, that sunny cascade swinging about her shoulders. "He looks like a Marmalade."

Marmalade? Nae. Cat would be most offended. Marmalade was sweet, and Cat most certainly was no'.

Fighting a grimace, he put on his beaver top hat. Blast but he preferred a tam. That sensible covering at least kept his head warm. *Laird,* how he missed wearing a leather vest and woolen kilt or trews, not all this refined popinjay falderol. Still, he'd chosen to leave the Highlands and become a proper man of business. These foppish trappings were part of the sacrifices he'd opted to make.

Yvette had been most adamant he couldn't parade about Stapleton Shipping and Supplies—or London, for that matter—bare-arsed, wearing a kilt, with a sword strapped to his hip and a dirk shoved in his boots, more was the pity. Nothing short of the archangel Gabriel appearing and demanding he do so would induce Gregor to forgo his dirk, however.

Withdrawing a key from his pocket, he wielded the iron toward the back entrance.

"That door's bolted from within, and I'll lock this one. Ye'll be safe as long as ye stay out of sight." Fastening the last button of his greatcoat, he canted his head. "Lass, I'll have yer word ye'll be here when I return. Dinna do somethin' foolish and go off on yer own. Santano has an ugly reputation."

Indecision warred in her eyes. Her situation was precarious either way. Forced to trust a complete stranger or risk being seen and apprehended by Santano's thugs when she tried to find her brother.

"What if someone comes in?" she asked, surprisingly pragmatic.

"Unlikely, but as I said, my cousin-in-law owns this establishment." He flicked a finger toward the window. "And several ships in yonder harbor as well. Anyone who has a key can be trusted. Now, what can I say to yer brother that he'll ken ye sent me?"

"Tell Kipp…, tell him Satan found us."

Gregor paused in pulling on his gloves, one eyebrow arched to his hairline. She wasn't dafty, was she? "*Satan?*"

For the first time, her mouth curled into some semblance of a smile, and he found himself staring once more. A man could fall in love with that smile. That face.

"Yes, Mr. McTavish. Satan. That's what we call Santano—the man who commandeered our father's ship, the *Mary Elizabeth* and is responsible for our parents' deaths."

Sarah Paine hesitated at the top of the stairs, still wondering if she'd made the right decision in trusting Gregor McTavish. For certain, she wasn't ready to reveal her real name to him as yet. Drawing a fortifying breath, she pushed the handle opening the door to his apartment.

Cat—*absurd name for a pet*—brushed past her before disappearing through one of the four doorways leading off the common room. The entire floor must be McTavish's private living quarters. Clearly a man's abode, for no signs of a feminine touch met her scrutiny, she stepped into a large, open-beamed room lined by windows on the far wall.

She hadn't even thought to ask if he was married. Relief swept her that no angry or confused wife met her on the stoop, demanding to know who she was and what she thought she was doing.

Two russet-toned wingback chairs and a braided rag rug sat before a cozy, blue-and-white tiled unlit fireplace. On the wall opposite the windows, a sofa, along with two side tables, formed a neat row. A painting of what must be the Scottish Highlands hung above the tobacco-brown brocade sofa.

At first glance, she'd assumed the Scot a Dane or Norseman—possibly a fierce Viking descendent. Actually, she'd thought him possibly the most powerfully-built man she'd ever seen. Mayhap one of the most attractive too.

No mayhap about it.

Ludicrous. Sarah gave herself a severe mental shake. She'd no business noticing such things when she literally feared for her life. Head angled, she studied the fairly-decent painting, the only decoration of any kind displayed in the room. Did the great blond Highlander pine for his homeland?

That she well understood, for not a day passed that she wasn't homesick for the tropical island where she and Christopher, her brother's real name, had been born. Truth to tell, she missed the vibrant turquoise ocean, the heavily-scented blossoms, and the bright green yellow-billed parrots, but little else.

Most especially not the snakes, spiders, crocodiles, and insufferable humidity.

Head still tilted, she studied the rugged emerald landscape so very different than Jamaica. Each held an entirely disparate type of beauty, neither more nor less appealing than the other.

Melancholy engulfed her. Would she ever see her homeland again? Yes. She must. There was unfinished business there. Chilled, she folded her arms and circled the room, impressed by its neatness.

Why she'd expected otherwise, she wasn't sure. Perchance because Papa and Chris weren't particularly tidy.

The office below had been organized, and except for two stacks of paper on a narrow table behind McTavish's desk, nothing lay strewn or stacked about. Stapleton Shipping and Supplies had an estimable reputation, and that—along with a great deal of desperation—had prompted her to bolt inside as she fled Santano's henchmen.

Her stomach growled and cramped, reminding her she and Chris hadn't eaten since fleeing their lodgings down the back stairwell yesterday morning. Barely escaping at that.

Poor, sweet Chris. He'd been asking for something to eat all morning.

How had Santano found them after all this time? Had she grown careless? Pressing two fingertips between her eyebrows, she closed her eyes and reflected back over the past few weeks.

No. She hadn't.

More likely, her landlord couldn't resist a bribe. Knowing Santano's thugs as she did, the hardly-more-than-a-closet-room she and Chris had called home for the past few months had undoubtedly been ransacked.

There'd be no returning. Not even to collect their meager belongings.

Three years ago, when calamity befell her parents, with nowhere else to go, and scared witless, they'd arrived in England. At once, although she'd never met them, Sarah sought her maternal grandparents, the Viscount and Viscountess Rolandson at their London house.

The self-important butler had coolly taken their measure from gaunt faces to soiled and wrinkled clothing. With a sneer curling his thin lips and elevating his hooked nose, he'd looked down upon them as if they smelled of pond scum or horse excrement and flatly refused them admittance. After announcing with a peculiar, haughty glee that Lord Rolandson had been dead a decade.

They *had* smelled and Sarah flushed in renewed humiliation.

When she'd attempted to press her point, and insisted she be allowed to speak to her grandmother, she'd been informed in no uncertain terms that she and Chris were to remove themselves at once. The dowager viscountess had no wish to see them, and if they dared to show their unwelcome persons again, the authorities would be called.

It seemed Grandmother Rolandson hadn't forgiven her gentle-bred daughter for refusing to marry the stuffy English lord her parents had selected for her. That explained the unopened letters returned to Mama over the years.

One of the few times Mama had spoken of her childhood, she'd mentioned the grand house she'd been raised in and which was unentailed. The mansion was settled upon the viscountess by her father when she wed. For whatever reason, Mama said, her mother preferred the house over the viscounty property in Mayfair.

Her mother rarely spoke of her elopement with Papa or her privileged upbringing. She'd never once complained about the long months Papa spent away sailing or about the hardships of living in the tropics.

In fact, Sarah had only discovered her grandmother's address when she opened the satchel Mama had stuffed into her hands as she ordered her and Chris to run and not turn back. Several letters, along with jewels, money, and a few other important documents lay inside the bag. She hadn't even been certain the dowager viscountess would be in residence.

Sarah gripped the hidden pocket she'd sewn into her trousers. Eyes closed, she rubbed her cheek against the sturdy wool collar of her coat. Papa's coat. His scent had long since disappeared, but the durable outerwear withstood England's harsh rain, wind, and cold.

The pocket she clutched held what few jewels and coins remained, and a couple of documents wrapped in leather, one of which was the deed of purchase for the *Mary Elizabeth*. The pouch contained a key as well, and she'd long suspected that was what Santano sought.

Even with her eyes tightly closed, Sarah couldn't block the memory of that awful day when her life crumbled apart.

"Find Captain Pritchard," Mama had ordered. "Tell him your father was right, and Santano's have commandeered the *Mary Elizabeth*. The captain will see you and Chris safely to England. The arrangements have all been made, my darling."

Her parents must've suspected Santano would betray Papa.

"No, Mama," Sarah had wept. "I cannot leave you."

Chapter Three

Weak as she had been, Mama had taken Sarah by the shoulders and kissed her forehead.

"You must, my darling girl. I don't believe Santano is above killing you and your brother. I shall only slow you down, and we both know my health is too fragile to travel. Now go, and always remember how much your father and I love you. Take care of Chris. He'll need you more than ever now."

A lone tear dribbled slowly over Sarah's cheek, and she hastily swiped it away.

For over three years she and Chris had hidden in the seedier parts of London, moving frequently, and using false names. She'd avoided the docks and other areas where sailors were wont to roam, with the exception of a weekly visit to a street urchin to learn if the *Mary Elizabeth* had laid anchor.

Twice, she'd learned the ship had put into port. The emaciated waif spying on her behalf earned a half-penny for his efforts and an extra for keeping silent about her inquiries. But last week, a wicked cough had kept Chris abed, and she hadn't been able to query about ship arrivals.

The one time she hadn't checked in all these long months, blister it, and Santano had slithered ashore. Eyes and fists squeezed hard, Sarah, released a frustrated groan. Despite all of her efforts, she hadn't been careful enough.

Santano. The despicable rotter.

He'd been father's closest friend, his first officer aboard the *Mary Elizabeth.* Until greed and thirst for power had overcome him, and the fiend had convinced other spineless traitors to mutiny. Everyone who'd stood with Papa now lay dead on the bottom of the Atlantic Ocean.

At least that's the story Sarah had parceled together.

With a ragged breath, she shook off her morose musings. There was nothing she could do about the past. *Yet.* For now, she must concentrate her efforts on avoiding Santano.

Taking a quick peek into the other four rooms, she discovered a kitchen area, two bedrooms, and what appeared to be a good-sized storage closet. Cat had made himself comfortable on one of the main room's windowsills and one striped leg pointed ceilingward, was engaged in a thorough grooming session.

Her stomach complained loudly again, and Sarah yielded to her hunger, cutting a thin slice of delicious-smelling brown bread and a small piece of hard cheese.

Standing off to the side of the multi-paned windows, she nibbled her simple meal and surveyed the wharf. Dock laborers rushed to and fro as wagons and carts laden with all manner of goods rumbled in both directions, first delivering products and then carting others away.

She shivered, her wet, woolen coat offering little warmth. Would she ever become accustomed to the damp grayness that shrouded England and penetrated her bones? How she longed for the Caribbean's fresh air, colorful flowers, and bird calls.

Naturally, now that Santano had found her, she'd have to leave London. Immediately.

The bread she'd been chewing dried on her tongue, but a wry smile curved her mouth. Where could she go? Strangers, especially a cripple, would draw unwanted attention in the villages and smaller towns.

She had lived frugally these past three years, but little of the money Mama had sent remained. Even before her grandmother had turned them away, she'd been afraid to seek employment. It was too easy to track her. Besides, she couldn't leave Chris alone while she worked. And the truth of it was, she possessed no skill beyond an average education that might gain her a respectable position.

A gust of wind splattered raindrops against the windowpanes, and careful to remain out of sight, she searched for any sign of Chris or Gregor McTavish. He hadn't been gone long, but neither was the cooper's very far.

There was no help for it. She must swallow her pride, temper her misgivings, and ask the giant Scot to help her leave London and mayhap find employment in her new local. Though why or how he'd do so, she couldn't fathom.

They were strangers, after all. But for whatever reason, she trusted the Highlander.

Over the years, she'd learned to rely on gut instinct above all else. And the plain, ugly truth was, she had no choice but to put her faith in him. Nevertheless, she didn't like it one jot.

Popping the last morsel of cheese into her mouth, she scowled. What was taking the Scot so long?

She bent forward, squinting at the docks, and several strands of lanky hair swung forward. Whilst running from Santano's men, she'd lost the ribbon tying it back. Her hair, in desperate need of washing, had dried in straggly tendrils. She flipped the strands over her shoulder, longing for days past when a warm, scented bath was the norm and not a wishful luxury.

When clean and her stomach full, she'd been able to sleep through the night without fear of someone breaking into their room. She'd taken to wearing men's clothing a scant fortnight after setting foot in England after continually being approached by men in search of female company. It was a wonder, really, that she hadn't been set upon or despoiled. The knife at her waist acted as a detriment to the less bold.

Her stomach tightened again, but not from hunger. She couldn't see the cooper's from here, but surely Gregor been able to find Chris by now. Unless Santano's goons had...

She tamped down the unthinkable notion. Chris was just hiding. She'd taught him well, and much like a fawn hidden by a doe, he'd learned not to budge until Sarah returned for him.

Another overloaded wagon rumbled through a puddle, its wheels spraying dirty water to the sides, and she bit her lip.

Should she go look for Chris herself?

No, confound it. She'd given her word she'd stay here. So stupid, to entrust him to a stranger.

Gregor had promised he'd find him. If she wasn't here, and he returned with Chris, her brother would panic for certain. He didn't deal well with change, and he'd grown progressively weaker these past months.

Twelve years his senior, Sarah had been thrilled when Mama delivered the skinny, sickly babe. His birth had been difficult, and for the first several weeks, they'd feared he'd die. Another couple of stressful months passed before anyone realized he'd never be quite normal.

As she'd told Gregor, Chris's was a trifle slow mentally, and his right leg dragged when he walked. His right arm bent slightly inward toward his torso as well. But he was sweet and kind and Sarah adored him. He was her beloved brother. She'd promised Mama to keep him safe and never to leave him, and she meant to keep that vow.

He was also the rightful heir to Bellewood House and the *Mary Elizabeth*, and someday, somehow, she'd see his inheritance restored to him or the properties sold and the monies used to ensure he never wanted for anything. And if she ever married—not likely, but not impossible—her husband would have to agree to allow Chris live with them. Always.

With one eye on the wharf as she awaited Gregor's return, she fingered the outline of the key hidden at her waist.

Did Santano truly know about the chest hidden in Bellewood's cellars? He must, but how had he come by the knowledge? As far as Sarah was aware, only she and her parents knew of its existence.

One time, about a year after Chris's birth, Papa had shown her a hidden chamber behind a rock wall beneath the house's main floor. Hardly larger than the pantry, he'd made her swear to tell no one about the small room. The hidey-hole contained a locked mid-sized chest, a few leather packets, several small coin pouches—which Mama had given her when Sarah fled Jamaica—two elaborate gold chalices as well as a few jewels.

At the time, Sarah hadn't questioned why Papa had revealed the hidden chamber. He'd made it clear because of Chris's mental and physical shortfalls, her brother would require care his entire life. The hideaway's contents were to be used toward that end.

As an adult nearing her fifth and twentieth birthday, Sarah now suspected Papa mightn't have come by the items completely honestly, and she never learned exactly what the chest contained. Pirates and privateers anchored in Port Royal by the dozens in the seventeenth century.

Had Papa found a buried treasure on Bellewood House's property? Or had he come by it another way?

She'd likely never know.

It was difficult to reconcile the idea that the kind man who seldom raised his voice in anger could've also been a buccaneer or privateer. If he had been, Santano, as his first mate, surely would've known about any treasure.

The window had grown steamy from her face nearly pressed to the cool glass, and Sarah drew away a few inches.

Once, when she'd been eighteen years old, she'd broached the subject of the room and its contents with her mother. Even then, Mama's constitution had been delicate. For as much as she loved her husband and enjoyed living in the tropics, neither the heat nor the insects suited her.

Her mother had given her a gentle smile, and after kissing Sarah on the forehead, patted her cheek. "Don't worry your pretty head about it, my dear. When the time is right, you'll know all. You know your father is a man of integrity, and he has insured that long after he and I are gone, you'll never have to worry about how to care for your brother."

Sarah gave the hidden bag a hard squeeze. She was exhausted—tired of running and living in fear, and yes, saddened, that her only living relative refused to acknowledge them. Mama claimed the Rolandsons' pride would be their downfall.

Sarah had hoped that time would have healed her grandparents' disappointment. But her grandfather had gone to his grave, a bitter curmudgeon, and her grandmother's reputation as a demanding, cantankerous snob was whispered about even amongst the lower orders.

Lady Rolandson also wasn't aware her daughter had died.

Scorching tears stung behind Sarah's eyes, and her heart twisted with grief. *Had Mama died?* There'd been no way to correspond with her.

The only person she'd trusted to deliver a letter had been Captain Pritchard. His ship had sunk shortly after he'd seen her and Chris safely to London. All hands had been lost, and Mama wouldn't be able to write her without an address.

No, if Mama were alive, she'd have written the viscountess. But given the many returned letters over the years, the effort would've been in vain.

"Grandmother, how can you be so cold-hearted? Have you no desire to meet your grandchildren? To know what became of your only daughter?"

Mayhap Sarah would try one last time to contact her grandmother.

Gregor might be persuaded to deliver a letter on her behalf. If Lady Rolandson still refused to see her then she'd make no attempt to contact the woman again. Right now, the most important thing was keeping Chris safe and escaping Santano's clutches.

Exhausted to the marrow of her bones, she rested her forehead against the window casement. Yes, she was fatigued, beyond words. Weary of always looking over her shoulder, wondering who might betray them next. Fearing that she would grow careless, and endanger their lives. Worrying that Chris would slip and forget what name he was going by at present or reveal his true identity. Or fall. Or become ill and require medical attention she could ill afford.

How long could she continue living like this?

Squaring her shoulders and jutting her chin upward, she tightened her jaw. *For as long as it takes, Sarah Elizabeth Martha Paine.* Santano would pay for his treachery—someday.

Perchance... just perchance Gregor McTavish with his connections to Stapleton Shipping and Supplies could help in that regard too. For Santano captained a stolen ship.

And she possessed the documentation to prove it.

Chapter Four

Gregor lounged against the wall outside the barrel-maker's shop. Pretending preoccupation in the cuff of his coat sleeve, he examined the many barrels from the corner of his eye. Passersby wouldn't notice anything out of the ordinary. Just another London dandy more concerned with his attire than the hardworking people nearby.

Och, nae one with eyes in their head would mistake my hulkin' form for a prissy cove.

His practiced eye detected no sign of the lad. Was he here, hidden in a barrel? Crouched behind one? Had he left? Ach, Gregor hoped not. What would he tell Sydney? Switching his attention to the bustling wharf, he searched for Santano's compatriots. Satisfied none loitered nearby, he adjusted his hat to partially shade his face.

How he loathed playing the part of a conceited fop. He hadn't a doubt, given his size, he looked utterly ridiculous.

"Kipp, laddie, yer sister sent me to fetch ye. Ye dinna ken me, and ye've nae reason to trust me." Not so much as a rustle met his quiet words. "Sydney said to tell ye that Satan has found ye, and ye're to come with me."

He nodded as two naval officers strode past, their cheerful blue uniforms neat and pristine.

The lid of the fourth barrel down shifted. Hazel eyes almost the exact shade as his sister's peeked between a one-inch gap.

Gregor gave the minutest inclination of his head to let the lad know he'd seen him. "She's safe and waitin' for us. She's verra worried about ye though."

Another swift survey of the docks eased his mind, and straightening, he motioned to the driver of a wagon laden with bags of grain and covered by a tarp. He and McGarry already had arranged a place between the grain sacks for Kipp to hide.

"Kipp, stay where ye are until yonder wagon parks in front of the barrels." Recalling what his sister had said about him, Gregor gave simple directions. "Ye need to crawl inside. There's a place prepared for ye. Be careful ye aren't seen. McGarry here is my friend. He'll take ye to my warehouse. That's where yer sister is."

The lid settled into place once more, and satisfied that the lad understood, Gregor crossed to meet McGarry.

With a click of his tongue, McGarry drove the wagon across the dock and positioned it at an angle so the rear faced the barrels. He climbed down from the driver's seat and after yanking the tarp halfway up the wagon bed, clasped Gregor's hand before moving to rest against the freight wagon's far side. One knee cocked, he jabbed a thumb toward the wagon load and wiped his brow with the back of his other hand. "Thirty sacks of oats for yer laird."

Ewan had no more need for oats than Gregor had need of bells on his boots. Nevertheless, he nodded and patted the horse's wither. The animal nickered softly and shifted his feet. He rubbed between the horse's ears. "Dinna be too hasty delivering them, McGarry. I'm takin' my time returnin' to the office, in case I'm bein' watched. Wait for me at the rear of the warehouse."

Gregor turned and slapped his palm atop a grain sack. He nodded once more, as if satisfied with his purchase, and shook McGarry's hand. Rounding the wagon, he caught the boy's eye. "Stay down, ye ken?"

Face pale and his gaze wary, the lad acknowledged the request with a slight shifting of his frightened eyes.

"Och, there's a good lad."

With a casual wave, Gregor pulled his collar higher against the wind as he sauntered off. He took his time returning to his offices, stopping to chat with several acquaintances along the way. The whole while he kept guarded and alert, watching for any indication he was followed.

At the Seven Seas, he ordered a warm, dark ale and sipped it slowly, probing every nook and cranny he could see for Santano and his men. Their absence likely meant they still searched for the Blanes.

As he strolled back to his lodgings, he pondered his impulse to help Sydney. In general, he wasn't a man given to indulging whims, much less rescuing damsels in distress. *Och, but this lass has sunshine in her hair and berries on her lips. And her eyes. Those eyes. Even a kelpie could drown in their beautiful pools.*

On the other hand, lowlife bullies like Santano and his cronies irritated Gregor. He flexed his gloved hands. Too many months of sitting at a desk and not enough riding, tramping through the Highlands, hunting, training, or some other sort of physical exertion at Craiglocky had him restless and itching for a good grapple.

How much longer would he procrastinate and delay the inevitable return to Scotland? A wee bit longer, it seemed, as he'd decided to help a lass and her brother.

If Sydney were to be believed, the rumors circulating about how Santano acquired the *Mary Elizabeth* were true. He wasn't the first ship's captain to tread the thin line between lawlessness and honest ventures.

At this moment, Gregor could point out half a dozen ships gently rocking in the Thames's waters, engaging in one form of questionable commerce or another. Privateering might be outlawed, but he as well as everyone else who worked the docks knew smuggling and raids continued.

Likely, Santano possessed forged documents giving him ownership of the vessel.

Stapleton's warehouse came into view, and a slight movement drew his attention to the upper story windows.

Sydney watched, and by thunder, she bloody well needed to take more care not to be seen.

Removing his hat, he looked overhead, squinting as if he examined the petulant sky then cast a casual glance about him, hoping to God no one else had noticed her.

Gregor hadn't quite decided what he was going to do with her and her brother, but once he'd determined to aid someone, he didn't turn his back on them. If any two people were in need of help, it was the Blanes.

That a bonnie lassie such as she managed to keep from being forced into prostitution or being set upon by the riffraff infesting London's docks, was a testament to her keen intellect and cunning.

Hopefully, he hadn't been an unsuspecting victim of both.

He unlocked the office door, and after stepping inside slid the bolt home once more. He'd yet to divest his outer wear before footsteps thumped upon the risers.

"Where is my brother?"

"Lass, stay out of sight."

"I sent you to fetch Chris, Highlander. Where. Is. He?" Panic riddled her voice.

"Dinna fash yerself. A friend of mine has the lad hidden in a wagon filled with bags of oats. They should be at warehouse doors, even now."

After removing his coat and hat then draping his gloves across another curved arm of the porcelain-tipped oak coat rack beside the door, he wandered in front of the window so that anybody observing the establishment wouldn't suspect anything. He stretched, flexing his spine and yawned. Selecting a ledger from his desk, he nonchalantly glanced to the window. Nothing. Flipping the journal open, he casually ambled toward the rear of the building.

"Was he all right?" she asked, only a hint of her earlier alarm evident in her voice.

Upon reflecting briefly, he said, "Aye, I think so. He looked well enough. A wee bit scared, but that's to be expected. I'm goin' to let yer brother inside. Remain out of sight and wait for the lad upstairs. We'll decide what to do with the two of ye while he's eatin'."

Chris gobbled the simple fare Gregor prepared. A piece of bread in one hand and a chicken leg in the other, his mouth bulging, he chomped away.

"Slow down. You're going to choke," Sarah fondly admonished.

Chris turned a boyish grin on her and, dropping the chicken, accepted the cup of water she offered.

"Lass, I need to speak with ye." *In private*, Gregor mouthed.

She squinted slightly at him, but his striking face and keen gaze gave nothing away. Fine lines creased the corners of his eyes, suggesting he was a man given often to mirth. "All right, Mr. McTavish." Patting Chris's shoulder, she gently reprimanded, "Slow down, darling. There's plenty of food."

For a change.

Taking a bite of cheese, Chris nodded, and continued to inhale the fare.

As she followed Gregor into the sitting room, she shivered and brushed her hands up and down her arms before taking a seat in one of the oversized chairs. At once, the cat began rubbing himself against her legs.

Gregor knelt before the hearth and after adding coal to the grate and lighting it, replaced the fender. She hadn't even had a fireplace or a stove in the one-room hovel they'd called home. Many a night, she'd wrapped Chris in her arms, holding him tight to still his quaking. And hers too.

That first winter had been the godawful worst. Accustomed to much warmer temperatures, even with hats, gloves, coats, and wrapped in two blankets, her very bones had ached with cold.

Cat continued to make little chirping noises and nudged her ankles.

"Come here." She gathered the tubby feline into her arms, burying her face in his fur.

Cat closed his eyes, and contented rumbles echoed from his fluffy chest.

"I've never had a pet, except for Biscuit, my yellow-billed parrot. I always wanted a dog though. Once, when I was a little girl, I saw a long, skinny dog with short legs at Port Royal. He was black with reddish-brown markings and looked like a long sausage with fat feet. He was the most adorable thing I've ever seen. If I ever have a dog, I want one like that," she declared with a firm nod.

Not much chance of that ever happening. Not when she could scarcely feed herself and Chris. Cutting Gregor a side-eyed peek through her lashes, mischievousness swept her. "And I shall name it Sausage."

The latter she declared to make the Highlander laugh and see if she'd been right about the lines framing his eyes.

He sliced her a disbelieving look and chuckled, the sound a mellow rustle deep in his chest, as he settled into the other chair.

She hid a grin in Cat's back. Very nice indeed. She quite liked his laugh.

Some men's were harsh and grating, but his reverberated in his chest, a welcoming, warm invitation to join in his humor. Sarah also liked his melodious brogue. It, too, invited one to listen to his lilting speech. To snuggle into his chest, place her ear upon the wide expanse, and melt into the sound.

"Biscuit? Ye named a bird *Biscuit?*" He slapped his knee and chortled again. "And ye want to name a dog Sausage?"

The bird's name wasn't *that* funny.

She raised an eyebrow. Her most reproachful one. "Must I remind you that you have a fat feline named *Cat*, Highlander? And you dare laugh because, as a little girl, I couldn't pronounce hibiscus?" Another wave of melancholy bathed her. "I had to leave her behind. I don't know what happened to her."

He'd removed his coat and rolled up his shirt sleeves. Resting his forearms on his knees, sympathy softened his face. "I am sorry, lass. Ye've no' had an easy time of it, but we need to decide what to do next. I dinna think Santano will easily give up lookin' for ye."

The coals glowed reddish-orange, their flames radiating delicious heat. The high sides of the chair captured the warmth, and for the first time in a long while, Sarah enjoyed a toasty fire as well as a small sense of contentment.

Keeping her expression carefully neutral, she threaded her fingers in Cat's fur. He arched his back, a contented kitty smile upon his wide face.

"I know we do, Mr. McTavish, and I don't wish to impose upon you further—"

He lifted a wide palm, halting her. "It's too late for second thoughts. I willnae abandon ye and yer brother now."

She hadn't even had to ask him. He'd volunteered of his own accord. It had been so long since anyone had cared about or helped her.

"But I do need to ken who ye really are." His tone changed the merest bit, and all signs of amusement fled his features. His blue-gray gaze probed hers, looking into the depths of her soul, and Sarah barely refrained from squirming.

Averting her attention, she swallowed twice. No one in England knew. Other than her grandmother and the viscountess's odious butler. "I concede you've no reason whatsoever to trust me," she said softly, still unwilling to take the final step and reveal her true identity.

Relaxing back in his chair, he hooked an ankle over his knee, totally at ease, watching her from beneath hooded eyes. "And ye've nae reason to trust me, either, but we're beyond that, dinna ye think?" The palms of both hands splayed open, his voice held no censure.

She acknowledged the truth of his words and lifted her chin a couple of inches, although her attention remained on the flames frolicking behind the grate.

"Let's begin again, shall we, lass?" He pressed a massive arm to his chest and dipped his chin in a mock semblance of a bow.

Eyebrows scrunched, she angled her head. What the devil was he about?

"I am Gregor Lieth Conall McTavish of Craiglocky Keep, cousin to the Laird Ewan McTavish, who is also Viscount Sethwick. His wife, Yvette, owns Stapleton Shipping and Supplies, and just under a year ago I left the Highlands to manage these London offices. I have a twin, Alasdair, and my parents Duncan and Kitta live at Craiglocky too."

He clasped a hand across his abdomen, drawing her reluctant attention to his muscled forearms once more. This was no weak fop. From his broad shoulders straining the fabric of his shirt, and the well-muscled thighs defined by his fawn-colored trousers, the Highlander was a fabulous specimen of masculine power and grace.

"Now, tell me who ye are." He rested his square chin with the merest hint of golden stubble on his fist. "And I'll have the truth this time, *Sassenach*."

Chapter Five

"*Sassenach?*" Sarah tried the odd word on her tongue. "What does it mean?"

"Saxon, and dinna try to change the subject."

She shouldn't be surprised he'd uncovered her secret. Continuing to withhold her identity was moot at this juncture. Particularly if he agreed to deliver a letter to Lady Rolandson on her behalf.

Burying her fingers in Cat's fur, she scanned his living quarters for the umpteenth time. More for a reason to stall than any lingering curiosity about his living quarters. How had she missed the massive sword propped in the corner by the door? Surely the monstrous thing was impossible to wield.

"Lass…?"

His persistence struck a discordant nerve, but Gregor was right. Santano had spies everywhere, and logic decreed it was only a matter of time before he found her and Chris if they remained in London. But to put her faith in this man she'd only known a couple of hours…

She must.

He'd kept his promise to bring Chris to her safely, surely that meant something.

Filling her lungs with air, she made her decision. "I'm Sarah Paine, and my brother is Christopher. My father was Captain Aaron Paine of the *Mary Elizabeth*. My mother Mary is—*was she still alive?* —was the only child of…aristocrats."

Anger surged through her toward her callous grandmother and the fiend responsible for her father's death. She squeezed her fists tight, her nails biting into her palms and forming crescents before forging onward.

"Santano and other miscreants commandeered my father's ship, killing everyone aboard who refused to join in their mutiny. Chris and I fled Jamaica, but our mother was too ill to travel. We've been hiding in London since under assumed identities. I fear Santano pillaged our home as well." Bitter tears burned her eyes as she wrestled to control her emotions.

Moments like these, when Sarah let her thoughts stray to Mama, and wondering if she yet lived, were almost unbearable. The not knowing gnawed at her peace of mind. And the guilt she carried. That was almost as awful.

Every day, she wished she'd insisted Mama leave too. Then her wiser self would argue; her mother wouldn't have survived the ocean voyage, and she'd known that. Not ill and recovering from a fever as she had been.

Sarah shifted, the weight of the hidden pocket pressing into her thigh. McTavish didn't need to know about the key or chest. Not yet, if ever. He'd already endangered his life by helping them. "As I said, Mr. McTavish, I don't wish to impose, but you are correct. It's far too late for that, I fear."

"And ye've nae relatives or friends who might take ye in?" His chin between his thumb and pointer finger, his astute gaze probed her, looking into her very soul.

A droll smile twisted Sarah's mouth. "My maternal grandmother refused to see Chris and me when we arrived in London. We were turned away at the door and ordered to never return."

Eyebrows pulled tight at the inner corners, Gregor scratched his jaw, his expression thoughtful. "Is it possible she didna ken ye'd called?"

"I suppose it is, but don't servants take orders from their employers? The butler vowed most emphatically that she wasn't at home to *us*. I'm sure you know that often means the homeowner may very well be peeking at their unwanted visitors from behind the draperies."

He acknowledged the truth of her words with a slight shifting of his eyes, more blue than gray at the moment. It must be his sky-blue double-breasted waistcoat that caused the color to change. "Who is yer grandmother?"

"The Viscountess Rolandson. Have you heard of her?"

Surprise well-seasoned with reservation flickered across Gregor's face. His reaction reconfirmed Sarah's own impression of her grandmother.

"Aye, though I've never met her personally." He rubbed one finger alongside his nose. "She has a reputation for bein'...starchy."

A nice way of saying she was a crotchety, unforgiving, demanding, grudge-holding old tabby. Not likely she'd be any more eager to meet her daughter's children now than she had been three years ago.

Changing the subject to a more immediate need, she said, "I'm not sure how Santano's men found us, but I'm positive our room has been searched." Ransacked. Their few possessions destroyed.

"So ye've nae place to go then, Miss Paine?"

She chuckled and swiped her stiff hair off her shoulder. "Don't you think it's a little late for formalities, Highlander? Please call me Sarah, and no, at the moment, Chris and I are without accommodations." Such a polite way of saying they were homeless.

"I'll only call ye by yer given name if ye do the same with me," he said.

She agreed with a brief inclination of her head

He gave a short, decisive nod as well. "Ye can stay with me for now. I ken it's no' at all proper, but I think it's the safest course. I have an extra chamber." Gregor angled a pickle-sized thumb to the doorway beside the kitchen. "As long as nae one kens ye are here, yer reputation shouldna suffer."

She laughed again, this time genuinely amused. Nearly five and twenty, she'd long since given up on society's strictures.

Not that she'd ever really followed them. Life in Jamaica was much different, much more relaxed and forgiving than stodgy England. Mama had seen that Sarah could conduct herself with poise and decorum in the stuffiest English drawing rooms, but given a choice, she'd prefer to be barefoot and bonnetless.

"I assure you, Gregor, I've stopped fretting about my reputation. In the past three years, Chris and I have lived in tenements where prostitutes entertained their patrons in the room next door. You know as well as I do, my repute is beyond salvaging."

An inarticulate sound of denial reverberated in his throat, but the truth rested in his honest gaze.

She lifted her shoulders, and Cat shot her a why-are-you-disturbing-my-sleep-by-moving-look. "I'm not feeling sorry for myself, because I'll manage somehow. But I do worry about Chris."

"As I said, lass, ye can stay here for now. Yer brother can sleep on the couch, and ye can take the bedroom. It locks from within." That almost seemed an afterthought to reassure her. He drummed his fingers, the nails square and clean, upon his broad knee. "I'm goin' to send letters 'round to friends and relatives and recruit a wee bit of help on yer behalf."

She crossed her ankles, very conscious of her holey socks and her breech's soiled, ragged edges. A long soak in the tub would be heaven. And a cup of steaming tea, liberally laced with milk and sugar. *Oh, my that sounds wonderful.* She scrunched her nose. "I thought all of your relatives lived in Scotland."

It was Gregor's turn to chuckle, that contagious rumble that called to her, and she couldn't help but smile in return. He scratched his temple, still grinning. "Och, only partially true. I'm either related by marriage or acquainted with a goodly number of peers who live in London or have residences within a day's ride."

Chris wandered in from the kitchen and made straight for the couch. Bluish shadows framed his eyes, a testament that he'd not been sleeping well either. Lying on his side, one hand nestled beneath his hollow cheek, his eyelids drifted closed.

She stood and crossed to her brother. After placing a throw pillow beneath his head, she brushed his hair off his brow. "Poor thing. He's exhausted."

"Na more than ye, I'd wager." Gregor rubbed his nape before saying, "I also advise ye to write yer grandmother, and tell her what has transpired. Unless she's completely without a heart, she'll nae turn away her grandchildren."

Sarah wasn't so certain the viscountess had ever possessed a heart and any organ in the woman's chest had long since turned to stone.

He considered Chris then rose and disappeared into one of the bed chambers for a moment. When he returned, he carried a blanket, which he tenderly laid across the already fast asleep child.

An unfamiliar sensation uncurled in Sarah's chest. A very dangerous thing for a woman relying on her wits and independence to survive. She'd no room for emotional entanglements. But this burly, attractive Highlander was proving to be the most kind, considerate man she'd ever met. The type of decent, honorable man a woman could fall in love with.

A woman not afraid for her life and responsible for a crippled child. A woman so accustomed to leeriness and mistrust, to living in a constant state of fear, she'd forgotten the happy, carefree woman she'd once been.

He ran his practiced gaze over her shoddy garments. "We also need to see ye attired in clothin' befittin' a viscountess's granddaughter. All the more reason I've decided to seek help from my female family and friends."

"I haven't the funds to spare to purchase clothing for myself or Chris." She refused to be embarrassed by that fact. She'd done well by her brother, keeping them fed, not always full, but they hadn't starved. She'd also kept a roof over their heads and managed to do so without compromising her virtue.

"Dinna worry about the funds. I'd offer to pay for them, but I can see by the independent spark in yer eye, ye'd refuse me and tell me to bugger myself, to boot."

"Right you are, Highlander." The small upward tick of her lips contradicted her rejoinder. She enjoyed bantering with him. Much more than she ought.

"Between Ewan's sisters and our friends, I've nae doubt they can spare everythin' ye need from the skin out," he said.

She couldn't prevent the blush scorching her cheeks at the mention of undergarments. Men simply didn't discuss something so intimate, but he continued on as if he hadn't crossed the mark or noticed her discomfiture.

"They'll be happy to do it too." He rolled his eyes. "Nothin' those noble ladies delight in more than a waif or an orphan to take under their protection."

"I hardly qualify as either," she retorted, her tone drier than flour.

Did he truly expect her to accept charity from women she didn't know? Her pride chafed mightily at the idea, but dash it to ribbons, he was right. Making a positive impression the first time she met her grandmother and entered Polite Society was imperative.

"By the way, Sarah, I saw ye peekin' from the window when I returned." He tempered his rebuke with a rakish smile. "Ye must be more careful."

Damn. She'd thought she'd been so cautious.

"Remind Chris to stay away from the windows too," he advised, turning to examine the long panels. "In fact, until we're sure that Santano is convinced yer no' here, let's leave the curtains drawn." He crossed to the windows and released the tiebacks on either side. With a whoosh and a rustle, the crimson velvet floated across the glass, obstructing the view.

Wouldn't that alert Santano or his thugs if they still watched the building?

"If ye're wonderin' if that'll make Santano's bounders suspicious, it willnae. I generally leave the draperies closed. I'm unused to neighbors and like my privacy," he said by way of an explanation. "My housekeeper opens them the days she cleans."

He'd read her mind—unnerving and disquieting. Exciting too.

"I intend to order a couple of warehouse workers to be extra vigilant and patrol the premises, just in case Santano or his men return. In the meanwhile, pen a letter to yer grandmother, and I'll make sure it's delivered."

He'd truly thought this through, hadn't he? But how long could she and Chris realistically stay here?

"However, there is one small kink in my plan, lass."

And here it came. The "but" she'd been anticipating.

"I'm sure ye noticed the other desk in the office," he said.

Sarah nodded, absently rubbing her hands up and down her arms. She had but had been too distraught to puzzle over it. "Yes, I thought it a bit odd that no one else worked in the office of an establishment this large."

"I do have a clerk, but he's been ill the past three days. I dinna want Baker to ken ye're here, so I'll have to contrive an excuse to keep him away." Gregor squatted before the fire and added more coal.

Convinced he did so on her account, another spark of gratitude fluttered in Sarah's chest.

Hearth broom in hand, he glanced over his shoulder. "As I mentioned, I've a woman who cleans twice a week, on Tuesdays and Fridays." He swept a smattering of coal dust into a small dust bin and dumped it into the fire. Once he'd replaced the tools, he began pacing the room, one hand on his nape and the other on his lean hip.

"I think I must decline your kind offer." Though what she would do instead, she couldn't fathom. It made her head hurt to contemplate. Made the knot in her stomach tangle impossibly tighter. Sarah pressed her fingers between her eyes. "At the very least, your clerk will be curious, and your housekeeper mustn't see us here. It would be no small task to keep Chris quiet in any event."

Gregor might have confidence in them, but Santano wasn't above trickery, bribery, or other devilment to gain information. His man, Yeates, hadn't believed the Highlander She was sure of it.

"Nae so fast, lass. Mrs. Smith winna come for a couple of days, and I'm hopeful I shall either have ye settled with yer grandmother or one of my friends by then."

Neither idea appealed overly much, truth to tell. They were strangers, after all.

"As for Baker, he's a trustworthy sort. He'd nae betray ye. Still, I dinna want him here." He snapped his fingers, and a grin lit his eyes. "I have it. I'll send him to Scotland with the letter for my cousin. I'll also have him deliver my other missives. It winna be the first time I've done so, and he'll have nae reason to believe anythin' out of the ordinary is goin' on."

"Gregor, you ought to be aware that you're putting your life in danger by continuing to help us." She slid a swift look to Chris, assuring herself he slept on. He'd never truly been able to grasp the peril they faced. "Santano killed my father, and he may have my mother as well. I don't doubt that he wouldn't hesitate to murder you too."

He slipped a wicked-looking knife from his boot, holding it up for her to see. "Och, never fear, lass. I can defend myself and ye, if need be. I never go anywhere without this." He pointed to the massive blade she'd spied earlier. "And trust me when I tell ye, I've some skill wieldin' a sword." He didn't boast, merely stated a fact.

"I have a feeling, Gregor McTavish, you're skilled in a great many things." Of its own volition, her gaze strayed to his mouth. Lord help her and the naughty path her thoughts dared to trundle down.

At that moment, Cat stretched and opened his eyes, giving her such an astute look followed by a feline smile, and she swore the beast knew exactly what she was thinking. She hadn't yet admitted to herself, but something far more than gratitude to the Highlander held her in thrall.

Chapter Six

Awareness of Sarah as a desirable woman assailed Gregor as she stared at his lips. When her small tongue darted out and moistened the corner of her mouth, he almost groaned aloud. He'd been without a woman since leaving Scotland.

The cold English misses held little appeal for him. Until this frail tropical flower had burst headlong into his life.

His mouth dried, his nostrils flared, and wild Highland ponies galloped through his middle. Not since Lily—*nae, not even then*—had a woman piqued his interest as acutely. Dressed in the first stare of fashion, her shimmering flaxen hair twisted into an elaborate coiffure, a little flesh softening the sharp angles of her bones, and Sarah Paine would turn many a man's eye.

Who was he fooling? She'd snared his attention dressed like a beggar and scared senseless. Keen of wit, unselfish, valiant as any warrior, and lovely of face and figure, a man wouldn't soon forget her.

His gut tightened sickeningly. Another reason to save her from Santano and the cretins working for him. Gregor had no doubt they'd ravish her before slitting her throat.

He scratched an eyebrow, noting Cat now lay splayed like an arrogant Egyptian Sphinx atop Chris as the lad slept. Traitorous beast.

Sarah's safety wasn't the only thing compelling him to ask her to stay. She intrigued him as no other ever had, and he hoped to know her better away from the constraints of society and family. When she trotted off to her grandmother's— as he truly hoped she'd be able to—he wouldn't likely have the opportunity.

He was no fool.

Granddaughters to viscountesses didn't associate with those smelling of the shop, and though his cousin Ewan might hold dual titles, one an English viscountcy himself, more commonly than not, the *ton's* denizens looked down their aristocratic noses at Scots.

Certainly, he was welcomed in the drawing rooms and gatherings of friends and family, but he seldom ventured into social circles beyond those. Neither highborn nor wealthy, he lacked two of the criteria that opened elitist *ton* doors.

If Lady Rolandson opted to recognize her grandchildren by inviting Sarah and Chris into her home, chances were, his association with Sarah would end. And he didn't want that to happen.

Not until he figured out why she fascinated him so, and he needed time to do that. With a silent sigh and single-minded purpose, he shoved his personal interest into a corner of his mind to be taken out and studied later at his leisure.

For now, although he'd known the lass mere hours, his foremost concern was keeping her hidden from Santano. He cleared his throat and scraped a hand through his hair. "I've a hip bath in the storage closet, if ye'd like to heat water. Ye'll find linens and all else ye need there as well."

Such thankfulness swept her face, one would think he might've offered her a palace. She clasped her hands and rocked back on her heels. "Oh, that sounds lovely." She plucked at her shabby shirt, scrunching her nose in a winsome manner. "But I'm loath to put on my soiled clothes again."

"Aye." He allowed himself an extended perusal of her form. His scrutiny only intensified his attraction. "Mine are too big for ye. For the lad too." Gregor skewed his mouth sideways. He couldn't risk purchasing clothing for a child or a woman.

"It's of no matter." She combed her fingers through her long locks. "A bath will still be much appreciated."

"Wait." He snapped his fingers again. "Yvette collects clothin' for the poor. There's a barrel in the warehouse that's meant for Craiglocky with the next load of supplies. I'm sure I can locate somethin' for ye in there."

Mayhap even a bar of perfumed soap in the supplies intended for home too.

He was positive Yvette wouldn't object if he confiscated a few of her personal toiletries. She could always order more, and as generous as she was, she wouldn't begrudge Sarah a cake of scented French soap.

"Prepare yer bathwater, and I'll see what I can pillage for ye to wear. Ye'll find a big pot in the storeroom to heat the water."

Shoes and undergarments might be an issue, but surely there was a discarded gown that would suit. It might not be the first stare of fashion, but given Sarah wore loose-fitting rags, he didn't think she'd complain.

At least until the ladies he intended to write swept in to rescue her. They'd soon have her decked head to toe in Almack patroness-approved attire.

"Gregor?"

He turned back from the door. "Aye, lass?"

Indecision flickered in her eyes before she drew her shoulders back and marched across the floor. "I cannot thank you enough for what you've done for Chris and me. I vow, someday, somehow I shall make it up to you."

Such sincerity rang in her voice he couldn't help but admire her gumption.

His gaze dropped to the rosy, plump lower lip she'd been torturing for the past half an hour. Likely, she wasn't even aware she chewed the tender flesh when nervous or upset. What he'd like to do above all else was ask for a kiss. Except, only the lowest cur bargained with a woman as desperate as her.

Still...

Slipping a handful of her hair over her shoulder, he gave her a naughty wink. "I can think of all sorts of creative ways ye might do that, my tropical flower, but I'll settle for a wee kiss from yer sweet mouth." He couldn't resist seeing her reaction. As he suspected, she wasn't immune to him either.

Her eyes rounded, filling with wonder, and her jaw slackened.

"I was but teasin' ye, lass." He gently pushed her mouth closed. "What kind of a blackguard do ye take me for?"

"Not a blackguard at all. You're a kind, decent, brave man." She thrust her hand out at him, and it was his turn to be taken aback. "I agree to your request."

No one need tell him a stupid ear-to-ear grin split his face. "Ye do?" He wrapped her small, rough hand in his and shook it.

"I do. But I choose when and where." She shoved his torso with her other palm. "Now find me suitable clothing, please. I cannot wait to bathe and wash my hair."

As Gregor thumped down the stairs, the vision of her naked and dripping wet sifted into his imagination, and he missed the next step, nearly tumbling head over arse. Good thing it was the second to the last stair or he might've broken his neck. "*Gude*, what's come over me?"

Another two days passed uneventfully, and Sarah stirred the porridge as she listened for sounds that Gregor or Chris had awoken. Humming, she browned the sausages then checked the steeping tea.

Wearing a stained apron over the simple plaid morning dress he'd procured for her, she'd cooked meals and performed other small tasks, trying in some small manner to repay Gregor's kindnesses. And to keep her mind off the irrefutable fact that her grandmother didn't want to see her or Chris.

Her letter, delivered by Gregor himself to the butler—possessed with a face homelier than an old mule's back end, according to the Highlander—had gone unanswered.

Again.

What would she have done if Gregor had turned out to be a scoundrel? She dismissed the unnerving thought. No sense fretting about something that hadn't come to pass, and she was quite confident at this juncture, wouldn't. That much she'd learned about him. Gregor McTavish was a man of honor.

Likewise, he awaited responses to the notes he'd sent, so she'd spent the past two days mending his clothing, tidying his already neat apartment, cooking, and reading from the pleasant and abundant assortment of books lining the shelves beside the window.

It had been so long since she relaxed and enjoyed a book, she felt wicked and indulgent.

Chris had been harder to keep amused. He could barely read, and grew bored easily. Cat kept him entertained part of the time, but he'd grown increasingly restless. After Gregor's daily outing yesterday to seek word about Santano's whereabouts, he had returned with a few toys.

With Christmastide just over three weeks away, it wasn't surprising he'd easily found trinkets for Chris's amusement. Not only were shop windows full of tempting displays, but street vendors also hawked their handmade wares.

At first, she'd fretted someone might've seen him, but he'd assured her he'd been discreet. A wagoner made the purchases and delivered them to Stapleton's warehouse, concealed in a freight wagon of supplies.

Although she hated being further indebted to Gregor, the joy on Chris's face as he'd sat upon the floor, opening the packages had reminded her very much of the Yuletides celebrated in Jamaica, and Sarah couldn't refuse the well-intended gifts.

She hadn't observed Christmastide whilst in London. Pauper poor and barely able to keep themselves fed, so pinch-penny was she with money that gifts had been out of the question. She blamed Santano for that too.

On his shopping sojourns, Gregor had obtained useful information.

The good news was the *Mary Elizabeth* was scheduled to sail in just over a week. Chances were, Santano wouldn't make port again for six months or more. The bad news, was that would make him much more desperate to find her and the key before he put to sea.

She'd avoided the blackguard for three years. Surely with Gregor's help she could manage another ten days. That gave her time to hatch a plan and leave London.

She couldn't argue that she found the Highlander deucedly attractive, and his appeal increased with each passing day. Larger than the men she was accustomed to, his ruggedly handsome face and hands bore evidence of time spent in the sun. He wore his hair—as light as hers, though more honey-toned than flaxen—unfashionably long and tied back in a queue.

Few men in the Caribbean had passed Papa's scrutiny or had been permitted to call upon her. Truth to tell, no more than she could count on one hand and none sparked more than a passing glance and a polite smile. Certainly, since arriving in London, romantic entanglements had been the last thing on her mind.

No, survival had been at the forefront of her thoughts for three years. For the first time since disembarking that fateful afternoon, she wasn't in a constant state of fear.

She owed Gregor McTavish much more than a promised kiss.

Touching the braid hanging over her right shoulder, she fingered the black ribbon.

He permitted her to borrow one of his, not wanting to raise questions by buying pins for her, although he might've asked one of his employees to do that as well. Except he told the worker who'd bought the toys for him that they were gifts for his kin. His claim rang true since Yuletide, though no longer illegal, was still strongly discouraged by the Scottish Kirk.

It seemed he'd thought of everything, constantly weighing the situation and the repercussions.

None of Santano's thugs had returned to the shop, but in case they did, the door to his living quarters remained locked at all times, and as Gregor had asked, she and Chris stayed away from the windows.

Sarah speared the drapery-covered windows a darkling look.

She'd much prefer the natural light, but would take no chances of discovery. She'd dared a peek outdoors this morning, and the sky lay heavy with a peculiar pinkish-gray cloud cover. As it had the past several mornings, a thick layer of frost and ice covered every surface.

Once again, appreciation swelled within her breast and tears in her eyes as well. Homeless, how would she and Chris have survived this freezing cold? They wouldn't have.

"I kent I smelled sausage."

Sarah whipped her attention to the doorway, very much aware of the virile man a few feet away.

Hair damp, and attired only in his boots, buckskins, and white lawn shirt, Gregor dominated the entrance. Lord, he was a gorgeous specimen of manhood. Under other circumstances, she might've been tempted to explore a relationship with him.

If he noticed her fascination, his mien in no way betrayed it. He inhaled a deep breath, patting his tummy. "I'm famished."

"You're always starving, Gregor." She ran another gaze over him and couldn't help but appreciate his well-muscled, masculine form.

His blue-gray eyes twinkled with mirth, and she vowed he knew exactly the wanton thoughts she entertained.

Heat swept upward from her middle to her neck then to her cheeks. To cover her embarrassment, she waved the spoon toward the table. "Sit down. The food's almost ready."

"Mrs. Smith is due this afternoon." He took a seat, dwarfing the sturdy chair. "I've decided ye and Chris should hide in the warehouse. I've already prepared a place for ye."

So that's why he was late to breakfast. "That's a good idea." She nodded as she poured his tea.

"I dinna want to do anythin' out of my normal routine to alert anyone that ye're here." He said by way an explanation as he lifted his knife and fork. "I expect responses to the letters I sent verra soon too."

As he tucked into his meal, Sarah once again tried to understand the enigmatic Highlander. Nothing seemed to shake his confidence. He remained optimistic and encouraging, still adamant her grandmother would come 'round.

A sad smile tipped her mouth, and she hid it behind the teacup raised to her lips. Too bad his optimism wasn't contagious.

The office bell clanged below.

Alert, his features tense, Gregor jerked his head up and put his finger to his lips. "*Shh.*"

Chapter Seven

Swallowing her fear, Sarah nodded and hands shaking, placed the cup back in its saucer. It took her a moment to settle it soundly and stop its clattering. Something as simple as an unexpected bell ringing and panic bubbled to the surface.

"Lock the door after me." Gregor patted her shoulder, his huge hand burning through the gown's thin fabric. The gesture had no doubt meant to soothe, but every time he touched her, sensual sparks lit.

No sooner had she turned the key in the lock than a sleepy-eyed Chris shuffled from the bedroom, rumpled and disheveled.

"Morning, sister."

"Good morning, darling. Did you sleep well?"

Yawning behind his hand, he nodded and blinked groggily.

Rather than take the bedchamber and have Chris sleep upon the sofa, Sarah had chosen to sleep on the floor at the foot of his bed.

For years, they'd shared the same uncomfortable mattresses, but she conceded, she appreciated not having his bony elbows in her ribs or being walloped during one of his bad dreams. Not only did he still have nightmares, but he also walked in his sleep. Though not likely, she couldn't take a chance of him wandering from Gregor's apartment.

After she spent the first night on the floor, a feather tick, a thick coverlet, and another pillow had appeared in the chamber for her use. She hadn't said a word, but Gregor had noticed.

That was another thing she admired about him; his attention to little details and his consideration for others. As if she needed something else to add to the growing list of things he'd done to impress her.

"Come along. Breakfast is ready." Wrapping an arm around Chris's shoulders, Sarah hugged him to her side and guided him toward the kitchen. While he ate, she meant to bundle her bedding into the storage closet to prevent the housekeeper from becoming suspicious.

Holding a brown spotted horse atop cherry-red wheels, his favorite of the playthings that Gregor had given him, he gave her a lopsided smile. "I like it here, sister." He gave her a toothy smile, and rubbed his left eye with the palm of his other hand. "I like Gregor and Cat too."

Sorrow and desolation whirled together, tightening her chest. She swallowed then cleared her throat before painting on a bright smile. "I do as well, darling, but I told you already, we cannot stay. It's not safe for us or for Gregor."

Well, not until the *Mary Elizabeth* set sail, in any event. Then she'd have a few months' reprieve. She fully intended to abscond to somewhere Santano would never find them.

A pout pulled Chris's usually cheerful mouth downward as he settled into the chair. Several strands of hair fell over his forehead, concealing his left eye. "Are we never going to have a home again, Sister? Will we ever see Mama again?"

I honestly don't know.

He knew about Papa, but not Mama. The truth of it was, she didn't know whether her mother still lived. A tiny spark of hope glimmered that she did.

Sarah couldn't tell him they mightn't ever have a home. Most likely wouldn't ever see their mother again, so she did what any loving sister would do and distracted him. "Have you named your pony yet?" She dipped her chin toward the toy horse he rolled back and forth before him.

"Yes. Brownie, 'cause he has brown spots." He pointed to the irregular circles.

"Most appropriate." If not entirely original.

Holding the toy up for her inspection, he broke into a wide grin. "Gregor promised to teach me to ride. I want to learn on a pony just like this."

Spooning porridge into his bowl, she glanced up. "He did? When was that?"

"While you bathed the other day." One of its wheels squeaking, he rolled the toy across the table again. "He showed me a big book with horse pictures. His cousin raises them."

Botheration. Gregor shouldn't be making promises of that nature. Chris didn't understand that sometimes people said things to be kind: things they didn't intend to or simply couldn't do.

The key rattled in the outer door lock, and she raised a finger to her lips, as she swiftly closed the kitchen door before placing Chris's food on the table. The unmistakable sound of the bolt sliding home reassured her, and she released the breath burning her lungs.

A moment later, Gregor swaggered in looking entirely too cocky and pleased with himself. "It's all right, lass, lad. Just a messenger, droppin' off an order for me. Truth to tell, I didnae expect him until later this mornin'."

She poured Gregor fresh tea before taking her seat again. Never had she known a man to drink more tea than Gregor McTavish, and he drank his brew sweet. Three lumps of sugar per cup.

Papa had preferred black coffee.

Grinning, as if he were Saint Nick himself, Gregor strode to the table, holding two large brown paper-wrapped bundles. "I have a surprise for ye."

My, the man did enjoy giving to others. She'd never known anyone with as generous a nature.

Chomping on a bite of sausage, Chris grinned. "What is it?"

"Chris, chew your food first then talk," Sarah gently admonished him. She turned the same starchy eye upon Gregor. "What have you done? I told you, I don't feel right accepting anything else from you. Besides, won't those raise suspicions?" She wiggled her fingers at the packages.

If anything, Gregor's grin grew bigger, pure delight sparking in his eyes.

She pressed a hand to her frolicking belly. *Gads,* when he smiled at her like that, it took all of her will to cobble together a coherent thought.

"Alas, that's the beauty of it." He gave a mischievous wink and patted Chris's shoulder. "I used the Yuletide as an excuse. I dinna ken why I didna think of it before. Dafty of me, really. I had a half dozen more packages wrapped and delivered to the kirk for the poor, so nae one kens the truth."

"But, Gregor, the Scots don't celebrate Christmastide." Even she knew that.

Drawing himself up, he sliced Chris—busily eating and playing with his horse—a sideways glance. "Och, but I'm in England now. Would ye begrudge me enjoyment of the tradition? I hear all sorts of savory foods and sweets are served." He patted his flat stomach.

Clever, endearing man.

"I ken there are kissin' boughs and mistletoe too." Rocking back on his heels, he hugged the packages, causing the stiff paper to crackle in protest. His devilish wink made her blood sidle warmer still, and heat stung her cheeks. "Should a lucky gentleman catch a bonnie lassie beneath either, he's entitled to a wee kiss."

Lord. A kiss from a man like him would no doubt set her blood afire and singe her hair.

"You're taking advantage of the situation, Gregor McTavish." She attempted to sound stern, but her voice came out rather breathier than she'd intended. "Your breakfast grows cold. Why don't you set those aside? We can open them later."

"Aye, lass." He winked again, obviously pleased as Punch with himself and enjoying this misadventure far too much. Before she could think of a suitable retort, he disappeared into the main room, returning shortly with letters between his forefinger and thumb. "I forgot to tell ye. I've had responses from Countesses Ramsbury and Clarendon and the Duchess of Harcourt."

Her confusion must've shown on her face.

"The countesses are Ewan's sisters and her grace is the wife of one of Ewan's closest chums," he explained as if it were the most common thing in the world to be on intimate terms with nobles.

"My, you do have lofty connections, don't you?" Sarah settled into her chair and after draping the serviette across her lap, cocked her head.

"Aye. I do." Gregor shied his eyebrows high up his forehead and chuckled. "I'm still waitin' to hear from the Baroness de Deavaux-Rousset, the Countess of Luxmoore, the Viscountess Warrick, and Lady Sethwick."

Spoon midway to her mouth, Sarah gaped. "Oh, my stars. You weren't jesting about knowing a goodly number of peeresses. Have you imposed upon all of them on my behalf?" She nearly groaned aloud from mortification. But if it benefited Chris, her damnable pride would have to suffer.

"Aye," he said, tea cup in hand and not the least bit repentant. "And a few noblemen too."

A humiliated groan did escape her then.

Two days ago, she'd believed he exaggerated. Knowing what she did about him now, she'd learned he was a man of his word. Having never spent any time in the company of aristocrats, the idea of doing so made her increasingly anxious. Imposing upon Gregor was one thing, but asking favors from high-ranking *haut ton* denizens?

That was quite another, and she wasn't altogether sure she'd measure up.

He cut a piece of sausage then speared it with his fork. "They're all either relatives or friends of Ewan who've become family friends as well."

"You're very close to your cousin, aren't you?" Sarah hadn't any cousins.

Mama had been an only child, and Papa rarely spoke of his family. He'd run away to the sea as a young boy. Once, he'd mentioned his drunkard of a father's ham-like fists and the beatings he'd endured. She had no idea if any of his relatives lived, and considering what little she knew of them, she wasn't keen to find out.

Chewing, Gregor nodded. "Aye. Even the Fergusons, my step-cousins, are as close as if they were my own flesh and blood." He aimed his fork toward the main room. "I want ye to see the surprise I have for ye." Impatient as a lad, he wiped his mouth. He stood and extended his hand.

Sarah stared at it for a moment. Ever so slowly, she fit hers into his great paw. His calloused palm swallowed her hand in a warm, comforting grip. Her logical side cautioned against imprudence. The woman who was increasingly taken with Gregor ignored wisdom. Leaving the dishes for later, she permitted him to urge her and Chris to sit upon the sofa.

Immediately upon spying her, Cat hopped from the windowsill and sauntered over. Giving Gregor a disdainful look, he twitched his whiskers and jumped into her lap.

"I believe ye've replaced me in his affections." Pleasure rather than envy tinged his observation.

Feeling only slightly guilty, for she enjoyed having a pet around, Sarah scratched Cat's ears. At once, his rumbling purr filled the room.

Chris ran a hand down Cat's side. He proceeded to make horse sounds as he rolled his toy along the sofa's arm.

Gregor handed her a package, requiring her to move Cat to the side to lay it atop her thighs.

White whiskers twitching, he gave her a haughty look, his green-yellow eyes narrowed peevishly.

His face animated with anticipation, Chris fidgeted beside Sarah.

"Here ye are, lad." Gregor passed him the smaller of the two bundles. "Let me ken if ye need help with the string."

One more thing to raise Gregor in her estimation. He offered to assist Chris, but always encouraged her brother to try everything on his own.

After a bit of fumbling, Chris managed to untie the string. He flipped the package over and unfolded the paper. Eyes wide with delight, he lifted a hunter green tailcoat trimmed in black velvet. A charcoal, jade green, and silver-striped waistcoat complimented the coat and black pantaloons. Stockings, a shiny new pair of shoes, along with a pristine white cravat, and new underthings lay beneath the suit.

Her brother ran his fingers over the fabric, his expression awed. "For me?"

"Aye, laddie." Gregor gave him a tender smile and ruffled his hair.

Chris sniffed and swiped the moisture from his face with his forearm, and Sarah thought her heart would burst from gratitude.

"What do you say, Chris?"

His eyes glistening, he gave Gregor one of his winning sideways smiles. "Thank you, Gregor."

"Ye're welcome, son. Now should yer sister open hers?"

Chris gave an eager nod, his wavy hair brushing his ratty collar. His hair needed trimming. Perhaps later today, she'd ask Gregor if he had a pair of scissors she could borrow.

Feeling somewhat self-conscious, Sarah untied her package. She couldn't suppress the gasp of pleasure upon turning the brown paper back to reveal a stunning gold and crimson gown—by far the loveliest she ever seen. Beneath the gown lay matching slippers, gloves, stockings, a fan, chemise, and short stays.

A blush heated her cheeks that he'd selected something so intimate for her.

"Ye might need to make alterations." He flicked a big hand over the garments. "I guessed on yer sizes based on what ye're wearin' now."

She glanced down at the apron covering her simple dress. The clothes he'd fetched from the donation barrel were every bit as appreciated as these lovely gifts, though in an entirely different way. It seemed his thoughtfulness knew no bounds.

As far as alterations went, Sarah possessed talent with a needle. "I've been remaking our clothes from cast-offs…" She faltered as humiliation brought a flush to her face. "What I mean to say is, I can easily manage any alterations required."

"I assumed as much." A smile bent his mouth revealing the straight row of his teeth as something more than appreciation kindled in his eyes. "I haven't thanked ye for mendin' my clothes."

Delicious heat bathed her and to hide her consternation, she ran her palm over the gown. "Gregor, this is lovely, just gorgeous." It truly was. "But wherever will I wear such a creation?" Her gaze questioning, she met Gregor's eyes. Pride and *affection?* shone there. She quailed to think how much the garments had cost. A warehouse supervisor didn't earn wages enough to be able to afford luxurious clothes such as these.

Had someone else paid for them?

Who?

Looking entirely too self-satisfied, he joined her on the couch and bold as brass took her hand in his and squeezed it. "That, *jo*, is part of the surprise. Ye ken those letters?"

The ones he'd just shown her a few minutes ago? Had he read them already?

"Yes," she agreed cautiously, setting the bundle on her lap aside.

"The Duchess of Harcourt is hostin' a Christmastide soirée in just under three weeks, and yer grandmother is invited. Trust me, given the Harcourts' influence and social standin', the dowager viscountess will attend. Her grace will see to it."

Proud as a peacock, he was. She almost expected him to puff out his chest. A dance and musicale? Sarah closed her eyes. Lord help her.

"Gregor, you must know, I've never spent so much as a minute in the company of an aristocrat. I shall embarrass us all, to be sure."

"Och, no' a bit of it. Ye'll be fine. They are kind people, Sarah," he assured her soothingly.

Hmph. There were degrees of kindness, and a gauche usurper plodding about their elegant homes with no knowledge of which spoon or fork ought to be used for what, surely wouldn't endear them to her pitiful cause.

"I have no voice nor can I play an instrument," she murmured, twisting her hands in her apron. How she hated this inferior feeling.

"I'll make sure ye aren't called upon to do either."

But she would be expected to dance. A lady of refinement might be excused the former for lack of talent or opportunity, but dancing? No. She was doomed. She flopped back against the sofa. "Gregor, I don't know how to dance."

Chapter Eight

"Och, lass, I'll teach ye." Gregor grasped Sarah's hand, and before she could object, pulled her to her feet.

A blush tinted her cheeks, but she didn't resist his urging.

"Now what would ye like to learn first? A Scottish Reel? A cotillion?" He dropped his voice to a husky whisper. "The deliciously wicked waltz?"

Her pretty hazel eyes wide, she blinked up at him. "I honestly have no idea."

He most definitely preferred the waltz. It gave him an excuse to hold her in his arms, but wisdom decreed he take a slower pace. "Let's start with somethin' simple then. The Hole in the Wall, I think. No' too difficult, even if we do require another couple to do it properly." His attention shifted to Chris. "Would ye care to learn, laddie?"

"Och, nae." Chris's vehement denial as well as his attempt at Scottish sent Sarah and Gregor into peals of mirth.

"It's to be just ye and me then." Gregor bent into a formal bow. "Madam."

Laughing, a bit self-consciously, she dipped into a less than graceful curtsy.

A minute frown pulled his eyebrows together. She'd no experience with dancing or curtsying? Because there was no opportunity, or because her parents didn't participate in social functions? What he knew about Jamaica's societal hierarchy wouldn't fill a salt spoon.

Several minutes passed as he hummed and counted, teaching her the steps and movements. An adept pupil, she soon caught on. The intense concentration pursing her mouth and crinkling her eyes gave way to pleasure as they circled and crossed the floor.

"This is fun," she exclaimed, as she stepped away with regal grace.

When was the last time she'd enjoyed herself? She hadn't done much of that these past few years, he suspected.

He chuckled to himself, drawing her attention.

A fine golden eyebrow arched, and she skewed her mouth sideways. "Am I really so inept?"

"Nothin' of the sort, *jo*. I'm just imaginin' what my brother and cousins would say if they could see me givin' dance lessons." He, one of Craiglocky's fiercest warriors. He'd never hear the end of it.

"I think it the noblest of gestures." She made an elegant turn, and passed him in the middle. "Although I must tell you, the idea of facing my grandmother when she's rejected every attempt to contact her sends a chill up my spine."

"Ye've nae need to fret, Sarah. For I am confident between all those ladies I mentioned and their husbands, we can contrive a solution to yer dilemma."

Her skeptical countenance suggested she wasn't so sure.

"I think ye've mastered this one. Let's try a quadrille, shall we? It's a wee bit more complicated." He held up a hand. "Take my hand." Sarah did so, and he said, "There are four couples for the set."

It was her turn to laugh. "I'm trying to picture you as a young man learning these steps. I'd be bound, at the time you'd rather have been climbing trees and such."

She had the right of it.

He'd complained often about learning the niceties required of Polite Society even in Scotland. Now though, as he swept an arm around her waist, leading her in a circle, he could kiss his mother for insisting he do so.

"Have ye ever given thought to visitin' Scotland?" His casual tone belied the question's importance.

What he truly wanted to know was if Sarah were offered a safe haven in the Highlands, would she go? And if she did, would he stay here in London? The Highlands had called to him more and more of late. His stint in London would soon come to an end. He could feel it in his pores. And if he and Sarah were both in Scotland...

Far too soon to be harboring those types of musings.

Wasn't it?

Instead of answering, her gaze confused yet hopeful, she stared up at him. Her work-worn hand clasped in his, he was unable to break eye contact. As he searched her eyes, seeing himself reflected in the blue and gold flecks, he couldn't identify what transpired, but in that moment, his life changed forever.

I swear leannan, I'll do whatever is necessary to keep ye and yer brother safe.

To see them off London's streets and settled someplace comfortably, as well. Mayhap...explore this ever-growing fascination.

"Sister, can't we go for a walk. Please?" Chris pulled a face and gazed longingly toward the window.

Poor lad. He needed exercise and fresh air.

"I think that's enough dancing lessons for today." Sarah withdrew her hand and stepped away, her eyes lowered. Caution had replaced her earlier enthusiasm.

She'd felt the connection too, and given the cool politesse that settled upon her, it frightened her. Sitting beside her brother, she fondly tussled his hair, several shades darker than hers. "No, darling, not right now. It's still not safe, and it's much too cold. Soon, though. I promise."

She glanced at Gregor for confirmation, and he hitched a shoulder, giving her an I'm-nae-sure-when-look. He'd be bound, given the pinkish glint to the sky, snow would soon cover London.

Had it snowed while she'd been in England other than a light blanketing?

He determined to take the boy's mind off his forced seclusion. "Tell me, lad. What's yer favorite part of Christmastide?"

Chris grinned, his face animated. "The food. Mama made gingerbread and plum pudding."

"I've never eaten either," Gregor admitted. "Although, I'm fond of black bun and clootie dumplin', which I'm told is verra similar to plum puddin'."

"Black bun?" Sarah asked. "Is that a sort of bread?

"Nae, it's a fruitcake covered with pastry, usually served for Hogmanay." He closed his eyes, the image blooming behind his eyelids of the trestle table in Craiglocky's great hall sagging under the succulent feast.

"That's your New Year's celebration?"

"Aye."

"Gregor, you obviously miss Scotland a great deal." Sarah stood a couple of Chris's toy soldiers on their feet. "Why do you stay here?"

"A man likes to be in charge of his own destiny. I will never have that at Craiglocky." Yet, he contemplated returning. In a different role. Not cousin to the laird and son to Ewan's second-in-command.

He settled in one of the chairs before the fire, and after a moment, Sarah sank into the other and tucked her feet beneath her. "If you could do anything at all, Gregor, what would it be?" She probed his gaze, her interest genuine.

"Become a doctor, but it's too late at my age."

"No. It's not." She gave a vehement shake of her head. "If it's your passion, you should pursue it."

Rather than argue, he asked her the same question. "What about ye, lass?"

"If I had the means, I'd open a school for those less fortunate." She sent her brother a fond look. "Perhaps an orphanage and a hospital, supported by wealthy and powerful patrons. There's little help for those afflicted with...*challenges.*"

Often no help at all. If they were lucky enough to be born into a family of means, they were shuttled off to the country, hidden away their entire lives.

She closed her eyes and rested her head in the corner of the chair. "Just imagine. A school for children like Chris and a hospital too. Why, you could treat patients there." Slowly, her lashes fluttered open, and he could almost grasp her dream.

Watching the cavorting flames, he idly rubbed his thumb and forefinger together. "I ken a number of people willin' to support such a cause, includin' Yvette McTavish."

Sarah perked up. "Truly?"

He nodded, and shifted his attention to her. "I forgot to tell ye. Yvette and Ewan should arrive in London within the week." He slapped his knees. "I say we propose such a venture to them."

The next afternoon, just as Sarah finished sewing a button onto Gregor's greatcoat, the bell ringing below revealed clients had entered Stapleton Shipping and Supplies. As she had the past three days, she checked that the bolt securing the door was in place, and on silent feet, rushed to keep Chris quiet.

"*Shh.*" She shook her head, one finger to her lips as her heart beat a hard, staccato rhythm. "You cannot play with your toys right now, Chris."

"'Cause we're hiding from Satan and the bad men still?"

"That's right, darling." She squatted beside him.

"Sister, why do they want to hurt us?" A bewildered scowl pulled his mouth down.

"I don't know." She had an inkling why, though.

Gregor's voice echoed in the stairwell, his deep brogue, now quite familiar and always welcome. He knocked softly two times rapidly followed by a single rap—the signal that all was well.

Giving her brother a reassuring smile, she patted her hair and ran her rough hands down the front of her gown. Until now—until Gregor—she hadn't cared all that much about her appearance. Her clothing and hairstyle had been practical, serviceable, and kept her gender hidden.

That was what had been important. What had kept them alive.

But now...

She couldn't lie to herself. She wanted to appear pretty, but without pins she could do little with her hair but plait it. And while the gown she wore was a vast improvement over her shoddy boy's attire, it fell far short of attractive, and the fit was dismal at best.

Chris resumed playing with his toy soldiers, his tongue caught between his lower teeth as he hummed to himself. What would become of him if she couldn't retrieve the chest and her grandmother didn't come 'round?

Cat, regally perched nearby, observed Chris's every move. The furry imp reached his paw out and batted a soldier over. Then another. He looked at Chris, blinked his big green eyes, and knocked over a third soldier.

Chris burst out laughing, and a gratified smile swept Sarah's mouth upward. It had been so long since he'd been this happy.

The door swung open, and Gregor stepped through, a look on his face she'd come to recognize meant he had another surprise. He quite liked surprises.

Behind him, filed in three of the most elegant women Sarah had ever laid eyes upon.

"Blimey," Chris breathed, his jaw practically banging his chest.

Cat on the other hand, appeared entirely unimpressed. After one bored, superior glance, he lifted a paw to his mouth—the same paw used to attack the soldiers—and begin grooming.

Chris's awed gaze flicked from lady to lady to lady then returned to Sarah. He stood and tried to smooth his thick, newly trimmed hair. "Coo, I ain't never seen the like afore, sister."

Trying not to wince at the slang he'd picked up whilst in London, Sarah corrected his grammar. "You haven't ever seen the like, Chris."

"That's what I just said. They're prettier than angels straight from heaven, aren't they?" As if he'd a notion of what angels looked like.

Gregor chuckled, and for some illogical reason, Sarah stifled the urge to tell him to hush. If she'd felt inferior a few moments ago, compared to these polished diamonds, she felt like a ragged beggarwoman now.

Not a hair out of place, their ensembles resembling garments straight from an Ackermann fashion plate, they whisked into the room, their friendly smiles only partially putting Sarah at ease.

"Allow me to introduce ye," Gregor said, pride shining in his eyes the color the sky before a storm.

Chapter Nine

Sarah permitted Gregor to draw her forward, kindness and understanding softening his face.

For the first time in her life, she wished the floor might swallow her up. Mustering every ounce of fortitude she possessed, she forced her mouth into a polite smile. It wasn't these lovely women's fault she lacked confidence or felt entirely out of her element. She mightn't be able to do a thing about her attire, but rag-mannered she'd not be.

In truth, she ought to be thanking them profusely for coming at all.

"Sarah, this is Her Grace, Alexandra, Duchess of Harcourt." Gregor motioned to an exotic black-haired beauty wearing violet gown and spencer trimmed with ebony lace and velvet. "Adaira, Countess of Clarendon." He indicated the extremely petite woman, resplendent in a pale blue traveling suit. "And, Isobel, Countess of Ramsbury."

The latter, attired in a soft plum and cream striped redingote was possibly the most beautiful woman Sarah had ever seen. Even she couldn't help but stare.

Practically beaming, Gregor completed the introductions. "Your Grace, my ladies, may I present Sarah Paine and her brother, Christopher?"

"Mums." Chris attempted a courtier's bow, earning him delighted cries and claps from the ladies.

Where had he learned to do that?

Ah, the other day when Gregor had bowed to her.

A credit to their kindness, none of the ladies mentioned his incorrect form of address. Likely Gregor had explained Chris's special needs as well as the complete lack of interaction the Paines had ever had with aristocrats.

"I am honored, Your Grace, your ladyships. I regret you've been discomposed on my behalf." Sarah curtsied, and as she rose in one lithe movement, couldn't prevent sending Gregor a triumphant smile.

Yes, she'd been practicing too.

He gave the subtlest wink of approval, and that lovely, addicting heat, like sweetened warm chocolate, spiraled outward from her middle.

The duchess made a shooing motion, her astute gaze inspecting Sarah from her braided hair to her scuffed shoes and saggy stockings, clearly visible beneath the too-short gown "You must call me Alexa. Any friend of Gregor's is a friend of mine."

He had told them she was his friend?

Sarah wasn't certain that was a good thing, given the acute curiosity the ladies' genial smiles and friendly greetings couldn't quite hide. Surely they didn't think...? *Oh God.* Did they believe she was a *special* friend to him? One of a less than reputable nature? *No. No*, she reassured herself. They wouldn't be here if they did. So how, precisely, had Gregor explained their relationship? She tossed him a considering look.

"Yes, please do call me, Addy," the Countess of Clarendon insisted, scrunching her nose in a winsome fashion. "I'm seldom addressed as Adaira."

"Aye, 'tis true and generally only when she's been embroiled in mischief of some sort," Gregor said, grinning, his tone light and teasing like a beloved sibling. "For instance, abductin' a laird of the realm. A certain earl renowned for his rigid adherence to decorum."

"Never say you did?" Sarah reassessed the small woman. Wasn't she the one who raised prize horses too? She might well have to rethink everything she'd previously believed about nobility.

Addy's wink was nothing short of vixenish. "I did, but it was a colossal misunderstanding. And in the end, Clarendon fell madly in love with me." She rolled a dainty shoulder. "So all's well that ends well."

Her sister, the Countess of Ramsbury, studied Sarah, her intelligent gaze contemplative. "Sarah, what Alexa says is true. Gregor's word is enough for us. You've no need to worry in that regard, and do call me Isobel."

Sarah didn't know what to say. Ladies didn't go about giving permission for commoners to address them by their first names. Mayhap she'd underestimated Gregor's position. Lord, had she insulted him by doing so? Her mind raced to recall any incident when she'd been less than respectful. *Dash it all.* Since the moment she plowed into his office, she'd treated him as her equal. He'd never indicated she should do otherwise.

The duchess glided forward and clasped Sarah's hand. "My dear, we are going to be the greatest of friends. I know it. Now, gather your things. We are going shopping."

The countesses bobbed their bonneted heads in agreement, eyes alight with excitement, and looking quite proud of themselves. Why, they were enjoying this intrigue.

Sarah sought Gregor's gaze. "Isn't that dangerous? For me to go out, I mean?"

The Countess of Clarendon—Addy—wandered to the window and peered at the dock below. "We alighted from a carriage out front, but we'll leave in one of the two waiting behind the building."

The duchess grinned, a twinkle in her eyes. "We need you suitably dressed for your first foray into society. I'm delighted to say, your grandmother has accepted an invitation to tea Monday next."

Sarah's heart stuttered. She believed she had until Christmas—almost three weeks—to prepare to meet her grandmother. But next Monday?

Ten short—*very short*—days?

Another unwelcome thought brought her up short. Just how much was this going to cost? *Too much.* She'd never been a gambler, and she wasn't certain spending money she couldn't spare on garments to impress Lady Rolandson was a wager she would win.

Adaira crossed to Chris. "I should very much like you to meet my children, Chris. My boys would be delighted for the company. You are of an age, I believe."

"May I, Sister?" Chris's countenance glowed from excitement. He'd never had a friend. Not even at Bellewood House.

Her gaze warm and welcoming, Adaira came to stand before Sarah. Several inches shorter, her height in no way diminished her presence. "We've discussed it." Her vibrant eyes, took in Gregor, Alexa, and Isobel. "If you're in agreement, Gregor will escort Chris to my house to play with my children while you, Alexa, and Isobel go shopping. Afterward, my husband and I would be honored if you and your brother would agree to stay with us until things are settled with Lady Rolandson. In the event that becomes a lengthy process, we'd be delighted to celebrate Christmas and Twelfth Night with you too. My husband and I host an annual Yuletide Ball, and I vow, no one makes a better plum pudding than Cook."

Mama had always made plum pudding on Stir-Up Sunday. She'd even gathered local greenery and made a sort of tropical kissing bough.

A tiny spark of discomfit gave Sarah pause. Or perchance, others taking control of her life was what disconcerted her most. She must entrust herself and her brother to women she'd just met on the advice of a man she scarcely knew any better. It wasn't easy to let go. To put her faith in strangers when she'd relied solely on herself for so long.

Isobel must've noticed her hesitation. "We only want to help, Sarah, and you needn't concern yourself with the cost. Consider the purchase our Christmastide gift to someone we would like to bless as we've been blessed."

Sarah swallowed against the tightness constricting her throat. Kindness such as this had been rare these past few years. Though it bordered on impudent, she must have an answer. "You don't know me; why would you extend such generosity?"

"Because Gregor asked us to." The Duchess of Harcourt lifted a hand toward the Scot solemnly observing the exchange. "And we have absolute trust in him and his judgment."

That said much about Gregor, that these women loved and respected him.

I could too.

She firmly tamped down the unbidden thought. This may be the chance that she had prayed for. Mayhap her only chance. Neither pride nor fear would prevent her from accepting their benevolence.

Yes, she'd go to the fittings. She'd allow the ladies to purchase her clothing, and pray that her grandmother would reimburse their expenses. If the Dowager Viscountess Rolandson still refused to acknowledge her grandchildren—

Well, Sarah wouldn't deny Chris one last, wonderful Yuletide.

Beyond that, she couldn't contemplate. The near future gleamed brightly, and what lay beyond that glow, she'd fret about when she must.

She stepped nearer to Adaira, and after a swift glance toward Chris, assuring he'd returned to his toys and wouldn't hear her, lowered her voice. "No doubt you've noticed Chris has some challenges. Are you certain you're comfortable taking him?"

Such an incredulous expression swept the countess's face Sarah was at once ashamed.

"I understand and admire your concern for your brother, Sarah. That makes you a caring sister. But I promise you, Chris will be treated with the utmost respect and gentleness. Gregor mentioned Chris's love of horses too. I have the gentlest pony that my sons ride. With your permission, I'd like to teach Chris to ride as well."

Chris might never be adept at the sport, but at least he'd be given an opportunity to try. He wasn't supposed to be able to walk either, but his tenacity proved the doctor wrong. Given the opportunity, who knew what he could do?

Once again, Sarah must rely on her woman's instinct, and though she admitted to being anxious, no alarm tunneled through her veins. Her nape hair didn't stand on end, nor did her stomach wobble in fear. Giving a slight nod, she acquiesced. "Very well. Thank you, and Chris would love to learn to ride."

Relief softened the corners of Gregor's eyes. Had he really thought she'd put up a fuss? Something like sorrow also deepened his eyes to slate blue. Was he saddened as much as she to part?

She'd miss him. Much more than she ought to after a mere three-day acquaintance. But Mama swore she'd known she'd loved Papa after their third meeting.

Love?

Was it possible to fall in love so quickly? Affection and interest—those were feasible. Even physical desire. But love?

No.

What about Mama and Papa?

They'd been devoted to each other, and if Mama ever regretted leaving her privileged lifestyle for that of the ship captain's wife, she never breathed a hint. It mattered not whether her parents had been in love. Sarah didn't have time for such distractions. Everything she did was to ensure Chris's future.

In short order, her few possessions, along with Chris and his toys, had been bundled into one of the waiting coaches accompanied by the lovely Countess of Clarendon.

Sarah couldn't contain her surprise at how readily her brother had accepted Adaira's hand and after a fond kiss on his forehead had been led from Gregor's apartment.

"I'll ride with the lad to Clarendons', just in case he needs a familiar face." Gregor draped a cloak around Sarah's shoulders. Likely another castoff from the charity bin. He handed her a plain straw poke bonnet.

"We'll wait for you in the carriage, Sarah." Alexa exchanged a telling look with Isobel.

Had they detected the undercurrent of attraction between her and Gregor?

Of course, it was only natural she felt gratitude toward him, and perhaps it had become infatuation as well. She'd been most careful to hide her interest, and she believed she'd done a satisfactory job.

Now wasn't the time for flirtations or romantic entanglements.

Would there ever be a time?

She'd faced that disconcerting truth some time ago. It would take a very special man to win her heart. Because he must accept that Chris would always be a part of their lives. Few men—none that she knew aside from Papa—would willingly take on such a burden.

Except for Gregor jesting about accepting a kiss in repayment, he'd been the perfect gentleman. She'd been the one who agreed to the terms and could not fault him in that regard.

"Thank you, Gregor. For everything."

He rested a hand on her shoulder, giving it a gentle squeeze. His voice slightly husky and his brogue a trace thicker he said, "It's been my pleasure, lass."

More emotional about their inevitable separation than she would've anticipated, Sarah struggled against tears. Eyes lowered, she managed a short nod.

"Nae tears, *jo*."

No tears, she silently chastised herself.

He lifted her chin, and swept a thumb across her damp cheek. "I promise ye, I'm no' desertin' ye. I vowed to see ye safely settled, and I am goin' to keep my oath." He flashed his charming grin. "Besides, Adaira invited me to dinner tonight."

Sarah smiled wide, uncaring he might guess why. "You've already done so much for us. I truly don't expect any more—"

"The truth is, I've enjoyed yer company, and I'll miss ye. Promise ye'll let me take ye on an outin' to Hyde Park tomorrow."

"All right." How could she say no?

He raised her hand, pressing a kiss to her knuckles, and a jolt of sensation streaked to her elbow then skittered up her shoulder.

This was a man she could care for. A man she'd risk much for. But there was Chris to consider.

Gregor pivoted her toward the door. "Now go, before they parade back up here to see what the delay is."

"I owe ye a kiss." On impulse, she stood on her toes, laid a palm against the broad plane of his chest, and touched her lips to his.

At first, he remained rigid and unmoving. Then with a groan deep in his chest, he urged her close and kissed her like a man long-starved. Breathing heavily, he angled away and growled, "Go. Now. Before I canna let ye."

With a last glance over her shoulder and a small wave, she turned her back, feeling almost as desolate as she had when fleeing Jamaica. Fighting tears and struggling to compose herself, she slipped into the coach.

The Duchess patted the seat beside her. "Sit here, my dear."

Sarah sank onto the plush bird's egg-blue seat, and Alexa wrapped her kid gloved fingers 'round Sarah's.

Isobel fished a delicate lace handkerchief from her reticule and passed the square across the carriage. She met Alexa's eyes as she settled into the squabs and put a finger to her chin. "I don't believe I've ever seen Gregor so entranced."

Sarah raised a startled glance. "I beg your pardon?"

"Leave it to us." Alexa patted her hand. "We'll have him coming 'round in no time."

Chapter Ten

Three days later, Gregor handed his hat to Ramsbury's majordomo.

Today, he'd been invited to a proper English tea. Hadn't he become the simpering fop? He brushed a cat hair off his buff coat. He reserved it, and the cherry and shimmering gold waistcoat he wore, for special occasions. What could be more special than seeing Sarah Paine again?

The three days since they'd parted felt like three interminable months. He'd thought of her constantly, had written to her daily, and his apartment was unbearably quiet and lonely now.

Cat even wandered around meowing plaintively.

The much-anticipated outing with her to Hyde Park had not manifested. After dinner at the Clarendon's, he'd returned home to find his living quarters ransacked. It hadn't taken a good deal of thought to figure out who was behind the break-in.

Yesterday, he'd interrogated Mrs. Smith, and the housekeeper tearfully confessed she'd seen a toy soldier beneath the couch when she last cleaned Gregor's quarters. A little more probing, and she admitted to accepting a few coins for sharing that tidbit with a scruffy, bearded man.

Yeates.

Mrs. Smith didn't think sharing that morsel would hurt anything, for she'd seen no other evidence of anything out of the ordinary. Her poor choice had earned her a dismissal, but Gregor had conceded to provide her with a reference and a purse to hold her over until she found another position.

A locksmith had been retained, and not only did Stapleton Shipping and Supplies now have new locks throughout, he'd hired two former soldiers to patrol the perimeter.

Thank God, Sarah and Chris had already left. He shuddered to think what would've happened had they been discovered.

Voices and laughter filtered from the drawing room. Having been here a few times before, he motioned for the butler to answer the new knock sounding at the door.

"I ken the way."

"Very good, sir."

Gregor lingered in the drawing room entrance, taking a few moments to savor his friends, family, and most of all, Sarah enjoying themselves. Previous visits had taught him that this room, as well as the rest of the house, would be decked out in holiday gaiety come Christmas Eve. Likely a few days beforehand since Isobel adored the holiday.

Wearing a lavender gown, a delicate lace fichu tucked into the bodice—unfortunately hiding the creamy bounty within—and amethyst and pearl earrings dangling from her dainty earlobes, Sarah looked every bit the lady of refinement. Her hair twisted into an intricate knot, she held a yellow chintz-patterned teacup as she smiled and made polite conversation.

A queer sensation kicked behind his ribs. *Gude,* he'd missed her. Missed her laugh and ready smile. Missed the gentle interaction with her brother. Missed her keen intellect, droll retorts, and the way her eyes rounded in wonder. He even missed the way her nose crinkled when he said something in Scots or Gaelic she didn't understand but was too polite to say so.

How had she and Chris wiggled their ways into his heart so quickly?

Ewan vowed he loved Yvette the minute he danced with her, but it had been two years before they met again.

Isobel spied him, and glided to the door. She looped her hand through the crook of his elbow and drew him forward. "I had begun to think you weren't coming, and that I'd misread your fascination with our dear Sarah."

Just what did she mean by that? He gave her a shrewd assessment, but she'd already turned away, leading him straight to Sarah.

Had he been that bloody obvious? Pointing his gaze ceilingward, he stifled unfamiliar chagrin. By God, he hadn't moped about like a moon-eyed milksop. He'd not even hinted his interest, so how did Isobel and the others know?

Women seemed to have an extra sense about these matters.

He knew the instant Sarah realized he stood beside her, though she hadn't glanced in his direction.

The faintest flush pinkened her cheeks, and she carefully set her teacup upon the table, before turning a radiant smile upon him. "Hello, Mr. McTavish."

How odd to have her address him so formally, but she'd not want to give rise to tattle. "Always a pleasure, Miss Paine." He inclined his head.

Lord and Lady Warrick entered the drawing room, and Isobel floated away to greet them.

Gregor eyed the dainty chair, the only remaining vacant seat near Sarah. He could either perch like an oversized bird upon its edge, or remain standing. For he hadn't a doubt that if he applied his full weight to the flimsy thing, the legs would give way, and he'd land on his arse.

Isobel clapped her hands, and her husband, Yancy, Earl of Ramsbury, joined her, and with a doting smile, she placed a hand on his forearm. "I have something special to show you." She gave the callers a mysterious smile. "Please follow me."

A swift perusal of the guests had Gregor's mouth twitching at the corners. Everyone, yes, every last one, was married except for him and Sarah.

So, the grand ladies—*and their husbands?* —played matchmakers, did they? Not subtly either, by God. He ought to have considered that he'd set himself up for their interference when he asked them to help a young woman of his acquaintance. Interestingly though, he didn't mind.

Nae, he didn't mind at all.

Adaira caught his eye, and whispered something in Clarendon's ear. The earl gave Gregor an apologetic shrug before guiding his wife from the room. Aye, the chaps were involved too. Likely inveigled into assisting their meddling wives.

On cue, the other couples filed from the room, leaving Gregor and Sarah to come last.

He mightn't have objections, but their disregard for her feelings rankled a jot. What if she noticed their ploy? Would she be offended? Humiliated? He offered Sarah his elbow, and she placed her gloved hand upon it.

"I received your note about the break-in, Gregor. I hope you were able to restore everything to order."

He couldn't prevent the satisfied curving of his mouth that she deemed to use his given name when others were out of earshot. Her perfume, mild, floral, a hint spicy with a touch of citrus, wafted upward. Had she borrowed the scent, or had his cousins purchased it for her?

"Aye, and I've added extra security as well," he said. Another waft of fragrance floated past. He almost bent to smell her shiny hair. Had she used scented soap to wash it? He reluctantly towed his errant thoughts back to the matter at hand.

"No doubt a good idea," she murmured a bit distractedly.

"Sarah, I believe Santano's thugs are still watchin' the offices, and I'd like to set a trap for them with yer permission, lass." He slowed their progress.

"A trap?" She cut a swift glance at those entering the conservatory.

Was she worried about the propriety of being alone with him? Now? When they'd spent days together? Well, Chris had always been there, but still...

"Aye." No help for it. He must speak with her privately and this was likely his only opportunity. He drew her to a halt. "I hope to apprehend the scoundrel before he sails. Several of the gentlemen in attendance here today are meetin' me at White's this afternoon to discuss the plan. But I wanted ye to be aware first. Do ye have any idea why he pursues ye, *jo*?"

Her tongue darted out to wet her lower lip, and she tucked her chin, causing her earrings to sway.

As he'd suspected, she'd been keeping something from him.

"I do. I possess a key my mother gave me. I believe it belongs to a chest hidden at Bellewood." She cut him a swift, almost guilty, glance before continuing. "That is—was—our home in Jamaica. I don't know what the chest contains, but my father showed it to me once and told me it was to ensure Chris's future. I can only presume the contents are of some value. I also don't know if Santano assumes I have the chest here and believes I've hidden it somewhere. I don't think he's found it yet, because he wouldn't continue to plague me otherwise."

"He must know what it contains then, and I'd wager the contents are very valuable." Gregor placed his hand over hers and gently squeezed her fingers. "What if we were to use another chest as bait?"

He squinted in concentration. Greedy sods like Santano lusted after wealth. Setting a snare for him and his henchmen shouldn't be all that difficult.

"Do you really think it would work?" Such hope lit Sarah's face, he longed to wrap her in his arms, pull her close, and assure her it would

He didn't dare, standing in the corridor, more was the pity.

Someday though...

"I do. Is that why he killed yer parents?"

Pain tightened her features, and the long, graceful column of her throat worked. "He killed my father for control of the *Mary Elizabeth*. I believe he may have killed my mother trying to find the chest, though I don't know that for certain."

"Sarah?" Placing his hands on her upper arms, Gregor turned her to face him. "Are you saying your mother might be alive?"

"Oh, Gregor." Her eyes glistened, her pain tearing at his heart. "I want it to be so with all my heart. But there hasn't been a word in three years. I keep hoping she's written my grandmother or could somehow make her way to England. But Mama was sickly when she forced Chris and me to leave her behind. If it hadn't been for Chris, I would've refused to go."

And she'd probably be dead now.

Gregor gathered her into his embrace and kissed the top of her head. Devil take what anybody had to say. Not knowing whether her mother lived or not must eat away like serrated, rusting blade every day.

"Lass, I ken ships that sail to the Caribbean—specifically Jamaica. I can have inquiries made so that ye'll know once and for all about yer mother." He dared press his mouth to her silky fragrant hair again. "It might bring ye peace."

She deserved peace. Deserved to have someone take care of her for a change.

Eyes closed, her breathing ragged and head bowed, she struggled for control. At last she whispered, "I want to know. I cannot ever find peace until I do."

"I'll see to it at once then."

Weighty silence filled the passageway.

Memories likely flooded Sarah's thoughts while Gregor calculated his next step. Clarendon, Warrick, and Ewan had worked as spies for the Home Office. He didn't doubt they'd have a clever idea or two that could help lead to Santano's capture and imprisonment.

A thought struck, and he asked, "Can ye prove yer father's ownership of the *Mary Elizabeth*?"

"Yes. I have the documentation. Mama thought to send it with me, and the deed to Bellewood too. But I expect Santano possessed forged documents claiming the ship is his."

Not hard to disprove with the right influence and resources, both of which Gregor had access to.

She'd been incredibly brave, very much like the women he'd introduced her to the other day. Someday, she'd have to hear their stories. He'd be bound she'd never believe the Duchess of Harcourt had once been a Highland gypsy. Or that Alexa had helped Isobel escape the band of rogue Highlanders who abducted her.

Aye, introducin' her to these braw, bonnie women is wise.

"While we have a moment alone, I wanted to invite ye to the theater tomorrow night." Gregor had no idea what the performance was, but every one of the lords now chatting in the conservatory had private boxes. For the second time in less than a week, he meant to take advantage of those connections. "And also if ye're agreeable, the Christmas Pantomime on Drury Lane on Boxin' Day, as well as

Astley's Christmas Spectacular. Chris is welcome too, of course."

"I've never been to any of them. They sound wonderful." She'd regained her composure and a half-smile curved her mouth. "I'm not sure Chris would appreciate the theater, but he so adores horses. I'm certain he'd enjoy Astley's."

Yancy poked his head around the door, cocking a reproving eyebrow at Gregor. "Are you coming? Isobel has a special surprise, just for Miss Paine."

"Aye." He took Sarah's elbow. Still far too thin. "Come along, *jo*."

"*Jo*? What does that mean?" Her bright eyes brimming with curiosity, she searched his face.

"Sweetheart or darlin'."

"Oh." Instead of blushing or dropping her gaze in a maidenly fashion, she grinned, joy blossoming across her face.

Gregor couldn't suppress a rather smug smile.

Upon entering the lush plant and flower-filled room, she released a delighted cry. Several parakeets flitted about, but it was the elaborate cage containing two green parrots that had her flying across the tiled floor.

"Oh, stars. They are yellow-billed parrots. Just like those in Jamaica."

"They are," Isobel agreed. "I acquired them a month ago from a traveling showman. They weren't being cared for well. When Gregor mentioned you'd had a pet one in Jamaica, I knew I had to introduce you before moving them to our country aviary."

"I confess, they make me homesick." Sarah gripped the cage, resting her forehead on the wires, a hint of sorrow shadowing her features.

Isobel pressed Sarah's hand. "You are welcome to visit them anytime whilst they are still here, and once we've moved them to the aviary as well."

"Isobel studies all manner of species of birds and other things." Gregor caught Ramsbury's attention. "Might I make use of yer theater box tomorrow? Miss Paine has agreed to attend with me."

More hearty approval followed his announcement. Because they were excited about the performance or that he'd asked Sarah to accompany him? The latter to be sure, for he'd not mentioned which theater. The performance might've been the rotund Prince Regent dancing naked atop a pink elephant, and they'd have agreed, if only to see the courtship's progression.

As Gregor had anticipated, all present invited themselves along.

Rather than look overwhelmed, Sarah seemed pleased.

He was too, but not only because her happiness brought him joy.

Shortly, he'd put the plan in place he'd spent days contriving. With Sarah's key and a fake chest as bait, Santano would soon be in the authorities' hands.

Chapter Eleven

Sitting in the Ramsburys' private box in the opulent Theatre Royal Drury Lane, Sarah scarcely knew what the current entertainment on stage was about. After the first performance—a rather depressing tragedy—the audience was now treated to a pantomime.

She didn't dare say so, but she found his antics more silly than humorous.

From the boisterous chortles and feminine titters, she might be alone in her observation, though from the sideways peeks she'd sent Gregor, he appeared more appalled than anything else.

A comedy now had the glittering crowd hooting and hollering. Those who weren't spying on others with their opera glasses, that was. However, as he had all evening, the riveting man at her side commandeered her attention.

She glanced down, smoothing her hand over the fine satin. As the garments commissioned for her wouldn't be ready for at least another week, she wore a gown borrowed from the Duchess of Harcourt. Sarah had never felt more regale Or more unequivocally out of place—as if she play-acted and pretended to be someone, something, she wasn't.

Every aspect of this seemed wrong on some level.

Why couldn't she just be Sarah, daughter of Captain and Mrs. Aaron Paine from Jamaica? Wasn't that good enough?

No. Not if she was to get into her grandmother's good graces. At this point, she wasn't even sure that was what she wanted anymore.

Gregor was her steadying rudder through it all, and her heart ached to think that soon they may go their separate ways. Scarcely over a week ago, panic had propelled her into his office. Now her circumstances were vastly improved, but every bit of the change was due, at least in part, to him.

His thoughtfulness. His connections. His perseverance. His goodness.

Seated on the far end of the box, every now and again, he ran his finger over the back of her hand resting in her lap. Brazen, considering the candles remained lit in their box. Only a few private boxes had extinguished their tapers.

Surely, everyone sitting nearby heard her heart knocking against her breastbone.

This gruff—much too attractive for her own good—Highlander was well on his way to capturing her heart.

Nonetheless, as long as Santano searched for her and Chris, she could never relax, never let down her guard. She couldn't be certain of their safety, even with a warrior like Gregor and his powerful friends vowing their protection. They couldn't know Santano was pure evil, and he seemed to have spies everywhere.

This evening as she descended from the coach, she'd caught sight of a vaguely familiar, shadowy figure lurking across the street from the theater. She couldn't be sure, of course. Not with poor lighting and her hurried glimpse. But something about his bearing caused her nape hairs to rise, and her instinct screamed danger.

Perhaps she was being paranoid, but only a fool failed to be cautious and dismissed something like that as chance. On the way home, she'd discuss her concerns with Gregor. For now, she'd enjoy his company and the rather awful performance upon the stage.

She squinted, leaning forward a couple of inches. Was that a man dressed as a buxom woman?

Gregor bent near, touching her hand again and whispering in her ear. "Enjoyin' yerself, lass?"

How could something as innocent as touching hands heighten her awareness of him? "Yes. Very much." Not because of the actors on the stage, however. No, another captured her interest. Feeling extremely daring, she laid her other hand atop his and squeezed his fingers.

He boldly returned the caress.

Someone behind them cleared her throat, and she withdrew her hand. Either they'd been caught in their indiscretion, or fate had intervened and brought her to her senses.

Encouraging him was unwise, as was indulging her growing infatuation. In a matter of days, she'd meet her grandmother at the duchess's tea, and Sarah would know one way or the other whether she and Chris would remain in London or move elsewhere.

She'd already conceived new identities for her brother and her, should the need arise, and she wouldn't hesitate to flee once again. Even if that meant not telling these kindhearted people where she was going. Much depended upon the success of the scheme Gregor and his friends had concocted to entrap Santano.

An hour later as they left the theater, the men sheltered the women from the curious onlookers and an occasional drunken reveler. His features stern and posture tense, Gregor guided her to the waiting carriages. "Look lively, lads. I've an uneasy feelin'."

So did she.

Even as the words left his mouth, Santano's three thugs rushed from the crowd directly toward her. Gregor neatly stepped in front of her, dispatching Yeates with a mighty blow to his jaw.

He dropped to the pavement like a soiled handkerchief.

Lords Clarendon and Ramsbury wrestled the smaller ruffian to the ground, but the third escaped.

Her heart pounding her throat, Sarah stared into Santano's hireling's hate-filled face, as he thrashed in the lordships' arms.

"Santano knows where you're stayin', bitch. Best be sayin' your prayers—"

Another well-placed punch from Gregor rendered him unconscious as well.

Sarah clutched Gregor's arm. "Chris!"

"Ramsbury, will ye see these bloody rotters are arrested?" Gregor asked as he handed her into the carriage.

"With immense pleasure." Ramsbury signaled his driver. The strapping fellow and Harcourt's drivers were binding the attackers' wrists and ankles as Sarah's conveyance pulled away from the throng.

Less than thirty minutes later, after a harrowing ride, her nerves tattered raw from worry, she closed Chris's bedchamber door. The servants assured her and Lord and Lady Clarendon that nothing out of the ordinary had transpired in their absence.

Allowing Gregor to lead her downstairs, Sarah pulled her shawl tighter about her shoulders. "Do you think Santano really knows we are here?"

Gregor drew her to halt, turning her so she faced him. "It's no' only possible, we want him to ken. As an extra precaution, I'll be stayin' here 'til the scunner's caught." His mouth quirked in that roguish manner she'd come to know. "Just think, *jo*, I can give ye more dancin' lessons."

Excitement and alarm swept her, not only that he would stay here, but that he'd tried sweeping her worry aside and changing the subject. She crossed her arms. "I presume you're going to explain those statements to me?"

"Dinna get yer feathers ruffled, lass. I'm no' keepin' secrets from ye." He kissed her forehead, right there for all to see, as if he were staking a claim on her. For a blissful instant, she forgot her fear.

Only an instant though before reality crashed upon her senses. "Good try, Highlander." She poked his chest. "I'll have the truth of it, and don't spare my sensibilities. In case you haven't noticed, I'm not a delicate flower or a swooning sort of female."

"Aye." He gave her a scorching glance that sent a frisson along her spine. "I noticed that about ye, and a lot more too." He made a slow work of raking his gaze over her from head to toe and back again.

"Gregor McTavish!" She didn't sound half so outraged as flattered at his seductive smile and the rakish glint hooding his turbulent gaze.

"Och, dinna fash yerself." He tapped her nose. "Today, word was deliberately spread around the places Santano and his sailors frequent that soon after my apartment was searched, a chest was delivered to Stapleton Shippin' and Supplies. If all goes as planned, Santano will attempt to steal it. Given I've added new security measures, I'm positive he'll take the bait. Once inside the warehouse, he'll find much more than a chest awaits him."

His low, slightly wicked chuckle sent shivers scuttling along her shoulders. Gregor McTavish wasn't a man to underestimate.

A few days later, Sarah inhaled a steadying breath and swallowed her nerves as she and Gregor entered the Harcourt's grand house. After passing the butler her new navy-blue silk bonnet and velvet-lined pelisse, she commanded her frolicking pulse to calm. As it was wont to do, the unruly thing completely ignored her dictate.

She must do this.

With Gregor by her side, she could.

"Has Lady Rolandson arrived yet, Tibbs?" Sarah couldn't wait an instant longer to ask the question burning the tip of her tongue.

"Yes, Miss Paine." The butler accepted Gregor's cane and hate as well.

She would've preferred to meet her grandmother for the first time in a private setting, but her ladyship's refusal to so much as speak to her had brought this public confrontation upon herself.

It had actually been quite brilliant of Alexa, truth to tell.

Gripping Gregor's arm as if it were a lifeline, Sarah allowed him to guide her down the passageway. Catching sight of them as they passed an ornate gilded mirror, a tiny smile bent her mouth. If she didn't know better, she'd suspect he'd picked his blue tartan waistcoat because it matched her midnight blue gown.

Both tall and blond, they did indeed make a most striking couple. Their children would be blond too, no doubt. Would their offspring have his blue-gray eyes or her hazel ones?

If only it might be so.

Those ruminations would have to wait. Her future was but a few feet away, and she intended to face it head on. She squared her shoulders, stiffened her spine, and elevated her chin.

Mustering her composure, and ordering whatever the rambunctious creature frolicking in her middle were to settle down, Sarah permitted Gregor to lead her into the drawing room.

"Smile, lass." He squeezed her arm. "Ye look like ye're goin' to a funeral. What's the worst that can happen?"

She was, in essence, facing a sort of death. For today she'd either forge a new future or slam the door on her past forever. As for the worst that could happen? Well, she wasn't certain where Gregor fit in either of those scenarios, and she very much wanted him to. Very much indeed.

He winked in that confident manner that never failed to charm a smile from her. "Ye and Chris can always come to Scotland with me."

Eyes narrowed the merest bit, she took his measure. Did he jest, or was he sincere? Then her mind stumbled upon the truth and dismay bludgeoned her. "You're returning to Scotland?"

"Aye," he agreed, his voice rather gravelly.

Dismay throttled up her throat. She'd become accustomed to his company. His dear face and roguish humor. And he was leaving.

"When?"

It wasn't any of her business. She'd hoped to see him after—that was *if*—things went well with her grandmother. Sarah lied to herself. She had counted on his being there, no matter the outcome. To think he wouldn't nearly undid her.

He rolled a shoulder nonchalantly. "It depends."

On what? She wanted to scream.

He canted his head in response to a handsome dark-haired man's greeting. "Yvette and Ewan are here, Sarah." He seemed inordinately pleased by that. "I'll introduce ye later."

With a small start, she realized who the man and the stunning blonde at his side were. Rumor had it, Yvette McTavish was the wealthiest woman in the whole of Britain. Sarah swept her gaze over the assembled guests, glittering in their high-fashion finery. Her grandmother was in this room somewhere.

She would have to wait to find out when Gregor intended to leave for Scotland. The moment she'd anticipated and dreaded was upon her. "I hope this isn't a colossal mistake," she whispered.

At once, Alexa glided to their sides.

Speaking quietly, she murmured, "Sarah, your grandmother is sitting by the window. I don't believe she saw you arrive, but I do have salts available in case she swoons." Her eyes crinkled in amusement. "She's known to do that on a regular basis."

Just perfect. Temperamental, mean-spirited, sharp-tongued, unforgiving, and given to the vapors. Had the dowager any redeeming qualities?

Digging her fingers into Gregor's forearm, Sarah marshalled every ounce of poise she possessed as the duchess wended her way across the drawing room, smiling and nodding to guests as she swept past.

Elegant, her mien superior and self-important, Lady Rolandson, attired in black from her lace cap to her gloves, was engaged in conversation with another distinguished grand dame near her age, also swathed in black from her sophisticated turban to her beaded, slippered toes.

Upon their approach, Lady Rolandson gave a disinterested upward sweep of her sparse lashes. Eyes widening, she froze, going perfectly still. The color draining from her face, she clutched at her throat as if choking. "Mary?"

Sarah shook her head, sinking onto the empty chair and offering a tremulous upward turn of her mouth. "No, I'm her daughter, Sarah Paine."

Almost at once, a plumpish prune-faced woman, perhaps in her fourth decade, rushed to her ladyship's side. Placing a hand on her shoulder, she patted gently, whilst glaring daggers at Sarah. "Calm yourself, Your Ladyship. Take deep breaths." All solicitous concern, she hovered above Grandmother. Rummaging in the reticule at her wrist, she asked, "Do you require your salts? 'Tis obvious *this person* has given you a most terrible upset."

Lady Rolandson speared the woman a sour look and shrugged the hand off her shoulder. "Stop coddling me, Bernice! You're my companion, not my nursemaid. I'll thank you to remember your place."

There was the temperamental harridan Sarah had been warned about.

Bernice's mouth cinched impossibly tighter as if she'd sucked a most unripe lemon. Something akin to fury tightened her plain features, and Sarah realized with an uncomfortable start, the companion's wrath was directed squarely at her. "But your heart, Your Ladyship," Bernice argued stiffly.

"Is now and has always been perfectly fine, *Miss Wattle*." After another scathing glance, Sarah's grandmother struggled to her feet, extending quaking hands. Eyes suspiciously moist, she offered a trembling smile. "My dear, why didn't you inform me you were in London? I'm beyond overcome, but so very delighted. I didn't even know of your existence."

Sarah stiffened, casting Gregor a flabbergasted look. It took all of her self-control not to condemn her grandmother for a liar right then and there. Was it possible he'd been right? That somehow, incredible as it seemed, her grandmother hadn't known about Sarah's many attempts to contact her?

With the slightest flexing of his eyes, he indicated she should go on.

Grandmother drew in a shaky breath, her focus sinking to the floor. In a small, weak voice, she said, "These many years, I never heard from your mother. I'd given up hope."

"I beg your pardon?" Outrage at the blatant tarradiddle sluiced Sarah from her head to her toes curled tight in her slippers.

Gregor's heavy, soothing hand on her shoulder calmed her a mite.

"Not a word." Grandmother shook her head. "I'd hoped and prayed, as did Rolandson, that she'd contact us. For nearly ten years, I checked the post every day. I gave up after that, you see. It was just too painful..." Her eyes grew misty, and her chin quivered. A heartbroken, fragile old woman had replaced the formidable dowager of a few moments ago. She dabbed an eye with her knuckle. "I finally realized Mary would never be able to forgive me."

Miss Wattle made a *tutting* sound, her tone and gaze condemning. "I must say, you've some nerve, Miss Paine, showing up unannounced and distressing her ladyship in this matter. In public too. For shame."

Who was this woman that she presumed order her and Grandmother about? Sarah bit the inside of her cheek from telling Miss Bernice Wattle precisely what she could do with her bloody disapproval. The suggestion might have something to do with a small body cavity.

"Might I advise you adjourn to a more private setting, my lady?" Alexa said as she cut Adaira a telling look.

The countess approached, concern pinching the corners of her eyes the merest bit.

Glancing around, Sarah encountered the curious glances of several other guests. Likely this gossip fodder would be whispered in drawing rooms and assemblies across London by day's end. It wasn't every day during a *le beau monde* tea that a peeress discovered the offspring she'd disowned decades before had a child.

Sarah's lips twitched. Grandmother might be allowed a fainting episode after all.

"Yes, yes, that would be wise, Your Grace. I should prefer to converse with my granddaughter alone." Lady Rolandson reached for Sarah's hand, and she reluctantly allowed the old woman to clasp it in her frail grasp.

Something was off here. Her grandmother didn't appear to be pretending her shock, so why would she claim that Mama had never written? Sarah possessed the returned letters.

"Yes, I too think it's wise to have this discussion in private and determine if this... *person* is who she claims she is. She might be impersonating your granddaughter in an attempt to swindle you." Accusation ringing in her words, Miss Wattle made to accompany them.

Balling a fist against the urge to slap the condescending smirk off Miss Wattle's chuffy face, Sarah forced herself to count to ten.

Gregor's hand lit upon her shoulder for a brief instant, once again calming her. He *knew*. Knew how hard put she was to bridle her tongue.

"Have you eyes in your empty head, Bernice?" Lady Rolandson swept a hand up and down Sarah. "She's the very image of her mother at that age, you twaddle-brain. You view Mary's portrait in the drawing room daily. Don't pretend you do not notice the resemblance," her ladyship snapped, whilst leveling Miss Wattle a peevish glare.

"I believe grandmother and granddaughter should be permitted this reunion in private, Miss Wattle." Alexa's demeanor clearly expressed that nothing else was acceptable.

"But... I don't...What if...?" Miss Wattle stuttered.

"There's no need for you to join us," Grandmother said with a dismissive wave of her hand. "I expect our discussion to become quite emotional."

"I'm not sure you should be alone with *this person*, your ladyship. After all, we know absolutely nothing about her." Miss Wattle could be given credit for her tenacity, if not her ragged manners.

"Come, Miss Wattle." Adaira looped the vexed companion's arm through hers. "Have you met my brother, Lord Sethwick and his lady wife?" Her side-eyed glance and slightly quirked mouth indicated she knew full well what Miss Wattle was about, and she wasn't having any of it.

"You won't leave, will you?" Sarah touched Gregor's arm.

"Nae. I'll be right here, waitin' for ye, *jo*." He crossed his arm over his chest. A gallant knight vowing his allegiance. "I swear."

Chapter Twelve

Silently, Sarah and her grandmother followed Alexa down the corridor and into a charming sitting room decorated in shades of pale blue and peach.

"Shall I request tea for you?" Alexa asked.

Meeting her grandmother's hazel eyes, so very much like her own, Sarah shook her head "I don't care for any, but perhaps her ladyship would—"

"No, thank you, Your Grace." Still appearing rather stunned, Grandmother patted Sarah's hand and gave a weak smile.

"I'll leave you then." With a sympathetic meshing of her lips, Alexa swept from the room.

For a long, awkward moment, her head cocked in an almost robin-like fashion, Sarah's grandmother stared. "I cannot believe it. I simply cannot believe it. Oh, if Rolandson had only lived to see this day. He would've been so very happy. The resemblance to your mother is uncanny, my dear."

"Papa always said so as well," Sarah admitted, feeling the familiar twist of her heart mentioning her beloved father brought.

Grandmother dashed a tear away from the corner of her eye, and a rather fragile smile replaced her drooping mouth. "I have a granddaughter."

"And grandson, too, my lady. His name is Christopher, he prefers Chris, and he's twelve years old." No need to tell her about Chris's difficulties just yet. She'd learn about them soon enough.

"Oh, my! A grandson." She clapped her hands once. "None of that *my lady* balderdash, either. I insist you call me Grandmama."

And, of course, no one told Lady Rolandson no.

Grandmama sank into a nearby chair, shaking her head back and forth, causing the jet earrings in her ears to sway with the motion. A few silvery curls peeked from beneath her crocheted cap. Had she been as blonde as Mama and her? Shoulders hunched, she put her hands to her face. "How I wish I could take back the harsh things I said to your mother," she sobbed. "My pride...My foolish, foolish pride and arrogance drove my darling daughter from me. I caused her to her hate me." Her voice, sounding like ancient parchment, cracked. "She never once tried to contact me in all these years."

Unable to resist comforting the weeping woman, Sarah sank to her knees. This wasn't the callous harridan she'd believed her grandmother was.

Another great sob shook her frail shoulders.

"Mama *did* write you. Many times. I have some of the unopened letters." She covered her grandmother's shaking shoulder. "Three years ago, Chris and I came to your house. We were turned away at the door. I wrote you recently, just over a week ago, and that messenger was also turned away."

Grandmother collapsed back into the chair, her expression aghast, one hand clutching at her throat. "No. No. That's not possible." She shook her head so frantically, her cap slipped to one side. "No one told me," she gasped, her gaze bouncing around the room like marbles in a shaken cup.

Did she think Sarah lied?

"I swear, it's true. Gregor McTavish delivered the letter himself. We presumed you wanted nothing to do with us."

After a bit of fumbling, her grandmother pulled a delicate handkerchief from her bodice. She dried her face and blew her nose. At last she managed, "I believe you, my dear. I do."

Remarkably pleased her grandmother should do so, Sarah's eyes misted.

An instant later, severe lines hardened Grandmother's lightly wrinkled face, giving Sarah a glimpse of the harsh woman she was reputed to be. Jerking upright, she slammed both palms onto the chair's arms. Forged steel replaced her earlier fragility. "That devious, conniving wench."

Sarah inched backward a jot, uncertain whether to admire or fear her grandmother. Lady Rolandson wasn't someone to cross. That much remained consistent with what she had heard about her grandmother.

Shrewdness narrowed the elderly woman's eyes. "Since Rolandson died and his nephew inherited the viscountcy, Bernice has hinted—quiet regularly I might add—that I ought to leave her a generous settlement. You see, until you surprised me today, it was thought that I had no heirs to leave my personal wealth and holdings to. I simply refuse to let the Crown seize my monies, so unbeknownst to her, I bequeathed all but a stipend for her and the other servants to charity." Her grandmother pinched her lips together. "*Hmph.* I'd best see about updating my will at once."

"I don't understand." Sarah sat back on her heels and furrowed her forehead.

"I'm onto Bernice and Stinkwiggon's dastardly scheme now, the unscrupulous fiends," Grandmama muttered to herself, pounding the unfortunate armchair again.

Stinkwiggon? Surely she had misheard. "Stinkwiggon?"

Grandmother spared her a starchy glance. "Stinkwiggon's my fusty, calculating butler. He and Wattle think I don't know they've been dallying with one another for years. I may be old, but I'm neither blind nor stupid." She tapped the fingers of one arthritic hand upon the carved wood, her vexation palpable. Her small frame quaked with outrage

"It was your butler who turned us away," Sarah said. Grandmother must be made aware of the truth. God only knew what else her butler and companion were capable of.

Likely, the conniving butler had intercepted her letters too. By returning Mama's correspondence, they made Mama believe her parents hadn't forgiven her. Things were starting to become quite clear.

"Yes, well," Grandmother huffed, her agitation turning her cheeks pink, "he'll be without a position as soon as I return home. So will Miss Bernice Wattle. She'll not find anyone willing retain her in of all of England. Neither will he, by God, by the time I'm done with them. Thought to pull the wool over my eyes, did they? Thought I was a dafty old tabby, did they? We'll see about that," she harrumphed.

Sarah almost felt sorry for the servants.

Almost.

She didn't doubt her grandmother's extensive influence, not to mention her far-reaching wrath, would prevent the pair from finding employment in London again. Or mayhap England, as she'd claimed.

"I've no doubt they've been intercepting letters intended for me with the intent of gaining an inheritance for themselves." Stuffing her handkerchief back into its hiding place, Grandmother pursed her mouth in displeasure.

"I think you must be right," Sarah agreed, her head slightly reeling with all she'd just learned.

Thanks to her devious servants, Grandmother had been as much a victim as she and Chris. Mama too. If Grandmother was right, Stinkwiggon and Miss Wattle deserved the consequences of their scurrilous actions.

Sarah rose, and after taking a seat in a nearby chair, pressed her lips together. "You should know that a very evil man is pursuing Chris and me. He killed our father, and we fled Jamaica, fearing for our lives."

Her almost invisible eyebrows skittering up her forehead, Grandmother whispered, "Dear God." She clasped Sarah's hand. "You poor, poor dear."

"Last week he found us, and if it hadn't been for Gregor McTavish's protection and kindheartedness, and that of several of the peeresses here today, as well as their husbands, Santano might've already abducted us." Or worse. "Mr. McTavish has devised a plan to entrap Santano, and hopefully he will be arrested soon."

"My darling girl, you've had such a time of it. It seems I owe Mr. McTavish a debt of gratitude, too." She peered at Sarah, a trifle too keenly for her comfort. "May I presume he is that giant of a man who escorted you today?"

"Yes." Sarah tipped her head in acknowledgment. She wasn't quite ready for grandmother to go poking around in that area when she herself didn't know exactly where she and Gregor stood with each other.

"Tell me…" Grandmother swallowed and patted another tear from the corner of her eye. "Does…" Her throat worked and a tear dribbled down her papery cheek. "Does my Mary live?"

Sorrow engulfed Sarah. "I honestly do not know, Grandmama." How strange it felt on her tongue to address the woman as such. "I hope she does with all my heart."

"As do I."

Fighting her own tears, and struggling for composure, Sarah glanced outside. "Why, it's snowing. I've never seen snow before."

Huge snowflakes fluttered from the sky, casting a fluffy white blanket on everything, even as she watched. Chris would be ecstatic.

"So it is." Grandmama turned her head. "It's been an unusually cold winter thus far. The trip home may be a bit of a challenge. We shouldn't delay overly long."

Did that mean she intended for Sarah to accompany her?

The dowager cleared her throat, drawing her attention. Trepidation shone in her grandmother's red-rimmed eyes. "Can you tell me what you do know?" Her gaze silently pleaded with Sarah.

"Mama was sickly when I left. She'd been frail for years. The tropical climate didn't agree with her all that well. When Santano commandeered Papa's ship, she made me take Chris and flee Jamaica. We scarcely had more than the clothes on our backs, but Mama and Papa had suspected Santano was up to something nefarious and had made arrangements for passage to England for us. She told me to contact you once we arrived three years ago. She sent a letter too." Hitching a shoulder, she dropped her gaze to her lap. "So, I don't know whether she lives or not."

Speaking those words out loud drove a dagger deep into her middle and twisted it. Sarah folded her hands, clasping her fingers tight, and crossed her ankles.

"Three years?" Agony etched the old woman's face. "Dear God. How have you and your brother managed to survive?"

"We had a few pieces of jewelry and some money." Sarah raised her chin. She would not be embarrassed nor would she accept condemnation. "We've scraped by, living in unsavory neighborhoods you've probably never even ridden a carriage through."

Grandmama closed her eyes, as if her shame were too great to even look upon Sarah. "This, what you and your brother have endured, is my fault. I tried to force Mary to wed a man she didn't love. A man too old for her. She didn't care about his title or wealth. She wanted love. How she must have suffered, and you children as well."

Sarah wouldn't deny it, not even to mollify her grandmother.

Mustering her composure, Grandmother offered a watery smile. "Well, if you'll permit me, my dear, I intend to make up for those years of neglect. You and Chris must come live with me. I've a rambling old house that has lacked laughter for far too long."

Relief washed over Sarah, as profound as if a lodestone had been lifted from her shoulders. Thank God Gregor had talked her into trying to contact her grandmother one more time. And thank God the Duchess of Harcourt had insisted on this tea party. For the first time in three years, she could actually anticipate Christmastide with a degree of joy.

"Thank you, Grandmother."

That trio of softly uttered words was all Sarah could achieve, so overcome with emotion was she. This was what she'd hoped and prayed for, and now that the moment was upon her, she couldn't quite conceive it was happening.

Even as the thought crossed her mind, another more sobering one did as well. What of her and Gregor? He meant to return to Scotland. Would she see him anymore?

You must, her heart cried. Even if that meant bolstering her courage, and telling him her feelings. Of her love. He felt something for her too. Nothing could convince her otherwise.

What did she have to lose by doing so?

She and Chris might've found a home with their grandmother, but Sarah's heart had already found a home with a blond Highlander possessing a wicked smile and rakish twinkle in his eye.

"My Fifi—she's my Pomeranian—may be a mite jealous of you at first." A self-deprecating smile tipped Grandmama's thin lips. "I fear I've rather spoiled her. Loneliness will do that to a person."

"I'm sure we'll march on splendidly. I've always wanted a pet dog. Chris has too."

"Then you must have one," Grandma's voice brooked no dissent. "Both of you. *Hmm*," she said, giving Sarah a speculative look. "We must find you a lady's maid, straightaway. It won't do for you to toddle about London unchaperoned, and I rarely attend functions these days. Though I might venture out a few times in the coming weeks to introduce you to Society."

"I have no need for a chaperone, Grandmama or a maid either." Her grandmother looked so disconcerted, Sarah softened her declaration with smile. "I'm almost five-and-twenty, and I assure you, given where Chris and I have lived, and the hardships we've endured, I don't give a whit what anyone else thinks of my reputation. I know the truth, and that's what counts."

"Very well, my dear," Grandmother conceded. "But you'll need a maid to help you dress. Today's fashions cannot always be managed by one's self. You can determine when and if she accompanies you on outings. Is that agreeable?"

She appeared so eager to please, Sarah didn't have the heart to deny her. On the other hand, Grandmama wasn't going to dictate to her. She'd been independent too long. "That's acceptable. If I have a say in who is hired for the position."

"Of course." Grandmother's face brightened, and she clasped her hands to her breast. "Oh, what a Christmastide this shall be. I haven't celebrated since your mother left all those years ago. We used to make plum pudding together."

"Mama always made Christmas pudding."

A single tear made a track down Grandmama's face. "And gingerbread? How Mary adored gingerbread."

"And...gingerbread." Sarah pressed a palm to her mouth, fearing the dam of emotions she'd kept at bay, had refused to yield to, could no longer be held back.

"Come here, Sarah." Grandmother opened her arms.

At once, she knelt before her, and burying her face in the crook of her grandmother's neck, smelling of lavender and roses, burst into tears.

"There, there, my dear." Grandmama made comforting sounds in her throat all the while patting Sarah's back. "We have each other now."

At last, her tears spent, Sarah sat up and retrieved her own handkerchief. As she composed herself, a twinkle entered her Grandmama's eyes. "Tell me about that Scot you came with. I believe you've a fondness for him? Did I hear he's related to Viscount Sethwick?"

"He's Gregor McTavish, and Viscount Sethwick's his cousin." Lest her grandmother have any ideas about dictating who she spent time with, Sarah squared her shoulders. "I am more than fond of him. I love him."

Chapter Thirteen

Gregor sat across from Sarah as the carriage rumbled through Mayfair's elite streets. The sprinkling of snow four days ago had long since melted. Too bad, since he'd hoped to take her and Chris for an outing complete with hot drinking chocolate and roasted chestnuts. Had they been in Scotland, he'd teach her to ice skate.

Extremely fetching in a raspberry-toned redingote trimmed in black fur with a matching hat and muff, she'd been quiet and preoccupied most of the ride. Every now and again, her lips twitched the merest bit, and she sighed softly.

Would he ever tire of watching her?

Not in a lifetime.

He'd called to take her on the promised ride through Hyde Park today, and when she'd descended the stairs, uncustomary nervousness pummeled him. Given Lady Rolandson's caustic reputation, he'd expected the dowager to eviscerate him with her hostile gaze, but instead, she welcomed him warmly and hadn't even balked at their lack of chaperone.

No doubt Sarah could be credited there. His tropical flower had turned out to be quite independent and strong-minded.

Permitting himself a thin, secret smile, he adjusted the cuff of his coat. He had something very special in store for Sarah. He only hoped he hadn't overstepped the mark. "Ye dinnae look as happy as I thought ye would with the news that Santano and his crew were arrested."

Gregor was well pleased that his plan had gone off with nary a hitch.

Last night, Santano had broken into the warehouse, only to be confronted by him, a half dozen Bow Street Runners, as well as Ewan, Clarendon, Warrick, Ramsbury, and Harcourt.

"Those two ruffians we caught that night at the theater couldn't wait to turn against Santano." In the unlikely event they were spared the hanging they deserved, for their testimony, the pair could expect to live the rest of their miserable lives in an Australian penal colony. "They provided enough information to have the mutinied crew members also arrested for murder, the Bow Street Runners informed me this morning."

Sarah brushed a hand over her thigh, her eyes more jade green than brown today. "I confess, I am profoundly relieved. Tonight, I shall sleep well for the first time in years." Her pretty bowed mouth tipped upward, and he yearned to taste those soft lips again. "I can never thank you enough, Gregor. And I'm very grateful for all that you've done, at great risk to yourself too."

Gratitude wasn't what he wanted from her. "Then what has ye lookin' so downtrodden, *leannan?*"

A sorrowful sigh escaped her, and she shifted on the seat. "This morning, my grandmother reminded me that we still don't know whether Mama lives." She palmed her tummy. "There's this persistent knot here, in my middle, that won't go away because I don't know." Her tongue darted out, moistening her lower lip. Throat convulsing, she turned her face away, obviously fighting tears.

Gregor couldn't bear her suffering and crossed the carriage to sit beside her. He gathered her into his embrace, and she immediately turned her face into his chest, wrapped her arms about his torso, and wept.

"*Shh, leannan, mo ghoal.*" Calling her *my love* wasn't so very bold, considering Sarah didn't speak Gaelic. He ran a hand up and down her spine, admiring the gently sloping curve even as he comforted her.

"Oh, Gregor." His greatcoat muffled her voice. "What would I do without you?"

"Dinna give up hope." He laid his cheek atop her head. "If I recall correctly, Captain Piermont is scheduled to sail to the Caribbean soon. I've already asked him to check on your mother." If all went as he intended, he'd be by Sarah's side for the rest of his life, and she'd never have to fend for herself again.

She tilted her face, her eyelashes adorably spiky, and her cheeks rosy from her cry. "I'll write a letter to send with him too. So that Mama knows Captain Piermont is trustworthy."

Resisting her slightly parted rosebud lips proved as futile as denying his growing homesickness for Scotland. Lifting her onto his lap, he cradled her in his arms and tasted her luscious mouth.

Sarah sighed again, only this was the sound of a contented woman. Twining her arms about his neck, she urged him closer. She opened her mouth to his tongue's gentle probing, and he deepened the kiss.

Desire, lust, and profound longing tunneled through his veins, filling every pore, and swelling within his heart. This woman had become something so precious in such a short period of time, he must convince her to marry him.

He *would* convince her.

After several more delicious minutes of exploring her mouth, he finally raised his head. The carriage had left the main part of London and bounced along a less busy lane on the town's outskirts. Good thing too, for his rash impulse wouldn't have served her reputation well had they been seen.

Cuddling her in his arms, he dropped a kiss atop her bonneted head.

The carriage hit a bump, and Sarah came down hard on Gregor's lap. At once, hot, intense desire flooded his groin. Gritting his teeth against the sweet torture, he shifted her onto the seat once more, then wiped away her tears with his thumbs.

His hair had come loose during their kiss, and she grasped a handful.

"I like that you haven't cut your hair. It suits the rugged Scotsman that you are far better than the Titus or Brutus." She giggled, holding a few tendrils out to the side and jiggling them up and down. "Or heaven forbid, the frightened owl."

Rotating a finger near his head, he chuckled. "Can ye imagine all of this styled in the frightened owl fashion?"

She dropped her focus to his fancy togs. "You might dress the perfect English gentleman, but at heart, you're Scot through and through, Gregor." Head to the side, she considered him. "I don't believe managing Stapleton Shipping and Supplies is what you're meant to do, no matter how good you might be at the position."

Neither did he.

"I think you should pursue becoming a doctor," she announced.

Edinburgh did have an outstanding medical school.

Sarah had grown up on a tropical island and more than once expressed how much she disliked England's drizzly, gray clime. Could he convince her to make Scotland, with its harsher weather, craggy terrain, and rugged people her home?

There'd be plenty of time to consider that later.

He'd reinforce his efforts to court her, and his surprise today was sure to earn him a place in her heart.

Rather than return to the opposite seat, he tucked her close to his side and took her hand in his. Yuletide was less than a week away, but he couldn't wait that long to give her the gift he'd found for her.

They traveled in silence for several minutes, and when he glanced down, it was to discover she'd fallen asleep, her head nestled against his shoulder.

She truly hadn't been sleeping well, fretting for her brother and herself. Now that her grandmother had acknowledged her, Sarah's life would be so much easier. Her mother was the final thing that plagued her peace.

Hopefully, Piermont would return with good news in the spring.

Stretching his legs out before him, Gregor rested his head against the squabs. He had more to overcome than Sarah's dislike of the climate. Her grandmother was a wealthy, powerful woman, and if he convinced her to marry him, though they'd never go without necessities, he wasn't in a position to shower fine things upon her.

He opened his eyes and touched his lips to the top of her bonnet. Nae, Sarah cared more about character and what was in a person's heart than being draped in fine silk and glittering jewels.

A few more minutes passed before the carriage juddered to a stop.

"Sarah?" Gregor gently shook her shoulders. "Sarah, wake up, lass. I've another surprise for ye. It's an early Yuletide present from me."

Blinking drowsily, she raised her sleepy gaze to his, and the tenderness there humbled him. Still sleep-drugged, her irises were a haunting shade somewhere between blue and green with gold flecks today. He loved that about her. Her eyes changed color depending on what she wore or her current mood.

"Another surprise? What have you done now, Highlander?" Excitement twinkled in the depths of her gaze, and she cast an inquisitive glance out the window. "Where are we?"

"You'll have to wait and see, *jo*." He gave her a seductive wink.

The carriage door swung open, and the driver lowered the steps.

Gregor descended first, then extended his hand to assist her from the carriage.

Her face awash with curiosity, she inspected the stately manor on London's perimeter.

After some lengthy inquiries, he had finally found what he sought. For a time, he feared the task he'd set himself impossible to complete, but with the help of Ramsbury, Harcourt, and Ewan he'd met with success.

"Why are we here?" Sarah took in her surroundings. "Am I meeting yet another titled relative?"

"Nae." Gregor lifted the knocker, and almost at once, a cheerful maid opened the door.

A secret in her eyes, she bobbed a curtsy. "Mr. Stallworth is expecting you, sir."

Sarah preceded him into the house and glanced around, her forehead furrowed with two neat rows.

"This way, please, Mr. McTavish, miss." The maid indicated they should follow her.

Completely bewildered Sarah asked, "Gregor, whatever are you about?"

"You'll just have to wait and see." Unfamiliar giddiness bubbled behind his ribs. He couldn't remember ever going to such efforts for a present before. And this would be the first Christmas gift he'd ever given.

True, he was giving it to Sarah early, but nonetheless...

The maid led them toward the back of the house, down a long corridor, then to a cozy room off the kitchen. A man rose from beside a short, wooden enclosure, and smiling, extended his hand.

"Mr. McTavish. It's a pleasure to see you again. I see you've brought the young lady you told me about."

"Sarah, this is Able Stallsworth," Gregor said. "Mr. Stallsworth, Miss Sarah Paine."

Squeaking and rustling from the enclosure hinted at Gregor's surprise.

Eyes going round in excitement and astonishment, her mouth formed a perfect little "o". She rushed to the box, and giggling, sank to her knees. "Oh, Gregor. Nothing could be more perfect." She scooped a wriggling black dachshund pup into each hand and held them against her cheeks. Cooing softly, she kissed their shiny heads. "Aren't you the most precious darlings?"

"Happy Christmas, Sarah," Gregor said, his throat oddly tight with sentiment.

She turned such a look of utter adoration on him, he didn't doubt she was meant to be his for all time. Everything that had happened, that had brought them to this point, had been part of a grand plan. She was his destiny as surely as snow was cold and fire burned hot.

Stallsworth gave a deferential half bow.

"You have your pick of the litter, Miss Paine. No one else has claimed a pup yet. It will be another two weeks before they are ready to leave their mother, however. Let me know which one you want, and I'll tie a ribbon around its neck. I'll give you a few minutes alone with them." At the door he turned back. "By the by, their mother's name is Elsa."

Such joy radiated from Sarah's face, Gregor could have watched her for hours.

Such a simple thing—the gift of a pup—and she reacted as if he'd presented her with a chest of jewels. Although, knowing her as he did, she preferred heartfelt gestures to gems and valuable trinkets.

She cast him an uncertain look then sucked her lower lip between her teeth. "Gregor?"

He joined her on the floor, accepting a pup to cuddle. The little devil promptly bit his nose. "Aye, lass?"

"There are only three, and I know Chris would love to have one as well. I cannot bear to think that a puppy will be left behind." Uncertainty made her hesitant. "May I... I know it's a lot to ask... And of course, Grandmother would have to be agreeable, as well as Mr. Stallworth. But might-I-be-permitted-*all*-of-them?" she finished in rush of words.

Gregor bent and kissed each cheek then boldly pressed his mouth to hers. "One for each Christmas ye've missed? Aye, that seems fair."

He laid his pup in his lap and lifted her hand to his lips. "I have a request of ye as well, my tropical flower."

"Yes?" Eyes shining, she cocked her head as she returned the three puppies to their worried mother.

"Will ye marry me, *mo ghaol*? I dinna ken where I'll be in a year, but I plan on applyin' to medical school in Scotland. We'll have to live at Craiglocky in the meanwhile, and I ken ye're no' used to the severe clime there. It will also mean leavin' yer grandmother, and ye've only just begun to ken her—"

"Do shush, Gregor."

He searched her face. "Is it too soon? I can give ye more time to get to ken me better."

"None of that other matters, silly man." She laid a palm against his cheek. "Since the day I barged into your office and you helped me without hesitation, I knew there was something special about you. With each passing day, my heart grew fuller, and though I kept telling myself it was impossible to already love you, my spirit said otherwise. I would follow you to the ends of the earth, Gregor McTavish."

He crushed her to his chest, laughing. "Thank God. I feared it was too soon. I love ye, Sarah. So much it frightens me as nothing ever has before."

"And I love you. I'll always remember this Yuletide as the one when a Highlander stole my heart." She smiled and whispered against his mouth. "Now kiss me."

Chapter Fourteen

London, England
Twenty-nine December, 1830

Sarah awoke slowly, rousing from a deep, comfortable slumber. Drowsily patting the mattress beside her, she came fully awake. Though warmth met her palm, Gregor's familiar form did not. She sat up, pushing the hair off her face and shivered. The fire burned low in the hearth, and the wind buffeting the windows revealed the winter storm that had threatened yesterday was fully upon them now.

Out of habit, she searched the chamber for him. He was wont to rise at all manner of hours over the past four years to study or take down a note for one reason or another. The room was empty, save the three lumps buried in their bed beside the wardrobe. Baron, Dickens, and Fergie slept on, oblivious to the storm buffeting the house.

In the end, Chris had confessed he preferred cats to dogs, and that's how Cat came to live with the Dowager Viscountess Rolandson. He'd grown impossibly more spoiled and pampered, which put him in good company with Fifi and the dachshunds.

Sarah grasped the coverlet, prepared to pull it aside, when the bedchamber door swung open.

Gregor, attired only in his trousers and shirt, slipped inside, cradling their fretting five-month-old son, Bryce. He closed the panel and pressed a kiss to his son's head. "The wee bairn thinks he's starvin'."

Though unfashionable, she'd elected to nurse her babe as she had Aaron, his almost two-year-old brother. Extending her arm, she gave a slight shake of her head and accepted her son's sturdy little body. She sank into the pile of pillows, and after unlacing the front of her gown, set Bryce to her breast. Bending, she kissed his satiny cheek and inhaled his sweet scent.

"How could I have not heard him?" she asked.

"He didna cry verra long. I only heard him because I was awake, thinkin' about the school and hospital." He chuckled and shook his head. "Yer mother and grandmother were already fussin' over him by the time I arrived. They changed his flannels too."

"I'm not surprised. They both adore helping." She raised an eyebrow and pushed her lower lip out a jot. "Why were you awake? Dr. McTavish, don't tell me you're nervous?"

"No' nervous, *mo ghaol.*"

Thanks to the generosity of his family and other wealthy peers' patronage, the dream she and Gregor had shared years ago to build an orphanage, a school, and a hospital for the physically incapacitated had become a reality.

New Hope Institution would officially open on January first, but seven-and-twenty children already occupied the hundred-bed orphanage, and the school had a waiting list as well. Chris would continue to live with Mama at Grandmother's but attend the school during the day.

After adding coal to the fire, Gregor shucked his shirt and trousers, and bare as the day he was born, climbed into the bed beside her. He, too, propped himself against the pillows before tugging her against the hard planes of his slightly hairy chest and dropping a kiss onto her forehead.

"Even after all this time, Gregor, whenever I see that scar on your side, my stomach twists sickeningly. To think, I might have lost you before I even found you."

"It disna even pain me anymore," he assured her.

Inserting his forefinger into Bryce's tiny fist, the babe's fingers hardly encircling half Gregor's pickle-sized digit, he chuckled as their son suckled voraciously. "He has an appetite like his brother."

Sarah looked above her and ran a hand over Gregor's bristly jaw. "Our sons have appetites like their father and Uncle Alasdair."

He chuckled, grazing her temple with his mouth. "Aye, they do. All the McTavish men eat like they're hollow to their feet."

Bryce's hazel-blue gaze shifted between Sarah and Gregor, and he grinned. A droplet of milk trailed from his mouth before he resumed his eager feasting.

Gregor brushed his fingertips up and down her arm. Even through her night rail's light fabric, the caress sent sensuous chills to more interesting places.

"Why weren't you sleeping at," she glanced to the bedside clock, "two in the morning, if you weren't worrying?

His boyish grin held a hint of bashfulness. "I'm already plannin' the second facility that Yvette is sponsorin' in Scotland. What do ye think about namin' it Second Hope Institution?"

"That's perfect, Gregor." She sighed and settled into his chest a bit deeper. "I knew there was a need, but I hadn't expected the overwhelming response we've seen. It makes me sad we can't do more."

"Och, we'll do what we can, and continue to advocate and ask others to." He turned his attention to their son still contentedly nursing. "Between yer mother and grandmother and my mother, I fear all our bairns will be spoiled."

"Not a bit of it. I don't believe a child can ever be loved too much." With her bent forefinger, she brushed the babe's cheek. "I can scarce fathom that Mama's been back in England almost as long as Chris and I were here without her. I'm so grateful, because I feared Grandmother would be horribly lonely when we married and returned to Scotland."

"Aye, and glad I am our bairns will ken her." Gregor whispered as he gently extracted his finger. "Our wee son's asleep, *jo*."

His tiny mouth slack, Bryce had succumbed to slumber once more.

A soft rap announced Mama had come to take her grandson back to the nursery. This had become a routine in recent weeks, while Sarah and Gregor stayed at Grandmama's until the finishing touches on New Hope were complete.

Two infants, four dogs, a pompous cat, and a mischievous parrot—yes, Biscuit had made the ocean voyage too—could be quite chaotic at times. Originally, Sarah and Gregor had planned on letting a house, but Grandmama wouldn't have it. She insisted all were welcome to stay with her and said a little excitement would do her good.

In fact, she thrived on the commotion and nearing her five-and-seventieth birthday, claimed to be healthier than she had been in decades. No longer having a broken heart or treacherous servants likely had much to do with her renewed vigor.

The last they'd heard, Miss Wattle and Stinkwiggon had boarded a ship for America. Grandmother's hand didn't reach that far. Yet.

Sarah couldn't deny Mama and Grandmama's help with an energetic toddler and an infant were most welcome.

"Here, let me have the laddie." Gregor accepted the small bundle, the same expression of awe on his face she'd observed every time he gazed at his children. That this brawny Highlander who dwarfed so many other men, became a gentle giant with their sons made her eyes misty.

After they'd wed, he'd confessed he hadn't thought to ever marry and have children. She'd never deny the path to their meeting had been a long, treacherous hard-won journey, but that made their love all the more wondrous.

Once Sarah secured the front of her gown, she slipped from the bed. Cuddling Bryce in the crook of her arm, she padded barefoot to the door. A quick glance over her shoulder assured her Gregor had pulled the bedcoverings to his chin, sparing Mama any blushes. Still, his naughty wink and suggestive smile sent Sarah's pulse skittering.

She opened the door, and as she expected, her mother waited there. Taking her grandson into her arms, a doting smile curving her mouth, she murmured, "I see a bit of your father's nose and jaw line."

Mama still grieved Papa's death.

"I do too." Sarah kissed her son's smooth forehead, inhaling a deep breath. Nothing smelled as wonderful as her children, except for perhaps, the brawny Scot waiting in bed. She hadn't missed the hunger in his eyes, but he could be patient a little longer.

Sarah bussed her mother's cheek, admonishing gently, "Don't stay up too long, Mama. You also need your sleep."

"Tish tosh." Mama shook her head. "I have years to sleep. This sweet one will only be little for a short time."

Leaning against the doorframe, Sarah watched as her mother, humming softly, wandered toward the nursery.

Overjoyed didn't begin to describe her emotion when the letter from Mama had arrived at Craiglocky Keep saying she was safe and well at Grandmama's house, along with Biscuit. When Santano had raided Bellewood, she and Ionie, their Jamaican housekeeper and cook, had huddled in the hidden chamber. Knowing he would likely return, Mama had secretly gone to live with Ionie in her village, taking the chamber's contents and burying the valuables.

Under the care of the village healer, Mama's health had gradually improved. Weekly, a nephew of Ionie's discreetly inquired at the harbor, seeking news of Sarah or Santano. That was how Mama learned of Piermont's arrival and Sarah's letter. She'd tried to talk Ionie into coming with her to England, but the servant wouldn't leave her family.

Chris would never have to worry about his future. The *Mary Elizabeth* had been sold to Stapleton Shipping and Supplies and the proceeds from the sale of Bellewood House had been invested on Christopher's behalf. As she'd suspected, the chest contained unimaginable treasure. Treasure, Mama adamantly maintained, Papa received for saving a privateer's life many years before. She would speak no more on the subject, giving Sarah cause to speculate there might've been other less honorable reasons they'd always lived in Jamaica.

Before climbing back in bed, she wandered to the window and pulled the drapery aside. "You're right, Gregor. There's quite a snowstorm outside."

When he didn't respond, she glanced to the bed.

He ran his appreciative gaze down her form, and she realized the firelight gave him a perfect view of her body silhouetted in the flowing gown. A more carnal visage replaced his admiration, and his facial features stood out sharply hewn, in what she'd come to recognize as desire.

Giving him a sultry smile, she unlaced her gown, slipped it off her shoulders, and wiggled free of its folds, allowing it to pool at her feet.

Inhaling a rasping breath, he opened his arms wide. "Come here, *leannan*."

She ran to the bed and threw herself into his waiting arms.

With a half-growl half-groan, in one deft movement, Gregor rolled her beneath him and entered her. All he ever had to do was glance at her with seduction in his gaze, and she was ready to receive him.

As he rose above her, passion sharpening his features, she wrapped her arms around his broad back and arched into his hips.

"I love you, my brawny Highlander."

"And I ye, my precious tropical flower."

The End

About Collette

USA Today Bestselling, award-winning author, COLLETTE CAMERON pens Scottish and Regency historicals, featuring rogues, rapscallions, rakes, and the intelligent, intrepid damsels who reform them. Blessed with fantastic fans as well as a compulsive, over-active, and witty Muse who won't stop whispering new romantic romps in her ear, she lives in Oregon with her mini-dachshunds, though she dreams of living in Scotland part-time. You'll always find dogs, birds, occasionally naughty humor, and a dash of inspiration in her sweet-to-spicy timeless romances®.

You can find details of her work at
www.ColletteCameron.com

One Enchanted Christmas

~ A Distinguished Rogues Novella ~

BY

Heather Boyd

Lady Margaret Stockwick is still mourning the loss of her beloved parents when her brother whisks her away from the family estate. Unbeknownst to Meg, Hector has no plans to allow her to return. Instead, he'll see her ensconced in London after the Christmas season to be married off as quickly as possible, thereby relieving himself of any further responsibility for her welfare. Meg is devastated; not only by her brother's betrayal, but at the prospect of spending the holidays with his best friend, the roguish Lord Clement.

Otis spends nearly all his days at his family's estate, the better to protect his mother and siblings. But his greatest wish is to remove them from beneath the thumb of his scheming father. Then Lord Vyne presents a wager—marry in three months, and Otis can win a bit of freedom for his family. It's a gamble Otis intends to win. But not with the chit his father's chosen, an arrangement based on financial gain. No. Otis is determined to marry for love and mutual respect…and it isn't long before he finds the lovely Meg inspiring both.

Chapter One

Lady Meg Stockwick covered her cold nose and mouth again and blew out a breath, hoping to warm her face a little bit. Meg was not used to traveling in the winter months. She was not used to traveling at all really. She was doing her best not to become an icicle.

Her brother was to blame for her discomfort, not that he seemed to care.

Until recently, she'd never had reason to venture from the family home on the coast of Dorset. But it was Hector's home now; her brother had assumed control of their father's estate and title upon his death, and she was supposed to obey the new viscount—even if she couldn't seem to stop questioning his decisions.

"It's not too late to turn back," Meg told him urgently as Hector's new traveling chariot began the slow descent into yet another blindingly white valley. "We could be home by Christmas morning."

"It certainly is too late. We're almost there," her brother assured her as he scrubbed the damp from the window with his fist. "You will enjoy yourself."

Meg doubted that as she huddled more deeply into her coverings. The sun had come out to shine at last and brought with it Hector's enthusiasm for new surroundings. He had been saying she'd enjoy herself repeatedly for the last day, and she was still quite sure he was wrong. Spending the anniversary of the worst month of her life in Derbyshire, at the home of a terrible rogue, was not her idea of fun.

"We should still celebrate Christmas the way we always have," Meg insisted, determined to win her brother over. "In our home. I had everything in hand before you arrived."

"Next year you can do as you wish," he promised. "But this year I have other plans than sitting in Dorset all alone."

Meg shivered, wishing her brother had stayed in London. His return had heralded an upset of all her plans for the holidays. And now she was here, far from home and all she'd ever known. Meg had heard nothing good about her brother's closest friend in the past few years and now she would be forced into close proximity with him for weeks.

She had known Lord Clement as a boy, but it had been a decade since she'd lain eyes on him. She had heard enough to form a clear picture of his character though. Lord Clement was often gallivanting about London with her brother, too important to visit their little coastal village. Meg believed him to be a terrible influence on her older brother.

She heaved a heavy sigh. There was only one thing to look forward to this holiday. Lady Vyne, the rogue's mother, was certain to be better company. Lady Vyne had written Meg many comforting letters in recent years following the death of her mother and then her father so soon after.

Hector suddenly began gathering his possessions—book, handkerchief, and a pouch of sweet meats he'd procured along the way—and stuffed them into a leather satchel he'd kept at his side for the entire trip.

Meg hugged her book close to her chest. "Mother and Father are still with us in spirit," she argued.

Hector shifted forward to stare at her, his expression grave. "If Mother and Father are spirits as you continue to claim, and watching over us as well, then surely they've heard our itinerary many times from your own lips and will have hitched a ride."

Meg wished that might be so. Did ghosts ever take a holiday? "That is how they met. Father climbed into the wrong carriage, and they fell in love."

"By the time they reached the fourth turnpike," Hector said softly.

"Love at first sight." Meg wanted so much to believe in the impossible right now. Even though she had Hector still, she felt very alone without her parents. There was no one to tell her secrets to and no one who gave her theirs to keep. Two years of death, first her mother and then her father, and the constant period of mourning had been hard to bear for everyone. Her closest friends had married and moved away to start new lives with their husbands already. She had lost touch with all but a few.

Hector had been away in London when their father had died, but he had rushed home to be with her for the burial. He had not stayed long, traveling back to London to meet with Lord Clement while she had mourned alone.

And now Hector insisted she must travel with him. In the winter!

"Cheer up, old thing," Hector said. "Who knows what might happen during the holidays."

Nothing good, she suspected. Not if Lord Clement was anywhere in the vicinity of her brother. She might not see much of Hector either. That was not how she wanted to see out the year.

Meg huddled farther beneath the warm furs, trying to resign herself to the fate her brother had forced upon her. "I'm still in mourning," she reminded him. "Even if you forbid me to be."

He shoved his satchel aside roughly. "It was past time!"

Meg glared at him. "Papa deserved to be mourned for a full year as we did with Mother. Six months is hardly long enough."

"Enough is enough," he cried, smacking his fist on his thigh. "You will do as I say, and be grateful I care enough to take you to visit my friends at all. I am the head of our family and you will enjoy yourself." Her brother scowled. "I insist you make merry."

Meg glared at him. "You cannot make me pretend."

Hector pinched the bridge of his nose, a sure sign she was trying his patience. "You will not embarrass me by spoiling Christmas for Lord Clement and me."

Meg pressed her lips together tightly, affronted that Hector thought more of Lord Clement's happiness than hers. "You don't seem to care what I want anymore," she grumbled even though knowing she was being difficult. This trip had been a tax on her nerves. She'd barely slept last night in yet another strange bed.

She slumped in her seat as her eyes pricked with the threat of tears. There were days she did not like her brother. He gambled away his fortune and spent far too many nights out in society. His improved situation had gone to his head. She'd also heard gossip he had a woman in London too—the sort Mama had whispered must never be acknowledged.

"I do care. Very much, and it is high time I did right by you and brought you out in society." Hector nodded. "Gentleman have to see you in order to ask to marry you."

Meg blushed at the idea of marrying a stranger. Hector was all for that. "You speak such nonsense. No one will notice me here."

"On the contrary, Lady Vyne is sure to host at least one dinner during our stay. There's a village not far from the manor house, too, and we will be here until after Twelfth Night don't forget. Anything can happen in that amount of time."

Meg turned up her nose. "That village has an alehouse, I assume?"

Hector grinned widely. "Every village tends to have at least one. Gentlemen come for miles around and some of them call on Lady Vyne, and Clement, too. They will assist with any introductions if they deem the connection suitable."

He had an answer for everything. "As if Lord Clement would stir himself on my behalf."

Hector chuckled. "He's a good friend."

"I thought I was that to you once," Meg grumbled.

"You're worse. You're my unmarried little sister. It is required that I adore you," Hector teased, grinning as he tapped her nose. "Even when you are out of sorts. If the signs of merriment bother you so much, just try not to scowl at everyone for the duration of our stay. Don't spoil Christmas for the rest of us. Mother and Father would hate to know you were so miserable."

She heaved a heavy sigh. Hector was probably right, but Mother and Father had made this time of year special. She had hoped to do the same but for Hector instead. "I will do my best. To honor their memory."

Hector turned his attention back to the view. "Excellent."

Meg glanced out the foggy windowpane, too. It wasn't Hector's way to let grief smother his good spirits. He had lived away from home for a long time. He'd not borne the worry of caring for either of their parents as they had declined.

He meant this trip as a way to end their mourning.

Meg might never end hers, no matter what happened. Her life had not been the same since her mother and then her father had passed, and it could never improve.

Frustrated that her breath had fogged the window again, she rubbed a circle on the pane with her fist and glared at the rolling fields of white powder until she realized she was looking down at their destination.

The manor on The Vynes estate, a widespread yellow stone structure, sat at the end of a long, winding road. Snowy mounds hiding what might be garden shrubbery dotted the landscape, bordered by low stone walls around the dwelling. But everything that could be pretty or green was hidden beneath inches of snow. There was no warmth here.

Meg desperately missed the rolling blue of the sea and the sound of crashing waves upon the shore near her home. It had been three days since she'd been bundled into this carriage, and two uncomfortable nights sleeping at posting houses along the way.

She focused her gaze back on the nearing house with a sense of foreboding. The family they were visiting were a good bit wealthier than they were, and it was a larger family, too. Lord Clement had a mother and father, Lord and Lady Vyne, a younger pair of unmarried sisters, and an infant brother as well. It was going to be a noisy few weeks in the country, and awkward to be with another family.

But Hector grinned as the carriage began to travel around the circular drive that would bring them to a stop before an impressive pair of oak doors. "Ready to dash inside and begin to make merry?"

"If my legs haven't gone numb yet." She smiled with false brightness. "As ready as I'll ever be."

But there was little chance this was going to be a happy Christmas. Meg was sure it might just be the worst ever.

Chapter Two

Otis considered the cards dealt him and then placed them face down on the comforter. "Your hand."

His father, the seventh Earl of Vyne, smirked as he drew the winnings across the bed. Father didn't even try to hide his glee anymore when he won the games they played—even when it was just a few pounds. "As always, Clement."

If only Vyne knew the truth of the matter. Otis played the part of a dutiful son but he kept his feelings about gambling and his father's lucky streaks strictly to himself. Otis was an expert card player. He could win the hands that mattered and lose others at will. But Father's health was declining rapidly, so Otis chose to let him feel lucky at least in this. "Another game?"

Father considered the suggestion, long and hard, and then shook his gray head. "I've reclaimed enough of my rightful inheritance back from you for one today."

Otis' inheritance, left to him by his grandfather in an unbreakable will, was a continual source of friction between them. Father had been unable to successfully challenge it, and he'd been furious with Otis ever since.

The fact that Otis' personal fortune now exceeded all expectations was unforgivable to Vyne. The earl had expected that money to be his upon the last earl's demise, and went out of his way to try to get every penny back.

Otis only played against Father, and lost often, so he might not be expelled from The Vynes again. He'd been banished to London for six months after the reading of the will. In that time, Father had made Mother's life hell, blaming her for everything and anything he did not like. For Mother's sake, and the happiness of his siblings, Otis had pledged to dower his sisters and committed additional funds to his younger brother's education.

Those small measures were all the concessions Grandfather's will had allowed Otis to make. He could give nothing to his father outright even if he had wanted to.

However, making those small commitments had been enough to be forgiven a little and allowed to return to the home he loved more than any other place in England.

Otis wished to keep a close eye on his siblings, and his mother, too. Mother was forbidden to leave the estate now, and so were the children. Father controlled everyone else here, even from the sick room, with an iron fist. Otis would gladly lose a little more money every now and then to keep the tyrant happy. "What shall we do then?"

Father's eyes narrowed. "I've been thinking about family."

Otis kept his face impassive as he waited for him to continue. Family was a topic that interested him greatly.

Father sat back, one thumb poised on the tip of his chin. "You do not ask the direction my thoughts have traveled, my son?"

The last time they had talked of "family" a sister's marriage had been arranged out of the blue in a fit of spite. Thankfully, the groom had been a decent enough fellow and had met with his sister's approval in the end. "Yes, of course I do."

"You must marry."

So Father had finally broached the subject Otis had been expecting for some time. Otis was already prepared. "I know."

Otis was six and twenty. Father was four and fifty. Mortality had become Father's greatest fear in recent years. "The succession must continue without interruption," Father announced pompously. "Unless you intend for your brother to inherit the estate."

Otis' brother was still a babe really. "I said I *will* marry."

"I want you settled before the season has begun," Lord Vyne insisted.

Otis sat back in his chair—stunned by the rush but unwilling to show it. "Wouldn't it be simpler for me to head to London for the season and choose from the cream of the crop?"

Father's expression grew sly. "My son has no reason to compete with the rabble of society. Not when I already have a well-dowered filly picked out for him."

Father believed that Otis shared his taste in women. Otis had quickly learned to play into that delusion over the years, but he would not when it came to choosing a wife. "I've no intention of competing with anyone. The ladies would be coming to me, not I to them, I'm sure."

Father grunted in agreement. "Be that as it may, I have taken it upon myself to issue an invitation for the holiday. My acquaintance has a suitable daughter in need of a husband. The family lacks a title but the girl's dowry is appropriately large. You will find her to your liking."

Good grief, Father was well advanced with this scheme. Even from bed he would try to direct Otis' life. Father had a number of friends. Otis loathed each and every one of them. Marrying one of their daughters was not in his best interests. "What is the chit's name?"

"Does it matter?"

Otis winced. He held women in the highest regard, while his father did not. "It does if I need to address her."

Father sat back with a sigh. "One of Milne's girls."

Milne was probably the best of the bunch. New money. Ambitious. Someone Otis had never truly warmed to though. Otis had honestly expected Father to suggest some duke's younger daughter or a widowed countess as his wife. The Milne chit he'd met was pretty, intelligent, but there were a few complications attached to her that did not suit Otis at all. "I think I recall meeting one. Dark hair, brown eyes. She had a fondness for yapping terriers if I recall correctly."

Otis was allergic to dogs, and Father knew it.

He frowned for a moment and then nodded. "If she is to be your countess, she must give up her small companions," Father decreed.

"Hardly kind."

"Only a fool pays attention to what a woman wants," Father claimed.

Otis was probably a fool then in Father's estimation. He stood, aiming to appear nonchalant, but his mind was racing as he took a few steps away from the bed toward the tall windows. He would not agree to marry just anyone Father chose. He may not know what exactly he wanted in a wife but possessing a large dowry held no lure for him.

Otis glanced out the window and caught sight of an unfamiliar traveling chariot pulling up before the manor. *Blast.* Was that the Milnes arriving already?

If so, Otis had little time to come up with a plan to turn them aside. Since Father's bed was too far away from the window to notice his guests had arrived yet, there was a chance Otis could pretend he hadn't, either.

As much as he was loath to leave the estate so suddenly, retreat might be his best option for the immediate future. He needed time to think of whom he might make a match with. If he could name a worthy alternative, he might yet have his way without too much of a struggle. He could leave for a day or two, avoid the Milnes, while he considered his options. Mother would understand his absence if he explained his reasons for going.

"I suggest you win Milne over first. I wager The Vynes you'll have a bride in hand before Christmas Day arrives."

Father's propensity for making wagers was why Grandfather had skipped over his eldest son in favor of leaving everything not entailed to a grandson—to Otis. Grandfather had valued Otis' intelligence and believed he would protect the family from the worst of Vyne's excesses. "This is not a decision I can make without due consideration."

"That is why they are coming to visit," Father insisted. "You will get to know one another very well indeed in the next days. If you are still unsure, test her mettle in the bedchamber if you must."

Otis stilled, disturbed by Father's suggestion. "I will do no such thing."

"Do you require further incentive to do as duty requires?" Father's eyes narrowed.

Just how low could Father get? "What are you suggesting?"

"As a reward for taking a bride, you may take your mother to the seaside for the summer," Father offered.

Father wielded absolute control over his family. He must want this alliance very badly indeed. "Mother would enjoy that, but only if the children could join her there, too."

It was a lot to hope for, but the more Otis considered the prize of the wager, Mother's freedom, the more he warmed to the idea of making such a deal. But only if the circumstances could be in his favor, too. Otis knew the Milne girl only a little and had never considered her in the role of wife before. Bedding a wife before any wedding, while reprehensible the way Father described it, might have been possible if they liked each other and he'd proposed first.

But a few days was not enough time in his opinion to decide on a bride, even if this was a chance to help his mother escape Father's control. If he pretended to consider Miss Milne and could prove she did not suit him, or the family, he would be free to choose another later. But he needed time for that.

"I'll take that wager," Otis said slowly. "On the condition that I am allowed an appropriate length of time for a proper courtship before any marriage takes place."

"What do you need to court her for? Just wed her and be done with it."

"No. I must know that the lady I marry feels more affection for me than my title."

Father snorted. "Engage a mistress and you will have a surfeit of attention."

"Mistresses love money, not the men they bed." He pursed his lips, disliking this discussion immensely. "Those are my terms."

"Don't be difficult about this."

"I have made a reasonable request so I may choose the best candidate to become a countess one day. The honor of the family demands it." Otis raised one brow. "Are you afraid that time will prove you've misjudged Miss Milne's suitability?"

Father glared. "Her dowry alone is worth the inconvenience of making a match without affection."

"Not to me." Otis shrugged. "But there's always London in the new year."

"No. You will wed Miss Milne. You have until Twelfth Night to propose."

Otis would not risk his own chance at happiness. "It cannot be done."

Father never liked to compromise, and his eyes narrowed. "You will court her."

"I can, but I make no promises about proposing."

Father stared at him. "Let me put it this way—if you fail to marry within three months, you'll never set foot here again until I'm dead."

Otis straightened. "No!"

Father smirked. "Exile, or a marriage in three months so you can take your mother and siblings away for as long as you'd like?"

Otis was thunderstruck. The price of failure was too bloody high.

Father extended his hand, his eyes alight with glee as he waited for Otis to accept his final terms. "Which is it to be?"

Otis, however, strode to the door and yanked it open. The footman jumped back at least a foot. "Fetch witnesses."

Father had never reneged on a bet, but there was always a first time. There must be written proof to ensure Mother could leave the estate when Otis tied the knot. Otis wouldn't hesitate to blackmail Father with it to get his way, if necessary.

When the steward entered, Otis explained what he wanted written down. The steward was pale by the end, but Otis asked for two copies to be made of the original. They signed all of them, and Otis tucked his copy into his pocket for safekeeping.

Thankfully, Father was so confident of winning that he never noticed the omission of Miss Milne's name in the terms of the wager. Otis was still free to marry anyone he chose, and still win that bet, but he only had three months to do it. Since that was the case, he would be heading to London after the holiday. Unfortunately, that meant he would have to meet with Miss Milne first.

He folded the last copy in half and handed it to the steward. "Keep that somewhere safe."

The steward knew Father well enough that Otis did not have to say to keep evidence of the wager anywhere Father could not get his hands on it. The man backed from the chamber with a deep bow and fled quickly.

Otis glanced out the window again, noting the carriage was drawing away toward the stables. Milne and his daughters must be in the drawing room with Mother by now.

He turned to his father. "Wasn't one of Milne's girls going to marry Lord Bellows?"

Father sneered. "I wager Milne would not allow his blood to mingle with that of a known imbecile, even if he *is* an earl."

"Is that right?" Otis nodded along, but disapproved of his father's attitude. Lord Bellows was not as smart as many people might want him to be. But he was genuine and a decent sort. Otis had thought it a smart match for the Bellows line. Miss Milne seemed intelligent. "A pity. "I thought her very fond of the man. She could have discretely guided Bellows, for the benefit of all involved. When might we expect the Milnes to arrive?"

"Not for a few days yet."

"That's a shame," he murmured…but wondered who was in the drawing room now with Mother?

Otis let out a quiet sigh. He had a reprieve of a few days from Miss Milne. He hadn't a moment to lose getting his affairs in order before he made the journey to London though. "I have to run a few errands. If you will excuse me, Father. I should be about my business."

"Yes, go, but make sure you are here when Milne arrives." Lord Vyne made an impatient gesture to dismiss Otis. "I promised the man an enjoyable holiday."

Otis fled. The Milnes were going to be disappointed.

Chapter Three

Meg did her best to curtsy to the Countess of Vyne despite her exhaustion. "Thank you for having us."

The countess drew close and placed her hands on Meg's frozen cheeks. "My dear, it is so good to see you again."

"The pleasure is ours," Meg assured her, trying not to shiver.

The countess impulsively embraced Meg then, enveloping her in sweet-smelling warmth. She drew back quickly and led Meg toward the great hearth where a large fire blazed. "Come to the fire and warm yourself. You look almost done for."

"No, I'm quite well," Meg promised, though she was eager for the warmth. She glanced back over her shoulder but her brother waved her away. "It is a bit colder than I'm used to."

"I know it is," the countess assured. The countess perched at her side. "I have looked forward to having you here since the day I read about your mother passing. I would have sent for you sooner if I thought you might have come."

"My father needed me," Meg murmured.

Father had taken the death of Meg's mother very badly indeed. He had only left the house to bury her, and then locked himself away from the world bereft of her vital presence. It had taken all of Meg's cunning to get him to eat, to sleep. He said he couldn't imagine a life without Mother and now he did not have to. Meg had done everything in her power to ease his mourning and it hadn't been enough. He'd slipped away a little more each day, until a sniff had become a cough, and then fever had set in despite her best efforts to have him cured.

"You did everything you could," the countess promised, and then smiled. "Now you are here, I am determined we will all have a lovely Christmas together. My daughters were particularly excited that you were coming, so too are the boys."

Not all the boys, surely.

Meg held her hands out to the flames and listened in silence as the countess described merriment that was planned for the coming weeks. The countess was enthusiastic but everything she mentioned reminded Meg of past Christmases with her parents, and that made her heart heavier.

She looked toward her brother just as a stranger rushed into the room. "What the devil are you doing here?"

"What do you mean? We were invited!" Hector exclaimed. "It's damn good to see you again, Clement."

Meg gaped, and then snapped her mouth shut. *That* was Lord Clement? She barely recognized him.

As a boy he'd been skinny with a shock of dark hair that he'd always been brushing from his eyes. Those longish locks were gone now, replaced by a shorter cropped style that revealed a pair of intelligent eyes set in an attractive face.

Meg glanced at Lady Vyne quickly, and discovered Lord Clement had grown up to resemble his mother. But he was far taller and broad shouldered than even her brother was. He was handsome now. More so than she'd ever imagined a man could be.

Lord Clement was unlike anything Meg was prepared to meet.

Meg averted her eyes as her cheeks suddenly heated.

But she couldn't help but peek again. Lord Clement and Hector embraced, shook hands vigorously, and expressed such joy to see each other that Meg immediately felt envious.

"And here I was merely hoping you would write me a letter before New Year," Lord Clement exclaimed.

"Well, we're here in the flesh," Hector said, throwing his arms wide. "Ready to make merry with you and yours."

Lord Clement glanced toward Meg and seemed to freeze in place for a moment. He quickly recovered and smiled at her. "And who is this beauty you have brought with you? I must have an introduction immediately."

"Surely you don't need to be introduced to my sister after all these years?" Hector teased with a hearty laugh that made Meg cringe.

She lifted her chin and looked Lord Clement in the eye, eager to get the greeting over and done with. "My lord."

Lord Clement's lips parted in obvious surprise. "Lady Margaret?"

"Meg," she said, nodding to him. "No one has called me by my full name since our mother passed."

Lord Clement shook his head suddenly. "Forgive me, but I would never have recognized you."

"I thought the same of you," she murmured, and then fidgeted under his startlingly direct gaze. The handsome devil had surprised her with his improved appearance but he was still a man to be wary of. He had kept her brother away from home for so much of the last few years.

Lord Clement drew closer, his smile growing wider as he came. "It is a surprise to see you but a happy one. Welcome to The Vynes, my lady."

She was about to dip into a curtsy but he reached for her hand instead. She placed her gloved hand in his larger one and looked up into the darkest, bluest eyes she'd ever seen and trembled. They reminded her of the sea, of her home shores, and she gulped in shock as he bowed over her hand in a courtly fashion. "Thank you, my lord."

He released her hand slowly, a look of puzzlement creeping into his expression as he drew back. His eyes narrowed on her face. "I say, are you warm enough?"

Meg was becoming entirely too warm with all the attention in the room fixed on her. She had kept her coat on despite being indoors but Lord Clement was having a heating affect on all parts of her body. "I believe so."

"Good. Good," he said, quickly glancing at Hector.

"About time too," Hector promised, slapping Lord Clement on the shoulder and drawing him back from Meg. "She kept promising me she'd turn into an icicle at every stop on the way here."

"I hardly blame her." Lord Clement frowned, glancing at Meg then away again. "It has been colder than usual for this time of year. I would not have subjected my sisters to such a journey."

Meg felt vindicated by Lord Clement's remark and glared at her brother. "I warned you it was entirely too cold for such a trip. The poor grooms must be frozen solid."

Lord Clement winced. "Your brother barely notices the weather. I'll make enquiries about your servants and make sure they are amply warmed."

"I would appreciate that."

Lord Clement stepped back farther and Hector began to regale him with the details of their journey, including the *charming* inns they'd stayed in along the way. Those inns had not been charming but frighteningly drafty in her opinion. She dreaded spending another night in them for the return journey home.

Meg inched closer to the countess' side but she felt Lord Clement's attention return to regard her. "Mother, why did you not tell me to expect my friends for Christmas?"

"I wanted to surprise you," she teased him. "Call it my Christmas wish for you to be with your friends again."

He shook his head and glanced at Meg. "I hate that I was the last to know."

"Not by much. Coming here was a surprise to me too," Meg said quickly. "I only learned what Hector planned the day before we left home."

"How very like him to leave everything until the last moment." Lord Clement shook his head. "Rest assured nothing has been left to chance in London. The new townhouse in Half-Moon Street will be ready to welcome you in the New Year."

Meg frowned at Lord Clement and then her brother. "What new townhouse?"

"Good grief, now you've gone and spoiled the surprise entirely," Hector complained to his friend.

Meg gulped. Surely he couldn't mean to leave her in Dorset to manage the estate alone. "Hector, what is going on?"

Lord Clement winced. "I am sorry. I thought you would have told her."

"I'll explain later," Hector warned Meg.

What had Hector done? "Why do you need a London townhouse?"

"Because we will be living in there soon. I cannot have a woman at my bachelor apartment on Clarges Street, even if she is a relation. Makes sense to establish a permanent residence before the season starts," he announced as he turned away. "How's that new horse of yours coming along, Clement?"

Meg gaped and then cast a quick glance at the countess. She tried to smile. London and the season, parties and pretty gowns and stumbling through reels and waltzes as if one were happy, was unthinkable right now. She was still in mourning, even if Hector believed otherwise.

Hector *had* broached the subject of finding a husband on the long journey from the coast but she had refused to consider it. Was he giving her no choice?

"Fine. Fine." Lord Clement glanced over his shoulder at Meg, frowning. "Don't look so worried. It is a lovely little spot. Very close to everything."

"Yes indeed," Hector promised. "She'll enjoy shopping and the parties very much."

"But Hector—"

"Later, Meg." Hector drew Lord Clement firmly away from her.

Meg's heart began to race with renewed anxiety. What else hadn't Hector told her about lately? This trip, and now a home in London. A season she hadn't asked for.

When Lord Clement glanced her way one more time, Meg studied her fingers. An uneasy sensation was growing in her stomach. She was supposed to do as her brother decided, the way she would have obeyed their father. The temptation to run away was very strong right now. If only she were a little older, she could make her own decisions.

Lady Vyne drew closer. "Have you done any preparation for the coming season?"

"No," she said in a tiny voice. She glanced at her brother, but he wouldn't meet her eye anymore. Panic began to overload her senses.

"Well, no matter. There's still plenty of time." The countess smiled warmly. "I think you might be warm enough now to venture upstairs to your bedchamber. I've had everything prepared for days. Come, let's get you settled. Do excuse us, gentlemen."

Hector nodded but Lord Clement murmured her name softly as she passed him by.

Once beyond the room, Meg's despair only grew worse as she shivered anew in the chill air of the hall. Hector should have confided in her.

"I wish I could be in London to support you finding a husband," Lady Vyne whispered. "Unfortunately, my husband is in poor health and I cannot leave."

Dread filled Meg at the news. "I am very sorry to hear that."

Having the countess by her side might have made the situation bearable.

"Not to worry. Your brother wrote of his intentions to bring you out when he accepted my invitation to come for the holiday, and I will be very happy, very honored, to offer any assistance I can to prepare you while you are with us."

"You're very kind," she said at last.

"Nonsense. It's the least I can do for my friend's daughter now that she has gone. I look forward to meeting your future husband one day, too."

Meg nodded miserably and started up the next flight of stairs at the countess' urging.

There was no reason to confess to the countess that the thought of a London season terrified her. Meg had hoped to marry one day, but not now. She felt the insult of her brother's rush very keenly.

She had seen the signs of Hector's restlessness and shrugged them off. How could she have been so blind to the truth—his unhappiness was with Meg's unmarried state!

The countess suddenly clucked her tongue. "Now who do we have here? Are you not supposed to be taking your lessons?"

Meg looked up in surprise. Three children, two pretty girls and a tiny boy, were looking down on them, their serious little faces pressed between the railings.

The girls rushed down to greet their mother and Meg, dragging the small boy with them. "We waited ever so long."

The countess smiled and gestured to Meg. "My dears, this is our good friend, Lady Margaret Stockwick. You must make Meg feel welcome."

The girls, Esther and Molly, curtsied and the little boy, Evan, made a bow when urged.

Meg couldn't help but smile at them all. They were adorable and reminded Meg of Lord Clement at that age. There had been another girl too, one closer to Meg's age, but she had been married off some time ago. "You are both so pretty," she murmured to the girls, and then looked at the boy. "And you, sir, are very handsome, too."

The children giggled, apparently delighted by her compliments. One of the girls took her hand and drew her along, surrounded by the Vyne family. She was taken into a bright room and then the children fled soundlessly.

Meg glanced around a bedchamber fit for royalty and stood gaping.

"I think this room will do very nicely for you. What do you think, my dear?"

This bedchamber exceeded her every expectation for comfort.

The walls were papered in yellow striped silk and a thick cornflower-blue silk comforter covered the bed. The room was warm and light and so much nicer than the one she'd left behind; nicer than any room she'd ever stayed in before for that matter. There was a fire already burning in the grate.

"It's lovely," she promised.

The maids had already begun unpacking Meg's trunks, storing her belongings in the tall oak chests that lined the walls. Meg collected a few of her more personal items and set them on the mirrored table between the tall sash windows. She glanced outside, noticing thick vines, though dormant now, bracketed her window.

She turned around to ask what flowers the vine would produce—until she noticed the maids were unpacking gowns she'd never seen before. She saw bright colors instead of the somber grays and lavender gowns she'd asked to be packed for this short holiday. Her familiar clothing was nowhere to be seen.

The countess asked a servant to add more fuel to the fire and then bid them all to go. She came to stand beside Meg. "Hector didn't mention moving to London, did he?"

"No."

"And you'd not intended to rejoin society yet."

She lifted her chin, determined not to fall to pieces in front of the countess. "I didn't."

"I am so sorry. All of this must be quite a shock. I know what it's like to have no voice, no say in any decision."

That was an understatement if ever she'd heard of one. "Three days ago, I had a home," Meg whispered.

"You will become accustomed to the change of pace in due time."

"Yes, I am sure one can grow accustomed to being treated as cattle, too." She swallowed the lump of horror that had lodged in her throat. "I think my brother will foist me off onto the first man who notices me."

"It won't be as bad as all that," the countess promised. "You'll make friends easily."

"What of the friends I have already?" She fought back tears. "He didn't even let me say goodbye to anyone."

The countess settled an arm around Meg's shoulders and drew her close. "He should have told you about the decision he made when your father died. What can we do? We women hardly ever have a say in our lives."

Meg allowed her tears to slide down her cheeks unchecked then. Hector had been planning to be rid of her for months and months and never told her. But he had certainly told the countess, and Lord Clement must know, too. They were best friends. Meg was nothing but a burden.

The countess rubbed Meg's arm briskly, trying to bolster her spirits. "It will be all right, I swear. I will do my best to help you. I will write to my friends and discover who will be in London when you are. They will help you if I ask."

It was a kind offer, but Meg didn't feel reassured. She had never felt so powerless before. She moved to the window and stared blindly at the view.

The Vynes was set in the center of the bowl-shaped valley, and she could see a small slice of it from this room's window. Everything was white and uninviting. "Has it been a harsh winter so far?"

"It has. I'm hoping the weather clears soon because it becomes quite dreadful when the children are shut up inside for excessive time."

"Yes, children do love their freedom," Meg agreed, wrapping her arms around her chest. She had lost hers when her father had died.

Chapter Four

Otis invaded his mother's bedchamber the next morning without knocking too loudly and risking waking his father in the next room. Mother customarily rose early while Father slept late. And he had a sour temper if anyone dared wake him earlier than elevenses.

Morning was the perfect time to see Mother. She'd been impossible to catch alone since the Stockwick siblings had arrived yesterday afternoon.

He glanced at the connecting door as he crossed the room just to be sure they were really alone. He kissed her cheek and sat beside her at the window overlooking the white gardens around the manor house. "It is going to be a beautiful day," he promised.

"I'm glad," she murmured. "The children could do with some fresh air."

"Not Evan," Otis warned. "His nurse said his nose was running like a brook all night."

Mother nodded. "Just us girls then."

Mother was already dressed for the outing, donning her warmest wool coat to keep away the chill. "Mother, what are Hector and Margaret Stockwick doing here," he demanded.

"Well, we couldn't very well invite Meg to stay without inviting Hector, too. I just couldn't bear to think of her alone in that huge house for one more Christmas."

"They do have servants."

Mother rubbed her hands together and blew on them. "You must guess how hard this year will be for her. Family must stick together."

"Yes, I'm aware of their growing estrangement, but the timing is troubling. Anyone can see just looking at her that she'd rather be anywhere else."

Mother sighed. "She's been in mourning since her mother died, and perhaps before that, too. Justine was ill for so long. It's too long for a girl her age to be sequestered away from society with just servants for company."

"She has a brother," Otis reminded her.

"But he's never there. You know he's not."

Otis sighed and glanced outside. "It's not my fault he prefers London. I have tried…"

"Her letters have torn at my heart and my conscience for too long." Mother settled her hand over his. "I don't blame you. I know you've done all you could to make him leave London and take care of his responsibilities at home, but it seems he will not do it."

"He's a stubborn bastard," Otis admitted. "The estate must be falling to wrack and ruin without a firm hand at the reins."

"Meg does what she can to keep the estate profitable."

"At least that is something." If only things were different. The Stockwicks' estate in Dorset had once thrived under the late Lord Stockwick, or it had before the mother had died.

"Be that as it may, I'm convinced Meg just needs a little reassurance that it is all right to set her mourning aside and think of the future. In a way, she will always be in mourning for the parents she loves and misses. But she had to face a life without them eventually. You'll hardly notice her. I promise."

That wasn't likely. The changes in Margaret Stockwick had knocked the wind out of his sails momentarily. She had not spoken very much at all yesterday, but she had once been bold and outspoken. Traits that had set her apart from other girls he'd known. As a child, she'd been intrepid, always following them around when he'd visited the Stockwicks' estate by the sea.

Otis raked a hand through his hair again. Margaret was miserable. He'd seen that very clearly. She was not as she once was, and that was a tragedy. "She has no idea how her brother intends to spend the next years, does she?"

"None at all, I'm afraid. We had a little chat when she was settling into her room last night. It's come as something of a shock that Hector is bringing her out of mourning early. I really thought he would tell her about moving to London before now, too."

Otis had seen Margaret's shock with his own eyes too at the mention of London. The poor girl—woman, he corrected himself—was practically reeling at the idea of entering the marriage mart. It had to be done, of course, it was the right thing to do, but obviously done the wrong way in Margaret's case. "I'll have a word with him."

"Not every gentleman worries about the happiness of women as you do," she said, in praise of him. "Would that your friend were the same. Meg has been so sad for such a long time. Losing both her parents in such a way has been very painful for her. You know how close she was to them. Hector's decision to force her into society like this is not the way."

Otis caught his mother's eye. "So you and Hector are conspiring against Margaret now. How long has this been going on?"

"It wasn't like that. I asked your father if she could come, expecting a refusal, and he had no objection for a change. I thought a short time away from home would do her the world of good, but I did not know then that Hector intended to sell the estate. What can be done to stop him if he does not like the place? Nothing, unfortunately."

"The estate has great potential. Selling now would be a mistake I intend to talk Hector out of," Otis decided. "It could be a very good situation if Hector would just apply himself."

Mother sighed. "Hector has no interest in managing a country estate, and you know it. He's happier gadding about in London with you and your friends."

"Well, those days are behind me. My life is here now with you and the children."

"I'm glad to see you here but you know you don't have to stay for us." Mother looked up at him and smiled quickly. "I'd like your promise that you will make Meg feel at home here during her stay."

Otis regarded his mother warily. "And how do you expect me to do that?"

"You could talk to her about the delights of London. She's lived a sheltered life by the sea, and everything will seem very strange and overwhelming at first."

"She is my best friend's sister. Men who pay too much attention to their best friend's sisters create discord and suspicion."

Mother regarded him with amusement. "Do you fear she will fall in love with you?"

"Don't be absurd. I would never allow that to happen."

"Love is always beyond our control, my son" she warned him, and then burst into a grin. "What would you do if she did set her sights on marrying you instead of preparing for a London season? Once upon a time, her mother and I thought something might happen between you."

"Something?" he asked, although he knew what Mother was about to say. She hoped for grandchildren as much as Father did. But she wanted him to wed happily, and with more love than she'd ever known in her marriage. And Mother was exceedingly fond of Margaret. It was not surprising she wished for a match between them.

Her brow arched. "Do you not think Meg is pretty?"

"That is a foolish question. Of course Margaret is a very pretty girl."

Mother smiled in delight at his answer. "Bright, too."

Not so clever as to realize her brother was keen to marry her off. "It is an unfortunate failing of yours to always wish for the impossible," he warned his mother.

"I wish for happiness, my son. For all of us. Especially Meg."

"Mother, you are a hopeless romantic but you are bound to be disappointed in me," he warned. Otis glanced at his mother quickly and forced a smile. "I have something to tell you?"

"You've made another foolish wager with your father."

Otis gaped. "How did you hear?"

"Your father gloated about it when he came to see me last night. I assume you know what you're doing?"

"I do have something of a plan, but only three months to marry someone good." Otis grasped his mother's hand quickly. "I'm sorry I did not consult with you first. I hope Father did not upset you."

"He tried," she said softly and wouldn't meet his eyes.

His parents' marriage had forever been volatile. "Mother, did he mention that the wager could have consequences for all of us? For you and the children too?"

"Yes, that part particularly pleased him." She sat back with a sigh. "He gloated that he'd backed you into a corner. He thinks to have his way."

"I am going to marry, Mother, but not the woman he's chosen for me." Otis' stomach clenched with worry though. "And I promised to look after you and the children. I will find a suitable bride and I will win your freedom in the end too."

She shook her head. "All I want is for you to be happy."

"Winning the wager will make me very happy."

Mother glanced toward the connecting door. "Once upon a time, I would have stayed with him out of affection."

Otis rubbed a hand over his face. "What can I do to make you smile?"

"Marry for love in your own time and move away," she replied. "What is done is done and the past cannot be changed. I have to live with the consequences of my decision to marry such a vindictive creature. Promise you will never become like him."

"I won't." Otis heard voices coming from his father's room. It must be nearing elevenses. "I have to go."

"Yes, your friends will be wondering where you are." Mother tilted her cheek up and Otis quickly pressed a kiss to her cool skin.

"Hector doesn't rise before noon."

She smiled quickly "Meg rises early, and she should be your friend, too. She will need you in the coming months. Help her where I cannot."

Otis sighed. He couldn't refuse his mother this one boon. He would be in London looking for a wife at the same time Meg was there too. "I'll do my best."

"You'll find her in the library at this hour, I expect." She stood and brushed her gown straight. "Now I had better go to the children before they come looking for me and earn a punishment from him."

Otis thought that an excellent idea. Father did not like to see his children anywhere but in the gardens or the nursery floor above. He bid his mother goodbye and turned in the direction of the library.

Chapter Five

The Vyne estate in Derbyshire was a bleak place in the middle of winter.

Meg huddled at one end of a large window seat in the vast library, under a thick wool blanket to keep the cold at bay. She stared out at the nonexistent view with a heavy heart. There was nothing to see but fog and snow-covered ground outside her window. At times it seemed like there were no clear skies on the horizon. She was surrounded by the weather and by a family that she didn't belong to.

Hector had abandoned her company almost as soon as they had arrived. He had disappeared with Lord Clement last night after dinner without saying when he'd return or when she might talk to him about London. She'd heard he'd ridden out early that day, despite the terrible weather.

She gritted her teeth. Her future had been decided for her. She would move to London, marry, and that was that. It hurt that Hector had run away from the conversation he'd promised her.

She pulled the blankets higher and settled deeper into the pillows behind her back. She had chosen a spot that afforded her a good view of the front drive and the stables. She might know the moment Hector returned. Until he did, there was nothing for her to do but wait.

The door creaked open slowly, and Meg froze as a presence entered the room slowly.

"Am I disturbing you?" Lord Clement asked softly.

Meg twisted around, grievously disappointed to see her brother was not standing there, too. "No. I was just about to leave."

Lord Clement quickly held up his hands. "No. No. Don't move from that lovely warm spot. I didn't intend to drive you from the room. I actually wanted to talk to you."

Meg regarded him warily. "What do you want from me?"

"Nothing," he said with a quick smile. He hovered by the door, but searched the room with his eyes. He put his hands behind his back and kept a distance. "I wanted to see if there was anything you might need."

"There is nothing I need," she promised, hoping he would go about his business soon and depart. "I have my book and your mother will send for me soon, I'm sure."

He looked around again. "Where is your maid?"

"I've never had one."

He shook his head and muttered something under his breath. "I'll have our Gladys assigned to you for your stay. She was with my other sister when she had her season. You'll find her invaluable."

"I don't need anything from you," she insisted, and then scowled at him. "Shouldn't you be with my brother?"

"He's up?" Lord Clement drew closer. "I assumed he would still be abed at this hour."

"He went out. I assumed he was with you."

"Not with me. I have responsibilities here that cannot be shirked even for visitors." He sighed. "But I am free now."

Meg was quite tired of lies, half-truths, and omissions. Lord Clement was a rogue, cut from the same cloth as her brother. "There's no need to pretend interest in me when you must long to be elsewhere. Hector has made it clear gentlemen have better things to do than sit about the countryside sipping tea."

"I'm not sure why your brother would include me in that statement, but I spend a great deal of time in the country sipping tea and enjoy it too. Actually, I only spend about six weeks in London each year, seeing the solicitor who manages my affairs and attending a few parties I cannot get out of. The rest of the year, I'm here. But I was forced to spend months away from the estate once. Hated every moment of it."

Meg studied Lord Clement, and then wet her lips. His statement seemed honest enough, but that would mean her brother had been lying to her. "Hector led me to believe he was with you in London for most of last year."

Lord Clement appeared surprised by that. "I was with him for only a few weeks and Hector can attest to my impatience to return home I'm sure."

She stared at him in astonishment. "Do you really prefer the country?"

"Indeed I do," he said and then winced. "Hector does not, however. Your brother has not accepted an invitation to visit The Vynes in an age. I am astonished that he came this year for the holiday."

"I see," Meg's eyes pricked with tears. If Hector hadn't been with Lord Clement in London then what had he been doing with his life? Obviously whatever it was, he didn't want her to know about it. Meg was stunned.

Meg looked away and brought her fingers to her lips. "Hector's comments have led me to believe you a bad influence on him. I blamed you for taking my brother away when I needed him most."

Lord Clement crossed the room to stand a few feet away. "If he'd spoken the truth, I must have seemed a heartless beast to you. I am sorry you were misinformed."

Meg frowned at the comment. "It is Hector who should apologize. Wherever he may be?"

"I can have him found and brought back if you like. We have enough servants to wrestle him out of any tavern." Lord Clement leaned her way to whisper. "It wouldn't be the first time, honestly."

"That will not be necessary," she said sadly. Her brother should want to be with her, and Hector would only resent her even more than he must already were he dragged back to The Vynes.

Lord Clement moved again, stopping at her side. She looked up into his eyes, so blue and kind as they held her gaze, and her heart fluttered for no good reason. He smiled slowly. "Are you sure there is nothing I can do for you? Another blanket or pillow, or a discussion of the best shops to patronize in London. Mother suggested I might help you prepare for your season."

"I assure you, I do not want to think about London right now but thank you for your kindness."

"Well, then. Another time perhaps. Have you been outside today?" Meg shook her head and Lord Clement's eyes lit up. "Mother is planning an outing with my sisters soon."

Meg dropped her gaze. "It is snowing," she noted. "And cold."

Lord Clement suddenly sat down beside her. "I adore this time of year here. When you are out amongst the snow as it falls, it is as if you are the only person in the world."

"That sounds lonely."

"Believe me, it's not when your sisters have been squabbling all morning." He pressed two fingers to his brow. "The noise can be quite overpowering."

"That would make a difference, I suppose," she conceded. "But I wouldn't know what that's like to fight with my sibling. Hector and I don't disagree very often."

She and Hector were as quiet as church mice, usually. And if they had a disagreement, she realized, as they did now, Hector tended to make himself scarce.

"You could join us for a short walk out," Lord Clement pressed. "I remember you were quite energetic when we were younger. And with such views as to be had in Dorset, I'd be surprised if you had grown tired of wandering the cliffs." He caught her eye, his expression hopeful.

She did not think he would recall anything of her nature after all this time. It had been years since he'd visited her home. She sighed. "Out to where?"

"Anywhere will do. Everything seems different when the world is covered in snow," he promised. "Even the pig pens can seem magical."

Meg laughed at that. "Except for the smell."

But a walk outside with others sounded like a pleasant way to pass the time given the way Lord Clement described it. Perhaps if she wasn't alone out there, she would not feel more lonely than she already was. But if she went out, she feared she could miss Hector's return. There were things they needed to talk about. "Perhaps tomorrow."

"Excellent. I will let my mother and sisters know that you might join us for the morning walk."

Meg nodded slowly.

"Is that a good book?" Lord Clement asked suddenly, gesturing to her lap. The blanket must have lowered upon his arrival to reveal the book she had placed there.

She glanced at it, and sighed. "It is quite terrible."

Lord Clement's face crinkled with confusion. "If it's dreadful, why are you holding it still? Do you want another?"

She revealed the book to him and spread her hands over the leather binding. "This was the last book my father and I were reading together. We made a pact to never not finish a book, even if it was terrible."

A look of understanding crossed his face. "I see, and you've been reading it all this time?"

"I try to. I just can't seem to finish," she confessed.

"May I?" he asked, holding out one hand.

Meg placed the book in his hand and watched the viscount skim through the early pages. He easily found her place midway through the book and turned it towards the light from the window.

Lord Clement began to read to her, his voice ringing out strongly in the quiet of the library.

And she was transported into the world that her father and her had once inhabited together. It really was a dreadful book, but fascinating all the same.

Lord Clement continued to read, turning two more pages before he finally looked up. "How far along did your father read before you took your turn?" he asked.

"We each took a chapter," she confessed, hoping he would not mind.

Lord Clement returned to the story, and Meg could not stop watching his expressive face.

She had not expected such kindness from him or his interest in her. He was unexpected. He was the last person Meg ever thought would do something just to make her happy. Her father had been like that. Always ready with a smile. Forever willing to lift her up when she was cast down.

It was hard to believe that the man sitting across from her was the same one she had dreaded spending Christmas with.

Meg felt peace wash over her at last and, for a moment, she stopped grieving for what was gone. But then she remembered so quick and so painfully that her eyes filled with tears. She looked away, and Lord Clement's voice died away slowly.

"I say, Margaret, are you all right?"

She nodded but she could not stop the tears that began to flow down her cheeks. She wiped them away quickly, but Lord Clement suddenly pressed his handkerchief into her hands.

"Here, use this instead," he whispered. "Can't have your fingers getting frostbite now, can we?"

"It's not quite that cold," she told him, and he laughed, his rich, deep voice filling the room with happiness. And she was cured of her melancholy for the moment. She found the strength to laugh along with him, too. Meg dabbed at her cheeks, and then she turned to face him. "Thank you," she whispered.

"You're very welcome," he promised.

His eyes were still kind, and she saw in him at last the young boy she had once known. She had called the boy by his given name—Otis. She did not remember when exactly she had stopped. But the pair were not so different. Both had made her laugh. She glanced at the handkerchief she was twisting in her hands, the one she'd been crying her tears over.

"Please keep it," Otis whispered. "You might need to use it to block your ears when my voice becomes intolerably hoarse."

He smiled as he turned the page to a new chapter and crossed his long legs and began to read again.

She leaned toward him and placed her hand on his arm. "You don't have to continue reading. You've done enough," she suggested.

"I need to find out what happens at the end of the story now," he told her, covering her hand with his. "I've already missed half the book. To stop now when there is more to go would be intolerable. I always like to know how a story ends."

Assured he meant it, Meg let him keep the book and sat back, resting her head against the wall behind her. Otis told a wonderful story, and she was soon enthralled in that world once more, but this time with none of the sadness she had experienced since her father's passing.

She could not account for how different she felt with Otis sitting beside her. Meg clutched the blanket closer around her body and lay her cheek upon her knees and was soon swept away by the soothing quality of his voice. There were so few men with such patience for storytelling. Hector had none. She appreciated Otis for his generous spirit more than words could say.

"My siblings routinely fall asleep when I read to them," Otis murmured with a quick glance in her direction. "I hope you're not in danger of doing the same."

"I'm not sleepy," she replied quickly, lest he stop altogether.

"Are you sure?" he asked in a teasing tone.

"I was just resting my eyes," she promised as she sat up straight. "See. Wide awake."

Determined not to succumb to the lull of his voice, she took the book from him, found the last words he'd spoken, and commenced to read aloud to him.

Otis inched closer, watching the page as she finished the chapter.

Continuing the story had felt better, too. Easier. She was not assailed by memories of Father reading to her that last final time he'd had the strength for it. Now she could remember Otis' voice and the comfort his kindness had brought her.

Otis sighed heavily. "Is that better?"

Meg nodded quickly and placed a scrap of paper inside the book to mark the place she had stopped and set it aside. "I can't thank you enough," she whispered. "I think I can continue on my own now."

Otis smiled widely, and captured her hands. His grip was firm, reassuring. "Oh, don't say you won't have my company again. I really must know what happens next. Perhaps after our walk with my siblings tomorrow, we can continue to read the next chapter. I'm quite eager to discover what happens next."

He sounded so sincere, Meg smiled. "Me too."

"It really is quite a dreadful book," he said suddenly. "I cannot thank you enough for allowing me the privilege of reading it with you."

Meg giggled, turning her hand over in Otis' grip. "You're welcome. I never really thought you had an interest in books. Hector has no patience to visit our small library."

"Oh, I am interested in quite a number of things. I dare say you will be pleasantly surprised once we become reacquainted properly," he promised. He leaned forward and pressed his lips to her temple suddenly. "It's good to see you smiling at last."

Meg shivered as he drew back. She met his gaze and saw shock in his. He was sitting so close that her breath faltered.

Otis cleared his throat. "I don't know why I did that."

"It meant nothing, I know," she assured him, looking down at their joined hands. He had kissed her as if she was one of his sisters. The women of his family were so lucky to have a warm man like this in their lives. But the last thing Meg wanted was awkwardness between them.

She lifted her gaze slowly. Otis was watching her face with a half smile playing over his lips. His grip on her fingers eased and then his fingers stroked over her palm. Meg's heart began to beat a little faster. She should push him away, but she couldn't seem to do what was expected of her. She wet her lips. "You should go," she suggested to him. "Before someone sees us together and misunderstands."

"I suppose I should."

Yet, Otis did not get up to leave. His fingers toyed with hers, gently stroking them until her face grew quite warm. "What are you doing," Meg asked softly. Otis confused her.

"I have no idea," he confessed. "You are my best friend's younger sister," he said finally as his light touch slid upward to her wrist, and then her arm. "Do you know I am not supposed to think of my friend's sisters as women, or," he smiled slowly as his eyes drifted over her features and down across her body before he looked up, "or to find them as attractive as I do you."

Meg's blush grew hotter until she was sure she couldn't blush any harder.

There was a strange tension between them now—and then Otis suddenly darted towards her and pressed his lips to hers. His kiss was sweet, soft, and oh so gentle. His fingertips lingered on her cheek, warm but gentle as he cupped her skull. A lingering pleasure that curled her toes in her slippers and made her senses soar to incredible heights. She leaned into the kiss, delighting in the forbidden thrill of attraction and desire, hoping it would never end.

She had been kissed before, but she did not remember enjoying those as much as she did Otis'. She was sorry when he drew back with a heavy sigh.

Meg frowned at him. "Why did you kiss me that time?"

Otis shook his head. "I don't know. I swear it will not happen again." He frowned so hard that deep lines appeared on his brow. "Um, excuse me. I had better go arrange for you to have that maid I promised. It's probably best you not be alone with me again."

"You might be right, my lord." Meg nodded, still a bit stunned by his kisses and how she felt about them. She was not offended or even upset with him. She wouldn't mind another too but Lord Clement quickly got to his feet and moved away.

He walked toward the door, but looked back over his shoulder a few times before he got there.

Meg noticed that he seemed unsettled by his actions. It made her like him even more. She would never have believed a rogue or a scoundrel would be ill at ease after kissing anyone. Perhaps he wasn't so bad after all.

He finally slipped from the room with one last lingering glance in her direction. Meg wrapped her arms about the book and laughed softly as she looked outside. A shaft of sunlight had fought through the clouds above The Vynes at last, and the estate was instantly warmer than it had once seemed.

Chapter Six

If he just pretended everything was normal, he would survive his latest indiscretion unscathed. That is what Otis told himself from the moment he woke the next morning until he faced Lady Margaret over breakfast. And when he saw her smile his way, Otis imagined any number of completely inappropriate thoughts revolving around kissing his friend's sister again.

Before his completely unprovoked kiss, he could have gone weeks and months without giving Lady Margaret Stockwick a second or even first thought. Before he'd kissed Margaret, he'd never imagined his best friend's sister might be worth risking a friendship over just so he could have the pleasure of kissing her again.

But as the breakfast progressed, and her eyes sought his time and again, he considered renewing his acquaintance with her a most intriguing opportunity. It had certainly been a while since he'd done anything without thinking the matter through properly. Considering the consequences and the needs of the family first had become second nature up until yesterday.

"I think I've had enough, thank you," Otis decided and allowed a servant to remove his breakfast plate. He sat back, noting Margaret requested more tea but ate little.

She looked so pretty that morning, dressed all in green velvet. She looked as if she had rested well last night, too, and she was smiling whenever Hector spoke to her.

Otis wished he could say he'd passed as good a night. He had been keenly aware that her bedchamber was not so very far away from his, and that he found her terribly attractive. He buried his nose in his teacup again, and scolded himself roundly. He would not kiss Margaret again—not without her permission or invitation.

Hector gobbled up one last slice of ham and glanced his way. "A word, Clement."

Otis nodded, wondering if Hector had already seen that he was paying attention to Margaret and meant to warn him off.

He drained the dregs of his tea, casting a casual eye over the waiting table as he rose. Mother seemed happy, but she always was when Father absented himself from dining with them. His siblings were content for the moment and not squabbling. His eyes were drawn back to Margaret but her expression filled him with unease. Would she have told Hector what he'd done with her lips yesterday?

Hector threw aside his napkin and strode out.

Fearing the worst, Otis joined him in the hall. "Where were you last night?"

"Renewing my acquaintance with George Moore," Hector said with a sly smile.

"And his sister too, I suppose," Otis murmured quietly. "She's trouble."

"After the year I've had, I enjoy that sort of trouble," Hector scowled. "For heaven's sake, don't go all *Meg* on me."

"What does that mean?"

"One mustn't have any fun. One must mourn forever," Hector said with an exaggerated feminine tone that might have been a poor attempt to imitate his sister.

Otis checked that the hall was still empty. He had no experience with losing a member of his family but he hoped he displayed more compassion to his loved ones than Hector seemed to. "Just a friendly warning."

"Anyone would think our father was a saint," Hector grumbled, rubbing the back of his neck. "He had a woman the year Mother fell ill."

Otis was surprised to hear it. Lady Stockwick had been very ill for a long time but he had thought the couple had been closer than ever. Margaret seemed to idolize her late father. She would be shattered to know he had not been faithful. "I assume your sister has no idea?"

"None. She'd never believe me."

Thank heavens for small mercies. "Telling her now would be cruel. Women tend to become emotional upon hearing about betrayals of that nature."

"And knowing my luck, it would turn her forever away from the idea of marriage. I'll never be rid of her if she found out." Hector smiled suddenly. "I was wondering if I might borrow a few pounds from you."

"What do you need money for?"

"George Moore."

"Why couldn't you leave it alone?" Otis murmured quietly. Hector gambled too often and recklessly for his taste. It was one of the reasons he was happy not to be in London with him very often.

"I have to try to win my money back." Hector nodded. "The bastard cheated me out of my money."

"If you didn't gamble while drinking it wouldn't be so easy." George Moore had a temper when there were winnings owed to him. Otis dug in his pocket to see what change he carried, hoping it would be enough. A few notes and a handful of coins was all he had right now. He held them out and Hector took all of it with a grin.

"I'll pay you back of course but I really must be on my way."

"So soon?"

"Meg seems to be settled in now with your mother and really doesn't need me," Hector announced.

"Of course Margaret needs you," Otis insisted, remembering yesterday's conversation. "You are her brother. The most important man in her life right now."

"She needs the company of other women. She also needs to prepare for her season and marriage. I cannot help with that. Lady Vyne has consented to take Mother's role in educating her on such matters. So I am going to absent myself until Christmas Day. After Twelfth Night, we'll head for London and I'll start introducing her around Town. With the dowry I'm prepared to bestow, I'm sure she will attract sufficient interest to find herself a husband."

Otis recoiled from Hector a little. There were days Otis did not understand Hector at all. He would never treat one of his sisters with so little consideration.

But Hector was right about the interest Margaret could stir up in London. She was pretty and bright and dowered, but she was not looking forward to the season the way many women did. He wished Mother could be in London with her then. She would keep any scoundrels away from her and steer her toward a good man.

If Otis found himself in London at that time, he could introduce her to any good men he knew.

After the emotional few years she'd experienced, she might need good friends as she made the most important decision of her life. Otis studied Hector warily. She clearly couldn't count on her brother to be patient. Otis was almost afraid Hector might just approve the first man who asked for her hand to be rid of her.

If Hector learned they had kissed, he might insist *Otis* marry Margaret, whether she wished to or not.

Although…if Otis did offer for Margaret, and was accepted, he would win the bet with his father with time to spare.

Otis turned at the sound of raised voices. His mother and sisters were finally leaving the morning room, while the boy was being dragged back upstairs by his nurse. Margaret was bringing up the rear.

Otis glanced around but found only empty air where Hector had stood.

"For heaven's sake," he cursed under his breath, and then smiled as the ladies joined him. He clapped his hands together once and rubbed them briskly. "So are we all ready to brave the outdoors at last?"

He looked at each of them. His sisters and mother exclaimed that they were. Margaret was quieter in her response, but she too agreed she was ready to face the outdoors. He was glad she could be coaxed outside with them at last.

"Well, then hurry up and get your coats," he told them all, moving as if he was about to rush outside without them. His siblings were usually quick, so they rushed for the waiting servants and began to rug up.

Margaret was first dressed and slid past him in the narrow hall without meeting his gaze. The sweet scent of honeysuckle left in her wake was utterly intoxicating. He'd found the scent on her skin most distracting yesterday, too.

Otis allowed everyone to file from the house ahead of him.

Mother was slowest, which ensured she and Otis brought up the rear together. Meg was swept away by the girls up the garden path, and that was for the best. He needed to talk to Mother without being overheard. "Stockwick intends to leave Margaret entirely to your care. He's slipped away again and won't be back until Christmas Day."

"Good."

He looked at his mother in surprise. "Good?"

Mother huffed. "She spent the whole of last night and this morning waiting to talk to him. If I can convince her he'll be gone for a few days, she might consent to having a little fun, or considering the future. Perhaps you can help with that."

He glanced at her with suspicion. "What did you have in mind?"

"Be attentive. Boost her confidence. Every woman wants to be admired by a gentleman of taste."

"I'm sure she knows her value."

"I'm not so sure anymore," Mother warned. "Did you know Meg once had a suitor?"

"Hector never mentioned that."

"Local lad. Hector introduced them. The fellow had ambitions that included leaving England. Meg was devastated when it was proved he was only interested in her for her dowry and planned to leave her behind as soon as their vows were spoken."

Knowing Margaret had been disappointed in love before did explain why she might be reluctant to venture onto the marriage mart. He would be, too, under those circumstances. "Is that why she never married, because her heart was broken?"

"That and losing the parents she adored to illness and grief. She hasn't had a chance to impress anyone since. Let's hope her next suitor has more staying power and a truer heart," Mother whispered and then strode forward.

Ahead, his sisters were whispering while Margaret walked alone. He had noticed the girls and Meg seemed to get along well this visit, almost as well as Margaret and Mother did. Margaret's devotion to her family was one quality they had in common.

He hurried to catch up to her.

Margaret seemed surprised when he fell into step with her. "Are you enjoying the walk?" he asked as she stopped and looked around for the rest of the group.

"Yes," she promised with a sigh. "This is just what I need. Peace and quiet."

"Yes, peace and…" Otis spun around quickly. Walks with his sisters were never quiet. And he could not see either one of them. Mother had fallen behind, nudging snow off a statue with the tip of her finger. All there was to see was snow-covered shrubbery.

His tension increased. It would be a surprise attack at any moment then.

Otis rushed toward Margaret, arms spread. "No, not today!" he cried out.

But it was too late. Balls of snow pelted down upon them in a thick white shower.

Margaret screamed in fright.

Thinking to protect her, Otis put his arms around her head and shoulders. "I'll punish them for this," he assured Margaret.

Margaret fell to the ground, and Otis moved to cover her as much as possible while the snowballs started striking his back in earnest.

Margaret broke away from him suddenly—and before he knew it, she was pelting handfuls of snow at his sisters.

He could not have been more surprised.

While he'd been protecting her, she had quickly lined up a series of balls unnoticed at their feet but was making very good use of them all now.

Otis hurried to make more, tossing out a few himself but handing most to Margaret. He was used to this sort of behavior from his occasionally brattish siblings, but he'd never expected any lady to want to join in with their usual method of winter warfare.

Margaret had a good arm, and soon it was his sisters' turn to shriek in terror and run and hide behind Mother for protection.

Otis looked up from his kneeling perch to see Margaret smiling as he'd never seen before. She was blinding, so happy and joyous right now.

Otis felt his attraction to her only increase.

Chapter Seven

Meg stepped from her steaming-hot bath, allowed her maid to wrap her in linen, and began to dry herself off before the blazing fire. Aside from the endless cold, it was easy living here, allowing servants to pamper her and fetch her anything her heart desired. Lady Vyne was emphatic that Meg make herself at home, and Meg had reluctantly agreed to because refusing seemed to make the lady unhappy.

She ducked behind a corner dressing screen to finish her drying off in private. "The weather seems much improved today," she called out.

"Yes, but heavy falls are expected before nightfall," Lady Vyne warned. "Make sure to wear your warmest gown for dinner."

"Yes, my lady."

Meg's new maid handed over thick woolen stockings that had been warmed by the fire, and then a chemise. To keep the chill at bay, Meg had taken to wearing as many undergarments as possible. It felt a bit constricting at times, but at least she was always warm.

She stepped out from behind the screen to allow the maid to help her into a day gown of burgundy wool and then sat before her mirror. The maid quickly brushed out her long hair and began styling. While she did, Meg observed her hostess. She often caught Lady Vyne frowning and today was no different. Something was on her mind that she would not talk about with Meg.

Lady Vyne drew closer, helping the maid insert a few of her more decorative pins to her hair. "You look lovely."

"Thank you," Meg said, hiding her smile. She felt a bit lovely, too. Despite the cold of The Vynes, she was happy to be here. She had not realized how much she had missed the company of another woman. Even the countess' children's antics appealed to her. The young boy was a sweet little gentleman, happy to perch on her lap occasionally, especially if it meant he was closer to the cakes placed on the tabletop.

The girls were playful, running here and there through the upper floor of the grand house. They were not allowed in any of the ground-floor rooms. Lord Vyne was said to prefer not to see his children more than once a week. Lady Vyne, however, was as devoted a mother as anyone could want.

Because of the absence of affection from their father, all held their older brother, Lord Clement, in the highest regard. He toted them around, played with them, admonishing them to be good or quiet when they became too rowdy. He was a wonderful older brother. He would make a kind husband and father one day too.

She turned away slightly as her face heated a little because she was thinking of him again.

Meg could not seem to forget that Lord Clement had kissed her, but had not tried to do it again since. She was not sure whether to be grateful or despondent about that. He was not avoiding her, but he was busy and always seemed rushed. She rather thought she might like another kiss from him if he was ever so inclined. After all, she was being forced to look for a husband in London. Why not be prepared to pick someone who kissed well? But in order to do that, Meg needed to be able to make a comparison.

"What are our plans for the afternoon?"

"We must wait." Lady Vyne moved to the window, and Meg dismissed the maid. "My husband has invited friends of his to join us for the holiday. They could arrive anytime now, I believe."

Meg was disappointed by the news that she must meet new people. "Who are they?"

"Mr. Xavier Milne. He is a prosperous merchant and quite wealthy, from London."

A prosperous husband might make a good husband too. "I see. Is Mr. Milne married, madam?"

"Indeed he is. His wife has given him several children."

Meg sagged with relief. For a moment, she feared Lady Vyne had invited the gentleman for the sole purpose of meeting her before the season began. Given the secrecy of everything that had gone before to get her here, she would not have been surprised if Hector had arranged something like that. "I do hope they are enjoying a smooth journey."

"Yes, but until they arrive, I am not quite certain how many members of his family will be joining us." Lady Vyne shrugged. "We shall see. Are you ready?"

"Yes." Meg snatched up a woolen shawl and wrapped it about her shoulders.

Lady Vyne smiled and led the way to the door.

They were in the morning room half an hour when a servant came with the news that a carriage was approaching the manor. Lady Vyne seemed displeased by the news but moved to the drawing room to receive them.

Meg was dragged along although she rather hoped she might have been excused. Lord Vyne was already in the drawing room, pacing. Meg had not seen her host more than once since her arrival. He was said to be ill and spent much of his day in bed. However, during the times she had been exposed to his company, she found him a cold and hard man, one with little conversation for Meg.

"I've sent for your son, madam," he said curtly.

Lady Vyne nodded.

Meg looked down at her fingers, feeling ill at ease that any search would be in vain. Lord Clement had left the manor before elevenses. Meg had waved to him from her upper bedchamber window when she'd seen his figure on the snowy lawn below. He'd waved back but continued on his way to the stables. She'd seen him ride off, too, but not return to the manor in the hours since.

"I will expect him to be attentive to all our guests," Lord Vyne informed his wife.

Lady Vyne nodded and arched her neck toward the door. "They are here."

The earl cast a baleful eye upon his wife. "I will speak with the boy later about his absence."

That did not sound very pleasant. Meg eased back as greetings were exchanged with Mr. Milne and a daughter. She seemed about Meg's age but with a polish Meg could never hope to imitate. Miss Milne was spectacularly pretty, with russet-red hair and a heart-shaped face. Meg rather thought she *knew* her looks were superior, too. The pair were very loud and exuberant. Meg did not like them very much.

Miss Milne glanced at Meg, frowning slightly at her presence.

Lady Vyne introduced Meg with a fond smile. "And this is our dear friend, Lady Margaret Stockwick."

"A pleasure, my lady."

"Miss Milne." Meg inclined her head. "I trust your journey was uneventful."

"Indeed it was," she replied, smiling at Lady Vyne.

They all sat down together, and Meg ended up beside Miss Milne. Being new acquaintances in the presence of old friends, Meg held her tongue and let others talk. Miss Milne felt no such compulsion. She added her pennies' worth at every opportunity, drawing all eyes in the room to look at her.

Miss Milne leaned closer suddenly and whispered, "Will Lord Clement be joining us soon do you think?"

"I cannot say," Meg whispered back.

"Have you been visiting long?"

"We arrived several days ago."

"You came with your brother?"

"Indeed. Do you know him?"

"Lord Stockwick and Lord Clement are the most desirable bachelors in all of England." Miss Milne smiled knowingly but Meg couldn't be more surprised about her brother's reputation. Could a man with so little patience be considered a catch?

The gentlemen suddenly excused themselves, announcing they would retire to the library for the afternoon to discuss important business matters. Meg was disappointed to discover that the library would be off limits until they were done. She had hoped to read the next chapter of her book with Lord Clement there upon his return from riding out.

She would have to wait until tomorrow, she supposed.

"It is a pleasure to be invited to stay at The Vynes. My father has been telling me all about the estate and the family's long history here."

"It is my family who once owned this estate but it became part of the Vyne estates upon my marriage." Lady Vyne's smile was strained, and then she gestured to the waiting servant and asked for tea. "Might I enquire after your family? Your mother and sisters are well, I trust?"

"Indeed they are, and very sorry to have missed the opportunity to travel to Derbyshire this year."

Meg leaned forward. "How many siblings are in your family?"

"Eight." Miss Milne eyed the cakes. "There were too many for even the largest of carriages so Papa said they must stay at home with Mama."

"Traveling as a family can be very trying on ones nerves," Lady Vyne remarked.

"Even when you only have the one sibling too," Meg murmured. "Men are so hard to amuse over long distances."

That earned her a laugh from Lady Vyne.

"I should like to have brought my sisters to meet everyone," Miss Milne said.

"It can be difficult to leave home," Lady Vyne replied, eyeing Miss Milne with a more sympathetic expression. "More tea?"

"Yes, please."

Lady Vyne asked Meg the same question but she declined a second cup.

"Cake," she offered next.

Miss Milne nodded quickly and took one slice of cake. Meg declined. She had enjoyed a good meal earlier in the day and needed nothing more.

Miss Milne, however, eyed the last piece hungrily. "May I have another?"

Lady Vyne agreed.

"Forgive me but I truly am famished," Miss Milne said when it was gone, too. "My father's impatience to reach the estate ensured our stops along the way were always brief."

"Some men never consider the needs of the ladies under their care," Lady Vyne murmured. "My son is not like that."

"No indeed. Lord Clement is very much concerned with everyone's happiness," Meg replied in full agreement.

"I am glad to hear it." Miss Milne nodded quickly.

Meg was not sure why she looked up when she did, but she found Lord Clement standing across the room, still as a post as he listened to her praise him. A funny smile teased his lips, then the smile grew.

Meg's cheeks began to tingle with the heat of a blush.

Lady Vyne and Miss Milne could not see him, and they talked on about the trials of pleasing a large family, with no idea their words were being overheard.

Meg held his gaze and scrunched her toes in her slippers. Lord Clement was finally back, and they might still read her book together that afternoon if he was free to do so.

He raised a finger to his lips, asking for her silence, and then backed quietly from the room without interrupting his mother.

Meg gaped. Why was he not joining them?

Lady Vyne must have seen something of Meg's disappointment in her expression then, because she whipped around to look behind her. "Is that you, my son?"

But Otis did not reappear, and Meg couldn't even hear his steps on the stairs.

Lady Vyne caught Meg's eye, her expression questioning. "I wonder what is keeping my son away?"

"I cannot imagine, my lady," she murmured.

Lady Vyne's gaze shifted ever so slightly to Miss Milne and a wry smile crossed her face. "I hope whatever it is doesn't keep him from joining us for dinner."

"I cannot imagine it would," Meg reassured her.

Lord Clement had never missed a meal since Meg had arrived. She had enjoyed his company immensely as his conversation had filled the void of emptiness inside her. He had enlivened every meal with his conversation in a way Hector never had. But with the Milnes visiting too, she would not be able to monopolize his time anymore.

Lady Vyne turned to Miss Milne. "Perhaps you'd like to retire to your room to recover from the journey for a short time before we meet again at dinner. If you are still hungry, I can have a tray of tea and sandwiches sent to your room."

Miss Milne beamed. "Thank you, my lady. I would indeed be grateful for some time alone with my thoughts if you can spare me."

Miss Milne left after reassurances were offered. Escorted by her maids and a footman to show her the way upstairs, Miss Milne swept out with a cheerful wave.

"She seems nice," Meg murmured.

Lady Vyne nodded. "One can only hope it lasts."

"Ah, there you are, Mother," Lord Clement exclaimed as he reappeared but at a different doorway than the one he'd used before.

His mother smiled in relief. "We were beginning to worry about you."

"I ventured upstairs to check on the boy. He's doing better I think."

"Did he jump all over you again?"

"Begged to be put on my shoulders and carried around." Lord Clement glanced her way with a smile. "How are you today, Lady Margaret. Warm enough, I trust?"

"Indeed I am."

His mother leaned forward. "I'm afraid you just missed meeting the new visitors."

Lord Clement's eyes widened in apparent surprise, and then he turned to Meg. "What visitors?"

Lady Vyne was only too happy to relate the particulars of the new guests.

"Well, I'm sorry to hear Miss Milne has retired for a while. Damn awful timing really. I was just about to suggest we all take another walk together." He turned to Meg suddenly, brows rising in question.

Meg grinned. "I'd be happy to join you today."

Chapter Eight

Otis rested his feet on the wall in the corner of the library and wet his finger, ready to turn the page. Meg's book was truly terrible but he couldn't rest until he'd caught up with the beginning of the story. He'd sent Lady Margaret a request for the loan of the book so he could catch up late last night, and his valet had delivered it to him at daybreak, before he'd managed to make plans to do anything else.

Beginning a story in the middle had been vastly unsatisfying to him, and he wanted to discuss the whole book with Lady Margaret the next time they met for a reading. Thankfully, he was a quick reader, and he was already a quarter of the way through the story. Unfortunately, his meeting with Meg to read together would be delayed because he was required to spend time with the Milnes that afternoon instead. Father had insisted on being present.

Otis was expected to meet with them at four in this room, resplendent to begin a courtship, but the story was much more interesting than sizing up any woman for marriage.

He lifted his eyes and rested the open book against his chest and gave thanks for Lady Margaret and her unusual choice of reading material. Otis found her utterly charming and far more interesting than Miss Milne. Lady Margaret was quite the surprise really, given the odd remarks Hector had said to her detriment in recent years. Very lively—now that she'd settled into the informal pace of the estate and its occupants. Much more talkative than upon her arrival, too, and spending time with her was no hardship. So entirely kissable that he didn't quite trust himself still.

It was clear that Mother's affection for Lady Margaret was reciprocated, and his siblings begged for her company constantly. Hector would obviously have no trouble finding her a husband once she was comfortable with the idea. She seemed a truly uncomplicated creature. That was a quality quite rare in his experience with women of the *ton*.

"Yes, I think we will all be very comfortable here," a man said suddenly to Otis' right.

"I hope so," a woman replied.

Otis risked a peek as the voices grew louder and louder. No doubt it was the Milnes prowling the house. They were drawing closer to the library and his hiding spot. He could not see them but because he'd left the door slightly ajar, what he soon heard was more than enough for one day.

He closed Meg's book and set it behind him.

"Vyne assures me he'll propose before the week is out," Mr. Milne boasted.

"Yes, Papa," Miss Milne agreed, but to Otis, she did not sound so confident about her chances.

Good.

The library door handle rattled, and then Mr. Milne pushed both doors wide to admit them.

Otis quietly set his feet on the floor. He had been hoping to avoid the Milnes for a little longer but it appeared his luck had run out. Mr. Milne strode to the center of the room and looked about as if he owned the place. "Impressive, isn't it?"

"There are so many books," Miss Milne exclaimed in wonder as she stared up at the walls. "We might finally get my sisters interested in serious matters at last."

"*When* you are mistress here," Mr. Milne said in a whisper.

Otis rolled his eyes. Presumptive prig! He'd not even spoken to the chit and they were making plans for after the wedding.

"Lord Bellows told me his library was much like this," Miss Milne noted.

Otis' ears pricked up at the mention of Miss Milne's former suitor.

"Not that he could read any of it," Mr. Milne said with a mocking laugh.

Otis was curious to know how Miss Milne considered her former suitor. Bellows was not very bright but he had been clearly besotted with this chit. Otis was certain he had seen affection for the earl when Miss Milne had been with the man.

"He does try very hard," she said briskly. But then Miss Milne turned around and spotted him in his corner. Her eyes widened, and she grasped her father's arm quickly.

Otis stood and tugged down his waistcoat. "Bellows does try extremely hard to hide his difficulties from others. Persistence and loyalty is what he is known best for though."

Miss Milne dipped into a deep curtsy worthy of a court appearance. "Lord Clement," she whispered in an unnaturally reverent tone. "We did not see you there."

"Miss Milne." He took in her appearance and bowed with the appropriate degree of respect for such a woman. This was the daughter he had met before. She was exactly as he remembered, elegant, delicate, somewhat vain, and he felt not a single stirring of attraction toward her still. He would not marry a woman he did not crave to be close to. "Welcome to The Vynes."

"The estate is lovely," Miss Milne gushed. "Your family has been so welcoming."

"I'm sure everyone will have done all that is required to make my father's guests enjoy their stay." He turned his attention on Mr. Milne. "Mr. Milne. I was led to believe that we were not to meet until four. You are somewhat early."

This pair had interrupted his musings about another lady. One he *was* finding himself very drawn to. He wanted them to go away while he considered what to do about Lady Margaret.

Mr. Milne adopted an apologetic expression. "My daughter was eager to see more of the manor. I'm sure you can understand why. Perhaps you would consent to show her around the rest of the house until our meeting."

He couldn't very well claim to be unavailable, so he nodded. "Have you viewed the family gallery?"

"Not yet."

"Please," he gestured toward the door as Mr. Milne hung back, urging him to join them. There was not a chance in hell he would conduct a private tour of the manor for just Miss Milne. "After you both."

Otis put his hands behind his back as they walked into the hall and turned toward the gallery. More than fifty paintings of unmatched size graced the walls, nestled between tall windows. Given it was snowing again, there was not much to see outside, but in springtime the gallery offered the best views of the garden.

"Oh, these are wonderful."

He pointed toward the wall. "One of my ancestors was prodigiously fond of painting the estate, as you see."

Miss Milne nodded. "Your mother told me your family has lived in this one valley for generations."

"Six generations, on both sides of the family, too. The Vynes and my mother's family, the Morgans, were once sworn enemies."

She smiled. "How was a peace brokered?"

"The usual way. Marriages were arranged between sons and daughters." He shrugged. "Not all unions ensured peace for the newlyweds."

"Yes, I've heard that can happen in arranged matches," Miss Milne murmured with a subtle glance over her shoulder.

Otis glanced behind them, too, and groaned. Mr. Milne was dragging his feet. "Mr. Milne, I think you will find this painting to your liking."

The man came forward slowly and stopped before a scene depicting a tannery. Milne had started out as an apprentice at such a place, he'd heard, but within twenty years had somehow amassed a fortune that had propelled the Milne family into the heart of the *ton*. "It is an impressive feat to rise from such honest labors. You made your fortune the right way in my opinion."

Mr. Milne colored deeply but Otis was not mocking him. There was no harm in offering the man his respect, given he'd come on a fool's errand.

"What is this one?" Miss Milne asked, pointing to the next painting.

Otis stepped up to it and smiled. "The house before improvements were made by my grandfather. It was quite a bit smaller in those days. This part of the house used to be outside—a walled garden and pond. Of course at this time of year, the pond was often so frozen it was skated upon."

Miss Milne laughed. "Lord Bellows once promised to teach me to skate."

"Surely there is still time for him to do so," he whispered, so her father did not hear the remark.

Miss Milne nodded slowly but her expression became strained. She flashed a smile that fell far short of sincerity. "Perhaps."

They moved along, and Otis answered every question Miss Milne put to him. He was well schooled in the family history to give the tour, even if he couldn't wait to get back to the book and Lady Margaret. Neither feat could be accomplished until after speaking with his father. But he was impressed by Miss Milne's intelligence. She would do very well for Bellows if Otis could turn her back in the earl's direction.

He glanced at his pocket watch and smiled. "Time to head to the library."

Miss Milne quickly availed herself of his arm. "Thank you," she whispered. "I hope Lord Bellows knows how good a friend you are to him."

"You can tell him, after you marry him," Otis suggested, leaning close. "He tends to get flustered when anyone does him a kindness."

"Well, well, well. This is what I had hoped to see," Mr. Milne exclaimed, grinning widely at the sight of them standing so close together.

Otis untangled himself from Miss Milne. "It's not what it looks like."

"Is it not?" Mr. Milne beamed, and then laid his finger beside his nose. "But I see and hear only that which makes my heart happy."

"We all see what we wish to see in others." He narrowed his gaze on Mr. Milne. "Did you know Lord Bellows was a good friend of mine before you dragged your daughter here? I could never bear to be the cause of his unhappiness."

Mr. Milne blinked. "She will do her duty."

"Marriage should be based on more than that. Respect. Affection and mutual interests." He caught Miss Milne's eye. "There are no dogs allowed around me. I'm allergic to them."

"Oh." Miss Milne stared. "That is unfortunate."

"Not for me." He gestured them toward the door that led back to the library impatiently. "We should not keep my father waiting longer than necessary. Delays are not good for his health."

He led the way to the library where Father was indeed waiting for them before the fire. Vyne brightened when he saw them arrive together but Otis made sure not to sit too close to the visitors. He would not encourage them to consider a marriage between himself and Miss Milne as a certainty.

It was anything but.

Chapter Nine

Meg took the chair closest to the fire to brush out her long hair, her thoughts fixed on Lord Clement. She had not seen him today but she'd heard he had met with Mr. Milne and his daughter that afternoon. She had hoped to see him at dinner tonight, but he had not appeared. No one seemed able to find him, or Hector either. "I hope nothing terrible has happened to him."

"I'm sure he'll turn up hale and hearty soon," Lady Vyne murmured, apparently unconcerned for the whereabouts of her son. "He has taken a great many responsibilities on his shoulders in recent years. I'm sure he's somewhere on the estate and fully occupied."

"I hope he is warm." The snowfall Lady Vyne had predicted yesterday had settled over them and continued still unabated. Night had fallen long ago, and there was snow piling up thickly on her window ledge. "Lord Vyne is very worried about his absence."

"True, but not for the reason you imagine," Lady Vyne advised.

"I imagine he must miss his son," Meg said.

"Well, you would be wrong," Lady Vyne murmured as she reclined in the opposite cozy chair by the fire, tipping her glass of wine high to drain the contents. The countess' children had long since gone to bed, Miss Milne had retired in a huff, and the gentlemen, Lord Vyne and Mr. Milne, were drinking in the library. Lady Vyne might be a little disguised at the moment. It was just the two of them in Meg's chambers tonight, talking together as usual before they went to bed.

Lady Vyne regarded her gravely as she set the glass aside. "I trust you will keep our family matters to yourself, but you must realize my son and husband are not close."

"Oh, I am sorry to hear that," Meg said quickly. "They have been together so rarely in the same room that I never noticed."

"I'm glad you were spared the tension." Lady Vyne rubbed her brow. "Neither ever hides their true feelings from me."

Meg nodded quickly, worried that to ask more questions would be presumptuous. "When fathers and sons quarrel, it is always hardest on the mothers."

"Of course, the money now is the source of discord."

"I am sorry to hear Lord Clement is a burden on the estate."

"Money is the least of my son's concerns." Lady Clement frowned at her. "Are you telling me you don't know about the inheritance he received from the late earl, his grandfather?"

Meg shook her head quickly. "Hector tells me very little that is the truth, I've come to realize. I thought Lord Clement's situation must be similar to Hector's, before he inherited my father's estate."

"Their situations were and are vastly different. Otis could afford to buy his own estate tomorrow, one grander than this one, if he chose to ever leave us."

Meg couldn't be more surprised. Otis did not act like he had pots of money. "Why doesn't he? He seems capable."

"He will not leave without us," Lady Vyne admitted, looking away guiltily.

Meg's estimation of Otis' character rose exponentially. He was a good man, more caring than her own brother, perhaps. "You are lucky to have such a son."

"I know."

Meg's comb suddenly caught on a lock of hair and when she removed it, she discovered a tooth had broken. She held it up, staring at its unhappy state. Since leaving home, it continued to break. She heaved a sigh. "At this rate, I might have to purchase a replacement before Christmas."

Lady Vyne shook her head. "I keep a second new comb laid aside for just such emergencies. I'll fetch it and bring it back to you shortly."

"It is not urgent," Meg protested but Lady Vyne was already out the door, a little unsteady on her feet.

Meg drew her knees up to her chest, made sure her legs were completely under her nightgown for warmth, and stared into the flames. It was comforting being with Lady Vyne, being here in the place she never thought she would ever enjoy herself. These quiet moments at night with another woman offered a companionship sadly lacking in her life since her mother's passing.

And the more she learned about Otis, the more ashamed she became. She had wronged him in her thoughts more times than she could count.

A window rattled suddenly, and a blast of cold air swept through the room, chilling her to the bone.

"What!" she exclaimed, turning towards the window as Otis climbed through it, his shoulders and hair dusted heavily with snow.

He put his finger across his lips to silence her again as he shut it—but then froze as footsteps hurried down the hall in their direction.

His mother's voice rang out, and he suddenly dived under her bed.

Meg bolted for the dressing screen and hastily pulled on her thick winter coat.

Lady Vyne sailed into the room, brandishing a new ivory comb. "I'm afraid I'll not be able to linger with you any longer tonight. I'm needed in the nursery."

"But Lord Clement—"

"Otis will be fine. Do not worry for his welfare so much, my dear," she suggested, and then frowned at Meg. "Were you really going to wear that coat to bed tonight?"

"I was thinking I might," Meg lied. She would wear the coat until Lord Clement left her room.

"I can have a maid deliver another blanket if you like."

A maid might discover Lord Clement. Meg quickly shook her head. "The coat will be enough."

"All right." Lady Vyne chuckled softly. "Well, good night my dear. Sleep well and perhaps dream of hot springs."

As soon as the countess was gone, she moved to the bed and peered under.

Lord Clement was hard to see in the shadows, but she had not imagined his arrival. "You cannot be here," she admonished. "What are you doing?"

"Every window and door downstairs was locked," Otis complained as he slid toward her. "I am very sorry about this."

Meg rushed to the window and looked down. "How did you get to my window?"

"The old vine is still quite sturdy," he answered in a soft voice, and then he glanced toward the door. "I had no idea my mother would be here when I started up."

"We talk together every night."

Otis grinned quickly. "What about?"

"Never you mind," she admonished again. "You had better go."

"True," he started toward the door, but when they both heard voices raised outside the room again, Meg froze and Otis hurtled himself across the bed and threw himself down on the opposite side.

Although impressed by his speed and agility, Meg hurried to the door and opened it a crack. "It is Miss Milne," she whispered to the viscount.

"Do not let her in!" he warned sternly.

Miss Milne and her maid appeared in no hurry to return to their room, though. The pair crept along the hall and, after listening at a closed door, Miss Milne slipped inside. The maid remained in the hall, appearing to be keeping watch.

Meg shut the door and locked it. Miss Milne's behavior disturbed her, but not enough to go out there and ask her what she was doing, creeping into another guest room.

Meg moved to the bed and clasped her hands together before her stomach. "The door is locked now," Meg informed Otis.

He poked his head up and placed his arms upon the bed. He smiled, and Meg was utterly charmed. "Thank you, Margaret," he whispered. "You have saved my life tonight."

"How did I do that?" she asked but felt a little thrill anyway. He was back and obviously well. She had worried for naught about him. But he could have frozen out there. She leaned down and grabbed his coat sleeve, discovering the fabric cold and damp under her fingers. "Oh, you must go to the fire before you catch a chill," she urged, pulling him up off the floor.

He moved slowly to the hearth, where a good fire burned, and sank down on his knees before the flames. He held his hands out and sighed in obvious pleasure. "I'm used to the cold you know, but I dreaded I might have to spend a night in the stables until I saw light at your window."

She nodded slowly and sank down on the nearest chair. "Where have you been?"

"Here and there about the estate. By the way, thank you for not letting Mother know that you saw me tonight, or in the drawing room yesterday."

"How do you know I kept yesterday a secret?"

"Instinct, and the fact that Mother called out my name and I still managed to slip away."

"Why were you hiding from her?"

He added another shovel of coal to the flames. "I do not hide from my mother."

Meg bit her lip. He was clearly not hiding from *her* either, so that just left... "Do you hide from Miss Milne?"

"Yes, but do not tell anyone I said so."

"You do not like her?"

"Not the way I like you." He grinned, and then schooled his features as if he'd not meant to confess that.

Meg couldn't hold back a smile. "She seems quite nice."

"I have nothing against her."

That was faint praise if ever she heard it.

"I had better leave you now," he whispered, as he climbed to his feet and dusted off his coat sleeves.

Meg caught his arm. "Will I see you tomorrow?"

He looked at her sharply. "Do you want to?"

"We were going to read my story together."

"So we were." He nodded. "The library will no doubt be occupied again tomorrow. My father likes to impress visitors with the size of his collection, not that he reads many of them these days. But there is a chamber on the floor above, right above it. The light is good, and no one should think of looking for either of us there. Will you meet me there at four o'clock?"

Lady Vyne took an hour of rest at that time, and Meg thought she could manage to slip away from her maid then, too. "I'll try."

"I'll wait for the hour. Come if you can," he whispered. "It's time to find out what happens next in your book."

Meg nodded...and when Lord Clement leaned down, she allowed him to kiss her again.

It was as lovely as the first time. Lord Clement cupped the back of her head as he peppered kisses over her willing lips. She felt the brush of his tongue across the seam of her lips and she parted them.

Lord Clement devoured her mouth then, and Meg submitted quite willingly. She lifted her hands to his coat and spread her fingers over his chest. A soft moan left her lips, and Otis drew back, blue eyes bright and full of questions.

Meg blushed hotly. "You should go."

He cupped her cheek in the palm of his hand and smiled. "I definitely should."

He crept to the door, turned the key and peered out—and then quickly shut the door again. "Does she *never* stay in her own room?"

"Town hours?" Meg suggested, and then yawned.

"I might have to wait her out." He bit his lip. "I don't want to inconvenience you but might I stay here a little longer? She has to go to her own bed sooner or later."

Meg considered what might happen if he stayed. He might kiss her again, but she did not believe he might try to do more than that. Having him here now already risked her reputation, but if he were seen leaving, and she was in her nightgown, it would be ten times worse. She nodded, knowing there was no other choice but to agree and hope for the best. The alternative, sending him back out the window was impossible. He might freeze. "You may stay."

"Again, you are saving my life," he assured her. "Take yourself to bed and don't mind me."

She glanced at him, and then at the narrow settee. "What are you going to do?"

"Wait by the door and hope I don't freeze. A pity you do not have a spare blanket lying around."

"I have all of them on the bed, but sitting by the door doesn't sound very comfortable or warm enough for you," she noted.

His brow rose. "Would you have me join you in bed instead?"

Meg gaped. "Otis!"

He chuckled softly. "We could always practice bundling."

"That is a terrible idea." She peeked out the door quickly and grinned. Miss Milne's maid was nowhere in sight and the hall was finally empty.

Otis joined her at the door, and she made room for him. She pushed. "Go."

"Until tomorrow," he said, and then slipped out of the room soundlessly.

Meg closed the door, grinning broadly. She was glad Lord Clement was a gentleman at heart rather than the rogue she'd imagined.

Chapter Ten

Otis flung himself from the carriage in the stable yard of the Lucky Chance Tavern. He glanced around carefully. There were four horses hanging their heads over the stalls inside the stables, one of which he instantly recognized by color and the blaze on its forehead. Lord Hector Stockwick was at the tavern, or nearby perhaps.

He turned toward the coachman. "Make sure the horses are given hay and cover them up while you wait. I'll try not to be too long."

"Yes, my lord."

Otis hurried toward the tavern, brushing snow from his shoulders, flanked by two of the burliest footmen from The Vynes. He'd come prepared for an argument, should Hector not wish to return home with Otis of his own free will.

As much as he'd like his arrival to pass unnoticed, the tavern drew customers from miles around. The taproom was full and loud. He gave the occupants a cursory glance but did not immediately see Hector in their number.

The tavern keeper saw him though and rushed over. "A table and ale, my lord?"

"Not today. I should like to speak with Lord Stockwick if he is here."

The fellow frowned. "I am sorry, my lord. There is no one here by that name."

Hector had a habit of hiding his identity when he was drinking in low places like this, so he would not become a target for thieves. "What about another name? A stranger to these parts. It is a matter of some urgency."

The innkeeper scratched his chin. "There's a fellow abed upstairs, but I never imagined him a friend of yours. He's been malingering here a few days."

The timing sounded right. Otis tried to recall what Hector had worn the last time he been seen. "He might have arrived wearing a blue coat, paler blue waistcoat, and riding boots. He has dark hair and is a little shorter than I. But I swear his horse is in your stable right now, unless he gambled it away."

The innkeeper nodded. "Might be my customer. He owes me money."

Otis sighed and dug in his pocket for coin. He counted out a number until the innkeeper smiled. Otis nodded, hiding his annoyance at the amount. "This is yours if the man upstairs turns out to be my friend."

"I'd be happy to take you to him." The innkeeper led the way, climbing the narrow stairs to an upper floor with a heavy tread. Otis followed, drawing his men with him.

The innkeeper banged on a bright yellow door at the end of the hall and hollered, "You've a visitor."

There was grumble of complaint inside, and Otis recognized the tone as belonging to Meg's brother. "That's him."

Otis handed over the money owed and asked his men to wait outside the door before going in.

He stepped through the doorway and squinted about the dingy little room, noting the décor hadn't improved since the last time he'd been forced to spend the night here due to bad weather. The same faded drapes still hung at the window, unpolished floorboards bare of any rugs graced the floor, and a narrow and untidy bed stood in the center of the room.

A large lump shifted under a faded quilt gracing the bed.

"Wake up, man," Otis demanded. "You've been here long enough."

"Bugger off," Hector complained. "Can't you see I'm busy?"

"Sleeping," Otis noted. "Don't make me drag you out by your heels."

A pair of dainty feet suddenly appeared on one of the pillows. "I think he means it, sir," a woman whispered.

Hector grumbled again and the bedding was flung back from one side. Hector had been sleeping upside down in the bed and, with a bit of effort, crawled out.

Otis averted his eyes from his nakedness. "For God's sake, cover up," he complained.

"S' your own fault for intruding," Hector taunted. "What brings you here so early?"

"It's midday."

"Oh, all right then," Hector agreed then began to look around. He seemed particularly unsteady, and the way he was scrubbing at his head made his hair stand on end even worse than before. "Be a good fellow and help me find my trousers."

Otis moved deeper into the room. He found Hector's discarded clothing scattered all about and a few items worn by a lady. He tossed each piece onto the bed where the woman still hid, saying not a word. Otis cared nothing about the lady, but his friend really should learn to be discreet. "I'll be waiting downstairs. Don't take long unless you'd like my men to truss you like a hog and tie you to the top of my carriage for the return home."

"I'm coming, I'm coming," Hector insisted as he put his trousers on backward. He jerked them back off and tried a second time. "I just need a moment."

Otis glanced at his pocket watch, struggling not to laugh. Hector was a difficult man, more so at this hour. Otis still had a little time to spare, but he was loath to be late today just because Hector couldn't don his trousers the right way round. Meg was expecting him.

The thought of her made him grin.

After last night's encounter and kiss, he was certain he was looking in the right direction for the woman who might be his bride.

"A storm is coming, and I'd like to be home before the roads become treacherous," he announced as he exited the room.

Otis left his men outside Hector's door, with strict instructions to bring Hector within ten minutes, dressed or not. He greeted a few of the locals and he departed the tavern, resisting the urge to linger. He would wait in the carriage.

The air was chilly, and he threw furs over his knees while he waited for Hector to make an appearance. In his head, he rehearsed what he would say to his friend. Asking for Meg's hand in marriage was a delicate business.

He was so close to winning the wager that he could taste the freedom to take his mother anywhere she wanted to go.

Eventually, Hector appeared at the tavern doorway, shading his eyes from the light. He stumbled across the stable yard with Otis' servants helping him along and into the carriage. Hector collapsed on the opposite bench seat with a groan.

Otis wasted no time. "Home," he called loudly as he thumped on the wall.

Hector flinched from the noise. "What is wrong with you?"

Otis studied his friend. He hadn't improved very much since Otis had found him. "Well, I'm not ape-drunk like you are, for one."

Hector pressed a hand to his brow. "I've had a very good time."

"No doubt."

Hector lowered his hand and squinted across the carriage. God, he looked terrible.

"So what's the crisis, man? Why did you come after me?" Hector demanded.

Otis nodded slowly. "My reason for disturbing you is a delicate matter best spoken of quietly. It concerns your sister."

Hector jerked upright. "Is she ill?"

"No, she is very well." He drew in a deep breath before he continued. "I want to speak to you about her future. Taking her to London might not be necessary after all."

Hector groaned. "What has Meg done now? Begged to return home…or wait, has she convinced your mother to let her stay at The Vynes? It is too much to ask for that she might have simply run off with some poor fool and saved me the expense of dowering her at all."

"Your sister has more sense than that, but you might be correct that she is willing to stay at The Vynes." He sighed. "She has asked for you every morning and every night, you know."

"I told you exactly when I would return." Hector's expression turned to alarm. "I'm not late, am I?"

"No. You were expected back tomorrow."

"Good. Then this can wait until tomorrow when my head is clear."

Otis shook his head. "Your clear head is needed at The Vynes now."

"Don't tell me you're lonely without me?"

"No, I have not missed you personally. But Meg does, and there is also Father's unexpected guests, Mr. Milne and his daughter, that you should meet with."

Hector's brows rose high. "How pleasant for you to have so many friends come to call, but I still don't understand?"

"It's Meg."

"You said there was nothing wrong with her." Hector drew close. "Why the urgency to speak of my sister all of a sudden?"

Otis drew a breath, and then wet his lips. "I know this might seem a hasty decision to you…but I wanted to ask for her hand in marriage."

Hector laughed. "Good God, you've a wicked sense of humor. Don't talk nonsense. You and Meg, an ill-matched pair if ever there was one. What is it you really want?"

"Your blessing."

Hector squinted. "But she's hated you for years?"

Otis reeled back. Hate was a very strong word. "That cannot be true."

"Oh, yes. You have no idea how much she disliked the idea of being under the same roof as you for the holiday. We argued about turning back for three days in a row."

Otis shook his head. Meg may have initially believed him responsible for Hector's prolonged stays in London, but he had set her straight days ago. Hector would know her opinion had changed if he'd not been preoccupied with his own amusements at the tavern. "I am convinced she understands now why you stayed away from home for so long. But I am still asking for your approval to court her."

Hector frowned. "Does your sudden change of heart have anything to do with the bet you made with your father? It's all the servants were talking about the day I left."

"What I feel for Meg has nothing at all to do with any wager."

"But in marrying her, you'll win. Why choose Meg over the Milne chit? A large dowry more than makes up for the disappointment of Meg's smaller one."

"The wager is beside the point. So too is the size of a dowry. I care about Meg."

Hector drew closer. "I knew you were desperate to win the wager, but to ask for my sisters hand and claim to love her is beyond the pale."

"I'm not sure it is love, but it is something important. After the last few days of becoming reacquainted, I think she would accept my proposal."

Hector seemed unconvinced still. "Does she know about the wager?"

"No," Otis admitted. "There wasn't time to tell her everything about my family."

Hector shook his head. "You've no chance then. My sister believes in love at first sight and all that romantic gibberish young women go on with. Once she learns about the wager...well, I'm sure you can imagine the likely response. She'll refuse you then, and so do I now. Don't waste your time and energy courting Meg. She was born stubborn."

Otis was not unduly alarmed at being refused but he definitely did not agree with Hector's opinion of her character. However, had Hector asked for one of his sister's hands in marriage, if they were the right age for marriage, he might have said no too at first. "I wager she won't."

Hector smiled coldly. "Care to put hard coin on that bet."

"I will not buy your approval. Meg's affections are priceless."

"I have told you no, and that is the end of it," Hector insisted. "We all promised to stay well-away from our sisters and if you know what's good for you, you will keep that promise."

"I cannot."

Hector glared, suddenly appearing very clearheaded and angry. "If you so much as touch one hair on her head, I'll throttle you."

Otis scowled. "How will you know what goes on between Meg and I? You're never around her. You make a bloody poor chaperone indeed."

"I will make up for any lapse just as soon as my head clears," Hector insisted.

"Oh good, and when you do, perhaps you could repay me what you owe me. There's the money you took to fund your little excursions to the tavern, to gamble with Moore, or so you said. Then there was more besides that was paid to the innkeeper for your stay. I assume you paid your female companion handsomely for her time, too."

"Of course I pay my way, you penny-pinching prig. I don't know why I bothered coming all this way to be subjected to your disapproval. I had enough of that when my father was alive."

"I hope your father's shade never learns that you abandoned your sister to spend Christmas rutting between a whore's thighs. You should be ashamed of yourself."

Hector's face paled suddenly, and he put his hand up to his mouth. "Stop the bloody carriage."

By the time Otis stepped out, Hector was hunched over and casting up his accounts with painful persistence. Otis watched in silence, but then when he was done and appeared weak, he strode over and helped Hector into the carriage.

"My thanks," Hector murmured as Otis tossed every blanket over him. "You are a true friend in my hour of need. I don't feel at all well. Let's forget we ever quarreled."

Otis shook his head, no longer amused. "I do this knowing Meg would want me to look after you as if you were part of my family already. You don't deserve an ounce of pity."

His complaint was met with a loud snore.

Chapter Eleven

Meg wandered The Vynes with a sense of anticipation building inside her. Casting an eye upon every clock as she moved from room to room, she checked the time to be certain that she would not be late for her meeting with Lord Clement at four. Meg had not seen him since last night, but that was not unusual. He was frequently busy about the estate, or he was with his younger siblings, doting on them.

She would never have believed Lord Clement a family man if she had not seen his good and steady influence on the children with her own eyes.

She stepped into another room, finding herself in the family gallery again. Of all the paintings hung upon the walls, she found the summer landscapes the most pleasing. This valley was so beautiful when bursting with green rather than smothered in white.

It was very possible that she just might see that transformation with her own eyes soon, if she had not misunderstood the intent behind Otis' exciting kisses.

Something had changed between her and the viscount last night. Developed beyond superficial curiosity about each other. She thought perhaps that Otis might be sincerely interested in her as a woman. One he might be willing to court if things continued to go well between them.

Meg was definitely interested in Otis, and not just because encouraging him might spare her from being dragged to London for the season. She had not been looking for a husband here, but she wondered if she might have stumbled upon one. She did not like to think Otis would bestow his affections in the hope of getting under her skirts. He would not do that to a friend's sister. She believed he had very honorable intentions toward her.

"Ah, there you are, my dear,' Lady Vyne cried as she burst into the gallery hall. "I've been looking for you everywhere."

"Here I am," she promised with a smile. One day, all going well, Lady Vyne might be family, a mother figure perhaps who she could count on for advice. "I was just walking about for the exercise."

"Miss Milne is doing the same, except upstairs."

There was not very much to see in the upstairs halls, unless one slipped into bedchambers that were not their own, as Miss Milne was wont to do. Meg preferred the lower rooms and the views to be found rather than snooping about. "Are the children still at their lessons?"

"I expect so," Lady Vyne said as she fell into step beside Meg. "Did you give any thought to my question of the other night?"

"Which one?" Meg asked, smiling. She honestly couldn't remember ever being asked so many questions about her likes and dislikes. The countess had questioned her thoroughly in the past few days. There were so many decisions she would have to make before she was fit to move about in society. Dresses, slippers, parasols, colors. If she married Otis, she might be spared most of that chore. He had claimed he spent most of his time here in Derbyshire with his family, and so would his wife, too. But he also moved in society a few weeks a year. Meg would have to navigate that world if her husband wished her to.

Lady Vyne moved so they could see each other. "I asked what sort of husband would do for you, young lady," she complained. "You said you would let me know, and yet I am still waiting. Well?"

Meg laughed softly and thought of Otis. "Someone I can admire."

"Someone handsome and important?"

"Kind at heart, and a gentleman who could make my toes curl in my slippers when we are together."

Lady Vyne laughed. "Ah, to be young and able to discover love anew. I envy you, and Otis too, in some respects. It is such a time of confusion and wonder. I do wish you all the best in your search for your husband, Meg. All your mother wanted for you was to be happy, and I aim to make that come true."

"I'll do my best to choose wisely," Meg promised, picturing Otis at her side as they spoke their vows.

Lady Vyne frowned suddenly as she looked about them. "I should have asked Miss Milne to join us, but I truly wish it could be us alone for a while. One grows so tired of being questioned constantly."

Meg's curiosity stirred. "Questioned? What about?"

"My absent son. Would that Otis had already chosen his bride."

She considered the countess, and what she might say if she learned Otis had stolen three kisses. Would she be happy? "What sort of woman do you wish your son to marry?"

"Someone that I like as much as I like you, but I will not hold my breath," the countess mused. "I just hope she is someone who understands the importance of family. You've seen how Otis is with his siblings. He treats them as if they were his own children rather than brother and sisters."

"I did notice he had some," Meg grinned impishly, "managing tendencies when they were around."

"He's very protective of all of us," Lady Vyne protested. "And that is exactly what you must have in your husband. You need someone you can depend upon."

Yes, a protective husband would be an advantage, but only if they valued her opinion, too. "I begin to wonder if my brother will ever marry."

"He will one day. As for my son, it is highly likely he'll marry Miss Milne before the season even begins."

Meg gasped, unable to hid her shock at that announcement. Otis couldn't marry that vain creature! And he had kissed Meg…but was that all it could be? "I had no idea he was courting her."

Lady Vyne raised a brow. "This is my husband's doing. Since his health has declined, he's become obsessed with Otis' situation. He invited the Milnes to ensure the match."

Meg wet her lips, her stomach clenching with disappointment. "So your husband wants Otis to wed."

"My husband expects a proposal to be made before Christmas Day arrives."

"I see." She looked around quickly, making sure they were still alone. "What does Otis—I mean, Lord Clement want?"

"He told me he intends to marry soon, and I believe him sincere."

"I understand." Meg nodded.

She could make Otis happy, if given the chance. She might even have become accustomed to being half frozen all the time just to please him, too. "He should marry someone who makes him happy," Meg murmured.

"I hope so, because when you marry without love it is an unending torment."

Meg looked at the countess quickly. She was slowly coming to understand that all was not as it seemed in this family. The earl and countess did not act as if they loved each other. Meg had assumed the pair were like her parents. Forever holding hands, making decisions together. Lord Vyne seemed disinterested in spending any time with his wife or his children. "Not everyone finds love," she suggested.

The countess' skin grew pink. "No, sometimes they throw their chance away to win a ridiculous wager," she bit out savagely.

Meg did not like how that sounded or the countess' apparent outrage, and didn't dare ask what she meant.

But Lady Vyne noticed her anxiety. "Can you believe my foolish son made a wager with his father to marry before the season even begins? I predict he will be made unhappy by any alliance made under those circumstances."

Lady Vyne caught her by the shoulder when she stepped back in shock. "I cannot believe he would do such a thing."

"Oh, don't worry, my dear girl. It will all be over soon enough, I expect. But never think I won't love you best. We will still write to each other, and one day when things have settled, I shall have you visit The Vynes again."

Any hopes Meg might have harbored in her heart of a mistake withered and died. No alliance made in haste, because of a bargain or an indiscretion, ever turns out well in the long run.

She stared at the nearby landscape and her heart tore in her chest. She could never return to The Vynes when Lord Clement was married. That would be too painful. She had foolishly fallen for him.

Lord Clement was not the man she'd imagined him to be, and she should have been more cautious about exposing her heart to a near stranger. However, in a way, she should be grateful to him. He had reminded her what it felt like to feel desirable and part of a larger group. He'd also taught her a valuable lesson—a rogue was a rogue, no matter how distinguished in name. Since her brother planned to launch her into society soon, she was sure she needed that clarity in the coming months as she assessed the gentlemen she was introduced to.

"Lady Vyne," Miss Milne called out suddenly. "Lady Vyne, are you there?"

The countess groaned softly and turned, smiling as her other guest appeared in the doorway. "Yes, Miss Milne."

"Oh, Lady Margaret. I did not see you," Miss Milne exclaimed with a silly giggle that made Meg cringe.

Miss Milne was wearing an exquisite gown of silk and lace that looked much too light for the drafts and chills of the manor. Meg glanced down at herself, realizing that there was no competing with such a well-turned-out creature. She didn't even want to try.

Miss Milne clapped her hands together. "I was thinking we might all take a walk out of doors together. I haven't yet seen the stables, and I would like to ride in the spring."

"Unfortunately, I must meet with my housekeeper," Lady Vyne said, her voice tinged with regret. "Perhaps it could wait until tomorrow."

"What of you, Lady Margaret. Will you walk outdoors with me?"

Lady Vyne laughed softly. "Coaxing our Meg out of doors when it is snowing would be quite an achievement."

Meg shrugged. "I don't care for snow."

"Then I think you must have visited at the worst time of year," Miss Milne exclaimed. "You simply must come back to visit in the summer, when it's warmer. The grounds are lovely then."

"I wasn't aware you had visited the estate before?"

"Oh, no. But I was talking with Lord Clement the other day, right in this very spot, and he described everything so well I have become enraptured. When he speaks, I can imagine the sights and scents of this beautiful place as if it were my home, too."

Meg shivered. "He has a pleasant speaking voice."

Meg had come to feel at home at The Vynes, too, because of Lord Clement's warm welcome, but she'd been utterly mistaken that he might have had any honorable intentions toward her. She rubbed her brow. "Would you excuse me, my lady? I think I have taken a chill."

Lady Vyne rushed toward her but Meg backed away. "I'm sure its nothing that a night in a warm bed cannot rectify. I am sure I will be fine in a few days."

Lady Vyne's face fell. "I'll send up your maid."

"I'd rather you didn't."

"How silly to refuse your maid?" Miss Milne said. "Who else will plump your pillows?"

Meg had managed quite well without a personal maid before, and there was no reason she could not do so again. "I'm just going to lie down and hope for sleep."

"I'll send up a tray with some tea and broth later," Lady Vyne decided. "Our housekeeper herself will attend you. I absolutely insist."

"I don't want to be a bother," Meg murmured. "If my brother should return tonight, would you let him know that I need to speak to him about London tomorrow? Tell him...I've had a change of heart."

Lady Vyne's eyes narrowed on her. "I'll do that as soon as I see him," she promised.

"I do hope you feel better soon, Lady Margaret," Miss Milne called. "I would hate you to miss the joy of the holiday. You never know what might come yet!"

A wedding—but not one she could look forward to.

"I'll ring when I wake, when I'm hungry, and if I am not better by morning, I'll summon your housekeeper." Meg backed away.

As soon as she was clear of the room, Meg rushed upstairs to hide in her bedchamber for the night.

Chapter Twelve

Otis crooked his finger at the maid to draw her toward his bedchamber door. "Well?"

"She *says* she's ill, my lord," the maid confessed.

"Is she?"

The maid glanced away. "I couldn't say, my lord."

Otis slumped back against the wall, wondering why Meg Stockwick would ever feel the need to pretend ill health. Mother said it came upon her suddenly, and he was concerned enough to send spies into her room to check on her welfare.

When the hour to meet with Meg to read together had come and gone with no sight of her, Otis had gone in search of Hector, thinking they might be together. But Hector was huddled in bed, claiming he was about to die, which was far from true.

Otis had sent his valet to care for Hector and then approached Mother, who passed along the message that Meg was so ill, she would not be joining them for dinner that night. He had endured dinner with his parents and the Milnes' company in a distracted state and fled as soon as he could.

He glanced at the maid again. "Did Lady Margaret ask for a tray to be sent to her room?"

"Yes, my lord, but she barely ate any of it."

Concerned, Otis looked down the hallway toward her distant bedchamber. He wanted to speak to Meg, to find out for himself how she fared, very much. "Does she know her brother has returned?"

"Not that I know of. She never asked about him."

Otis nodded. It was likely Hector would be recovering for a few days like the last time he'd overindulged. It was a blessing that Meg would never know just how bad he got at times. "Thank you, you may go."

The maid bobbed a curtsy. "Yes, my lord."

When the maid was gone down the servants' staircase, he stepped back into the hall and closed the door on his room. He was probably expected to return downstairs soon to join the Milnes and his parents, but he could not. His heart was not willing to wait another minute to see Meg.

He put her book under arm and, aiming for nonchalance, sauntered down the hall. When he was level with Meg's door, he stopped, knocked and ducked inside quickly.

Meg was curled up under a blanket by the fire, sniffling into a gentleman's handkerchief.

Her eyes widened at seeing him in her room again. "You shouldn't be here."

Despite the impropriety, he hurried across the room and fell to his knees. "I was worried about you."

"There's no need to concern yourself with me," she said, drawing back from him.

He smiled quickly and pressed his hand to her cheek and then her brow. "There is when you feel unwell. At least you don't appear fevered."

She moved her face out of reach. "Shouldn't you be with your family and guests?"

"The Milnes can wait," he said as he sat back on his heels. Meg's eyes were a bit red, and so was her nose, but otherwise, aside from a little sniff now and then, she seemed well enough to his eye. "It was a quiet dinner without you tonight."

"Was Miss Milne not entertainment enough?"

"She might have been if I could pay attention."

Meg's expression hardened. "Is that how you will be with her?"

"Probably. If she expected more, she should have married Lord Bellows last year when he was courting her."

"Obviously she found him lacking," Meg insisted. "Is he another rogue?"

"Bellows? Hardly. And denying that you love someone just because they are not smart enough to please your family is a mark against her in my book." He frowned. "Why are we talking about Miss Milne when it's you I want to hear about?"

"We are talking about Miss Milne because you are going to marry her."

"No, I'm not!"

Meg frowned. "Your mother told me you were."

"Then she is very wrong."

Meg's eyes narrowed on him. "Was she wrong about the wager too?"

"Ah, no." He raked a hand through his hair. "I was going to mention that."

"How could you have made a wager to marry Miss Milne and then kiss *me*? Your family and hers expect a proposal!"

"I made a wager with my father to be married within three months. I never specified *who* I would propose to because I did not know at that time. My plan all along was to find someone who I can talk to, worry about, and have them feel the same about me. I think I've found her at last."

"I see," she said, looking ill at ease.

"Rediscovered her." He grinned. Did she really not know she'd captured all of his attention? His heart too. Perhaps he'd have to be more obvious about his interest in her. "As to the timing of any marriage to meet the terms of the wager, I thought three months would be long enough for you to decide to accept me or not."

Her brow furrowed. "Accept you?"

He swallowed down his anxiety. Since he was already kneeling, he freed Meg's hand from the smothering warmth of her many blankets and held it. "My dear Margaret."

"Meg," she murmured.

"My dearest Meg then." He took a steadying breath. "We barely know each other but the moment I saw you, I think I knew my heart would be yours."

Meg gaped. "You want to marry *me*?"

He nodded. "Very much."

"I don't know what to say," Meg said as her eyes widened even more. "Why me?"

"Why not you? I ordinarily don't go around kissing intelligent, funny and stunningly beautiful women all the time or stealing away to read her favorite book together." He produced her copy and laid it on her lap. "There are a few more chapters in this one still, but The Vynes library is vast and largely unread. Or we could purchase our own books together after."

"After you win the wager?"

"Yes. I don't want to leave my mother and siblings behind."

"You expect me to live here?"

"Not necessarily. If we did marry, I hoped we could spend the summer by the sea and have my mother and siblings join us there, too. The warmer air would be better for you and my little brother." Since an agreement seemed a long way off, he shrugged. "I only ask that you consider me. Take as much time as you need to decide one way or the other. In the meantime, I have brought your brother back to the estate since you've missed him so much."

"You left the estate to get him for me?"

"A short jaunt to the village tavern. While I was with your brother, I did ask his permission to court you. He refused."

"On what grounds?"

"Pigheadedness, most likely." Otis winced. "And he was a cup shot at the time. I did not perhaps choose the best moment to broach the subject. I am hoping he will reconsider. I am prepared to wait and ask your brother again and again, until he changes his mind."

Meg bit her lip. "No, don't do that."

"Meg, I must have his permission...or is *no* your answer?"

Meg suddenly smiled. "It is my birthday next month."

"I did know it fell not long into the New Year. But you won't be here then. You'll be in London getting ready to be courted by dozens of bachelors with very good taste in women. You'll be lured to dark corners and kissed by other men."

"I find that highly unlikely. I never wanted to go to London. I'll be one and twenty on this birthday, and you know what that means."

"You'll not need his permission to marry anyone soon!" Otis sat forward and gripped her hand tightly. "Hector led me to believe you were a year younger!"

"Hector never remembers my age. He always forgets my birthday, too, and that has been a blessing when it came to discussions about the future. If he had realized my real age, he might have been even more desperate to marry me off."

"I'm glad he has not." He kissed the back of her hand. "Will you think about it and let me know."

"Yes," she promised.

Otis nodded. "Thank you. I hope you feel better soon."

"Good news has a way of healing the worst hurts. Otis, that was *the* yes!" Meg leaned forward, and suddenly her lips were pressed against his.

Otis groaned and pulled her closer. That wasn't easy because she bundled up all warm and snug. He couldn't get close enough for his liking, so he moved some of the blankets aside and slid under them to sit at her side.

Meg laughed softly and wrapped her arms about his neck and held him tightly. "I was so upset to imagine I might never kiss you again."

"Did you pretend to be ill because you thought I would marry Miss Milne?"

Meg's face turned pink and she looked away. "Miss Milne is everything I'm not."

Otis cupped her cheek, his heart bursting with joy. Meg really did care about him. "She's in love with a friend of mind, not that she will admit it."

Meg silenced him with her lips. Otis didn't want to hear another word about Miss Milne, either. She was happy, and Otis was happy, too. She drew back slowly, drinking in the stirring look in his eye. "I like this," she said softly. "Being with you. Kissing you."

"I can tell," he teased, and then brought his lips to her cheek. "There's nothing better for me, either."

He moved along her jaw, peppering her skin with tiny kisses. Meg tilted her head and invited him to continue. Otis did, and she shivered.

He chuckled softly. "Do you want me to stop so you can huddle back under your blankets? I should probably go. We can discuss what we do next tomorrow."

"Don't go yet," she whispered. "I want you to myself for as long as possible. When everyone learns we intend to marry, we might never be alone until our wedding day. I need a few more kisses from you."

Meg kissed him again with flattering enthusiasm. As Otis wrapped his hands around her waist and lifted her closer, almost onto his lap, he was breathless with anticipation. He began to caress her body, and she did the same, spreading her hands over his shoulders, touching his face as they kissed. Soon she had wriggled fully onto his lap.

She even pushed back some of the blankets to get closer.

Otis slowly lowered one hand down her side and then farther along her leg. His touch was light, careful. He desired her but he would not rush her into making love to him.

Meg suddenly covered his hand with her own. "I like it when you touch me."

He nuzzled her neck. "I could continue if you lifted your hand."

She lifted it, and that was all the proof he needed that his attentions were welcomed.

His slid his fingers softly over her ankle and thick stockings. As he moved his hand under the edge of her nightgown, skimming her woolen stockings until he reached bare skin, she gasped and writhed delightfully.

He pressed his lips to her brow and then caught her face in his hand. "I shouldn't take liberties. Not until our wedding night."

"What if I think I've been a spinster long enough? Would you believe me wanton if I admit to being very curious about the pleasures to be found in the marriage bed?"

"Never." His brows rose. "Such a boon would be more than I deserve."

She grinned back at him. "I've heard that ladies enjoy intimacies. I desperately wish to know if that's true."

He tightened his grip on her head. "You'll enjoy everything about our life together, I swear it."

Meg got up from the settee and held out her hand to him. "Show me."

Otis was on his feet in a second and swept her up into his arms to carry her across the room. When they reached the bed, he pulled back the covers and placed her atop the sheet gently then kicked off his shoes and untied his cravat before joining her.

Meg pulled him down on top of her, a little nervous laugh escaping her lips until he kissed her. He settled on the bed at her side as they continued, exploring each other with their hands. Meg pressed her body into Otis, anticipation thrumming through him.

He lifted her nightgown slowly, caressing her thighs as it rose higher.

When his fingers slid into her curls and he touched her intimately, she moaned and parted her legs wider.

Otis delved between her folds, touching her in a way that could only bring her pleasure. She held on to his shoulders and started to rock against his fingers.

He liked that she displayed no hesitation or doubt. She could not still her body, as she writhed against him constantly. He slid his fingers lower and found her damp core. Moving as slow as he could, he slipped his fingers into her tight channel. She seemed not the least bit worried that he was taking her innocence. She was enjoying what they did far too much for doubt.

"Otis," she whispered desperately.

"Soon, darling, let me tease you a little longer."

Otis teased his fingers into her again and again, biding his time. He wanted to see her give herself over to pleasure. He ached to feel her around him too.

Otis drew back to loosen the buttons on his trousers and drag his shirt over his head. When he moved closer to Meg, she threaded her fingers in his hair and kissed him again. "You. Are. So. Warm," she noted between kisses.

"So that's why you like me so much?"

"That and a few other things," she promised.

Her fingers slid down his bare back, a little cold, and he shivered. "Such as?"

Meg stilled and then her fingers slid beneath the waistband of his trousers at the small of his back. She pressed him tighter against her lower body. Another moan escaped her lips. "That is one."

Otis brushed his erection against her sex more firmly, and then he brought them closer together as he shoved his trousers out of the way.

She gasped as he eased into her body, and her grip tightened on his backside even more as he started moving inside her.

He leaned his brow against hers as they rocked together. It felt so good. Almost too good. He would not last. Otis slipped his fingers between them and teased her clit. She stiffened suddenly, and then she cried out.

Otis quickly covered her mouth with his lips to stifle the sound, and a few moments later he groaned, his body jerking as he found his own release too.

They gasped for air and slowly parted.

Firelight danced over the ceiling above them and Meg whispered, "That was lovely."

"Indeed," Otis said as he drew Meg against his side. She burrowed closer to his warmth as he drew a deep calming breath. He was going to marry Meg and he couldn't be happier. He nuzzled her hair—content and replete. "The perfume you wear reminds me of the summer I spent at your home as a boy. As intoxicating as making love to you."

"I could never imagine being so happy," she responded.

"Neither could I, until you. Are you warm enough?"

"Yes," she whispered. "Very warm with you beside me."

He nuzzled her neck. "May I stay a little longer?"

"Yes, Otis," she whispered, and then laughed. "You are the most remarkable bed warmer I've ever had."

"Happy to be of service," he whispered. "I'll warm your bed every night if you want me to."

For an answer, she pulled him close and kissed him again.

Chapter Thirteen

Meg was in the portrait gallery the following morning, bundled up from head to toe in her thickest coat, wool scarf and felt cap to keep the ever-present chill at bay, when Otis strolled up to her. She had been alone, waiting for breakfast to be served in a nearby room, and Otis wasted no time in pulling her into his arms, tilting her backward, and kissing her witless.

When he allowed her to rise, his cheeks were flushed and his eyes were bright. "Good morning, Meg. Merry Christmas."

"Merry Christmas," she answered, blushing hotly. She patted his broad chest, still astonished by the way she felt when he held her close. "I trust you slept well."

"I didn't even try," he told her, slipping an arm around her shoulders. He drew her along to the far end of the long room. "Someone very particular was on my mind this morning."

"Who could that have been?"

He stopped and cupped her face. "The woman I think I might love." Meg blushed as he kissed her again, but he drew back too soon. "I have something I want to give you."

From his pocket he produced a small silver case.

She turned it over in her hands, completely baffled. "What is it?"

"Something I think you might find invaluable in the coming years when you are cold."

Meg carefully opened it and found, not jewels, but matches.

She started laughing as she removed one slender, sulfur-tipped match. "A priceless gift for me." But Meg felt bad. "I have nothing to give you. Hector did not give me time to make or purchase anything for someone like you."

"Having you say yes to me is enough of a present for this year," he promised. He kissed her cheek, and then sighed. "I have to talk to Hector today. Set things in motion."

"Ah, yes, Hector," she said, and then pulled a face. "If he puts in an appearance."

"Oh, he certainly will show himself this morning." Otis grinned. "I snuck into his room earlier, laid out his clothes, put his fire out and opened a window to let the winter in. I'm sure he'll be downstairs and complaining at any moment that he is starving."

Meg laughed. "Why didn't I think of that?"

Otis squeezed her to his side. "You're not as cruel as I am to him."

Perhaps that is what had been wrong with her life all along. She had tried to look after her brother and he clearly didn't want to be coddled by her. "Are you sure we're not rushing into this?"

Otis grew quiet but then he grinned. "We probably have rushed things a little, but I don't believe I will regret anything about us. Are you having doubts now?"

"Not really. But I am a little worried about you, and what your father will say? He's not going to be happy that you're going against his wishes."

"One problem at a time," he suggested as he squeezed her shoulder again.

Otis had fully explained the wager, shown her proof that there was no particular bride included in the bet. He was free to marry anyone he chose and would win if they married within three months. After last night, Meg had little incentive to delay the marriage. She'd chosen Otis to be her husband when they'd shared her bed last night, and liked what they did together too. And there was the anticipation, unexpressed, that she might soon be carrying Otis' child. Meg desperately wanted to make a family of her own with Otis.

When they reached the doorway to the breakfast room, everything was ready. Otis bid her enter first. Otis' siblings were squabbling over which chairs they would sit on but Otis drew her to the other end of the room and held out a chair. "You take your tea with milk, don't you?"

"Yes, I..." She looked at him in surprise. "You take yours the same."

He winked. "I noticed that, too."

The London newssheet from last week was on the table near them and Otis offered it to her first. "Not today, but thank you for asking."

When Otis moved to the sideboard and loaded up two plates, Meg sighed a little. Christmas had always been her favorite season and now she had even more reason to love it. Otis would make a very attentive husband. He made her so happy already.

They talked quietly for most of the meal but then Hector arrived. He seemed grossly put out, not to mention unwell. Puffy eyed and pale, he squinted at the food as he loaded a plate for himself. When he sank into the opposite chair and groaned, Meg considered her chances of engaging in a reasonable conversation with him were slim.

So she ignored her brother, ate well, and chatted with Otis, relishing the small seemingly random brushes of his arm against hers. Eventually, the children left the room and it was just the three of them enjoying breakfast together.

She glanced across at her brother and then drew in a deep breath. She really wanted to marry Otis but she had to have her brother's permission first.

Otis spoke before Meg could think of a way to start that conversation. "Are you feeling better now?"

Hector scowled at him. "I'm fine."

"Good," Otis said. "Perhaps we might continue our conversation from yesterday."

Hector's scowl only deepened, never a good sign. "What conversation?"

"The one we were having before you cast up your accounts beside my carriage?"

Meg gasped. "You never told me he was ill."

"It is the sort of illness that only time can cure." He chuckled softly, settling his hand lightly over hers. "More tea?"

"Yes, please," Meg murmured, deciding not to press for particulars. She didn't want to drive her brother away. At least, not until he agreed to let her marry Otis. After that, she might not mind ever seeing him again. He didn't exactly inspire her loyalty.

Otis refilled his cup too. "I haven't changed my mind. I want to marry her."

"To win a bloody wager," Hector exclaimed, throwing her a warning look. "Can you believe this?"

Meg felt Otis' touch on her back. She grinned slowly, even wriggled back against him. "I know all about the wager, Hector, and I think he's been very clever. When he wins, he'll take his mother and siblings on a holiday. Somewhere much warmer I hope."

"Definitely somewhere warmer," Otis promised.

Otis' father entered the room. This was the first time Meg had seen him in the morning room at this hour. Lord Vyne seemed a bit pale and a servant hurried to seat him and serve him.

Once he had a plate of food before him he dismissed the servant and looked across at Otis. "You will accompany the Milne's into town and show them around."

"I'm afraid that is impossible," Otis replied. "I have other plans today."

"What other plans could you have more important than engaging in a courtship," Lord Vyne nodded. "Milne is expecting you to be attentive to his daughter."

Meg sucked in a shocked breath that Lord Vyne would speak so boldly of such a matter while she and her brother was still in the room.

She glanced first at Otis and then at her brother. Surely Hector would prefer Otis to marry someone he really wanted and not Lord Vyne's choice.

Otis caught up her fingers and held her hand under the table. "I cannot do that."

Hector slowly lowered his fork down, his gaze speculative on Meg and then his gaze dipped a little. He shook his head and a smile appeared. "Hmm, yes I suppose we do have quite a lot to talk about today. Lord Vyne, Lord Clement has asked for my sister's hand in marriage and I am giving them my blessing. We have yet to decide the wedding date."

Meg couldn't contain her smile, and tears formed in her eyes. Hector would let her marry Otis after all. She wanted to hug him, thank him, but she didn't want to let go of Otis' hand quite yet.

Lord Vyne gaped. "What?"

"He asked quite boldly too. Would not take no for an answer." Hector offered her a smile. "I guess that means it was love at first, or is it second, sight."

Lord Vyne suddenly smiled. "Well, well, well. So you've finally given up. I'll have the carriage brought around immediately."

Otis' grip tightened on Meg's hand. "Whatever for?"

"The terms of our wager were very clear," Lord Vyne seemed positively smug. "If I win, you leave."

"Those were indeed the terms but I have not lost or conceded you the victory. I was to begin a courtship and marry within three months. Stockwick has approved my suit and has agreed to a wedding as soon as possible."

Lord Vyne's eyes narrowed. "But you chose the wrong woman, my son. No offence intended Lady Margaret."

"None taken," Meg murmured.

Otis threw a smile her way. "Oh, I definitely chose the right woman to be my wife. I chose with my heart. The terms of our wager did not specify the lady I must wed. Perhaps if you read the wager again more closely you will see I am right. It says nothing about who I would marry just that I must."

The earl shot to his feet and stormed out.

The silence in his wake was deafening. Otis raised Meg's hand to his lips and kissed her. "That went better than I expected. Thank you for your timely intervention, Stockwick. I promise my mother will be much more enthusiastic about our news than my father just was."

"We should go and tell her the happy news soon. I'd rather Lady Vyne hear it from us than from your father." Meg glanced at her brother who was watching her through squinted eyes.

Hector was nodding slowly. "So that's that?"

Meg blushed. "You *did* want me to marry."

Hector grunted. "Now if only I could be rid of the estate as easily."

Otis stood. He pulled Meg to her feet and led them both toward the drawing room. "I actually wanted to talk to you about that, Stockwick. I think I may have a solution that makes perfect sense for both of us."

Hector glanced up at a bunch of mistletoe hanging over the threshold of the drawing room now and sidled around it. "Really?"

"Obviously we cannot stay here year round. It's much too cold for Meg."

"I will stay if you wanted me to," Meg promised Otis but then she noticed the drawing room had changed. "Oh my."

She moved away from Otis and her brother. There was a tree almost reaching as high as the ceiling in one corner, decorated with ornaments hanging from the branches. Something she'd heard royalty did, but she'd never seen it done before. Other things were far more familiar and brought a smile to her lips. A Yule log burned in the great hearth and although night was a long way off, the mantle blazed with a dozen or more candles. It was an enchanting scene that reminded her so much of Christmas' past.

"I thought I might purchase your estate and make a home there for our family," Otis was saying.

Meg spun around to stare at him in astonishment. "Really?"

He nodded quickly. "I knew the first day I saw you again that I would do anything to make you happy. But there is a benefit to me too. I want to see the estate prosper again."

Meg bit her lip and stared at her brother. "You truly don't want to live there do you?"

"Not for even one more night." He nodded slowly and then held out his hand. "We can discuss your purchase of the estate tomorrow when we begin to draw up the marriage contract."

Meg laughed as the deal was struck. "This is the happiest holiday of my life."

Hector cleared his throat loudly. "I don't hear a *thank you, Hector?*"

"Thank you," she cried. Meg rushed to her brother and gave him a quick hug then threw herself into Otis' waiting arms. "I've never been happier to be so wrong. This is the best Christmas ever."

Epilogue

Meg hurried down the stairs of The Vynes, mortified that she had overslept on the most important day in her life. At her side was the woman who would be her mother as soon as the ceremony concluded. Her brother was pacing at the bottom of the stairs.

He looked up scowling. "What time do you call this?" he complained.

"Every woman is entitled to be a little late for her own wedding," Lady Vyne argued. "Now say something nice, Hector, or don't say another word."

Hector wisely buttoned his lips shut.

The countess seemed the only person he ever listened to, especially about the wedding. She faced Meg and teased another two tendrils of hair free to frame her face. "Your mother would be so proud if she could see you today. If she were here, she'd say there had never been a lovelier bride."

"Thank you," she whispered, fighting back tears. She still missed her mother desperately, but having the countess standing in for her made the pain of loss lessen. She impulsively kissed her cheek. "Thank you for all you have done to make today so special."

"You've done more for me than you'll ever know, too."

Lady Vyne was coming with them to Dorset and taking her children with her for a long holiday. After a brief argument between the couple, and a few threats of locked doors and cold dinners, the earl had relented to uphold his end of the wager as long as she promised to return. Lady Vyne had agreed but not stated when that day might be. She had learned a little something from her son's example.

"You'll have a wonderful holiday with us," Meg promised. "Are you packed and ready to go?"

The countess nodded quickly. "And very keen to see a new horizon and a new home."

Lady Vyne hurried into the drawing room with a little wave. Left just with Hector now, Meg smiled brightly. After today, she did not know when she would see her brother again. He was headed to London to enjoy life as a bachelor with no responsibilities whatsoever. She tugged on his sleeve. "You were right all along. I never knew what good would come of taking this holiday. I should have thanked you before now, but I am grateful that you brought me here. I've had a wonderful Christmas."

"I didn't expect you to marry him when I wrote to the countess." Hector nodded. "But now that you are about to marry, I can say I am glad to be spared the expense of a London season."

Meg punched his shoulder. "Miser."

"I'll have you know I intended to spoil you terribly," he admitted. "To make up for Mother and Father not being with us anymore, I was prepared to spend a fortune on clothes and carriages so you would feel you belonged. The best shops to patronize are in London, my dear."

"I don't need to be spoiled to feel loved. I don't think you know how happy Otis makes me." A shadow passed over Meg, and she shivered. "Oh, the drafts in this place."

She was quite done with the cold and snow that forever shrouded this valley in mist, at least for this year. She might have to live here when Otis inherited this estate upon his father's death, but she hoped that was a long way off.

He pressed a kiss to her brow suddenly, and then held out his arm. "Come along, sister dear, your betrothed awaits his beautiful bride. Probably most impatiently, too."

Pleased by Hector's behavior, Meg slipped her arm through her brother's.

Hector walked her steadily toward Otis but all she wanted to do was run into his arms. As she took her place beside her betrothed, a shiver raced over her skin again. She stumbled through her vows in a state of acute excitement. When the ceremony was over, and she had taken her husband's name, Hector approached her again, but Meg's eyes were drawn to a shimmer of light beside him.

For a moment, she could swear her parents were staring back at her...and then the shimmer was gone.

Meg shivered.

Otis wrapped his arms about her. "Have you become cold again, my love?"

She turned to look up at her husband's grinning face and realized he'd not seen anything amiss. "A little, but I was just thinking of my parents and wishing they could have been with us."

"Who says they were not?" He kissed her cheek and then her lips. "Spirits have been known to haunt The Vynes. There have actually been several sightings in the library. Maybe your parents took their own holiday here to keep an eye on you."

Meg laughed at the idea but hoped that if it were possible, they had. If so, then her father would know how the book ended, and that Meg and Otis' story was just beginning. She couldn't wait for what happened next.

The End

About Heather

Determined to escape the Aussie sun on a scorching camping holiday, Heather picked up a pen and notebook from a corner store and started writing her very first novel—Chills. Years later, she is the author of over thirty sexy regency historical romances. Addicted to all things tech (never again will Heather write a novel longhand) and fascinated by English society of the early 1800's, Heather spends her days getting her characters in and out of trouble and into bed together (if they make it that far). She lives on the edge of beautiful Lake Macquarie, Australia with her trio of mischievous rogues (husband and two sons) along with one rescued cat whose only interest in her career is that it provides him with food on demand and a new puppy that is proving a big distraction.

You can find details of her work at
www.Heather-Boyd.com

Mistletoe and Kisses

~ A Duke of Strathmore Novella ~

By

Sasha Cottman

When love is staring you straight in the face…

Lord Hugh Radley is handsome, clever, and not short of a penny. He is also at times more than a little vague, often lost in his own world.

For the past two years professor's daughter Mary Gray has worked alongside him while he completed his studies at Cambridge University. She has brought him coffee and toast for supper most nights.

Somewhere along the way, she also secretly gave him her heart.

Christmas 1790 looms large with life changes for both of them. Hugh has completed his degree and has a bright future ahead of him.

For Mary, she faces a bleaker Christmas. It will be her first without her beloved father, and she will be alone.

A mislaid book sees Hugh returning to the university in time to discover the secret that Mary has been keeping from him. She has been evicted from her long-time home.

Hugh is outraged at the treatment Mary has received, but while he is busy being angry, his sister Adelaide steps in and invites Mary to spend Christmas with the Radley family at Strathmore Castle in Scotland.

In the wilds of chilly Scotland, Hugh finally faces up to the truth that he has long given over his heart to Mary. He makes the fateful decision to ask Mary for her hand in marriage.

Being Hugh however he is clueless about the minds of women and he makes a mess of things. With the clock ticking down to New Year's Eve, he knows that if he doesn't secure Mary's love by then, he will lose her forever.

Cupid's little helpers are meanwhile busy at work.

With the aid of the time old tradition of kissing under the mistletoe, Hugh and Mary make tentative steps toward finding their happily ever after.

One kiss at a time.

Chapter One

Cambridge,
December 1790

Lord Hugh Radley closed his travel trunk one last time, silently reassuring himself that he had indeed got everything he would need for the trip to Scotland. He turned and groaned. There, sitting on the end of his bed, was the pair of boots he was certain he had already packed.

"You would forget your head if it wasn't attached," he muttered.

He would be needing the boots for the ice-covered roads around his family home in Scotland. After adding the boots and closing the lid of the travel trunk once more, he stepped back and allowed the porters to take his luggage.

He had been looking forward to this day for months. Christmas at the Radley clan's ancestral home, Strathmore Castle, was always a special time. Hugh was champing at the bit to see his family.

He would be making the trip north this year, along with two of his sisters and their respective spouses. With all of them in the one coach, it was going to be a cramped four-day journey. He had packed several books in his travel bag, intending to bury his nose in them rather than attempt hours of small talk. As much as he loved his family, he had important documents he needed to study and commit to memory before he returned to England in the new year.

"When the coach arrives, could you make sure my luggage is safely loaded onto it? If my family asks, please tell them I have to see a friend before I leave, but I won't be long." He followed the porters out of his private rooms and locked the door behind him.

For a moment, he stood with the palm of his hand laid against the solid oak door. It would be the last time he touched it. He was no longer a student at St John's College, Cambridge University. His days of living on the campus of the hallowed halls of learning were now at an end.

"Lord Hugh Radley, BA Theology. Fancy that," he said.

He crossed the college courtyard then strolled along a walkway with edges bordered by tall white rose bushes before finally arriving at a black door with a brass nameplate.

Professor J. L. Gray.

He knocked on the door and opened it. Professor Gray's rooms were never locked.

"Mary, it's Hugh. I've come to say farewell," he cheerfully called out.

A hand rose from behind a pile of old exam papers and waved. "Down here."

Stepping around a neat stack of books, he found her. Mary Gray was kneeling on the floor, dust pan and brush in hand.

"What are you doing?" he asked.

"A spot of cleaning. I moved a few more of Papa's piles of papers this morning and actually found the floor. I dread to think the last time the stone flagging saw daylight," she replied.

He held a hand out to her and helped Mary to her feet. Her gaze took in his coat and scarf, and she smiled.

"So, you are off to Scotland for Christmas?

"Yes, the travel coach will be here shortly. I have sent the porters and my luggage out to the main courtyard to await its arrival," he replied.

She looked around the room, then back to him. "It must feel a little odd to be leaving here for the last time."

He had thought it would be his last time, but earlier in the week he had been given the news that he still had some minor studies to complete before he could take up his post as curate at St Martins-in-the-Fields in central London.

"Actually, it's not the *very* last time I shall be on campus. I have to come back after Christmas for a week. I will stay at one of the inns in town, but I shall drop by and say hello," he replied.

Mary nodded, a tight smile sat briefly on her lips. She picked up another pile of papers and straightened them. He sensed she was nervous.

"Is your sister Adelaide making the trip with her newborn? I remember when she visited at half term and she was complaining about how swollen her ankles were," said Mary. She put the papers down again and stood, tapping her fingers on the top of the pile.

Mary always fidgeted when she was uncomfortable about something.

Adelaide and Charles Alexandre had been blessed with the birth of a son, William, in early October. Hugh was dreading the prospect of sharing a cramped travel coach with a wailing infant but needs must.

"Yes, she is. My brother, Ewan, has commanded that as many members of the family as possible should make the trip this year. My sister Anne and her new husband, the Duke of Mowbray, are also going to be travelling with us," he said. His other sister Davina, the Countess of Shale, was with child and unable to travel.

Mary wiped her hands on her apron. "Do you have time for a cup of coffee before you go?"

Hugh shook his head. "No. The coach will be here soon, and I shouldn't keep them waiting. I just wanted to come by and wish you a merry Christmas."

At his words, her face lit up. She quickly scuttled from the room, then returned with a small parcel in her hands. She offered it to Hugh. He set down his travel bag, along with the book he was carrying, and took it.

"Merry Christmas, Hugh. It's not much; just a little gift," she said.

He accepted the present with a sinking feeling in the pit of his stomach. He had been so disorganized and muddleheaded when it came to making ready for the journey to Scotland that he had completely forgotten to buy her a Christmas present.

Poor form, Radley. Too busy thinking about yourself, and not enough about her.

With the death of her father earlier in the year, Mary would be spending her first Christmas without her beloved papa. Hugh felt the heat of embarrassment burning on his cheeks. "Oh, I am so sorry. I completely forgot to get you a gift. I am the very worst of friends," he said.

She nodded at the parcel in his hands. "That's perfectly alright. You have been busy studying. Christmas no doubt crept up on you," she replied.

Hugh opened the present and his discomfort deepened. Inside was a bar of beautifully wrapped French soap, and a small bottle of gentleman's cologne. It must have cost Mary a good deal of money. Money, he suspected she did not have in abundance.

"You shouldn't have," he said.

She smiled. "Nonsense. As soon as I saw them in the shop, I thought of you. I hope you like them."

"I do, and I promise I shall bring you back a special gift from Scotland when I return after Christmas. I cannot believe that I could be so absentminded to forget about getting you something. I am mortified," he replied.

Mary reached out and placed a hand on Hugh's cheek. "It's fine. The fact that you like my present is reward enough."

The warmth of her hand on his face stirred once more to life the longing he had held for her these past two years. Somewhere in the endless nights of her bringing him toast and coffee for supper while he studied alongside her father, his thoughts of Mary had changed from those of friendship to those of love.

But with her father being the head of theology and divinity, and the man directly responsible for the conferring of Hugh's degree, he had not dared to move on those feelings.

Now, the temptation to pull her into his arms and kiss her senseless was almost too strong to resist. The heavenly scent of her perfume filled his senses. His fingers twitched with anticipation.

When she withdrew her hand and turned away, Hugh was left to battle emotions of regret and relief. She had never shown any sign of being interested in him in a romantic way, so it was best that he not act on those impulses. With her father now gone, only a cad of the lowest kind would press his attentions on a vulnerable young woman.

"So, when are you leaving to visit with your mother's family?" he asked. He prayed she did not hear the shake in his voice as he spoke.

"Oh, sometime later in the week. I am yet to make final arrangements," she replied.

"And you will be back after the new year? I only ask because when I return, I would like for us to have a conversation."

A conversation that he hoped would involve him declaring his love for her, and Mary, in turn, considering that a future shared with him might not be the worst thing she could imagine doing with her life.

A knock at the door interrupted them, but as he turned away, Hugh caught a glimpse of Mary. She was biting down on her bottom lip.

It stopped him in his tracks.

Chapter Two

"We thought we might find you here. Hello Mary."

Hugh's sister Adelaide and her husband, Charles, stepped through the doorway. Charles's held a small bundle in his arms—a bundle which was making gurgling and snuffling sounds.

"Did the porter manage to get my luggage to the coach?" asked Hugh, stirring from his thoughts of Mary.

Adelaide snorted. "And hello to you too, dearest brother."

Mary stifled a grin. For all his intelligence, Hugh Radley was at times a tad clueless when it came to social situations. His oversight in having not gotten her a Christmas present was so very typical of Hugh.

She understood it, and was sure to forgive him, but it still hurt. The private moment they had shared when she'd touched his face meant more to her than any shop-bought gift could. He had leaned in toward her, and for the briefest of moments she'd imagined he was about to kiss her.

Yet again, her hopes for Hugh to see her as more than just a friend had vanished like the morning mist.

He is the son of a duke, and you are merely the daughter of a deceased university professor. Hugh Radley would never think to love someone like you, let alone marry her.

"Hello Adelaide. How was the trip up from London?" said Mary.

Adelaide stepped past her brother, giving him a small disapproving shake of the head. She greeted Mary with a hug. "Good. William slept most of the way. We also got a good night's sleep at the inn where we stopped in Sandy last night. We should all pray that he keeps this up for the rest of the journey north," she replied.

Hugh turned to Charles. "Where are Anne and Mowbray?"

Charles and Adelaide exchanged a look. Baby Will stirred in his father's arms, and Adelaide hurried over to him.

"I think it is time for your morning feed. Mary, do you have a chair or somewhere that I can nurse Will?" she asked.

Mary pointed to the doorway of her father's old study. "There is a comfortable rocking chair in the corner if you wish."

Adelaide took Will from his father, and Mary ushered them into the room. In between scattered piles of books and papers, the room also somehow managed to hold the chair and a large desk. Until recent days, the desk had been buried under a pile of midterm papers her father had succeeded in marking before his sudden passing. Mary had managed to clear the papers away earlier in the week, and like the floor in the front room, the top of the desk now saw the light of day.

While Adelaide settled into the chair and allowed Will to latch on, Mary took a seat behind her father's desk and sat with her hands gently clasped.

"I am sorry about your father," said Adelaide.

"Thank you. And thank you for the lovely letter you sent. I appreciated it greatly," replied Mary.

Adelaide Alexandre, nee Radley, had always made a point of calling in to see Mary and her father whenever she was visiting her brother. For a duke's daughter, Adelaide had a surprisingly pleasant affinity with people across all social classes.

"May I ask what you are doing for Christmas? Are you staying here alone at the college? It would be a terrible pity if you were," Adelaide said.

Mary tightened her fingers together. Thankfully she had shown Adelaide into the study, rather than her bedroom. There was little evidence in this room that she was about to vacate the apartment for good.

"I am due to visit with family for Christmas. I am just waiting for their letter to confirm the arrangements," she replied, holding onto the lie she had already given to Hugh.

Will began to fuss, and it was to Mary's relief that Adelaide became too distracted with breastfeeding her son to press for further details of her family.

"Could I offer you a cup of tea?" Mary asked.

"Thank you, Mary, that would be lovely. Though we can't stay long; Charles wants to make good time once we leave Cambridge. The road through to Stilton might be difficult in the fading light if we leave too late," replied Adelaide.

Mary looked at William and immediately understood Charles' concerns. The last thing any new parent wanted was to find themselves stuck in a carriage late at night with a tired and hungry infant.

After their final farewells to Mary, Hugh and the Alexandre family climbed aboard the travel coach. Hugh pulled down the window and waved to Mary as she stood on the side of the street. It was only when she was finally lost from sight that he drew up the glass and sat back in his seat.

"So why did Anne and Mowbray cry off from coming to Scotland?" he asked.

He hadn't thought it polite to press for further details about the obvious absence of his sister and her husband, Clifford, the Duke of Mowbray, in front of Mary.

Charles rolled his eyes. "They are not coming for Christmas. And for that we should all be truly grateful."

Adelaide kissed her baby son on the forehead and cooed. "Your uncle is not coming because he says he is a *bloody* duke, with his own *bloody* castle, and he does not see why he should have to travel all the way to *bloody* Scotland for Christmas. Isn't that right, my beautiful boy?"

"If the first word that our son speaks is *bloody*, I shall blame Mowbray. I cannot deny that I am glad he is not coming for Christmas," replied Charles.

Hugh was not the least surprised that Anne and Mowbray were not making the trip. In the short time that they had been married, the Duke and Duchess of Mowbray had established themselves as being in a near-constant state of war with one another. When they were not going into battle, they were being sickeningly sweet to each other. Having witnessed both forms of behavior in the newlyweds, Hugh was not completely certain which one he disliked the most.

He was ashamed to be relieved that Anne and Mowbray were not making the journey with them, but he knew he shared Charles's sentiments.

"Oh well, that leaves more room for us in the coach." He could now spread out his study papers and books without fear of getting an elbow in the ribs from the Duke of Mowbray.

Chapter Three

Mary walked back to her rooms and closed the door behind her. She had watched the coach until it had disappeared from sight, crushed by the knowledge that it would be the last time she would ever see Hugh leave the cramped but homely rooms at St John's College, which she and her father had always called home.

She wiped a tear away, gritting her teeth to force back any others that may have threatened. Crying would not change her circumstances, and she knew from many bitter, lonely nights that it would not bring her father back. She was now on her own in the world.

She had cleaned the main room from top to bottom over the past few days, intending that the new tenant should have a fresh start when they arrived early in the new year. Never would she have it said that the rooms had been left in anything but workable condition. Her father's valuable papers and books she would entrust to the next head of theology and divinity. His clothes had been gratefully received by the head grounds keeper who promised to find each item a suitable new home.

In her tiny bedroom, she squeezed between the wall and her single bed. The linen was freshly laundered, and the mattress had been hung out in the late afternoon sun the previous day to air. On top of the small nightstand was a travel bag, and next to it, her long red wool coat.

Picking up the coat, she put it on and buttoned it all the way to the neck. The first snow had fallen in the previous week, and the air outside was icy.

Travel bag in hand, she stepped out of her bedroom before glancing back one last time. She would never sleep in this room again. It was another final goodbye.

"Come on, Mary. If you keep this up, you will be here all day. You cannot say farewell to every single room and object," she muttered.

She indulged in one final tour of the apartment. She had cleaned her father's study earlier in the week, and shed a million tears as she did so, grateful that Hugh had been too busy to visit that day.

Hugh.

He had been her father's star pupil. A man destined for greatness in the Church of England, perhaps someday even becoming the Archbishop of Canterbury. With the Duke of Strathmore as his older brother, Hugh Radley had enough connections and talent to make that a reality.

Mary set her bag down and then collected the empty cups and plates from where her visitors had left them, taking them over to the washbowl near the fire. After washing and drying them, she carefully placed them on a nearby shelf.

For some inexplicable reason she left Hugh's cup for last. She washed it in the warm soapy water, and then held it. She pretended to herself that it was still warm from when Hugh had last touched it. She raised it to her lips and kissed the cup where she knew his lips had been.

So close, yet so far away.

It was a simple coffee cup with a red, gold, and blue mosaic pattern on white china. It was a one-of-a-kind in her home. Nearly every day for the past two and a half years she had made Hugh a cup of coffee in it and brought it to him as he studied late into the night.

Mary chuckled softly. Hugh liked his coffee thick and mud-like. No sugar, and just a dash of milk. The cup would sit untouched for hours while Hugh and her father engaged in long philosophical discussions, often only being finally drained when the coffee had long gone cold.

Opening her bag, she pulled out a woolen scarf and wrapped it around the cup. She would keep it as a memento of all those wonderful days.

When Hugh returned to Cambridge after Christmas, she would meet him somewhere else in the town and patiently wait for him to tell her of his exciting plans for the future. She would share the news of her own changed circumstances as a mere afterthought, something to be noted and then never mentioned again.

She carefully placed the cup into her bag. Then with one final tearful look, she bid farewell to the only home she had ever known. "Time to go, Mary Gray. Time to put the past behind you."

She closed the door of the rooms for the last time and locked it. After returning the key to the groundkeeper's office, she crossed over the cloisters and headed toward the main entrance of St John's College. It took all her willpower not to look back, not to cry.

Thank God Hugh was not there to see her leave.

Chapter Four

"Oh, blast," muttered Hugh.

He put his hand back into his travel bag one more time and rummaged around, but his prayers were not answered. The book was nowhere to be found. He had already emptied and repacked his leather satchel twice in his desperate search; the travel bag had been his last hope. He slumped back on the bench and huffed with frustration. Yet again, he had misplaced something.

"What's the matter?" asked Adelaide. She held a sleeping William in her arms, the infant having dozed off after his mother had fed him at the college.

Charles held out his hands and took his son from her. Will did not stir as his father tucked him into the crook of his arm.

"I had a book on ecclesiastical law that I needed to study while I was in Scotland. I must have left it behind in my room," Hugh replied.

"If it is important, could you perhaps secure a copy in Edinburgh?" asked Charles.

Hugh shook his head. "It's a Church of England lawbook. Edinburgh comes under the Church of Scotland. I doubt very much if I would be able to find a copy in Edinburgh. I'm sorry to have to ask this of you both, but I need that book."

Adelaide gave him a sisterly, knowing look. Hugh had a long history of losing things, finding them again, and then losing them once more.

"Well at least we are not far from Cambridge. It won't take us too long to return and collect it," replied Adelaide.

Charles covered his son's ears as Hugh stood and rapped on the roof of the coach. To the relief of all, the sleeping Will did not stir. After giving quick instructions to the driver, Hugh sat down in his seat and gave a sigh of relief as the coach made a turn in the road and headed back toward Cambridge.

"I think I know exactly where I left it. I swear I picked it up three times this morning, intending to put it in my bag," he eventually said.

He raked his fingers through his hair, frustrated and a little more than angry with himself. He had set the book down when Mary had given him the Christmas gift. The book was still on top of a pile of marked exam papers in Professor Gray's old rooms.

Once they reached St John's College, Hugh jumped down from the coach. "I won't be long. I shall say a brief, polite hello and goodbye again to Mary, then be back."

He hurried across the grounds, through the cloisters, and with a quick knock on the door, took hold of the handle.

The handle did not budge. He rattled it several times, thinking it must be stuck. When it finally dawned on him that the door was indeed locked, he frowned. The Grays rarely, if ever, locked their door.

"Mary!" he called out. Where on earth could she have gone? He needed that book.

"Lord Radley?"

He turned and when he caught sight of one of the college groundskeepers, he could have cried.

"Please tell me you have your set of keys upon your person; I need to access Professor Gray's rooms," he said.

The groundskeeper scowled. No groundskeeper worth his salt would be wandering the university grounds without his master set of keys. "Of course, I have my keys. Though they are no longer Professor Gray's rooms," replied the man.

Hugh nodded. He was in too much of a hurry to discuss the passing of his old professor. In his mind, as long as Mary remained in residence, they would always be Professor Gray's rooms.

The groundskeeper unlocked the door, then, after promising to come back and lock it again once Hugh was gone, he took his leave.

Hugh hurried into the room, sighing with relief as he spotted his book.

"Thank heavens for that," he muttered, as he picked it up.

He paused for a moment; something in the room was different. He looked at the piles of books and papers. They were stacked and arranged neater than he had ever seen them. He had not noticed the changes when he had been here earlier with Mary, his interest focused on her. He slowly took in the rest of the room.

Papers which were normally haphazardly thrown together had been put into neat bundles and tied off with string. The bookshelves were now full. Mary had made mention of having been cleaning, but until this moment, Hugh had not thought to ask why. The professor had always liked the messy look of his rooms, and Mary had sworn to keep them exactly as he had left them for at least the first year after his passing.

He poked his head inside Professor Gray's old study and was surprised to be greeted with the sight of a tidy room. Hugh had never seen the top of the professor's desk before. The sight was disconcerting.

Now that is odd. What have you been doing, Mary?

He steeled himself as he opened Mary's bedroom door. He was invading her privacy, but his concerns held his mind. As he saw the bedding which had been folded and put to one side, a rising sense of panic gripped him. The cupboard where her clothes should hang was empty.

"Calm down, Radley. She has just been getting things ship-shape before leaving to visit her mother's family," he told himself.

His words, however, were cold comfort. Not more than an hour ago, Mary had told him she had not had confirmation of her visit from her relatives. Yet she had clearly gone somewhere and taken all of her possessions with her.

Stepping back into the main room, he found the groundskeeper waiting. "Did you find what you were looking for, my lord?"

Hugh frowned. He barely noticed the book in his hand.

"Yes and no," he replied.

"It's a pity about the Professor and Miss Gray. They were always kind to the staff around here," said the groundskeeper.

Hugh tightened his hold on the book. "What do you mean?"

"Not that it's my place, but it would have been nice if Miss Gray could have stayed on at the university for a little while longer. But I suppose they needed the rooms for the new professor, and she had to go." The groundskeeper nervously jangled the ring of keys he held in his hand. University staff were meant to be seen and not heard.

Cold, hard realization settled heavily on Hugh's shoulders. Mary was not visiting relatives; she had left St John's College for good. And she hadn't told him. *Think. Think what to do.*

He rallied his thoughts. "You wouldn't by any chance know where Miss Gray has gone, would you?" he asked.

The groundskeeper shook his head. "Not exactly. Though, she did make mention that she had found a room in a boarding house not far from the market square when she visited the office just before she left."

"How long ago did she leave?"

"Not a quarter of the hour ago, I would say. She may not have got that far from the college grounds," replied the groundskeeper.

After slipping the man a coin and wishing him a merry Christmas, Hugh raced outside and to the waiting travel coach. He flung open the door.

"They have thrown Mary out!" he cried.

Adelaide's eyes grew wide. It took an instant for Hugh to realize that it wasn't so much about his revelation, as the volume at which he had delivered it. Charles put a finger to his lips. William stirred in his sleep and let out a soft whimper.

Everyone held their breaths. To the relief of all, William remained asleep.

"What do you mean?" replied Charles quietly.

Hugh caught the attention of the coach driver and issued brief instructions. He then climbed aboard and closed the door.

"The university needed the rooms for the new professor, and Mary has had to vacate them. One of the groundskeepers told me Mary left only a short while ago. I've asked the coach driver to head down toward the market square and see if we can spot her," he explained.

Charles took up a position on one side of the coach, while Hugh sat at the other window. He dropped the glass window down and poked his head outside.

"Where are you?" he muttered.

As the coach entered Bridge Street, it slowed to a crawl. Being the week before Christmas, everyone was out in the town center. And all, it would appear, were headed toward Cambridge Market Square. Hugh snarled his frustration. They would never find Mary in this crush of carriages and people.

He rapped on the roof of the coach and instructed the driver to pull over to the side of the street.

"What are you doing?" asked Charles.

"If you keep going and continue to look out on the other side of the street, I will see if I can make headway on foot. Just remember she will be wearing red," Hugh replied.

He hurried away from the coach, frantically looking for any sign of a red coat and Mary. He was met with a sea of black, brown, and gray. Breaking into a run, he slipped between the gaps of other pedestrians as he fought to make his way through the Christmas crowds.

He had gone only a few yards before a hand thumped him on the back. Turning, he found a breathless Charles standing before him.

"She is on the other side, fifty yards on."

Hugh nodded his thanks and made a mad dash across the street. He narrowly avoided being run over by a heavily laden mail coach which was travelling in the other direction.

His reckless pursuit, however, was immediately rewarded with the sight of Mary's red coat as she turned into Market Street.

"Mary!"

She kept walking. Hugh broke into a full run, grabbing hold of the back of her coat when he finally caught up.

"Mary, didn't you hear me?"

She turned, and as their gazes met a look of shock appeared on her face. She was clearly not expecting to see him.

"Hugh? What . . . what are you doing here?" she stammered.

"I forgot a book . . . I mean, what are you doing *here*?! Why didn't you tell me you had been evicted?" His relief at finding her was quickly replaced with the anger he had managed to keep at bay since discovering the truth of her deception. He continued to hold fast to her coat.

Her head and shoulders dropped. "I was going to tell you, but with everything else happening in your life, it didn't seem important."

He released his grip on her coat and stood staring at her. "How could you not think you were important to me?"

Chapter Five

Mary's heart sank. She had been waiting patiently for weeks until Hugh had left for Scotland so she could quietly pack her things and leave the university. Her earlier relief at his departure was now crushed by seeing him standing before her. The look of angry disappointment on his face added to her woes.

She had hoped to avoid this conversation until after Christmas, because knowing Hugh and his ingrained sense of justice, she had a strong inkling as to how he would react to the news that she was now living in a boarding house.

She straightened her back and steeled herself for the inevitable conversation. "I have taken a room at number sixty-two Market Street, and I plan to tutor students from there during each college term," she replied, nodding toward the green door of her new lodgings.

His eyes narrowed. She could almost hear his brain processing her words. When he looked at the bag containing all her worldly goods which she clutched in her hands, Mary held her breath.

"But they threw you out? Put you on the street without a thought for your future? he said.

"Not in so many words, but yes, I was asked to vacate the rooms. The new professor will be coming sometime after Christmas," she replied.

Hugh's face darkened. "Your father gave the university thirty-three years of faithful service, and yet they cannot even see their way to allow his daughter to remain in the only home she has ever known. And to top it all off, it is Christmas!" he said.

Mary sensed one of Hugh's rants about the spirit of Christmas and the true meaning of the holy celebration was imminent. When she saw Charles Alexandre climb down from the coach, holding his infant son in his arms, she almost cheered. No matter how angry he was, Hugh would not dare make a scene in public, and especially not in front of his family.

She was wrong.

Hugh immediately turned to his brother in law. "Do you know what those cads at the university have done, the week before Christmas?" he said.

Charles looked from Hugh to Mary, then down at his sleeping son. He stopped and kept his distance a yard or so away.

"They have thrown her out!" bellowed Hugh.

Charles took a step back. "Yes, you had already mentioned that. I might just leave this to my wife."

Charles retreated back toward the peaceful sanctuary of the coach. Adelaide's head appeared in the doorway and the couple exchanged a few brief words. Even from where she stood, Mary could see that the news of her changed abode had not been well received. Bless the Radley family and their need to preserve the sanctity of Christmas.

Adelaide hurried down from the coach and marched over to where Hugh and Mary stood.

"Is it true? They have evicted you?" asked Adelaide.

Mary lifted her travel bag and held it close against her stomach. Hugh and Adelaide were her friends, but even as they both rose in her defense, she felt the need for protection. "Yes. No. I mean. Oh."

If she didn't take the heat out of the moment, the pot was about to boil over. She had a vivid image of both Hugh and Adelaide marching up to the faculty dean and giving him a piece of their collective mind. Charles and Will would no doubt be pressganged into service to support the cause.

Mary took a deep breath and summoned her courage. The last thing she needed was for the Radley siblings to stir up a fight with the head of the school whose students she was relying upon to make her future living.

"They asked me to vacate some months ago. I dillydallied about it until they were forced to send me a second letter earlier this month. It is all my fault I am having to make the change so close to Christmas," she said.

The truth was, she had ignored much of what had happened during the year; her father's sudden passing left her numb to nearly everything other than the absolute necessities of marking overflow exam papers, some sleep, and bringing Hugh his supper each night. She had not had the strength to consider leaving the only home she had ever known. To know that she would no longer be counted as a member of the university family was beyond her grief-clouded mind.

Adelaide, bless her, was having none of it. While Hugh seemed to have calmed down a notch, his sister was just getting riled up.

"So, what you are saying is that you will be spending Christmas alone in a boarding house room with no family," said Adelaide.

Mary clutched the bag tighter to herself, suddenly feeling very alone in the world. She should have written to her mother's family in Devon and asked to visit for Christmas. Not that she actually knew them, but still, she chided herself for the oversight.

"Hugh, take Mary's travel bag. Mary, come with us and get into the coach. You are coming to Scotland. We will not allow you to spend Christmas on your own."

Words of feeble protest struggled to her lips, but when Mary saw Hugh's tight-set jaw as he stepped forward and took a hold of the bag, she knew they would be to no avail. She released her grip on the travel bag, giving him a wan smile as he tucked it under his arm.

"Good. That is settled. When we return after Christmas, I shall have a word with the dean," he said.

Mary followed Adelaide and Hugh back to the coach. As she took her seat inside, Charles leaned forward. "You weren't seriously thinking that they were going to let you spend Christmas on your own, were you? The Radley family's Christmas motto is that no one gets left behind."

"Unless of course you are a *bloody* stubborn duke," muttered Adelaide.

Chapter Six

With Mary now on board the travel coach, and Hugh's missing book safely in his hands, they set out across country to meet the Great North Road and continue their journey to Scotland.

While Adelaide and Mary were making polite conversation about the baby and how well he was doing, Hugh was lost in his own thoughts, most of which consisted of him raging at himself. By the time they made their final stop for the day at the Bell Inn in Stilton, he had worked himself into such a foul mood that he cried off supper and went for a long walk instead.

With his hands stuffed deep into the pockets of his greatcoat, he trudged through the snow-covered streets of the town. There were only so many ways a man could be angry with himself, but Hugh Radley was determined to work his way through the list. He passed several taverns on the road and was tempted to go inside and have a pint, but he knew he would need more than alcohol to take the edge off his self-loathing.

The walk finally began to have its desired effect and his mood lifted. As he turned and started to head back to the inn, his thoughts returned to Mary. It was a relief to know that she would not be spending Christmas on her own, that she was coming to Scotland with him. He had much to atone for when it came to her.

Mary had not only been dealing with grief over the death of her father, but the impending loss of her home. He, meanwhile, had been so preoccupied with his final exams and career progression that he had failed to see what was happening under his very nose. He had not been there for her when she needed a friend.

"And to top it all off, you forgot to get her a Christmas present. Hugh Radley you are a selfish blackguard," he muttered.

Back at the inn, he found Charles rugged up in a greatcoat and seated in front of an open fire outside in the rear mews, his back against the wall of the stables. His head was buried in a newspaper. He didn't look up until Hugh sat down beside him.

Hugh glanced at the newspaper. It was the *L'Ami du Peuple;* a radical popular newspaper from Paris. With the French king in custody, and the whole of France in turmoil, émigrés such as Charles were constantly in search of news from their homeland.

"What is happening in France?" asked Hugh.

Charles folded the paper up and sat it on his lap. While his hands remained steady, his boot was tapping hard on the stone ground. He sighed. "They have given all French citizens who are living abroad a deadline to return home or forfeit any land that they hold in France. I shall have to sell everything I own within the next twelve months or lose it all. I tell you, Hugh, France is going to hell."

For the second time that day, Hugh was sharply reminded that the world did not revolve around his studies or himself. Charles had been an open supporter of King Louis, but with the king and his family now under arrest, Charles dared not return home. His brother-in-law was trapped in exile in England.

Charles pulled two cheroots from his pocket and lit them using a lighted taper from the fire. He handed one to Hugh.

"I'm sorry, Charles. It must be so hard to be this close to home but know that you cannot risk going back."

"If it was only me, I might chance it, but I have a wife and a child to consider now. I would never put Adelaide through that sort of worry, knowing that I might never return. People have started disappearing in France, and I have a feeling that we are only just at the beginning of something terrible," he said.

Hugh drew back deeply on his cheroot, then held the smoke in his mouth for a moment before pushing it out with his tongue. A pale gray smoke ring formed and hung in the still night air. Charles snorted his appreciation of the trick.

"*Astuce,*" he said.

Hugh settled back against the stone wall of the stables. It was good to be headed home to Scotland. He had missed Christmas the previous year, being too busy with exams and preparation for his last year at university, and he had spent the last twelve months regretting it.

"I hope you didn't mind Adelaide and I inviting Mary to come with us. We both got a little riled up over her having to find a new home after all those years living at the university," he said.

Charles was a decent man, his calm nature a balm to his wife's sometime skittish behavior. His sister had chosen her partner in life wisely.

"Is that what you are telling yourself? That the only reason you raced after Mary in the middle of Cambridge was out of some sense of righting an injustice? Please, let me know when you actually start to believe that *coq et taureau* story," replied Charles.

Hugh didn't answer. He could proclaim his actions were all in aid of a young woman unfairly treated, but they both knew there was more to it than that. He and Adelaide could have gone to speak with the dean before leaving Cambridge; matters could have been resolved. But that would have left Mary still in Cambridge, and he on the road to Scotland.

He drew back once more on the cheroot, silently grateful when Charles opened his newspaper once more and went back to reading.

Today had been a day of unexpected revelations. He'd experienced genuine fear when he discovered that Mary had been evicted from her home. Of greater concern was the fact that she had not confided in him. That she had decided her own overwhelming problems were too insignificant to share.

That she somehow thought he didn't care.

"How long are you planning to stay at Strathmore Castle?" asked Charles.

"Christmas, then Hogmanay, finally finishing up on Handsel Monday." Hugh counted the days out on his fingers. If they arrived on the twenty-third of December, then stayed to Handsel Monday on the seventeenth, he would have just under a month in Scotland.

He wanted to get back to England earlier, but knew his older brother, Ewan, would insist he stayed for the annual handing over of gifts to all the castle staff on Handsel Monday.

"I will be leaving early on the eighteenth of January," he replied.

Charles nodded. "Well, dear brother, you may think you have plenty of time in which to sort out the Mary Gray situation on your own. But I would counsel you to make haste if you want the decision to be yours alone."

Hugh understood the underlying meaning of his brother-in-law's words. The previous year, the dowager duchess, Lady Alison, and Great Aunt Maude had shamelessly played cupid. On Christmas Day, the Duke of Strathmore had made Lady Caroline Hastings his wife.

Knowing his mother and great aunt, as soon as they set eyes on Mary, they would be looking to replicate their success. Two Christmases; two weddings. He couldn't fault the logic. He wouldn't be disappointed if indeed that was what transpired, but only if Mary was willing to take a chance with her heart.

Hugh broke off the burning end of his cheroot, and after butting it out in a small patch of snow, he put the remainder in his coat pocket. He got to his feet.

"I shall bid you a good night, Charles," he said.

"I won't be long out here. Adelaide is settling William down, and I shall go up to our room shortly. Good night, Hugh."

Hugh snorted. Charles would do anything to avoid being exposed to the smell of his son's soiled linen clout before bedtime.

As he walked back into the inn and sought the warmth of his bed, Hugh Radley was struck with a thought. Earlier in the day he had sent prayers to heaven about finding his book and they had been answered. With the unexpected addition of Mary to the group headed for Scotland, perhaps another of his longtime entreaties had finally been heard.

Chapter Seven

Mary looked at the price tag on the long emerald and blue scarf and put it back on the table. It was beautifully made, the thread around its edges no doubt real gold. The silk scarf was worth more than the cost of all the clothes on her back.

"That's nice. It suits you—it matches your enchanting green eyes."

Mary saw the smile on Adelaide's face. Her remark about Mary's looks was the latest in a slowly growing list of small kind ones Adelaide had been offering since they'd left Cambridge.

Mary nodded, then turned to look at another shelf of goods in the shop.

They were in High Street, Edinburgh, along the Royal Mile, undertaking a morning of shopping before leaving on the last leg of their journey to Strathmore Castle.

Mary wasn't particularly interested in shopping; the small number of coins in her possession had all been earmarked for living expenses. She could not risk spending money on non-essential items until she had managed to secure a regular group of students in need of her tutoring. Building that client base, however, would take time. And in the meantime, she still needed to pay rent and feed herself.

Still, it was good to be out of the travel coach. Three days from Cambridge to Edinburgh in even a spacious coach, such as the one hired by Charles Alexandre, had played havoc with her back and hips.

Hugh had not helped matters either, constantly asking her how she was to survive going forward. Making lists of people he would speak to on her behalf at the college to get her old living quarters back. Then a shorter list of people he would speak to if his first overtures failed. By the time he had finished mentioning yet again that his brother was the Duke of Strathmore and his brother-in-law the Duke of Mowbray, Mary had developed a headache which lasted two whole days.

She quietly chided herself. At least she wasn't spending Christmas alone in the bedsit of a boarding house. Hugh and the Alexandres had no connection to her beyond mere friendship, and they were under no obligation to render her assistance. She should be grateful that they wanted to help at all.

"So where else do you have in mind to visit today?" asked Mary.

Adelaide shrugged. It was the first day she had let Charles take their son off her hands for more than an hour. Mary had noted that every so often, Adelaide would look down at her empty arms and sigh. She was missing her baby.

"We will be leaving early tomorrow for Strathmore Castle, so if you wish to walk the street at the bottom of Edinburgh Castle and wander into a few more shops, I can meet you back at the inn in time for supper. I have a private errand to undertake in the meantime; I have something to collect," replied Adelaide.

Having never visited Scotland before, Mary was keen to take in a few more of the sights of the great city of Edinburgh. There was every chance she may not get the opportunity again.

With Adelaide off on her secret mission, Mary was surprised as to how quickly she welcomed the time alone. The one thing she did not welcome, however, was the biting wind which pierced her coat. Cambridge was cold in winter, but a thick scarf and her trusty red coat had seen her through the worst of the chilly days. Here in Scotland, her English attire failed against the onslaught of an icy Scottish breeze. Standing outside a drapery, peering in through the window, she hugged herself in an effort to stay warm.

"Stockings—that is what I need. Thick wool ones," she muttered.

Hugh dropped the last of his Christmas gifts into his leather satchel and gave himself a silent cheer. "Ewan, Caroline, David, Mama, Great Aunt Maude, Adelaide, Charles, and William. Not that the baby will actually do anything with his gift, but it's the thought that counts," he said.

His Christmas shopping was complete. At the bottom of the satchel lay two other gifts. One was a special Christmas present for Mary, the other a small box.

It was the item inside the small box which had taken Hugh most of the morning to choose. He had thought to ask Adelaide's opinion, but decided it was best if he kept his own counsel. He had already failed Mary enough times without adding the pressure of his family's expectations to her worries.

When the time was right, he would speak to her.

Stepping out into High Street, he turned in the direction of the inn and began to walk. His morning had been a success. Apart from all the gifts, he had also bought two new bottles of black writing ink and some extra parchment. He had even remembered to get the small silk bags that Ewan had requested for giving coins to the castle staff on Handsel Monday.

He was quietly pleased with himself; for once he was organized for Christmas. He did, however, make a mental note to write out a long list once he got back to the inn— just in case he had stayed true to form and forgotten something of importance.

Crossing over High Street, he spied McNally's sweet shop. His stomach rumbled at the thought of Scottish tablet, and he made a beeline for the front door.

"Hugh."

A sudden voice from his right stirred him from his single-minded mission. Coming toward him was Mary, a small parcel tucked under her arm. He gave her a friendly greeting. "Hello."

He nodded toward the parcel. "Anything exciting?"

She shook her head. "No. Just woolen stockings. I never realized Scotland would be this cold."

As she neared, he could see she was holding the parcel close to herself, and her shoulders were scrunched up. A wave of pity swept over him the instant he realized Mary was shivering. He ached to pull her into his arms and protect her from the wind.

If she was suffering in the relative warmth of Edinburgh, Mary was in for a miserable time in the frigid climes of Strathmore Mountain. He smiled as a thought came to him. He now had the perfect opportunity to try and make up for some of his thoughtless behavior—to show Mary that she was indeed important to him.

"Did you by chance get an opportunity to go to Butlers with Adelaide?" he asked. Butlers in Edinburgh sold all manner of clothing, from hats and scarfs, through to greatcoats and boots, and everything in between.

"No. We passed it on the way through to some other shops and she pointed it out to me. They are by royal appointment to the king, are they not?" she replied.

"And the Duke of Strathmore," he said.

The look of delighted surprise on her face made his heart beat a little faster.

Hugh offered Mary his arm. "Come. You cannot visit Edinburgh without setting foot inside Butlers, especially when you are a guest of one of its patrons."

She took his arm and his heart soared. They had walked together through the university grounds over the years, but never once had he dared dream that he would be walking arm in arm with her in the middle of Edinburgh.

With her hand on his arm, he knew she was where she was meant to be. He nodded his greetings to other people as they headed back up the Royal Mile, all the while indulging in a pleasant fantasy that they were a married couple, and this was something they did every day.

The short walk to Butlers soon had Hugh's mind racing with other ideas. He would buy Mary a pair of sensible wool-lined leather gloves. Yes, that would do. No. A thick scarf and gloves was what she needed. And a coat.

By the time the doorman at Butlers ushered them inside, Hugh had a plan firmly set in his mind. Mary would not feel the cold for one moment if he had anything to say about it.

As a nearby shop assistant made his way toward them, Hugh straightened his shoulders and turned to Mary.

"I am so sorry," he said.

She scowled. "What for?"

"For being an ass. I forgot your Christmas present in Cambridge because I was too caught up in my concerns. And I wasn't there for you when you were asked to leave the university. It was selfish of me. So, I am begging your indulgence to allow me to make a small step toward the restitution of our friendship," he said.

"Oh, Hugh," she murmured.

The shop assistant stopped in front of them and bowed low. "Welcome to Butlers. How may I be of assistance to you today?"

Hugh turned and smiled at the man. "Good morning, I am Lord Hugh Radley, and this is my friend Miss Mary Gray. Miss Gray is staying with my family at Strathmore Castle for Christmas. As her wardrobe is more suited to the warmer climes of England, I was thinking she might need kitting out with a full Scottish wardrobe. What do you think?"

Mary's mouth opened, but Hugh ignored her attempted protest.

The shop assistant held his hands together tightly; a nice Christmas commission would come from such a sale. "I could not agree more, my lord. May I suggest we begin with a pair of tackety half-boots to ensure Miss Gray has a sure footing in the snow, and then move on to the woolens section?"

"Perfect."

Mary's cheeks continued to burn until they finally left Butlers several hours later. In that time, Hugh had spent, in her opinion, an outrageous sum of money on a new wardrobe for her. Her second attempt at protesting over his extravagance was ignored by both Hugh and the shop assistant; they were too busy deciding on the color of the hat which was to go with her new coat.

But it was not just the amount of money Hugh had spent on her which had Mary's heart racing. It was the brief and often light touches of his hand whenever he drew near. When he handed her a pair of kid leather gloves, she felt the heat of his fingers as they brushed against hers. She trembled at his touch.

When he reached out and tucked a wayward curl behind her ear after she had finished trying on a hat, Mary didn't know where to look. A pair of piercing blue eyes met her gaze. The smile which accompanied them took her breath away.

"Since you cannot choose between the forest green one and the chocolate brown one, I think we should take both," he said. He was so close to her that she caught the hint of musk and jasmine. Hugh was wearing the cologne she had given to him.

She pretended not to look at the price tag of the hat, having already been gently scolded for wincing when she looked at the price of the coat Hugh had chosen for her earlier. He was determined to spoil her, and she knew nothing that she said would have the slightest effect on him completing his mission.

When they returned to the inn later that afternoon, Mary's faint hopes of hearing Adelaide censure her brother over his prodigality were immediately dashed.

"Oh my, aren't you the kick!" exclaimed Adelaide, her gaze moving up from Mary's green coat to her matching hat.

Mary was tempted to pinch Hugh when she saw the sly smile which sat on his lips. He seemed so very pleased with himself. Happiness made him even more handsome.

"It took the combined efforts of myself and an enthusiastic shop assistant at Butlers to win the day, but I think we all did well. Including Mary," he said.

"Yes, you did, and Mary, you look wonderful. I must confess I was going to go through the tall cupboards at the castle and see what spare winter clothes we had so that you would not freeze. It is hard to eat supper when your teeth are continually chattering," said Adelaide.

Charles appeared in the room, carrying a smiling Will. Adelaide hurriedly scooped her son up into her arms. "Did your papa rescue you from a long sleep?" she cooed.

"Actually, we both had a very long sleep. I put him down and went to have a five-minute *sieste* on the bed; the next thing I knew, it was three hours later," replied Charles.

Charles looked at Mary and her new attire, then looked back to his wife. Mary caught the slight raise of an eyebrow as he and Adelaide exchanged a knowing look.

"Well, that is good. It means you will be able to get up to him in the middle of the night and I might get some sleep," replied Adelaide.

Hugh cleared his throat. "Speaking of sleep, I thought we might like to have an early supper this evening so we can be on the road at first light. I have reserved a private dining room."

If his efforts at shopping earlier in the day had been a surprise, the fact that Hugh had made arrangements of any sort was a revelation to Mary. He was forever forgetting to eat, so much so that she suspected the toast she regularly made for him in the evenings was the only meal he ate some days.

The Hugh Radley who now stood beside her was revealing himself to be a different man to the one she had thought she knew over the last two or so years. There was something in his manner that she couldn't quite put her finger on. It intrigued her.

She had developed a habit of chancing a look in his direction every so often, continuing her ongoing private study of him. But over the past few days, there had been several occasions when she had turned to Hugh, intent on sneaking a glance, only to find him looking at her.

Just as he was doing this very moment.

She forced herself to look away, fearful that if she continued to hold his gaze that he may finally see what she was certain was written all over her face.

She was hopelessly and irretrievably in love with him.

Chapter Eight

Mary had lived a sheltered life. Her knowledge of the world, and even England for that matter, came mostly from books. With her father devoting his time to the university, there had been little opportunity for them to travel outside Cambridge. She had been to London once, but that had been for a series of lectures given by her father, and apart from a short visit to Westminster Abbey, she had seen nothing of the great city.

The trip to Scotland was proving an eye-opening experience. Edinburgh, with its cobbled streets and imposing castle, had captured her imagination. She made a promise to herself that if she was able to make her work as a tutor a success, she would set aside a little money each week so that at least once a year she could afford to travel outside of Cambridge. She longed to see more of the world.

She looked around the travel coach. Adelaide and Charles were busy with William. Charles softly singing a French lullaby to his son, while his wife held Will in her arms and stared lovingly at her husband. Mary felt her heart swell as she watched the devoted couple and their baby. From the happy gurgles of Will, it was obvious he enjoyed hearing his father's dulcet tones.

Hugh sat beside Mary on the bench. For once he did not have his nose in a book. He was staring out the window, the hint of a smile on his face.

The coach had turned off the main road not far from Falkirk several hours earlier, and as they made their way along the narrow side road which led to Strathmore Mountain, Mary could see the landscape changing. The wooded Lowlands gave way to sweeping snow-covered meadows framed by towering mountains. The peaks of the mountains were hidden from view by low gray clouds.

Adelaide handed Will to his father and both she and Hugh pressed their faces to the window of the coach. At one point, they exchanged an excited giggle. Mary sat bemused at the sight, while Charles simply smiled.

"Walls!" cried Adelaide.

Hugh snorted. "No! Where?"

His sister held her finger to the glass. "Between the tallest of those trees. There it is again. I win."

Adelaide sat back in her seat and grinned at Hugh. "When will you ever learn? I know the exact point on the road."

A less-than-impressed-looking Hugh shook his head. "Alright, you win. *Again.*"

He turned his gaze from his sister and looked blankly at Mary. He blinked, and the vague expression on his face changed. He had registered her presence.

"Come, look," he said.

He got up and after Mary had shuffled along the bench and taken a position at the window, Hugh sat down on the other side of her. He pointed to two tall trees which stood in the middle of a nearby wood.

"There. Can you see the gray walls? Keep watching; it will come into full view any moment now," he said.

Mary peered out and she caught sight of a solid patch of gray between the trees. As the coach turned, the wood was left behind. She then got a clear view of what Adelaide and Hugh had been searching for.

Across the distance of a mile or so, beyond a small village loomed a towering Norman era stronghold. Strathmore Castle, home of the Duke of Strathmore and the Radley family.

Her mouth dropped open.

Hugh chuckled, and Adelaide clapped her hands. "Over five hundred years, never been taken," they chorused.

She had seen pictures of castles in books, and there were several real ones in the area around Cambridge, but none of them were anything like what Mary now saw. There were no ornate towers or flying buttresses. This was a stone behemoth built to withstand attack from bloodthirsty invaders.

"That is Strathmore village. Most of the castle servants live in the village and walk up the hill each morning to come to work," explained Hugh, pointing to the small collection of buildings in front of the castle.

Mighty though the imposing structure was, Mary's gaze was now drawn to the mountain beyond the castle. It dominated all that lay before it. Strathmore Mountain rose high into the sky. Its snow-capped shoulders were visible, but its peak was shrouded in thick, menacing cloud.

Mary shivered, imagining how bitterly cold it would be up on the mountain. She looked back at Hugh. "I now understand why you were so insistent on buying me that fur-lined hat."

Hugh's generous gift of winter clothing would be put to good use during her stay at Strathmore Castle.

After passing through the village, where the coach slowed down to make way for the local inhabitants on foot, and where Hugh waved out the window to everyone, they crossed over the castle's heavy wooden drawbridge and through the gateway.

Adelaide fussed with her hair as the coach entered the courtyard and drew to a halt in front of the main steps of the keep. "How do I look?"

Her husband leaned over and placed a kiss on her cheek. "*Enchanteur comme toujours,*" he murmured.

Mary felt close to tears. Charles thought his wife enchanting. With such sweet endearments, it was little wonder that a minor nobleman from France had managed to capture the heart of a duke's daughter.

The door of the coach was opened by a heavily set gentleman with a long white and gray beard, who poked his head inside. Mary sat back in alarm; he must have been close to seven feet tall. A giant of a man.

"Wylcome. Well then, who would we be a havin' here?" he asked.

Hugh leaned forward. "A son and daughter of the house. Family and friend."

The gentleman looked around the carriage and stood for a moment, scratching his beard. "Hmm. I canna sae I know you. The only other son of the house was lost long ago," he replied.

Mary cast her gaze from the gentleman to Hugh and back again. She suspected there was some sort of byplay happening, but everyone was keeping a straight face.

Hugh broke first. "One Christmas. I missed one Christmas—am I never to be forgiven?"

He launched himself out of the carriage and into the embrace of the huge man, who wrapped him in a bear hug.

"Lord Hugh? Why, I didn't recognize ya. The prodigal son has returned!" he cried.

Charles climbed out next and then helped Adelaide down. She held Will in her arms. At the sight of her, the man-mountain set Hugh aside and bowed low.

"Wylcome home, Lady Adelaide," he said.

Adelaide immediately handed her firstborn over to him. As Will's eyes settled on the hulking stranger who held him, Mary gripped the door of the carriage. Any moment now she expected the infant to be registering his protest. Instead, he softly gurgled and wrapped his hand as best as he could around one of the man's thick fingers.

"So, this is William. He is a fine bairn. He is as hairy as a wild mountain boar!"

Mary laughed, but her mirth quickly died when the man mountain caught her eye. With Will still safely held in the crook of his arm, he reached out a hand to her. A blushing Mary took it and stepped down into the castle courtyard.

A murmur rippled through the other castle servants who had gathered over the past minute or so. Mary caught a whispered, "Who is that?"

It only took a sideways glance from him in the direction of the gathered servants, and they all fell silent.

"Wylcome to Strathmore Castle," he said.

Hugh hurried to Mary's side. "Master Crowdie, may I present my guest, Miss Mary Gray of Cambridge."

Having never met many lords or ladies, Mary was not completely au fait with the rules of noble society, but she knew enough to understand that if Hugh was addressing Master Crowdie in such a manner, then he must be an important man.

"Mary, Master Crowdie is the steward of Strathmore Castle. Nothing happens within the walls of the castle and the village without his say so," explained Hugh.

"Really? And here was I thinking I was in charge." A tall fair-haired man stepped up to Hugh and slapped him hard on the back.

Hugh embraced the interloper. "Brother."

Ewan Radley, Duke of Strathmore, was dressed exactly how Mary had imagined a Scottish lord would be, right down to the tartan kilt and thick black coat. She recognized the black, gray, and blue of the Strathmore plaid from the scarf which Hugh regularly wore.

"And you brought a surprise for me—excellent," said Ewan.

Mary dipped into her best curtsey as the duke caught her gaze. Her left knee wavered as she rose, and Ewan stepped forward to stop her from toppling over. He held her gaze as well as her arm, and she immediately noticed the similarity between him and Hugh. There was no mistaking that they were brothers.

"Your grace," she said.

"So, you are Miss Gray. I have heard a lot about you over the past few years. May I offer my condolences on the passing of your father."

She accepted his kind words with a smile. "Thank you."

Ewan then looked to Adelaide. "Unless you have a duke and duchess hidden in your luggage, I take it that Anne and Mowbray will not be joining us for Christmas?"

Adelaide shook her head. "Don't get me started on the pair of them. With their constant rows, I am glad that Mowbray threw a tantrum and refused to come. I am certain I would have murdered the pair of them within an hour of us leaving London if they had graced us with their company."

Hugh offered Mary his arm and the travel party followed Ewan over to the steps of the keep. Assembled on the steps was a trio of women. All three wore Strathmore tartan sashes over blue woolen gowns.

The youngest of the women, who Mary guessed was Caroline, the Duchess of Strathmore, was holding a wriggling toddler in her arms. As the arrivals approached, she handed the child over to a nursemaid and headed down the stairs. She greeted her family members with hugs and kisses before fussing over baby Will who had been safely retrieved by his father.

"It is so good to see you all. I hope the journey north wasn't too taxing on you," she said. Her eyes were fixed on Will as she spoke the words.

"He slept most of the way, for which I am eternally grateful," replied Adelaide.

"Wait until he is a toddler. David has almost inexhaustible energy," replied Caroline.

When Caroline turned to Hugh, he stepped forward with Mary. At that moment, the other women made their way down to them.

"Your graces, Lady Maude, may I present Miss Mary Gray of Cambridge. Mary is joining us for Christmas and Hogmanay," he said.

The matching smiles which appeared on their faces had Mary suddenly feeling like she was the cream and they were a pounce of cats.

"Mary. A pleasure to meet you. I am Caroline, Duchess of Strathmore. This is Lady Alison, the Dowager Duchess of Strathmore, and Lady Maude, her sister-in-law."

Mary looked down at Caroline's offered hand. She had never met a duchess before, let alone two. She dipped into another deep curtesy, holding tightly onto Hugh's hand, and prayed that her legs would not fail her this time.

"Hugh, you made it," said Lady Alison.

Hugh placed a dutiful kiss on his mother's cheek. "Mama."

She snorted. "A whole year away from home and all I get is a peck on the cheek. Unhand your lady friend and give your mother a proper greeting."

Mary caught the blush on Hugh's cheeks as he released her hand and embraced his mother. Lady Maude then stepped up for her hug, followed by Caroline. If he had thought he was going to make an understated return home, the womenfolk of the castle clearly had other ideas.

Her own soft chortle ended as soon as she saw Lady Alison's arms held out in greeting to her. "Come now. If you are a friend of my son, you shall also be greeted properly."

With no choice but to accept the welcome hugs from Hugh's female relatives, Mary submitted. Lady Alison's embrace was a little longer than the others, and the smile which sat on the dowager duchess's face when they finally parted was enough to give Mary pause.

Her unwed son had brought a young woman home for Christmas, and Lady Alison had drawn an obvious conclusion.

As Mary took Hugh's offered arm once more, and they followed the rest of the Radley family into the castle keep, Mary pondered the prudency of having come to Strathmore Castle. Hugh might be blind to her love for him, but having now met his mother, she doubted that Lady Alison was cursed with the same affliction.

As Lady Alison glanced back over her shoulder at her son and then to her, Mary wondered how long it would be before the dowager duchess took her aside and began to ask probing questions. From the glint in Lady Alison's eyes, she deduced it would not be long.

Chapter Nine

Mary's first encounter with having her own maid was a touch awkward. Having gone back to the coach to retrieve her travel bag, she was politely informed that all her things had been brought inside and were waiting for her in her room.

Her room within the castle, it transpired, was more of a small apartment than a simple bedroom. It had a separate sitting room as well as two bedrooms. The walls were decorated with wallpaper in the Strathmore tartan. Mary was grateful that the imposing theme did not carry to the plush blue carpet on the floor.

A maid was busy unwrapping the parcels of clothes that Hugh had bought for Mary in Edinburgh. As soon as she saw the maid untying the string which held the parcels together, Mary hurried over.

"Oh, please, let me do that. You don't need to," she said.

The maid frowned. "It's nae bother, miss; this is ma job. I won't take long. I will hang your things up in the wardrobe and then be leavin'. If you need anything else after that, either pull on the bell here or find a footman. There is always someone about the castle who can help."

Mary's hopes to unwrap the new clothes herself and spend time admiring them were scuttled by her unexpected social status of being an honored guest of the house.

Making short work of unpacking Mary's things, the maid hung everything in the oversized oak wardrobe, she then gave a quick bob of a curtsey before leaving.

With the maid finally gone, a slightly frazzled Mary sat down on the well-appointed sofa which graced her sitting room. The furnishings of the room spoke of an opulent lifestyle she could only imagine living. After pulling off her gloves, she let her fingers touch the soft black leather. With her fingertips barely skimming the surface of the sofa, she lay back and closed her eyes.

"This is bliss," she whispered to herself

A soft tap on the door roused her some time later. Blinking, and wiping sleep from her eyes, she opened it. Hugh was standing on the threshold.

"Do you have everything you need? Has your maid been in to attend to your garments?" he asked.

"Yes, I have everything, thank you. But I wasn't sure what I was supposed to do with the maid, do I pay her?" she replied. Her greatest fear was that she would somehow put a foot wrong and have the castle staff think her rude. Was she supposed to tip the staff like porters at a hotel? She had heard that was the proper thing to do. She would leave a coin for the maid next time just to be sure.

"Just let them go about their work; they are here to help you. You only have to ask. And no, you don't need to pay her," he said.

It was nice to have a maid, but she was not comfortable with the idea. A few weeks in Scotland would spoil her for the life she had waiting for her back in Cambridge. No one would be pressing her gowns for her once she returned to England. The furniture in her cramped bedsit would consist of a small bed and a single chair.

Hugh's gaze went to her hair, and the hint of a shy smile appeared on his face. "I was waiting in the great hall for you to make an appearance, but when you didn't, I thought I should come and find you. You look like you took the opportunity for a nap."

She put a hand to her hair. The soft chignon she had fashioned that morning had fallen, and badly needed repair. "I sat to rest my eyes and must have fallen asleep."

Hugh stopped a passing footman and murmured instructions. The footman nodded, then hurried away.

"I have asked that your maid attend to you and fix your hair. I thought you might like to take a stroll around the castle once you are ready. Make sure you dress warm."

Mary frowned. She had been managing her hair since she was a little girl; the thought of sitting while a maid attended to it struck her as odd.

Hugh leaned in and took hold of her hand. "Enjoy your time here and let the castle servants assist you. If you don't, then they will think they have done something wrong. And then we shall have Master Crowdie having a word with my brother, and eventually I will be taken aside and spoken to. So please, let your maid, whose name is Heather, fix your hair."

After Hugh made the proper introductions, he left Mary and Heather to overcome their initial awkward start. While Heather set Mary's hair, they discussed a daily routine which would suit them both. Once Mary's chignon had been set to right, she retrieved her new fur hat from the cupboard.

"Do you have any hatpins, miss?" asked Heather

"No. I forgot them." Her only good hatpin had recently broken, and she had decided replacing it could wait until she had more money.

"I shall see if I can find you some, but in the meantime, you will have tae watch out for the wind. It does loves tae steal the hat from your head," said Heather.

Heather left the room singing a happy little ditty, leaving Mary to finish dressing for her walk with Hugh. With her new thick coat buttoned to the neck, Mary was as warm as toast. She stuffed her gloves into her pockets, then stood back and looked at herself in the mirror.

She cut a fine figure in her new, expensive clothes. Perhaps now Hugh would notice her. His efforts in Edinburgh had given her the first real glimmer of hope that he did see the Mary beyond the girl who brought him coffee and toast.

The clothes were wonderful. But it was the attention Hugh had given her all that afternoon, the words of encouragement for every item she tried on, and the small affectionate touches of his hand that had set her heart racing.

"Don't be silly, and don't get your hopes up. This is Hugh," she cautioned herself.

At some point, he would break her heart and, knowing the sweet and often baffle-headed man that he was, Hugh would likely have no idea what he had done.

She met him downstairs a short time later. The great hall reminded her of the dining halls at St John's College, though the long dining tables were missing. The hall itself was divided up into several living areas, with large tapestries hanging from the roof to create the illusion of separate rooms.

Hugh nodded at the tapestries. "My father had them installed. He decided that the castle no longer needed to be a great meeting place, but rather somewhere that his family could live. We move all the furniture out of the way and replace it with tables for events such as Hogmanay," he explained.

"And Christmas?"

He shook his head. "Not in Scotland. Christmas is not celebrated widely here. The Church of Scotland doesn't hold with the holy day, so the Radley family celebrates it privately, and then hosts the big celebration over New Year's."

Hugh had never struck her as being a typical Scotsman. He didn't have much of a lilt in his voice, and only the use of the occasional Scottish word indicated that he was anything other than a full-blooded Englishman.

"Come. Let me show you the castle. The weather is still fine, but Master Crowdie tells me we will be in for a major frost overnight, and possibly snow."

Mary followed him out of the great hall, expecting to turn right and venture into the courtyard, but Hugh turned left and headed for a set of nearby stone steps.

"You will want your gloves and hat held on tight where we are going," he said.

"And where is that?"

"The ramparts."

He put one foot on the bottom stone step, then held out his hand to her. Mary took it. If she had thought he was being a little overprotective about her climbing the steps, she soon understood his reasoning.

The steps wound tightly around the staircase, hugging close to the wall. In some places the stones had been worn away so badly that she had to avoid the step and take two at a time. She was hot and huffing by the time they finally reached the top of the castle.

Hugh stopped at a huge door made from hard elm and looked back the way they had come. When he let go of her hand, Mary sensed the loss. His strong grip as he led her up the stairs had been an interesting revelation. The quiet, bookish Hugh Radley was a man of unknown physical strength.

"Ewan is going to get a stonemason over from Glasgow to look at rebuilding the steps. They may have served their purpose when this was a fortified castle, but now they just make it difficult to carry things up and down," said Hugh.

He pushed on the door and stepped through it. Mary followed him out into bright sunshine. She held her hand up to shield her eyes from the sun. At the same time, a sudden blast of chill wind tore at her hat. It flew from her head and landed on the stone rampart, where the wind quickly picked it up once more and skipped it out of reach.

"Oh!" She went to step past Hugh to rescue her hat, but he moved in front of her.

Bent low, he chased after it. His sure-footed leaps from one side of the narrow ramparts to the next showed how much at home he was on top of the castle.

With a deftly timed sweep of his hand, he finally caught Mary's hat. She applauded his success as he spun around on one foot and held it up, a triumphant smile on his face.

"Well done, Hugh."

He trotted back to her and with a flourish, returned the hat to its rightful owner. A familiar flash of heat raced down her spine as their gazes met. Mary held the tight smile she had perfected for such moments with him; she dared not reveal the full smile her heart so desperately craved to give him. *A heart not risked is a heart not broken.*

She held the hat firmly in her hand, not wanting to add its loss to the cost of replacing her hatpin.

The wind on the ramparts was fierce and unrelenting, but Hugh did not seem to mind. While Mary was busy trying to keep her hair out of her face and protect her ears from the stinging cold, he went about with only a coat and scarf to keep the elements at bay.

When they finally managed to find a spot out of the wind, it took her a good minute or so to pin her hair back. Heather's earlier efforts at fixing Mary's hairstyle had been blown away.

"If you look over there, you can see Castle Hill. On top of it is Stirling Castle. That's where a number of the kings and queens of Scotland were crowned," he said, pointing to a tall crag in the distance.

"Including Mary Queen of Scots," replied Mary. She may not have travelled much in her life, but she knew her history. Access to the extensive library was one of the privileges of having grown up at Cambridge University.

"Now that I have a better understanding of where Strathmore Castle is situated, I realize there are a number of significant historical sites around here. Bannockburn, where Robert the Bruce defeated the English, must be only a few miles away," she added.

"That's it there. It's about fifteen miles as the crow flies," Hugh replied, pointing to a flat area toward one side of another hill. "The Bruce used Strathmore Castle as a staging ground for his troops before the battle of Bannockburn, though it was not as complete a castle then as it is now."

Mary heard the fierce pride in Hugh's voice as he spoke. Every moment that she spent with him in this place showed him in a different light. And every moment, her love for him grew.

She turned away from the view over the battlements and forced herself to take several long deep breaths.

"I am glad you came. I hadn't realized how much it would mean to me to show you my home," said Hugh.

Mary nodded, incapable of speech. The next few weeks here with him at the castle were going to be a trial for her heart. The way he made her feel, she feared she may not survive it.

Chapter Ten

Hugh had initially thought to simply show Mary around the castle and introduce her to a few of the castle stalwarts—people he trusted and loved—but by the time they returned to the keep, he sensed something else was at play. From the moment he had taken her by the hand and led her up the castle steps, his perception of her had begun to change.

Several times over the past days he had caught her staring at him, an odd expression on her face, as if she was studying him. And then at other times when he looked, she seemed distant and closed off from him, as if lost in herself.

He recognized himself in that behavior, knowing that he often retreated into his own thoughts to escape from the world. *And what is it that you seek to escape from Miss Mary Gray?*

"Ah, there you are. We were speculating as to where you had got to," said Ewan.

As Hugh and Mary entered the great hall, he saw the rest of the Radley family members all gathered near one of the castle fireplaces. A fire was burning in the huge iron grate, but even at ten feet from one side of the hearth to the other, it struggled to create much warmth in the cavernous space.

"I was just showing Mary the view from the ramparts," Hugh replied. He ignored the small shared looks that he saw exchanged between Adelaide and Charles, but the look that passed between Lady Alison and Aunt Maude gave him pause.

Not you as well. Please don't meddle.

He had expected his sister and brother-in-law to try and play cupid—Adelaide was never one for subtly—but he was more concerned by his mother and aunt's apparent interest in Mary and himself.

When he looked to Ewan, he was greeted with a raised eyebrow. He sighed, relieved that at least his brother and Lady Caroline were being sensible about things. Mary was his friend, and a guest at the castle. Whatever else developed between them from her stay in Scotland, he wanted it to be fresh and unencumbered. He had not brought her all this way simply to use the time alone with her as a means to seduce her into marriage.

He pushed his tongue against the back of his teeth, but a little voice in his brain told him it would take more than that to believe the lie he had just told himself. He wanted Mary; the question was, did she want him?

"We are heading to the village to buy some tablet if the two of you would like to come," said Adelaide.

Hugh noted the use of the term "the two of you? and suspected it would not be the last time he heard it over the Christmas period.

He looked to Mary. She blinked, then put a hand to her face and wiped something away from her eye. *Was that a tear?*

His family were making more of the relationship between him and Mary than currently existed. A quiet word or two might need to be had to calm the matchmakers down. He did not need his family interfering with his plans, or making Mary feel uncomfortable.

"The road to the village is icy, so you will all require your tackety boots today," said Ewan.

Hugh could have hugged his brother for the delicate change of subject.

"Well then, it is fortunate that Hugh procured Mary a pair of boots along with a number of other items of clothing while we were in Edinburgh," said Adelaide.

Hugh could have swatted his sister for the not-so-delicate remark.

"Right then. So, if everyone who needs to change their boots can go and do so, the rest of us will wait here and then we can all walk to the village together," said Aunt Maude.

Hugh watched with interest as Mary made her first tentative steps in her new boots. "How do they feel on your feet?" he asked.

"A little strange when I place my feet on the road, but they are comfortable. I never thought to actually wear boots with metal plates and nails in them," replied Mary.

"That's because you have never been to Scotland and had to walk on black ice," said Aunt Maude.

The party of six, Caroline and Ewan having stayed behind at the castle, were making their way down the road to Strathmore village. The walk, if it could be described as such, was a constant game of sidestepping hazards. The road surface was covered with icy patches, interspersed with frozen puddles of muddy water. Every step held the promise of a hard and wet landing for an unsure foot.

Hugh had offered Mary his arm, but she told him she needed to learn to walk in her new boots. He accepted her reasons with good grace, but still walked close enough so that he could rescue her if she did slip.

While he had often turned to Mary for assistance while he was at Cambridge, he now found himself in possession of a growing need to protect her. With her father gone, she was all alone in the world. Every time he thought that she had nearly spent Christmas by herself in a boarding house, he grew angry with himself again. He had abandoned her.

Adelaide and Charles had taken the lead in the walking party, with Lady Alison and Aunt Maude following close behind. Hugh and Mary were left to bring up the rear. His family members marched on ahead, creating an ever-growing gap between them.

Mary slipped but managed to steady herself. "Oops, nearly," she said. Hugh reached out and took her arm. He looked down and saw the patch of black ice she was standing on.

"Here, step toward me. There are some drier spots over this way," he said.

She took a step toward him, but the black ice caught her a second time. As her feet went out from under her, Hugh steadied himself and wrapped his arms around her.

They stood in silence for a moment. A little white cloud of condensation hung between them as they both breathed heavily in the cold air.

"Thank you. I am glad you are surer of foot than me," she finally said.

Her head rose, and in that instant, Hugh was certain he had been clubbed with the hilt of a highland dirk. The green eyes which held him were mesmerizing. He blinked hard. Who was this enchantress who had stolen the body of kind, helpful Mary? His love for her had coalesced into something deeper, something more powerful.

Pure. Raw. Desire.

He brushed a hand on her cheek and leaned in close. His heart was hammering in his chest. Closer. She batted her long eyelashes. Closer. Her lips parted. *Closer*.

"Come on, you two, we need to get to Dunn's before nightfall!" bellowed Maude.

Hugh muttered several very un-Christmas-like words under his breath as Mary turned her head away. He waved to his family, who he was not surprised to see were all staring daggers at Maude.

"Coming," he replied through gritted teeth.

In the village, they headed for the local store: Dunn's. As soon as she stepped inside, Mary felt immediately at home. Unlike the fancy shops in Edinburgh, Dunn's was more like the usual places where Mary shopped in Cambridge. A one-stop shop for most things.

"Have you ever tried tablet before?" asked Hugh.

"No. What is it?" replied Mary.

"It's made from sugar and cream," said Hugh, handing her a piece.

"And a dram of whisky if you have any self-respect," added Maude.

Mary popped the tablet into her mouth. The buttery confection was a delight. So chewy and yet so soft. She hummed with happiness.

She wiped the sugary crumbs from her lips, then licked her finger. "That was marvelous," she said.

Hugh offered her another piece. Then, for some inexplicable reason, he stood and watched her eat it. When she licked her fingers again, she was certain she heard him swallow deep. The barest hint of a moan escaped his lips.

He quickly returned to the counter and purchased another two bags of tablet, handing them both to Mary who put them into the pocket of her new coat.

Before they left the village shop, Mary made a mental note of some inexpensive items which would make suitable Christmas gifts. With a little more practice in her hobnail boots, she felt confident that in time she could make the trip back to the village on her own.

"Thank you, Mister Dunn. As always, it is a pleasure to visit your shop," said Lady Alison, as they finalized their purchases and made for the door. Aunt Maude stuffed a boiled sweet into her mouth and nodded her agreement.

Mary allowed Hugh to take her arm for the return walk home. She told herself it was purely for safety's sake and to please Hugh. She was his guest and should not refuse him any kindness he wished to bestow upon her.

She pulled the bag of tablet from out of her coat pocket and offered it to him. With a polite 'thank you' and a smile which had her blinking hard, he took out two pieces. He handed the largest piece to Mary and popped the other one into his mouth.

"Thank you," she said.

"For what?"

"For the delicious tablet. For saving me on the road earlier. Just everything." As she placed her arm once more in his, Mary made a fateful decision. She would not hold back from enjoying this Christmas. Wherever she spent her next Christmas, she would always have this one to remember him by. A happy memory of a treasured friendship. Of a love that, though it was unrequited, still gave her joy.

After New Year's she would return to England, and she would let him go.

As Hugh and Mary led the way home, Lady Alison took a hold of her daughter's arm. She smiled at Adelaide.

"It is lovely to have you home, my darling. And wonderful to be able to hold my new grandson. You and I need to catch up on so much."

Adelaide raised an eyebrow. "Thank you, Mama. It is wonderful to be home in Scotland. Is there anything particularly pressing that you wish to discuss with me?"

Lady Alison leaned in close. "Well, since you asked. May I enquire as to whether you were able to secure a particular item in Edinburgh?"

Adelaide gently patted her mother's arm. "You didn't think I would dare to arrive without it, did you? Charles had it well hidden in our luggage."

Lady Alison softly chortled. "Well done, my dear. Now it just remains to see if we can make magic happen a second time."

Aunt Maude followed behind, tucking into her bag of boiled sweets before offering one to Charles who walked alongside her.

"Witchcraft at Christmas, hmm," she gruffly remarked.

Chapter Eleven

The whisky hit the back of Mary's throat, and she held a hand to her chest. Heat coursed through her body, right to her toes.

"I have had a hot toddy before, but never straight whisky. I can see why you would need a bottle or two of it here to see you through winter," she said.

After their visit to the village, Mary had been stolen away from Hugh and pressed into service by the women. While the great hall was to be utilized by the family for a small Christmas gathering, its main purpose was as a place for all the castle staff and villagers to gather for Hogmanay at New Year's.

"It is not officially Hogmanay until you can smell the wild boar roasting over the fire pits in the center of the castle courtyard," said Lady Alison.

Aunt Maude rubbed her hands. "I cannae wait."

Mary was surprised to see the Radley women dressed in simple brown woolen gowns with aprons. The dowager duchess held a broom in her hand, and she was sweeping ash from around the fireplace.

Maude was seated in a chair, tying together bundles of what appeared to be small branches of juniper. Beside her on the floor sat an impressive pile of completed work.

"Hogmanay traditions are to be kept. The first one is for the women of the family to clean the castle from top to bottom. It's like spring cleaning in England, only the redding is done in preparation for New Year's Day," explained Lady Alison.

"Redding?" replied Mary.

"We clean the house now, then at Hogmanay we sweep all the ash from the fireplace so that our home is clean for the start of the new year. We light the juniper bundles and walk them around the castle to ward off bad spirits from the old year. The other bundles are for the villagers to take with them and perform the ceremony in their homes."

Lady Alison handed Mary the broom and pointed to the back of the great hall. Mary was used to cleaning the small apartment at the university, so domestic work was not an issue. What did have her gripping the broom handle tight was the notion that she was considered a member of the family.

"If you would like to start sweeping from the back, I will get another broom and work in from the sides. Oh, and don't fret over the rest of the castle; it was all done last week. I wouldn't press you into service in such a way on your first Christmas here," she said.

First Christmas.

Mary caught the remark. It sounded like Lady Alison expected to see her at Strathmore Castle in future years; not just this one. If only that could be.

Adelaide and Lady Caroline appeared at the foot of the stairs. Adelaide carried a red box in her hands, holding it with obvious reverence as she walked into the great hall. Mary could only imagine what precious treasure was contained within.

Adelaide set the box down on a table out of the way of where the women were working. "Nearly time," she said.

Lady Caroline took a seat in a nearby chair while Adelaide picked up a dust cloth and began to bustle about the great hall, dusting and polishing every surface as she went. Lady Alison came and spoke to Lady Caroline, who said only a few words before rising from her chair and leaving the room.

As she passed, Mary could see that she was pale, and her features drawn. She gave Mary a wan smile as she made her way to the stairs. The duchess had been quiet the whole time, barely saying anything beyond the minimum required by good manners.

Two castle servants appeared at the front door of the great hall. One carried a wooden step and hammer, while his companion had a large coil of rope hanging over his shoulder and a piece of wood in his hand.

They bowed to Lady Alison, and she pointed toward a spot on the floor. "That should do nicely. If I recall, that is the same spot we used last year."

The man with the rope took the piece of wood and tied them together. He then stood on the stool and began to throw the wood up toward one of the oak beams which supported the roof of the great hall. His colleague held onto the other end of the rope.

Mary stopped her sweeping and, along with the others, watched in silent fascination at the goings on. On the fourth attempt, the wood cleared the beam and then came rattling back toward the floor. The servant holding the rope pulled back, stopping the wood before it could hit the ground. He tied off a knot in the rope, but left the wood hanging.

With this piece of work now complete, the two men stood back from the stool.

Adelaide put down her dust cloth and retrieved the box she had brought with her. With a curtsy to her mother, she handed it over.

"Lady Caroline is indisposed this afternoon and has asked that I continue my role for this year," announced Lady Alison.

Mary set her broom aside and walked over to where the others stood. She was eager to see what item of importance lay within the box that warranted such a ceremony.

Lady Alison removed the black ribbons which held the box closed and handed them to Adelaide. With great reverence, the lid was lifted. Mary and Aunt Maude both leaned in close, peaking over the side of the box.

A golden ball of mistletoe sat before them.

Aunt Maude and Lady Alison both gasped. The castle servants turned and bowed low to Adelaide.

Mary didn't know where to look. All this had been for a branch of mistletoe. She stifled a nervous laugh.

"Absolutely magnificent. Adelaide, you have done your family proud," whispered Lady Alison. A soft smile sat on Aunt Maude's face.

Mary's clear lack of understanding of the significance of the moment, together with her embarrassment, were saved by the arrival of Ewan, Hugh, and Charles through the front doors of the great hall.

With a solemn look on his face, the Duke of Strathmore strode over to where the mistletoe lay in the box. He looked down, paused for a moment, then nodded. "Near-perfect formation. Bright coloring. And just the right amount of branch on the end. I couldn't have chosen better myself."

"I know," replied Adelaide.

Ewan chuckled at his sister's words. "Now to get this beast up where it belongs."

After the hammer and a nail were handed to him, Ewan set to work attaching the branch of the mistletoe to the piece of wood. Several more nails were added before he stood back and declared that the job was done.

Everyone watched while the wood was hauled back into the air, coming to rest some ten feet above the floor. The rope was then tied off a second time with a firm knot.

Hugh came to Mary's side. "The hanging of the mistletoe is a very important part of the annual festivities. I am glad you were here to be able to witness it," he said.

She felt safe enough to ask him the obvious question. "I know people in England see it as a fun part of Christmas—most everyone has kissed under the mistletoe — but why is it so important here?"

"Because it holds real magic," he whispered.

She met his eyes. Hugh was about to become a curate for the Church of England, and yet here he was talking about magic. She had never known him to be anything other than serious about matters of his faith and life's calling.

"It's alright; I won't get thrown out of the church for respecting old customs and ways. All forms of religion have a degree of believing in something we don't fully understand," he said.

If her father could hear Hugh right now, he would be frowning with disapproval. Professor James Gray had been strict to the letter in his observance of the scriptures.

"This is Scotland; we do things a little differently here," he added.

With the mistletoe now in place, eager looks passed between the members of the gathering.

Charles slipped an arm around Adelaide's waist and drew her to him. She pretended to bat away his amorous advances but did not put up a fight when her husband steered her in the direction of the mistletoe.

"Just remember that with great power comes great responsibility. We expect to hear word of a new arrival from the two of you if you dare to kiss under the Strathmore mistletoe," said Ewan.

Charles laughed, and taking his wife in his arms, he gave her a soft, loving kiss.

Applause rippled throughout the great hall. The mistletoe had captured its first couple.

"And there will be many more before it comes down after Hogmanay. I wonder who will be next," said Adelaide.

Mary kept her gaze fixed on the rest of the group, quietly praying that Hugh did not see the heat which she felt burning on her cheeks. She could only pray that she was one of those whom the magic of the mistletoe would touch.

Chapter Twelve

Hugh hadn't failed to see the bright red of Mary's cheeks as she watched Charles and Adelaide embrace.

No one who witnessed the kiss could have been left unaffected. French-born Charles Alexandre wore his passion for his wife on his sleeve. Hugh sensed a small pang of jealousy toward his sister and her joyful union, but he chided himself for it. Adelaide had found Charles after a long period of heartbreak and deserved every moment of happiness.

After the mistletoe ceremony, Mary slipped from the great hall. Hugh spent the rest of the afternoon in Ewan's study, discussing estate matters. He was not the duke, but as the second son of the house, and heir presumptive, he still had his duties to perform.

"Now I have tallied up the heads to receive Handsel Monday coin purses, and it stands at fifty-seven. Master Crowdie has confirmed the number," said Ewan.

Hugh sat and stared at his hands; his mind was completely elsewhere. His thoughts focused solely on Mary.

"I thought we should give every man one hundred pounds."

One hundred pounds.

"What?!" replied Hugh.

Ewan sat and stared at his brother. "I thought that might get your attention. I know you find estate matters a tad boring, but if you could just concentrate for a few minutes, then you can go back into the hall and continue to make doe eyes at Miss Mary Gray."

Hugh had been caught daydreaming, a fact he could not deny. "Is it that obvious?"

Ewan chuckled. "Yes. Do you remember when I had a small thing for Lord Stirling's daughter some years ago? Well, the look I wore on my face all that summer is the very same one you have had plastered to your face since you got here. I'm surprised that the two of you are not already betrothed."

"Her father was my professor, and so pursuing his daughter would not have been proper. And now that she is alone, it is going to be difficult to convince her that I am acting beyond mere pity for her changed circumstances. Add to that the fact that I do not know if she holds any romantic feelings for me, and you will have an understanding of how complicated this situation actually is," replied Hugh.

Ewan sat back in his chair with a look of serious contemplation on his face. If anyone had an appreciation of dealing with a complicated love life, it was him. He had thrown Lady Caroline Hastings over in order to marry her sister, only to be jilted by his fiancée who had died while giving birth to his illegitimate son. It was a miracle he had managed to win Caroline back and secure her hand in marriage.

"The only advice I can give you, if you are asking for it, is to be honest with her. It took some time for me to come to that realization when Caroline and I were estranged. Make a promise to yourself that before New Year's, you will talk to Mary and tell her how you feel. It was the only thing that brought Caroline back to me in the end."

"Yes."

"Oh, and don't let Mama or any of the others try to play cupid. They got away with it, last Christmas, but that is because they had my infant son David to wave under Caroline's nose. You don't have the luxury of a sweet-faced bairn to win Mary over to you."

"Try just a bite."

Mary looked at the ladle and screwed up her face. Hugh tried not to laugh. It had taken more than a little coaxing to get her to consider attempting a mouthful of haggis. But now that it sat before her on the spoon, she hesitated.

"Couldn't I have another piece of the blackbun instead?" she said.

"No. The rest of the blackbun is for Hogmanay. We only got to try some today because cook had made an extra batch. Come on, you have to try a spot of haggis; it is the law." He waved the ladle under her nose, laughing when she finally opened her mouth and let him feed her. She didn't chew for a moment, a look of distaste evident on her face. Offal was not to everyone's liking.

Then, to his delight, her face changed.

As she chewed, her eyes grew wide. She swallowed. "That was not at all what I expected. It was nutty and peppery."

"Cook adds a lot of spices to it. Once you get over the idea that it is the heart, liver, and lungs of the sheep, it's quite a good meat," he replied.

He offered her a second spoonful and grinned when she accepted it without hesitation. For someone who had lived a sheltered life at the university, he was pleased to see that Mary was open to embracing new experiences.

The family were gathered in the great hall for supper. The great space had been cleaned from top to bottom. A roaring fire burned in the giant stone fireplace.

The room was a sea of Strathmore family tartan. One-year-old David was decked out in a kilt which had once been his father's, while baby Will was wrapped up warmly in a tartan shawl. Everyone wore the family plaid. Everyone except Mary.

Hugh had broached the subject of giving Mary a Strathmore tartan stole to wear, but Ewan had refused. Only family could wear it. Hugh understood his brother's message loud and clear. If he wanted Mary to wear the tartan, he had to make her one of the family.

Lady Caroline finally made an appearance in the great hall just before supper. She looked brighter than she had been earlier in the day but was still pale. As she came to her husband's side, Ewan drew her in close and spoke to her. She smiled and nodded.

"Could I please have your attention for a moment," announced Ewan.

He bent down and lifted David into his arms. Lady Caroline stood close.

"This time last year, I was fortunate to make Caroline my wife. In doing so, David gained a mother, and the castle its new duchess. Today, I am happy to announce that Caroline and I are to have our first child together in the new year."

Ewan's words had the immediate effect of Adelaide squealing with delight, Lady Alison giving a knowing nod of the head, and Aunt Maude searching her pockets for a handkerchief. Mary stood with her hands clasped together, held to her lips.

Before anyone had the chance to step forward and congratulate the expectant mother, her husband gently steered her to the place under the mistletoe. Charles took David from his father.

"You have made this first year of our marriage the happiest year of my life. Thank you for making me your husband." Ewan placed his hands on Caroline's cheeks and bent his head. Caroline wrapped her arms around his waist and gave herself up to the kiss.

Hugh discovered there was something in his eye and quickly wiped it away, noting that he was not the only one who had experienced a sudden eye irritation.

"Oh," Mary softly sighed.

He tore his gaze from the amorous couple and looked at her. The longing he saw in her eyes had him swallowing the lump which had formed in his throat. She too wiped away tears.

"You have such a loving family," she said, turning to him.

Hugh studied her face for a moment. How many times had he seen that same look on Mary's countenance as she brought him toast and coffee? It was there every time she had encouraged him to study a little later, to make his university paper better.

And until this moment, he had not understood it. A bolt of sudden awareness hit him.

He was not alone in wishing for love.

He stayed close to Mary for the rest of the evening, ensuring she was included in all the family celebrations. He forced himself to maintain the faint smile on his face, with the result that by the time he retired for the night his cheeks hurt.

Once back in his room, the smile swiftly disappeared. He sent his valet away, unable to maintain his polite manner for a single minute longer.

The past few days had been a slow and uncomfortable revelation of how poorly he had treated Mary. While all the time she had looked at him with love and longing in her eyes, he had been more concerned with his studies and his career. He had kept her at arm's length.

She deserved better than the mere thanks he had given her every time she had shown him kindness. And she should have received far more from him than the occasional "sorry" after her father's death. Little wonder she had kept such an important issue as the loss of her home from him when he had shown so little regard for her feelings. He had made a mockery of the word *love*.

He looked down at his kilt, running his fingers along the lines of the tartan. The blue and black had been proudly taken back up by the family as soon as the ban on wearing tartan had been lifted. His hand dropped to his side; he was unworthy to wear the plaid.

Mary had a whole new winter wardrobe thanks to his need to assuage his guilt, but it was not enough. She should be wearing the Strathmore family tartan.

"I'll be damned if you are not wearing the plaid come Hogmanay night."

Now he just had to figure out a way to get Mary to understand that she held his heart, and that from now on, she would always come first.

Chapter Thirteen

Mary wondered if she could ever be comfortable in the freezing Scottish winter.

As soon as she and Hugh left the protection of the high castle walls the following morning and headed onto the lower slopes of Strathmore Mountain, the wind attacked them. Its cruel fingers pinched her face and bit through to her bones.

The chilly weather, however, was only one of her problems. The other was the odd mood which she discovered Hugh was in the moment she met him downstairs at breakfast that morning. His greeting for her was a terse "Good morning, Mary."

He'd barely acknowledged the rest of the family seated around the breakfast table, reserving his responses to their questions of him to one or two words at best.

Something was seriously amiss. She knew enough of him to know that he usually only became this taciturn during exams, and that was due to lack of sleep. But he was here, at home with his family, and he should be happy, not lost in a dark mood. She had only accepted his offer to take a stroll on the side of Strathmore Mountain so she could be alone with him and try to get to the bottom of what troubled him. She hoped he would confide in her.

"It's a brisk morning," she said, trying to lighten the mood but failing.

He nodded and gave her a curt, "Yes."

She followed him as he walked the narrow track which meandered along the side of the mountain. At one point, it broke into two sections. One track looked like it eventually became a bigger road which continued on and then disappeared to one side of the mountain. The other led up onto Strathmore Mountain.

When Hugh made to continue along the path which crossed the mountain, Mary stopped. If he wanted to share his foul mood with her, then she would rather it be somewhere warm.

He took a few more steps before he turned and look back at her. "Are you coming?"

"No. Not if you are going to be a misery guts for the duration of our walk. If I am going to freeze to death, I would prefer it was with a smile on my face. I don't know what is bothering you this morning, Hugh. If you don't tell me what is wrong, then I shall return to the castle, and you can keep your own company." Mary stood her ground. She knew her words were harsh, but her experience of Hugh was that sometimes he only responded to a gruff approach.

She nodded with some relief when his stiff shoulders slouched. Her words had reached him.

He walked back to her. "I'm sorry. I lay awake all night trying to resolve a problem. I'm still not sure if I have found the right solution."

"Try me. You know I am always someone you can turn to for advice," she replied.

A brittle hint of his usual self appeared on his face. "Yes, you are. That is another of your many wonderful traits, Mary. Though I am not so certain that you are the right person in whom I should confide, seeing as the problem concerns you."

She should have seen it coming. Hugh had held off on doing anything about the issue of the university and her living arrangements. But now, it appeared after speaking with his brother, he had come to the conclusion that there was little, if anything, he could do about it.

"You don't need to go into battle for me with the head of St John's College. You have your new appointment at St Martin-in-the-Fields to worry about. Just let things stay as they are," she replied.

He huffed in clear annoyance at her reply. "That matter is not yet settled, but it is not what vexes me this morning."

She waited. If there was one thing, she had in abundance from dealing with students all her life, it was patience. Bitterly cold, evil wind and all, she could stand on the side of a mountain and wait him out.

His gaze drifted from her to a nearby barn. He pointed toward it. "Let's at least get out of the wind so we can talk."

When the barn door closed behind them, Mary put a hand to her ears. Her winter bonnet had kept most of her head warm, but her poor ears were stinging. "Remind me to never complain about an English winter ever again. How do you people survive?"

"Actually, it is barely winter yet. Come January, the mountain will be lost under a thick layer of snow, and even the road into the village will become impassable at times," Hugh replied.

Mary found herself a nice pile of warm, dry straw on which to sit and plopped down on it. Hugh remained standing. After pulling off one of his gloves, he rubbed it over his face.

A chill of worry settled in her stomach. It was unusual to see Hugh in such a troubled state.

She patted the straw next to her. "Come and sit down. Tell me your troubles."

With an uncertain huff, he wandered over and dropped down beside her. "Alright. Here goes nothing."

He fell silent for a time. As the seconds stretched into minutes, Mary began to wonder if he had changed his mind about confiding in her. He startled her when he finally spoke again.

"You and I are friends, are we not?" he ventured.

"Yes. I hope so," she replied.

He was laying the ground for whatever difficult conversation lay ahead. Mary picked up a piece of straw and began to nervously wrap it around her finger.

"Well, I don't want us to be friends. I mean, not just friends."

"What do you mean?"

He moved to face her, taking her hand in his. "I want you to consider becoming my wife."

Under most any other circumstance she would have rejoiced at his words, but only disappointment stirred within. Hugh had obviously thought long and hard about her perilous situation and decided that the obvious solution was to offer her marriage.

In his world, it no doubt made perfect sense. They were already friends, and with his family's wealth at his disposal, he could offer her a life of security and comfort. Problem solved.

She would be mad not to seriously consider the offer, yet her heart demanded more.

"I see," she replied.

If she married Hugh, she would have a home, and likely a family in the years to come. She would no longer be alone in the world.

But she would be alone in her love for him.

"Will you at least consider it?" he said.

She shivered, the barn no longer holding the warmth it once had. Hugh's marriage proposal, if it could be considered as one, was as cold as the chill winds on the mountain.

She tried to console herself with the knowledge that many other people had practical marriages based purely on friendship. Many of those unions seemed to work.

The challenge she now faced would be deciding if she could spend the rest of her life with him knowing he would never feel anything more than a warm regard for her. Her love for him would remain unrequited.

"I may need some time," she replied. Mary got to her feet. A dull ache of sadness sat heavy in her heart. "You have never once shown me any indication of affection, so I am going to have to assume that your reasons for offering me marriage are purely practical ones. If so then mores the pity, because my father always said that a marriage created without any heat or passion to sustain it, would eventually falter when faced with the madness that life throws at us all," she said.

She headed for the door, leaving Hugh to sit on the straw and ponder her words. She could only pray that he had it in his heart to offer her more.

"I shall see you at supper," she said.

She slipped through the barn door and headed back to the castle.

Chapter Fourteen

As Mary disappeared, Hugh uttered a number of words that would get him thrown out of Sunday mass if anyone was to overhear them.

Mary, of course, was right. He had put as much emotion into his marriage proposal as he did when asking her for a cup of coffee. He should be counting his blessings that she had not given him a straight out *no* to his pathetic offer.

If his feeble attempt had been a university paper, he knew he would be pulling an all-night study session and resubmitting it in the morning. He could just imagine what the professor would have written on the front page in large black ink.

"D minus, lacking in effort. See me after class," he muttered.

His brother's words now came back to haunt him.

He should have been honest with her and confessed his love. If she didn't feel the same for him, then he would at least finally know the truth of where their relationship stood. But what if she did care for him? By not being brave and offering his heart, he risked never getting the chance to hear her tell him she loved him.

She couldn't be held to blame for choosing to protect her heart if she decided Hugh did not hold it in high enough regard. Love was precious.

He got to his feet. Mary hadn't said no, which was at least some small comfort. She had, however, made it clear that if he thought to marry her for the sake of convenience, he may not like her answer.

Opening the barn door, he stepped out into the fierce wind. He looked at the path which led up onto the mountain and nodded. If there was one thing the wild Scottish winter was good for, it was blowing some sense into a clouded mind. He pulled up the collar of his coat and headed up the track.

Chapter Fifteen

Hugh felt like he was treading on eggshells. Mary was polite, but cool whenever he tried to talk to her. It was a side of her he had not seen before, and if he was honest, it scared him just a little, yet it was also oddly encouraging.

If the rest of the family had noticed any difficulty between him and Mary, they were keeping it to themselves.

Toasting forks sat around the fireplace, along with a huge pot of tea. These were the nights Hugh treasured the most. Hogmanay, with its huge bonfires, whisky, and roasted wild boar was a wonderful experience, but nothing compared to the quiet evenings spent with his family in the lead up to the end-of-year celebrations.

I should have made the effort to come home last Christmas. I won't make that mistake again. And next year, I shall bring my wife with me.

Mary sat close by, nursing David on her lap. He was a bubbly little boy, full of life. He had a vocabulary of a good dozen words now, and each day he added new ones. Every time he looked at Caroline, he would point to her stomach and say "baby."

Hugh finished his first cup of tea, then stood and went to get another.

Ewan met him by the fireside. "So, can I take it from the frosty relations between the two of you that things are not going well on the wooing front?"

Hugh looked down at his empty cup. "I think I made a bit of a hash of things today, so yes things are not how I would like. I mentioned marriage and she said she would think about it."

Ewan winced. "Give yourself credit, dear brother. From the daggers that Mary is staring at you, I would suggest you have made a complete mess of things. But at least she didn't refuse you outright."

The mirth that he saw threatening on his brother's face did not help with Hugh's mood. "I am glad you find it amusing."

Ewan glanced over at Mary, then looked back. "I would hazard a guess that she is angry with you because you haven't gone about courting her in the right way, not because you asked her to marry you. You might want to question how you intend to woo her."

Standing on the side of Strathmore Mountain earlier that morning, Hugh had been blessed with the epiphany he so badly needed. If she was angry over the lack of romance he had shown during their encounter in the barn, it must have been because she expected him to woo her. And by wanting him to woo her, that meant she must feel something for him. He took that piece of insightful logic a step further—Mary being angry was actually a good thing.

Ewan gave him a brotherly pat on the shoulder and smiled. "Take heart from the knowledge that you are not the first of the Radley lads to have made a mess of their attempt to secure a wife. Now you just have to find a way to show her a different side of your relationship. One that takes things further than simply being friends, if you get my meaning?"

David's nursemaid came and took him from Mary. Ewan nodded as Caroline waved him over. "I shall see you in the morning."

Ewan escorted his wife from the room. Charles picked up a sleeping Will and led Adelaide and Lady Alison toward the stone steps, bidding everyone a good night as they departed.

Eventually only Hugh, Mary, and Aunt Maude were left. Aunt Maude was fast asleep in a high-backed chair in front of the fire, her hands resting gently in her lap.

Hugh decided it was time to make another attempt to speak to Mary. He rose from his seat and came to stand in front of her. "May I join you?"

Mary looked up, then across to Aunt Maude.

Hugh followed her gaze. "Don't worry about Maude; she always falls asleep in front of the fire. She sleeps the sleep of the dead. Her maid and a footman will eventually come to escort her upstairs."

He needed time to talk to Mary, so he was happy to let sleeping aunts lie.

He took a seat on the sofa next to Mary. "I must apologize for this morning. It was thoughtless of me."

"Yes, it was. Perhaps we might be better off if we forget about it completely," she replied.

"No. I don't want us to forget about it. I want another chance. Give me the days until Hogmanay to show you what really does lie between us. If your answer after that is no then I will accept it," he said.

She looked at him, and he was dismayed to see sadness in her eyes. She wasn't angry with him; she was hurt.

He took hold of her hand, relieved when she did not pull away. "Please."

"Yes, Hugh. You have until New Year's Eve, but I am not sure if that will make any difference." Mary rose from the sofa. "I need to go to bed now. It's been a long day."

He followed her as she headed toward the steps which led up to the private family apartments. "Mary, wait," he said.

She stopped and turned. Hugh pointed to the mistletoe hanging overhead.

She shook her head. "I think we will need more than a little old-fashioned Christmas magic."

Hugh came to her side and leaned in to place a brief kiss on her cheek. "I am going to use all means at my disposal. If a little magic helps with my quest, then so be it."

Chapter Sixteen

Mary leaned back against the door of her bedroom and closed her eyes. She had taken a risk with Hugh and so far, it had worked. But to claim his heart, she knew she would have to hold her nerve steady.

Her fingertips touched the place on her cheek where he had kissed her. Two years and an unknown number of months she had waited for a kiss.

"It was a peck, but it's a start."

She had slyly watched him all evening, taking heart from his obvious discomfort at her holding him at arm's-length. While playing with David, she had seen Hugh speak to his brother. When Ewan ventured a look in her direction, their gazes met, and he had offered up the hint of a smile before turning back to Hugh. The Duke of Strathmore's silent approval gave her the encouragement she needed in order to stand her ground.

Hugh had asked for a few days to show her how well they would suit before expecting her answer to his proposal. She could only hope that he felt enough for her to be able to manage more than a small kiss on the cheek.

"Come on, Hugh, don't fail me. Don't fail us."

The following day had an unexpected start for Mary. No one had mentioned that most of the menfolk would be out on the mountain hunting wild boar for the better part of the day. Hugh had gone with the hunting party when it set out at first light and not returned until supper.

Mary had spent the day with the Radley women, making more juniper bundles. By the time supper came around, her aching fingers had her wishing never to see another bundle of juniper in her life.

It was late when Mary and Hugh finally got a moment alone. Everyone else, except Aunt Maude, had retired to bed. Maude was in her usual spot in front of the fire, fast asleep.

Hugh, seated in the chair opposite to Mary, was nursing a badly bruised leg from the hunt.

"What did you do exactly?" she asked, pointing at his leg.

He huffed. "Nothing heroic unfortunately. I tripped over a branch on the mountain and landed heavily. I don't know which is more bruised: my leg or my pride. The rest of the hunting party had a grand laugh when they saw me go head over heels into the heather."

"I could rub some comfrey cream into it if you like," she offered, trying not to laugh.

Hugh smiled warmly, reflecting the amusement she knew was on her own face. He rose from the chair and came to sit beside her.

An awkward silence settled between them for a moment before he finally spoke. "I know why I fell over this morning; I was busy thinking about you and not looking where I was going. To be honest, I have been thinking a lot about you since we left England."

He reached out and took hold of her hand. She shuddered as he raised it to his lips and kissed her palm. Their gazes met.

"My brother thinks you are in love with me. He says he has watched you and your eyes rarely leave me when we are in the same room. I thought he was mistaken, but I watched you tonight, and I think he might be right," he said.

"And?" Mary prayed his answer would be a swift one—if she held her breath for any longer, she may faint.

"And I need to know if you do feel something for me, because I have to tell you, my affections toward you are not those merely of a friend. They haven't been for some time," he said.

It was a good thing that they were seated away from the fireplace, as the whoosh of air which left her lungs would surely have threatened to put out the flames.

"You . . . you love me?" A trickle of a tear rolled down her cheek. The love she saw shining in his eyes threatened to bring on more tears.

"Yes, Mary, I do love you," he whispered. He speared his fingers into her hair and drew her to him, placing a searing kiss on her lips. The heady scent of his cologne, the same one she had gifted him, filled her senses.

Their tongues met in a soft dance. Every kiss he offered invited her to respond—to show her love for him. Mary was determined to hold nothing back.

Aunt Maude stirred in her chair.

They released one another from the kiss and sat with their foreheads touching while they both regained their breath.

A shy smile sat on Mary's face. "I love you, Hugh. I always have."

He took hold of her hands. "I was a fool not to have spoken my heart to you a long time ago. I promise I won't ever hold my love from you again."

Aunt Maude grumbled in her sleep and yawned.

Hugh cast his eye in her direction, then looked back at Mary.

"Come with me." He took her by the hand and led her toward the steps. When they arrived under the mistletoe, he stopped.

Mary waited, expecting another soft, chaste kiss on the cheek.

"We don't need magic, but I think we should still avail ourselves of it just to be sure." He let out a growl before pulling her to him, swiftly taking her lips in another kiss which was anything but chaste. She clung to him as he plundered her mouth, meeting his hungry need with her own.

When he finally released her from the kiss, he held her close. His eyes burned bright with desire—desire she knew was for her.

"I can walk you to your room and we can say good night, or you can come with me and we can greet the dawn together. Either way, we will be making an announcement tomorrow morning," he said, his voice gruff with barely restrained passion.

Mary nodded. "The dawn sounds perfect." She placed her hand in his and they walked from the great hall.

As they disappeared up the steps, Lady Maude Radley rose from her chair. She crossed to the sofa where Hugh and Mary had been sitting. From behind one of the cushions, she retrieved a sprig of mistletoe. She held it up and softly chuckled.

"Old-fashioned Christmas magic always goes a long way."

Chapter Seventeen

Hugh and Mary stole into his private apartment, and Hugh locked the door behind them. He pulled her into his embrace again and kissed her with the urgency and passion she sensed he had barely held in check back in the great hall.

"Are you sure you want to be here with me tonight? I will understand if you wish to wait," he said.

Matters between them were moving fast but Mary had lain awake too many nights, imaging what she would do if she was ever given the chance to lie with Hugh, to even consider holding back at this pivotal moment.

Laying her hands on his stubbled cheeks, she drew him to her, and placed tender, inviting kisses on his lips. "I have waited long enough for you, Lord Hugh Radley. Tonight, you become mine."

"And you mine. But first thing's first," he said, releasing her hands.

Hugh crossed to the tallboy which sat in the corner of his room and opened the top drawer. Mary took a deep breath and prayed that if this was indeed a dream, she would never wake from it.

He returned, stealing a warm kiss from her.

"We have to do this properly," he said. With her hand held in his, he went down on bended knee. "I can be blind to some things at times; it is a fault in my nature. But my love for you has always been there, and always will be. You know my shortcomings better than anyone. And as my partner in this life, I empower you to take me to task if you ever feel that I am being anything less than fully supportive of you," he said.

With a wry grin, Mary nodded. "I shall hold you to that, Hugh Radley."

"Good. Mary Margaret Gray, I love you and want to spend the rest of my life with you. Will you do me the greatest honor possible and become my wife?"

There were a dozen other words she could have used at that moment, including *finally* and *about time*, but her heart was so full of love for the man who knelt before her that Mary could only think of one. "*Yes.*"

He got to his feet and slipped a diamond ring on her finger. The oval-shaped stone was set in gold with a delicate filigree pattern etched into it. It was perfect in its elegance and simplicity. Hugh knew her better than she realized.

"Edinburgh has some fine jewelers as well as clothing stores," he whispered.

"Oh, Hugh."

And she had thought he'd only been worried about keeping her warm. The wicked man had been planning to ask her to marry him all along.

She looked down at the ring and sighed. "This is the most beautiful Christmas gift anyone could ever receive. Thank you."

Hugh slipped his hand around her waist. "The ring is a betrothal gift, my love. I have something else planned for my fiancée for Christmas Day, but you will have to wait."

He was the most handsome, wonderful, and at times infuriating man she had ever met, but she would not have exchanged him for anyone else. Hugh Radley was exactly the man for her.

She wiped away a tear, then, emboldened by his declaration of love, she stole one kiss. Then another. By the time she was ready for a third touch of his lips, Hugh had tightened his grip about her waist and pulled her hard against him. His low growl of need set her heart racing.

Until now, her private fantasies of this moment had been enough to keep her satisfied. With his heated touch, her desire raced to a dangerous level.

He stepped back from her, and with what she imagined was an unintended overly dramatic flourish, tore his scarf from his neck. With the mixture of nerves and the humor of his look, she snorted a laugh. He raised an eyebrow in her direction as he tossed the scarf on a nearby sofa. His jacket quickly followed.

"Your turn," he murmured.

Mary looked at Hugh's clothes laying in a pile. Seeing them now brought home the reality of the situation. She was tempted to pinch herself; this was really happening. Never had she dared to imagine that her secret dreams of being with him would come to fruition. Now they were.

A worried look appeared on his face when she didn't move. For her, this moment was more than a simple physical encounter. Her love for him ran to her very soul.

She held out a hand and was reassured when he took it and drew himself closer once more. "Hugh," she murmured, offering up her mouth to his. He nipped at her bottom lip, teasing. She nipped him back, her breath shuddering.

No longer needing any invitation, she placed her hands on his face, drawing him down to her. Their mouths locked in a fiery embrace, tongues tangled. It was a wicked dance.

When she finally released him from the kiss, Mary knew the time had come. Time for her to follow his lead.

With a deft shrug, she let her wool shawl fall to the floor. She resisted the temptation to follow Hugh's example and toss it away. She had a terrible throwing arm and the shawl was more likely to end up in the fireplace than on the sofa. She kicked it safely aside.

After sliding a finger under the top of her gown sleeve, she pulled it down. Her intention of revealing a hint of shoulder failed miserably in the attempt. The sleeve wouldn't budge. She silently rued the sensible nature of Scottish clothing. They both chuck

"You may have to help me with the fastenings," she said.

He turned her to face away from him, then began to undo the ties on the back of her gown. For every knot he untied, he placed a kiss on the nape of her neck. Mary shivered with anticipation.

"For my sake, you might want to have a word with your maid about how tight she ties these laces. This could take a while."

When she was finally free of her binds, Mary stepped out of her gown. Hugh rewarded her with yet another kiss.

His shirt was next to go. Mary made quick work of the button at the top and watched with bated breath as she got her first glimpse of his hair-dusted chest.

She lay a hand over his heart, feeling its steady beat. A heart she knew beat for her. "You are the most . . ."

He brushed a hand on her cheek as she stood, lost for words. Hugh lifted his shirt free from the top of his kilt and pulled it over his head.

With his bare torso and striking blue and gray kilt, he looked for all the world like a rugged Scottish highlander—one she was hoping would soon ravish her. He took hold of the buckle of his belt and gave her another saucy grin.

He took his hand away and she mewed with disappointment. Her elusive prize remained hidden under layers of heavy wool. When he met her eyes, she saw all humor had disappeared from his face.

"I want you to do this; that way, you are in control. Nothing happens from this moment on without your express permission," he said.

She lay her trembling fingers on the buckle of his belt. His words were perfect in their reverence. They would have a lifetime of knowing each another, but there would only ever be one first time. A moment to treasure always.

She looked deep into his piercing blue eyes as she separated the leather belt from the buckle and dropped it to the floor. His kilt quickly followed.

Her gaze drifted lower, taking in the sight of Hugh in all his splendor. She sucked in a hesitant breath. She knew enough from overhearing the not-so-scholarly discussions in the meals hall at college to understand the state of his manhood and what it meant.

He wanted her.

"May I?" he asked, taking hold of the sides of her shift.

"Please."

As her shift joined the rest of the scattered garments on the floor, Mary resisted the instinctive reaction to cover herself. She was about to become his woman; this moment demanded full honesty between them. She let her hands fall to her sides.

"Come," he said, offering her his hand.

Hugh drew her to the bed and pulled back the covers before laying her down on the soft linen sheets. He soon joined her, rolling over so that they faced one another. She shivered as he reached out and cupped one of her breasts. Her whole world tilted as Hugh bent his head and, drawing a nipple into his mouth, gently nipped at it with his teeth.

"Oh, my sweet . . ." she murmured.

She clutched at the bedclothes as he slipped a finger into her heat and began to stroke. He sucked hard on her nipple, and Mary whimpered. The torture was exquisite.

When he finally released her nipple from his masterful attention, he rose over her, and gave her a kiss that made her toes curl.

She groaned as he slipped a second finger into her, and when his thumb began to rub against her sensitive bud, she sobbed. Her need for release built with every stroke.

"Is that good? Tell me if you want me to change anything. I can go harder or deeper; I am at your command," he said.

"Don't stop," Mary pleaded.

"I love you," he said.

She was beyond words at this moment, unable to reciprocate his declaration, consumed by the driving need to find her sexual release.

He slowed his strokes and murmured in her ear. "I want you come, but I need to be inside you when you do."

She opened her eyes as he released her from his touch. He moved between her legs, his hard erection brushing the side of her inner thigh.

"This may sting for a second, but I need you to stay with me. As soon as your body accepts me, I will make it enjoyable again," he said.

Placing the bulk of his weight on one arm, he lowered himself over her before slowly parting her slick folds with his cock. Mary winced at the sensation of Hugh stretching her and held her breath.

He stilled, patiently waiting for her body to adjust. The discomfort eased and she slowly breathed out.

"Does it still hurt?"

"No," she replied.

He began to move within her, slowly at first then quickening as his strokes deepened. With her hands gripping either side of his hips, she urged him on. The tension began to build within her once more. Her need to reach the peak came with every one of his thrusts. His groans of pleasure added to her own.

She crashed through on the end of one of his deep and powerful thrusts, sobbing his name as she came. Hugh buried his face into the base of her neck. She felt the nip of his teeth on her skin before he let out a shout. He shuddered, then collapsed on top of her, pressing her into the mattress.

Mary wrapped her arms and legs around him and held him to her, promising to herself that she would never let this man go.

Chapter Eighteen

"Is that everything?"

Hugh looked inside the basket Mary held in her hands, pointing at each of the items. "Bread, blackbun, and salt for food. A bottle of whisky for your host's good health... Oh, I forgot the coin." He opened his sporran and pulled out a gold coin. "This is for wealth. This is a pistole; the last of the coins minted for Scotland."

He dropped it into the basket, stealing a kiss from his wife in the process. "Now you are ready."

The love she saw shining in his eyes was the same she had beheld on Christmas Eve as she and Hugh had stood facing one another to speak their marriage vows in the castle chapel. Ewan had escorted her down the aisle to the tune of a single bagpipe, beaming as he placed her hand in Hugh's.

The Radley family had, of course, been delighted when a sheepish Hugh and Mary appeared at breakfast the morning after spending their first night together and announced their betrothal. Master Crowdie had overseen a flurry of activity in the castle and village, which saw Hugh and Mary married that same day.

Aunt Maude gave the bride a family heirloom wedding band, which matched Mary's engagement ring to perfection. The Duchess and Dowager Duchess of Strathmore presented Mary with a blue woolen gown and a matching Strathmore tartan sash and shawl. Mary Radley was now one of the family.

It was New Year's Eve, Hogmanay in Scotland, and in a break with tradition, Mary had been chosen to conduct the ancient First Foot ceremony.

Earlier in the evening, she and Hugh had led the castle staff down to the village and shared a hot supper with them. Her welcome into the Strathmore Castle and village family had been so heartfelt that she'd felt close to tears at many moments during the day. Only Hugh's constant presence—he was never far from her—kept her from dissolving into a weeping mess.

Master Crowdie strode into the village tavern with a large brass bell in his hand. A hush fell over the gathering before he swung the bell high and rang it loudly. He then turned and marched out the door.

Hugh offered Mary his arm and they followed. A happy, chatting group of villagers took up the rear. Flaming torches held on spikes were dotted along the road to light the way back to the castle.

Walking arm in arm with her husband, Mary felt sure of her future, and thanks to her trusty tackety boots, also of her footing. Her Strathmore tartan shawl kept the bitter night wind at bay.

As they crossed over the drawbridge and into the castle bailey, a loud cheer rose from the assembly. Hugh smiled at her. "The cheers are for you, my love."

They waited until everyone from the village had arrived and gathered around them in the courtyard. Master Crowdie pulled out his pocket watch and checked it. He nodded toward Mary. Hugh let go of her arm and stood back, a huge smile of pride on his face.

She gave him one last nervous look, then climbed the steps of the keep. A hush descended on the crowd. All eyes were fixed on Master Crowdie.

He held his hand up and then dropped it to his side. The bells in the village church began to peal. The castle chapel bell rang in time. The crowd looked to where Mary stood on the steps of the castle keep.

She took hold of the door knocker and raised it before hitting it hard on the wood. The knock echoed in the still night air.

She did it a second time, and then a third.

After the third knock, the door of the keep slowly opened. Ewan Radley stood in the doorway, a glass of whisky in his hand.

Mary cleared her throat. "A happy new year and good tidings to you and yours," she said.

She handed him the basket, and Ewan gave her the glass of whisky in exchange. He stepped back and she crossed the threshold. Inside the great hall, all the Radley family, her family, were gathered. The heady scent of burnt juniper filled her nostrils.

Ewan shrugged. "Evil spirits only leave if you burn enough juniper to have everyone's eyes watering."

At the sound of steps on the stone flagging behind her, she turned and saw Hugh race in the door, just ahead of the rest of the castle staff and villagers. He grabbed hold of the door and after swinging it fully open, stood and held it for the crowd which quickly filed through.

The great hall was filled with lit torches, and on the first table was a mass of cups—all full of whisky from the look of it. One by one, the villagers took up a cup. Then, with their whisky untouched, they stood back and waited.

When every last cup of whisky had been taken, Ewan Radley climbed up on one of the roughly hewn wooden tables. Master Crowdie held up his hand once more. Silence descended on the great hall.

The Duke of Strathmore was about to speak.

Chapter Nineteen

"Wylcome to you all, this most special of days. May the new year find you blessed by good fortune and good health," he said.

Some of the younger members of the gathering went to raise their cups to drink, but a growl from Master Crowdie had those same cups quickly lowered.

Ewan shook his head, a smile still on his lips. "Now some of you may have noticed that our First Foot tonight was indeed a woman. But she is of dark hair and also a member of the Radley family, so I think the sprits of Hogmanay will forgive my trespass," he said.

Hugh caught a sideways glance at his new bride. Mary's eyes shone bright with happiness. The touch of her fingers met his, and he leaned in and brushed a soft kiss on her cheek. A soft "ah" rippled through the gathering.

"I see I am going to have to make this a short speech," Ewan added, looking directly at his brother.

Hugh grinned back at him. He was a newlywed, and that entitled him to a healthy degree of leeway.

"As I was saying, my family and I welcome you all to our home tonight. And to Mary, a special welcome on the occasion of not only your first Hogmanay, but your first as my brother Hugh's wife. Thank you for your First Foot gifts; we shall put them to good use. To the rest of the Strathmore family, I am both honored and humbled to serve as your laird. I raise my glass to you and yours. May the new year be a good one and your health stay hearty. *Slainte!*"

"*Slainte!*"

The sound of cups and glasses being clinked together echoed through the great hall, followed by loud cheers of "Happy New Year!"

With the formalities over, Hugh pulled Mary into his arms and gave her the kiss he had been aching to give to her all evening. Her soft lips met his as she melted into his embrace. Holding her in his arms was as natural as breathing

"Happy New Year, Husband," she said.

"Happy New Year, my wife, my love," said Hugh.

Waking up beside her that morning had been a gift beyond words. He'd been humbled when she had welcomed him into her arms, and they'd made love. With the new year would come a new life for the both of them. Knowing that every day he would be blessed with her love had him lost for words.

"Come," she said.

He let her lead him over to where the mistletoe still hung.

"I love you," she said, wrapping her arms around his neck.

Hugh did the only thing a newlywed man could do. He pulled his wife into his arms and, ignoring the cheers of the crowd, kissed her senseless.

With his loving wife to support him, Hugh Radley did make a success of his career in the Church of England, rising to one of its highest positions of rank, eventually becoming the Bishop of London.

And every year he, along with Mary and their children, would arrive at Strathmore Castle a few days before Christmas, bringing with them a red box.

Inside that box would be a perfect branch of mistletoe, ready to weave its magic.

The End

About Sasha

Born in England, but raised in Australia, Sasha has a love for both countries. Having her heart in two places has created a love for travel, which at last count was to over 55 countries. A travel guide is always on her pile of new books to read.

Her first published novel, Letter from a Rake was a finalist for the 2014 Romantic Book of the Year. Sasha lives with her husband, daughter and a cat who demands a starring role in the next book. She is always seeking new hiding spots for her secret chocolate stash.

Sasha's novels are set around the Regency period in England, Scotland, and France. Her books are centered on the themes of love, honor, and family.

You can find details of her work at
www.SashaCottman.com

Must Love Majors

By

Samantha Grace

He longs for the past...

Major Phillip Rowland has one objective when he returns from war, retreat to the country with his dog—which is quite impossible when a debutante has kidnapped him. Determined to rescue his pet, Phillip charges into a Christmas house party only to discover he's intruded on a private marriage mart. When unexpected events leave him stranded at the party, Phillip is confronted with the truth. He doesn't know how to rejoin a world where he no longer feels he belongs.

She is his hope for the future...

Lady Ambrosia Everly promised to select a husband by Christmas, but a certain major has become a major distraction since his arrival at Everly Manor. She knows nothing about warfare, but the man should prepare for the fight of his life if he thinks she will surrender her beloved dog. When the lines between enemies and lovers become blurred, however, Ambrosia faces her own personal battle. Should she give her heart to the major or marry a man of her parents' choosing?

Chapter One

Everly Manor, Kent
2 December 1816

It had been one year, seven months, and ten days since Cupid's arrows had struck Lady Ambrosia Everly. As her eldest sister Mercedes was fond of saying, 'Love finds you when you least expect it.' For Ammie, love had found her in an alley behind Madame Delannoy's fashionable London dress shop—or more aptly, she'd found *him*.

"There's my Mr. Perky," she cooed as a footman escorted her beloved into the cozy drawing room. "I missed you, Perky Poo. Yes, I did. Yes, I *did*."

Her sisters groaned when she abandoned their game of whist to shower her sweetheart with affection, scratching behind his ears and making smooching noises with her mouth. Mr. Perkins, her adorable whisky-colored springer spaniel, wagged his stubby tail and licked her face as if they had been separated for weeks instead of fifteen minutes.

"Ew!" Calliope, Ammie's youngest sister, crinkled her pert nose in disgust. The light dusting of freckles sprinkled across the bridge of her nose and cheeks made her appear even younger than thirteen. "Do you have any idea where that dog's mouth has been today?"

"Of course she doesn't," Octavia said. "She has no idea where Sir Edmund's mouth has been either, but I'll wager she will grant him a kiss under the mistletoe all the same."

"Quiet, you pests." Ammie laughed softly and ruffled Mr. Perkins's ears. He flashed her a grin like only a dog could—mouth open, brown eyes sparkling.

Ammie's twin sister piped up from across the table, "You must admit the youngsters make good points."

"Aren't you supposed to be on my side?" Ammie asked.

Laurel smiled and shrugged.

Octavia leaned toward Ammie and lowered her voice. "We want details afterward. Sir Edmund looks like a marvelous kisser."

"Pardon?" Their mother glanced up from the book she was reading on the green velvet sofa.

"I barely know Sir Edmund, Mama." Ammie kicked her sister under the table. Octavia grunted and laughed. "I have no intention of allowing him to kiss me."

"Mm-hmm." Mama narrowed her eyes. "Should I remind you and Laurel what is considered proper behavior before the guests arrive for the house party?"

"No, Mama," Ammie and her twin said in unison. They could have saved themselves the trouble of answering, because once again their mother launched into 'The Dreaded Dressing Down', as Octavia had dubbed the tiresome lecture.

"No man shall be allowed liberties until *after* he has proposed. And you two"—Mama wagged her finger toward Octavia and Calliope—"what are the rules?"

"We are not to venture from our governess's side for any reason," the youngest girls recited in monotone voices.

"It appears you were listening after all." Their mother returned to her reading, her dark blonde brow arching in amusement. "No need to look glum, girls. Your brothers are under similar instructions for the coming Christmas festivities."

"Four more years of lectures," Octavia muttered. "How will I ever survive?"

Ammie chuckled. "You will endure. You always do."

She leaned down to kiss the top of the spaniel's head once more before retrieving her cards from the table.

"Thank you for taking Mr. Perkins outside," she said to the footman standing by awaiting further orders.

"He's a right good dog, he is." Charlie attempted to maintain decorum by standing up taller when addressed, but a beaming smile broke across his face. "It be my pleasure to take Mr. Perkins for a walk, milady."

"It *is* my pleasure," Mama corrected without looking up. "Proper grammar is not optional, Charlie. A footman is a reflection of his employer."

Charlie dropped his head, blushing. "Yes, milady."

"Pleasure or not," Ammie said, attempting to temper the young man's embarrassment, "I am grateful to you for taking Mr. Perkins outside in my stead. Octavia and Calliope threatened to riot if I left before finishing the game." Ammie tossed a card on the table when it was her turn.

"Only because we are *winning*." Laurel reached to tweak their baby sister's plump cheek, and Calliope smacked her hand away.

"Stop it! You are ahead because you cheat."

"It isn't cheating if Ammie and I are able to read each other's minds," Laurel teased. "It is the gift of being twins."

Fire flashed in Calliope's brown eyes. The poor girl was terribly easy to rile. She slapped her cards on the table and jutted her chin. "You are a cheat *and* a liar. Ammie told me there is no gift."

"Girls."

Their mother nailed Ammie's sisters with an imperious glower then flicked her gaze toward the footman. The message was clear. *No arguing when the help is present.*

Laurel and Calliope snapped their mouths closed and dutifully lifted their cards.

Octavia, seemingly untroubled by the bickering or their mother's reprimand, tapped her finger against the table. "It is your turn to lead."

Ammie selected a card and addressed Charlie. "Mr. Perkins appears content for the moment." Her pampered dog had already made a bed by the fire and was softly snoring. "You may leave him with me and return to your duties."

"Yes, milady."

Once the servant had gone, Laurel cocked her head. Her sable hair slid over one shoulder in a silky waterfall. "You don't seem particularly enthused by the prospect of seeing Sir Edmund again."

No one who met Laurel and Ammie believed they were twins. They looked nothing alike. Out of ten offspring, Ammie was the only one to inherit her maternal grandmother's green eyes and auburn hair. For the longest time, her older brothers tried to convince her that gypsies had left her in a basket on Everly Manor's doorstep. Sometimes, she'd believed them.

"I am optimistic but cautious when it comes to the gentleman."

Sir Edmund was an uncommonly handsome man with golden hair, a regal nose, and eyes as pale blue as the winter sky, but she'd only made his acquaintance at the end of the Season. A week wasn't long enough to know if she wanted to spend the rest of her life with him.

Ammie won the hand and swept the cards into a pile. "Sir Edmund must earn Mr. Perkins's approval before he wins my heart."

Laurel tsked. "I pity any man who believes he can usurp that dog's place in your heart."

"I cling to my scruples," Ammie said with a shrug.

"How noble."

While Ammie would never actually favor Mr. Perkins over a husband, she did believe how a man treated animals revealed his true character. She cut her gaze toward Mama and lowered her voice. "It would be best if my future husband recognized his place sooner, rather than later. Wouldn't you agree?"

"Only if he values his manhood," Octavia said.

Calliope giggled into her cards.

There had never been a question about who ruled the household. Mama was queen and Papa, her loyal subject. Any man brave enough to marry into the family would have quite the battle ahead if he attempted to dethrone the Marchioness of Seabrook.

Ammie and her sisters were nearing the end of their game when their father stalked into the room with a sheet of paper in his hand.

"There you are," he said to Mama without greeting anyone in the room. "Do you recall Lord Grandstern's son, Major Phillip Rowland?"

Mama closed her book and set it aside. "I seem to recall Lord Grandstern has two sons commissioned in the Army. Which one is the major?"

"He is the older of the two." Papa joined Mama on the sofa. "Phillip Rowland is with the King's Hussars. His regiment was deployed to Spain and later he fought in the Battle of Waterloo. The 13th and 15th Regiments were responsible for driving back the *Cuirassiers*."

"A war hero? Impressive. Lord Grandstern must be very proud."

"Indeed." Papa sighed and passed what appeared to be a letter to Mama. "His hero status will only complicate matters, I fear."

Ammie was only half-listening while she dealt cards around the table. It wasn't unusual for her parents to have lengthy conversations about people she had never met, and eavesdropping rarely proved interesting. She and her sisters played through the hand and counted points at the end.

Octavia scribbled the numbers on a piece of paper and calculated the total score. "For heaven's sake, Calliope." She dropped the pencil on the table. "You overestimated your hand, and they beat us again."

Their youngest sister puffed up, sputtering. "It-it's not *my* fault. They cheat. I know they do."

Her accusation wasn't true. Ammie doubted Calliope believed it herself, but her pride had been stung. Since Ammie had always been partial to her baby sister, she offered to partner with her next time. This seemed to mollify Calliope, and she stacked the cards, neatly lining up the edges.

Mama and Papa were whispering together as Ammie and her sisters dispersed to pursue individual interests. Ammie whistled for Mr. Perkins, but he only opened his eyes briefly before closing them again.

"Are you being lazy, you pampered pooch?" She crossed to where he'd made his bed and crouched to pet him. "It is rather nice by the fire. I suppose I'll leave you to it then."

She stood and started toward the door.

"Stay for a moment, Ammie," her mother said. "This matter with Major Rowland concerns you."

Ammie frowned. "I don't see how. I have never met the man."

She hoped it wasn't another request to court her. She and Laurel had been inundated with offers during the Season, but Mama was shrewd at discerning the character and intentions of potential suitors and had insisted their father refuse the men.

Gold diggers and rakes are blights upon Society and do not deserve a wife of quality. How many times had she heard Mama repeat this sentiment? The occasions were too numerous to count. Mercedes's husband hunt had played out similarly. Her eldest sister hadn't received an acceptable offer until her second Season.

Her father abandoned his place on the sofa. "Perhaps you should have a seat next to your mother, love."

The dire looks on her parents' faces elicited a trickle of unease beneath her skin. Her legs trembled as she lowered to the sofa.

"What is wrong, Mama? Please, put an end to my worries."

Her mother cleared her throat. "Darling..."

Ammie's alarm multiplied. Her mother didn't use endearments freely. Something was very wrong.

"Major Rowland's letter states he has a claim to Mr. Perkins. He possesses a bill of sale to prove ownership." Mama reached for her hand while Ammie's heart threatened to beat through her breastbone. "Dearest, the major wants his dog returned."

Her mother's words made no sense. Mr. Perkins was Ammie's dog. She had cared for him for over a year. She adored him.

"The major is mistaken," she said. "I found Mr. Perkins in the alley. The dog was starving and scared, and his fur hadn't been tended for weeks. I *saved* him, Mama. If the major had any love for animals, Mr. Perkins would not have been in the state he was in."

"Ammie," Papa said, "you must realize not everyone's love for animals matches your own. Mr. Perkins is a hunting dog. I am certain the major paid handsomely for him. The spaniel looks as if he comes from good stock."

"Can we purchase Mr. Perkins from him?" Ammie appealed to her mother. "Use all of my pin money for next year if you must. Please, I cannot bear to part with him."

"I realize you have a soft spot in your heart for animals, Ambrosia."

"No, Mama, it is more than my love for animals. Mr. Perkins is..." Tears burned the backs of her eyes. How could she explain what the dog meant to her without sounding like a crackpot? "He is Mr. Perkins," she finished lamely.

In a home with ten children, Ammie often felt invisible—just another mouth to feed and body to clothe in the middle of the pack. She had never doubted her parents' love for her and her siblings, but their attention and approval was hard won with so many competing for it.

It was different with Mr. Perkins.

Whether she was away for one minute or an entire day, the dog was ecstatic to see her whenever she returned, as if he'd believed she would be gone forever. His adoration was unconditional and belonged to her alone.

"We tried to find his owner," Ammie said. "No one at the assemblies knew of anyone missing a dog. I've taken care of Mr. Perkins to the best of my ability, and he loves me. How can Major Rowland come forward now?"

Her father grunted. "The major was at war. You cannot fault the man for not knowing his dog was missing."

"No, of course not."

She bit her lower lip when it trembled and took a deep breath to calm her riotous emotions. When she had better control, she spoke.

"I understand that he couldn't have known Mr. Perkins was missing, but he should have made better arrangements for the dog. Mr. Perkins's keeper failed him, and he was in a sorry state when I found him. You know it is true."

Mama's tsk sounded sympathetic, but Ammie didn't want pity. She needed her mother to be the champion she had always been.

"You did wonders for the dog, Ambrosia," Mama said. "No doubt the major will be grateful to you, which might allow us to strike a bargain with him." Mama's face lost its motherly softness, and she was back to business once again.

"Seabrook, write to Major Rowland and invite him to join the Christmas house party. I am certain once the man realizes how happy the dog is with Ammie, he will agree to the sale. Good hunting dogs are easy enough to come by if one knows where to look." Mama turned to Ammie. "I will write to your Uncle Gunther and request that Major Rowland be allowed the pick of the litter when Gunther's hound whelps this year."

"Excellent suggestion, Lady Seabrook," Papa said. "No man in his right mind would turn down such an offer."

Mama lightly slapped her hands on her thighs and smiled. "There we go. We will offer Major Rowland a bargain he cannot resist, and all will be well."

Unable to contain her happiness and relief, Ammie launched from her spot at the opposite end of the sofa and threw her arms around her mother's neck. "Thank you, Mama. *Thank* you."

"Oh, Ambrosia. Really, such a fuss."

Despite her mother's scolding tone, she held on to Ammie just a little bit longer than necessary, once again spoiling the illusion that a cold heart resided beneath her hard exterior.

Chapter Two

Major Phillip Rowland paced Lord Seabrook's study, growing increasingly impatient with the marquess's tardiness. The entire affair annoyed him, from the ridiculous invitation he had received to attend the Seabrook's Yuletide party, to the guests' laughter filtering through the walls.

Phillip hadn't come to Everly Manor to frolic or make merry for the holiday, and he certainly hadn't agreed to participate in the private marriage mart the marquess and marchioness had arranged for their twin daughters. Had he known he would be intruding on such an affair, he would have ignored propriety and arrived to collect his dog earlier in the month without giving notice.

The muffled sound of a lively fiddle came from somewhere close. "God's blood," he mumbled.

After ten years of being surrounded by the men in his Regiment, he needed the quiet and solitude of home before rejoining them in Hounslow. He longed to take his springer spaniel on walks through the frozen meadow and relive simpler days, before he had lost good men on the battlefield.

He eyed the decanter of brandy and two glasses displayed on a small silver tray placed on the corner of the marquess's desk. It was tempting to pour a couple of fingers to dull his senses, but it was also unwise. Lord Seabrook's reputation as a shrewd negotiator preceded him. It was unlikely Phillip would be allowed to leave Everly Manor with Orion without it costing him something.

Someone cleared a throat behind him.

Phillip yelped and spun to face the intruder, instinctively raising his fists. A lovely young woman with the roundest, greenest eyes he'd ever seen stared back at him. They were ridiculously large for her delicate pixie-sized face.

He dropped his arms to his sides, belatedly realizing she posed no threat and feeling foolish.

"Faith," he said. "Sorry about the"—he lifted one fist briefly before dropping it again—"Uh, sorry."

She exhaled, laughing softly. Wispy strands of copper hair floated around her heart-shaped face. "Major Rowland, I presume?"

Behind her was a solid wall covered in gold leaf. The decor was excessive and vulgar, and the gold shimmered in the sunlight falling through the window like the entrance to a magical realm.

"You presume correctly. And what are you, some type of fairy appearing from thin air? Give her a spin, if you will?"

Her brow furrowed as if he spoke a different language, but she slowly twirled in a circle, keeping him within her sight.

"Hmm, very curious." He made a show of examining her from across the room. "I see no wings, therefore, I must conclude you were hiding here the whole time. Were you spying on me?"

"Yes, I was disguised as a plant, genius." She rolled her large expressive eyes, which was poorly done of her, but it was the most honest reaction he'd received since returning home.

Everyone at the club treated him as if they didn't know how to engage in normal conversation anymore. All they ever wanted to discuss was the war, and if one more person referred to him as a hero, he swore his head would explode. Even his family behaved differently. They had been treading too gingerly around him ever since he'd confronted his brother for being careless with Orion. Phillip was growing to despise being revered by strangers and his loved ones handling him like a powder keg.

The young woman knew who he was—she had called him by name—and she didn't care. Her refreshing approach improved his mood.

"Very well, wood nymph, I can play along." He maintained a respectful distance, certain she was one of Seabrook's daughters—possibly the one he sought. He sat on the edge of the marquess's desk, his legs stretched long and crossed at the ankles. "What is your name?"

She rolled her shoulders and stood taller. She was a nice height for a lady—not too short, not too tall. The perfect dancing partner for a man of above average height like himself. "You, sir, are addressing Lady Ambrosia Everly."

The thief herself. "I've come to understand you are in possession of my property."

Her expression soured. "Mr. Perkins cannot be owned," she snipped. "He is a wonderful, loving animal with feelings. How dare you insinuate—"

"Mr. Perkins? Good Lord, do not tell me you named him after the butler."

Her mouth opened and closed without any sound.

"You did, didn't you?" Phillip chuckled. "The dog cannot be owned, but he can be in service to the great Lady Ambrosia Everly. Is that how it is?"

"I did *not* name him after a servant. I named him after someone I admire." When he started to respond, she jabbed her finger in his direction. "Not the butler, although he is a good man in his own right. I've come to tell you I will not be surrendering Mr. Perkins, especially to the likes of you."

"The spaniel's name is Orion, and I haven't come to Everly Manor to ask your permission, little fairy." Phillip pushed away from the desk and came to stand inches from the precocious thief. Her round eyes flared even wider. "I chose him from a litter of six," he said, "and I paid the breeder's fee. That makes him mine."

Her hands landed on her hips, her face tipped toward him in challenge. "Well, Mr. Perkins chose *me*."

His proximity didn't appear to trouble her in the least while he quickly realized his mistake in coming too close. The scent of her soap reminded him of melted butter and honey on a warm piece of bread. It beckoned him to come closer, inviting him to stay a while. The scowl on her face, however, was far from welcoming and brought him to his senses.

Remember, she is the enemy. He retreated a few steps and returned her glower. "Orion is loyal to whomever feeds him. You are not special."

She snorted, clearly not believing him. "As far as I can tell, Major Rowland, you are unfit to own a dog."

"Unfit?" His laughter lacked humor. "I was second in command of a squadron, Lady Ambrosia. England is free of tyranny because of my men's bravery at Waterloo. I believe I am more than capable of being master to a dog."

"While I offer my gratitude for your honorable service, sir, I cannot applaud your efforts at arranging for Mr. Perkins's care while you were gone."

Phillip's chest tightened with indignation; he thrust it out. Although he was still angry with his brother for neglecting Orion, family loyalty came first. "I've done nothing to deserve the charge you level against me. I left my dog in my brother's care. Orion was in capable hands while I was abroad—at least he was until you *stole* him."

"Ha! Mr. Perkins was running the streets when I found him. He was as thin as any poor creature could be and still be alive. I rescued him, sir. I am not a thief."

Phillip narrowed his eyes. His older brother never would have allowed Orion to run free. If Phillip's precious dog had slipped out of the garden gate on his own while left unattended, Jeremy wouldn't have lied about it, would he? Phillip had thought they were past such silliness.

"I don't believe you," he said, stubbornly clinging to loyalty to his brother.

"It is true, Major," a feminine voice said behind him.

For the second time that day, Phillip was startled. He turned toward the study entrance, inwardly cringing when he spotted Lord and Lady Seabrook standing inside the threshold. The marchioness was a handsome woman with graying blond hair, broad shoulders, and the proud bearing of a warrior. Her icy glare could freeze a man's blood, and it was fixed on him.

"Ambrosia, your father and I said we would speak with the major on your behalf. How do you think it would appear if a guest stumbled across you and Major Rowland in a clandestine meeting?"

"I never agreed to a meeting with her," Phillip said.

Lady Seabrook sighed as if she were dealing with a child. "This is about appearances, Major Rowland, not intentions."

The marquess frowned but held his tongue. Phillip's father had told him Lord Seabrook was henpecked, but he was shoulder to shoulder with his wife—her partner. Together they formed a wall, blocking Phillip's escape.

Damnation.

If the little thief and trickster had set a trap to secure a husband, he'd charged straight into it. No more than a foot separated him and Lady Ambrosia. The scent of honey rose from her fragrant skin, lingering in the space between them. He ached to stand closer yet, because her scent reminded him of home, a place he'd dreamed of returning to for too long.

Lady Ambrosia sighed and lowered her head. "I'm sorry, Mama. My only thought was for Mr. Perkins."

"*Orion*," Phillip said through his teeth, quiet enough for Lady Ambrosia's ears alone.

Lady Seabrook addressed her daughter as if he weren't in the room. "I understand the dog means a lot to you, but if you wish to marry a man of your choosing, you must practice restraint. We can only do so much to protect you from opportunists."

"Opportunist? Now see here, madam. I-I am not—" Phillip snapped his mouth closed. He appeared to be on the verge of blustering. His father, the Earl of Grandstern, blustered. *He* did not.

"Oh, calm yourself," Lady Ambrosia muttered. "My mother wasn't referring to you."

She swept past him to claim a seat on an upholstered bench that was nestled into a nook created by two large bookshelves. Her peach skirts complimented the ivory velvet. "Please, may I stay for the negotiations, Papa?"

"I suppose there is no point in sending you away. You have a stake in the outcome." Lord Seabrook invited Phillip to sit in the chair closest to his desk while his wife joined Lady Ambrosia on the bench.

There were no negotiations to be had. Orion was Phillip's dog, and he wasn't leaving without the pooch. Nevertheless, he had promised his father that he would mind his temper and behave like a gentleman, even though neither had ever been a problem for him. His argument was Jeremy had been born of righteous anger, not a lack of self-governance.

Phillip accepted Lord Seabrook's invitation to sit, eager to have this business behind him. "Please allow me to extend my gratitude for the excellent care Orion received while I was abroad. I will have a stern word with my brother for his carelessness."

His gratitude was sincerely. When Phillip had returned to England to discover his beloved dog had been missing for over a year, he'd despaired of ever recovering him. He'd imagined all sorts of horrible fates befalling the dog, and his thoughts had promptly traveled back to the atrocities he had experienced on the Continent.

"How did you track the spaniel to our door?" Lord Seabrook's question mercifully jerked Phillip back to the present.

Lady Ambrosia fired another question his direction before he could answer her father. "How do you know Mr. Perkins is even yours?"

Her mother shushed her.

Phillip took a deep cleansing breath. Lady Ambrosia's judgmental tone vexed him to no end, but her inquiry was not without merit. "Does the dog have any unusual markings? Perhaps he is tricolored with copper eyebrows?"

Lady Ambrosia's own eyebrows shot up, answering his question.

"You walked him often when you were in London," he said.

"Every day."

"You were noticed, as was Orion."

Her cupid bow mouth puckered as if she wanted to correct him but suspected it was pointless. She was astute. To Phillip, the dog would always be Orion.

"I am not sure that explains how you traced the dog back to our daughter," Lord Seabrook said.

Phillip dragged his gaze from her lips. His disappointment at being interrupted was like an irritating itch he couldn't reach. He wished he and Lady Ambrosia were alone again to engage in verbal sparring without interference.

"My father would not like me sharing his secrets," Phillip said, focusing his attention on her father, "but you've asked a direct question, and I am an honest man."

Lady Ambrosia snorted softly. He refused to look in her direction.

"My father is a founding member of the Mayfair Secret Society of Sleuthhounds, my lord. The men use deductive reasoning and investigative skills to solve mysteries. The members were happy to assist me in locating Orion."

Lord Seabrook's eyes gleamed with interest. "A secret society of sleuthhounds? Are they accepting new members?"

His wife cleared her throat, loudly.

"Yes, well..." The marquess shuffled a few papers on his desk and stacked them with edges lined, avoiding eye contact with anyone. "We can discuss that later."

Lady Seabrook took control of the conversation. "Our daughter has become quite attached to the dog, and we fear her heart will be broken if you take him. We will purchase him from you."

"With all due respect, my lady, Orion is not for sale."

The marchioness straightened her spine and looked down her nose at him. "I am afraid you misunderstood, sir. You will allow us to buy *Mr. Perkins* or you will leave empty-handed. Either way, you are not taking the dog."

Her daughter gasped. "But Mama, what about Uncle Gunther's hounds? You said Major Rowland could have pick of whelps from the next litter."

Phillip gritted his teeth, finding it much harder to mind his manners than he had anticipated. "I. Want. *My*. Dog."

Lady Seabrook scoffed. "How can I recommend him to Gunther when he is completely irrational?"

"This is ridiculous." Phillip shoved out of the chair and straightened his jacket. "Bring me Orion, so I may be on my way."

Lord Seabrook sighed, squeezing his eyes closed and pinching the bridge of his nose. "Could everyone please take a moment to calm down? We needn't be hasty or make this process contentious. Major Rowland, will you allow us a few more moments of your time?"

Phillip was accustomed to delivering and receiving orders. Perhaps the novelty of being asked and having the freedom to decline held sway over him. He complied with the marquess's request and resumed his seat.

"Thank you." Lord Seabrook inclined his head. "You must forgive my wife for speaking out of hand. She is motivated by a mother's love. Our Ammie has grown attached to the spaniel, and we are exceedingly fond of our daughter."

Phillip slanted a glance toward the lovely thief. She had scooted to the edge of the bench and clasped her hands in her lap. Her peaches and cream complexion was paler and anxiety softly lined her forehead.

"What can I do to make this easier?" The question fell from Phillip's lips unbidden. His jaw twitched. He didn't want to feel sympathy for her, or anyone. *Faith*! He didn't want to *feel*.

"Allow Ammie a proper good-bye," Lord Seabrook said.

"Papa, no!" Lady Ambrosia bolted from the bench and came to her father's side. "Please, Papa. Don't allow him to take my dog."

Phillip suppressed the desire to remind her that she did not own Orion. Obviously, Lord Seabrook was a reasonable man who saw the wisdom in returning another man's property.

Lord Seabrook patted his daughter's hand where she was gripping his sleeve and murmured soothing words about trust. He seemed to have the right touch, because even though Lady Ambrosia still appeared miserable, she released his arm.

The marquess's smile was grim when he addressed Phillip. "Stay the night, enjoy the festivities, and allow our daughter to spend her last moments with the dog."

"It is the least she deserves after the excellent care she has given him," her mother piped up.

Phillip couldn't tear his gaze away from Lady Ambrosia's face or ignore the stabbing guilt in his gut when tears welled in her eyes.

"Very well," he said. "I will stay one night, but I want Orion returned tomorrow at dawn. We have a long journey ahead of us."

Chapter Three

After the meeting with Major Rowland, Ammie trudged back to her chambers. Heartache weighed her down, and even Papa's promise to resolve the issue did nothing to lift her spirits. Major Rowland seemed as unmovable as the walls surrounding the Tower of London.

She sighed as she pulled the bedchamber door closed behind her. Mr. Perkins popped up his head. He'd been napping at the foot of the bed when she'd left to ambush Major Rowland. The hidden passages behind the walls had allowed her to catch her enemy by surprise—not that it had given her the advantage she'd hoped.

She smiled at Mr. Perkins, her troubles forgotten for the moment. "Did I wake you, sweet boy?"

The dog jumped from his perch and came to greet her with his own smile, his little tail wagging with a swish.

"There's my sweet boy," she cooed as she bent to pet him.

Mr. Perkins flopped on his side, exposing his belly for scratching. Ammie knelt beside him to shower him with attention, the ache in her heart intensifying. This might be the last time he would come to greet her. She swiped at the dampness gathering in her eyes.

"I promised you a walk outdoors, didn't I?"

His ears twitched when he heard one of his favorite words, but he was enjoying the belly rub too much to move. The bedchamber door swung open and Laurel stepped inside, closing it softly behind her. She and Ammie shared a room and had all their lives. When the time came for either of them to marry, it would be hard separating from her twin.

"How was your talk with the major?" Laurel asked. "Is he allowing you to keep Mr. Perkins?"

The back of Ammie's throat thickened. She pressed her lips together, not trusting herself to answer lest she burst into tears.

"Law! He told you no?" Laurel dropped to her knees on the other side of Mr. Perkins and scratched behind his ears. "Did you tell him about Uncle Gunther's hounds?"

Ammie swallowed hard and nodded. "He only wants *his* dog."

"Surely you've ruined Mr. Perkins for hunting by pampering him as you have," Laurel said.

"I'm not certain Major Rowland cares."

Ammie's twin frowned. "I don't understand."

"Neither do I. Papa persuaded him to allow me one more night with Mr. Perkins, but I'm expected to surrender him tomorrow morning."

"Oh, Ammie. I am so sorry." Laurel nibbled her bottom lip, her gaze on the little dog. "Major Rowland must be fatigued from his journey. Perhaps he will reconsider after a good night's sleep."

Her sister's reassurance was like a gentle breeze to a flame, and hope flickered to life in her once more. "He did seem a bit surly. Perhaps you are right." She pushed up from the floor. "I promised Mr. Perkins a walk outdoors. Would you like to accompany us?"

"*Yes.*" Laurel half groaned, half laughed. "Anything to escape the crush for a while. Guests are still arriving by the hordes, and the neighbors are housing even more. Before long, we won't be able to move without tripping over each other. Should we invite William and Hugh? They have been annoying Julius and his friends all afternoon."

Their two younger brothers were notorious for getting into mischief when they grew bored. It was to everyone's advantage that the young men stay busy.

"Julius will owe us," Ammie said.

While Laurel retrieved their brothers, Ammie gathered her and Laurel's outerwear from the wardrobe. Perhaps her older brother could come to her aid. Julius rarely lost at cards. Was the major a gambling man? Would he dare to wager the little dog's papers? He didn't strike her as the undisciplined sort.

Ammie summoned Mr. Perkins with a click of her tongue. The spaniel dashed into the corridor ahead of her and trotted down the stairs. Laurel was waiting in the foyer, and their younger brothers arrived shortly dressed for the elements.

A fine snow had begun to fall that morning, stopping and starting several times throughout the day. Barley enough to form a snowball, but nothing would stop eleven-year-old Hugh from enjoying what little snow there was. He hurried across the terrace, purposely sliding on the slippery spots with his arms thrust out for balance.

Hugh's eyes glittered with excitement, his face still round with youth. "Cook's knees are aching, and you know what that means. More snow! I hope we get ten feet."

"That might solve my problem," Ammie said. "Temporarily at least."

William cocked his head. "What problem would that be?"

At age fifteen, he considered himself a man and believed he should be kept abreast of family matters.

"I met with Major Rowland this afternoon," Ammie said.

She, Laurel, and William left their little brother crouched on the lawn to scrape what little snow he could find into a pile with his mittens. She provided an abbreviated version of her encounter with the major. William frowned when she revealed the outcome.

"He cannot mean to take Mr. Perkins from you," he said.

Ammie nodded. "Major Rowland was quite clear about his intentions."

Boot falls pounded the ground behind them, approaching fast. Hugh raced past, wheeled, and flung a snowball at William. Reflexively, William spun and the wet ball smacked him between the shoulder blades. Icy spray hit Ammie and her sister. They yelped.

"Hugh!"

"You little rat!"

William grinned before tearing after him. Hugh led him on a chase into the pasture. Mr. Perkins sprinted ahead, his ears flapping, before circling back to bark at the boys. When William tackled Hugh and wrestled him into submission, they were both laughing. Laurel scolded them for ruining their Yuletide attire, but neither boy paid attention as they exchanged playful blows.

Ammie chuckled. She loved her family, her home, and the surrounding countryside. In the spring, the pasture would be vibrant with yellow and blue wildflowers, and the barren copse of trees on the hill would grow flush with leaves. She regretted that she must miss out on the splendor come springtime, but she intended to fulfill her familial duty and choose a husband by the Christmas ball.

In London, the ballrooms had been overwhelming. Ammie hadn't been able to keep straight which suitors earned her parents' approval and which ones she should avoid. Additionally, she couldn't imagine accepting any man's proposal without first introducing him to Mr. Perkins, and she couldn't very well tote her dog to Almack's or the theatre.

The house party would simplify matters. Only acceptable gentlemen had been invited to attend, and she had Mr. Perkins at her disposal—at least for the moment. She tried not to dwell on what would happen tomorrow if Major Rowland's mind remained unchanged.

As Ammie and her siblings walked further into the pasture, a figure topped the hill in the distance, a man.

"Who is that coming this way?" Hugh asked.

Ammie shook her head. "I cannot make out his face."

Laurel ventured it was one of the guests lodging with the neighbors. The spaniel froze in place, his gaze locked on the man, muscles tense.

"There, there, sweet boy." Ammie spoke soothingly as she eased toward him. The dog was protective of his people, and although he'd never bitten anyone, she didn't know how he might react to a stranger in his territory.

The moment her fingers grazed his fur, he darted across the frozen grass, headed toward the intruder. "Mr. Perkins, *no!*" Ammie grabbed fistfuls of her skirts and gave chase. "Stop him!"

Her brothers, who were much faster, shot past her.

Mr. Perkins sprinted up the hill, his speed impressive. They would never reach him in time. The man spoke seconds before Mr. Perkins leapt at him. Ammie's heart jammed in her throat; she stopped, gaping in horror. Several moments passed before she realized Mr. Perkins wasn't launching an attack.

Her lips parted in surprise. "He is *playing.*"

The man bent forward to lightly wrestle him. Robust laughter carried on the air. Mr. Perkins broke free of the man's hold and danced around him.

Ammie's fear drained away, leaving her body limp. The stranger's laughter was a balm to her nerves. She smiled.

Laurel linked their arms and dragged Ammie toward the hill. "Let's go meet your future husband."

"I-I b-beg your pardon?"

How foolish did her sister think she was? She would never marry a man based on first impressions. Even if he met one of the most important requirements on her list: *Must Love Dogs.*

Hugh and William had slowed to a walk and appeared to be introducing themselves to the stranger. When William pointed toward Laurel and Ammie at the foot of the hill, the man turned. Ammie caught a good look of his face.

"Law," she grumbled. "It is Major Rowland."

"*That* is the major? Twit." Laurel pinched her arm hard.

"Ow!" Ammie jerked away. "Why did you do that?"

Her twin sniffed. "You never said he was handsome."

"Are you mad? He is the *enemy*. Who cares about his appearance? He has come to take Mr. Perkins."

"Yes, there is that." Laurel tucked a strand of windblown hair into her bonnet. "You must admit he is not a bit hard on the eyes, though."

"Traitor," Ammie said under her breath.

Her sister chuckled. "I can enjoy the view and still be on your side."

Ammie studied the major, trying to see him as her sister did, and the changes in his appearance were startling. In her father's study, his jawline had been too severe and square, his arresting blue stare too hard, and his thick dark brows, which sat low over those glacial eyes, made him look curmudgeonly. Even his mouth had been pinched, like he was stingy with kind words.

Somehow, his features had lost their sharp edges since the earlier encounter in her father's study. She could forgive her twin for finding him attractive, but she would not be tricked by his outward transformation. The man was a blackguard through and through.

Hugh chattered all the way down the hill as the small party came to intercept Laurel and Ammie. "Do you own a sword?"

"Every Hussar is armed with a saber," the major said.

Hugh's eyes lit. "May I see it?"

"I only carry it on the battlefield, Lord Hugh." Major Rowland met Ammie's gaze. "I trust we are not at war at Everly Manor."

Hugh guffawed, doubling over and slapping his own knee. Ammie was not amused. She narrowed her eyes on her enemy.

"My father has a rifle," Hugh said after he recovered from laughing. "Do you hunt grouse?"

"Not any longer. I prefer quiet walks in the countryside." The major was responding to Hugh's questions with impressive patience. Her brother could worry a person endlessly and never satisfy his curiosity.

"My sister takes Orion for walks all the time," Hugh said.

Ammie smiled tightly. "You mean Mr. Perkins."

"Major Rowland said his name was Orion before you found him and changed it. I like Orion. It's a better name."

Ammie expected the major to gloat about winning her brother to his side. Instead, he squeezed Hugh's shoulder in a fatherly fashion. "Mr. Perkins is a fine name, and your sister has taken excellent care of him in my absence. She has earned my gratitude."

Hugh grinned. "Do you want to walk with us?"

No! Ammie's gut clenched. She didn't want to spend time another moment in the major's company. It was requiring every ounce of restraint to curb her tongue as it was.

"Thank you for the kind offer, Lord Hugh, but it would be rude to intrude on your sister's time with Mr. Perkins."

"Ammie doesn't care if—"

Major Rowland sketched a bow, cutting off Hugh's argument. "Ladies, my lords. I bid you a good day."

Ammie and her siblings turned to watch him walk in the direction of the house.

"The major seems nice, too," Laurel murmured. "You really don't find him handsome? "

"You cannot be serious." The man was intent on ripping out Ammie's heart. "Major Rowland is the worst."

Chapter Four

Phillip woke at dawn to discover a metamorphosis had occurred overnight. The brittle grass-covered hills he'd walked the day prior were buried beneath a blanket of snow, tinged blue by the early morning light. Fluffy snowflakes twirled like amateur ballerinas on gentle gusts and clumsily plopped on the window ledge.

A wintery English countryside was a beautiful sight. The peaceful quiet soothed his soul. Many times over the years, he'd wondered if he would ever see another winter at home. Under different circumstances, he would enjoy admiring Mother Nature's handiwork a bit longer, but he needed to gather Orion and set off before the roads became impassable.

Heaving a sigh laden with regret, he turned away from the window. Was it too much to hope Lady Ambrosia would turn over his dog without making him feel like the most callus blackguard on earth? He had underestimated how difficult it would be to reclaim his dog from the young lady.

When his father reported a noblewoman had taken Orion, Phillip had expected her to be like many of those he'd encountered in London over the years—the ones who toted their pooch around like an accessory and lost interest in the creature once the novelty had worn off. Lady Ambrosia clearly loved the spaniel, though, and Phillip derived no pleasure from being responsible for her heartache.

When her father had announced she must surrender Orion, the mournful look in her eyes had pricked Phillip's conscience. The memory had been troubling him ever since, and his guilt had burgeoned when Lady Ambrosia was missing from the supper table last night. Asking after her welfare had earned him a glower from her mother and a snide comment about Lady Ambrosia cherishing the last moments with *her* dog.

He hadn't wanted to argue or make the situation more contentious, so he'd held his tongue and suffered through the long evening of baleful stares from Lady Ambrosia's family and tiresome conversation from the other guests. Every time someone mentioned the war or dubbed him a hero, he was reminded that he no longer belonged in High Society. It really was for the best that he was rejoining his regiment where no one asked about his experiences abroad. The questions never arose, because his fellow officers had seen and done everything he had in service to England. None of them wished to talk about it either.

"Hop to it, then," he mumbled to himself and retreated to the small oak wardrobe to gather his clothing.

He'd sent his batman ahead to set up living quarters in Hounslow, which meant Phillip was without a valet for now. He planned to rejoin his company at the camp after the holiday, and he trusted Davis to have everything in order when he arrived. There might not be much time to set up house otherwise. With tensions growing in the Midlands, Phillip expected he and his men would be sent north eventually to be on hand if the conflict between laborers and factory owners turned violent.

He could manage without his trusted man for a few weeks, more if necessary. While he was away at war, he'd learned to live without many luxuries, but a strong cup of tea in the morning was an indulgence he refused to give up.

He rang for a footman and set himself to the task of dressing, his thoughts once again preoccupied with Lady Ambrosia. His beautiful nemesis had caught him by surprise in the pasture yesterday. With her cheeks pinked by the cold, she had been the picture of vitality. Her laughter had carried to him over the hill, her merriment warming his bones and restoring his good humor. Her own mood had soured, however, when she recognized him.

Not wishing to upset her more than necessary or intrude on her time with Orion, Phillip had excused himself as soon as he could without appearing rude to her younger brother. Lord Hugh was an enthusiastic lad, full of curiosity. Phillip imagined Lady Ambrosia's brother could get up to mischief easily enough, which elicited feelings of fondness in Phillip for the boy. He had been much the same when he was young.

He was finished dressing and growing restless when a knock came at the door.

"Enter," he called.

A gangly footman no older than fifteen slowly opened the door and hesitated in the threshold. "You rang, sir?"

"I did, yes." Phillip refrained from chastising the youngster for his tardiness. He wasn't a soldier under Phillip's command, and he was unexpectedly pleased the lad would likely never know the hardships of such a life. "A dish of tea, if you will, before I take my leave, young man."

The footman's prominent Adam's apple bobbed. "Erm... I would do your bidding, Major, 'cept—" Red bloomed in his cheeks, and he cleared his throat before correcting himself. "*Except* Lady Seabrook has requested your presence in the breakfast room. I am not to withdraw from the bedchamber until you accept, sir."

"I see."

Tightness traveled from Phillip's jaw to his temple as he ground his teeth. Lady Seabrook was a most trying woman he had ever met. He suspected the marchioness desired his company even less than he did hers, but he couldn't decline the invitation without offending his host and hostess, and he wanted to get on his way without stirring up trouble.

"Lead the way, lad."

"It's Charlie."

"Pardon?"

"Er, Charlie." The footman nervously tugged on a lock of blond hair. He needed a haircut. "It is my name."

"Yes, well, Charlie, I require directions to the breakfast room."

The boy smiled and stood up straighter. "Yes, sir. This way, please."

As Phillip followed the servant to the breakfast room, he mentally prepared for an ambush. Would Lady Seabrook offer him one of her brother's hounds again? Perhaps two? The marchioness didn't understand that a hundred dogs could never replace Orion.

Phillip loved *his* dog. No other would do. Orion had become his hope and solace during a chaotic war that had claimed too many of his friends. The prospect of reuniting with his dog had given him the will to survive.

When Phillip and the footman reached the breakfast room, he took a cleansing breath, schooled his expression, and entered. Lady Ambrosia froze in the act of taking a bite from her bread. A speck of butter dotted her top lip.

Her mother turned in her chair to face him. "Major Rowland, how good of you to join us at last. Regretfully, Lord Seabrook is occupied with an urgent matter. He would have been here to greet you otherwise."

Her chatter was like the chirp of crickets in summer. He was vaguely aware the marchioness spoke, but her voice faded into the background. Lady Ambrosia and the speck of butter had ensnared him. Warily, she held his gaze and returned the bread to its plate without taking a bite. When she swept her tongue across her lips to lick away the butter, he almost moaned aloud.

"Does he speak?" someone to his left murmured.

Phillip blinked, bringing the occupants seated around the table into focus. He'd made Lady Laurel's acquaintance already and assumed the two younger girls were also Lady Ambrosia's sisters. They looked very much like Lady Laurel—dark hair, expressive eyes, and regal bearing. The Seabrook girls were all lovely in their own rights, but Lady Ambrosia was like an exotic bird in their midst. He had a hell of a time not staring at her.

She cleared her throat. "Mr. Perkins is having his breakfast in the kitchen. Perhaps you should return later." She added under her breath, "Or not at all."

"Now, now." The marchioness covered her daughter's hand where it rested on the table between them. "I have invited the major to break his fast with us."

"Whatever for?" Lady Ambrosia winced the moment she blurted the question. She extracted her hand from beneath her mother's and lowered her gaze to the floor. If she could disappear without anyone taking notice, Phillip suspected she would dive under the table.

A small smile slipped past his defenses. How refreshing it was to encounter a woman with so little skill at hiding her emotions.

Her mother's expression was less easy to read. "Major Rowland must be made to feel welcome. After all, it appears the major will remain at Everly Manor for an extended time as our guest."

"Actually," Phillip said, "I will take my leave within the hour."

The marchioness cocked her head. "Will you?"

"You may rely on it, my lady."

Lady Seabrook's face puckered as she spooned jam onto a piece of bread. "I cannot say I approve of your recklessness, sir. Did you look out your bedchamber window this morning?"

"A little snow doesn't concern a solider. I expect the weather will improve further south."

Lady Ambrosia stole a peek at him with her head still slightly lowered. "Papa said you are traveling home to Alfriston?"

"That is correct. I'm not expected to report to Hounslow for a few weeks."

"Do take a seat, Major Rowland." The marchioness impatiently gestured toward the empty chair closest to Lady Ambrosia. "It is impolite to force one to strain one's neck while conversing."

Phillip bit his tongue and offered what he hoped passed for a smile. Was the woman trying to goad him? Force him to cause a scene for her entertainment? If so, he would be a disappointment. Phillip had never been one to become overly excited or throw tantrums, even before his training as an officer had taught him to remain calm and strategize when faced with a foe.

He turned to speak with Charlie the footman. "Have the butler send word to my driver to prepare for departure."

"Yes, sir." The lad ducked his head and hurried from the room.

Phillip sat in the chair as the marchioness wished and directed his attention toward Lady Ambrosia. An older footman placed a full plate on the table in front of him.

"I should take this moment to offer my sincere gratitude to you for taking care of Ori—" Phillip stopped himself. There was no harm in allowing her to call the dog whatever she liked, and he didn't wish to part with her thinking him cantankerous. "Mr. Perkins looked very well yesterday. Do you take him for walks frequently?"

"Every day." She pursed her cupid bow lips, apparently displeased by his inquiry. "A dog requires regular activity, Major Rowland. I do hope you will have time to continue the practice once you resume your duties. Mr. Perkins is prone to mischief if he is not exercised."

Her concern and love for the dog elicited a flicker of guilt in Phillip. No doubt, she would feel the loss keenly once the spaniel was gone.

"I assure you," he said, "your Mr. Perkins will have little opportunity to misbehave since he will accompany me to the training field daily."

She fiddled with the bread on her plate, not meeting his eyes. "And if you are sent abroad? Who will keep watch over him?"

"Not my brother or his servants." A hint of steel crept into his voice. *Irresponsible prats.* "I wonder, Lady Ambrosia, would it be an imposition if I called on *you* to care for Mr. Perkins in my absence?"

His suggestion seemed to disarm her as much as it surprised him. She met his gaze at last and graced him with a smile that reached inside his chest and accelerated his heartbeat. It was fortunate that he was leaving within the hour, or he might find himself fawning over the lady and making a fool of himself.

As he had learned at supper last night, Lady Ambrosia already had a suitor, one that met with her parents' approval. Her mother made certain Phillip knew Sir Edmund Throckmorton had been chosen for her daughter and a betrothal was imminent. Therefore, she'd warned Phillip to guard his heart. He'd deemed the woman mad and politely taken his leave, but perhaps the marchioness was more adept at recognizing his weaknesses than he was.

"I would be delighted to have Mr. Perkins return to my care," Lady Ambrosia said then frowned. "Oh, dear. I don't wish to see you sent to war, sir. That was not my meaning."

The furrowing of her brow was adorable, her concern sweet. His fingers itched to reach out to smooth away her worries, which was his signal to go. He pushed away from the table, prepared to thank the marchioness for her hospitality when Lord Seabrook trod into the room. His cheeks were red and his hair windblown as if he'd been out for a morning ride.

"Good morning, Major Rowland," he said. "My butler informs me that you wish to take your leave."

Phillip inclined his head, acknowledging Lord Seabrook's greeting. "I intend to join my family for Christmas, my lord, before my regiment needs me."

"Huh." Lord Seabrook sat across from his wife at the round table and placed a napkin across his lap. "Was your father aware of your plans?"

"Yes, of course. He sent the carriage to London to carry me here." A sense of foreboding stirred in Phillip's belly. "Why do you ask?"

"That is peculiar then." Lord Seabrook grinned when the footman placed a plate in front of him. He leaned forward to inhale the apple pastry and sat up slowly with a happy sigh. "Cinnamon. How divine. I believe Mrs. Shiers has outdone herself again."

"You must limit yourself to one," his wife said.

"You worry too much, Lady Seabrook. Two pastries for breakfast never hurt a man."

While the couple negotiated, Phillip bounced his leg and waited for an opportunity to ask Lord Seabrook what he found peculiar. The marquess and marchioness settled on a compromise, one and a half pastries.

"My lord, what—?"

Lord Seabrook interrupted. "According to the stable master, your father's travel coach continued to East Sussex yesterday. The driver and coachmen took refreshment in the kitchens before setting off again. I assumed you had changed your mind about staying."

Phillip gaped, waiting for the marquess to crack a smile and admit he was joking. When he dug into his meal with the gusto of a man who'd just engaged in vigorous exercise, Phillip realized Lord Seabrook was serious.

"How? Wh—?" He shook his head to clear his thinking. "I must speak with the stable master. There has been a mistake."

"Suit yourself," Lord Seabrook said with a shrug. "Although I can attest to an empty stable yard. We would be in a pickle if we needed to travel. I sent my driver and coachmen to retrieve our daughter and her husband yesterday. They have been on holiday at his family's estate, but they must be home for Christmas."

"Mercedes's husband is the parish parson." Lady Seabrook's thin eyebrows rose toward her hairline as if expecting a response.

"His parents must be very proud." Phillip's answer seemed to satisfy her; she smiled and returned to eating her breakfast. Lady Ambrosia snorted softly, her eyes bright with amusement. Again, Phillip was captivated. What was it about this woman that enthralled him so?

"Perhaps the stable master misunderstood," he said, "and my father's men are lodging in the village. May I borrow a horse to ride to the inn, my lord?"

Lord Seabrook shrugged again. "You are our guest. The stables are at your disposal."

"You must eat first," the marchioness said. "Wastefulness is not an honorable trait."

Phillip agreed and dutifully cleaned his plate before taking his leave. Unfortunately, the ride into the village proved as fruitless as it was miserably cold. His father's men and coach were nowhere to be found. Worse, the owner of the coaching inn told him all the carriages for hire were carrying passengers elsewhere, and the post coach wasn't expected for another week. Phillip discarded the option of traveling by horseback. He had Orion to consider.

Phillip resigned himself to remaining at Everly Manor as Lord and Lady Seabrook's guest, at least for now. And God's blood, the prospect pleased him.

Chapter Five

Ammie had been given a reprieve, and she intended to use the next few days to her advantage. An army camp was no place for a cherished pet. Surely, Major Rowland was not too stubborn to deny the truth.

What if Mr. Perkins became caught beneath horse's hooves, or one of the soldiers accidentally shot him? The risks far outnumbered any benefits the dog would receive from the vigorous exercise he was likely to get from military life. He belonged with Ammie where he would be kept safe and received the pampering to which he had become accustomed.

She really had spoiled the spaniel and made him soft. Perhaps over the next few days, Major Rowland would see that Mr. Perkins was no longer the dog he'd left behind. The major was unlikely to reach that conclusion, however, without a bit of help, which was the reason she was lurking outside her father's study. She required an ally, and her father was her best candidate.

Papa's study door was cracked open a sliver, allowing her a view of him at his desk. His head was bent over a sheet of paper lying on the surface; his spectacles sat low on his nose. She took a deep breath to calm the flutters in her belly and knocked.

"Enter," her father called.

When she pushed the door open, his eyes flared. "Ammie, what a surprise."

"Papa, may I speak with you a moment?"

"Eh, yes. Of course, please come inside." He sat up straight and placed the paper in the desk drawer. "Correspondence," he muttered.

Ammie closed the door. She didn't want Mama hearing about her private audience with her father. Otherwise, Ammie wouldn't know a moment's peace until she revealed every detail of their conversation, including her father's reactions. Ammie had never had the misfortune of being interrogated in a courtroom, but she imagined the experience was as equally terrifying as being called before her mother.

Papa motioned to the ornate needlepoint chair in front of his desk. "Have a seat."

Since she didn't know how long they might have before they were discovered, she launched into the business at hand. "I believe I can persuade Major Rowland to leave Mr. Perkins in my care."

"Oh?" The corners of Papa's mouth twitched as if he was struggling not to laugh. Perhaps he found her optimism naive, *amusing*.

She pressed her lips together to contain the impetuous words rising at the back of her throat. When she gained control of her tongue, she scooted to the edge of the chair. "Please, hear me out, Papa. At breakfast, Major Rowland asked if I would watch over Mr. Perkins if the major is called to duty, which leads me to believe he is not as intractable as he seemed yesterday. If I am allowed to speak with him, I may be able to convince him that it is in the dog's best interests to remain with me. Major Rowland may call whenever he likes."

Her father tilted his head to the side and drummed his fingers on the desk. "You would make an empty promise to a man who has dedicated his life to serving England?"

"No, sir. I am sincere about welcoming him. I might have misjudged him initially, but as you've pointed out, he is a war hero. Surely, there is some good in him." Grudgingly, she admitted he would probably have many good qualities if she allowed herself to get to know him. She could find no fault in how he'd interacted with Mr. Perkins or her brother yesterday.

"Your husband might feel differently about welcoming a strange man into his home," Papa said. "You have not forgotten the purpose of the house party, have you? Your mother is eager to see you and your sister betrothed by Christmas."

"Oh." His reminder was a bucket of cold water dousing the fire in her belly. In the excitement of Major Rowland's arrival and fear of losing Mr. Perkins, she'd not given husband hunting a thought. She lifted her chin. "My husband will love Mr. Perkins as much as I do. Otherwise, I will not choose him. He will understand why it is necessary to open his doors to the major."

Her father shook his head. "You think it is easy to bend a man to your will. I blame your mother. She believes she has me wrapped around her finger."

Ammie's eyebrows shot toward her hairline.

He laughed. "Yes, it is true. She does, but only because I am mad for her. If you can make a love match like we did, I expect you will have better success at persuading your husband to see everything your way. I understand from your mother that you favor Sir Edmund."

Ammie shrugged. "We haven't spent enough time together for me to form an opinion. He is handsome and kind enough, but I would need to see how Mr. Perkins likes him first."

"I advise you to see to it then. Christmas is a week away." Papa reclined in his leather chair and formed a steeple with his hands. "If you believe you can change Rowland's mind, I will arrange another meeting with him. Allow me to consult with your mother. It might be difficult to find a time that doesn't interfere with her hostess duties."

"Yes, but perhaps..." Ammie caught her bottom lip between her teeth and struggled to find the right words. She didn't want to appear disrespectful or ungrateful.

"You may speak freely," Papa said. When she remained silent, he smiled ruefully. "I think I understand. Your mother can be trying at times, and you would prefer not to involve her."

"Or you, Papa," Ammie blurted.

Her father started.

She rushed to explain. "I believe my chances will be improved if Major Rowland doesn't feel he is being ambushed. I wish to approach him alone. Perhaps if he sees me with Mr. Perkins again, he will realize I truly have the dog's best interest at heart. I would like to invite him to accompany me on a walk."

Her father's face twisted in horror. "Alone and without a chaperone?"

"No Papa, nothing scandalous. Hugh and William could accompany us. They are less threatening than you and Mama. We will remain within sight of the manor house." She clasped her hands, prepared to beg if necessary.

Her father pursed his lips. "Your mother would never approve."

"Please, Papa. I must try to change Major Rowland's mind. Otherwise, I will never forgive myself if something terrible befalls Mr. Perkins in Hounslow."

"Ammie." Her father signed and rubbed his temples as if her request caused his head to ache. "Why has everything become complicated?"

"I'm sorry." Truly, she was. She had always tried to comply with anything her parents asked of her, but Mr. Perkins was too important. She had to fight for him.

Her father uttered a mild curse. "I suppose I did promise to help resolve the issue, although I am not convinced granting my permission is wise. Your attention should be focused on selecting a mate."

"I will. As soon as I see to Mr. Perkins's wellbeing, I will throw myself into finding a husband."

Papa grimaced. "Your mother will have my head for agreeing, but I see you need a resolution before you can consider any gentleman's suit. Be quick about it. I won't be able to keep this from your mother for long."

Ammie was out of her chair and rounding the desk to hug him before he finished talking. "Thank you, Papa. Thank you, thank you."

Her display would have earned her a reprimand from her mother, but her father chuckled and allowed her to kiss his doughy cheek. "Remember, you must have one or more brothers with you always," he said. "If you can enlist one of your older brothers, that would be preferable."

"You have my promise." And she meant it. Heaven forbid that an act of carelessness should bind her to the major for life instead of a lovely gentleman like Sir Edmund.

She hugged her father once more and practically skipped toward the door.

"*One* walk," her father called.

"Yes sir."

When she returned to her chamber, she wrote a brief note and rang for a footman. Charlie answered her call, as usual. Mr. Perkins lifted his head briefly and wagged his tail when he saw his friend before resuming his nap at the foot of her bed.

"Close the door behind you." She waved the young servant into the room. "I have a secret task for you, Charlie. No one must intercept this message, and you cannot speak a word of it to anyone. Are you the right man for the job?"

The boy's dark eyes glittered with what she assumed was interest. "I know how to be invisible when I should. I reckon I'm better at it than all the other fellas."

"I am pleased to hear it." Ammie smiled at his boastfulness. He sounded like William or Hugh, who seemed to believe they excelled at everything. She held out the folded sheet of paper. "Deliver this to Major Rowland and wait for a reply. I place my full trust in you."

The sparkle in Charlie's eyes dimmed. "Are you asking me to deliver a message to a gentleman? I don't know if I should, milady. Lady Seabrook will sack me for sure if she finds out."

"You needn't worry about Mama," Ammie said. "I have my father's permission to speak with the major. However, it is imperative you practice discretion. This is a private matter that doesn't concern the other houseguests."

Charlie gulped and his complexion paled. "What if I am caught and make a mess of it?"

"You will do fine. I am placing my reputation in your hands. Would I take a chance if I thought you would be questioned?"

"I don't know. Probably not?"

Ammie's conscience niggled at her for worrying him. "You have been assigned to act as Major Rowland's valet, have you not?"

Charlie nodded and fidgeted with his coat sleeves. "Lady Seabrook said I must give him my help, even if he doesn't want it."

The young servant was untrained as a valet and likely to make a mess of the task. She hoped Major Rowland wouldn't be too stern with Charlie because of his inexperience. It wasn't his fault. Ammie suspected her mother had selected the servant to attend Major Rowland as a small act of revenge. Despite her crusty demeanor, Mama loved Ammie and her siblings in her own way, and the mother hen did not take kindly to anyone upsetting one of her chicks.

"I am certain the major will find your assistance very useful," Ammie said to reassure the boy. "And you needn't worry about anyone questioning what you are doing in the major's chamber. You are meant to be there."

A tentative smile eased across his face. "I didn't think of that." He accepted the note and tucked it into his waistband. "I promise not to let you down, milady."

"I know you won't, Charlie. Thank you."

When the footman slipped into the corridor, Ammie retrieved a bonnet and her heavy wool pelisse in anticipation of Major Rowland accepting her invitation. She saw no reason for him to refuse.

Charlie returned a few moments later with the major's acceptance. The rendezvous point was the pasture again, and she would take Hugh along. Her youngest brother had been impressed with the major yesterday, so he would be eager to accompany her. As a bonus, he was an inattentive child. If their mother questioned him later, Hugh was unlikely to recall any part of the conversation between Ammie and Major Rowland.

She clapped her hands. "Come, Mr. Perkins."

The spaniel hopped from the bed and followed when she headed to the schoolroom to collect her youngest brother. Hugh was reluctant to leave the tower he was building from blocks until he learned they were meeting the major. Their small party hadn't traveled far from the manor house before she spotted Major Rowland crossing the snow-covered lawn en route to intercept them. Mr. Perkins wagged his stubby tail and trotted forward to welcome him.

As Laurel had reminded her before bed last night, Ammie was more likely to achieve her objective through kindness than squaring off with a seasoned warrior. When he reached the edge of the pasture, she pasted on a pleasant smile and called to him. "Good afternoon, sir."

Hugh popped up from the ground, abandoning the snowball he had been forming, and ran in the major's direction.

"Major Rowland, you've come at last." Her brother began firing questions before the major could return her greeting. "Did you bring your war horse home to England? What about Napoleon? Did you ever see him in battle? Does he have devil's horns like Mama says? I've never seen them in pictures, but Mama said he hides them beneath his hat. Is she telling the truth?"

Major Rowland grinned at her brother and knelt to ruffle the dog's fur. "I never saw Little Boney myself, Lord Hugh. And my horse is being cared for at the camp. "

"Who cares for him? How many hands is he? Will he allow anyone to ride him, or only you?"

Major Rowland chuckled. "You are an inquisitive lad." His mild tone suggested he was simply offering an observation rather than a criticism. "Have you thought of becoming a barrister?"

Hugh snorted. "I want to be an officer like you."

The major's smile faltered. Mr. Perkins launched his small body at him and almost knocked him off balance. Major Rowland laughed. "You little rascal. Are you looking for a tussle?" He playfully wrestled with the spaniel while answering Hugh's questions.

Mr. Perkins seemed to enjoy the rough play and jumped on the major relentlessly until he stood and pulled a small brown ball from the pocket of his greatcoat. The dog dropped to his haunches, his eyes on the ball. When the major hurled it through the air, Mr. Perkins shot across the snow in pursuit. Hugh raced after the spaniel, shouting for him to fetch.

Mr. Perkins snatched the ball from the ground and ran toward Hugh with it in his mouth. At the last moment, he veered out of reach. Hugh hollered at the sky then chased him up the hill. With her brother occupied and entertained for the moment, Ammie fell into step with Major Rowland.

"I was sorry to hear about your carriage troubles," she said, not bothering to hide a gloating smile. "It must have been disappointing to have your plans thwarted."

He glanced sideways at her, his expression unreadable. "You know what they say, one must bend or break when confronted with the unexpected, my lady."

"I have never heard that saying."

"Of course you have. I just said it."

Ammie stopped in her tracks. He smirked, roguishly baiting her. She rolled her eyes. "No one of consequence, then."

He laughed. "Touché, Lady Ambrosia."

"One must bend or break," she mused. "It is a solid philosophy when given proper consideration."

"I have always found it helpful." He clasped his hands behind his back as they resumed trailing Hugh and Mr. Perkins, albeit at a more leisurely pace. "I assume you didn't summon me to discuss life philosophies, though."

"Are you always this direct, sir?"

"Yes." The corners of his mouth twitched as he fought not to smile. She was beginning to suspect his boorish presentation was more facade than substance. "Some have accused me of lacking finesse, but in my defense, I find it exhausting to be charming all the time."

"How well rested you must be," she said. "I don't believe I have seen you employ charm since your arrival."

"You didn't attend supper last night. If you had, you would know I had the crowd eating from the palm of my hand."

"Did someone break the china plates?"

"You are a cheeky one, Lady Ambrosia, and a masterful banterer." His smile was like a ray of blinding light when turned full force on her. The sight briefly stunned her. She blinked, willing herself not to be tricked by his appearance. He was still the man who wished to steal her happiness.

"Considering your aversion to social graces," she said, "I will not expect you for charades this evening—or any other festivities."

"Perhaps I will surprise you." He tapped a finger to his temple and grinned. "I like to keep a watchful eye on my foes."

The slight crinkle at the corners of his blue eyes lent him a boyish charm that made him seem much more approachable today.

"About us being foes," she said, "must we be? I can see no reason we shouldn't attempt to get along while you are staying as my father's guest. We have at least one thing in common. We both love dogs."

"I love a *specific* dog, my lady. I hope you aren't suggesting I accept a hound from your uncle to replace him. Orion cannot be replaced in my heart."

His answer should have been discouraging, but it elevated him in her eyes. *Blast it all!* She didn't want to like him.

"The dog in question is named Mr. Perkins," she teased, "but for the sake of keeping the peace, I will overlook your blunder."

"Did I mention you are stubborn, too?"

She laughed, enjoying their tête-à-tête more than she should.

Watch your step, a voice in her head warned. *He isn't a man to be trifled with.* Uneasy with the thought he might think she wanted something more than a civilized talk, she rushed to fill the silence. "I feel the same as you about Mr. Perkins. Orion Perkins? Maybe we could call him Opie. Should we call him Opie?"

"Opie?"

"It is simply a suggestion," she said and flicked her hand, "a compromise of sorts."

He tested the name aloud. "I'm not sure it suits him. It is not as dignified as Orion, or even Mr. Perkins."

She snorted. "Dignified? Have you seen him bathe himself?"

The moment the mortifying words left her mouth, she prayed the ground would open and swallow her. He had the decency to stare straight ahead to allow her to squirm in her scalding pool of embarrassment in private.

"Opie it is," he said. "Was that all you wished to discuss? A common name for the dog?"

She cleared her throat, wondering if she should apologize for her own lack of social finesse. "No, there is more."

It seemed prudent to take care with her strategy when it came to Major Rowland. He had the fortitude to withstand and deflect a direct attack.

"I would like to suggest sharing the dog while you are a guest," she said. "We could alternate nights—one night he sleeps in your chambers, the next in mine. We could share responsibility for exercising him. Daily walks perhaps?"

He stopped. She reluctantly halted, took a deep breath, and turned to face him. His gaze pierced through her. Hugh praised the dog in the distance. Major Rowland's attention didn't waver. Her mouth grew dry when he didn't so much as blink. It was as if he could see into her soul and know every thought, dream, and fear she had. No one ever looked at her, not like someone who wished to memorize every inch of her and uncover her vulnerabilities. She felt stripped bare by his gaze, her emotions raw. His face blurred and her chin quivered.

"I am unprepared to say good-bye to Mr. Perkins." She fluttered her lashes frantically, attempting to hold back tears. "Please, sir, allow me to enjoy his companionship a while longer."

Major Rowland's razor jaw lost softened, and the stern set of his mouth slacked. When he spoke, his voice was soothing, slightly husky. "I can see you hold a tender spot for him in your heart."

She nodded, swallowing to ease the tight ache in her throat. "H-he notices when I enter a room, and he's always happy to see me, like I am important and special."

Law. Her most rewarding relationship was with a dog. How silly and pathetic she sounded. She braced herself for mockery.

Major Rowland sighed, his breath creating a cloud in the frigid air. "I understand, Lady Ambrosia," he murmured. "I do."

His sincerity knocked her off balance. She no longer recognized her enemy, and it frightened her.

"How do we decide which bedchamber Opie will stay in tonight?" he asked.

Ammie laughed, her relief too great to bottle. "Perhaps we should settle the matter with a round of whist when we return to the house?"

"I prefer chess."

"You would."

She shrugged to indicate she didn't care how the matter was decided, and she didn't. Although she would probably lose to the major, she had gained valuable ground today. Besides, Mr. Perkins had stayed with her last night. It was only fair that Major Rowland should get his turn.

When it was time to return to the house, Ammie slid a look in his direction. "You seem different from when we met," she said. "More at ease."

"I prefer the outdoors. I always have."

"Me too," she murmured. "You are very patient with Hugh."

"He is a good boy, I think, just eager. I have encountered lads much like him in the Army. It requires patience to train them properly."

"I hope you will be as understanding with the valet my mother chose for you. Charlie is one of my favorites."

"You have my word," he said. "I will treat the lad well, but don't expect me to show *you* any mercy during our chess match. I am not that nice."

She chuckled. "Yesterday's news, Major Rowland. Yesterday's news."

Chapter Six

Phillip arrived late for partner charades and claimed a place at the back of the room where he could be a spectator. Lady Ambrosia had pegged him correctly during their walk earlier. He had been planning to avoid the holiday festivities as much as possible during his stay—that is until he realized the unthinkable. The pleasure derived from her company outweighed his distaste for large gatherings.

He had enjoyed matching wits with her this afternoon, but her vulnerability with him had been humbling. How anyone as uniquely beautiful as she could feel invisible when she entered a room was perplexing. Every time he saw her, he lit from within, and a sliver of who he had been before the war felt revived. He couldn't ignore her even if he wanted.

His gaze repeatedly strayed to where she sat on a settee with her twin sister. Orion was curled on her lap, dozing as she stroked his head. Surprisingly, the lady was allowed to tote the dog wherever she wished at Everly Manor, and aside from supper, she had kept the spaniel close all evening.

Phillip's turn with the dog would come later, thanks to his skill at chess. Despite a sound trouncing, Lady Ambrosia had accepted the defeat with an impressive measure of goodwill and congratulated him. Many men could take lessons in graciousness from her.

Reluctantly, Phillip dragged his attention away from her before someone caught him staring and tried to make sense out of what the couple at the front of the room was trying to convey. Miss Evans and Lord Pepperton were engaged in some indiscernible activity while audience members shouted incorrect guesses. When they exhausted all the typical things one might do at Christmas, the players moved on to the ridiculous.

"Shoeing a horse!"

"Apprehending a thief!"

Thankfully, the players' turn ended when the last grain of sand slipped through the hourglass. Lady Ambrosia's brother Julius was in charge of keeping the game moving along.

"Time is up," he called.

Miss Evans huffed and stomped her foot. The blonde curls at her temples bounced, emphasizing her frustration. "We are hanging *garland*." Her tone suggested she thought everyone in the room was a dolt, aside from herself.

"You did a lovely job, Miss Evans," Lord Julius said before singling one of his younger sisters. "Octavia, pick your partner."

Lady Octavia enlisted her eldest sister's help. Lady Mercedes was married to the parson, Mr. Taylor, and Lord Seabrook had recommended him for the position when he married his daughter. Phillip was slightly embarrassed by his interest in Lady Ambrosia's family and attempted to convince himself that he only gathered facts about them to know his enemy better.

As the sisters bent their heads together to discuss their strategy, Sir Edmund and Merritt Bartley, the Earl of Warford, entered the room, stopping inside the threshold. The earl nodded a greeting to Phillip before continuing his conversation with the younger man. Warford had been one of the older students at Oxford when Phillip entered University. They had never been more than acquaintances, and Phillip was content to keep his distance. Normally, Phillip would have no interest in anything the gossip had to say, but his ears pricked when he heard Warford mention Lady Ambrosia.

"I heard a rumor you intend to court her," Warford said to his companion.

Sir Edmund mumbled what sounded like an affirmative. With his back to Phillip, he couldn't be certain.

"We met in London at the end of the Season," Sir Edmund said. "I would have offered for her hand months ago if my uncle hadn't fallen ill and summoned me back to the country. I wrote to her father as soon as I was able, declaring my devotion to her."

"Seems rash given the brevity of your association," Warford said, "but you are no different from most young men your age. Always rushing headlong into marriage without giving it proper thought."

In the abstract, Phillip agreed with Warford about the foolishness of youth, but Lady Ambrosia's appeal was hard to deny. Falling under her spell would be easy, possibly even unintentional.

"You are wrong about me," Sir Edmund said. "I've thought of nothing else since we parted. She is the most delightfully charming creature I have ever encountered, and I must have her for my wife."

Warford crossed his arms, his stance challenging. "Are you certain it isn't her dowry you find dazzling? It is no secret you enjoy the gaming tables."

The young man shoulders stiffened, and a blush crept up the back of his neck. "I made mistakes in my past, my lord, but I am reformed. My debts are paid."

"Nevertheless, her fortune must hold some appeal."

Sir Edmund snapped, "You dishonor the lady by suggesting she is less valuable than her dowry. Continue in this vein to your peril, sir."

Phillip was on the verge of intervening when Warford clapped the younger man on the shoulder. "Congratulations, Sir Edmund. Her mother will be satisfied by this good report."

"Did Lady Seabrook ask you to speak with me?" Instead of being properly offended by the marchioness's interference, Sir Edmund sounded as if he'd been handed a gift. "Does she support my courtship?"

Warford nodded. "As will her father, I have been told."

The earl caught Phillip's eye over the other man's shoulder. Phillip looked away. Lady Ambrosia's future marriage prospects were none of his concern, even if the sudden tightness in his chest said otherwise.

"When should I seek an audience with Lady Ambrosia? Tomorrow? No, *tonight*, I should speak with her tonight."

Before Sir Edmund could charge across the room in his eagerness, Warford caught his arm above the elbow. "Fools rush in, remember?"

"What do you mean?"

"You might have her parents' approval, but more importantly, you need her dog's blessing." Warford caught Phillip gawking again and raised a dark blond eyebrow. "*Some* men understand that is the way to her heart."

"The dog," Sir Edmund repeated. "Yes, of course." He thanked Warford for the advice and melded into the crowd.

The Earl of Warford remained at the back of the room. "Phillip Rowland, it has been a long time. Where have you been keeping yourself?"

"No place worth mentioning," he said. It was Christmas—peace on earth, good will to men. Nothing spoiled the holiday spirit faster than talk of war. "It seems Lady Seabrook employs spies. Why am I not surprised?"

Warford chuckled and shrugged with his arms extended at his sides in a self-effacing manner. "One does what one must for family. Astrid is a distant cousin. She wishes to do right by her daughters."

Phillip held his tongue. Sir Edmund seemed like a decent man. He would make a good husband for any young woman, and Phillip had no right to entertain thoughts of thrashing him for wanting to marry Lady Ambrosia. He indulged his imagination anyway.

Warford gained his attention with an unexpected revelation. "I saw you walking with Ambrosia this afternoon. You looked cozy together."

The earl had always been a repugnant gossip, one who seemed unlikely to allow a small thing like being related to the Seabrooks stop him from spreading tales. Phillip felt justified in telling a white lie to protect Lady Ambrosia's reputation.

"I crossed paths with her and her younger brother. It was quite by accident. We walked a short distance, and I asked after her dog to be polite."

Warford clicked his tongue as if he saw through Phillip's lies. "As I told Sir Edmund, some men are natural born strategists. How long did it take you to determine the way to Ambrosia's heart is through her beloved pet?"

Phillip scowled, tempted to knock the saccharine smile from Lord Warford's face. "If I were interested in courting the lady, I would be straightforward about it, not pretend to like her dog to manipulate her into loving me."

"It is a relief to hear you've not set your sites on the girl," Warford said. "I wasn't looking forward to reporting your activities to Lady Seabrook."

"My *activities* are none of the marchioness's concern."

"If they involve her daughter, I am afraid she'll not see it your way."

Phillip doubted Lady Seabrook would see anything his way. She had taken an instant dislike to him, and her animosity was like a burr in his boot. "Tell me, Lord Warford. What is her objection to me? I am a man of my word; I have no vices. Lady Ambrosia would marry into a good family, and she would always be treated with the respect she deserves."

"For someone who claims to have no intentions toward Ambrosia, you seem eager to argue your suitability."

Phillip snapped his mouth closed. He didn't have a ready defense or a clear understanding of why he felt driven to win Lady Seabrook's approval. Thankfully,

Warford abandoned the topic and announced he was retreating to Lord Seabrook's study where some of the men were gathering for brandy and cheroots. He didn't invite Phillip.

When Warford was gone, Phillip realized he was clenching his teeth. He exhaled and willed the tension to drain from his body. Lady Ambrosia's eldest brother Clive, heir to the marquessate, shouted the answer to the latest charade and took his place at the front to choose a partner.

"Laurel?"

Lady Ambrosia's twin hopped from the settee to join her brother. The Seabrook's offspring were dominating the game. They must have entertained each other many long winter nights through the years, honing their skills. Their camaraderie was unmistakable, even when they bickered.

Phillip felt a tug of wistfulness. He'd come from a small family—only three sons, and he and his brothers hadn't rubbed well together when they were young. A strong sense of competitiveness between them had often led to violent rows and the occasional bloody nose. After years apart fighting a real enemy, their differences seemed petty now. Phillip was even willing to overlook his brother Jeremy's negligence in caring for Orion, since no harm had come to the dog.

His gaze strayed toward Lady Ambrosia again. Sir Edmund took advantage of the vacated seat next to her and plopped down beside her. When he reached to pet Orion, the spaniel growled. Sir Edmund jerked back his hand.

"Good dog," Phillip muttered and smiled.

Chapter Seven

The young footman Charlie arrived at Phillip's door half an hour after he'd retired to his chamber with Orion in tow. The spaniel rushed the room and danced a circle around Phillip.

"What a good boy you are," he said, showering the dog with attention. The lad stepped inside and closed the door.

"Lady Ambrosia wishes you a restful sleep, sir."

"She is very thoughtful."

Phillip hadn't known whether she would keep her promise to surrender Orion come nightfall. She'd given no indication she noticed Phillip in the great room. She had seemed too preoccupied by Sir Edmund's attempts to woo her through the dog. When she had rewarded the pretender with a brilliant smile, Phillip's gut had soured.

"Would you like help readying for bed?" Charlie asked.

Phillip considered declining the boy's assistance then thought better of it. It would be good experience for Charlie to learn a valet's duties and improve his chances of promotion down the road. What Lady Seabrook surely meant as an insult to Phillip, he could turn into a good deed. If he pleased Lady Ambrosia in the process, he would consider it a bonus.

Phillip removed his jacket and began loosening his cravat. "You can assist with removing my boots and polish them properly for tomorrow."

"Yes, sir."

Charlie hopped to the task when Phillip sat on the edge of the bed. He instructed the lad in how to care for his boots, applying the same patience and demand for quality that he did with new soldiers under his command. When Charlie had them gleaming, Phillip offered a simple word of praise and dismissed him. The valet lessons could resume in the morning.

Alone at last, Phillip discarded his waistcoat and sat on the bed again. It had been a long day. That morning he'd risen from bed expecting to be halfway home, but here he was sharing custody of *his* dog. He chuckled and patted the spot beside him. Orion jumped on the bed and playfully tried to bite Phillip's sleeves. Phillip wrestled the dog onto his back and scratched his belly. Orion stopped fighting; his tongue lolled from the side of his mouth.

"I think Lady Ambrosia spoiled you while I was gone. You're a very lucky dog. You found a good keeper."

Phillip's mind drifted as he continued to pet Orion. He needed to warn Lady Ambrosia that they had been spotted walking together without a chaperone earlier today. Since the Earl of Warford was her relation, he would be less likely to spread the rumor, but it was too risky to continue the arrangement.

"Damnation." He exhaled, his shoulders slowly sinking toward the floor. He'd been looking forward to spending time with her again without her eager suitor Sir Edmund underfoot.

Orion wiggled to a seated position, looked up at him, and whined.

"What is it, boy?"

The dog hopped from the bed and approached the door to paw it. He turned back toward Phillip with imploring amber eyes.

"Do you need to go outside?"

Orion whimpered.

Phillip retrieved his boots and cursed Sir Edmund for sneaking the dog too many treats. He had to hand it to the man; he was innovative in his approach to winning Orion's approval—sweet-talking the cook into allowing him to raid the kitchen. *Roast beef, indeed.* The blighter wasn't the one taking the dog out for midnight walks.

"Let's go," Phillip murmured and opened the door. The spaniel shot into the dark corridor, heading away from the stairs.

"Orion, heel," he hissed. The dog either couldn't hear the command or had forgotten everything he had been taught.

As quietly as possible, Phillip pursued him over creaky floorboards. Lady Ambrosia would have his head if he lost the dog the first night in his care. Orion stayed several steps ahead, ignoring Phillip's furiously whispered command for him to come. She had turned the spaniel into a disobedient rascal, ruined him. Phillip would have to retrain the dog in Hounslow, and God only knew when there would be time.

Orion disappeared around a corner. Phillip hurried his step, grateful for the thick carpet to muffle his footfalls. When he caught up to Orion, he was scratching at one of the closed doors.

"No!" Phillip lunged for Orion as the door opened; the dog bolted inside.

Phillip froze, crouching at a lady's feet. He needn't look up to know her identity. Her scent was recognizable, even if he hadn't already worked out that the dog was returning to sleep in his own bed.

Slowly, he rose to face Lady Ambrosia. Before he could whisper an apology, she laid her finger to his lips to shush him. Of course, she wouldn't want to be discovered with him. He'd felt the same when she had surprised him in her father's study. When had the notion of becoming trapped into marriage lose its sense of horror?

She grasped his wrist and drew him inside. The door closed softly behind him. When she lifted to her toes to whisper in his ear, an urge to embrace and keep her close washed over him. He didn't move.

Her breath was as light as a fairy wing fluttering over his skin, her hand warm and comforting resting on his shoulder. "Laurel is sleeping."

Through the fog of his enchantment, her words filtered into his consciousness and he became aware of his surroundings. Airy snores were coming from the canopied bed. A steady flame leisurely consumed the logs stacked in the hearth, bathing the feminine room in a warm glow. Orion was curled into a ball at Lady Laurel's feet, fast asleep already.

Defector. Phillip smiled. How could he blame the rascal for preferring the company of ladies?

Ambrosia remained tucked against his side. Her body heat and subtle vanilla fragrance surrounded him. "Is something wrong?" she whispered.

He nodded, eager to prolong their contact. Besides, he might not get another chance to warn her that they might be the subjects of gossip tomorrow.

She tapped his shoulder. "Come with me."

"Where?" he hissed.

She didn't answer and headed for the dressing screen in the corner. When she passed in front of the fire, every lovely slope of her body stood out in relief beneath her cotton gown. Her legs were long and trim, her waist and breasts small. The view was an intimacy meant for a husband's eyes alone, but he was powerless to look away.

"I should leave—"

She shushed him and retrieved the wrapper left draped over the screen. After she donned slippers and lit a candle with the fire in the hearth, she motioned him to follow. She slipped behind the dressing screen and pressed a place on the wall. A panel sprang open to a hidden passage. She led the way, her candle casting flickering light over the stone walls. The temperature dropped the further they traveled.

"Wait." He shrugged off his jacket to place it around her shoulders. "You will catch a chill."

She frowned. "Are you impervious to the cold, sir? Perhaps you fancy yourself immortal?"

Not immortal but luckier than most. "I have survived worse."

She huffed. "I am warm enough, and your chivalry is worthless if *you* catch a chill." She tried to return his jacket.

"Keep it, Ambrosia." He draped it around her again.

She pursed her lips but accepted his offering. They had walked several paces when she said, "Everyone who knows me calls me Ammie."

It appeared she had no objection to his familiar use of her name. He accepted her allowance as a small victory. "I prefer Ambrosia," he said. "It is a woman's name."

She grumbled to herself, but the shy tilt of her head suggested she might like being regarded as a woman in his eyes. She stopped in front of a slide lock on the wall, handed him the candle, and opened the secret door. When he stepped through the threshold, he found himself back in his bedchamber.

"This is how you surprised me in your father's study."

She didn't confirm or deny his observation.

He extinguished the candle and placed the holder on a side table. There was very little seating in his room, so he offered her the chair and sat on the footstool far enough away as to not alarm her. Her gaze was direct, and her posture composed when she addressed him.

"You brought Mr. Perkins to me. Did you change your mind about our arrangement?"

He laughed softly. "Your Mr. Perkins has his own ideas about our arrangement. It seems he prefers your company at night."

The dog's show of favoritism would have bothered him yesterday, but Phillip was feeling generous. He forgave Orion's defection. It had led to this beautiful woman visiting his bedchamber. After a single afternoon of basking in her undivided attention, Phillip craved more.

She sighed; her mouth formed a sympathetic moue. "I'm sorry. I thought Mr. Perkins would have no trouble adjusting to the change. It is obvious he remembers and loves you."

He didn't like to see her sad, even on his behalf. "I thought we agreed to call him Opie," he said, trying to tease her into a happier mood.

"Opie." She wrinkled her nose. "Perhaps you were correct. It is an undignified moniker."

He would rather suggest she call *him* by his given name, but he suspected the attraction he felt was one-sided. Her eye seemed firmly fixed on Sir Edmund.

"You do realize Mr. Perkins only warmed to Sir Edmund, because he was sneaking the dog bites of roast beef."

Ambrosia recoiled. "No! Is that true?"

"I caught him in the act. I assume he returned to the kitchen sometime during charades."

"Oh, my word!" Her green eyes sparked in the lamplight. Whether from amusement or irritation, Phillip didn't know. He hoped the latter. "No wonder Mr. Perkins warmed to him so quickly. He doesn't take to strangers, but you must know that already."

"Your Mr. Perkins is a careful judge of character," he said evenly.

She sank into the chair with a smile teasing her lips. "It is rather sweet, isn't it? Sir Edmund seeking Mr. Perkins's approval?"

"Don't be foolish," he snapped. "You cannot believe Sir Edmund cares what a dog thinks of him. His only aim is to win *you*."

Her gaze cut toward him, her smile long gone. "Perhaps you've never courted a lady, Major Rowland, but we do appreciate a bit of effort."

"The man is manipulating you."

"At least Sir Edmund is showing initiative, and he already has my parents' approval. He never would have been invited to Everly Manor otherwise."

Her defense of the man was irksome. "I suppose you find him handsome, too. He meets every requirement on your short list, I wager."

"I do not appreciate your tone, sir, nor having my judgment challenged."

She might be speaking in a harsh whisper, but there was no doubt she was shouting at him. "Yes, I prefer a husband who is pleasing to the eye, and I will not apologize for desiring my parents' blessing or seeking a man capable of loving a vulnerable animal."

He held up his hands in surrender. "It is your life."

"I *know* it's my life." She scooted to the edge of the chair and extended her finger, ticking off each point as she made it. "One, my parents' approval will bode well for my future happiness. I love my mother, but she is difficult. If she tries to pick apart the man I have chosen, I cannot stand by quietly or allow the abuse to continue, and I would rather not be forced to avoid my family. Two, a man who shows tenderness to animals reveals a good heart. I believe he will be a loving husband and father."

"Consider this, Ambrosia." Phillip scooted closer, too, his knees bumping against hers. "What manner of man must hide meat in his pocket to make a dog like him?"

"I— He wants..." She clenched her fists and a sound of frustration rumbled deep in her throat. "Why are you carrying on about this? No one is asking *you* to marry Sir Edmund."

"I don't trust him," Phillip said, "and I will not leave Orion in your care when I am called to duty if you marry him."

A furious blush had invaded her cheeks, and her eyes appeared nearly black. If he could recall his words, he would do so immediately. The ultimatum had been an act of impulsivity.

She narrowed her eyes. "If you truly cared about your Orion, you wouldn't take him to an army camp. It is too dangerous for a little dog. You are only thinking of yourself. Why am I arguing with you? You are impossible."

She pushed from the chair and tripped over his legs in her haste. He bolted from the footstool and caught her around the waist before she fell. Her weight settled against him, her breasts flattened on his chest. His hand rested on the small of her back; his fingers unintentionally splayed on the swell of her bottom.

A familiar tightening invaded his lower belly. He'd have a raging cockstand in a matter of seconds. She didn't pull away; he didn't release her.

Her lips were very close. If he tilted his head, he could taste them. Her gaze was locked with his, her breath ragged.

Desire for her thrummed in his ears, through his veins, pumping hard in his chest. He placed his mouth to her ear, longing to capture the velvet button lobe gently between his teeth and coax a sigh of pleasure from her. "I could give it up for you," he murmured. "Sell my commission to keep from worrying you."

His suggestion startled him, but as soon as he heard himself speak the words, he knew it was true. The heaviness he always carried inside him lifted. He was weary of war and ready to make a home with a beautiful, spirited woman like the one he held in his arms.

He heard her swallow hard. A slight pressure from her fingertips cooled his ardor. He eased away and released her.

"It is late," he said. "I shouldn't keep you. "

She wet her lips. "Will you be joining us for breakfast again?"

Perhaps she dreaded facing him in the light of day, or maybe she feared her mother seeing them together and realizing something improper had occurred tonight. A need to protect her welled inside him.

"I am accustomed to lighter fare," he said. "I had planned to break my fast in my chamber."

She exhaled as if she'd been holding her breath waiting for his reply. He imagined a shadow of disappointment pass across her eyes, but it had to be a trick of the light. She tightened the sash of her wrapper. When she spoke, her tone was clipped. "Tomorrow in the meadow then. We agreed to nine o'clock."

Do you want to see me again? The question stuck in his throat. If he asked it, he must accept her answer, and he wasn't prepared for an end to their association.

He busied himself with removing the lamp chimney to light her candle. When he opened the secret door to escort her to her bedchamber, she reached for the candleholder. He relinquished it.

"I know the way." She stepped into the tunnel, closed the door, and slid the lock into place.

Chapter Eight

Ammie slept poorly after her midnight adventure with Major Rowland. Disorienting images and a sense of urgency had hounded her in her dreams. She'd climbed from bed that morning in a drowsy haze with just as many unanswered questions as she'd had after fleeing his chamber.

He offered to give up his career for me.

No matter how many times she had relived the moment word for word, she couldn't make sense of it. If he sold his commission, she would no longer have a reason to protest him taking Mr. Perkins away. Perhaps she would never see her dog again. Major Rowland had rendered her only weapon useless with the ease of a whisper.

He had won the battle.

Why, then, had he held her close, gazing at her as if only she could quench a thirst in him she couldn't fully comprehend? Was everything a tactic designed to lower her guard, a type of emotional warfare? Surely, he wouldn't be so coldhearted and cruel.

Please, let his intentions be pure. Please.

Last night she had discovered that she had no defenses against a man who caused her pulse to race with his nearness, and being wedged into the back seat of a six-person sleigh with him currently wasn't helping.

"Yaw!" Her older brother Julius snapped the reins, driving the horse faster.

The sleigh flew over a snowy hill, and for a terrifying moment, Ammie and Mr. Perkins were airborne. She squealed, hugging the dog against her chest. Her bum landed hard on the seat.

Major Rowland's scowl was as fierce as she'd ever seen. "Have a care, or I will commandeer the sleigh." He barked the order like a man accustomed to being obeyed, but Julius had been born with a reckless and wild streak that refused be tamed by anyone.

Her older brother flicked a glanced over the seat and smirked. "Calm yourself, Major. I am in full control."

Laurel shared the front seat with Julius; Hugh was tucked between them. Ammie's twin reached around their youngest brother and pinched Julius's ear.

"Faith, Laurel!" He jerked free of her punishing grip. "Do you want us to wreck? You are worse than Mrs. Turner."

"And you learned nothing from our contrary nanny," Laurel shot back. "Show some respect your elders and slow down."

Not one to be left out of any ruckus, Hugh tugged off his mitten and grabbed for his older brother's hat, knocking it askew.

"Watch it, runt." Julius resettled his hat. "I have no qualms about leaving *you* behind."

Ammie's siblings bickered in the front seat, but Julius eased back on the reins.

The major's scowl faded as he scratched behind the dog's ears. When he lifted his gaze toward Ammie, his indigo blue eyes crinkled at the corners. "Was your sister implying I am old?"

Her mouth was dry, and her lips didn't want to work properly.

"How old *are* you, Major?" Hugh asked, saving Ammie from having to respond.

William, who sat on Ammie's right, leaned forward to see around her, his jaw working back and forth while he studied the major. "I think old enough to have a wife," he said eventually. "Why haven't you married yet?"

Major Rowland's eyes twinkled with a hint of good humor. "Perhaps answering questions posed by nosy lads has left me no time for courting."

Ammie was too distracted by the thrilling swoop in her belly anytime the major looked at her to join in the playful banter. Since they had set off from Everly Manor, she'd been teetering between wanting to dance with joy and a fear of tossing up her accounts. It really could go either way. Had her parents known about her budding attraction to Major Rowland, she doubted they would have planned this morning's outing.

Yesterday, someone had seen her and the major together, so their daily walks had been cancelled. Mama and Papa were determined to silence any rumors of an agreement existing between Ammie and Major Rowland before her real suitors became discouraged. Nevertheless, her parents were sympathetic to her plight and wished to help, which is how Ammie, the major, and her four siblings came to be spending the day at the cottage by the lake—a quarter of an hour ride from the manor house.

Hidden from prying eyes, Mama had said with a suggestive lift of her eyebrows.

In her parents' minds, they were allowing Ammie one last chance to persuade the major to leave Mr. Perkins with her. She looked at it as an opportunity to find clarity, and she was looking forward to spending the day away from Everly Manor.

The lake cottage had always been Ammie's favorite among her father's properties. She often spent summer days reading or dreaming up her own stories on the grassy bank beneath an ancient Ash tree. Over the years, the house had provided refuge from the chaos that often erupted at the family home with too many occupants and not enough space to breathe. Papa seemed to understand Ammie's need for solitude best, and often kept her siblings from disturbing her when she wished for time alone.

As soon as Julius stopped the sleigh in front of the cottage, Hugh scrambled over Laurel and raced toward the front door. "I'll find the skates."

"He cannot find the nose on his face," William said before sauntering after him.

Ammie lowered Mr. Perkins to the floor, and he leapt from the sleigh. As he dashed around the snow-covered lawn, he stopped every few feet to sniff a bush or tree stump. He was a regular visitor to the cottage and followed the same routine every time.

"I think he loves this place as much as I," she said to the major. "I will miss it when I leave home."

He smiled kindly. "I hope you will be allowed to return often."

With the manor house full of guests, every servant had been called to duty, leaving the small stable unmanned. Major Rowland's training and comfort with horses was evident as he unharnessed the mare from the sleigh.

"I will see to her now," Julius said and led the mare toward the barn.

Ammie and her sister were left alone with the major. Laurel exchanged a look with her, silently coaxing Ammie to take the lead. She mentally grappled with finding something clever to say, but words failed her. When the silence was becoming awkward, Laurel rescued her.

"Do you know how to skate, sir?"

"I did when I was a boy, but I haven't been on the ice for years."

Ammie piped up. "Skating is a skill you never forget." She felt proud of her ability to string several words together without them sounding like gibberish.

"I hope that is true, Lady Ambrosia. A broken leg would pose a problem at the Christmas ball."

"Balderdash! You don't need two good legs to brood at the back of the room, sir."

"Me, brood? Never."

"Hmm, I must have mistaken another gentleman for you at charades last night. The poor man looked miserable."

He grinned. "Perhaps he has no skill for charades and didn't wish to embarrass himself. I expect he is an accomplished dancer, though. I imagine his mother made certain he received the best instruction available."

She laughed softly, the erratic flutters in her belly lessening as they settled into a comfortable banter. "In that case, I hope he asks to sign my dance card. It is often a challenge to find a gentleman with any skill for dancing."

"How could he resist? I suspect it has been a long time since he has stood up with a lady, and he intends to make the most of the opportunity."

Ammie lapsed into silence. She didn't much like the thought of him dancing with other ladies.

Laurel picked up the conversation. "Here they come—William and Hugh. Shall we put your skill on the ice to the test, Major?"

After the heavy snowfall two nights earlier, the servants had cleared a large circle on the ice. Hugh and William loved skating, and it was in everyone's best interests to encourage their passion. Tired younger brothers became *well-behaved* younger brothers.

Julius returned from the stable when Ammie, Laurel, and the major were moving onto the ice. William and Hugh had hurried through strapping the blades to their boots and were chasing each other around the circle.

Major Rowland seemed a little unsure on skates at first. When his feet tried to get away from him, he thrust out his arms to regain his balance. "Whoa!"

She chuckled. "You are not on a horse, sir."

"I am well aware, fairy."

Ammie skated a wide circle around him to avoid their skates becoming tangled if he took a spill. "Surely, you are not too old to remember what you are doing."

His glower was comical given he was as unsure on his feet as a newborn colt. "I am one and thirty. You tell me, does that make me too old for you?"

Her body flushed with heat. She had wondered at their age difference, although she had only meant to goad him into trying harder. "You are doing a fine job," she murmured.

He was gentlemanly enough not to draw notice to her change of subject. Soon his body seemed to recall the feel of balancing on the thin blades. She took his hands when it appeared he was no longer in danger of falling and skated backwards slowly, providing instruction and praise as he grew more accustomed to the movement.

Hugh and William flew by several times while leaving enough space for Ammie to teach the major without fear of a collision. Even Laurel and Julius kept their distance.

After completing a lap around the circle, Major Rowland was steadier on his feet. "I think I am ready to try it on my own," he said.

"Perhaps it is better if I stay close for a couple of turns to guard against that broken leg."

"Very wise, my lady."

She spun so they were facing the same direction. "Last night you were calling me Ambrosia. Are you having second thoughts about our friendship?"

He must feel it, too—this electric current tethering them to one another. To call it a friendship sounded like a mockery, but she lacked the courage to acknowledge the truth.

He slanted a wary look in her direction. "About last night..."

Oh, dear. She placed her hand over her thumping heart to keep it from breaking free of her body.

"Faith, Ambrosia." He forcefully exhaled and removed his hat to push his hand through his hair. "My behavior was unacceptable. I never should have said what I did about Sir Edmund or thrown down the gauntlet. I might not like the gent for you, but I will not keep your Mr. Perkins from you if you choose Sir Edmund."

She reached out to stop his forward momentum and turned to face him. "I'm sorry, too. I overreacted, and you were right to call my attention to what Sir Edmund was doing. It was sneaky and dishonest of him, although I do not believe he meant any harm."

His eyes shuttered. "As I said, I will not stand in the way of your happiness."

A lump formed in her throat. Was he trying to tell her to look elsewhere for love? It certainly felt as if he was pushing her away.

"I thought maybe." She swallowed around the hard knot crowding her throat and tried to gather her courage. She lost it at the last second. "It is Christmas. Perhaps we can enjoy one another's company for an afternoon without discussing our dog."

"I think it is possible." An easy smile spread across his face, the warmth of it filtering into his eyes. "*My* friends call me Phillip. Perhaps you would do me the honor of using my given name, too."

"Yes, Phillip, I will."

Chapter Nine

An ache had taken up residence in the middle of Phillip's chest after the small ice skating party returned to Everly Manor, and he said good-bye to Ambrosia. After spending the entire day together yesterday, he felt the loss of her company more keenly.

He only had himself to blame for her parents curtailing their daily walks to exercise the dog, but he had taken the honorable path. His conscience had demanded he shield Ambrosia from any unpleasantness or speculation, so he'd warned her parents about them having been seen together. Lord and Lady Seabrook's decision hadn't come as a surprise, but it was a blow all the same.

And he truly ached.

The hurt was soul deep and steeped in urgency, as if he couldn't be near her again—now—he might come apart. Therefore, he'd pushed aside his discomfort with large gatherings to join a group of carolers intent on serenading the neighbors.

He'd counted thirty-four singers brave enough to venture into the cold night before they set off from Everly Manor.

Ambrosia was the only one who mattered.

He walked alongside her, the sound of crisp snow crunching beneath thirty-four sets of boots underscoring happy chatter. Servants walked alongside the guests with lanterns raised to light the way.

"I wouldn't have pegged you for a songbird, Major Rowland," Sir Edmund piped up from his place at Ambrosia's other side.

Phillip tempered his response. Instead of telling the intruder to shut his trap so Phillip could forget he was there, he said, "I am a man of hidden talents."

He didn't have a voice to make angels weep, but he'd been told it was pleasant enough.

Sir Edmund's laugh held a hint of mockery. "Do enlighten us, Major. What gifts do you possess aside from your obvious talent for warfare? You are a war hero, are you not?"

Phillip's spine stiffened. Inevitably, someone who had no sense of what it meant to fight for England wanted to make light of war. He'd been the same at one time, romanticizing patriotism and acts of heroism.

Ambrosia turned toward Sir Edmund. "I believe Major Rowland used the word hidden, because he doesn't reveal his talents to everyone. Do you have any special skills, sir?"

Sir Edmund puffed out his chest. "I am a member of the Four Horse Club."

"A useful skill, indeed," Ambrosia said. "I wouldn't know the first thing about driving a barouche. Well done, sir."

Phillip clamped his lips tightly, stewing. Must she sound so admiring?

"My brother Julius is a member."

"I have seen him at meetings." Sir Edmund practically crowed over stealing her attention. "His bays are exquisite. Their strong trot is enviable. I would give my left arm for an introduction to the breeder."

Ambrosia tittered as if he was the cleverest man she had ever met. Phillip's scowl deepened.

"An appendage will not be necessary, Sir Edmund. Julius would be happy to provide a letter of introduction." She called her brother's name. "May I intrude a moment?"

Lord Julius, who had been engrossed in flirting with a seasoned widow, kissed her hand and promised to find her later. His easy smile appeared genuine as he approached. "How may I be of service, dear sister?"

"Sir Edmund was admiring your horses. I understand you and he belong to the same driving club. Perhaps you could tell him more about your breeder now."

"Splendid. Shall we?" Her brother clapped a strong arm around Sir Edmund's shoulders and dragged him away. "Nothing gets my blood flowing faster than talk of horseflesh."

Phillip detected a note of sarcasm from him, most likely aimed at his sister and her inopportune timing. Nevertheless, Lord Julius obliged her request and ignored Sir Edmund's subtle protest.

"Should we discuss this later, my lord?"

"No no, you aren't a bother in the least." Lord Julius spoke quickly, making it impossible for Sir Edmund to interject without appearing rude, and widened the gap between his sister and her suitor.

Unwanted suitor? "Did you fob off Sir Edmund on your poor brother?" Phillip murmured.

"Don't be ridiculous." She averted her gaze and picked up her pace.

"You *did*, but you do not want to admit it."

"Balderdash."

Phillip chuckled as she stalked ahead of him. "Otherwise, you wouldn't be running away."

She stopped, crossing her arms impatiently while he caught up. "It is cold. I am trying to warm up, and we've fallen behind."

"I know how to warm you." He stood facing her, much too close for propriety and not near enough to satisfy the longing she'd awakened in him. "May I touch you?"

A small breath cloud drifted from her parted lips. He waited, holding still. Talking and laughter from the other guests grew fainter as the gap widened. The lantern light dimmed. Soon they would be left in darkness, but he waited.

Her voice was barely more than a whisper. "You may."

He removed his gloves, tucked them into his greatcoat pocket, and slowly reached for the top frog on her pelisse. She had neglected to fasten it. The backs of his fingers brushed against the luxurious velvet. She swayed toward him. He slid his hand to cup her cold cheek, his fingertips tucking into her winter bonnet to touch her silken hair.

"Is that better, my lady?"

"Yes," she answered breathlessly.

The drive to kiss her surged through his veins and trembled in his limbs. Once again, he found himself in a predicament. Ambrosia must choose him, definitively.

He couldn't make assumptions.

"Thank you for sending Sir Edmund away," he murmured.

"You are not fond of him and I sensed..." Her tongue nervously flicked over her lips. "Is it uncomfortable to speak of the war, Phillip?"

Her inquiry was sincere and sensitive, but the memories it stirred weren't conducive to romance. He sighed and withdrew his hand. "I prefer not to dwell on my time abroad, but it depends on who asks. Sir Edmund is a stranger."

She blinked and dropped her gaze. "Yes, of course. I'm sorry for prying."

He should offer reassurance and explain he didn't view her as he did Sir Edmund, but it was easier to change the subject. "We should join the others before they send a search party." He offered his arm, not wishing to leave her with the impression she had angered him, and injected as much humor into his tone as he could muster. "I might have to take more drastic measures to warm you while we wait to be found."

"How ominous that sounds." She linked arms with Phillip, feigning a shiver for dramatic effect, and spoke of lighter topics. "No one asked about *my* talents."

"An unpardonable oversight that I would like to correct. What are your special talents, my lady?" *Aside from casting a spell on a man from the moment he meets you?*

"I'm not sure I should say. Only my sisters know."

"Then I am doubly honored you are bringing me into your confidence."

She laughed—a tentative, nervous sound—and leaned her head against his shoulder. "I write stories for children, about Mr. Perkins and his adventures."

"That is a marvelous talent. Why do you keep it secret?"

She shook her head and laughed again. "I don't know. Maybe because I am afraid my writing is rubbish."

"I assume your sisters have read your stories. What do they say?"

"What any good sisters would say. They love Mr. Perkins's adventures. Laurel thinks I should ask Papa to help find a publisher for my stories, but I know they are not good enough for publication."

He drew her closer as a wave of protectiveness swelled beneath his breastbone. "I suspect you are too close to the project to be objective. Perhaps you would allow me to read your books. I already love the protagonist. How could I not enjoy his adventures?"

"Maybe I will, someday."

Someday hinted they had a future. He would accept it.

When they caught up to the others outside of the neighbors' home, the carolers were starting the first song. Phillip and Ambrosia lent their voices to *God Rest You Merry, Gentlemen* midway through the first verse. She was possibly one of the worst singers he had ever heard, but she was enthusiastic, smiling, and undeniably adorable.

And another piece of his heart was lost to her.

After three songs, the neighbors invited the carolers inside for refreshments. Welcoming fires crackled in the great room hearths, and a long table adorned with the finest white linens had been set up in the middle of one wall. Silver trays and china platters held an assortment of petit fours, biscuits, and sandwiches.

A pianoforte had been set up in the corner. A young woman, possibly one of the daughters of the house, sat on the bench to play lightly while everyone filled plates and mingled with one another. Sir Edmund found Ambrosia to resume conversation, and although she was polite and charming, she only strayed from Phillip's side when her sister Laurel requested her. He lost sight of the women when they headed into the corridor.

Sir Edmund's pleasant smile vanished. "I believe pressing my suit would be an ill use of my time," he said without rancor. "I am standing down. No need to thank me."

Phillip ground his teeth. For a man who'd professed his devotion to the lady forty-eight hours earlier, Sir Edmund's surrender had come too easily. His lack of fortitude and arrogance reinforced Phillip's poor opinion of him.

"Perhaps it is in the lady's best interests," he said evenly. "Lady Ambrosia deserves a steadfast mate."

Sir Edmund shrugged off the challenge to his character. "I am certain she will have one."

Turning on his heel, he strolled toward the young woman sitting at the pianoforte. When Ambrosia returned, she didn't seem to notice his absence. She hooked Phillip's arm.

"Come with me. I want to introduce you to our hosts."

He hesitated a moment before giving himself over to Ambrosia's care, trusting her to guide him into a world that felt foreign now. Her ease with social graces and ability to engage with the other guests melted the frozen knot in his chest, and although he couldn't say he was enjoying himself, socializing was easier with her at his side. By evening's end, he'd begun to relax and was disappointed when it was time to say goodnight to her.

The lad Charlie was waiting for him when Phillip retired to his bedchamber. His valet apprentice was a quick study, and he set to work helping Phillip remove his boots and polished them until they gleamed. After Charlie left, Phillip removed his cravat and was hanging his jacket and waistcoat in the wardrobe when the lock to the hidden passage dragged against wood.

Orion dashed inside and leapt on the bed. Ambrosia stood in the opening, dressed for bed and a sheath of papers clutched to her chest. "Since I had my turn the last two nights, it only seemed fair to bring Mr. Perkins to you."

She held back, biting her bottom lip.

His heart expanded. "Have you come to read me a bedtime story?"

"I don't know. Maybe." She frowned. "It has been a long day. Should I go?"

He crossed the room and took her hand to coax her inside. "You should definitely stay. I'll not be able to rest knowing I missed a chance to hear you read of Mr. Perkins's adventures."

A pink blush infused her cheeks. He longed to kiss her until she forgot to be nervous, but once he started, he wasn't certain he could stop. She trusted him like he had placed his faith in her earlier. He wanted to be as worthy of that trust as she.

"You have nothing to fear, Ambrosia. I will love your story." How could he not when he was so deeply smitten with the author?

Chapter Ten

Ammie woke with Mr. Perkins softly snoring at the foot of the bed. The room was cold, and she'd fallen asleep on top of the counterpane. Sunlight fell across her face and illuminated the unfamiliar burgundy wall coverings. She blinked, disoriented by the changes in her bedchamber. As the haziness of sleep began to clear, she gasped and bolted upright.

Phillip leapt from the bed with a guttural growl, his fists raised. His gaze shot wildly around the room. Sleep had rumpled his shirt and trousers and left his dark brown hair flattened on one side. The rest rose like spikes from his head.

"Phillip, it is Ambrosia. We fell asleep."

As recognition filtered across his face, he dropped his fists.

She swung her legs over the side of the bed and woke the dog, too. "I need to hurry before Laurel wakes. Where are my papers?"

Phillip plowed his hand through his hair, turning toward the side table by the chair. "Over here." His voice was rough from sleep. They had been up most of the night talking.

He gathered the sheets of her story while Ammie found her slippers. She had been too shy to read her stories aloud, so Phillip had done the honors, reading all four, one right after the other. Afterward, he'd spent a good hour singing her praises and asking about her ideas for future stories. She had been flattered by his genuine interest and stunned that he believed a publisher would be eager to put her words into print.

If you write a few more, he'd said, *they could be published in a collection.* He had connections at a publishing house he could contact on her behalf. Additionally, his close friend was a talented sketch artist.

But they are written for children, she had argued.

A good children's tale enchants the young, and the young at heart.

Ammie hadn't dreamed anything would ever come of her writing. Laurel was encouraging, of course, but Ammie's sister was hardly objective. When Phillip spoke enthusiastically about a future in publishing, she began to believe it was possible.

Phillip met her at the foot of the bed and passed the sheath of papers to her. "Thank you for sharing these with me," he said. "I am honored and serious about helping you."

Impulsively, she threw her arms around his neck and hugged him. "Thank you, Phillip. You have no idea how grateful I am."

His arms circled her, and they held each other longer than necessary. "I really should go," she said, reluctant to end the hug first.

He released her and smiled. "Yes, no more stalling. I am officially tossing you from my chambers." Gently, he turned her around by her shoulders and nudged her toward the hidden passage.

Mr. Perkins realized she was leaving and followed. "Your dog loves me better," she whispered, teasing.

He grinned. With his hair mussed, his smile lent him a boyish charm. "You spoil him terribly. How can I compete?"

Perhaps competition was unnecessary. If they were to marry...

The flicker of hope in her heart snuffed out as quickly as it had sparked. Her parents personally selected every bachelor attending the house party after a careful examination of reputations, finances, and connections. Every unmarried gentleman had received prior approval—all except Phillip. And Mama had taken a dislike to him immediately.

The backs of her eyes stung. "Leave the door open to light the way." She slipped into the dim corridor, not waiting for him to light a candle.

"Ambrosia, wait."

She hurried down the hidden passage, worried he might have seen tears building behind her eyes and not wishing to answer questions. At the secret entrance to her room, she took pains to open the wall panel slowly so it wouldn't creak. The curtains were drawn, and Laurel was lying still beneath the covers. Ammie tiptoed into the bedchamber. Mr. Perkins hopped on the bed.

"Where have you been?"

Ammie jumped. "Oh! D-did I wake you? I needed the chamber pot."

"I woke awhile ago"—Laurel sat up, tucking the covers beneath her arm—"and you were missing. Where did you go in your nightclothes?"

Ammie's body flushed with heat. She never lied to her twin, and to be caught out made her cringe. With a resigned sigh, she sat on the edge of the bed and dropped her writing on the counterpane. "The major wanted to read my stories. I only meant to take Mr. Perkins to spend the night in his chambers and leave my manuscript, but Mr. Perkins wouldn't stay without me. Phillip and I fell asleep talking."

Laurel's dark eyebrows shot toward her hairline. "Phillip, is it?"

"It appears our truce has turned into friendship."

"You were happy at the lake cottage," Laurel said, "and I believe Major Rowland put that smile on your face. Are you certain it is only a friendship?"

"I'm not sure of anything anymore." Ammie fell backward across the bed and stared at the rose and green floral canopy. Mr. Perkins curled next to her, laying his head on her shoulder. "I think I might be falling in love with him. I don't know. It is too quick to fall in love, isn't it?"

Her twin smoothed her hand over Ammie's hair. Ever since they were little girls, they had comforted each other in this way. "The heart cannot tell time," Laurel said. "Perhaps you should trust that it knows what it wants."

"I fear it is leading me toward heartbreak."

"How so?" As her sister's hand made another pass over her head, tension in her body began to melt.

"Papa would never approve of the match," Ammie said. "Phillip is not one of the suitors chosen for us, and it is obvious Mama does not care for him."

Laurel frowned. "She has been uncommonly rude to the major. Still, you have no idea what Papa will say until you speak with him."

Ammie rubbed her eyes; they felt gritty from too little sleep. "Law, I'm getting ahead of myself. Maybe Phillip doesn't feel the same about me. Why poke the bee hive for no reason?"

"Well, there you are wrong," Laurel said. "Even Julius noticed the major is smitten, and our brother is oblivious to anything that doesn't involve him."

"He is rather boorish at times." Ammie blinked her sister's upside down face into focus. "Tell me what to do, please. Is it wise to take a chance on Phillip? He hinted he would be willing to sell his commission, but what if he doesn't? I would worry myself sick if he was sent abroad. Maybe it would be best to encourage Sir Edmund's suit and protect my heart."

"Do you want to marry Sir Edmund?"

In London, she'd thought she could learn to care for him, and even though the gentleman had done nothing wrong, she would never feel for him what she did for Phillip. "No," Ammie murmured. "I don't want to marry him."

"Then you mustn't."

Ammie and her sister were silent for several moments, each lost in their own thoughts. "It would not be good for Phillip either," she said eventually, "being sent abroad again. He doesn't talk about the war, but I think it still haunts him."

"If you are truly seeking my advice, you should talk to the major. Ask if he plans to sell his commission and share your worries. And do it for *him*, whether you have a future or not. As you said, you are friends. He might not realize what the war has done to him."

As usual, her sister was right, but it wouldn't be an easy conversation. She reached for Laurel's hand and drew it to her lips for a kiss. "Thank you. You always steer me toward the correct course."

Her sister's shoulders drooped and her face fell. "I wish I knew the right one for me."

"What is wrong?" Ammie sat up. She'd been no better than Julius, thinking only of herself. "Oh, dear. Forgive me. I've been too wrapped up in my own troubles lately."

"No, it is silly." Her sister drew the sleeve of her nightrail across her eyes to dry them. "I am tired. That is all."

"You always do this." She shook her sister's arm to get her attention. Laurel lifted her gaze. "Let me help you for once."

Laurel scoffed. "Unless you have a love potion hidden someplace, there is nothing you can do."

"To use on you or someone else?" Admittedly, Ammie hadn't been paying close attention, but she couldn't recall seeing Laurel more than once with any of the gentlemen staying at Everly Manor.

"For *me*." Laurel rolled her eyes. "I think a magic spell is my only hope. Not a single man here seems capable of carrying on a decent conversation. All they wish to discuss is the weather or how flattering blue or green or yellow is on me. The other night Lord Kensingly wouldn't stop fussing over my gown, so I offered to loan it to him."

A shocked laugh burst from Ammie. Her sister smiled.

"I would have loved to have seen the look on his face," Ammie said.

"It was rather fun. I better understand why Octavia is always so cheeky. "

"It doesn't hurt that our younger sister is able to get away with it either." Ammie sobered thinking about their situation. "I don't want to appear ungrateful for this opportunity Papa and Mama arranged for us, but perhaps we should be honest about the men they have chosen. Knowing how close our parents are, I cannot imagine they would want to see us settle for unfulfilling matches."

"No, of course they wouldn't, although it will be disappointing news." Laurel twined a strand of her own hair around her finger, a sign of her nerves trying to get the better of her. "Do you think they will listen?"

"If we stand together, I believe they will." Ammie climbed from bed to summon their lady's maid. Their family would be gathering in the breakfast room soon, and tardiness would invite questions she didn't care to answer. "Shall we request an audience after breakfast?"

"Yes." Laurel's exhale seemed shaky. "I suppose it is better to resolve the matter quickly."

Ammie and her sister never had a chance to pose the request, however, because they were ordered to their father's study before they left their bedchamber. Ammie was first to be called on the carpet.

Mama crossed her arms, her face very stern. "Did you and Sir Edmund have a row?"

The question knocked her off center and she stammered a denial.

"Are you certain?" Mama narrowed her eyes; Ammie's temper flared.

"Whatever would we find to argue about, Mama? We don't know each other well enough to become cross with one another."

"Then perhaps you have another explanation for Sir Edmund leaving early this morning. The stable boy reported his carriage left at dawn."

Ammie gaped. He'd said nothing to her about his plans.

Laurel cleared her throat, coming to Ammie's rescue. "Perhaps he and Miss Raby reached an agreement last night. Once Sarah was seated at the pianoforte, Sir Edmund couldn't keep his eyes off her. He lingered after everyone else returned to Everly Manor."

"Did he?" Ammie murmured. She hadn't given him another thought after she and Laurel sought out the retiring room. In truth, she hadn't even noticed his absence when they left the Rabys' house last night.

"That deceitful cow!" Mama bolted from her chair and paced to the window, presumably to glower in the direction of the neighbors' house. "I should march in there and tell Mrs. Raby what I think of her. She promised to wait until you and Laurel made your choices before parading out her daughter, but I see she cannot be trusted."

Papa left his seat to speak with her in soothing tones. "Let's not start a feud with our neighbors just yet, love. The Rabys are housing several of our guests."

Ammie didn't wish to be the cause of any dispute with their neighbors, especially when the news of Sir Edmund's departure came as a relief. "I, for one, am happy for Sarah and Sir Edmund if they found one another. Although he and I didn't suit, I believe he is a decent man."

"Your father and I are aware of the caliber of gentlemen in attendance," Mama snipped. "They have all been thoroughly curated."

Neither Ammie nor Laurel was allowed to speak again. Mama was on a tear, lecturing them about duty to the family and reminding them of the sacrifices made to create a private marriage mart where they each had their pick of men.

All except the one Ammie truly wanted.

"Join your siblings for breakfast," Mama ordered at the end of her tirade. "The servants have other responsibilities today. It is rude to interfere with their schedules."

Papa nodded his agreement and dismissed Ammie and her sister.

"I'm sorry," Laurel mumbled when they reached the study door. "I thought I was helping."

"I know." Ammie opened the door and came up short. Phillip was standing in the corridor. Her sister slipped from the study and Ammie hurriedly pulled the door closed behind them.

"What are you doing here?" she whispered to him.

"I was summoned."

"Why?"

"I wasn't informed of the reason."

Her stomach turned; a sour taste rose at the back of her throat. Did her parents know she had spent the night in his chambers? Would he insist it was innocent? Her parents wouldn't believe him, of course, but she had never lied to them. "I-I should come with you."

Laurel linked arms with her, her grip tight. "We should do as we were told. Don't make trouble for yourselves. Wait until you know what our parents want with the major."

Ammie's heart was pounding in her ears. "If they ask you to leave, promise you will find me first."

He nodded, his expression grim.

The study door flew open. Papa grunted in surprise. "Laurel and Ammie, run along to breakfast."

When Ammie hesitated, Laurel tugged her arm, leaving her no choice except to walk away.

Chapter Eleven

A brutal northwesterly wind had arrived sometime in the night, prompting partygoers to seek refuge indoors that afternoon. In anticipation, the great room had been transformed into a gaming area with various sized tables and mismatched chairs interrupting the flow of foot traffic. Fires blazed in two large iron stoves located at opposite ends of the room. Heat rolled off the ornate behemoths, making the air heavy in the overcrowded space.

Suppressing his urge to retreat to someplace quieter, Phillip headed for the gaming tables to search for Ambrosia. She found him first.

"*Where* have you been? I have been waiting forever for you to arrive."

"I was reading in my bedchamber."

She huffed. "Oh, for Pete's sake! You must know I was on edge all morning. Let's find somewhere with less people, unless you enjoy shouting."

"Not particularly." He followed her into an empty alcove where three chessboards had been set up.

"I demand a rematch"—she claimed one of the chairs, coyly gazing up at him with her chin lowered—"or perhaps a lesson. I am not very good."

The move made her seem vulnerable and flirtatious at the same time. He didn't know whether to kiss her or come to her rescue. Since the former would be inappropriate and possibly unwelcome, he sat on the ladder-back chair across from her.

"Do you really want a lesson in chess," he asked, "or are we engaging in a charade for onlookers?"

"How easily you have seen through my ruse." Smiling, she grabbed the queen-rook-pawn to move it two spaces. "Perhaps you've come to know me better than I realized."

Not as well as I'd like.

She leaned over the board. Her large green eyes glimmered in the brightly lit room; an apprehensive furrow had formed between her brows. "Why did my father summon you?" she whispered. "Does he know about last night?"

"No, it was nothing." The bewildering meeting with her parents had been brief and without a purpose as far as he could tell. He'd expected to be warned to stay away from Ambrosia today, so she could become better acquainted with the gentlemen who had come to court her, especially now that Sir Edmund had taken his leave. "Your parents asked if I found my lodgings comfortable."

"Oh no." Color drained from her face; she plopped against the chair back. "They know."

Phillip reached across the board to take her hand for comfort and thought better of it. He grabbed his knight instead.

"I don't believe they are aware you visited my chambers. Otherwise, they would be demanding we marry." He took a moment to govern himself, not wishing to appear too eager in the event she found the idea distasteful. "We spent the night together, Ambrosia. It was innocent, but honor dictates I should offer for your hand."

Her frown deepened. "Must you?"

Her rejection came as hard and fast as a fist to the gut. He physically recoiled, curling inward. "It is your turn," he said more brusquely than intended.

She studied him from her reclined position. Eventually, she sat upright and moved her rook to the vacant square behind the pawn. "May I ask you something personal, Phillip?"

He didn't trust himself to speak. His jaw was twitching, and clenching his teeth did nothing to stop the involuntary spasms. She didn't wait for his consent.

"Did you mean what you said about selling your commission?"

"I—" He swallowed hard. She was treading too close to a topic he wished to avoid, but he owed it to her to answer. If she asked about his experience in the war, he would direct the conversation elsewhere. "I believed the Army was where I belonged, but when I heard myself promise to walk away, I felt..."

He hesitated. Would admitting the truth make him sound like a traitor?

"What did you feel?" She rested her arm on the table; her fingertips accidentally brushed his. "Please, you may tell me anything."

"Relief," he said softly. "I felt relieved."

"Oh, Phillip." She rewarded his honesty with a smile that reached into his chest to cradle his heart. Every moment in her presence strengthened the notion he'd found where he really belonged. "Perhaps you should trust that part of yourself to know what is best."

"Perhaps I should." He turned his palm up and she placed her hand in his. "Thank you, Ambrosia."

"Why would you thank me?"

"For listening without judgment." Gently, he squeezed her fingers then reached for the king-bishop-pawn.

She absently grabbed the rook and illegally jumped her own pawn. He didn't correct her. "What do you want to do after you sell your commission, or haven't you given it any thought?"

"I don't know," he lied.

She raised her eyebrows in challenge. "I find that hard to believe. Isn't there anything that stirs your passion?"

Aside from you?

She pointed toward his telltale smile. "I knew it. Something does excite you. Please, tell me. I confided in you about my writing."

"I've thought about breeding spaniels and training them to hunt."

She gasped, raised her hands in front of her sternum, and clapped her hands in a miniature round of applause. "What a perfect choice! You will make a marvelous trainer."

He chuckled, delighted by her enthusiasm, however overdone it was. "How do you know? I could be a complete failure."

"Don't pretend modesty. Mr. Perkins received excellent training. I haven't kept it up like you would have, but I tried."

She randomly moved another pawn, no longer taking turns. It didn't matter. The chess game was simply a façade to allow them to speak without interruption.

"We realized Mr. Perkins wasn't a stray when I brought him home," she said. "My father and brothers tried to find the owner, but no one claimed him. Now I understand the reason. You were out of the country."

Had his older brother not been preoccupied with his mistress, perhaps he would have realized Phillip's dog had gone missing sooner and been aware the Seabrooks had taken in Orion. But then Phillip wouldn't have met Ambrosia. For that reason alone, he could forgive Jeremy for being an irresponsible lout.

"Tell me more about your thoughts on becoming a breeder," Ambrosia said. "Do you have land available?"

He didn't, but his father provided an ample yearly income for him and his brothers from their mother's inheritance. Phillip had been in a position to purchase his own commission, much to his father's distress. He had hoped Phillip or Phillip's younger brother would choose the clergy, but neither of them was suited to that profession. Phillip and Nathaniel had always been too physical to spend hours pouring over their studies.

"I might let a country house with land," he said.

"How lovely would it be to find a place nearby? London isn't so far away for gentlemen to travel for a dog, and Mr. Perkins has been very happy here. A happy dog must make for a good hunter."

"Actually, that is an excellent thought."

The next hour was spent contemplating his plans and discussing strategy with her. He found he quite liked sharing this private part of himself, and her excitement fueled his own. Two gentlemen joined them in the alcove and played a match of chess during that hour, but they seemed to lose interest after one round.

When Phillip and Ambrosia were alone again, she said, "I've been thinking about your advice to write a collection and seek publication. The prospect scares me silly, but maybe it will be worth the risk."

"There is little risk involved. You are a gifted writer."

Her cheeks pinked. "I still have much to learn."

"There is always more to learn in anything one undertakes. Wise people recognize this truth."

He loved the way her pixie nose crinkled when she laughed. "Did you just compliment me, or yourself?"

He grinned. "That didn't come across as I had hoped. Allow me to pose a personal question to you. Why did you choose the name Mr. Perkins? Who is this mystery man you admire, and should I be jealous?"

"Very," she teased. "Reginald Perkins was the smartest man I've ever met. He took an interest in me early on—or rather, he took an interest in my learning. Mr. Perkins was my older brothers' tutor, but when I began loitering around the schoolroom, Mr. Perkins demanded I grab a slate and have a seat. If I was going to make a nuisance of myself, the least I could do was become an *educated* nuisance.

He was a bit of a curmudgeon, but we got on well enough. He is responsible for me taking up writing, although his form of encouragement might not be to everyone's tastes. I believe his exact words to me were 'stop talking about the blasted ducks and put your words to paper.'"

Phillip lifted an eyebrow. "Ducks?"

"My first stories were about the mallards that gathered on the pond every year. They weren't very interesting."

"I've always found ducks to be dull conversationalists."

She laughed again, and it was the happiest sound he'd ever heard. How could one ever be blue when she provided an endless supply of joy?

"Well, we have exhausted that topic." She tipped her head, signaling a subject change. "Last night you mentioned your friend is a gifted artist. Do you really think he would be interested in illustrating my book?"

Phillip's smile froze. He'd spoken in haste last night, and in that moment, Phillip had been remembering his longtime friend as he used to be—not as Gabriel was when he returned home from war. Perhaps Gabe no longer practiced his art. Nevertheless, Phillip had recommended his friend, and Ambrosia was excited about pursuing her passion. He couldn't disappoint her.

"Captain Brazier is at his family's estate in Northumberland," he said. "I could write to him after the holiday if you like. If he is not available for the task, I will help you find someone else."

"Thank you, that is a kind offer, although I do hope the captain agrees. I would feel better working with an artist you know rather than a stranger."

There was a good chance Gabe wouldn't respond to any letter Phillip sent. He had reached out to his friend after their Regiment returned to England in May, but Phillip never received a word in return.

Their last contact had become seared into Phillip's memory. Mercifully, Gabe was too addled by laudanum at the time to realize his leg had been too mangled to save. Phillip, on the other hand, couldn't forget anything about the field hospital— not the wailing or moaning, not the stench, and not his role in the suffering all around him.

Ambrosia's warm touch on his arm startled him. The furrow between her brows was back. "Where did you go just now?"

He shook his head and chuckled. It sounded strained. "I've been here with you the past hour. Where else would I be?"

"Yes, of course. Silly me." Her smile wavered and never reached her eyes, and the most terrifying thought crossed his mind. Once she met Gabe, she would know what Phillip really was.

Chapter Twelve

Later that evening, Ammie and Phillip sat side-by-side to watch the Christmas pageant her oldest sister had arranged. Mercedes recruited her husband to narrate the story and impressed Ammie's siblings into service. In the past, Ammie and Laurel would have been included in the cast, whether they agreed or not, but Mercedes had allowed them a reprieve this year.

Despite Phillip smiling and commenting at the appropriate moments, Ammie sensed his distraction. He hadn't been the same since their conversation in the alcove. The shift in mood had occurred when he'd spoken of Captain Brazier, whom she assumed had served alongside him on the Peninsula, and possibly at Waterloo. She couldn't work out what might have brought about the change in him, no matter how many times she turned it over in her head.

"What if Phillip regrets offering his assistance?" Ammie was pacing the bedchamber she shared with her sister and speaking aloud to sort out her thoughts. She wasn't expecting an answer.

"Go to him."

She shot an irritated glance in Laurel's direction. "If he helps negotiate with the publishing house and hires the illustrator, our association could go on indefinitely. Maybe he realized he wants to be rid of me. I don't think he loves me. If he did, would he talk of honor when discussing offering for my hand? He certainly didn't seem eager about the prospect."

"You should go to him," Laurel repeated. She was sitting at the dressing table, calmly brushing her long sable hair.

Ammie wrinkled her nose at her sister's reflection in the oval looking glass. "Is that the only advice you have to give? You told me the same thing earlier."

"It is the only *good* advice I have. Now, stop arguing. You know you'll get nowhere talking to me about your concerns. Go to the source for answers."

Ammie held her arms out at her sides, putting her plain ivory attire on display. "I've already donned my nightrail. Maybe I will seek him out tomorrow."

"And what will you do if you are given no privacy?" Laurel swiveled on the padded bench to face her. "We'll be having this conversation again tomorrow night. It is best to have the matter settled. If Major Rowland has no love for you, it is better to know now, so you can turn your attentions toward a different man."

Ammie half groaned, half growled. "Why do you always have to be so irritatingly logical?"

"Because you are a mess and a half lately," her sister retorted. "*One* of us must use common sense."

"Well, I want a turn at being the logical one." Ammie snatched a wrapper from a peg in the wardrobe and shoved her arms in the sleeves before stepping into her satin slippers. "How are you faring? Did anyone catch your fancy today?"

Laurel rolled her eyes.

"Don't abandon hope." Ammie's platitude was rote and felt hollow, but she had no experience with matters of the heart to offer useful advice. She was barely muddling through herself.

Since Mr. Perkins was fast asleep at the foot of the bed, she didn't wake him. She turned to look over her shoulder at the dressing screen. "I don't know how long I will be gone."

"I will turn the lock and tend the fire if needed. No one will know you've left the room."

Ammie left the candle for her sister and carefully felt her way along the dark passage. At Phillip's door, she knocked softly before sliding the latch and opening it. The room appeared empty at first glance. Then she heard counting.

"Eighty-seven, eighty-eight."

The sound was a little louder than a whisper. She followed it to the foot of the bed and came up short as her lungs seized. Barebacked and slick with sweat, Phillip was stretched out, balancing on his hands and feet. He counted, bending his arms and lowering his body toward the floor before raising it again.

She gaped in fascination. He was lean and well formed in a way she'd never imagined a man could be—broad across the shoulders, waist tapered, firm derrière. His body appeared to be made of stone covered by a shimmering expanse of skin that told the story of a warrior. A thin, pale scar wrapped around his side. Possibly inflicted by the downward swing of a saber. There were smaller red raised marks as well—two on his muscular bicep, another across his shoulder.

War had always been an abstract notion to her, but reality stared her in the face. Nausea welled at the back of her throat. The horrors of what he must have experienced overwhelmed her. Was it any wonder he didn't want to remember? A sob built in her chest. She tried to smother it with her hands, but it slipped through her fingers.

His head snapped toward her. "Ambrosia!"

Her heart was too full of hurt for him to contain. The pain spilled over into tears.

He jumped to his feet and came to wrap his arm around her shoulders. "What is wrong? Has something happened?"

Unable to speak, she shook her head.

He gathered her against his chest and tenderly placed a kiss to her forehead. She closed her eyes and nestled her face into the crook of his neck. His tone was soothing as he murmured words to comfort her and caressed the length of her back. "I am here, my darling. I have you. No need to cry anymore."

His gentleness intensified her ache. Why must someone as good and loving as Phillip endure the type of hell he'd been through? Why must anyone? She found the raised scar on his side and ran her fingers along the ridge.

"What have they done to you?" she whispered.

Phillip's body grew rigid; he set her away. "You should have told me you were coming tonight." He turned away, grabbed his discarded shirt from the chair, and pulled it over his head. "It has been a long day. Return to your chamber so we both may rest."

His abrupt dismissal stung. The urge to runaway was strong, but her sister would be awake still, and she would have questions. Knowing Laurel, she would send Ambrosia back with orders to face her troubles with Phillip before they were allowed to fester.

Blast her for being the wise one.

Her tears had stopped, and she wiped the dampness from her cheeks. "I am staying. We need to talk."

His glower would be frightening if she didn't know him better. Any man who loved animals the way he did was good at his core. No one would ever persuade her otherwise. And like a wounded animal himself, he lashed out.

"We've been together all day. What more is there to say?"

"Plenty." She perched on the end of the bed and patted the place beside her. Her hands shook. "I will go first."

His thick brows were dangerously low over his steely blue eyes. He crossed his arms over his chest. His body was closed off, but she wouldn't allow his invisible armor to deter her. Setting aside the last shred of her pride, she pleaded.

"Please, Phillip. This is not easy for me either."

For a moment, she thought he might force her to leave. His frown deepened, and he sat on the bed stiff-backed, arms still crossed. What words could she offer to a man who'd suffered as he had? Her life had been easy. She'd always had plenty of everything, had lost no one, and no one had ever mistreated her. She was acutely aware of how naive and pampered she'd been.

"I only now realize the reasons you do not talk about the war," she murmured. "I am sorry for mentioning Captain Brazier today. I suspect our conversation stirred up memories you would rather forget."

He met her gaze. She rushed to fill the silence.

"We could find a different illustrator, someone without a personal connection. I will save my pin money and purchase an advertisement in the news-sheet. I would want your help in interviewing the candidates."

His arms drifted to his sides; his lips parted as bewildered by her rambling. It confused her as well, but she couldn't stop talking.

"We should wait until the new year, or perhaps in the spring. No one will want to travel before the ice thaws and the mud dries. There is nothing worse than being stranded on the side of the road, what with highway men running amok these days."

Soundlessly, his mouth opened and closed.

"We will want to wait until the roads clear to start the kennel, too, although it might take a while for us to select a healthy lady dog." She cocked her head. "Or will more be required? Do we begin with a single litter, or is it best to have a few? We should really decide soon, don't you think?"

Mercifully, he placed his hand over hers on the bed and gently shushed her. She stopped babbling; a deluge of heat engulfed her body. He brushed his thumb across her cheek and pushed a strand of hair behind her ear before stroking the length of her braid. It hung heavily down the middle of her back.

The hard anger that had lined his face was gone. His eyes were dull now, and she sensed his sadness. It seeped through her skin, threatening to overpower her hope.

"The Christmas ball will be held in two days, Ambrosia. You must select a husband. He will help you interview illustrators. We will not see each other again."

"No, you are wrong. I have no future with any of the men my parents invited." Her stomach roiled; her tongue felt gritty. Fear whispered in her ears.

He doesn't want you. He will laugh at you. You will look like a fool.

She chose to be brave. "I love you," she whispered.

He didn't laugh.

"I love you," she repeated in a louder voice. "I only want to be with you."

"If you knew everything I have done, you wouldn't say that." He closed his eyes, squeezing tightly. "War changes a man; it makes him into something he doesn't recognize anymore."

"I know all I need to know." She caught his hand between hers to anchor him to the bed. "You fought against England's greatest enemy and saved us from invasion. You are a hero."

"I am not a hero," he snapped. "Why must everyone keep using that word?"

He broke free of her fragile hold and paced to the fireplace to rest his arms and head on the mantle. "You don't understand, Ambrosia. Men *died* under my command. I committed atrocities that turn me inside out to think about now. My best friend lost his leg in battle, because I ordered the charge. How does any of that make me a hero?"

She didn't know how to respond and feared she would say something wrong, but her silence would be unforgivably cruel. Taking a deep breath for fortification, she said, "You did what any solider must do. You served your country."

A shudder passed through him. Ammie left the bed to try to ease his pain, even though she didn't know how to offer solace to a man whose experiences were worse than anything she could imagine. Tentatively, she reached to slick a curl behind his ear. His hair was the color of the precious cocoa kept locked in the larder.

When he didn't shy away from her touch, she lifted to her toes and gingerly kissed his cheek. A shadow darkened his strong jawline; his whiskers were rough beneath her lips.

"You survived," she murmured. "Your task was to stay alive and come home to your family."

He held very still. The air around him vibrated. The tension was exciting in a way she couldn't explain. Goose flesh rippled along her arms. Her heart knocked against her breastbone.

"You are good, Phillip." Emboldened, she kissed the corner of his mouth. "You have a beautiful soul."

He turned his face toward her. His eyes were the deepest blue, like the sky at twilight. "How do you know?" he whispered.

Cradling his face, she kissed the tip of his nose and chin, and held his unwavering gaze. "I wouldn't love you as I do if your heart was not pure."

"Ambrosia." He spoke her name with a reverence she didn't deserve when compared to him, but she basked in it. The huskiness of his voice caressed her body, causing a shocking pulse between her legs.

He stood upright and encircled her waist. His strong hands linked at the small of her back. She twined her arms around his neck. The soft hair at his nape brushed her wrists, and she shivered with pleasure.

"I see you, Phillip—all of you—and I love you. I want to spend the rest of our lives together, but not out of a sense of duty or honor. I must be loved in return."

A small pressure at the curve of her back urged her closer. She leaned into him and offered herself. His lips skimmed hers, the contact too brief to be satisfying. A whimpered plea reached her ears. It took a moment to realize the sound had come from her.

With a weak groan, he claimed her mouth.

Chapter Thirteen

Ambrosia's acceptance of him, even after he'd confessed his transgressions, was a gift Phillip couldn't refuse. He buried his fingers in her silky hair and splayed his hand on her back. Her heat penetrated the thin cotton of her wrapper and nightrail. She rose on her toes, pressing her sweet body into his.

A hunger to see and touch her ravaged him. He yanked the sash around her waist loose. Her wrapper fell open, and he shoved the garment off her shoulders. Breaking the kiss, she dropped her arms from around his neck.

Hellfire. What was he doing? He halted, not daring to move for fear of spooking her more than he likely already had. Ragged breaths passed their lips, their chests rising and falling in perfect rhythm. His throat thickened as she stared up at him. A storm was building behind her eyes. He tried to form an apology, but he couldn't speak.

Slowly, she slid a finger beneath the hem of his shirt, hesitating a heartbeat to search his face before continuing her exploration. The snow-white fabric gathered at the waistband of his trousers. When the pad of her finger touched his feverish skin, his abdomen contracted. He sucked in a sharp breath.

Triumph curved the corners of her plump mouth, and she flattened her palm against his lower belly. He smothered a groan as blood ripped through his veins. His cock grew heavy and sensitive to the barest brush with his trousers.

Grabbing the edge of his shirt in her fists, she drew it higher on his chest. He bent forward to allow her to tug the garment over his head before settling his hands on her waist. Her gaze roamed his body, her fingers following the same path over rugged planes and the swell of muscles. Her caress caused an ache deep in his bones, and he trapped her hand when she covered his heart. Closing his eyes, he leaned his forehead against hers.

"I adore you," he murmured. "I think I loved you from the second I saw you, but I didn't allow myself to believe you could ever love me back."

"You were wrong."

He smiled. She never censored herself with him, and he would never doubt her words of kindness when she delivered her less favorable opinions with the same sincerity and conviction. "I want to be with you forever, Ambrosia."

Her beautiful eyes glittered in the candlelight. "I want it, too."

"Will you marry me?"

"Yes *yes!*"

She planted a smacking kiss on his mouth. He gently captured her behind her head before she could pull away, and deepened the kiss. With a pleasurable sigh, she melted against him, parting her lips while he tasted her. She was sweet like the ambrosia for which she was named. Unable to satisfy his hunger fully, he devoured her. She clutched his biceps and met him kiss for kiss.

He stripped away the wrapper; the garment dropped in a puddle at her feet. When she raised her arms, he tore the nightrail over her head. Her braid fell heavily against her back. They hung apart, time suspended. A rosy flush covered her chest and cheeks. Her nipples pebbled under his intense stare. When she draped her arm across her breasts and slid her hand down to cover her sex, the movements were innocent and erotic at once.

"You are beautiful, my love," he said. "Will you allow me to see you?"

Seemingly hesitant at first, she uncovered her breasts. They were pert and firm and perfect for her slender frame. Her blush intensified, but she didn't look away.

His heart expanded, claiming all the space in his chest. He had never loved anyone more than he loved her. "Thank you. You truly are perfection."

The worried furrow between her brows faded away, and she dropped both hands at her sides. A low rumble sounded in his chest. He swept her in his arms, lifting her as he kissed her again. She wrapped her legs around his waist, returning his kisses with a desperation that matched his own. He cradled her arse and stumbled toward the bed. They landed on the edge of the soft mattress, both laughing from the shock. He fumbled with the front fall of his trousers and stood long enough to shed them.

Her laughter waned, and her already large eyes seemed twice their size as she gawked at his nude body. For a brief moment, he had his own bout of shyness. He'd not stood bare before a woman since his return from Belgium, and his body was no longer what it had been. He had grown more muscular and lean in his years abroad, and he had scars. Some were no more than small nicks sustained in training; others, larger gashes earned in battle.

"*You* are perfection," she said breathlessly.

Her admiration restored his confidence. Grinning, he cupped his hands around her rib cage and tossed her higher on the bed before climbing over her. He settled between her thighs and smoothed loose strands of auburn hair away from her face. Their kisses were more leisurely and sensual. When he drew back to feast on the sight of her lovely face, she caught her bottom lip between her teeth, worrying it.

"Something is wrong," he guessed. "Do you wish to stop?"

She shook her head. "But I-I am a virgin."

"I know, sweetheart." He smiled and placed a tender kiss on her cheek. "When our wedding night arrives, I promise to be gentle."

"Our wedding night?" Her glare bordered on being comical. "Are you suggesting we *wait*, after all this?"

"I think we should delay consummation until our vows have been spoken, yes."

She huffed. "Then what is the point in both of us being naked and flustered? Law." She planted her hand in the middle of his chest to push him away. "I don't need this frustration, Major. Please, move."

Chuckling, he captured her hand and lifted her palm to his lips. "There are other ways to make love, fairy, all very pleasurable."

She narrowed her eyes. "Is that true?"

"I swear it. I could prove it if you like."

Her eyebrow arched and interest lit her jade green eyes. "By all means, Major Rowland, show me, and don't leave out any details. I appreciate a man who is thorough."

Phillip was nothing if not attentive. He caressed and kissed almost every inch of Ammie until she was quivering. He propped himself up on his elbow and allowed his gaze to lazily sweep over her body. No longer embarrassed by her state of undress, she stretched and practically purred for him.

When his fingertips glided around her belly button and grazed the edge of her curls on a path to her thigh, she moaned. She ached from wanting him.

"You are torturing me, Phillip."

"Am I?"

His eyes held a wicked twinkled as he bent toward her and blew a stream of cool air across her sensitive nipple; his fingers walked up the inside of her leg. She shifted on the covers, restlessness spreading through her body.

"*Phillip.*"

He grinned. "I'm sorry, sweetheart, but you told me to be thorough."

"Please, get on with it. I cannot take the anticipation anymore."

Granting mercy, he closed his mouth over the tip of her breast, swirled his tongue around the bud, and lightly sucked. Ammie gasped. She could feel the pull deep in her core. He kissed her breasts, giving them the same consideration the rest of her body had received thus far.

When his fingers reached the apex between her thighs, and he touched her at last, she sank into the bed with a cry of relief. He played with her, skimming his hand over her hot skin before inserting his finger inside her. On his second pass over her sex, his fingers were slick and glided effortlessly over her flesh. He touched an especially pleasurable spot, and she moaned.

"Does that feel good?" His voice had grown husky; his face had lost all traces of playfulness.

"Mm-hmm, marvelously good."

His fingers stilled. He kissed her slowly. When he drew back, his eyes were a smoky blue. "Do you want more?"

"Yes," she whispered. "Please, don't stop."

He held her gaze and delved two fingers inside her. When he brushed his hand over the same sensitive spot, she arched her back, gasping.

"That's right, love. I want you to come for me."

Yes, yes, anything you want. Her mind was too dazzled by the pleasurable sensations coursing through her to ask what he meant. With each touch, tension spread from her lower belly. She was losing control; she didn't care. Her breath churned, her chest rising and falling rapidly.

He matched her increased pace, his hand driving her toward a place she had never dreamed existed. A pleasant pressure expanded into her chest, nearing a point where it couldn't be contained. One more flick to that lovely spot he'd discovered and she burst into a thousand pieces, again and again, wave after wave of the most amazing sensations she had ever experienced.

Afterward, Phillip held her, stroking her damp brow while she drifted back from heaven. Her heartbeat began to slow again, and a pleasantly tingling elasticity lingered in her limbs. Languidly, she turned in his embrace and rested her chin on his chest.

"Dear lord," she said breathlessly, "I might never leave our marriage bed."

Chapter Fourteen

Ammie stifled a yawn as she and Phillip waited for her parents in her father's study. They had spent the night pleasuring each other, dozing for short periods before reaching for each other again.

They sat side by side on the same bench she had shared with her mother a few days earlier. It felt like a lifetime ago.

"Does it seem like we've known each other forever?" she asked. "I cannot remember what life was like before I met you."

"Yes and no." Phillip smoothed his hand from her nape to the small of her back and kissed her temple. "I feel we have always belonged together, but I know how long it has taken to find you. My life is unquestionably better with you."

She swiveled toward him, her knees touching his. "Promise you will fight for us. No matter what my parents say, we belong together. Please, stand with me on this."

He leaned his forehead against hers. "Whatever it takes to win their approval, I will do it. I love you, Ambrosia. I cannot bear to lose you."

The study door, swollen over time, flew open with a scrape and loud crack. Ammie and Phillip jumped apart. Her father stood in the threshold, frowning at the doorframe. "I thought Robbie repaired this."

Her mother clicked her tongue and waved away his concern as she slipped past him to enter the room. Phillip stood.

"It is an old house. What more can be done?" Mama smiled when she spotted Ammie and Phillip together. "Good morning daughter, Major Rowland."

"Good morning," Ammie and Phillip mumbled in unison. Mama was unusually cheerful, and Ammie hated to spoil her pleasant mood.

Her mother sat in her father's chair behind his desk and folded her hands on the surface. "Let's get on with it, shall we? I have much to do and little time to spare."

Ammie and Phillip exchanged a look. His perplexed expression mirrored her state of mind. Ammie cleared her throat. "Get on with what, Mama?"

"The reason you requested a meeting, of course."

Ammie's father came to stand behind her mother and rested his hands on her shoulders.

"I assume you've reached a compromise regarding Mr. Perkins, one that is pleasing to both parties," Mama said.

"Um..." Ammie stumbled over her words, starting and stopping a couple of times. Her stomach twisted in knots.

"We have." Phillip's voice was strong, his bearing confident. He offered his hand to Ammie and murmured, "We stand together, always."

His reassuring smile bolstered her courage. She placed her hand in his and they approached the desk together. Neither of them released each other when they stopped to stand in front of her parents to accept their judgment.

"Ambrosia and I are in love." Phillip squeezed her hand; she held on tightly. "We wish to marry."

Her mother's face lit up. "Bravo, Major Rowland!"

"An excellent compromise, indeed," her father added and flashed a rare smile. "Exactly what we had hoped."

"I-I do not understand," Phillip said.

Ammie frowned. "Neither do I. Mama has been disapproving of Phillip since he arrived."

Her father leaned forward to squeeze her mother's shoulders. "A marvelous performance, Lady Seabrook. I knew you had it in you."

"It is good my best efforts bore fruit, and quickly. I expected the major to be a tougher nut to crack."

Ammie's parents kept up their side conversation, ignoring her and Phillip, until Ammie slapped her hand on the desktop. Her parents flinched then stared as if she had lost her mind. "For heaven's sake, would one of you tell us what is happening? Are you saying you approved of Phillip all along?"

Her mother smirked. "Why would we disapprove of the major? His family is well regarded, his reputation is above reproach, and his yearly income is more than adequate to support a wife. Do you think it is easy to find a suitor who loves dogs as much as you do? You cannot imagine our relief when Lord Grandstern wrote to inform us the dog you'd found belonged to the major and suggested a marriage match to resolve the situation."

"My father arranged for the coach to leave without me," Phillip murmured. "I should have known he had a hand in me becoming stranded."

Papa puffed out his chest. "Your father does not deserve all the credit. It was not an easy task riding into the village to hire out all the travel coaches before you set off."

"Lord Seabrook is not an early riser," Mama said.

Good heavens! The lengths her parents had gone to in order to orchestrate this entire affair... They had practically trapped Phillip into marrying her.

Ammie swayed on her feet as a wave of nausea swept through her. Would Phillip believe she was ignorant of the scheme or blame her for manipulating him?

His arm circled her waist. "Come sit before you fall."

She leaned on him, allowing him to help her to the chair closest to the desk. He lowered her gently when her shaky legs buckled. She couldn't meet his gaze. He perched on the armrest and draped his arm along the back.

"Please allow me to offer my gratitude," he said. "I never would have found her without your intervention."

Ammie jerked her head up. He smiled down at her. Her humiliation lessened.

"As I said before, my lord, we are in love and wish to be together forever. Ambrosia has accepted my proposal and now I must humbly ask for your blessing. Will you grant your daughter's hand in marriage?"

"Gladly, but we must hear her say that she has chosen you. You've done most of the talking thus far." Both of her parents looked to her in askance.

Ammie blinked, still in a slight daze from lack of sleep and shock. "Yes, of course. I choose Phillip."

"Splendid." Her father started toward Phillip to offer congratulations, but her mother grabbed his arm to stop him.

"Let's not be hasty, Lord Seabrook. There are still a couple of conditions Major Rowland must agree to before you grant permission."

"Mama," Ammie protested, but Phillip reassured her that he would agree to whatever conditions they felt were necessary to ensure her happiness.

"Firstly," her mother said, "we'd not like to see our daughter become a young widow or abandoned when you are called to duty. Therefore, you must sell your commission and settle into the business of being a husband."

"Is this condition my father's doing? No, do not answer. It doesn't matter. I have already decided to sell my commission. Ambrosia and I have discussed breeding spaniels and training them, and she will continue writing her stories."

Ammie's mother clapped her hands in a rare show of delight. "Oh, how lovely! He really was the perfect choice, Seabrook."

"Yes, marchioness. Your judgment was spot on," her father said before addressing Phillip. "I expect the next condition will be easy enough to fulfill. It is important that Ammie and her sister Laurel are not too far from one another. They have a special bond. Therefore, we are gifting the lake cottage and twelve acres to Ammie."

She gasped, covering her mouth with her hand.

"After the wedding," Papa said, "you may set up house and make use of the land for your new venture."

Phillip turned to her. "What do you say, love? Should we make the cottage our home?"

Ammie nodded, her eyes misting with tears of happiness. "The cottage used to be my favorite place in the world."

"What, don't you like it anymore?"

"I love the cottage"—she reached to cup his cheek, her heart overflowing with tenderness for this wonderful man she adored—"but my favorite place will always be with you."

The next few days Ammie's mother was high on the ropes planning Ammie and Phillip's wedding. Her older sister's husband, being the local parish clergyman, had granted them a common license to marry and would perform the ceremony Christmas morning. By the night of the Christmas ball, the newlywed couple would be presented to the guests. Her mother was beside herself with excitement to have another daughter making a love match.

"I knew Major Rowland was the perfect choice," she crowed as she dipped her spoon into an eggcup.

Ammie was partaking in her last breakfast as an unmarried woman. She was happy to have this time alone with her mother and four sisters while Phillip and Papa were away inspecting minor repairs being made to the cottage.

"Did you, Mama?" Ammie asked. "As I recall, you were uncommonly rude to him."

Her mother covered her heart as if wounded. "I told you it was all an act."

"Yes," Laurel said from her place across from Ammie, "but you never explained the reason for the charade."

Mama pursed her lips and sniffed. "What kind of parents would we be if we forced any of our beloved children into a marriage he or she didn't want? You, of all people, should understand perfectly."

"I will never hear the end of it, will I?" Laurel looked toward the ceiling as if appealing for help from above and stuffed a piece of bread into her mouth. Despite her grumbling, Ammie's twin was very grateful to their parents.

When Laurel had finally gathered the courage to tell Mama and Papa she didn't fancy any of the bachelors they had invited to the party, their parents had surprised her. They had been understanding and reassured her that she needn't rush into a decision. Laurel would be allowed another Season to search for the right man who would keep her happy.

"Besides," Mama said, "the Earl of Grandstern advised us not to say anything to lead the major to believe he was a candidate. He thought it best to allow Major Rowland and Ammie to decide if they suited one another without our interference. Your father and I agreed."

Octavia snorted. "You and Papa arranged an all day outing for the two of them and made them believe a marriage between them was forbidden. If that is not interference, what would you call it?"

"Assistance," Mama snipped. "Every relationship could use a little nudge in the beginning."

Mercedes, who sat next to their mother, chuckled and patted her hand. "Don't listen to any of them, Mama. They will be happy for your intervention someday. I know Matthew and I are grateful. I cannot imagine my life without him."

Mama's face relaxed into a smile. "He is a good husband to you, my dear."

Mercedes had always had the right touch when it came to their mother.

"Will the major's family arrive in time?" Calliope piped up from Ammie's right. "I thought they were due to arrive yesterday."

"No," Ammie said. "Lord and Lady Grandstern and Phillip's oldest brother will arrive sometime this afternoon."

Their stay had been prearranged before Phillip's arrival at Everly Manor.

Our parents are an arrogant lot, planning our futures without asking us, she had said to Phillip last night before retiring to her own bed. She missed snuggling beneath the covers with him, but they had agreed to a moratorium on spending the night together until they were married. Phillip hadn't wanted to tempt fate since her parents approved of their union.

I would be lost if they withdrew permission now, he'd said.

Ammie didn't believe they would be that cruel, but Phillip had seemed truly worried, so she had been honoring his wishes.

Calliope's smooth brow puckered. "Will his youngest brother miss out on Christmas?"

"Don't be silly," Octavia said. "It will still be Christmas wherever he is deployed."

"I wouldn't like to be away from family at Christmas." Calliope's eyes misted and her voice quivered. "I never want to leave home."

"Well, if Mama has her way," Octavia said, "none of us will ever move beyond the village."

Their mother's smug smile acknowledged the truth.

Ammie put her arm around her youngest sister's shoulders. The poor girl had cried when she'd heard Ammie would be leaving home. "I hope you know you can call on Phillip, Mr. Perkins, and me whenever you like. I'm sure Phillip will welcome your help after the first pups arrive. They will need lots of love and cuddles to grow into good hunting dogs."

"She is right."

Ammie perked up at the sound of Phillip's voice. He and Papa were back and came to join the ladies at the table. Phillip was so very handsome in his buckskins and dark blue jacket, and the color matched his eyes perfectly. She barely suppressed a dreamy sigh

He smiled and leaned down to place a kiss on her hair before sitting in the vacant chair next to her. "I am convinced love is the secret ingredient to success."

Octavia made a gagging noise. "Your sweet talk is spoiling my appetite."

Phillip whispered in Ammie's ear, "And I am ravenous for *you*, my love." He gave her a secret wink before draping a napkin over his lap.

Heat washed over her as images of their one night together flooded her memory. As far as she was concerned, their wedding night couldn't arrive soon enough. She met his gaze and silently formed the words, 'I love you."

Epilogue

Phillip found his wife reclining beneath the sprawling branches of her favorite Ash tree. A summer wind whipped across the lake, rippling the water's surface and agitating the leaves overhead. The sweet aroma of rain wafted on the air.

"I thought I would find you lazing away the day," he teased.

Ambrosia shaded her eyes with her hand and turned to watch his approach. It had been six months since they had spoken their vows, and she grew more beautiful by the day.

He sat on the grass beside her and leaned down to steal a kiss. "Are you creating a new adventure for Mr. Orion Perkins out here?"

The subject of her soon-to-be published children's stories was busy sniffing a patch of tall grass at the water's edge. He flushed out a toad, but he wasn't quick enough to catch it before it plopped in the lake. His lady dog, as Ambrosia insisted on calling the female springer spaniel chosen for his mate, was napping in the sun.

"I am creating your offspring." Ambrosia smiled and caressed her belly. "Surely, that warrants a rest now and then."

"A brief wink or two, at least." He laid his palm over the back of her hand and laced their fingers. Signs of their child had only begun to show last week, barely noticeable to anyone besides Phillip who knew her body intimately.

She had donned a simple pink day gown that morning and worn her auburn hair loose around her shoulders like he preferred. Her silky locks were spread out around her on the grass like a magical halo.

"New drawings have arrived for you, fairy."

"Oh?" She scrambled to a seated position. "Are they as good as the others?"

He playfully narrowed his eyes. "Is this a trap? You know I never open Gabe's post anymore."

She had been so disappointed when the first sketches arrived and Phillip had opened them while she was calling on her sisters at Everly Manor. He had given his word to never peek at Gabe's work again until she had seen it first.

"Let's open it together." She sprang to her feet, as if no one had ever told her a woman with child should slow down.

"If your mother saw you hopping about like that, she would demand my head," he said.

"If you tell her, *I'll* be the one demanding your head." With an impish smile, she lifted to her toes and planted a smacking kiss on his cheek.

He chuckled and held her hand as they strolled toward the cottage.

As promised, Phillip had written to Captain Gabriel Brazier after the wedding and told him about Ambrosia's project. Phillip's closest friend had responded within days with an invitation to bring his bride to Northumberland to allow Gabe the honor of an introduction.

Phillip and Ambrosia had traveled north early in the spring. He hadn't known what to expect, exactly, but he'd been gobsmacked when Gabe walked out to meet the carriage. His friend had been fitted with a prosthetic leg, and even though he used a cane and had a pronounced limp, he was still the same old Gabe that Phillip had known most of his life.

As expected, Ambrosia had charmed Phillip's childhood pal before the servants had unloaded the trunks, and the two had become bosom friends by suppertime. When Ambrosia and the other ladies of the house retired to the drawing room after supper, Phillip and Gabe had found a quiet place to talk.

Gabe apologized for never responding to Phillip's letter when he returned home. He admitted to suffering from crippling guilt at the time for abandoning the Regiment and leaving Phillip to fight on his own. Gabe's revelation had been stunning. Phillip had never imagined they would share the same feelings. He, too, had been carrying his own guilt for escaping the war unscathed.

The wounds no one except Ambrosia had been able to see in Phillip began to heal that night. He and Gabe had had many conversations about the war in the three weeks Phillip and Ambrosia stayed as house guests. Somehow, retelling their stories seemed to help them both, as did keeping up correspondence about how they wanted their new stories to unfold.

Gabe's parcel was waiting on the Louis XV walnut writing desk Phillip had given his wife as a wedding gift. She'd gushed over his thoughtful selection, insisting it was a thousand times better than jewelry, which she rarely wore. In his eyes, she didn't need any adornments besides the ones God had given her. And he didn't require any gift besides her.

Phillip cut the twine holding the parcel together with a knife and urged her to hurry. Her excitement was contagious.

Ambrosia gasped with pleasure and held up the first drawing of their springer spaniel in a hat. "It's Mr. Perkins on his wedding day. Just as I imagined."

Gabe had a way of animating the dog's face that was both charming and amusing, just like Ambrosia's writing.

She shuffled the papers and pulled out another sketch. "And here is Lady Dog. Look at her. Is she not beautiful?"

"Her name is Nova," Phillip said, feigning a glower.

"You and your silly names."

"What is silly about Nova?"

A coy smile played across her lips. "What isn't silly about it? I hope you do not expect to have all the say in naming our child."

"Our child will be out of leading strings before we agree on a name." Phillip slipped his arms around her waist from behind and rested his chin on top of her head. "How about a compromise? If we have a daughter, I will choose the name, and if we have a son, you will do the honors."

"Oh, I do like that compromise." Ambrosia turned in his embrace so they were face to face. "I'll name him after someone I greatly admire."

"If you say Reginald Perkins, I will kiss you until you cannot remember your own name."

Her green eyes lit with interest, and she tipped her head at a flirtatious angle. "And if I say it is the butler?"

"I will definitely kiss you senseless." Phillip drew her close, following through on his threat, and forgot everything except how much he loved his adorable wife.

The End

About Samantha

Samantha Grace's storytelling has received starred reviews from PW and critical acclaim from Booklist, RT Book Reviews, and Library Journal. She has written over fifteen Regency historical romance books and enjoys using her degree in behavioral psychology to create engaging, multidimensional characters. Her novel IN BED WITH A ROGUE earned her a RITA nomination, and LORD MARGRAVE'S SECRET DESIRE was nominated for a RONE award. A lifelong romantic, Samantha first caught a case of the warm fuzzies while watching Disney's animated version of Robin Hood at age four. She has never looked for a cure. Samantha lives in Wisconsin with her real life hero, daughter, and Holo the Husky.

You can find details of her work at
www.SamanthaGraceAuthor.com

A Twelfth Night to Remember

~ BOOK 3 OF THE MATCHMAKING EARL SERIES ~

BY

Donna Cummings

High-spirited Grace Nettleton had once believed in exciting escapades and magic—so much so, she eloped with a man who promised both. But her husband offered little beyond betrayal and heartache, except for their son, Oliver, the one good and pure thing to come from their union. Now widowed, Grace has returned to Hartstone Hall, resuming a position in the kitchens and setting aside her former fanciful notions of adventure in order to provide stability for her son.

Rhys Wilton, Grace's dearest childhood friend, has loved her all his life, but his position as third son of a noble family seemed an insurmountable obstacle in their youth. Putting Grace's happiness first meant silently stepping aside when she departed to begin a life with someone else, despite the blow to Rhys' soul. With her return, he will not make the same mistake twice. Finding his place in Grace's and Oliver's hearts is easy. Convincing her to ignore their stations, and embrace a new adventure as his wife, will require all the magic of the season.

Chapter One

Late November

Grace wrapped her arms tighter around her sleeping son, trying to protect him from the jostling of the carriage. It had been worth the extra coins to sit inside the crowded conveyance instead of up top. She had little to give Oliver this holiday season, but she had at least managed that.

She gazed at the wintry countryside through the frosted glass. The bare tree limbs and dreary gray sky matched her mood. She had dreaded returning home, waiting as long as possible, not even writing ahead of time to announce her arrival. She knew already what her mother would say. "Did I not tell you that man would ruin your life? You should have stayed here instead of going off to see the world."

Now there was nowhere else for her to go. She would endure her mother's disapproval because her son needed a home. He had no father anymore. The only thing he had was a mother who was at her wits' end fretting about providing for him.

She pressed a tender kiss to his forehead. Oliver was the only reason she had not lost hope completely.

It was not long before they were deposited on the drive of Hartstone Hall, an impressive building designed centuries ago to display the family's wealth and power. Her mother had served as Lord Hartstone's cook for many years. Grace had helped in the kitchens, loving the moment when she had been grown enough to move from helper to being in charge of baking whatever she wanted to create. Those were some of her best memories.

As well as those involving Rhys, her lifelong friend.

He had been the only one to encourage her improbable dreams of seeing what the rest of the world offered. So she had taken the opportunity her late husband Ben had dangled in front of her. She had seen more than the county she had been born in, and discovered numerous delights—as well as an unexpected bit of heartache.

"Mama, where are we?"

Oliver looked up at her, curious but not fearful. She gripped his gloved hand in hers, drawing strength from his trusting expression, and headed for the servants' entrance.

"This is where your mama was raised."

"In a castle? It looks like it's magical."

She grinned at the awe on his sweet face. "I can show you where the magic was truly made. In the kitchens."

Grace did her best not to fall back against the well-worn kitchen table. "She's gone?

My mother's gone?"

"Yes, she is. Oh, but not like you think." Susanna, a kitchen maid who was one of Grace's favorites, grinned in her usual saucy fashion. "She had her head turned a few months back by one of the vendors who came by all the time. Next thing you know, they were wed and she was off to have a grand adventure, as she called it."

Grace nearly snorted her disbelief. Her mother, the one who had chided Grace constantly about her desire to seek out adventure rather than stay in one spot the remainder of her life—*she* was the one off on a lark while Grace had been forced to return to where she'd started. The one place she had never expected to see again.

"The Fates certainly do have an unusual sense of humor," she muttered.

She had no idea what to do now. She had hoped to prevail upon her mother to allow them to stay, at least until Grace could find a position somewhere. But now, with the woman traipsing the countryside with her new husband...

Grace felt a lump rising in her throat. This holiday season was turning out to be a bit more than she could endure. Yet she had to remain strong for Oliver. In his four years, he had yet to know what it was like to spend Christmastide with his family. It was a tradition she had hoped would start here, this year, and now it was yet another to add to her dashed hopes.

There was a bit of clatter on the stone steps leading into the kitchens. Grace glanced up, and then stood up straight, as did all of the other servants who had been enjoying a rare break with a cup of tea.

"My lord," they said in unison, adding a curtsey.

"Is this Grace? Grace Nettleton?" Lord Hartstone's eyes lit up. "It has been ages since we have seen you. How are you doing?"

"Very well, my lord. I apologize. I did not mean to impede the staff's efforts—"

"Not at all," he said graciously. "Are you here to stay?"

Before she could answer, Oliver peeked around her skirts and announced, "My mama said they make magic here."

Lord Hartstone grinned. "She is absolutely correct. In truth, she made the most magical desserts. I still dream of the fig tarts she used to create."

Oliver looked up at her as if he expected her to snap her fingers and produce those very tarts.

"You are too kind, my lord."

"I am too selfish," he said with another laugh. "I hope you are staying long enough to make a large batch."

"I would be happy to." A burst of bravery born of desperation made her add, "I understand you are in need of a cook. I could make those tarts every day if you like."

She held her breath. Most cooks did not bring a young son as part of their situation. Lord Hartstone was likely to decline her bold offer due to the difficulties it entailed.

To her relief, he gave her a quick wink that only she could see. "I cannot think of a better solution for my current dilemma." He glanced at Oliver. "How clever of you to bring an assistant. There will be a great deal of cooking for all of the upcoming festivities. We shall need every available set of hands to accomplish it all."

Oliver was too young to do more than get underfoot, despite his eagerness to help, but she would find a way to make it work, no matter what.

"We can get started straight away," Grace answered, her heart beating with more hopefulness than she could recently remember.

"Wonderful! Make sure fig tarts are the first item on the list." Lord Hartstone turned as if to leave, and then halted. "Oh, your mother's quarters are still available," he continued. "I hope that will suit the both of you."

Grace had always appreciated his kindness, and now it made her blink away tears, grateful that he had taken away the last of her concerns.

"You have just ensured I shall be baking tarts for you day and night, my lord."

Lord Hartstone chuckled, they all bobbed him another curtsey, and then he departed.

Grace dropped into a chair, her legs wobbly from all of the excitement coursing through her. Oliver climbed onto her lap. "When do we get to make some magic, Mama?"

"Soon, my love," she answered, brushing his blond hair away from his forehead. "Very soon."

Yet she had already experienced more of it than she had expected. Her son had a home for the foreseeable future. She had a position that would allow her to provide for him. She could once more do what she loved, surrounded by those she had known most of her life, and who genuinely seemed glad she had returned.

What a wonderful, miraculous day it had turned out to be.

That afternoon

Rhys Wilton slowed his pace, calling fruitlessly for his dog Bodhi to heel. The animal, a mere pup, dashed down the hill as soon as he sighted Lord Hartstone, confident the man would have some sort of treat in his pocket.

Hartstone grinned as he reined in his horse and dismounted. He ruffled the dog's fur and scratched the beast's head by the ears.

"You have made it impossible for me to train him for anything useful," Rhys said.

"I apologize. But he is such a wonderful dog." Martin knelt and dug something out of his coat pocket. The dog lapped it up and then stuck his nose in Martin's pocket.

"Yes, wonderful," Rhys said drily. "If you want to assure you do not have any lint lingering in your coat."

Martin merely laughed. "Growing up with numerous younger siblings, and every one of us with a dog, I cannot imagine having merely one. Perhaps you should add another."

"This one is more than enough."

Rhys envied his friend's boisterous upbringing, and knew that as much as Martin bemoaned the constant commotion, he loved his family dearly. Rhys' family was a great deal more staid and formal, as if needing to constantly remind society they had been here since the days of William the Conqueror.

It was no wonder Rhys had preferred spending his time at Hartstone Hall when he was a boy. He still did.

Martin stood and gave the pup one last pat. "Sorry, old man. You have depleted my supply."

The hound gave him a look of utter disappointment and then walked away slowly, until something rustled in the nearby grass, setting him off on a new chase.

Martin took the reins of his horse and he and Rhys continued their trek towards Hartstone Hall.

"Whyever did you choose Bodhi for a name? It is not the typical sort of thing for a hunting dog."

"I came across it in a philosophy text, and thought it might prove aspirational. It means 'enlightenment'." Rhys grinned. "Now I fear I have burdened the poor beast with a name he can never live up to."

"Perhaps he shall surprise you one day. Oh, speaking of surprises, I nearly forgot. You will never guess who has returned."

"There are so few who have departed this place. Surely it cannot be too difficult—"

Grace.

It had to be Grace. Rhys had been disappointed when she had married and gleefully set off for her adventurous new life several years ago. Yet he had also completely understood her desire to leave.

He had only wished it had been with him.

"Grace Nettleton," Martin announced, unaware of Rhys' musings.

"But why? Her mother no longer lives here."

"Grace is my new cook."

Rhys halted in the middle of the path. "She is staying? How did you convince her to accept the position?"

Martin chuckled. "She appeared on my doorstep and convinced *me.*"

It was something Rhys could see Grace doing. He wondered why, though, unless she had had her fill of traveling the world. He could not imagine it. She was so full of life, and ambition, and an optimism that had always inspired him.

As selfish as it was, he was glad she had returned.

Had her husband accompanied her? Rhys peppered Martin with questions, but the man simply smiled and said, "You should come round and see for yourself."

"Perhaps I shall."

Martin got back on his horse and turned towards Hartstone Hall. "Do not forget. You are expected to be part of the upcoming Christmas festivities."

"How can I forget? It is the only enjoyable aspect of the season, spending it with your family instead of mine."

Martin grinned and then nudged his horse forward. Rhys half expected Bodhi to chase them, but the errant pup apparently thought better of it.

Rhys was tempted to follow Martin to Hartstone Hall, but instead he headed towards his own home, deciding it was more prudent not to rush to see Grace just then.

Their difference in station had not seemed a hindrance when they were younger. Or he had not truly been aware of it. She had had less freedom than he, of course, and her days had been consumed with innumerable tasks that his had not. Yet they had still managed to find time to explore the surrounding woods and ponds, making grandiose plans that never came to fruition.

Grace had always made him seem important. Whenever he was in her presence, he was not merely the third son, one who served no purpose short of a disaster befalling the heir and the spare.

Before he could divulge his growing feelings for her, though, she had married and set off for a new life. It had taken a long while to become accustomed to her absence. He had truly never expected to set eyes on her again.

Now she had returned, almost like some sort of Yuletide miracle. His heart pounded with anticipation at seeing her once more, followed by wariness at reviving the heartache he had overcome.

Still, there was no reason they could not spend a few moments reminiscing about their childhood friendship, and the many fond memories they had created over the years.

What would she remember most about those halcyon days?

Chapter Two

The next morning

"You put a frog in my hair!" Grace exclaimed.

She started to slap Rhys playfully on the arm, as she had done when they were children, but she halted herself just in time. "I must have washed my hair ten times before I removed all traces of it."

She did her best to appear stern, but it was next to impossible. She had been startled by his appearance at the back door of the kitchens, and then elated, and then swamped with memories of how much he had been part of her daily life when they were growing up.

He was as handsome as ever, his dark curls longer than she remembered, but suiting him perfectly. He wore an elegant greatcoat, emphasizing his broad shoulders, while his buckskin breeches displayed even more of his muscular frame.

Rhys grinned. It was a devilish expression, a silent invitation to join him in mischief. It had been hard to resist when she was younger. How could she hope to withstand it now?

She had no choice, however. She had her child's welfare to consider, not just her own.

"I apologized for the frog," Rhys reminded her. "Though I truly did not expect it to end in your hair. I meant to put it close to your face and it just leapt—"

She laughed. "So I should be thankful it landed in my hair instead of on my face?"

"It does seem the more palatable option."

"When the frogs are plentiful again, I shall test this theory of yours. On you."

His blue eyes lit up. As if he enjoyed the thought of her being here at another season.

They strolled through the kitchen gardens, most of it barren, all of it covered with a light dusting of snow. She had been glad to take a few minutes away from her duties to chat with her lifelong friend. To her surprise, there was no awkwardness between them. It was as if they had spoken moments earlier rather than several years ago.

"I cannot wait to hear of your adventures," Rhys said, his voice filled with envy. "We had always imagined what the rest of the world was like, and you have actually seen some of it."

"Did you not go on a Grand Tour? I thought all young nobles were required to do so," she teased.

"I had planned to, but it had to be postponed as Charles and Henry both came down with an illness at the same time. It was the only time there was genuine concern for my welfare, since for a few weeks it appeared as though I might end up being the heir."

His tone held a touch of asperity, and Grace's heart softened a bit more. He did not complain about his status, but she knew how restrictive it was. Nearly as confining as hers, though in a different fashion. His family was as unaware of what he desired in life as hers had been.

No wonder they had become such fast friends. Yet ultimately that was frowned upon, for fear it might blossom into something more, a liaison too scandalous to be borne. Leaving had been Grace's best option, before she could begin to hope for something that could never be.

"I shall regale you with some of my tales one day," she said lightly. "I am still in shock that my mother is apparently a world traveler, after constantly chiding me for my wish to be one. It is not as easy now that I am a widow, though."

Rhys blinked as he registered what she was confessing. "I am sorry to hear that, Grace. I had always hoped your life away from here was filled with happiness."

The tenderness in his gaze caused an unexpected fluttering in Grace's stomach. She had to put a halt to it. There was no sense in letting her long-ago feelings for Rhys surface, becoming even more inconvenient than they had been before.

"There was a great deal of joy," she managed. "In truth—"

"Mama! Where are you?"

They both spun around, Rhys clearly puzzled, while Grace hastened to greet her child.

"I am right here. Can you not see me? Oh dear. I forgot to remove the spell." She waved her arms over her head and spun around. "There!"

Oliver ran toward her with outstretched arms and wrapped them around her knees, giggling. "You said the magic was in the kitchens."

"Magic is everywhere. The kitchens are just part of it." She deposited a brief kiss on the top of his head. "Oliver, I want to introduce you to someone I knew when I was your age."

Oliver stepped back, clearly curious at the notion of his mother being any age than what she was now. Grace saw Rhys watching them with a mixture of emotions on his face: surprise, awe, a bit of envy even.

"Rhys, this is my son, Oliver. Oliver, this is Mr. Wilton."

"Oliver, it is my pleasure."

Rhys knelt on one knee so he was at eye level with Oliver. Her son tilted his head, slightly confused, since he was not used to adults putting him on equal footing. Yet she could see it impressed him.

"My mama said someone put a frog in her hair once. Was that you?"

Rhys' lips twitched, and he fought to keep his expression a remorseful one, but he lost the battle. "Yes, it was me," he confessed. "But as I was just trying to explain, I was merely introducing her to the frog, and it decided to jump."

Oliver giggled. "You are lucky it was not a spider. She hates spiders."

"I remember that, as well. Do you like them?"

Oliver's head bobbed vigorously. "I like dogs better. Do you have a dog?"

"I do. I can bring him around some time, if you'd like." Rhys glanced at Grace, silently asking permission.

She hesitated, but for the briefest of moments. How could she deny Oliver his heart's desire? She gave Rhys a quick nod.

"I'll have to warn you, Oliver," Rhys continued. "The beast loves treats, and he is not above searching all your pockets for them."

Oliver's nose scrunched up as he began to plot. Grace knew his pockets were bound to be bulging with everything he could scrounge in the kitchens.

"He will insist I add additional pockets to his clothing now," Grace said with a laugh. Oliver's expression grew hopeful. "No, you cannot have more pockets. We shall find another solution. Now go. It is time for your tea. Susanna will have it ready for you."

Oliver turned, ready to dash to the kitchens. He halted and returned to Rhys, who had just started to rise from his kneeling position. He stayed in place.

"Mr. Wilton. What is your dog's name?"

"Bodhi."

Oliver grinned, as if Rhys had given the correct response to one of his riddles. He skipped towards the kitchen, repeating the dog's name in a singsong fashion, clearly content with his life in that moment.

Rhys stood and they both watched Oliver dart through the kitchen door, calling out to Susanna about the dog Bodhi that was going to visit him soon.

"What an absolutely delightful child," Rhys said. "He is so like you—"

Grace chuckled. "At that age, perhaps. I have lost that sort of exuberance as I've grown older."

"That is a shame."

He gazed at her with a blend of compassion and regret that made Grace wish she had continued believing daily life was something to relish. She knew why she had come to such a conclusion, and was not even sure it was possible to return to her previous way of thinking. But Rhys' expression made her feel a distinct sense of loss. Even worse, it seemed he felt that same loss.

She shook her head, banishing such glum thoughts. "I should return. There is much I must do to prepare for the upcoming festivities."

"Martin is expecting a great deal of those fig tarts." He grinned. "He could not stop talking about them during our brief walk yesterday. He is nearly as bad as Bodhi when it comes to treats."

"I shall make sure his pockets are lined with them." A spark of her old self prompted her to add, "Shall I set some aside for you?"

"I can think of nothing I would enjoy more."

Grace had to fight off a shiver. His words were about her baking prowess, but there was no mistaking the underlying emotion—he wanted to see her once more, possibly to explore whatever emotions had resurfaced now that they were together again.

It would be wise to refuse such an invitation, unspoken as it was, or to pretend she was unaware of the undercurrents between them. What was the point of indulging such feelings when she knew beforehand there was no happy outcome?

Apparently wisdom was in exceedingly short supply just then, for Grace replied, "I would enjoy it as well."

That night Grace snuggled with Oliver, an indulgence she permitted herself each evening before putting him in his own bed. His sleep was seemingly filled with adventures, his legs kicking and his arms flailing, as if he were racing about, enjoying every one of life's treasures even while sleeping.

"Mama," he said, his voice not even a little bit sleepy. "When can I have my own dog?"

They had had this conversation almost since the moment he could put sentences together. She did not want to disappoint him, but there was not a possibility of adding a dog to their current living arrangements. Perhaps one day, when they had their own home, a cottage that could accommodate her adventure-seeking son and a menagerie of animals.

He tilted his head back to scan her face for the answer he was seeking. "When I am six years old?"

"That could be a possibility." He would be five soon, so that gave her at least a year's reprieve. "It is a lot of responsibility, taking care of a dog."

"What does that mean?"

"It means you have to ensure the dog has food, and water, and lots of exercise to keep him healthy." She tickled him, treasuring his giggles. "It is a lot like taking care of a little boy."

"I would give my dog a lot of love. Like you do for me."

"Yes, that is one of the most important parts. Of course, it is easy to give you lots of love. Because you are the most loveable little boy in the world."

"When I am six years old, I can do all of that."

Grace tried to keep her words non-committal. She did not want him to latch onto a promise she had no ability to keep, despite her wish to do so.

"It gives you plenty of time to decide what sort of dog would be best, as well as the proper name."

"I can help Mr. Wilton with Bodhi until then. He would probably want someone to help."

She squeezed her adorable boy. "We'll have to find out, won't we?"

To her surprise, he yawned and then gave her cheek a quick kiss. "I love you, Mama." He climbed down and got into his own bed, without any prompting from her.

"I love you, too, Oliver."

It was not long before he was asleep, his soft snores the only sound in the darkened room. Oliver would always be her favorite Christmas gift. This year she was grateful she was able to provide him with a home, especially when it had seemed it might not be possible. One day she would allow herself to hope for more, as she did when she was younger, but for now she was content to enjoy some stability.

She turned and pulled the blanket over her shoulders. Her thoughts drifted towards Rhys, and how enjoyable it had been to see him again, resuming their friendship as if they had never parted. It almost made her believe her fears about returning had been unfounded.

Yet just a few moments with Rhys had also stirred up the longing she had tried to suppress years ago. It was pure folly to wonder what life might hold in store now that she and Rhys could see each other every day.

Still, as foolhardy as it was, Grace could not halt herself from thinking about it as she drifted off to sleep.

Chapter Three

"Are you certain you do not mind Lord Hartstone giving me the position of cook?"

Susanna laughed heartily. "Oh dear me, no. I enjoy my position here, but I have no desire to be in charge of everything. It was like a prayer being answered when you appeared that day."

Grace blew out a breath of relief. "I was so grateful for his offer, I did not even consider you might have had your heart set on it."

"I have my heart set on something else entirely." Susanna winked and went back to stirring the bowl in front of her.

"I should probably not ask," Grace said with a laugh. She had always enjoyed Susanna's high-spirited nature. They had been conspirators at one time, with Susanna helping Grace sneak out of the kitchens on occasion to meet up with the man she had ultimately wed.

"No, it is probably best if you do not know," Susanna agreed, joining in the laughter. "Is your heart set on Mr. Wilton?"

"Of course not." The protest was instantaneous, but not precisely truthful. "I have fond memories of our youth, and he was so gracious to Oliver. How could I not be glad to see him?"

"Will you want to see him again?" Susanna asked. It was done in a nonchalant tone, but Grace could see the young woman biting back a smile.

Grace was not sure how to answer. She had fallen asleep filled with anticipation at seeing Rhys again, but wakened with the memory of why it was foolish to indulge such thoughts. She had tried once before to pretend that friendship with Rhys could be enough since no other future was permitted, but it had been well nigh unbearable.

This time, though, she did not have the luxury of running away.

She deflected Susanna's question with a teasing one of her own. "Are you attempting to play matchmaker? You may want to select someone else, if you want success."

Alice, one of the newer kitchen maids, a young girl with red curls and freckles, piped up. "They call Lord Hartstone the matchmaking earl. He's matched two couples already. One was at this very house, at a Valentine party."

"Is that so?" Grace raised her eyebrows. "You have some competition, Susanna."

"Or another conspirator." Susanna grinned. "Time will tell."

They all laughed and then Grace set them to their tasks. They had plenty to prepare for this evening's feast, a dinner for Lord Hartstone's friends and neighbors. And then tomorrow it would be Stir Up Sunday, where they would prepare the Christmas pudding. There was so much to do she would not have a spare moment to let her thoughts drift to Rhys, and how handsome he looked after all these years, and how intoxicating it was when his eyes could not seem to drink enough of her in...

Susanna chuckled, bringing Grace back to the tasks at hand.

"So much to plan," Grace attempted.

"Indeed," Susanna replied. "Perhaps I can help with all that planning."

Grace knew the minx was talking about something other than the logistics for the holiday events. She could only hope no one else was able to deduce Grace's thoughts as easily.

"Susanna, I will always be grateful for your help. And I want to thank you for your assistance with Oliver. It's wonderful being able to count on that."

Susanna blushed, a rare occurrence. "I adore the little mite. And I know it cannot be easy taking care of him all by yourself. I am in awe of what you do."

"Thankfully I do not have to do it all myself now." She gave Susanna a grin. "Now *you* can explain to him how many days it is until he is old enough to have his own dog."

Susanna's groan was a theatrical one. "He is relentless on that topic! How can one little boy love every critter and beast he sees?"

"It is why I hope to one day have a little cottage of our own, so he can play in the woods and meadows even more than I did. He is sure to appreciate the woodland animals a great deal more, too."

"Maybe Father Christmas will deliver you such a gift," Susanna said.

"I would not count on it. Though I cannot help but wonder what he might bring for you."

Susanna's eyes danced with merriment. "I have created a list to assist him. It is topped with a handsome man who works in the village, with the darkest hair and bluest eyes." She fluttered her own eyes. "I am certain I could love him."

"Have you even spoken to him?"

"I let my eyes speak for me," she answered with a laugh.

Grace snorted. "I hope he does not misinterpret the message your eyes are delivering."

"That is not possible. The last time I saw him, I also blew a kiss in his direction."

"Susanna! You are incorrigible. I may have to lock you in the kitchens to ensure all of the men in town are safe from your seductive wiles."

"That might be wise." She grinned. "But I am not sure it will be successful."

That evening

Rhys pretended to listen to his dinner companion while she prattled on about...something. He had no interest in anything but seeing Grace again. She was truly the only one he enjoyed conversing with, probably because she was interested in more than the polite society blatherings that passed for conversation.

She had always wanted to discuss everything she saw, and what she hoped to see, doing her best to make her world larger and more adventurous. Even when she was constricted by her station in life, she had found a way to explore.

Now it seemed that aspect of her had been diminished. Did she still grieve for her husband? She was the sole support for her son, which was bound to bring its own set of worries. Or perhaps she was filled with regret at returning home after trying to leave it behind forever.

Yet Rhys could not deny she appeared genuinely happy to see him again. Their conversation was as lively and enjoyable as anything they had experienced years ago, making it seem there had been little passage of time—at least until Grace had introduced him to her son. Oliver possessed the same blond hair and mischievous blue eyes as his mother, as well as the buoyant high spirits Rhys always associated with Grace.

His heart had found it remarkably easy to crave more with Grace, ignoring the ache such desires had caused previously...

A discreet cough brought him back to his duties as a guest. "My apologies," he said. "I did not hear your question."

"I merely wondered," the dowager said in a loud voice, "why you have yet to marry."

He nearly sputtered at the impertinence, but the elderly woman was known for such brash statements. It would be churlish to put her in her place. He saw Hartstone at the end of the table, lifting his glass in salute, giving him a sympathetic shrug.

"There is no need to rush into matrimony," Rhys answered, forcing a smile. "After all, I am merely a third son, and the line of succession is secure without my efforts."

"It is a wonder you have not bought a commission, or joined the clergy." She gave him a thorough looking-over, filled with approval. "You do not appear to be a layabout. So surely you are doing something useful with yourself."

He laughed. "I am not suited for battle, and I would be even worse at trying to save wayward souls. I spend my time assisting with the running of the estate, since I discovered I have an affinity for it."

"Even though it will never be yours?"

"Perhaps I shall take the knowledge and experience and use it elsewhere one day."

The dowager sniffed, as if unable to comprehend such a decision on his part, and then turned her attention to the person sitting to the other side of her. Rhys sighed with relief.

He much preferred to devote his thoughts to Grace. It was torturous knowing she was nearby, but at such a distance that he could not see her, or speak with her. It was yet another reminder of the difficulties that separated them: he was a guest at Hartstone Hall, while she toiled in the kitchens.

Still, despite that, he was eager to speak with her soon. He had a gift for Oliver, and he hoped she would permit him to give it to her son. Surely she would not find it amiss if Rhys presented it on St. Nicholas Day.

Until then, he would enjoy the food adorning the table, knowing it had been prepared by Grace. That brought a secretive smile to his face. The remaining portion of the evening was a great deal more bearable with thoughts of Grace to keep him company.

Chapter Four

Rhys approached the kitchen door, his heart thudding with a bit of apprehension. Would Grace consider him impertinent, giving her child the small gift? He hoped not. In truth, he was eager to see Oliver's expression, so it was as much a gift for Rhys as anything else.

Before he reached the entrance, Grace came out, her wool cloak draped around her. Her face brightened as soon as she saw him, but the joy was quickly banished.

He felt a moment's dismay that she felt the need to hide her happiness. In the next instant, he was nearly bowled over by the implication: he was not the only one with strong emotions.

"Rhys," she began, and then gave him a rueful smile. "I suppose I really should address you as Mr. Wilton."

He pretended to frown. "I might fly into a rage if you do."

Her delightful laugh filled the air. "You have never flown into a rage. I do not ever recall seeing you angry. Perhaps exasperated at times. And often with me."

"Exasperated only because you would not heed my warnings about the dangers of certain situations."

"Fortunately that was when I was young, and impatient, and in a rush to discover those things you warned me to avoid."

Her grin let him know she was teasing, and it warmed his heart. "Then hopefully you will have a moment to attend me when I explain myself now."

Her eyebrows shot up. Was she worried he meant to warn her away from him? Or perhaps she was even more concerned he might declare himself.

The warmth his heart had just experienced drained away. He had hoped, foolishly it seemed, that there was a reciprocal feeling on her part. Perhaps he had mistaken the depth of their bond, just as he had years ago, when she had chosen a reckless young man to be her husband and fellow adventurer.

"I have brought a small gift for Oliver." He knew his voice sounded stiff, but it seemed the better course of action just then. "I do not mean to presume, but it was something I hoped he might find enjoyable."

Grace nibbled at her bottom lip, but kept her eyes on his. He could see the wariness fighting with the joy of him treating her son with such compassion. After a few moments, she said, "Could you tell me what it is?"

Rhys dug in the pocket of his coat and extracted the gift, which he had loosely wrapped in a colorful cloth. He peeled back the corners to display a small dog he had carved. He held it in his outstretched hand. "Since he loves dogs so much…"

Grace gasped, but quickly covered her mouth with both hands. He saw her eyes fill with tears, and his heart ached that he was the cause of her distress.

"I apologize, Grace. I did not mean anything untoward." He hastily began rewrapping the carving, but her hand shot out, halting him.

"It is delightful. As are you for thinking of my son's happiness."

I am also thinking of yours, he managed to leave unsaid.

She dashed a hand over her eyes, and blinked away the remnants of tears. Her sunny smile returned. "Let me fetch Oliver. He will be overjoyed when he sees this."

She got up on her tiptoes and placed a brief kiss to his cheek. The warmth of her face against his, her tantalizing body so close to his own, made his heart thunder with emotion. He wanted to turn slightly, to have her lips brush against his, but it was madness to even consider it. She knew it, too, since she stepped back, her cheeks blushing, and then she dashed towards the door, calling for Oliver.

Rhys quickly re-wrapped the gift, pondering the one Grace had just given him. Unfortunately it made him yearn for more from her, and he had no reason to believe it would ever be possible.

Grace chided herself for her impulsive action. She had not even realized she was going to kiss Rhys until she had done it. Fortunately, she had only kissed his cheek. Unfortunately, it had set off a longing for more kisses, and her imagination was able to create a dazzling set of kisses she could enjoy with Rhys.

She thrust those impractical thoughts aside, striding through the kitchens until she found her son sitting in a chair, watching as Susanna removed a large pan from the oven.

"Oliver, love, I have a surprise for you. Actually, Mr. Wilton does—"

"Did he bring Bodhi?" He slid down from his chair in record time. "I hope he brought Bodhi."

She held out her hand. "Let us see what he brought."

Her heart raced as they returned to Rhys. His expression seemed slightly worried, until he saw them exiting the kitchen door, and then it was as if he were watching his prayers being answered. There were so many reasons why they could not indulge whatever these emotions were, and just as many reasons why she wanted to eradicate the obstacles between them.

Oliver ran the last few steps to reach Rhys. "Where's Bodhi? My mama said you had a surprise."

Rhys knelt again, so he was the same height as Oliver. "Bodhi had to stay home today. He got himself in a bit of trouble, I'm afraid."

"What did he do?"

"He is a bit too exuberant at times, when he thinks someone might be hiding a treat that he considers his. My brother was not at all pleased when Bodhi tore off not one, but *both* of his pockets. From his favorite hunting jacket, no less."

That set Oliver off into peals of laughter. "I like Bodhi."

Rhys leaned in to whisper, "I do, too. Charles can be a bit stuffy, and I was glad to see Bodhi give him his comeuppance."

Grace ahemed, but she had to fight to keep from laughing. Especially when Rhys looked up and gave her a conspiratorial wink.

"I brought you something," Rhys said to Oliver. He handed the wrapped gift to her son. "Something I made for you."

Oliver's eyes lit up with obvious excitement. He glanced at Grace, asking for permission, and when she nodded, he began to unwrap the gift.

"It's a dog! My very own dog!" He clasped it close to him, and then threw himself at Rhys for an unexpected embrace. "Thank you, Mr. Wilton."

Rhys did not even falter. He returned the hug, adding several pats to Oliver's back. There was no mistaking the happiness in Rhys' face at the unexpected affection bestowed on him.

Oliver extracted himself so he could race to his mother and show her his dog. "It's beautiful," she said. And it was a stunning piece of work. She had forgotten Rhys' talent, one he had discovered in childhood, and clearly improved upon through the years.

"I have to call him Bodhi," Oliver announced, returning to Rhys' side.

"Of course," Rhys said. "Though I suspect this one will be much better behaved than its namesake."

Grace chuckled as the two of them discussed the particulars of the carved dog, and how much it resembled the original Bodhi. She could feel her heart swelling with emotion. She should have realized how perfect Rhys would be with Oliver.

"Mama, Mr. Wilton says we can go for a sleigh ride the next time it snows. I want to do that. When will it snow again?"

Grace pretended to groan. "He shall be as relentless as Bodhi is about treats."

Rhys tossed her another one of his devilish grins. "Sometimes relentlessness is an admirable trait to possess."

"Is it one you possess?" she teased.

"At times, yes. When it is something I want dearly."

She was not sure how to respond. Fortunately Oliver changed the conversation, in his reliably persistent fashion.

"When will you bring Bodhi, Mr. Wilton? I want him to see this Bodhi." He held up the wooden dog. "But I will make sure he does not try to eat it."

"That is an excellent plan." Rhys glanced at Grace. "I know your duties keep you quite busy, but if you have a spare hour soon—"

"We would love for you to bring Bodhi for a visit. In fact, we will gather some treats to distract him from the wonderful gift you brought today."

Oliver scampered off to the kitchens. Grace smiled as she watched him. "He will be showing the new Bodhi to everyone he comes into contact with. I suspect he will insist on sleeping with it as well."

"I am truly glad he enjoys it. I was not sure how it might be received."

It was the perfect opening, a chance to explain to Rhys why she could not welcome his attentions, much as she relished them. Their difference in station had not changed. She was the cook at Hartstone Hall, while he was a nobleman from the neighboring estate, a friend of her employer. Time had not obliterated that particular obstacle. It had actually intensified it.

But a spark of hopeful defiance pushed those thoughts aside. It was pure folly to expect more, yet that yearning would not go away. It was as insistent as anything else they'd discussed that day.

She glanced quickly from side to side, and seeing they were still alone, she brushed her lips quickly against his.

"You need never fear how you will be received, Rhys."

Before she could confess anything more, she turned and hurried back to the kitchens.

Rhys stood rooted to the spot. He watched Grace until he could no longer see her, yet still he waited, perhaps hoping she would return and grant him even more of her delicious kisses. Or maybe he wanted to ensure he was not in the midst of some dream, before waking to the terrible reality that he had merely imagined Grace's lips on his.

He slowly made his way out of the kitchen garden. He was still a bit dazed, not just from the kisses, but at seeing the Grace he feared had been lost to him forever. He understood she had had to set aside the bold nature of her youth. She was a parent now, and the sole person responsible for her delightful son, Oliver. It was no wonder she had to suppress the impulsive nature that had been her driving force when she was younger.

How could he persuade her that he wanted to not only encourage the return of her boldness, but to be a part of her future? He was already growing fond of Oliver. If he let his thoughts go wild, it was easy to imagine raising him as his own son, with Grace traipsing along with them through the marshes while chasing frogs.

But not spiders. He grinned. She would never abide those.

"There is the face of a happy man."

Rhys glanced up, so lost in his mental meanderings, he had not realized Martin had joined him. They continued walking together.

"I have just come from seeing Grace, and Oliver."

"No wonder you are so overjoyed."

"Yes, though it is not easy to escape the difficulties of the situation. Not that there is a situation. Nothing that Grace has explicitly offered."

Martin's grin was infectious. "I understand your need for caution. But perhaps it is not called for in this instance. I am not certain it was called for previously with Grace."

His words stunned Rhys. "There may be no other choice. We are of different stations, and it is difficult to overcome that particular obstacle."

Martin continued his climb of the hill leading away from his house. "Difficult, yes. Impossible? I cannot see why."

Rhys pondered his friend's words as they silently trod together. Finally, he ventured, "I chose caution previously with Grace because—well, because she seemed so happy with the choice she had made. I did not wish to wreak havoc with her plans by revealing my feelings for her. Especially if they were not reciprocated."

"Understandable, and probably quite noble." His tone suggested he did not consider it at all noble. Before Rhys could protest, Martin added, "Yet if you never divulged the depth of your feelings, how could she have chosen differently?"

Rhys wanted to grumble, but Martin's words made sense. Rhys did not wish to squander this new opportunity he had been given. He needed to know if a life together was something Grace truly desired, or if it was a dream cherished by him alone.

"It is possible she will not wish to change her current situation."

"There is that possibility." Martin's eyes twinkled. "But you have the next weeks to woo this woman you adore. If you are talented, and if the Fates decide to smile upon your efforts, Grace will realize you are the future she has always wanted."

"I am both heartened and disheartened by your little speech. It sounds as though it depends most heavily on the Fates being charitable."

"From what I have seen of your wooing abilities," Martin chuckled, "we can only hope the Fates are eager to help things along."

Rhys gasped, and then grabbed a handful of snow. Martin's eyes widened and he began to run, but his laughter kept him from getting too far ahead. Rhys caught up and did his best to dump the snow down Martin's neck, although without success. His valet had tied his cravat expertly and the form-fitting coat left no room for an unwanted handful of snow.

"So much for my attempts at revenge."

They both laughed again and continued their walk. "Let us spend the time working on your wooing skills," Martin said. "After all, I am called the matchmaking earl. Surely I can assist in your romantic endeavors."

"I had forgotten about that. Here I am with an expert as a friend, and I have not seen fit to utilize your skills. The Fates are indeed smiling on me."

"It would seem they are."

Chapter Five

The Fates were laughing at him.

Rhys grimaced as he looked outside. The sky was darkening, a sure sign it was likely to snow, yet it held off, thwarting his plans for a sleigh ride with Oliver and Grace.

It had been an eternity since his last visit with her, though his calendar marked it as a mere two days. While he was anxious to see Grace again, he was loath to appear overeager by visiting too soon, or too often. Nor could he simply loiter by the kitchen door, waiting for her to appear when she had a respite from her duties.

The sleigh ride had seemed the perfect solution—until the snow had chosen not to cooperate.

Rhys glanced through the window once more. He did not want Oliver to be disappointed that the promised sleigh ride had not yet happened. Rhys remembered being an eager young child and how excruciating it could be to wait for something he wanted so badly.

He laughed. He felt that way now.

Rhys dashed out of the study and headed for the stables. On the way he whistled for Bodhi. Surely there was no harm in a quick visit to Hartstone Hall with Oliver's favorite dog. He had promised Oliver he would bring Bodhi, so why not now, when the weather was proving obstinate and hindering his original plan?

Of course, it would also provide an opportunity to see Grace, a pleasure he did not wish to deny himself any longer.

Perhaps the Fates would smile upon his efforts to woo this woman who held his heart. If not, he would at least do his best to keep them amused.

Rhys tied up his horse outside the wall of the kitchen garden. Bodhi snuffled in the surrounding grass, his tail wagging cheerfully, clearly not winded by the trek from their home.

"You are a boundless source of energy," he marveled. Bodhi looked up and his expression was joyous. It was hard not to think the pup was smiling. It made Rhys' happiness soar just to look at him.

He had fashioned a leash to rein in Bodhi's more exuberant impulses, not wanting him to bowl over Oliver. He slipped it over Bodhi's head, expecting resistance, but got none.

They walked through the frosted-over garden. Or at least Rhys attempted it, except Bodhi was intrigued by every single tuft of greenery, digging his nose into several places that must have been fragrant to the dog.

After what seemed like an hour of the dog's explorations, they made it to the kitchen door. Rhys felt his heart racing as he rapped the door several times.

Susanna peeked through the window before opening the door, a brilliant smile on her face. "Good afternoon, Mr. Wilton. Would you care to come in?"

"Actually, no." He nodded towards Bodhi. "I can only imagine the chaos that would ensue if he were to get inside. I was hoping Grace, er, Mrs. Nettleton and Oliver might have a spare moment."

"I'll just fetch them both." She gave Bodhi's head a quick rub. "Such a sweet animal."

Bodhi licked her hand, as if wanting to show his gratitude at her generous characterization. Susanna giggled and then headed back into the house.

Rhys knelt and gave Bodhi a short lecture on proper behavior. "Remember, he's just a young lad, quite like yourself. But you have a lot more strength and can easily overpower Oliver. So you need to try to curb your boisterous impulses. Do you think you can manage that? I would very much appreciate it if you could."

Bodhi tilted his head as if considering the request. Then he shook his head vigorously, finishing with an elaborate yawn. Clearly he believed Rhys' admonishments were unnecessary.

"Bodhi!"

Rhys stood as soon as he heard Oliver's excited voice. It was a good thing he did, for he would have been flattened by the young boy racing to get to the dog. Oliver threw his arms around Bodhi, who surprisingly stayed put instead of greeting the young boy in an equally exuberant fashion. Bodhi looked just as happy, however, as if he had found his soul mate.

Grace raced out the door, clearly concerned about Oliver. "Rhys, I apologize. I had just finished counseling him about not frightening Bodhi with his exuberance."

Rhys laughed. "I had just done the same with Bodhi. For once, the contrary animal heeded my advice."

"I wish my son had the same ability. Some days I wonder if I am having any effect at all on his behavior."

"Grace, you have nothing to fret about. He is happy and joyous and filled with wonder. I cannot imagine there could be a better child in this world."

Grace's expression softened, but before she could respond, Oliver asked, "Can I walk with Bodhi?"

The boy held the leash in one hand and Bodhi stood, not impatiently as usual, but content to follow Oliver's commands.

"I can hardly believe it," Rhys said, "but it seems Oliver has tamed Bodhi's wildest impulses. I am confident it is safe to allow them to walk about together here."

Grace nodded. "We have a brief spell before it will be time to prepare for the next meal. Would you care to take a walk a little further afield?"

Rhys did not even try to disguise his happiness. "I would be delighted."

Grace told Oliver to wait where he was so she could grab a hat and gloves for him, as well as her cloak. In minutes she had returned wearing her red wool cloak, the color highlighting her blonde curls. She quickly overruled her son's objections to having his head covered, though she did it in a playful manner that kept Oliver's protests to a minimum.

"We shall have to return in thirty minutes," Grace said. "I am lucky to have even that amount of time."

"We will make the most of what we have."

They set out, with Oliver and Bodhi in the lead. Rhys had wanted to offer his arm to Grace, but had decided against it. To his surprise, and utter delight, she tucked her hand in the crook of his elbow.

"I hope you do not mind," she said, smiling up at him.

"It is my pleasure." He hesitated, before adding, "I must confess I am never quite sure what to do when I am with you, Grace. I fear I am constantly making the wrong choice because of my fear of making the wrong choice."

She chuckled. "I understand completely. I find myself dithering, trying to decide if I am flying headlong into a disastrous mistake, or if I am setting myself up for disappointment by my failure to act."

"What are we to do then? I am not keen on letting fear be my guide."

"Nor am I." She glanced ahead at Oliver, happily traipsing through the frosted grass. "Nor do I wish Oliver to lose his sense of wonder because he fears the consequences of every action."

He could see from her expression she knew she had succumbed to such a fate, and was regretful of it. He gave her hand a quick squeeze to reassure her.

"Know that you have nothing to fear when you are with me. Tell me what you are thinking, what you are wishing for, anything that causes you doubt. Remember how we were when we were younger, when I relied on you, and you did the same with me."

"Can it be like that now? When so much has changed?" She nibbled at her lip. "When it also seems as though nothing has changed."

Rhys did not have a chance to respond. Bodhi chose that moment to give chase to something, possibly a rabbit, or more likely a scent or sound only he could sense. Oliver tried to keep up but was forced to drop the leash. Unfortunately it was after he had tumbled to the ground.

Grace rushed to her son, with Rhys on her heels. "Oliver! Are you hurt?" She gathered him into her arms, frantically checking to see if he had come to harm anywhere. His bottom lip quivered, and Rhys felt his heart begin to ache when the boy's eyes filled with tears. He better understood Grace's constant concern for the young boy since he was now experiencing it himself firsthand.

"Bodhi was too fast for me," Oliver said. "I wanted to go with him but I could not run like he does."

Grace and Rhys both expelled sighs of relief. Oliver was not physically harmed, merely disappointed in what he perceived as his shortcomings.

"I find it impossible to keep up with Bodhi once he starts to run," Rhys said. "Sometimes I just give him a wave as he races off, reminding him to come back to see me when he has finished all of his tasks."

Oliver giggled as he dashed a hand over his eyes. "What tasks does he have?"

"Oh, probably more than we will ever know. I suspect he feels responsible for rooting out every single rabbit trying to burrow in for the winter. And then there's every phantom scent that wafts across the fields. It's a wonder he has a speck of energy left once he has seen to all of that."

Grace gave Rhys a grateful look and then set Oliver on his feet, brushing off some snow stuck to his coat. "He sounds just like a little boy I know, constantly racing around, inspecting and exploring until I think he has surely tired himself out. Yet he is wide awake when it is time for him to sleep."

Oliver cackled. "That little boy is *me*. Isn't it, Mama?"

She pretended to ponder the question. "Yes, you are quite correct. That little boy is indeed you. Though it seems you are growing so fast every day, we won't be able to call you little for much longer."

That brought a smile of pride to Oliver's face. He made a roaring sound and then set off after Bodhi, calling the dog's name, his cheerfulness completely restored.

"What an amazing transformation," Rhys said. "As well as a reminder not to dwell on life's unexpected foibles."

"I learn more from him each day than I teach him. I am certain of it."

Rhys glanced at her and to his immense surprise, she leaned towards him, her eyes closed. He did not hesitate. He pulled her into his arms and pressed a heated kiss against her lips. He knew it was a stolen moment, one that could not last very long, even though they could not be spied upon by anyone.

He also knew it was one to treasure as it happened. He teased her lips open and she responded with passion. Her arms circled his neck, keeping him close while their mouths melded together.

Too soon, Grace broke off the kiss. Her breath created a cloud of fog, the heat mingling with the cold air surrounding them, and it made her lips curve up in a smile. He placed a tender kiss at the corner of her mouth.

"I am glad you have returned, Grace. I cannot think of a better gift than this."

"I am glad I have returned, too, Rhys. I did not realize just how much I missed you until I saw you again."

Her words made hope shoot through every particle of Rhys' being. "You do not need to miss me, ever again."

She smiled at him, clearly comforted by his words. She gave him another quick kiss. He wanted more but knew the impossibility of it happening just then.

"Mama! Mr. Wilton! Look."

Oliver marched towards them, his face beaming, holding Bodhi's leash in a triumphant fashion. The dog walked alongside as if it was what he had decided to do all along.

"Is it just me," Grace asked with a bemused voice, "or is Bodhi smiling right now?"

Rhys laughed and tucked Grace's hand in the crook of his arm once more. "I fear the animal is not only smiling, he is celebrating having outsmarted us all. Even worse, he is likely to continue, despite our efforts."

"Well, I cannot complain, since he is allowing Oliver to believe he is the one who outsmarted Bodhi. He will be crowing about that for several days at least. And I shall have to pretend to be amazed each time I hear the tale."

"Just as you did with me," Rhys said. "I could never figure out why my tales seemed to enthrall you each time when I was certain I had already regaled you with them."

"I *was* enthralled by your tales, and the way you told them. I had no choice but to pretend I had not heard them. You might have stopped telling them to me if I had."

"I suspected it, but now I know for certain. You are a devious one, Grace."

"Not always." Her eyes twinkled. "Only when necessary."

Rhys laughed, his heart filled with contentment. They joined Oliver and Bodhi and turned back to Hartstone Hall. Oliver chattered happily about all manner of things, and Rhys genuinely enjoyed every word he uttered.

Even more enjoyable was when Oliver slipped his hand into Rhys' as they continued their trek homeward. It was a display of trust that Rhys had not expected, yet knew he would treasure for the rest of his born days.

Grace plopped down into one of the wooden chairs surrounding the kitchen table. She had a list of tasks she needed to accomplish, but she also needed a brief moment to collect her thoughts after the whirlwind outing with Rhys and Oliver.

Her heart pounded at the memory of the kisses she and Rhys had shared. They were filled with promise, and passion, and it made her impatient for more of them. There was no longer any doubt that Rhys desired her, and he had made it clear he was interested in whatever she might offer.

Her heart urged her to ponder the tantalizing possibilities, yet her mind cautioned her to remember the obstacles. Now there were not only her emotions to consider, but also Oliver's. She did not wish to bring heartache to her son, not when he trusted her to see to his welfare, but it was likely if a liaison with Rhys ended badly.

And how could it end any other way? There was even less chance of a future than when she had left previously.

She dropped her head in her hands and groaned. "What am I to do?"

"A cup of tea will help you sort it out," Susanna said.

Grace lifted her head and gratefully accepted the cup her friend offered. "I do not know what I would do without you. Is Oliver settled?"

"Yes, he is napping. Though he had so much to talk about, I thought he might never fall asleep. He is quite enamored of Bodhi. As well as Mr. Wilton."

Grace sighed. "My heart nearly melted when Oliver slipped his hand into Rhys'. I had never anticipated my childhood friend would become my own child's friend."

Susanna sat down, sipping on her cup of tea. "Perhaps your childhood friend is meant to be more than a friend."

"I wonder that, too. Especially when I am kissing him."

Susanna's eyebrows shot up. "You have had a busy afternoon indeed." Her grin turned mischievous. "Will there be more than kissing in the future?"

Grace took a gulp of tea to avoid answering. Susanna patiently waited her out.

"I want there to be more than kissing," Grace finally admitted. "I have thought of it many times. Yet I am having trouble convincing myself to take that step."

"Why? It is clear he is besotted with you."

"Or perhaps he is merely grateful to reignite a friendship that brought us both a great deal of happiness during times that were a bit trying."

Susanna snorted. "I am amazed how you are so unwilling to acknowledge what is right in front of you. Have you never wondered why he is not wed?"

"No," Grace murmured, though it was a lie. She had wondered why he had chosen to remain unmarried, and at times had felt guilty that he had done so while she had wed and had a child. "Besides, there is no need to rush into anything. I am not going anywhere for the foreseeable future, and he is likely not either."

"I worry you plan to content yourself with a few stolen kisses until you are in your dotage."

Grace laughed. "While I have no fear you will be impertinent even when you are in your dotage."

"I will also have many tales to think upon when I am in my rocking chair, my shawl wrapped around my frail body, cackling about all the handsome young men who gave their hearts to me."

Grace sighed again. "I was like that once. When I was the old Grace, the one who could not resist an adventure, no matter the outcome. Now, the new Grace—"

"Is in danger of becoming a fusty old maid," Susanna finished.

Grace gasped. "I should banish you to the larder and force you to inventory every single item in there. And then do it again when you have finished."

Susanna took Grace's empty cup and sashayed to the sink, clearly not afraid of Grace's empty threat. "Except you need me here to banish the new Grace and encourage the old Grace."

"I am doing my best to be a respectable widow, as well as the mother Oliver needs."

"And does that mean your wishes mean nothing? I cannot believe anyone benefits from that."

Grace couldn't argue with that profound statement. She repeated the phrase she had used earlier. "Susanna, I do not know what I would do without you."

"You would do nothing fun or enjoyable, and would continue to talk yourself out of enjoying a handsome man that is devoted to you." Susanna dug into the pocket of her apron. "I was going to save this for Boxing Day, but there is no time to waste."

Grace took the small paper packet wrapped with a thin bright ribbon. "What is this?"

Susanna grinned. "You can unwrap it and find out."

Grace pretended to give her cheeky friend a fierce stare. "You can only hope Father Christmas does not punish you for your impertinence."

Susanna's snort demonstrated how little she feared that outcome.

Grace opened the package and stared at the key sitting atop the paper wrapping. She was completely puzzled. "Are you certain this is meant for me?"

"My gran is visiting with some friends for the holidays and she asked me to look after her little cottage. I am certain to be busy with other activities, so I hoped you might help me with this task." Another wink appeared. "The bedchamber is sure to need some seeing to."

Grace was touched by the gesture. It was all well and good to bemoan the numerous difficulties of the situation with Rhys. But now she would have to decide if she was brave enough to confront another impediment: her fear of exposing her heart for what was bound to be a brief affair.

She closed her palm around the key. "This is not likely to change anything, not permanently."

"Not many things do." Susanna grinned once more. "Which is why we are given new choices every day. What will yours be?"

Grace tucked the key into her own apron pocket. Did she continue to resist her desire for Rhys, spending the rest of her life wishing and wondering what might have been? She had been given a second opportunity with him, one that she never would have expected to present itself.

In the past she had selected what seemed the safest option. Now her heart counseled her to be bold, to do what she should have done years ago, despite all the hurdles.

There would always be hurdles. And obstacles. And impediments.

Right now she seemed to be the biggest of them all.

"My choice?" Grace gave her outspoken friend a brief hug. "I say we'd best get to work on those seduction tarts."

Susanna giggled. "I recommend we double the recipe. That handsome man in the village will have need of them, too."

They laughed and then started putting large bowls onto the wooden table, gathering eggs and flour, and debating on which flavor was most likely to prove irresistible. Grace sighed with contentment, happy with her lot in life, her friends, and the hopefulness of the days ahead of her.

It was bound to be the best Christmastide she had ever experienced. She would not allow it to be anything else.

Chapter Six

Grace had tied the key to a ribbon and hung it around her neck. She was not certain when she would put it to use, but she kept it close for when the moment presented itself as the right one. She had sneaked away one afternoon to look the cottage over, and ever since, she had imagined Rhys in her embrace before the fireplace, Rhys in the bed with her...

She shook her head to clear her thoughts. If she did not, there was no telling what might be missing from the hamper she was packing for the long-awaited sleigh excursion.

"Mama, have you been in a sleigh before? Does it go fast? I hope Bodhi will like it. Do you think he will?"

She did not even try to answer the barrage of questions. Oliver was content to spill them as they appeared in his mind. It kept him occupied while she gathered everything they would need that day.

Susanna grinned as she wrapped the hot bricks to keep their feet warm. "I have tucked a few more blankets in here for you as well." She gave a lascivious wink. "You never know if they will be needed."

Grace shushed her, nodding her head towards Oliver.

Susanna's eyes widened with faux innocence. "I merely meant it was additional protection against the chill air outside."

Grace bit back a laugh. "I must make something extra special for Lord Hartstone when I return. He has been so indulgent. What other cook do you know who would be given such privileges as I enjoy?"

"He wishes to extend his success as a matchmaker, no doubt. And not just for your sake, but for Mr. Wilton. Besides, you are also gathering the greenery we need for decorations. You are employed in a most important undertaking."

It eased some of Grace's concerns, though it seemed as soon as one worry was vanquished, another popped up to take its place.

Oliver stood at the window, bouncing with his excitement. "There is so much snow. Where did it all come from? Mama, have you ever seen so much snow on the ground?"

"It has been many years," she answered, wrapping him in her arms and giving him a kiss. "Let me see if your coat is buttoned up so you will stay warm."

"Bodhi is lucky he does not have to wear a coat."

"Bodhi wears his coat all the time," she reminded him. "Even during the hottest of summer days when he wishes he could remove it."

Oliver giggled. In the next instant, his expression lit up. "Mama, Mr. Wilton is here."

Grace opened the door and could not keep her heart from racing when she saw Rhys, his eyes filled with elation at seeing her. She self-consciously brushed at a stray lock of hair that had escaped her bonnet. She was not certain how to handle the myriad of emotions between her and Rhys, yet there was nothing she wanted more than to explore every single one.

"We have so many things to bring with us," she said when Rhys halted at the doorway. "I hope your sleigh is able to accommodate all of it."

He glanced at the basket she had filled with provisions, and the container with bricks, as well as the blankets folded into a neat pile. "I think we shall manage. Oliver, if you could take Bodhi's lead, I will bring these outside."

Oliver beamed at being charged with Bodhi's care. He gave Grace a knowing look, as if to remind her he was able to be responsible for a dog, and then he set out for the sleigh.

Rhys picked up the container with the bricks, and tucked the blankets under his arm. Grace grabbed the hamper. She began to follow him but Susanna tugged at her sleeve, so she halted while Rhys headed for the sleigh.

"Which Grace is going on this expedition?" Susanna teased.

"The old Grace." She placed a hand over the key nestled inside her bodice. "The one who is consumed with thoughts that are likely to melt every bit of snow and ice we encounter today."

"Perfect. When those bricks cool down, you can be put to good use."

Grace laughed. "You are wickedly impertinent, and I love you for it."

Susanna shooed her out the door. "Go enjoy your outing. And make sure Mr. Oliver is worn out when he returns, so he will sleep through the night."

Grace nodded, her heart racing at the import of Susanna's words: unless Grace lost her nerve, she would not be sleeping a wink that night. Nor would Rhys.

"Mama! Look. I am driving the sleigh, all by myself."

Rhys tossed Grace a wink, treasuring the smile she returned. Oliver stood in front of Rhys, gripping the reins, unaware that Rhys kept his knees near the little boy so he could not take a tumble. He was not about to take a chance with Oliver's safety.

Yet he knew how important it was for the lad to believe he was in charge of the vehicle.

"You are a magnificent driver, Oliver," Grace said.

Bodhi let out a bark from his perch in the back of the sleigh.

"Even Bodhi agrees with that assessment," Rhys added.

They continued their smooth ride over the snow, some of it swirling around and landing on their clothes. A few errant snowflakes began to drift down from the sky. Grace tipped her head back to catch them on her tongue, laughing with delight.

Rhys laughed, too, filled with happiness for the first time in ages. He had thought spending the Christmas season with Martin's family had been delightful, but now he had discovered something much better. Something that made him crave his own family, one of his creation, and one that would bring him and Grace and Oliver happiness for many years to come.

He knew the obstacles standing in the way of such a desire. Yet he would thrust those aside for now. He was not willing to let the difficulties dampen the day's joyful moments.

After several miles, Rhys asked Oliver to tug back on the reins to slow the horse. "If we are to gather some of the greenery to decorate the house, I know the perfect spot."

Oliver leaned back, pulling as hard as he could, and Rhys subtly added his own strength to finish the job. Oliver beamed, convinced he had done it all by himself. Grace applauded, adding to Oliver's joy.

Rhys jumped down from the sleigh then turned, holding up his arms. "Come, Oliver. Once you are settled, I will get Bodhi—"

The pup leapt from the sleigh and disappeared in a pile of snow. He popped up, his nose covered in white and then circled the sleigh, barking happily. Oliver giggled and then vaulted fearlessly into Rhys' arms. Rhys clutched him tightly before setting the boy on the ground. Seconds later Oliver and Bodhi began running to some destination only the pair of them knew.

He turned to see Grace smiling at him. "I tell myself to be prepared for whatever happens when they are together," he said, "and I believe I am. But they surprise me at every turn."

"I feel the same. Though it does my heart glad to see how joyously they embrace everything they encounter."

"A lesson for us, perhaps?"

"Perhaps. Though now that we are older, and presumably wiser, it is too easy to let the hindrances hold sway."

"Not today," Rhys vowed. "We can leave that to a day when we are even older. Decades from now."

She laughed. "I agree. Now let us see to finding some holly and pine branches. We shall need a great deal of it to adorn all of Hartstone Hall on Christmas Eve."

He took her hand in his and led her in the direction Oliver and Bodhi had run. "I wonder if we shall find some mistletoe as well."

"I best not decorate the house with that. Susanna is bound to cause commotion whenever it is near."

Rhys chuckled. "I wish I had had her boldness when I was younger. I would have carried a sprig in my pocket, ready to call it into service whenever you came to see me."

Grace halted, her expression serious, but before he could apologize, she said, "Rhys, I wish I had been bolder then, too. I hope to be so now, and at times I believe I am, yet there are still so many barriers—"

"Not today," he repeated. He kissed her lightly. "There is nothing impeding us today. We have all of this day to ignore the difficulties."

Grace's expression turned from worry to genuine happiness. "I shall heed your wise counsel. Not forever, of course."

He laughed. "I am happy for any moments you share with me."

Grace squeezed his hand, signaling she understood the vow contained in his words. The excitement shining in her eyes was also a promise to him.

"Mama, I am hungry. Bodhi is hungry, too."

Grace tore her gaze from watching Rhys, who had just finished piling the pine boughs in the back of the sleigh, along with numerous branches of holly. She looked at her son, who had done his best to assist Rhys, handing him a single branch at a time. Now the young lad was famished from his efforts.

"You are fortunate I brought a feast for us," she said. "Now we just need to find a spot so we can sit and eat."

She twirled around, but there was nothing that seemed suitable, not with snow everywhere and the trees blotting out the sun. They would be close to frozen in no time.

"I have something in mind," Rhys said, a secretive smile curving his lips.

Her stomach fluttered once more. It was a marvel that she had been able to resist the allure of him when she was younger and more impulsive. She could barely do so now. It seemed the old Grace and the new Grace had become co-conspirators, ensuring she would always want Rhys in her life, and in her embrace.

"Mama?"

Oliver stood inside the sleigh, reins in hand, while Bodhi sat next to him. Rhys waited to help her into the conveyance.

"My apologies. My mind was wandering, trying to remember: did I truly bring anything for us to eat?"

Oliver gasped until he realized she was teasing. His face relaxed into a smile. "If you did forget, you can make something with magic. You said it is everywhere."

"So true," Rhys agreed. He held his hand out to Grace to assist her into the sleigh. When their gloved hands touched, Grace swore she felt a spark of something flow between them.

How could she deny the possibility of magic on this delightful day?

Grace could not halt her squeal of excitement as soon as Rhys stopped the sleigh. "This is an absolutely perfect spot, Rhys. I cannot believe I did not remember it."

Oliver frowned at the sight of the frozen pond. "We did not bring skates, Mama."

Rhys extended his hand to Oliver, who quickly took it, and they headed toward an open area to the right side of the pond. There were several logs gathered in a semi-circle, surrounding what had clearly been utilized in the past as a fire pit.

"This is where your mama and I looked for frogs. In the springtime, of course. They are not here now."

Oliver grinned, clearly enjoying being brought someplace he had heard about before. "We can come back when the frogs are here. Mr. Wilton, you know where they like to hide, don't you?"

Grace held her breath for a moment, but there was no need, since Rhys answered happily, "I do indeed know where they like to hide." He lowered his voice to a conspiratorial tone. "I know where the best jumpers are, too, but do not let your mother know about that."

Oliver beamed.

"Before you two conspire any further, I believe it is time to eat."

"Conspiring does work up an appetite," Rhys teased.

"It does," Oliver agreed loudly, though he had no idea what conspiring was. It was clear he was happy to be part of something, and it warmed Grace's heart that he had found it with Rhys.

If she weren't already half in love with the man...

She started. She had tried so hard not to admit her feelings for Rhys. They had complicated her life before, and were bound to complicate it even further now. She brushed the thoughts away. Time to concentrate on their winter picnic.

Grace had Oliver clear the snow from the logs that would serve as their chairs while Rhys set about building a fire.

"Your skills from long ago have not failed you," she teased.

"I have not done this in a while," he said, "so I was not entirely sure my skills were intact. Fortunately I shall be able to keep us from freezing."

Grace helped Oliver finish his task, and then they stacked the blankets atop the logs. She set the hamper on the ground that had been cleared of snow and began to extract a bevy of things she had stowed earlier: meat pies, cheeses, bread. Bodhi raced over, ready to plop his head inside the basket, but Oliver grabbed him just in time.

"That is not for dogs," Oliver said. "I have something just for you."

Grace's heart nearly melted when she saw her young son take something out of his pocket, obviously tucked there beforehand, and fed it to Bodhi. How had the pup not discovered it before now?

Rhys grinned, and then gave her a wink. She did not know it was possible to feel so much happiness. It was another form of magic, and it surrounded them all completely. She could only hope it was an inexhaustible supply, for she knew she would desire it the rest of her born days.

Rhys watched as Grace slowly extracted one last item from the hamper. Oliver's eyes were wide as he waited to see what she would produce. She carefully unwrapped it and set it on the makeshift table before them.

"A Twelfth Night cake?" Rhys asked.

"It is a practice cake. I wanted to ensure the one I create for the actual holiday is perfect. So it meant I had to make one ahead of time."

It was sheer perfection. The smooth white icing was topped with intricate decorations made of sugar. He could only imagine the time that had gone into making it.

"We are the lucky ones, aren't we, Oliver?"

"Yes!"

Bodhi whimpered, laying his head on his paws. Rhys pulled something out of his pocket and tossed it towards Bodhi, who snapped it up without hesitation. Oliver went into peals of laughter.

"I planned ahead, too," Rhys said, chuckling.

Grace joined in their merriment, the picture of happiness, and Rhys knew it was a magical moment he would remember for the rest of his life. He was more determined than ever to have more of these moments.

Grace carefully sliced the cake and placed it on the small plates she had brought, handing one to Rhys, and another to Oliver.

"If you find the bean inside," Oliver explained, "it means you are the king of Twelfth Night. A real king. You can tell everyone what they have to do."

"I remember that," Rhys answered. He put his fork into the cake and immediately felt it hit something solid. "Oliver, would you mind retrieving a napkin from the hamper for me? I will hold your plate."

Oliver jumped up and Rhys grabbed his plate just in time. While the boy ran to the hamper sitting next to his mother, Rhys switched the plates.

"Thank you, my good sir," he said when Oliver returned with the linen. "I dare not let crumbs fall or Bodhi will attack me, mercilessly."

Oliver nodded sagely. "He cannot help himself when it comes to treats."

Once Oliver was settled again, Rhys handed him the plate that had been Rhys'. The boy tucked into the cake and then his eyes widened. "I found it! I have the bean. That means I am the king now."

"Oh dear," Grace muttered, doing her best to hide a smile. "We are in for it now."

Rhys tsked. "Surely it cannot be so bad."

"I had no idea how devilish the lad could be." Rhys was gratified to see Oliver asleep at last, wrapped in a blanket in Grace's arms, as they traveled homeward. "And imaginative. I do not know that I would ever come up with so many fiendish tasks as he assigned to me."

"I was particularly fond of the one-legged jumping while spinning in a circle. You did quite well with that one," Grace said with a chuckle. "It was very thoughtful of you, giving him the chance to be the Twelfth Night king."

"It was my pleasure. I know what it is like to want something but feel overlooked."

Grace gasped, her countenance stricken. "You believe that is what I did with you?"

"No, not at all," he hastened to reassure her. "I meant my own family. Not you, Grace. You have always treated me as though I was someone important."

"You are. Though I have not always demonstrated it, particularly when I left—"

"You made the right choice then, Grace. I am convinced of it."

Her expression demonstrated she was not completely persuaded by his words, but he did not press her any further. They rode in silence for a while, the sleigh gliding across the snow, a companionable quiet between them.

Rhys wondered what thoughts were spinning through Grace's mind. Was she contemplating, as he was, how they had been given another chance to plan a future together? Years ago it had seemed improbable, but after today--

"Rhys, I must ask you something."

"Of course." Since her voice was a bit more tentative than usual, he steeled himself for a request he did not want to hear, even knowing he would respect her wishes, whatever she might ask of him. "What do you wish to know?"

"If you had been the king of Twelfth Night, what would you have decreed?"

Rhys gulped, not sure he could answer since his heart was firmly lodged in his throat. He tossed a hungry gaze in her direction, and fortunately it said everything he was afraid to voice just then.

Grace's eyes widened for a moment and then her lips curved into a smile he found impossibly seductive. "Yes, I thought so." She leaned forward and placed a kiss against his cheek. "Would tonight be too soon?"

Surely Grace had cast a spell, and she was whispering something mundane about the weather while his poor addled brain had transformed it into a beguiling offer. Whatever magic she possessed, he did not want it to end. He would happily be held captive by her for all time.

"Tonight cannot arrive soon enough," he answered.

Grace tucked her arm in his, moving herself even closer, and rested her head against him. Rhys wished he had mastered the art of driving one-handed. If he had, he could put his arm around her, cradling her while she held Oliver, adding one more to the delightful memories they had created that day.

He shot a glance at the sky, glad the sun was descending towards the horizon. He was impatient to commence this night, one he wanted to ensure Grace would always remember.

If the Fates were smiling upon him, this would be the first of many such blissful nights.

Chapter Seven

Later that evening

Grace clasped her hands, and then unclasped them. She stood in the middle of the cottage's main room, completely nervous now that she and Rhys were alone, even though she had been consumed by the notion the entire afternoon. When they had returned to the house, Susanna had taken the sleeping Oliver, tossing Grace a saucy wink as she wished her a most pleasant evening.

Grace was not accustomed to being in this situation. She began to seek out a task to accomplish, but there were none.

"I shall get the fire going," Rhys said. He seemed as nervous as she was just then. It helped to ease her own concerns.

"You have been charged with this assignment twice today," she teased. "You may not wish to accompany me on excursions if you must labor this much."

"It is not a labor to provide you with comfort, Grace. Or pleasure. I can assure you it is a joy for me to do so."

He returned to his task. Grace took the opportunity to remove her hat, and her cloak, albeit with trembling hands. Were they rushing into something they should not even contemplate? Would this be a mistake for both of them?

She must have said the words aloud, or more likely, Rhys had seen her pacing and understood the reason for the nervous response.

He stood in front of her, and held her face in both hands, brushing her skin with his thumbs. "Grace, I understand if you want to change your mind. I am content to sit by the fire and talk to you for hours on end. I do not wish to be on your list of regrets."

"There is not a list," she said with a laugh. "And if there were, you would only be there because of my cowardice."

He scoffed. "You are braver than anyone I have ever encountered. Just look at all you have borne. It has not bested you. I do not believe there is anything in life that will."

His words reassured her like nothing else could. "Now I must live up to your lofty belief in me. I cannot bear to disappoint you."

He grinned, right before he kissed her very tenderly. "There is no possibility of that."

Grace returned the kiss, softly at first and then more passionately. She had been afraid to let her feelings for Rhys rise to the surface but now there was no reason to quell them. She halted the kiss, to remind him this was likely their only night together, but once again he knew her thoughts. He shook his head quickly and then teased her lips open.

There was no hope of resisting him. It was as exciting being in his embrace as she had imagined. She knew he would care for her, see to her every need, just as he had done all his life. Why had she ever doubted him?

Grace plucked at his cravat. He held her in his arms while she untied the linen. "I can see you do not mean to provide me any assistance," she teased.

"None at all. I am content to watch as you disrobe me."

"As long as you return the favor, when I am done here."

"Of course. Though do not feel as though you must rush. I plan to take my time, when it is my turn."

She shivered at the erotic promise in his words. Still, she managed to prolong her delightful task, unbuttoning his waistcoat with deliberate slowness, punctuating it with leisurely kisses until they were both dizzy with need.

His waistcoat soon dropped to the floor, joining the cravat already there. She tugged at his shirt until it was free from his breeches so her hands could skim over his chest. He inhaled sharply at the contact and then leaned in for an open-mouth kiss that completely stole her breath. At the same time he reached for the back of his shirt and quickly broke off the kiss so he could pull the shirt over his head.

In the next instant he placed her hands back on his chest. "You have no impediments to anything you wish to do now."

Grace swallowed. He would always know what she was thinking and feeling. Even more remarkable, he seemed to present the solution when she insisted on dwelling on the problem.

"How do I deserve you?" she asked. "I want you so desperately, yet I struggle to believe I have earned the right."

He gazed at her with something akin to awe. "You have taken the words from my very soul, Grace. I have told myself many times over the years I can never prove myself worthy of you. Yet it does not stop this need, this desire. I shall always feel it for you."

She gave him another heartfelt kiss. "Then, as undeserving as we believe ourselves to be, let us both enjoy this guilty pleasure."

"When should we feel guilty?" He grinned. "Before the pleasure, or after?"

"Why not during? It may heighten the pleasure, after all."

He pulled her into his arms. "I adore you, Grace." He whispered it, as if he was not certain he should say it aloud.

It made her braver, and she boldly stepped back, her arms to her sides. "Where shall you start?"

He pretended to ponder the question, walking around her, eyeing every portion of her ensemble. She shivered under his very appreciative gaze.

"I must return before the sun rises," she reminded him.

"I warned you I meant to take my time. You know I am a man of my word."

Indeed he was. She was nearly giddy when he finally stopped his intimate perusal and began to loosen the tie of her bodice. The back of his hand brushed against her exposed skin and it sent a thrill through her entire being. His lips curved up at her response. She saw his head lower, but not to kiss her lips. No, he gently placed his mouth against her throat, lavishing it with heated kisses.

She grabbed the back of his head, afraid he might retreat before she had experienced enough, but he was indeed a man of his word. He took his time kissing the curve of her breast, as if he had been blessed with an eternity for just that task. He slowly removed the bodice, and the chemise, and she felt a moment of coolness against her skin.

Until his lips covered her nipple.

She cried out his name, holding him so close she feared for a moment she might smother him. He continued to drive her to the brink of madness, tempting her to shred her clothing so he might devote his attention to other, equally aroused, parts of her body.

She counseled herself to remain patient. They had both waited too long to rush through this moment. For all she knew, this would be the only one they were given. She banished that unwelcome thought. It made more sense to help remove more of his clothing while he did the same with hers.

She reached for the buttons of his breeches but was distracted by the hard length displayed by the tight-fitting material. She had intended a quick brush of her hand, to demonstrate her appreciation, but Rhys expelled her name in a soft hiss. His head was thrown back, his expression nearly beatific.

She smoothed her hand over him once more, and then again. She reached for the buttons, needing to liberate him, but his hand gripped hers.

"Grace, if there has ever been a time when I hope you will heed my warnings, it would be now."

"I have always heeded your warnings," she said with a laugh. "I just have not always followed the advice contained in them."

He chuckled as he let his hand drop from hers. "I shall not expect it now then."

She shook her head and continued her quest. Soon his breeches were completely unfastened. They rested momentarily on his hipbones, but then impatience got the best of Rhys. He pushed them down and stepped out of them.

Grace gazed at him with awe and then slowly circled him, the same way he had done with her earlier. "Now I understand why you insisted on taking your time. There is so much to appreciate. To revere, even."

He growled but it merely made her laugh. Clearly he enjoyed her viewing him in this way. Her laughter halted when she was behind him. Grace wrapped her arms around him, resting her cheek against his muscled back.

"I adore you, Rhys," she whispered against his skin. "I always will."

Rhys knew he was not meant to hear her confession, but he was too acutely attuned to Grace not to hear the words. It warmed every fiber of his being, knowing how she felt. He had spent so many years hoping for those very words.

Now he had to demonstrate to Grace how much he treasured her, and always would.

He slowly turned until he was facing her. She tilted her head back so she could see into his eyes. Her smile melted him on the spot. It was a blend of happiness, and mischief, and something so seductive.

He kissed her cheekbones, and the shell of her ear, and down the column of her throat. He wanted to memorize every sensation while also ensuring Grace could not bear this to be their only night together. He would use all of the passionate wiles at his disposal.

He loved Grace. He did not know how to handle the thought of her being with anyone else but him. Not now.

"I fear I have lost a fair amount of patience," he said. "I may need your aid in getting you out of this garment."

She wriggled out of it, needing his assistance with some pins holding things in place, and then the fabric was draped on the rug. Grace was standing in front of him, completely nude, nibbling at her lip while she watched him.

He was bereft of words, so he showed her with his touch how beautiful she was to him. His fingertip traced the outline of her lips...until she gave him a playful bite.

He grinned and continued his exploration, cupping her breasts in both hands, teasing the nipples until they tightened. His hands slowly moved over her waist, smoothing over her rounded hips. He grabbed her luscious bottom and pulled her against his very hard body.

She gave a small murmur that aroused him even further. When she moved slowly, rubbing her softest parts against his impossibly hard arousal...

He quickly picked her up in his arms and strode toward the bed. She kissed him the entire time, as if unable to be parted from him for even a moment. It matched his own emotions. He laid her onto the mattress and then stayed atop her.

She quickly wrapped her legs around him, silently inviting him to enter her, but he held off.

"Rhys," she said, her tone a blend of pleading and chiding.

"Soon," he promised. He continued caressing and kissing, relishing the feel of her legs surrounding him, the sight of her hair spread across the pillows.

"I fear we do not have the same notion of 'soon'." She wriggled against him, tempting him beyond measure. "I would prefer you use my definition."

He gave her hardened nipple a quick kiss. "I am inclined to utilize mine instead." At her mock frown, he added as contritely as he could manage, "I shall feel intensely guilty about it, though."

Her eyes narrowed in a mock frown and he knew she would do everything possible to win this battle. Fortunately it meant both of them would ultimately prove victorious.

Grace slid her hands down Rhys' back. She halted at the base of his spine, watching his expression. He silently dared her to continue, knowing she was unable to resist such a challenge. It was one of many reasons he adored her, his fearless adventuress.

Her hands began their relentless pursuit once more. They smoothed over his backside, causing him to shudder from the sheer pleasure of it. Naturally she had to torment him numerous times.

"Grace," he said with a soft warning tone.

"I am feeling intensely guilty," she answered pertly. "So it is permitted, correct?"

He nipped at her bottom lip, partly to keep from laughing at her using his own words against him. She opened her mouth, though, inviting him in. He knew it was a distraction but he could not deny the request. He could not deny anything Grace desired.

It was why he had been able to wish her well when she had left previously, when it was the last thing he wanted.

He shook his head to rid himself of the unpleasant reminder of how ephemeral their connection could be, much as he would try to prevent it from happening again.

"Rhys?"

He kissed Grace, a bit more passionately than he had intended, but she answered it with an equal ferocity. His fear of losing her once more, combined with her impatience, proved to be too much for him. He needed to know she was his, for at least this brief moment.

"Grace," he murmured. She seemed to understand what he could not explain aloud. He entered her as slowly as he could, so she could grow accustomed to the sensation of being joined with him, but her cry of joy prodded him to go deeper. She arched into him, her legs clamped around him as if fearful he might retreat, until she realized he would not. She rocked against his body, the rhythm as natural as if they had been together like this throughout time.

Time.

He needed more of it. He needed to spend every waking moment with Grace, loving her, caressing her, laughing with her, bringing her immeasurable joy.

He muttered a little prayer that such a wish could be granted, vowing to cherish the gift she would be in his life. Her movements began to speed up and become more frenzied. She clutched at his back, tightening her legs, and then began a slow moan. He increased the rhythm, knowing what she needed, and then he felt her squeezing him at the same time she began to wail his name.

He fought to hold off until she found her release, and when she did, he followed her into that blissful oblivion.

Grace held on to Rhys while they both tried to catch their breath. She kept her eyes closed, unwilling to leave the pure perfection she had experienced. She was not certain she could speak if needed. Her body tingled everywhere, especially where Rhys' skin touched hers.

He finally lifted his head and she opened her eyes. His concern melted away when he saw her smiling at him. He gave her a lingering kiss that made her feel the stirrings of arousal again.

"Not this time," he teased, moving to the other side of the bed and lying on his back. "You must think I have no control at all, as easily as you had me succumbing before."

"I enjoyed you succumbing, as I am sure you know." She rolled onto her side and began a slow caressing of his chest. "But if you wish to demonstrate your self-control later, I will prove to be the most avid audience."

He grinned and brushed her hair back over her shoulder. "You always have been."

Grace snuggled against his chest, and he wrapped his arm around her, pulling her tight against him. She had never felt so treasured, so comforted, so happy.

"Now it is my turn to be an avid audience," he said, slowly stroking her arm. "Tell me of some of your travels. Where did you go first? What was your favorite locale? Where would you return?"

"So many questions. Let me try to answer them in order. The first is the easiest. Scotland."

"Really?"

"It is where eloping couples go, of course. I was not quite enamored of their food, so it does not qualify as my favorite locale, or somewhere I would rush to return to. Yet I am glad I went. The scenery is magnificent, and the castles are ancient, filled with mystery and something quite mystical."

"From your glowing description, I find it hard to believe it is not your favorite." When she leaned back to look at him, he brushed a kiss against her lips. "You have quite made me feel as though I was there, as well."

"I wish you had been." She hesitated before confessing with a frown, "It was not long into our wedding journey that I learned my husband's true nature."

Rhys tightened his hold on her. "He did not harm you, did he?"

"No, not physically."

"Was he not loving?"

"Oh, he was very loving. So loving that he had to share himself with the entire female population of every place we visited. Any female that responded with a smile to his blandishments was favored with his 'loving nature'."

Rhys sat up and wrapped her in a quilt before carrying her to a chair near the fire. Once she was seated, he rummaged through the cupboards until he found a bottle of brandy. He returned and handed her the bottle. In the next instant, he was in the chair, and she was on his lap.

She took a measured sip of the spirits. Rhys waited patiently, giving her bare shoulder a tender kiss. Grace knew he wanted her to tell her tale, and he was providing her with a comforting setting to do so.

"I did not mourn his death," she said, handing Rhys the brandy. "I had already grieved previously, when I knew I was married to a man who could not love only me."

"He was a complete fool." Rhys took a quick swig from the bottle and then his lips lifted in a wicked smile. "Tell me you did not bring about his demise, poisoning his dinner one evening, or skewering him while he tended the fire."

"I did none of those things! I merely thought about them. No, his philandering nature brought about his own demise, or an angry husband did, most likely. He returned from carousing one evening, beaten and bruised, insisting he had been set upon by footpads. It was not the first time, either. I had packed my belongings, and Oliver's, but agreed to nurse him back to health, once more." She took the bottle from Rhys for another drink, a longer one this time. "I know I should have left sooner—"

There was nothing but compassion and understanding in his gaze. "You had Oliver to care for."

"He is the only reason I do not regret the marriage, as ill-fated as it was."

"It is because you find magic wherever you go, Grace. In truth, I believe you are a sorceress, creating magic when there is none, or even any hope of it. I have been the beneficiary so many times."

His words made her catch her breath. She nearly spilled the emotions in her heart just then, but the strength of her feelings frightened her. He seemed to sense her confusion, for he tightened his arms around her, and she rested her head against his steadily beating heart.

"Tell me which locale was your favorite," he murmured.

Here, she almost blurted. *This bewitching cottage, isolated from everyone, wrapped in your embrace.*

Instead, she said, "I was enamored of Paris. There is definitely some sort of enchantment there."

"Would you return if you could?"

"Oh, yes, definitely. I was also quite taken with Italy. There was a particular glow to the sunshine, very hard to describe, and the endless warmth produced wines beyond compare."

She snuggled in his arms, content to be travel guide for him, wishing they would have the chance to explore it together. It had been her most ardent wish when it was her turn at Stir Up Sunday.

"I am glad you had the chance to travel," Rhys said, brushing her hair with a kiss. "And even more glad you have returned to tell me about it."

"I should ask about your adventures," Grace said, "but I do not know that I could bear the jealousy it would bring me."

"Why would—oh, you mean amorous adventures." He flashed his roguish grin. "I was a veritable saint all those years."

She narrowed her eyes in a mock glare.

"Truly. There is a plaque in the village chapel extolling my piety and virtue." Rhys struggled to keep the merriment from his expression. "It has become a pilgrimage, of sorts, with visitors from all the surrounding shires. I would be happy to take you to see it, though I must warn you, some days the queues are rather long."

"While it does sound appealing, I want to devote my efforts to something else entirely." She grinned and pulled his head towards hers for a kiss. "It may mean the loss of your sainthood."

He deepened the kiss, stealing her breath, and then whispered against her lips, "Precisely what I prayed for all those years."

Chapter Eight

Twelfth Night

Each night was more blissful than the previous one, and each morning Grace struggled to leave, to return to the daily chores awaiting her. Rhys was much too tempting, and he did everything he could to persuade her to linger in his arms.

"I cannot afford to lose my position," she reminded him. "Lord Hartstone has been more than indulgent, but once the new year arrives, I cannot count on that to continue."

Rhys grumbled but thankfully he did not mention the possibility of a different life in the year to come. She had promised herself to revel in the stolen moments they shared, holding tightly to the happiness within her grasp right now, for however long it lasted. Yet at times, she could not help but yearn for more than an affair that must remain secret.

Rhys slowly donned his clothing and assisted her into hers. He saddled his horse and then swung onto it, leaning down to lift her in front of him. She cherished the feel of his arms holding her protectively, all while wishing they could gallop into a different future, one that held promise for a man and woman of such different stations in life.

Too soon they were at the edge of the kitchen garden. The sun was peeking through the last of the darkness, reminding her reality could be held at bay no longer. Rhys dismounted and then lifted her off the horse, holding her close as she descended. She would have kissed him, but there was a distinct throat clearing behind them.

They broke apart quickly. Grace brushed at her hair while Rhys tugged at his coat. Lord Hartstone greeted them with a broad smile.

Grace blushed, wanting nothing more than to dart into the kitchens. Surely Lord Hartstone knew they had spent the night together, but as he had not yet sent her packing, perhaps he remained unaware.

"Rhys, what great timing. I was on my way to remind you—we are anticipating you will join the Twelfth Night festivities this evening."

"Of course," Rhys answered, almost absentmindedly. "I had nearly forgotten which day it was."

Grace fought off a blush. She had trouble remembering which day it was, too, thanks to the nights spent in Rhys' arms.

"Good, good," Lord Hartstone said. "I am glad you shall be attending." He turned and beamed at her. "I know Grace will be making the most wondrous food for us. She always does. I cannot imagine what our feasts would be like if she were not here."

Grace felt her heart sink into her stomach. Despite Lord Hartstone's enthusiastic praise, it emphasized she was, and always would be, the cook. A servant who prepared the festivities, not one who could ever participate in them.

Rhys would continue to be invited as a guest, while Grace would ensure that Hartstone Hall's revelers were well taken care of.

"I have a great deal to do today," Grace said, her throat tight with anguish. She turned to Rhys. "Mr. Wilton, I must thank you for providing me a ride home. When I turned my ankle, I was not at all certain I could make it back safely. Fortunately your rescue was particularly well timed."

She could see Rhys understood she was attempting to save face, for the both of them. Still, he gave her a pleading look, while Lord Hartstone appeared confused. Grace gave her employer a brief curtsey, and Rhys a quick nod, and then she disappeared into the kitchens, cursing herself for being such a hopeless fool.

Rhys groaned, wishing he could thrash his friend in that moment. "What were you about, Hartstone?"

"What do you mean? I did not let on that I knew about your secret liaison. I had no wish to cause Grace any distress."

"But you have done just that! It seemed the Fates have been smiling on my wooing efforts, yet just when I have nearly persuaded Grace to contemplate a future with me—" He growled in frustration.

Martin's face fell as he realized his mistake. "I emphasized just how wide the chasm between the two of you is. Dash it all! Surely I can repair this. Let me prove I am a much better matchmaker than this, when I am not accidentally causing mayhem, I mean. I shall speak with her."

"No, I beg of you, do not. I will plead my case with her once more, this evening."

Rhys muttered a prayer to any deity who might favor a heartsick man such as he, and headed home, doing his best to believe he would prevail.

Yet if ever he needed a large dose of magic, it was surely tonight.

Late that evening, Grace wrapped her wool cloak around her and strolled into the kitchen garden. She lit the way with a lantern, even though she was likely able to do it without any light, having traversed it so many times before. The party upstairs was in full swing, while the servants were enjoying their own celebration. Oliver had been allowed to stay up a bit longer to participate in the revelry, but soon she would bring him to his bed, putting him down for the night.

He would wake to a secure future tomorrow, and every day thereafter. It was precisely why she had returned. Spending the nights in Rhys' embrace had made her forget that goal. Fortunately, Lord Hartstone had reminded her, and she would not soon erase it from her thoughts.

"Grace."

Rhys stepped out of the shadows and her heart lurched at the sight of him. She forced herself to stay in place, even as her heart urged her to race into the comfort of his arms.

"Rhys. Why aren't you at the party?"

"It is not particularly festive for me, not when I wish to be with you." He moved closer, slowly, studying her expression. "Grace, come away with me."

"Tonight?" She shook her head. "I cannot. There is still much I must do."

"No, not tonight. Every night. I want you with me every single moment."

She bit back a cry. "It is impossible, Rhys."

"Why, Grace? Why is it impossible?"

"It has been since we were born. You are a member of a noble clan, while I am the class designed to serve." She attempted a half-hearted smile. "If I possessed the magic to change it, I would. But we will both be better off once we accept this is how it must be."

Even as she said it, her spirit rebelled. The unfairness of the situation would always cause her pain. Maybe it would be different for Oliver one day…If so, then she could believe it was well worth the unhappiness swamping her now.

"Grace, if you care about me—"

"I do! It is why I cannot have you saddled with a lowly cook the rest of your days, the object of ridicule everywhere you go."

"Saddled? I would count it as the greatest blessing of my life were you to be my bride."

She shook her head. "You would see the error of your ways one day. I could not bear to have you change your mind."

"When have I ever changed my mind where you are concerned?"

The truthfulness of his words nearly choked her. It was a long moment before she could say, "I do not doubt the sincerity of your feelings, Rhys. I just do not believe they can overcome all of the difficulties we are bound to face."

"I thought it was unbearable losing you before," Rhys said quietly. "But it is nothing compared to the anguish of losing you now. At least then you were choosing adventure. Now you are choosing to forego it."

"I am choosing security," she protested. "And certainty."

"But at what cost?" He tenderly brushed a tendril from her forehead, and she could not help but react to his touch. "Will your heart cry out some day in the future wishing for something more? You create magic for everyone around you, but are unwilling to believe it is possible in your own life."

His words were more piercing because of the gentleness with which he uttered them. There was no anger, or pity, nor were there recriminations for her decision which altered his future happiness.

Just as it had done once before.

He waited patiently, his eyes hopeful, but she forced herself to remain silent. His shoulders sagged and he finally turned away. Grace knew without him saying it aloud this would be the last time they saw each other. As heartbreaking as that was, she knew it would be even worse to see him marry one day and have a family he adored.

Her heart splintered. "Rhys."

He turned slowly to face her. He lifted her hand and gave it a brief kiss. "My heart is yours, Grace. It has been since the first moment we met."

He waited a moment, as if hoping she would change her mind. When she did not, he gave her a bleak smile and then left.

Chapter Nine

January 13

Grace was grateful the holiday festivities were finally concluded. It was all she could do to maintain a pleasant demeanor while she carried out her daily tasks. The decorations had come down, the greenery burned before midnight to keep bad luck from visiting them. In truth, it felt as though it had anyway.

Oliver chattered as he usually did, although sometimes she had to ask him to repeat his questions because she had been so wrapped up in her morose thoughts, she had no idea how to answer him.

Oliver was not happy that it had been several days since Rhys and Bodhi had been by for a visit. Thankfully she had managed to convince Oliver they were travelling, hoping the lie would not be discovered. She was not sure how she would put him off in future when he realized they would not be returning.

For now, she needed to concentrate on finishing the baking. Even without holiday events, there were still many meals to prepare each day. It did not bring her the joy it had in the past. Nothing did, except for Oliver. Too many times, though, she remembered her son with his favorite dog, and Rhys' gentle, caring manner with Oliver...

She placed a hand to her heart. Would this feeling of loss ever subside? Now she had brought it into Oliver's life, when she had tried to prevent it from happening.

She dug into the bag sitting on the table in front of her and tossed a handful into the bowl.

"You do not want to put salt in there. It is sugar you need."

Grace glanced up, shocked to see her mother standing in the kitchens. "When did you return?" She raced around the table to give her a hug. "How long will you be staying?"

Her mother squeezed her more heartily than Grace expected. She relished it, though, needing comfort from the heartache that was bound to be her constant companion. Any other time she might be tempted to rail at her parent for enjoying everything she had once chided Grace for wanting, but not today.

"We are not staying long," her mother answered. "But I wanted to see everyone. I certainly did not expect to see my own daughter here."

"I had not expected to see me here, either," Grace admitted.

Grace fixed them some tea, and they sat quietly, sipping it. Her mother glanced around the kitchen and gave an approving smile. "You have made it yours.

I hardly recognize it even though I spent so many years here."

It made Grace happy to hear the words. "It was easy to make that transition, since it was perfectly organized and ready to take over when I came here. Lord Hartstone still reminisces about the meals you made. I find myself competing with your legend."

Her mother smiled at the praise, and then the silence continued a while longer before she spoke again. "Grace, I know you have a lot you want to say, but I have a few things I must tell you first."

Grace tilted her head, waiting politely for the lecture that was sure to come. Did one ever grow too old to be instructed by her mother on how to improve her life?

"I know you thought I was heartless, stifling your dreams of wanting more from life than cooking for someone else. I thought I was doing what a mother should, preventing you from suffering heartache. It seems I only caused it to appear in a different fashion."

Grace felt some of her resentment easing. "I have similar feelings for my own child's happiness," she said. "So even though I could not comprehend when I was younger, I do now." She flashed a quick smile. "I still have to admit I was stunned to learn you chose the life of world traveler after doing your best to keep me tied to this place."

Her mother's lips twisted into a wry expression. "You are not the only one. One day, after you left, I was scrubbing this very table and I could hear you in my mind, asking why it was so impossible to consider moving beyond our station. You asked, with such conviction, 'Is a seed told it must stay a seed, when it has the potential to become nourishment? A frog does not start as a frog. It is a tadpole, changing along the way until it becomes what it was meant to be. Why is it not then possible for a cook to aspire to more in life?'"

Grace sat back, stunned. She had completely forgotten those impassioned thoughts. "I did not realize my words would have such an effect."

"Oh, but they did! I was envious once you left. I am ashamed to admit that. Yet I finally understood that, just like you, I wanted more than what was in these kitchens. When Mr. Jenkins kept wooing me so persistently, I decided I was ready to be as brave as my daughter had been."

"And now we have switched places," Grace mused. "I could not have predicted that occurring."

Her mother patted her hand. "There will be more adventures for you again. I am confident of it."

"I am not so sure." Her voice wavered. "Yet I want my son to have more, too. He is so full of joy, and an exuberance that I never want to see diminished by the harsh realities of this world."

"Then why have you returned?" Her mother's expression brightened. "Was it because of Mr. Wilton? You two were inseparable. I always expected the two of you to elope, not you and Mr. Nettleton."

"I know everyone thought I was an adventuress when I married Ben." She took a sip of tea. "In truth, it was the more prudent choice. Rhys and I had no future, our stations in life sealing us to a path neither of us could change. If I had stayed—"

"You would have been faced with the impossibility of it on a daily basis."

Grace nodded, sniffing to keep the tears at bay. "Both of us would have. Fortunately that will not happen now. I am certain Rhys will be leaving soon for his much-delayed quest for adventure."

"'Tis a shame he must go alone. With you being an adventuress and all."

"A former adventuress," Grace amended with a brief smile. "My life requires more stability now that I have a child. Rhys is sure to understand why I declined his offer."

Her mother frowned. "I cannot think of anything more stable than exploring the world with a man who puts my happiness before his own. Who obviously did so when the woman he adores married someone else."

Grace blinked several times as she absorbed her mother's words. She had always feared that Rhys' love could not withstand the difficulties the world would throw at them. Yet his devotion had never faltered, even when she tested it at every turn. He demonstrated each day, and every blissful night, that her happiness was paramount to him.

Even when she turned him away once again.

"There is no one as constant as Rhys. He has proved it time and again, yet I continue to make such a muddle of everything where he is concerned."

"We all do our best to protect our hearts, Grace. Sometimes our attempts are misguided, or have results we cannot anticipate. Fortunately, when you realize your mistake, you have a choice, just like with a recipe." She added a wink. "You can try to fix it, or start over completely."

Grace laughed, the simplicity of her mother's advice soothing her earlier anguish. She loved Rhys. They had been given a chance to start over, and she had nearly let it slip through her hands.

It was time now to choose the life she truly desired, just as she should have done years ago when she had convinced her own mother a cook could aspire to more in life.

"I should warn you," Grace said with a grin, "I am likely to bring scandal down upon us."

Her mother clucked her tongue. "I can tell you about a handful of scandals that occurred after you left, yet the world still continues on, day after day. Besides, what will I care? I shall be travelling the world, and will not be here to listen to envious gossip about my beautiful adventuress daughter and the man she loves."

Grace chuckled at her mother's cheeky response.

"Now where is Oliver? I cannot wait to finally meet him." Her mother's eyes twinkled. "That was the most difficult thing to endure—not being able to see my very own grandson."

Oliver burst into the room, as if they had summoned him, laughing and clutching his wooden toy Bodhi. It went everywhere with him. "Mama! Is Mr. Wilton bringing Bodhi today? I miss them. I need to walk Bodhi so he can get his exercise."

Her mother gasped and then covered her mouth with one hand. Her eyes teared up as she watched her grandson, and any resentment Grace had harbored long ago melted away.

"Oliver, remember how I told you about someone you would love the moment you met them?" When he nodded vigorously, she added, "This is who I meant. Your grandmama."

Oliver grinned as he rushed into his grandmama's arms. "I'm Oliver. And this is Bodhi. Mr. Wilton made him for me, and it looks just like the real Bodhi. Except the real Bodhi can run and lick my face."

Her mother rocked Oliver in her arms and laughed and cried at the same time. Grace wiped away a happy tear or two to see her mother and son together.

Susanna walked in, and Oliver announced proudly, "This is my grandmama."

"Would you believe I knew your grandmama a long time ago? Before you were even born."

Oliver's eyes widened, trying to puzzle that one out.

Susanna chuckled and set the kettle on the stove. "I shall see to Mr. Oliver's tea while Mrs. Jenkins and I catch up." She gave Grace a knowing look. "I think there are some things you need to attend to."

"You were eavesdropping, weren't you? Just when I think you cannot be more impossible--" Grace gave Susanna a quick hug. "Wish me luck. Though if I am successful, you may find yourself in charge here."

Susanna added a saucy wink. "Maybe that was my plan all along."

"Here, Bodhi. Fetch the stick."

Rhys hurled it and waited for Bodhi to scamper after it with his usual enthusiasm. The branch hit the ground with a resounding thud but Bodhi did not move. He gave it a disinterested glance and then lay down, his head on his paws.

"I sympathize, Bodhi. But we cannot spend the rest of our days moping about."

Perhaps it had been a mistake to leave Grace without trying once more to dispel her fears. Yet he did not know how to do so. He did not wish to plead with her if her heart remained resistant.

Still, he remembered her whispered confession, their very first night together. He knew she adored him. Though she had not told him directly, she had proven it to him many times. Unfortunately it did not provide the result he desired. Instead it reminded him he was once more third in line, behind Grace's need for security, and stability.

He understood those needs, and it saddened him that he could not provide her the assurances she required.

It was time for him to set off on his own travels. He should have done so long ago. Had he stayed, hoping Grace would return? If so, there was no reason to remain now. He had to move forward, carrying Grace in his heart, but not in his embrace, nor his future. He could only hope the rightness of his decision would one day banish the melancholy swamping him now.

"Come, Bodhi, let us head home. We may as well plan our next steps."

Bodhi's ears perked up, and he lifted his head, but he was not paying attention to Rhys. Bodhi leapt to his feet, his tail wagging mightily, and then he began racing forward, barking.

Rhys turned, expecting to see Martin, but it was Grace heading his direction, her stride determined, not at all tentative. Still, he refused to let hopefulness seep into his heart. He had just started the task of becoming accustomed to Grace as a bittersweet memory. He could not bear to have his hopes dashed anew.

"Rhys, I am on the verge of making the biggest mistake of my life. I need your wise counsel." Her gaze was earnest, making it difficult not to rush to her aid, as he had always done before.

"How can I help?" He kept his voice neutral, as if she were merely asking directions to the next village.

"Many years ago, I fell in love with a man—"

"Yes, I know. You married him."

"No, I did not. I wish I had married the man I loved. The one I love to this very day. But I was afraid of the obstacles we would encounter, and I chose to believe they were insurmountable."

His heart beat a little more hopefully at her admission that she loved him. "Why did you believe them insurmountable?"

"How many cooks do you know who fall in love with a nobleman? It is a cautionary tale from beginning to end, guaranteed to conclude with heartache. I was also well aware of the scandal it would cause your family—"

"The scandal is they scarcely realize I exist. Not unless Charles sneezes twice in a row, or Henry complains about a tickle in his throat." He took a tentative step closer. "It is the curse of being a third son, I suppose. A talented cook would be understandably wary of an alliance with someone of so few prospects."

"Except he was the most important part of her entire life growing up. A steadying influence as well as a kindred adventuring soul." She inhaled deeply, as if gathering her courage, and then continued. "I fear it may be too late to make amends, to commence what should have begun years ago. Yet I am also irrationally hopeful that we will be given that chance. That you are willing to take that chance with me."

Rhys could not resist the heartfelt plea in her eyes. His heart swelled at the bravery she exhibited. It gave him strength to make his own confession.

"You were not the only one who was fearful, Grace. When you left, it was easy to convince myself I had mistakenly inflated your regard for me. I was grateful I had not declared myself to you, as I had originally planned." He paused. "I was afraid to believe you could truly love me."

Grace did not even hesitate. She threw herself into his arms, wrapping hers tightly around him. He thought his heart would melt when she said, "You shall fear that no longer, Rhys, for I love you with my entire being. I only wish I had acted on it years ago."

He halted her words with another kiss. "Neither of us were ready then," he murmured against her mouth. "The important thing is we are now, and we have a lifetime to spend together."

"We have Oliver and Bodhi now, too. Our lives are bound to be filled with happiness. Though there will likely still be difficulties—"

"Nothing could be as difficult as a future without you."

She gave him one last kiss and then grabbed his hand. "Come. Let's find the rest of our family and tell them the happy news."

Rhys grinned and followed her, dazzled by her happiness, and how it so easily multiplied his own.

Grace watched as Bodhi raced ahead of them towards Hartstone Hall. She kept her hand in Rhys', needing his touch, almost unable to believe they would spend the rest of their days together.

At last they were at the entrance to the kitchen garden. Rhys pulled her into his embrace, and this time she did not protest. What did she care about scandal? She was in love. She was loved. There was no reason to hide her joy from anyone who happened to wander by.

She lost herself in his kisses, each more ardent than the previous one. She broke away, just to catch her breath, and to remind herself they had many plans to implement.

As if on cue, Oliver and Bodhi raced up to them, Oliver giggling, and Bodhi panting happily.

"It seems as if they were meant to be together," she said happily.

"We all are," Rhys agreed.

"Mr. Wilton, Bodhi found something really smelly and I tried to get him away from it, but he was too strong for me." Oliver's expression was slightly horrified when he added, "He even rolled his whole body in it."

Grace bit back a laugh, and admired Rhys' ability to keep his expression bland in the face of Bodhi's aroma, and Oliver's dismay.

"Fortunately, we can toss a bucket or two of water over Bodhi. It's the only solution, since it is impossible to prevent him from doing something when his mind is set on it."

Grace pretended to frown at her son. "Why does that sound like someone else I know?"

Oliver giggled, giving her one of his fierce hugs. He turned when Rhys said, "Oliver, I wonder if I could ask you something very important."

Oliver nodded, and Rhys squatted down in front of him. "I love your mother very much. I plan to ask her to marry me, but I want to be assured that you agree with this decision."

Oliver nibbled on his bottom lip as he pondered the question. Grace wondered what was going through his mind just then. She did not have long to wait, however.

"Does this means Bodhi would be my dog?"

Grace could not hold back her laugh this time. The little scamp had found a way around her restrictions, but she could not help but admire his tenacity.

"Of course he would be your dog," Rhys answered. "In truth, Bodhi believes he is your dog now. He merely resides at my house."

Oliver threw his arms around Rhys' neck and squeezed tightly. "Yes, I want you to marry my mama. Then Bodhi can live at my house." He stepped back and added solemnly, "You can live with us, too."

"I appreciate your generosity, Oliver." Rhys grinned. "I think we shall find a new house, one that all of us will choose together."

Oliver laughed. "Bodhi, I wish you smelled better so I could give you a hug, since you're my dog now. Mostly."

Rhys chuckled. "Let's see if we can persuade Susanna to donate some water from the kitchens so we can get Bodhi back to smelling as good as new."

"Yes! Come on, Bodhi." Oliver and his new dog raced to the kitchen door, intent on completing their mission.

Grace leaned against Rhys and he wrapped his arm around her waist. "You know you have just signed on to a grand adventure."

"Life became an adventure the first day I met you, Grace. It has been one magical episode after another since then."

She turned so she could circle her arms about his neck. "Where should this next magical adventure start?"

He kissed her sweetly, making her heart sing. "Right here."

Epilogue

Martin carefully refolded the letter, smiling as he tucked it inside his jacket pocket.

Rhys and Grace were settling in at the villa in Italy Martin had purchased with them in mind. He had persuaded Rhys that his management skills were desperately needed, and it would be the perfect place for Oliver and Bodhi to roam free. Grace would be able to work her magic with the olives and grapes and everything else that grew there in such abundance.

He could only imagine the wondrous Twelfth Night celebrations they were bound to have. Perhaps they would invite him to attend next year's festivities.

In time, Martin would have the deed transferred to the newlyweds—once they had settled in so much they could not consider anywhere else to be home.

He sighed with contentment. Fortunately they had married before setting off for Italy. He would have hated missing such a joyous wedding. Everyone would have. Well, except for the Wiltons, but their absence had scarce been noticed.

Best of all, this latest success cemented Martin's reputation as the matchmaking earl. There was a moment, though, when he had nearly spoiled it. That had not happened with his two previous attempts, a good reminder of just how difficult this matchmaking business could be.

It was why he was in no rush to make a match for himself. There was still plenty of time for that. Until then, he could celebrate his triumphs, and ponder who might be the next to benefit from his talent for finding a perfect match.

The End

About Donna

I have worked as an attorney, winery tasting room manager, and retail business owner, but nothing beats the thrill of writing humorously-ever-after romances.

I reside in New England, although I fantasize about spending the rest of my days in a tropical locale, wearing flip flops year-round, or in Regency London, scandalizing the *ton*.

You can find details of her work at
www.AllAboutTheWriting.com

A Kiss Upon the Wind

~ A Scandalous Kisses Novella ~

BY

Barbara Monajem

Twice-widowed Lady Isolde Doncaster doesn't want to remarry, but her parents will stop at nothing to find her a new husband. Even the family ghost, a dashing Cavalier, insists she must wed again. When a masked stranger at the Christmas masquerade helps Isolde avoid her suitors, she is grateful—until she realizes he is the son of the neighboring family, come to steal a pendant their mothers have feuded over for years.

Gawain Burke sneaked into the Christmas masquerade with one goal: to retrieve the pendant that rightfully belongs to his mother. But his chivalrous instincts come to the fore, and protecting Isolde from lecherous men becomes his primary concern. He's not a suitor for her hand. She has sworn never to marry again. They'll just work together to return the pendant and stop the feud.

But neither of them reckons with the ghost, who has a far better ending in mind.

Chapter One

"I told you not to wear that costume," the ghost of the Cavalier said.

Ever since he had started speaking to Lady Isolde Doncaster, the Cavalier had shown himself to be an I-told-you-so sort of ghost, full of advice and admonitions. But she'd had enough of that lately from her parents. A widow had the right to take charge of her own life, and Isolde intended to do so.

"You didn't tell me until after I had already left my bedchamber," she whispered from behind a bust on a pedestal in the ballroom at Statham Court. She was taking a well-deserved respite from the Christmastide masquerade, but she doubted this method of escaping attention would work for long.

The faint form of the ghost, barely visible in this dim corner, stiffened in haughty dignity. "My dear child, it would have been improper of me to enter your chamber whilst you were unclad."

She appreciated this, for while married she'd had enough of being leered at—although perhaps the Cavalier was too proper, or simply too dead, to wish to do so. "It was kind of you to warn me, but I was trying to convey a message with this costume." She'd copied it as exactly as possible from a scandalous caricature of herself dressed as the Greek enchantress Circe, carrying her cup of poison—the only difference being that Isolde's costume wasn't transparent like the one in the horrid drawing. "That I would poison my suitors rather than marry again."

The Cavalier chuckled. "Circe turned men into swine with her potion, but she was also a seductress—a message gentlemen were far more likely to heed."

Isolde sighed. She had been married twice. She should know by now how gentlemen's minds worked. The female guests, as well as a few starchy males, had been shocked, but she'd been besieged by lascivious men. She'd refused several dances, used a hatpin to fend off attempts to kiss and paw her, and thrown the contents of her goblet in Lord Cape's face—a waste of a perfectly good tisane.

Very much like the one she'd given her first husband, Simon Doncaster, who had died of his stomach pains despite the healing tisanes she'd given him—but the truth didn't prevent the speculation that she had poisoned him, hence the caricatures. "My suitors are proving to be swine without any help from me," she said.

It couldn't get much worse. Her mother would be even more hysterical than usual after tonight, and her father, the Earl of Statham, even more determined to marry her off again. He had invited three prospective suitors—respected older men he approved of—to spend a fortnight at his estate, and was offering ten thousand pounds to whoever won her hand. She hadn't the slightest intention of wedding any of them—or anyone else, for that matter. She'd put up with the first two husbands her father had insisted upon. She couldn't count on a third convenient demise.

As if he'd read her mind, the ghost said, "You must not marry one of those chosen by your father."

"There we agree," she muttered, but Christmas was over, New Year's past as well, and now Twelfth Night, after which all the guests would leave, loomed far too close. Each day her suitors became more fervent—or perhaps more desperate was a better description.

"I shall inform you when a worthy lover arrives," the ghost said.

She sighed again, but didn't reply. The ghost was a poet, so obsessed with love that he composed volumes of poetry about it. He simply didn't understand that nothing could make so-called love—in other words, lust—palatable to her.

She peered around the pedestal. She'd had enough of drunken lechers. She'd stabbed one with her trusty hatpin only five minutes ago, at which the ghost had cheered. What a pity no one else could hear him. Or see him for that matter, but he was visible only in the dark, and then only when he chose to be seen.

She just wanted to get away, but mistletoe still decked every doorway, making escape difficult. One would think that in one's own father's house, one could count on protection from unwanted advances. No such luck. Her brothers were celebrating Christmas elsewhere. James, her favorite, now lived far away in the north of England with his bride. And Isolde's father actually *hoped* one of the three suitors would seduce her—as if that would force her to wed.

Sir Andrew Dirks, unoriginally costumed as Henry VIII, marched up to her. *Not again.* "Waltz with me, goddess!"

"I haven't changed my mind since the last time you asked, Sir Andrew."

He pouted. "The correct form of address is Your Majesty."

"Your Majesty may go to the devil," she snapped.

He heaved a brandy-fueled sigh. "This time I come at the express request of your father."

My father may go to the devil, too. Before she could get the hatpin out, he had his arm around her waist, her wrist firmly in his grip.

The Cavalier roared with rage, drawing his ghostly sword. "Let be, dastard!" he cried, which was noble but utterly useless. She had to fend for herself.

"You won't fool me with that trick twice." Sir Andrew leaned in for a kiss.

She turned her head, struggling. "Stop it. We're not under the mistletoe."

He was too drunk to care. She was about to shriek like a banshee, more scandal be damned, when a peremptory voice said, "My dance, I believe."

A fist caught Sir Andrew on the jaw, and he crumpled to the floor. Isolde gazed in astonishment at the man who had so swiftly saved her. Behind him, the Cavalier cried, "Huzzah!"

"Unless you'd rather not." Her rescuer was Charles II, or perhaps the Earl of Rochester—in any event, one of those libertines with a long curly wig.

"Now *this* is a true gentleman," the Cavalier said. "A praiseworthy lover." Fortunately, her rescuer couldn't hear the ghost's embarrassing comment.

Who *was* he? His mask covered much of his face. "We might stroll around the room instead," he suggested. "Or share cakes and wine."

His voice was vaguely familiar, but she couldn't quite place him.

"Unless you need to refill your cup of poison?" Her rescuer sounded amused—no surprise about that. Meanwhile, Sir Andrew lay where he had fallen, out like a snuffed candle. She beckoned to a footman to move the unconscious man out of the way.

She didn't intend to thank Charles-or-Rochester, for doubtless he would prove to be as bad as the rest. "Only if it is your ambition to become a swine."

He chuckled. "Not at all. You are perfectly safe with me."

She shrugged and placed her hand on his proffered arm. She didn't believe him, but as long as he wasn't pawing, squeezing, groping, or forcing a kiss on her, she would put up with him.

And yet her curiosity was piqued. "Then why did you rescue me? Chivalry is long since dead, and Sir Andrew could hardly rape me in the ballroom." That sort of plain speaking should do the trick. Either he would shy away out of outraged propriety, or get rapidly worse. If the latter, it was best to get it over with.

"I must be a last bastion of chivalry," Charles-or-Rochester said. "I wouldn't have let that cur inconvenience you under any circumstances. But I confess that I was hoping for a chance to speak with you."

She grimaced with distaste. "If you're another suitor, you may as well know straightaway that I don't intend to remarry."

"No? Then why the ten-thousand-pound prize for winning your hand?"

"That was my father's notion." She hadn't known a thing about it. She'd been pondering going north to visit James, perhaps even to live there, if she proved to get on well with his wife. But when Mama had begged her to come home to Statham Court for Christmas, and Papa had cajoled, pleading Mama's fragile state of mind, Isolde hadn't had the heart to refuse.

What a mistake! No sooner had they arrived than so did the three suitors, along with a few other guests, for a fortnight-long party—at which point it was far too late for her to flounce back to London in a rage. How dare Papa foist these men onto her, insisting that he knew best, as if she were still an innocent girl?

"I'm not a suitor," the stranger said. She must have appeared skeptical, for he added, "Believe me, I know all about parents eager to push one into marriage. You have my wholehearted sympathy."

An ordinary libertine then, hence the costume. "So what do you want from me?" *Just get it over with.*

"I should like to learn about the Statham ghost."

That was a surprise. She eyed him, still wondering who he might be.

"The dashing Cavalier," he elaborated. "With his plumed hat and embroidered gauntlets, sword at the ready—or so I've heard. I hoped to have a chance to learn more about him, perhaps even see him for myself."

A ghost enthusiast, was he? The masquerade was a clever way to get into the Court, since Papa invariably refused to allow such people access. However, she owed Charles-or-Rochester a favor. "That depends on whether the ghost wishes to be seen." She jutted her chin toward the doorway with its sprig of mistletoe. "If you can get me safely out of the ballroom, I'll see if I can persuade him—"

"Isolde darling! There you are. I thought you were to dance with Sir Andrew." Her mother scurried up, her twitchy, birdlike gaze darting between Isolde and her companion.

"He became unwell," Isolde said through her teeth.

"*Isolde*," she whispered. "Pray watch what you *say*." Mama appeared poised, but Isolde could tell she was on the verge of hysteria. "Mr. Nebley, who is by far my favorite of your suitors, begs to dance with you." With a distracted nod at Charles-or-Rochester, she bore Isolde away. "Who was that?"

"I have no idea," Isolde said, although she felt that, in fact, she *should* know. Perhaps she'd met him in London sometime.

"That is the problem with masquerades," Mama said. "Even the riffraff gets in."

This was unfair. "He wasn't riffraff, Mama. He spoke like a gentleman, and more important, he rescued me from Sir Andrew's odious advances."

"Sir Andrew is a suitor for your *hand*," her mother said. "His advances are *honorable*." Her voice trembled. "How *could* you wear such a dreadful costume, when you are already a subject of scandal and innuendo? You are fortunate indeed that anyone is willing to marry you."

Willing to take Papa's ten thousand pounds was more like it. "The scandal wasn't my fault," she retorted, a waste of breath, but she couldn't help it. Her first husband had paraded her like a trophy, sharing vulgar confidences about his enjoyment of her in bed, which inspired a number of disgusting caricatures. Her second husband would doubtless have been worse. Fortunately, he too was dead, but the broadsheets still featured caricatures of her whenever no juicier subject offered. Gossips abounded, here and everywhere; there was probably at least one informant at this masquerade. Lord Cape with her potion dripping from his cravat would no doubt appear in an upcoming print; Sir Andrew too, ousted by a libertine whose arm she had supposedly taken with libidinous glee.

She might not mind quite so much if she had any libido to speak of. Whatever she'd started out with had vanished long ago.

"Hush," her mother whispered. "You must rise above the gossip, not contribute to it. If you will only choose one of your suitors and remarry, all will be well again."

Gawain Burke didn't consider himself a vain sort of man, and he'd disguised himself well on purpose—and yet, it piqued him that Lady Isolde didn't know who he was.

Which was absurd, for why should she? They had met often during childhood, as their fathers' estates bordered one another, but after that he'd been at Oxford and then on the town. Not only that, since a dispute over a heart-shaped pendant a few years ago, the two families were sworn enemies. They crossed to the opposite sides of the street to avoid one another—although he and James Blakely, Isolde's brother, remained friends regardless. But when James had approached Isolde with him during her first season, Lady Statham had intervened, hissing, "We do not speak to *those people*," and hustled Isolde away.

A pity, for she'd changed from a gangly, tangle-haired girl to a lively blonde beauty. Under better circumstances he might have pursued the undeniable attraction, but she'd soon been married off to that lascivious old bore, Simon

Doncaster. And then, when Simon died a year or so later, to his cousin Alan. That marriage had lasted all of three hours. No wonder they called her Lady Luckless—or a rather cruder play on the name related to the way Alan had died.

Damn Lady Statham, both for ending their conversation—but he could find a way to pick up where they'd left off—and for having so little sympathy for her daughter, who'd been the subject of vulgar gossip started by her own husband.

Isolde had confirmed what he already knew about the ghost's appearance, so he needn't speak to her again. It would be safer not to, for if she recognized him, he would find himself in the soup.

Very well—but he would content himself with one chivalrous act.

The mistletoe was gone.

"Your lover took it down," the Cavalier's voice came from beside Isolde. "I told you he was worthy."

She blinked at the bare doorway, disbelieving. *He's not my lover.* She didn't say it aloud, for it was pointless to argue with the ghost.

With the unmasking completed, the masquerade was drawing to an end. It had begun fitfully to snow, and most neighboring guests had already gone, hoping to arrive home before the snow fell in earnest. A few guests still played cards and billiards, whilst others had already retired for the night. Isolde hoped to reach her bedchamber undisturbed by drunken suitors, her disappointed mother, or her irate father. But what if her so-called lover's assistance came at a price?

"Fear not, for he seeks only to help you escape," the ghost said.

She sighed, longing to believe this. Mr. Nebley, her mother's notion of a perfect gentleman, hadn't proven as difficult as some of the others. He was costumed as a Roman emperor, which suited his condescending attitude. How dare he act as if he were doing her a favor? On the other hand, there'd been no need to fight him off.

She'd put up with his starchiness for the rest of the evening, smothering her yawns as best she could, and once he'd finished prosing, she'd politely refused—for the fourth or fifth time—his offer of marriage. When he'd stormed off to complain to her father, she'd fled, craving peace, quiet, and solitude.

"Quickly," the Cavalier said. "Now is your best chance."

Despite the assurances from both the ghost and Charles-or-Rochester himself that he wouldn't harm her, she hesitated. "Is he waiting for me?"

"To protect you." He added smugly, "He will kiss you when the time is right, with or without mistletoe."

She huffed. She didn't intend to kiss anyone, but she owed her rescuer a brief—very brief—conversation about the ghost. She made a dash for the doorway and found him standing in the mercifully empty Great Hall, contemplating a suit of armor festively decked with fir boughs and holly. The tip of a sprig of mistletoe protruded from its helmet.

She couldn't help but chuckle, and the intruder grinned. Something about that smile reminded her...of whom, she couldn't recall. He still wore his mask.

"Thank you for hiding the mistletoe," she said. "What do you wish to know about the ghost?"

"Never mind that. You'd best hurry upstairs. Your father looks ready to take a switch to you."

"He will scold, but he won't actually beat me." She sighed. Perhaps if he did beat her, she would gather the resolve to defy him once and for all. But he was rightly worried about poor Mama, who grew more distraught with each passing day. "Walk with me, and I'll answer your questions."

"That may cause gossip," he said.

"Everything I do causes gossip." She lit a bedroom candle and started up the stairs.

He followed. "And speculation, to which I am averse."

"You don't want your identity revealed."

"Preferably not."

How intriguing. "Then you shouldn't linger. Masks aren't allowed after the unmasking." Evidently the risk of exposure wouldn't stop him, for when she reached the first landing, he passed her and continued languidly upward, his cloak swishing gently.

"What do you wish to know?" she asked.

"Where he walks, and when. Whether he wails or moans, or anything of the sort."

She shuddered, recalling the one instance when she'd heard the ghost moan. "Only if one enters the north attic. There, he wails and moans and rattles his chains."

"He's in chains?"

"When in the attic, he is, and bleeding from dreadful wounds. He never speaks about it, but as far as we know, he was wounded at war and returned only to die. Ever since one of my brothers fell down the stairs after going in there on a dare, we are forbidden to enter the north attic, day or night."

He snorted.

"Do not view it as a challenge," she said. "I went there once to escape a beating, and it was almost worse."

"Almost?"

She nodded. "He was truly dreadful to look at. I believe he took pity on me because I was weeping, and only a girl. He motioned me to a corner, and when one of the servants came seeking me, he groaned and rattled his chains, and the poor man left in a hurry, certain I couldn't possibly be up there. I was so frightened that I didn't stay long—enough that my father forgot to beat me, though."

"Brave girl."

She grimaced. She didn't feel brave anymore. "When not in the attic, he has no wounds or chains. He roams throughout the house, and he's quite friendly. He speaks, but most people can't hear him."

"And you can?"

"Yes, although when my brother James lived here, he spoke mostly to him. He used to spend hours with him, dictating..." She broke off; she must be overwrought, for she had almost revealed the ghost's secret—which was bad enough, but to a man whose identity she didn't even know, which was far worse.

"Dictating…?"

"Nothing," she said, and a cold breeze down her back, the ghost's calling card, made her shiver.

"Nothing?" the Cavalier bellowed in her ear. "How dare you denigrate my poems?"

"I do beg your pardon," she muttered. "What I meant was that I am not permitted to explain it to our guest."

"He is no guest, but your lover."

Heat flooded her cheeks. "He is not! I don't even know who he is."

The ghost huffed and was gone. She bumped into the stranger, who had turned to stare.

A horrid premonition assailed her. "Well now," she said bitterly, "how convenient. You can tell the caricaturists not only about my antics with the hatpin and cup of poison, but you can also report that I have gone mad and argued with thin air." She stormed past him, shame and fury colliding within her. Usually she knew better than to betray herself to an informant.

He followed, speaking softly. "I'm not here to transmit gossip."

For some odd reason, she believed him—not that she could do anything about it either way.

"You were speaking to the ghost? He's right here?"

"Not anymore. I insulted his—uh, him—and he stalked away in a dudgeon."

"I did no such thing," said the ghost, beside her once again. "You have my permission to discuss my poetry with your lover."

"If I ever have one," she retorted, "perhaps I shall."

"Have one what?" Charles-or-Rochester didn't appear disconcerted by the exchange of which he could only hear one side; rather, he seemed amused. Again. "Is it not dark enough for me to see him?"

"Maybe he doesn't want to show himself. In any event, our conversation was none of your business." At last she reached her bedchamber and opened the door. "Thank you for escorting me to safety. I wish you luck seeing the ghost."

"Do not dismiss him!" the Cavalier cried. "A lustful man awaits."

"What?" She turned to the stranger and proffered her candle. "Please inspect my room for intruders, if you would be so kind."

"Delighted," the man said grimly. He stalked in, holding the candle high.

A married house guest lay sprawled across the bed, naked and all too obviously aroused.

"Mr. Denton! Have you run mad?" Isolde demanded.

He sprang up, aghast at the sight of the masked stranger, and hurriedly pulled the sheet over his erection. "I—I beg your pardon, Lady Isolde. If I had known you already had a lover, I assure you, I wouldn't have—

"I don't!" she began, about to deny his assumption, but the stranger interrupted.

"Get out," Charles-or-Rochester snapped. "And keep your mouth shut, or you will regret it."

"I beg your pardon, sir!" the naked man protested. "I merely wished to help

Lady Isolde. Her costume is a clear indication of what she craves. After those two old men she married, she must be desperate for a real f—"

The stranger threw him into the corridor, sheet and all.

"Bravo!" cried the ghost.

The masked man gathered the intruder's clothing and tossed it out after him. "Ring for your maid, Lady Isolde. I shall wait out of sight down the passageway until she arrives."

"Thank you," she said. He left, closing the door softly behind him.

Once the maid was safely in Isolde's room, Gawain retreated to his hideaway in the lumber room at the end of the corridor. He knew a little about Statham Court, thanks to his childhood friendship with Isolde's brother James, who, luckily, now lived in the North of England with his wife. Gawain didn't want James implicated in what he was about to do; he was already estranged from his parents for marrying the woman he loved, rather than the heiress of his father's choice.

All the Earl of Statham cared about was money—the more the better—regardless of other considerations, such as the happiness of the parties involved. Isolde had been married off to two wealthy older men, who had no doubt paid well for the privilege—more than enough to cover the ten thousand Statham was prepared to pay now.

It was all quite disgusting. He hoped Isolde would manage to escape her father's clutches.

As for the heart-shaped pendant, Lady Statham had as good as stolen the damned thing. That was years ago, and although James had tried to persuade his mother to give it back, Lady Statham had refused. She was known to be a hysteric, but this blatant theft was unacceptable. Lord Statham could have overridden her and insisted on returning it, but he hadn't—unsurprising, given his relentless greed.

Enough. Gawain was home for the holiday, so what better gift for his mother than to take back the heart-shaped pendant? The masquerade made access to Statham Court a simple matter. All he had to do was find the pendant—and he was almost sure he knew where it was, thanks to a game he and James had played one afternoon long ago.

He removed his mask, wrapped himself in his greatcoat, and settled in a moth-eaten armchair to doze until the household slept. When he woke shivering a while later, all was dark and quiet.

He changed into the Cavalier costume he had brought with him—tall boots, a longish coat with wide tails, and an ancient sword. His hat had a magnificent plume. He traced a mustache and beard on his face with a bit of charcoal. It was probably awry, since he had no looking-glass, but hopefully it would suffice should someone chance upon him in a dark corridor. A menacing expression and a drawn sword should frighten someone off.

He checked for his tinderbox, shuttered his lantern, and slipped quietly into the passageway. Light from the ormolu sconces in the Great Hall helped him make his silent way to Lady Statham's suite of rooms. He paused outside her bedchamber door and glanced up and down the passageway. All clear...

No, not clear. Several doors down, a candle flickered. A man set his hand on Lady Isolde's door. Unsheathing his sword, Gawain marched down the passage.

Chapter Two

A terrified yowl woke Isolde. She sat up in bed, heart galloping, and shoved the curtains aside.

A low, eerie growl penetrated the door. "Begone, foul murderer!"

The yowl erupted again. "I wasn't going to kill her," a desperate voice babbled. "Oh God, oh God, it's the ghost come to get me!" That sounded like Lord Cape. He was known to be superstitious. He'd hung a horseshoe over his bedchamber door for luck in his quest to marry her. A waste of effort, for there wasn't the slightest chance she would go to his room, and he wouldn't have any luck if he came to hers.

"Begone," the low voice said again.

A series of thuds followed—someone running down the stairs. By this time the maid, Millicent, had woken. "Wha—what is it, my lady?"

"I think someone saw our ghost and was frightened." By whom? That eerie voice was definitely not the ghost's, and Lord Cape wouldn't have heard him even if it had been.

Was her rescuer prowling the house, keeping watch over her sleep? Much as she would like to imagine him hovering nearby, ready to fend off all comers, that was absurd.

"More fool he for creeping about the passageway at night," Millicent said. "One of those gentlemen wanting to wed you, I daresay."

"Accosting me in the middle of the night is not the way to convince me to wed," Isolde retorted.

"But you would have no choice, my lady!" Millicent said. "If you were caught with one of them, what else could you do?"

"I could just say *no*," Isolde said, "and to Hades with the scandalmongers."

The maid shook her head and tutted. "I must say, my lady, I wish you would get married again, so we could be comfortable once more." She stretched and turned over on the truckle bed.

Everyone wanted Isolde married—her mother because she was afraid nothing else would keep Isolde safe from scandal, her father because he feared for her mother's sanity, and now Millicent, because she didn't want to spend a few nights on a narrow bed. *What about me?* thought Isolde grumpily. She got out of bed, stuck her feet into her slippers, and put on her wrapper.

"Surely you won't go out there, my lady!" Millicent quavered. "What if the ghost is still there?"

"I'm not afraid of the ghost." She opened the door and peered up and down the dark corridor. "Whoever it was, he's gone." She peered over the balustrade, shivering in the draft. Heavens, the front door was wide open! She muffled a snort of laughter. Lord Cape had fled into the snowy night.

"Come back to bed, please, my lady," Millicent whispered from the doorway.

A door opened down the passageway. Her father! She scurried back to her bedchamber, but he had already seen her. He stomped to her door, glowering in the light of a candle.

"What are you up to now, Isolde?" he said.

"Nothing at all," she retorted. "Someone made a ghastly noise in the passage and woke me. I believe it was Lord Cape, for he was babbling about the ghost."

"That's nothing to make a fuss about," her father said. "You haven't been at it with your hatpin again, have you?"

She clenched her teeth to stifle a scream of frustration. "I was *asleep*," she said, "and if Lord Cape had entered my bedchamber with a fell purpose, I would have defended myself with far more than a hatpin."

Her father huffed. "A less rough and ready method of acquiring you would be preferable, but your suitors have become impatient, and rightly so. They will use fair means or foul in their efforts to win you."

"And the ten-thousand-pound carrot you are dangling before them." *Asses that they are.*

"That too, but think of the advantages of accepting one of them. Once you remarry, you needn't fear nocturnal visitors."

"Except my husband," she snapped.

"Yes, of course, for it would be his right." Papa pushed past her into the room and spied the maid, who dropped a hasty curtsey. "What's she doing here?"

"Helping to keep the lechers at bay. When I came upstairs tonight, Mr. Denton was in my bed, stark naked."

"Denton? A married man with his wife here in the house—how indiscreet." He shook his head. "It's a pity a few silly fools got the wrong idea, but what did you expect? First those scandalous broadsheets, and tonight that horrendous costume. If only you had accepted Mr. Nebley's proposal, we would have announced your betrothal at the unmasking and all would be well."

Not for me. "I'd be stuck with that starchy man for the rest of a very short life—for I would surely die of boredom from listening to him prose on and on and on."

"I sincerely hope you die *before* your husband next time." He grimaced as he realized what he'd said. He noticed the maid again and waved her away. "Back to your garret, Millicent. Her ladyship is perfectly safe with me."

He waited impatiently while the maid gathered up her blankets and left, then motioned Isolde to a chair by the banked fire. He stirred the coals and cleared his throat. "My dear child, you know I didn't mean that, but think of your poor mother. The scandal is making her ill. Every time a new broadsheet featuring you is published, she takes to her bed for days. It might kill her if Alan Doncaster's accusation were to come to light."

"Why should it? He's dead. No one knows why I agreed to wed him."

"But now someone is sure to wonder if there is some truth to the gossip, thanks to your very ill-judged costume this evening."

"Let the idiots wonder all they like." She knew perfectly well that her potions hadn't hastened Simon's death. As for Alan, they'd only been married a few hours, during which she hadn't given him anything to drink. She crossed her arms, glaring at him. "I refuse to be forced into marriage again."

"Wipe that mulish expression off your face and think of your mother," Papa said.

She took a deep breath and tried to look less hostile, but kept her arms crossed as a compromise.

"For pity's sake, child, she's already hysterical much of the time because of that damned pendant. It's not even a pretty piece—it hangs askew, as if the jeweler who made it was drunk. She believes it has brought us bad luck." He huffed. "Absurd, but her weak woman's mind cannot help but succumb to superstition."

Isolde opened her mouth and shut it again. She didn't intend to argue about women's minds, for on that score she would never win. Besides, she couldn't blame him for thinking that about her mother. Just not about *her*.

"You must marry speedily to scotch the scandal. There is no other choice."

"There *is* another choice!" she cried. "If Mama would but return the pendant to Lady Burke, she would realize that it has no effect at all on our luck and would therefore be more rational regarding my situation."

"Impossible," her father said. "We've been cutting the Burke family publicly for years. It would amount to admitting we were in the wrong. Imagine the spiteful gossip! No, it simply can't be done."

"Why not? James is still friendly with Gawain—" A startling notion assailed her.

"James never had any respect for older and wiser minds," Lord Statham growled. "Haring off without so much as a by-your-leave to marry the daughter of that old fool, Walt Warren..." Although Thomasina Warren was an heiress and the marriage had taken place almost a year earlier, Papa still wasn't reconciled to a match he hadn't arranged himself.

Isolde hardly heard him through her surprise. She thought she knew—no, she was suddenly sure who Charles-or-Rochester really was.

No wonder he hadn't removed his mask. What a kerfuffle that would have caused! The Burkes were no longer permitted on Papa's land, much less across the hallowed threshold of Statham Court. Her parents refused to discuss how it had come about. All Isolde knew was that each lady claimed ownership of the heart-shaped pendant. The two families were now sworn enemies.

So much for her foolish wish that her rescuer was watching over her, keeping her safe. Gawain Burke's chivalrous intervention had been a ruse to speak with her, to ask about the ghost's habits so he could safely prowl about the house.

Because he had come to take the heart-shaped pendant?

He wouldn't find it. No one but Papa knew where it was kept.

"As usual, you're not listening," Papa said testily. "James' traitorous friendship with Gawain Burke is irrelevant. The pendant stays here."

Hurriedly, she composed herself and said simply, "I miss James."

"I daresay," he said, a gruff note in his voice the only indication of feelings to which he would never admit. "But nothing can be done about that either."

Which was ridiculous. Not about James—of course they would miss him—but about the pendant. Just because her father would do nothing, it didn't mean *she* couldn't. She wasn't sure quite what, though…

"You owe it to your mother to marry again," he said. "She gave you life. Now it is your responsibility to save hers."

Gawain chased Lord Cape out the front door and returned to the Great Hall just as the Earl of Statham reached Isolde's bedchamber door. He hovered while Statham went into the room and the maid scurried out, then quickly mounted the staircase. That fool Cape was still cowering out in the snow. Hopefully he really believed Gawain was a ghost.

He should have found a quieter method of getting rid of him. He wasn't usually so hasty, but he couldn't leave Lady Isolde to fend for herself.

He would have to, though. Best to get the job done tonight. He crept to Lady Statham's door and listened. Silence. He opened it and peered inside. Soft snores greeted him from behind the bed curtains. Good; apparently the commotion hadn't wakened her.

He tiptoed in and shut the door behind him. The snoring stopped. He held his breath. At last came the sound of Lady Statham turning over and settling to sleep again. He looked about; her dressing table must be in the next room. He crept to the adjoining door and slipped through. Lady Statham's dressing room adjoined his lordship's own chambers, but with luck, Gawain would find what he sought and be gone before Lord Statham returned to bed.

He unshuttered his lantern and got to work. The drawers yielded nothing of interest, but in a dressing-case were various necklaces, bracelets, rings, and earbobs, plenty to interest a thief, which he wasn't. All he wanted was his mother's pendant, and to get it, he needed the key to the box that contained it. Since Lord Statham was known to boast about how well hidden it was, he didn't seriously expect to find the pendant itself in this room.

He searched the shelves, taking care not to disturb bottles of perfume and pots of potions and creams. Perhaps the key was in the cupboard where other clothes were kept. There were shoes on the lower shelves, and nightgowns, stays and chemises on the upper. He handled these gingerly, not wishing to violate Lady Statham's privacy except in one small way. Finding nothing there, nor in the pockets of her cloaks, he turned.

And gasped, stumbling in his surprise, and saved himself from falling by grabbing a cloak hanging on the door. The ghost of the Cavalier scowled down at him, a hand on the hilt of his sword. He shook his head and pointed toward the door to the earl's rooms. His spectral mouth spoke silent words.

Trying to tell Gawain to leave, no doubt. Too bad, for he hadn't finished searching. He ignored the ghost and opened the clothes press. With painstaking care, he felt between the layers of clothing all the way to the bottom, but found nothing. He closed the lid, hoping her ladyship's maid wouldn't notice any disturbance in her orderly packing of the garments.

Where next? Meanwhile, the ghost still hovered, eyeing him balefully. Suddenly, his stance changed, and he made shooing motions at Gawain.

"There's no point trying to drive me away," Gawain whispered. "I suppose you're loyal to this family, but if you had any sense of justice you would—"

"Statham! Statham, oh help, oh murder, oh help!"

That was Lady Statham's voice. She must have heard something. Gawain made for the window and flung the casement open. No, that was hopeless—no drainpipe, no ivy, nothing. He wasn't quite that desperate. He closed the window. The ghost glowered at him, hands spread, in an I-told-you-so sort of pose. An astonishing thought occurred. Had he been warning Gawain to leave?

Any second now, Lord Statham would come through from his own chamber, and the game would be up. Gawain couldn't bring himself to harm a man as old or older than his own father... The ghost rolled his spectral eyes and pointed again toward the door to Lord Statham's room. *Yes, yes, I know he's coming....*

Just before shuttering the lantern, he saw it—a tiny key hanging on a hook on the door itself. Eureka! He pocketed the key. He would dash through Lady Statham's room and down the corridor, and—

"Hush, Heloise. Quiet, my love. You'll wake the guests."

That was Lord Statham's voice...coming from his wife's bedchamber. Seemingly, he hadn't returned to bed yet, and had entered her room from the corridor. Perhaps he'd been scolding poor Isolde all this time. He continued to speak to his wife, more softly now.

Gawain crept to the door and put his ear against the panel.

"It was only a dream, dearest," the Earl said. "You're perfectly safe."

She whimpered. "Death stalks us, and all because of the pendant."

"Now, now, darling," the earl said. "The pendant is safe and sound, and no one wants to kill you."

Lady Statham broke into hysterical sobs. "Not me! It's not me they'll kill, but my little Isolde!"

Who would want to kill Isolde? Gawain wondered. And why?

"Nonsense," Lord Statham said. "Isolde didn't poison either of them. Everyone knows it's just gossip. In any event, she'll marry again soon, the scandal will die down, and all will be well." A pause. "I've just come from speaking to her, Heloise. She understands what she owes you and will wed swiftly."

"Truly?" Her voice rose in desperate hope. "When?"

Who in Hades had Isolde agreed to wed? Gawain found it hard to believe she had chosen any of the guests, but the old man might have brought intolerable pressure to bear. Damnation, it simply wasn't right—and all to placate his delusional wife.

"As soon as I can arrange it," Lord Statham said, "but in the meantime we can't have the guests whispering about the state of your health. You must continue to control yourself, like a good girl. Now, take a couple of these drops and go back to sleep."

Gawain turned to leave while he had the chance. He crept through the connecting door into Lord Statham's dressing room, and thence through his bedchamber to the corridor. Back in the lumber room, he pried open the molding at one end of the mantelpiece and removed the tiny metal box concealed inside. The key fit perfectly. He opened the box and took out the pendant—a beautifully-wrought gold filigree heart on a golden chain.

As easy as that.

A cold breeze, sudden and intense, shivered its way down his back. The Cavalier hovered before him, pointing at the pendant, saying something again.

Gawain clutched the pendant. "Sorry, but I'm taking it. It belongs to my mother."

The ghost rolled his spectral eyes—a ghoulish sight—and said something again. He moved his hands together, twisting a little—and then apart.

Gawain shrugged. "I don't know what you're trying to say."

The ghost reached for the pendant. His cold hand mimed grasping the heart, then performed the same movements as before. Hand 'holding' the heart toward the other hand, twisting a little, then away again.

His face contorted, and a spectral tear trickled down his cheek. He jabbed his ghostly finger into Gawain's chest. It was unsubstantial but icy cold, sending a chill to his heart. *What the devil?*

"Fool!" cried the Cavalier. Gawain didn't hear him, but it was all too obvious what he'd said. The ghost threw up his hands and vanished.

Shuddering despite himself, Gawain pocketed the pendant again. He had no idea what the ghost wanted and didn't care. He locked the box and restored it to its place, tossed the plumed hat and sword into a corner amongst all the other odds and ends in the room, and left. Only one more task remained: to return the key to the dressing room so there would be no sign a theft had taken place.

He waited an agonizingly sleepy half hour, then returned to listen at Lady Statham's door. All was silent. He crept through to the dressing room, hung the key on its hook, and left again, scarcely daring to breathe.

Below in the Great Hall, the front door was now locked and barred. No matter; he preferred to leave by the side door in the direction of home, and likely no one would notice that it had been unlocked part of the night.

As he neared Lady Isolde's bedchamber, he spied the Cavalier blocking her doorway, arms crossed. Standing guard, but Isolde needed more than a ghost to protect her. Had the maid not returned? Probably not; she'd left carrying her blankets. Lord Statham had left his daughter alone and vulnerable once again. Either he thought his presence in the house should be protection enough, or—dastardly man—that if she must be forced into marriage, so be it.

Which meant Gawain couldn't go home just yet. A pity he couldn't enter and guard her in person, but for too many reasons, that was impossible. He smiled, thinking ruefully of the most appealing of them. Not appealing to her, though; she'd done her best to drive all comers away. Besides, he must keep his identity a secret. Eventually the loss of the heart-shaped pendant would be discovered, but hopefully not for a while.

"Come get me if she is in danger," he whispered to the ghost. He returned to the lumber room and settled himself in the old chair again, leaving the door ajar. If

Lady Isolde cried for help, he would hear—or if not, the ghost would come and find him.

Isolde slept fitfully for most of the night. She wasn't afraid of intruders, for she had shoved a small but heavy clothes press against the door. It made a dreadful noise scraping across the floor. She would hear if someone tried to enter her room.

She was far more afraid of what she might have to do. When Mama had cried out in her sleep—which happened far too often—Papa had left in a hurry to quiet her. She'd held her breath, wondering if he would discover Gawain Burke, but no commotion erupted.

Which was a relief, but it only postponed deciding on a course of action. To stave Papa off, she had promised to consider the suitors of his choice, but she couldn't, simply couldn't marry any of them. Yes, Mama (and Papa) had given her life. She loved her mother and wanted her to be well and happy, but there had to be a better way than another miserable marriage for herself.

Her duty was plain: to tell Papa that Gawain had come to the masquerade in disguise. He would make sure Gawain had no chance to steal the pendant. And yet, what if Gawain—or his mother, rather—was in the right? Not that Mama was a thief, exactly, but she had a habit of interpreting things to her own benefit. What would cause her more harm—keeping the pendant and worrying about bad luck, or losing it and her pride along with it?

Isolde tossed and turned, fretting both awake and asleep, and roused at last to the ghost's urgent voice. "Wake up! It's almost dawn, and I must dictate."

"Now?" she groaned, but he would pester until she gave in—rightly so, since she was only here for Christmastide. He had to make use of her while he could. She got the fire going, brought out pen, ink, and paper, and sat at her desk to write. He dictated a particularly fervent love poem. As usual, he wrote of love and loss, maundering on and on about the pain in his heart and the tears he shed, but this time he went down on his ghostly knees and prayed for a way to make amends and join the sundered hearts once again.

Reading it over, she had to admit it would make an excellent addition to the next volume of his poems. They were quite a publishing success—anonymous, of course, first by way of James, and now through her.

"Your lover guarded you throughout the night," the Cavalier said, fading as morning approached. "You must show him my poem."

"He's not my lover," she muttered, but the ghost had already gone. She dragged the clothes press back where it belonged, rang for Millicent, and went to look out the window.

The world lay blanketed in snow, pristine in the wintry dawn. No one had ventured outdoors yet, it seemed....

Ah. Off to the right, a single track of footprints led from the far wing in the direction of Burke Hall. Whether or not Gawain really had guarded her, as the ghost said, he had gone home now. Had he found the pendant?

She doubted it. It wasn't in her mother's rooms. Only the key to the box that held it was there, where her mother could see it every day and reassure herself the pendant was safe.

Isolde couldn't bring herself to betray Gawain, but she had to do *something*. If only it weren't for this stupid feud...

A brilliant notion descended upon her. When Millicent lumbered into the room with a jug of hot water, she said, "Get out my warmest clothes. I'm going for a walk in the snow."

Chapter Three

The heart-shaped pendant burned like a hot coal in Gawain's pocket. He'd arrived home and eaten a huge, well-deserved breakfast, waiting for his mother to wake. She thought he had sneaked into the masquerade for a jest. He couldn't wait to surprise her with the pendant.

And yet, something was bothering him. He wasn't ashamed of retrieving the pendant, for it belonged to his mother, so what could it be? He poured himself another cup of coffee and gazed out the breakfast parlor window into the snowy morning.

A woman stood on the rise that divided his father's land from Lord Statham's. Robed in a dark cloak and a red cap and muffler, the woman was tying a white cloth—a pillowslip, perhaps—to the bare branch of a sapling.

A sign of surrender. Or truce. Or a desire to negotiate. He and James and other boys had once used it in their mock wars. If it was Lady Isolde—he was almost sure it was—it meant two things: one, the theft of the pendant had been discovered, and two, she knew that he was the thief.

But if she had told her father about him, she wouldn't be using their sacrosanct childhood method of indicating a desire to parley. What if Isolde intended to trap him somehow? He shook his head. He couldn't believe that of her. She was a forthright sort of girl. In any event, involving a parent would amount to another breach of sacred childhood etiquette.

Very well, he would hold off giving the pendant to his mother—but not for long.

Isolde went down to breakfast hungry after her walk in the snow. With any luck, Gawain would see her flag of truce and find a way to speak with her. In the meantime, she must do her best to pretend to seriously consider the three bores.

"Who would like to stroll to the village shops?" she asked brightly. That should be safe enough. Hopefully they wouldn't encounter Sir Wally and Lady Burke, for she refused to give them the cut direct—but if she so much as nodded at them, her disloyalty would be reported to her parents. Heavens, what if Gawain ignored the flag of truce? She would feel such a fool. Disappointed, too. And sad. Gawain had always been kind to her when they were children, and she, in her girlish way, had been madly in love with him.

She walked to the village with Sir Andrew Dirks, who was somewhat better behaved when hung over, the starchy Mr. Nebley, the adulterous Mr. Denton, his pleasant-faced wife, and their daughter Jane, who at sixteen was not yet out. Mr.

Denton's eyes had widened with trepidation when she'd suggested that they all stroll together. Did he think she was about to tattle on him? It would serve him right, but she would never so mortify his wife and daughter, even if they weren't dear friends. The Dentons had been invited for Mama's sake—they wouldn't gossip about Mama's dreadful state of nerves—and also to add a few female guests.

The village street bustled with activity. The scents of baking filled the frosty air. Twelfth Night involved the blessing of the apple orchards, so everything apple-related was included in the celebration—cakes, tarts, ciders, and her favorite holiday beverage, lamb's wool. Years ago, when they'd been friends with the Burkes, the whole village had shared a huge cauldron of it, but since the feud, Statham Court kept its lamb's wool for itself. It wasn't much fun anymore.

Well, at least they could enjoy the festive mood in the village. Children ran back and forth, shouting, throwing snowballs at one another, and being scolded by their parents. Sir Andrew growled, Mr. Nebley looked down his nose, Mr. Denton dithered, and Isolde and the Denton ladies strolled from one shop window to the next, admiring hats, gloves, and a magnificent clump of mistletoe decked with red ribbons.

"It's enormous," Jane Denton giggled. "Imagine being kissed under it! It deserves a very special kiss."

"Tsk," her mother said, but Jane was right—one couldn't help but imagine a kiss worthy of that bough. A perfect kiss from a perfect lover.

What nonsense.

She turned from the shop window and found herself face to face with Gawain Burke. A blush rose to her cheeks. She'd hadn't seen him this close for years—except last night, of course, which was different, for he'd been in disguise. How well she remembered that intelligent grey gaze and that mouth that always hinted at a smile! She had missed him, she realized suddenly. Such a beloved childhood friend—who had grown into a handsome, virile man.

Where had *that* thought come from? She had no interest in virility. None whatsoever!

Gawain said nothing, merely eyeing her warily as if he anticipated being ignored, too.

She pulled herself together and put out a gloved hand. "Mr. Burke! How delightful to have the opportunity to wish you a Happy New Year."

He took the hand and brushed it with his lips. "And you, Lady Isolde." A twinkle softened the wariness in his eyes.

She introduced her companions. Mr. and Mrs. Denton were uneasily polite, their daughter blushed and giggled, Mr. Nebley scowled, and Sir Andrew looked daggers at Gawain. Did he think he was confronting a rival for her hand?

She muffled a snort. Sir Andrew still didn't understand that he wasn't in the running. No one was.

"I'll wager you could use a pint of our local brew," Gawain said to the three men. "Why not leave the ladies to their shopping and go across to the inn?" He steered the menfolk away.

Jane Denton gazed wide-eyed at Isolde. "What about the feud? Your family never speaks to the Burkes."

"Tsk," her mother said. "It's none of our business."

"But everyone *knows*," Miss Denton said.

"Nevertheless," her mother said, "it is ill-mannered to discuss it."

"But everyone *does*," Miss Denton said.

"Not in the presence of either family," her exasperated mother said. "I do apologize, Lady Isolde."

"No need," Isolde said. "My brother James and Mr. Burke are still friends. They refuse to let our parents' dispute affect them. Not only that, it's Christmastide. What about 'on earth peace, goodwill toward men'?"

"Quite right, my dear, quite right," Mrs. Denton said. "But I fear your mother will be distressed when she learns of this."

"Then I must hope she won't," Isolde said.

"I certainly shan't tell," Mrs. Denton said, "and nor will Jane." She bent a stern gaze on her daughter. "I shall suggest to my husband that it would be unwise, but you know what men are like. And I cannot speak for Sir Andrew or Mr. Nebley, although they are more likely to bring it up with your father than your poor mama."

"It doesn't matter," Isolde said. "I refuse to let a feud ruin the season."

"Good for you," Mrs. Denton said, and Jane blushed a violent red—because handsome, virile Gawain Burke was beside them again.

"I left them nursing their ale." He offered his arm to Isolde. "Let us take a stroll and demonstrate the Christmas spirit to the villagers."

"An excellent notion." Isolde took his arm.

"Tsk." Mrs. Denton shook her head. "Come, Jane, let us look more closely at those hats."

And just like that, Isolde and Gawain were alone—or as close to alone as they could be on a busy village street. They ambled along as if they hadn't a care in the world. As if they weren't likely to incur wrath and reproachful tears from parents on both sides.

Isolde took a deep breath and let it out with a sigh. "Thank you for rescuing me last night. More than once, I think."

"It was my pleasure," he said, adding after a pause, "You wished to speak with me?"

"Yes," she murmured, "but not where everyone can hear. It's about the pendant."

"I thought so," he said. "I'm sorry, but—"

She shook her head. "I'm sick of this feud, and although I hate to be disloyal, I wonder if perhaps your mother is in the right."

Another pause, and then: "You do?"

"It was hers to begin with, or at least your family's. And my mother is..." Oh, dear. How to avoid being disloyal? "She has a tendency to hysteria, particularly when things don't go her way."

He said nothing, either because he was guiding them through a knot of villagers, or because it would be impolite to agree.

They passed the last of the shops. A few cottages lined the street now, but they could speak more easily.

She stopped and turned to him. "I would like to hear your mother's version of what happened." She put up a hand. "Not from your mother, but from you. And not now, but somewhere private. If we are seen speaking at length, it will cause talk."

"We are already causing talk," he said ruefully.

"That can't be helped." She frowned up at him, trying to gauge his feelings, worried she was asking too much. "Would you please sneak into the Court again tonight?"

Gawain gazed down at her lovely face and wondered if Isolde realized what she was asking. He was perfectly willing to play along—which was reprehensible of him, perhaps, since he already had the pendant. He couldn't decide. No, he couldn't *resist.*

It wasn't unacceptable for a widow to take a lover, as long as they were discreet. Unfortunately, she expected, or rather, *trusted* him to behave in a gentlemanly way. She probably had no idea how much he desired her. She thought of him only as her brother's friend.

A pity, but he would keep his hands to himself, because despite all the scurrilous gossip, she seemed uninterested in physical passion to the point of avoiding harmless kisses under the mistletoe. Why? he wondered. She'd been full of fun as a girl. She was undeniably beautiful, but her liveliness had dimmed, which suited her as little as the dove-grey mourning gown she wore. A sop to the conventions, for she couldn't possibly mourn an old man she'd been wed to for only a few hours. As for her previous husband, he'd been dead well over a year.

Judging by her face, her figure, her sensual air, her forthright, energetic nature, Isolde seemed made for bed sport....

Well, at least from a man's point of view. He might blame her lack of interest on the age of the Doncaster cousins, which might have made them inadequate lovers for a young woman, but it might not be that simple. Had Simon mistreated her? Why had she chosen to marry his cousin? Alan had been even older than Simon, and not a pleasant sort of man.

Money, he assumed. Lord Statham had insisted that all his children marry wealth.

"I'll leave the library window unlocked," Isolde said. "Please?"

"Yes, I'll come," he said, but before she could suggest they meet in her bedchamber, which would not help quench his desire, he added, "I'll be in the lumber room at midnight."

"Thank you!" She smiled, and his heart turned over. He gazed down at her, rapt.

A whistle from up the street shattered the moment. One of the village lads, his cohorts at his heels, pointed gleefully above their heads at an oak tree bedecked by nature with mistletoe.

Damn. If he didn't kiss her, they would be pelted with snowballs—which was good fun—and cause some gossip, which wasn't, and it would hurt her far more than it would him. If she disliked passion, she must have a good reason, but no one was likely to understand or respect that.

"It's up to you, Isolde—if you don't mind the snowballs and the gossip, nor do I. I know you're averse to the custom of kissing under the mistletoe."

She wrinkled her nose. "I'm not *quite* as averse if it's you."

He burst into laughter. "What a compliment that was!" He swooped in and kissed her.

Oh, how sweet. Astonished at the thought and embarrassed as well, she dropped her eyes. The boys were cheering and throwing snowballs anyway. Gawain tossed a few back, then tucked her arm in his again for the walk back up the street.

"I didn't mean it that way!" she said softly. "It's just that—"

He was still laughing. "You didn't hurt my feelings. I expect you'll receive a scold at home, but the unpleasant gossip will be less than if you hadn't allowed me to kiss you."

"That's true, but now some of the other gentlemen will claim the same privilege." She grimaced. "I'll tell them I only kiss young, handsome men." She smiled up at him. "That was a better compliment, I think."

He grinned—that charming smile she'd almost recognized last night—and restored her to the Denton ladies with a bow. He walked away whistling.

"He kissed you!" Jane Denton whispered. "Was it lovely?"

"Very," Isolde said, surprised to find that she meant it.

"Tsk," Mrs. Denton said. "Not that I blame you—you didn't have much choice—but this will surely get back to your parents."

"I'm not a young girl anymore," Isolde said. "I'm twice a widow, and a friendly kiss under the mistletoe means nothing."

Except that it did, although she wasn't sure what.

"You're young for a widow," Mrs. Denton said. "And you don't wish to upset your dear parents, I'm sure."

"Nor do I wish to appear shrewish before the entire village," Isolde said, "and so I shall tell them."

She spent the rest of the day in a state of pleasant expectation. How childish, she thought, but nevertheless the notion of meeting a forbidden friend in the middle of the night got her blood running.

This enjoyable state of distraction made it easier to put up with her suitors. On the way home, she tried *I only kiss young, handsome men* on the lecherous Sir Andrew, who narrowed his eyes and said, "I only kiss young, beautiful women."

She should have known better. She should have known better about last night's costume, too. She seemed to be utterly unable to discourage annoying men. She turned away with a shudder—not that it did the least bit of good. It only seemed to deepen the heat in his gaze.

Mr. Nebley, on the other hand, warned her about the chastisement she could expect at home, as he, for one, intended to inform Lord Statham of the entire business.

She rolled her eyes. "What business? It was a kiss under the mistletoe."

"You gave Mr. Burke the opportunity to kiss you by stopping under the oak tree whilst on his arm."

She hadn't thought of it like that. She couldn't suppress the beginning of a smile.

"That amuses you? I am appalled," Mr. Nebley pronounced. "You should have given him the cut direct. Your poor mother will be distraught."

Too bad, thought Isolde, but a twinge of guilt assailed her all the same.

"I believed you to be above such disloyalty, Lady Isolde."

"Then it's a good thing I refused your offer, for you wouldn't want to marry a disloyal sort of woman." Which she was proving to be. Her conscience pricked, but in a desultory way, as if it was as confused as the rest of her.

"You wouldn't be disloyal to *me*," Mr. Nebley said with absolute but misplaced conviction.

As for Lord Cape, he had caught a chill, but would he keep to his bed like any reasonable man? When evening drew in, he ordered hot rum, covered himself in a rug by the drawing room fire, and regaled anyone who would listen with his tale of meeting the ghost. He explained his unwillingness to remain in his bedchamber by swearing that the ghost had accosted him there.

"I didn't accost him, but perhaps I shall," the Cavalier whispered in Isolde's ear.

She shook her head. Lord Cape wasn't likely to bother her now that he was ill.

"Don't shake your head at me, Isolde," her father said. "Come to the library. I wish to speak with you."

She hadn't been paying attention; it was more fun looking forward to a midnight rendezvous. Mr. Nebley had come into the room behind her father. His smug expression as he seated himself, and the prospect of a thundering scold from Papa, couldn't dispel her pleasurable anticipation.

"Of course, Papa." She followed him down the passageway.

"Your lover dispatched Lord Cape most handily," the Cavalier whispered. "He is a worthy gentleman. I shall compose a sonnet about your midnight assignation."

She sighed. There wouldn't be any romantic dalliance tonight, but she couldn't prevent the ghost from imagining it.

"Don't sigh at me, Isolde." Her father closed the library door and pointed to a hard chair. She sat on the soft, comfortable sofa instead. In her childhood, that would have earned her a birching.

Now, Papa just scowled. "You promised to encourage your suitors, and look what you did instead—you let that blackguard Burke kiss you!"

"He's not a blackguard, but a well-mannered gentleman and a friend of James." As her father drew breath to launch into a harangue, she added, "I promised to *consider* my suitors." Which she was doing, but she refrained from telling him precisely *what* she considered them. *Asses or swine, take your choice.*

"I shall break the news about Burke to your mother. I should prefer not to tell her, but some busybody is sure to do so. She will need time to compose herself." He narrowed his eyes. "In the meantime, if one of the guests seeks to kiss you under the mistletoe, you are now obliged to comply." He paused. "Except Lord Cape. I would not wish you to catch his cold."

She considered retorting *I only kiss young, handsome men*, but wisely refrained. She would just have to keep to herself.

Or get rid of the mistletoe. No one had noticed that one bough was already missing, and the Christmas season was almost over. She slipped down the backstairs to the kitchen in search of a footman.

And bumped into one. In the doorway. With mistletoe above them.

The footman wasn't young and handsome, but he was a dear soul. Perhaps she should change her mistletoe excuse to *I only kiss kind-hearted men*. Papa wouldn't approve of that either, but she reached up and kissed the footman anyway. "Marcus, I need a favor."

He smiled down at her. "I shan't tell anyone you kissed me, my lady." He glowered at Cook, who was brandishing her rolling pin. "And nor will anyone else."

"Thank you," she said, smiling at the cook, and whispered in the footman's ear. "Please get rid of whatever mistletoe you can without being caught." She glanced up. "Not this one, though."

Marcus promised to do his best. By evening, several doorways sported holly or nothing at all, and she had successfully avoided kisses from both Mr. Nebley and Sir Andrew Dirks. Mr. Nebley's affronted gaze didn't disturb her; the frustration and anger in Sir Andrew's did. She had only escaped him this time because Mrs. Denton was nearby.

She made sure to take Millicent with her when she went to her bedchamber, but this time no one waited in ambush. Once she was ready for bed, she sent the grateful maid to her own room. She pushed the clothes press against the door again, snuggled in a *bergère* chair by the fire, and picked up a novel.

"Wake up!"

She started, opening her eyes. The novel lay in her lap. The candle was guttering, the fire had died down, and the Cavalier hovered over her. "Your lover awaits, fearing you have jilted him!"

Dear God, she'd fallen asleep. What time was it? The clock on the mantel said twenty minutes past twelve—not so very bad. Since Gawain *wasn't* her lover, he wouldn't worry about being jilted, but nevertheless he might think she had changed her mind or set a trap for him, as one might do to an enemy....

She hoped he didn't think of her as any kind of enemy. She valued him, his friendship, his *esteem*.

She put that unsettling thought aside and lit another candle, donned a pair of slippers, and moved the clothes press just far enough that she could squeeze through the door. Mercifully, the corridor was empty of lascivious suitors.

It was also bone-chilling cold. She tiptoed down the passageway, her heart beating uncomfortably fast, which was absurd. She wasn't afraid of Gawain. The door to the lumber room was ajar. She slipped inside.

At first, she didn't see him. "Gawain?" she whispered.

"Over here." He rose from a tattered old chair in the far corner, yawning. So much for the ghost's fretting.

"Sorry I'm late," she said anyway. "I fell asleep by the fire." Gawain was dressed as the Cavalier in an ancient coat and plumed hat, with a sword belted at his hip.

"Is that what you wore to scare Lord Cape last night? He caught a chill."

"Serves him right," Gawain said with a grin.

She beckoned. "Let's go."

"Go where?"

"To my bedchamber, of course. It's freezing in here. I don't know why I didn't suggest it this morning."

Chapter Four

She was already out in the corridor, leading the way, so Gawain had no choice but to follow. He would certainly welcome a few minutes by the fire, but...

"Push the clothes press against the door, please. It keeps unwanted visitors out." She bustled over to the fireplace. "If anyone tries to sneak in, I shall hear."

He obeyed, annoyed that she had to resort to such shifts to protect herself. It was obvious why she hadn't kept her maid in the room with her tonight, but what about after he left? And future nights? "You don't have a key to your door?"

"Mama is terrified of house fires, so to calm her, Papa took our keys away years ago. There may be one on the housekeeper's ring, but I didn't need it until now."

Lady Statham was proving to be a damned nuisance. Except that...if she hadn't stolen the heart-shaped pendant, he wouldn't be here now, alone with Isolde. In her bedchamber. In the middle of the night.

He had always liked her as a girl...but as a woman, she was unbelievably alluring.

She motioned him to the sofa. "I had my maid bring some milk earlier, as well as my usual tisane." She set two small pots on the hob to warm up. "There's plenty for us both, or brandy if you would prefer. I never drink it, for I do not tolerate alcohol well, but I sneaked some from the decanter in Papa's library in case you wanted some."

"Warm milk is fine," he said, bewildered by this housewifely behavior. She seemed to consider him a guest rather than a barely-tolerated enemy. Definitely not a prospective lover, alas. "With a dash of brandy."

"You needn't worry that my maid will suspect because of the milk," she said. "It sometimes works better than my tisane for—for sleepless nights."

"Are you often sleepless?"

She made a face. "When I am wondering how to...how to do what I wish without upsetting my parents. They simply can't accept that I don't want to marry again."

"That bad, was it?"

She shrugged and turned away, a clear indication that she didn't intend to discuss it. He settled back on the sofa to ponder her as she bustled about. She had every right to refuse marriage. By what he understood, she had a tolerable jointure and therefore wasn't obliged to remain at Statham Court. But setting up on her own would cause even more scandal and result in more pressure from both genuine suitors and mere lechers. He'd never thought about it before: there were disadvantages to being a beautiful, sensual widow.

Especially if the sensual side didn't really exist. Or had been smothered...

At last she passed him a mug of milk and sat at the opposite end of the sofa, cradling her mug in her hands. "Thank you so much for coming. I hope a frank discussion will benefit us both."

So did he. Unsurprisingly, there wasn't even a hint of innuendo in her voice. And yet, in the uncertain light cast by the fire and a few candles, he thought he detected a blush. He smiled—hopefully friendly and charming without seeming even faintly lascivious. "I hope so, too."

She clasped her hands in her lap. She looked so *uneasy*. Had he let his desire for her show in his voice? He was doing his damnedest not to. "You wished to hear my mother's side of the story," he said.

"Yes. I was at school in Bath when it happened, and my parents refuse to discuss it. All I know is that it was a dispute over whether your mother gave mine the pendant or only loaned it to her."

"Your parents came to an evening party at Burke Hall," Gawain said. "Lady Statham's necklace broke just as she arrived, and my mother loaned her the pendant to wear instead, expecting that it would be returned within the next day or two. Instead, Lady Statham claimed that my mother had given her the pendant to keep."

"That doesn't sound like something Mama would do." Isolde flushed. "I'm not denying that your mother told the truth. I'm sure she did. I just don't understand why Mama would make such a claim."

"I don't mean to distress you," Gawain said, "but you did ask for my mother's side of the story."

She nodded. "Please go on. I need to know what really happened."

"My mother was shocked and hurt," he said, "and called on her, hoping it was just a misunderstanding. Your butler tried to say that Lady Statham was not at home, but my mother marched right past him and into the drawing room." He ran a hand over his face. "I wasn't there, of course, but I gather it was a most unpleasant scene. Lady Statham insisted that the pendant was now hers, after which my mother told Lady Statham precisely what she thought of her. My mother is not one to make a fuss, so you may judge by that how upset she was."

"Yes," Isolde said. "Lady Burke is such a kindhearted lady. I'm—I'm so very sorry."

"It wasn't your fault," Gawain said. "Just as my mother was about make a dignified exit, yours burst into tears and said, 'The pendant belongs at Statham because the ghost of the Cavalier told me so.' After which my mother abandoned all pretension to dignity and slammed the door behind her on the way out."

Isolde's brows knit. "What an absurd excuse to give, and so unlikely. My mother and the Cavalier are not on speaking terms."

"She can hear him?"

She grimaced. "Oh yes, she can hear him very well. I expect that's where James and I came by the ability, for my father and other siblings cannot. But she absolutely loathes the ghost, and their dislike is mutual. He calls her 'that hysterical fool.' He gave up on her when we were very small and transferred his attention to James."

"Perhaps she was telling the truth. Maybe the ghost had a reason to tell her to keep the pendant."

"But why would she obey him? She must have known it would cause a dreadful fuss."

"And yet she won't discuss it."

Isolde shook her head. "Now that I know what happened, I'm not surprised she won't talk to me about it, nor would she explain to James. Maybe she feared we would ask the ghost and find out that she had lied." Isolde stood and paced before the fire. "When I ask, she says I'm an ungrateful daughter, and it's impossible to press her. One feels so guilt-ridden." She sighed. "Even if she believes the pendant belongs to us, the way she kept it amounts to theft." She turned, twisting her hands together. "Perhaps that seems disloyal." She paused. "I don't want to be disloyal. I'm not the disloyal sort. I was loyal to S—"

She shouldn't have said that. She clamped her mouth shut, but it was too late. Gawain would finish the sentence: ...*Simon?* And she would feel obliged to explain. Either that, or to say it was none of his business, in which case, why had she brought it up? Something about Gawain made her want to talk. To let out all her frustrations. To blurt about matters that were none of his business.

"I don't see it as disloyal," Gawain said placidly, with no hint of curiosity on his features. "There's nothing wrong with wanting to get to the truth." He was so solid and at ease, so comforting in his warmth and kindness. If only she could be at ease, but she couldn't be comfortable until she knew for sure what to do.

"That's why I asked you here—so I can explain my mother's situation and you can explain yours." She paused, and when he said nothing, she ploughed forward. "My mother is constantly overset. She spends much of her time prostrate. At the moment, she frets mostly about me, about the scandal and the broadsheets. She fears..." No. That wasn't relevant. "She thinks that if I remarry, the scandal will go away."

Gawain shrugged. "Maybe so." He chuckled. "Unless your third husband should suddenly die, particularly under mysterious and gossip-worthy circumstances."

"It's not funny!" But it was, in a horrid way, and she gave a choked little giggle in response to his sympathetic grin. "The costume was meant as a warning to my horrid suitors, but it didn't deter them at all. Most of the others were shocked, as if I really were like Circe. How absurd. Would I masquerade as a poisoner if I truly were one?"

He contemplated her, the corners of his mouth turning up again. "A devious sort of person might."

"I'm not devious," she said, and suddenly recalled: "But you are. You and James both."

He laughed. "Indeed." Was she imagining it, or did he seem slightly abashed?

"What is the *matter* with me?" she grumped. "I don't want to discuss my husbands or my suitors, but the stupid topic keeps arising despite me." She paused. "Poor Simon. I felt sorry for him."

"That's extraordinarily charitable of you, considering his scurrilous boasting."

"He wasn't...*incapable.*" She blushed in shame at such boldness; this wasn't the sort of subject a lady discussed. She hastened to explain. "At least not at first, but he became ill soon after we married. It would have been not only disloyal, but cruel of me to contradict him. In any case, I could never have brought myself to mention such an improper topic." So why was she doing it now?

"Then I suppose I shouldn't ask why, since you had an unpleasant time with Simon Doncaster, you agreed to marry his equally disagreeable cousin."

"No, you shouldn't." She pressed her lips together. If James were here, she would have confided in him, and Gawain was as close to James as she could get. Like a brother to her.

Except not really. She never thought of her brothers as virile men. They were, of course, but she didn't see them that way.

"Then I shan't," he said with a twitch of the lips that seemed to imply, *At least, not yet.*

Drat the man, he wasn't asking because he had no need to. She was about to blurt it out anyway. "If you must know, I married Alan because he threatened to say I had poisoned Simon. Mama was hysterical with fear, and Papa said it was my duty, so I gave in." She swiveled, fists clenched. "It was stupid of me, but I was afraid for my mother's health, even her life."

Gawain's silence, coupled with a dubious expression, forced her to explain further.

"It's not as absurd as it seems. She knows I make various herbal tisanes. I shouldn't have mentioned to her that I had tried several on Simon, for she saw that as the proof that would hang me."

Gawain blew out a breath. "And now she is afraid that someone will learn of Alan's threat, and that you will be formally accused of murder."

She nodded. "Especially since Alan died unexpectedly, too."

"Highly unlikely," he said. "Simon was not a young man when you married him and died over a year ago, and Alan had an apoplectic fit after imbibing too much at the wedding breakfast."

A hot blush rose to her cheeks. How kind of him not to repeat what the scandal sheets said—that Alan had died while in bed with her. Unfortunately, that was the exact truth, regardless of her family's official version of events. She took a deep breath to recover her composure.

"The caricatures are merely an artist's lurid imaginings, and in any event, your father is far too influential to permit you to be arrested," he went on. "At the worst, there would be more food for scandal."

"That may not seem dreadful to you, but it does to my mother." So why, she wondered again, had Mama kept the pendant? That had caused plenty of scandal, too. It seemed so unlike her.

"She lives in desperate hope that you will marry soon, sink into obscurity as a respectable wife, and therefore be safe from gossip again," Gawain said.

"That's it in a nutshell," she said glumly.

"But what has that to do with the pendant?"

"Only that she is torn between superstition that the pendant is bringing us bad luck, and fear that if she returns it to your mother, disaster will strike. My father believes that if she loses the pendant, her mind will become unhinged."

"It sounds to me as if she already is unhinged." He grimaced. "Or merely suffering from a guilty conscience."

"Perhaps both." She gave a sad little laugh. "You don't mince words, do you?"

"Would you rather I did?"

She put up a hand. "No, your frankness is most welcome." It certainly made her own openness less shameful, and for that she was grateful. She took a deep breath and returned to the sofa. She clasped her hands. "Her beliefs about bad luck aren't entirely unfounded. Ever since she took the pendant, she has been plagued with nightmares, and my parents' plans go awry. James refused to wed any of our father's choices of bride and was banished from Statham. We all miss him, but Papa won't forgive him, for that would mean admitting he was wrong. He pushed me into two frightful marriages, but he won't accept that that was a mistake, too." She paused. "Although from his point of view, they weren't frightful, for he profited from both of them. Giving in to Alan for Mama's sake didn't mean not negotiating a good financial arrangement." She sighed. "My father cares about money more than anything, and also firmly believes that he is always right."

Saying that about her father *was* disloyal. Time to change the subject. "What about *your* mother?" she asked.

"My mother simply feels that the pendant is ours, since it was passed down to her by my paternal grandmother, and to her by the previous Lady Burke, and so on for well over a hundred years." His brows drew together. "But since both our families have lived here a long time, it's quite possible that the pendant once belonged to yours, and that one of my family members purloined it long ago."

That was only kindness on his part, to alleviate her embarrassment at her parents' behavior. "Perhaps, but we have no proof of that, and in the meantime—"

"Maybe we can have proof," he said. "There is someone who has been here far longer than anyone, and supposedly he told your mother to keep the pendant. Why not ask him why?"

Gawain let the suggestion hang in the air. This charade was beginning to disturb him. Isolde was sincerely distressed, while he was merely playing a game for his own enjoyment. Regardless of the truth, he didn't intend to return the heart-shaped pendant.

So why had he suggested the ghost, who might ruin his little game?

"The Cavalier?" she said. "I doubt if he'll answer. All we know is that he was Earl of Statham at the time of Charles I. He ignores most questions."

"And dictates a flurry of poetry instead, I expect," Gawain said. There, confessing that he knew about the ghost's poems made him feel a little less duplicitous.

"James told you about the poetry? It was supposed to be a strict secret! Even I didn't know until James left and the ghost turned to me."

"He told me bitterly and at length. Does the ghost dictate to you now?"

"Yes, whenever I'm here, and it's rather fun." For the first time, she gave a genuine smile. "I deal with the publisher too, in secret needless to say. Mostly the poems are laments. Have you read any of them?"

"All of them, at James's request. My mother and sister adore them." Luckily, they didn't know their source. Nor did they—or anyone but James—know that Gawain wrote poetry of his own.

For a while, Isolde sipped her warm milk and said nothing. He watched her, drinking in her loveliness, loath to break the companionable silence.

At last she said, "The ghost asked me to show you his latest poem."

Gawain blinked at that. "He did? I wonder why."

"Because he approves of you," she said darkly, and Gawain wondered if she were blushing again. She stood and opened the drawer of her dressing table, pulling out a sheaf of papers. "What a pity I can't remain at Statham. I don't know to whom he'll dictate after I leave."

He had to ask. To know. "Because you will marry again soon?"

"No! Whatever gave you that idea?"

"Last night, I searched your mother's dressing room and overheard your father speaking to her. I left in a hurry, but not before hearing him say you had promised to choose one of your suitors. Lady Statham expects you to marry almost immediately."

Isolde gasped. "How dare he! I only said I would *consider* them, to make him stop pestering me." She took to pacing again. "That is the last straw. He simply won't accept that I refuse to be forced into marriage *again*."

Gawain let out a long, relieved breath.

"I should never have come to Statham for Christmas. I shall leave immediately after Twelfth Night to live with James and his wife."

Oh, no, Gawain thought. *Please don't go.*

The Cavalier appeared, full of wrathful indignation. "You may not depart!" he thundered—at least, it seemed loud to Isolde, although Gawain of course heard nothing.

He saw the ghost, though, evidenced by his polite bow.

"I shall leave if I wish," she retorted. "If this is about your poems, I'm very sorry, but if I were to marry one of those bores, you would lose my assistance just the same."

The ghost glowered. "How dare you desert your lover so callously!"

"He's not my—" Drat, she felt herself blushing again. Worse, Gawain was watching their exchange far too closely.

"But he wants to be," the ghost said. "Ask him, and you'll see."

"I cannot possibly—" She turned to Gawain. "He says you would rather I didn't leave Statham."

He nodded, his smile rueful. "Such a pity, don't you think, when we're just getting to know one another again?"

She dropped her eyes, putting her hands to her heated cheeks. Whatever Gawain felt for her, she would rather not know.

"Coward," muttered the ghost.

"Which of us?" she hissed back. "Him or me?"

"Which of us what?" asked Gawain.

She swiveled. "The ghost and I are speaking. Kindly ignore us."

He laughed. "It's a trifle difficult."

"You are the coward," the Cavalier told her. "He is behaving in a gentlemanly manner, for which I honor him."

"What about me behaving like a lady?"

"He does not wish to distress you and therefore says nothing, but he is overwhelmed with longing for your kiss. It is for you to take the first step."

She shut her eyes and let out a ragged breath. Fine, maybe Gawain did want her—and his kiss had indeed been wonderful—but what was the point? Even if their families weren't sworn enemies, she loathed all the pawing and groping and...and everything else that went on.

"Isolde?"

She opened her eyes. Gawain's gaze was so very kind.

"I don't know what he said to distress you, but please don't be," he said. "Give me the poem, and I'll go."

"He may not leave," the Cavalier said. "For safety's sake, he must remain."

"I am perfectly safe," she hissed at the Cavalier. "Mr. Burke must leave before he is caught."

The Cavalier shrugged this off at the same moment that Gawain rolled his eyes. The two men, living and dead, grinned at one another.

"He is a valiant lover," the ghost said. "He fears no one."

"I daresay, but you're just trying to—" She stopped herself just in time. She took a deep breath.

"To make you see sense," the ghost said sternly. "You may not give him the poem."

Isolde threw up her hands. "What? You asked me to show it to him."

"Indeed. He must read it here."

"Why? He can read it perfectly well at home." The ghost's tactic was clear—to make Gawain stay as long as possible. She put her hands on her hips. "What if I just give it to him? You can't stop me."

"No, alas, I am powerless. Are you not ashamed to be so unkind to a poor, helpless ghost, who wants only what is best for you?"

He was as bad as her parents. She clenched and unclenched her fists. "You're not playing *fair*. Go *away*."

"'The rules of fair play do not apply in love and war,'" the ghost quoted—and vanished.

She clenched her fists and let out a long shudder of frustration. "Even the ghost will not let me be!"

Gawain watched her stalk back and forth before the fire, cursing softly under her breath.

"This is neither love nor war, confound it." She glanced at Gawain, muttered, "I beg your pardon," and kept on pacing.

He wished he could take her in his arms to soothe and comfort her, but that would make her retreat even more. At last she heaved a great, frustrated sigh, and although her bosom swelled delightfully when she took a deep breath, her dislike of carnal relations marred his own pleasure at the sight.

"Does the ghost often annoy you so much?" Gawain was getting used to the spectral presence—although if he ever had the good fortune to share a bed with Isolde, he hoped the Cavalier would make himself scarce.

"Not usually." She let out another furious huff. "At the moment he's as bad as my father, ordering me about, deciding what's good for me." She took another of those lovely deep breaths. "He insists that you read the poem here."

"And he also insists that you are in danger."

"It's all just a ruse to—" She stopped in mid-sentence and shut her eyes. Tears leaked from the corners.

"Isolde," he said helplessly, reaching for her, then dropping his hands. "Please don't cry."

"He doesn't really know me," she raged. "He doesn't understand me. He only knows what *he* understands, which is antiquated and unfair." She slumped, dashing the tears away. "He may be right about danger, though. Sir Andrew hasn't given up yet. I hate the...the predatory way he looks at me."

So do I. "The ghost wants me to stay to protect you, and therefore I shall. Go to bed and get some sleep, Isolde. I'll sit here and read the poem."

"That's—that's most kind of you, but it's not *right*," she said.

"I won't do anything untoward," he said. "I'll just *be* here."

"I know, but it's not *fair*."

"In what possible way? I'm happy to stand guard."

She swallowed, so clearly steeling herself that his heart twisted. She clenched her fists. "The ghost says you want me," she said, adding after a miserable pause, "In bed, I mean."

He wasn't about to lie. "Yes, you're very desirable, but that's irrelevant."

"It's not irrelevant, but I am unwilling, so you must go."

"I'm perfectly fine, Isolde, and regardless of what I would like, I'm not leaving you to be preyed upon by the likes of Sir Andrew." He took her hands. "Sweet Isolde, the one it's not fair to is *you*."

Isolde gave a shuddering sob and got herself under control. She withdrew her hands. "I'm perfectly fine as well, I assure you."

He must know this wasn't true, but he didn't contradict her. He watched her calmly, and somehow his very tranquility helped her maintain her own composure—yet she couldn't meet his gaze, doubtless because of the mortifying topic at hand.

Best to get it over with, then. "I don't wish to remarry, and I don't wish to take a lover, regardless of what the ghost says. It was improper of me to invite you to my bedchamber, although it was just for the sake of privacy. I apologize."

He shook his head. "Come, let's sit on the sofa. We have to talk."

"No, we—" She huffed. He was right. They hadn't decided what to do about the pendant. She sat down, and he poured a dollop of brandy into her empty mug. "Drink up. It'll give you a boost."

He leaned against the back of the sofa, watching her again. She sipped the brandy slowly, trying to marshal her thoughts on the question of the pendant. The brandy warmed her gullet. Warmed her belly. She sank against the cushions, calmer now, but too tired to think, or maybe too...something. She wasn't sure what.

So she sipped, and he watched, and slowly she sipped some more. Warmth and ease crept over her. She leaned against the sofa and sighed.

He removed the cup from her hand. "Isolde, the joining of husband and wife is meant to be enjoyable for both parties," he said. "Ecstatic, even."

"Ha!" she said before she could stop herself.

"You've been deprived of that pleasure—or maybe even harmed—so you no longer want what's natural and right. That's what's not fair."

This wasn't the topic she meant to address. "I wasn't harmed, and I don't want to talk about it."

He kept on watching her. Good God, did he actually expect her to confide in him? She'd already said far too much.

"Have some more brandy." He added another dollop to her mug.

It crossed her tired and slightly muzzy mind that he might be trying to get her intoxicated for his own devious ends. She knew how to put a stop to that. She set the mug down.

"Very well, if you must know, I was disgusted." Pause. "Or just sick and tired of it." Another pause. "Or simply bored out of my mind." She picked up the mug and took another sip of brandy. "All that grunting, like a pig." She made a face. "I think Alan would have been even worse. He pinched and leered, and then panted and heaved, red-faced and horrid, and then suddenly he flopped onto me, heavy as lead—not surprising, I suppose, since he was dead."

"Disconcerting."

"Yes, for a few moments, and then, ah, such blissful relief." She shouldn't have said that. It was the sort of confession that fueled caricatures. If she hadn't drunk the brandy, she wouldn't have been so indiscreet. She set the mug down again and crossed her arms. "You'd better go."

He didn't. He simply sat there, watching her, saying nothing. After a while he got up and put more coals on the fire. She should be mortified at what she'd said, but she was too weary and too befuddled to care. She should insist that he leave, but it would be a waste of breath. Clearly, he wasn't going anywhere.

"I don't think I grunt," Gawain said pensively, "but I can't say for sure. My experience is limited, but no one's ever accused me of it."

"How fortunate for you," she retorted. At least, she meant it as a retort, but it came out as an exhausted mutter.

"Nor do I pinch, and I don't think I leer, but gazing with lustful eyes upon a beautiful female form is almost unavoidable."

That made her wonder if women ever gazed with lustful eyes upon a male form. She pondered what Gawain would look like without his clothing. Better than either Simon or Alan, of that she was sure. "I appreciate your truthfulness," she said.

He smiled at her, but she didn't detect any lust in his gaze, only kindness and concern. She yawned. Once, twice, her eyelids fell shut, and she jerked them open again. He was still there, leaning back on the sofa cushions, staring at the fire.

He turned his head, meeting her eyes. "I think you were just unlucky."

She scowled, or tried to. "I refuse to risk that sort of bad luck again."

"Marriage isn't the only way to find out," he said.

Chapter Five

"Where were you all night?"

Gawain opened one eye. That was his mother's voice. Judging by the way he felt, he'd only been asleep a few minutes. He shut his eye again. One's mother wasn't supposed to ask that sort of question of a grown man.

"You sneaked into the Court again, didn't you?"

How typically motherly to ask him a question to which she already knew the answer. He grunted, stubbornly refusing to open his eyes.

"And you didn't return until dawn." Lady Burke pulled the coverlet down. "Not only that, you came through the kitchen, of all foolish entrances to choose. The cook, a footman, and the scullery maid all saw you, and it's causing talk."

That didn't worry him. He'd been seen at the Court by both a visiting valet and one of the Statham footmen. Perhaps the game was up—but he'd also gained an ally. "What does it matter?"

"It matters because you kissed Lady Isolde in the village yesterday. Most unwise, as I told you the instant I learned of it."

"It would have been worse not to," Gawain said. "Besides, I enjoyed it." He let a smile play across his face.

"I daresay," Lady Burke said. "She's a beautiful woman, but you must keep your distance from now on."

"Why? I like her. She suffered with two unpleasant husbands, not to mention the scandal. She deserves a kind-hearted friend." He yawned.

"Dressing up as Circe was hardly the ideal way to prevent further gossip," his mother said. "It will be in the broadsheets by next week."

He opened his eyes at last and rolled to face her. "She was trying to warn her suitors away. She dislikes them all, but her father is determined to force her into another arranged marriage." He pulled the coverlet back up to his chin.

"And willing to pay ten thousand pounds for it, I hear. Who has he chosen this time?"

"A fool, a bore, and a relentless lecher. She won't agree to any of them. She's had enough of marriage and means to live with James and his wife, but until then, I intend to protect her from unwanted advances. She was reduced to barricading her door last night."

His mother tutted. "How unconscionable of Lord Statham." Her features relaxed into resigned understanding. "You're planning to spend every night there until then?"

"I am," he said. "Statham is encouraging the suitors to seduce her, and knowing Sir Andrew Dirks, he won't stop at seduction, if that doesn't get him what he wants."

"How horrid. Very well, but please be careful, Gawain. Sneaking into a masquerade for a jest was fine, but think how unpleasant not only for us, but for Isolde, if you were caught. Scandal upon scandal, poor child."

His mother left, but it was a while before sleep claimed him again. He had enjoyed guarding Isolde. He'd warmed a hot brick for her bed and carried her there, tucking the covers around her. Then he'd read the poem as instructed, and kept watch as she slept through the rest of the night. At last the sounds of servants starting their day had told him it was time to leave.

He had a feeling she wouldn't agree to a guard every night. Fortunately, they both wanted to know more about the pendant's history, which provided him with an excuse to see her. Meanwhile, the Cavalier seemed to have plans of his own....

Gawain fell asleep at last, looking forward to the coming night.

Her maid's voice woke Isolde. "My lady? What is blocking the door?"

Daylight showed through the crack between the bed curtains. For a long moment she lay under the covers...and then the events of the night woke her properly.

She sat up and parted the curtains. Gawain was gone, thank heavens, but when had he left? "Just a moment, Millicent." She got out of bed and padded over to the door. Somehow, Gawain had managed to squeeze his way out of the room, leaving only a small space between the clothes press and the door. She dragged it out of the way.

Millicent bustled in. "Whatever is your clothes press doing here?"

"Keeping my suitors out." Isolde yawned and crawled back under the covers. "I don't sleep well if I have to worry that one of them will creep in during the night."

The maid tutted. "If you don't mind my saying so, my lady, his lordship should have chosen more respectful suitors for you." She crossed to the fireplace. "But nothing can be done about that. Her ladyship ordered me to wake you. She says you are neglecting the guests, and that will never do."

Isolde groaned. She tried to remember what had happened last night. She and Gawain had been discussing the pendant....

No, they'd been discussing a much more mortifying subject: bed sport. She'd babbled about Simon. And Alan, oh, *God*. She should never have touched the brandy. He'd offered it to her on purpose, hadn't he? Devious man, trying to get her to talk....

More than that. He'd said something about marriage not being the only way to find out....

Which was nothing but a blatant attempt at seduction on his part.

That was when she'd decided to stop fighting sleep. If she were asleep, he wouldn't have an opportunity to wax more persuasive, or kiss her, or... She sat up. She didn't recall going to bed. She was still wearing her wrapper over her nightdress. Had Gawain carried her? Tucked her in? How embarrassing, as if she were a child—and yet, how typically kind of him.

The papers with the ghost's latest poem sat in a tidy pile on her bedside table. Seemingly, he had read them before leaving. She picked them up, wondering why the Cavalier had wanted him to do so.

At the bottom of the first page was a penciled stanza of verse:

Until tonight, my Christmas dove
I blow a kiss upon the wind
That it 'cross snowy fields may find
Thy lips to tell thee of my love.

She sat up and read it again. She certainly hadn't written that down. The pencil must have been Gawain's....

The Cavalier had dictated a poem to Gawain instead of to her!

"The fire's going good and strong now, my lady. Let's get you dressed."

Isolde folded the sheets of paper and put them away in her secrétaire. She felt hurt and even a little betrayed by the Cavalier, who hadn't even tried to see things from her point of view. *It doesn't matter,* she told herself. She would leave soon, so he would have to find someone else to dictate to in any event.

She let Millicent dress her as she chose, for her mind kept returning to the poem. Such a sweet sentiment, the sort she would adore to receive if ever she had an assignation with a lover. Except that she hadn't and didn't want one. But the poem reawakened her memory of Gawain's kiss, making it blossom in her mind.

Which was sheer foolishness. Love in that poetic context meant lust, nothing more. And they weren't really lovers. They were just old friends.

Except that he had kissed her, and would like to kiss her again. Did he mean to return again tonight? They hadn't decided what to do about the pendant, so perhaps he would.

She entered the breakfast parlor just as Lord Cape said, "My valet saw the ghost shortly before dawn. He had gone to the kitchen to brew me a hot posset, and on his way up the stairs, the ghost suddenly loomed before him. It was a dreadful shock, he tells me. His hands shook so much he almost dropped the tray. Fortunately, one of your footmen arrived to help him, and by then the ghost had vanished."

Her father snorted, and Sir Andrew guffawed. Heavens, what if the ghost was Gawain, and the footman had seen him? Isolde hoped her anxiety didn't show.

She mustered her composure and served herself from the sideboard. "That is the risk one takes when walking about the house at night," she said. "As you know to your cost, my lord."

Cape reddened, and Sir Andrew laughed again. "He wouldn't scare *me,*" he said, his assessing gaze on her, and Isolde feared he was right.

"You won't laugh when he chases you out of the house," Lord Cape snarled.

"The ghost at my brother's house in the north of England," Isolde said, "has a reputation for murder. He is known to have pushed one man off the battlements, another down the tower stairs, and chased another into a field, where he was gored by a bull. I look forward to visiting there, so I can meet such a fascinating ghost." There, that set the stage for her departure a few days hence.

Lord Cape goggled. "You want to meet a murderous ghost? Dash it all, that seems frightfully hazardous."

Sir Andrew made a rude noise. "Ghosts can't kill people."

"My brother says there are death masks to prove it," Isolde said. "I can't *wait* to see them."

"Nonsense, Isolde," her father said. "Your future husband will never agree to such a foolish start."

I won't have a husband, she said to herself. *But if I did, he would be happy to visit my favorite brother. Like Gawain. He certainly wouldn't be afraid of ghosts. Like Gawain.*

What was she *thinking?*

She wasn't going to marry—and Gawain wasn't interested in marrying her in any event. He wasn't a suitor; he'd said so when still in disguise. He just wanted to take her to bed, and in the process show her that being married mightn't be so very bad. She didn't believe that for a minute, and yet she couldn't stop thinking about him.

She went for a stroll in the garden with Mrs. Denton and Jane, consumed all the while by the memory of Gawain's kiss. Its sweetness, its warmth. Her lips tingled as if each wintry gust truly could carry a kiss from him to her.

She could have more such kisses, if she chose.

If he even came again tonight. If he knew one of the footmen had seen him, he might not.

But if Gawain did come…he might expect far more than kisses. He'd said he didn't grunt. Or pinch. But he would want to touch her everywhere. He would want to see her naked. He hadn't promised not to leer. Which was frank and truthful, and therefore oddly comforting.

What was *wrong* with her? She didn't care about the family enmity—a friend of James was her friend, too—but her parents would be deeply offended if they learned that she had dallied with Gawain. So would his, which actually mattered far more. They were good people, generous and kind, and didn't deserve that Gawain should betray them with the daughter of the enemy.

Finally, the day was over—a long unpleasant day of evading Sir Andrew Dirks. He made a point of brushing against her whenever he had the chance, and then apologizing with a knowing leer. Worst of all was when he'd murmured in her ear, "This coyness makes me want you all the more, Isolde."

She'd shuddered at that, and as she turned away, he'd added softly, "I'll get you in the end." She'd armed herself with a penknife after that.

But at least she had received no scold or awkward questions from Papa, so perhaps the footman hadn't recognized Gawain—in which case, he might come again tonight. She hoped so; it would be a long, anxious night without him. She slipped out of the drawing room with the excuse of fetching her embroidery, but went straight to the library to make sure the window was unlocked—and found Marcus the footman bolting it shut. She gasped, a hand to her thundering heart. Did her father *know?*

Marcus glanced about. "Never fear, my lady," he murmured. "I'll leave the side door unlocked instead."

She gaped at him, disbelieving. "What if my father finds out? He'll dismiss you!"

"I wouldn't do this for anyone else, but Master Gawain asked me to. He is a true gentleman who will protect you." He reddened. "Begging your pardon, my lady, but it fair riles me that his lordship cares so little for your comfort and happiness."

"Thank you, Marcus," she whispered and fled. What the footman must think of her! Although perhaps he thought Gawain meant to marry her, and she hadn't the courage to disabuse him of this belief. He would find out soon enough.

Relieved that Gawain planned to come, she fetched her embroidery and spent the rest of the evening awhirl with anticipation. Fortunately, discussing recent numbers of *The Lady's Monthly Museum* with Mama, Mrs. Denton, and Jane wasn't a taxing sort of occupation.

At last she was alone in her bedchamber, waiting, alive with...longing. She hadn't seen the Cavalier all evening. Perhaps he had taken offense and didn't wish to speak to her. Saddened by his absence, she read the long, mournful poem again, trying to understand why the Cavalier had insisted that Gawain read it, too. It didn't say anything that would spark love, or rather, lust; he repented his folly and stupidity, begged forgiveness for his many sins, and fervently hoped that two hearts would soon be joined again.

"I don't understand," she murmured. If the poem wasn't part of the Cavalier's campaign to get her to take a lover, what was it? "Why was Gawain supposed to read this?"

"Because it's the only way I can speak to him," the ghost said, and she jumped. She'd felt so alone, and yet he was right here.

"What, you changed your mind about abandoning me?" Her voice quavered. "You dictated a poem to him last night."

"I, write such drivel?" he said. "Never, not even if he could hear me dictate."

She stared at him. If she'd been thinking clearly, she would have known that he couldn't have dictated the poem to someone who didn't hear him. "*Gawain* wrote it?"

"His poetry is trumpery stuff, not the equal of mine, but it proves his love." She was still staring when he added, "Dear child, I shall not abandon you. Rather, in place of your father, I give you to a man who will love and care for you."

She took a deep breath. Like Papa, he thought he knew best. But he meant well. And Gawain had written the poem!

"I beg you, do not abandon me in your turn." He raised a gauntleted hand. "Hearken, your lover comes!"

He vanished, and almost immediately a soft tapping had her scurrying to move the clothes press away from the door.

Gawain slipped inside, closed the door behind him, and shoved the clothes press into place. He turned, smiling. "Darling Isolde."

"Gawain," she whispered. She couldn't think what to say.

She didn't need to, for he pulled her into his arms and kissed her. His lips were cold but his breath was warm. "I've been waiting all day for this," he said. "Wind kisses are all very well, but they don't compare with the real thing."

Then he kissed her again, and without thinking she put her arms around his neck and kissed him back.

Oh. Such heaven...

She must get a hold of herself. Soon his hands would stray to her derriere, and God only knew where after that. She pulled back. "*You* wrote that poem."

He laughed, but continued to hold her gently in the circle of his arms. "My secret is out."

She closed her eyes. She mustn't let this comfort and delight overwhelm her. He'd spoken of love...but in poetry, it usually meant lust. All he wanted was to bed her. And to show her that it could be pleasant. He didn't intend anything else.

A gentle hand caressed her cheek, slipped a strand of hair behind her ear. "Lovely Isolde, I could kiss you forever, but we have work to do tonight. Or at least I have, if you'd rather not."

"Rather not what?"

"Go up to the north attic," he said.

"Good God, *why?*" she cried.

A fist pounded on the door. "Isolde! Open this door immediately!"

It was Papa! Isolde put her hands to her cheeks and whispered, "Quickly, you must hide!"

Gawain hesitated, scowling. "I'd prefer to confront him."

"Please don't." She raised her voice. "What do you want, Papa?"

"Who is in there with you?"

Gawain strode across to the window, flung open the casement, and climbed out. "Close it behind me," he mouthed.

"Papa, there's no one." Drat, why must her voice tremble? She dashed over to the window. Gawain was climbing down the drainpipe.

She shut the window, drew the curtains, and hastened to the door.

"I heard you talking." Her father pushed on the door, but it scarcely budged, thanks to the clothes press. "What is the meaning of this? Open the door, girl."

"Just a moment." She dragged the clothes press an inch or two away from the door at the same moment as her father shoved hard. She tumbled to the floor in a heap.

"What the deuce?" Her father stormed in, saw her sprawled on the carpet, and put out a hand to help her up. He glanced about the room, his glower...more like a smirk. "Who is in here with you?"

"No one except the Cavalier. He's gone now."

"Then why the clothes press?" He got down on his knees, candle in hand, and peered under the bed. He came up looking disappointed.

She put her hands on her hips. "To prevent my suitors from getting in."

He huffed. "You're a widow, not an innocent."

"Yes, and I don't want them in my bedchamber!" She almost shrieked it. "You're my father. You should protect me, not aid and abet men I dislike to accost me."

"I don't know how else to get you married off," he muttered. "If you insist on being missish, why didn't you have Millicent sleep here again?"

"You ordered her out the night before last, Papa." She blew out a breath. "If I push the clothes press against the door, anyone who tries to get in will make a frightful amount of noise."

"Humph." His brows drew together. "Nebley says he saw a man prowling in the corridor and heard knocking."

"Mr. Nebley was spying on me? How dare he!"

"He was, ah, concerned for your safety," Papa said grumpily. "He fetched me."

"Concerned that someone else would get the ten thousand pounds, you mean. He's an interfering busybody, and I wouldn't marry him if he were the last man alive." She had an idea. "By the bye, the Cavalier doesn't approve of any of the suitors you chose."

"That ghost," her father said, "has made your mother's life a misery. If he weren't dead already, I would gladly run him through."

"Did he really tell her to keep the pendant?" Isolde asked.

"So she says," her father growled. "Hogwash, if you ask me, but it's caused nothing but trouble." At the sound of footsteps, he glanced into the passageway. "Go back to bed, Nebley. She's well, and if you had any bollocks, you would have tried seducing her yourself."

Mr. Nebley murmured something low and bitter. His footsteps retreated.

Papa turned back to Isolde and narrowed his eyes, but a hint of that smirk still marred his disapproving expression. "Are you sure there was no one here, miss?"

She clenched and unclenched her fists, doing her best to control her annoyance at being called *miss* as if she were still a child. "Who could possibly be here? Lord Cape? He's too ill. Sir Andrew? He's loathsome. And Mr. Denton, if you recall, is a married man."

Papa glowered. "Aye, that's all very well, but whom did Nebley see?"

"The ghost, I assume. Lord Cape and his valet have both seen him."

Papa digested this. "Cape is a fool." He paused. "But so is Nebley—a jealous one. Still, if you're sure you don't want him—"

"I'm sure." Heavens, was Papa actually considering her opinion?

"I don't see what's so unpalatable about Dirks. He's an excellent fellow in the prime of life."

"His advances make me ill," she retorted.

"Tsk," her father said. "You're becoming irrational like your mother, which just goes to show you need a firm, guiding hand. Dirks is a man like any other, and a handsome one, too. Cape isn't a bad fellow, either."

Two seconds ago, he'd said Lord Cape was a fool. If anyone was as irrational as Mama...

Isolde sighed, and Papa shook his finger at her. "For everyone's sake, you must marry again soon. As for nocturnal visitors, you had better be telling the truth, young lady. Dirks wants you badly, and I won't hold it against you if you bed him before the vows are said."

Somehow, she managed not to shriek, and at last he left.

Chapter Six

Gawain hastened around to the servants' quarters to find Marcus, meanwhile pondering his next move. He had sought out his father that afternoon and put his proposal before him. "What do you say to my marrying Lady Isolde?"

After a pause, Sir Wally had said, "That must have been an outstanding kiss."

Gawain grinned. "She's a lovely girl. I liked her as a child, and now I find her irresistible."

"Have you asked her?"

"Not yet," Gawain said. "It will take some persuading. She's dead set against marrying again."

"Hardly surprising," said his father. "What about Statham's feelings on the matter?"

Gawain shrugged. "If she's willing, I'll take her whichever way I must, but it would be preferable if you and he were in accord."

Sir Wally grunted. "I don't think much of him, but it's his lunatic wife who caused this stupid feud."

"Both Isolde and I want the feud to end, but I haven't yet suggested to her that marriage might be the way to accomplish it."

"I daresay your mother will be agreeable, as long as she gets the pendant back," Sir Wally said. "She never mentions it, but she was deeply hurt by Lady Statham's deception. Does Lady Isolde understand that?"

"She does, and she wants to do what is right, but for now she's at her wits' end trying to pacify her mother and show respect to her father, while fending off the advances of several greedy men." He took a breath; just the thought of her suitors got him riled. "As I told Mama, she has decided to go north to live with James and his wife. If she refuses me, I'll insist on escorting her there. I can't allow her to go running off on her own."

Sir Wally chuckled. "My knight-in-shining-armor son. You were well named. May you succeed in your quest."

Gawain felt himself reddening. "Thank you, Father. I hope I shall."

Now, he pondered their kisses and his chances of success. He returned from the servants' quarters just as Isolde reappeared at the window. She opened it, craning her neck in the direction of Burke Hall.

He said softly, "I'm right here." He blew on his fingers to warm them and made his way up the drainpipe again.

"Why didn't you leave while you had the chance?" She giggled as he toppled into her bedchamber. "You're out of your mind."

He shut the window and took her in his arms, shaking with silent laughter, and suddenly she was laughing too, and clinging to him in return.

"You're so cold!" She ran her hands up his back, and he laughed again with sheer joy "Shh!" she whispered. "We must be very quiet, or he'll hear us."

Gawain should, at this point, have turned his mind to practical matters. Instead, he said, "I know a good way to keep quiet," and kissed her.

The moment Isolde gave in was one of sheer, lunatic delight. Not simply the pleasure of kissing him, but of realizing she was *excited* about going to bed with him. Hesitant still, but not disgusted in even the tiniest way.

Not even when the tip of his tongue touched hers. In fact, that tentative greeting from his mouth to hers sent a shock of desire straight to her privates.

He let her go and rubbed his hands together. "The ghost and his problems will just have to wait. Let's get into bed and warm up." He took off his shoes and stockings and then his coat.

She watched him, suddenly unsure. She wasn't quite ready to remove her nightdress. What if he leered?

He reached into the pocket of his coat and pulled out a key, then strode to the door and locked it.

She gaped. "How?"

"I tapped on the window of the butler's pantry, and Marcus brought it out to me. Took him all day to get it, he said."

She couldn't help laughing. Both Marcus and the Cavalier were doing their best to give her to Gawain.

"He wanted to sneak me upstairs, but I told him climbing the drainpipe was more romantic."

He was absolutely right about that. She didn't need a mirror to know she was smiling like a besotted fool.

He tossed his coat onto the sofa and motioned toward the bed. "Coming?" He slipped under the covers, still wearing his shirt and breeches.

Her heart beat chaotically. "With so many clothes on?"

He held the covers open for her to climb in beside him. "Let's get properly warm before we start thinking about taking our clothes off."

"I can't help but think about it." She snuggled close and put her arms around him. He was cold, but she was the one who shivered...from nerves. "Oh, Gawain. One moment I'm excited, and the next I just don't know."

"Patience, my love, my darling. We have all the time in the world."

My love. My darling. She mustn't let those sweet words make this more than it was. He was a dear friend and would be her lover for a night. That was all.

He pressed a lingering kiss on her forehead. "Now. About the north attic."

"Thinking about *that* won't warm me up."

She felt his smile against her temple. His mouth feathered gently lower. "I believe the Cavalier kept people away from there on purpose. I think he's protecting something there."

"Such as what?"

He nuzzled her ear. "Another pendant—or rather, the missing half."

He was a distraction and a challenge. She noted every pleasurable reaction as if she couldn't quite believe them. "Missing half?"

"Yes. There's something unusual about that pendant. My mother loved the gold filigree but lamented that the heart hung lopsidedly rather than upright as it should—as if the jeweler had placed the loop for the chain in the wrong spot. But because it was old, she was reluctant to risk having it repaired. I think there were two hearts that, if hooked together, would hang properly."

"Whatever gave you that idea?"

"The Cavalier's poem mentions his longing for the joining of two hearts once again. If I recall correctly, there is a space in the filigree work that could easily accommodate a hook of sorts." He looked as if he would have said more, but instead pressed his lips to the corner of hers, a delicate touch that made her moan. Her heartbeat quickened, and she blushed at his mastery over her senses. With Simon, she had never, ever experienced anything like this.

He withdrew and said, "What if the other heart is in the attic somewhere, stowed away in a box or a trunk, and he has been protecting it all these years?"

"But why? Surely if he'd told me, I would have searched for it and asked my father to get the pendant, so we could join them together again."

Gawain pondered. "I don't have an answer for that. But it does explain why he wanted Lady Statham to keep my mother's pendant. Once it was here, he wanted it to stay. He can't retrieve the other half, either. That's up to us."

"He called himself a poor, helpless ghost, which I thought was flummery, but maybe it's the absolute truth." She pushed herself up on one elbow. "Let's suppose your brilliant idea is correct."

He shrugged, looking adorably abashed. "Well, we shall see."

"Seriously, Gawain. Suppose there is another heart, and we find it and join the two together. Then what?"

His warm hand ran delicately down her spine to rest on her hip. She tensed, not sure whether this was good anticipation or bad. "Then I will have to find a new excuse to visit you," he said.

"That's not what I meant," she said with an uneasy laugh.

"I know," he said. "But I don't care much about your ghost. I care about *you*, Isolde."

That made it even worse. She didn't know what he meant. "You're very kind."

"Nonsense." He rolled onto his back and lifted her atop him.

A mistake, Gawain thought immediately, for she tensed again. "I—I don't know, Gawain."

"What don't you know, sweetheart?" He did his best not to squirm under her, although she couldn't help but feel his erection.

"Whether I can do this."

"It's not a question of whether you can, but of whether you want to." He took a breath and concentrated on remaining still. "Stop thinking about what happened in the past. Concentrate on what your private parts are telling you now."

"Um…"

Her uncertainty tugged at his heart, and meanwhile, he was so hard it hurt.

"Close your eyes, Isolde." She did as he asked, but in the dim light from the fire her eyelids fluttered as if she still wasn't sure.

"Let your body enjoy its proximity to mine, as it's meant to do. Let it take pleasure from the heat between us. Let it tell you what to do." Hades, it took all his control to rest his hands gently on her hips, to refrain from running them down to her soft, round, luscious bum. Or up to her breasts, to caress and suckle.

He groaned, and her eyes flew open. *Damn.* "Sorry."

She shook her head. "It's telling me to kiss you."

This wasn't precisely true, but it was close enough. She enjoyed kissing him so very much. She had never kissed Simon voluntarily, and as for Alan…

Stop thinking about them.

She kissed Gawain tentatively at first, then opened her mouth just a fraction to the temptation of his tongue. As before, it sent arrows of pleasure straight to her privates… *Oh.*

And it wasn't only her privates, but now her breasts ached strangely, as if they begged to be touched. So astonishing, because with Simon…

Don't think about him. She leaned close, brushing her nipples against Gawain's shirt.

"Mmm," he said. Until now, his hands had rested hot and firm on her hips. Now the back of one hand moved gently against her nipple through the fabric of her nightdress. She let out a sigh of helpless delight and squirmed against him without meaning to. He made a soft sound of pleasure in his throat, and that excited her, too. Strange again, because she'd never found Simon's pleasure the least bit arousing, and as for Alan…

Stop stop stop. This was a lesson, she reminded herself. A way to learn that carnal knowledge could be pleasurable. It didn't really matter if the lesson wasn't entirely successful. She knew better than to expect a miracle, but hope dawned despite her justified cynicism.

What she'd experienced so far tonight was definitely better than before. Which was good, but it didn't mean she had to marry again, even if she decided it mightn't be too bad after all.

"Touch my breasts," she said. "If you don't mind."

"Such a sacrifice on my part," he said, even while those hot hands lifted her nightdress. For a startled second, she feared he might remove it, but he merely shifted the fabric enough to access her breasts. He palmed them gently. "A perfect fit."

A flush swarmed from her nipples to her belly and below. She rubbed herself against his erection before she even realized what she was doing.

He smiled and pulled her down to kiss him, one hand gently caressing her breast, the other moving to her hip. Her mouth responded of its own accord, opening to his in something approaching abandon. She rubbed against him again, her privates throbbing in the most astonishing way.

"Oh, Gawain," she whispered. "I had no idea."

He smiled and kissed her again. "Now it's time to remove our clothing," he said.

He moved her off him and set about stripping himself quickly, before she became uneasy again. Would his nakedness encourage or frighten her? He couldn't do much about his rampant erection.

He hesitated before lowering his smalls. "We can blow out the candle, if you prefer." It would effectively prevent him from leering.

"No." She bit her lip. "I want you to enjoy yourself."

His heart turned over. "Oh, my sweet."

She'd never considered Simon's enjoyment, or at least not much. She'd been too caught up in her own discomfort.

"I'll enjoy myself either way," he said. "But, thank you." He removed his smalls and quickly took hold of her nightdress, as if he feared she would change her mind.

She wouldn't, not now. That would be cowardly, and she'd had enough of giving in to fear, even though most of the fears had been her mother's.

"May I?" he asked.

"Please." She raised her arms to help him pull the nightdress over her head. She closed her eyes—drat, a moment of cowardice—and opened them again.

A small smile curved his lips. His eyes lit with appreciation. "My beautiful Isolde." He pulled her down next to him, and they lay facing one another. "Where may I touch you?"

Astonishment made her reckless. "Anywhere you like." She closed her eyes.

"Oh, love," he said, and she gave in to the sensations of his hands and lips, touching her everywhere, *adoring* her. His lips on her breast. His hands hot on her derriere, sliding softly between her legs, brushing her inner thighs.

She shuddered with pleasure and clung to him, opening without reservation to his questing hands. She moaned when he touched her sweet spot. How odd, because she'd felt absolutely nothing when Simon had touched her there. Once she'd got past the revulsion, that is, to just putting up with it.

"You're thinking about them again, aren't you?"

"Sorry," she said, and he laughed and kissed her and played with her until she couldn't take it anymore.

"For God's sake, put it inside me before I go mad," she said.

"With pleasure." He guided himself into her and sighed. "Another perfect fit." He rolled them over, still joined, and palmed her breasts again. "Ride me, sweetheart."

This was something she knew how to do—but it was different with Gawain. Not a chore like before, but a privilege to watch his beloved face, to feast on his delight. And as she rode, he caressed and played with her, until they were both so far gone that they could do nothing but move in unison, until she crested and broke, and he spent himself inside her.

When she woke, it was still dark. Beside her, Gawain slept. She got out of bed, lit a candle, and checked the clock on the mantel. Almost morning. Gawain must leave.

What a pity. Sleeping beside him felt so comfortable. So right. She sighed, donned her nightdress, and crossed the room to push the clothes press in front of the door, and then remembered that Gawain had locked it.

But where was the key? It wasn't in the lock. Maybe he had put it in his coat—an automatic sort of thing to do. She padded over to the sofa, reached into one of the pockets, and pulled out—the heart-shaped pendant.

What? Why?

A soft curse came from the bed. He propped himself up on one elbow. Even in the dim light of the candle, his anxiety showed.

She'd never seen him anxious before. It was strangely endearing. "You had it all the time, didn't you?"

He cleared his throat. "Since the first night."

Now she remembered that he'd seemed abashed. "Devious man." So much for Papa's secret hiding place. James probably knew of it and had shown it to him when they were children. "Why did you return?"

"Mostly so I could see you again."

She thought about that. "What about the rest—the not-mostly part of your reason?"

He sat up and ran his hands through his hair. "I went home, fully intending to give it to my mother, but…" He shrugged. "It didn't feel like the right thing to do."

She found herself gazing at his naked torso, enjoying the way his muscles shifted when he shrugged.

"Then you signaled, and I assumed the pendant's absence had already been discovered, but we met and talked…and then I kissed you. After that, all I really cared about was seeing you again."

"Thank you," she said simply.

"You're not angry with me." A statement, not a question.

"It was a good kind of deviousness." She came to a decision and returned the pendant to his pocket. "For heaven's sake, don't lose it."

"You're trusting me with it?"

"I trusted you with myself." She retrieved the key from the other pocket. "You'd better get dressed and go. The servants will be up and about any moment."

"You're not completely averse to marriage anymore." In this statement, there was a bit of a question.

"No, not completely averse." *Not when it's you.* But she couldn't say that aloud. She had loved him all her life, but he was only her friend—nothing more.

"Good." He got out of bed, and again she found herself gazing. More than that, *staring* at his lean, powerful body, at his quiescent member against its nest of dark hair.

"Can it be that you are leering?" He grinned at her, laughing, and so did she, blushing like an innocent. Which she had been, really, until now.

He dressed swiftly. "Since I'm being frank, I should confess that when I found the pendant, your ghost mimed something I didn't understand until I read the poem. I realized he was miming joining the two hearts. I'm not quite as brilliant as you clearly assumed."

She laughed. "You are *so* devious. From now on, I shall know how to interpret an abashed expression."

He chuckled. "I'll return tonight to search the north attic."

"And to leer at me?" she asked.

Isolde locked the door behind Gawain and snuggled under the still-warm covers. She breathed in the scent of Gawain. The scent of their lovemaking.

The ghost burst into the room. "I was mistaken. Your lover is a dishonorable man."

Isolde rolled over, so astonished she couldn't frame a sentence.

The Cavalier loomed over her, scowling. "Why did he not ask you to wed him?"

Oh, for heaven's *sake*. She sat up, clutching the covers around herself. "He is not obliged to marry me. It is entirely acceptable for a widow to take a lover, as long as she is discreet."

"Nonsense. You are an innocent—or rather, you were until last night. That dastard has made you little better than a whore, and so I told him." He clenched his fists. "Or tried, but he cannot hear me."

Furious now, she snapped, "How dare you? Gawain is a kind and honorable man. What happens between him and me is none of your business."

"It is indeed, for I brought it about." He clamped his spectral mouth shut, as if he'd said too much.

"You did, did you?" She thought about it and narrowed her eyes. "Is it true, then, that you told my mother to keep the pendant?"

He glared down his nose. "I needed it here. When she came home with it, it was like a miracle. After endless years of wishing and hoping, I couldn't allow her to return it to Lady Burke."

Which supported Gawain's theory. "I suppose you insisted and insisted until she gave in."

"One uses what meager tools are at one's disposal."

Poor Mama. She'd never had much force of mind, but she didn't deserve to be persecuted by this odious ghost. "You owe her an apology. You did her a great deal of harm. She was always nervous, but you have made her hysterical."

"Apologize for her stupidity? She should have pretended it was lost and offered to pay for it, leaving me to get on with my plans. Instead, she told an obvious lie, and as if that wasn't foolish enough, she followed it with the truth, which nobody believed. She created a rupture between the very two families..." Again, he shut his mouth.

She stared. "The very two families you seek to…to reconcile?" But that made no sense; how would keeping the pendant here, even if it had been done secretly, reconcile two families who had already been tolerably friendly? "You sought to unite our families?"

He nodded sulkily.

"By way of Gawain and me? Why?"

"It has been obvious since childhood that you and he were destined for one another." His mouth worked. "Or so I thought until now." A pause. "He loves you, but he is yet young and heedless. He must be made to honor his obligation to you."

"Gawain is not heedless!" He would make an excellent husband for some…some deserving lady. "I repeat, it is none of your business. I refuse to allow him to be pushed into marrying me."

"Now, now, child. I am in the place of a father to you, and I know best."

"You are as bad as my own father." She got out of bed and yanked hard on the bell for Millicent. "Did you ever have a daughter? Did you cause her as much unhappiness as my father has caused me?"

The ghost reared back as if slapped—and vanished.

What had she said to cause that? She wondered for a few bewildered moments—and then knew where to look: the old family Bible. Once she was dressed, she hurried down to the library. She'd read all the entries in it years ago, pondering her ancestors. Surely there was mention of a young woman who had fallen from a window and died….

Yes, here she was: Maria Blakely. Isolde remembered her from wandering the churchyard as a child, reading the inscriptions, placing dandelions and bluebells on the graves. Maria was the only child of Thomas Blakely, then Earl of Statham. Thomas had been gravely wounded during the Civil War and died soon after, and since then had haunted Statham Court.

Why would Maria have fallen from a window, unless she'd been trying to climb out of it? Gawain's feat of climbing last night hadn't been very safe, but he was strong and nimble, while a young woman would be hampered by skirts…. Isolde's stomach twisted at the thought. Had Maria been locked in and attempting to escape…to a lover?

This seemed plausible, but it didn't explain why reconciling the two families mattered so very much—unless the lover was a Burke, of which there were many in the churchyard. The most interesting inscription by far, though…

Oh! She hadn't been there for years, but now she remembered—the inscription for Thomas Blakely was a poem of sorts. A couplet…

She rang for Millicent and set out with her for the churchyard. She wouldn't risk being *anywhere* alone as long as Sir Andrew Dirks was near. They tromped through the soggy snow. Millicent whined about her wet feet and the chilly wind. "Why must we do this now, my lady? The gravestones aren't going anywhere, nor those who are buried here."

Isolde ignored her, intent on her quest. There it was: Thomas Blakely, 3rd Earl of Statham. Next to him lay his wife, who had died a few years earlier, and his daughter, Maria, a year earlier still.

Beneath his name was the couplet:
Until two hearts be joined again
In chains of penance I remain.

What a strange epitaph. As he lay dying of his wounds, had Thomas Blakely written this couplet for his own gravestone? Was it an oath? It sounded more like a curse.

She returned to the house, pondering the meaning of the couplet, wishing she could discuss it with Gawain.... No, it would be better by far if he didn't return tonight, because the ghost would interfere and do his best to force them to marry. She had upset the Cavalier, but he wasn't the sort to give up.

Maybe she could send a message to Gawain by way of Marcus, asking him not to return.

But he had the pendant.

So...she would find the missing heart and send Marcus to Burke Hall with it. There would no longer be any need for Gawain to return. Tears burned behind her eyes. She ordered herself not to be a maudlin fool.

Chapter Seven

"I'll need you to stand guard," Isolde said as she mounted the attic stairs, lantern in hand. With breakfast over, she had a little time to herself.

"Up there?" Millicent's voice trembled. "I'm sorry I complained about the graveyard, my lady, but it's more than my life is worth to go into that attic." Belatedly, she added, "Truly, you mustn't go up there either, my lady. It's not safe."

"What's not *safe*," Isolde said, "is for me to be alone anywhere in this house as long as Sir Andrew is here. You needn't come into the attic. Just stand guard and warn me if anyone approaches."

"But my lady, the ghost—"

"Don't argue with me, Millicent. I'm not afraid of the ghost. I'll be fine."

She continued up the steep staircase and steeled herself. She hated to hear the Cavalier moan, to see him so helpless and in anguish, even though she was furious at him for trying to order her life for her.

She heaved a sigh. Perhaps she should try to be more understanding. She knew how it felt to be misunderstood, to have one's wishes ignored.

A bloodcurdling moan greeted her. From the bottom of the stairs, Millicent shrieked, "Oh, my lady!"

"Hush, Millicent!" Isolde lowered her voice to speak to the ghost. "Stop moaning. If you're really concerned for my safety, don't frighten my maid away."

The Cavalier lay in chains with his gaping wounds, almost transparent. He wouldn't be visible at all if it wasn't so dark in the attic. In a thread of a voice, he said, "For pity's sake, child, don't search for the other heart."

"Why not?"

"Not yet. I am not worthy." He groaned again, and fell back exhausted on his spectral deathbed. Below, Millicent whimpered.

"Millicent, I'm fine," Isolde repeated, and turned on the ghost. "Why is it that most people can't hear you speak, but they all hear you moan and groan?"

"Because I must protect the heart until I have made amends." One of his gauntlets had fallen off, and blood trickled from his bare hand. "I do what I must, even if it saps my strength unto death."

Which seemed like a strange statement from a dead man, but she let it pass. "One heart belonged to your daughter—the heart you are hiding here—and the other to her lover. Is that correct?"

He turned his face away. After a long pause, he whispered, "Yes."

"Your daughter fell from a window whilst trying to escape to him?"

"Must you put my shame into words?" he cried, his anguished gaze meeting hers.

"I'm just trying to understand," she said. "If your daughter is the one who fell from a window, I'm sure you feel dreadful about it, but it was a hundred and fifty years and more ago. Surely she has forgiven you by now."

"Yes, she is a dear child. Her lover died in the war, so they were soon reunited."

She pondered more, thinking of the lovelorn Cavalier's poetry, stanzas upon stanzas where he longed for his beloved. "Is it her mother, perhaps, who will not forgive you?"

He closed his eyes. "She, too, forgives me, but I swore to make amends, and therefore I am bound by these chains until I do so."

How typically male to make up one's mind to something and refuse to ever change it. So stubborn and pointless! And hypocritical, too, it seemed. "You're not in chains all the time—only when you are protecting the pendant."

He shrugged. "I soon realized that if I did nothing, nothing would ever happen."

Isolde put her hands on her hips. "I am willing to bet that your wife would rather you just forgot the whole thing."

His expression turned mulish—no surprise. "When a man takes an oath, he must fulfill it. I hoped James, or even better, Gawain would notice that the pendant is only half of a piece of jewelry. Countless times, I spoke of sundered hearts in my poetry, but did either of them realize what it meant? No! Instead, James published my poems and didn't even name me as the author."

Oh, for heaven's sake. "No one would have believed the poems were written by a ghost. If James had published them openly, they would have assumed he'd written them. He is an honorable man who would not wish to take credit for work not his." Actually, James wouldn't be caught dead writing poetry. "Anyway, Gawain worked out what you were saying."

"Yes, after I fed it to him like a baby," the Cavalier grumbled.

"I don't see why you didn't come right out and say what needed to be done," she said. "To my mother, to James, to me, or to whomever."

"Because everything had gone awry. What was the point of joining two trumpery pieces of gold if the two hearts they represented were not united as well?"

"They don't represent me and Gawain. They represent your daughter and her lover of long ago."

He gestured with one bloody hand. "Both," he said. "Both theirs and now yours, which is my way of making amends."

She wondered if the blood on his hands today—usually, the blood was on his torso—represented the blood of his daughter. When he wasn't lauding carnal knowledge in his poems, he maundered on, coupling blood with love and with loss. Such symbols, the stuff of poetry, were beginning to annoy her. She intended to get back to reality—that she wasn't obliged to marry Gawain.

"Just because you think you must unite the two families by way of a marriage, it doesn't mean it's so. Why not by way of friendship?"

He crossed his spectral arms across his chest in a gesture reminiscent of her father. "Because I say so. You must agree to marry your lover first, and then search for the heart."

"Why? Surely you will not be so unreasonable as to demand that I marry only to serve your ends. That is as bad as my father's plans. I can't marry Gawain just because a ghost tells me to."

"You must marry him because you love him."

"I don't..." But she did love him. She always had. "Maybe, but he has to love me, too."

An unpleasant male voice interrupted her thoughts. "Who has to love you, darling Isolde?"

She whirled. Sir Andrew Dirks grinned at her from the attic doorway. He approached hungrily and put out a finger to caress her cheek. "At last, I find you alone."

She shrank away. "My future husband has to love me—and that is definitely not *you*." She tried to pass him, but he blocked the way.

"Cape and Nebley have conceded, and your father sent me to find you," Sir Andrew said. "He accepted my offer for your hand."

Her heart thudded. "But *I* did not accept it."

"Come now, darling. All I have to do is tell your father I seduced you." He smirked. "Right here and right now, I think." He prowled closer. "We're all alone. What could be better?"

She jabbed him in the chest. Her voice shook. "Nothing you can do will make me wed you, and—"

His gaze traveled past her. "What the devil is that?"

The Cavalier rose from his bed, groaning, rattling his spectral chains. Sir Andrew backed away. Isolde dodged past him and tore down the stairs. Millicent was nowhere to be seen. Isolde hurried down the next flight toward people and safety. Behind her, she heard Sir Andrew tumble, then curse and howl in pain.

The ghost followed her, invisible and cold as ice. "I will apologize to Lady Statham," he whispered, "but I beg of you, consider my plight."

"Very well." She didn't have much choice. He had just saved her—for although she wouldn't have allowed Sir Andrew to force her to marry him by rape or any other means, what would it have done to her newfound love for Gawain, and his feelings for her, whatever they might be?

She didn't know. She didn't want to know, either. She ran into Marcus, coming up the stairs two at a time.

"Millicent fetched me," he panted.

"I'm fine," she said. "I'll go sit with my mother, where I'll be safe." Marcus accompanied her to the drawing room, dear man. Her mother, Mrs. Denton, and Jane were gossiping around tea and cakes.

"Darling!" Her mother's wide smile tore at Isolde's heart. "Papa says you have agreed to marry Sir Andrew."

"No, Mama," Isolde said firmly. "Papa and Sir Andrew are doing their best to force the issue, but they will not succeed. I will not marry him."

Lady Statham's face fell. She dropped her teacup with a clatter. "But *Isolde...*"

"I shall marry for love," Isolde said, "and for no other reason."

"I'm glad to hear that," Mrs. Denton said. "I don't think you would have been happy with Sir Andrew."

"*I* think you should marry that handsome Mr. Burke," Jane said.

Isolde felt a blush rising to her cheeks. Hopefully, she was already somewhat red from exertion.

"Jane!" Mrs. Denton cried. "You *must* learn to hold your tongue."

"But Mama, he is *marvelously* good-looking. I would marry him if he asked me."

Isolde composed herself. "Mr. Burke is handsome, isn't he? But I don't believe he has asked anyone. Perhaps he isn't ready to marry yet." The ghost hissed in her ear, and she ignored it, addressing Mrs. Denton and Jane. "I beg your pardon, ladies, but I must speak to my mother in private."

Mrs. Denton glanced at Lady Statham, who was fighting tears. "I quite understand. Come, Jane."

Isolde shut the drawing room door behind them. She sat next to her mother on the sofa and took her hands. "I'm so sorry, Mama."

"Oh, Isolde." Her voice quivered, and now tears began to flow. "Your Papa *said* you agreed to marry Sir Andrew."

"He lied, Mama, and he should be ashamed of himself." She passed a handkerchief to her mother and waited as she wiped her eyes. "The Cavalier confessed to me that he told you to keep the pendant."

"That evil, *evil* ghost."

"He is not evil, and he wants to apologize," Isolde said. "Cavalier, are you here?"

"Yes," whispered the ghost. "I apologize."

Lady Statham glared—not that anyone could see him with daylight streaming through the window. "Speak up. You could at least have the decency to apologize out loud."

"I don't think he can, Mama. He just exhausted himself saving me from Sir Andrew's horrid advances."

Her mother continued to address the ghost. "Then go *away*."

"He will, once he has finished," Isolde said. "It was an unkind and unreasonable request to make of you, and he regrets it. Is that not so, Cavalier?"

"Yes," whispered the ghost. "I should have known better."

"And when you didn't want to do as he asked, he shouldn't have pestered you."

"No, I shouldn't have pestered." The ghost sighed. "May I leave now?"

Lady Statham's face suffused with rage. "Didn't you hear me? Go!"

"Don't forget your promise," the ghost whispered in Isolde's ear, and then was gone.

Lady Statham blew her nose. "He did far more than pester," she said bitterly. "He terrified me. He said I would lose you if I didn't keep the pendant, so I did as he asked, but everything went wrong, and now you are in danger of your life." She wailed. "Why won't you marry again?"

"I'm not in danger," Isolde said. "Papa would never allow me to be arrested. Surely you know that."

She frowned, twisting the handkerchief in her trembling hands. "Then why didn't he say so? Why did he insist that you marry Alan Doncaster?"

"Because he was worried about you, dearest Mama. He wanted you to feel comfortable and safe." And also, she was sure, because of a beneficial financial arrangement.

"If he wanted that, he would have given the pendant back. I want nothing more than to get rid of the horrid thing, and yet your Papa says no, we cannot."

Isolde took this with a grain of salt. Mama habitually tried to shift the blame. Witness how she'd insisted Lady Burke had given her the pendant, rather than simply pretending she'd lost it.

"I wish I knew where it was, for I would gladly return it myself. But he says no, once a decision has been made, one must never change one's mind."

"That sounds like Papa—stubborn to the core." Just like the Cavalier.

"I quite liked Lady Burke, you know, and it's my fault we're no longer friends."

Maybe Mama really did want to give the pendant back—and now, Isolde and Gawain were in a position to do so.

"He doesn't understand me," Mama said mournfully, dabbing at her eyes. "He never has. He decides what will make me happy, but often as not it doesn't."

"Don't worry, Mama. We'll give the pendant back, and all will be well."

Isolde only wished she believed that herself. How could she help her mother and the ghost as well?

Gawain and his father were leaving the stables at Burke Hall for a morning ride when they spied Marcus the footman, running across the snowy fields toward them.

"Damnation." Gawain spurred his steed forward. "What is it, Marcus?"

"It's Lord Statham and that Sir Andrew," the footman panted. "They decided between them that Lady Isolde must marry Sir Andrew. She refused and ran to her ladyship, but there's no telling what them two villains might do next." He reddened. "Begging your pardon, sir, for saying such a thing of my master, but it fair burns me what he's done to Lady Isolde."

"He'll never do it again," Gawain said. With a word of thanks, he galloped the short distance to Statham Court, Sir Wally by his side.

"What the devil? No, you may not let them in. We no longer receive the Burkes."

Isolde paused outside her father's library, stunned. That was her father's voice. She had left her mother once more ensconced with Lady Denton and Jane, and was looking for Marcus. She would have him guard her while she searched for the pendant. Unlike Millicent, he wouldn't run at the first ghostly moan, or obey a dastard—for that was exactly what Millicent had done. She'd left her post immediately when Sir Andrew ordered her to do so.

But at least she'd had the sense to run for Marcus. Sir Andrew had twisted his ankle hurrying down the attic stairs, which should prevent any further overtures, but she couldn't take the risk.

"They are already in, my lord," the butler said apologetically. "I tried to stop them, but Mr. Gawain pushed past me, Sir Wally right behind. They are waiting in the Great Hall."

"Throw them out," Lord Statham said. When the poor butler dithered, he added, "Stop whining, man. Get a footman or two, and toss them into the snow."

Isolde continued to the Great Hall, where Gawain paced back and forth, eager to march into her father's presence without further ado.

"Isolde!" he cried, taking her hands. "You're unharmed." He blew out a breath. "Thank God."

She disengaged herself, trying unsuccessfully not to be exhilarated. He'd come to rescue her! Not that she really needed saving, but how dashing of him. "Thank the ghost, actually. He frightened Sir Andrew." She curtseyed to Sir Wally. "Good morning, sir."

Sir Wally twinkled at her. "My son and I wish to speak with your father, but I expect he will refuse. What do you advise?"

"Storm the bastions," she said. "He has already ordered the butler to have you thrown out."

Gawain planted a clenched fist in his other hand. "He'll agree to my demands or else," he said and stalked toward the library.

She hastened after him, Sir Wally following placidly behind. "What demands?" she asked.

"Either he agrees to what I propose, or I shall take you to James," Gawain said.

"I don't need anyone to take me to James. I can go on my own."

"While your father conspires with fools and villains to marry you off? God only knows what might happen, with no one to protect you but a servant or two. You're going with me, even if I have to abduct you."

She blushed at the thought of this rough-and-ready approach, which was entirely improper and wonderfully exciting. She forced the excitement down, reminding herself that he wasn't in love with her. He was a kindly childhood friend, nothing more. She'd known from the start that he wasn't meant for her, regardless of what the ghost wished. She had to accept that.

She hurried ahead and tapped on the door to her father's library. "Papa, may I come in?"

Her father barked a furious acquiescence, and she opened the door and went in. On the sofa by the fire, Sir Andrew sat with his injured foot on a stool, looking as if he would gladly strangle her.

"Come to apologize, have you?" her father bellowed. "How dare you disobey my commands? I gave you to Sir Andrew. I shall not go back on my word." He spied the two Burkes behind her and ceased one tirade to begin another. "Unspeakable gall! Get out of my house!"

Isolde closed the door. "Papa, Gawain intends to speak with you whether you like it or not. As for your promise to Sir Andrew, you have no right to betroth me without my consent."

"You promised that you would consider your suitors. After Cape and Nebley proved themselves unworthy, you have no choice but to take Sir Andrew."

She strove to speak calmly. "I promised to *consider* them, which I did. It would be rude to say exactly *what* I consider them."

Gawain snorted, and Sir Wally laughed out loud. Papa shouted, "Go, damn you!" but neither of the Burkes moved.

How lovely to have two such staunch supporters. "Suffice it to say that none of them were acceptable to me. You will just have to go back on your word, which you had no right to give in the first place."

Her father grew purple with fury. Fortunately, this prevented further shouting, at least for the moment. He glared at Gawain, who took this for consent to speak.

"Lord Statham, I have come to ask your permission to court Lady Isolde," he said.

What?

"Needless to say, this is only a formality, as Lady Isolde's consent is all that matters. However, my father and I agreed that I should attempt to approach you politely, regardless of the anticipated response."

Sir Wally nodded, looking amused.

Papa regained his ability to shout. "To *court* her? *You?*"

Gawain bowed. "Lady Isolde is understandably reluctant to marry again, but I hope to convince her to take a chance on me. If she accepts, I shall love and cherish her for the rest of our lives."

What in heaven's name had possessed Gawain? He didn't want to marry her. He had never considered such an outcome of their intimacy, and nor had she expected it.

"No," Lord Statham said, "I do *not* consent. Such a match would devastate Lady Statham."

Not to mention your pride, thought Isolde. Why was Gawain doing this? Perhaps to make it more acceptable for her to agree to his escort to James…?

Did that make sense? She wasn't sure. Perhaps not. But why…?

Oh, God, what to *do*?

"There is no need to make a decision now, Lady Isolde," Gawain said. "I simply wished to make my intentions clear before you were pushed into making another unhappy alliance."

She let out a sigh of relief. Gawain was giving her a way out, while at the same time saving her from Sir Andrew and others like him. "Thank you, Mr. Burke," she said politely. "I shall *consider* your offer."

She hoped her emphasis on that one word made it clear to him that she didn't mean to accept it.

Gawain did his best to hide his dismay. Not that he'd really expected Isolde to leap into his arms, but she was so plainly aghast at the thought of wedding him that it tore his heart.

Sir Andrew's snarl broke into his somber thoughts. He jabbed a finger in the direction of his host. "You owe me the ten thousand, Statham. You gave your word."

"Apparently my word carries no weight with my daughter," the Earl said savagely. "As you well know, I cannot legally force her to marry you." He scowled at Gawain. "Or prevent her from marrying some scoundrel." He narrowed his eyes at Isolde. "A scoundrel who was in her bedchamber last night. You lied to me, daughter."

A telltale flush rose to Isolde's cheeks.

Statham's accusing glance swung toward Gawain. "And you, foul libertine—you imposed on my hapless daughter!"

Before Gawain could muster a response, Sir Wally intervened. "My son is no libertine," he said softly. "I suggest you unsay those words, Statham."

Isolde put up a hand. "Don't let my father's ill-mannered outburst disturb you, Sir Wally. He is merely unused to being gainsaid. He was willing to let any one of my suitors seduce me, so playing the Puritan like this is absurd. Gawain is an honorable gentleman, worth a thousand of them."

"Thank you, Lady Isolde," Gawain said glumly, for what was the use of being so worthy if she didn't want to marry him?

Unsurprisingly, Statham ignored his daughter and sneered at Gawain. "If you think your licentious behavior has won you the ten thousand, think again, Burke." He gave a little crow of a laugh. "*Now* tell me if you want to court her."

"I don't want your money," Gawain said. "I want Isolde—but only if she wants me."

Sir Andrew struggled up from the sofa. "Fine, take the bitch, but that money is rightfully mine!"

"Bollocks," his lordship answered crudely. "It's a damned good thing you're not marrying my daughter. You would have wasted my money and then battened on me for the rest of your life. Have your man pack your bags. You are no longer welcome here."

Sir Andrew hobbled to the door and turned. "Good luck to you, Burke. She may be pretty, but she's cold as ice."

Gawain forced himself to say mildly, "What a pity your injury prohibits me from planting you a facer, Sir Andrew."

"Just you wait," Sir Andrew said. "She'll poison you like she did the others." He limped out, shouting for his valet.

Isolde let out a whoosh of relief, but Papa immediately returned his attention to Gawain. "You burst into my house for nothing. Isolde loves her mother. She would never agree to marry a Burke."

"Why not? I think it's an excellent notion."

Isolde whirled at the sound of her mother's voice. Lady Statham stood in the doorway, with Mrs. Denton and Jane behind her.

"Damnation, Heloise!" cried Lord Statham. "What the devil has got into you?"

"All I want is my Isolde's happiness." She entered the drawing room. "How delightful to see you, Sir Wally, and dear Gawain. Are you acquainted with Mrs. Denton and her daughter, Jane?"

Once the introductions were performed, she smiled contentedly. "What excellent news. There is nothing better than a love match."

Appalled, Isolde gathered her wandering wits. "I haven't agreed to marry anyone, Mama."

"Come now, child, I'm not blind. I wondered why you were blushing earlier, and now I know. It's obvious that you're in love with dear Gawain, and he with you."

Isolde caught Gawain's eye. He nodded gravely. He was so kind, and chivalrous too, but while Mama might be able to read her own daughter aright, she couldn't know Gawain's mind.

"Gawain has asked to court me, that is all. I repeat: I have not agreed to wed him or anyone else."

"He wants to *marry* you?" Jane cried. "Oh, you lucky, lucky thing!" She flushed to the roots of her hair, clapped her hands to her burning cheeks, and ran from the room.

"Please excuse her," murmured Mrs. Denton. "She is very young." She followed, doubtless as much to escape what threatened to be a rousing quarrel as to remonstrate with her daughter.

Papa had been staring in astonishment at his wife, but now he recovered himself. "You are forgetting something, Heloise. Even if this absurd match were to take place, there is the little matter of a disputed pendant. Which family will have it after we are gone?"

"Both," Mama said, beaming. "For the two families will be joined."

"Ha!" Papa said. "If Isolde is so deluded as to accept this offer, she will become a Burke. Think about it, Heloise."

"I am thinking about it," Mama said. "Isolde will live nearby. I shall see her often. I shan't lose her, as I have done James."

"That's the consequence of his folly, my love." Papa dismissed James—and Mama's sadness—with a flick of the wrist, and instantly Isolde decided to bring Mama with her to visit James.

"I believe I should return the pendant," Mama said, "as a gesture of friendship and goodwill. I wouldn't have kept it at all if the ghost hadn't pestered me half to death. But now he has apologized. I think I should apologize, too."

"A Statham, apologize? Never! Not that it would do the least good. Lady Burke will never forgive you for keeping the pendant in the first place."

Sir Wally's usually cheerful countenance darkened, and Gawain sucked in a breath.

Mama pouted. "Nevertheless, I wish to return it. When Isolde and Gawain marry, we shall all be friends once more."

Papa crossed his arms. "Think, my love. If Isolde marries young Burke, his mother will have the ideal weapon of revenge. She will prevail upon her son to prevent you from seeing Isolde ever again."

Mama burst into tears.

Chapter Eight

Pandemonium broke loose. Gawain leapt forward to restrain his father. Sir Wally roared furiously and would have punched Lord Statham, if Gawain hadn't held him back. "Ignore him, Father. He's an old brute."

Isolde ran to her mother's side. "Gawain would never do that, and nor would Lady Burke."

"Of course not," Gawain said in disgust. "My mother would be happy to see the feud come to an end and cordial relations resume. She is a kind-hearted woman. It would never occur to her to separate a mother from her child."

Isolde led Lady Statham to the door. "Go to your bedchamber, Mama, and have your maid bring you a composer. I'll be up soon to reassure you."

"Indeed you will, daughter. It is your duty to inform your mother that you will not marry that libertine," Lord Statham added in a feeble attempt to regain control.

Isolde didn't respond. Did that mean she never would marry him? Gawain wondered.

Or that she didn't intend to indulge in a fruitless argument with her father? He hoped that was the case.

"Let's go, Gawain," Sir Wally said, "before I pummel Statham into insensibility." This was no empty threat, for he was still strong and fit—far more so than Lord Statham—but a fistfight would only make matters worse.

Gawain sent a tentative glance to Isolde. Regardless of whether she chose to marry him, they could clear up the problem of the pendant immediately, if what he suspected about the missing heart was true.

She returned the slightest of nods. "Pray accept my apologies for my father. I'm so sorry that what should have been a civil conversation degenerated into a horrid quarrel. Allow me to escort you to the door."

They left the library, shutting the door behind them, and once they were out of earshot, Isolde said softly, "Gawain, we should search for the pendant while we have the chance. Papa won't know you haven't left the premises if we go by the back stairs."

He smiled at her. He couldn't help it. He was besotted, damn it all, for better or worse. "An excellent notion. Go on home, Father, and I'll follow soon."

Isolde braced herself for an extremely uncomfortable conversation. Difficult though it might be, she was grateful for the necessity of seeking the pendant, for it forced her to make her position regarding marriage completely clear.

And yet she found herself hesitating. Rehearsing her words. After that first moment of relief, matters had become rapidly worse. Mama supported the proposed marriage, and so did Gawain's father. Noble, chivalrous Gawain might feel obliged to persist in his suit.

They fetched a lantern and a branch of candles. She hurried ahead of him up the stairs. Perhaps if she simply concentrated on searching for the pendant, he would realize she was serious about not wedding him.

Or maybe they could pretend to court for a short while...but no, that would be *torture*, and it would also be dishonorable with regard to the ghost. Best to settle the matter now and avoid Gawain in future, as the most effective method of falling out of love.

Ah! If she fled to James and brought Mama along, he couldn't insist on coming, for she wouldn't be alone.

Now that was an *idiotic* notion. He would merely insist on escorting them both. On the other hand, he wouldn't be able to wangle his way into her bed again with Mama there.

For she was no fool, and his alternate suggestion to courtship would have provided him with ample opportunity to persuade her how very pleasant marriage could be.

She stifled a sob.

"Isolde?" He was right behind her, and he'd heard it.

"Let's get this over with, shall we?" She pushed open the door to the attic and moved aside to let Gawain pass, but the lantern hardly pierced the darkness. Directly ahead, chained bleeding on a ghostly bed, was the Cavalier—mercifully silent for now. She doubted he would remain so if he realized she still had no intention of marrying Gawain.

"He does look ghastly," Gawain said.

"At least he's not moaning. We'll put the candles on that old chair." She shoved aside the cobwebs that festooned the space and marched past the ghost. There was little furniture in this section of the attic, which contained mostly ancient luggage, as well as discarded swords, a battered shield, and a couple of old clocks. The trunks were intact, the valises less so, and the bandboxes had been chewed to bits by vermin or used as nests. She set the candlestick down and returned to take the lantern from Gawain, who still contemplated the ghost.

She lit the branch of candles. "Ignore him. He's long dead. He no longer suffers from those wounds."

"Some wounds never heal," the ghost whispered.

She glared at him. "Hush! That's your fault and no one else's."

Gawain frowned, then realized. "He's speaking to you again."

"As I said, don't pay him any heed." She scowled at several trunks—some of which, she realized now, were directly under the ghost. The Cavalier had returned to Statham from war, then died at home of his festering wounds. Why would his ghost choose to lie above these very trunks unless to keep people away from them?

She gritted her teeth. The ghost was cold to the touch—far worse than the chilly breeze he often used to announce his presence—but she refused to let him prevent her from searching. "I'll wager the other heart is in one of those trunks."

"Stay away," the ghost hissed. "You may not search until you agree to marry your lover."

"I will search them if I want to," she retorted. "You, like my father, will just have to stop being stubborn and accept that friendship and agreement fulfills the requirements of your oath."

"What oath?" Gawain asked.

She explained about the poem on the Cavalier's grave, and the star-crossed lovers of more than a hundred and fifty years earlier. "I assume his daughter's lover was a member of your family who subsequently died fighting against the parliamentary forces."

"Or *for* Parliament," Gawain said. "The Burkes were very much divided on that score."

"Puritanical young fool," the ghost said. "Unworthy of a Blakely woman." He paused. "Or so I thought, to my chagrin."

Gawain looked a question. "He's bemoaning his error of judgment regarding his daughter and her lover," Isolde said. "I wish he would consider his error of judgment regarding *me*."

Immediately, the ghost reassumed his stubborn pose.

Gawain said mildly, "It doesn't look as though he's going to get out of the way."

"I don't care." She marched right up to the ghost. Frigid air met her. "Stop it. You can't make me go away." She shivered, but got down on her hands and knees. She felt around until she found a handle at one end of a trunk. She grasped it—oh, it was deathly cold.

The Cavalier let out a frightful wail.

"Maybe he can't get out of the way," Gawain said. "He is in chains, after all."

"They are chains of his own making." Isolde dragged the trunk inch by frigid inch from under the ghost. She let go of the handle, shaking her fingers to warm them. "You could at least have the—ugh—decency to help me!"

"I'm rather torn between you and the Cavalier," Gawain said. "You're in distress, but so is he. He will calm down if you stop tormenting him, but what, I ask myself, will calm you?"

She stood, furious. "I'm tormenting him? What do you think he's doing to me?" She clenched her fists. "Getting this *over* with will calm me!"

"And then what?"

"Then I will leave for the North. With my mother, if I can persuade her. And without you."

"I beg your pardon," Gawain said, struggling to control his anguish. "I didn't mean to distress you, Isolde. I was trying to protect you."

"Yes, you are all that is chivalrous and kind, but you don't want to marry. You told me so when you were in disguise—that you knew all about parents pushing one into marriage."

"Not *my* parents," he said. "I was thinking of you and James."

"But you *implied...*" She paused. "Don't try to convince me you were being devious. I won't believe it."

"I was trying to reassure you that you were safe with me. I never said I didn't wish to marry."

"So very kind of you, but truly, you mustn't persist in this folly," she cried. "Now my mother expects me to marry you, and your father does, too."

"Our parents have no say in this." Gawain clenched his jaw, but his voice shook nevertheless. "I want no unwilling bride."

Her face crumpled. "I'm sorry, I'm sorry. I didn't mean to hurt your feelings. It's just that..."

She whirled, facing the ghost. "Stop it! Yes, you say you mean well, but all you really care about is an oath you made ages and ages ago." A silence, and then, "It doesn't matter what I want." Another silence. "Oh, come now. We don't all want the same thing."

"Maybe we do," Gawain said, taking a hopeful guess at the side of the conversation he couldn't hear. "I'm not being chivalrous, Isolde. I'm in love with you."

Told you so, whispered the Cavalier.

Isolde wanted desperately to believe Gawain, but she couldn't. "You're *most* kind, but after you helped me avoid being married against my will, how could I possibly inflict the same fate on you? It would be *damnable*."

"Sweetheart." He drew her into his arms, and she subsided against him. It felt so good. And warm. And right.

He caressed her hair. "You're not inflicting anything on me. If anything, I'm the one doing the inflicting. I would have asked you to marry me last night, but I thought it was too soon. I wanted to give you some time to get accustomed. Then Marcus came and told me your father had betrothed you to Sir Andrew. I had to intervene immediately, come what may."

"He is a noble lover," the ghost said. "I apologize for thinking him dishonorable." With a sigh, he added, "It is yet another stain on my character."

"Don't be maudlin," she retorted, reluctantly pushing herself away from Gawain. "We all make mistakes."

Gawain stilled, then blew out a breath. "The ghost again?"

She nodded. "He had temporarily reversed his favorable opinion of you, and now he regrets it. He insists that we agree to marry before we search for the pendant. He is as stubborn as my father. It's not right for him to insist on compromising my honor to satisfy his."

"No," Gawain said, "it's not."

The ghost moaned. "I shall never, ever make amends."

Isolde buried her face in her hands. "I don't know what to *do*."

"I do," Gawain said. He addressed the Cavalier. "Sir, you have more than satisfied the requirements of honor. I humbly request that you withdraw and allow me to court Lady Isolde in my own way, without hindrance, however well-meant."

The ghost eyed Gawain for a long moment, then heaved a sigh. He rolled over, bloody wounds, chains, and all, and was gone.

Isolde raised her head. "As easy as that?"

"He is more able to appreciate my point of view than yours."

"And to believe you, too. If only my father were so easy to sway."

"Lord Statham knows full well he shouldn't have made a promise he couldn't keep. Once he thinks it through, honor will require him to change his mind—with your mother's help, no doubt. He is a stubborn old coot, but he loves her in his hidebound way."

She frowned, but more in thought than disagreement, Gawain judged. He reached for the trunk Isolde had partly pulled from under the ghost. The clasps were rusted shut. He pried them open with one of the old swords. He beckoned to Isolde, who looked more worried than ever.

"What does this have to do with courting me?" she asked.

"Everything," he said.

Doggedly, Isolde set about searching for the missing heart. The sturdy leather trunk had kept out the larger sort of vermin, and lavender and other herbs had discouraged insects. Carefully, she unfolded a blanket scarcely touched by moths, and pulled out yellowed linen shirts, stockings in dire need of mending, and a pair of immaculately embroidered gauntlets. Then a well-worn Book of Hours, which must be very old and worth far more than the second heart.

But not to the ghost.

She was about to give up and go on to another trunk when she saw it—a tiny bag so worn and dark with age that it was almost invisible in the bottom of the trunk. The drawstring fell to pieces when she opened the bag.

She tipped the contents into her palm. The little golden heart gleamed cheerfully in the candlelight. Sure enough, it was the opposite of the stolen heart, with a tiny hook that would fit into a hole in the filigree of the other.

Gawain removed the stolen heart from his pocket. "What now?"

"You return that to your mother, I suppose," she said. "And my mother can keep this one."

"If you wish," he said, "but I think they'll both be disappointed."

"Why? They can't feud if they each have one."

"No, because, like me, they are both in favor of—forgive me for waxing poetic—two hearts joined by love."

She bit her lip. Resisting Gawain was so very, very hard.

"Last night at dinner, when I told my mother of my intentions, she advised me to warn you about my poetry. 'Make sure Isolde knows you will inflict it on her for the rest of her life,' she said."

Helplessly, Isolde laughed. "That wouldn't be inflicting." She paused to collect her thoughts. "You decided you wished to marry me before you...before you came to me last night?"

"Yes, I asked for my father's approval yesterday. He twitted me about kissing you under the mistletoe and gave me his best wishes for success."

"And before everything that happened today." Obviously, but she wanted to be sure.

He nodded.

"So...so you truly don't feel obliged in any way?"

"No, I feel besotted. Completely, hopefully, helplessly in love with you."

She moaned. This was far too good to be true. "Are you sure? I'm scandalous. There will be a lot of talk."

"Well, as long as you don't poison me..."

"Gawain, I'm serious. Maybe you should take some time to think about it."

"I have thought about it." He held her away from him and gazed down at her. She couldn't meet his eyes.

"Look at me," he said.

"Gawain..."

"Do you love me?" he asked. "The truth, now."

She swallowed. She took a deep breath. She shouldn't be afraid, and yet she was. But of what? She knew Gawain, had known him forever. She had loved him all her life. "Gawain, I..."

He put a finger under her chin and raised her eyes to his. Oh, God, the worry in his gaze...

And then it became clear: if she'd been an innocent girl, she would have accepted his proposal with eager delight. She mustn't let her previous marriages affect her decision. It wasn't fair to her—or to him.

"Yes," she said. "I love you with all my heart."

After a great many kisses and a few brief words, Isolde and Gawain decided to join the hearts immediately. The little hook locked perfectly into place. Gawain clasped the chains around Isolde's neck. The two hearts lay glowing on her breast.

"It's lovely," she said, "but I don't trust my father not to try to keep it." She unclasped it and put it in Gawain's hand. "Give it to your mother as a gesture of goodwill, to hold until our wedding. I shall explain to my mother."

Which she did, and found her father grumpy but resigned. "You could do worse, I suppose," was all he said when she announced her intention of marrying Gawain as soon as possible. Which might not have sounded like an apology from anyone else's mouth, but Isolde knew her father.

Or maybe she didn't, for to her astonishment, he immediately reinstated the old custom of gathering all the villagers on Twelfth Night, to toast the apple trees for a fruitful crop in the year to come.

A huge cauldron of lamb's wool was carried to the orchard that evening. Gawain and Isolde announced their engagement and were duly celebrated with toasts and well-wishes. Lady Statham and Lady Burke beamed side by side, and if Lord Statham and Sir Wally weren't exactly cordial to one another, they put up a good pretense.

"Look!" Isolde said as the hubbub died down. Far back in the orchard, an otherworldly tableau took shape. The Cavalier strolled forward, a ghostly matron on his arm. He raised a spectral tankard in a toast of his own, and gestured behind…to a ghost in the garb of a Puritan soldier with a young woman, lithe and graceful, at his side.

As suddenly as the ghosts had come, they were gone, and the villagers marveled or shuddered according to their respective natures.

"Do you think they are gone forever?" Gawain asked.

"No," Isolde said dryly, for the Cavalier had spoken to her earlier, and lingered now, invisible. "I'm afraid not."

He smiled down at her. "What now?"

"The Cavalier says that although you are an honorable man and a worthy husband for me, your poetry is execrable. You need a tutor, and therefore, he has no choice but to remain."

Gawain gave a shout of laughter. "As long as he promises to stay out of our bedchamber, that's fine by me."

"You have my word," said the ghost of the Cavalier.

The End

About Barbara

Winner of the Holt Medallion, Maggie, Daphne du Maurier, Reviewer's Choice and Epic awards, Barbara Monajem wrote her first story at eight years old about apple tree gnomes. She published a middle-grade fantasy when her children were young, then moved on to paranormal mysteries and Regency romances with intrepid heroines and long-suffering heroes (or vice versa). Regency mysteries are next on the agenda.

Barbara loves to cook, especially soups. She used to have two items on her bucket list: to make asparagus pudding (because it was too weird to resist) and to succeed at knitting socks. She managed the first (it was dreadful) but doubts she'll ever accomplish the second. This is not a bid for immortality but merely the dismal truth. She lives near Atlanta, Georgia with an ever-shifting population of relatives, friends, and feline strays.

You can find details of her work at
www.BarbaraMonajem.com

Miss Hathaway's Wish

~ BOOK 4 OF THE HATHAWAY HEIRS SERIES ~

BY

Suzanna Medeiros

Will Emily Hathaway get her Christmas Wish?

Emily Hathaway wants to marry for love, but after three unsuccessful seasons she's given up on finding the same happiness her brothers found in their marriages.

Sir Jonah Stanton has returned to England after ten years abroad. A Christmas party at Hathaway Manor provides the perfect opportunity to ease back into English society. But one thing has changed since Jonah's been away. His friend's little sister is now a young woman, and he finds himself appreciating her in ways he'd never imagined possible.

As Emily becomes reacquainted with Jonah, she discovers the feelings she'd attributed to friendship run far deeper. Is it possible Jonah might be the man she's been looking for all along?

Chapter One

December 15, 1816

Emily Hathaway could barely contain her excitement as she made her way to the Hathaway manor house. She'd taken care to bundle up, so the cold air that nipped at her nose didn't dampen her spirits.

It was ten days before Christmas, and her eldest brother had agreed to host a ball the following evening. Some of the guests who lived far away would begin to arrive this afternoon, and Emily's thoughts had been filled with nothing else for the past month. The entire event would only last three days and two evenings, but it was, essentially, a house party. She'd never imagined such an event would take place under her brother's roof.

James had become Viscount Hathaway four years before, when their uncle died without an heir, but he'd never lost his preference for avoiding social gatherings. He attended only those events he felt were necessary and declined all other invitations. Of course, that only resulted in his favor being courted by all, his attendance at a soiree a prize many sought to claim.

Her brother had loathed every second he'd spent in London over the past few years. He and Sarah had escorted her for what had proven to be three very long seasons during which James had scowled at any man brave enough to approach her. That Sarah had somehow convinced him to host this gathering spoke volumes about how much he loved his wife.

Emily quickened her pace, looking forward to spending the morning with the two women who had made her brothers so happy. She imagined Sarah would already have things well in hand, but there were always last-minute details that needed to be taken care of.

When she reached the manor house, she didn't bother to wait for the butler to open the door and let her in. Nonetheless, he appeared instantly as she closed the door against the sharp breeze. She visited so often she might as well be living here. If Mama hadn't insisted on staying at the dower house when James first inherited the viscountcy, she'd be living in the manor house now. But she hadn't wanted to leave her mother alone when she was still reeling from the sudden change in their social status, and now Emily was comfortable with the arrangement.

She smiled at the older man as she removed her hat and cloak and handed him the garments. "It's a beautiful morning despite the cold, isn't it, Dalton?"

He inclined his head by way of response, but the corners of his mouth lifted in an ever-so-slight smile. "Lady Hathaway is waiting for you in the library."

"Thank you," she said, then rushed down the hall to the room that was near the back of the house.

When she crossed the threshold, she saw that Grace was also present. Both she and Sarah were seated on a settee placed near the blazing fireplace, their fair heads bent together in conversation. She was grateful for the tendrils of heat she could feel reaching out across the room.

She'd known Sarah since she and James had wed four years before. She'd only been sixteen then, but they'd taken an instant liking to one another and had become friends from the start.

Grace was a newer addition to the family. When her brother Edward had returned to England the year before after serving in the war against Napoleon, he'd met Grace in Somerset and fallen in love. They'd been expecting Edward's arrival in Northampton and had been shocked to receive an invitation to Somerset for his wedding to a young woman named Grace Kent. They now lived in a small house bordering James's estate, and Edward helped with Hathaway Stables, continuing the business their father had started before any of them had been born.

Sarah turned to Grace as Emily made her way to the fireplace to warm her hands. "I told you she would be early."

"I may be new to this family, but I could have predicted that for myself," Grace said.

Emily only smiled in response as she waited for both women to stand so she could give them each her customary hug by way of greeting. It wasn't the first time they'd teased her about her exuberance, but who could blame her? They were about to host an event she'd thought would never take place in this house.

She pulled back after hugging Sarah and gave her head a slight shake. "I still can't believe James actually agreed to host a house party. Everyone can see that he loves you, but my brother has got to be one of the most stubborn men in existence." As far back as she could remember, James had always insisted he'd never allow himself to be forced to stay under the same roof with strangers who would expect him to dance attendance on them. He hardly tolerated a dinner party, and his behavior when in London was barely civilized. "You must share your secret."

Sarah laughed as she and Grace sank back onto the settee. She waited for Emily to join them before saying, "Well, to begin, don't call it a house party in his presence. We're referring to it as a Christmas ball and not mentioning the fact that some of the guests will be staying for two nights."

Emily fought the urge to roll her eyes. "Changing the name of the event doesn't change what it is."

"You and I both know that. But James is terrified we're going to have a snowstorm and all the guests will be trapped here for days on end. As for how I convinced him to host a ball in the first place..." She shared a look with Grace before continuing. "I shouldn't tell you this since it takes the shine off my accomplishment, but it was actually Grace's idea."

Emily lowered herself onto the settee next to Grace, barely managing to keep her expression even as all manner of unwelcome thoughts threatened to surface.

She'd walked in on each of her brothers and their wives several times in what could only be called a heated embrace, and she now regretted asking the question. "If this has anything to do with what you get up to in the bedroom when you're alone with your husbands, I'd rather not hear the details."

Grace and Sarah laughed again, and she realized she hadn't been successful in holding back her slight grimace.

"If you really want to know, it involves you actually," Grace said when their amusement died down.

"Me?" Emily was now more confused than ever. James would never agree to host a ball—especially not so near to Christmas—for her.

"I'm almost afraid to tell you." Grace cast a sheepish glance at Sarah before facing her again. "You might not be happy when you hear this."

Emily waved a hand in dismissal at Grace's concern. "You might as well tell me straight away and get it over with. Even if I am annoyed, we all know I'll forgive you soon enough as long as your intentions weren't malicious."

"Oh no, never that. It's just that... Well, you'll reach your age of majority just before your next season starts."

This time Emily didn't even try to hold back her frown. She tried not to think about the fact that she'd already had three unsuccessful seasons and was almost one-and-twenty with nary a marriage prospect in sight. After this year she feared she'd be firmly on the shelf.

"Which means," Grace said with an arch smile, "that you will no longer need your brother's approval to wed."

Sarah jumped in to add, "I've assured Grace that James would never withhold your dowry to force you to fall in line with his wishes. He never approved of the way his father was cut off when he began breeding and selling horses, after all. James would never be so heavy-handed in dealing with his own family."

Grace nodded. "That means you'll be free to wed whomever you wish."

Emily couldn't see how her upcoming birthday had anything to do with hosting a ball, especially since she couldn't imagine running off with anyone, and said as much.

Sarah shook her head in exasperation, her blond curls swinging with the movement. "This will be the last opportunity James has to choose someone *suitable* for you. Or at least to have a say in whom you choose. When I pointed that out to him, he relented and agreed to host this party. Of course, he also insisted on providing me with a list of suitable candidates."

A sense of dread settled over Emily as she imagined all the staid, boring men who would be paraded before her like prized cattle over the next two days. She'd seen clearly enough the type of man of whom her brother approved, and none had held even a faint interest for her.

What had once seemed like an enjoyable occasion had now become a vain attempt to find her a husband. And the last thing she wanted was another reminder that she was destined to remain a spinster since she refused to settle for anything less than the happiness her brothers had found for themselves.

Emily leaned back against the cushions of the settee and closed her eyes. "I know you meant well, but the two of you have done me no favors."

"Don't fret," Grace said, reaching over to pat her hand. "Sarah and I might have slipped in a few invitations about which our husbands know nothing. There will be several men here who never show their faces in London during the season. You'll have the opportunity to meet someone new."

"And," Sarah added, "there will be no expectation placed upon you—or on these men—to circle each other, looking for a potential marriage partner. You can be yourselves without all those constraints."

Emily opened her eyes and stared right at the woman who'd just spoken such nonsense. "Clearly you don't know my brother as well as you think you do. He *loves* constraints. He's always trying to rein in my 'indiscriminate enthusiasm.' And won't it seem a little odd if it's just us and a whole house filled with men?"

She had to close her eyes again as the awfulness of the situation settled over her. How humiliating. Everyone present would know exactly what Sarah and Grace were trying to do. Find a spouse for their almost-spinster sister-by-marriage whom no man wanted.

Although that wasn't strictly true. Plenty of men had wanted her, but they'd wanted her generous dowry more. Anyone with enough wealth that the money to be settled on her when she wed wouldn't be the main enticement was either already wed or utterly boring. Or old. She didn't want to think about all the men who'd already buried wives and were looking for another young woman to take their place. And now she'd have to deal with them under this roof.

Thank the heavens she resided at the dower house with her mother. At least she could escape there when the situation became too insufferable at the manor house.

She realized it was too quiet and opened her eyes to see what Grace and Sarah were doing. She found them staring at her, twin expressions of exasperation on their faces.

"There will be plenty of women here as well—both wed and unwed. You needn't worry about being uncomfortable."

Emily could feel the heat creeping up her face. "You can hardly blame me for my reaction. You could have assured me this wouldn't appear to be a gathering put together to rid yourselves of me before you mentioned all the men you plan to parade me before."

Grace gave Emily's hand another brief squeeze. "You can hardly blame us for wanting to secure for you the same happiness we've found."

"And as you recall," Sarah continued, "I was forced into this marriage with James and wasn't at all happy about it. But it turned out well for everyone involved."

"If you say so," Emily said, trying her best not to allow her dismay to cloud her former enthusiasm. Things wouldn't be so bad if she made sure to stay close to her family or members of her own sex during the ball.

Sarah was quiet for several moments, and Emily knew she wanted to reassure her again, but instead she stood and moved over to the table that acted as her desk. Three chairs had been placed around it, and she settled into one and lifted a page from one of the neatly separated piles. "The menus have been planned, but I haven't been able to make up my mind about what activities should be made available for this afternoon and tomorrow before the guests who are staying here return to their rooms to dress for the ball. This might be the shortest house party any of them have ever attended, and while they might not expect much, I'd like to ensure everyone isn't bored to tears."

Guilt settled over Emily when she saw the way Sarah's brows had drawn together as she dropped the page she was holding and concentrated on a second pile. Pushing aside her doubts about any embarrassment she might suffer, Emily stood and, together with Grace, joined Sarah to give their opinions and to reassure her everything was well in hand.

Chapter Two

Jonah Stanton wasn't sure how he'd allowed himself to be talked into attending this ball. But after spending the past ten years away from home and earning his fortune, he supposed his attendance at such events was inevitable now that he was back in England. All it had taken was one disappointed look from his mother before he'd readily agreed to accompany her to this house party. He might be twenty-eight, but it was clear he was sorely out of practice when it came to holding out against maternal guilt.

Of course, there was also the fact that he was trying to make up for his absence when his father died the year before. By the time he finally learned of his father's death, several months had already passed. It had taken another six months before he was able to return home.

He told himself this would be a good opportunity to become acquainted again with English society. He'd been away for so long he wasn't sure anyone would remember him.

It was late morning when they finally arrived at the Hathaway estate. The carriage deposited them at the dower house where his mother would be staying with her good friend Mrs. Hathaway. Or would she now be considered the dowager Lady Hathaway? Could one be a dowager when they'd never held the title of Lady Hathaway?

So much had changed since he'd left. James now held the title of Viscount Hathaway, and the entire family had moved from Newmarket, where they'd been neighbors, to Northampton. They'd grown up together, however, and Jonah was looking forward to the upcoming reunion.

After seeing his mother settled, he made his way on foot to the manor house where he would be staying with the other guests. He could have settled back into the carriage for the short distance, but he'd already been cooped up in its interior for the past day minus the few hours they'd spent at an inn along the way. Despite the cold, he welcomed the opportunity to stretch his legs and breathe in the fresh air. It was decidedly brisker than that to which he was accustomed after spending the past ten years in India. Still, he was back in England to stay now and would need to become reacclimated to cold winters and to the damp weather the rest of the year.

He was about halfway through his walk when he noticed a small figure approaching. He'd been told Emily Hathaway lived with her mother in the dower house, but since the woman coming toward him was bundled up against the cold, it was difficult to tell if she was the young girl he'd once known.

He did a few quick calculations in his head and realized Emily would now be a young woman.

The approaching figure was covered from the neck down in a voluminous cloak that was sky blue in color, and her hair was tucked away beneath a dark-colored hat that could only be called practical. A few strands of dark hair had escaped to frame her face, adding an allure to her appearance that sparked his interest.

As she neared and looked up at him with sparkling blue eyes, he could see this was none other than Emily Hathaway. It was almost impossible to believe she was all grown up.

The way her head tilted to the side and her face scrunched up as she tried to place how she knew him reminded him of the lively child he'd once known. It wasn't difficult to tell when she recognized him, for a large smile spread across her face and her eyes lit with happiness.

"Jonah? What are you doing here? Aren't you supposed to be away in India?" She gave her head a slight shake as though to remind herself to curb her tendency toward exuberance. He'd almost forgotten that about her. "No one told me you were coming."

"Actually, it's Sir Jonah now. It seems that when one comes from an old family with ties to nobility and becomes personally responsible for ensuring the royal kitchens are equipped with enough exotic spices to satisfy the regent's palate and impress all manner of visiting dignitaries, the crown can be very generous."

"You'll have to excuse me for my ignorance, *Sir Jonah*," Emily said before dipping into a deep curtsy. He didn't miss the twinkle in her eye when she straightened. "I am but a humble woman. Tell me, do you possess a ring I should be kissing? I wouldn't wish to offend you by not offering you all the courtesies you're owed."

"I see you're as precocious as ever," he said, his tone dry.

Her laugh still had the ability to make him smile, and he found himself doing so now as she let forth a peal of delight.

"James and Edward will be so happy to see you! I'm going to have to box their ears for not telling me to expect you."

She turned and headed back toward the manor house, and he fell into step beside her.

"Well, in the interest of saving them a little pain, I should confess that they didn't know I was coming."

She glanced sideways at him, and her eyes narrowed. "Did Sarah invite you?"

"Would it be a problem if she had?" He couldn't understand why her jaw tensed at that. "Actually, it was Lady Hathaway—your mother—who extended the invitation. I don't believe she was aware I'd returned when she invited my mother. Mother, of course, wrote back, and together they decided that she shouldn't travel so far alone. *Et voilà*, you now have to endure my company."

"That's nice. Mama did say something about Mrs. Stanton coming to stay with us over Christmas." She stopped and looked up at him. "Oh, that means you'll be staying as well. We'll be able to become reacquainted properly after the ball when the guests leave."

"Yes, it's all been settled," he said as they resumed their walk.

"I wonder why Sarah didn't mention it?"

"She probably has a lot on her mind with the ball being so close to Christmas. Mother will be staying at the dower house with you and Lady Hathaway, and I'll be at the main house with the rest of the guests."

"Mama really doesn't like being called Lady Hathaway. She's still struggling with just how much our lives have changed since James inherited."

Jonah gave her words some thought, but in the end shook his head. "If I'm to adjust to being back here again, I have to practice my manners. I've become lax over the past few years, so I'm going to have to insist on formality so I don't embarrass myself—or your family—around others."

"I suppose that means I'll have to call you Sir Jonah now, and of course you'll insist on calling me Miss Hathaway."

They'd reached the house and Emily stopped again. Jonah took a moment to admire the sheer size of the manor, marveling at just how much his friends' lives had changed in the past few years. Their former home was large, but certainly not anywhere near the scale of the house before him now.

He turned to face Emily, detecting a slight frown on her face that had him wondering as to its cause. "Is something the matter?"

"Oh no," she said, giving her head a vigorous shake and smiling at him. "I was just thinking how strange it is that I feel as though I know you so well when I don't. Not really. You're my brother's friend, and it's been ages since I last saw you."

"It's been ten years since I moved to India and you were… ten years of age, was it?"

"Heavens, I feel so old now. Mama always goes on about how time goes by more quickly as one ages, and now I understand what she means. It doesn't feel as though ten years have passed. I was still a child the last time we spoke."

"I must admit, I find it difficult to imagine you're all grown up, especially since I can't see what you look like under that hat and cloak."

Emily laughed again, no doubt thinking he was jesting, but he was completely serious. She was taller than the last time he'd seen her, but at over six feet in height, he still towered over her. She'd always been outgoing and loved tagging along after her brothers, much to their chagrin. He hadn't minded since he didn't have any brothers or sisters and had enjoyed her penchant for trying to make them all laugh. But he found it almost impossible to picture what she'd look like when she removed her cloak and hat. From what he could tell, her personality hadn't changed much from that outgoing girl he'd once known, although he had to admit she'd developed a sense of wit that he found charming.

"You'll have to wait a little longer to sate your curiosity," she said, giving him a small push toward the door.

"What? You're going to leave me here all alone?"

"Hardly alone," she said. "My brothers are home. You can become reacquainted with them and meet their wives. Enjoy the quiet before most of the male population of England starts arriving later this afternoon. I'll be back then to help greet them."

He raised a brow at that. "Just the male population?"

"Well, my sisters-in-law insist that won't be the case, but I'm afraid they're matchmaking."

He gave a sympathetic wince, knowing he'd soon be facing the same thing next year when the season began. Only he wanted to get married, he told himself.

"At any rate, enjoy the peace until then. I'll return with Mama and Mrs. Stanton this afternoon and will stay through dinner."

With a small wave, she turned and walked away. Jonah watched her for a full minute, allowing his curiosity about what she looked like under that cloak to take hold of his imagination. Catching himself, he gave his head a shake to clear his thoughts and turned back to the house. Emily wasn't wrong that he was looking forward to the relative peace before the other guests arrived. The ball tomorrow evening would be his official return to society.

Chapter Three

Emily waited for the carriage door to open, impatient with the formality of having to take the conveyance when the manor was only a mile from the dower house. She didn't complain, however, because she knew it was important to her mother that they keep up appearances. Despite the fact they'd all settled into their elevated station in society, it was something about which her mother still worried.

"Emily..."

The note of warning in her mother's voice brought Emily out of her reverie. She hadn't even realized she was tapping her foot.

"Oh, leave the poor girl," Mrs. Stanton said with a fond smile. "She's excited, and who can blame her."

Mama gave her head a small shake. "I'll never understand where she gets her energy and her love for all manner of social events. It certainly wasn't from her father or me."

The carriage door swung open, and Emily let out a sigh of relief. She waited as the young footman—a new member of her brother's staff whose name she hadn't yet learned—helped her mother and Mrs. Stanton out of the carriage. And then, finally, he was handing her down as well.

Even though she was wary about her family's matchmaking efforts, Emily couldn't deny that her mother had been correct. She was still excited about the upcoming ball.

They'd scarce entered the manor before Sarah descended on them. She greeted them warmly and waited while Mama introduced her to Mrs. Stanton.

"Thank goodness you're here," she said, her voice low. "A number of guests have already arrived, and I'm afraid I'm being run ragged."

"Is something the matter?" Mama asked, her lips tightening in concern.

"I don't believe so. It's just that it's much more intimidating than I imagined, overseeing the well-being of houseguests with whom one has only a passing acquaintance. I can't imagine why I thought this was a good idea."

"Nonsense," Emily said, drawing her arm through Sarah's. "Now that we're here, you can delegate and we'll help you. Tell me, has my brother gone into hiding yet?"

Sarah gave a small laugh, but Emily could sense the tension behind her composure. "Not for lack of trying. The first guest arrived one hour ago, and I've already caught him trying to sneak away to his study three times! As punishment, I've set him up in the drawing room where he is now surrounded by would-be friends whose names I'm sure he can't remember."

Emily wasn't surprised, especially since she still couldn't believe her brother had agreed to host this event. But not only had he agreed, now he was engaging in polite conversation with strangers? He must be desperate to see her settled. But despite her unease, she vowed to enjoy this once-in-a-lifetime experience. After all, it wasn't entirely outside the realm of possibility that she'd meet her future husband over the next two days.

Chapter Four

James found her in the library several hours later, browsing the bookshelves for a distraction.

He came to a stop next to her. "We seem to have switched personalities. Why is it I'm out there and you're hiding away in here?"

She glanced toward the doorway, and when she saw the door was open, she crossed the room to close it. She leaned against it and let out a breath. "Lord Kirby has been relentless. Every time I turn around, he's there. I just needed ten minutes to myself before it's time to head in for dinner."

James lifted one hand to rub at the back of his neck. "About that..."

Emily narrowed her eyes. "What did you do?"

"He's a good man. You should give him a chance. Everyone speaks very highly of him."

Emily sighed, telling herself that her brother meant well. But she couldn't help cringing as she imagined the conversation he and Lord Kirby would have had that led the latter to believe he was her brother's choice of a husband for her.

"Getting to know him is one thing, but he's scarce given me a moment to breathe since we've been introduced."

"That's a good thing, is it not? It means he likes you."

James looked so confused. Emily wanted to tell him that she felt no spark of interest for Lord Kirby, but perhaps her brother was right. His own wife had been in love with another man when they'd wed, and look at how well their marriage had turned out.

She nodded and took his arm, allowing him to lead her back to the drawing room. The moment Lord Kirby spotted her, he started in her direction. The man was fair-haired, and she had to admit he was attractive, even if his pale blue eyes were a little unsettling.

Emily took a deep breath and greeted him with what she hoped was a warm smile. Then she spotted Jonah entering the room and no longer had to pretend to be happy.

"Sir Jonah," she called out in greeting. "Please join us."

Jonah's head swiveled in her direction, and she watched as his dark eyes swept over her. She remembered their earlier conversation and how he'd joked about not being able to imagine what she looked like under her cloak.

She took the opportunity to examine him as well. He'd been slimmer all those years ago, but now he filled out his navy-colored jacket in a most becoming manner. His hair was the same sandy brown, the lightened ends just touching the edge of his cravat. She remembered how his hair had always been a wild mess and felt the urge to tousle the strands from their current immaculate state.

One corner of his mouth tilted up. "Miss Hathaway," he said when he reached the small group. He gave her a formal bow before greeting her brother and Lord Kirby.

"It is *so* good to see you," she said. "Where have you been hiding?"

"Lady Hathaway introduced me to her and James's sons, and I've been keeping them company in the nursery. I'm afraid I might have bored them with tales of India."

Emily laughed. "That's highly unlikely. I'm sure William and George talked your ear off and barely allowed you to get in a word."

"You've caught out my lie." His mouth turned down in an exaggerated grimace as he turned to James. "Were we that rambunctious as youths? It's a wonder our parents survived."

"We were worse," James said.

"Well, I for one would love to hear about your adventures abroad," Emily said, ignoring the small frown that appeared on Lord Kirby's face before he excused himself and turned away from the group.

"Emily." James's tone told her he didn't approve of her silent dismissal of the other man.

She lifted one shoulder. "I haven't seen Jonah since I was ten! We have so much to talk about."

She took Jonah's arm and he led them to one of one the new settees Sarah had arranged for the comfort of the guests.

"Where would you like me to start?" he asked.

She considered his question for a moment but didn't know what to ask. She couldn't imagine visiting such an exotic location, let alone living there for ten years. "Tell me everything."

Chapter Five

Jonah followed the sound of laughter down the path to what he was told would be a small pond.

It was deuced cold that morning—certainly too cold for him to be outside—but that hadn't deterred Emily from deciding to go ice-skating. The activity wasn't on the approved list of entertainments for the guests, but that hadn't stopped her from volunteering to take her two nephews outdoors to work off some of their excess energy.

Jonah had almost decided against the outing, but when Mrs. Hathaway mentioned over breakfast that she expected Lord Kirby would want to join her daughter, he'd wasted no time donning his outerwear and searching them out.

He'd watched Kirby fawning all over Emily the evening before during dinner, and the display had bothered him more than a little. Kirby was far too boring for Emily, and it irked him to no end that James seemed to be pushing for a union between the two. It was also clear it was a match Emily didn't want, and he could hardly be considered a friend if he didn't help her avoid being alone with the man.

He paused to take in the sight before him when he rounded the last bend. He scanned the area and felt his tense muscles loosen when he didn't see Lord Kirby. The boys' nurse—an older, matronly woman—stood off to the side, watching the group with what looked like trepidation. Jonah couldn't blame her. He himself had never participated in this particular sport.

William—who had taken great pride in telling him the day before that he would be three in a month's time—was already gliding over the smooth surface of the pond with a casual confidence that indicated this wasn't his first time skating.

George—the younger of James's two sons—wasn't as successful. Emily was skating backward while holding both of his hands in hers. He watched as she released one hand, only to grasp it again when the boy lost his balance atop the slim blades that were attached to his boots.

William glided to a stop beside Emily and George and placed his hands on his hips. "Hurry up and learn how to skate so we can have a proper race. It's no fun racing Aunt Emily. She never lets me win."

Emily laughed. "When you're all grown and have surpassed me in height, I'm sure you'll have your revenge. I need to win now while I still can."

She glanced up and caught sight of where Jonah was watching them from off to one side. Her eyes lit and her genuine smile made him revise his misgivings about braving the cold.

"Well, this is a rare treat. Have you come to join us, Sir Jonah?"

William and George turned to look at him. William's eyes lit up at the prospect of having another playmate while George pressed closer to Emily's side.

"You seem to have things well in hand. Besides, I don't have any skates."

He couldn't tell who was more crestfallen by his statement... William or Emily.

"I'm not very good," a little voice called out from amid Emily's skirts.

"Oh, George, you'll learn. William wasn't very good the first time I took him skating last year, but now look at him!"

George didn't look as though he believed her, and it was obvious from the aghast expression on William's face that he didn't either.

Jonah crouched down near the edge of the lake and met the youngest Hathaway's eyes. "Do you want to know a secret?" He glanced at William and could see he'd caught the older boy's attention as well.

George nodded.

"I never learned how to skate. Your grandmother told me I could borrow a pair of blades to attach to my boots if I was coming out here to join you, but I didn't want to embarrass myself by falling."

George loosened his grip on Emily's skirts and stood straighter. "I fell a few times."

Jonah nodded and kept his tone serious. "Everyone falls when they first learn how to skate."

"Aunt Emily can teach you," William said. "Nurse says she has the patience of a saint."

George nodded. "She said William was awful when she taught him, but I don't believe her."

"I'm a natural," William said, his chest puffed out with pride. "But I know George will be too."

"Yes, they are," Jonah said with a smile as he rose to stand. "Then it seems I'll be the only one who doesn't know how to skate."

"You don't actually need blades to slide around on the ice," Emily said.

His gaze caught hers, and he could see the mischievous twinkle she wasn't even trying to hide.

"That's how I started," George added. "I'm good with my boots."

Jonah narrowed his eyes at her. It wasn't bad enough that he was going to freeze to death out here—and why wasn't everyone as bundled up as he was?—but now she had to humiliate him.

"I'm sure it will make George feel better if he's not the only person learning to skate." Her innocent expression vanished, her voice taking on a decidedly evil lilt. "I'm sure you wouldn't want to disappoint the boys."

Well, this was really his fault. He should have stayed indoors. He didn't know why the thought of Kirby being out here with Emily had bothered him so much, but he should have ignored his urge to race out and make sure they weren't alone together.

"Besides," Emily added, "you're so well padded, I'm sure it won't hurt if you do fall."

Jonah couldn't hold back his bark of laughter at her witty observation. Living in India for the past ten years had left him with zero tolerance for the cold. Emily and her nephews were wearing coats and mittens but no scarves or hats. He'd once been impervious to England's cooler weather, but that had been a lifetime ago. He wasn't sure he'd ever get used to it again.

"I'll do my best," he said, stepping onto the ice with exaggerated care and smiling widely at the two boys when he didn't immediately fall. He wasn't sure how long he'd be able to hold on to his dignity, but in that moment he didn't really care.

He watched as Emily resumed her careful guidance of George. This time when she released one hand, he wobbled only once before straightening and continuing to skate next to her. He wasn't sure whether George or his brother was more excited by the feat.

"See, I told you that you could do it!" William said.

Feeling foolish standing rooted to the spot while everyone else was having fun, Jonah pushed off, ignoring the warning bells in his mind that told him this endeavor wouldn't end well. It might have been a decade since he'd last had to navigate ice, but surely his body would remember how it was done.

He'd underestimated how difficult it would be to stop and found himself windmilling his arms to keep his balance as he made for the edge of the pond. He counted it a win when he stumbled onto firm ground again before his feet slid out from under him.

Emily's laughter trailed after him. He turned to glare at her but couldn't hold his expression of mock indignation when he saw how beautiful she looked. Her cheeks were flushed from the outdoor activity and the cold, her blue eyes dancing with amusement. And he realized that he wanted to kiss her.

He looked away from her lest he betray his inconvenient discovery and watched as William came to a stop beside his aunt.

"I'm hungry," he said.

"Me too," George added.

The boys' nurse stepped forward at that, but she was careful to avoid the slick surface of the lake. "I'll help you with the skates and we can head back."

Emily helped George skate to the woman's side and started to kneel to unstrap the blades from his boots, but the woman shooed her away.

"I'll help George. Can you ensure William doesn't cut himself with his blades again?"

Jonah winced imagining that.

Emily nodded and lowered herself onto a log next to her older nephew.

"I can do this myself," William said, a hint of stubbornness in his voice.

Emily began to work on the straps that tied her skates to her boots, but Jonah didn't miss the way she watched her nephew out of the corner of her eye. "Of course you can. But it's Miss Abigail's job to worry about you, so you can understand why she'd ask me to watch you."

"I suppose." William's tongue poked out of the corner of his mouth as he worked at undoing his straps, and soon enough he'd removed both blades. "See?"

"You're such a big boy," Emily said, snatching the blades away from him and passing them to the nurse.

"Thank you, Miss Hathaway," the woman said as she took both pairs of skates.

Emily made no move to join the group when they turned to head toward the house.

The older woman's brows drew together and she glanced between Emily and Jonah. "Are you joining us?"

"You go on ahead, Miss Abigail. Jonah and I will follow shortly." The woman looked like she was about to protest, so Emily added, "It will give Jonah and me time to catch up. We grew up together back in Newmarket, but Jonah has been away from England for a few years. He's almost another brother to me."

The woman looked as though she wanted to argue, but instead gave a curt nod and started after the boys who were already racing toward the manor house.

Jonah waited for her to disappear around the bend in the path before speaking. "I'm like a brother?"

Emily shrugged. "That depends on how overbearing you are. I'd like to think we're friends, but I know Miss Abigail wouldn't want to leave me unchaperoned. In fact, I wouldn't be surprised if she sent my maid out as soon as she reaches the house."

Emily lowered herself onto the log again, and Jonah took a seat next to her, careful to leave a respectable distance between them.

"You can't blame her. The house is filled with strangers, and as you told William, it is her job to worry."

Emily rolled her eyes. "You'd think I was still a child the way she fusses. The way they all do."

"They care about you. That isn't a bad thing."

"No, I know it isn't. Please excuse me, I'm just feeling a little disappointed."

Her statement surprised him. Emily had always been outgoing and loved meeting people. "If memory serves, there was never a stranger you didn't want to turn into a friend. Don't tell me you've developed James's hatred for social events."

Her sigh had him imagining that that was exactly what had happened, but then she confused him by saying, "I *love* balls."

"Are you afraid this one isn't large enough? I can assure you that while you've been out here, a steady stream of guests have been arriving. I'm surprised the manor has enough bedrooms for everyone."

Emily shook her head. "No, it's just that what I thought was to be a lovely event—one I never imagined James would ever agree to host—has turned into another attempt to find me a husband. And after three unsuccessful seasons, I'd like to enjoy one ball without everyone in my family watching me to see if I'll find a suitor."

Jonah couldn't hold back his laughter.

"You find my dismay amusing, *Sir Jonah*?" Emily folded her arms across her chest and glared at him. He could tell she wasn't genuinely angry, however.

"I imagine there is no end of men lining up to court you."

She sighed and relaxed her arms so they were resting on her lap again. "You're correct, of course. Who wouldn't want to court a passably attractive young woman with a sizable dowry?"

He could only shake his head in bewilderment. "I imagine your dowry might be an inducement for some, but trust me when I say it isn't the only thing they want."

Wanting to put an end to this conversation, Emily reached down for her skates, which were resting behind the log, and stood. "We should head back before my maid arrives to chaperone us."

He fell into step beside her, and they walked in companionable silence for a full minute before Emily spoke again. "How did you know to find us here?"

He didn't want to ruin the morning by mentioning the real reason he'd come out, so instead said, "Your mother mentioned it. I'll admit I was worried you might be overdoing it in the cold. Speaking of which, I feel as though I should be offering you my coat, but I'm afraid I'd freeze on the spot if I removed it."

"Poor Jonah. Has India ruined you for England? Are you planning to return once this party is over?"

Jonah shook his head. "My days living abroad are over. I'm here to stay now."

His heart lightened at the look of relief on her face.

"I'm glad. I'd hate to have to say goodbye again to a friend. At least now you can visit and we'll see each other often."

Jonah didn't reply, but he knew that wouldn't be happening if she met someone at the ball later tonight. When she married, she'd be spending her days with her future husband's family and wouldn't have time for him.

He pushed aside his disappointment at the thought.

Chapter Six

Emily's dancing slippers were beginning to pinch her feet. Unless she was mistaken, she'd danced with every man at the ball once, but she was far from tired. She'd have to find a proper way to thank Sarah and Grace for keeping true to their word. While there were several eligible men present—many of whom would never be seen in London during the season—there wasn't that same air of desperation surrounding this event. All in all, she was enjoying herself more than she'd thought she would.

That didn't mean she hadn't noticed the looks of interest from some of the men. But when she didn't encourage their attention, they moved on readily enough.

Unfortunately, the same wasn't true of Lord Kirby, who seemed oblivious to the fact she was avoiding him. Bolstered by the knowledge that James was clearly in favor of a match between them, he'd been relentless in his pursuit.

The man was becoming a problem. His confidence that he'd win her hand despite the fact she'd been careful not to encourage him was beginning to annoy her as the evening wore on. She'd taken to moving from group to group when she spotted him approaching her, unable to spend more than a few minutes in one place.

She'd just taken refuge with Sarah when James joined them.

"Have you been avoiding Lord Kirby?" His voice was low, but Emily glanced at those around them to ensure they hadn't overheard. "I thought we'd agreed you would get to know him. He's smart, titled, and well-off. And from the way several of the other women are looking at him, quite handsome. You don't want to miss your chance with him."

Emily didn't want to have this conversation on the edge of the ballroom floor where anyone could overhear them. She cast another look around them before replying. "If you're so enamored, maybe you should pursue a relationship with him."

James's mouth dropped open in shock, and Sarah's amused laughter broke the tense silence that followed her statement. Sarah sobered soon enough, whispering, "Speak of the devil..."

Emily turned to find Lord Kirby fast approaching. Her gaze went back to her brother, who was grinning at her in satisfaction. She found that she much preferred James when he was glowering at any man who dared approach her.

Lord Kirby greeted them with what she imagined, for him, was great enthusiasm since the man rarely showed even a hint of emotion.

She glared at James when he took his leave, dragging Sarah onto the dance floor with him.

"Is something the matter?" Lord Kirby asked.

"Oh no," Emily said, managing a polite smile. "My brother was just teasing me. You know how siblings can be."

"I'm afraid I am an only child."

That explained so much. If ever there was a man in need of a sibling to shake up his unflappable reserve, it was the one standing before her now. Although Jonah was also an only child, he wasn't quite so unemotional.

Lord Kirby's arms were clasped behind his back, and he looked down at her from his greater height, his pale blue eyes sending a shiver through her. When he cleared his throat, she knew what was coming. He was going to ask for leave to court her. She frantically searched for an excuse to put him off, but nothing came to mind. She stood there, frozen, as he began to speak.

"I'm so glad to have caught up with you. There was something I wanted to discuss—"

"Emily, there you are. I wondered where you'd been hiding."

Lord Kirby frowned at Jonah's familiar use of her given name, but Emily couldn't find it within herself to care. In fact, at that moment she wanted nothing more than to embrace him.

Chapter Seven

Jonah could sense Emily's relief and so pressed on. "After our dance together, you promised me a turn about the room. I've come to collect."

He ignored the way Kirby glared at him, instead offering Emily his arm. She clutched it with a little more enthusiasm than was seemly and took her leave of the man who'd been hovering over her moments before.

"Thank you," she said when they were out of Lord Kirby's hearing. "I think he was about to ask for leave to court me." The way her brows drew together told him she wouldn't have welcomed the man's interest.

"You didn't seem to be enjoying yourself, so I decided to intervene."

"Oh no," she said. "Do you think he noticed? I don't wish to hurt his feelings."

He wasn't surprised the young woman he'd once known as a sensitive, carefree child was more concerned about someone else's feelings than her own. "I'm sure he's fine. If he realized you didn't care for his company, he wouldn't have been hovering over you."

The words left a sour taste in his mouth, but he tried to ignore his displeasure at the thought of Kirby—or any man—courting Emily. He'd known her since she was a child, so it was natural he'd feel protective of her. He didn't wish to see her unhappy.

"Of course," she said with a soft sigh.

She didn't say anything else, and neither did he when he realized she was leading them out of the room. It was a pity it was too cold for the doors to the garden to be open. Instead, they'd have to wander along the hallway where others had also sought escape from the crowded confines of the ballroom.

He knew his next question was overstepping the bounds of propriety, but he couldn't hold back his curiosity. "Is there already someone for whom you have a *tendre*? I can't imagine a young woman as beautiful as you doesn't already have an understanding with an equally handsome young man."

She cast a sideways glance at him, an odd expression on her face. "You think I'm beautiful?"

One corner of his mouth tilted up. "As do most of the men here. I'm hardly alone in that thought."

Emily winced at the reminder of her would-be suitor. "To answer your question, no, there isn't anyone."

He ignored the surge of pleasure her admission brought since he was certain it wouldn't be true for long.

"Do you wish to return to the ballroom?" He didn't want their brief time together to come to an end, but she had told him she loved balls earlier that morning. He could have taken her into one of the other first-floor rooms that were open to guests but found himself reluctant to release her to the company of yet another man who was eager to capture her attention. He'd seen clearly enough that Kirby wasn't the only man interested in getting to know Emily better. The thought shouldn't have bothered him as much as it did.

Being with Emily was comforting. He knew he'd have to begin his own search for a bride soon. That was, after all, one of the reasons he'd decided not to return to his life abroad. But first he needed to readjust to society here. Yes, he'd been surrounded by Englishmen and women while in India, but things were decidedly different there. Freer. He'd almost forgotten all the constraints that were placed upon one here in his home country.

Even this brief stroll would cause tongues to wag despite the fact there was nothing untoward between them. They were friends, their comfort in one another's company aided by long familiarity.

Emily nodded toward the end of the hall and he hesitated, thinking she was going to lead him into James's study, the one room on this floor that wasn't currently open to the public and was sure to be empty. She cast him a curious look and he began moving again.

Unable to stop himself, his thoughts went to what sort of mischief they could get up to behind those closed doors. What shocked him most about the wayward direction of his thoughts was the fact he wasn't disgusted with himself. No, he found he *wanted* to be alone with Emily.

Her brothers were going to beat him to a bloody pulp, but as she led him the rest of the distance, he couldn't bring himself to care.

He was so distracted, so intent on his own imaginings about what was going to happen, that he almost didn't stop when she tugged him over to the side. Only then did he see that chairs had been placed in the hallway for those who wanted a moment of relative, but not true, privacy.

Disappointment crashed over him.

He'd been away from polite society far too long if he believed Emily Hathaway was leading him away for a romantic assignation. But in that moment he realized he wanted more than friendship from her.

Emily withdrew her hand from his arm and lowered herself onto one of the chairs. After she was settled, he did the same.

"My family means well. But between James pushing me toward a staid, respectable union and Sarah and Grace going to great lengths to ensure there were a few eligible men present, I feel as though I am something of a disappointment to them."

He could understand not wanting to be pushed into a union one didn't desire, but surely Emily didn't wish to remain a spinster. He chose his words with great care when he asked her just that.

"You don't wish to wed?"

"Oh no, it's not that. It's just that I never thought it would be so *difficult* to find someone."

He raised a brow at that but didn't have to ask the obvious question.

"Yes, well, perhaps it isn't quite that difficult to find a husband. But I want what my brothers found. I want love."

He had to hold back his impulse to laugh. Of course Emily would be stuck on such a romantic notion.

"Sometimes love comes later. From what James told me, he didn't expect Sarah would ever come to care for him."

"That may be true, but he was smitten with her from the start and willing to take the risk that their union would come to mean more. But I haven't felt that emotion for *anyone*. Oh, I like many of them well enough, but I don't feel a spark of interest, let alone anything that approaches love. The closest I've come to feeling any heat are the moments my anger is sparked when I realize they care more for my dowry that they ever would for me."

"I hate to tell you this"—and he found that he really did—"but there are more than a few men here who have absolutely no need of your dowry."

Emily blew out a breath. "They may not need it, but you can trust me when I say they want it nonetheless." She shook her head as if to clear her mind of the current subject and smiled up at him. "Well, now that you've learned my secret Christmas wish, you have to share yours. Tell me, *Sir* Jonah. What is it you're hoping to receive this Christmas?"

What was he hoping for? He couldn't shake the feeling that there was something missing in his life, but he ascribed that to the sensation of being unmoored now that he was back in England. He didn't know what he was going to do to fill his days, and that thought unsettled him.

"I don't know yet."

Emily laid a hand over his and gave it a brief squeeze before releasing it again. He was surprised at the unguarded show of compassion, but what unnerved him more was his desire to reach for her hand again, peel the glove from her fingers, and clasp it within his.

Emily stood then, saving him from doing something foolish, and he followed suit. "Come," she said. "We should head back now before tongues start wagging."

"If you want to start a few rumors, you should dance with me a second time."

He'd been joking, but Emily leaped at the suggestion. "Maybe Lord Kirby will think you're courting me. You can do that, right? Feign interest in me to keep him at bay?"

Jonah felt a strange sensation in his belly at her words. He ascribed it to nerves at the reminder that soon he'd be entering the marriage mart himself. He wasn't sure about the wisdom of Emily's suggestion, but he found himself powerless to disappoint her. "I think I can manage that."

He held out his arm and Emily took it, smiling up at him in a way that had him feeling ten feet tall as they made their way back to the ballroom.

Chapter Eight

Emily could feel the tension in the air when she entered the breakfast room to find the only occupants were Jonah and Lord Kirby. It was almost midday, and she'd hoped to avoid her would-be suitor by arriving after he'd departed, but clearly she hadn't waited long enough.

Jonah was leaning casually against a wall, his arms folded across his chest and an expression of extreme boredom on his face. Lord Kirby, on the other hand, was glaring at her partner in crime from his seat at the table. She could see that Jonah hadn't been exaggerating after they'd returned to the ballroom when he told her the other man hated him. He'd suggested it was because of their pretend courtship, but Emily couldn't help but wonder if there wasn't more to the story than he was willing to share.

She only had a moment to take in Jonah's appearance, her foolish heart giving a small leap at how handsome he looked in his maroon coat and waistcoat and buff breeches, before he noticed her. The corners of his mouth lifted and a spark of mischief danced behind his eyes. She almost pitied Lord Kirby in that moment and suspected Jonah was doing everything in his power to stir up the other man's temper.

Lord Kirby leaped to his feet when he realized he and Jonah were no longer alone. "Miss Hathaway, I am so happy to see you this morning," he said, greeting her with a cautious smile. "I was afraid the time would come for me to depart before I had the opportunity to bid you adieu. Or to tell you how beautiful you look."

"That would have been a tragedy."

Jonah's interruption caused Lord Kirby to clench his jaw, but the unwelcome audience didn't deter him from his task. Lord Kirby closed the distance between them and gazed down at her.

Emily could almost see the wheels turning in his mind. She'd avoided this moment the night before when Jonah had come to her rescue, but it was clear the man wouldn't be deterred.

She managed to keep a polite smile on her face when Lord Kirby reached for her hand and dropped a kiss on the back. She'd been through this same situation enough times now to ensure she always wore gloves as a barrier.

He released her hand with reluctance. "Will you be in town this coming spring?"

She took a discreet step back, allowing her smile to widen the tiniest fraction so he wouldn't take offense at her retreat. "I believe that's the current plan." She didn't offer him any encouragement, but she knew he would take her polite response as an attempt on her part at coyness.

"I look forward to seeing you there then. Perhaps you'll spare me a few moments of your delightful company when your attention isn't quite so consumed by old acquaintances who make unwelcome demands of your time."

She said nothing to that, knowing full well he was referring to Jonah. But the only acquaintance who was pressing upon her time was him and all the others who saw her only as a means of attaching themselves to a wealthy family.

She dipped into a brief curtsy, making sure to break eye contact, and sighed with relief when he took it as the dismissal it was meant to be. He stepped back but didn't depart just yet.

She chanced another glance at his face and noticed the slight crease that had formed between his brows as he glanced in Jonah's direction. She knew then that he'd learned Jonah and his mother would be staying with them through Christmas and the beginning of the new year. Longer, perhaps, if it snowed and the roads become impassable.

If it wouldn't be a breach of decorum, she suspected Lord Kirby would have pressed for a longer stay himself. She was grateful that the house party hadn't been planned for the actual Christmas holiday as Emily had originally wanted before she learned it would become yet another attempt by her family to find her a husband. No doubt that was James's doing, and for once Emily was glad her brother avoided society whenever possible.

She glanced at Jonah and wasn't surprised to see what could only be called a self-satisfied smirk on his face. He appeared to be taking an inordinate amount of pleasure in Lord Kirby's distress. It was too bad, really, that his show of triumph over the man was merely an act. What would it be like to have two men fighting for her attention—especially if one of those men was Jonah?

"Yes, I've enjoyed our opportunity to become reacquainted," Jonah said, his tone rife with insincerity. Emily was glad Sarah wasn't there to witness it since she was so concerned about ensuring each of their guests enjoyed their stay. "But if those heavy clouds are anything to go by, we'll soon have snow, and we'd hate for you to be stuck here with us over the holidays. You really should leave now if you want to make it home. It would be a shame to find yourself stranded at an inn on Christmas morning."

Emily managed not to laugh at the frown that crossed Lord Kirby's face before he gave them both another bow and turned to leave. She counted it a tremendous feat of restraint when she held back her mirth for a full ten seconds after the man left the room.

"You are so evil," she said when she managed to catch her breath again after her amusement died down. "The poor man looked as though he wanted to strangle you."

A corner of Jonah's mouth tilted upward in a more genuine smile. "I'm quite certain that's exactly what he wanted to do. If you hadn't arrived when you did, I'm sure he would have called me out merely for the offense of existing."

Emily gave her head a slight shake, wincing slightly as she wondered whether Lord Kirby had heard her laughter. Oh well, it was too late to worry about it now.

"Kirby was right about one thing," Jonah said. "May I say that you look lovely today, Miss Hathaway? Of course, you always do."

At his formality, Emily glanced toward the doorway to see who was witnessing their exchange. When she realized they were still alone, she cast a sideways glance at him and made her way to the sideboard.

"You can save your teasing for others, *Sir Jonah*. These past few days have been trying enough."

She expected him to join her as she reached for a plate. When he didn't, she realized he must have already eaten. "You needn't stay to keep me company. I'm sure someone else will be along shortly."

She'd given him permission to escape but was glad when he didn't take the opportunity. Instead, he waited for her to finish loading up her plate—she felt a sense of relief that she could eat her fill without worrying about appearing gluttonous—and followed her to the table.

"There is no place I'd rather be," he said, lowering himself into the seat next to her.

How was a girl to keep her thoughts from scattering in the presence of such a formidable opponent? With his classically handsome features and wit, Sir Jonah Stanton would have no difficulty finding a bride this upcoming season. He was going to have to carve his way through the crowds of hopeful young women vying to capture his attention.

Needing to divert her thoughts from their current path, she grasped for the one subject she knew would unsettle him. "Tell me more about Lord Kirby."

Jonah's frown told her she'd succeeded in distracting him from his teasing. She had to look away lest she betray her amusement.

"I thought you weren't interested in knowing more about him."

She lifted one shoulder but kept her gaze averted. She hoped he'd take it as shyness on her part, but in truth she feared she would burst into laughter again. It appeared Lord Kirby's dislike of Jonah wasn't one-sided.

"You and he are of an age, are you not?"

"Yes." Jonah's reply was curt.

She met his eyes and somehow managed to keep a straight face. She raised a brow, and Jonah folded his arms across his chest.

"You are not going to entertain his suit. He's far too annoying and dull for someone like you."

"Someone like me? James seems to think we'd make a good match, and he is not one to give his consent lightly."

"You know what I mean. You are far too full of life to saddle yourself with someone so stolid."

"It sounds like I'm just what he needs then. Someone to show him the joy life has to offer."

Jonah scowled at that. "I sincerely hope you're joking."

Emily could no longer hold back her laughter. "I wish you could see the look on your face." She attempted to arrange her features into a similar scowl but gave up and chuckled when his frown deepened.

"To set your mind at ease, I'll admit that I won't be entertaining Lord Kirby's suit. My interest in him stems solely from my curiosity about the animosity between the two of you. Were you rivals at school?"

Jonah shook his head, and Emily was glad when his expression softened. "Nothing quite so dramatic, although we did know one another back at Eton. We've never been anything more than acquaintances, but I've always found him to be a little too full of himself."

"So you weren't onetime friends who had a falling-out?"

"Definitely not. I told you this last night, but apparently you didn't believe me. Kirby means to have you for himself, and he can't abide the sight of me because he thinks I'm standing in his way."

Emily took a sip of her tea as she contemplated Jonah's words. Lord Kirby wasn't the first man to have set his sights on gaining her hand in marriage.

"So I take it his fortune is limited and he needs my dowry?"

Jonah hesitated, and for a moment she didn't think he was going to reply. Finally he shrugged. "I don't think so. Really, Emily, you must see that you hold a great deal of worth beyond the amount James will be settling on you when you wed. You are smart, generous, have a lively wit, and you brighten every room you walk into with merely a smile."

Emily found herself at a loss for words. It almost seemed as though Jonah admired her. But no, she was letting her imagination get away from her.

"It's too bad you won't be able to be my protector during the upcoming season," she said when she could speak again. "Although it shouldn't be too difficult to convince my brother to forgo the affair entirely. I'll just have to figure out a way to keep Sarah from changing his mind again."

"I remain ever at your service, Miss Hathaway." He grinned at her, and Emily felt her foolish heart lighten at his obvious good mood.

She had to force her thoughts back to reality instead of allowing herself to get caught up in foolish daydreams. "You forget that I know you're planning to look for a wife. You can hardly do that while pretending to court me to keep unwanted suiters at bay."

Jonah held her gaze for several seconds before speaking. "I don't know. If my luck holds, I may not need to worry about that. But only if you promise to come to London in the spring. How else would I be able to court you properly?"

Emily's stomach did an odd little flip at his words. She had no witty comeback and could only watch, struggling to keep her jaw from dropping open, as he rose and strolled from the breakfast room.

It wasn't possible he'd spoken in earnest. No, he was teasing her again. Jonah didn't need her fortune, and they'd known each other much too long for him to be interested in her romantically.

That thought shouldn't have depressed her as much as it did.

Chapter Nine

Despite her best efforts, Emily couldn't stop thinking about her conversation with Jonah. No matter how hard she tried, her thoughts kept circling back to what it would be like to have Sir Jonah Stanton court her.

He'd woo her with flowers and drives through Hyde Park, but he wouldn't be content to follow the traditional path quite so strictly. He'd find moments to take her aside and kiss her whenever he could. No, not just one kiss but several. Whenever the opportunity presented itself.

Emily had to give her head a sharp shake to keep from getting carried away with her fantasy. Her feelings for Jonah were being muddled by the role he'd played during the ball the night before. And after his teasing that morning, it was becoming difficult to separate fantasy from reality.

It was possible Jonah was also caught up in the same trap. But come spring he'd be over any inclination he might have had to court her.

She made her way to James's study, wanting to thank him properly for agreeing to host the Christmas ball. He might have had ulterior motives, but in the end she'd enjoyed herself tremendously. Perhaps he'd like to go for a ride. It seemed an age since the two of them had gone riding together, and she needed to distract herself from thoughts of Jonah.

She let herself into the study after a quick knock. "It's safe to come out now, James—"

She stopped abruptly when she realized her brother wasn't alone. In fact, he and Sarah were in the midst of a heated embrace.

He spun them around, his broad back shielding his wife so Emily couldn't see what was happening, something for which she was infinitely grateful.

"How many times have I asked you to knock first, Emily?"

Fumbling for the door latch, she let herself back out with a hurried, "I didn't see anything. In fact, I wasn't even here."

She released a shaky chuckle once she'd escaped the room. Well, it appeared James had found another way to celebrate his newfound freedom from unwelcome houseguests.

Never mind—there was always Edward or Grace. Setting out in search of them, she made her way to the library and cautiously opened the door.

And stood frozen in shock for several seconds when she realized Edward was lying over Grace on the settee, his mouth traveling down the column of her throat while his wife let out a little sound that spoke volumes about how much she was enjoying her husband's attentions.

They hadn't noticed her entrance, so when she could move again, Emily closed the door as quietly as possible. She leaned against the wall and closed her eyes, unable to forget that little sound.

More than anything, she wanted the type of relationship her brothers had both found. Maybe she should take Jonah up on his offer and allow him to court her in earnest before he changed his mind.

She decided the safest course of action was to return to the dower house since she was unlikely to run into anyone engaged in a heated embrace there.

Chapter Ten

With the way her day was going, Emily wasn't surprised to find Jonah at the dower house. His mother was staying there, after all, so it made sense he would visit. But she couldn't help wondering if the universe was conspiring against her that morning, going out of its way to dangle before her everything she would never have.

Jonah, who was seated in a comfortable armchair, stood when she entered the morning room, which was her mother's favorite room in the house. She wasn't sure why they called it that since it faced south and was filled with natural light for most of the day. Mama and Mrs. Stanton were sitting together on the settee, both engaged with their needlework.

"We didn't expect you back so soon," her mother said, lowering the square of fabric onto her lap. Mrs. Stanton looked up from her embroidery as Emily moved farther into the room.

"Everyone was busy at the manor." She really didn't want to explain what they'd been so busy doing, so she turned the conversation to them. "What were you discussing? I heard laughter from all the way down the hall."

"Jonah was just telling us about some of the adventures he had while in India." Mrs. Stanton gazed fondly at her son. "He has the most amusing stories—I'd almost forgotten how he could entertain his father and me for hours."

"I'm sure he does," Emily said in reply, grateful for the change in subject.

"What was everyone busy doing?" Jonah asked.

Emily was going to kill him. She turned to meet his questioning gaze and didn't miss the amusement lurking there, as though he knew exactly what was going on at the main house. Now that she thought about it, maybe that was way he'd chosen to visit his mother. "Certainly nothing that required my attention."

She narrowed her eyes slightly, promising retribution if he pursued the current subject. Fortunately, he understood her unspoken threat and didn't say anything further.

"You're welcome to join us," Mama said. "I can call for some tea to help warm you. I know how cold it is out. Thank heavens we won't have to make the trip back and forth to the main house after today."

Emily lowered herself onto the settee next to her mother. From the look on both her and Mrs. Stanton's faces, it was clear they were holding something back.

"Are you going to make me beg, or are you going to tell me what has you both so happy?"

Mama laughed and gave her a pat on the knee. "I never could keep anything from Emily. She's far too adept at reading my expressions."

Emily merely waited, not bothering to comment on what they could all see for themselves. Her mother was terrible at keeping a secret, a trait that Emily knew she shared. Her mother's eyes danced with delight, and it was obvious to everyone that she was excited.

Jonah took his seat again and answered her question. "It appears you're going to be moving to the main house for the week leading up to Christmas."

"I thought it would make a nice change of pace to spend the Christmas season together, especially since Jonah will be there. And I'll admit I'm looking forward to seeing George and William every day."

Somehow Emily kept from bouncing in her seat. She gave her mother a quick hug. "Really? Oh, I must tell my maid what to pack. Although if I forget something, it won't be too onerous a task to fetch it."

When her gaze moved back to Jonah, she noted the fond smile on his face as he took in her excitement. Anticipation shot through her when their eyes met. They were going to be seeing much more of one another in the next week, which would give them both the opportunity to discover whether their pretend courtship could develop into something more.

And in that moment, Emily knew what she had to do. She needed to discover whether she and Jonah were physically compatible. Some might say she was acting with ill-advised haste, but there was only one way to learn what a marriage to Jonah would entail. They were already friends... Could they be more?

Logically she knew she might come to regret her hasty decision, but she'd always trusted her instincts and they'd never led her astray. And the more she got to know him, the more she began to believe that Jonah might be the man she'd been looking for all along.

"Actually, I just remembered that there was something I needed to discuss with *Sir* Jonah."

Jonah raised a brow at the way she emphasized his title. "I am ever at your disposal, Miss Hathaway."

The hint of amusement in his voice reminded her of all the reasons they were good together. They shared a sense of humor, and Jonah understood her in a way many others who'd sought her favor hadn't. Surely it wasn't too much to hope that perhaps they could have more than friendship.

She looked directly at her mother, doing everything in her power to keep her expression impassive.

"This is something we need to discuss in private, Mama."

Her mother gave her a penetrating stare, and for a moment Emily feared she'd be able to read her mind. She forced herself not to look away lest she betray the fact that she had ulterior motives for wanting to have a private conversation with Jonah.

"May I inquire as to the subject of this discussion?"

Emily didn't want to lie to her mother, so she opted for evasion instead. "It's the week before Christmas and I need his assistance with a few matters."

Strictly speaking, both statements were true. Hopefully her mother would think she wanted to talk to Jonah about a Christmas gift for Mrs. Stanton.

Jonah's mother caught Mama's eye, a strange look passing between them, before she turned to her son. "Of course. You and Emily are practically siblings, so I know there won't be anything untoward happening."

Emily tried her best to conceal her displeasure at Mrs. Stanton's characterization of their relationship. Did everyone see them as such? She certainly didn't see him in the same light as her brothers.

Jonah followed her into the hallway. They'd scarce crossed the threshold when he spoke, his voice low so their mothers wouldn't overhear. "I most definitely do not consider you a sister."

Emily's heart soared, and she couldn't hold back her relief. "Well, that's good. I find that two overprotective brothers are more than enough."

She didn't say anything else until they reached the drawing room, which was far enough away from the morning room that they could speak freely. To ensure none of the staff would interrupt them, she pulled the door until it was almost closed.

Jonah stood in the middle of the room, waiting for her to sit. Instead of doing so, she came within a few feet of him and took a deep breath.

"There's a matter I need to discuss with you, but I don't know how you'll take it."

Chapter Eleven

Jonah's thoughts leaped to scenarios too unpleasant to contemplate, the foremost of which was that, despite her protestations to the contrary, her affections were already engaged elsewhere.

"You're secretly betrothed to another."

"What?" Emily's nose scrunched at his statement. "No, of course not. Why would you think that?"

"What else would you have to tell me that I won't like? Unless... Did Kirby return? He didn't press his unwanted attention on you, did he?" He frowned as it occurred to him that perhaps Kirby's courtship wouldn't be quite as unwelcome as she'd led him to believe.

"No, nothing like that. You saw him take his leave. He was already on his way before you disappeared yourself." She tilted her head. "Why didn't you tell me you were planning to visit your mother?"

Jonah didn't know how to reply to that. He wasn't about to tell Emily that he'd shared his desire to court her with their mothers, who'd both been delighted by the news. He wasn't quite ready to share that information with James or Edward—not until he knew whether Emily reciprocated his feelings—but he'd wanted their mothers' support. He needed to approach this with care, for it had suddenly become far too important to him that Emily see him as more than just an old family friend. Or as a brother.

"Why don't you tell me what you wanted to say before I jump to any more conclusions? I assure you, my imagination can be very fruitful."

He'd hoped to elicit a laugh from her, but instead Emily gave a sigh and looked away. He waited, resisting the urge to press her.

"Has Edward told you about his courtship of Grace?"

Now she had him truly confused. He could in no way imagine how her brother's relationship with his wife had anything to do with him or Emily.

"I know they met when he was delivering a letter to her written by a friend who passed away at the end of the war."

She examined him closely for several seconds. "Nothing beyond that?"

"No, of course not. Edward is hardly the type to share the details of his relationship. I do know, however, that he cares for her a great deal."

Emily sighed. "He does. And James also loves Sarah."

He remembered her Christmas wish that she also find love and felt a pang when he realized he wanted that as well. He'd told her he didn't know what he wanted for Christmas, but that was no longer true. He wanted Emily.

He didn't reply and Emily continued.

"Sarah didn't want to wed James. Their union was agreed to by her father, and for reasons she's never shared with me, she agreed to it. But she'd imagined herself in love with someone else at the time."

He winced, imagining the disappointment that knowledge must have cost James. "But they moved beyond that."

"Yes. But they were lucky."

"Many find happiness with their spouses when presented with similar circumstances."

"Yes, and many despise one another, while others merely tolerate their husband or wife."

"What do you know of such marriages? I was under the impression your parents were happy as well."

"They were," Emily said with a sigh.

She sank onto the settee, and Jonah hesitated only a moment before taking a seat in one of the armchairs. He wanted to sit next to her, but it was too soon for that.

"What is bothering you?"

He'd almost asked her if she was worried about his declaration that he wanted to court her, but something held him back. Was it possible the beautiful, lively young woman seated before him felt none of the same emotions currently plaguing him? Was she trying to convince herself that a practical union with him would be enough? While he'd expected to enter into such an arrangement when it came time to wed, he found that was the last thing he wanted with Emily. Still, the knowledge that James and Sarah's love had come after they'd wed gave him some hope.

"During my time in London, I've seen too many people who are unhappy in their marriages. Sarah has pointed out to me every married woman who has approached James about engaging in an affair. He never would, of course—he turns them down and has told Sarah whenever it happens—but his unavailability seems to make him all the more attractive in their eyes."

Well, good for James that he could share that information with his wife. It went a long way toward confirming that his friend had chosen well in his marriage despite their unsteady beginnings.

"It happens, but that's not the type of marriage I want either. My own parents were happy together before my father's death."

Emily's gaze softened as she gazed at him, and he had to hold back his desire to bridge the distance between them and kiss her. Before he could do anything, she had to tell him why she needed to speak to him in private.

"James and Sarah were very fortunate, but I'm not willing to risk my future happiness on luck."

"Not even if you consider your future spouse a friend? Surely that weighs the odds more favorably."

Emily shook her head, and Jonah felt that denial like a blow. Still, the battle for Emily's heart wasn't over yet, and he refused to concede before he'd even entered the fray.

"I think Grace had the right of it."

She stood and he followed suit, gazing at her with confusion as she crossed to the door. For a moment he thought she was going to leave without telling him the reason for this conversation.

Emily opened the door slightly, and he realized she was checking to make sure no one was present to overhear what she was going to say.

"And what was this idea of hers?"

Emily approached him, but this time she didn't sit. "She and Edward had a tryst before they were wed."

Jonah's heart began to race as he realized what she was suggesting. Still, he wasn't going to assume. He wanted—no, he *needed*—to hear her say it.

"Go on."

"I think we should do the same, you and me. That way we'll know if a future marriage between us has the potential to be as happy as what my brothers have found."

His heart screamed yes at the suggestion, but his head cautioned him otherwise. If he hadn't missed his guess, Emily was a maiden. What if their first time together was filled with more pain than pleasure? It was entirely possible she'd renounce him completely if that happened.

He also knew that her brothers wouldn't be pleased with Emily's plan if they learned of it.

"And how exactly would we enact this plan of yours?"

Emily waved a hand. "That's simple enough. The manor house is quite large. I'm sure we could find a quiet corner. Or we could come here since Mama and Mrs. Stanton won't be in residence."

He wanted to agree, but still he hesitated.

Emily took a step closer. "I need to know if we can find the same happiness in our own marriage. Given how happy James and Edward are, I don't want to settle for mere friendship. I like you, Jonah, a great deal. I believe we have a chance at happiness together, but I need to be certain."

Jonah didn't really want to fight her on this anymore, not when it was what he wanted too. "Your brothers are going to kill me. I foresee that I won't live to see our wedding day if we go through with this plan of yours."

"You'll do it?" Emily's eyes lit up.

"Was there ever any doubt?"

"There was some doubt." Emily looked away for a moment before meeting his gaze again and continuing. "I feared you might have been teasing me earlier when you said you wanted to court me."

He smiled down at her. "I would never tease about something like that. What would be the point?"

"It was such a surprise. And, well, I found I liked the idea more than I thought wise. Thank you, Jonah."

She reached up to place a hand on his arm but stopped short. Her uncharacteristic awkwardness had him reaching out to take her hand in his. As he dropped a kiss on the back of her hand, he noticed she'd removed her gloves and remembered that another man had made the same gesture earlier that morning. He took heart from the fact she didn't remove her hand from his and enjoyed the feel of her skin under his own.

Emily gave her head a small shake. "I don't know what to say now. I hadn't planned this far ahead."

"Well," Jonah said, running his thumb along the back of her hand and taking pleasure in the way she shivered at the contact, "I think I can take it from here."

"I'd like that," she said with an eagerness that touched him deeply.

"I'm going to show you exactly what you've been missing, Emily Hathaway. But first you must agree to my suit in earnest."

Emily tilted her head to the side. She glanced at him from under her lashes. "That depends on what you show me, doesn't it?"

Jonah gave her hand a sharp tug, and with a small squeak of surprise, Emily fell against him. "Should we seal our pact with a kiss?"

Emily searched his expression before giving a wordless nod.

Jonah needed no further encouragement and lowered his mouth to hers. He still held her hand in his as he tried to keep from advancing too quickly, too soon. His mouth moved softly against hers, but he couldn't hold back his groan when she threaded the fingers of her other hand in the hair at his nape.

He didn't even realize he'd thrust his tongue into her mouth until he heard her small gasp of surprise. He tried to pull back, but then she was returning his kiss in earnest. He released her hand and brought her body flush against his as he explored her mouth. He fought the urge to take their embrace further, and it was with great reluctance that he slowed the kiss and stepped back.

Emily's breathing was as shaky as his when she looked up at him, wonder in her expression. "In the interest of full honesty, I should tell you that wasn't my first kiss. But it was by far the best."

He said nothing in reply, not wanting to ruin the priceless moment by calling attention to his own past experiences. But he realized the same was also true for him.

Chapter Twelve

Emily's maid was pinning her hair up with quick, efficient movements when her two sisters-in-law entered her bedroom.

"Am I late?" Emily asked.

Tonight was to be their first dinner together, just the Hathaways, Jonah, and Mrs. Stanton. She couldn't help thinking that if things went well between her and Jonah, they'd soon be one large family.

Grace shook her head. "No, we're a little early. Although the men have already gone downstairs."

While they waited for the maid to finish, the two women perched on the edge of her bed and chatted about how it was infinitely more difficult to host a house party than to be a guest.

Her maid tucked the last few pins in her hair and took her leave. When Emily turned in her seat at the dressing table, she saw that Sarah and Grace were looking at her with great interest. She had to hold back her sigh.

Hoping to forestall further speculation on their part, she said, "No, I will not be encouraging Lord Kirby."

Sarah tilted her head to one side, her gaze sharp. "Forget about Lord Kirby. I know James wants to see you settled with someone solid, but to him that means boring. Lord Kirby would smother the very life from you."

Why did everyone think they knew her so well? "Perhaps I'd liven him up, make him more outgoing."

"Perhaps," Grace said. "But it's been my observation that men rarely change once they've reached adulthood."

Grace met Sarah's gaze. The two of them had a plan in mind, and she was almost afraid to find out what it was.

"Perhaps we should go down—" Emily started.

Sarah continued as though she hadn't spoken. "How do you feel about Sir Jonah?"

Grace nodded in agreement. "We know you've been acquainted with him since you were a child, but he's been away for so long. Edward thinks you consider him a brother, but perhaps there could be something more?"

Emily sighed. These two were relentless in their desire to find her a husband. She knew their meddling came from a place of love though and couldn't be angry with them. And if she was being completely honest, she wanted to share her secret with them. But she couldn't tell them what she was planning. They wouldn't tell her brothers if she asked them not to, but she was loath to ask them to do something that would anger their husbands.

"I'll consider it." She laughed when she saw the twin expressions of disbelief on both Sarah's and Grace's faces. "Come, let's not keep everyone waiting."

"You can't just say that and leave," Sarah said following her to the bedroom door.

Grace was right behind her. "I never realized before today that you have a mean streak. Surely you're going to tell us more."

"I'll tell you more when there's more to say." That wasn't strictly true, but Emily didn't know what to think about the current situation herself. How could she talk about her feelings when they confused her so much?

She'd relived her conversation—and kiss—with Jonah over and over in her mind. But before she shared any details with the two women who'd come to mean so much to her, she needed to explore her newfound feelings. Given her lack of luck when it came to finding love, she was afraid speaking of them would somehow jinx her and Jonah's relationship before it even started.

The three of them entered the drawing room together to find everyone else already present. The men were standing by the fireplace, discussing something in low, earnest tones while Mama and Mrs. Stanton sat on the settee, equally engrossed in conversation.

It took all of Emily's self-restraint not to stare at Jonah lest she betray her interest to the other occupants of the room. James had already cornered her before she'd gone upstairs to change for dinner to ask her how she felt about Lord Kirby. He hadn't been surprised when she replied that he seemed pleasant enough and that she was sure he'd make some *other* woman a fine husband. The last thing she wanted was to draw his attention to a potential alliance with the man who'd remained behind.

She wondered if it had ever occurred to James to consider a match between her and Jonah. They'd been friends for most of their lives since the Stantons' estate bordered their former home in Newmarket. She was so much younger than Jonah and couldn't be considered a contemporary, not with an eight-year age gap between them. But what seemed unthinkable at ten and eighteen would scarcely be considered much of a difference now that they were twenty and twenty-eight.

Despite Emily's attempt to appear casual in his presence, it was impossible to ignore how handsome Jonah looked. He was slightly taller than her brothers, and of the three anyone would agree he was the most handsome. He was dressed in deep blue, and it occurred to her that since she also wore blue, they matched.

She watched her brothers move to greet their wives, telling them how beautiful they looked. Really, you'd think they hadn't seen one another in a month, but Emily knew what they'd been up to earlier in the day after the last guest had departed.

Emily wanted that type of relationship so much it almost hurt.

She was so taken by the display of marital affection displayed before her that she didn't notice Jonah approaching until he was standing next to her.

"How is it possible that you grow more beautiful each time I see you?"

His voice was low, for her ears only, and Emily felt her heart skip. She would have thought he was teasing her—poking fun at the display her brothers were giving them—but the intensity of his expression told her otherwise. She hadn't forgotten he'd called her beautiful and wasn't ashamed to admit she'd dressed to capture his attention, the bodice of her dress lower than what she normally wore.

She gave a slight curtsy, trying to hide the effect his words had on her. "Thank you, kind sir." She was about to pay him a compliment as well, but she became aware of other eyes on them and chose to remain silent.

"It is so good to have everyone gone." The relief in James's voice was almost comical. "I haven't been able to enjoy a meal properly in days."

Sarah wound her arm through her husband's. "Not even when you snuck away and locked yourself in your study? I'm sure I saw at least one of the footmen bring you some food."

Emily tilted her head, the picture of innocence, and asked, "Was there anyone here who *didn't* expect that to happen?"

James replied with a shrug. "I may have agreed to host the thing, but I never said I'd dance attendance on the guests every hour of the day. That's why the rest of you were here."

"Well, for once, I actually agree with my brother." Emily gave an exaggerated shudder. "I thought Lord Kirby was going to call out poor Jonah."

"Whose idea was that?" Edward asked. "To have Jonah pretend to be a suitor?"

Emily felt a twinge of annoyance at the unvoiced implication that Jonah would never be interested in her but ignored it. It *had* started as pretend after all.

Jonah replied for her. "It was Emily's, of course."

She shrugged. "You can hardly blame me."

James expelled a breath, but in the end he gave her a nod. "*Touché.* You cleverly outmaneuvered us all."

He cast a speculative glance at Jonah, and Emily held her breath, wondering if he suspected there was something more than pretense behind their actions. Fortunately, the dinner bell rang and he turned away from them to lead his wife from the room.

Jonah leaned down and said softly, "I hope you don't mind that I'm going to escort my mother in."

"Oh no, of course not. We don't want to risk everyone asking questions if you didn't."

"I'm not going to keep my interest in you a secret forever, Emily."

She knew that if anyone was watching them now, the soft smile she gave him would betray her growing feelings for him. "We'll discover very soon if there's something real between us."

Jonah looked as though he wanted to argue, but instead he gave a small nod and started to turn away.

Emily hesitated but decided it was better to be seen handing Jonah a note than to be caught passing him one in secret. James and Edward had already led their wives from the room, and before Jonah could reach his mother's side, she called his name.

He turned back to her, one brow raised.

"I wanted to give you that list I promised you."

She took a small, folded note from where she'd stashed it in the palm of her glove and handed it to Jonah. To his credit, he said nothing, simply tucking the note in an inner pocket of his tailcoat.

"What was that?" Mrs. Stanton asked as she placed a hand on her son's arm.

"Emily's playing matchmaker. She knows I'll be in London in the spring," he said before leading his mother from the room.

He hadn't lied, she'd give Jonah that. But the note she'd given him had nothing to do with his search for a bride, containing instead the location where they'd meet later that night.

It was just her and Mama alone in the room. Emily had started to follow the others when her mother laid a hand on her arm. And just like that, she knew her mother hadn't been fooled.

"I trust you and Jonah, but please be careful."

Emily stared at her for several seconds, then nodded silently in reply. Arranging what she'd hoped would be a secret encounter with Jonah was hardly a topic she wanted to discuss with her mother, after all.

When she entered the dining room, her gaze met Jonah's. She said nothing when the footman pulled out the empty seat next to him, and she found herself wondering if everyone realized there was something more than friendship between the two of them.

Her gaze swept over the group. She believed every woman present knew, or at least suspected. She was certain James had no idea, and Edward was an enigma. But when the younger of her two brothers gave her a half smile that told her he was vastly amused and looked to Jonah, then her, she almost groaned aloud.

Hoping to draw attention away from her and Jonah, she turned to James as the footmen began serving the soup. "What were the three of you discussing when we came down to dinner? It seemed serious."

James's brows drew into a frown. "I think we're going to have to sell the old stables."

Mama gasped, and Emily felt a small pang of loss. Papa had established those stables, and they'd always been a part of their lives. But when her brother inherited and moved to Northampton four years before, he'd moved their primary horse-breeding establishment here. He and Edward ran it together, with the latter taking control when James was too busy with estate matters. They'd kept the old stables running, however, with help.

"Fraser feels he's getting too old to run the Newmarket stables," Edward said. "He plans to retire soon, and we can't run it ourselves. Frankly, we're loath to trust it to someone we don't know. It would be better to sell it outright while it's still successful."

"Your father loved those stables." Mama's voice was so small. She wouldn't berate her brothers for their decision since she trusted their judgment, but it was clear she was disappointed.

"I might know someone who can run the stables for you."

All eyes turned to Jonah.

"Well, don't keep it a secret," James said.

Jonah chuckled. "Me."

Emily felt her heart give a small leap. Jonah had said he wasn't planning to return to India, and while she'd wanted to believe him, she realized a part of her had been unsure about his commitment to remaining in England. He'd been actively involved in trade for the past ten years and wasn't the type of man to enjoy a life of idle leisure.

But if he helped run one of their stables, that would keep him engaged. It also meant she wouldn't have to worry about leaving England if they wed. Emily hadn't even realized a small part of her had worried about that happening until it was no longer a concern.

Her gaze swung to James and Edward. They were looking at each other, smiles tugging at the corners of their mouths.

"It's been many years since you used to visit us at the stables and help out," Edward said.

"But you always did have a knack for handling horses," James added.

Emily was almost bouncing in her seat. "And his work for the past few years means he has experience running a business."

James's eyes narrowed at Emily's staunch endorsement of his old friend. Fortunately, Jonah's next statement distracted him.

"I'd be willing to purchase the stables outright, but we all know the Hathaway name has undeniable weight when it comes to the business of breeding and raising horses."

Emily watched as her brothers looked at one another again. She had no idea how they did it, but they'd always been able to communicate with few—or even no—words. When she glanced at Jonah again, his expression betrayed no doubt. He already knew how this would go.

It was Edward who broke the silence. "James and I will discuss the details with you after dinner, but I think we can come to an agreement."

Jonah's eyes flickered to hers before he looked away, but in the second their gazes had met, she could see their entire future.

Chapter Thirteen

Jonah glanced down at the note Emily had given him one final time to ensure he'd memorized its contents before tossing it into the fireplace. He watched the edges of the paper begin to darken and curl before it caught flame. When it was nothing but ashes, he stooped to bank the fire.

He left his bedroom and started along the route Emily had laid out for him. Given how protective her brothers were, he wasn't surprised she'd thought of everything. His route would take him near the kitchen, giving him an excuse if he should run into anyone since he could always claim he'd lost his way in a quest for something to eat.

Just before reaching the stairs that led down to the kitchen and servants' quarters, he veered left down another hallway, his goal the last room on the right. He hadn't been in this wing of the house before, and he suspected it was normally kept closed.

He was surprised when he opened the door and found he was in what appeared to be a storage room filled with bedroom furniture. Old, ornate furniture that was heavily covered in gilt.

He closed the door and when he turned around, Emily popped out from behind a wardrobe. She was a vision. Her dark hair was down, but she still wore the blue dress she'd donned for dinner. He turned back to the door and locked it.

"Where are we?"

Emily closed the distance between them. "This was the furniture in James's bedroom when he first moved in. You should have seen the house. There was gold everywhere. I imagine it would have rivaled the palace of Versailles."

Jonah could imagine how his friend had taken that. He wasn't one to swan about, and he would have hated the ostentation Emily described.

"You made sure you weren't followed?"

Jonah reached for her hand and drew her close. "No one saw me. And if they did, they probably thought I was heading to the kitchen for some food. Although given how much we ate over dinner, they would have to think I possess a bottomless pit for a stomach."

Emily's mouth twisted into a delightful little pout at his teasing. "It was the only thing I could think of to ensure we weren't discovered."

"Speaking of which… Were you hoping to get me killed by passing me that note in front of our mothers? What if one of them said something to your brothers?"

Emily hesitated, a hint of worry creeping into her eyes. "I think everyone knows about us. Everyone except James, that is. I believe even Edward suspects, but I can't be certain."

He resisted the urge to jump back and place some distance between them. "About tonight?" He could just imagine the chaos that would ensue if her brothers decided to break down the door he'd just locked. He could hold his own against James or Edward, but against the two of them together? It was too gruesome to think about. "Maybe we should postpone our little experiment. I can still ask James for permission to court you properly first."

She tried to draw her hand back, but he didn't release it. "You don't have to stay if you don't want to."

"I haven't changed my mind, Emily. I just don't want you to be forced into something you don't want. I don't care if the entire household storms through that door and demands we wed tomorrow, but I know that isn't what you want."

He took a deep breath when she closed the distance between them and pressed her body against his. His hands settled on her waist, and he reveled in the anticipation that surged through him when she grasped his upper arms.

"I wanted to tell you earlier how handsome you looked, but I didn't want to attract more speculation. But I must say, I enjoy seeing you in just your shirt and waistcoat." Her hands roamed up and down his arms while her eyes remained on his. "You're very muscular. I find that I like that."

Jonah was done with words. He claimed her lips in a kiss that rivaled the heat of the one they'd shared earlier. Emily's arms went around his neck as she threw herself into the embrace.

His palms itched with the need to draw up her skirts, but first he needed to know just how much restraint he should show.

He broke their kiss. She followed the backward movement of his head, trying to keep their mouths pressed together, but he had the advantage of height on his side.

"I don't want to stop," Emily said, her breathing ragged.

Jonah was powerless to deny her. "I have no intention of stopping, but I need to know... Have you made this offer to other men?"

A little *V* formed between her brows. "And if I have? Would that be enough to make you change your mind about me?"

He dropped a quick kiss onto her forehead, hoping to erase that crease. "That would be the height of hypocrisy on my part. I don't care if I'm your first as long as I'm your last. But I do need to know whether I should be careful. Often there's pain the first time a man lies with a woman, and I would spare you as much of that as possible."

Emily raised a hand to his cheek and met his eyes, a slow smile blossoming on her face. "I haven't lain with anyone else—I haven't wanted to before you. You'll be my first and hopefully my last."

Jonah closed his eyes for a moment. It turned out he was a hypocrite after all, for her admission pleased him more than it should.

He nodded toward the bed that was jammed into the corner of the room. From the haphazard piles of objects strewn on the floor next to it, he imagined Emily must have cleared the surface of the bed before he arrived. "Do you think that will hold our weight? It looks very insubstantial."

Emily lifted one shoulder. "I have no idea. Want to test our luck?"

James laughed. "I'm feeling like the luckiest man in the world right now."

Emily squeaked, then clapped one hand over her mouth when he lifted her into his arms and tossed her onto the bed.

Chapter Fourteen

Expectation rose within her when Jonah followed her onto the bed. Emily inched backward, making room for him. She'd thought she'd be filled with nerves when this moment finally arrived, but instead she felt nothing but anticipation. The way Jonah stared down at her as he braced himself over her on his elbows set her heart racing.

She'd seen similar looks on other men's faces, and now she knew what the expression was... desire. Perhaps Jonah had been correct when he told her that other men wanted her for more than just her dowry. But that knowledge changed nothing, because there was only one man she wanted, and he was here with her right now.

She reached for him the same moment he lowered his head. This time he moved with care, his mouth exploring hers slowly, but somehow that only made her want him more. When he settled the length of his body over hers, most of his weight braced on one arm bent by her head, a delicious heat consumed her.

This was what she wanted, what she needed. This surfeit of emotion and sensation that threatened to overwhelm her. She'd never imagined Jonah would be the man to call it forth. She'd always liked him, but now she felt so much more.

She needed to let him know.

When he moved to kiss along her throat, she was surprised at how good it felt to have his lips pressed there. She'd never realized just how sensitive her neck could be.

Somehow she managed to speak. "We don't have to do this."

He lifted his head and looked down at her. She didn't miss the way he lifted his body so it was no longer pressed against hers, and she wanted to weep at the loss.

"Have you changed your mind?"

She shook her head. "No, I find that I want to continue more than I'd thought possible."

He searched her eyes, trying to decipher the truth behind her words. "Then why do you want to stop? If you're not ready—"

"No, it's not that. I need to tell you something first."

He shifted so he was lying on his side next to her, leaning on one arm. The other rested on her hip as though he too needed to maintain that connection with her. He said nothing, waiting for her to continue.

She shifted onto her side so they were now facing one another and brought her hand up to his face. Running her fingers along his jaw, she marveled at how Jonah was now so dear to her. "I've been very picky when it comes to men because I wanted to ensure I had the same type of marriage as my siblings found."

Jonah shifted his head and pressed a kiss in her palm. "Something for which I am infinitely grateful."

She smiled as she ran a thumb over his lower lip. "I approached this as a sort of test, but I've realized I don't need it. I know you're the only man for me."

He captured her hand and rolled so he was over her again. His gaze was intense as he stared down at her. "I love you, Emily Hathaway. But please don't tell me I have to stop now and ask for permission to court you first."

Emily didn't hold back her delighted laughter. She knew Jonah would wait if she asked him to, but that was the last thing she wanted.

"I love you too, Sir Jonah. Now please compromise me so my family will have no choice but to agree to your suit."

Neither of them believed that would be necessary. Her brothers were protective, yes, but they liked Jonah a great deal. Still, if that lie was needed to overcome any qualms he might have about continuing, she'd tell it again and again.

He answered with a smile that could only be called wicked, one that had all her senses on high alert.

"Your wish is my command," he said before kissing her again.

They continued to kiss, and she had to concentrate to undo the buttons of his waistcoat. When she succeeded in tugging open the material, she made a small sound of satisfaction and placed her hand on his chest over the lawn shirt. That sound turned into a surprised moan when she realized he'd used the hand on her hip to inch up her skirts.

He drew back and slid his hand along her outer thigh. "Are you fine with this?"

In reply, she tugged his shirt from his trousers. When she burrowed underneath and ran her fingers over his abdomen, he let out a small hiss.

"I'm going to take that as a yes."

He rose onto his haunches, and Emily watched with wonder as he removed his waistcoat and dragged his shirt over his head before tossing both garments onto the floor. When he lowered himself over her again, she took great satisfaction in running her hands over the exposed skin. He was harder than she'd expected, and his skin gave off enough heat to compensate for the lack of a lit fire in the room.

She stiffened in surprise when he moved his hand to her inner thigh but then forced herself to relax. She wanted this, after all. It was normal to be a little nervous about what was to come, but she most definitely did not want to stop.

She wasn't wearing any smallclothes, which Jonah clearly liked from the look of surprised wonder on his face.

She yelped in surprise when he rolled them over again so she was lying on top of him. He used his legs to spread hers farther apart, and she didn't resist. When his mouth clasped the peak of her breast through her dress, a bolt of pure sensation streaked through her. It only intensified when he moved his hand between her legs.

"Jonah..." His name was a long, low moan on her lips. When she thought about the intimacies that took place between a man and a woman, she'd expected to feel embarrassment, but instead she felt only eagerness to experience more.

His touch was pure magic, and the pull of his mouth on first one breast then the other had her making sounds that were decidedly unladylike. She allowed herself to sink into the world of sensation she was experiencing through Jonah's touch. There would be time later for her to bring him to equal heights, after he showed her what to do.

Once she stopped worrying about what she should be doing, it took little time for her to reach crisis. One pure, unexpected moment where all thoughts left her and she could only feel.

When she called out his name, it was louder than she'd expected, but Jonah covered her lips and silenced her cry of pleasure.

His movements slowed and she sagged on top of him, her head on his chest and her breathing ragged. It took her a minute before she found her voice. "I can see now what all the fuss is about."

Jonah chuckled, but the sound was cut off with a strangled moan when she reached down and cupped his manhood. She was shocked at how hard he was.

Jonah dropped a kiss atop her head. "I'd ask you if you want to stop now, but I'm afraid you'll say yes."

She lifted her head to meet his gaze. "I don't want to stop. I want to experience everything with you."

He shifted their positions so he was over her again. "Good." His brows drew together. "This might hurt at first."

"I know." But given how much Sarah and Grace seemed to enjoy their husbands' company, she also knew that it would pass. If not tonight, then the next time they were together.

She'd worn a dress with a low bodice and a half corset, thinking only to entice Jonah. It hadn't occurred to her that it would take just a quick tug for him to expose her breasts before he captured one peak in his mouth again. The feel of his warm, silken mouth on the bare skin of her breast was infinitely better than when he'd teased her through the fabric of her dress.

She was determined to give him as much pleasure as he was showing her. Her fingers had gone to his hair, where they combed through the thick sandy-brown strands. Needing to touch every inch of him she could reach, she lowered her hands first to his shoulders, then stroked the heated skin of his upper back. When he lifted his head and began to kiss her again, she was able to reach his waist and she dipped her hands beneath the fabric that still covered his hips.

He groaned and tore his mouth from hers. "I'm not sure how much longer I can wait."

"I'm ready now, Jonah."

He searched her face as if to assure himself she wasn't just saying the words to give him what he wanted. In response, she started to unbutton the fall of his trousers. He remained unnaturally still, as though he were afraid to move, but when she reached to encircle his manhood with her hand, he let out his breath with a stuttering exhale.

Jonah took over then, positioning her legs so he could brush his hardness against her folds. Then he moved forward, entering her with great care.

She'd expected pain, but she was so slick with desire it didn't hurt beyond the initial pinch at his invasion. Still, Jonah stopped his movements and gave her time to adjust to him, concentrating again on kissing her. Emily would never tire of the feel of his mouth against hers, but soon the ache where they were joined had her lifting her legs to encircle his hips. A spark where Jonah had touched her earlier had her gasping in pleasure, and she started to thrust her hips against him, chasing the earlier sensations.

He gazed down at her, one corner of his mouth tilted upward. "I take it this isn't unbearably painful for you?"

From the tight set of his jaw, Emily guessed that his determination to be careful was costing him dearly and her heart expanded.

"Is this all there is?"

In response, Jonah pulled out and then moved back in. The smooth glide of his body within hers had her releasing a small "ooh" of surprise and delight.

There were no words after that. When Emily reached her second peak, she stifled her moans against his shoulder. Jonah gave a small grunt and pulled out of her, spilling onto the sheets. She knew it was prudent, but a small part of her could hardly wait until they wouldn't need to worry about preventing a pregnancy.

Jonah rolled to one side and took Emily with him. They lay together, the only sound that of their mixed breaths for several minutes.

It was Jonah who broke the silence. "How soon do you think we can wed? After all, once I declare my intentions, James will no doubt have a footman guarding you. We might not get another opportunity to be alone together."

Emily laid a hand along his cheek, savoring the knowledge that when the day of their wedding arrived, she'd be able to touch him whenever she wanted. "Then we should make proper use of tonight."

His smile was wicked. "I like the way you think, Miss Hathaway."

Epilogue

No longer content to hide his feelings, Jonah asked James for permission to court her the day after their tryst. They wouldn't need her brother's blessing once she turned twenty-one in the spring, but they both wanted it anyway.

Once James granted it, Emily took great joy in being able to show her affection openly. But Jonah had been correct when he said her brother would have someone watching him like a hawk at all times to ensure he didn't overstep the bounds of propriety with her. Fortunately, she'd earned the affection of most of the household staff, and they were willing to look the other way when she and Jonah wanted to be alone together for brief periods of time. It also helped that Sarah was more than willing to distract her husband.

At Jonah's insistence, they didn't make love again. He wanted to wait until they were wed, and Emily was currently in negotiations with her family about how soon she and Jonah could marry without stirring gossip about unseemly haste.

It was Christmas morning, and Emily's patience was starting to wear thin. She managed to grab a seat next to Jonah in the breakfast room, where they'd all gathered before they would go into the drawing room to open their gifts. James's brows drew together when Jonah reached for her hand, which was resting on the table next to her plate. She was relieved when her brother didn't say anything.

"What do you think about a March wedding?" Sarah didn't look up from the task of buttering her toast.

Emily's heart leaped. Her preference was for Jonah to fetch a special license so they could be wed soon, but she realized that wasn't going to happen. And calling the banns over the next three weeks had also been vetoed. Fortunately, March wasn't so far away.

"I don't see why we need to rush." James's voice was a petulant grumble, suggesting he and Sarah had argued about the matter and he'd lost.

Emily frowned. "First you wanted to throw me at Lord Kirby, a stranger, and now you have reservations about my marrying someone you know, whom you respect and call a friend?"

James had the courtesy to look abashed at her rebuke. "I have no reservations about Jonah. It's just difficult for me to think of you as a grown woman who will be leaving us soon."

"The distance between Newmarket and Northampton isn't that far," Jonah said. "Besides, we're also going to be business partners, and I've always found it preferable to conduct business in person rather than relying solely on correspondence. Have no fear, James. We'll be here so often you'll soon tire of seeing my face."

James made a small harrumph. "That's a gruesome thought."

Everyone broke into laughter since they all knew that of the three men present, Jonah was the only one whose features could be considered classically handsome.

Jonah squeezed her hand and she met his gaze. "It's only three months."

Emily released a soft breath. "I've never been very patient. But I've already waited three endless seasons to find the love of my life. What's three more months?"

She knew the smile she gave Jonah would be considered overly sentimental, but she didn't care because she meant every word.

"With that settled, we should head into the drawing room," Sarah said. "I'll go collect the boys so we can open presents. I'm sure they're driving their nurse crazy."

"Well, I already have my gift," Edward said. All eyes turned to him as he dropped a kiss on the back of his wife's hand. "Grace and I are expecting our first child."

Emily leaped from her chair to congratulate her brother and his wife but had to wait her turn to offer them each a hug since the other women had done the same.

They were making their way to the drawing room—minus Sarah, who'd gone up to the nursery—when Mrs. Stanton spoke. "Perhaps by next Christmas Emily will be able to give me a grandchild as well."

That was all it took for James to position himself between her and Jonah. "Just make sure there are no surprises before then," he said with a low growl.

Emily couldn't hold back her laughter, and soon everyone else was joining in.

When Sarah returned with her two nephews several minutes later, Emily found her heart was full. Jonah had already fulfilled her Christmas wish. Anything else she received that day would pale in comparison.

The End

About Suzanna

Suzanna Medeiros was born and raised in Toronto, Canada. Her love for the written word led her to pursue a degree in English Literature from the University of Toronto. She went on to earn a Bachelor of Education degree, but graduated at a time when no teaching jobs were available. After working at a number of interesting places, including a federal inquiry, a youth probation office, and the Office of the Fire Marshal of Ontario, she decided to pursue her first love—writing.

Suzanna is married to her own hero and is the proud mother of twin daughters. She is an avowed romantic who enjoys spending her days writing love stories.

She would like to thank her parents for showing her that love at first sight and happily ever after really do exist.

You can find details of her work at
www.SuzannaMedeiros.com

The Earl from Christmas Past

BY

Wendy Vella

Gabriel, Lord Lockhart, is shocked by the woman his childhood friend has become. Distant and aloof, Maddie's beguiling beauty remains, but she is nothing like the mouthy hellion he remembers. That is until the day he finds her on a dirty street in one of the seediest areas in London, championing children.

He soon realizes how wrong he's been about her, and that his long-buried feelings for her have reignited into something even more powerful. Now all he has to do is keep her safe!

Miss Madeline Spencer loathes society, but has promised her parents she will behave so she can keep her freedom. Everything is going to plan until Gabe stomps back into her life. He uncovers her secret, and demands she stop taking risks. She soon realizes that the gentle boy she once loved is now a passionate man with an iron will. But she can't allow him to deter her from what must be done. Even if it means she can't be with the man she loves.

Chapter One

"Oh, this cannot be good."

Gabriel, the Earl of Lockhart, heard the muttered words as he approached Lord Haswell's study.

"Not good at all... in fact, terrible. If I was to compare this moment to a food, it would be jellied eel."

Gabriel knew who that voice belonged to. Looking in the room, however, he couldn't see her. He stepped inside, letting the light from the wall sconce behind him cast its glow.

"Jellied eel, and quite possibly gruel also. Why anyone would eat either willingly is beyond me."

He cleared his throat, and the muttering stopped. A head popped up from behind the large oak desk. It was quickly followed by a body, and he found himself facing Miss Madeline Spencer. Society darling. Cherished youngest daughter of Viscount Spencer, and one of the most annoying women Gabe knew.

Once they'd been childhood friends; now they were mere acquaintances, and not very good ones at that.

"Gabe.... L-Lord Lockhart?"

Her beauty reached out and hit a man square in the face. Her hair, which was the color of burnished gold, was thick and long when released from whatever elaborate creation it was pinned into most evenings. Gabe knew this because when they were children it was often loose, the morning's ribbons consigned to nature, and by day's end it was usually tousled with hay, dirt, and leaves. Her mother had been forever scolding her for her hoydenish ways.

He'd very much liked the young version of the woman who stood before him. This one, however, was silly. She giggled a great deal and appeared to have little to say that was worth listening to.

Most evenings she wore demure gowns that were anything but demure on her body. The woman was a walking siren, and Gabe hated that he was not immune to the pull of her beauty. Hated it even more considering their history.

Men stared at her constantly, and many had offered for her hand. This he knew as their mothers were close friends. She had accepted none of the requests thus far, and he believed this was because only a marquess or duke would do. Madeline, in his opinion, was waiting for the wealth and status that she believed she deserved.

"What are you doing in here, Gabriel?"

"I think the more important question is, what are you doing here, Madeline?"

"I-I asked first." Her voice had lost its usual melodious tone and sounded high-pitched and panicky.

A memory of her saying just those words slipped through Gabe's head. He dismissed it. This woman was as different as night was to day from the child he'd known.

She'd always hated jellied eel, however.

"I was just taking a walk. Now, tell me why you are here alone in this study, muttering about jellied eel and gruel, Madeline?"

Now he thought about it, that was extremely odd. She was usually surrounded by her minions, who hung on her every word. Even if many had already left to spend the festive season with their families at estates across England, there must be some still in London.

It was nauseating how infatuated both women and men were with Madeline. She'd once loathed how her elder sister behaved, the perfect society miss, and yet now she was an exact replica.

"Ah... well, I am lost." She said the last four words in a rush. They were a lie. Gabe knew this, as her head tilted slightly to the right. She'd always done that.

"I find it hard to believe you would get lost in a house you have frequented before, Madeline. I think you're lying to me."

It was cold in there, and he could see she was shivering. December in London could reach low temperatures, and a flimsy gown would provide little protection. White, with silver threaded through the hem and bodice, it floated around her lush curves and made her look like an angel... an extremely annoying one.

"I came here so long ago." She waved a hand about in a vague manner. "But enough of that. How is your dear mother? I have not seen her in weeks."

"So long ago?" he said, ignoring her question. "Surely you came to the performance by Lyndovsky at the beginning of the season? The violinist," he added, in case she'd forgotten who he was.

"Ah yes, of course. I had forgotten about that." She giggled inanely, which made him want to gnash his teeth. *Brainless twit.* He'd once had great hopes for this woman. Once, he'd even wondered if she would be his wife one day.

"What's going on, Madeline?"

She started, looked over his left shoulder at the door.

"Madeline, is there a problem you wish help with?" Reluctant as he was to utter those words, he was a gentleman and his mother would likely be furious with him if he did not offer to assist her. "Have you broken a shoe ribbon or torn a hem?" His sigh was loud in the small room.

This was her first season, and yes, he hadn't seen her for years, as they'd drifted apart when he left for Eton, but he'd been looking forward to meeting her again when his mother told him she was in London. That had changed when she'd treated him like a stranger, then proceeded to ignore him while gushing over everyone else.

"Madeline?" Gabe prompted when she said nothing.

"No, I need no help, and my shoe ribbons are in excellent health, as is my hem. I have told you, I simply became disorientated." She straightened the seams of her gloves, avoiding his eyes. "Now, excuse me, I must leave as my dance card is, of course, full." She raised her chin and glided past him. Gabe stopped her, wrapping his fingers around her wrist.

"What are you up to?" Something was off here; he just couldn't quite tell what.

She trilled out a hideous laugh. "I became disorientated, nothing more. Now I really must return. Please excuse me."

She jerked her arm free with surprising force and then left. The woman didn't even walk like other people; she glided.

Gone was the girl who had swum, jumped, and run over their estates as children. This one was perfect in every way... except one. She wasn't real anymore.

"No, excuse me," Gabe muttered. He drew in a deep, steadying breath and inhaled her scent. Elusive, a soft floral musk that she no doubt paid a fortune to have created. "God save me from precious women."

Dismissing her and the nagging sense of disappointment in the woman she had become, Gabe moved behind the desk. Dropping to his knees, he looked underneath.

There was something there. Reaching out, his fingers touched a piece of paper. Retrieving it, he headed back out the door to stand beside the light.

It was an official document of some kind with Lord Haswell's seal on the bottom—a deed of sale for a property in London. The location was in Spitalfields.

Haswell was one of the old generation of noblemen who did not believe in being anything but a gentleman. They lived off their titles and whatever their ancestors had left them. So why did he own this property in such an area?

Memorizing the contents, he took it back into the room and placed it in a desk drawer, then made his way back to the ballroom.

What the hell would Madeline Spencer want with such a document? Gabe was certain she'd been searching for something, and as this was where she'd been looking, it added up that this was what she'd been seeking.

Entering the ballroom, he was immediately bombarded with noise. Music, voices, and a riot of color. With Christmas Day not far away, those who had not retired to their estates were here tonight enjoying the Haswells' hospitality on a bitter London evening.

Fires roared, throwing out heat, and when combined with the overperfumed guests, the scent was not always pleasant. Above hung chandeliers lit with hundreds of candles dripping wax on those dancing below.

"But what could possibly make you frown on such a joyous evening, my dear Lord Lockhart?"

"Good evening, Lady Glimley." Gabe bowed before her. Married to the aging Lord Glimley, who spent more time with his friends than her, she was always on the prowl for a new bed partner. Her eyes had been focused on Gabe recently.

"I do believe I have a dance free in the third set." She leaned forward so he could see down her bodice.

"I fear I must leave shortly, my lady. Perhaps next time."

She patted his chest in a way that suggested she was far more familiar with his body than she should be, then sailed away in a cloud of heavy scent.

"That woman would take you in her bed any way she could get you."

Mr. Elliot Yates moved to Gabe's side. They had been friends for many years, and there was no one he trusted more. Shorter, and balding, the man had married a woman because his parents had dictated he should. As luck would have it, he also loved her.

"And yet I still resist."

"God's truth, I'm unsure why. Her prowess is legendary."

When Gabe said nothing, Elliot, who liked to talk, moved on to his next topic of conversation.

"That idiot Hawkins needs shooting."

"Why?" Gabe searched for Madeline and found her surrounded by men and women. Popularity had not been a problem for the youngest Spencer sibling since she'd entered society.

"Other than the fact he has that thing with his fingers, he also speaks as if everyone around him is hard of hearing, and sniffs constantly."

"What thing with his fingers?" Gabe kept his eyes on Madeline as she smiled and played the pretty with the people around her.

"Don't tell me you haven't noticed how he snaps his fingers in your face to make a point. Verbrook told me next time Hawkins did it, he would stuff them up his nose—which would solve both annoying habits."

"Yes, not the easiest person to converse with, I'll give you that."

"He just has to walk into a room to annoy me," Elliot added. "There is also the matter of his belief Miss Spencer is toying with him, but one day will see the error of her ways and marry him."

"Why do you care who she marries?" Gabe dragged his eyes from Madeline. Strangely, his heart had started to thud harder inside his chest.

Promise you will love no one but me, Gabe. She'd once said those words to him.

"I couldn't give a fig about that woman, but for some reason my wife does."

"Where is your Lyndy?"

"Home. She is poorly."

"Poorly how?" Gabe looked at Elliot. The man was blushing and wore a foolish smile. "She's with child," Gabe guessed.

"I never said that!"

"You didn't have to, the glow and besotted look on your face told me."

"Well, it is rather exciting."

"Extremely. Congratulations, my friend, I am happy for you both."

"Thank you. Lyndy wants you to be its godfather because you are supposedly my only sensible friend."

Something warm and heavy settled in Gabe's chest.

"I would be honored. Let's hope it has her hairline and temperament."

"A great many women love bald men. And what's wrong with my temperament?" Elliot glared at him.

"It's fiery, and that's me being polite."

"Well, rather that than sullen. You scare everyone off with your scowl, Gabe, and gruff ways."

"Gruff ways? Oh, now I do protest." Madeline was now taking the floor with the sniffing finger-flicking Hawkins. Light from above made her dress shimmer as she walked.

What the hell was she doing in that room looking at that deed?

"You have a fearsome reputation, even if it is not warranted," Elliot added.

"Harsh." *But true,* Gabe added silently. He hadn't always been that way, but life had changed him, and not always for the better.

"Yes, well, you will never get a wife if you do not learn to smile. Apparently, according to mine, you are something of a catch, but women are terrified of you."

"What utter rot," Gabe said, once again looking at Madeline. She was laughing at something Hawkins said. In turn, he was gazing at her adoringly.

"I'll just say Miss Hindle to strengthen my point."

"She tripped on her shoe ribbon," Gabe snapped. "I said nothing to her, but she made the entire event into a production. She did not faint because of my savage scowl."

"If you insist."

"I do. Now tell me what you know of Miss Spencer."

"As in?"

"As in what do you know of her, Elliot. Not a terribly taxing question, even for you."

"I'm not sure why I put up with you."

"Because no one else will have you."

"Why the interest in Miss Divine?"

"Is that what they're calling her?" She moved with grace. Dainty hands held her skirts as she sank into a curtsey. "And I am merely curious, not interested, Elliot."

"I thought your families were close and you spent time together as children? Shouldn't you know more about her than I?"

"Children, Elliot, not adults. We are now strangers." Gabe watched as she turned and her eyes caught his. She stumbled, which he found an interesting reaction. Madeline was never clumsy.

"I don't know anything about her, actually, which is strange. I mean, people always talk, and I of course am an excellent listener."

"You're a gossip," Gabe added.

"But there is rarely anything interesting said about Miss Spencer, other than that she is sweet and polite."

"Sweet?" Gabe scoffed. "The woman's after the loftiest title and biggest estate she can lay her hands on through marriage."

"Lyndy gets angry if I speak like that, as she likes Miss Spencer."

"That seems odd, considering your wife is usually a woman of intelligence. If my memory serves, marrying you was her only lapse in judgement."

"I don't actually know," Elliot said, not taking offence. They'd been tormenting each other with insults since they met one drunken night a few years ago. "She always says things like 'there's a lot more to Miss Spencer that people don't see.' It's all very vague, and when I question her further, she won't add anything."

Miss Spencer gave her dance partner a blinding smile that had him stumbling.

If I was to compare this moment to a food, it would be jellied eel.

The old Maddie, as he'd once called her, would have said something like that, but not this one... well, he'd not thought she would. Clearly he was wrong.

"Come." Gabe pushed off the walls. "Let's leave before people start behaving badly, as they tend to do after too many libations. We'll visit the club. It'll probably be our last time before we leave for my estate."

Elliot and Lyndy had chosen to spend the festive season with Gabe and his family rather than their own.

"Yes, but I cannot be late, as I need to check on Lyndy."

"You're not going to fuss around her for the entire nine months, are you?"

"Probably, and it's only six now."

Gabe threw a last look at Madeline Spencer. She lifted her head as if sensing him. Their eyes caught and held again, and then she quickly looked away.

Shrugging off the ripple of awareness, he followed Elliot from the room. Whatever had put Madeline in that room had nothing to do with him.

Nothing at all.

Chapter Two

Maddie tapped her spoon against the cup as she thought about that deed of sale she'd found last night in Haswell's study.

"You will desist at once, Madeline. That sound should not be heard at the breakfast table... or any table, for that matter."

"Sorry, Verity." She lowered her spoon as her sister scowled at her.

"You are even more preoccupied than normal this morning."

Maddie muttered something and continued to stare into her cup of tea.

She'd needed that document but had not been able to reach it under the desk after it had fallen from her hands. That fiend Lord Snotty had stopped her from retrieving it. How dared he looked down his nose at her.

Once she'd hung on every word he uttered. Once, Maddie had believed he would be the man she'd marry. Of course, at twelve years old she hadn't really known what she wanted, but still, Gabriel had been her hero.

"You sighed, Madeline. If you are not going to share with us why, then desist that also."

"Sorry, Verity."

He'd approached her at the beginning of the season when she'd been attending her first ball, so handsome and assured. Maddie's shock at seeing the changes in her old friend had tied her tongue into knots. He was no longer the thin, shy boy she'd known.

Once she'd loved this man, or at least the boy he'd been, to the depths of her innocent heart. Now he was a cold, aloof stranger with piercing blue eyes that seemed to look right through her.

He'd tried to talk to her. Maddie had replied with foolish giggles and a few silly comments she managed to get out of her dry mouth. He'd then bowed and walked away from her after a few minutes of strained silence. They'd not spoken again.

She'd spent plenty of time observing the earl when he wasn't looking during the nights they frequented the same society gatherings.

Maddie often wanted to gnash her teeth at the young ladies of her acquaintance as they constantly sighed or twittered about him. "He's so handsome." "His eyes are like the sky on a cloudless summer day." "He sits a horse like no other." On and on it went. She found it nauseating and disturbing at the same time. The latter because somewhere deep inside her she still felt slightly proprietorial about Gabriel. Foolish, she knew, but nonetheless it was there. He'd once been very important in her life, and she'd never been able to shake that.

Handsome seemed too simple a word for what Gabe had grown into. Thick brown hair, piercing blue eyes, and a large, solid body that he clothed elegantly.

"Must you stare vacantly into your cup, Maddie? It makes you appear simple. But perhaps you are thinking about someone you met last night? Which gentleman has captured your interest? Lord Silvers, perhaps? I believe he is quite enamored with you. Or

Lord Lockhart. You and he once believed you would marry. Has the time come to renew your acquaintance with him?"

Maddie didn't like her eldest sister very much. Love her, yes, but like... definitely not. Engaged to an earl who was equally as pompous as she, Verity rarely let an opportunity pass to annoy Maddie with her lofty opinions.

Maddie watched as Verity lifted her teacup and sipped a mouthful, her movements dainty, as proper young ladies should be. Verity never did anything that wasn't proper.

"I'm tired, Verity, nothing more. And I have no wish to marry either of those men."

Especially not the last one.

"Yes, well, not everyone has the stamina for an evening in society. I, of course, was something of an incomparable before I became engaged to Stephen. 'Tis a shame you will not follow in my footsteps."

"Verity." The caution came from her mother, who had been silent until that moment, reading her newspaper.

Verity thought reading the newspaper unfitting for a lady, but she was not brave enough to challenge their mother.

"I'm just talking, Mama."

Verity wore a thick shawl around her shoulders to ward off the bitter chill that hung in the air. Golden haired, brown eyed, she was beautiful like their mother. Maddie had often heard men talking about her, and it was always flattering and nauseating. Maddie would rather be known for her wit or intelligence than the style of her hair.

"No. You are deliberately baiting your sister. I wish you to stop at once, Verity."

"I was merely pointing out that she—"

"Do you ever tire of that?" Maddie cut her sister off.

"Maddie." She ignored the caution in her mother's tone.

"Tire of what?" Verity flicked a curl over her shoulder, then nibbled on a corner of toast.

"Being a sharp-tongued shrew."

Their mother's groan did not deter Maddie.

"How dare you speak to me in such a way!" Verity's mouth formed a thin, angry line. "Mama, I insist you discipline her!"

"How dare I?" Maddie got to her feet. "You're always insulting someone. One hopes you show your fiancé your true colors before you marry, so he can run for the hills! You have the airs and graces of a princess... which I assure you, you definitely are not. What you are is a rude, spoiled, self-indulgent brat."

"Is it too much to ask for peace at the breakfast table?" Lady Spencer closed her paper with a crisp snap. "Stop this at once if you please, girls."

Maddie was too far into this to heed her mother's words. She'd had enough of Verity's pointed barbs.

"How dare you!" Verity's face was puce with rage now.

"Girls." Lady Spencer was out of her seat now. "That will do."

"You've said that already, Verity." Maddie was not to be deterred. Her sister had been poking at her for weeks, and she was done with it. "Quite frankly, I've had enough of your sanctimonious ways."

"Mama, you must deal with her at once!" Verity threw her toast at Maddie. She caught it and took a large bite, chewing slowly while looking at her sister.

"Desist!" Lady Spencer demanded. "Both of you will be quiet. You are giving me indigestion."

Maddie glared at her sister one last time and then threw the toast back harder. It hit her sister in the forehead. Luckily, it was coated in strawberry preserve.

She then walked from the room.

Stomping back to her bedroom, Maddie prepared for her outing. She and then made her way down to the front door.

"Verity is different from you, Madeline."

Searching for her mother, she found her under the stairs, looking at the paintings of her father's ancestors.

"How did you know I was leaving the house?"

"Because when you're angry you want to get away from Verity in case you do her bodily harm."

"I would never physically harm her, Mama."

"I know, darling. Sometimes I look at you both and wonder how you can be sisters. You are strong and always challenging something or someone. Verity is quite content to simply be a young woman in society. She does not want more and is happy to be marrying Stephen, knowing he will care for her."

"She's nasty." Maddie moved closer, and her mother wrapped an arm around her waist.

"No, she's not; you provoke her into being nasty. Verity is unsure how to communicate with you, as she feels there is no common ground between you. You should try harder with her."

Maddie thought about that as she looked up at the painting.

"Why are we looking at him?"

"He's an austere-looking chap, but it was his mustache I was looking at. Your father had one of those when I first met him. I made him remove it."

"You miss him very much, don't you?"

"Very much," Lady Spencer said quietly. "But he shall be home soon, and finally we can leave for the estate."

Ian, Lord Spencer was a wonderful father; however, he spent a great deal of time helping run the country. She could not fault him in his duty, even if sometimes she wished he'd be selfish and spend more time with them.

"Now, where are you off to today?" Her mother motioned her back to the front door, where a maid stood. "And don't lie to me, I'll know."

"I wouldn't lie to you!" Maddie tried to look outraged.

"Yes, you would if it suited your purpose."

"You know me too well."

"Because you are just like me."

"I had thought to get some small gifts to give the staff before we leave London."

"That's very kind of you, sweetheart, but where else are you going?" Her mother leveled her with the look that said she wasn't moving until she had the truth.

"I thought to visit Margaret and then go to the bookstore." It was a lie, but it was better her mother was not aware of her youngest daughter's actual intended location.

"You will take James."

"Penny will be with me. I do not need anyone else—"

"James!" Her mother walked to the stairs and yelled in a very unladylike manner. Seconds later a large footman appeared.

"Mother, really, there is—"

"You called, my lady?"

"I want you to accompany my daughter... this one." She pointed to Maddie, who was not amused. "You will stay at her side at all times."

James hurried down the stairs. Big and burly, he had been with the Spencer household for five years now. Maddie and he had an understanding of sorts. He didn't give away her secrets, and she paid him handsomely for that. Usually in treats like candy or pies. James liked food.

"I do not need to take James away from his work, Mama," Maddie protested. "I will hardly get into trouble in a bookstore."

James cleared his throat, knowing very well there would be no bookstore visited today.

"Then you will not go." Her mother's smile told her she had lost.

"Oh, very well."

"That's my grateful daughter. Now, James, should my daughter get into trouble and refuse to follow your direction, you have my permission to throw her over your shoulder."

"Very well, my lady." The footman's eyes didn't betray what he was thinking.

"Very amusing," Maddie said.

"Yes, well, you'll forgive me if I don't have complete faith in your ability to stay out of trouble," Lady Spencer said. "There was that incident with the pony—"

"I was ten."

"And the man on the street who was mistreating the horse."

"Yes, well, that happened only a few weeks ago. But he was being unkind and needed that pointed out to him."

Lady Spencer laughed. "I think he understood your meaning, dear."

Maddie kissed her mother's cheek.

"I need you to think about what I said, Maddie. You and Verity are different, but you are sisters. You're strong and determined; she is equally so, but in other ways. This household will run in a far more harmonious fashion were you to at least attempt to find a common ground with her."

"Are you having this talk with her also?"

"Of course."

Maddie sighed. "I am the epitome of a well-behaved woman every evening, Mama. Surely you cannot expect me to be that way in the day as well."

"The perfect miss, do you mean?"

Maddie nodded.

"It is quite amazing how you can be two different people. Your father thinks some man is going to get quite a shock one day when he realizes the woman he has married is actually a mouthy little baggage full of purpose and determination."

"I don't think I want to marry, Mama." Maddie pushed the vision of Gabe aside. He was not the boy she'd once loved.

"One day you will find the right man, but for now simply enjoy being young. Now go and enjoy your outing but behave yourself. Remember, the reason I do not stop you from leaving the house is because I know you need to have things to occupy you, but if you break my trust that will stop."

Guilt settled heavily around her shoulders as Maddie left the house.

Chapter Three

"The day was bleak. A flurry of snow was in the air, and it made the streets icy, so the carriage trip was a slow one. London in December was never a pleasant time, as the streets were often turned to sludge by the rain and ice. The Spencer women were awaiting Lord Spencer's return from his government business so they could leave for Chasten, their estate, before Christmas Eve. Maddie couldn't wait to start the celebrations, beginning with decorating the house and lighting the yule candle.

She had not told her mother the entire truth about where she was to go, as she would have been forbidden from leaving the house. Maddie knew she would be in a huge amount of trouble were the truth to ever come out, but the risk was worth it. This was something she needed to do.

"She'll find out one day, Miss Spencer."

"But not today, Penny," Maddie told her maid, who sat across from her wrapped up warmly in her winter coat.

On her second day in London, Maddie had stumbled across a young girl lying in a doorway. Blind, she'd been huddled in a tight ball attempting to escape the cold. That girl's name had been Hetty. Everything had changed for Maddie from that moment on.

"But what can be done for the people in Spoke House if they must leave, Miss Spencer?"

"I'm unsure as yet, Penny, but I will think of something," Maddie said hoping she was right.

Spoke House was in Spitalfields, where Hetty lived. A run-down old house where children went when they had nowhere else to run to. Often only a few were there when Maddie arrived, but some days there were as many as twenty.

The problem they were now facing was that the landlord had given them an eviction notice, and Maddie had little time to find an alternative arrangement for the children before she left London.

"It is sickening to think that house will become a brothel." Penny shuddered.

"I won't let them be evicted without a fight," Maddie said. There had to be something she could do.

Maddie had found this piece of information out through the man who looked after the property for her.

"Come, Penny, we cannot dwell on that at the moment. We have lessons to give," Maddie said as the carriage pulled up outside what had once been a grand old house. James opened the door for her.

"Bring the hampers, please, James." The footman nodded.

She'd had to sneak those out, paying more servants to keep silent, and Mrs. Fitch, her mother's cook, for the leftovers she often contributed.

All around them were buildings in various sizes. Smoke billowed from some chimneys, others had broken windows and missing boards. People scurried about on the filthy streets trying to get out of the cold. The once prosperous Spitalfields was now a desperate place that housed people of dire circumstance. It was many miles in both distance and circumstance from where she lived in Mayfair.

"This place is dreary," Penny said. "Thick black dust and dirt is everywhere. Have a care where you step, Miss Spencer."

"Yes. We are the lucky ones, living in the luxury we do."

Walking across the road, she had nearly reached her destination when she heard the clip-clop of hooves. Of course, there was nothing unusual in that, but Maddie, who was inherently nosy, had to look.

Her eyes found the tall, erect form of Lord Lockhart. She quickly looked away. *What is he doing in such a place?*

She doubted he had seen her, and even if he did, he would not be stopping. He wouldn't give a fig that she was here in Spitalfields.

The old Gabe would have. He'd cared about everything she'd said and done.

Maddie hurried in through the doors of a building and out of the bitterly cold day.

"Well, well, well, if it isn't the sweet little do-gooder."

Maddie didn't hate many people in the world, but this man was an exception.

"You'll leave here at once and not approach my mistress again, Blackley." James moved to her side.

Frank Blackley. Local thug who believed he and his family controlled this area of Spitalfields. She avoided him where possible, but that was not always the case.

"You are trespassing, Mr. Blackley," Maddie said.

"I want payment for you being here. The others pay, you should be no different."

Maddie's fingers itched to slap the smug smile off his face. *Loathsome beast.*

"Leave now," James said in a menacing tone that made Maddie relieved her mother had insisted he accompany her.

"I have told you, you will receive no money from me, Mr. Blackley. I am not intimidated by the likes of you, nor do I live in this area. I am immune to your brand of intimidation and blackmail." Maddie kept her voice calm.

His eyes narrowed and he leaned closer. James pushed him roughly back. He didn't retreat far.

"Oh, you'll pay all right, don't you worry about that. Remember to look over your shoulder, sweetheart, because I'll extract that payment when you least expect it."

"That man is dangerous," James said, watching him walk from the building. "It's not safe here for you, Miss Spencer. Next time you'll need to have both me and Peter with you."

"He will not harm a nobleman's daughter," Maddie said with a confidence she was far from feeling.

"Him and his sort don't play by the rules you live by, Miss Spencer. Please remember that."

With her heart still thudding hard inside her chest, Maddie started up the stairs.

The building no longer held traces of the grand place that had once been inhabited by a family many years before.

"It's icy in here today, Miss Spencer," Penny said, following.

"It is, and the children will be feeling it."

Pushing open the door that led into the rooms she'd set up for teaching, she found them all seated in their chairs around a fireplace. They turned and greeted her with genuine enthusiasm. It had taken her many weeks to gain their trust, but now she had it was a wonderful thing. She had just taken a step closer when she heard his voice.

"Madeline? What in God's name are you doing here?"

Chapter Four

Gabe looked at Madeline, then around the room to the children who were seated watching them.

What the hell is she doing here?

Intrigued after reading the address on that deed of sale last night, he'd decided to ride past today. Gabe had been shocked to see Madeline walking across the road, even considering he'd found her in that office last night.

"Go away, Gabriel; this does not concern you."

She turned from him and waved the footman, holding two baskets, forward.

He watched as she opened one and began to hand out food.

"Madeline, I insist you answer me." Gabe moved closer.

"You can insist all you like, but I shall refuse as this is no concern of yours, Lord Lockhart. Now, take your polished boots out of here before they get dirty. This is no place for you."

"Don't you dare dismiss me." Gabe stalked closer.

She straightened, the gentle smile she'd been giving a young girl falling from her face. She shot him a look before addressing the children.

"Penny is to take today's lesson. I hope you have all been practicing your letters," she said, her eyes on Gabe.

There was a chorus of yeses, and then the woman with Maddie, presumably Penny, moved to the front of the seats and began to read from a book she held.

Maddie ignored him and went between the children, handing out things from the baskets.

Gabe only had so much patience.

"Maddie," he said with more force. "I want to speak with you at once."

"Why are you still here?" She threw him a frustrated look. "Leave, please."

She looked different today, less... less elegant? Less like the untouchable beauty he'd come to know... or thought he knew.

Dressed in a deep blue velvet cloak, her hair, beneath the matching velvet bonnet, was in a simple bun at her nape, and her boots were a serviceable black leather.

"What are you doing here, is more to the point?" Gabe replied.

"She looks after us," one of the children said. "She's our angel, is Miss Spencer."

She was blind, he realized, her eyes sightless as her head turned his way.

"Maddie loves me."

"Yes, I do." Maddie hugged the girl. "Now listen to Penny's story, Hetty."

He couldn't take it in. The obnoxious Miss Spencer here in Spitalfields helping these young children.

I hate that we have so much, Gabe, and some have so little.

He remembered she used to say things like that constantly when they were children.

"Madeline." He tried to draw her away so he could question her, but she ignored him and shook her arm free.

"Will you just go away please?" Her tone was flat and cold.

"Why are you here?" Gabe countered.

"That is none of your business, Gabriel. Now please leave."

"Why are you helping these children, Madeline? I demand you answer me."

"Someone has to," she snapped, in a tone that the other inhabitants in the room would not overhear.

"But why are you doing this...?" His words fell away as her eyes narrowed.

"Should I perhaps simper and curtsey to them? Play the piano and sing? Oh dear." She pressed a hand to her lips. "There is no piano here, how will I cope?"

"Maddie, stop now," Gabe snapped. "I'm merely attempting to understand what is—"

"Or perhaps pat them on the head and hope they do not freeze or starve to death when they walk out into the brutal world they inhabit," she interrupted him. "You know those twelve days of Christmas our families always looked forward to, Gabriel? The dancing and balls. The boughs of greenery and burning the Yule. Well, these children have no idea of such things. They have rarely if ever known joy or a full stomach. They had no idea there was goodness in this world."

"So, what? You're providing them with some goodness? You, a young woman who should know better than to venture into Spitalfields." Gabe's anger climbed at the realization of what she was doing. "How can you be so reckless, Madeline? I'm sure your parents—"

"Leave them out of this," she hissed. "This has nothing to do with them."

"Because you haven't told them what you are doing," Gabe said, knowing he was right when she looked away.

"Just leave, and don't come back. There is nothing for you here. Go back to your cosseted life, Lord Lockhart."

"Don't dismiss me, you little baggage." He felt the leash on his temper slip. She'd always been able to get a rise out of him with very little effort. "You will allow me some confusion. The woman I have come to know this season—"

"You know nothing of me, nor do I wish you to!"

"I just—"

"I do not want to hear anything you have to say, Gabriel. Why can you not understand that? This," she waved a hand about, "is something I must do. I have not asked for your help, nor do I want you here. Leave at once."

"I merely—" Gabe cut himself off and covered her mouth with his hand when she opened it to interrupt him once more.

"If I may actually be allowed to finish a sentence, I will explain that you must admit, this," he looked at the children, "is not something I would have thought you involved in. Once, but not now."

She bit him.

"Ouch!"

"Your hand was cold."

"How? It's in my glove." Gabe shook his hand hard to stop the sting of pain.

"Look." She exhaled slowly through her teeth. "We don't like each other anymore, so I think it best you forget about anything you have seen, and we can carry on with our lives, avoiding each other."

"You think I can simply walk away and leave you here? Carry on with my day as if this has not occurred?" Gabe couldn't believe she thought him capable of that.

"Of course you can," she scoffed. "Is it not your belief I have changed beyond recognition also? After all, your attitude toward me has been dismissive from that night we met at the ball."

"Because of your attitude," Gabe said with a calm he was far from feeling.

Her brows drew together. "My attitude? What about yours?"

"What about me? I simply greeted my old childhood friend," Gabe said. "You treated me like a stranger. Giggled inanely, then said some ridiculous, extremely feather-brained things. I could not leave fast enough."

He watched as she drew in a large breath, then released it slowly before speaking.

"You said, 'it seems you have changed a great deal, Madeline,' in a tone that suggested it was not for the better." She gritted out the words. "You could not even see I was nervous at meeting you again after so long. The man who once.... Well, never mind. The point is I was nervous, overawed at my first ball, and feeling like I was about to cast up my accounts on your polished evening shoes."

He hadn't believed her nervous... hadn't even contemplated that fact. Perhaps he should have.

"I am the same person, Madeline."

She barked out a laugh that held no humor. "You are nothing like the gentle, sensitive boy I once knew. You're snooty, and your attitude suggests you think yourself superior to everyone else. Most of the women, married and not, are enamored with you, but terrified to even smile at you as you're usually scowling. The men are in awe of you, the formidable earl with the ruthless reputation."

"I beg your pardon?" Gabe wasn't going to lie, her opinion of him was a surprise. It was also uncomfortably close to what Elliot had said last night. Yes, he wasn't one for social chitchat, but he wasn't rude... or hadn't thought he was.

"I'm not repeating myself when clearly you heard." Maddie folded her arms.

"Well, if it's a character assassination that you want, let me oblige," Gabe said, feeling nettled. "You're obnoxious and parade around the ballroom with your minions most evenings as if you were a bloody princess."

"I beg your pardon?" She looked outraged now.

"I'm not repeating myself, as clearly you heard." He threw her words back at her.

They glared at each other.

He didn't want to notice her beauty at that particular moment, but angry color filled her cheeks. And her brown eyes were darker, almost black now. Her skin was like porcelain, soft to the touch, he was sure. Her top lip had a perfect bow shape to it. Gabe had heard men waxing on about her beauty, and it was even more evident this close and in such a drab setting.

"I loathe you. Now leave," she muttered as someone started coughing behind her. "There now, Jody." She hurried back to the young girl and handed over a handkerchief she dug out of her cloak. "Take some slow, deep breaths for me."

"Can you fix my doll's hair?"

Gabe located that voice and found a little girl holding up a pile of rags for him to inspect.

"'Tis knotted."

He looked to where Madeline crouched beside the other girl. She didn't appear to be moving to help.

"Pleassssse," she begged.

He couldn't just ignore her; nor could he leave. No way was he leaving Madeline here in such a place, even if she was a mouthy little baggage.

"What is your doll's name?" He moved closer, whispering so the story listeners would not be disturbed.

"Maddie!"

"It is a name for a sweet-natured lady," he said with a heavy dose of mockery in his tone. Maddie ignored him.

"And I am Emma."

"Hello, Emma, I am Gabriel."

"Can you untangle it?"

He took the grubby doll but couldn't achieve what he needed to with his gloves on, so he handed it back and removed them.

"It's quite tangled."

"I should brush it more, like Maddie says I should brush mine too. Bath day is for that, me ma says."

"Very likely," Gabe muttered as he wrestled with the knots... of which there were several. Twisted lumps in the material that had been that way for some time, he guessed.

"Do you live here, Emma?"

"Sometimes when Ma has visitors, she lets me come here to sleep."

Gabe didn't want to know who those "visitors" were. He wasn't immune to the plight of others and gave money on the streets where he could. He sat in the House of Lords and played his part in getting laws passed to make things better for those less fortunate than himself. But he could do more.

The truth was, whatever Maddie was doing here would no doubt put him to shame. Although he'd never admit that to her.

"I can do that." A hand reached around him to grab the doll.

"I have it." He lifted it out of Maddie's way.

"But there is no need as I am here now, and surely you have no wish to sully your hands with such a job."

Handing the doll back to Emma with a smile, he turned to face Maddie. She didn't look happy.

"Your opinion of me is very lowering, Madeline."

"As yours is of me."

She didn't back away, wasn't cowed by the scowl that was very likely on his face now.

"Is it spelling time now?"

The question interrupted their stare down.

"Soon, Jay. Let me just see Lord Lockhart to the door."

"I will stay for spelling time," Gabe found himself saying.

"Why?"

"Because I was always a great deal more proficient at it than you."

If she could breathe fire, now would be the time. Stomping away, she muttered something unflattering he didn't catch.

He moved to stand beside two boys as they attempted to form letters on the paper Maddie had obviously supplied them.

"You will find it easier if you hold the pencil like this."

After a few aborted attempts, the boys got the hang of holding it the right way. He helped them form the letter *A*, and their smiles told him they were happy with the results.

"Have you met the Duke of Wellington?"

"I have." Gabe nodded.

"Is he short?"

"Ah, well, shorter than me at least."

"I heard he sleeps in his uniform."

"Very unlikely, as the sword would be extremely uncomfortable, surely, and what of the hat?"

The boys snuffled out a laugh. Unlike his nephews and nieces who laughed loud and free, these two were more subdued.

Gabe felt it then. Guilt, that he had so much and they so little. He wondered if this was what prompted Maddie to do what she had.

"I want to meet him," one of the boys said. Like the rest of the children in this room, he was thin-faced, large-eyed, and grubby. "Maddie says if we learn well, maybe one day we will."

Gabe doubted that but didn't speak the words. "Very likely," he lied.

Deciding that he needed to inspect this place Madeline was clearly spending time in, he left the children to their letters and, without looking her way, slipped out the door.

Once a family of prosperous Huguenots had lived here, he was sure. So much had changed over the years, and now the grand house was cold and empty.

He found beds in a room, and a table and chairs. Every other room on the lower floor was empty.

What the hell are you doing in this place, Madeline Spencer?

Chapter Five

Maddie finished the lesson, and still Gabriel had not returned. Making sure everyone had food, she had James stoke the fire.

"Another story, please, Penny. I shall return shortly."

Her maid nodded, and she left the room to look for the large, dark lord. She doubted he'd left the building, no matter how much she wished it was so.

She had at least told him how she felt now, as he had her. It surprised her that Gabriel believed she had changed so much from the girl he'd known. She'd fooled everyone, just as her mother wanted her to. She and her mother had struck a bargain when she entered society. She behaved in public, and her mother would allow her some freedom, as long as she didn't get into trouble.

Until she'd visited Spoke House, she'd kept to her part of the bargain.

Was she wrong about Gabriel? Could some of the boy she'd once known be in there somewhere? He'd certainly been gentle with Hetty and the boys.

Taking the stairs down, she found him wandering through the deserted rooms. Ignoring the small jolt she received looking at him, Maddie approached.

"Why are you still here?"

"Why were you in Lord Haswell's study looking at the Deed of Sale for this property, Madeline?"

So, he had found what she'd been looking for that night.

He was tapping his hat idly against one large thigh, for all appearances mildly curious. Maddie knew better; Gabriel had an inquiring mind and not much escaped him. He was also fiercely determined. If he wanted answers, he would ensure he got them.

Folding her arms once more, she refused to answer him. He smiled and simply looked at her. That was something they'd always had in common. Stubbornness.

His overcoat was black and hung open, revealing a jacket of deep green. His collar was a crisp white, and his breeches the same. The man was ridiculously handsome. Miss Little had said he should be painted or immortalized in ivory. Maddie had wanted to throw up.

His eyes were unusual, a blue so pale they were piercing in their intensity when focused on you… as they were now. Maddie had never seen another with that color. She'd loved to look at them when she was a silly, naïve young girl. She'd spent nights dreaming about them one day looking at her with longing and love.

They were now narrowed and cool.

"I have nowhere to be, Maddie, and can stand here or follow you around all day if need be."

"This is my business, not yours."

"As you have already said. However, I want to make it my business. Perhaps I could ask Lord Haswell?"

"You wouldn't!" That would be a catastrophe.

"Then tell me what I want to know." He stood there comfortable with the knowledge he held all the power. A man of title and substance. A man who did not rely on anyone for his survival. A man she'd once called friend.

"I don't understand why you care!" Frustrated, Maddie only just refrained from stomping her foot.

He didn't speak, just looked at her in that steady way he had. Her father had the same look. Maddie had never been able to perfect it because she couldn't stay quiet or still for that long.

"All right!" His smile had her wanting to hurl something at him, but nothing was at hand. "I offer these children a place to come. I help teach them to read and write, and when they cannot go home, they stay here. They come and go, some don't return, and I don't ask where they have gone for fear they are dead. But this house is for the children no one but me cares about." Her voice rose as emotion took over. She was passionate about these children, and she would not let him stop her doing what she did.

"Does your family know?"

She ignored his question.

"Lord Haswell intends to sell the house to another, and they will turn this place in to a brothel," she said instead.

She'd surprised him, she knew, as his eyes widened. It was the only reaction he made. Again, unlike her; she would have at least gasped.

Maddie's family was always trying to get her to think before she spoke or acted. But as she'd told them, she did that most evenings, she couldn't be expected to continue doing so during the day also.

"I doubt a brothel in Spitalfields—"

"Are you calling me a liar?"

"Is there any chance I could finish what I am saying, Madeline?"

She fell silent.

"Would be a popular choice, but it would depend on the type of brothel and what it offers."

"I don't care about that! I want him to stop his plans to sell. We pay him a decent rent—"

"We?"

"Now who is interrupting."

He snapped his teeth together.

"He is just being greedy and has no need to sell it but will not discuss the matter with us. I cannot approach him because I am a woman, and therefore supposedly without sense or the ability to discuss such things."

"Well, to be fair, the woman you are in society vastly differs from the one before me today. In fact, appearances suggested to me you were without sense," he said in a reasonable tone that had her wanting to slap him. "However, it seems you are still the old Maddie, if a little different on the outside."

"I am not without sense!"

"I said you *appeared* to be without sense. Please note the difference."

"Don't you dare use that bloody sanctimonious tone with me, Gabriel."

"How is it you manage to keep all that fire hidden from society? The simpering and gushing must be extremely taxing on you, the woman who can't let a person finish a conversation without voicing her opinion. You must spend most evenings gnashing your teeth in frustration at some of the foolish conversations going on around you."

"We are all hiding in some way, Gabriel, even you. And I recite Greek mythology when things get too taxing. It calms me."

He barked out a laugh.

Maddie dug her feet into her practical black boots as he walked closer, stopping a mere handful of inches away.

"How do you know Haswell is not in need of money, Maddie? Perhaps that is why he is selling."

"I just do."

"Which tells me nothing, so please continue."

"Don't use that tone on me!"

A black brow rose. "Tone? I merely asked a question."

Which she did not want to answer, so she changed the subject and took a different route to get him to stop prying and leave the building. The flattery one.

"Thank you for helping my children. It was very kind of you, Gabriel." She even forced a smile onto her face.

"I am not a monster, Maddie. I have family members who are children. Surprisingly, I can even spend time with them and enjoy myself. Even more surprising is they seem to like my company. I would have hoped you realized I was capable of such behavior."

"As I would have hoped you knew me better."

His sigh was loud.

"Tell me how you became involved in this, Maddie, please?"

Maddie thought through her options. They were extremely limited. He knew about Spoke House now and could make things extremely difficult for her and the residents if he chose to tell anyone what he had learned. Her hands were tied, and it seemed she had no choice but to tell him the truth.

"I'm sure I don't need to tell you to keep this information to yourself."

"Continue," he said in a tone that had her hackles rising.

"I am not a member of your staff; pray do not treat me like one."

His smile was small. "You really haven't changed much, have you? The mouthy little baggage who used to torment me just has a polished veneer now and has learned to act like the perfect lady in front of her peers."

Choosing to ignore that comment, Maddie continued with her story.

"I stumbled across Hetty shivering outside a shop one afternoon not long after I'd arrived in London. She told me she was lost. I asked where she lived, and she directed me here. This was the place she stayed when she could not go home."

"Hetty is the sightless girl?"

"Yes. When I got her back here, I came inside. The place was a mess. The door broken, no furniture, and little to keep her warm. There were three children here that day, living here in terrible conditions."

Maddie remembered how she'd felt seeing the misery, especially considering she lived in such luxury.

"I found out who owned the building and offered some money to rent it. Then I helped make it comfortable for those that needed a place to stay. The other children started arriving a week later."

"Your aunt May left you money upon her death, if I remember correctly. Are you using that to fund this?"

She nodded. "I contacted my father's man of affairs—"

"Mr. Thompson," Gabriel said. "I remember him."

"Yes, but actually it's the younger Mr. Thompson, his son, who looks after my money. He is a liberal-thinking man, and it was he who found out who the owner of this building was. He also negotiated the rent."

He watched her silently.

"Have I shocked you, Gabriel? Imagine a young woman my age having money of her own and the ability to do as she wishes with it."

"You have no idea what I am thinking, Maddie. I am of course surprised, as you are not who I thought you were, and this is not something I would have thought, or wanted, you to be involved in."

"But I am," she said firmly.

"And is Mr. Thompson also the one who found out Lord Haswell does not need the money?"

Maddie nodded.

"Returning to my earlier question. Does your family know?"

She shook her head.

"Your father would lock you up and throw away the key, and Verity would take to her bed for weeks."

She nodded.

"Where do they think you go?"

"I am an exceedingly good liar, which I'm sure you remember."

"I do. Tell me, Maddie. What were you hoping to achieve by stealing the deed to this place?"

Maddie wasn't really sure how to answer that, as she'd simply reacted, which was a fault of hers. But she had no wish to tell him that.

"You did have a plan, I hope? Or were you acting without thinking, which from memory was a particular failing of yours."

"Of course I knew what I was doing," Maddie lied.

He balanced his weight on one leg, which told her he wasn't going anywhere soon.

"Well, let's hear it then."

"I don't have to tell you anything. I just want you to leave and tell no one about what you've learned today. Surely that is not too much to ask. After all, like I have already stated, we are merely acquaintances now and mean nothing to each other."

Saying the words made her chest hurt.

He didn't speak, simply looked at her again. It was starting to get irritating. "Well?"

"You still don't like silence very much, do you, Maddie?"

She loathed it. It made her uncomfortable, especially if she was in the presence of someone like this man.

"I don't know what you are thinking," Maddie said.

"And that makes you uncomfortable?"

"Very much, as the fate of this place could very well be in your hands now."

"That is very dramatic of you, but I take your meaning. For now, you may rest easy. I have no wish to toss your people out on the street or alert Lord Haswell to your nefarious activities."

Maddie exhaled loudly. "But what of my family? Will you keep my secret from them also?"

"I will... for now. And I do like you, Maddie, I just didn't understand how you could have changed so much."

"It is the same for me, Gabriel."

"The last thing I would like to say on the matter of this house is that you will not come here alone again."

Chapter Six

"I beg your pardon?"

Gabe thought she may explode if the color filling her face was any indication.

"I saw that man who walked out when you entered, Maddie. He looked dangerous. This is not a place for a young, innocent woman who cannot defend herself."

"I can defend myself!"

He rushed her, wrapping his arms around her, and holding her close.

"Oh really, how?"

She lifted a knee, and Gabe only just managed to twist so the blow landed beside his groin. She stomped on his foot next, then jabbed him in the gut. Winded, he released her.

"Satisfied?"

As he was attempting to breathe, it would take him a moment to answer that question. But he would, in detail.

"Also, I have this."

Straightening, he felt the color leach from his face as she pointed a small pistol at him.

"God's blood, are you mad!" Gabe wrenched the pistol from her fingers. "Where did you get this?"

"I purchased it. Now give it back!"

"May the Lord preserve me from brainless twits," he muttered, pocketing the pistol. "Do you even know how it works? Have you fired it?"

Her head tilted slightly.

"I thought not. I will teach you, but until then you are not carrying it."

"That's all right, I have a knife."

Gabe watched, horrified, as she turned and lifted her skirts. When she turned back, she held a knife with a wicked-looking little blade.

"Give me that!"

"No!" She backed away. Lifted her skirts, attempting to replace it.

He grabbed her from behind and reached for her hand to remove it. His gloveless fingers ran up the stockinged skin of one thigh and froze.

"R-release me." Her words were shaky.

He did, backing away.

"You cannot walk about with knives and guns, Maddie."

Gabe attempted to regain his composure. He'd touched her thigh, nothing more, and the reaction had sent heat through his entire body. His hand felt like it was on fire.

"I-I can if they protect me. James told me how to use the knife, and it was he who taught me how to defend myself."

He was pleased to see she was at least a little breathless, because he was seriously unsettled.

"James?" Gabe did not like the jealousy that bolted through him at the thought of another man getting close to her.

"The footman who accompanies me."

"You haven't changed at all from that headstrong, reckless hellion you were, have you?"

"I am not reckless, but I will acknowledge the other two descriptions proudly."

He wouldn't laugh at the defiant tilt of her chin, but he wanted to. Why did he feel lighter inside just knowing she was still his Maddie?

His Maddie?

It was a strange, Gabe thought, how intriguing he suddenly found his old friend. Before she'd created mild annoyance inside him, easily dismissed when he left her presence, but now... well, now she was something entirely different. He'd always thought her beautiful, but now she was that and also so much more.

"What you are doing is admirable, Maddie, even if it is foolish."

"It is not foolish." Anger lit her eyes, and he wondered again how she'd hidden all that fire from everyone. Most evenings some fool made him angry at least twice.

"You should not have tried to steal that title deed for this property."

"I did what I thought was right and will continue to do so."

"It wasn't right, it was reckless. And I meant what I said about coming here, Maddie. You will not do so alone again." Gabe cut off her words. He needed her to understand this. Just the thought of her here with a single footman and maid made his blood run cold.

"I bloody well will."

"Don't use that language."

"Go away, then you won't have to hear it."

If he grabbed her and shook hard, no one would fault him. Instead he tried to speak calmly and rationally.

"Had anything happened to you, your family would have had no idea where you were."

"I have my maid and footman with me."

"Yes, we've established that already, but as they do exactly what you say they are not going to question you when you do something foolish."

She did not lower her eyes or look guilty, but he was quite sure he was right. Gabe doubted she was above bribing her staff to achieve what she wanted.

"I've deduced that you attempted to steal that document from Lord Haswell to stall any sale he may have?"

"It seemed like a good idea."

"It would not have stalled him for long."

"I had to at least try."

"Maddie, I'm not sure this is a fight you will win—unless you can buy the building yourself?"

"I cannot afford that."

"Then find another place for your children," Gabe said. "Surely there are any number of empty buildings about London."

She gave him a look that suggested he was a simpleton. He didn't like it.

"I have, of course, tried to do so, but it is not easy to find such a place, and now I have run out of time. Don't you see, we are to leave London soon, and the sale will go through at the end of December. These children will perish on the streets!"

"And I am to blame for this?" Gabe felt his temper tweak as she yelled at him. "Stop roaring at me and converse like an adult."

Frustration tightened her pretty features.

"I'm an adult attempting to help people! I'm sorry if your considerable ego is tweaked, Gabriel, but I do not have time to pander to it today. Good day, I must see to my children, but before I do so, I must ask again that you keep your silence about Spoke House."

He grabbed her arm as she began to walk away from him, turning her back to face him.

"I do not have a considerable ego," he snapped. "And don't dismiss me, you little baggage."

"Let me go." Her chin rose.

He pulled her closer, so close that her breasts brushed his chest.

"I am going to watch you closely from now on, Maddie."

Her face flushed with color. Those lovely lips opened and closed twice before sound came out.

"Why?"

"Because you are playing a dangerous game coming here, and I will not have that on my conscience when something happens to you."

"What will happen, for pity's sake? Please, Gabriel, you must see there is no danger. I walk in the door from the carriage and out of it when it draws up outside."

He touched her cheek simply because he wanted to test the texture of her skin.

"I don't trust you and believe it would not take a great deal of provocation to have you doing something foolish, Maddie. Especially if it involves the occupants of this place."

"Clearly you have an unflattering opinion of me, Lord Lockhart, but let me educate you on something." She tried to shake her arm free, but Gabe simply tightened his grip. "I don't give a fig what you think of me. Now release me."

Gabe let his eyes run over her face, settling on her lips. "You are a beautiful woman, Maddie."

"Verity is beautiful." The words had lost their fire and were said softly, her eyes focused on his.

"No. Yours is a true beauty, deep inside the bones." Gabe traced a finger along the ridge of one cheekbone.

"Gabe, please...."

"Please what, Maddie?"

She didn't speak or move, instead lifted her face to take his kiss.

She tasted like heaven, and he lost all thought but one.

More.

He angled her head so he could take the kiss deeper, drinking from the sweetness of her mouth as his arms slipped around her waist. She didn't pull away, her hands clutching the lapels of his jacket, holding him as close as he was holding her.

Their first kiss, and he knew now it would be far from their last.

He wasn't sure how long they stood there in each other's arms. A minute or ten; Gabe lost all track of time and only knew that in his arms was a woman who felt right.

Maddie.

A loud bang above them had her jumping free. They stood facing each other, both breathless, and yes, shocked over what had just happened. The hand she raised to her mouth trembled.

"Maddie...." He didn't know what to say. His head was a jumbled mass of thoughts that he struggled to clear.

"Leave now and never return." She ran around him and in seconds had disappeared.

Gabe did not follow.

Chapter Seven

Maddie spent time with the children upon her return and tried to make sense of her treacherous thoughts. Why had Gabe kissed her? Why had she wanted him to kiss her? Was she a hussy? A woman of loose morals who wished for a man's touch?

Surely not.

She had never wanted it before. But in that moment when Gabe pulled her close, she'd felt desperate to have his lips on hers. The need to feel his arms around her had urged her to grip his jacket and hold him tight.

God Lord, what does this mean?

"It is time for us to leave now, Miss Spencer."

Remembering her mother's warning, she nodded and collected her things, pleased to push her thoughts aside, no matter how briefly.

"You will stay warm in here and keep the fire going," Maddie said before departing. The children nodded, but she didn't hold out much hope they'd all be there when she returned.

Thankfully, there was no sign of either Gabe or Frank Blackley when they left Spoke House.

Maddie directed the carriage to stop briefly at a shop on the return journey. She dashed in and purchased the gifts she'd told her mother were the reason for leaving the house today. She then directed James, who sat beside the driver, to take her home.

Touching her lips, Maddie could still not believe Gabe had kissed her. The man she'd thought cold and snooty had placed his lips on hers, and she'd felt anything but cold. In fact, warmth had filled her body from her toes to her fingertips.

She'd once hoped for this. Believed they were meant to be together—but not now. Now they were strangers... or so she'd thought. Today had turned that belief on its head.

When he'd grabbed her and his hand touched her thigh, Gabriel had been as shocked as she was. The look on his face when he'd released her had confirmed that.

"A cup of tea will ward off the chill, I think, Miss Spencer," Penny said as they left the carriage and made their way up the four front steps to the Spencer townhouse.

"Indeed, Penny, that sounds just the thing."

Maddie pushed Gabriel from her mind. She had more important matters to think about and needed to focus on Spoke House now.

"Good day to you, Phillips." She handed the butler her bonnet and cloak.

"Good day, Miss Spencer. Your mother has asked that you attend her in the morning parlor upon your return."

Maddie bit back a groan. Clearly, they had a visitor.

"Penny, can you please take my things up to my room."

She didn't exactly stomp to the parlor, but it was a near thing. Her mother had many friends, as did Verity, so they often had callers. The rumble of a deep voice greeted her as she opened the door. Maddie thought seriously about retreating when she saw who was chatting to Verity and her mother.

"Maddie, dear. Look who has come to visit us today."

"How wonderful." The insincerity in her voice was noticed only by Gabriel. "And on such a cold day, Lord Lockhart. We are indeed honored."

He was on his feet bowing when she reached him. She sent him a foul look; his reply was a wide smile that flashed his white, straight teeth.

"You promised," she mouthed before joining her mother on the sofa.

"Gabriel has asked us to join him at the pantomime this evening, dear. Isn't that wonderful?"

"Exceedingly," Maddie muttered.

"Of course, my fiancé has a box so I will be with him, but I am grateful for your invitation, Gabriel," Verity simpered.

Maddie gnashed her teeth.

"And when do you leave London, Lord Lockhart?" she asked with an insincere smile on her lips.

"Gabriel or Gabe, please; we are old friends, after all." He smiled back.

"Gabriel," she managed to get out without choking.

"I am unsure as yet. I have business to finish before I leave. Something unexpected has turned up that may delay me."

He's talking about me. She didn't want him to stay in London and meddle in her affairs.

"And what of you, Lady Spencer. When will you leave for Chasten?"

"As soon as my husband returns, Gabriel. He is at present attending meetings on government business."

"Of course, and we are grateful for all his work on our behalf. And now I must leave you, as I too have business to attend to, but will see you tonight."

"Maddie, see Gabriel out, please."

"Yes, Mama."

Closing the door behind her, she walked Gabe toward the front door.

"My intention for coming here was genuine, Maddie. I thought you and your family would like to go to the pantomime this evening."

"And yet before today you have kept your distance from us."

"Because I was disappointed in the person you appeared to have become. That was wrong of me, I see that now. I should have tried harder to speak with you, but I didn't. You were new to London, I wasn't. Forgive me."

She hadn't expected an apology.

"Perhaps I should have tried harder also," Maddie conceded.

"Perhaps?" He was teasing her now.

"Just perhaps at this stage, Gabriel."

Phillips appeared when they reached the front door and handed Gabe his coat and hat.

"I shall see you tonight then, Maddie."

"Yes."

He moved closer so only she heard what he said next.

"Promise me you won't go back to Spitalfields alone."

"I can't promise you that, but what I will promise is that I will always have two people with me and will show caution."

His eyes ran over her face briefly.

"I don't think you know how to show caution."

"I have promised you that I will try. Is that not enough for now?"

"Not nearly enough." He touched her chin, and then he was gone, leaving her wondering what had happened to her life since she'd opened her eyes that morning.

Suddenly she felt off-balance. As if something monumental and life changing had happened.

Shaking her head, Maddie headed up to her room, where she found her maid sobbing.

"Penny. What has happened?" Maddie took her hands, gripping them hard.

"My br-brother's boy, he's missing. James said my other nephew came to the rear entrance to tell me. He's been gone four days now."

"Oh dear, that's terrible."

"He's been running with a bad crowd, Miss Spencer. My brother, Fred, has six children, and Lewis is the eldest. Fred works long hours, and his wife has the others to watch over."

"And Lewis cannot be watched all the time?"

Penny nodded.

"What do you believe has happened to him?"

"I fear he's been caught doing something he shouldn't and they've put him in prison. I worry he'll be deported." Penny sniffed.

"What is being done to find him?"

"Fred is spending his evenings searching, but so far nothing."

"I'm so sorry. If you need to go and be with your family, please do so."

Her maid sniffed. "Thank you, but there is little I can do at the moment but pray."

Maddie couldn't imagine how it would feel to have a child go missing. She worried constantly for the children of Spoke House and what could happen to them, but they were not of her blood.

"I'm sure all will go well, Penny." Her words sounded empty, but Maddie could think of no other way to help her maid. She would give the matter some thought, but for now she had to prepare for an evening in Gabriel's company.

The thought should not be as pleasing as it was.

Chapter Eight

Maddie still had not come up with a resolution for Spoke House as she readied herself for the pantomime.

Would Gabe help? Dared she asked him to? Wouldn't he have offered if he wanted to?

"Oh, Miss Spencer!"

Penny rushed in, clasping a note in her hands.

"What have you heard? Is it about Lewis?"

"He is in prison because he was caught stealing a fob watch. Fred tried to get him released but was informed that was impossible, and in all likelihood he would end up on a ship bound for the colonies."

"Your poor family, they must be distraught."

"Yes. B-but we have no one to turn to, no one who will help. He is a criminal, and as such he will be punished," Penny cried.

Maddie wasn't sure how she could help, but knew she had to try.

"Firstly, Penny, you must go to your brother and his family after I have left for the evening," Maddie said. "I will not return until late as I must attend the pantomime at the Theatre Royal."

"Thank you, I-I would like to support them." Penny sniffed.

"Of course. And I will think about what can be done. I may have to rise early and go to the prison myself, before the household wakes, to see if I can secure Lewis's release."

"You're never going to the prison, Miss Spencer!" Penny looked shocked. "I could not live with myself if something happened to you."

"I will tell James I want the carriage early and take him with me. Surely there must be someone there I can discuss Lewis's release with?"

Hope flared in Penny's eyes.

"Once I have your nephew, I shall return him home and then be back here before anyone realizes I have left." *Hopefully.* "But you must keep quiet about this, Penny. If any of my family hear, they will not be pleased."

"But you've never been to such a place! Surely it is dangerous? How will you know who to speak with?" Penny's words echoed Maddie's thoughts. Although she sounded confident, inside she was far from it.

"I shall be fine with James at my side. But I cannot promise unequivocally that I will be able to get Lewis released, Penny, so do not tell your family anything yet."

"I don't know how to thank you, Miss Spencer."

"Say nothing more. Now go and get James for me, please."

Penny nodded and went to summon the footman.

He was not pleased.

"It's folly to go to such a place, Miss Spencer."

"Very likely, but a little boy is depending on me, James. We must try something."

"And I'll say again, 'tis folly," the footman muttered before walking away, leaving Maddie to wonder if indeed he was right.

Maddie, Verity, and their mother arrived at the Pantomime to a light flurry of snow. Verity was soon claimed by her fiancé and went off at his side giggling, which Maddie found nauseating.

"Don't scowl, Maddie."

"Sorry, Mama, but I fear my head is sore this evening." She planted the seed that would allow her to sleep late tomorrow. Should anything go amiss at the prison and she was delayed returning, no one would bother her, especially if she locked her door. "These late nights are catching up on me."

"Then you must sleep late tomorrow, darling."

"I believe I will, Mama."

Of course, everything could go amiss at the prison, and she wondered what she could do to aid Lewis's release—if anything. This was unknown territory for Maddie. The problem was, she had no one to ask for help. Her mother would be horrified, and her father was not home.

Dare she asked Gabe?

"If your head pain increases, Maddie, we shall leave, and Stephen will see Verity home, I am sure."

"Very well, thank you, Mother." Maddie pushed down the guilt.

"Lady Spencer, Madeline. How beautiful you both look this evening."

Stay calm. Maddie looked at Gabriel, who had sneaked up on her. He wore a black jacket and waistcoat teamed with the white of his shirt; it was a contrast that only added to the impact of this man.

Before, the only emotion he'd stirred inside her had been irritation and perhaps disappointment, and yet now, since this morning, there was so much more.

"Good evening, Gabriel," Maddie said slowly.

"Why are you frowning?"

"She has a sore head, but it is not bad enough for us to return home," Lady Spencer answered him. "Excuse me one moment, I see someone I need to speak with."

"Who?" Maddie looked around them, but her mother did not answer and had soon disappeared.

"Can I get you anything, Maddie?"

"No, thank you."

"I was being solicitous."

"And I am grateful for your solicitousness."

"I always find that an extremely long word and one that is hard to get your tongue around."

"I'm sure it is a hard word for some to say," Maddie said.

He placed a hand against her spine and nudged her to a wall a few feet away so they were not constantly being bumped into.

"You really should be nicer to me, considering what I know about you, Maddie."

"I was teasing you, and you promised to keep my secret. You are a fiend to suggest otherwise. Now I really must return to my mother." Maddie only managed two steps before a hand gripped her skirts, stopping further progress.

"What are you doing?" Her whisper was furious.

"Stopping you, as I have not finished our conversation," he drawled.

No one could see what he was doing, but if she tried to wrench free, they would.

"Now turn around, Maddie."

"I can't believe you did that." She turned to face him. "Are you quite mad?"

He looked far too happy with himself.

"Perhaps, but then you do bring out the worst in me."

Maddie laughed. He'd often said that when they were children.

"Can I ask you a question, Gabriel?"

"Of course. My considerable knowledge is at your service."

"Your arrogance is showing."

"Can I help that my intellect is vast?"

Maddie didn't reply to that.

"If someone is restrained in an institution—"

"Like a prison such as Newgate?"

"Yes, exactly. How would you go about securing their release, Gabe?"

He lost his relaxed stance and was suddenly alert.

"Who is in prison?"

"Oh, no one I know, it was simply a question."

"It's a very strange question to simply ask. Now tell me why you really want to know." His brows drew together as he frowned at her.

"I like to know things," Maddie said vaguely. "But you are right, it is a silly conversation." She quickly skirted around him and hurried to where her mother stood before he could stop her again.

"What were you and Gabriel discussing, Madeline?"

"Nothing, Mama."

"It did not look like nothing, in fact it looked very much like something. And can I add that once I thought you and he would one day marry. Perhaps now that you seem to be talking once more, that may happen. He would make you a wonderful husband."

Bloody, bothering hell!

"No, Mother, he would not. Now please do not discuss this again."

"And here he comes to take us to our seats. I was just saying to Maddie how wonderful it is to have you back in our lives, Gabriel. You and she were once such close friends, after all."

"We were." His voice gave none of what he was feeing away.

"I shall have to write to your mother tomorrow; she will be as happy as I when she hears you and Maddie have reconnected."

I am doomed.

Chapter Nine

Why had she asked him that question? Gabe mulled it over as he watched the pantomime. It made no sense to him—unless one of her children was in trouble.

Surely she wouldn't be foolish enough to go anywhere near a prison? The thought of Maddie attempting to secure the release of someone from such a place made him feel ill. Was he being dramatic? Had she just asked the question out of curiosity?

Gabe had been there and it was not suitable for gently bred ladies... in fact, any lady.

He looked at Maddie, who was watching the performance, and apparently enjoying it if her smile and the clapping was any indication.

Was he wrong, and she had simply been curious? Lord, he hoped so.

Tonight's dress was a soft rose color. Demure, without too many bows or frills, it made Gabe's hands itch to touch her. He wanted to run them over her body and have no barrier between them. He wanted to kiss her again, had thought of little else since leaving her.

Maddie Spencer had thrown Gabe off-balance, and that didn't sit well. He was a man who liked to be in control at all times.

Looking at the two curls that sat on her slender shoulder, he wondered at their texture and had to clench his fists to stop from reaching for one.

When intermission came, she rose, stating she needed to visit Verity. Minutes later, she hadn't made an appearance in the box two along from Gabe's, where her sister and her fiancé sat with his family.

Lady Spencer was busy chatting with someone to her left and hadn't noticed, so Gabe went to find Maddie. He nodded and forced a smile onto his face, as apparently he scared people otherwise, but saw no sign of her.

Where are you?

He walked down the hallway, eyes searching the guests, and finally found her standing beside a painting.

"How is your head?"

"Gabriel!" She clutched her chest dramatically, which told him she'd been deep in thought and not heard him approaching.

"The very one. Why are you standing here alone looking at this painting of a pantomime when the live one is about to restart?"

"I was hoping the walk and air would ease the ache in here." She tapped the side of her head.

"What air? You're inside a theatre."

"But it is less crowded out here."

"Have you looked at the many people milling at your back?"

"I forgot that about you."

"What?"

"The need to question everything. The need to point out the faults in every sentence. The need to always be right."

"I like things to be factually correct." Gabe shrugged.

"How pompous of you."

"Maddie. What are you up to?"

"What?" She shot him a look. "Nothing," she added far too quickly before returning her eyes to the painting.

"Why did you ask me about the prison earlier? It has made me extremely nervous." Her laugh was stilted.

"There is no need, I was just curious. My maid mentioned that her nephew was in there. I just wondered what the process would be for his father to get him out."

It was a perfectly plausible explanation... so why then did the hair on his neck suddenly rise?

"Maddie, I have spent time at Newgate for various reasons— "

"Have your nefarious activities caught up with you, Gabriel?"

"Ha, no. It is not a place for a woman such as you... in fact, any woman."

"Why would I go there? Good Lord, Gabriel, have you gone mad?"

Her eyes looked innocent, and her head hadn't tilted, so perhaps he was wrong and her question had been innocent.

"Excellent. And can you assure me you are not about to invade someone else's study to rifle through their desk drawers?"

"You know why I did that, Gabriel, and have seen Spoke House."

"You appear to be telling the truth. I see none of the little telltale signs you give when you are not."

"Don't be ridiculous! You can have no idea the person I have become. We've barely conversed."

"You're shrieking," he said reasonably. "And you definitely used to do that when you were cornered."

Her mouth closed with a snap of her teeth.

"And we may not have conversed a great deal of late, but after what we shared today, I feel we know each other a great deal better than we did yesterday."

Color filled her cheeks.

"Do not mention that kiss. It should not have happened and will not again."

"What upsets you the most, Maddie, that you enjoyed our kisses, or that it was with me... the man who you have lately found stuffy?"

"Desist in this line of questioning," she hissed, looking over her shoulder. "And I did not enjoy those kisses."

Gabe saw just the place to prove her wrong. Nudging her backward a few steps, he had her in the small alcove before she realized it.

"What— "

He swallowed the rest of her words. He felt it again, the surge of emotion. Slipping his hand around her back, he pressed her close, loving the feel of her body against his. He wanted more of this woman. The emotion pulsing through him was nothing like he'd felt as a sixteen-year-old. This was so much more.

"Please." She pressed a trembling hand to his mouth when he pulled back to take a breath. "This must stop."

"Look up."

She did and saw the mistletoe.

"We are allowed to kiss under that." Gabe tried to lighten the mood, because he was off-balance himself. He'd disliked the woman Maddie had become, but today everything had changed, and now he wanted her desperately.

"We cannot do this again, Gabriel."

He lifted her chin so he could read her expression. He saw the heat in her eyes; she wanted this as much as he did.

"Everything changed between us today, Maddie. You know that, as I do."

"No."

"Yes." He kissed her again, a soft brush of his mouth over hers.

"My m-mother, she will wonder where we are."

He ran his thumb down her cheek.

"Gabe, please let me go." She pushed against his chest. "Please, I have no wish for anyone to see us."

"All right, but I meant what I said. Everything has changed between us now, Maddie."

"I know" was all she whispered.

He could see she was unsettled, as was he, so he took her back to the box.

The pantomime was loud, with plenty of participation from the audience. Maddie smiled and chatted with her mother, but didn't look at Gabe again. He spent the remainder of the evening looking at her and wondering how his feelings toward her could have changed irrevocably in the space of a day

"That was wonderful, Gabriel."

"I'm glad you enjoyed it, Lady Spencer." Gabe assisted her out of her chair when the show finished.

"I will collect Verity and meet you in the foyer."

"I'll get her, Mother."

But Lady Spencer had already left the box. Gabe took Maddie's arm and followed.

"I want to call on you tomorrow, Maddie. I have some things I wish to discuss in relation to Spoke House."

"What things?" She looked worried.

"Nothing bad, I assure you."

"Very well."

"I meant what I said, Maddie. I don't want you going there without me."

"Gabe, we've discussed this, and I have no wish to do so further tonight. The day has been a long and tiring one."

Which did nothing to ease his mind. Maddie could be reckless, as evidenced by the fact she'd traveled to Spoke House alone many times already. He would leave it alone for now, but tomorrow they would be having a talk, and he would be telling her quite clearly what he expected.

"Come then, I will walk you to your carriage." He guided her down the hallway.

"Hold on to Gabriel, darling. I would hate for you to faint on the way to the carriage because of your poor head."

These words came from behind them.

"I am quite well, Mother. There is no need to fuss."

"But we would hate for anything to harm you, dear Madeline," Gabe teased.

She dug her nails into his sleeve, but as she wore long gloves and he a shirt and jacket, the effect was not felt.

"Tut tut, play nice, Maddie."

"I'm extremely grateful, Gabriel, for your kindness to my dear daughter."

"Mother, he merely escorted us to our carriage," Maddie said in a sharp tone that had Gabe swallowing another smile.

He'd thought her submissive and a society miss who would be a pliant and biddable wife for some man one day. He'd been wrong. She was very much still the young spirited girl he'd known.

"Yes, well, it was still kind, and to take us into his box at the theatre, Maddie. We must not forget that." Lady Spencer gave her daughter a look that he'd received many times from his own mother, suggesting she was displeased.

"Good evening, Gabriel." She turned and batted her eyelashes at him. "Thank you for taking the time to walk me *all the way* to our carriage."

She whispered "all the way" so only he heard the sarcasm.

"You are most welcome, Madeline, and if it is acceptable, I would like to call on you tomorrow, to see if your head is better."

He said the words loudly so Lady Spencer heard them. As he was helping Maddie into the carriage, she could not glare at him.

"Lovely! We shall await you tomorrow then, Gabriel. Good evening."

Gabe waited for Lady Spencer to nudge her daughters firmly onto a seat, then he closed the door. He watched the carriage roll away and tried to understand what he was feeling, and he came to the conclusion that it was something he'd never felt before.

Interest, yes, but there was more. When he'd seen Maddie tonight, he'd felt something warm settle inside his chest.

Smiling, he decided to make for his club. Once there, he and Elliot would discuss the business they must attend to early tomorrow morning, and then he would be paying a call on a certain Miss Spencer. The thought made him ridiculously happy.

Chapter Ten

Maddie held a handkerchief to her nose as the man with the foul-smelling breath remained adamant in his refusal to release Lewis.

"He's not being released, and that's my final word. It's not my decision to make."

"Then tell me who I must speak with?" She'd asked him this question several times already; as yet he had not given her an answer.

She'd risen before the sun and arrived at Newgate early, only to confront this man who did not understand the concept of bathing.

Dear God, what was that running across her feet... a rat, perhaps? Fighting back the scream that had threatened to make an appearance at least twice since she entered the dark, dreary walls of Newgate prison, Maddie tried again to persuade the jailer, one Mr. Stint, to release Lewis into her care.

"But surely if I pay you handsomely you can look the other way, Mr. Stint. I will whisk Lewis from your care without another soul aware of my intentions. I can assure you no one will hear of these events."

Maddie's heart sank further as the large man before her crossed his big, beefy arms and shook his shaggy head.

Looking around the damp walls, she wondered how the little boy fared in such a dismal place. Was he scared? Crying for his mother? How many boys his age were in here? The thought was a sobering one.

"Are you telling me you won't be bribed, Mr. Stint? That you are above such things? Come, we all know everyone is in need of more money." Maddie went for the friendly approach. "I have plenty here in my purse should you just agree to let Lewis Brown, the boy put in here four days ago, out. He stole that watch so he could sell it to feed his family. Can you be so heartless you do not understand that, Mr. Stint?"

Perhaps she should not have left James outside? Would he be able to reason with this man?

"You need to leave here now," Mr. Stint said. "Bloody do-gooders, always thinking they can help those less fortunate than themselves. The boy's a thief, and he'll be punished for his crimes."

"Do you have children of your own, Mr. Stint?" Dismayed, Maddie watched him shake his shaggy head.

Dear Lord, was that something crawling down his shoulder? *Focus, Maddie.* This was not the time to notice the man's hygiene or lack thereof.

"Well, perhaps a niece or nephew?" Again, he shook his head but remained silent. Maddie furiously tried to search for something to bribe Mr. Stint with.

"You are being unreasonable, sir. That boy cannot leave London. How would his family see him again? It would be a gross miscarriage of justice were he deported for such a petty crime."

"He's not being released. Now take your do-gooding ways and get out of here. Bloody nobles."

"How do you know I'm a noble?"

"They've got a certain look, and you have it."

Maddie wasn't sure if she was offended by that statement or not.

"Is there anything I can do or say to persuade you to release Lewis, Mr. Stint?" Maddie tried one last time. If not, she would leave and regroup. Perhaps she would then seek Gabe's help.

Maddie felt her flesh crawl as the large man's demeanor suddenly changed. Those beady eyes ran over her body. Not that he could see much, as she wore a thick coat, but still, it unsettled her further.

"Of course, I might be willing to release the brat if...."

"Certainly not. How dare you suggest what I think you have just suggested!"

Mr. Stint suddenly advanced on her. Oh dear, this was not good, not good at all. She was here alone in a prison with a large, filthy man. It was then Maddie felt the full folly of her impulsive actions, which was what usually happened. Act first and think later seemed to be the motto she'd lived most of her life by.

No one but James knew she was inside, and he would not hear her screams. Her eyes searched for a weapon or somewhere to run, but found nothing. The door was not a great distance, but still, he'd grab her before she reached it. "I... um... I think I can come up with more money, sir, if that is what you wish."

"I've never laid with a proper lady," he said, moving closer.

His foul breath nearly made Maddie retch as she pushed against his chest. She was just about to lift her leg into the man's groin when a voice stopped her.

"I see no reason for your education to change today, Mr. Stint. If you will kindly unhand Miss Spencer, I will think seriously about sparing your life."

Maddie exhaled a breath of relief as Mr. Stint released her and staggered back a step. The fist that followed drove the man back into the wall with considerable force.

With a feeling of impending doom, she turned from Mr. Stint, who was now groaning in agony on the floor, to look at the man behind her.

The anger radiating from his large body was so strong it filled the room. One look into his eyes and she saw he was in a towering rage.

"Get up off the floor, Stint. I did not put as much force as I wanted behind that punch, as we have business to discuss. I will leave my associate to do that while I return Miss Spencer to the safety of her carriage."

Gabriel's words were cold enough to form ice.

"What associate?" Maddie said, attempting to look behind him.

"That would be me." Mr. Elliot Yates entered the room. "Are you all right, Miss Spencer?"

"I am, thank—"

Before she could finish the sentence, a large hand banded around her wrist and dragged her from the room. She was then lifted off her feet and carried down the long, smelly corridor under his arm.

"Unhand me!" She tried to prize his fingers from her waist, but the effort was futile. "I insist you unhand me at once!"

The cold air caught in the back of Maddie's throat as they reached the outer door. She coughed several times. Even this failed to gain a response from Gabriel; instead he kept walking until he reached his carriage.

Wrenching the door open, he threw her inside. Maddie landed in a heap on the soft seat. She struggled to right herself and her bonnet, which was now covering her eyes.

A hand shoved it back.

Finally free, Maddie looked to where Gabriel stood in the carriage doorway.

His large body filled the space, eyes blazing with fury. Hands opened and closed, almost as if he wished he had something clasped between them, namely her neck. Maddie swallowed several times. She would not be intimidated by him. She had something to do and must see it done.

"I am going back inside the prison, Gabriel. It is imperative to the safety of a small boy."

"Be quiet!"

"I will not!" Maddie tried to get off the seat, but he merely nudged her back onto it.

"Gabriel, please, you need to understand—"

"For the love of God, woman, be quiet! I am this close to shaking you so hard your teeth will rattle, but as that would be wrong, I am instead attempting to calm down."

Maddie closed her mouth.

Chapter Eleven

Gabe had been angry in his life before, there were not many who hadn't. He'd even known rage, but this.... God, he wanted to shake her. Then he'd hold her until the emotions inside him had eased, and never let her go.

If he'd been in any doubt that he'd begun to think about this woman in a different light, his reaction to what he'd just witnessed confirmed it.

Seeing her in the clutches of Stint within the filthy walls of Newgate Prison was beyond anything Gabe had ever experienced. He wanted quite simply to kill the man who had threatened Maddie, but as he could not, he needed to find the calm he was known for.

Gabe watched as she struggled to straighten her skirts, and with each movement he thought of Stint touching her and his anger grew.

"Please let me go back in there, Gabriel. I must, don't you see?"

He saw the desperation in her lovely eyes as she begged him, and imagined Stint lying on top of her with his mouth against hers, those lush lips screaming in terror. He clenched his hands into fists to stop them shaking.

When he spoke, it was slow and deliberate, each word chosen with extreme care.

"You will stay in this carriage, and if, Madam, you disobey this order then I will be forced to take action. Do you understand?"

She opened her mouth but shut it again as she darted a quick look at his face.

"Repeat after me: I will not leave this carriage or Gabriel will inform my father of my actions today," he said.

"You would not dare!" she cried.

"Say it, Madeline... now," Gabe ordered.

"I must save my maid's nephew, Gabriel. I-I was not in there for social reasons!"

"No. You were in there because you are a bloody fool who has no regard for her safety. My mistake was believing you had merely asked me that question last night to ease your curiosity. Now repeat the words, Maddie."

"I will not." She crossed her arms.

"'I will not leave this carriage or Gabriel will inform my father of my actions today.' Say the words, Maddie, or by God, I will stand here until you do."

She looked away.

"I cannot save the boy if you do not say them."

"Will you? Oh, Gabe, thank you."

He did not weaken at the glisten of tears in her eyes, he had to deal with Stint and find the boy. If he touched her now, he'd never leave.

"Say the words, as I do not trust that you will stay in here while I do what I must."

"I will!"

He didn't speak.

"I will not leave this carriage or Gabriel will inform my father of my actions today."

"Tell me about the boy."

She did so quickly. With a curt nod, Gabe pulled the curtains across the windows and slammed the door with enough force that the carriage swayed.

He spoke to his driver. "Adam, do you still have that length of rope beneath your seat?"

"I do, my lord."

"If Miss Spencer opens that door, you are to tie her hands and feet, is that understood?"

"Ah, yes, my lord," came the confused reply.

Ignoring the outraged cry from his carriage, Gabe walked back inside the jail.

Twenty minutes later, he handed the small, terrified Lewis Brown into the carriage beside Elliot. He was dirty and cold, but none the worse for his experience.

"Take him home in Miss Spencer's carriage, Elliot, and I will return her to her parents. I shall contact you later today."

"Be gentle with her, Gabe. She was incredibly brave to do what she did," his friend said.

"She was incredibly foolish!" Gabe still felt the bite of anger. Shutting the door, he turned to address the footman who was hovering nearby.

"You should never have brought your mistress to such a place. It was only luck that we arrived when we did."

"I tried to tell her not to come, my lord, but she said if I didn't bring her, she would find another way to get here."

Gabe's bark of laughter held little amusement. He just bet she did, the little shrew. "Not the easiest of mistresses, then?"

"No, my lord, but the very best and kindest," the footman added.

"Take the boy to his mother now, and then Mr. Yates to his address, please. I will return your mistress to her home safely."

The footman climbed up beside the driver and then the carriage rolled away.

Looking at the sky, he thought they had perhaps a few hours before her household rose.

Gabe opened the door of his carriage and felt the last of his rage flee as he looked at the slumbering form of Maddie. She'd taken off her bonnet and lay on her side with her hands beneath her chin. Long lashes resting on her pale cheeks, she looked like an angel sleeping peacefully. Climbing inside, he shut the door and turned up the lamps, then took the seat opposite her and watched her eyes open as the carriage began to move.

Confusion clouded the dark depths, and then clarity as she remembered where she was. Sitting upright, she looked at him.

"The boy?" Her whispered words were desperate.

"He is safe and at this moment on his way home with Elliot."

She nodded, her relief evident. He watched as the long lashes closed fleetingly. "Thank you."

Gabe felt his anger flare to life.

"Why did you not tell the truth at the pantomime? I could have helped you. Dear God, Maddie, have you any idea of the danger you placed yourself in going to the prison alone? Had I not arrived when I did, you could have been raped and beaten, then left for dead."

The color drained from her cheeks. He didn't want to hurt her, but she needed to understand what could have happened. Needed to know she could not simply walk blindly into situations without a thought to the consequences.

"I did what I had to do, what anyone would have done were they in my position."

He was having none of it. She may look like a delightfully rumpled angel, but he was still bloody furious that she had put herself in so much danger. And he would get her to acknowledge what she'd done was wrong if it killed him.

"Perhaps, but anyone with a lick of sense would have sought help in their endeavors."

"Who was I to ask?"

"Me!"

"I do not know you well enough to do so." She looked away.

"After today, yes, you do, Maddie. What you did was reckless and merely reinforces my belief you cannot be left alone... or, for that matter, trusted."

Dark eyes spat fire back at him.

"I do not answer to you! You may have the right to vote and educate yourself, but that does not make you any more intelligent than me. You cannot treat me as if I were a... a simpleton. You do not have the right to tell me what I can and cannot do!"

Gabe actually blinked. Where the hell had all that come from?

Bracing his booted feet on the seat opposite, he folded his arms in a pose designed to infuriate his beautiful companion further. She was here, safe with him; he was beginning to feel calmer. Maddie had been easy to niggle when they were children, and he found he wanted to see if that was the same now. He needed some retribution for what she'd put him through tonight.

"Come now, Maddie, surely you can see that men have a far superior emotional and intellectual capacity than women?"

She let out a little screech of outrage, her fists clenching as if she'd like to strike him. *Direct hit.*

"Utter rubbish. From an early age, women are forced to face life's realities, while men swan around behaving like small boys until they are in their dotage."

She had a point there, Gabe conceded silently.

"But I do not make the rules, Maddie. Furthermore, this has little to do with your irresponsible behavior. If you think your actions this morning in any way strengthen your argument, then I suggest you think again."

Maddie glared at him, then spoiled the effect entirely by sniffing. He watched her small white teeth clamp around that full bottom lip to stop it from trembling.

She had to have been terrified when Stint grabbed her. He had no idea how she'd found the strength to even walk inside that jail, but she had, and he remembered again the strong girl he'd once known.

"I'm sorry that man scared you today." He'd tormented her enough. "Will you let me hold you? Only then will I know you are truly safe."

She flew across the carriage and into his arms, and Gabe crushed her against him.

"You scared me this morning, and I do not scare easily," he whispered into her hair. "You must promise me that you will never attempt anything so foolhardy again." Soft curls brushed his chin as she nodded.

"I promise," she sighed. "And I am sorry to have scared you. To be honest, I was scared a great deal more."

"I wish I could believe you." Gabe enjoyed the feel of her in his arms. "I think I shall just have to oversee your movements personally from now on."

"I cannot turn my back on someone who needs my help. So many have no one to turn to."

"I understand that, but you cannot continue to do these things alone. There is too much risk. The thought of you going to Spoke House was terrifying enough, but now I will be haunted with visions of you visiting prisons too."

"I will not change who I am or what I do because of what happened, Gabe. But I promise to show more caution."

That would do for now. He knew they would have several heated debates about her actions in the future, but for now he simply wanted to hold her.

"How came you to be at Newgate prison this morning, Gabe?"

He'd known this question was coming but still had not rehearsed the answer, so he settled on the truth.

Chapter Twelve

"Three years ago, Elliot ran over a boy in his carriage. His name was Luke and he was twelve years old. Horrified at what he'd done, and unsure what to do with the child, he brought him to my house. He was not badly hurt but had suffered a sprained ankle and lots of bruising. Luke was very agitated and most insistent that he leave; upon further questioning I realized why."

Maddie didn't want to leave the comfort of Gabe's arms, yet knew it was the correct thing to do.

"I shall return to my seat."

"I'm not letting you go. Now, be quiet and listen. You asked me a question, and I'm answering it."

It did not take much to convince her to stay. She rested her head on his chest, and his chin brushed the top of her head.

Did Verity feel this way when she sat close to Stephen? Maddie hoped so, because it was a wonderful feeling.

There was something powerful stirring inside her for this man, and Maddie had a feeling she knew exactly what it was, but she'd think more about it later. For now, she wanted to hear his story.

"Luke was the sole caregiver for his brothers and sisters, of which there were four."

Gabe went on to explain that their father had died and their mother had abandoned them. It was a story like so many others.

"What are you doing?" she asked when he leaned over her.

"Getting a blanket." He reached under the seat. "I'm cold, so I'm sure you must be."

He wrapped it around her.

"Gabe, I don't think this is right."

"It feels right." he looked down at her.

It did feel right. It felt amazing.

"The abbreviated version of an incredibly long story is that we have set up several houses out of London for families and children who have nowhere to go."

"What a wonderful thing you and Elliot are doing, Gabe."

"Are you weeping, Maddie?"

"Of course not, I don't weep."

"What, never?" he teased. "How terribly hardhearted of you, Miss Spencer."

"I am sorry that I doubted you for so very long, Gabe."

She could see her words had confused him.

"Sorry I doubted your ability to be the man I wanted you to be. The man who the boy I cared for had grown into."

Silence greeted this statement; the only sound was the clip-clop of horses' hooves.

His eyes held hers, the blue depths intent and seeking. "I feel the same way about you. I loathed the woman I thought you had become. This one is so much nicer." His finger traced the line of her nose.

"I'm glad neither of us have changed so much."

"Amen," he whispered. His eyes ran over her face slowly and settled on her lips. "I want you so much, Maddie."

She closed her eyes as he lowered his head, and the kiss that followed was everything she wanted and so much more.

The emotions of the past few hours drove them on; passions rose and consumed them. He drank from her lips, his tongue teasing hers, stroking the inside of her mouth, and Maddie kissed him, holding nothing back.

She felt his fingers on the buttons of her coat. He opened them slowly, then parted the edges.

"I want to touch you, Maddie." The rasp of need in his voice made her shiver.

"I want that too."

Gabe lowered her to the seat and then pulled the bodice of her gown down until her breasts were free. Maddie should be shocked; she wasn't. Her body ached for more.

"You're beautiful." His hands cupped her breasts, fingers stroking her nipples. "You could incite a man to murder. Don't be afraid, Maddie."

"I'm not afraid, Gabe. I know you would never hurt me."

Insecurities forgotten, maidenly shyness pushed aside, her own needs soon matched his. Reaching for him, Maddie pushed his overcoat and jacket from his shoulders. After removing his necktie, she began unbuttoning his shirt, as eager to see him as he was her. Desperate to touch his body.

She traced the hard planes of his chest, her fingers brushing his nipples. Gabe shuddered, so she did it again.

"Your skin feels so good to touch, all slopes and hard planes... and warm... so very warm." Maddie watched her hands as they mapped his chest.

"Your touch is like heaven and hell combined," Gabe gritted out.

Lowering his head, he kissed her again, this one more intense than the last. It spoke of the tension that was building inside them.

His lips moved down her neck, igniting where they touched. Reaching her breasts, Gabe licked the sensitive curve on one, and then gently grazed his teeth over her nipple. Maddie cried out as delicious shivers coursed through her body.

"So responsive, my sweet Maddie. I should have known it would be like this between us. Our connection has never quite severed."

His hand moved under her skirts. One palm stroked her leg through the wool of her stockings as it traveled up her thigh, exposing her to his gaze with every inch her hem rose. The tension inside Maddie was almost unbearable now. She'd never felt this way before; the wicked heat licking at her senses had her writhing beneath Gabe's hands.

She tensed as cool air touched her exposed skin.

"Trust me," he whispered against her lips. His kiss was soft and searching, touching her soul.

Maddie's eyes closed as he stroked a finger softly over the curls only she had ever touched before. A moan tore from her lips as he moved lower. The first brush of his hand had her arching off the seat.

"Gabe?"

"Trust me, Maddie." His voice was hoarse with a need that matched hers.

He touched the hard bud between her thighs, and she shuddered. His lips found her breast as he pushed a finger inside her tight sheath.

"Let go for me, my sweet." He thrust in and out, and the sensations climbed. She arched off the bench, shattering in ecstasy seconds later.

"Christ, Maddie, you're beautiful." He kissed her hard. "I want you, sweetheart. Do you understand what that means?"

She touched his jaw. Clenched tight, the muscles bunched as he spoke. "Now, Gabe. I want you now."

"It will hurt, sweetheart."

"I know. Penny, my maid, told me about what happens between a man and woman."

His laugh was a gruff bark as he released his breaches. "I don't want to know what she told you."

"That it can hurt... ah, especially if the woman is not ready."

"You are." He touched her again, his hand cupping her breast. "I would never hurt you, Maddie."

"I know that."

He moved over her, bracing his hands on either side of her head. Maddie felt him there, pressing against her entrance. His eyes held hers, the blue depths intent. As he eased inside, she felt a small sting of pain and then, her body accepted him inch by inch until, he was there, seated deep and high.

"Tell me what you feel, Maddie."

"I feel as if you are part of me now." She lifted her arms and wrapped them tight around his neck.

"How is the pain?" he gritted out, tension in every line of his body.

"It eases."

He slowly withdrew, and then reentered.

"That feels... well, it's quite wonderful," Maddie whispered.

His grunt sounded as if he was in pain.

"Gabe?"

He kissed her hard, then thrust back inside her once more. Maddie felt the wonderful tension build inside her again.

"Let go again, Maddie. Do it for me, sweetheart."

She did, flying once more, and with a final thrust, Gabe followed her.

Chapter Thirteen

Gabe rode his horse toward the Spencer town house, impatient to see Maddie.

He'd managed to smuggle her back inside the house undetected two days ago, with the promise that he would call on her today. Her smile had been a secret lover's smile, the kind Gabe had seen Elliot and Lyndy share when she left him.

He'd had a business meeting that he couldn't postpone yesterday but had spent the entire time thinking of her.

Maddie, his love.

He loved her, there could be no other word for the feelings inside him. He wanted to spend the rest of his life with Madeline Spencer and was certain she felt the same. She would never have made love with him in his carriage if she did not.

Just thinking about what they'd shared in the early hours of that morning made his body stir. So passionate for someone who had been an innocent. She'd touched him, and his body had responded as it never had before.

He smiled as he thought about the years ahead of them. They would argue and debate and then he'd take her to bed and hold her the entire night. The thought had his smile growing.

Patting his breast pocket, he felt the rustle of paper. This was his gift to her, and he knew no flowers or jewels would make her happier.

Knocking on the front door, he waited impatiently for someone to answer.

"I wish to speak with Miss Madeline Spencer. Please tell her Lord Lockhart has called," he told the butler when the door finally opened.

"I'm afraid she is unable to accept callers today, my lord."

"What? Why?"

"I cannot say, my lord."

"I wish to speak with Lady Spencer at once then."

"If you will come this way, I shall see if she is receiving callers."

Gabe paced the small confines of the parlor he'd been placed in. Was Maddie sick?

"Gabriel?"

Lady Spencer entered the room, and one look at her red eyes told him something was very wrong.

"My Lady, are you well?"

"I am thank you. My husband has recently returned to London, and I am expecting him home from his club shortly."

Which told him nothing.

"Something has happened to upset you, perhaps I can help in some way?

Lady Spencer collapsed into a chair and started weeping.

"Where is Maddie?" The words came out with more force than he'd intended, but something told him that whatever was going on in the Spencer household, it involved Maddie. "Please, my lady. Tell me what has caused your distress?"

"She and Henry had a terrible fight. I do not know all the details, only that he was very angry with her. Then just moments ago a letter arrived demanding money for Maddie's return. She has been kidnapped, Gabriel!"

"What?" Gabe's body went cold. Not his Maddie. He couldn't lose her now that he'd only just found her again.

"She left the house without our knowledge after Henry told her she was forbidden to leave her room. Oh, Gabriel." Lady Spencer staggered to her feet and collapsed against him. "My darling girl is in danger."

Gabe held Maddie's mother while he grappled with what must be done. He had to find her, but where did he start? Maddie needed him to be controlled now; this was what he usually excelled at.

"I will find her." Gabe released her. "Stay here and try to remain calm. I will send word."

"H-Henry will arrive soon and know what to do."

"Very likely, but I cannot sit here and wait for him. I must go and find her now.

"B-but how will you know where to go?"

"I will find her," Gabe said with a confidence he was far from feeling. "But first I need to speak to your footman."

"Which one? Why?"

"Bring them in here. I have no time to explain."

Minutes later he was speaking with the one he wanted.

"You are James, correct?"

"I am, my lord."

"And you know your mistress is missing?"

"Yes, I know what has happened." The footman's face was clenched with worry. "But she left the house without me. If I'd known she was leaving, I'd have gone."

"I understand, and be assured this is not your fault," Gabe said. "Do you know who dropped off the ransom note, James?"

"A boy, but he fled before we could question him," the footman said.

"Who would want to hurt her, James?" Gabe wanted to roar. He wanted to run out onto the street and not stop running until he'd found Maddie. But he couldn't help her that way.

"Frank Blackley and his brothers."

"Why?"

"He's always there trying to get money out of her, and she won't pay him. Not Miss Spencer; she won't be intimidated."

Gabe saw the respect on the footman's face.

"Gabriel, what has you here today?" The parlor door opened, and in walked Lord Spencer.

"Oh, Henry!" Lady Spencer ran to her husband. "Maddie has been kidnapped."

"What!"

"She left the house after you forbade her to do s-so."

"Good God!" Lord Spencer staggered back with his wife and fell onto the sofa.

"Why had you forbidden her from leaving the house, Spencer?" Gabe asked.

"Tell him, Henry. He and Maddie have grown closer," Lady Spencer urged her husband.

"My solicitor contacted me. It seems Maddie has been involving herself in things she should not. I came home to sort that out. I confronted her, told her I knew what she was up to. We argued, I am ashamed to say, then I forbade her from leaving the house."

Maddie would be distraught if her father kept her from Spoke House, but he had no time to worry about that now. He had to find her.

"I know what you speak of," Gabe said. "And it is there I'm going now, as I believe she would have visited Spoke House today."

"You knew?" Lord Spencer got out of his seat. "You should have told me, Gabriel."

"I have only just learned of it myself and was taking steps to stop her going there."

Lord Spencer paced across the room.

"She mentioned you, and at the time I didn't understand. She said you'd betrayed her."

It made him angry that she thought him capable of telling her father about Spoke House after what they'd shared. But he had no time to think about that now; he would deal with her lack of faith in him when he found her.

"I am going to find her and I'm taking your footman with me, Spencer."

"I will come with you."

"It will be easier if I go alone."

Her father wanted to argue, but to his credit he simply nodded. "I will go to Watch House and get the money in case it should be needed."

"I will succeed," Gabe vowed.

"Bring her back to us, please," Lady Spencer begged.

He left the house, directing his driver to take him to Spoke House. James sat silently opposite him in the carriage, looking worried.

"How did she manage to get you to accompany her to Spoke House, James?" Gabe needed to talk, or he'd go mad. The thought of anyone hurting Maddie was not to be borne.

"She bribes me with food. But I would go even if she didn't, just to keep her safe."

"Tell me more about this Blackley."

"I don't know much about him, only what the children told me when I questioned them. Seems he and his brothers believe they have control over that part of London. They extort money out of people. Protection money, they call it. If they don't pay it, the Blackleys hurt family members until it's paid."

Gabe didn't want to contemplate Maddie in the hands of such men.

He was out of the carriage and running up the steps into Spoke House seconds after it stopped. He found several of the children there. Gabe dragged a chair before them and sat so his size didn't intimidate them.

"I need your help, so please listen carefully."

They all nodded, watching him wide-eyed.

"Miss Spencer has gone missing. When did you last see her?"

They were visibly upset by his news, but he could not take the time to comfort them. All that mattered was getting Maddie back.

"She was here for a bit this morning, but she was upset and said she had to leave."

She was upset because she believed he'd told her father about Spoke House.

"A ransom note was sent to her family, and James believes that Frank Blackley is behind her kidnapping. I must find her, but I will need your help to do so."

Horror was etched on the children's faces now.

"Them Blackleys are bad!"

"What do you know, Hetty?"

"They didn't see me, but I heard them a few days ago. I was in the doorway two along, hiding when I heard their footsteps. They were talking about her... Maddie."

"What were they saying, Hetty?" Gabe crouched beside the little girl.

"That she was looking for trouble coming here alone. That she'd fetch a pretty price if they took her. I told Maddie. Told her to have a care."

"We need to find her."

"Where do we search for her? Where would the Blackleys have taken her?" Gabe looked around the worried faces.

"I know, follow me."

"What's your name?" Gabe asked the boy who had spoken.

"I'm Graham, and these are Jack and Paul."

He and James followed the three boys who had volunteered to find Maddie out onto the streets and started running.

I'm coming, Maddie. Stay safe until I reach you.

Chapter Fourteen

"Let me go!" Maddie yelled, as she had many times since she'd arrived here. Wherever here was. "You can't hope to hold me here! My father will find you; then you'll know fear!"

Maddie swallowed down the terror that clawed at her throat. Terror and despair. *Gabe had betrayed her.*

Had she been thinking clearly, she would never have allowed Frank Blackley to grab her, but her thoughts had been on Gabe's betrayal.

Her father had told her someone he knew and respected had alerted him to Maddie's involvement in Spoke House. There were plenty of people who were aware of what she did there, but none who would betray her or surely, they would have done so by now. Gabe had known for only a matter of days, and he'd told her he didn't want her going back there. Maddie believed this was how he intended to ensure that. The realization of his betrayal hurt so much it was almost a physical pain.

She'd fallen in love with the fiend and believed he could love her back. And yet he'd made love to her as if he cared and then betrayed her. Now she would have to live with her foolishness. She'd never love or trust again, Maddie vowed. That was, if she got out of here alive.

"Cad!"

She'd waited until her father left the house, forbidding his youngest daughter to even leave her room, and then had defiantly slipped out.

After leaving Spoke House, where the children had asked her what was wrong, she'd been grabbed from behind, a sack thrown over her head, and bundled into a cart. The rest was a blur.

She was bound hand and foot, a blindfold placed over her eyes, and transported to this warehouse by a rowboat. Clearly, she was by the Thames somewhere, and likely down at the docks. She just had no idea where or how anyone would find her now.

They'd left her on the cold floor, wrenched off her blindfold, and walked away, leaving her still bound hand and foot.

There was no furniture, not even a barrel or a crate, only Maddie and the dark, murky waters of the Thames beyond the dock that was a few feet away from where she sat.

She'd moved around on her knees, and hopped, but found nothing to cut the ropes from her wrists or a way to leave. She'd drown if she went into the water, which her captors knew when they'd placed her here.

Slumping down the wall to the cold floor once more, Maddie watched the water as daylight slowly dwindled into darkness and tried to fight back the panic that clawed at her throat. The place seemed even more sinister now that the only light she had was from the moon as it cast shadows over the water.

It was damp, and the cold had slipped into her bones and stayed there. Clenching and unclenching her fingers, she tried to warm them up, but the job was hopeless.

She'd been alone in here for hours. Alone with her thoughts, and they were not good company.

Focus on that perfidious fiend, Gabriel Lockhart. The rage will warm you up.

Her father's rage had been worse than any she'd encountered before, and there had been times when she tested him... but this was worse.

He'd threatened to send her back to Chasten and leave her there forever. His disappointment in her for what she'd done, looking after those children and renting Spoke House, had cut deep. Maddie had tried to explain, but he'd not wanted to listen.

There had also been dire warnings about a convent before he left, slamming the door behind him.

The sound of footsteps had her struggling to her feet, using the wall at her back as a prop. She would not cower to Frank Blackley, the man who walked toward her.

"I wish for food." Maddie wouldn't let him see her fear.

"You'll get it when I'm ready." He moved closer. She stood her ground. "I've always wondered if it would be different with a lady."

Maddie didn't want to contemplate what "it" meant but had a terrible feeling she already knew.

"You do realize, of course, what the penalty for kidnapping the daughter of one of England's most respected peers will be, don't you, Mr. Blackley?"

He leered at her, his eyes settling on her breasts.

"Let me educate you, Miss Spencer. We don't care about you or your family. We only care about the money you'll bring us. No one will find us if we don't want to be found, and that goes for you also."

"My father will never give you money without seeing me first."

Her skin was literally crawling at the look in this man's eyes as they traveled over her. But Maddie would not let him see her fear, only her disdain.

"We'll just have to send him a little incentive then, won't we."

Before she could stop him, he'd ripped open her cloak, the heavy material falling from her shoulders, and wrenched the necklace from her neck. Maddie lunged at him, but as she was bound, she fell to the floor.

She welcomed the anger, because it gave her strength. Forcing herself into a sitting position she glared at him, then made herself laugh.

"I will be in the front row for your hanging, Mr. Blackley. And I shall enjoy the moment immensely."

The surprise on his face made her force out another laugh. She was not laughing a moment later when he kicked her in the thigh. But she did not whimper. She would never show this man fear.

The slap she took to her left cheek, however, made her cry.

Chapter Fifteen

"They have a place there." Graham pointed to a narrow building that looked uninhabited. Boards were loose or rusted, and it had a general air of decay.

"Are you sure?" Gabe asked the boy.

Graham nodded. "It's a warehouse with an open end and a dock, which allows them to do any number of underhand dealings as no one can see what comes in by boat."

He and his friend Becks, who they'd picked up at their second stop, had been James and Gabe's guide for the last few hours.

They'd gone from place to place, meeting people and getting information or any clue as to where the Blackleys were holding Maddie.

God, she has to be safe and unharmed.

Desperation clawed at Gabe. She was out here somewhere, and he couldn't find her—and when he did it may be too late.

No! He couldn't allow himself to contemplate that. He had to find her. He couldn't live without her now.

The weather was cold now that night was settling around them. An icy cold that chilled your cheeks and formed puffs of white when you spoke.

"I'm going inside the warehouse. James, you take the boys and wait by the entrance, but stay out of sight."

"I'd advise strongly against that, my lord."

"And yet that's what I am doing."

The footman tried to argue, but Gabe was determined. If he was to get inside that warehouse undetected, he needed to do so quietly. He also needed someone outside to carry on looking for Maddie should something happen to him. He kept that to himself, however.

The darkness hid him as he walked around the building searching for the entrance. Pushing the door so it was just wide enough to slip inside, Gabe then pressed his back to the wall.

Pulling out his pistol, he moved slowly down the building. He could see weak light coming from somewhere up ahead. Passing wooden crates, he listened for any sound that would tell him someone was in the building. More importantly, was Maddie in here? When he got her back, he was never letting her go.

He heard no voices, but that didn't mean he was alone.

"Take another step and it will be your last."

Gabe froze as the muzzle of a gun pressed into his spine.

"We have company!" He was pushed forward. "Hand over the gun and walk."

He did as he was told and started moving. Gabe could not help Maddie if he was dead.

"Left."

He tracked left and soon found himself near the end of the warehouse. He could hear the lap of water.

"Let me go!"

Fear locked every muscle in his body rigid as he took the two paces needed to bring Maddie into his line of vision. Her lovely eyes filled with tears as she saw him.

"Gabriel!"

Ignoring the man behind him and the one who stood beside Maddie, Gabe walked toward her.

"Who the hell is this?" the man with her demanded.

"I don't know. He was inside the warehouse with a gun, Frank. So, my guess, he's come looking for her."

"You'll stop now!"

"You'll have to shoot me." Gabe reached Maddie and pulled her into his arms. Relief filled him that she was alive and he was holding her once more. "Because my fiancée is terrified and I am going to comfort her."

She was cold, her body shaking as he held her close. Her cheek was bruised, and he'd make someone pay for her pain, but they held weapons. He did not. Retribution would have to wait. Getting her out of here was his main priority now. To do that, he must keep calm.

"You should not have come," she whispered in his ear.

"How could I not? I love you, Maddie."

"You lie!" Her whisper was furious.

"What is your name?"

Gabe looked at the man who spoke, recognizing him as the man who had been at Spoke House that day. Frank Blackley.

"I am Lord Lockhart, Blackley, and you will pay for hurting the woman I love." The man laughed.

"I like your bravery, even if it is hopeless. Therefore, I am willing to indulge you with a final farewell to your beloved. After all, tonight will be the last time you see each other."

"You would shoot an earl and a viscount's daughter?" He pulled Maddie closer and whispered in her ear, "Trust me." Only she could hear his words.

"I care nothing for your birth, only the money she will bring me. You can be found floating in the Thames, and it will be a terrible accident that you've drowned." Blackley laughed. "Although perhaps you will net me more?"

No. It would not end here, Gabe vowed silently, pressing his face into her hair. They would live to raise their children and grow old in each other's arms. He would ensure it.

"Release her now and move away."

"A final goodbye, please, I beg of you," Gabe said, injecting desperation into his tone.

The men laughed at him as he wrapped both arms around her.

"Start crying loudly," Gabe said into the shell of her ear.

Her sobs were real, Gabe knew that, and loud enough to make him wince. "When I say jump, you jump into the water, Maddie, and start swimming. I will make sure you are safe."

She didn't acknowledge him, and Gabe knew what he asked of her was terrifying. She was bound hand and foot and would drown in seconds without him.

"Very touching. Now step away from Miss Spencer."

"I cannot," Gabe said, his words anguished. "Have you no mercy?"

As he spoke, he crept slowly backward with Maddie until they were inches from the water.

"Take a big breath." Gabe clutched Maddie close to him. "Now jump!"

Curses rent the air behind them as they both fell into the icy water. Gabe felt a bullet graze his arm, but he didn't stop. Grabbing Maddie's arm, he towed her down with him under the water. He knew she was struggling with the weight of her clothes. Panic would be clawing at her as she fought against her bonds.

The darkness would cover them when they left the warehouse, but Gabe wanted them out into the Thames, where hopefully the tide would sweep them away from the Blackley brothers. She gasped in a huge breath of air as he pushed her upward and they broke free of the water.

"I have you now." Gabe pulled her into his arms, keeping her afloat as they began to move swiftly with the current.

"Un-untie me, we will drown!"

"I can't stop to do that now!"

Gripping her under the arms, he kept them both afloat and angled toward the bank.

"A few more minutes, Maddie," he said as the bank drew nearer, and then his feet touched. Grabbing her waist, he sat her on the edge, and then followed, pulling himself out beside her.

Removing the knife from his boot, he quickly cut the ties from her hands and ankles. She was shivering, great shudders of cold wracking her body. He was no better.

"We need to move before they find us, Maddie. James is around here somewhere with your boys."

"Wh-which b-boys?'

"Does it matter?"

Gabe lifted Maddie to her feet and tried to take her in his arms again, but she pushed away. The force behind the slap she gave his cheek was weak, but it still stung.

"What the hell was that for?"

"Y-you betrayed me."

Chapter Sixteen

Just looking at him hurt. When he'd walked into the warehouse with one of Blackleys holding him at gunpoint, Maddie had known real fear... and pain. Lots of pain. She'd wanted to yell at him to run, even considering what he'd done, because she loved him.

"Maddie, we have no time for hysterics now. We must leave."

"I h-hate you."

"I just rescued you!"

"Th-thank you for that. I st-still hate you."

He grabbed her upper arms and pulled her close until she stood on her toes... so close his cold nose now touched hers.

"I didn't betray you."

"My father—"

"Your father's solicitor found information in his son's papers. It was he who wrote and told your father what you were doing, not I."

"B-but—"

"Shut up and listen to me." Gabe gave her a little shake. "We have to get out of here or one of those Blackleys will put a bullet through us, and if that doesn't happen, the cold will finish us off."

"Are y-you telling me the truth?"

He sighed. "Yes. I told you I would not tell your father. Have a little faith, woman."

She couldn't help it, Maddie burst into tears.

"Shhh, have mercy, woman. Can you not weep softly?" Gabe pulled her into his chest, pressing her against his cold body, but Maddie didn't care. He hadn't betrayed her after all.

"Maddie, my love. I want to spend the rest of my life with you, but to do that we need to get away from here. To do that, we need to move now."

"I-I know... it's just that—"

He put his hand over her mouth. "I need you to be quiet now. Do you understand?"

Maddie nodded.

He took her hand and towed her along the bank. She couldn't see anything and hoped Gabe was leading them away from danger and the Blackley brothers.

He stopped, then pulled her behind him.

"We've got to find them."

Maddie knew only relief at the voice up ahead of them.

"We are here, James," Gabe said, taking her hand once more.

"My lord, have you found her?"

"I have."

Maddie couldn't speak, she was so cold.

"She's extremely cold. We had to jump in the water to escape."

"Here's my jacket."

Maddie nearly moaned at the bliss she felt as Gabe wrapped James's jacket around her shoulders.

"We must get her home."

After that everything became a blur for Maddie. They hurried from the docks with the boys.

Somehow Graham found a cart, and she was placed on that, seated in Gabe's lap. He wrapped her in his arms, both now shivering and chilled to the bone. The cart slowly rolled through London, taking them home.

"Nearly there, sweetheart." He kissed the top of her head. "My brave girl."

"I-I'm sorry I thought you'd b-betrayed me, Gabe."

"Such little faith in the man you love, Maddie. We will have to work on that."

She looked up at him, his handsome face smiling down at her.

"How d-do you know I love you?"

"Because you always have."

There was nothing she could say to that, because his words were the absolute truth.

Christmas Eve at Chasten was a festive affair. The house was decorated with evergreen boughs of holly, ivy, hawthorn, rosemary, and hellebore, sending sweet scent into the air. The Yule log had been lit, and games played. It was quite simply the best Christmas Eve Maddie had ever experienced—because Gabe was here.

After her kidnapping he'd asked her father for her hand in marriage, right there in the entrance of their London townhouse. Her father had agreed gladly. Gabe said that was because he was relieved he no longer had to worry about his reckless daughter.

Verity had surprised her too. Crushing her in a hug, she'd told Maddie she loved her and had been terrified at the thought they may never see each other again. Since that day they'd grown closer.

In a week she and Gabe would marry, here on her father's estate, and she wanted that so much now. He was her life, as she was his.

Retiring for the evening, Maddie lay in bed thinking of the life she would have as his wife. She could not wait. He had bought Spoke House for her, and together they would work at making it a safe place for the children to come. Together, they would have many more houses situated around England for those who had no one else to care for their welfare.

Maddie heard the door to her room open. Seconds later, the rustle of clothes followed, and then he was there beside the bed, sliding beneath the sheets.

"I should be shocked."

His laugh was a soft rumble as he slid his arms around her and settled her against his body.

"Hello, my sweet, and biddable fiancée."

This time she laughed.

"You looked so beautiful tonight, Maddie, that I wanted to plant my fist in any man who looked your way."

"Wonderful, then my plan worked."

"Shrew." He rolled her onto her back and kissed her.

"This love, Gabe, does it scare you?" Maddie cupped the cheek above her.

"No. It warms me and makes me stronger."

"But it is also a strange thing. I thought very closely about hurling my eclair at Lady Helen when she patted your arm and batted her lashes at you, and I love eclairs."

"Jealousy is new to me also, my sweet."

She looked up at him, the weak moonlight letting her study each and every feature on his handsome face.

"I love you, Gabe. I love your strength and your kindness. I love the boy I once knew and the man I am still learning about. Never leave me."

"Never," he breathed against Maddie's lips. Then there was no need of words as they set about showing each other their love.

The End

About Wendy

Wendy Vella is a bestselling author of contemporary and historical romances that have sold more than a million copies worldwide. Join her mailing list at wendyvella.com/subscribe for free reads, extra scenes and reader goodies.

Known for compelling and uplifting stories laced with witty humor, sensuality and intrigue, Wendy has hit the bestseller ranks many times with reader favorites, the Langley Sister series, Lords of Night Street series, Sinclair & Raven series, and contemporary small-town series' Lake Howling and Ryker Falls.

An incurable romantic, Wendy found writing romance a natural fit. When her children were small, she would find writing time in the early hours of the morning, sitting quietly with her grandfather's old typewriter while the family slept. These works, however, she says, will never see the light of day! Wendy joined Romance Writers of New Zealand and started honing her craft, and after years of contests and conferences, she was finally ready to publish her first book in 2013.

Born and raised in a rural area in the North Island of New Zealand, she shares her life with one adorable husband, two delightful adult children and their partners, four delicious grandchildren, and too many cantankerous farm animals.

You can find details of her work at
www.WendyVella.com

The Duke She Despised

BY

Alina K. Field

The new Duke of Kinmarty has lost everyone who mattered and gained naught but a title, and debt, and an old pile of a castle. Then a fetching new housekeeper appears on his doorstep, frantic to ready the place for the Yuletide, and he seizes the chance for a respite from grieving and pretends to be the new duke's estate factor.

When a vicar's widow learns that her cousin's children are arriving from India to reside with their dreadful uncle, the new Duke of Kinmarty, the man who years ago sabotaged her own chance for happiness, she hides her identity to take the position of his housekeeper. Overwhelmed by a castle understaffed and in disarray, she forges a bond with the new duke's charming but not very competent factor, not knowing that he's hiding something as well.

When allies become lovers, each senses the truth may rip them apart. Can their love survive when she discovers he's the duke she despised?

Chapter One

London,
June 1811

"He's ruined it for you, Minny."

Filomena Grant barely felt the warm squeeze of her cousin's plump hand on her arm. Penelope Grant—no, Penelope was a MacDonal now—was as prone to drama as to the unpunctuality that had made her more than an hour late.

Mr. Swinton was late as well. He was meant to arrive at the same time as the newly married Penelope, who was serving as chaperone for an afternoon visit while her godmother took a much-needed rest.

Mr. Swinton hadn't appeared, nor had he sent a note.

A cold haze formed, numbing Filomena, much like the day when Godmama brought the news of her parents' deaths. She fisted her hands, trying to bring back the feeling in them.

A tear trickled down Penelope's cheek. "How pretty you are today, Minny. The pink muslin brings out the rose in your skin."

Penelope rarely awarded compliments, Filomena being younger, and browner, and plainer.

"And you've taken more care with your hair, and—" Penelope sobbed.

Filomena took in a deep breath and willed her heart to not burst. "Who's ruined what?"

"Has Mr. Swinton sent his regrets for tonight?"

Her godmother was hosting a dinner that night honoring the newlyweds, and Mr. Swinton was to be one of the guests. "No."

"He will. Or he'll be a complete boor and just won't appear. Evan is furious. He's cut ties with Andrew completely."

Filomena's heart thudded into her stomach. Andrew MacDonal was Penelope's new brother-in-law, and only one thing could be ruined—her chance at a respectable marriage. "How? Why? He's never even *met* me. He's never *seen* me." Evan's wretched brother dodged most society events and anything to do with the marriage mart, and he had pointedly refused to attend the wedding of his brother to the unsuitable Penelope Grant.

"Andrew disparaged us, you and me, at his club. 'Not good *ton*. Social climbing upstarts. Shabby genteel twits.'" Penelope shook her head. "Mr. Swinton was present. In fact Andrew made sure Mr. Swinton would hear."

Filomena steadied herself while the room tilted. Black dots spotted her cousin's face and the tears streaming there.

Now Penelope would cry? She'd married a man whose only family had fiercely opposed the match. The harm was done, and the cost would have to be counted. Unfortunately, Filomena would be paying it.

Blasted Andrew. How could he?

When her cousin sobbed harder, Filomena eased in a breath, trying to right herself, reaching for patience and a plan. Perhaps she could spend the next season in London with Penelope and Evan.

"Stop crying. You still have Godmama, and me, and your dowry. You won't starve, and Evan will still inherit the dukedom someday."

Penelope shook her head. "Of course, there's the title, one day, but until then I won't have you and Godmama, dear Minny. I won't see you for ages after we depart."

"*Depart?*"

"We won't be at dinner. We are leaving tonight for Rotherhithe."

"Rotherhithe," Filomena said dumbly. "The docks?"

"Yes. We are bound for India. Evan said his brother has gone too far. Besides, he has an opportunity there, and my dowry paid for our passage."

"*India.*" The black dots appeared in Filomena's vision again and a weight pushed the air out of her lungs. Staggering to her feet, she stumbled to an armchair, plopping down with a creak that shook the room. "You are l-leaving."

Their godmother required rest most of the time now. The only family Filomena had of any account was her cousin, who'd married well. To a duke's heir.

And now she was leaving.

Filomena's chance at a good marriage this season—or any other—was ruined. Her life was ruined. Mr. Swinton was no paragon of noble looks, but he *was* the younger son of a viscount. It was too late in the season for another match. No other gentleman of the *ton* would seek her out, not after Andrew MacDonal's insults.

She pressed a hand to her chest, trying to breathe. It was true, she wasn't good *ton*, but she was a gentleman's daughter, well-brought up by her godmother, not a social climber exactly, and not a twit. She certainly had more good sense and manners than Andrew MacDonal.

But she *was* too poor, and her future ducal connection was sailing for India. When her godmother died, she'd have to take humble rooms, or worse, find work as a governess or companion.

Because Andrew MacDonal hated her.

She struggled to her feet and summoned some air, trying to quell a rising panic. "Go then, if you must." The door seemed miles away, but she found her way to it.

"Minny, don't be like this. It's my husband's wish to go. I must. It's, it's not my fault."

Filomena squeezed her eyes shut on hot tears, thinking of all the scrapes Penelope had led them into over the years. This latest, her sudden marriage with its whiff of scandal, had incited the *ton's* gossips. Not just Evan's brother, but also his cousin, the Duke of Kinmarty, had cut ties with him. Oh, Evan would inherit one day, the duke couldn't stop that, but the old man had made his displeasure clear.

"When did you make these plans?" One didn't up and board a ship for India on a whim.

Penelope shrugged. "Do not fret, Minny. Once we are settled, we will send for you."

The door latch was cold in Filomena's hand. Her dreams of travel had not extended beyond Bath or Brighton. All she'd ever wanted was a secure home and a true family.

"Englishmen are desperate for English women there, Evan says. We shall find you a husband quite easily."

OH. Her knuckles went white around the ornate metal. So, a man would have to be desperate to see a social-climber like herself as a suitable wife. Andrew MacDonal and the entire *ton* believed so.

She eased in a breath. "I will go and tell Godmama to come down and say her farewells. *Bon voyage,* cousin."

"You must write to me, Minny," Penelope called. "And I will write back."

Except for secret notes smuggled to Evan, Penelope didn't write letters. Their scant correspondence had always been Filomena's task. That she would pretend to promise letters now was one more blow. "Do not bother." Filomena closed the door and leaned against the corridor wall.

She would not write to her cousin. At least not right away. Heavens—it would be years before she could forgive her.

And Mr. Swinton's desertion? She squeezed her eyes shut. He'd made no real promises, had he? Oh, but he'd courted her, and everyone knew of it. A pox on him for raising her hopes and dashing them with such public humiliation.

She found her way to the bedchamber she'd once shared with Penelope, and gave full vent to her tears.

Godmama would die and Penelope had always been unreliable, but she'd been counting on Mr. Swinton, or if not him, some other gentleman in need of a sensible wife.

Instead, she'd have to make her way all alone, because of one beastly man's slander, the arrogant, overbearing, heartless Andrew MacDonal.

Him she would never forgive.

Chapter Two

The Scottish Highlands,
21 December 1821

Filomena Marlowe tucked her chin, pinning her shawl to her neck before the wind could lift it away and blow frozen wet flakes right down into her bodice.

Her foot slipped on an icy patch, and she rebalanced her valise in one hand and the large covered basket in the other.

It was slippery as Michaelmas goose fat on the road to Kinmarty Castle, true, but a stout donkey and cart could have navigated it, freighting her trunk and the basket of food the village innkeeper had urged on her. She would gladly have walked alongside a cart, for the chance to have all her things with her.

But no. While she'd haggled with the innkeeper over a cart, news arrived that the new duke was dismissing the old duke's factor. Ale flowed freely with the rejoicing, and no one would offer the new duke's new housekeeper anything more than winks, knowing glances, and from the tavern wench, a whispered warning.

Yes, Filomena had heard the lore of the Lairds of Kinmarty and their housekeepers. She, however, would take a poker to the man before she'd let the current duke lay a hand on her.

And a celebration it was by the villagers, the volume of which—both in noise and in tankards of ale—had been rising while she'd sorted out storage for her trunk and directions to the Castle. And with the factor gone, who would be there to greet her? The agent who'd hired her had confided he'd been searching in vain for a butler. She'd somehow have to manage the entire staff of footmen and maids of a duke's castle on her own.

She reached a turn in the road and saw the two massive pillars the innkeeper promised would signal the lane. It was a scant mile walk from here, though the castle itself wouldn't come into view until she was almost upon it, he'd said.

Or she thought that was what he'd said. Between his thick Scottish accent and her own impatience… Heavens, she must just keep going or she'd freeze in place.

Stands of yew bushes dotted the fields and lined the narrow lane. Unkempt it was, and yet breathtaking in its grand expanse. She hurried along, skirting holes, jumping over chasms, and dodging the errant branches threatening to smack her.

With her head muffled and her gaze to the ground, the rider was almost upon her before she saw him. Just in time, she jumped clear of him and his shouted curse, landing bottom first in a drift of new snow.

Blasted coxcomb. Had that been the dismissed factor or the dratted new duke himself?

She struggled to her feet and brushed off the snow, wishing the new duke to Hades and reminding herself of her mission. She must make Kinmarty ready because the children were coming for Christmas.

Just past a dense growth of yew and pine trees, the lane curved and the Castle rose before her, taking her breath away.

Two towers flanked the grand entry of the great stone edifice, and others rose behind. Oh, it was *magnificent*. Snow fog shrouded battlements with their crenellations and loopholes, and windows dotted the high walls stretching out on both wings. She'd not had the chance to see this on her childhood visits to Kinmarty. An ogre like Andrew MacDonal could not be so bad in a castle this grand.

It was a true castle, a stronghold to guard against fear, a fortress where old hatreds might heal, a place where her own small dreams might come true.

The children would love it.

"Well, I've done it, George. I've dismissed the bastard."

Andrew MacDonal, new Duke of Kinmarty, tugged at his neckcloth, tearing off the constricting cloth and tossing it aside.

His friend, the Honorable George Lovelace, handed him a glass of brandy, and raised his own in salute. "And just how bad are things, your grace?"

Andrew waved a hand at a desk scattered with ledgers. "Look for yourself. And cease with the 'your-gracing'. Would that I was still plain Mr. Andrew MacDonal, enjoying my spartan bachelor rooms."

George settled into the massive desk chair and moved the lamp closer.

Andrew poured himself another drink. "I'd hoped to leave before Hogmanay. But looking at those ledgers, looking at the condition of this old heap and the village—I'm guessing Kinmarty has had a rough go under Haskill's stewardship."

He should have been here to help the old duke. Why hadn't he come?

Because he'd been too angry, too selfish, too utterly bereft after Evan's departure for India. He'd filled his time with every jolly manly pursuit he could drum up—cards, women, drink, and pretended it was enough. And now he was truly, totally, completely bereft. Now he had no one at all, except the multitude of mouths dependent upon him.

"I'll stay at least through Hogmanay and give the tenants a proper New Year's celebration." They'd have a grand bonfire, one that would honor the old duke and the duke who should have been, his brother, Evan. "Then I'll find a competent factor to help sort out this tangle, and I'll go south to see about finding money."

Would that he could go back to his old life and wake up from this nightmare that had started with news of Evan's death.

George opened a ledger. "You'll be required to put on your robes and coronet and take your seat in the Lords."

"Those fusty Scots nobles never cast a vote for Old Horace. Neither will they elect me to represent them in Lords." Dear God, he hoped not.

"And then there's the matter of an heir. You'll need a proper wife for that. Preferably one with a fat dowry."

"Bite your tongue."

George smirked. "There'll be plenty of stuffed purses willing to dangle their daughters for the title of duchess. And you're a handsome devil, so the ladies of London tell me."

"I was better off being an untitled devil." He waved toward the books again. "So, what do you think?"

George and his brother were crack managers of their father's wealth. George would have spotted in five minutes what had taken himself half the day to uncover.

"If it was only a factor you wanted, you might have left the old one in place. There isn't much more for him to embezzle."

"Bloody thief. How old Horace didn't catch him...tight as a drum, the man was..."

George traced down a column of figures. "He'd been ill, you said."

"Aye. I suppose that was it." Old Horace had been a skinflint to beat them all. Looking at the books, he understood why. Poor rents, poor crops, and a village populated with shoy-hoys only fit to scare away birds.

He swiped a hand through his hair and went to throw on another one of the logs they'd scrounged, moving by rote. "Good of you to come along and offer moral support, George."

George had been with him when the letter dooming him arrived. They'd been hoisting toasts to Old Horace upon his passing, and to the new duke, his brother Evan. He'd been drowning his guilt over his neglect of the old man and rejoicing that Evan would have to return from India. Then he and his brother could reconcile. He'd do whatever it took to make peace. He wanted his brother back.

The letter had dashed all his hopes.

He poured another brandy, trying to shake the bleak memories.

"Shall you call in the magistrate?"

"No. Haskill can claim the old duke knew all and approved. Or claim his own incompetence."

"At least send an express to the bank and the solicitor letting them know what you've found. You might also reconsider your order to cancel the hiring of the housekeeper and butler. If you decide you must let the Castle, it might be more appealing to have staff in place. Not to mention, there's much upkeep needed before you even consider offering it."

"I'll winkle out the old butler. He retired hereabouts. He might know of a competent replacement for Haskill." *If* he could convince the old butler, Forbes, to help him. His hand shook around the glass, and this time the brandy soured his stomach.

He was hungry, was all.

"What are we to eat *tonight*, George? I'm afraid my skills go no further than toasting some of that stale bread from the larder. You did far better with the eggs you discovered. For two farthings, I'd hand you this whole bloody dukedom and let *you* play cook, factor, and lord of the manor all in one."

"Tut-tut. No self-pity, not with so many prime acres for stalking."

Andrew glanced toward the window. Outside, thick snowflakes danced in the waning light. "And I shall grant you that stalking I promised, if you don't mind being knee-deep in snow."

A faint pounding started up. Andrew rubbed at his temple. "Another one of the bloody banging shutters that kept me up all night, do you suppose? Or might that be one of the legendary ghosts?"

George raised an eyebrow. "Or might it be someone at the door?"

Andrew tilted his head to listen, bile rising in him. "I locked Haskill out not a quarter of an hour ago and barred the door. Did the bastard forget something?" He looked around for his castoff neck cloth.

Never mind. If this was Haskill at the door, he wouldn't risk bloodying the thing when he kicked the man out on his arse again.

Chapter Three

Cold air overwhelmed him in the hall, the sort of damp chill oozed by a medieval pile left unheated for years. He wished for his overcoat, flung over a chair in the study, since neither he nor George had brought so much as a groom.

They'd tended their horses themselves as well, and washed in the ice-cold buckets they'd had to carry up. George, though, had managed a shave and fresh linens, the pompous ass.

George wasn't the one who'd been plunged into despair. George hadn't just been encumbered with a crumbling castle and a bankrupt estate. George hadn't just learned he'd lost his only brother months and months earlier to a fever.

Andrew rubbed at his chin. No neckcloth and two days-worth of beard—this had better not be a social caller.

He unbarred the door and yanked the heavy wood open.

In the half-light a woman stood, ramrod straight despite her shivering, swathed in dark wool.

"I beg your pardon," she said. "I knocked at the servant's door but no one answered."

By God, she was an Englishwoman, and she didn't speak like a servant.

Her wrap slipped, and he peered closer, his interest stirring. She was youngish, and from what he could see, attractive.

"I'm the new housekeeper."

A blur of dark fur shot through the door and they both jumped.

"I believe that was a cat." She peered around him.

"I've never seen it before." The bloody thing scurried off toward the bowels of the Castle and out of sight.

"May I come in?" She cleared her throat. *"No one is answering the servants' door."*

A sharp gust of wind blasted him. He apologized, stepping back, watching her enter.

The heavy wrap outlined a shapely woman. She put him in mind of Mrs. Ramsey, Old Horace's faithful housekeeper for so many years. 'Twas whispered that she had been more than a servant, and perhaps it was true given the old man's sharp decline after her death.

The new housekeeper placed a valise and a basket on the black and white tile.

"Are these all your belongings, or have you left a driver out in the snow?"

"I walked and—"

"Walked? In this weather?" Either she was of hardy stock, or he'd soon have to call the apothecary to treat her.

"Yes," she said. "I've a trunk at the inn, to be brought up when the weather eases."

He scoffed. "Next spring, then, perhaps."

She sent him an arch look and slipped the shawl back from her head, taking a bonnet with it and revealing errant dark locks that curled about her cheeks and dangled on her shoulder.

Her attention traveled over the dark paneling and up to the painted cornice with its scenes of medieval knights and their ladies. She gasped. "It's astonishing. Like...like a fairy tale castle."

A fairy tale castle? Was she mad?

The scenes might have once fascinated his childish heart, but he'd outgrown such nonsense.

She leveled a gaze at him. "What is your name, young man?"

His name? He blinked. *Young man?* He was likely older than her.

A chuckle bubbled up, the first moment of lightness he'd experienced in days. She thought he was a servant. A servant in a fairy tale castle.

Well, well. How would a lackey behave toward an arriving housekeeper?

"Never mind." She reached for her basket. "Just show me the way to the servant's—"

He snatched up the hamper. The aroma of stewed meat escaped from under the heavy cloth, making his mouth water. "You must first be introduced. Come along. The duke conducts business in the study."

Her hand went to her disheveled hair. "I must—"

"You are fine as you are." As he nudged her along, a beam of light caught her features.

His prickle of interest bloomed into full-fledged awareness. Full lips, porcelain skin, and a determined little chin—his new housekeeper was more than fine, and she spoke like a Mayfair matron. A youngish one. The urge to become better acquainted overwhelmed him.

Except, he was a duke now. Blast it. Why did Evan have to die and leave him this burden?

He reached up to tug his neckcloth and found it missing. Her frown showed she'd noticed, and that made him smile again.

"No one expected a bonny housekeeper."

Dark eyes glinted at his impertinence.

So much for the letter he'd sent to cancel her hiring. He was keeping her, at least through Hogmanay. "I fear we are all at sixes and sevens here," he said.

She pursed her lips. "I see that. You've lost your neckcloth, your razor, and your comb."

He squashed another grin. "I'll just carry this basket along out of the way of the resident mice."

Those full lips pinched tighter, raising his spirits even higher. She thought he was the duke's naughty retainer. Well, he could be. He wouldn't need her around for much longer than a few weeks, and as a footman...no, not a footman. He could play the new factor. A factor could spar with her the way a duke—or a footman, for that matter—never could. He'd do her no harm.

"Do not worry. You'll find that most of the vermin have sought warmer abodes than Castle Kinmarty though I suppose we now have a cat to contend with any remaining. We've only opened one floor in the south wing, as it's the newest, being only a century or so old. Besides bedchambers, it has the convenience of the old duke's study and a small parlor."

He took her arm as they climbed the stairs. Her step was graceful, her face alight and intelligent, and the feminine scent of lavender wafted up from her dampness.

George was right. He needed staff to prepare the Castle for a tenant. And she was an Englishwoman, a pretty one with the foresight to bring food.

If Evan had been the duke...well, his brother wouldn't scruple to try his luck with a woman this lovely.

He shook off the thought. He wasn't Evan and damned if he could think straight this night.

When he led the new housekeeper into the study, George lifted his dark head from the books spread before him, frowning. He said not a word of greeting, nor did he rise.

He was fully immersed in the ignominy of Old Horace's household accounts.

The new housekeeper curtsied and lifted her chin, sending George a bold gaze, and one none too friendly for a menial. Perhaps she thought George would steal her basket of food and send her back into the night. Andrew swallowed a chuckle.

"Good evening, your grace," she said addressing George. "My name is Marlowe. I was engaged to be your new housekeeper. I've traveled here in all haste, as requested."

That speech, directed at George in a cultured, melodious alto, stirred the devil in him.

He sent George a wink. "Your grace," he said. "Miss Marlowe has come armed with a supper basket."

She glanced his way. "If you please, it is *Mrs.* Marlowe."

He peered closer. He *did* please. Might the *Mrs.* be a mere housekeeper's honorific? "You are married?"

She blinked, glancing back to George, whose frown had deepened. Pulled from the entrails of a financial tangle to impersonating a duke, George was trying to catch up.

"I am recently widowed," she said. "Your grace—"

"I beg your pardon," Andrew said. "I am, er, Andrews, Mr. Andrews, his grace's factor. New factor. The old one has just departed."

"I see." She nodded and turned back to George. "The basket is—or was—a hot meal from the inn. I'll take it down to your cook for warming."

"There is no cook," Andrew said.

She blinked, took in the cluttered desk, the round table littered with dishes, and the blazing warm fire. "Shall I prepare a supper tray for you to dine here?"

"That would be satisfactory," George said.

She curtsied and reached for the basket.

Andrew's fingers closed over hers. "I shall carry it down for you."

Color rose in her cheeks. At the door, she cast one last glare at George and a rumble emerged from her throat.

Lips clamped, eyes narrowed, shoulders squared—no, this was something stronger than irritation, and what the devil was this about?

Intrigued, he closed the door and caught her arm. "I apologize, Mrs. Marlowe. We only arrived yesterday and Castle Kinmarty is not in the condition the duke remembered." He led her along the corridor. "For one thing, at present we've only been able to secure enough wood for the kitchen hearth and this floor of the south wing." Inspiration struck him and he stopped at a door and pushed on the latch. "Consequently, I'll ask you to occupy this bedchamber."

Another gasp escaped her. "It's far too elegant for me, and..." She glanced at the doors lining the passage. "The duke's bedchamber is along this corridor?"

"Yes." In fact, the duke's bedchamber was the very next one with an unobtrusive door connecting to hers.

She shook her head. "No. It is no trouble for me to sleep—"

"In the housekeeper's quarters? First of all, there is no bed there, not even a humble cot. And second of all, you will risk freezing again. That I will not allow."

"But—"

"Do not worry. The duke will be the soul of propriety."

A mulish look stole over her. "You can speak for the duke?" she muttered. "The man has a...a questionable reputation."

Andrew's heart jumped. This was a bold woman, considering they'd only just met.

And who had maligned his reputation with her?

"Most assuredly I can speak for him." He'd never molested a servant. Never. And the ladies who'd succumbed to his charms had been more than willing to fall. "I'll carry up your valise for you later. And now, let me show you the kitchen."

Chapter Four

Filomena surveyed the cavernous kitchen with a rising sense of despair. In the upper rooms, a good airing and cleaning would uncover the Castle's elegance. Here, though, crusted crockery cluttered the wooden table and counters. The lone pot hanging over the fire looked none too clean. If Kinmarty was a fairy tale castle, this might be the monster's lair.

The duke had lost not only his cook but all of the kitchen maids.

At least she'd survived her introduction to the man. His disgraceful grace had barely looked at her. There'd been no recognition in his brief glance and *thank goodness*. She'd worried about explaining why the former Filomena Grant, the woman he'd called a twit, had appeared as his housekeeper. Not that he'd set eyes upon her ten years ago, but he might recognize her Christian name if he'd required her to reveal it.

The chatty estate manager was another matter. Andrews had been all self-assured courtesy, showing her the bedchamber, pointing her to the water closet—thankfully indoors—and giving her directions to the kitchen. She'd found him there, poking hot embers to life before toting out wood, promising to kindle the fire in her bedchamber.

She must be careful of him. He was as handsome as the duke and far more charming.

She set about heating water, finding clean dishes, and preparing a tray. She'd played the role of a vicar's contented wife for ten years—she could certainly pretend to be a housekeeper for a few weeks. And never mind the duke. She knew her purpose here. Evan MacDonal was dead, Penelope was widowed, and homeless, and heading straight for Castle Kinmarty and a man who hated her. He hated Filomena as well, curse his dark heart.

Andrew MacDonal could go to the devil. She'd simply stay out of his way and see to her business. When Penelope and her children arrived, they'd find Castle Kinmarty ready for them.

Back in the study, Andrew called a greeting and George looked up.

"Are you mad?" George pushed away from the desk and filled his tumbler again.

"Yes, perhaps. But I'll need your help. You'll play along with me."

That had been his first ducal command—well his second after banishing the thieving factor.

Though George was a friend, not an underling to be ordered around.

"Please, George."

"Why?"

"Didn't you see her? She's lovely. I've been pondering her face all the way up the stairs. She looks familiar, like someone I might have seen in town. Not recently. Some time ago. She doesn't speak at all like a servant."

"If she's a lady fallen on hard times, the kindest thing is to leave her alone. Pay her off and send her away. Or keep her here temporarily through Hogmanay and then let her go."

"As you suggested, the house needs a good cleaning. It will be pleasant to have a lovely woman around organizing that."

"A gentleman doesn't—"

"She has a backbone." One that ran to a lovely bottom under all that dark wool, or his name wasn't Andrew MacDonal. "She chided me on my lack of a neckcloth."

George scoffed.

"My failure to shave as well."

"Why not mention your hair standing out on all sides?"

"She did." He laughed and poured a drink. "You see, she's a challenge. It's only temporary, as you said. It will just be a bit of harmless fun and then I'll reveal all."

"She'll take offense and scamper off before all the layers of grime have been lifted."

"In Scotland? In the dead of winter? If she's fallen on hard times, she'll *have* to stay here."

That thought brought up visions of Old Horace and Mrs. Ramsey and the rumors about them. In only his second day here, he began to understand the old duke's temptation.

"You'll not do it, Andrew. You'll not seduce a servant. That's beneath even you."

"That's a low blow, George. You know my reputation is not earned."

George huffed.

"I only flirt with ladies who enjoy it." And sometimes he ended up bedding them, but only when they were willing.

"I'll not do it, not if you plan to seduce your housekeeper."

A tree branch slapped the windowpane. Snow pelted the landscape, a fierce Scottish snow like the ones he knew from Yuletide visits. Outside the weather would rage, and inside, Mrs. Ramsey would have games, piles of oatcakes and buckets of pudding at the ready, a refuge from the bleakness.

She'd been a force at Kinmarty. Perhaps Mrs. Marlowe had some of that same spirit.

If Ramsey had truly been the old duke's leman since the early death of his young duchess and daughters—well, what of it? 'Twas a tradition of Kinmarty clan chieftains, the locals said.

Not that he wished to keep to the old ways, but Marlowe had piqued his curiosity. He needed to find out why, he wanted to know her better, and he couldn't do any of that as the duke.

"I won't harm her. You know my plans, George. I won't stay on here longer than the time required to hire a manager and set the estate to rights. I shall tell her very soon."

"She'll puzzle it out when the neighbors call."

"Neighbors?" He pinched the bridge of his nose. "Blast it. I'd forgotten Strachney." Not a quarter hour after their arrival in Kinmarty, Strachney had managed to send a servant with a note. According to Haskill, Benedict Strachney was a recent retiree from the Indian Service with a well-dowered young daughter.

With any luck, the bloody snow would keep the man away.

"The nabob and his eligible daughter will call on you soon. You could do far worse."

He could also do far better. The gaggle of young virgins on the marriage mart had never appealed, not even when he'd occasionally had the itch to contemplate looking. A fat dowry and a pretty face weren't enough. If he were to marry, it would have to be to a woman who could hold his interest for more than the time needed to beget an heir. Was that too much to ask?

"I'd rather marry the lovely housekeeper than snatch a girl from the schoolroom." He plopped into a chair. "George, you're always ready to advise me on my behavior. You're a nobleman's son, whereas my father was a plain mister. This is an opportunity for you to show me how to conduct myself as a proper peer."

George eyed him closely, one finger drumming the desk. "You would like me to teach you? Tempting."

Andrew smiled, knowing he'd won this battle.

A muffled bump sent him rushing to open the door. Mrs. Marlowe struggled under the weight of a laden tray.

He reached for the burden and she hurried to ready the table.

"You've found a clean tablecloth," he said.

"There are a few linens," she said. "Not many."

She'd managed a teapot and chipped china as well.

Where had all the good china gone? Was that more of Haskill's thieving?

"Your grace, shall I pour your tea?" she asked briskly.

George eyed her under droopy lids, scowling. "Black."

She pressed her lips together as she poured and passed him a cup.

"Milk and sugar for me," Andrew said.

"No milk. It curdled." She stirred sugar into a cup, handed it to him, and filled bowls with thick stew.

"This is our supper?" George grimaced.

"If you'll provide me a list of preferred foods, I'll go into the village tomorrow."

"I'll make the list, duke." Andrew dug into his bowl. "Inn fare, but tolerable for our first hot meal. Thank you, Mrs. Marlowe."

"I'll come for the tray when you ring." She curtsied and steadied herself with a hand on the back of a chair.

Fatigue smudged the skin under her eyes, and she gripped her shawl. She was tired, and cold, and probably still wet from that long walk. Someone should have driven her. The innkeeper might have sent a note and he could have fetched her on his horse.

And she was likely hungry as well.

"Go, have your own meal, and turn in," he said. "I'll carry the dishes down."

She looked from him to George, nodded, and slipped out.

George raised an eyebrow. "How very courteous of you, Mr. Andrews."

"You were rather rude."

"I was playing Andrew MacDonal."

"A bit higher in the instep than I truly am."

"Hmm." George's smile was sly. "Perhaps I'll enjoy this role after all."

Chapter Five

In her bedchamber, Filomena huddled near the growing fire, her damp cloak draping her.

Here she was, housekeeper in a duke's castle, one with a meager supply of linens, chipped crockery, very little fuel for heating and cooking, and not a single servant besides herself.

She'd completely underestimated the difficulties of this challenge.

Oh, but the Castle was beautiful, magical almost, and this room was a godsend, and she was determined to be grateful. It was far finer than her cozy bedchamber at the vicarage, and undoubtedly meant for a high-ranking guest or family member, perhaps even the duchess herself.

Two windows were grimy, but they faced west, allowing for views of glorious sunsets. The fireplace with its carved wood and marble mantel shared a wall with an adjoining chamber. Whether a dressing room or bedchamber, she couldn't determine. The entry door blended so well with the paneling that the locked latch had been almost invisible.

On the bed and windows, the faded curtains and hangings had once been a rich blue brocade. And this chair, though lumpy, had deep wings that held in the heat from the fireplace and kept the draftiness at bay.

Mr. Andrews had kept his promise and started a fire, thank goodness, and he must have set out the sheets for the bed. She'd snatched a few spoonfuls of the stringy mutton stew before coming up to retire. Passing the library, the low murmurs of the men's voices had tempted her, but she'd resisted the urge to press her ear to the door.

The last thing she needed was to draw the duke's attention to a lone woman under his roof. She'd hurried down the corridor, stirred the fire, made up her bed, and found the heavy nightgown stuffed into her valise.

After so many days without proper sleep, she was weary to her bones, but anxiety kept her awake.

It had been sheer chance to learn of the position of housekeeper at Kinmarty. Marlowe's death last summer had been unexpected, leaving her casting about for a purpose. She'd had to vacate the vicarage for rented rooms and begin playing her new role of grieving widow until Marlowe's estate was settled. Once she'd learned that she'd be able to support herself on her inheritance, she'd pondered her new freedom. On a whim, she'd gone up to London, inquiring with an agent about a position as governess or companion for a family traveling to the Continent.

It was then that news came of the old duke's death, and she knew she couldn't leave England. Evan and Penelope would surely come home to take up the title. She'd returned to her village, praying for a chance to make peace with them, to be a family again.

Some days later, the papers reported Evan's death, and the hiring agent sent word of the housekeeper's position in Kinmarty.

She stood and fed the fire. How many days until Penelope's arrival? All she knew were the snippets gleaned from the gossipy agent.

It had been after the new duke's departure for Scotland when his solicitor received word of Penelope's plans. He'd sent an express to the new duke, and commanded that the Castle be staffed as quickly as possible for the duke and his family. No experienced London servants wanted to work in the Highlands. The agent was desperate. She'd barely had time to pack a trunk.

It had all been a whirlwind, because of the children. Penelope had children and she was bringing them home.

Tears pricked her eyes. Her ten years of marriage had been childless, and she faced a future stretching in unending loneliness. Penelope's girls, the chance to know them, made all of this subterfuge and speed, and sacrifice worthwhile.

Sea travel could be unpredictable, but the hope was for the children to reach Kinmarty in time for the sort of Christmas their father had enjoyed there.

Did Penelope know her host would be an old enemy, Andrew MacDonal? She and the girls must have set out months before news of the old duke's death could have reached them. The thought of her cousin facing Andrew alone with her children in tow had made Filomena's decision to play housekeeper easy.

The logs crackled and popped, and another noise intruded. Someone scratched at her door.

Pulling the cloak around her, she reached for the poker. When she eased the door open, a dark shape brushed by her. The cat.

The intruder hopped into the chair, licked itself a few times, and curled up.

The boldness cheered her. "I suppose you may have my seat. I've warmed it up for you." When she reached out a hand, the creature froze.

Wisely. The cat didn't know her. It was hedging its trust as she must do also.

The next morning, the sound of a door closing woke her. A warm weight pressed against her and she lifted her head to find two green eyes watching her.

"Are we friends now?" she asked.

The cat meowed. Drawing her hand from under the covers, she reached out and rubbed the top of its head, inciting a deep comforting purr.

"When it's this beastly cold, friends must stay warm together." Filomena pushed back the covers shivering, hurriedly dressed, and went down to the kitchen, noting that, in the light of day, worn carpets, loose balusters, and layers of dust were all too apparent.

In the kitchen, a kettle of water steamed on the hearth. As she went to find a cup, the outside door popped open, letting in bright sunlight.

"Ah. You are up." Mr. Andrews said. "Good morning."

His smile lit the room. A square jaw, a prominent nose, and merry eyes all came together to make her breath catch. He would make for a good First Foot, the dark-haired man to be first across the threshold at the New Year's Hogmanay celebration. Penelope's girls would love the tradition.

Mr. Andrews advanced into the room. "It's a fine morning after all that snow."

His trousers hugged his thighs over well-made riding boots. Warmth curled through her into her cheeks, and she lifted her gaze.

In the clear beam of sunlight, the mossy green of his eyes glinted with humor.

As if he'd read her interest.

"The, er, duke and I are going riding."

His gaze shifted away, but her pulse didn't ease.

The castle was grimy, the larders bare and they had no staff, and he was going riding? "Should you not be seeing to hiring more servants? There is maintenance to be done, as well as the cleaning."

"Yes, it's a miserable old pile, isn't it?" he said cheerfully.

"No. Not at all. You mustn't say that. Castle Kinmarty is lovely, it's…it's breathtaking, really and filled with so many astonishing details."

"A fairy tale castle you said last night."

That had been her first thought when she'd spotted it from the lane, and then when she'd seen the depictions of knights in the hall. "Yes, and it needs servants."

"Is it not your job to see to the servants, Mrs. Marlowe?" He reached a hand into his coat and rummaged there.

"Housemaids, certainly. But a butler, footmen—I should think you would want to manage that."

"The agent was supposed to hire the butler."

"He confided that no one wanted to come so far north. Perhaps you might find someone within the local area."

"Ah, here it is." Andrews pulled out a slip of paper. "You might check in the village for Forbes. He was the old duke's butler."

Hire the housemaids, and the butler? What work did Mr. Andrews plan to do?

Before she could blurt out that question, he reached for her hand, sending a spark of lightning up her arm. He pressed the paper into her palm, a small smile quirking his lips.

Breathe. She reined in her pulse. Her purpose here was clear. She was here for the children, and Penelope, too, of course.

When he released her, she glanced at the paper, avoiding his gaze. It was the promised list of the duke's favorite foods.

He'd wisely added nothing too exotic for Kinmarty.

Finding a cook would be her first priority. "What salaries might I offer?"

"As much as is required to fill the position. I shall leave that to your discretion."

"Mr. Andrews, I have only just arrived. I've yet to tour the whole castle and evaluate the, er, challenges. You have only just met me. As the duke's factor you should—"

"I should do what the duke commands." He grinned again. "And today, he commands me to go riding with him." He leaned in perilously close. "We are touring the estate boundaries, and he awaits me in the stables."

Straightening, he walked to a cabinet, retrieved a flask she hadn't noticed, and sent her a parting smile.

She poked at the fire and threw on a piece of wood from the dwindling pile.

They would need manservants sooner rather than later if they were to not freeze to death in their beds. For certain, the duke would not chop wood, nor would his handsome, cheeky factor.

What she'd seen of the inn patrons—men in shabby coats and scuffed boots—told her that work in Kinmarty might be scarce. Surely there were villagers here needing work.

Back in Hertfordshire, Mr. Marlowe had left household management to her, and she knew what it took to employ good staff. The best servants wanted a respectable household and good wages. She would offer good wages. Anyone willing to work at Castle Kinmarty would be decently paid.

Respectability of the household was another matter. She could only hope that with the title of duke, Andrew MacDonal would behave honorably.

A tour of the castle and an inventory of household items could wait until later that day. She hurried through her breakfast and pulled on her cloak.

The rare, late afternoon sun was descending as they turned down the lane toward the stone-walled stable.

"You've real prospects here," George said. "The Castle is old but impressive."

George was as optimistic as the housekeeper. "A fairy tale castle?"

George sent him a sidewise glance. "What?"

He shook his head. "Nothing. You'll have me seeing opportunities here."

"There are opportunities. The hunting lodge can be let. And there's iron ore, perhaps. I'll write to my brother and have him send up a man to conduct a survey."

"That would be capital, providing the cost is not too dear."

"Consider it a speculative investment on my part. For a percentage share if the ground yields ore, of course."

Andrew laughed. "And a permanent invitation to hunt. If this weather holds, we'll track down that stag. Perhaps tomorrow."

George patted his horse's neck. "I'd best check this fellow over before planning anything. He's been limping since the last turning."

They entered the stable yard and Andrew reined up. A wagon stood near the kitchen entrance, with two men offloading cordwood onto a neat pile. They doffed their caps and bent back to their task.

A boy hurried out from the stables and reached for the horses.

"You've acquired servants," George said.

Andrew glanced at his friend. "Is this your doing?"

They'd stopped at an outlying cottage and bought oatcakes and surprisingly good ale from the crofter and his wife, mentioning that the new duke was hiring staff. Perhaps George had slipped the man some extra coin.

"Not this quickly," George said.

His heart lifted. It must be Mrs. Marlowe's doing.

They dismounted and Andrew handed over his reins.

"Go on, I'll catch up with you," George said.

Andrew made his way to the kitchen where the scent of savory meat, onions, and yeasty bread sent his stomach growling.

Someone had worked another miracle here. The dirty crockery had vanished, and the sideboards held bulging sacks of foodstuffs and casks of drink. A stout woman turned away from a mound of dough and curtsied. A girl pumping water did the same, and a young boy darted out from a storeroom and bowed.

"Good day to you," Andrew said, "have you anything ready to eat?"

The stout woman dipped her head. "Good hot bread, sir, and some ham. We can send up—"

"Slice some up for me now. And some for the, er, duke who'll be here in a moment."

They scurried around and moments later the girl wobbled a plate into his hand. She was a scrawny thing, no more than thirteen, shabbily dressed but scrubbed pink down to her fingernails, and she seemed to be studying his mud-speckled boots.

And, praise Juno, they now had a boot boy.

He thanked the girl, and she scooted away.

Marlowe had done well. "Where is the housekeeper, Cook?"

"Do you know, Duff?" The cook directed her question to the boy.

"Aye. Jest carried up wood to the nursery."

"The nursery?"

Whatever would she be doing in the nursery? There were no children in residence at Castle Kinmarty, nor would there be. No matter what George said, he had no plans to get leg-shackled.

"Aye. And she wants more. I kin show you the way."

Andrew knew where the nursery was. He and Evan had spent many happy hours there.

"Beggin' your pardon sir, but Duff has pots to scrub," the cook said.

The boy bit his lip, and gazed up through pale red eyelashes, his gaze hopeful.

Andrew swallowed a smile. Duff was no more than eight or nine. The nursery held hobby horses, and games, books and toys, and a grand set of tin soldiers. Putting those in order would be more fun than scrubbing pots.

He pulled a stool out. "Tap me some of that ale or whatever you might have. I'll make quick work of my bread and ham while Duff gathers that wood."

The cook's eyebrows shot up, the boy grinned and scurried off, and a cup appeared on the table before him. He savored the warm bread, his compliments sending the fat cheeks into a blush, and pondered the miracles a good woman could accomplish.

Moments later he took the bundle of wood from the struggling boy. "Onward, Duff," he said. "Lead the way up the stairs."

"Here they are, miss."

Filomena joined the girl bending over the open trunk in the nursery storeroom.

"Oh, well done, Kyla." She'd been hoping there'd be dolls in the nursery from some long-ago MacDonal lass. "I'm so glad you found them."

The girl's blue eyes widened as she lifted a small figure from the trunk. Richly dressed in century old blue brocade, the doll's hair was the same pale gold as Kyla's, her eyes a similar shade of blue, like Penelope's. Perhaps Penelope's girls shared her coloring and would appreciate this doll.

Though Kyla was at least twelve or thirteen, she handled the toy with the reverence 0f a much younger child, as well she should. Such a toy might set a villager back a year's wages.

Filomena's heart twisted. Her doll, Berenice, had been as fine as this one. One night, she'd woken to a flaming row between her father and mother, one that left her trembling under her covers. Berenice had disappeared the next day, along with her mother's jewelry and her father's prized paintings.

She shook off the memory and straightened. "And what have we here?"

Wedged at the back of the chest was a framed drawing. Two laughing boys gazed out of the gilt frame, their features sketched in bold pencil strokes.

This was surely Evan and his brother in a happier time. His girls might find it as cheerful as she did.

She set it aside and stood. She must somewhere find bed linens. "Why don't you inspect all the dolls and check their gowns. We may need to make repairs before the children arrive."

"What children would that be?"

The deep baritone sent a shiver through her and she turned, heat rising into her cheeks.

Chapter Six

Mr. Andrews stood in the doorway, the corner of his mouth twisted up, his hand gripping a tote full of firewood. A red head popped into view next to him—the kitchen boy. What was his name?

"Duff," Mr. Andrews said, "can you manage this while I speak to Mrs. Marlowe?"

Duff took the bundle and Mr. Andrews ruffled the boy's hair, sending it every which way. Like his own.

His hair was in disarray, his coat was dusty, and his cheeks were ruddy under his late afternoon stubble. He looked wild and fresh and incredibly masculine, and he made her toes curl in her boots.

"Have we visitors coming that I'm not aware of, Mrs. Marlowe?"

He didn't know they were coming?

Kyla moved up next to her, clutching the doll. Her freckles all but disappeared as she blushed a pretty shade of pink.

The factor was too handsome for everyone's good.

"Mr. Andrews, this is Kyla Forbes, a new maid."

"Welcome, Kyla." He bestowed a kind glance on the girl.

Filomena shooed her back to work and nudged Mr. Andrews out into the playroom.

It required a poke to a very firm bicep, a poke that sent a spark from her fingertip all the way to her racing heart. She shook herself and turned to Duff who was slowly arranging the wood.

"Well, done, Duff." She couldn't blame him for dawdling in the nursery, but there was work to be done elsewhere. "Have you finished your pots yet?"

"Not yet, miss."

"Go on then, and come back when you're finished."

As he left, the longing glance he cast back at the toy chest made her smile.

Mr. Andrews crossed his arms over his chest.

She stood taller. "Good news. We've a cook. She comes highly recommended, and she's able to read. We discovered a copy of Mrs. Glasse's book of cookery here. Once settled in, she'll attempt some fashionable dishes."

"I have sampled the cook's baking."

"And?"

"Satisfactory, so far. Now, please tell me about these children you're expecting."

She chewed on her lip. The agent had said an express had been sent. Surely the duke knew of Penelope's plans?

Or…the letter had been misdirected and hadn't yet reached him? The men had only arrived the day before yesterday, and with the dreadful weather, it was possible the letter hadn't yet turned up.

He tipped his head near, filling the air with the scent of the starch used on his neckcloth. "Mrs. Marlowe?"

She swallowed. He was too close, his lips mere inches from her own. "The duke's elder brother passed away."

"Yes. Which is why he is now duke."

"His brother left behind a widow."

"I am aware of his widow. She is in India."

Another thought occurred to her. "The duke didn't tell you."

He blinked. "Tell me what? I am sure that if the duke knew, I would know."

She remembered Mr. Andrews' casual appearance and his easy confidence the night before. He and the duke were steadfast friends. "Of course. He would have told you." She let out a breath. "Then he doesn't know either."

"Yes, now you are following along." He swiped a hand through his hair and a chunk of it stood at attention. "What the devil is it the duke is supposed to know?"

"*Language*, sir. The duke is supposed to know that his brother's widow, Penel—er, Mrs. MacDonal, is on her way to Kinmarty."

He reared back and glanced toward the window where late afternoon light streamed in. The green-eyed cat, sunning itself on the window ledge, lifted its head.

With an arrogant flick, Mr. Andrews attacked an imaginary piece of lint. "It will be months before she arrives."

She shook her head. "She left India immediately after her husband's death. She plans to be here by Christmas. Which is in two days."

As she spoke, his eyes widened, and despite the chill in the room, moisture beaded his forehead.

Her heart thudded. The duke's factor knew Penelope, or at least he knew of her. And if the duke told him everything, then he knew the duke hated Penelope. He was dreading the duke's reaction.

She gripped fistfuls of her work smock. "I'm told the duke's late brother especially wanted her to bring the children here."

His head jerked up. "What. Children?"

The affable Mr. Andrews had punched each syllable.

She held in a shiver and lifted her chin. "The duke's nieces, of course."

With another swipe to his head that sent more hair awry, he stomped to the window. The cat jumped away, making a hasty retreat from the fist that pounded the window ledge.

Mr. Andrews was in a state.

Not that he frightened her. She'd deal with him. She'd deal with the duke himself. If either man thought to keep children away from their ancestral home— well, she would, she would...

What *would* she do? She would shame them into submission.

"I can see this news has upset you."

He didn't answer.

"Surely the duke won't refuse to take in his sister-in-law and nieces? Once he recovers from the unexpected surprise—if it is a surprise and not just a failure of the duke to inform you—he'll be pleased. Children are a blessing, and they bring such innocent joy to feast days. Someday the duke will fill this nursery and this glorious castle and grounds with his own babes. Why not start with hospitality to his own flesh and blood?"

His back went straighter, indignation radiating in hot waves.

Mr. Andrews had shown kindness to both children she'd just employed, but no doubt the duke wouldn't, and he knew it.

She sighed. "Very well. We will do our best to make sure they're not underfoot."

A log cracked in the fireplace and the silence stretched on.

Ignore her, would he? "I was told the duke and his sister-in-law were not on good terms. Is that the reason for *your* displeasure?"

The glare he sent over his shoulder sliced through her.

She crossed her arms. "I was told the duke didn't favor the marriage and went so far as to disparage the lady…" She took in a tight breath. "And *all of her family*, causing a rift with his own brother."

When he turned, he'd schooled his face into an unemotional mask, as frozen as the ice crystals coating the window. "The duke doesn't plan to stay at Kinmarty through the entire Yuletide."

That would be just as well. But…

Oh, this selfish cad. Now she understood a part of the problem.

"You had hoped to have no one but staff underfoot?"

He scowled. "What?"

"The duke will give you the charge of Kinmarty when he leaves. You are the factor here, are you not?"

He studied her a long moment before clearing his throat. "Castle Kinmarty conveyed with debt and little income. It may have to be let." He grimaced. "Why am I telling *you* that? Do not share that with the servants or they'll be out of the door tomorrow." He nodded curtly and stomped out.

Filomena let out a long breath. She'd seen the poverty of the adjoining village, but letting this glorious castle to strangers… It was too sad.

Not only might the duke be unwilling to help Penelope, he might be unable to.

With her own small income, they could all squeeze into a cottage, perhaps in Leith or Dalkeith, on the outskirts of Edinburgh. She'd find a way.

If Penelope wanted to live with her. If they could reconcile.

She pressed a hand to her chest. The children would at least spend Christmas and Hogmanay here. The duke wouldn't find a tenant before then, and he just couldn't send the children or their mother away. He couldn't be that dishonorable.

She went to check on Kyla, who had all the dolls lined up on the bare mattress of the narrow bed.

"Just a few repairs needed, ma'am." She pulled out the full skirt of a dark-haired doll. "If you've a needle and thread, I can sew up these small tears."

Filomena grabbed an empty basket and handed it to the girl. "Gather them up. I'll fetch my sewing kit and look for some linens to make up these beds." At the door, she turned back. "I've brought a supply of ribbon up from London. We'll give them each a festive bow, shall we?"

"Red, ma'am?"

"Yes. And tomorrow, we'll begin decorating the great hall for Christmas."

Penelope's children might have only one Yuletide at Castle Kinmarty, but she would see that it was a memorable one.

And the duke? He could enjoy himself, or not.

Andrew flew down the stairs, his heart pounding.

You are the factor here, are you not?

For a moment he'd thought Mrs. Marlowe had caught him out, she with her smug self-assurance about blasted Penelope MacDonal's arrival.

With children. His brother and the heartless harpy had produced children and had never told him.

Of course, Evan wouldn't have told him. They'd had a terrible row after Evan's betrothal, and again, the day of his wedding, which he'd refused to attend. And then one more time, after the wedding, when Evan accused him of besmirching his bride's reputation at White's.

Everyone thought Penelope was a sweet girl, too sweet for Evan who they'd whispered had ruined her, and too poor to marry a duke's heir. As it had turned out, she was not too poor to pay their passage to India, and neither was she too sweet to corner Andrew before the wedding and rail at him about refusing to support their nuptials.

A pox on her and the sickly cousin who'd hid at home while Penelope swanned about London entrapping his foolish brother.

He paused at the study door, his hand on the latch, and took in a deep breath.

Hell. He'd tried to persuade Penelope to cast Evan off. He'd tried a cold dash of the truth—that his brother had no temperance with either gambling or drink and especially not with women. She'd refused to listen. She'd set her cap firmly. She was in love.

In love with his brother's chance at a dukedom. Evan had needed a bride with money. A rich society widow craving a duchess' coronet would have done, one young enough to produce an heir, and worldly enough to let Evan go about his own worldly ways.

How many children was Penelope conveying to his care? Had Evan left means to support them or would they now add to the burden of the Duke of Kinmarty? Because of course, *of course* he would do his duty to them.

Someday he'd want to fill the nursery with his own babes? He shuddered.

Marlowe had said they were girls. That must be, or else it would be the new duke arriving in Kinmarty for Yuletide.

He entered the study and sighed in relief that George wasn't here.

With a glass of the fine local whisky to stiffen his resolve, he opened the deep drawer of the desk, lifting out piles of correspondence, the same piles of paper he'd wrenched out of Haskill's hands before he'd kicked him out.

He'd caught the man preparing to burn them.

Flipping through papers he found second and third requests for payment, heaps of them, some for tailors and candle makers, others for grocers and mercers, drapers and blacksmiths. Hadn't the tradesmen talked to each other before advancing the man credit?

He rubbed his eyes and glanced at the stack of ledgers. Likely these totals matched those marked paid. During the months of Old Horace's illness, Haskill had bought goods on the duke's credit, sold them, and pocketed everyone's money.

Damn it all. The old duke deserved better than the shame of these old debts.

Perhaps he really *must* find a tenant for Castle Kinmarty. Though he'd discussed it with George—and promptly rejected the notion in his heart, he'd only spouted that bit of bravado to wipe the smug look from Mrs. Marlowe's face.

It had succeeded, more shame to him. What sort of man wouldn't see to the needs of his family, albeit an unpleasant sister-in-law who hated him?

He shoved away from the desk and went for another drink. He should have locked Haskill in the cellar instead of letting him go, to hell with the scandal. The man had an account somewhere with Kinmarty money. Everyone had suffered, the duke, the servants, and especially the tenants and local tradesmen. He'd need a sharp factor to help him. In the interim, he could rely on George's assistance, but this wasn't George's problem. It was his own.

A shallower drawer held more letters. This correspondence he'd removed from the duke's frigid bedchamber and stashed here himself.

There were notes from the neighbors, messages of sympathy at the death of Mrs. Ramsey. His neighbors had known how close the old duke was to his housekeeper. The old duke had saved these, and Haskill, apparently hadn't discovered them.

Under all those he found it—a letter from his brother, addressed to the Duke of Kinmarty many months earlier.

Chapter Seven

His heart thumped at the familiar signature that lurched across the paper more violently than when Evan was younger. Fortunately, the letter had been penned by someone with a slightly better hand. He squinted, deciphering it.

My dear duke,

I write to inform you that I am ill, gravely ill, according to my physicians, and am not likely to return home. I think with great fondness upon the holidays spent in your good and patient care. I beseech you, as a man speaking from his deathbed, to offer hospitality to my wife. It is my fervent wish that my children be raised at Kinmarty with you and the good Mrs. Ramsey, and Penelope has agreed to take them there.

Penelope had agreed to take them there. How oddly worded that was. They were her children, were they not?

Or…He read through the letter again, but found no evidence to confirm what could only be an unfounded suspicion.

More shame ate at him, opening the door for a wave of grief. Evan hadn't written to *him*, his own brother, for help. He'd died without once contacting him. Evan was gone, as was Mrs. Ramsey, and the crusty old man who'd been their only father figure.

The people he'd cared for.

George came through the door calling a greeting. "Tackling that correspondence, are you? Well, here's another piece, just delivered." He slid over a square of folded paper. "Why the long face? You look like you've seen the family ghost."

He picked up the new missive. "You remember I spoke of my elder brother?"

"Of course. The deceased heir. I never had the pleasure of meeting him."

"His wife is returning to England. She's traveling to Kinmarty for Christmas."

George raised an eyebrow and his mouth quirked. "As I recall, you said you were not on the best of terms with the happy couple."

That didn't bear a reply. He cracked the wafer on the latest letter and scanned the brief note, his stomach churning.

"More bad news?"

"The promised visit from the nabob. He and his daughter will pay a call tomorrow. Is the messenger still here?"

"He flew back down the road as soon as he handed it off. Why not just have done with it? You must meet them sooner or later."

"Later it will be. I won't be home tomorrow. Perhaps you could—"

"I won't play the duke for an influential neighbor who may well be your future father-in-law. Send the housekeeper off to the village to find more servants. I noticed she hasn't yet been able to conjure a butler. What happened to the old one? Did he die as well?"

His mind had stalled on the word *father-in-law*. The last thing he'd do was allow George to arrange a marriage for him. He'd find his own bride when the time was right. What else had George said?

Oh, yes: the old butler. "Forbes is retired, not dead." There'd been a note of condolence from him in the pile. "Now, go." He picked up a letter and flapped it in a shooing motion. "Go back to the stables, or up to your bedchamber. Or go down to the weapons room and see what the old duke has for our stalking."

George grinned. "I believe I'll visit the kitchen and tell the cook to hurry with dinner. I'm famished."

"Don't spoil your appetite on the biscuits."

George laughed. "I heard that enough as a child."

He rubbed at his aching jaw. "You'll hear it again. My sister-in-law is arriving with children."

"*Well.*" George's eyebrows shot up. "Girls. You'll have dresses and ribbons and coming out balls to think about. Beaus to fend off and marriages to arrange."

"Bite your tongue."

George wagged a finger. "You'll set thing straight with the housekeeper before then. Don't think I will play uncle to them."

Andrew sighed. "Is it so horrible being me?"

With a laugh, George shook his head and departed.

George was right. It was time to end his charade. He'd bollocksed things up with Evan those many years ago, and now, with Mrs. Marlowe, a worthy woman if ever there was one. Handsome also, with worthy curves. And he was never allowed to touch them.

He let out a long breath. He must set things straight with her as soon as possible and hope for the best. He'd need her help if he was to fend off an angry sister-in-law.

How the devil was he supposed to support everybody with a bankrupt estate, in a crumbling castle?

A fairy tale castle. Women loved their romantic ruins, and everything here was certainly old and worn.

The toys, as well. The visit to the nursery had raked up fierce memories. The soldiers tumbled into the box under the window after pretend battles, the rocking horse that so often had thrown them off laughing, the creaky window he'd dangled from, Evan clutching his ankles. Even the blasted cat who now wandered the corridors trying to trip him—Ramsey had always had one or two cats to take on the mice.

Grief snared him, circling his heart and squeezing. He eased in one breath, and then another before settling back in his chair.

Enough of self-pity. He must deal with the worthy Mrs. Marlowe. He'd seek her out after dinner, raise her wages if need be, and somehow explain his asinine deception.

A manservant served their beef roast and peas, and between courses tugged at his tight gloves and his ancient ill-fitting livery. If he wasn't mistaken, this was one of the men who'd been stacking wood. In addition to a butler, Kinmarty would need proper footmen, no matter who lived here.

When the table was cleared, they shared more of the spirits from Old Horace's stores and discussed the condition of George's horse and the prospects for a good hunt in the next few days. Then George went off to see to his own correspondence, and Andrew went to find Mrs. Marlowe.

The kitchen had been cleaned, the fire banked, and no one was there. No chatter came from the servants' hall either. He'd have to ask Marlowe where she'd put all the servants.

He peeked into the housekeeper's quarters on the off chance she'd had a bed moved down. The room was bare.

In the south wing, he crept past the study where George was working, moving down the corridor to the bedchamber next to his own.

A rap on the door brought no answer.

His hand went to the latch, but he pulled it away. She'd likely fallen asleep, and he'd promised her she wouldn't be molested. Asleep or not, she wouldn't appreciate him invading her room in either persona, factor or duke.

Too restless to turn in, he found himself moving up the next flight of stairs to the nursery rooms tucked under the attic. There were ghosts in that nursery, the ghost of his brother, the ghost of Mrs. Ramsey bringing them oatcakes, the ghost of the boy he had been.

At the landing, he spotted a light glowing through the open nursery door.

His heart lifted. He knew who was there.

Andrew stood in the doorway, observing. Marlowe's cheek touched the back of the rocker. Curled up on her lap was the tabby cat, awake and staring languidly at him through eyes the same shade of green as his own.

At some point Marlowe had lost her white cap, and dark hair spilled out from the loose bun at the back of her head, reflecting the lamplight in shades of deep chestnut. A sleepy pout puckered her lips, and her bosom moved up and down in deep slumber.

The plump nursery maid he remembered here had never looked so fetching.

Other memories niggled at him, making him smile. At about the same time, he and Evan would sneak out for a late-night raid on the larder, or better yet, they'd deposit a frog in the nursemaid's pocket. How many times had they pulled off such nonsense on a girl worn out from chasing two nodcocks all day?

She stirred in the chair, moving her head to the other side, displaying a length of creamy neck and a pulse that begged to be kissed.

She's your housekeeper. You can't kiss her there. Or at all.

He cleared his throat, and a deep sigh escaped her, the corners of her mouth twitching with a contented dream.

Parts of him were twitching as well. He'd seen her response to him. He knew when a woman was feeling desire. He could pursue her. At the very least, he could steal a kiss.

Or he could throw aside decorum and go after much, much more.

He thought of the rumors about Ramsey and Old Horace and shoved down his yearning. Mrs. Ramsey had suffered withering gossip by neighbors for those rumors. It wouldn't be proper, nor fair, not as the duke, nor as the duke's factor.

"There you are," he said loudly.

Marlowe's eyes flew open. Her hands slapped the chair arms, gripping them. Shaken, the cat leapt away.

"I beg your pardon, my dear. I didn't mean to startle you."

Her gaze searched the gloom, and she shivered, not yet spotting him.

When he stepped into the room, she sucked in a deep breath.

"*Mr. Andrews.*"

"It is I."

"I fell asleep."

"I see that." The last flames of fire had burnt down to red embers, and a spool of dark ribbon lay nearby on the floor. "Many a nursery maid has settled into that rocker for only a minute. We are lucky your ribbons didn't fall into the flames and burn down this fairy tale castle."

The chair creaked on its rockers as she pushed herself up rubbing her eyes like a child woken from slumber. She pushed hair behind her ears, caught herself and clutched her hands at her waist.

By God, she was lovely.

"Was dinner satisfactory?" she asked.

"Quite."

"The duke was pleased?"

He took a deep breath. He must tell her the truth. "About that…"

"Oh." Her lips pressed together. "He didn't like it. I should expect he would not."

"Why?"

She shook her head. "He's…" She shuddered. "Difficult."

He wasn't difficult. Most of the time. "Once you become acquainted with him—"

"He's unpleasant."

He moved closer. "Who told you that?"

She opened her mouth, closed it, and opened it again.

"Was it the agency that hired you?"

"No."

"The duke's solicitor?"

"No."

"Who then?"

"It was, er…" She licked her lips. "My late husband."

"Your late husband had dealings with the new duke?" He searched his memory for a Marlowe. All the Marlowes of his acquaintance were still very much alive as far as he knew. "Was he a tradesman?"

"N-no."

In truth, he knew little of Marlowe's background. The appearance of an attractive, intelligent woman ready to serve him had dazzled him so, he hadn't asked proper questions. "Was he a gentleman, fallen on hard times?"

She sighed, surrendering, and he knew what she was about to say would be the truth. "He was a clergyman."

Mrs. Marlowe was a clergyman's widow? Oh, *that* was disappointing. *That* explained her quick efficiency though. She'd been one of those vicars' wives running about doing whatever was needed to keep the faithful in line, when they could spare time from their offspring.

"Do you have children?"

"No."

Which might explain her interest in filling the nursery. Dare he ask why not? Most vicars had a houseful, being obliged to abstain from other diversions. Either she was sterile, or he had been. Or perhaps…perhaps he'd been indifferent. Though what husband would not take Marlowe to his bed?

She chewed on her lip, hiding something.

"And how did Mr. Marlowe know the duke?"

She clucked her tongue. "He didn't. He'd merely heard in the course of his work about…about the duke's difficult demeanor."

Andrew MacDonal had been the topic of conversation among the clergy. How odd. This was a woman with secrets.

Her gaze shifted away and then back, and the spark of defiance there stirred an urge to laugh.

Marlowe was the widow of a man of the cloth, not much used to prevaricating. The vicar's widow was being wicked. She was lying.

A sheen of moisture appeared on her cheeks and her lips pressed together, suppressing a tremble.

She was delicious. He took a step closer and watched her eyes widen.

"*Sir.*"

Chapter Eight

He left her plenty of room to retreat. She held her position.

A potent mix of curiosity, amusement, and desire brewed in him. "Your husband, the gossiping vicar, what, pray tell, caused his demise?"

"He suffered an apoplexy."

"An apoplexy? He was elderly?"

She huffed. "He was...he had just turned one and sixty. Really, Mr. Andrews, this is—"

"None of my business? You don't think the duke will want to know that his housekeeper's late husband spread slander about him?"

She gasped. "That is not—"

"He values loyalty."

"Loyalty?" She scoffed. "Hmm. And he shall have mine. Am I not trying to see to his comforts? Is it disloyalty for a servant to want to know what irritates her master and what pleases him?"

His head dipped closer and her pulse jumped as strong hands curved around her forearms.

A choking breath brought a woodsy male scent sparking shivers all the way to the soles of her half boots. *Ack.* He'd startled her into clumsy lies.

And she should not have mentioned that notion of *pleasing.* Their gazes locked.

His mouth parted. He blinked, his eyes catching the gleam of the lamp.

"Are you...are you quite all right, Mr. Andrews?"

When he drew closer, her heart took off in a wild gallop. Might he...would he...

His lips touched hers, briefly, sweetly, and then he lifted his head away, still watching her.

Warmth unfurled in her, misting her eyes. The few kisses she'd shared with her long-ago suitor had never been so gentle or caring. His look of wonder, of frank admiration heated her as much as the kiss had.

She went up on her toes, freeing her hands to thread through the wild hair at his nape, and when he hooked a hand at her waist and slanted his mouth over hers, she parted her lips for a wholehearted kiss. Desire burst inside her like the pent-up waters of a damn breaking, and the moments stretched on and on.

When he moved her head to his shoulder, his heart pounded in time with her own.

That had been a real kiss.

"I suppose that was quite improper." The whispered breath tickled her ear. "You must think me a villain."

He stepped back, his hands sliding along her arms as he released her.

Heat flooded her cheeks, and she blinked away tears. The kiss had been astonishing, and far too brief.

But she must not even contemplate a liaison with the duke's handsome factor. She was a widow, but not one seeking scandal. She must come to her senses.

"Mr. Andrews, it's late and..."

He'd averted his eyes, his gaze sweeping around the room like he was gathering sweet memories. The tender kiss, the longing look—Mr. Andrews was a gentleman. Perhaps he'd grown up in a nursery like this, with a nursery maid he was fond of. Perhaps he himself was the son of a gentleman fallen on hard times.

She longed to ask, but prying might only open some wound in him. It might also reopen more awkward questioning about her own past.

He walked to the mantle and picked up the framed portrait she'd found earlier, holding it up to the lamp.

For long moments he lingered over it, saying nothing.

"I found it in storage," she said. "Might it be the duke and his brother?"

He sent her a quizzical look.

"If you think he'll be troubled, please don't show him it. I only thought his nieces might find it comforting. I hope he can come to know how lucky he is to have these children in his life. It's my job to make Castle Kinmarty a comfortable home for him and his family. If you can see a way, as his friend, to help him come to know how blessed he is to have this wondrous, grand, home, and tenants who are eager to work with him and for him, and how much he has to be grateful for in his brother's children..."

As she spoke, his lips grew steadily firmer. The sudden chill reminded her she was merely a servant. How the duke saw his circumstances was not her concern.

She sighed. "You didn't tell me the duke's complaint about dinner."

He settled the drawing atop the mantle, one corner of his mouth quirking. "The footman in the ill-fitting coat. Was he not the same fellow stacking wood today?"

"Yes, he was." They were back to the difficult duke's snobbery. "We are in the Highland wilds now, not London." She bit her lip. *And if he wanted to be waited on hand and foot, he would have to take servants as he found them.* "He's a willing fellow, and a good butler can bring him up to snuff. I've yet to find proper livery. I'll have Kyla search tomorrow while I go into the village to inquire about more servants."

"More servants," he mused, turning his gaze back to the shadowed corner with the toys.

The fire had gone out completely, the cold penetrating the wool of her shawl. She fetched her ribbon from the floor and pulled her wrap tighter.

"I believe I will turn in."

That brought him out of his musing. "I'll escort you down."

He offered his arm. Under the fine wool of his coat, the firm muscle was solid, and she shivered again as they descended the stairs.

"You're trembling." He set a hand to her waist guiding her, his hot touch radiating through her. "Don't be frightened." Her ears tingled from the whispered words. "I won't follow you into your bedchamber."

They'd reached her door. "I'm not afraid," she lied. "I'm chilled to the bone."

It wasn't Andrews who frightened her—it was herself, and her smoldering reaction. No man had ever triggered such feelings—certainly not the late Mr. Marlowe.

"Chilled to the bone?" He raised an eyebrow. "Rightly so. I hope Duff restocked your wood." His gaze heated. "Mrs. Marlowe, I shouldn't have kissed you, though I found I couldn't resist. I hope you'll forgive me."

Her heart pounded as she worried over her reply. Indignation would be yet another lie. Telling him it was nothing would mean she thought dallying was fine—and that wasn't true either.

The kiss had meant a great deal. The kiss had been a warm spark lighting up her soul. And he politely hadn't mentioned that she had kissed him back, fiercely.

The way his gaze softened and his eyes darkened told her the kiss had meant something to him as well.

"What...what is your Christian name, Marlowe?"

Her Christian name? A thread of suspicion snaked through her, making her hesitate. Her name was unusual. He might tell the duke, and the duke might recall a Filomena who'd been briefly the subject of a scandal—one he'd caused by his meddling—so many years ago.

But she supposed, a factor ought to know the housekeeper's full name.

"Filomena," she whispered. She hurried into her bedchamber, closing the door and leaning against it.

Filomena.

Andrew stared at the closed door. The name niggled at him. There'd been a girl named Filomena at some time in his past. Something noteworthy had happened to her.

"We need to talk." George appeared at his elbow, grumbling the words.

What now? He followed his friend down the corridor to the study.

Inside, George rounded on him. "You shouldn't have *kissed* her? What the devil was that about?"

He walked to the sideboard and poured a drink. "Spur of the moment. It was all in innocence. A mere touch of the lips, like you might kiss your great-aunt."

"A gentleman does not—"

"Yes, I know. Seduce his housekeeper." Although apparently old Horace had done so, and he could now understand why. Perhaps he was a chip off the old Castle Kinmarty block after all.

"Mrs. Marlowe has done well for you. Dinner was more than palatable, there's a good supply of firewood in each room and someone to carry up more, and we're spared rising at dawn to see to the cattle. She's performed miracles of housekeeping in one day."

"She has, hasn't she?"

She'd arrived one day and achieved all that the next. His fairy tale castle was taking shape. She'd even got him to review the blasted correspondence he'd put aside.

He forced a laugh. "She's a managing sort of female, and her Christian name is Filomena. Tell me, George, does the name Filomena Marlowe sound familiar to you?"

"It's not particularly common."

"Have you ever heard tell of a clergyman named Marlowe?"

"Her husband?"

"So she says. An older fellow who must have married her out of the schoolroom. She can't be more than thirty. I know her from somewhere. Or I've heard of her."

George scowled with more emotion than he usually displayed.

"Listen, your *grace*, I'm serious. A penniless clergyman's widow? If that's what she truly is, I won't stand by and watch you play with her feelings."

"You don't think she's telling the truth?"

"How would we know without an inquiry? Let her alone."

"Or what? Will you call me out?"

His friend's scowl darkened.

"I won't play the rake with her. Though she's damned pretty."

"For now, she's your housekeeper, and possibly a competent one. You're in the wilds of Scotland—don't dally and distract her. You still need someone to find you a butler. She has as good a chance as anyone."

He eased onto the wide leather-upholstered chair at the desk and drummed his fingers on the stack of letters there. "I told her about Forbes, the old duke's butler. If she spoke to him today, he must have said no. Perhaps *I* can lure him back, or at least get his help for a time."

"Capital idea."

"I'll pay him a visit tomorrow."

"The nabob is coming tomorrow."

"I know."

"You're impossible." With a shake of his head, George left.

Andrew let his mount meander through the dense woods at the edge of the castle grounds, skirting the main drive, in part to avoid his visitors, and in part to make a more direct approach to where Forbes's cottage should be.

He'd spent a good part of the night ruminating about Marlowe. Eager to see her in the flesh, he'd risen early, only to find she'd already left the Castle.

The same faux footman had poured his coffee for him, and the young maid he'd met in the nursery had cheerfully delivered a platter of eggs. Marlowe had introduced her as Kyla Forbes. She was surely kin to the old butler.

On her first full day of residence at Castle Kinmarty, Marlowe had taken the bit of information he'd given her and found her way to the Forbes family. Did she have ties in Kinmarty? Could that be why the name Filomena was so familiar? As lads, he and Evan had attended a few village festivals, ones where the children ran wild, but they'd never made friends here.

He smiled at the memories of raucous games on the green. In later times, Evan pursued every pretty milkmaid and wench who'd look twice at him—and being the duke's heir and a hale fellow, there'd been plenty. His own task had been keeping the fool out of real trouble and getting him home before Ramsey set a footman to find them.

Gad, it had taken a few years of growing before he understood the appeal of the lasses, but until then he'd thought his brother an utter numbskull.

He turned his mount to a line of trees and heard the rush of the water. So, the burn hadn't frozen, in spite of the frigid weather.

Dismounting, he led his horse closer. The stream was shallow here, the water brisk and foaming. Even in summer, it was bone-chilling for anyone with the misfortune to fall in. One August day while hunting for Evan, he'd hauled out a lass who'd been looking for the girl his brother was meeting.

He shivered with the memory...

A long wail pierced the bushes straggling alongside the stream. On the rocky bank opposite a girl, a skinny thing, stared down at a place where the water pooled. Something silky and blue floated there.

A bright flash of yellow crashed into the pool with a colossal splash.

"What the—"

She'd jumped.

He wiped the drenching from his eyes. Yellow ballooned all about her. In the clear water, bare legs thrashed in time with her arms.

He laughed. "You look just like a duck."

Her head whipped around. "What have you done with her?"

"Who?"

She threw back her head, sucked in a long breath, and rolled forward, until her grimy bare feet stuck out.

A girl. He'd never seen anything like it.

Oh, he'd seen Evan plunge into water, but he was a boy. He'd never seen a girl in a great bulky dress try to—

Her head crested. She spluttered and splashed, churning water and bobbing like a sea monster had hold of her skirts and was...

Her skirts. She was in the bloody middle of the stream and couldn't touch the bottom.

"Nodcock girl."

Hell, she'd soaked him already anyway. He yanked off his hat, boots and coat, and jumped in.

Cold sliced him, freezing his breath.

Her head slipped under. With a great kick he reached her and yanked her up.

She gulped air and went under again, pulling him with her, down and down. In the clear water, the stark look of fear made his heart race.

His foot touched the bottom. He shot up, still gripping her, kicking like mad, towing her. He found purchase not five feet from where she'd been drowning and half dragged her into a patch of weeds.

Her lips were purple, her skin a pale shade of gray, but she was breathing.

She'd scared the wits out of him. He wanted to smack her.

"Do you have stones in your pockets?" A tiny thing, she was younger than him, with no titties yet. "What the devil were you doing, brat? You might have drowned."

She pinched up her mouth and said "Shut up."

"I just saved your life. That is beyond rude."

With her dark hair plastered all over her cheeks she looked ridiculous.

"Thank you." Her teeth chattered all over the words.

"Did that hurt? No. And now I'll get a beating for going home soaked."

He laughed out loud. That girl had pluck, whoever she was.

Much good it had done him saving her. Late for dinner, and him sopping wet, he'd taken an equal punishment with Evan. Perhaps Ramsey had somehow heard of his heroics because that night there'd been butter on his own ration of bread.

He'd never seen the duck again. Never wanted to. He hoped the little nodcock had suffered her own punishment for almost drowning the both of them.

His mount picked its way over snow-covered trails before reaching the side road that led west, into the rolling hills that fronted the Cairngorms. Gad, Marlowe had the right of it. The land was magnificent and the castle was lovely, at least from a distance.

Years ago, there'd been a cottage near this burn belonging to the butler's kin. He and Evan had stumbled across the dwelling and been welcomed and well-treated. He'd start his search for Forbes there.

As he neared a small path that veered off toward the water, he heard voices among the trees, a woman's warm laugh, and a man's heartier one.

The tones rang with a familiarity that lifted his spirits. He dismounted again and went to investigate.

The silhouette of a bothy appeared through the thicket. He searched his memory—he and Evan had walked every inch of Kinmarty along this burn, and he didn't remember this structure. The tidy stone-walled building with its thatched roof looked new.

Just short of the small clearing, his breath caught. Smoke puffed from the bothy's chimney. An old man, his face sparkling with good humor, sat perched on a downed log, pouring a drink into the tin cup held by the woman beside him.

"A wee drop more will warm you straight to your toes," Forbes said.

The gravelly voice brought a wash of memories. To two fatherless boys, Forbes had been as much a force as Mrs. Ramsey. And he'd often covered for them, understanding a boy's need to break free and roam now and again.

"Aye," the woman said. "The last sip only reached as far as my knees." She laughed, tipped back the cup, and wiped the back of her gloved hand across her mouth. "'Tis a good brew, Mr. Forbes."

Andrew's pulse pounded. She might be *ayeing* and *'tising*, but that was most certainly Filomena Marlowe, his housekeeper, drinking whisky, and—he glanced at the sky through the trees—it not yet noon.

Chapter Nine

He cleared his throat and both heads swiveled his way.

Alarm turned Marlowe's cheeks pink. She broke into a tense smile and stood. "We've been caught out, Mr. Forbes."

Under her bravado was a smidgeon of embarrassment.

"A good day to you, sir." Forbes rose, smiling. Deep lines crinkled the corners of the old butler's mouth, and his blue eyes sparkled.

Jealousy niggled at him. Forbes looked like a man relaxed and happy with his lot and the day's surprises. Was his good mood from seeing Andrew, or did his interlude with Marlowe have him glowing?

Marlowe had married an old man once before, and Forbes, despite all the gray hair and wrinkles, was still a hardy and fit specimen.

"Mr. Forbes," Marlowe said, "Allow me to introduce Mr. Andrews, the new duke's factor. You can see, he's a difficult taskmaster, having tracked me all the way to your...er...enterprise. Mr. Andrews, this is Mr. Forbes, the late duke's butler, and the best whisky-maker in all of Scotland, I'm told."

Forbes preened under the compliment and gave her a little bow. God help him, Marlowe was flirting with the old codger.

"I'll leave you gentlemen now, as I have another call to make, but please do send a barrel up to the Castle, Mr. Forbes. If the new duke cannot appreciate your elixir, the staff surely will."

She flounced off through the trees like a lady heading off to the shops on Oxford Street. Andrew watched her go, speechless.

"*Mr. Andrews* is it?"

Relief flooded him. It had been a good dozen years, but Forbes had known him on sight.

"What the devil are you up to Master Andrew?"

"I couldn't fool you, could I?"

"Aye, and I've heard a tale or two about you since the last time we met. What are you aboot, laddie, pretending to be someone else?"

He picked up the cup she'd left. "May *I* have a wee dram?"

"'Tis a fine woman you've hired in Mrs. Marlowe. I would that you'd treat her well." Forbes picked up the pitcher and poured without spilling a drop.

The honeyed scent warmed his nose as he sniffed it. It wasn't a fashionable drink in town, but he was growing fond of the local brew. "I'm *aboot* nothing nefarious. I merely had a mad moment of...of..."

Why had he done it? He couldn't seem to remember what he'd been thinking two days ago.

"Fear?"

Always perceptive, was Forbes.

"Wheest, boy. That's a fine woman, is Mrs. Marlowe."

"You've said that already."

He was destined to be chastised. He might as well sit back and take it like his eight-year-old self had learned to do.

At least he had whisky to help him cope now. Tipping the cup, he let the liquid pool on his tongue as he savored the rich notes and, finally, swallowed.

The smooth burn didn't quite reach his toes, but it was brilliant. "Is this truly your brew, Forbes?"

"Aye." The old man crossed his arms on his chest. "I heard of yer brother's death. I am sorry. Life doesn'a always seem fair, but it's time to stop feeling sorry for yourself and face up to who ye are now."

"I beg your pardon."

"Beg my pardon all ye wish. Since ye were a wee lad, all ye did was dash about after yer fool brother. Ye were always the steadier fellow until he left and ye fell all apart. What were the chances Master Evan would die in that godforsaken land leavin' ye to inherit? Damn good, I said, and so did Ramsey. She pressed the duke to bring ye home and train ye. And when he finally came 'round to it, ye didn'a wish it. Refused to lift a finger to help. As stubborn and prideful as the old man, ye were."

Andrew's chest squeezed and his tongue froze along with his heart. He'd prefer the lash to this. Forbes had never spoken so boldly. Retirement had loosened *his* tongue.

Not that he *didn'a* deserve it. He *had* gone to pieces when Evan left. He'd had enough income to plunge into a bachelor life in the ton, enough wit not to gamble all his money away, and enough charm to access both ballrooms and bedchambers. And when ennui sat in as it always did, he made sure he got himself roaring drunk. He'd been a man with no redeeming purpose. Now and then he'd thought about heading north to Kinmarty, but once he'd refused the duke's summons, the old man had cut ties with him.

Forbes's grim look told him there was more. He steeled himself.

"'Tis a pity yer brother didn'a want the title either, rushing off to India as he did. The old duke woulda come around to his marriage. He might've brought his bride to Kinmarty and learned a thing or two. Better yet, he might've brought ye, Master Andrew. Might've spared us the reign of that devil Haskill."

The old pain flared in him, and a gnawing started in his belly. Perhaps he might have warmed to the unsuitable Penelope Grant, if only Evan had stayed, and given him time to adjust.

"Or ye might have come when the old man asked for ye."

Evan had left England in a cloud of anger, and he had proclaimed himself freed from what he'd painted as the shackles of family.

God, but he missed his brother, and the old duke, as well. He'd managed without them, and been lonely as hell.

Stubborn and prideful, he was. Forbes had the right of it.

He took in a deep breath of the crisp air, tinged with the wood smoke from the still. He'd never be able to make things right with Evan or the old duke, but he could make things right for Evan's children and the people of Kinmarty. If he'd been here, if he'd come, he might've learned of Evan's girls, brought them here sooner. He would've nipped Haskill's thieving before more people suffered.

And how badly had their people suffered?

"Tell me about Haskill, Forbes. Tell me what happened here."

"That I shall do. Come with me, if you will."

The snug Forbes cottage still stood on a rise above the burn. All was quiet as they approached. The children who'd lived here had, like him, grown up.

"Was it your wife and your children living here, Forbes?"

"Never took a wife, not yet anyway. 'Twas my elder sister, gone this last year. Her daughter and her family live here now, but they're oot and aboot this morn."

Forbes led him into the warm kitchen and stirred the red embers at the hearth, setting about preparing them tea.

"When did Haskill begin stealing from Old Horace? Did he suppose he would never be caught?"

"He was counting on yer brother making a slow voyage from India. Thought it might be a year, maybe two before he arrived. The old duke had set him over Kinmarty until then."

Andrew accepted the cup of tea. "A wee drop of the whisky wouldn't go amiss, especially with this story."

Forbes obliged him, topping off his cup. "And a story it is. Since his arrival in Kinmarty, Haskill badgered the duke to clear out the tenants and bring in sheep."

"Like the Sutherlands." Lady Sutherland had forced thousands of tenants away to clear the land for wool cultivation.

"Aye. The old duke opposed it."

"Was that Mrs. Ramsey's influence?"

"Mayhap, it was. She and Haskill were at loggerheads much of the time. Tried to sully her name, he did. I'll not hear any ill spoken of her."

He took a hearty drink. The rumors of the duke and Ramsey had taken root long before Haskill arrived, but no matter. "Don't worry. Mrs. Ramsey was dear to me."

Forbes grunted, topped off his cup again, and told him about the tenants threatened with eviction, families that were kin to the dukes of Kinmarty going back generations, clansmen and clanswomen who owed fealty and service and should be able to expect loyalty in return.

"I'd left before she passed on, though I went back to be with her and the old duke those last few days. After that, most of the old servants departed, and upon the old duke's death, all but Haskill's toadies were let go." Forbes shoved his own cup away. "Have ye looked at the leases yet?"

"No."

"I ought to have gone straight to ye the first day ye arrived."

"Whose leases did he cancel?"

"None yet as I know about, but he'd threatened all the families."

The old duke's will might have given Haskill the running of Kinmarty, but the duke's solicitor seemed a competent man. Surely Old Horace's will would've designated his heir as the one deciding the fate of the tenants and the future of the land. It was another matter to look into.

"Forbes, I need you. Will you come up to the Castle for a time until I can hire a butler?" He rubbed at his jaw. "Though it's nothing like the grand old days. You'll have to manage without the silver, and china, and the best of the linens. Haskill stole all of that, and God knows I've no money for replacements."

Forbes drew in a deep breath. "About that, duke… Do me another kindness and follow me into my wee cellar. I've something else to show ye."

Less than an hour later, Andrew was humming a tune as he steered his mount to the village that had been Marlowe's destination.

He had a butler, albeit a temporary one, and Forbes had promised to contact an acquaintance, a man from Kinmarty in service in Glasgow who was eager to come home. Better, he'd promised to train the new staff Marlowe was hiring.

Best of all, he'd led Andrew to the Kinmarty silver and china stashed away in his cellar. He and the last of the duke's loyal servants had spared most of it from Haskill's greed.

He patted his pocket. Forbes had also safeguarded Ramsey's dearest possessions, to be kept out of Haskill's hands and passed on to the new duke.

Not that the new duke had any plans for any of the valuables, certainly not a grand dinner party. In London, society matrons showered him with invitations, but as a bachelor living in rooms, he'd never hosted such affairs. Arranging dinners and such was a woman's business.

The silver was valuable, though. If anyone were to melt it down for the King's tax, it ought to be the duke himself.

He prayed it wouldn't come to that. Expedient it might be for a time, but he'd only have to find something else to sell for the next bill. Not himself though, nor his freedom.

The creak of carriage wheels behind him made him rein up.

Blast it. He'd forgotten the nabob.

Chapter Ten

He turned his mount toward a gap in the trees, but he'd been too late.

"What, ho." A sturdy carriage pulled by two horses came up next to him, the two occupants bundled against the cold like Egyptian mummies.

"There you are."

There was too much delight in that deep-throated greeting.

Andrew took in a breath. "Good day to you. I'll just move aside and you may—"

"Kinmarty, are you not?" The driver brought the horses to a stop, and the speaker threw off his rug, clambering out.

He was a large man—large in width, shorter in height—with skin the color of walnuts topped by a white crop of hair. He looked like a man who'd spent too much time in the bright sun of India gorging himself on curry and chickpeas.

Andrew glanced toward the thicket. He could be through those bushes in seconds, galloping across the hills on the other side.

But to where? No doubt the nabob would turn around and follow him back to the Castle.

Forbes had been right. It was time to face up to who he was.

He dipped his head, and the other man beamed.

"Happy to meet you, duke. Benedict Strachney, here. I've just come from Kinmarty. Found your friend Lovelace in the stables tending his horse. I've two good mounts you may borrow. Have my groom bring them over tomorrow and he can look at that leg. A dab hand with horses, he is. Er...may I present my daughter, Ann?"

The remaining bundle of rugs lifted a gloved hand and waved. Andrew swallowed a groan and bowed from his saddle.

Strachney cocked his head. "Did you not receive my note that I was paying a call?"

Irritation bristled in him, churning the third helping of whisky he'd shared with old Forbes.

No social-climbing nabob would bully him, not as Mr. Andrew MacDonal, and certainly not as the Duke of Kinmarty.

"Your man scurried off before I could send my regrets." He swallowed his annoyance, remembering that, though a duke may lord it over his neighbors, his was a poor dukedom and this particular neighbor was as rich as Croesus. He might need his help one day. Best to keep good relations. "I hope you weren't too inconvenienced."

"Oh?" Strachney said. "Oh well, we've had a dose of fresh air, haven't we, Ann? Helps me to thicken my blood after so many years away. Though my Ann is used to it, aren't you love? Ann remained here with her mother during my travels, living with my sister in Edinburgh."

"I see."

"She's well-suited to wild Scottish weather, you'll find."

Good Lord. "Yes, well, I must be on my way, and well-suited or not, I'm sure neither of you wants to remain in the cold."

"I look forward to becoming better acquainted when I see you tomorrow night."

"I beg your pardon?"

"For dinner. Lovelace extended the invitation to your Christmas Eve dinner party. Said you were eager to meet your neighbors. Very kind of you to include my daughter and me."

Anger took hold of his throat and constricted it. George had arranged a dinner party? Of all the meddling, interfering, managing...

He swallowed his bile and took a deep breath. "Please also include Mrs. Strachney, your lady wife."

Strachney's gaze dropped in a moment of feigned mourning. "How very good-hearted of you, your grace. I'm afraid Mrs. Strachney has been gone these many years."

"I am sorry. Well, then, until we meet again."

He turned his horse and crashed through the brush, but instead of the gallop across the snow-covered country his blood called for, he found himself picking his way over hidden dangers, careful of his mount's footing. No need to incur a social debt to the nabob for the loan of a mount. When the horses arrived on the morrow, George could damned well ride both of them. He could marry the damned heiress as well.

He fumed his way through fields and small copses, letting the sound of the chaise wheels fade into the soft silence of the winter landscape, counting his blessings that the man hadn't planned to return to the Castle.

After an hour of meandering, his anger had lifted, and he found himself again admiring—*admiring*—the country and the view of the castle peeking through trees as he approached. Marlowe truly did have the right of it—it was magnificent, as glorious as it had been the very first time he'd arrived in Kinmarty, a small boy in need of a fortress.

As he came around to the back, he found himself in a thicket of yew and evergreens on a hill a short walk from the stables. A figure moving in the trees brought him to alert.

An animal brayed, and a woman shushed it. Moving closer, he saw a donkey strapped with panniers that were bursting with evergreen boughs.

The woman moved into his field of vision and his heart swelled. What the devil was Marlowe up to now?

Borrowing the donkey had, perhaps, been a mistake. The temperamental creature walked when it was meant to stand, and balked when it should move on. No wonder the innkeeper had been happy to loan the beast at no cost. It had taken all of an hour to coax it to this stand of bushes that Mr. Forbes told her about and find a spot to its liking.

And now the donkey appeared eager to move on, baring its yellow teeth, shaking its long ears, and *hee-hawing* at her.

"Shush now." Filomena clutched her shears under her arm and squeezed the freshly cut pine branch in among the others. "Only a few more and we'll head for the stables and your supper."

She should have brought Duff and Kyla to help her, as she'd promised the children yesterday, but that would have required returning to the Castle after her visit to the village and…and she needed to be alone. She needed the bracing cold air and some distance from Castle Kinmarty, and most especially some distance from Mr. Andrews.

Her cheeks heated remembering the kiss in the nursery, his lips, surprisingly soft upon hers. And there'd been his hand burning into her waist as he'd guided her down the dark staircase.

The duke's voice had rumbled through her closed bedchamber door greeting Mr. Andrews. He'd been close enough to observe their goodnights. She prayed he'd not heard mention of that kiss.

That kiss. Once upon a time, she'd been a young girl aflame from a man's touch. Mr. Andrews stirred those ancient memories, reminding her of her dreams of marriage, of the young man who'd courted her, a young man she'd been prepared to love. What a fool she'd been.

She shook the snow from a promising branch, jumping back as it showered her skirts.

Andrew MacDonal had ruined that. He'd called her a twit, a social-climber. He'd planted doubts. Her suitor had dumped her.

She'd slunk back to Hertfordshire, grieving over lost dreams, regretting her break with Penelope, and dreading her godmother's coming demise. When a neighbor's visiting brother offered for her, she'd accepted, never mind that he was three decades older.

With his new parish, Mr. Marlowe had needed a wife to run the vicarage, to organize the ladies' societies, to tend to the poor, and to see to any other need that might possibly draw him out of his library. He'd been mostly kind and completely uninterested in her person. They'd never shared a bed. He'd never once kissed her.

She pressed a hand to her chest and lifted her chin, gulping in great breaths of cold air. Oh, what she must have missed in the marriage bed. Mr. Andrews had given her a hint of it. His touch had made her withered heart bloom.

And what poetic nonsense that was. She wasn't a girl anymore.

She knew there was much, much more she'd missed out on. Mr. Marlowe might have been a clergyman, but on the top shelves of his library, she'd found his forbidden books and looked at every last illustration.

She was simply feeling carnal desire. A widow of the *haute ton* was free to explore what marriage might have denied her. A clergyman's widow, not so, unless she was willing to risk much.

The donkey hee-hawed at her and sneered. She stuck out her tongue at the beast.

She'd been daring enough to come to Castle Kinmarty and hide her relationship to Penelope. Would striking a romance with Mr. Andrews be too reckless?

It all depended on what happened after Penelope arrived, and she must remember her purpose. She was here for her cousin. Most of all, she was here for

Penelope's children. The more she thought of them, the dearer they seemed.

She glanced at the horizon and the waning light and then assessed the fruits of her labor. This would do for a good start on the Great Hall.

The wind soughed through the trees, rubbing branches together, sending a chill through her scarf.

"Good day again, Mrs. Marlowe."

She whipped around and her heart rose into her throat. Mr. Andrews sat atop a magnificent black horse, his muscular legs gripping the side of his mount.

Sudden heat flooded her. As if she'd conjured him, he'd appeared.

"Cutting pine boughs, are you? Do we not have a servant for that?"

A servant? Oh, how he addled her wits. She took a few quick breaths, summoning Mrs. Marlowe, the vicar's demure wife, before speaking.

"In many homes, gathering the Yuletide greenery is a family affair. In any case, I *am* a servant, Mr. Andrews. And since the innkeeper loaned me this donkey, I thought I might just as well load it up on my way back to the Castle."

He studied her, making her shiver as if she'd shed all of her clothing right down to her chemise.

Perhaps he'd forgotten that he was a servant also, after a fashion. She lifted her chin and stared back at him, letting her gaze roam over the tight fit of his breeches and tall polished boots.

His lips twitched. "Very well."

He swung one leg over and dismounted, as graceful as she was awkward. How could she ever imagine he'd have any interest in her?

"You make a very good point. I have fond memories of gathering greenery with my brother at Yuletide."

Oh, blast it, what had she started with her boldness? She shooed him back. "I'm just finishing. Go on to the castle. You're not dressed warmly enough."

"And neither are you." He trudged through the snow in her direction. "Come, let me help you." He reached for the shears and her fingers tightened reflexively on the handle.

Heat poured from him as he cupped her hand and peeled back her thumb.

"Even your fingers are frozen, my dear."

The low rumbled words fogged around her and filled the air with the honeyed scent of Mr. Forbes's brew. Under his gentle touch, each of her traitorous fingers surrendered, one by one, until he took possession of the shears, sliding his thumb and two fingers into the finger holes.

He smoothed his free hand up her arm, frowning. "We should talk about that kiss, Filomena Marlowe."

Alarm rose in her. "Did the duke hear your apology?"

He blinked. "What?"

"Last night. I heard the duke join you outside my door. Did he mention our kiss?"

His lips parted and his eyes widened. "He...he didn't."

A tingle went through her. She'd organized more than one parish party for rowdy children, and she knew that look—Mr. Andrews was lying.

Which meant trouble was coming.

Chapter Eleven

Not only had she kissed Mr. Andrews, she'd given the handsome rascal her Christian name, and that had been within the duke's hearing. As soon as Andrew MacDonal remembered her from a decade ago, and he would, of that she had no doubt, she'd be dismissed.

Oh, she expected to be dismissed once her cousin arrived and the duke discovered her own deception, but she was counting on the opportunity to make peace with Penelope and plans for the children before being sent packing.

Or…there might be a worse possibility. The scandal sheets had occasionally featured Andrew MacDonal's affairs of the heart, especially with widows. He might come after her himself.

The mere memory of kissing Mr. Andrews made her heart almost burst, but the duke? The thought of intimacy with him made her skin crawl.

She pulled away and went to untie the donkey. "The kiss last night was pleasant, but it truly was nothing and won't happen again. I shall tell the duke the same thing if he asks."

"It was nothing?"

"No. If you please, stow the shears in the pannier. The new footmen can cut more boughs tomorrow."

"We have new footmen?" He packed the shears away and brushed against her in passing, sparking a new flood of warmth.

"Y-yes. And they come highly recommended by Mr. Forbes." When she jiggled the donkey's lead, the creature sneered at her and stiffened.

"Blast you." Could a beast be this obstinate? "Come along then."

In a few steps, the lead strained. The animal pulled its lips back with a baleful braying that sounded pained.

"What is wrong? Is a branch poking you?" She moved to the animal's side and fumbled with the pannier. "Is your load unbalanced?"

Andrews chuckle tickled her ear. "It's pure stubbornness. A good smack on the—*Oof.*"

Her feet flew out from under her, and she landed flat on her back in a soft mound of snow with Mr. Andrews atop her.

Her heart all but stopped. His weight…his heat…the scent of his shaving soap…

The snow, her insides, everything began to thaw. She'd vanish into a puddle like the time she'd almost drowned in the burn. They'd not find her body until spring.

He raised up on one elbow and rubbed at his backside. "The bloody beast kicked *me.*"

"Are you injured?" She struggled, finding no purchase in the soft snow.

"Only my manly pride. It was a glancing blow. He was aiming at you." The corner of his mouth lifted.

Braced above her, his eyes glazed and he dipped his head closer, close enough to share a breath.

Oh. Oh, she was mad. This was madness.

And she didn't care. She lifted her head, anyway. His lips were chilled, his nose cold, the snow around them freezing, but everywhere else she was afire, and so was he. She matched him kiss for kiss, tongues twining, hands searching, losing herself in the heat and the need, in his hands moving over her breasts. Desire flamed even through the layers of clothing. She wanted more, she wanted everything, and—

Bracing cold touched the bare skin of her leg above her garter. Gasping, she came to her senses and called out his name.

His head came up. He looked around, blinking away his bedazzlement, hastily pulling her skirts down, and helping her to her feet.

"That was...that was...Are you well, Mrs. Marlowe?" He brushed snow from her back. "Oh, my dear. Let me put you up on my mount."

The donkey hee-hawed.

"I should apologize. Not about that kiss." He took in a sharp breath. "*That kiss.*" His eyes held a look of wonderment. "I mean I shouldn't have tumbled you into the snow."

Heart pounding, she grasped at the donkey's lead. If it weren't for the snow, if it had been a fine day...

She found a breath and shook her head. They couldn't continue down that amorous path. "It was a mistake."

"This was our second, er, *encounter*, and it didn't feel like a mistake. It felt damned good."

"*Language*, sir. You know there must not be a third. I have my reputation to look after and so do you. You must go on ahead to the Castle. Don't wait for me. Now, come along, donkey." She tugged.

Hands on his hips, Andrews studied the beast then inched behind it. "Pull...*now*." He tapped the broad rump, dodging the sharp kick that followed.

His boyish grin made her cheeks flame again, and she stepped out coaxing the animal. The donkey took a few plodding steps and then a few more. She slackened the lead and rubbed the dark shock of hair between the huge ears, laughing. That clump of hair reminded her ever so much of Mr. Andrews' unkempt locks.

"Thank you," she called over her shoulder. "And you," she muttered to the donkey, "you need to move faster." The heavy steps, the snorts, the rattling of the panniers all hid the movements of the man behind her, but she could feel his persistent presence.

He was a danger to a woman like her, as handsome as any of the knights who might once have defended Kinmarty. He could never be her knight, though, and she must remember that.

Moments later she reached the drive and the castle came into view. Pausing, she pressed a hand to her chest. The late afternoon gloaming shrouded the old stonework in mystery.

He stepped up next to her, leading his horse.

"You're right, Mrs. Marlowe. Castle Kinmarty is magnificent. I am lucky to…to live here." His hand settled on her back. "Let me put you up on my mount and I'll lead both my horse and Lucius here."

"Lucius?"

"Lucius of *The Golden Ass*. A Roman story of a man changed into a donkey. Do you know it? This is a male donkey, you know, and Lucius is as good a name as any for the creature."

"You studied Latin."

"Yes, of course. And Greek."

Of course, because he was gentry, just like herself. But unlike her, he had a family, a brother he'd said. And someone had taught him kindness as well. He'd been genial with Kyla and Duff, and he'd found a way into the Cook's heart.

"Yet you've taken this position. You were not from a family of wealth?"

He stopped and turned his full gaze on her. "How very astute of you. I was not. But for the charity of others, I would not have read the story of Lucius."

"Were you at school with the duke then? Is that how you made his acquaintance?"

"About that…" He lifted his hat and plopped it back down again. "About that, Mrs. Marlowe—"

"*What, ho!*"

Good God. It was the second time that day he'd been hailed thusly.

He turned to see a pony cart coming up the drive.

He'd been so absorbed in the woman beside him and the confession he needed to make, and that kiss… That kiss that had been such a mauling his privy counsellor was still all aflame—well, he hadn't heard the creak of the wheels.

Forbes sat in the cart's box, pulling his pony up.

Andrew's stomach roiled. He'd waited too long to tell Marlowe the truth.

Forbes lifted an eyebrow.

Oh, devil take it. Marlowe had just been about to pry into his past, anyway. Best get it done with. Forbes would reveal his guilt and he must just stiffen his backside and take the thrashing he deserved. Sooner or later, Marlowe had to learn that he was a fraud.

"Forbes." Andrew grinned, relieved the old man would do the difficult task of unmasking him, and relieved he would be nearby should the lady decide to wallop him—or worse, try to leave Kinmarty. "I didn't expect to see you until the morrow."

"The whisky delivery could have waited," Marlowe said. "It will be full dark soon. I'd not have you picking your way all alone down this lane."

"Well, then, ye've no need to worry. I'll be staying the night at Castle Kinmarty."

"Staying the night?" The smile that bloomed on Marlowe's face made him glance at the old man. Forbes beamed back at the both of them.

He was flaunting Marlowe's admiration, but at least he hadn't hurled a *your-grace*. Forbes hadn't given him away, not yet, anyway.

"Coming to work, I am." Forbes nodded at Andrew.

Andrew roused himself from the complicated swirl of emotions. "I didn't have a chance to tell you, Mrs. Marlowe. While you were busy hiring footmen, I hired a butler."

"And uncovered the Kinmarty plate, which I've brought along in the cart, seeing as how ye'll be hosting a grand dinner tomorrow night."

She blinked. "The plate. *You* had the plate, Mr. Forbes?"

"It's a bit of a tale," he said. "I'll let the, er, *factor* do the telling."

He let out a long breath. Forbes would spare him her fury until later. But he mustn't wait too much later. He must talk to her that very night.

Mrs. Marlowe gasped. Loudly. "A grand dinner?"

She'd just absorbed that bit of news.

"Tomorrow night? How many guests? How many courses?" She tightened her grip on Lucius' lead, evoking an equine snort. "No one has told me of this."

"I just learned of it myself. I believe it's only a neighbor, Mr. Strachney, and his daughter coming. I encountered them on the road. The invitation had been extended today while we were absent."

"I hope the duke isn't given to such slapdash, spur of the moment..." She bit her lip.

If she were the Duchess of Kinmarty herself and the King had been spotted in the village about to pop by, she couldn't have looked more alarmed.

"Oh, aye," Forbes chuckled. "The new duke will be full of surprises."

She gathered her skirts. "He'll want a good table for his first dinner party. And the house not yet decorated for Christmas. I'll be up half the night. Do you know these guests, Mr. Forbes?"

"Aye. Stopped by today for a case."

Strachney had stopped by and crowed to Forbes about the invitation.

"Tell us about Strachney." he said.

"Made his wealth in the India trade. Came home last year and took the lease for Glenthistle. Eager to get his daughter well-married, so he keeps a good table and likes a good whisky."

Andrews raised an eyebrow. "One of your regular customers, is he?"

Forbes chuckled. "Tried to hire me to set up a still for him."

"But you'd have none of it."

"That's right. I'm a Kinmarty man."

"And he hasn't set the King's gaugers onto you yet?"

"Nay. Not as yet." He grinned. "And best he doesn't. I've a duke on my side."

"A dinner party," Mrs. Marlowe said. "Gentlemen, I must hurry on before the light fades altogether."

Knowing his secret was still safe with Forbes, Andrew left the old butler and a fretting Marlowe sorting out the unloading and storage of the plate, and the arrangements for the party the next night.

He found his so-called friend, George, ensconced in a wing chair in the study, his boots propped on the fireplace fender. George closed his book and set it aside, his weaselly smile infuriating.

"You'll thank me later," George said.

The cat stared up at him from his desk chair. "You again." He shooed the creature away and flopped onto the seat. A new stack of missives awaited him.

"How could you?" He gripped the pile, the urge to fling all of them into the fire almost overwhelming.

Flipping through them, he saw letters from tradesmen, notes likely from more neighbors threatening to pay calls, and another official-looking envelope, a tax dun, he supposed.

A second formal post, made his breath tighten. It was an express from his solicitor. What now?

He broke the seal and unfolded a scripted letter with a piece of delicate paper that slipped out. He scanned the brief letter and then turned to the feminine handwriting on the thinner sheet.

This note was dated one day after Evan's death. In a hurry to get this post on a ship departing that day, Penelope MacDonal wrote that she would be leaving India as soon as Evan was buried, and upon her arrival in England, would travel directly to Castle Kinmarty with the children as Evan had requested in his previous letter.

"There's another tax bill in that stack," George said.

"How could you possibly know that?"

The other man chuckled. "All the letters from the Exchequer look the same. When I saw the post come in, and then encountered your nabob in the yard, I had a stroke of inspiration. The daughter didn't look awful, what I could see of her. You'll enjoy having company to dinner. You were never one to brood in your rooms."

He'd brooded plenty, but that wasn't his public face. Not even a good friend like George knew his private moods, but they hadn't become acquainted until a few years ago.

And George knew the duke couldn't very well shirk his own party, not without a wife or sister or some other female relative to carry on hosting in his absence.

If only Marlowe could join them at table.

He shook off the thought. Dukes didn't sit down to dinner with their housekeepers.

Perhaps Penelope would arrive on the morrow and make herself useful managing the guests. She might even have met the nabob during her sojourn in India.

England abounded with nabobs. Might Evan have also found riches there? Might he have left his widow a fortune? Not that he would ever consider marrying his late brother's wife, even if it were legal in Scotland, but he might prefer her financial help to the nabob's, if they could get over their feud.

"There might be other well-dowered candidates, but you must at least meet this one."

George's gaze narrowed. "Trust me, Andrew, you mustn't encourage the housekeeper. She fancies you already. Once she learns you're the real duke, she'll appear at your bedchamber every night."

That image cheered him.

"Stop grinning."

He laughed. "What say you, George? Must it be marrying a purse, or might there be hope of another way? I'm not one for extravagant living. Can I shut down part of this heap? Run hunting parties? Mine for ore? Might there be a way to make Castle Kinmarty solvent? I'm finding I rather like the old pile and the company."

George scoffed. "The company, as in Mrs. Marlowe? I've been thinking. What respectable Vicar's widow takes a job as a housekeeper and then carries on with the factor? She's well-spoken? What of it? I've met soiled doves who could pass for nobility."

"She's not a lightskirt, George."

"I'll commence trifling with her and we'll see how quickly she turns her attentions away from the lowly factor and onto the duke."

His hands curled into fists. "You'll leave Mrs. Marlowe alone." If he couldn't have her—and he couldn't, everyone said he couldn't—he wouldn't have George importuning her.

"You have no money and a grand title to save. Marrying an heiress is your easiest choice." George stood. "I'm off to check those weapons again. We'll have venison for Hogmanay, just you wait."

When the door closed, he buried his face in his hands. Marry to save a grand title he'd never wanted?

He thought of his last near duel over a harmless bit of flirting with a cit's daughter. The impoverished earl her dowry had saved fretted endlessly over his generations of family honor and his necessary marriage, dismissive of the pretty bride who had to tolerate all that pomposity.

Kinmarty was an old title, as well. He'd fret also if after securing Strachney's daughter's dowry he spent forever being bullied by the old man. He wouldn't do it. He'd rather marry the housekeeper, and let the *ton* laugh at him as they'd laughed at Old Horace. He'd at least be keeping the family tradition.

He sighed and picked up the tax notice. Christmas was the day after next, and he had a dukedom that needed a duke who was supposed to be himself; a friend who wanted to play matchmaker; and a housekeeper frantic to make a home for children who no one had ever heard of, girls who would run wild and fall into the burn like the one he'd rescued so many years ago.

He'd have children underfoot, perhaps for the next decade or two. Mrs. Marlowe had done much in two days to prepare for them. She'd done much to help him accommodate the notion of them. It was lovely of her.

Filomena. He tapped the letter on the desktop. Perhaps if he hadn't drunk himself silly for so many years, he'd have puzzled out the mystery of that name by now. What was the memory niggling at him?

Chapter Twelve

"To bed with you, Mr. Forbes." Filomena climbed down from the ladder and rubbed her eyes. "We've done well here." They'd tied ribbons, and hung boughs, and made the great hall and the parlor jolly for the Yuletide. The other servants had gone off to bed, and it was now the wee hours.

Forbes set aside the stepladder. "This I'll carry away. But first…" He pointed to the sprig of mistletoe she'd just hung in the doorway.

She laughed and presented her cheek for the quick touch of his dry lips.

"Now go on."

"Aye, and doan't ye linger, either. It's not many hours until daybreak."

"I'll be right up." She'd spend a last night in her grand bedchamber, and tomorrow, she'd move to the housekeeper's room. "Let me just gather my things."

She was curling up the remaining ribbon when a whisper of air touched her neck.

"What are you doing up so late?"

Filomena jumped, her blood turning to ice and then heating in anger. She bit her tongue against asking the Duke of Kinmarty what he himself was doing wandering about the castle at this hour.

His gaze traveled around the room. "You've decorated for Christmas."

There was no friendliness in his haughty tone.

"Yes." *Yes your grace*, she should say, but as tired as she was she feared saying more. Her tongue might get the best of her and deliver ten years of pent-up wrath.

"Is all ready for tomorrow night's dinner?"

"It will be." She took in a breath. "Though it was fearfully short notice."

"Oh? You seem quite efficient, Marlowe. Yet you're not prepared for the unexpected?" He took a step closer and his lip curled as if a smile might form.

She stepped into the doorway. "I should rather say *you* are not prepared, sir, since it is your household." She pressed her lips together on even more insolent words. *Don't get yourself dismissed just yet, Filomena.*

He moved closer, his eyes brightening. "Mr. Andrews didn't provide you with sufficient staff."

Drat and blast. She did not wish to see Andrews lose his position, or be sent away.

The duke would leave soon, Andrews had said. If the duke went, and Andrews stayed, and herself…

The possibilities made her heart thrum. She would like to explore another kiss, and more than that. She would like to feel where his hand had been wandering today, albeit in a warmer and dryer setting.

The duke watched her. She cleared her throat. "Mr. Andrews has found an excellent butler in Mr. Forbes. Everything will go smoothly tomorrow night. We'll make sure of it." She curtsied and turned, trying not to flee.

He touched her elbow, ever so softly, and dread snaked up to her shoulder. "Just a moment."

The press of his lips to her cheek was soft and disarmingly cold. She ducked, choking back a rising panic. He'd caught her out under the mistletoe.

The blasted mistletoe had seemed like such a good idea when Forbes pulled it out of his pouch.

"And a good night to you," she muttered, hurrying off.

The mistletoe. Both Mr. Forbes and the duke had kissed her under it.

The man whose kissing she wanted more of hadn't bothered to make an appearance.

Andrew awoke with a quill in his hand.

Ink blotted his cuff and his cheek ached from being pressed to the pile of letters.

He pushed against the chair back and stretched. The clock said he had long ago missed breakfast, and a glance out of the window showed the day had turned dank and gray, threatening snow.

The letter he'd been penning to his solicitor mocked him. It ought to be about the matter of Kinmarty's taxes, or the impossible bills, or even about hiring a permanent butler.

Instead, he was asking the man to make inquiries about Filomena Marlowe.

He crumpled the paper and flung it into the grate. Last night, lured by the voices and laughter, he'd broken away from his business letters and wandered down to the great hall, knowing she'd be in the midst of the hubbub. He'd found her surrounded by their few servants stringing greenery and other decorations.

The rich timbre of her laugh stuck with him. Her laugh and the trim set of her ankles on the stepladder, and the sparkle of candlelight in her uncovered hair still warmed him. She didn't conduct herself like a housekeeper to the quality, but she wasn't a mere commoner either. She was some gentleman's daughter, one who ought to be stringing the holly and ribbons at her own hearth.

Who was she? The letter had seemed like a good idea the previous night. He rubbed his jaw, bristly with overnight scruff.

In the gray light of day, the shabby state of the room was apparent, and he remembered Forbes's admonishment. For certain, Marlowe had secrets., but it was time to put his attention on Kinmarty and his duties as duke. Perhaps when he shared his secret, she would tell him hers. If not, there would be time to investigate later.

The door squeaked open and George peered in. "Finally up? Strachney's cattle have arrived. Care to ride out? Your servants are bustling about everywhere. Best to get out from underfoot of the new butler and our Mrs. Marlowe."

"*Our* Mrs. Marlowe?"

"She and Forbes were up half the night decorating. I did, however, corner her under the mistletoe and managed to steal a kiss of my own."

Anger blazed in him. George had *cornered* her?

He took a deep breath, recognizing the goading note in his friend's voice. Tamping down his ire, he forced a yawn.

"I hope she planted you a facer."

"Well, you'd be disappointed. As it was, I was next in line after Forbes."

His hand fisted reflexively, and he forced the fingers to open, to spread flat on the desk.

What was wrong with him? Of course, Forbes and George would have a go at kissing a handsome woman like Marlowe. He himself had kissed plenty of ladies under the mistletoe. It was all innocent fun.

He pushed himself up from the chair.

"I'd best find a fresh shirt and some breakfast. Go on without me."

"You might wish to shave as well."

He rubbed his chin again. Would it be better to take the time to scrape off his beard and be freshly shaved when he confessed to Filomena Marlowe? Or was he only delaying the inevitable again?

He strode out of the room. He would shave, and change his shirt, and be done with this.

Distressed at the late hour of her rising, Filomena hastened to dress and hurried downstairs.

In the kitchen, two new maids stood at the board chopping and kneading, while the cook barked orders. Mr. Forbes, they said, had sent for the extra help as well as the fish and the fowl needed for the dishes she and the cook had agreed on the night before. Cook insisted on feeding her breakfast while they went over each new dish the kitchen staff was attempting.

Finally free, she looked for Forbes in the dining room, and found the two new footmen spreading a pressed tablecloth over the long cherrywood table. China plates sat stacked on a sideboard next to the polished silver, and on another, the candelabra stood ready, fitted with fresh tapers. Mr. Forbes had given instructions for these preparations as well.

The duke's ancestors gazed down from portraits hung round the room, men in kilts, and a lady in a panniered gown and powdered hair. She hadn't toured this room in the light of day, and the largest of portraits made her pause. With his strong jaw and nose, and his burning gaze, there was a familiarity about the middle-aged man in the portrait.

"'Tis a good likeness," one of the young footmen said.

Her new hires were locals. "Is that the last duke then?"

"Aye. As he looked years a'fore I was born."

The white cloth floated over the table, and she left them straightening the corners. Forbes would inspect this work later, she was sure.

In the entrance hall, Kyla perched on the staircase, cleaning and polishing the balusters, while Duff brushed the stair runner.

"Mr. Forbes put us to cleaning here," Kyla said. "After we readied the green bedchamber. Said the duke's sister was coming."

Filomena had shared that news with Forbes just last night.

Duff glanced at the length of still dusty stairs and groaned. "Is there aught else you'd have us do? There's a carpet to brush in the nursery."

The poor lad. He'd happily get lost in the box of toys there.

"I'm sorry, Duff. The duke won't be entertaining his dinner guests in the nursery, so we must leave that carpet for another day. Thank you for staying late to help last night. Did you get enough rest?"

"Oh, aye." Kyla smiled. "And Mr. Forbes said it put him in mind of the old days, when the staff decorated the Castle for Yuletide."

"Where *is* Mr. Forbes?" Filomena asked.

"In the dining room," Kyla said.

"No." Duff shook his head. "He went to check on the wine."

Kyla nodded. "Mayhap in the cellar, then."

She'd found no wine in the cellar, but in her tour the day after her arrival, she'd seen a few bottles in the butler's pantry.

She promised the children an extra penny for their hard work and went to find Forbes.

When a knock on the pantry door brought no answer, she tried the latch.

"Mr. Forbes," she called, peeking in.

A lamp lit the room, shimmering off the silver tureen and dusty crystal stacked on the shelf. This lot would be cleaned before being stored, yet Forbes had performed miracles here also, transforming the cluttered space into a proper pantry as it must have been in the old days.

If she were the duchess presiding here, she'd convince Forbes to stay on forever. Mrs. Marlowe the housekeeper could never match his efficiency.

But of course, she'd never be any lord's permanent housekeeper. She was only here to ease the way for the children, and Penelope of course.

The duke's kiss under the mistletoe was a portent of doom. He'd finally noticed her. Should he try to do more, to take more, she'd have to find a way to put him off. She was staying until Penelope and the children arrived. With any luck, she might even have a chance to discover what might be possible between her and Andrews.

No, no, she must remember, nothing was possible where he and she were concerned.

Sadness crept over her, a sense of loss greater than Mr. Marlowe's passing. When the shock of his death had ebbed, when the will and her income had been resolved, she'd shed tears of relief. No more would she need to carry on as if she wasn't half the time dead inside, and the other half itching with need for something she couldn't fathom.

She'd settled for far less with Marlowe because Mr. Swinton's jilting had taught her to give up dreaming of more. Leaving Kinmarty, as she certainly must do once Penelope arrived and her identity was uncovered, meant giving up dreaming again, at least where romance was concerned.

She wiped a tear from her cheek and traced the finger over the rim of a goblet, making it sing. She must remember the children. This was for them.

But Mr. Andrews…oh, the man had given her a taste of…of what *could* be between a man and a woman. She wanted more, someday, somehow…

If the duke truly would dismiss her after Penelope arrived, then perhaps she ought to take one more risk, perhaps tonight after dinner, or tomorrow…

She went down the row of goblets trying to make each one sing.

It was madness to think such thoughts, and wicked to boot. But heavens, when she left Kinmarty and *him*, she might carry away a sweet memory of being loved by a man she desired.

The sound ebbed and died, and she picked up a damp towel from the wash basin and polished each goblet.

It was a fool's dream, of course. Perhaps she might take a cottage near Kinmarty, near the children, and Penelope, and Mr. Forbes, who'd been awfully kind to her, and so efficient. Forbes would keep Kinmarty running, and Andrews would learn much from the old butler, and needed to.

His skills as a factor might need improvement, but if the duke required a gentleman with looks and affability, one who could move smoothly among the quality, Mr. Andrews was the man.

How had he fallen in with the duke? Perhaps they'd banged about town together, Mr. Andrews pinching his pennies and enjoying his friend's benevolence, another genteel near-charity case, just like herself.

"Why, Mrs. Marlowe. Fancy encountering you again."

The oily tone slithered along her spine and her breath tightened. The only way out of this nook was the one doorway—she glanced over her shoulder—now blocked by the duke.

Chapter Thirteen

She grudgingly turned and curtsied and wished him a good morning.

It had been mere hours ago that he'd kissed her under the mistletoe. Had he slept? His starched and brushed handsome looks distinguished him from Mr. Andrews' usually rumpled ones, but the new duke was utterly lacking in the warmth and good humor his factor exuded.

And right now, the predatory look in his eyes sent chills through her.

"Mr. Forbes...er...asked me to join him here." She crossed her fingers behind her skirts. "He'll be along in a moment."

He swept a gaze over the pile of silver. "Odd, isn't it, that Forbes reappears with the ducal silver?" His sharp gaze pierced her. "Perhaps I should call in the magistrate."

Good heavens. He was threatening Forbes now?

"I should say not." She drew herself up taller. He was shorter than Mr. Andrews, and she could almost send his neckcloth a level glare. She had no idea how the old butler had laid hands on the duke's valuables, but she could surmise. "I imagine Mr. Forbes more likely *rescued* your silver and safeguarded it. You should be grateful to him."

The blue eyes glinted. "I should be grateful, Mrs. Marlowe? Yes, I suppose so." He took a step toward her. "I'd like to be grateful to you, as well. Will you let me show you my gratitude? This is a cozy chamber, and we don't need mistletoe for what I have in mind."

Heat flamed in her cheeks. Loathing—and no small amount of fear—swept through her. Scanning the room, she spotted a great carving knife. She reached for it, then drew her hand back, a lurid newspaper headline flashing in her imagination—*Duke slain by vicar's widow posing as housekeeper.*

Not keen on a hanging, she clutched her trembling hands together. Servants were bustling about everywhere today. With one scream, someone would come running from the kitchen.

"Or perhaps my bedchamber will be a better locale. I hear it is a tradition of the Duke of Kinmarty to keep his housekeeper as more than just—"

"You think to ask me to be your...your...?" Her breath caught as hot anger pounded through her. "*That is quite enough nonsense, duke.*"

Humor twitched on the man's lips. She opened her mouth to berate him again when a hand gripped his shoulder and spun him into the corridor.

"The lady is right."

Oh, thank God. Andrews shoved the duke against the corridor wall. "You'll leave off with your insults."

"Remove your hands, *Andrews*." The duke, if he was nonplussed, didn't show it. His lips still twitched as if he were squelching a grin.

Chest heaving, Mr. Andrews gave the duke one last shake and complied, stepping back. "You'd best leave."

"And you'd best consider your position in this household." Smiling, the duke glanced her way. "And that of Mrs. Marlowe." He strode down the corridor, laughing.

Andrews glared after him.

When he turned back to her his eyes still glowed in a way that took her breath away.

He swept her back into the butler's pantry and into his arms, into a tight embrace, like she was precious, like she was dear, like he would never let her go. Under his coats, his heart beat a brisk tattoo, and each gulp of air raised and lowered his chest against hers. She melted into him for a long moment until her senses finally returned.

She'd bungled this, and Andrews would suffer the duke's wrath, and he knew it. She choked in a breath. "That reprobate."

She also would suffer. The duke would dismiss her immediately. Why he hadn't done so already, she didn't know. Perhaps he planned to renew his assault on her person before letting her go.

"I'm sorry. Surely he won't dismiss *you*."

Anger burned in his cheeks, sending guilt and regret tumbling through her. He would quarrel more with the duke and lose his position. This was her fault, except it wasn't, not entirely.

"Andrew MacDonal is a beast," she said. "I detest him."

His eyes widened. "What?"

"He's your friend, I know, but...how well do you truly know the man?"

He looked stunned. Of course, he did. The duke was his bosom friend, and he might lose this position he desperately needed.

Because of her. Her lies and secrets might even stir trouble for Penelope and the children.

He stepped back, taking her hands. "I must...must speak with you, Mrs. Marlowe."

Oh, *that* had been heartfelt. He was kind. He would treat Penelope honorably, no matter how dastardly the duke behaved. He would see the children well-cared for. She felt it in her bones. She felt other things bone-deep as well.

His masculine touch. The pleasure he stirred by a simple touch. If only she might be able to stay.

When she left Kinmarty, surely his confrontation with the duke would blow over. But she must make sure he understood the duke's dislike for Penelope, so he could intercede in her behalf.

She would tell him the truth about who she was, and let him reject her if he would. And if he didn't, perhaps...perhaps someday they could meet again somewhere private. The thought made her want to weep. Oh, how she would miss him.

He cupped her face with his hand, his thumb sweeping over her cheek.

Or…the private meeting could be right now, and it wouldn't matter if he rejected her after he learned the truth. She was used to men turning away.

The duke's dinner was well in hand, and there was no telling whether the children would arrive before she herself was dismissed. She might risk losing the chance to know them.

Yet, the children weren't here, and there was no way to know if Penelope would allow her the chance to know them.

And Mr. Andrews was right here, right now. She'd been brave enough to come to Kinmarty. She must take one more risk.

Footsteps resounded in the corridor, and they heard Forbes's distant tones from the kitchens.

Heart racing, she covered his hand with her own. "You are right. We must speak, but not here."

His nerves still pounding from his run-in with George, Andrew held onto Marlowe's hand as she raced quickly and silently up the servants' stairs and down the corridor that led to the study. She halted midway, cocking her head. The distant voices of the boy and the young maid chattering filtered their way. No one else was about.

She opened a door and pulled him in.

To her bedchamber.

"*Marlowe*—"

"Shhh." Keeping a grip on his hand, she turned the key in the lock and put a finger to his lips.

As if he had any need to be more conscious of how closely they stood, the warm pad of her finger slid over his cheek and her chest heaved against his.

She ripped the cap from her head. Thick locks of hair the color of dark mahogany tumbled from her loosely pinned bun.

"Thank you for rescuing me, Mr. Andrews. For certain I won't be the duke's lover."

His heart lurched. George could bloody well keep his hands off her. She was his.

She drew in a frantic breath. "But his factor's…" Her gaze sent his cock to full alert. "*Your* l-lover, that is another matter."

Heat roared through him, pressing the air from his chest. He cleared his throat, as inarticulate as a lovesick schoolboy. He, Andrew MacDonal, with some claim as an accomplished lover. Other women, experienced women, professional women, had solicited his favors. Those women had stirred his, er, manhood. None had ever stolen his breath like Mrs. Marlowe, her with her visions of fairy tale castles.

Or perhaps it was his heart that had gone missing.

The duke would not dismiss Marlowe. He would not allow it…but…

Blast it, *he* was the duke.

He was the duke, and he could have any woman in Kinmarty he wanted, if he wanted to sacrifice all honor, and he didn't. Filomena Marlowe deserved better.

She blinked and bit her lip.

When he reached for her, she backed up, her bottom hitting the door.

"*No*," he said and "*I'm s-sorry*," she stuttered at the same time.

He couldn't allow her to feel shame for the honor she offered. He drew her into his arms, meaning to comfort her, and instead soothing himself with the lavender scent of her tangled hair.

He'd sought her out for the truth, he reminded himself. Why was he being such a bloody coward?

Because you care for her. Because you don't want to hurt her or worse, lose her.

"It…it wouldn't be fair to you." Marlowe deserved her own home, her own nursery filled with children.

She took a trembling breath and raised her chin. "Have I misunderstood? Are you truly unaffected? I should like you to be honest."

He should lie and tell her he had no desire at all for her. Or tell the truth that *he* was the duke she despised.

The words wouldn't come. He would lose her. He'd lost everyone who mattered. *Please, not her also.*

He smoothed his hands down her sides. If he pulled her hips tight against his own, she would know how much he wanted her. That part of his body could say what his lips couldn't and shouldn't, and that part of his body wouldn't be lying. Lust was the most honest emotion.

She felt it as well. Her eyes had darkened to glistening midnight and pink tinged her cheeks. She wasn't acting, and he couldn't resist.

He kissed her, first gently, and then with more warmth, easing her lips apart. She fell into him, and his tongue slipped between her lips, searching and tangling.

She was equally honest, answering in kind, growing bolder, more heated, her passion unschooled. He whipped her around, and put his back to the door, pulling her to him the length of their bodies, to the length of his privy counsellor.

When her eyes widened, he froze.

He traced a finger over her silky cheek, silently counting to ten, and then twenty. That had been a great deal of surprise for a woman married ten years and widowed.

Ten years wedded didn't mean ten years bedded.

Might she still be a virgin? If that were the case, would it be wrong to take her now?

Virgin or not, of course it's wrong. She's your housekeeper.

Marlowe apparently couldn't hear his conscience shouting at him. She pulled him down into a kiss until all the voices were silenced and his only cogent thought was how to undo her bodice and find his way to her breasts.

Soft footsteps resounded down the corridor and they paused, exchanging hot breaths until the danger moved past.

He gazed into the dark pools of her eyes. She was so lovely, so vulnerable.

His housekeeper. He couldn't do it.

"I won't ruin you."

"I'm a widow."

"A clergyman's widow, and as housekeeper, you still have a reputation to maintain."

"The duke only has to hint that I came to his bed. Anyone might have heard his speech to me. You did. My reputation is already destroyed. You know that as well."

His insides quaked, knowing it was true. A word dropped here or there, and everyone would believe she'd slept with the duke.

With him.

Dear God. He set her back and swiped a hand through his hair.

"I am not who you think I am," he said.

Her chin shot up. "Nor am I. And I don't care. Today, we are only a man and a woman." She reached for his hand. "The truth? As I told you, I'm a clergyman's widow. I have a small income. I've never been in service, and I don't need to be. When I leave here, I have means to live quietly and simply."

Her lips were plump from their kissing, her eyes shiny with unshed tears, slowing his brain as he picked through her words.

"You're a gentlewoman?"

"Yes."

"Not one fallen on difficult times?"

"I was a gentleman's daughter. As a young girl, I had a season in London. When I leave here, I plan to live quietly, perhaps on the outskirts of Edinburgh."

While his mind raced, the male part of him argued that she was his for the taking, now, and perhaps later if they found her a cottage nearby.

He mopped his face with his hands. No. He wouldn't do it. Not like this, not without honesty.

"We'll soon part ways." Her eyes pooled again and she ducked her head. "I won't jeopardize your position. Give me this one hour of yourself, Mr. Andrews. Forbes has the staff well in hand, and the duke will only know what we've done if you tell him."

His conscience reared. "Marlowe, I…I'm not who you think I am. I'm not—"

"The knight?"

"What?"

"The knight in shining armor riding his destrier to rescue the maiden in the fairy tale castle?"

What in blazes was she talking about?

More footsteps trod down the corridor.

Tears brimmed in her eyes. "You can be my knight, today, this moment. Tell me your secrets later." She touched the back of his head and pulled him to her.

Tell her later…he could do that. He would do that. His hands found their way to her bottom.

She was a widow, one who'd claimed to have had a season which made her at least well-to-do gentry.

He was a duke. Dukes married as they pleased. He could marry her.

Dukes with money marry as they please, not poor sods like you.

Shut up, he shouted back in his head, and then he swept her up into his arms, his heart soaring.

Chapter Fourteen

Andrew carried her to the bed where she settled onto the mattress with a startled gasp.

"Shhh," He sat next to her, cradling her cheek, studying her.

Wide-eyed, her breath coming in short gasps, she looked…frightened. No—she was terrified.

Hot blood rose in her cheeks while he sorted through the problem.

Marlowe had been a faithful wife. "You've never done this before, have you?"

"What?" That came on a tight breath with another frightened look.

"Dallying. Having an affair. Having a tumble."

She struggled up, bracing herself on her elbows.

"It's true." An edge of defiance sharpened the words. "But I learn quickly." She reached for his neckcloth and loosened the knot.

Color swept up her neck again, to her cheeks and all the while she chewed her lower lip.

She hadn't done this before. She learned quickly. She was in high color and worried, even while her hands trembled with need and desire and…

She glanced at him from under long dark lashes. There it was again: fear.

Marlowe's husband had somehow broken this part of her.

What would it take to repair that? Because he wanted to. He wanted to make her whole again.

That couldn't be done in a quick afternoon tumble. That would require a long night, many long nights.

He eased her chin up and dropped a kiss on her mouth, urging his numbed brain to take control from his baser self.

He couldn't dishonor her. And yet, and yet…

On its own accord, his hand strayed to her bodice and began working the fastenings. She would be angry when she learned he was the duke. Not a friend of the duke, not his factor, not a bloody fairy tale knight. The duke.

She might want to leave, but she needed to stay. He needed her to stay.

He nibbled a path down her cheek to her neck, making her wriggle. Her bodice dropped open and her chest heaved with a startled breath.

Full breasts swelled against the top of her stays, begging to be touched. Andrew ripped at the stays and pulled out the knot in her chemise, easing the lace edging down, laying her bare. The silk of her skin was warm on his lips.

Need raged through him, hard, desperate. He raised his head and gazed into her glazed eyes.

"Yes," she said.

NO, his conscience shouted.

He was a man, only a bloody man, and she was a woman, the woman he wanted, now and forever.

He would marry her. He would find a way.

Dark and hooded, his gaze burned into her, stoking the pleasure his lips and fingers had kindled, wave after wave of pleasure.

How had she allowed herself to miss this? How had she settled for a marriage utterly lacking in carnal desire?

When she fingered his jaw, his gaze softened.

Tears clouded her vision. Her heart lurched and swelled and pounded.

She'd missed this with Mr. Marlowe. She'd have missed it with Mr. Swinton as well. Because she hadn't loved either man.

She loved Mr. Andrews.

Andrews was kind, and mostly responsible, and a good friend to the miserable duke.

He didn't love her, but he wanted her, he truly did. She had this one moment and it must be enough for the rest of her life, because this…this desire, this had bloomed in her heart, rare and beautiful. This might never come again.

She fumbled his neckcloth loose, and in a few swift moves, he tore off his coats, then drew her up to her feet, and in moments she wore only her chemise and her stockings, and the hot gaze that made her shiver with power and triumph. He truly wanted her.

She ran a hand down his chest.

The hard length of him moved under his tight trousers.

"Marlowe." He lifted her hand away. "You'll make me blush."

That sent heat back to her own cheeks, but she took a step closer and shoved his shirt up, over his head.

She'd seen men without shirts, laborers mostly, but she'd never looked closely, she'd never *touched*. She pressed her lips there, to the curling hair, and the soft skin over hard muscles.

Then she was floating again, then falling gently onto the counterpane. He stretched out next to her and rolled her to him.

The midday light limned the contours of his strong jaw and lips and forehead. His arm, corded with muscles, settled around her waist.

"You are so beautiful," he whispered.

Some of her joy ebbed. She didn't want lies.

"Your eyes always harbor a hint of wariness, of mystery, that makes me want to explore."

His hand settled upon her breast, making her wriggle.

"And then there are these sensitive mounds. And your lips."

The kiss he bestowed was gentle, and then firmer.

"Beautiful," he murmured again kissing his way down her neck.

Desire warred with suspicion. "I'd rather you didn't lie."

He pulled back and looked at her, pushing the hair back from her face, blinking. "What?"

"I know I'm plain."

His gaze went from alarmed to angry. "Who told you that? Your husband?"

"No. It was my...my cousin. She was beautiful and next to her...well, I *was* plain."

He fell back and stared up at the canopy. "Men will say things—but that's not the case here." He rolled back to her. "The moment I opened the front door to greet you, I was very nearly smitten." He settled a warm palm upon her left breast. "You're beautiful here, as well, Filomena Marlowe, here where it counts the most. Surely your husband noticed that."

"Oh." Drat. She was weeping again. "No."

Mr. Marlowe had noticed whether his dinner was hot and his linens were clean.

She stroked his cheek, finding a swathe of whiskers he'd missed when he shaved. "Are we supposed to be talking this much?"

He laughed, and then he blinked, turning back to study her.

Her face heated. *Stupid Filomena, you've just given yourself away.*

Never mind. She wouldn't give up now. She sent him her most challenging gaze, hoping he found it alluring.

"Marlowe. Dear Marlowe." He plundered her mouth then, stroking her leg, his fingers inching and circling, each delicate swirl unfurling sweet bursts that resonated between her legs, finally finding his way to her center where the touch of his thumb sent her arching against him.

His finger slid into her. She gasped, and he froze.

"Did I hurt you?"

"No." Truly, she felt joy, excitement, anticipation, not pain.

"Good."

His finger, his hand, his lips worked magic, inciting more flurries within her. He inserted a second finger, stretching her.

She jumped and squeaked.

Again, he stilled. "Are you well?"

"Yes, only...only a bit startled."

She opened her eyes to a tender smile.

"Let me startle you more."

Then the rhythm of his hand pressing, his fingers moving altered and quickened and sent her arching to meet him, the pleasure building and growing and bursting, sending her over the edge in an explosion of bliss.

The stroke of his finger on her breast brought her around.

"That was...that was astonishing." She raised her head. He still wore his trousers.

The chill of the room seeped into her. That...whatever that was, that climax of sensations had dazed her but she knew there was more that involved him. She'd seen the drawings.

Her gaze traveled up to his face and the tight, almost angry look there. She gripped a handful of the counterpane, dread pooling inside her, draining the last bits of exhilaration.

"Will you not take off your trousers?"

His mouth firmed, and her heart sank in a flood of shame. He would be another man turning away.

Yes, he wanted to scream the word. He wanted to rip off the blasted trousers and plunge into her again and again, but he'd just summoned the brainpower to puzzle out her secret, and enough willpower to take the honorable path.

Mrs. Marlowe was an innocent. Her husband had treated her shabbily.

He wanted her. She was as taken with romance as many women, but more sensible than most. She was also sweet and responsive, and so lovely. He had things to teach her, mysteries to explore with her.

He didn't want her to leave, ever, most certainly not because he'd been in her bed. He dearly wanted to spend more time there.

If she would have him, after she knew who he truly was. And if he could do so honorably.

He pushed a lock of hair back and stroked her cheek. "Mrs. Marlowe."

Would she admit to the truth?

"What was wrong with Marlowe that he didn't perform his husbandly duties?"

Her mouth formed a mulish pout even while her eyes glistened. "You don't want me, either."

"Oh, my love."

His heart swelled and pounded. It was true. He loved her.

He locked an arm about her. "I wanted you the moment you walked through the castle doorway and chided me about my lack of a neckcloth. Please, tell me. Was there truly a Mr. Marlowe?"

"There was."

"Was he sickly? Or overly spiritual? Or did he prefer his fellows?"

"He would never discuss the reason for his disinterest." She squeezed a fistful of blanket. "After his death—which was quite sudden, I found a collection of...er...books."

"Naughty books?"

"Yes."

"With pictures?"

She nodded.

"You read them?"

She firmed her lips on a smile, lifted a shoulder, and he wanted to laugh.

"Why did you marry him?"

Her smile faded, and he cursed himself. She married as many women—and men, even dukes—did, to keep a roof over her head.

"His new patron required him to be married, to be an example to his parishioners. I didn't know until our wedding night that we wouldn't share a bed, in any sense. He thought that would make me happy."

"Did it?"

"I was relieved at first. But as the years stretched on, it angered me. I realized that unless I committed adultery, I would never have children."

And Marlowe liked children, that point was obvious.

"Will you not make love to me? You need not worry I would importune you if...if...I would send word to you. Not to make demands, but only so that you would know."

"Send word?" She was talking again about leaving.

"If there was a child. Even if the duke doesn't dismiss me, I fear I c-can't stay here, seeing you every day."

The duke. She'd spoken ill of him from the first day. He reached for her hand.

"Why do you hate the duke so?"

"You d-don't want me." She sat up and arranged her chemise, covering her breasts.

He rested his chin on her shoulder, inhaling her fragrance. "I do. But honorably."

If she would have him. And once she discovered who he really was... And he would tell her the truth. In a moment.

"Why, Marlowe? Why do you hate him?"

She pulled out of his embrace and slid from the bed, struggling into her stays. The way they lifted her breasts addled his wits. He had to look away, or he'd lose the battle with his honor.

"Why, Marlowe?"

"Andrew MacDonal ruined my life."

His head snapped up, anger flooding him.

That was a lie, an outright lie. He'd never flirted with virgins, never run off to the gardens with one. He'd never been with a virgin either. Not until now.

Good Lord. He *had* nearly ruined her.

He managed a breath. "How so?"

She turned away, fastening the front of her gown, and he wondered what emotion she was hiding and whether she was assembling a lie.

He drew on his shirt, waiting.

"He blackened my name with a suitor."

No. He'd never done that, had he?

"I was seventeen. My godmother arranged a season in London, at great expense, in the hope my cousin and I would both make good matches. A viscount's son courted me, but something Andrew MacDonal said turned him off me."

His mind raced, searching for a memory of something he might have said. Those early years in London were a blur of brandy and betting and the occasional brothel. If it had been after Evan's hasty marriage, he could add rage at his brother and new wife to his mix of befuddlement.

"When was this?"

"Ten years past."

So, whatever he'd done, it had happened that season when his world fell apart.

"And your marriage to Marlowe?"

"Godmama arranged that just before she passed away."

When he'd lost his brother to India and the duke to his own stubbornness, he'd grieved as much as when his parents died. But at least he hadn't been forced to marry in order to survive.

"You had no other family?"

"My parents died long ago."

"They made no provision for you?"

She sighed. "My father gambled heavily. The little that was left came to me."

"But you have a cousin. What of your aunt and uncle?"

"Also gone."

"Good heavens. Your cousin as well? Was she not of an age with you?"

"We are…we are estranged."

Like him, she had no one.

Except…he had Evan's children. And he would welcome them because he'd learned to see them as a blessing by looking through Marlowe's eyes.

If he married Marlowe, they would be her nieces also. But how could he marry her and also take care of his family, his estate?

And if he didn't marry her, how could he keep her underfoot and stay out of her bed, assuming she would even want him when she learned the truth.

"Do you still harbor a tendre for this viscount's son?"

"No." She paused in tying her bootlaces and scoffed. "He married a rich cit's daughter days after spurning me and locked her away in the country. He would have done the same to me."

A viscount's younger son dropping one girl and making a hasty marriage to a cit's daughter because of something *he'd* said—that sounded a bit familiar. As she twisted her hair, pinned it, and covered it with the ugly white cap, he sorted through his brandy-fogged memory of the *ton's* ancient gossip and drew a blank.

He hastily tied his neckcloth and pulled on his waistcoat. It would come to him later.

Marlowe frowned. "You must think me a wanton, throwing myself at you." The words sounded tight and painful.

"No. Never. This is not finished between us."

"It must be. I will leave after the children arrive, unless the duke sends me away sooner."

The duke. It was time to muster his courage and tell her the truth. He was the worst sort of reprobate and still he couldn't let her go, not even if she hated him.

After all, she'd come here to serve him as his housekeeper, and…

"Marlowe, if you didn't *need* to take employment, if you hate Andrew MacDonal, why did you come to Kinmarty?"

She went to the window and rested her forehead against the wavy glass. He joined her there.

"Someone might see you through the window," she hissed.

"And so?"

She moved in front of him and stood taller as if that would block the world's view of them together in her bedchamber.

"What aren't you telling me, Mrs. Marlowe?"

"Wasn't there something *you* were going to confess to *me*?" she asked.

Oh hell.

He must tell her. Good God, he'd just almost made love to her.

He could tell her later, after the blasted dinner party…except, after the blasted dinner party, she would already know. Strachney and his daughter would be your-gracing *him*, not George, and Marlowe would hear, flitting about making sure the dinner went smoothly.

Damn, damn, damn.

He took her shoulders and nudged her around. "Mrs. Marlowe, I am n-not the duke's factor. I am—"

A sharp rap on the door rescued him.

"Visitors on the drive," Forbes said loudly.

Outside, a rider pounded up the lane, and one of the new servants trotted down the steps to greet him. In the distance, a carriage—no two carriages and a heavily laden wagon tooled along toward the Castle with outriders following.

"Surely those are not the dinner guests." Marlowe opened the window letting in a blast of cold air that made her shiver. He wrapped her in his arms and peered over her shoulder.

The rider sported a heavy gray beard and a tightly wrapped black turban.

Marlowe gasped. "It's Penelope."

Chapter Fifteen

She turned in his arms and looked up. Wonder and something like fear lit her face.

"Whoever you really are, Andrews, you've stolen my heart. I'll never forget you." She pressed her lips to his cheek.

When she tried to pull away, he bent his head and poured all of what he was feeling into a proper kiss, until she squirmed away, flushed and dazed.

"Marlowe, we must talk."

She shook her head, and she rushed out the door.

While he yanked on his boots and his coat and hurried out behind her, his addled brain sorted through the facts. "It's Penelope" she had said, not, "the duke's sister-in-law is arriving," or "Mrs. MacDonal and the children are here."

"It's Penelope."

She knew his brother's wife, Penelope.

Penelope had been an orphan with a guardian and...

She'd had a cousin, a sickly thing. He'd never known her name, and she'd disappeared from society shortly after Evan sailed for India.

Filomena Marlowe was surely that cousin.

She hadn't come here for revenge on Andrew MacDonal. She'd come here to meet Penelope. She was a liar but not a villain.

He was the villain, and he was about to embarrass her in a very public way, unless he could get to her first.

He found her in the grand hall where she huddled with Forbes, who raised an eyebrow at him even as he bowed.

"I must speak to you for a moment, Mrs. Marlowe," Andrew said.

A footman rushed in and she beckoned him. "Go and find the duke," she said. "Tell him he must come. His sister-in-law is arriving."

"Marlowe—"

"Not now, Mr. Andrews. What of the nursery, Mr. Forbes?"

"I'll check on preparations and ye may speak to the...er...gentleman here."

"No. Mr. Andrews can wait until later."

The young maid hurried in with the red-headed boot boy.

"What are we to do now, Uncle?" the girl asked.

"We are on duty, my dear. Ye must call me Mr. Forbes."

"Sorry, sir. What are we to do now, Mr. Forbes, Mrs. Marlowe?"

"Have you laid a fire in the nursery?" Marlowe asked.

"Yes, mum."

"And...did you say you'd readied the green bedchamber?"

"Yes, mum. It's aired and cleaned, with fresh bedding, and firewood carried up."

Forbes sidled closer to him. "Best straighten yer neck cloth. Would ye like me to assist?"

Andrew let out a sigh. "No."

"Ye didn't tell her," the old butler murmured.

Marlowe glanced back at Forbes. "How much time have we?" she asked.

Forbes sent him a pointed look. "Enough, if ye hurry."

Andrew stepped up and grasped her elbow. "We must talk, now, Mrs. Marlowe."

He steered her away from the grouping of servants, which unfortunately brought them closer to the door.

"Don't ruin this," she said. "I want all to go well. And you are—"

"I am telling you something important that—"

"You are distracting me now when—"

"Something important that will save you embarrassment when—"

The door swung on creaky hinges, cold air freezing his words and hers.

George stepped up next to them and nodded to Andrew over Marlowe's head. The turbaned servant helped a lady up the few steps and across the threshold, and he found himself staring into the blue eyes of an old enemy.

Speech momentarily failed him. In the ten years since he'd seen Penelope Grant, she'd aged, and somehow, she was hiding the animosity she felt, not just for his past sins, but for supplanting her late husband as Duke of Kinmarty.

The Castle should have been hers to run. He could never deny her residence here.

Her gaze moved on to the lady next to him and her eyes widened and pooled with tears. She dropped all forbearance and threw herself into Mrs. Marlowe's arms.

"Oh, Minny," Penelope sobbed.

Minny? Mrs. Marlowe was Minny?

The duck's name had been Minny. Minny had been the girl who'd plunged into the burn after another girl.

Tears had begun to fall, buckets of them. Head swimming, his hand went to a pocket where there should have been a handkerchief and came up empty. George silently handed him his.

"What the devil is going on?" George muttered.

Penelope was babbling. "You came," she said, and "Oh, Minny," and, "What did I do without you?" all the while Minny—Mrs. Marlowe—made soothing noises and patted Penelope's back.

Marlowe turned a sheepish glance toward George, and Andrew handed over the handkerchief.

She took it without looking at him, her attention still focused on his friend.

"Mrs. MacDonal and I are cousins, duke." Marlowe smiled kindly at the new arrival. "Penelope, my dear, though you are already acquainted, allow me to introduce you again to the Duke of Kinmarty." She swept a hand out toward George, her back turned to Andrew.

Penelope paused in dabbing her eyes and glanced from George to him. Her mouth dropped open and her gaze raked over him, probably appalled at his rumpled appearance, all the while strangling the damp square of linen.

And there it was: a flash of the anger he'd been expecting.

"Oh, my dear." Penelope turned to Marlowe, her face softening to a pity that riled him.

Hell and damnation. This was his fault. All his fault. What had he been playing at? "Marlowe—"

"No, Minny." Penelope's lips thinned as she cut him off and pointed, her finger like the barrel of a fine Manton pistol. "*That* is Andrew MacDonal, the new Duke of Kinmarty."

In the hush that followed all he could hear was Marlowe's panicked breath and the clanging of his own pulse.

What flashed in her eyes wasn't anger but something else, something he couldn't read. He needed to talk to her.

"And who are you, sir?" Penelope directed the question to George who had the good grace to introduce himself like a proper gentleman.

Before he could summon breath to join the conversation, the door opened again, and a servant ushered in a woman swathed in yards and yards of bright cloth and two bundled children.

Penelope beamed at them. "Take off your cloaks, boys."

Unwrapping the layers of wool revealed two children; two children with straight black hair and darker-toned skin.

Penelope's golden locks caught the lamplight and glittered. These were not Penelope's children, at least not by blood, but love shown in her eyes.

"Your grace," she said. "I am pleased to introduce to you your nephews. Arun is six years old, and Ravi is four. Boys, greet your uncle, his grace, the Duke of Kinmarty."

They glanced at each other, mischief sparking between them.

It was as if two Evans had sprung to life in front of him. His eyes misted, and he willed away the moisture.

Arun bent grandly, one arm at his waist. "Pleased to meet you, uncle, your grace." Ravi parroted his brother and giggled.

He crouched down and shook each of their hands. As in the childhood portrait of Evan on the nursery mantel, they had Evan's square jaw and the start of his great beak of a nose, and eyes that glinted with his thirst for merriment.

He understood why Evan would want them brought here. He didn't understand why Penelope had agreed, but gratitude made his heart race and his eyes fill again.

He cleared his throat. "Welcome, Arun and Ravi. Your father and I had grand times here at Castle Kinmarty and so will you, if you follow the rules."

Gad, he sounded as pompous as Old Horace.

He squelched a smile. "And the first rule is this: you are not to call me 'your grace'. You are to call me Uncle Andrew."

"You look like our papa," Arun said.

"As do the both of you."

Ravi grinned, squirming and scratching his belly and arms. Either they'd picked up bugs at an inn on the way, or the skeleton suits they wore itched.

This time he did smile.

"But Papa had blue eyes," Arun said. "Yours are a funny color."

"Uncle Andrew's eyes are green." Penelope tugged Marlowe closer, crowding him. "and this is your Aunt Minny, who has brown eyes like yours."

Marlowe bent and gave each boy a hug.

Tears shone in those lovely eyes, and she swallowed hard holding them back.

She'd been shocked into more tears this day, and he still needed to speak to her. "You boys will want to see the toys in the nursery that your Papa and I played with."

Marlowe took in a deep breath and beckoned Kyla and Duff while Penelope called over the foreign woman.

"This is Sitara," Penelope said, "Arun and Ravi's cousin, who graciously agreed to accompany us."

Ravi's tiny finger shot out pointing at Duff. "Why is your hair orange?"

Duff's blush swallowed his freckles. "Me mam said I was tooched by the fairies."

"Will you show us these fairies?" Arun asked.

"No," Duff said, "But I'll show you the toy soldiers."

They both latched onto Duff and the train of small boys rushed to the stairs, Kyla and Sitara following. Once they disappeared at the first landing, the hurried steps turned into stomping feet and laughter that reverberated in the grand entry.

It would be like the old days of Castle Kinmarty, with mayhem and mischief and life. Instead of the crotchety old Horace, he'd preside as the duke. Forbes would be here for a time. Ramsey was gone, but Marlowe, dear Marlowe...

She couldn't leave. He must talk to her. "Penelope—may I call you by your Christian name? I'm sure you'll want to have a rest. We have guests coming tonight for Christmas Eve dinner and you absolutely must join us. Forbes, would you kindly show Mrs. MacDonal to her rooms?"

"I'll do that," Marlowe said.

Her arch tone threw up a challenge. "No, Mrs. Marlowe. You may join your cousin in a few moments. First you and I must speak."

The firm set of her mouth signaled a skirmish ahead.

Penelope touched her arm. "The duke is right. Come join me when you have finished."

He snatched up Marlowe's hand and tugged her along to the first door he found.

Chapter Sixteen

The tiny, dank room might have been an old receiving room for unwanted visitors, or a resting place for a porter from the days when the Castle employed one. A small patch of light poured through the grimy pane highlighting a table and two ladder-back chairs.

Marlowe stood shivering near the door as he closed it. The grate was bare, no fuel to start a fire even if she granted him the few minutes it would require.

Best get right to it, as he should already have done. "I'm sorry, my dear."

She allowed him to keep hold of her hand.

"I lied, Marlowe. I lied about who I was. Who I am. I don't deserve…this title should have been my brother's. The old duke died, and I thought, thank heavens, Evan is coming home. And then the news arrived. He was dead, had been dead for months."

Blast it, his eyes were moist again. He squeezed them shut. Men did not cry, not even dukes.

"I have no excuse, Marlowe, except that…as I told you, I was completely at sixes and sevens. I'd only arrived and seen almost immediately that the factor was embezzling, and…then you appeared, and you were so fetching and, you had already mistaken me for a servant and, well, I asked George to play the duke for a few days. I'm sorry." He bit his lip. "About lying, that is, not about the kisses or what happened between us in your bedchamber today."

She drew in air through rounded lips. "All right," she said, not meeting his eyes.

"Whatever I said so many years ago to cause you grief—"

His breath caught. Of course. He remembered now. He'd got himself roaring drunk at White's. He'd lashed out at Penelope Grant and her cousin. "Oh hell." He swiped a hand through his hair. "I was so angry then. Not at you. I didn't know you. Except…except I did know you, didn't I, *Minny?* I'd met you that time when we were children. You were the duck. It was you I fished out of the burn."

She frowned up at him while more memories rushed him.

Why did you jump in the water with a stupid dress on?
You daft boy, I was rescuing someone. I saw the shawl. I thought she fell in.

Her eyes widened. He squeezed her hand. Their lives had intertwined before, and fate had brought them here together.

"I'm sorry about what I said at White's. I'm sorry that it hurt you."

But any man who would walk away from you because of my drunken ravings was a weak fool.

He didn't say that. He couldn't say that, not yet, anyway.

She studied the worn carpet that stretched under the few pieces of furniture. No screaming. No raging anger. In his experience, that wasn't a good sign.

But neither had she threatened to leave him again. Because Penelope was here and that meant Marlowe would want to stay. Not for him, but never mind. He would still have a chance with her.

"I understand now that you came here for your cousin and her children. You were afraid I would be unwelcoming, but I won't be, not to her or to my brother's…" He laughed. "Boys. We were all fooled. Boys, not girls."

"You don't mind?"

He knew what she meant: you don't mind that they're by-blows?

"No. They are certainly my nephews. Do you mind?"

She swallowed hard, sniffed, and shook her head.

"I'm glad that whatever estrangement you had with your cousin has been healed."

His last talk with Evan came to him—there'd been raging aplenty on both sides. He dropped her hand and walked to the small patch of glass and the weak light that trickled in. Out of pure arrogance, he'd bungled everything, with Evan, with the old duke, and now, with Marlowe.

Forbes had called it fear, and he hadn't been wrong. He'd lost his brother forever, as well as Old Horace. He couldn't lose Marlowe.

"You have every right to be angry. But please stay, my love. Please do not leave because of my stupidity."

When he turned, he caught her watching. She'd recovered, and her eyes told him nothing.

She could hide her true feelings well when she wished to. She would make a marvelous duchess, would Mrs. Marlowe.

He wasn't Mr. Andrews the factor; he was Andrew MacDonal, the Duke of Kinmarty, and she was the one he wanted. He wanted Filomena Marlowe to be his duchess.

Filomena watched the proud angles of his shoulders framed in the window, all the while trying to make sense of his words.

He'd lied to her. He'd made her an object of pity to Penelope and the staff. He'd nearly made love to her.

He'd stopped but he hadn't rejected her outright, not yet.

Outside the light was waning and the need to be elsewhere nagged at her. With the short days and long nights, they'd set their dinner for country hours, and the guests would arrive soon. She wanted some moments with Penelope before then.

And Mr. Forbes—she was letting him down. She'd left him all the preparation and gone off for a tumble with…with the duke.

Dear God, she'd been intimate with the Duke of Kinmarty. They hadn't done the full deed only because Andrew MacDonal was not truly a scoundrel. He had a sense of honor.

As had that skinny rude boy who'd saved her from drowning so many years ago. Had it truly been him? That meant the boy with him had been his brother,

Evan. No wonder Penelope fell so quickly for Evan in London—she'd been renewing an old romance.

Filomena fisted her hands in her skirts. Ten years past, Andrew had ruined her chances at a good marriage, called her a social-climber, a shabby genteel twit.

And before that, he'd saved her life, for she truly would have drowned.

And today, he'd almost made love to her.

Her heart ached, and she squeezed her eyes tight. She'd been wrong about him. Could she truly forgive him? The words that cost her a marriage had been spoken in anger, but not at her. His brother had deserted him as Penelope had done to her.

"You have every right to be angry. But please stay, my love. Please do not leave because of my stupidity."

She'd thought she had every right to *be angry,* in fact she *had* hated him, and for years. Somehow, her anger had melted away.

And—*my love. Oh.*

Yet she couldn't stay here. If he appeared in her bedchamber, she'd never conjure the willpower to tell him to leave.

Why tell him to leave? Why not let him stay? The voice of temptation perched on her shoulder and whispered the words, coaxing her to go against a lifetime of rules.

It would be wrong in so many ways, and what would Penelope say?

Yet…Arun and Ravi were surely Evan MacDonal's by-blows, and her cousin had taken them in as her own.

Perhaps Penelope wouldn't care about her and the duke.

Oh, but *she* would care when the duke married, and he would have to. He needed an heir. To take this affair any further would mean more heartache than she'd borne in all of her years with Marlowe. If she loved Andrew MacDonal— and she did—she must let him go, and for her own sake it must be now.

When the duke in question finally turned away from the window anguish drew his lips tight and furrowed his brow.

Her heart ached with his pain. His brother's loss was fresh and raw, and he was still grieving. Penelope had returned to her, but he'd lost Evan forever.

The effort to tame the anguish strained him. He wasn't that good of an actor— he'd fooled her only because she'd been blinded by bias.

She took a step forward and his chin shot up, and he was once again the cocky boy who'd pulled her out of the burn, who'd called her a brat, who'd told her she looked like a duck. He'd had enough sense of her pride to not coddle her then.

Oh, how she loved him.

She straightened her shoulders. "Pretending to be the factor was an addlepated prank. Not at all worthy of a duke."

He let out a long breath. "You are so right, Marlowe."

She touched his hand. "I forgive you. But I'm not at all certain I can ever forgive Mr. Lovelace."

Someone knocked at the door. She dropped his hand and went to answer.

Forbes glanced from her to the Duke.

"I've not harmed this nodcock, Forbes. Is Mrs. MacDonal settled?"

"Yes, she is."

"Duke." She curtsied. "I would speak with my cousin before your guests arrive."

Andrew watched her walk off. "Forbes," he said. "Mrs. Marlowe cannot be allowed to leave. She's a fine woman."

"Aye, as I told ye before."

Shadows smudged the old butler's eyes, but a twinkle caught in the light.

"Did you mean what you said, Forbes, that you're a Kinmarty man?"

"Aye, duke. Of course."

"Would you consider a partner in your distillery?"

Forbes smiled. "One as has come to his senses, mayhap."

"I'll need you to set another place for this dinner."

"For Mrs. MacDonal, aye, I've seen to it."

"Yes, and you must add one more. Come with me." He would need the old butler's help for this plan to succeed.

In the green bedchamber, Filomena found a lady's maid unpacking clothing. Penelope had gone to the nursery to check on the children, the maid said.

In the nursery, the boys sat at the small table, eating biscuits, attended by Duff who was helping himself to the feast as well. The cat stretched in the window watching them.

"You have a cat," Ravi said around a mouthful of biscuit. "We want to see the Yule log."

"The cat won't let us touch him," Arun said. "Duff said the log is as big as my uncle, and there will be singing and cakes tonight."

"You will have no cakes," Sitara said, "if you do not finish eating and take your rest."

Filomena told them to give the cat time to become acquainted and to mind Sitara, and she made a mental note to talk to Cook about refreshments for the children after the more formal dinner.

She inquired after Penelope and learned her cousin had left the nursery moments before.

Heading back to her bedchamber, she spotted a footman exiting the parlor.

"Is Mrs. MacDonal there?" she asked.

"Aye, ma'am. I've just brought in a tray."

Heart racing, she paused at the door. Penelope must think her a fool, being bamboozled by the duke and that lascivious wretch, Lovelace. If Penelope only knew how her heart ached...

She shook off the thought and paused in the open doorway. Penelope looked up from pouring a cup for Mr. Lovelace, who stood when he spotted her.

"Minny, come join us," Penelope said. "Mr. Lovelace has just been explaining to me about your charade."

"*My* charade?"

"Yes." She patted the spot on the sofa next to her. "Come. Do you still take milk and sugar?"

"Yes, but...but, no thank you, not now. My charade is not truly a charade. I really did take the position of housekeeper at Castle Kinmarty."

"Please do join us," Lovelace said.

She glared at the smug villain. "Perhaps you would like to discuss *your* charade, Mr. Lovelace."

"About that, I apologize." That came with a smile.

A smile—the arrogant fool.

"For everything," he added.

Penelope raised her eyebrows.

Behind her, a throat cleared.

"Mrs. Marlowe." Forbes had found her again. "You're wanted in the kitchen."

It was just as well. She couldn't talk intimately with Lovelace present.

"Penelope, I dearly want to speak with you later. For now, I'm not at all sure I should leave you alone with this man. Shall I send for your maid?"

Penelope laughed, and Lovelace blushed, the beast.

"I will not misbehave again, Mrs. Marlowe," he said. "I promise."

Through the partially open door of his bedchamber, Andrew watched Marlowe pass down the corridor, and then went to join the others in the parlor.

Penelope nodded by way of greeting. "What exactly is between you and my cousin, Andrew?"

He closed the door. "I understand you're the only family she has."

"That's true."

"In which case, I must speak with you."

"Oh?" She sent him an arch look. The giggling girl his brother ran off with had matured into a formidable matron. A necessary thing, he supposed, to survive living so far from home and putting up with his brother's disloyalty.

That was a story for later, and only when she was ready to share it.

"Mr. Lovelace has told me about your dinner guests, Mr. Strachney and his daughter, and her sizeable dowry. Which takes me back to my question: what is between you and my cousin, Andrew?"

"An excellent question," George said.

The arrogant ass. "Damn it, George, I'm not marrying Miss Strachney. You are free to pursue her dowry yourself, with my blessing. You may dine with them every night at Glenthistle instead of taking it upon yourself to invite them to my table. Penelope, I would speak with you *privately*."

George stood. "It would have been the easiest resolution to your problems, old man, but if you won't marry for money, I have some excellent ideas for making Kinmarty financially solvent."

"Kinmarty needs money?" Penelope asked.

"Taxes," George said. "Unpaid bills. A crumbling edifice."

"I see."

"Yes, thank you Lovelace, for sharing that, and I do hope you restrain yourself from going into those details with Strachney tonight. Now—"

"Now I really will take my leave." George flashed him a grin and closed the door silently.

He walked to the fireplace, trying to formulate his words. "First, let me apologize for interfering in your marriage so many years ago. It was wrong of me to—"

"You were perfectly within your rights. Stop apologizing, and be seated. What's done, is done, and I've reconciled myself to the past. Why your brother chose me as a wife, well, I suppose I was the pliable one, the girl lacking a male relative to impose some restraint. And more importantly, I had enough dowry to fund our passage to India. And you were right about him, Andrew. Like most men, he was incapable of being faithful to only one woman." She sighed. "To his great disappointment and mine, I was incapable of giving him a live child."

She stared at her empty cup, her long pause leaving him speechless. His brother had been a rake, not so different from many other men he knew, and Penelope was not so different from many of their wives, except for her generosity towards his offspring.

He'd never thought much about fidelity in a marriage, but he believed it was possible…with the right partner. Someone like Marlowe.

"When the children's mother passed away, her closest family shunned the boys. Only Sitara came for them and, for their sake, she and I reached an agreement to see how they did here. I couldn't turn my back on them, though Evan was willing to do so." Her voice cracked, and she took in a long breath.

He remembered the letter he'd found in the study. "At least he had the good grace to write to the duke about taking them in."

She shook her head. "I wrote that letter and made him sign it."

He plopped into the chair vacated by George and rubbed his head. He'd followed his brother on some of his escapades, but he'd always been more careful than Evan. To the best of his knowledge, he had no by-blows running about, paying the price for his moments of pleasure.

It had been a near thing that day with Marlowe.

"Now, what of my cousin? What have you done to Minny, and what do you intend to do?"

He raked his hands through his hair. He intended to finish what they'd started today, that very night, if possible. He intended to make love to her again, and again, and again.

He loved her.

He couldn't say that to Marlowe's cousin, not until he'd told Marlowe first.

He stared at the teapot, a laugh bubbling up in him. As matters stood, once the taxes and tradesmen were paid, he'd not have two farthings to rub together, but here he was with three new dependents and in love with a woman who couldn't possibly save Kinmarty.

But she could save him.

"Andrew." Penelope rapped on the table. "I am not without means. Let us negotiate."

He looked at her then, really looked at her. The hot sun of India had taken a toll on her blonde beauty, but her dress was of the finest quality and height of fashion, her hair intricately styled, and around her neck hung a ruby as large as a robin's egg. Yes, it appeared she did have means, but he wasn't here to ask for money.

"I haven't come to negotiate," he said. "I've come to beg for your help."

Chapter Seventeen

"Hunting," George said, "and whisky production. I'll talk to Forbes when he has a free moment."

Andrew arranged the crisply starched neck cloth with more care than usual. "Not hunting," he said.

"Most definitely hunting. And for a hefty fee. Gordon asks eight thousand pounds for the privilege of fishing for salmon in his stream." He squinted. "Are there salmon in the burn?"

He rolled his eyes. "I envision a horde of prosperous cits descending on Kinmarty expecting wine, women, and song. It won't be good for the boys."

"They'll be away at school."

He glared at his friend who laughed. "Fine, Andrew. You've a hunting lodge on the property as I recall."

"A lodge that is falling down."

"A few repairs and it will serve. Or, we can get the word out to the wives about the haunted castle—*The Castle of Otranto*—and invite the ladies to accompany their husbands and stay here in the medieval wing for a larger fee."

A shudder went through him. "The whisky distilling is more palatable." He grabbed his freshly brushed coat—Forbes had mercifully set a servant to tend to his clothing—and pulled it on.

Then Forbes himself appeared to announce that the guests had been spotted on the drive.

His heart pounded with a sense of exhilaration, and he strode out past the butler.

Downstairs, George stood by him as he greeted the Strachneys and the footman carried away cloaks and scarves.

He ushered them into the great hall and poured drinks.

"I see Kinmarty is ready for a proper Yuletide," Strachney said, looking around.

Marlowe had outdone herself with greenery and ribbons and the huge log ready to be set aflame.

"Yes, indeed. In fact, we'll be making a family party of it after dinner. My sister-in-law has just arrived with my brother's children, and they'll join us for lighting the Yule log."

"Your sister-in-law? I believe I met her and your brother once at a Company dinner. Come to keep the holiday with you, have they?"

"They're newly returned from India. They'll be living here at Castle Kinmarty."

Strachney's brows furrowed. "Didn't know your brother had children."

Andrew wanted to laugh. Strachney was assessing the impact on his daughter when she became the future duchess. Perhaps he even worried about a rivalry with Penelope.

"You must be happy they've joined you, your grace." Miss Strachney colored and dropped her gaze to his boots. "Children always make for a more pleasant Yuletide."

The girl was either fearfully shy, or embarrassed by her oaf of a father. Besides the generous dowry, perhaps she had a spot of good sense.

He still wouldn't marry her.

George, who was a middle son of a baron in a family of ten offspring, hovered near her bending her ear, recounting memories of his large family's Christmases past until he had her laughing.

Strachney's frown deepened, but before he could interfere, Forbes ushered in the ladies.

Penelope had linked arms with Marlowe, and it appeared there might have been some wrestling required getting her down to the great hall.

But Marlowe was here, and as she approached his pulse quickened. In her green gown with the choker of emeralds and diamonds circling her elegant neck, she was lovely beyond belief.

Strachney's mouth dropped. "Two ladies," he muttered.

Forbes led Filomena to the foot of the table and pulled out the chair.

"I cannot possibly sit here," she hissed.

"You must, Mrs. Marlowe," the duke called from his place at the head. "Mrs. Marlowe has been serving as my hostess," he told Miss Strachney. "Very kind of her. Very helpful. I could not have managed without her."

Such utter rubbish. Filomena pressed her lips together and allowed Forbes to seat her, watching as Strachney helped Penelope into the seat on her left and Mr. Lovelace seated Miss Strachney at the duke's left, and then seated himself on Filomena's right.

The duke beamed a smile her way. Forbes, still hovering near her elbow, cleared his throat.

"Shall I bring in the first course, Madame?" Forbes asked.

She sighed. Not an hour before, she'd been summoned to Penelope's bedchamber, rapidly stripped of her practical work attire, pinned into the most beautiful gown she'd ever beheld, and had her unruly hair arranged by Penelope's maid into an intricate arrangement of curls, all while being subjected to a steady, insistent discourse by Penelope.

She fingered the jewels at her neck. Penelope had fastened those on as well.

Her cousin had insisted she wear the dress and the jewels because she would join them for dinner tonight not as a servant but as a member of the party, by order of the duke.

And here was Forbes, making it clear that she was actually the evening's hostess.

"Yes, please, Mr. Forbes. By all means we must eat, and the cook has prepared an excellent feast for us."

Which she knew because she had been about the business of tasting the soup when Penelope summoned her.

Strachney studied her from his place next to Penelope, and she gritted her teeth, waiting for him to call her out as Kinmarty's housekeeper.

"Where do you hail from, Mrs. Marlowe?" Strachney asked.

"My cousin and I are from Hertfordshire," Penelope said. "Though we spent time in London. It's where I met my late husband."

Strachney leaned over his plate, peering around Penelope, his beady eyes glowing. "And is Mr. Marlowe planning to join the family here for the Yuletide?"

"Mr. Marlowe is deceased," the duke said, dipping his head in a sympathetic gesture. "Mrs. Marlowe is also widowed."

Strachney's mouth turned down. That had been unwelcome news.

"I've spent little time in London, myself," Strachney said. "I suppose your family and the duke's were well-acquainted from your time there?"

He'd directed his question to Filomena. She took a spoonful of pea soup stalling.

"Perhaps well-acquainted would be putting it too strongly," Penelope said. "But as I said I met the duke and his brother there."

She remembered all too well. Godmama had wangled an invitation to an important ball, but sick with nerves, she'd come down with a cold that left her too ill to attend. Penelope had gone though, returning home with a dreamy look, a mysterious neck bruise, and a torn chemise.

"Actually," the duke said. "We all met here at Kinmarty, many years earlier when we were children."

His warm gaze from the other end of the table sent heat to her cheeks.

"Do you remember, Minny?" The words floated softly down the table, wrapping her in their warmth, meant only for her, as if no one else was present. The tenderness stirred memories of their afternoon. Good heavens—that very afternoon, when he'd almost made love to her.

She shook herself and forced a laugh. "Yes. We spent a summer near here, and I fell in the burn, and the duke—the future duke—very kindly rescued me." She signaled, and the footmen began clearing plates. "I fear I have always been clumsy. I was the girl stepping on toes, turning the wrong way in a dance, and spilling ratafia on my gown. Or worse—on Penelope's."

Penelope reached for her hand and squeezed it. "And I never minded. Not once."

She managed a laugh, and the others joined in, and then the footmen served the baked grayling.

"Do you plan to make Kinmarty your home, Mrs. MacDonal?" Lovelace asked.

"I should love to, if the duke will allow it."

"He most certainly will," Andrew said. "And the children. Their father and I had our happiest times here with the old duke."

"How old are the children?" Miss Strachney asked.

"They are six and four." Penelope smiled, her fondness evident.

Her cousin had softened during her years spent in India.

"You shall meet them later," Penelope added. "They're joining us—after all, it's Christmas eve."

"Such a lovely age." Miss Strachney sounded wistful.

She liked children. If the duke were to marry her, she would be a kind aunt to the boys.

"Do you have brothers and sisters?" Filomena asked her.

"No, but I grew up with younger cousins. They're in Edinburgh."

The girl's sad tone hinted at her loneliness.

"You must come and visit the children any time you wish," Penelope said. "They would delight in your company."

"Very kind," Strachney said.

Penelope asked Strachney about his residence in India, his return to Scotland, and his plans for the future. It became clear he'd yanked the girl from the only family she'd known with a scheme to help him advance socially.

Lovelace turned the conversation to business and the industry in the area, also probing Strachney for his plans.

Forbes's army served course after course, the roasted lamb, the ham, the French beans, puddings, and more peas. Conversation swirled around her, and every time she looked up, she was trapped in the duke's thoughtful gaze and a smile meant only for her.

Mr. Strachney ate heartily, complimenting the dishes he favored, and discussing his cook's version of the ones he cared less for. His daughter picked at her food, out of nerves or dislike for the dishes, Filomena wasn't sure.

She doubted the girl had been long out of the schoolroom. She might be no more than eighteen years, perhaps younger.

She toyed with her own food watching to see when the last guest sat back from the table before asking the ladies if they'd like to retire to the great hall.

"Bravo, Mrs. Marlowe." The duke was smiling again. "It was an excellent Christmas Eve dinner. I hope that you too will deign to make Kinmarty your home."

He rose and strode down the table to pull out her chair, setting her cheeks aflame. He might as well publicly declare his intent to make her his mistress. And what of the girl at the table who was meant to be his wife?

While Mr. Lovelace distracted Miss Strachney, her father's frown turned ugly.

The duke was oblivious to the emotional currents. "Mr. Strachney, Lovelace, you may stay and smoke your cigars if you wish. I will join the ladies and the children in the great hall."

He took her hand and set it upon his arm.

When Penelope beamed a smile at them, suspicion twisted in her.

And perhaps, perhaps...hope. She glanced up and his gaze trapped her again.

At his gentle tug, she fell into step with him. "Have you lost your mind?" she whispered.

He smiled and tapped his chest leaning close. "My heart." The words rumbled through her on a cloud of bergamot scent, melting her defenses.

Forbes held the door for them to enter the great hall.

The room was ablaze with light, and a table held cakes and biscuits, bowls of frumenty, and glasses of syllabub. In the fireplace, the tinder and kindling sat ready to spark the great log to life.

Andrew pulled her along with him to the hearth. Pounding on the stairs and excited shrieking signaled the children's arrival.

"You're just in time, lads." He lifted a long taper from a branch of candles and touched it to the bunched tinder, sparking the flame and loud whoops.

As the sparks licked and spread, Filomena let out a breath. Given the snowfall, she'd worried the log would be wet. It was bad luck for the flame to go out, but this fire was blazing stronger, as it ought to do.

Andrew backed away from the hearth, a boy attached to each leg, as naturally as if they were his own sons. She'd misjudged Andrew MacDonal.

She turned away and saw Mr. Strachney's glare fixed on Andrew and the boys. Miss Strachney's mouth hung open.

Penelope sent Filomena a conspiratorial smile.

She was enjoying the shock she'd engendered. Her cousin had always been one to flout convention. Perhaps she'd needed that streak of defiance to endure her marriage to Evan.

"Bravo, Uncle Andrew," Penelope called. "Come, Ravi and Arun, and be introduced to Miss Strachney who particularly wants to meet you, and then you may enjoy the treats Aunt Minny has arranged for you."

Penelope and Lovelace bustled the children and Miss Strachney over to the table and Andrew went to join them.

Which left her with Mr. Strachney.

His eyes flashed anger. "I know who you are, Mrs. Marlowe. I make it my business to know everyone hereabouts. You're the duke's housekeeper."

Chapter Eighteen

She eased in a breath.

"His housekeeper sitting at table with respectable guests. And those boys…I don't know what he's playing at, but if he means to foist baseborn blacks on society with the children of the quality and keep you the way the old duke kept his housekeeper, well it won't stand."

Anger crushed the air out of her. She glanced back at the rest of their party loading up plates, then gritted her teeth and tugged the vile man closer to the door. If she'd truly been Kinmarty's hostess, she'd have called for the footmen to toss him directly out into the cold night.

She eased in a breath, and then another, struggling for control, and giving up.

"A pox on your insults about me and the duke. And those dear children being raised by their uncle—why would anyone care?" she asked. "He is, after all, a duke."

His gaze narrowed on her. "A poor one. One who's about to lose his land to taxes. There are those of us with the means to buy it up entirely, if we can, and if we can't, to buy out the leases and clear out the tenants for sheep." His mouth firmed. "A man without money is a man without power. I couldn't have my daughter living here with two colored by-blows under the same roof."

The daughter in question had pulled Ravi onto her lap and was laughing at something he said.

Filomena's heart skipped a beat. Miss Strachney would make a sensible duchess and give Andrew the money he needed to save Kinmarty.

She herself would have to leave, but not before she gave this bully a piece of her mind.

"If you wish to help your daughter become a duchess, you *will* mind your tongue. Those boys are the duke's only family. You had best accommodate yourself to their presence here and cease insulting them."

He turned a curious look on her. "You are a bold one, Mrs. Marlowe. If you would help me achieve my goal, I could make it worth your while." His gaze swept over her from the top of her head to her toes and back up again, like a snake winding itself around her.

"I wouldn't be helping *you*." *You loathsome toad.* "Your daughter seems a kind and sensible girl." *And getting her away from you would be a great kindness to her.* "But the duke is his own man and I have no sway over him. Can you not buy your daughter a noble title in Edinburgh where she has family and would be happy?"

"Women think too much of happiness. With my money, he can buy her a house in Edinburgh. He is a virile fellow, I'd guess, and will do as well as any to give her a child or two that she can spoil."

She squeezed her eyes shut on the image of Andrew bedding Miss Strachney, her heart twisting with hot jealousy.

When she looked, Miss Strachney was skipping off to the fire, a child in each hand.

Mr. Strachney grumbled low in his throat. "I do not like it. I do not like it at all."

The duke followed the young lady and the boys, and the girl smiled up at him. Filomena's heart sank to her stomach, churning it until bile rose.

Andrew was not for her.

She'd known that when she'd brought him into her chamber, thinking he was merely the duke's factor. There had been no hope for her then, just as there was none now. She wouldn't stay on as his leman while he installed his wife in another bedchamber.

"If I can help your daughter, I will do so," she said. "But you are to stay away from those children. And me."

Penelope stood locked in conversation with Mr. Lovelace. The refreshments were waning.

She slipped out of the great hall and made her way to the kitchens.

"Not so close." Andrew snagged the collar of Ravi's robe and pulled him back from the flames.

Miss Strachney smiled up at him. "I've a cousin who caught his neck cloth on fire once." She laughed. "My aunt poured the pot of tea—which fortunately had gone cold—over him, and no harm was done."

While Arun and Ravi demanded to know all the details of her story, he turned away, seeking Marlowe.

He'd been busy with the children, but had kept an eye on what looked to be a tense conversation between her and the nabob.

And now, the nabob stood by the door, a calculating look in his eye, and Marlowe had disappeared.

He caught Penelope's attention. Frowning, she glanced around, signaled to Forbes who'd just entered the room, and came to link arms with Andrew.

"We shall give that blasted man something else to fret about," she whispered.

"Boys," Andrew announced loudly, "tell Miss Strachney good night. Miss Strachney, Mr. Strachney, Forbes has sent for your carriage." The nabob frowned, but to hell with him. "We wish you safe travels home and a Merry Christmas."

While Miss Strachney hugged each of the boys, Strachney bestirred himself and approached to shake hands with Andrew and Lovelace.

Sitara appeared as stealthily as a wraith, ignoring the nabob's glare as she took each boy by the hand.

"Daughter," Strachney pressed, "our invitation?"

"Yes, of course. Father has invited some of the best families in the area for dinner on Friday next. We should like you to join us, your grace." She nodded at the others. "You and your party."

"Thank you." He fixed a gaze on Strachney. "I shall have to ask Mrs. Marlowe if she has arranged anything else for that day, though I know she'll be pleased by the invitation."

The nabob colored deeply. "Sir, I don't think—"

"Mrs. Marlowe will send a note."

"Mrs. MacDonal's cousin is most welcome as well." Miss Strachney's look dared her father to contradict her and he silently cheered.

"Bravo, Miss Strachney," Penelope said. "Hospitality is so important in Highland society, is it not, Andrew?"

"It is."

The departure dragged on, but they finally waved farewell and closed the door on their guests.

"Dreadful man," George said. "The daughter, on the other hand, is—"

"A child," Andrew said.

"Yes." Penelope said. "But not a fool. And I don't think she's determined to be the next duchess."

Neither was Marlowe. And Marlowe's conversation with Strachney had upset her. He'd observed her discomfort, but he'd also seen the man eyeing the boys with distaste. He'd wanted to go to her rescue, but remaining with Arun and Ravi sent a signal to the old blunderbuss that the boys were family and they would stay.

Now he had to find Marlowe and convince her she should as well.

Hovering nearby, Forbes cleared his throat. "I believe Mrs. Marlowe went below stairs."

Andrew flew down the narrow servant staircase and through the service corridor spotting a light through the partially open door in the pantry—the same pantry where George had cornered Marlowe.

At his touch, the door moved silently and his breath caught.

A white smock covered the emerald dress, the strings tied at the waist of a back that had gone stiff. She'd discerned his entry and frozen in place, though the curls piled atop her head trembled.

He came up behind her.

"The nabob and his daughter have left."

Her shoulders sank with a long exhale, and her elbows moved as she dried the silver, piece by piece.

"Leave off this task, my dear."

"They'll spot."

"Let them." He pulled the apron string and lifted the garment, knocking out a comb and sending a lock of hair tumbling.

Her lips bent in a determined frown. "Miss Strachney was very kind to the—"

"No. I will not marry her."

"She was kind to the children. She would make you a suitable wife. In time—"

"No." He nudged her around and took her hands. "I want to marry you. I fear I've loved you since you jumped into the burn."

"I didn't. I fell. I was—"

"Clumsy. Yes, I heard your story. But I was there. You jumped, thinking your cousin was under the water. I was in awe of your pluck. When you floundered I had to save you."

"You called me a nodcock and a brat."

"Of course. I was all of eleven years old."

"I could have saved myself but for that blasted new gown."

He swept a finger over her cheek where, despite all her eye-scrunching, a tear was making a path over the silky skin.

"No doubt you could have. And now you can save me, if you will. I love you, Minny. Filomena. Marlowe. By whatever name, I love you. Will you please marry me?"

Her eyes flashed and more tears flowed before she slowly shook her head. "You can't think only of love. You must also think of Kinmarty, and Kinmarty needs money."

"Is my lack of money your only objection?"

Filomena caught the humor in his eyes and hope rose in her.

He loved her. Could it possibly be true?

Despite his losses, despite the burdens placed on him, he had kept his capacity for humor. It was early days though, wasn't it? Mightn't he grow sullen when the money ran out completely?

She wasn't a fool, but oh, how she longed to be in his arms again, forever.

"You're teasing me, duke. You know I'm speaking of my own lack. I have only enough to live quietly with a servant or two."

"And you would choose that over becoming a duchess and chatelaine of a fairy tale castle?"

Hope thrummed within her. "There's that, I suppose."

His eyes lit and darkened. "And there's also the matter of our unfinished business today."

The hot gaze sparked flames in her, as if she herself was the Yule log catching fire, and his smile made her want to weep again.

"Do you have any other objections?"

No, she wanted to shout. But one of them must be sensible. They couldn't maintain Kinmarty on only her income and their love.

Love. She loved him, and he loved her. The miracle of it made her choke.

She managed a breath. "There's the matter of gossip."

"Do you really care about that?"

She shook her head. "Honestly, the problem is money, Andrew. Mr. Strachney threatened to turn the whole county against you, to use his money to ruin Kinmarty, to buy up the land and clear out the tenants. You have the boys to look out for and educate, and..." Her hand went to her belly. If they married, there might be more children.

Oh, how she wished there might be more children.

He pulled her into his arms and kissed her, tasting of sweet lemon syllabub, and she had no power to resist. Her arms came around him and she tilted her head welcoming him.

He could be hers. She could kiss him like this every night.

His gaze darkened to a deep forest green. "I'll take that kiss as a yes."

"I...no, Andrew."

"Come." He took her hand. "We'll have a practical talk up in the study where I'll persuade you with sensible words."

In the study, Penelope and Lovelace sat on either side of the large desk, Lovelace scribbling with a quill and Penelope examining pages of writing under an oil lamp. Forbes was there also, standing off to the side.

"Perhaps we should go elsewhere, Andrew," Filomena whispered.

"Well?" Penelope asked without looking up. "Did you ask her?"

She drew in a sharp breath. It was as she had suspected. They had conspired together.

Penelope finally raised her gaze to them. "You didn't tell her, Andrew."

He turned Filomena to face him. "What I said, is the truth. I love you and I wanted to make a proper proposal. The subject of money is not very romantic. Not that I mind you bringing it up."

"Money is always romantic," Lovelace said.

Andrew fumbled in his pocket and brought his hand out, fisted around something. "You have a dowry, quite a sizeable one, and..." he uncurled his fingers "a proper ring."

Her heart pounded. An emerald set in gold and surrounded by diamonds, twinkled up at her. The ring matched her necklace.

"I couldn't take Penelope's jewelry."

"It's not my jewelry," Penelope said, "and don't go missish on us, or I'll pull that emerald necklace—which isn't mine either—tighter around your neck. The jewels are from Andrew."

"Actually, they're Mrs. Ramsey's," Andrew said. "Her wedding gift from the old duke."

"Wedding gift?" Filomena asked.

"Forbes, will you explain?"

Forbes stepped out of the shadow. "The old duke couldn't let Mrs. Ramsey go into the hereafter without setting things right. Before she died, he married her."

"But...is that commonly known?"

Forbes shrugged. "It's known by me and the other two servants who witnessed it. She bade us not share the news, should it cause the duke embarrassment, and we honored our word to her."

"You witnessed it?"

"Aye. Under Scottish law, all that's required is a Scottish citizen to witness a man and a woman's vows."

"Marrying over the anvil," she whispered. The ring winked at her.

When she lifted her head, four pairs of eyes bore into her.

"Forbes is a Scottish citizen," Andrew said.

No. No, no, no. They expected her to marry Andrew tonight, here, in this very room.

"Evan did well in India, and all his money came to me. I am very rich." Penelope laughed. "Far richer than Strachney. Wait until that dratted man finds out. Lovelace has some excellent schemes, and I plan to invest in Kinmarty, but first I will help my cousin and dearest friend in all the world by giving her a proper dowry."

"Penelope—"

"You mustn't refuse. Lovelace is on the last page of the marriage agreement, and it is very nicely done."

"Thank you," Lovelace said, and his pen commenced scratching again.

Her mind reeled. She would have a dowry sufficient to marry a duke—the duke she'd despised for much of her adult life, a man who'd posed as someone else, just to make a joke of her.

No, that wasn't right. He'd been making a joke of himself, and she'd been lying to him, as well.

He slipped an arm around her and bent close. "I wanted you as my duchess even without Penelope's money. I would have sold the emeralds if needed, but I very much want you to have them."

His face lit with a smile before becoming serious again. "Like the old duke, I fell in love with my housekeeper." He traced a finger down her cheek. "But he held onto convention too long. He should have married Ramsey when they were younger. She might have borne him an heir, and you and I might have found each other at a ball during your season and been plain Mr. and Mrs. MacDonal. But, Minny, we can't help what has gone before, and we don't have to repeat old mistakes."

Her heart stirred mightily. This was the boy who'd jumped in without hesitation and saved her. He'd borne the loss of his brother—not just in the past few weeks, but for years and years. He'd been alone, as had she, for so very long.

They'd both broken with the people they loved. They'd both made mistakes. She wouldn't make another.

"Yes," she said. "Yes, I will marry you, Andrew."

He lifted her up and spun her around until she was dizzy and laughing with him.

"You must sign this contract first," Penelope called.

Back on her feet, she staggered against him. "But, we will marry in the kirk as well and all of Kinmarty will come."

"Agreed." He dropped a kiss on her cheek and escorted her to the desk.

As she bent over the papers, the cat leapt up next to them.

"Ah, Mungo is here for the nuptials," Forbes said. "How appropriate."

"Mungo? Is that truly his name?" she asked. "We've become fast friends." She gave him a pat and then scratched her name across the bottom of the page.

Andrew took the pen next. "And why is it appropriate for Mungo to join us?"

"Mungo was present when the old duke wed Mrs. Ramsey," Forbes said. "He was her favorite mouser. It feels like the old girl herself is here with us."

"Well, then." Andrew signed and waved the feather at the cat's nose. "Tell your mistress I've found her a worthy successor, Mungo."

The cat fixed them both with a haughty look, then settled upon his haunches and meowed.

Forbes chuckled. "Mungo says it's time. Let us begin."

Fifteen minutes later...

The whisky from one last toast was still burning a path down her throat when Andrew swept her into his arms.

"Goodnight all," he said. "And a merry Christmas." He nuzzled her ear. "And a merry Christmas to you, duchess."

Duchess? She'd awoken that morning as a housekeeper and now she was a duchess. It made her head spin.

She clung to him as he stumbled into the corridor. "Put me down, duke."

"Duke? I like the way that sounds on your lips." He stopped at a door and juggled her while he reached for the latch.

"This is the wrong room, duke. My door is the next one down."

Ignoring her, he carried her through, and set her on her feet for a long kiss. And then his fingers flew, pulling out combs and hairpins, spinning her around to work the fastenings on her gown.

This chamber was the mirror of her own, except the bed was larger, the curtains darker. A man's razor and a masculine brush lay on the dressing table. A man's coats draped one of the chairs. The fireplace backed the one in her chamber, and next to it was a door...

The same unobtrusive door in her bedchamber that she'd found locked.

"*You.*" She pressed her hands to his cheeks. "You lodged me in the bedchamber adjacent to your own."

"Yes. Kick off your slippers, love."

She obeyed, blindly. "With a connecting door."

He grinned. "I cannot tell you how I struggled to resist temptation." Under his skilled fingers, her bodice loosened. "It was a near thing. Had I known earlier how strongly you returned my interest I might have thrown off all caution before you seduced me."

"Andrew." Her cheeks flamed.

"You're a bold one, duchess."

"Bold? I..."

The room chilled as her gown fell around her and he helped her step out of it.

"Yes, bold. Bold enough to jump into the burn. Bold enough to take a position with a man you hated. Bold enough to bring that man to his senses. And thank God for it." He loosened her stays. "And thank God for you. I love you. We shall have a good life. I'll do my best to see to it."

Her throat clogged with wonder. Unable to speak, she opened her arms and he crushed her to him.

"I love you as well, Andrew MacDonal." She pulled back and lifted her gaze. "And why are you still fully dressed?"

His laughter filled her heart, filled the room, filled the entire castle and all of Kinmarty.

Epilogue

One week later...

The bonfire was the largest anyone had seen in years, or so the local villagers told the duke and duchess when their graces walked out to the meadow to greet their people and join in the caelidh.

It was nearing midnight when Andrew and Filomena returned to the Castle. Inside the great hall, the local gentry had gathered for a more sedate party which, under the influence of the duke's wine, brandy, and whisky, had livened up.

At a quarter of twelve, Filomena sent for the children. Andrew had decreed that Arun and Ravi might come down for the fireworks at midnight.

At ten minutes of, she heard the clatter of boys on the stairs. The guests gathered round as Andrew and Penelope greeted the children, and Mr. Lovelace pushed up to join them.

"Have you decided upon our First Foot?" Filomena asked.

Arun raised his hand. "I want to do it. I have black hair."

"Me, too," Ravi said.

"You're not tall enough, lads," one of the neighbors said.

"Should it not be the duke?" someone else asked.

"Or Mr. Lovelace?" Filomena smiled. She'd reconciled with the scapegrace.

Lovelace bowed to her, smiling back. "The duke and I will draw straws."

"Though I am the taller," Andrew said.

Filomena glanced again at the pocket watch Andrew had loaned her. "Decide quickly. Midnight is almost upon us. Why not have two?"

"I want to do it, uncle," Arun moaned.

"How much time now, duchess?"

Someone had opened the door, and a blast of cold wind hit her. Her hand trembled around the timepiece. "Two minutes."

"We must hurry then." Andrew sent her a wink. "The duchess has made an excellent suggestion. Come Lovelace." He tightened the belt on Ravi's dressing gown. "You too, lads." He took both boys by the hands and escorted them outside.

All around her, the crowd murmured. Forbes added another glass to the tray set with whisky and cakes near the door.

"One minute," Filomena called and then the assembly began to count down the seconds.

At midnight, the door opened to cheering, and Andrew and Lovelace bumped over the threshold together, each of them with a wiggling boy on his shoulders.

Miss Strachney clapped her hands together. "Four dark-haired handsome males. You'll have luck in abundance, duchess."

She gave the young lady a quick hug while Forbes brought the tray.

Filomena handed each boy a cake and held out the traditional glass of whisky for each of the men. Andrew flipped a giggling Ravi to the floor, setting him on his feet. Then he accepted the glass, tossed back his drink, and pulled her into an embrace.

He raised his head and began to sing: "*Should auld acquaintance be forgot and never brought to mind...*"

Inside and outside, their servants, their clansmen and clanswomen, their neighbors, and all of their guests joined in, and Filomena sang also, resting her cheek on Andrew's damp shoulder.

"You're crying, my love?" Andrew's smile heated her while the sweep of his thumb over her cheek made her shiver.

She'd come to Kinmarty prepared to do battle with a man she disliked, and here she was, in his arms, celebrating a new life. Could she possibly get any luckier in the year to come?

"Tears of happiness, duke."

"Duke?" He scoffed, grinning.

"Very well. My beloved duke." She dropped a kiss on his cheek and bit back a smile.

With a low growl in his throat, the Duke of Kinmarty swept his new Duchess into a New Year's kiss that the people of Kinmarty talked about for years to come.

The End

About Alina

Award winning author Alina K. Field earned a Bachelor of Arts Degree in English and German literature, but her true passion is the much happier world of romance fiction. Though her roots are in the Midwestern U.S., after six very, very, very cold years in Chicago, she moved to Southern California and hasn't looked back. She shares a midcentury home with her husband, her spunky, blonde, rescued terrier, and the blue-eyed cat who conned his way in for dinner one day and decided the food was too good to leave.

She is the author of several Regency romances, including the 2014 Book Buyer's Best winner, *Rosalyn's Ring*. She is hard at work on her next series of Regency romances, but loves to hear from readers!

You can find details of her work at
www.AlinaKField.com

Dear Reader

Thank you so much for reading Winter Wishes. We truly hope you enjoyed our stories and that we kept you entertained for a good long while. If you liked the stories a lot, we'd appreciate you sharing your opinion with friends by way of review or recommendation wherever you can.

Much love and all our best for the holiday,

The Ladies of Regency Historical Romance.